John H. C. Coffin, United States Naval Observatory, Thomas Jefferson Page

Zones of Stars

observed at the United States Naval Observatory with the mural circle in the years

1846, 1847, 1848, and 1849

John H. C. Coffin, United States Naval Observatory, Thomas Jefferson Page

Zones of Stars
observed at the United States Naval Observatory with the mural circle in the years 1846, 1847, 1848, and 1849

ISBN/EAN: 9783337405847

Printed in Europe, USA, Canada, Australia, Japan

Cover: Foto ©Andreas Hilbeck / pixelio.de

More available books at **www.hansebooks.com**

NES OF STARS

OBSERVED AT

IE UNITED STATES NAVAL OBSERVATORY

WITH

THE MURAL CIRCLE

IN

THE YEARS 1846, 1847, 1848, AND 1849.

BY

Professor J. H. C. COFFIN, U. S. N.
Lieutenant T. J. PAGE, U. S. N.
Lieutenant CHARLES STEEDMAN, U. S. N.

PUBLISHED BY AUTHORITY OF THE
HON. SECRETARY OF THE NAVY.

REAR-ADMIRAL B. F. SANDS, U. S. N.,
SUPERINTENDENT.

WASHINGTON:
GOVERNMENT PRINTING OFFICE.
1872.

TABLE OF CONTENTS.

INTRODUCTION.

Soon after the establishment of the Naval Observatory a plan was formed for making an extensive catalogue of stars. An account of this plan may be found at pp. [39] to [42] of the Appendix to the annual volume of the Observatory for 1845. The work was begun in 1846, with three meridian instruments, the Mural and Meridian Circles and the Transit Instrument. The zones observed in 1846, below 30° south, were usually gone over but once, the Mural Circle and Transit Instrument taking alternate belts. Those in following years were gone over twice, and generally with different instruments.

The observations of zones of stars were discontinued in July, 1849, as it was then found that the astronomical force of the Observatory was not sufficient to perform the current and necessary duties of such an institution, and at the same time to complete the vast work of cataloguing stars which had been undertaken. In the mean time the professors in charge of the several instruments had prepared formulæ for the reduction of the zones, had determined and tabulated the various instrumental corrections necessary for making the reductions, and had begun the work of reducing. These reductions, however, were soon interrupted by the detachment from the Observatory of some of the officers, and by the ill-health of others, and nothing further was done until 1859. In that year the reduction of the zone observations was resumed by Mr. James Ferguson, late assistant astronomer, who reduced the zones observed with the Meridian Circle in 1846, and which were published in 1860. In the summer of 1861 copies of all the observations of zones were made under the care of Mr. Ferguson, and they were put into the hands of Dr. B. A. Gould to revise the work already done and complete the reductions. He returned them ready for printing in July, 1867.

The stars embraced in these zones are all in southern declination, and for the most part between the parallels of twenty and forty-five degrees, and in regions where as yet very few of the smaller stars had been observed. The observing-books indicate that a large part of the observations with the Mural Circle were carefully made. It has been decided, therefore, to publish the zones observed with that instrument, and also in a succeeding year those observed with the Transit Instrument, these two instruments having been employed conjointly. The following pages, 1 to 331, contain the observations of the zones observed with the Mural Circle in the years 1846, 1847, 1848, and 1849, with the reductions and the deduced positions of the stars. The declinations were prepared by Professor Coffin, except for a portion of the zones in 1849, as also the reductions to mean of wires for the Transit observations in 1846 and 1847, and the preliminary tables for the right ascensions for the whole period, except the portions involving clock and instrumental corrections.

THE INSTRUMENT.

The following description of the Mural Circle, the instrument employed in making the observations, is taken, with slight changes, from the annual volume of the Observatory for 1846:

The Mural Circle was constructed by Troughton & Simms, of London.

During the time of the zone observations it remained in the *east* observing-room, and upon the eastern face of the sandstone pier, to which it was removed in the latter part of 1845. This pier is nine feet four inches high, six feet from north to south, and three feet three inches from east to west. The axis of the instrument reaches entirely across the pier, through an archway of thirty-two inches span and twenty-one inches pitch.

The circle is placed upon the eastern end of the axis, which is sustained in part on friction-rollers supported by counterpoises. It is five feet in diameter. The divisions are upon the periphery of the rim, cut upon a band of gold, and 5' apart. They are read off by means of six of "Troughton's Reading

Microscopes," mounted firmly upon the face of the pier, and adjusted, as nearly as practicable, 60° from each other. These microscopes are designated in the observations by the letters A, B, C, D, E, F. They are arranged as in the accompanying diagram, A being on the north side of the pier, and the line through the center joining A and B being horizontal. By this arrangement

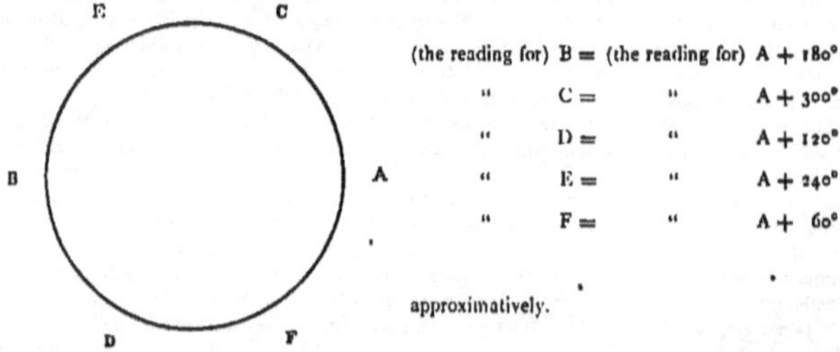

(the reading for) B = (the reading for) A + 180°

"   C =   "   A + 300°

"   D =   "   A + 120°

"   E =   "   A + 240°

"   F =   "   A + 60°

approximatively.

These microscopes are adjusted, as to focal length, so that five revolutions of the micrometer-screw of each may measure one space, or 5' of the circle. The micrometer heads are divided into sixty parts—reading, therefore, directly to *seconds*, or, by subdivisions easily made, to *tenths* of seconds. In general, in making readings of the circle, the *seconds* and *parts* are read from each of the six microscopes, and to these are prefixed the *degrees* and *minutes* from A alone. The mean of these six readings constitutes the "Circle Reading."

For illuminating the graduated limb, a lamp is placed behind the pier in a line with the axis of the instrument; the light from this lamp passes through six holes, bored through the pier, directly to the reflectors attached to the several microscopes. In this way a less variable illumination is secured than formerly by means of lamps carried in the hands. The object aimed at has been to have the same illumination for the readings of the circle, both in the observation of a star and in the determination of the "Nadir Point" which is to be employed in its reduction.

The circle is adjusted to a vertical position by means of a plummet suspended on a fine silver wire, with the aid of appendages, attached to the telescope known as "Ramsden's Ghosts," and to its position in the meridian by observations of the transits of circumpolar stars.

The telescope of this instrument has an object-glass of four inches clear aperture, with a focal length of five feet. It is attached to an independent axis, moving within the axis of the circle, and may be moved to any position with reference to the graduations. The ends of the tube, or the cells supporting the object-glass and the micrometer, are firmly clamped to the rim of the circle.

The eye-end of the telescope is furnished with a fixed diaphragm, containing seven vertical wires, designated I, II, III, &c., nearly equidistant, and at an average interval apart of $15^s.4$, (in time,) and one horizontal wire, which it is found convenient to call the *fixed wire*. The adjustments of this diaphragm have consisted in placing it in the principal focus of the object-glass—turning it so that an equatorial star will exactly traverse the *fixed wire*—and, the circle being adjusted to an exact vertical position and the telescope directed to the nadir, moving the diaphragm so that the *vertical wire* IV will coincide with its image reflected from a surface of quicksilver and seen by means of the collimating eye-piece.

In connection with the fixed diaphragm is another, movable, with a micrometer-screw, and furnished at the commencement of the year (1846) with one wire or spider's line only. In the latter part of February, in order to adapt the instrument to the work of cataloguing, this diaphragm was furnished with *eight* additional wires parallel to the original one, and distributed on each side of it at distances equivalent to five revolutions of the micrometer-screw. Subsequently the four nearest to the middle or original one were removed, those which remained being respectively *five, fifteen, fifteen, five* revolutions apart. These were changed in May, 1849, to intervals of *five, ten, ten, five* revolutions. In the record of the work in which they have been employed they are numbered **1, 2, 3, 4, 5**, in the order of the micrometer-scale, *i. e.*, commencing in the southern part of the field of view. To render available so large an extent of field in declination as is embraced in this system of wires, the eye-piece was also provided with a vertical motion. The adjustment of this diaphragm consists in making *wire 3* parallel to the *fixed wire*.

The head of the telescope-micrometer is divided into 100 parts, and is usually read to *thousandths* of a revolution. It is adjusted so that when *wire 3* is moved into coincidence with the *fixed wire*, the micrometer reading shall be nearly 30ʳ.000, 30ʳ. indicating the notch of the micrometer-scale which is intersected by the *fixed wire*. In making a micrometer reading that notch of the scale is noted which the wire used in the observation has passed.

§ 3.

METHOD OF OBSERVING AND OBSERVERS.

The instrument was clamped at a division of the circle, or midway between two divisions, and the microscopes were read, (on two sets of division when the circle was set between them,) and also the meteorological instruments. These readings were generally repeated several times during the observation of a zone. The transits were observed by the eye and ear method. The bisections for declination were made at one of the transit wires I, II, III, IV, &c., with one of the micrometer wires **1, 2, 3, 4, 5.** The observations were recorded in blank-books, the form of which is given in the Appendix of the annual volume for 1845, under the heads *O* and *P.* The following notes are taken from one of Professor Coffin's observing-books:

a. "The transit wire on which the micrometer bisection is made is the IV wire if the transits were observed upon it or upon wires both sides of IV; otherwise the wire observed on nearest IV. The exceptions are noted."

b. "The micrometer wire when not noted is wire **3**."

c. "The minute belongs to the first transit wire observed."

The above rules were followed by Professor Coffin in all his observations, and it appears that the other observers followed the same rule with regard to the minute of the transit.

The observers were Professor J. H. C. Coffin, U. S. N., who observed from the beginning until the end of the work in 1849; Lieutenant T. J. Page, U. S. N., who observed from the beginning until January 4, 1848; and Lieutenant Charles Steedman, U. S. N., who observed from December 15, 1847, until June 21, 1849. The initial of the observer is placed at the beginning of the zone together with the date of observation.

The adjustments of the instrument were made by Professor Coffin, who also made the observations for determining the value of a revolution of the telescope micrometer and the corrections of the micrometer wires.

Professor Coffin furnishes the following corrections to be applied to the micrometer readings, derived from the published volumes of the Observatory for the years 1846 to 1850:

1. Corrections on Account of Eccentricity of the Micrometer-Head.[*]

Mic. Reading.	Correction.	Mic. Reading.	Correction.	Mic. Reading.	Correction.
.00	− 0ʳ.0000	.35	− 0ʳ.0029	.70	− 0ʳ.0001
.05	05	.40	28	.75	+ 04
.10	10	.45	27	.80	09
.15	15	.50	23	.85	10
.20	20	.55	19	.90	09
.25	24	.60	14	.95	06
.30	− 28	.65	− 05	.00	+ 00

[*] Washington Astronomical Observations, 1846, Introduction, p. xviii.

2. *Reductions of Wire 3 to Parallelism with the Horizon.*

These are given at transit wire III; the same numerical values answer for V; for II and VI, they are to be multiplied by 2; and for I and VII they are to be multiplied by 3; and the signs changed for V, VI, and VII. The reduction at IV is o.

Year.	From—	To—	Corr.	Remarks.
1846	April 4	April 23	+ 0ʳ.0004	
	April 24	May 14	12	
	May 15	June 8	05	
	June 9	June 30	19	
	July 1	July 31	05	
	Aug. 1	Aug. 31	11	
	Sept. 1	Oct. 5	06	
	Oct. 6	Nov. 20	19	Nov. 17. Re-adjustments.
	Nov. 21	Dec. 31	26	
1847	Jan. 5	Feb. 6	32	Feb. 10. Wires disturbed.
	Feb. 12	April 13	50	
	April 14	May 25	65	April 14. Wires disturbed.
	Aug. 5	Sept. 6	37	
	Oct. 15	Dec. 3	48	Dec. 4. New wires put in.
	Dec. 18	Jan. 22	+ 0ʳ.0002	
1848	Feb. 1	Mar. 24	− 0ʳ.0016	Feb. 1. New VII and 3.
	Mar. 29	May 22	12	March 26. Wires disturbed, and re-adjusted.
	May 23	Aug. 11	17	
	Aug. 11	Aug. 15	21	
	Aug. 16	Sept. 19	31	Sept. 19 and 26. Diaphragms taken out and replaced.
	Sept. 26	Oct. 5	03	Oct. 5. Re-adjustments.
	Oct. 6	Oct. 11	18	
	Nov. 21	Dec. 31	− 0ʳ.0018	
1849	Jan. 4	Jan. 27	+ 0ʳ.0008	
	Feb. 3	Feb. 10	14	
	Mar. 10	Mar. 31	16	
	April 3	April 30	12	
	May 2	May 14	13	
	May 17	May 18	143	May 20. 3 had been disturbed. New set of wires put in.
	June 4	June 22	+ 0ʳ.0014	June 27. Re-adjustments.
	July 2	July 30	− 0ʳ.0005	

3. *Reduction of the other Micrometer Wires to Wire 3.*

These reduce the readings for observations with the several wires to what they would have been if wire 3 had been used.

During 1846 and 1847 wire 5 could not be brought into coincidence with the fixed wire, so that the reductions for it have not been determined; and, therefore, except in the earlier zones of those years, that wire has not been used. In a few of the earlier observations of Lieutenant Steedman he has used a wire which he calls 6, of which there is no account. The declinations derived from observations with these two wires are, therefore, imperfectly determined; so also from observations with wire 1, in zones 158–161 and 178–187.

The periods of the following table are those in which there was no known disturbance of the wires, and the several determinations agree satisfactorily with each other.

In 1846 and 1847,	from 12 determinations,	$\Delta R =$	$+ 0^r.0020$
In 1848, before September,	" 2 "		$+ 0^r.0025$
In 1848,	" 2 "		$- 0^r.0022$
In 1849,	" 4 "		$+ 0^r.0010$

Its value would probably be affected whenever the telescope was unclamped from the rim of the circle and moved. This was done January 2 and September 19, 1848, and January 1, 1849.

The determination of the nadir point was made by means of the collimating eye-piece. The telescope being directed downward, the circle was moved by one of the tangent-screws until the fixed wire, illuminated by means of this eye-piece, coincided with its image reflected from a surface of mercury; then the circle reading corrected for runs and errors of division constitutes the nadir point. Each determination consists of several such coincidences and circle readings, the wire and its image being brought into coincidence from opposite sides.

Corrections of Clock.

Date.		Corr.	Hourly rate.
1846.	h.	s.	s.
April 6,	12	+ 63.261	l. 0.014
9,	10	65.036	l. 0.025
13,	12	67.851	l. 0.032
14,	12	8.139	l. 0.001
15,	12	8.214	l. 0.004
16,	12	8.190	l. 0.006
17,	12	8.564	l. 0.008
18,	12	9.100	l. 0.009
20,	12	9.353	l. 0.008
27,	12	11.051	l. 0.028
May 4,	12	16.495	l. 0.028
19,	12	29.708	l. 0.026
20,	16	29.991	l. 0.018
21,	16	30.231	l. 0.021
25,	16	33.686	l. 0.044
27,	16	35.269	l. 0.038
June 3,	16	42.761	l. 0.008
4,	16	43.204	l. 0.010
6,	16	43.146	l. 0.013
15,	16	47.338	l. 0.020
16,	16	48.354	l. 0.021
17,	16	48.420	l. 0.025
18,	16	49.390	l. 0.020
22,	16	50.529	l. 0.004
24,	13	50.453	l. 0.002
July 1,	13	55.312	l. 0.034
7,	12	59.985	g. 0.022
9,	12	59.630	g. 0.004
10,	17	59.557	g. 0.000
11,	17	59.647	g. 0.005
14,	17	58.886	g. 0.011
15,	17	59.483	g. 0.010
24,	17	8.856	l. 0.003
29,	17	9.228	l. 0.009
Aug. 5,	17	9.142	l. 0.005
11,	18	+ 10.685	g. 0.003

Date.		Corr.	Hourly rate.
1846.	h.	s.	s.
Aug. 12,	20	+ 10.387	g. 0.009
13,	20	10.132	g. 0.012
18,	20	7.943	g. 0.017
29,	21	7.935	l. 0.010
31,	21	7.367	l. 0.006
Sept. 9,	22	4.777	g. 0.021
13,	22	3.439	g. 0.020
14,	22	3.248	g. 0.024
15,	22	2.484	g. 0.021
16,	22	1.622	g. 0.027
19,	18	+ 0.030	g. 0.019
21,	18	− 0.419	g. 0.020
23,	18	1.513	g. 0.011
24,	20	1.620	g. 0.015
29,	22	4.226	g. 0.018
Oct. 7,	21	4.757	l. 0.013
8,	21	4.427	l. 0.010
9,	21	4.288	g. 0.004
11,	21	4.896	g. 0.008
16,	22	5.709	g. 0.010
19,	22	6.303	g. 0.018
26,	22	. .	g. 0.012
28,	22	10.649	g. 0.012
Nov. 16,	0	7.609	g. 0.032
21,	0	11.589	g. 0.032
Dec. 4,	0	22.074	g. 0.024
26,	0	− 35.364	g. 0.023
1847.			
Jan. 6,	5	− 40.73	g. 0.027
22,	2	45.92	g. 0.007
Feb. 1,	10	46.65	0.000
5,	4	46.00	g. 0.009
6,	2	45.86	g. 0.011
12,	4	48.27	g. 0.014
23,	5	− 49.12	g. 0.010

Date.		Corr.	Hourly rate.
1847.	h.	s.	s.
Mar. 5,	5	− 50.77	g. 0.004
10,	6	+ 10.02	g. 0.020
18,	6	5.83	g. 0.012
22,	8	4.02	g. 0.015
24,	6	+ 4.51	g. 0.018
April 3,	7	− 1.77	g. 0.010
7,	15	4.10	g. 0.028
9,	6	5.05	g. 0.024
13,	6	8.17	g. 0.026
15,	20	9.45	g. 0.028
20,	14	11.86	g. 0.020
May 4,	17	18.40	g. 0.020
6,	8	19.27	g. 0.022
17,	14	19.20	g. 0.026
29,	14	22.26	g. 0.008
June 11,	20	24.87	g. 0.020
15,	14	26.91	g. 0.028
17,	14	28.19	g. 0.020
24,	12	28.71	l. 0.005
July 16,	19	33.92	g. 0.020
18,	1	34.81	g. 0.021
Aug. 2,	18	41.71	g. 0.006
5,	18	43.31	g. 0.015
20,	19	50.03	g. 0.040
26,	16	55.22	g. 0.035
30,	23	− 58.07	g. 0.024
Sept. 6,	19	+ 19.61	g. 0.040
14,	17	13.11	g. 0.046
16,	18	10.63	g. 0.035
21,	19	8.34	g. 0.028
27,	20	4.71	g. 0.036
29,	19	+ 2.96	g. 0.048
Oct. 15,	19	− 12.41	g. 0.055
16,	19	13.61	g. 0.050
18,	19	15.40	g. 0.020
26,	20	− 21.64	g. 0.045

Corrections of Clock—Continued.

Date.	h.	Corr.	Hourly rate.
1847.	h.	s.	s.
Oct. 27,	22	− 22.43	g. 0.040
28,		. .	g. 0.040
Nov. 2,	20	24.49	g. 0.024
16,	1	36.47	g. 0.060
27,	19	44.80	g. 0.040
Dec. 18,		− 57.35	g. 0.044
1848.			
Jan. 4,	4	− 71.313	g. 0.044
18,	9	80.672	g. 0.023
20,	3	2.240	l. 0.005
22,	3	3.378	g. 0.029
Mar. 7,	7	37.892	g. 0.031
24,	8	21.290	
29,	8	24.040	g. 0.024
April 1,	7	− 25.456	g. 0.033
20,	8	+ 8.420	l. 0.007
May 27,	18	18.682	l. 0.008
30,	15	18.381	g. 0.005
June 12,	15	17.300	g. 0.018
16,	19	16.091	l. 0.008
23,	17	19.493	l. 0.002
26,	19	18.866	g. 0.009
July 10,	16	21.152	l. 0.047
11,	17	23.470	l. 0.047
17,	21	23.326	g. 0.018
19,	15	23.152	0.000
20,	16	+ 23.719	l. 0.008

Date.	h.	Corr.	Hourly rate.
1848.	h.	s.	s.
July 24,	19	+ 24.440	l. 0.008
Aug. 1,	20	24.483	g. 0.008
4,	19	22.739	g. 0.002
7,	7	22.907	g. 0.030
14,	19	23.845	l. 0.013
16,	16	24.640	g. 0.000
18,	0	23.806	g. 0.023
24,	20	19.786	g. 0.018
29,	21	19.686	l. 0.002
30,	19	18.913	g. 0.015
31,	20	18.965	g. 0.021
Sept. 2,	21	17.264	g. 0.033
7,	20	14.145	g. 0.028
18,	23	8.540	g. 0.019
Oct. 7,	19	4.589	g. 0.039
11,	21	+ 2.020	g. 0.028
Nov. 28,	3	− 12.987	g. 0.014
Dec. 2,	1	14.545	g. 0.014
4,	17	15.151	g. 0.018
18,	19	15.900	l. 0.009
30,	5	− 19.084	g. 0.011
1849.			
Jan. 23,	4	− 23.645	g. 0.018
27,	1	25.090*	g. 0.027
Feb. 9,	7	30.932	g. 0.018
10,	6	31.371	g. 0.017
15,	12	− 31.722	l. 0.008

Date.	h.	Corr.	Hourly rate.
1849.	h.	s.	s.
Feb. 16,	6	− 31.467	l. 0.009
19,	5	33.867	g. 0.015
23,	5	33.163	l. 0.008
Mar. 7,	9	23.356	g. 0.007
19,	6	28.832	g. 0.025
22,	11	29.583	g. 0.018
30,	8	33.717	g. 0.020
April 2,	8	36.210	g. 0.040
5,	12	39.125	g. 0.038
10,	10	32.583	l. 0.011
11,	8	32.288	l. 0.009
14,	10	32.413	0.000
16,	8	32.296	l. 0.004
19,	10	31.753	l. 0.012
21,	5	30.873	l. 0.010
May 2,	8	20.920	l. 0.003
11,	2	− 17.949	l. 0.016
June 14,	4	+ 3.404	l. 0.022
17,	5	5.244	l. 0.021
18,	15	5.256	l. 0.004
21,	4	6.339	l. 0.015
22,	13	6.705	l. 0.015
July 2,	16	9.760	l. 0.016
11,	7	16.736	l. 0.016
17,	16	+ 17.436	l. 0.009

Coincidence of Wires, Value of Micrometer-Screw, and Observed Values of Zenith Point.

Date.	Coincidence.	R_o	Zenith Point.	Zone.
1846.	r.	″	° ′ ″	
April 6	30.003	62.74	359 59 59.55	1
9	29.998	62.74	60.37	2
13	30.007	62.74	59.77	3
14	30.006	62.74	60.73	4
15	30.007	62.74	60.34	5
16	30.005	62.74	60.62	6
16	30.005	62.74	60.48	7
17	30.008	62.74	60.90	8
18	30.006	62.74	61.88	9
20	30.005	62.74	62.10	10
27	30.006	62.75	62.00	11
May 4	30.002	62.75	62.35	12
19	30.006	62.75	62.59	13
20	30.001	62.75	62.48	14
21	30.000	62.75	62.18	15
25	29.909	62.75	62.25	16
27	30.005	62.75	62.73	17
27	30.005	62.75	· 62.73	18
June 3	30.002	62.75	62.46	19
4	29.097	62.75	62.90	20
6	30.009	62.75	62.46	21
15	30.005	62.75	62.12	22
16	30.006	62.75	63.00	23
17	30.005	62.75	62.45	24
18	30.006	62.75	62.60	25
22	30.004	62.76	62.43	26
24	30.008	62.76	359 59 62.40	27
July 1	30.001	62.76	0 0 2.44	28
7	30.004	62.76	2.57	29
7	30.004	62.76	2.57	30
9	30.003	62.76	3.41	31
10	30.002	62.76	2.73	32
10	30.002	62.76	2.73	33
11	30.002	62.76	2.52	34
14	30.005	62.76	2.89	35
14	30.005	62.76	2.89	36
15	30.006	62.76	2.60	37
24	30.005	62.76	2.16	38
29	30.006	62.76	2.50	39
29	30.006	62.76	2.50	40
Aug. 5	30.002	62.76	2.50	41
11	30.006	62.76	2.20	42
11	30.006	62.76	2.20	43
12	30.002	62.76	2.40	44
13	30.002	62.76	2.17	45
13	30.002	62.76	2.17	46
18	30.016	62.76	0 0 2.09	47

Coincidence of Wires, Value of Micrometer-Screw, and Observed Values of Zenith Point—Continued.

Date.	Coincidence.	R_o	Zenith Point.	Zone.
1846.	r.	"	° ′ "	
Aug. 20	30.005	62.76	0 0 2.54	48
29	30.010	62.76	1.84	49
31	30.007	62.76	1.81	50
Sept. 9	30.011	62.75	1.59	51
9	30.011	62.75	1.59	52
13	30.004	62.75	1.40	53
14	30.008	62.75	1.30	54
14	30.008	62.75	1.30	55
15	29.996	62.75	1.79	56
16	30.006	62.75	0.54	57
19	30.006	62.75	0.95	58
19	30.006	62.75	0.95	59
21	30.000	62.75	1.40	60
23	30.008	62.75	0.20	61
24	30.007	62.75	1.40	62
24	30.007	62.75	1.40	63
28	30.006	62.75	0.70	64
28	30.006	62.75	0.70	65
30	30.004	62.75	0 0 1.21	66
Oct. 6	30.005	62.75	359 59 55.62	67
7	30.006	62.75	55.62	68
8	30.004	62.75	55.73	69
9	30.005	62.75	55.67	70
10	30.005	62.75	55.76	71
16	30.006	62.75	55.85	72
16	30.006	62.75	55.85	73
17	30.005	62.75	55.85	74
19	30.009	62.75	56.28	75
26	30.010	62.75	53.71	76
28	30.011	62.75	54.27	77
28	30.011	62.75	54.27	78
Nov. 16	30.010	62.75	359 59 55.91	79
20	29.990	62.75	0 0 4.55	80
20	29.990	62.75	4.55	81
21	29.989	62.75	4.56	82
Dec. 3	29.993	62.75	3.27	83
4	29.982	62.75	2.77	84
23	29.993	62.75	1.74	85
1847.				
Jan. 6	(29.996)	62.75	2.79	86
22	30.0015	62.75	2.26	87
27	30.0025	62.75	1.92	88
Feb. 1	29.9983	62.75	1.29	89
5	30.0104	62.75	1.02	90
6	30.0075	62.75	0.93	91
12	30.0106	62.75	1.01	92
12	30.0106	62.75	1.01	93
14	30.0162	62.75	0 0 1.16	94

Coincidence of Wires, Value of Micrometer-Screw, and Observed Values of Zenith Point—Continued.

Date.	Coincidence.	R_s	Zenith Point.	Zone.
1847.	r.	'	° ' ''	
Feb. 23	30.0162	62.75	0 0 1.17	95
23	30.0162	62.75	1.17	96
23	30.0162	62.75	0 0 1.17	97
Mar. 5	30.0155	62.75	359 59 59.74	98
5	30.0155	62.75	359 59 59.74	99
10	30.0146	62.75	0 0 0.67	100
18	(30.015)	62.75	0 0 0.06	101
22	30.0137	62.75	359 59 59.58	102
24	30.0122	62.75	0 0 0.44	103
April 3	30.0103	62.75	359 59 59.75	104
7	30.0112	62.75	59.38	105
7	30.0112	62.75	59.38	106
9	30.0125	62.75	59.62	107
9	30.0125	62.75	59.62	108
13	30.0156	62.75	60.26	109
16	30.0275	62.75	59.97	110
21	30.0247	62.75	62.28	111
May 4	(30.026)	62.75	61.58	112
6	30.0260	62.75	61.00	113
6	30.0260	62.75	60.81	114
17	(30.025)	62.75	61.89	115
29	30.0236	62.75	62.77	116
June 11	30.0250	62.75	62.11	117
14	30.0253	62.75	62.76	118
14	30.0253	62.75	62.76	119
17	30.0274	62.75	62.36	120
17	30.0274	62.75	62.36	121
24	(30.020)	62.75	63.08	122
July 17	(30.022)	62.75	62.63	123
19	30.0218	62.75	62.30	124
Aug. 2	30.0495	62.75	64.12	125
5	30.0462	62.75	63.60	126
20	30.0480	62.75	64.82	127
26	30.0510	62.75	63.52	128
30	30.0500	62.75	64.24	129
Sept. 6	30.0474	62.75	65.70	130
14	30.0518	62.75	64.48	131
16	30.0500	62.75	63.98	132
16	30.0500	62.75	63.98	133
21	30.0505	62.75	65.06	134
27	30.0085	62.75	62.04	135
27	30.0085	62.75	62.04	136
29	30.0123	62.75	62.26	137
Oct. 15	30.0177	62.75	60.89	138
16	30.0140	62.75	60.59	139
18	30.0471	62.75	62.45	140
18	30.0471	62.75	62.45	141
26	(30.045)	62.75	359 59 63.14	142

Coincidence of Wires, Value of Micrometer-Screw, and Observed Values of Zenith Point—Continued.

Date.	Coincidence.	R_o	Zenith Point.	Zone.
1847.	r.	"	° ′ ″	
Oct. 27	30.0475	62.75	359 59 63.39	143
28	30.0455	62.75	62.42	144
28	30.0455	62.75	62.42	145
Nov. 2	30.0438	62.75	62.22	146
15	30.0534	62.75	61.76	147
20	30.0391	62.75	62.38	148
Dec. 18	29.9900	62.80	359 59 60.31	149
1848.				
Jan. 3	29.9876	62.76	9 59 59.74	150
4	29.9930	62.76	58.30	151
4	29.9930	62.76	58.30	152
18	29.9820	62.76	57.07	153
18	29.9820	62.76	57.07	154
19	29.9858	62.76	56.59	155
20	(29.985)	62.76	57.11	156
22	(29.986)	62.76	56.13	157
Mar. 6	29.9876	62.824	61.73	158
7	(29.984)	62.824	60.99	159
24	29.9819	62.824	54.27	160
29	30.0035	62.824	55.39	161
April 1	30.0060	62.824	56.92	162
20	30.0131	62.824	57.28	163
May 3	30.0089	62.824	56.82	164
27	29.9238	62.824	61.48	165
30	(29.925)	62.824	61.08	166
June 2	29.9255	62.824	61.01	167
3	29.9968	62.824	61.47	168
5	29.9986	62.824	61.34	169
6	(29.999)	62.824	61.21	170
12	(30.002)	62.824	64.08	171
15	29.9945	62.824	61.83	172
16	(29.997)	62.824	60.65	173
20	30.0010	62.824	64 93	174
24	30.0043	62.824	64.58	175
26	(29.999)	62.824	62.20	176
27	30.0004	62.824	64.19	177
July 10	30.0001	62.824	62.40	178
11	30.0021	62.824	63.49	179
17	(30.003)	62.824	63.77	180
18	30.0029	62.824	63.99	181-180
19	30.0014	62.824	62.21	181
20	30.0010	62.824	63.32	182
20	30.0010	62.824	63.32	183
24	(30.001)	62.824	62.89	184
Aug. 1	30.0038	62.824	64.10	185
4	(30.001)	62.824	63.36	186
7	(30.002)	62.824	62.78	187
14	(30.000)	62.824	9 59 73.01	188

Coincidence of Wires, Value of Micrometer-Screw, and Observed Values of Zenith Point—Continued.

Date.	Coincidence.	R.	Zenith Point.	Zone.
	r.	"	° ′ "	
1848.				
Aug. 15	30.1597	62.824	9 59 73.83	189 .
16	30.0100	62.824	60.10	190
16	30.0100	62.824	60.10	191
18	(30.006)	62.824	61.75	192
24	30.0070	62.824	62.66	193
29	30.0118	62.824	61.99	194
30	30.0139	62.824	60.73	195
30	30.0139	62.824	60 73	196
30	30.0139	62.824	60.73	197
31	30.0094	62.824	61.86	198
31	30.0094	62.824	61.86 ·	199
Sept. 1	30.0101	62.824	60.81	200
1	30.0101	62.824 ·	60.81	201
2	30.0105	62.824	62.47	202
7	30.0134	62.824	63.37	203
18	30.0150	62.824	62.48	204
Oct. 7	30.0067	62.824	63.45	205
10	30.0051	62.824	61.99	206
11	30.0139	62.824	62.86	207
14	(30.014)	62.824	61.28	208
Nov. 28	30.0131	62.820	57.23	209
28	30.0131	62.820	57.23	210
Dec. 2	30.0086	62.820	55.94	211
4	30.0057	62.820	55.26	212
18	30.0057	62.820	56.82	213
30	30.0095	62.820	9 59 54.68	214
1849.				
Jan. 23	*30.7957	62.819	20 0 0.00	215
23	30.7957	62.819	0.00	216
23	30.7957	62.819	0.00	217
27	30.7779	62.819	0.00	218
27	30.7779	62.819	0.00	219
Feb 9	(30.7900)	62.819	0.00	220
9	(30.7900)	62.819	0.00	221
10	30.7896	62.819	0.00	222
13	(30.8055)	62.819	0.00	223
13	(30.8055)	62.819	0.00	224
15	(30.8210)	62.819	0.00	225
16	30.8215	62.819	0.00	226
16	30.8215	62.819	0.00	227
16	30.8215	62.819	0.00	228
19	30.8240	62.819	0.00	229
19	30.8240	62.819	0.00	230
23	30.8259	62.819	0.00	231
Mar. 7	(30.8202)	62.811	0.00	232
12	(30.8174)	62.811	20 0 0.00	233

* In 1849 nadir point was observed by moving micrometer wire 3 to coincidence with its image. The micrometer reading was then reduced to correspond with circle reading 207° 0′ 00″.

Coincidence of Wires, Value of Micrometer-Screw, and Observed Values of Zenith Point—Continued.

Date.	Coincidence.	R_s	Zenith Point.	Zone.
1849.	r.	"	° ′ ″	
Mar. 16	(30.8149)	62.811	20 0 0.00	234
16	(30.8149)	62.811	0.00	235
19	30.8083	62.811	0.00	236
22	(30.8063)	62.811	0.00	237
22	(30.8063)	62.811	0.00	238
23	30.8056	62.811	0.00	239
23	30.8056	62.811	0.00	240
29	30.8223	62.811	0.00	241
30	(30.8249)	62.811	0.00	242
April 2	(30.8232)	62.811	0.00	243
5	30.8165	62.811	0.00	244
5	30.8165	62.811	0.00	245
10	(30.8095)	62.811	0.00	246
11	30.8123	62.811	0.00	247
12	36.6523	62.811	0.00	248
14	. . .	62.811	0.00	249
16	. . .	62.811	0.00	250
20	30.8078	62.811	0.00	251
May 2	30.7736	62.811	0.00	252
11	30.7445	62.811	0.00	253
June 16	30.6722	62.849	0.00	254
18	30.6655	62.849	0.00	255
19	30.6633	62.849	0.00	256
20	30.6632	62.849	0.00	257
21	30.6563	62.849	0.00	258
22	30.6645	62.849	0.00	259
22	30.6645	62.849	0.00	260
July 2	30.6073	62.845	0.00	261
3	30.5669	62.845	0.00	262
5	30.5774	62.845	0.00	263
5	30.5774	62.845	0.00	264
11	(30.5719)	62.845	0.00	265
17	(30.5566)	62.845	0.00	266
17	(30.5566)	62.845	20 0 0.00	267

§ 5.

METHOD OF REDUCTION.

The magnitudes of the stars, the seconds of the observed times of transit in the columns I, II, III, &c., the micrometer readings, the micrometer wires used, and the transit wires at which the bisections were made, have been taken from the observing-books, and the proofs compared directly with them and corrected to agree with the records of the observers. The minutes of the transits have been changed, when necessary, so as to adapt them to the "mean of wires."

The method of reduction, as arranged by Professors Coffin and Hubbard, is nearly the same as that described by Mr. Ferguson in his Introduction to the Meridian Circle Zones of 1846, published in 1860. The differences arise from the different construction of the two instruments.

1. The times of transit of a star were first reduced to the mean of wires, using for each wire the reduction for the zone in the part of the field indicated by the micrometer reading;

T, representing the clock times of transit of the mean of wires;

k, the clock correction at that time;

I, the reduction of the mean of wires to the meridian for the middle of the field, or at 30^r of the micrometer;

M, the reduction to 1850.0 for the right ascension and declination of the middle of the field;

ΔI and ΔM, the variations of I and M for the distance of the star in declination from the middle of the field, or, $- (m - 30^r)$ in terms of the micrometer, m being the micrometer reading;

and putting

$$a_1 = k + M, \qquad a_2 = I + \Delta I + \Delta M$$

the right ascension of the star is

$$a = T + a_1 + a_2$$

The preliminary work consisted in the preparation of tables for each zone containing a_1 for each 10^m of clock-time, and a_2 for each 5 or 10 revolutions of the micrometer, and at such intervals of time as was requisite. The columns a_1 and a_2 were then readily filled by an easy interpolation.

The column a_1, which is printed, includes corrections for erroneous values of k used in the earlier zones in forming the tables of a_1; and in some zones a constant appears to have been added to one and subtracted from the other so that the signs should be uniform.

2. C, representing the first circle reading for a zone;

Z, the zenith point;

r, the refraction for the zenith distance $(C - Z)$ and the first readings of the barometer and thermometer;

M, the reduction to 1850.0 for the declination of the middle of the zone, or 30^r, and the right ascension of its commencement, or an exact 10^m preceding;

m_0 the micrometer reading for coincidence of ▩ with the fixed wire; or, in 1849, the reading of ▩ to correspond with $Z = 20^\circ\ 0'\ 0''$:

the constant of declination for the zone is

$$D_0 = 38^\circ\ 53'\ 39''.25 - (C - Z) - 62''.75\,(m_0 - 30^r) - r + M + 30' + n' + n''$$

$30'$ and the arbitrary constants n' and n'' being added so that all the reductions shall have the same sign as D_0. Omitting these, D_0 is the mean declination of wire ▩ at the commencement of the zone and for the micrometer reading $30^r.000$. n' and n'' were omitted from the copy prepared for the printing, and the papers containing them are missing.

The micrometer reading for each star was corrected for eccentricity of the micrometer-head, and reduced from the recorded micrometer and transit wires to wire ▩ at transit wire IV, and to the meridian by means of the tables, pages ix and x.

m, representing this corrected reading;

$$i = - [62''.75\,(m - 30^r) + 0''.0025\,(m - 30^x)^2 + 30']$$

A table for each $0^r.01$ of m facilitated the preparation of this column.

ΔC, representing the change in the circle reading C;

Δr, the change of refraction for changes of the barometer and thermometer;

ΔM, the change of M for difference of right ascension;

$\Delta_1 r$, the difference of refraction; and

$\Delta_1 M$, the difference of M, for the distance of the star in declination from the middle of the field, or $-(m - 30^r)$;

$$d_1 = -\,[\Delta C + \Delta r - \Delta M + n']$$

$$d_2 = -\,[(R_0 - 62''.75)\,(m - 30^r) + (\Delta R - 0''.0025)\,(m - 30^r)^2 + \Delta_1 r - \Delta_1 M + n']$$

ΔR and R_0 are given on pages xi and xiii–xviii.

The declination of the star is

$$\delta = D_0 + i + d_1 + d_2$$

The preliminary work for each zone consisted in computing D_0 and preparing tables of d_1 for each 10^m of clock-time, and of d_2 for each 5^r or 10^r of m, and at such intervals of time as was requisite. These columns were then readily filled by interpolation.

The columns i and of right ascension and declination include also corrections for errors of exact revolutions of the micrometer, and of minutes or exact seconds in the times of transit, which Dr. Gould, in the thorough scrutiny which he made, detected by comparison with other zones or catalogues. Such cases are noted in the margin. Some of the few errors of the copyist were detected by him in the same way and corrected.

Notes by the observers of doubtful observations are indicated in the text by a ?; but the degree of doubt, as 1^s or 10^s in a transit, or of 1^r of the micrometer, are omitted; so also are notes of other stars seen whose positions were only estimated. The numbers of stars identified in the British Association Catalogue, and in Oeltzen's Catalogue of Argelander's southern zones, which were added by Dr. Gould, are also omitted, as it was inconvenient to print them; and, moreover, these catalogues and the zones being referred to the same epoch, the stars which are common to them may be recognized with little trouble.

The quantities of reduction and the deduced positions of the stars have been printed as in the completed copy returned by Dr. Gould.

It having been decided to publish the Zones observed with the Mural Circle and Transit Instrument, the supervision of the work was put into my hands by Admiral Sands, Superintendent of the Naval Observatory, in April, 1871. It has been my endeavor to give, in the first place, an exact copy of the observations. For this purpose the proofs were compared, as has been already mentioned, with the hand-books of the observers. The results deduced by Dr. Gould, and his notes to the observations, have been printed without any change. A few cases occur where the results will be changed on account of changes in the copy, but in nearly every case the correction will be indicated by a comparison of the notes and the observations. It was also the intention to print the tables of reduction which had been prepared for each zone, but, unfortunately, up to the present time, these tables cannot be found; should they be found hereafter they will be published either with the Transit Zones or in a separate Appendix.

In reading the proofs I have been assisted from page 1 to 57 by Mr. O. Stone, from page 57 to 73 by Mr. Harrison, and from page 96 to the end by Mr. A. N. Skinner.

I am much indebted to Professor J. H. C. Coffin, Superintendent of the Nautical Almanac, for information concerning the Zones, and for assistance in preparing the Introduction.

A. HALL,

Professor of Mathematics, United States Navy.

FEBRUARY 10, 1872.

INDEX OF ZONES.

In the following Index, D denotes the declination of the middle of the zone, and the following columns give the extent in right ascension, and the number of the zone, the page on which it will be found, and the number of stars it contains.

The whole number of observations of stars in these zones is 14,804; of which—

Professor Coffin made 6,796
Lieutenant Page made 4,721
Lieutenant Steedman made 3,287

D=−40° 5'.

Right Ascension.	Zone.	Page.	No. Stars.
h. m. h. m.			
16 9 to 18 10	34	39	41
21 29 to 22 2	72	77	10
21 9 to 23 28	74	78	33
9 36 to 13 31	247	299	123

D=−39° 30'.

Right Ascension.	Zone.	Page.	No. Stars.
14 3 to 16 3	1	3	25
8 44 to 11 19	2	3	35
10 7 to 12 3	3	4	49
9 22 to 10 32	4	5	19

D=−38° 50'.

Right Ascension.	Zone.	Page.	No. Stars.
9 11 to 11 2	5	6	25
13 30 to 17 39	15	17	70
20 25 to 0 6	57	63	50
19 19 to 20 25	62	69	13

D=−38° 15'.

Right Ascension.	Zone.	Page.	No. Stars.
12 45 to 14 22	245	297	51

D=−37° 35'.

Right Ascension.	Zone.	Page.	No. Stars.
9 55 to 11 50	6	6	41
14 11 to 15 23	7	7	24
13 34 to 15 27	17	20	42
19 25 to 19 34	18	21	3
14 57 to 18 8	24	27	67
19 41 to 21 6	60	66	52
22 5 to 0 11	69	75	19
7 32 to 10 6	234	278	97
18 3 to 19 42	48	55	42

D=−37° 5'.

Right Ascension.	Zone.	Page.	No. Stars.
h. m. h. m.			
11 39 to 14 46	242	290	114

D=−36° 20'.

Right Ascension.	Zone.	Page.	No. Stars.
9 4 to 12 6	8	8	42
13 9 to 18 19	16	18	80
18 17 to 21 3	49	56	57
20 57 to 23 2	55	60	40
23 2 to 0 30	71	76	29
0 44 to 1 44	80	83	6

D=−35° 40'.

Right Ascension.	Zone.	Page.	No. Stars.
17 30 to 17 44	35	40	11
8 10 to 10 58	237	282	111

D=−35° 5'.

Right Ascension.	Zone.	Page.	No. Stars.
9 28 to 11 30	9	9	48
13 36 to 16 59	14	15	82
17 4 to 18 53	33	38	62
19 25 to 23 57	53	58	57
18 19 to 20 15	54	59	26
0 1 to 1 51	83	84	27
7 47 to 9 53	232	275	95
11 18 to 12 40	235	280	40
9 59 to 13 19	243	292	125

D=−34° 30'.

Right Ascension.	Zone.	Page.	No. Stars.
12 24 to 14 17	238	284	62

D=−34° 10'.

Right Ascension.	Zone.	Page.	No. Stars.
15 0 to 18 8	22	24	114

D = —33° 50'.

Right Ascension.				Zone.	Page.	No. Stars.
h.	m.	h.	m.			
9	39	to 12	44	10	10	114
14	32	to 15	13	20	23	13
17	5	to 17	34	26	31	13
17	59	to 20	31	36	41	75
20	29	to 0	1	59	65	47
0	0	to 0	13	82	83	7
23	49	to 0	23	84	84	15
0	3	to 2	7	85	85	30

D = —33° 15'.

Right Ascension.				Zone.	Page.	No. Stars.
9	32	to 11	12	239	285	66
12	39	to 14	47	240	287	75

D = —32° 35'.

Right Ascension.				Zone.	Page.	No. Stars.
9	51	to 11	59	11	12	41
13	30	to 14	16	21	24	18
14	15	to 15	27	23	27	18
15	26	to 21	1	25	28	110
19	26	to 20	11	51	57	14
20	55	to 22	6	52	58	25
22	41	to 23	30	67	74	12
22	3	to 23	8	68	74	25
23	11	to 23	34	73	77	11
22	59	to 0	16	77	80	32
1	49	to 4	2	78	81	38
7	50	to 10	3	223	262	113
11	43	to 13	41	224	264	81

D = —31° 20'.

Right Ascension.				Zone.	Page.	No. Stars.
10	43	to 12	45	12	13	57
12	52	to 17	23	19	21	118
21	30	to 23	6	38	44	24
18	0	to 18	43	39	45	30
19	46	to 20	47	40	46	31
17	22	to 21	39	44	49	89
23	0	to 0	29	75	78	27
2	3	to 3	28	81	83	23
3	54	to 4	31	87	87	14
3	29	to 5	36	89	89	44
8	36	to 11	3	107	113	100
12	22	to 14	8	108	115	63
5	22	to 9	2	225	266	88
6	12	to 7	21	227	268	42
7	27	to 8	40	230	271	65
6	0	to 8	27	231	273	101
17	9	to 17	30	266	330	21

D = —30° 40'.

Right Ascension.				Zone.	Page.	No. Stars.
h.	m.	h.	m.			
2	3	to 5	6	86	86	62
5	30	to 7	2	95	98	50
7	55	to 9	7	96	99	51
10	20	to 11	22	97	101	39
6	58	to 7	10	100	104	9
7	11	to 9	7	101	104	23
15	3	to 19	1	120	133	143
19	47	to 21	1	121	136	21
22	1	to 0	31	139	160	100
11	1	to 12	11	236	281	42
11	55	to 12	8	246	298	12

D = —30° 5'.

Right Ascension.				Zone.	Page.	No. Stars.
13	30	to 15	27	13	14	34
15	30	to 16	47	28	33	45
16	21	to 16	52	32	37	17
16	44	to 19	53	37	42	104
19	31	to 20	22	58	65	19
20	0	to 23	5	61	67	89
22	51	to 2	20	76	79	53
4	9	to 8	0	88	87	100
6	22	to 6	43	92	94	11
8	37	to 9	45	93	94	34
7	53	to 12	4	103	106	116
18	39	to 23	59	131	147	142
2	1	to 2	9	214	252	5
6	19	to 7	52	216	253	77
11	52	to 13	50	241	288	80

D = —29° 45'.

Right Ascension.				Zone.	Page.	No. Stars.
15	48	to 16	25	262	326	25

D = —29° 25'.

Right Ascension.				Zone.	Page.	No. Stars.
7	28	to 11	42	90	90	75
4	1	to 7	41	91	92	90
9	41	to 10	23	109	117	24
12	8	to 13	30	115	124	19
18	56	to 0	1	132	150	198
1	49	to 3	0	133	154	37
5	22	to 5	59	215	253	25
5	46	to 6	42	229	270	35
18	1	to 19	10	261	325	58
15	50	to 16	26	263	327	26

D = −28° 50′.

Right Ascension				Zone.	Page.	No. Stars.
h.	m.	h.	m.			
14	31	to 18	58	27	31	64
17	59	to 21	4	47	53	79
21	1	to 0	31	63	70	75
1	42	to 3	39	79	82	42
7	32	to 9	9	102	105	68
17	28	to 18	5	124	139	20
19	3	to 21	8	130	146	68
14	5	to 14	49	168	193	20
15	50	to 16	59	173	200	36
17	49	to 19	27	182	213	69
6	1	to 7	41	210	246	86
9	2	to 10	0	217	255	47
4	42	to 6	31	220	258	75
3	36	to 5	2	222	261	50

D = −28° 10′.

Right Ascension				Zone.	Page.	No. Stars.
6	9	to 8	18	98	102	95
10	26	to 11	1	99	104	10
8	15	to 10	31	104	109	52
14	16	to 18	14	117	126	139
18	18	to 21	44	128	142	136
22	56	to 2	26	140	162	85
3	56	to 5	6	141	164	19
10	59	to 12	20	158	181	30
12	16	to 15	0	164	168	70
2	19	to 5	52	213	250	125

D = −27° 35′.

Right Ascension				Zone.	Page.	No. Stars.
15	35	to 17	17	29	34	55
19	41	to 21	1	30	35	26
17	16	to 17	45	41	46	8
17	53	to 19	48	45	51	60
21	0	to 21	31	65	72	14
21	30	to 0	29	66	72	66
4	44	to 9	15	94	95	150
9	7	to 12	38	105	110	125
15	6	to 16	3	106	112	28
10	5	to 10	52	110	117	21
13	0	to 15	0	116	125	70
16	0	to 17	24	118	129	53
18	10	to 20	59	119	130	107
2	9	to 4	1	151	173	44
0	27	to 4	25	209	243	108

D = −26° 55′.

Right Ascension				Zone.	Page.	No. Stars.
h.	m.	h.	m.			
10	26	to 10	42	111	118	5
11	47	to 14	24	112	118	84
20	31	to 21	0	136	158	9
22	58	to 0	6	138	159	33
6	34	to 7	5	152	174	18
9	59	to 12	4	162	185	64
14	31	to 16	22	172	199	48
16	33	to 20	4	176	204	95
7	42	to 9	1	221	259	64
8	25	to 9	19	233	277	33

D = −26° 20′.

Right Ascension				Zone.	Page.	No. Stars.
15	51	to 19	13	31	35	98
19	12	to 19	24	50	57	3
19	12	to 0	0	56	61	117
23	59	to 2	25	70	75	53
11	36	to 15	0	113	120	125
16	0	to 18	19	114	122	75
18	14	to 19	29	127	140	55
19	18	to 21	6	129	145	47
4	20	to 5	36	153	174	25
5	37	to 7	3	154	175	32
4	59	to 9	2	157	179	97
9	13	to 12	55	161	183	66
14	48	to 16	37	169	194	54
20	42	to 21	44	191	223	24
9	11	to 11	47	244	295	101

D = −25° 40′.

Right Ascension				Zone.	Page.	No. Stars.
15	58	to 17	4	122	136	38
17	2	to 21	33	123	137	96
23	48	to 2	2	149	171	60
9	4	to 10	26	159	182	32
9	14	to 10	49	160	182	41
10	42	to 14	5	163	186	99
14	48	to 17	3	167	192	70
20	31	to 23	59	208	241	106
4	57	to 5	58	226	267	40
14	14	to 15	49	253	311	66

$D = -25°\ 5'$.

Right Ascension	Zone	Page	No. Stars
h. m. h. m.			
17 38 to 19 49	42	47	72
21 23 to 22 28	43	48	20
20 1 to 20 47	64	71	25
20 1 to 0 1	134	155	125
13 2 to 15 46	165	190	67
16 12 to 17 46	166	191	37
17 44 to 19 16	190	221	56
10 49 to 13 3	251	308	97

$D = -24°\ 25'$.

Right Ascension	Zone	Page	No. Stars
23 33 to 0 6	147	170	17
15 39 to 19 52	170	195	97
19 32 to 20 10	198	227	6
19 32 to 22 7	202	232	60
9 40 to 14 23	248	301	107
10 30 to 12 22	249	304	54

$D = -23°\ 45'$.

Right Ascension	Zone	Page	No. Stars
20 3 to 22 2	46	52	38
21 0 to 21 24	142	164	9
1 58 to 3 50	143	165	59
21 23 to 0 0	144	166	96
1 33 to 1 53	145	168	7
23 52 to 0 56	148	171	22
1 49 to 2 9	150	173	7
2 2 to 4 0	155	176	44
4 47 to 8 49	156	177	108
16 55 to 19 12	171	197	60
15 1 to 17 23	174	201	78
20 12 to 22 52	183	214	44
19 7 to 20 21	195	225	36
3 59 to 4 50	218	256	32
6 19 to 7 4	219	257	50
8 1 to 9 0	228	269	42

$D = -23°\ 10'$.

Right Ascension	Zone	Page	No. Stars
21 31 to 0 2	146	168	77
15 1 to 18 4	175	202	91
17 41 to 18 9	178	206	15
18 3 to 18 23	179	207	10
18 7 to 19 24	180	207	30
19 7 to 21 48	192	223	66
9 52 to 13 38	250	305	136

$D = -22°\ 35'$.

Right Ascension	Zone	Page	No. Stars
h. m. h. m.			
16 13 to 16 29	177	206	5
15 51 to 20 6	180-181	208	120
20 2 to 22 0	186	216	39
23 20 to 1 23	211	248	75

$D = -21°\ 55'$.

Right Ascension	Zone	Page	No. Stars
17 41 to 21 9	181	210	123
23 1 to 23 31	194	225	11
21 4 to 23 9	203	233	41
14 48 to 16 6	252	310	62
15 47 to 17 36	256	316	48
17 29 to 18 2	267	331	28

$D = -21°\ 20'$.

Right Ascension	Zone	Page	No. Stars
20 14 to 21 48	184	215	35
17 50 to 18 5	185	216	11
3 15 to 4 2	212	249	23
14 43 to 17 1	255	314	99
16 54 to 17 18	264	328	25
17 3 to 19 2	265	328	100

$D = -20°\ 40'$.

Right Ascension	Zone	Page	No. Stars
18 29 to 22 27	187	217	99
22 26 to 23 16	193	225	14
22 26 to 0 52	199	228	31
23 12 to 0 59	201	231	44
16 4 to 15 41	257	317	100
15 3 to 16 34	259	322	47

$D = -20°\ 5'$.

Right Ascension	Zone	Page	No. Stars
18 58 to 20 44	188	219	42
20 43 to 22 1	196	226	29
22 43 to 23 41	197	227	25
15 33 to 17 12	254	313	62
16 58 to 19 4	260	323	107

$D = -19°\ 25'$.

Right Ascension	Zone	Page	No. Stars
18 0 to 19 9	189	220	51
19 13 to 22 1	200	229	94
16 11 to 19 28	258	319	124

D = −18′ 45′.				D = −14° 30′.			
Right Ascension.	Zone.	Page.	No. Star.	Right Ascension.	Zone.	Page.	No. Star.
h. m. h. m.				h. m. h. m.			
19 19 to 22 10	204	234	73	19 41 to 20 4	135	158	10
D = −18° 10′.				19 45 to 20 6	137	158	11
22 49 to 3 24	206	236	139	**D = −5′ 50′.**			
D = −16° 55′.				16 32 to 16 49	125	140	7
22 35 to 0 0	205	236	27	**D = −4′ 35′.**			
20 32 to 22 42	207	239	86	16 45 to 17 15	126	140	12

ERRATA.

In printing the "seconds of transit" in the zones observed by Lieutenant Page in 1846 the ciphers should have been omitted, as they do not occur in the observing-book. It appears that both Lieutenant Page and Lieutenant Steedman at first were inexperienced in observing transits, and in their earlier zones only the even second was observed.

In the case of Zone 107 several circle readings were omitted by the copyist, and in the single one copied an error of − 20″ was made in copying the reading of microscope F, thus introducing an error of − 3″.3 into this circle reading. It is probable that all the declinations of this zone are systematically in error by this amount.

In numbering the zones the number 180 is repeated at the end of Zone 181, and Zone 182 is called 181, and so on to the end.

Page 3, under "Rémarks" in the last note, omit the 25.

Pages 11 and 12, under micrometer, for E. W. read F. W., which denotes the fixed wire.

Page 72, for September 24 read September 28.

Pages 173 to 217, under the head of corrections, the 0ʰ should have been omitted.

ZONES OF STARS

OBSERVED AT THE NAVAL OBSERVATORY

WITH

THE MURAL CIRCLE

IN THE

YEARS 1846–'47–'48–'49.

1—z

ZONES OF STARS

OBSERVED WITH THE

MURAL CIRCLE AT THE NAVAL OBSERVATORY IN THE YEARS 1846–'47–'48–'49.

ZONE 1. APRIL 6. C. $D_0 = -38°\ 56'\ 30''$.

No.	Mag.	I	II.	III.	IV.	V.	VI.	VII.
1	10		41.0	1.2				
2	9						40.0	59.5
3	7	19.5		59.5	19.2	39.0	56.9	18.9
4	7	36.5	56.2	16.2	37.0	57.0	16.8	36.5
5	7	6.7	26.5			26.7	46.2	6.4
6	9	5.0						
7	7		24.5	44.0	4.0	24.0	43.8	
8	8	1.2	21.0		0.8	20.5	40.0	0.0
9	7		8.2		43.0	8.2	27.9	
10	8						54.5	14.5
11	8	10.0	30.0		10.0		49.7	9.5
12	10							
13	9					4.5	24.5	14.0
14	9					6.5		
15	8			23.5	43.4		23.0	
16	9						43.0?	3.0?
17	9						3.0	23.0
18	10	27.0						
19	7				4.0	24.5	44.0	
20	9	49.8	9.8					
21	9					12.0	33.0	54.0
22	8		16.2	36.0	56.0	16.0	36.0	
23	9	10.0	30.0		10.0			
24	9	5.5				24.0		
25	9		37.0			37.8		18.0

No.	T. (h m s)	a_1	a_2	Mic.	n	r	i	d_1	d_2	Mean Right Ascension, 1850.0 (h m s)	Mean Declination, 1850.0
1	14 2 20.92	+71.22	+1.52	III.	4	44.128	−15 11.9	−20.1	−4.5	14 3 33.66	−39 12 6.5
2	3 0.08	71.24	1.46	VI.	4	40.102	19 23.7	20.0	6.1	4 12.78	16 19.8
3	16 19.21	71.46	1.65	IV.	4	40.592	14 44.5	18.9	4.8	17 32.32	11 38.2
4	20 36.60	71.54	1.22	IV.	2	14.874	45 50.5	18.5	16.3	21 49.36	42 55.3
5	26 6.50	71.63	1.49	IV.	3	24.129	36 8.4	17.9	12.4	27 19.62	33 8.7
6	31 4.50	71.71	1.95	II.	4	42.886	16 29.7	17.3	5.0	32 18.16	13 22.0
7	37 4.09	71.82	1.96	IV.	3	38.868	20 43.4	16.6	6.6	38 17.87	17 36.6
8	43 0.61	71.91	2.22	IV.	4	48.185	10 57.1	15.9	3.0	44 14.74	7 46.0
9	47 48.13	72.00	2.10	IV.	3	38.605	21 0.1	15.2	6.7	49 2.23	17 52.0
10	49 14.89	72.02	2.25	VI.	4	44.400	14 53.8	15.0	4.4	50 29.16	11 43.2
11	14 54 9.85	72.10	2.10	IV.	3	33.162	26 41.7	14.3	8.8	14 55 24.05	23 34.8
12	15 4 . .	72.27	2.50	III.	4	46.712	12 29.5	12.8	3.5	15 5 . .	9 15.0
13	6 44.60	72.31	2.41	V.	3	41.000	18 29.5	12.4	5.7	7 59.32	15 17.6
14	10 46.53	72.38	2.25	V.	3	29.260	30 46.5	11.7	10.4	12 1.16	27 38.6
15	13 43.37	72.42	2.63	IV.	4	45.768	13 28.7	11.2	3.9	14 58.42	10 13.8
16	15 3.26	72.45	2.44	VI.	3	35.282	24 28.3	11.0	8.0	16 18.15	21 17.3
17	17 23.32	72.48	2.59	VI.	3	40.661	18 50.6	10.6	5.9	18 38.39	15 37.1
18	22 26.88	72.57								23 . .	30 . .
19	23 4.23	72.57	2.34	IV.	2	23.941	36 22.1	9.5	12.6	24 19.14	33 14.2
20	26 49.71	72.64	2.33	II.	2	20.776	39 40.3	8.8	13.9	28 4.68	36 33.0
21	26 53.20	72.64	2.61	V.	3	34.961	24 48.6	8.7	8.1	28 8.45	21 35.4
22	29 56.05	72.68	2.50	IV.	3	27.506	32 36.6	8.1	11.1	31 11.23	29 25.8
23	34 9.81	72.75	2.60	IV.	3	38.650	20 57.2	7.2	6.7	35 25.36	17 41.1
24	15 44 4.53	72.90	3.14	IV.	4	48.360	10 46.2	5.2	2.9	15 45 20.57	7 24.3
25	16 1 17.66	+73.16	+3.12	IV.	4	35.564	−24 9.1	−1.8	−7.9	16 2 33.94	−39 20 49.1

ZONE 2. APRIL 9. P. $D = -39°\ 1'\ 10''$.

No.	Mag.	I	II.	III.	IV.	V.	VI.	VII.
1	8	54.0		34.0	54.0			
2	8	56.0		36.0	50.0			
3	6		57.0	17.0	37.0			37.5
4	8		30.0		10.0			
5			26.0		7.0			
6	8	42.0	2.0	22.0	42.0			
7	8		45.0	5.0	25.0			
8	8			57.0	16.0			
9	10	55.0	15.0	35.0	56.0			
10	7		14.0	34.0	54.0			

No.	T. (h m s)	a_1	a_2	Mic.	n	r	i	d_1	d_2	Mean Right Ascension, 1850.0 (h m s)	Mean Declination, 1850.0
1	8 42 54.02	+70.41	+0.25	IV.	2	16.326	−44 19.7	−5.6	−17.7	8 44 4.68	−39 45 53.0
2	9 9 55.89	70.53	0.22	IV.	3	31.936	27 58.5	12.5	11.2	9 11 6.64	29 32.2
3	23 37.18	70.61	0.19	IV.	2	13.765	47 0.0	15.8	18.7	24 47.95	48 44.5
4	33 9.96	70.68	0.18	IV.	4	38.460	21 7.7	18.0	8.6	34 20.82	22 44.3
5	38 6.46	70.71	0.17	IV.	3	33.860	25 57.7	19.1	10.5	39 17.34	27 37.3
6	42 41.90	70.75	0.17	IV.	3	33.260	26 35.6	20.1	10.6	43 52.82	28 16.5
7	45 24.91	70.77	0.16	IV.	3	43.197	16 10.3	20.7	6.7	46 35.84	17 47.7
8	47 16.50	70.78	0.17	IV.	3	31.285	28 39.5	21.2	11.5	48 27.45	30 22.2
9	50 54.85	70.81	0.16	IV.	3	33.885	25 56.2	21.9	10.4	52 5.82	27 38.5
10	9 56 53.91	+70.86	+0.16	IV.	4	45.667	−13 22.5	−23.2	−5.7	9 56 4.93	−39 15 1.4

CORRECTIONS.

Date		Corr. of Clock	Hourly rate	m	n	c	Zenith Point	Mic. Co.
1846.	h.	s.	s.	s.	s.	s.	° ' ''	r.
April 6,	12	+ 63.261	+ 0.014	+ 0.521	− 0.342	+ 0.246	359 59 59.55	30.003
9,	10	+ 65.036	+ 0.025	+ 0.521	− 0.342	+ 0.246	359 59 60.37	29.998

REMARKS.

April 6. At 14ʰ clear; bright moonlight.
April 9. 9ʰ to 10ʰ, thin clouds. Suspended work from 10ʰ 42ᵐ to 10ʰ 50ᵐ.
(1) 3. Mic. reading assumed as 44'.592, to agree with Transit Z., 1846, April 6, and Mural, May 21.
(1) 24. At 15ʰ clouds rising.
(1) 25. Illumination of wires at times very unsteady.

INSTRUMENT READINGS.

	Date	A.	B.	C.	D.	E.	F.	Mean.	Barom.	At.	Ex.	U.	L.	I.
	1846. (h. m.)	° ' ''						''	In.	°	°	°	°	°
Zone 1	April 6, 14	78 14 59.0	59.0	62.0	57.0	66.7	63.9	61.27	30.408	54.0	50.1	52.8	53.0	53.0
	14 20										49.9			
	14 43										48.5			
	15	58.7	59.4	62.0	57.8	66.6	64.2	61.45	30.386	52.6	48.0	52.0	51.8	
	15 22										47.5			
	15 44										47.2			
	16	58.0	59.9	62.0	57.1	66.9	62.9	61.13	30.372	52.0	48.5	51.3	51.2	53.0

Zone 2. April 9. P. $D_0 = -39°\ 1'\ 10''$—Continued.

No.	Mag.	I.	II.	III.	IV.	V.	VI.	VII.	T.	a_1	a_2	Micr.	n	r.	i	d_1	d_2	Mean Right Ascension 1850.0	Mean Declination 1850.0
									h. m. s.	s.	s.			r.				h. m. s.	° ' "
11	8			9.0	29.0				9 58 28.98	+70.85	+0.15	IV.	4	40.633	−18 51.2	−23.6	−7.8	9 59 40.01	−39 20 32.6
12	9	56.0		37.0		17.0			10 1 56.55	70.91	0.13	IV.	2	17.985	42 35.5	24.2	16.9	10 3 7.59	44 26.6
13	.			9.0		49.0			4 28.95	70.93	0.12	III.	2	14.440	46 18.0	24.8	18.4	5 40.00	48 11.2
14	7					32.0			6 11.98	70.95	0.13	V.	3	25.710	34 29.0	25.2	13.7	7 23.06	36 7.9
15	7								6 . .	70.95	.	VII.+	3	27.760	32 19.2	25.3	12.9	8 . .	34 7.4
16	9							12.0	8 12.10	70.97	0.13	VII.	3	26.216	33 56.7	25.5	13.6	9 23.20	35 45.8
17	10					48.0		28.0	10 28.10	70.99	0.12	V.	3	32.245	27 39.2	26.0	11.2	11 39.21	29 26.4
18	10				19.0				13 38.99	71.02	0.11	III.	2	19.933	40 33.4	26.6	16.1	14 50.12	42 26.1
19	12	15.0		55.0	15.0				17 14.91	71.05	0.11	IV.	3	32.430	27 27.7	27.5	11.1	18 26.07	29 16.3
20	12	7.0	27.0	47.0					21 6.85	71.09	0.10	IV.	3	32.544	27 20.5	28.0	11.0	22 18.04	29 9.5
21	10	39.0		19.0	39.0				23 38.92	71.12	0.10	IV.	3	31.925	27 59.2	28.4	11.2	24 50.14	29 48.8
22	7	43.0	2.5	23.0	42.5				25 42.64	71.14	0.10	IV.	3	33.783	27 2.6	28.8	10.5	26 53.85	27 51.9
23	8	58.0		58.0	58.0				30 58.07	71.19	0.08	IV.	1	9.338	51 34.5	29.8	20.5	32 9.34	53 34.6
24	12	11.0		51.0					36 10.75	71.25	0.09	IV.	4	42.930	16 26.9	30.7	6.8	37 22.09	18 14.4
25	12											IV.	3	33.260	26 35.5	30.9	10.6	(43) . .	28 27.0
26	10				25.0				50 21.97	71.41	0.08	IV.	3	53.077	5 51.5	33.0	3.0	51 36.40	7 37.5
27	8						7.0		52 27.05	71.44	0.05	VI.	2	20.770	39 40.3	33.3	15.8	53 38.54	41 39.4
28	9				18.0			58.5	10 55 58.35	71.48	0.06	I.	3	31.770	28 8.8	33.8	11.3	10 57 9.89	30 3.9
29	12	53.0			53.0				11 0 52.97	71.54	0.04	I.	3	23.922	36 20.2	34.5	14.5	11 2 4.55	38 19.2
30	10	37.0		18.0	38.0				9 38.00	71.65	0.02	I.	2	17.62	42 57.9	35.8	17.1	10 49.67	45 0.8
31	9	57.0						50.0	11 5. .	71.67	0.03	VII.	3	34.24	25 33.2	36.1	10.3	12 16. .	27 29.6
32	8								12 . .			VII.	2	21.58	38 49.0	36.1	15.4	13 . .	40 50.5
33	.	28.0		9.0	29.0				15 29.02	71.72	0.01	I.	3	21.26	39 9.7	36.5	15.5	16 40.75	41 11.7
34	.		53.0						17 32.85	71.75	0.02	II.	3	35.345	24 24.3	36.8	9.9	18 44.62	26 21.0
35	10					55.0		35.0	11 17 35.09	+71.75	+0.02	V.	3	31.035	−28 55.0	−36.8	−11.6	11 18 46.86	−39 30 53.4

Zone 3. April 13. C. $D_0 = -39°\ 1'\ 30''$.

No.	Mag.	I.	II.	III.	IV.	V.	VI.	VII.	T.	a_1	a_2	Micr.	n	r.	i	d_1	d_2	Mean Right Ascension 1850.0	Mean Declination 1850.0
1	7	8.5	29.0	49.0		28.0	48.2	9.0	10 6 8.61	+73.97	+0.41	IV.	3	25.745	−34 26.9	−7.6	−11.9	10 7 22.99	−39 36 16.4
2	7	19.0	38.8	58.5	18.5	39.0	58.7	18.5	6 18.71	73.97	0.40	V.	3	27.827	32 16.2	7.6	11.1	7 33.08	34 4.9
3	8					29.0	49.0		8 9.05	73.99	0.41	V.	3	26.259	33 54.8	8.0	11.7	9 23.45	35 44.5
4	8,9			45.0	5.0				10 24.91	74.01	0.40	III.	3	32.306	27 35.4	8.5	9.2	11 39.32	29 23.1
5	7		55.5	14.7	35.0	55.5	15.0		13 35.15	74.03	0.43	IV.	2	19.926	40 33.7	9.2	14.3	14 49.61	42 27.2
6	9		32.0		12.0				17 11.96	74.07	0.42	IV.	3	32.462	27 25.7	10.0	9.2	18 26.45	29 14.9
7	9					31.5			20 51.54	74.10	0.44	VI.	2	19.491	41 0.7	10.8	14.5	22 6.08	42 50.0
8	8				35.0		15.0		22 35.10	74.12	0.42	IV.	3	32.915	26 57.0	11.1	9.0	24 49.64	28 47.1
9	7		59.2	19.0	39.0	59.5	19.0		25 39.15	74.15	0.42	IV.	3	33.767	26 3.6	11.8	8.7	26 53.72	27 54.1
10	9				40.0		20.0		31 40.11	74.21	0.42	IV.	3	33.799	26 1.6	13.0	8.7	32 54.74	27 53.3
11	9				7.0	27.0	47.0		36 6.97	74.26	0.41	VII.	4	42.959	16 25.1	13.9	4.7	37 21.64	18 13.7
12	9							8.5	37 8.69	74.27	0.43	VII.	3	33.389	26 26.6	14.2	8.6	38 23.39	28 19.6
13	7				39.5			39.0	44 39.31	74.35	0.47	IV.	3	20.745	39 42.5	15.8	14.0	45 54.13	41 42.3
14	7				0.5		41.0		45 0.82	74.36	0.47	VII.+	3	24.910	35 17.2	15.9	12.2	46 15.65	37 15.3
15	8,9					21.0	41.0	1.0	46 1.24	74.39	9.43	V.	4	44.206	15 6.5	16.6	4.5	49 16.06	16 57.6
16	9							2.0	48 42.27	74.40	0.40	VI.	4	42. .	17 . .	. .	. .	49 57.07	19 . .
17	7	11.7	31.8	52.0	11.7	31.0	51.2		52 11.53	74.44	0.46	IV.	3	35.039	24 43.6	17.5	8.2	53 26.43	26 39.5
18	9		43.0	3.0	23.0	43.0			54 22.96	74.46	0.44	IV.	3	43.390	15 59.7	18.0	4.9	55 37.86	17 52.6
19	7				55.0	15.0	35.0	54.9	55 55.07	74.48	0.47	IV.	3	31.844	28 4.3	18.3	9.4	10 57 10.02	30 2.0
20	9				28.0	48.0			10 59 28.06	+74.52	+0.46	IV.	3	37.853	−21 47.1	19.2	−7.0	11 0 43.04	−39 23 43.3

CORRECTIONS.

Date.		Corr. of Clock.	Hourly rate.	m	n	c	Zenith Point.	Mic. Co.
		s.	s.	s.	s.	s.	° ' "	r.
1846, April 9.	19h	+ 65.036	+ 0.025	+ 0.521	− 0.342	+ 0.246	359 59 60.37	29.998
13.	12	+ 67.851	+ 0.032	+ 0.521	− 0.342	+ 0.246	359 59 59.77	30.007

INSTRUMENT READINGS.

	Date.	A.	B.	C.	D.	E.	F.	Mean.	Barom.	At.	Ex.	U.	L.	I.
	1846, h. m.	° ' "						"	in.	°	°	°	°	°
Zone 2	April 9. 8	78 19 61.0	59.0	63.5	58.3	67.0	65.5	62.38	30.536	61.5	48.0			50.0
	11 20	78 19 59.0	60.0	62.7	57.6	65.0	62.3	61.10	30.370	51.0	46.0	53.0		50.0
Zone 3	13. 10 6	78 19 60.2	61.9	62.9	60.9	65.4	65.4	62.78	30.014	50.5	41.0	49.4	50.9	57.5
	10 37												39.8	
	11 2												37.8	

REMARKS.

April 13. Night clear; numerous faint stars which would not bear illumination.
(3) 8. Minute assumed as 23, not 22.

ZONE 3. APRIL 13. C. $D_0 = -39°\ 1'\ 30''$ — Continued.

No.	Mag.	I.	II.	III.	IV.	V.	VI.	VII.	T. (h. m. s.)	θ_1	θ_2	Mic.	n	r	i	d	d_2	Mean R.A. 1850.0 (h. m. s.)	Mean Decl. 1850.0 (° ′ ″)
21	9	58.0		39.0					11 2 58.47	+74.56	+0.50	III.	3	19.060	−41 26.0	−19.7	−14.7	11 4 13.53	−39 43 30.4
22	9							30.0	3 30.33	74.57	0.45	VII.	4	43.978	15 19.4	19.8	4.6	4 45.35	17 13.8
23	9.10							13.0	6 13.36	74.60	0.46	VII.	4	46.568	12 36.8	20.3	3.6	7 28.42	14 30.7
24	8			14.0	34.0				9 34.02	74.64	0.52	IV.	2	17.682	42 54.6	20.7	15.3	10 49.18	45 0.6
25	6.7				47.0	7.0	26.5	46.5	10 46.78	74.66	0.52	IV.	3	21.662	38 43.0	20.9	13.6	12 1.96	40 47.5
26	9	25.5	45.0	5.0	25.0				15 25.11	74.73	0.52	IV.	3	21.258	39 8.5	21.5	13.8	16 40.35	41 13.8
27	8.9			1.8	21.7	41.7			16 41.72	74.73	0.52	IV.	3	25.012	35 12.9	21.7	12.2	17 56.97	37 16.8
28	8					49.0	9.0	29.0	17 29.15	74.74	0.50	V.	3	35.415	24 20.3	21.8	6.0	18 44.39	26 20.1
29	9						12.0	32.2	17 32.25	74.74	0.51	VII.+	3	31.111	28 47.9	21.8	9.7	18 47.50	30 49.4
30	9		38.0	58.0					21 17.85	74.79	0.48	III.	4	48.619	10 30.0	22.3	2.8	22 33.12	12 25.1
31	8		48.5	8.0	28.5				24 28.27	74.83	0.50	IV.	3	40.329	19 11.9	22.7	6.1	25 43.60	21 10.7
32	5				3.0	23.0	43.5	3.5	25 3.24	74.84	0.54	IV.	2	17.166	43 26.9	22.8	15.5	26 18.62	45 35.2
33	9			9.0?					27 28.98	74.87	0.54	III.	3	21.502	38 53.0	24.4	13.7	28 44.39	41 1.1
34	7	9.0	29.5	49.5	9.5	29.5	49.5		30 9.52	74.91	0.51	IV.	3	33.572	26 16.0	23.5	8.7	31 24.94	28 18.2
35	9	11.0	31.0						32 11.00	74.94	0.54	II.	3	18.375	37 10.1	23.7	15.0	33 26.48	39 18.8
36	9					15.0	35.0		33 55.05	74.96	0.54	V.	3	26.629	33 31.5	23.9	11.6	35 10.55	35 37.0
37	7			22.8		2.5		42.5	36 42.60	75.00	0.55	IV.	3	21.498	38 53.4	24.2	13.7	37 58.15	41 1.3
38	5			48.0	7.5		47.5		38 7.70	75.01	0.55	IV.	3	21.471	38 55.1	24.4	13.7	39 23.26	41 3.2
39	8						54.5	14.7	39 14.80	75.03	0.53	VI.	3	34.451	25 20.5	24.6	8.4	40 30.36	27 23.5
40	8				13.5	33.0	53.0		41 13.27	75.06	0.53	IV.	3	35.274	24 29.2	24.8	8.1	42 28.86	26 32.1
41	8			34.0	53.7	14.0			43 53.91	75.15	0.53	IV.	3	33.572	26 16.0	25.1	8.8	44 9.59	28 19.9
42	6		3.7	23.0					47 43.27	75.15	0.55	III.	3	30.484	29 29.6	25.6	10.0	48 58.97	31 35.2
43	9						37.0		47 57.12	75.15	0.55	VI.	3	29.169	30 51.9	25.6	10.5	49 12.82	32 58.0
44	9						36.0?		47 56.10	75.15	0.56	VI.	3	27.	33			49 11.81	34
45	8.9				28.7	48.7			50 28.70	75.19	0.57	IV.	3	20.092	40 21.5	25.9	14.2	51 44.46	42 31.6
46	9.10								52	75.22		IV.	3	20.574	39 51.3	26.1	14.0	53	42 1.4
47	9	27.0	47.0						56 26.83	75.27	0.50	II.	3	.748	32 21.3	26.6	10.2	57 42.66	34 28.1
48	9		8.0	27.0				8.0	11 57 7.58	75.28	0.55	III.	4	37.291	22 21.3	26.7	7.3	11 59 23.41	24 25.3
49	9	13.5				1.0			12 1 43.71	+75.32	+0.59	III.	3	18.723	−41 47.2	−27.2	−14.8	12 2 59.62	−39 43 59.2

ZONE 4. APRIL 14. P. $D_0 = -39°\ 1'\ 10''$.

No.	Mag.	I.	II.	III.	IV.	V.	VI.	VII.	T. (h. m. s.)	θ_1	θ_2	Mic.	n	r	i	d	d_2	Mean R.A. 1850.0 (h. m. s.)	Mean Decl. 1850.0 (° ′ ″)
1	9	17.0	37.0	57.0	17.0				9 22 16.89	+12.52	+1.67	IV.	3	34.065	−25 44.8	−6.6	−9.2	9 22 31.06	−39 27 10.8
2	9					45.0	8.0		23 28.18	12.53	1.88	VI.	4	41.820	17 35.6	7.1	6.2	23 42.59	18 58.9
																		25 (38)	
3	10							16.0	25 16	12.54									
4	10	16.0	36.0	56.0	16.0				29 15.92	12.56	1.53	IV.	3	29.615	30 24.2	8.5	10.9	29 30.01	31 53.6
5	9			41.0	2.0				33 1.50?	12.58	1.47	IV.	3	27.780	32 19.3	9.4	11.7	33 15.55	33 50.4
6	9				34.0				37 34.04	12.61	1.73	IV.	4	37.730	21 53.4	10.5	7.8	37 48.38	23 21.7
7	7	39.0	59.0	18.5	39.0				43 38.78	12.65	1.59	IV.	3	32.730	26 37.3	12.0	9.7	43 53.02	28 9.0
8	8	22.0		1.0	21.0				46 21.17	12.67	1.87	IV.	4	43.103	16 16.1	12.6	5.7	46 35.71	17 44.4
9	8		33.0		13.0				48 14.97	12.68	1.54	II.	3	31.203	28 44.6	13.0	10.3	48 27.19	30 17.9
10	9				25.0			4.0	49 4.49?	12.69	1.21	VI.	3	18.690	41 50.8	13.2	15.3	49 18.39	43 29.3
11	8			46.0	6.0	25.0			9 59 25.60?	12.77	1.80	IV.	4	40.720	18 45.7	15.5	6.6	9 59 40.17	20 17.8
12	9	25.0			25.0				10 5 25.05	12.81	1.05	IV.	2	14.376	46 22.0	16.8	17.1	10 5 39.91	48 5.9
13	7	29.0	49.0	9.0					7 8.99	12.83	1.37	IV.	3	25.650	34 32.9	17.2	12.5	7 23.19	36 12.6
14	7		59.0	19.0					7 19.01	12.83	1.43	VII.	3	27.685	32 24.4	17.2	11.7	7 33.27	34 3.3
15	3			6.0	26.0				11 20.00	12.87	1.54	IV.	3	32.125	27 46.7	18.1	9.9	11 40.41	29 24.7
16	8				35.0				10 14 35.05	+12.89	+1.20	IV.	3	19.835	−40 39.5	−19.8	−14.9	10 14 49.14	−39 42 23.2

CORRECTIONS.

Date		Corr. of Clock	Hourly rate	m	n		Zenith Point	Mic. Co.
	h.	s.	s.	s.	s.	s.	° ′ ″	r.
1846, April 14	12	+ 8.139	+ 0.001	0.521	− 0.342	+ 0.246	0 0 1.42	29.999

REMARKS.

(3) 39. Min. of T. one smaller than Transit Z., April 13.

(3) 41. Minute assumed as 42 instead of 43.

(3) 48. Transits probably over I and II, and minute 56 instead of 57.

April 14. At 10ʰ clouds forming; some stars may have been missed in consequence; missed none that were seen above the 9th mag.

(4) 7. Micrometer reading assumed as 33″.230 instead of 32″.730. (See Zone 2, No. 6.)

INSTRUMENT READINGS.

	Date		CIRCLE.						Mean	Barom.	THERMOM.				
			A.	B.	C.	D.	E.	F.			At.	Ex.	U.	L.	I.
	1846, h. m.		° ′ ″						″	in.	°				
Zone 3	April 13, 11 43													37.5	
	12 1		78 19 59.6	62.9	64.4	61.3	67.1	63.3	63.10	30.056	46.5	36.8	46.0	46.5	57.0
Zone 4	14, 9 22		78 19 57.7	58.4	63.0	57.0	65.0	61.0	60.35	29.990	53.0	50.5	51.5	53.0	
	10 31									29.994	53.0	49.2			

Zone 4. April 14. P. $D_o = -39°\ 1'\ 10''$—Continued.

No.	Mag.	I.	II.	III.	IV.	V.	VI.	VII.	T. (h. m. s.)	a_1 (s.)	a_2 (s.)	MICROMETER.		r.	i	d_1	d_2	Mean Right Ascension, 1850.0 (h. m. s.)	Mean Declination, 1850.0 (° ' ")
17	8				35.0				10 24 35.05	+12.98	+1.51	IV.	3	31.774	−28 8.7	−20.7	−10.1	10 24 49.54	−39 29 49.5
18	8	39.0	59.0	19.0	39.0				26 38.90	13.00	1.56	IV.	3	33.595	26 14.5	21.2	9.4	26 53.46	27 55.1
19	8							54.0	10 31 53.88	+13.05	+0.89	IV.	1	9.270	−51 38.7	−22.4	−19.2	10 32 7.82	−39 53 30.3

Zone 5. April 15. P. $D_2 = -38°\ 21'\ 0''$.

No.	Mag.	I.	II.	III.	IV.	V.	VI.	VII.	T. (h. m. s.)	a_1 (s.)	a_2 (s.)	MICROMETER.		r.	i	d_1	d_2	Mean Right Ascension, 1850.0 (h. m. s.)	Mean Declination, 1850.0 (° ' ")
1	6	51.0	11.0	30.5	50.5			49.5	9 10 50.34	+13.32	+0.96	IV.	3	34.545	−25 14.9	−5.6	−8.4	9 11 4.62	−38 46 28.9
2	10			27.0	24.0				15 23.92	13.34	0.52	IV.	2	18.303	42 15.8	6.7	14.2	15 37.78	39 3 36.7
3	9					49.0			16 29.10	13.35	0.40	IV.	1	13.753	46 57.8	7.0	10.1	16 42.85	39 8 20.9
4	6				5.0		44.0		18 4.78	13.35	0.92	IV.	3	34.155	25 39.4	7.4	8.5	18 19.05	38 46 55.3
5	6				11.0			50.0	26 51.15	13.40	1.22	V.	5	51.985	7 6.6	9.6	1.9	27 5.77	28 12.2
6	7	23.5	43.5	3.5					32 23.04	13.44	0.63	III.	3	25.377	34 50.1	11.0	11.7	32 37.11	56 12.8
7	5					27.0	26.5	47.0	33 47.31	13.44	0.74	V.	3	30.105	29 53.3	11.3	10.0	34 1.49	51 14.6
8	7	55.0	15.0	34.5	54.3				37 54.35	13.47	0.69	IV.	3	28.363	31 42.9	12.3	10.5	38 8.51	53 5.7
9	6	26.0	45.5	5.0	24.5				40 24.66	13.48	1.05	IV.	4	42.833	16 33.0	12.9	5.2	40 39.19	37 51.1
10	7	31.0	51.0	10.5	30.0			29.5	49 30.26	13.55	0.70	IV.	3	30.870	29 5.4	15.0	9.7	49 44.51	50 30.7
11	6		3.0	22.5	42.0				54 42.26	13.58	0.84	IV.	3	37.155	22 31.1	16.2	7.4	54 56.78	43 54.7
12	5						15.0	35.0	54 35.76	13.58	0.95	V.	3	41.125	18 21.7	16.2	5.9	54 50.29	39 43.8
13	6			32.0	52.0				56 32.16	13.60	0.89	IV.	3	38.895	20 41.7	16.6	6.8	56 46.65	42 5.1
14	7						50.0	9.5	9 57 10.56	13.60	1.08	VI.	4	47.193	11 55.5	16.7	3.8	9 57 25.24	38 33 19.0
15	9			23.5	43.0				10 2 43.17	13.64	0.26	IV.	2	16.100	44 33.7	17.9	15.0	10 2 57.07	39 6 6.6
16	9				50.0				4 50.04	13.66	0.90	IV.	4	40.973	18 29.8	18.4	6.0	5 4.60	38 39 54.2
17	7	33.0	52.5	12.5	32.0				7 32.03	13.68	0.98	IV.	4	44.600	14 42.7	19.0	4.8	7 46.69	36 5.9
18	8				57.0				8 57.00	13.69	1.05	IV.	4	47.730	11 25.5	19.3	3.7	9 11.74	32 48.5
19	6	22.0	42.0	2.0	22.0				13 21.67	13.73	0.44	IV.	3	24.707	35 32.1	20.2	11.9	13 35.84	57 4.2
20	9		36.5		16.0				24 15.97	13.82	0.95	IV.	4	46.330	12 53.6	22.3	4.2	24 30.74	34 20.1
21	9			19.0					26 19.05	13.84	0.42	IV.	2	26.310	33 53.7	22.8	11.4	26 33.31	55 27.9
22	5			59.0	19.0		58.5	18.0	28 18.91	13.86	0.60	IV.	3	34.005	25 48.7	23.2	8.5	28 33.37	47 20.4
23	9			40.0	6.0				35 5.91	13.92	0.53	IV.	3	32.385	27 30.5	24.5	9.1	35 20.36	38 49 4.1
24	9	13.0	33.0	53.0	12.5				10 57 12.58	14.15	0.08	IV.	2	21.323	30 6.5	28.1	13.2	10 57 26.81	39 0 48.1
25	7	53.5	13.0	33.0	52.5				11 1 52.70	+14.20	+0.58	IV.	4	41.410	−18 2.5	−29.1	−5.9	11 2 7.48	−38 39 37.5

Zone 6. April 16. C. $D_2 = -37°\ 5'\ 50''$.

No.	Mag.	I.	II.	III.	IV.	V.	VI.	VII.	T. (h. m. s.)	a_1 (s.)	a_2 (s.)	MICROMETER.		r.	i	d_1	d_2	Mean Right Ascension, 1850.0 (h. m. s.)	Mean Declination, 1850.0 (° ' ")
1	7				17.0	6.5	26.0	45.7	9 54 47.26	+14.68	+0.05	IV.	4	42.721	−16 40.0	−0.9	−10.0	9 55 1.99	−37 22 40.9
2	7	17.5	36.5	55.0			35.0		10 1 15.53	14.73	−0.03	IV.	3	28.479	31 35.6	2.3	14.3	10 1 30.23	37 42.2
3	9.10				41.0?			30.0?	3 41.43?	14.75	+0.05	IV.	3	37.384	12 16.8	2.6	11.6	3 56.23	18 20.2
4	7							30.0	5 31.74	14.76	0.00	VII.	3	29.309	30 42.7	3.2	14.0	5 46.50	36 49.9
5	8				16.0		36.5		7 37.71	14.78	0.01	VI.	3	29.615	30 23.9	3.6	13.9	7 52.50	36 31.4
6	7	37.2	57.0?	16.5		54.7		33.5	37 35.48	15.03	0.26	IV.	4	44.112	15 12.8	9.2	9.6	37 50.77	21 21.6
7	8		26.0		4.5				41 4.77	15.06	0.06	IV.	2	16.336	44 19.1	9.8	18.0	41 19.09	50 36.9
8	7			23.0				1.2	42 3.28	15.07	0.21	V.	3	34.807	24 58.2	10.0	12.4	42 18.56	31 10.6
9	8	17.0			55.5?		31.5		46 55.70	15.11	0.30	IV.	4	42.526	16 52.4	10.8	10.0	47 11.11	23 3.2
10	7								47 .	15.12			2	12.	49 .			48 .	55 .
11	7.8			35.7	55.7		35.5	55.0	50 56.00	15.15	0.05	IV.	2	12.436	48 23.4	11.4	19.2	51 11.23	54 44.0
12	7.8				33.5	53.5			52 55.03	15.17	0.29	VI.	3	37.097	22 34.4	11.7	11.7	53 10.49	28 47.8
13	9								10 57 .	+15.22	+0.26	IV.	3	30.561	−29 24.9	−12.4	−13.6	10 58 .	−37 35 40.9

CORRECTIONS.

Date.	Corr. of Clock.	Hourly rate.	m	n	ϵ	Zenith Point.	Mic. Co.
1846, April 15, 12h	+8.214 s.	+0.004 s.	+0.521 s.	−0.342 s.	+0.246 s.	0 0 0.47	30.007 r.

REMARKS.

April 15. Very clear.
April 16. Clear, except cloud-bank near horizon; wind fresh, causing the lamp to flare, and rendering the illumination of the wires very unsteady; magnitudes consequently doubtful, and several stars missed.

INSTRUMENT READINGS.

	Date.	CIRCLE. A.	B.	C.	D.	E.	F.	Mean.	Barom. (in.)	THERMOM. At.	Ex.	U.	L.	I.
Zone 5	1846. April 15, 9 11	77 39 57.5	59.5	63.5	57.5	66.8	62.5	61.22	30.235	56.0	50.0			
	10	77 39 56	58	62	56	65.3	61	59.72						
	11 1	55	57	61	55	64.3	60	58.72	30.282	52.0	43.0	54.0	50.0	
Zone 6	16, 9 50	76 24 60.6	61.1	64.0	60.1	67.9	63.0	62.78	30.324	52.0	46.7	50.0	50.3	52.2
	10 30	60.1	61.3	64.0	60.0	67.5	62.7	62.60	30.334	51.0	46.1	49.7	49.8	

Zone 6. April 16. C. $D_1 = -37°$ 5' 50"—Continued.

No.	Mag.	I.	II.	III.	IV.	V.	VI.	VII.	T. (h m s)	a_1	a_2	MICROMETER		r.	i.	d_1	d_2	Mean Right Ascension, 1850.0	Mean Declination, 1850.0
14	6	35.0	54.0	13.5		52.5			11 0 33.00	+15.25	+0.26	IV.	3	30.461	−29 31.2	−12.8	−13.7	11 0 48.51	−37 35 47.7
15	9							48.7	0 50.40	15.25	0.23	IV.	3	26.066	34 6.9	12.9	15.0	1 5.88	40 24.6
16	8				9.2			7.5	3 9.25	15.27	0.28	IV.	3	31.660	28 15.9	13.2	13.3	3 24.80	34 32.4
17	8.9								3 ..	15.27	0.30	IV.	3	33.551	26 17.3	13.2	12.7	4 ..	32 33.2
18	8	53.7	12.5						7 51.52	15.32	0.36	II.	3	38.862	20 43.3	13.9	11.2	8 7.20	26 58.4
19	7			50.6	10.0				8 10.01	15.33	0.36	IV.	3	39.350	20 13.4	13.9	11.0	8 25.70	26 28.3
20	7			9.0	28.2	47.5		7.0?	9 28.23?	15.34	0.31	IV.	3	31.321	28 37.3	14.1	13.4	9 43.88?	34 54.8
21	8				12.7	33.0		11.0	10 13.01	15.35	0.33	IV.	3	32.338	27 33.5	14.2	13.1	10 28.70	33 50.8
22	7		20.7	40.0	59.2	18.7			13 59.35	15.39	0.37	IV.	3	36.692	23 0.1	14.7	11.6	14 15.11	29 16.6
23	8			58.3		37.6			16 17.93	15.41	0.32	IV.	3	26.831	33 18.8	15.0	14.8	16 33.66	39 38.6
24	7			32.0	51.7		30.0	49.2	18 51.39	15.44	0.46	IV.	4	45.490	13 46.3	15.3	9.2	19 7.29	20 0.8
25	8						39.0	58.2	19 0.16	15.44	0.47	VI.	3	38.388	21 13.5	15.4	11.3	19 16.01	27 30.2
26	6		30.3	49.3	8.7		17.5	7.0	22 8.81	15.48	0.36	IV.	3	28.549	31 31.2	15.7	14.2	22 24.65	37 51.1
27	8			36.0		16.0			26 55.94	15.53	0.21	IV.	2	10.398	50 31.1	16.3	19.9	27 11.68	56 57.3
28	8.9							44.7	27 46.18	15.54	0.22	IV.	2	8.882	52 5.7	16.4	20.4	28 1.04	58 32.5
29	8		4.5	24.0		3.2			30 43.54	15.57	0.38	IV.	3	27.578	38 32.0	16.7	14.6	30 59.49	38 53.3
30	7			59.0	18.7		57.0	16.2	32 18.30	15.59	0.56	IV.	4	48.771	10 20.2	16.9	8.2	32 34.45	16 35.3
31	8				29.2	49.0			34 29.40	15.62	0.46	IV.	3	35.420	24 20.1	17.1	12.2	34 45.48	30 39.4
32	8.9							7.5	34 9.33	15.61	0.49	VII.	3	38.419	21 11.0	17.0	11.3	34 25.43	27 29.3
33	8					38.0			37 18.57	15.65	0.47	V.	3	35.244	24 31.0	17.4	12.2	37 34.69	30 50.6
34	8					37.5		14.0	39 17.?	15.66	0.57	V.	4	46.970	12 12.8	17.5	8.7	38 (33.)?	18 29.0
35	9							47.5	38 49.44	15.67	0.56	VII.	4	46.234	12 57.9	17.5	9.0	39 5.67	19 14.4
36	9				57.5				41 57.50	15.70	0.58	IV.	4	45.841	13 24.1	17.8	9.1	42 13.78	19 41.0
37	8	41.5						35.0	44 ? ?	15.71	0.61	IV.	4	49.598	9 28.4	18.0	8.0	44 ..	15 44.4
38	6.7				58.2	17.5	36.2		44 57.93	15.74	0.51	IV.	3	35.762	23 58.4	18.1	12.1	45 14.18	30 18.6
39	7					19.7	38.5	58.5	46 0.03	15.75	0.48	IV.	3	29.763	30 14.8	18.2	13.9	46 16.26	36 36.9
40	8			36.0	55.7				48 55.57	15.79	0.53		3	36.	24 ..			49 11.89	30 ..
41	6.7				38.0		17.0	36.2	11 49 38.04	+15.79	+0.46	IV.	3	26.709	−33 20.8	−18.6	−14.8	11 49 54.29	−37 39 44.2

Zone 7. April 16. C. $D_2 = -37°$ 5' 50".

No.	Mag.	I.	II.	III.	IV.	V.	VI.	VII.	T. (h m s)	a_1	a_2	MICROMETER		r.	i.	d_1	d_2	Mean Right Ascension, 1850.0	Mean Declination, 1850.0
1	6	11.1	30.5	49.5	9.0	28.2	47.7	6.5	14 11 8.91	+17.76	+0.81	IV.	4	53.630	−5 15.2	−17.0	−6.4	14 11 27.51	−37 11 28.7
2	8				57.0				18 57.05	17.87	0.36	IV.	1	14.781	46 31.2	16.3	18.6	19 15.28	52 56.1
3	7				44.5	4.0	23.7		21 44.57	17.91	0.36	IV.	2	13.811	46 57.1	16.0	18.9	22 2.84	53 22.0
4	7		4.2		43.2		22.0		25 43.17	17.97	0.38	IV.	2	16.414	44 14.2	15.5	18.1	26 1.52	50 37.8
5	8.9							6.0	29 8.04	18.02	0.83	VII.	4	54.885	3 54.7	15.2	6.3	29 26.89	10 6.2
6	5.6				1.5	21.2	59.9	19.1	32 21.11	18.07	0.84	IV.	4	56.204	2 33.7	14.7	6.0	32 40.02	8 44.4
7	9.10					53.0			34 33.59	18.10	0.61	V.	3	35.972	23 45.1	14.5	12.0	34 52.29	30 1.6
8	7		44.2		23.2	43.0	2.3	21.8	37 23.36	18.14	0.51	IV.	3	27.267	32 51.6	14.2	14.6	37 42.01	39 10.4
9	9	23.0	42.8						40 21.36	18.19	0.34	IV.	2	12.665	48 9.0	13.8	19.2	40 39.89	54 32.0
10	9				37.5	57.0			41 37.53	18.20	0.44	IV.	2	21.904	39 29.8	13.6	16.4	41 56.17	44 49.8
11	7				32.7	52.2		30.8	43 32.67	18.23	0.51	IV.	3	28.261	31 49.3	13.4	14.1	43 51.41	38 7.0
12	9						35.5		44 56.66	18.25	0.51	V.	3	27.888	32 12.3	13.2	14.5	45 15.42	38 30.0
13	9							4.0	45 15.73	18.25	0.52	VII.	3	29.750	30 52.6	13.1	14.1	45 34.50	37 9.8
14	9				5.7	25.6		4.2	49 15.00	18.31	0.46	IV.	3	23.796	36 29.1	12.6	15.8	49 34.67	42 47.4
15	7							25.7	40 27.66	18.32	0.75	VII.	4	48.746	10 20.1	12.6	8.1	49 46.73	16 30.8
16	7.8					44.0	3.5	22.8	51 24.67	18.35	0.62	IV.	3	38.377	21 14.5	12.3	11.3	51 43.64	27 28.1
17	7.8		37.0	56.6	15.7		54.6	13.7	14 57 15.80	18.43	0.69	IV.	4	43.920	15 24.7	11.4	9.6	14 57 34.92	21 35.7
18	9				24.0	43.7	2.2		15 0 43.56?	18.48	0.64	IV.	3	39.669	19 53.2	11.0	10.9	15 1 2.68?	26 5.1
19	7.8				14.7	34.5	53.0		15 4 14.58	+18.53	+0.31	IV.	2	11.691	−49 10.0	−10.5	−19.5	15 4 33.42	−37 55 30.0

CORRECTIONS.

Date.		Corr. of Clock.	Hourly rate.	m	n	c	Zenith Point.	Mic. Co.
		s.	s.	s.	s.	s.	° ' "	r.
1846. April 16,	h. 12	+ 8.190	+ 0.006	+ 0.521	− 0.342	+ 0.246	0 0 0.60	30.005
16,	15						0 0 0.47	30.005

INSTRUMENT READINGS.

	Date.		CIRCLE.							Barom.	THERMOM.				
			A.	B.	C.	D.	E.	F.	Mean.		At.	Ex.	U.	L.	I.
	1846.	h. m.	° '							in.	°	°	°	°	°
Zone 6	April 16,	11 49	76 24	59.6	60.3	61.1	60.1	67.5	62.0 62.27	30.320	50.7	45.6	49.9	50.0	52.2
		13 55		57.0	59.3	61.2	58.6	65.0	59.2 60.05				47.8	48.5	52.2
Zone 7		14 11								30.302	49.0	43.2			
		14 57										43.3			
		15 22								30.300	48.0	42.1			
		15 30	55.9	60.0	61.3	57.9	65.7	58.0	59.80				48.1	48.2	52.0

REMARKS.

April 16. 12^h moved circle for other observations.
14^h 0^m to 14^h 22^m cap on.
15^h 20^m cloud bank rising; soon after obscured.

ZONE 7. APRIL 16. C. $D_z = -37°\ 5'\ 50''$ — Continued.

No.	Mag.	I.	II.	III.	IV.	V.	VI.	VII.	T. (h m s)	a_1	a_2
20	7.8	··	24.7	43.4	3.5	··	··	2.5	15 7 3.41?	+18.57	+0.35
21	7	34.5	53.3	12.7	31.7	50.3	9.8	29.7	11 31.85	18.63	0.49
22	7.8	··	27.7	47.7	7.0	··	··	5.7	15 7.04	18.68	0.51
23	8	18.5	38.	··	16.5	36.5	··	15.3	15 16.83	18.68	0.32
24	7	··	49.5	9.0	28.2	··	··	26.5	15 22 28.31	+18.79	+0.56

No.	MICROMETER			i (′ ″)	d_1	d_2	Mean Right Ascension, 1850.0 (h m s)	Mean Declination, 1850.0 (° ′ ″)
20	IV.	2	13.804	−46 57.5	−10.1	−18.8	15 7 22.33	−37 53 16.4
21	IV.	3	26.132	34 2.7	9.5	15.0	11 50.97	40 17.2
22	IV.	3	28.389	31 41.3	9.0	14.2	15 26.23	37 54.5
23	IV.	3	28.969	31 4.7	9.0	14.1	15 36.03	37 17.8
24	IV.	3	32.748	−27 7.5	−8.0	−12.9	15 22 47.66	−37 33 18.4

ZONE 8. APRIL 17. P. $D_z = -35°\ 50'\ 10''$.

No.	Mag.	I.	II.	III.	IV.	V.	VI.	VII.	T. (h m s)	a_1	a_2
1	8	22.0	41.0	··	··	19.0	··	··	9 4 19.13	+13.94	+0.88
2	8	··	··	··	··	54.0	··	··	13 54.06	13.98	0.87
3	8	··	··	··	··	··	52.0	··	18 32.90	14.00	0.90
4	9.10	··	··	··	··	0.0	··	··	21 0.00	14.01	
5	8	··	··	32.5	51.5	··	··	··	23 51.59	14.02	0.87
6	7	··	··	··	··	··	25.0	··	25 5.94	14.03	0.95
7	8	··	··	··	··	55.0	··	52.0	27 54.91	14.04	0.93
8	7	32.0	51.0	10.0	29.0	··	··	··	31 29.13	14.06	0.92
9	7	17.5	36.5	56.0	15.0	··	··	··	34 14.95	14.07	0.88
10	8	··	··	··	13.0	32.5	··	··	35 32.32	14.08	0.89
11	6	58.5	17.0	37.0	56.0	··	··	53.0	42 55.78	14.11	0.88
12	7	56.0	··	34.0	53.5	··	··	··	47 53.38	14.14	0.87
13	8	··	··	18.0	37.0	··	··	15.0?	52 37.30	14.17	1.01
14	8	··	··	24.5	44.0	3.0	··	··	9 58 43.82	+14.21	1.03
15	7	21.0	40.5	59.5	18.5	··	··	16.0	10 1 18.67	14.22	0.89
16	8	··	··	··	··	7.0	··	··	3 7.00	14.24	1.01
17	8	··	··	··	··	53.0	··	··	7 52.97	14.27	0.05
18	7	··	··	··	··	52.0	11.0	30.0	8 32.80	14.28	0.00
19	6	··	··	28.0	47.0	6.0	··	··	11 47.00	14.30	0.03
20	9	··	··	··	5.0	··	··	··	14 24.12	14.32	0.06
21	8	18.0	37.0	56.0	15.0	··	··	··	20 15.19	14.36	0.95
22	9	··	··	··	··	··	··	6.0	22 8.80	14.37	1.03
23	6	21.0	40.0	59.5	18.0	··	··	··	27 18.38	14.42	0.93
24	7	··	··	··	9.0	28.0	47.5	··	28 28.16	14.43	0.94
25	8	13.0	32.0	··	··	··	··	··	37 10.08	14.50	1.08
26	6	35.0	··	··	··	··	10.0	29.0	37 31.95	14.50	1.05
27	8	··	··	··	··	··	21.0	40.0	38 42.86	14.51	1.05
28	8	··	24.0	··	2.0	··	··	··	44 2.09	14.55	1.06
29	3	31.0	50.0	9.5	28.5	47.5	6.5	25.7	49 28.38	14.60	1.03
30	7	··	··	39.0	58.0	17.0	··	··	10 56 57.98	14.67	1.13
31	9	··	··	··	30.0	··	8.0	27.0	11 10 29.85	14.80	1.06
32	9	··	2.5	21.6	40.5	··	··	··	18 40.67	14.88	1.06
33	8	··	··	··	··	··	13.0	32.0	20 34.82	14.90	1.09
34	10	··	··	··	··	··	47.0	··	29 8.90	14.97	1.12
35	8	4.6	24.0	43.0	··	21.0	··	··	29 2.02	14.99	1.08
36	9	··	··	··	··	8.5	··	47.0	31 49.40	15.02	1.04
37	6	46.5	5.5	24.7	43.5	2.5	22.0	41.0	35 43.77	15.06	1.10
38	9	25.4	44.6	··	··	41.0	··	··	43 22.28	15.15	1.17
39	10	··	··	··	··	54.0	··	··	52 54.04	15.26	1.06
40	9	··	··	52.0	··	30.0	··	··	11 57 30.25	15.31	1.05
41	10	··	··	··	55.0	··	··	12.0	12 2 14.40	15.37	1.14
42	9	··	··	··	45.0	4.0	··	··	12 5 4.10	+15.40	+1.07

No.	MICROMETER			i (′ ″)	d_1	d_2	Mean Right Ascension, 1850.0 (h m s)	Mean Declination, 1850.0 (° ′ ″)
1	IV.	3	35.955	−23 47.5	−1.4	−10.3	9 4 33.95	−36 14 9.2
2	IV.	3	31.000	28 57.3	3.0	11.5	14 8.91	19 22.6
3	IV.	3	36.280	23 26.1	4.9	10.2	18 47.80	13 51.2
4							21(14).	
5	IV.	3	24.703	35 32.3	6.2	13.1	24 6.48	26 1.6
6	IV.	3	44.250	15 5.7	6.5	8.3	25 20.92	5 30.4
7	IV.	4	39.960	19 33.4	7.2	9.3	28 9.88	9 59.9
8	IV.	3	34.880	24 53.7	8.1	10.5	31 44.11	15 22.3
9	IV.	3	22.850	37 28.5	8.6	13.6	34 29.90	28 0.7
10	IV.	3	26.610	33 32.8	8.9	12.7	35 47.29	24 4.4
11	IV.	2	21.566	38 51.1	10.6	13.9	43 10.77	29 25.6
12	IV.	2	16.365	44 17.2	11.7	15.3	48 8.39	34 54.2
13	IV.	5	45.240	10 55.6	12.8	7.1	52 52.48	36 1 25.5
14	IV.	5	52.753	6 12.5	14.1	5.9	9 58 59.06	35 56 42.5
15	IV.	5	15.205	43 30.0	14.6	15.5	10 1 33.78	36 30 10.1
16	IV.	5	47.590	11 34.4	15.0	7.4	3 22.25	36 2 6.8
17	IV.	5	54.870	3 59.7	16.0	5.4	8 8.29	35 54 31.1
18	V.	4	40.203	19 17.9	16.1	9.2	8 48.08	36 9 53.2
19	IV.	5	46.350	12 54.2	16.8	7.6	12 2.33	3 28.6
20	IV.	3	27.955	32 8.3	17.3	12.3	14 39.40	22 47.9
21	IV.	3	23.674	36 36.8	18.5	13.4	20 30.50	27 18.7
22	VII.	4	41.570	17 50.8	18.8	8.9	22 24.20	8 28.5
23	IV.	2	14.624	46 6.4	19.8	15.7	27 33.73	36 51.9
24	IV.	2	16.185	44 28.4	20.0	15.3	28 43.53	35 53.7
25	II.	4	47.291	11 53.4	21.6	7.5	37 25.66	2 32.5
26	IV.	4	41.507	17 56.5	21.6	8.9	37 47.50	8 37.0
27	VI.	4	40.764	18 42.1	21.8	9.1	38 55.42	9 23.0
28	IV.	4	40.440	19 3.4	22.8	9.2	44 17.70	9 45.4
29	IV.	3	30.756	29 12.5	23.7	11.6	49 44.01	36 19 57.8
30	IV.	5	54.530	4 21.0	24.9	5.5	10 57 13.78	35 55 1.4
31	VII.	3	28.600	31 27.2	26.9	12.1	11 10 45.71	36 22 16.2
32	IV.	3.	26.458	33 42.0	28.0	12.7	18 56.61	24 32.7
33	VII.	3	34.950	24 48.6	28.2	10.5	20 50.81	15 37.3
34	VI.	3	37.880	21 45.2	29.0	9.8	29 24.99	12 34.0
35	IV.	3	26.300	33 52.3	29.3	12.7	29 18.09	24 44.3
36	VII.	1	15.474	45 9.2	29.6	15.5	32 5.46	36 4.3
37	V.	3	29.454	30 34.4	30.1	11.9	35 59.93	21 26.4
38	V.	4	44.026	15 17.8	30.9	8.3	43 38.60	6 7.0
39	IV.	2	12.070	47 49.2	31.9	16.1	53 10.36	38 47.2
40	IV.	1	8.890	52 2.3	32.3	17.2	11 57 46.61	43 1.8
41	VII.	3	29.390	30 37.7	32.7	11.9	12 2 30.91	21 32.3
42	IV.	1	10.220	−50 39.2	−33.0	−16.8	12 5 20.57	−36 41 39.0

CORRECTIONS.

Date.	Corr. of Clock.	Hourly rate.	m (″)	n (″)	c	Zenith Point.	Mic. Co.
1846. April 17,	12h + 8.564 s	+ 0.008 s	+ 0.521 s	− 0.312 s	+ 0.246 s	0 0 1.04	r 30.008

INSTRUMENT READINGS.

Date.	CIRCLE.							Barom.	THERMOM.				
		A.	B.	C.	D.	E.	F.	Mean.	(In.)	At.	Ex.	U.	L.	I.
Zone 8 April 17, 9 4 (h m)	75 9 61.4	57.6	64.2	56.7	66.4	63.4	61.62	30.200	61.0	64.5			
10 38	··	··	··	··	··	··	··	30.220	61.5	63.5			
12 5	75 9 61.4	57.6	64.2	56.7	66.4	63.4	61.62	30.222	63.5	61.5			

REMARKS.

ZONE 9. APRIL 18. C. $D_0 = -34°\ 35'\ 0''$.

No.	Mag.	I.	II.	III.	IV.	V.	VI.	VII.	T.	a_1	a	Mic.		r	i	d_1	d_2	Mean Right Ascension, 1850.0	Mean Declination, 1850.0
									h. m. s.	s.	s.			$r.$	′ ″	″	″	h. m. s.	° ′ ″
1	7		4.8	22.7	41.7	0.7		38.2	9 28 41.75	+15.71	+0.31	IV.	3	25.865	−34 19.4	−0.5	6.2	9 28 57.77	−35 9 26.1
2	7			38.0		16.8		53.5	30 57.18	15.72	0.19	IV.	2	10.621	50 17.0	1.1	9.4	31 13.08	25 27.5
3	9		26.0	57.0					34 5.	15.73	0.28	III.	3	20.778	39 38.3	1.9	7.2	34 (20).	14 47.4
4	8			19.5		57.0	15.6	34.5	34 38.06	15.74	0.23	IV.	3	14.646	46 2.9	2.0	8.5	34 54.03	21 13.4
5	8							4.0?	36 7.52	15.74	0.32	VII.	3	25.022	35 11.5	2.4	6.3	36 23.58	10 20.2
6	7.8			4.9	22.8	42.0	0.8		39 23.22	15.76	0.32	IV.	3	25.071	35 9.3	3.3	6.3	39 39.30	10 18.9
7	9		3.2		43.0		19.2		42 41.22	15.78	0.29	IV.	2	19.802	40 41.6	4.1	7.4	42 57.29	15 53.1
8	9			7.0		41.6		20.0	46 22.10	15.80	0.30	IV.	2	19.849	40 38.6	5.0	7.4	46 38.20	35 15 51.0
9	9					35.0	53.0		49 15.87	15.81	0.46	V.	4	39.300	20 14.6	5.7	3.3	49 32.14	34 55 23.6
10	6.7		32.6		10.0		48.0	6.7	52 10.22	15.83	0.36	IV.	3	24.915	35 18.9	6.3	6.4	52 26.41	35 10 31.6
11	9				25.0	44.5	2.8	21.3	53 25.12	15.83	0.29	IV.	3	16.163	44 27.8	6.6	8.2	53 41.24	19 42.6
12	9		40.0		18.5				58 59.22	15.86	0.35	IV.	3	20.829	39 35.2	7.9	7.2	59 15.43	14 50.3
13	9							55.0	9 58 58.58	15.86	0.43	VII.	3	31.035	28 54.3	7.9	5.0	9 59 14.87	4 7.2
14	9						17.3	36.0	10 0 39.69	15.87	0.45	VI.	3	33.579	26 15.2	8.2	4.5	10 0 56.01	1 27.9
15	7			29.0	48.0	6.7	25.1	44.0	2 47.75	15.89	0.40	IV.	3	27.949	32 8.7	8.6	5.7	3 4.04	7 23.0
16	9		37.0	56.0					6 14.79	15.91	0.31	III.	2	16.112	44 33.0	9.4	8.2	6 31.01	35 19 50.6
17	9		2.8	22.0	41.0		18.5		8 40.80	15.93	0.60	IV.	4	50.056	8 59.6	9.9	1.1	8 57.33	34 44 10.6
18	8			22.0	40.5	59.2	18.2	36.6	11 40.52	15.95	0.48	IV.	3	34.369	25 26.0	10.5	4.3	11 56.95	35 0 40.8
19	9		42.0	1.0		48.7			17 19.76	15.98	0.55	IV.	3	41.341	18 8.4	11.5	2.9	17 36.29	34 53 22.8
20	7.8		37.0?		15.7	35.2		12.7	21 15.96	16.01	0.29	IV.	2	9.031	51 56.4	12.3	9.8	21 32.26	35 27 18.5
21	8		49.7	8.6		46.7			26 27.55	16.05	0.38	IV.	3	18.162	42 22.5	13.2	7.8	26 43.98	35 17 43.5
22	7			18.0	36.5	55.0	14.5	32.7	30 36.58	16.08	0.56	IV.	3	38.342	21 16.7	13.9	3.5	30 53.22	34 56 34.1
23	7.8		7.0	25.5	44.2		22.0	41.0	33 44.45	16.10	0.56	IV.	3	37.324	22 20.6	14.5	3.7	34 1.11	57 38.8
24	7		55.0	14.0	32.2	41.2		19.2	34 32.58	16.11	0.57	IV.	3	38.011	21 37.3	14.6	3.6	34 49.26	34 56 55.5
25	8.9		12.0	30.2	49.3		27.0	46.0	39 49.38	16.15	0.40	IV.	2	17.505	43 5.8	15.5	7.9	40 5.93	35 18 29.2
26	8.9			25.0	44.2				40 44.04	16.16	0.40	IV.	3	15.839	44 48.1	15.6	8.3	41 0.60	20 12.0
27	9			34.0		12.0		48.7	42 52.77	16.17	0.55	IV.	3	34.432	25 22.1	16.0	4.3	43 9.49	35 0 42.4
28	9						17.5	35.5	43 39.54	16.18	0.57	VI.	3	35.954	23 46.0	16.1	4.0	43 56.29	34 59 6.1
29	7				46.2	5.0	23.5	42.5	45 46.21	16.20	0.72	VI.	4	52.641	6 16.4	16.5	0.6	46 3.13	41 33.5
30	9					40.0	59.4		48 2.91	16.22	0.73	VI.	4	52.334	6 35.9	16.8	0.6	48 19.86	41 53.3
31	9						10.2	29.0	50 32.75	16.24	0.66	VI.	3	44.250	15 5.0	17.2	2.3	50 49.65	50 24.5
32	9		17.0		13.0				50 54.40	16.24	0.65	IV.	3	42.630	16 47.3	17.2	2.6	51 11.29	52 7.1
33	9				50.0			27.7	53 31.36	16.26	0.71	V.	3	49.100	10 1.1	17.6	1.3	53 48.33	45 20.0
34	9	17.57							56 13.69	16.29	0.67	I.	3	43.844	15 30.1	18.0	2.1	56 30.65	50 50.5
35	5.6		55.0	14.0	32.8		10.6	29.2	10 57 32.83	16.30	0.60	IV.	3	35.311	24 26.9	18.2	4.1	10 57 49.73	34 59 49.2
36	9		19.8	39.0	42.0			41.2	11 2 43.	16.34	0.48	IV.	2	18.981	41 33.1	18.9	7.6	11 2 (59)	35 16 59.6
37	9							36.0	2 39.21	16.34	0.53	VII.	2	24.381	35 53.6	18.9	6.4	2 56.08	11 18.9
38	9	18.2			14.7		52.8		7 14.87	16.38	0.49	IV.	2	18.208	42 21.7	19.5	7.7	7 31.74	35 17 48.9
39	9				27.0				8 8.25	16.39	0.78	V.	4	52.544	6 23.1	19.6	0.6	8 25.42	34 41 43.3
40	7.8	14.7	33.0	52.0			29.0	48.2	12 51.80	16.44	0.53	IV.	3	21.046	39 21.6	20.3	7.2	13 8.77	35 14 49.1
41	7.8		0.1		38.0			15.0	13 37.75	16.44	0.79	IV.	4	52.072	6 53.1	20.3	0.7	13 54.98	34 42 14.1
42	6.7							38.0	15 41.41	16.46	0.48	V.	1	15.569	45 4.0	20.6	8.3	15 58.35	35 20 32.9
43	7			38.0	57.2	16.0	34.2	53.2	17 56.89	16.48	0.54	IV.	2	21.469	38 57.3	20.8	7.1	18 13.91	35 14 25.2
44	9		43.0	1.2		39.0	57.5	16.5	20 20.23	16.50	0.80	IV.	4	50.884	8 7.5	21.2	0.9	20 37.53	34 43 29.6
45	9		59.0		35.7		13.0		23 35.61	16.54	0.75	IV.	4	45.402	13 51.9	21.5	2.1	23 52.00	34 49 15.5
46	7		37.2	56.8		34.2	53.5		25 15.41	16.55	0.50	IV.	3	13.471	47 16.6	21.7	8.8	25 32.46	35 22 47.1
47	8.9				23.5	42.8		1.2	26 23.31	16.56	0.50	IV.	3	13.761	46 58.2	21.8	8.7	26 40.37	22 28.7
48	8		16.8	35.5	54.3		32.1	51.2	11 28 54.46	+16.59	+0.55	IV.	3	18.529	−41 59.6	−22.1	−7.7	11 29 11.60	−35 17 29.4

CORRECTIONS.

Date.	Corr. of Clock.	Hourly rate.	m	n	c	Zenith Point.	Mic. Co.
	h.	s.	s.	s.	s.	° ′ ″	$r.$
1846. April 18,	12	+ 9.100	+ 0.009	+ 0.521	− 0.342	+ 0.246	0 0 2.02	30.006

REMARKS.

April 18. Cloudy near horizon; lamp flaring badly at times, rendering transits of small stars doubtful.

(9) 36. Transits discordant.

(9) 41.47. Transits over T. VI assumed as recorded over T. VII.

INSTRUMENT READINGS.

	Date.	CIRCLE.							Barom.	THERMOM.				
		A.	B.	C.	D.	E.	F.	Mean.		At.	Ex.	U.	L.	I.
		° ′ ″						″	in.					
Zone 9	1846. April 18, 9 28	73 54 60.4	57.1	61.4	58.9	59.8	55.8	58.90	30.076	67.2	70.0	69.4	65.4	61.3
	10 6										67.6			
	10 15	73 54 60.9	67.4	61.9	69.3	60.3	65.0	59.13				69	66	
	10 30								30.098	68.8	67.6			
	11 2										67.6			
	11 28	60.6	67.0	61.1	69.0	60.1	66.1	58.98	30.082	69.0	67.5	68.4	66.4	62.0

ZONE 10. APRIL 20. P. D. = −33° 19′ 50″.

Columns I–VII are SECONDS OF TRANSIT.

No.	Mag.	I	II	III	IV	V	VI	VII	T	a_1	a_2	Mic.	n	r	i	d_1	d_2	Mean Right Ascension, 1850.0	Mean Declination, 1850.0
									h. m. s.	s.	s.			r.	′ ″	″	″	h. m. s.	° ′ ″
1	8	13.0		50.0	8.5				9 39 8.57	+16.16	−0.02	IV.	3	22.540	−37 48.0	−7.2	−6.9	9 39 24.71	−33 57 52.1
2	9		31.0		14.0				42 14.00	16.17	+0.13	IV.	4	42.600	16 47.7	7.8	3.1	42 30.30	36 48.6
3	8				19.0				43 19.06	16.18	0.04	IV.	3	28.490	31 34.9	8.1	5.8	43 35.28	51 38.8
4	9				37.0				46 37.05	16.20	0.05	IV.	3	27.810	32 17.4	8.8	5.9	46 53.30	52 22.1
5	8				8.0			3.0	49 7.75	16.21	+0.08	IV.	3	33.800	26 1.5	9.4	4.8	49 24.04	33 46, 5.7
6	7					32.0	51.0	9.5	50 13.70	16.21	−0.04	V.	2	18.960	41 34.2	9.6	7.6	50 29.87	34 1 41.4
7	7	27.0	46.0	4.0	22.0				54 22.56	16.23	+0.04	IV.	3	25.625	34 34.5	10.5	6.3	54 38.83	33 54 41.3
8	6			41.0			36.0	55.0	54 59.31	16.24	0.10	IV.	3	33.810	26 0.9	10.6	4.8	55 15.65	46 6.3
9	7	57.0		35.0					57 53.02	16.25	+0.06	III.	3	28.040	32 3.0	11.2	5.9	58 9.33	33 52 10.1
10	6				37.5	56.0	14.0	33.0	9 58 37.23	16.25	−0.07	V.	2	11.690	49 9.8	11.4	9.1	9 58 53.41	34 9 20.3
11	8	10.0	29.0	47.0					10 2 5.80	16.27	−0.09	III.	1	9.315	51 35.9	12.2	9.5	10 2 22.04	34 11 47.6
12	8						41.0	0.0	2 4.25	16.27	+0.13	VI.	3	36.407	23 17.8	12.1	4.3	2 20.65	33 43 24.2
13	8	58.0	16.0	35.0					4 53.28	16.29	+0.20	III.	3	43.800	15 33.7	12.7	2.9	5 9.77	33 35 39.5
14	8						8.0	27.0	4 31.09	16.29	0.00	IV.	2	17.630	42 57.9	12.6	7.9	4 47.38	34 3 8.4
15	6											IV.	4	43.800	15 32.2	13.	2.9	(6)	33 35 (38)
16	8			43.0					8 1.56	16.31	−0.06	III.	1	9.210	51 42.5	13.3	9.6	8 17.81	34 11 55.4
17	8					2.0	21.0		8 43.74	16.31	+0.13	V.	3	34.340	25 27.8	13.5	4.7	8 0.18	33 45 35.0
18	8						5.0		9 28.01	16.32	0.12	VI.	3	33.100	26 45.2	13.7	4.9	9 44.45	46 53.8
19	7					45.0	3.0		10 26.28	16.32	0.18	V.	3	39.650	19 54.4	13.9	3.7	10 42.78	40 2.0
20	7		37.0	55.0	13.5				12 13.72	16.33	0.09	IV.	3	28.220	31 51.8	14.2	5.8	12 30.14	52 1.8
21	8				47.0				11 28.50	16.33	0.19	V.	4	39.600	19 55.5	14.0	3.7	11 45.02	40 3.2
22	8					27.0	45.0		13 8.24	16.34	0.14	V.	4	34.280	25 29.7	14.4	4.7	13 24.72	33 45 38.8
23	8						47.5	6.0	14 10.36	16.34	0.02	VI.	3	18.595	41 55.1	14.6	7.7	14 26.72	34 2 7.4
24	8					58.0		34.0	16 39.07	16.36	0.24	V.	4	48.490	10 37.6	15.1	2.0	16 55.67	33 30 44.7
25	8	37.0		15.0		10.0			20 33.02	16.38	0.07	IV.	3	24.110	36 9.5	15.8	6.6	20 49.47	56 21.9
26	8	38.0		16.0					20 34.02	16.38	0.12	III.	3	30.440	29 32.5	15.8	5.4	20 50.52	49 43.7
27	6					5.0	23.0		20 46.29	16.38	0.21	V.	4	41.540	17 53.9	15.9	3.3	21 2.88	38 3.1
28	8						56.0		21 19.13	16.39	0.26	V.	5	47.750	11 26.4	16.0	2.2	21 35.78	31 34.6
29	8							52.0	21 56.56	16.39	0.24	VII.	5	44.890	14 25.8	16.1	2.7	22 13.19	34 34.6
30	7		19.0	38.0					24 56.25	16.41	+0.23	III.	1	42.180	17 14.4	16.6	3.2	25 12.89	33 37 24.2
31	9		14.0						25 51.25	16.42	−0.04	II.	1	8.800	52 7.7	16.8	9.6	26 7.63	34 12 24.1
32	9					39.0			28 20.37	16.43	+0.02	V.	2	14.710	46 0.7	17.3	8.4	28 36.82	34 6 16.4
33	7				54.0	12.0			29 53.74	16.44	0.10	IV.	3	25.900	35 1.3	17.6	6.4	30 10.28	33 55 15.3
34	8	58.0		35.0					31 53.57	16.46	0.10	III.	3	22.890	37 25.9	18.0	6.9	32 10.13	57 40.8
35	8						12.0	31.0	31 35.26	16.46	+0.21	VI.	4	37.30	22 19.7	17.9	4.1	31 51.93	33 42 31.7
36	7	4.0	22.0						31 59.52	16.46	−0.02	II.	2	8.185	52 46.4	18.	9.8	32 15.96	34 13 (4.)
37	8		42.0		19.0				37 18.99	16.49	+0.30	IV.	5	50.780	8 16.3	18.0	1.8	37 35.78	33 28 27.0
38	7		29.0						39 6.13	16.51	0.09	II.	2	20.390	40 4.7	19.3	7.3	39 22.73	34 0 21.3
39	7	52.0	11.0	30.0					39 48.02	16.51	0.15	III.	3	28.300	31 40.8	19.4	5.8	40 14.68	33 52 2.0
40	7				43.0		19.0		40 42.52	16.52	0.18	IV.	3	31.750	28 10.2	19.5	5.2	40 59.22	33 48 24.9
41	8			11.0					42 29.56	16.53	0.03	III.	1	11.940	48 51.4	19.8	9.0	42 46.12	34 9 10.2
42	7				29.0				43 29.02	16.54	0.23	IV.	3	37.400	22 15.8	20.0	4.1	43 45.79	33 42 29.9
43	7				17.0	36.0			44 17.25	16.54	0.21	IV.	3	35.420	24 20.1	20.1	4.5	44 34.00	44 34.7
44	6	44.0	2.5	21.0					46 39.49	16.56	0.23	III.	3	36.930	22 45.1	20.6	4.2	46 50.28	33 42 59.9
45	7					20.0	38.0		47 1.08	16.57	0.03	V.	1	11.220	49 36.5	20.6	9.2	47 17.68	34 9 56.3
46	7			55.5		32.0			49 13.75	16.58	0.21	IV.	3	34.140	25 40.3	21.0	4.7	49 30.54	33 45 56.0
47	7	42.0	0.0						51 37.20	16.60	0.25	II.	3	38.180	21 26.3	21.1	3.9	51 54.05	41 41.6
48	7	45.0	4.0						51 40.78	16.60	0.20	IV.	3	30.800	29 9.8	21.4	5.3	51 57.58	49 26.5
49	8						23.0	41.0	10 51 45.84	+16.60	+0.31	VI.	4	45.550	−13 41.6	−21.4	−2.6	10 52 2.75	−33 33 55.6

CORRECTIONS.

Date	Corr. of Clock	Hourly rate	m	n	c	Zenith Point	Mic. Co.
	h.	s.	s.	s.	s.	s.	° ′ ″	r.
1846, April 20,	12	+ 9.353	+ 0.008	+ 0.521	− 0.342	+ 0.246	0 0 2.10	30.005

REMARKS. April 20. Readings of Bar. and Thers., opposite (309) made at 9h 20m.

INSTRUMENT READINGS.

Date	A.	B.	C.	D.	E.	F.	Mean.	Barom.	At.	Ex.	U.	L.	I.
	° ′ ″						″	in.	°	°	°	°	°
Zone 10, 1846 April 20, 9 30	72 39 64.0	63.0	66.5	64.3	62.4	57.0	62.87	30.340	66.0	60.0			
10 29								30.332	64.4	59.5			
11 44								30.304	62.0	55.1			
12 43	72 39 64.4	63.0	66.5	64.3	62.4	57.0	62.93	30.286	60.6	54.2			

Zone 10. April 20. P. D.$_2$ = −33° 19′ 50″—Continued.

No.	Mag.	I.	II.	III.	IV.	V.	VI.	VII.	T. (h. m. s.)	a_1	a_2	Mic.	n	r.	i	d_1	d_2	Mean Right Ascension, 1850.0 (h. m. s.)	Mean Declination, 1850.0 (° ′ ″)
50	8		51.0				24.0	42.5	10 51 47.12	+16.60	+0.33	VI.	5	49.020	−10 6.7	−21.4	−1.9	10 52 4.05	−33 30 20.0
51	9		51.0					46.0	58 28.01	16.65	0.34	II.	5	52.710	6 15.2	22.5	1.3	58 45.00	33 26 29.0
52	8							46.0	10 58 50.26	16.66	0.11	IV.	2	16.955	43 40.0	22.5	8.0	10 59 7.05	34 4 0.5
53				1.0					11 1 19. .	16.68								11 1 (35.)	
54	9							35.0	1 39.47	16.68	0.26	VII.	3	35.610	24 7.4	23.0	4.4	1 56.41	33 44 24.8
55	7	26.0	45.0	3.5					4 21.94	16.70	0.14	III.	2	20.580	39 53.0	23.4	7.3	4 38.78	34 0 13.7
56	7			4.0	22.0				4 22.25	16.70	0.32	IV.	3	44.270	15 4.5	23.4	2.8	4 39.27	33 35 20.7
57	7		8.0	27.0	45.0				6 45.21	16.72	0.23	IV.	3	31.300	28 38.6	23.8	5.2	7 2.16	33 48 57.6
58	7						32.0		6 54.84	16.72	0.07	VI.	1	11.325	49 29.6	23.8	9.1	7 11.63	34 9 52.5
59	6		13.0	31.5	50.5			46.0	8 50.26	16.74	0.22	IV.	3	29.330	30 42.2	24.1	5.6	9 7.22	33 51 1.9
60	6	13.0	32.0	51.0	9.0		46.0	4.0	10 8.93	16.75	0.19	IV.	3	25.420	34 47.5	24.2	6.1	10 25.87	55 8.1
61	8		41.0						14 18.02	16.79	0.41	II.	5	53.120	5 49.	24.6	1.0	14 35.22	26 (5.)
62	7				21.0				15 21.06	16.79	0.23	IV.	3	29.845	30 9.7	25.0	5.5	15 38.08	50 30.2
63	7			2.5	21.0	39.5			16 39.55	16.81	0.24	IV.	3	29.660	30 21.4	25.1	5.6	16 56.60	50 42.1
64	6					14.5	33.0	51.0	16 55.94	16.81	0.40	V.	5	51.400	7 37.4	25.1	2.2	17 13.15	33 27 54.7
65	7					49.0			18 49.04	16.82	0.09	IV.	1	9.950	50 55.9	25.1	9.4	19 5.95	34 11 20.7
66	8			9.0	46.0				23 46.00	16.87	0.40	IV.	5	48.730	10 24.9	26.1	1.7	24 3.27	33 30 42.7
67	7		56.0		33.0				25 33.07	16.89	0.21	IV.	3	24.320	35 56.5	26.3	6.6	25 50.17	33 56 19.4
68	8				27.0			24.0	24 27.68	16.88	0.18	VII.	3	19.655	40 46.3	26.2	7.5	24 44.74	34 1 10.0
69	7			49.0		26.0			29 7.49	16.92	0.21	IV.	3	23.240	37 4.2	26.7	6.8	29 24.62	33 57 27.7
70	7								29				3	33.190	26 40.	27.	4.9	29	47 (2.)
71	7						35.0	53.0	28 57.70	16.92	0.28	VI.	3	31.000	28 56.9	26.7	5.3	29 14.90	49 18.9
72	8					6.0	24.0		30 47.37	16.93	0.46	VI.	5	55.280	3 33.9	27.0	0.6	31 4.76	23 51.5
73	5			11.0	29.0				32 29.30	16.95	0.24	IV.	3	25.755	34 26.3	27.1	6.3	32 46.49	54 49.7
74	7			14.0	33.0				33 32.75	16.96	0.34	IV.	4	39.780	19 44.7	27.3	3.6	33 50.05	40 5.6
75	8							26.0	33 49.03	16.96	0.34	IV.	4	36.710	22 57.4	27.3	4.2	34 6.33	43 18.9
76	8		52.0		29.0				36 29.00	16.99	0.37	IV.	5	41.570	17 54.1	27.6	3.2	36 46.36	38 14.9
77	8					50.0			37 31.40	17.00	0.23	V.	3	22.110	38 15.0	27.7	7.0	37 48.63	58 39.7
78	6					52.5	10.5	20.0	38 33.58	17.01	0.25	V.	3	25.470	34 44.3	27.8	6.1	38 50.84	55 8.5
79	8							44.5	39 49.03	17.02	0.38	VII.	4	42.670	16 41.7	27.9	3.1	40 6.43	33 37 2.7
80	8		0.0						44 37.20	17.06	0.16	II.	1	12.020	49 46.1	28.4	9.0	44 54.42	34 9 13.5
81	6				17.5	36.0			45 36.05	17.07	0.12	IV.	1	7.610	53 22.5	28.5	9.9	45 53.24	34 13 50.9
82	6						51.0	10.0	46 14.20	17.08	0.32	VI.	3	31.150	28 47.6	28.6	5.3	46 31.60	33 49 11.5
83	8			7.5	26.0				47 44.52	17.10	0.34	III.	3	34.310	25 29.7	28.7	4.7	48 1.96	33 45 53.1
84	8				12.0				49 12.05	17.11	0.21	IV.	2	17.140	43 28.6	28.9	8.0	49 29.37	34 3 55.5
85	8			10.0					52 28.51	17.14	0.28	III.	3	24.365	35 53.6	29.1	6.6	52 45.93	33 56 19.3
86	6			14.0	33.0	51.5			53 51.38	17 16	0.32	IV.	3	31.400	28 32.3	29.3	5.2	54 8.86	48 56.8
87	7			48.0					54 48.02	17.17	0.37	IV.	3	37.360	22 18.3	29.3	4.1	55 5.56	42 41.7
88	7			36.0	54.0				55 54.30	17.18	0.26	IV.	2	22.410	37 58.3	29.4	7.0	56 11.74	58 24.7
89	7					52.0	10.5		56 51.99	17.19	0.28	IV.	2	24.120	36 10.9	29.5	6.6	57 9.46	56 37.0
90	6						34.0	53.0	11 58 15.79	17.20	0.42	V.	4	41.590	17 50.7	29.6	3.3	11 58 33.41	38 13.6
91	6			42.0	0.5	19.0	36.0		12 0 19.14	17.22	0.33	IV.	E W	30.004	29 59.7	29.8	5.5	12 0 36.69	50 25.0
92	6	5.0	24.0	42.5	1.0				2 0.92	17.24	0.31	IV.	3	28.355	31 43.4	29.9	5.8	2 18.47	52 9.1
93	8							2.0	2 25.01	17.24	0.36	VI.	3	34.190	25 36.9	29.9	4.7	2 42.61	46 1.5
94	8				19.0	56.0			4 19.06	17.26	0.52	VI.	5	52.390	6 35.2	30.1	1.1	4 36.84	26 56.4
95	8	17.0	35.0	54.0					8 12.23	17.30	0.54	III.	5	54.270	5 40.0	30.3	0.8	8 30.07	26 1.1
96	8		46.0		23.0				9 23.00	17.31	0.43	IV.	4	39.660	19 52.3	30.4	3.7	9 40.74	40 16.4
97	8		30.5		8.0				15 7.75	17.38	0.48	IV.	5	45.060	14 15.1	30.7	2.5	15 25.61	34 38.3
98	8		10.0	29.0	47.5				12 10 47.33	+17.39	+0.51	IV.	5	49.220	− 9 54.1	−30.9	−1.7	12 17 5.22	−33 30 16.7

CORRECTIONS.

Date	Corr. of Clock.	Hourly rate.	m	n	c	Zenith Point.	Mic. Co.
	h. s.	s.	s.	s.	s.	° ′ ″	r.
1846.							

REMARKS.

(10) 56. Min. of T. 1 smaller than Transit Z., April 20.
(10) 95. Micrometer reading assumed as 53.270 instead of 54.270.

INSTRUMENT READINGS.

Date	A.	B.	C.	D.	E.	F.	Mean.	Barom.	At.	Ex.	U.	L.	I.
				CIRCLE.							THERMOM.		
1846. h. m.	° ′ ″						″	in.	°	°	°		°

ZONE 10. APRIL 20. P. $D_0 = -33°\ 19'\ 50''$—Continued.

No.	Mag.	I.	II.	III.	IV.	V.	VI.	VII.	T. (h. m. s.)	a_1 (s.)	a_2 (s.)
99	8						52.0		12 17 15.17	+17.40	+0.54
100	8					9.0		47.0	18 50.79	17.41	0.24
101	6			36.0	54.5				20 54.55	17.44	0.31
102	7			32.0	51.0				21 50.80	17.45	0.33
103	8							45.0	21 49.50	17.45	0.45
104	7	10.5	28.5	47.5	4.0				25 5.91	17.48	0.38
105	8					41.0			26 22.43	17.50	0.36
106	8				19.0		56.0		27 18.98	17.51	0.30
107	8						33.0		28 55.79	17.52	0.21
108	9	30.5	49.0	7.5					34 26.00	17.54	0.45
109	9						7.0		34 29.91	17.59	0.33
110	9	46.5	5.0	23.5					38 42.05	17.63	0.40
111	9	42.0	9.0						40 46.00	17.66	0.46
112	7			48.0	6.5	25.5			41 6.67	17.66	0.37
113	9						6.0	25.0	41 29.38	17.66	0.58
114	6				30.0	48.5	7.0		12 43 29.88	+17.69	+0.24

No.	MICROMETER		r	i (' '')	d_1 ('')	d_2 ('')	Mean Right Ascension, 1850.0 (h. m. s.)	Mean Declination, 1850.0 (° ' '')
99	VI.	5	52.680	− 6 17.1	−30.9	− 1.0	12 17 33.11	−33 26 39.0
100	V.	1	12.790	47 58.0	31.0	8.8	19 8.44	34 8 27.8
101	IV.	2	20.735	39 43.1	31.0	7.3	21 12.30	34 0 11.4
102	IV.	2	22.600	37 46.3	31.1	6.9	22 8.58	33 58 14.3
103	VII.	3	39.750	19 47.4	31.1	3.7	22 7.40	40 12.2
104	IV.	3	30.350	29 38.2	31.2	5.4	25 23.77	50 4.8
105	V.	3	26.180	33 59.7	31.3	6.2	26 40.29	33 54 27.2
106	IV.	3	18.900	41 36.1	31.3	7.6	27 36.79	34 2 5.0
107	IV.	1	5.750	55 18.9	31.4	10.2	29 13.52	34 15 50.5
108	III.	3	35.090	24 40.6	31.5	4.5	34 43.99	33 45 6.6
109	VI.	2	19.130	41 23.2	31.6	7.6	34 47.83	34 1 52.4
110	IV.	3	27.135	32 59.8	31.7	6.1	39 0.08	33 53 27.6
111	IV.	3	36.255	23 27.6	31.7	4.3	41 4.12	53 53.6
112	IV.	2	22.475	37 54.2	31.7	6.9	41 24.70	58 22.8
113	VII.	4	50.215	8 48.2	31.7	1.7	41 47.62	33 29 11.6
114	IV.	1	5.630	−55 26.5	−31.6	−10.3	12 43 47.81	−34 15 58.6

ZONE 11. APRIL 27. P. $D_0 = -31°\ 59'\ 40''$.

No.	Mag.	I.	II.	III.	IV.	V.	VI.	VII.	T. (h. m. s.)	a_1 (s.)	a_2 (s.)
1				40.0	58.0				9 50 58.17	+15.90	+2.00
2	9			55.0		32.0			54 13.49	15.91	1.96
3	6		53.0	11.0	30.0				56 29.63	15.92	1.96
4	6	45.0	3.0	21.5	39.5				9 58 40.72	15.93	1.94
5	9	44.0	4.0		42.0				10 0 40.	15.91	1.92
6	7			36.0					1 54.22	15.95	1.89
7	7				10.0				2 10.00	15.95	1.88
8	7					54.0			2 35.78	15.95	1.87
9	9							56.0	3 1.28	15.95	1.87
10	6	35.0	53.5	11.5	29.5				6 29.73	15.97	1.84
11	8	10.0	28.5	47.0					8 5.07	15.98	1.86
12	9					0.0		36.0	8 41.41	15.98	1.84
13	8	56.0		33.0					11 51.03	16.00	1.81
14	8	0.0		37.0					11 55.02	16.00	1.81
15	6		35.0	53.0	11.5				13 11.41	16.01	1.70
16	7	41.0	59.0	17.5	35.5				17 35.74	16.03	1.77
17	7	27.5	46.0	4.5					22 22.60	16.06	1.73
18	7				31.0	40.0			24 30.88	16.07	1.67
19	8					0.5		37.0	25 42.14	16.08	1.70
20	7	30.5	49.0	7.5	25.5				29 25.54	16.10	1.65
21	7	46.0	4.0	22.5	41.0				32 40.90	16.12	1.64
22	9				9.0				39 9.05	16.16	1.55
23										16.16	
24	9				31.0		7.0		47 30.77	16.22	1.46
25	6	15.0	34.0	52.0		46.0			52 9.98	16.25	1.40
26	8	17.0	36.0	54.0		48.0			52 11.98	16.25	1.40
27	6	33.0		10.0	28.0				56 28.08	16.28	1.40
28	6	51.0	9.0	28.0	45.5				10 59 45.87	16.30	1.39
29	7							26.0	11 7 31.17	+16.36	+1.31

No.	MICROMETER		r	i (' '')	d_1 ('')	d_2 ('')	Mean Right Ascension, 1850.0 (h. m. s.)	Mean Declination, 1850.0 (° ' '')
1	IV. :	3	26.630	−33 31.5	− 0.3	− 6.9	9 51 16.07	−32 33 18.7
2	V.	4	35.650	24 3.7	0.9	5.4	54 31.36	23 50.0
3	IV.	3	28.948	31 6.0	1.4	6.5	56 47.51	30 53.9
4	IV.	2	20.443	40 1.6	1.8	8.0	9 58 58.59	39 51.4
5	IV.	3	28.850	31 12.1	2.2	6.5	10 0 (57.)?	31 0.8
6	III.	5	50.400	8 40.1	2.4	2.8	2 12.06	8 25.3
7	IV.	4	44.750	14 32.6	2.5	3.6	2 27.83	14 18.9
8	V.	5	51.850	7 9.1	2.5	2.5	2 53.60	6 54.1
9	VII.	4	42.660	16 42.4	2.7	4.2	3 19.10	16 29.3
10	IV.	4	41.620	17 49.2	3.3	4.3	6 47.54	17 36.8
11	III.	3	20.900	39 30.6	3.6	8.0	8 22.91	39 22.2
12	VII.	3	27.880	32 13.8	3.8	6.7	8 59.23	32 4.3
13	III. 'E W		30.006		4.3	6.3	12 8.84	29 50.2
14	III.	3	31.965	27 56.6	4.3	6.0	12 12.83	27 46.9
15	IV.	3	36.890	22 47.6	4.6	5.2	13 29.21	22 37.4
16	IV.	2	16.690	43 56.7	5.4	8.7	17 53.54	43 50.8
17	III.	2	21.783	38 37.4	6.3	7.8	22 40.39	38 31.5
18	IV.	4	41.463	17 59.2	6.6	4.1	24 48.62	17 50.2
19	VII.	3	24.240	36 0.0	6.8	7.3	25 59.02	35 55.0
20	IV.	3	30.160	29 50.1	7.5	6.1	29 43.29	29 43.7
21	IV.	1	10.850	49 59.6	8.0	9.7	32 58.66	49 57.3
22	IV.	3	27.840	32 15.5	9.1	6.7	39 26.76	32 11.3
23								
24	VI.	4	35.640	24 5.0	10.4	5.4	47 48.45	21 1.7
25	IV.	4	42.920	16 27.5	11.2	4.1	52 27.03	16 22.8
26	IV.	4	44.625	14 40.5	11.2	3.8	52 29.63	14 35.5
27	IV.	3	22.170	38 11.3	11.8	7.7	10 56 45.76	36 10.8
28	IV.	2	16.060	44 36.2	12.3	8.8	11 0 3.56	44 37.3
29	VII.	3	29.860	−30 8.2	−13.4	6.1	11 7 48.84	−32 30 8.0

CORRECTIONS.

Date.	Corr. of Clock.	Hourly rate.	m	n	c	Zenith Point.	Mic. Co.
1846, April 27,	h. 12	s. + 11.051	s. + 0.028	s. + 0.521	s. − 0.342	s. + 0.246	° ' '' 0 0 2.01	r. 30.006

INSTRUMENT READINGS.

	Date.	CIRCLE.							Barom.	THERMOM.				
		A.	B.	C.	D.	E.	F.	Mean.		At.	Ex.	U.	L.	I.
Zone 11	1846 April 27, h. m. 9 50								in. 29.914	62.0	57.5			
	10 52								29.914	61.2	57.0			
	11 30								29.910	60.0	54.2			
	11 58	71 19 60.6	59.2	64.2	61.2	59.2	52.5	59.48	29.912	60.0	53.0	62.0	62.0	60.0

REMARKS.

April 27. Some stars may have been obscured by the light barely visible clouds.

Zone 11. April 27. P. $D_0 = -31° 59' 40''$.—Continued.

No.	Mag.	I.	II.	III.	IV.	V.	VI.	VII.	T.	a_1	a_2	Micrometer	r	i	d_1	d_2	Mean Right Ascension, 1850.0	Mean Declination, 1850.0
									h. m. s.	s.	s.		r.	′ ″	″	″	h. m. s.	° ′ ″
30	7				5.0	24.0	42.0		11 9 5.36	+16.37	+1.30	V. 2	17.787	−42 47.8	−13.6	− 8.6	11 9 23.03	−32 42 50.0
31	7	21.0	40.0	57.5	16.0		52.5	10.7	14 15.91	16.41	1.24	IV. 3	31.140	28 48.6	14.4	6.1	14 33.56	28 49.1
32	9	50.0		28.3	47.0				21 46.72	16.47	1.15	IV. 3	38.593	21 0.8	15.4	1.9	22 4.34	21 1.1
33	7			36.5	54.5	13.0			24 54.66	16.49	1.11	IV. 5	51.775	7 13.8	15.8	2.5	25 12.26	7 12.1
34	6	56.0	14.3	32.7	51.0				28 51.00	16.52	1.13	IV. 2	16.400	44 15.1	16.4	8.7	29 8.65	44 20.2
35	7	42.0	00.0	18.5	37.0				30 36.83	16.54	1.12	IV. 2	14.330	46 24.8	16.6	9.1	30 54.49	46 30.5
36	6	17.0	35.2	53.7	12.0				32 11.92	16.55	1.09	IV. 1	23.290	37 1.1	16.8	7.5	32 29.56	37 5.4
37	8					17.5			32 59.19	16.56	1.08	VII. 3	23.020	37 17.3	16.8	7.6	33 16.83	37 21.7
38	7	57.0	15.0	33.5	52.0				42 51.74	16.64	0.95	IV. 4	41.030	18 26.3	17.0	4.1	43 9.33	18 28.6
39	7	39.0	57.0	15.0		52.0			47 33.57	16.68	0.94	IV. 3	23.470	36 49.0	18.4	7.5	47 51.19	36 55.7
40	7			50.5	8.5	27.0			49 8.68	16.70	0.91	IV. 3	31.200	29 16.3	18.5	6.1	49 26.29	29 20.9
41	7	10.5	28.7	47.0	5.5				11 58 5.24	+16.78	+0.79	IV. 5	51.846	− 7 9.4	−19.3	− 3.5	11 58 22.81	−32 7 11.2

Zone 12. May 4. P. $D_0 = -30° 49' 40''$.

No.	Mag.	I.	II.	III.	IV.	V.	VI.	VII.	T.	a_1	a_2	Micrometer	r	i	d_1	d_2	Mean Right Ascension, 1850.0	Mean Declination, 1850.0
1	8				55.0				10 42 55.03	+23.80	+1.09	IV. 4	40.535	−18 57.4	− 9.0	− 2.4	10 43 19.92	−31 8 48.8
2	7	38.0	56.0	13.5	31.5				45 31.74	23.81	1.10	IV. 3	37.440	22 13.3	9.4	2.8	45 56.65	12 5.5
3	7					38.0	56.0	14.0	46 19.90	23.82	1.12	VII. 2	18.680	41 51.1	9.5	5.8	46 44.84	31 31 46.4
4	6					39.5	57.5	15.5	48 21.59	23.83	1.07	V. 5	49.560	9 32.0	9.8	1.0	48 46.49	30 50 22.8
5	8	35.0	54.0			29.0	47.0	5.0	52 10.94	23.85	1.06	IV. 4	23.880	36 23.8	10.4	5.0	52 35.85	31 26 19.2
6	6								53	23.85	1.05	IV. 4	46.660	12 32.7	10.7	1.4	53	2 24.8
7	6		7.0	25.0	43.0	1.0			10 55 43.01	23.87	1.05	IV. 3	40.225	19 18.4	10.9	2.4	10 56 7.91	9 11.7
8	8	45.5		22.0	39.0				11 0 39.53	23.90	1.06	IV. 3	33.245	26 36.5	11.6	3.5	11 1 4.49	16 31.6
9	9				7.0	26.0			1 7.32	23.91	1.09	V. 2	19.670	40 49.8	11.6	5.6	1 32.32	30 46.0
10	5		41.0	59.0		35.0			2 17.03	23.91	1.09	IV. 2	17.290	43 19.3	11.8	6.0	2 42.03	33 17.1
11	6		1.0	19.3	37.0	55.3			4 37.18	23.93	1.09	IV. 1	43.540	47 11.3	12.1	6.6	5 2.20	37 10.0
12	8	26.0	44.0	2.0	20.0				8 20.08	23.95	1.08	IV. 2	17.406	43 12.0	12.6	6.0	8 45.11	31 33 10.6
13	6	34.0	52.0	10.0	28.0				10 27.92	23.96	1.01	IV. 5	52.848	6 6.5	12.9	0.5	10 52.89	30 55 59.9
14	6	55.0	13.0	31.0	49.0			43.0	12 49.00	23.98	1.04	IV. 3	32.905	26 57.7	13.1	3.6	13 14.02	31 16 54.4
15	9	34.5		10.0		46.0			16 28.50	24.00	1.00	V. 5	51.945	7 3.2	13.6	0.6	16 52.50	30 56 57.4
16	8				15.0	33.0	50.5		17 14.81	24.01	1.04	IV. 3	24.180	36 5.2	13.7	4.8	17 39.86	31 26 3.7
17	7	1.0	19.0	37.0	55.0				19 55.02	24.03	1.03	IV. 3	30.470	29 30.7	14.0	3.9	20 20.08	19 28.6
18	7				43.5	1.5	19.0		20 43.38	24.03	1.00	VI. 4	47.250	11 56.4	14.1	1.3	21 8.41	1 51.8
19	9		32.0						25 8.00	24.06	1.01	II. 3	34.890	24 52.7	14.6	3.2	25 33.07	14 50.5
20	4			55.0	13.0			7.0	25 13.02	24.06	0.99	IV. 4	47.428	11 44.7	14.6	1.3	25 38.07	1 40.6
21	9						35.0		26 59.08	24.08	0.99	VII. 4	42.950	16 24.3	14.8	2.0	27 24.15	6 21.1
22	9			6.0					29 24.05	24.09	1.03	III. 2	11.590	48 57.4	15.2	6.9	29 49.17	38 59.5
23	4								34	24.13	1.02	VII.+ 1	10.860	49 59.3	15.	7.0	34	31 40 (0.)
24	7			50.0	7.5				37 7.71	24.15	0.96	IV. 5	52.175	6 48.7	15.8	0.6	37 32.82	30 56 45.1
25	7						23.0		37 46.97	24.15	1.00	VI. 3	24.440	35 48.8	15.9	4.9	38 12.12	31 25 49.6
26	7							31.0	38 35.87	24.16	1.01	VII. 3	20.890	39 30.9	16.0	5.4	39 2.04	29 32.3
27	7	52.0	10.0	28.0			22.0	40.0	41 46.01	24.18	1.00	III. 3	14.100	46 39.1	16.3	6.5	42 11.19	30 41.9
28	9				58.0				43 58.02	24.20	0.95	IV. 4	43.300	16 3.9	16.5	2.4	44 23.17	6 2.4
29	8		1.0	19.0	37.0				46 37.03	24.22	0.96	IV. 3	32.400	27 29.6	16.7	3.6	47 2.21	17 29.9
30	7	48.0	6.0	24.0	42.0			36.0	48 42.02	24.24	0.97	IV. 3	24.328	35 56.0	16.9	4.9	49 7.23	25 57.8
31	7	50.0	8.0	26.0	44.0			38.0	48 44.02	24.24	0.97	IV. 3	24.328	35 56.0	16.9	4.9	49 9.23	25 57.8
32	7	59.0	17.0	35.0	53.0				52 52.98	24.27	0.93	IV. 3	36.345	21 16.5	17.2	2.7	53 18.18	11 16.4
33	7	33.0	51.0	9.5					11 55 27.21	+24.29	+0.96	III. 3	24.980	−35 21.0	−17.4	− 4.8	11 55 52.46	−31 25 23.2

CORRECTIONS.

Date.	Corr. of Clock.	Hourly rate.	m	n	c	Zenith Point.	Mic. Co.
	h.	s.	s.	s.	s.	° ′ ″	r.
1846. May 4,	12 + 16.495	+ 0.028	+ 0.590	+ 0.458	+ 0.207	0 0 2.35	30.002

REMARKS.

(11) 40. Mic. reading assumed as 30′.700 instead of 31′.200.

(12) 15. Transit over T. VI assumed as recorded over T. VII.

INSTRUMENT READINGS.

	Date.	CIRCLE.							Barom.	THERMOM.				
		A.	B.	C.	D.	E.	F.	Mean.		At.	Ex.	U.	L.	I.
		° ′ ″						″	in.	°	°	°	°	°
Zone 12	1846 May 4, 10 42	70 10 70.0							30.070	68.8	63.3			
	12 45		8.3	13.0	9.5	8.5	3.6	8.82	30.090	67.0	60.5			65.0

ZONE 12. MAY 4. P. $D_s = -30° 49' 40''$—Continued.

No.	Mag.	I.	II.	III.	IV.	V.	VI.	VII.	T.	a₁	a₂
									h. m. s.	s.	s.
34	8			52.0	10.0	28.0			11 56 9.96	+24.30	+0.94
35	8	57.0	15.0	33.5	51.0				12 5 51.21	24.37	0.94
36	8	47.0		23.5					8 41.32	24.40	0.93
37	7	55.5	13.0	31.0	49.0				13 49.09	24.44	0.88
38	8	4.0	22.0	40.0	58.0				15 58.07	24.45	0.92
39	8	4.0	22.0	40.0					17 57.94	24.47	0.89
40	8							39.0	17 43.13	24.47	0.86
41	9						57.0		19 20.94	24.48	0.91
42	7		7.5	25.7	43.0				20 43.42	24.49	0.88
43	7	34.0	58.0	10.0					23 27.94	24.52	0.85
44	5					2.0	19.5		23 43.60	24.52	0.90
45	8						50.0		24 13.88	24.52	0.90
46	7					8.0	26.0		25 50.00	24.54	0.86
47	8						58.0	16.0	26 22.09	24.54	0.86
48	7			11.0	29.0	47.0			28 29.01	24.56	0.86
49	7		59.0	17.0	35.0				32 34.97	24.60	0.82
50	8				42.0	1.0			33 42.50	24.61	0.82
51	9							59.0	34 5.15	24.61	0.81
52	8	34.0	52.0						37 27.91	24.64	0.82
53	7				36.0	53.0			37 35.50	24.64	0.82
54	8						33.0	51.0	37 57.13	24.64	0.82
55	7				48.0		24.0		39 48.00	24.66	0.87
56	8	17.0	35.0	53.0	11.0				43 10.99	24.69	0.82
57	8				27.0	45.0			12 44 27.01	+24.70	+0.81

No.	MICROMETER.		r.	i	d₁	d₂	Mean Right Ascension, 1850.0.	Mean Declination, 1850.0.
			r.	' ''	''	''	h. m. s.	° ' ''
34	IV	3	33.570	-26 16.1	-17.5	-3.4	11 56 35.20	-31 16 17.0
35	IV	2	17.540	43 3.6	18.1	6.0	12 6 16.52	33 7.7
36	III	2	19.540	40 58.2	18.3	5.6	9 6.65	31 2.1
37	IV	4	42.900	16 28.9	18.6	2.0	14 14.41	6 29.5
38	IV	2	20.730	39 43.5	18.7	5.4	16 23.44	29 47.6
39	III	3	30.795	29 9.9	18.8	3.9	18 23.30	31 19 12.6
40	VII	5	52.450	6 31.5	18.8	0.6	18 8.46	30 56 30.9
41	VI	2	20.600	39 51.2	18.9	5.5	19 46.33	31 29 55.6
42	IV	2	35.995	23 43.8	19.0	3.1	21 8.79	13 45.9
43	III	4	44.250	15 4.3	19.1	1.8	23 53.31	5 5.2
44	V	1	8.760	52 10.4	19.1	7.3	24 9.02	42 16.8
45	VI	2	12.760	48 2.5	19.1	6.7	24 39.30	38 8.3
46	V	3	33.940	25 52.7	19.2	3.4	26 15.40	15 55.3
47	VI	4	46.830	12 21.2	19.2	1.4	26 47.49	2 21.8
48	IV	4	29.185	30 51.2	19.3	4.1	28 54.43	31 20 54.6
49	IV	5	54.950	4 57.4	19.4	0.2	33 0.39	30 54 57.0
50	IV	4	49.470	9 36.5	19.4	1.0	34 7.93	59 36.9
51	VII	4	55.525	3 18.6	19.2	0.1	34 30.57	30 53 17.9
52	II	4	45.090	14 11.5	19.5	1.7	37 53.37	31 4 12.7
53	IV	5	52.340	6 38.4	19.5	0.7	38 0.96	30 56 38.6
54	VI	5	50.245	8 49.8	19.5	0.9	38 22.59	30 58 50.2
55	IV	2	20.270	40 12.4	19.6	5.5	40 13.53	31 30 17.5
56	IV	3	36.137	23 35.0	19.6	3.0	43 36.50	13 37.6
57	IV	4	46.800	-12 23.9	-19.7	-1.4	12 44 52.52	-31 2 25.0

ZONE 13. MAY 19. Iᵖ. $D_s = -29° 34' 30'$.

No.	Mag.	I.	II.	III.	IV.	V.	VI.	VII.	T.	a₁	a₂
1	8			39.0					13 29 56.78	+37.84	+0.70
2	7				20.5				36 20.48	37.89	0.48
3	7							10.5	37 7.30	37.89	0.50
4	5					30.0			39 12.21	37.91	0.73
5	6						24.0	42.0	39 48.59	37.91	0.70
6	8				57.0				41 57.00	37.93	0.59
7	6	47.0	4.5	22.0	40.0				46 39.98	37.96	0.62
8	7		51.0	9.0	27.0				48 26.84	37.98	1.02
9	8		4.0	22.0				33.0	13 48 39.67	37.98	0.94
10	7	59.0		35.0	53.0				14 0 52.65	38.07	0.71
11	7		44.0		20.0				5 19.85	38.11	1.07
12	8		44.0		20.0				7 19.84	38.12	1.00
13	8	41.0	59.0	17.0					15 34.55	38.19	0.90
14							43.0		16 7. .	38.20	
15	4	45.0	2.5	20.3	38.3			31.5	23 38.19	38.25	0.86
16	7	58.0		33.5	51.0				30 51.15	38.30	0.74
17	6		41.0	59.0	16.0				32 16.49	38.32	1.08
18	8			17.0	35.0				33 34.84	38.33	0.61
19	8					5.0			34 47.18	38.34	0.97
20	9					6.0			34 48.15	38.34	1.04
21	8	8.0	26.0		2.0				14 42 1.69	+38.39	+1.07

No.	MICROMETER.		r.	i	d₁	d₂	Mean Right Ascension, 1850.0.	Mean Declination, 1850.0.
1	III	3	35.635	-24 6.3	-18.5	-4.2	13 30 35.32	-29 58 59.0
2	IV	5	52.585	6 23.0	18.1	2.0	36 58.85	41 13.1
3	VII	4	50.660	8 20.3	18.0	2.2	37 45.69	43 10.5
4	VII	3	34.790	24 58.9	18.0	4.3	39 50.85	59 51.2
5	VII	3	36.903	22 46.3	17.9	4.0	40 27.20	57 38.2
6	V	4	44.970	14 17.2	17.8	3.0	42 35.52	49 8.0
7	IV	4	43.788	15 33.0	17.3	3.1	47 18.56	29 50 23.5
8	IV	3	15.625	45 3.6	17.3	7.0	49 5.84	30 19 57.9
9	III	3	21.580	38 47.7	17.3	6.2	13 49 18.59	30 13 41.2
10	IV	4	39.935	19 35.0	16.3	3.6	14 1 31.43	29 54 24.9
11	IV	2	14.860	45 51.4	16.0	7.1	5 59.03	30 20 44.5
12	IV	3	19.860	40 37.9	15.8	6.4	7 58.96	15 30.1
13	III	3	27.965	32 7.5	15.0	5.3	16 13.64	6 57.8
14					15.0		16 (45.)	
15	IV	3	31.900	28 0.7	14.1	4.7	24 17.30	30 2 49.5
16	IV	4	41.080	18 23.1	13.3	3.5	31 30.19	29 53 9.9
17	IV	2	18.220	42 20.9	13.1	6.6	32 55.89	30 17 10.6
18	IV	3	50.900	8 6.5	13.0	2.2	34 13.78	29 42 51.7
19	V	3	25.470	34 44.3	12.8	5.6	35 26.49	30 9 32.7
20	V	3	21.190	39 12.7	12.8	6.2	35 27.53	14 1.7
21	IV	2	20.190	-40 17.4	-12.0	-6.3	14 42 41.15	-30 15 5.7

CORRECTIONS.

Date.		Corr. of Clock.	Hourly rate.	m	n	c	Zenith Point.	Mic. Co.
1846.	h.	s.	s.	s.	s.	s.	° ' ''	r.
May 19.	12	+ 29.708	+ 0.026	+ 0.505	+ 0.353	+ 0.207	0 0 2.72	30.006

REMARKS.

(12) 49. Mic. reading assumed as 53."950, not 54."950.

May 19. Interrupted at times by very faint clouds, barely visible.

(13) 3. Transit over T. VII assumed as 0".5 instead of 10".5.

INSTRUMENT READINGS.

	Date.		CIRCLE.							Barom.	THERMOM.				
			A.	B.	C.	D.	E.	F.	Mean.		At.	Ex.	U.	L.	I.
		h. m.	° ' ''	''	''	''	''	''	''	in.	°	°	°	°	°
Zone 13	1846. May 19,	13 29	68 55 6.0	8.7	15.5	7.0	9.7	0.0	8.15	30.046	59.5	50.5			
		14 59								30.058	58.5	50.7			
		15 26								30.052	58.5	51.0			

ZONE 13. MAY 19. P. $D_o = -29°\ 34'\ 30''$—Continued.

No.	Mag.	I.	II.	III.	IV.	V.	VI.	VII.	T.	a_1	a_2
									h. m. s.	s.	s.
22	8			53.0	11.0				14 43 10.92	+38.40	+1.22
23	5										
24	7	47.0	4.0			58.0			46 40.06	38.43	1.08
25	4	54.5		29.7	47.5			41.0	49 47.61	38.45	0.92
26	7	12.3	29.5	47.5	5.5				53 5.32	38.48	0.78
27	6	57.0	15.0	33.0	50.5				55 50.52	38.50	0.86
28	8	35.0	53.0			45.0			56 28.30	38.50	0.74
29	4							42.0	56 48.52	38.51	1.16
30	7		45.5	3.0	21.0			14.5	14 59 21.01	38.53	0.98
31	8		46.5	5.0	22.0				15 2 22.33	38.55	1.16
32	8					52.0			3 14.17	38.56	1.06
33	7	23.0	41.0						6 16.46	38.58	1.04
34	8			6.0					15 20 23.79	+38.73	1.01

No.	MICROMETER			i	d_1	d_2	Mean Right Ascension, 1850.0	Mean Declination, 1850.0
				′ ″	″	″	h. m. s.	° ′ ″
22	IV.	1	10.380	−50 29.3	−11.8	−7.7	14 43 50.54	−30 25 18.8
23		3	37.120	22 33.3	11.5	4.0	.45	29 57 18.8
24	II.	2	19.420	41 5.6	11.3	6.5	47 19.57	30 15 53.4
25	IV.	3	28.445	31 37.7	10.9	5.2	50 20.98	30 6 23.8
26	IV.	4	41.363	18 5.5	10.4	3.4	53 44.58	29 52 49.3
27	IV.	3	36.470	23 14.1	10.0	4.1	56 29.88	57 58.2
28	IV.	4	44.095	15 13.8	9.9	3.1	57 7.54	29 49 56.8
29	VII.	2	15.550	45 7.4	9.9	7.0	14 57 28.19	30 19 54.3
30	IV.	3	28.730	31 19.7	9.5	5.2	15 0 0.52	6 4.4
31	IV.	2	16.720	43 54.8	9.0	6.9	3 2.04	18 40.7
32	V.	3	24.270	35 59.6	8.9	5.8	3 53.79	10 44.3
33	II.	3	24.955	35 16.0	8.3	5.7	6 56.08	10 0.0
34	III.	3	30.240	−29 45.0	−5.1	−4.9	15 27 3.53	−30 4 25.0

ZONE 14. MAY 20. C. $D_o = -34°\ 34'\ 50'$.

No.	Mag.	I.	II.	III.	IV.	V.	VI.	VII.	T.	a_1	a_2
									h. m. s.	s.	s.
1	8		30.0	49.3	8.0		45.5	4.5	13 36 7.94	+38.19	+1.15
2	7			33.0	52.0	11.5	31.0		37 33.58	38.20	0.97
3	7.8		20.0	38.5	57.2	16.0	35.0		39 38.58	38.22	1.26
4	7		30.6	49.5	8.0	26.3	45.6	4.5	44 8.00	38.27	1.26
5	9							4.0	44 7.68	38.27	1.26
6	9				9.0		46.0	5.0	46 8.67	38.28	1.16
7	9			43.5	2.6	21.0			48 2.36	38.30	1.34
8	8		6.5		44.0		22.4	41.0	50 44.40	38.33	1.17
9	8			41.0		18.8	37.6		50 59.94	38.33	1.17
10	7.8				51.0	10.4	29.0		52 51.24	38.35	0.92
11	8			46.5	5.5	24.0	43.0		55 5.39	38.37	1.22
12	7.8		58.0	17.0	35.7	54.0	13.0	31.5	57 35.50	38.39	1.30
13	9				53.0		31.5		13 57 53.53	38.40	1.23
14	9			18.0	37.5		16.0		14 10 37.00?	38.52	1.28
15	9				3.2		37.5		11 3.24	38.52	1.15
16	8.9				29.0	48.4	7.0		13 29.36	38.55	1.13
17	8				48.0	7.0	25.5		17 48.11	38.59	1.22
18	9.10					4.0			21 45.26	38.62	1.27
19	7		20.5	39.7	58.2	17.0	35.6		24 58.23	38.66	1.20
20	8		18.7	37.0	56.0	15.0	33.5		27 56.06	38.68	1.15
21	7.8			48.0	7.0	26.0			29 7.01	38.69	1.10
22	6			51.5	10.0	29.0			31 10.13	38.71	0.80
23	7		49.0	8.0	27.0	46.0			35 26.94	38.75	0.77
24	7		0.0	19.0	37.6	56.5	15.7		38 37.97	38.78	0.93
25	8						45.0	4.0	39 7.60	38.79	1.08
26	9.10					32.0			46 13.23	38.86	1.13
27	7.8			17.0	36.0	55.0	13.2		47 35.94	38.87	1.12
28	7.8				59.2	18.5	37.0		49 59.35	38.89	0.78
29	9						30.5		50 52.84	38.90	0.88
30	7			14.0	32.5	51.6	10.0		53 32.59	38.92	0.80
31	9					45.0		24.0	54 45.67	38.94	0.81
32	7.8		59.1	17.8	37.0	56.0	14.6		14 59 36.90	+38.98	+0.82

No.	MICROMETER			i	d_1	d_2	Mean Right Ascension, 1850.0	Mean Declination, 1850.0
				′ ″	″	″	h. m. s.	° ′ ″
1	IV.	3	25.607	−34 35.7	−31.6	−8.0	13 36 47.28	−35 10 5.3
2	IV.	1	6.690	54 20.1	31.5	12.3	38 12.75	35 29 53.9
3	IV.	2	38.271	21 21.1	31.5	5.2	40 18.06	34 56 47.8
4	IV.	3	39.727	19 49.6	31.3	5.0	44 47.53	55 15.9
5	V.	3	40.740	18 45.9	31.3	4.7	44 47.21	34 54 11.9
6	FW		30.002	29 59.9	31.2	7.0	46 48.11	35 5 28.1
7	IV.	4	51.018	7 59.2	31.1	3.5	48 42.00	34 43 22.8
8	IV.	3	32.501	27 23.2	30.9	6.4	51 23.90	35 2 50.5
9	IV.	3	32.060	27 50.8	30.9	6.5	51 39.44	3 18.2
10	IV.	1	8.352	52 36.2	30.8	12.0	53 30.51	35 28 9.0
11	IV.	3	39.671	19 53.1	30.7	4.9	55 44.98	34 55 18.7
12	IV.	1	48.119	11 1.2	30.5	3.0	58 15.19	46 24.7
13	V.	3	40.648	18 51.8	30.5	4.7	13 58 33.16	54 17.0
14	IV.	4	52.489	6 27.0	29.4	2.2	14 11 17.40?	41 48.6
15	IV.	3	37.770	21 52.4	29.3	5.3	11 42.91	57 17.0
16	IV.	3	35.355	24 24.1	29.1	5.8	14 9.04	59 49.0
17	IV.	4	48.469	10 39.3	28.6	3.0	18 27.92	46 0.9
18	V.	4	53.938	4 55.5	28.2	1.8	22 25.15	40 15.5
19	IV.	4	46.629	12 34.7	27.9	3.4	25 38.09	47 56.0
20	IV.	4	42.991	16 23.1	27.6	4.2	28 35.89	51 44.9
21	IV.	3	38.649	20 57.3	27.5	5.1	29 40.80	34 56 19.9
22	IV.	1	7.304	53 41.8	27.2	12.1	31 49.64	35 29 11.1
23	IV.	1	5.965	55 7.0	28.0	12.4	36 6.46	50 37.4
24	IV.	3	23.105	37 12.5	26.4	8.5	39 17.68	35 12 37.4
25	VI.	4	39.702	19 48.7	26.3	4.9	39 47.47	34 55 9.9
26	V.	4	47.944	11 11.8	25.3	3.1	46 53.22	46 30.2
27	IV.	4	47.971	11 10.4	25.2	3.1	48 15.93	34 46 28.7
28	IV.	2	10.772	50 7.4	24.8	11.3	49 39.02	35 25 33.5
29	VI.	3	22.092	38 15.8	24.7	8.3	51 32.62	13 39.3
30	IV.	2	15.130	45 34.6	24.3	10.3	54 12.31	20 59.2
31	VI.	2	15.940	44 43.2	24.1	10.2	14 55 25.42	20 7.5
32	IV.	2	18.659	−41 53.3	−23.4	−9.6	15 0 16.70	−35 17 16.3

CORRECTIONS.

Date.		Corr. of Clock.	Hourly rate.	m	n	r	Zenith Point.	Mic. Co.
1846. May 20,	h. 16	s. + 29.991	s. + 0.018	s. + 0.505	s. + 0.353	s. + 0.207	0 0 2.48	r. 30.001

INSTRUMENT READINGS.

	Date.	CIRCLE.							Barom.	THERMOM.				
		A.	B.	C.	D.	E.	F.	Mean.		At.	Ex.	U.	L.	I.
		° ′ ″							in.	°	°	°	°	°
Zone 14	1846, May 20, 13 30	73 54 60.4	60.2	65.1	63.8	59.8	50.6	59.98				65.0	64.9	64.0
	13 36								29.908	66.0	60.7			
	13 57										60.0			
	14 10								29.916	65.0				
	14 20	59.6	60.9	65.6	64.7	59.9	50.1	60.13				63.5	63.5	
	14 31										60.7			
	14 59								29.928	64.0	60.1			
	15 20	58.9	60.8	65.0	63.6	59.1	50.0	59.57				62.0	62.4	

REMARKS.

May 20. Night clear, bright, and beautiful.

(13) 26. Minutes assumed as 54 instead of 53.

(13) 32. Transit over T. V assumed as 22ˢ instead of 32ˢ to agree with Arg. Z. 384 : 23.

(14) 18. Discordant from Transit Zone of same date.

(14) 26. R. A. discordant from Transit Zone of same date.

(14) 28. Min. assumed as 48 instead of 49.

Zone 14. May 20. C. $D_0 = -34^\circ\,34'\,50''$—Continued.

No.	Mag.	I.	II.	III.	IV.	V.	VI.	VII.	T. (h. m. s.)	a_1 (s.)	a_2 (s.)	MICROMETER.		r.	i (′ ″)	d_1 (″)	d_2 (″)	Mean Right Ascension, 1850.0 (h. m. s.)	Mean Declination, 1850.0 (° ′ ″)
33	8.9		8.5		45.7				15 1 45.90	+39.00	+1.02	IV.	3	40.148	−19 23.2	−23.1	−4.8	15 2 25.92	−34 54 41.1
34	9				42.0	1.0			3 42.08	39.02	0.82	IV.	2	19.850	40 38.6	22.8	9.3	4 21.92	35 16 0.7
35	9			52.0	12.5	31.2			9 12.45	39.07	0.84	IV.	3	26.291	33 52.9	22.0	7.8	9 52.36	9 12.7
36	9						13.0		9 35.43	39.07	0.91	VI.	3	32.022	27 52.8	21.9	6.6	10 15.41	3 11.3
37	7.8		52.8	11.4	30.7	49.7	8.0		14 30.52	39.12	0.73	IV.	2	13.378	47 24.4	21.2	10.8	15 10.37	22 46.4
38	7.8		58.0	16.8	35.6	54.5	13.1		16 35.60	39.14	0.79	IV.	3	20.856	39 33.5	20.9	9.1	17 15.53	35 14 53.5
39	8.9		38.0	56.2	15.2	34.0	53.0		19 15.31	39.16	0.93	IV.	4	42.014	17 24.4	20.5	4.4	19 55.45	34 52 39.3
40	8		13.0	32.0	51.5	10.4	29.0		20 51.19	39.18	0.84	IV.	3	28.250	31 50.0	20.2	7.4	21 31.21	35 7 7.6
41	9					56.0			21 37.19	39.18	0.88	V.	3	33.396	26 27.1	20.1	6.3	22 17.25	35 1 43.5
42	8			13.7	32.5	52.1			30 32.78	39.26	0.91	IV.	3	38.869	20 43.4	18.7	5.1	31 12.95	34 55 57.2
43	8.9				12.8	32.0			32 12.98	39.28	0.73	IV.	2	19.479	41 2.0	18.5	9.4	32 52.99	35 16 19.9
44	9						20.0	38.9	32 42.65	39.28	1.00	VI.	4	48.831	10 15.5	18.4	2.9	33 22.93	34 45 26.8
45	8			32.0	50.5	9.0	28.0		34 50.54	39.30	1.06	IV.	4	56.563	2 11.9	18.0	1.3	35 30.90	34 37 21.2
46	8		8.2	27.0	46.2	5.4	23.8	42.5	35 46.13	39.31	0.83	IV.	3	32.916	26 57.0	17.9	6.1	36 26.27	35 2 11.3
47	8.9		10.2	29.3	48.5	8.0	25.8	45.0	35 48.41	39.31	0.83	IV.	3	32.444	27 26.8	17.9	6.5	36 28.55	2 41.2
48	9				31.5		38.5		44 1.21	39.38	0.75	IV.	3	26.151	34 1.6	16.6	7.9	44 41.34	9 16.1
49	8				28.7			25.5	45 28.86	39.40	0.70	IV.	3	21.822	38 32.9	16.4	8.8	46 8.96	13 48.1
50	8					11.3	0.0	19.4	49 22.68	39.43	0.60	V.	2	11.621	49 14.2	15.0	11.2	50 2.71	24 31.2
51	9.10								52		0.60	IV.	2	13.132	47 39.8	15.4	10.8	52	22 56.0
52	8				45.0	4.0	22.5		53 45.06	39.47	0.77	IV.	3	33.401	26 26.8	15.2	6.2	54 25.30	35 1 38.2
53	9		30.0			26.0			58 7.40	39.51	0.92	IV.	4	48.869	10 14.0	14.5	2.9	58 47.83	34 45 21.4
54	9				52.0	10.0			58 51.61	39.51	0.73	IV.	3	29.	31			15 59 31.85	35 0
55	8.9				34.0	52.1			15 59 33.63	39.52	0.65	IV.	3	21.389	39 0.3	14.2	9.0	16 0 13.80	14 13.5
56	9			7.0	25.6	44.5	3.5		16 1 25.74	39.53	0.67	IV.	3	22.928	37 23.6	14.0	8.6	2 5.94	12 36.2
57	9.10			57.2					3 16.05	39.55	0.56	III.	2	11.652	49 12.4	13.6	11.2	3 56.16	24 27.2
58	9.10							34.0	3 37.40	39.55	0.57	VII.	2	13.489	47 16.4	13.6	10.7	4 17.52	22 30.7
59	7.8		11.1	30.2	49.0		26.5		8 48.92	39.60	0.69	IV.	3	28.178	31 54.4	12.7	7.4	9 29.21	7 4.5
60	9								8		0.74	VI.	3	33.000	26 51.4	12.6	6.3	9	35 2 0.5
61	8		25.0	43.5	2.5	21.0			14 2.40	39.64	0.83	IV.	4	45.159	14 7.1	11.7	3.7	14 42.87	34 49 12.5
62	8		4.0			59.5			15 41.17	39.65	0.92	IV.	4	56.021	2 45.9	11.4	1.4	16 21.74	34 37 48.7
63	8		36.0	55.0	14.0	33.0			18 13.93	39.67	0.54	IV.	2	14.957	45 45.4	10.9	10.4	18 54.14	35 20 56.7
64	8.9			24.0		1.5		38.0	18 42.69	39.68	0.65	IV.	3	27.279	32 50.9	10.9	7.6	19 23.02	7 59.4
65	8.9		41.6	0.4	19.4	38.0	56.0		23 19.29	39.71	0.58	IV.	3	22.352	37 59.9	10.6	8.7	23 59.58	13 8.6
66	7			21.0	39.8		17.7		24 39.88	39.72	0.49	IV.	2	11.752	49 6.1	9.7	11.1	25 20.09	35 24 16.9
67	6						27.5	46.0	25 49.83	39.73	0.73	VI.	3	38.251	21 22.0	9.5	5.2	26 30.29	34 56 26.7
68	9		41.2	0.6	19.0	39.0			29 19.10	39.76	0.70	IV.	3	37.521	22 8.2	8.8	5.3	29 59.56	34 57 12.3
69	7					21.5	42.1		30 2.45	39.77	0.48	V.	3	12.804	48 0.1	8.7	10.9	30 42.70	35 23 9.7
70	9				10.0	34.5			32 34.70	39.79	0.49	IV.	2	13.622	47 9.1	8.1	10.6	33 14.98	22 18.0
71	9				10.7		7.0		35 29.42	39.81	0.49	IV.	3	15.802	44 52.4	7.6	10.2	36 4.72	20 0.2
72	9.10				52.0				39 10.81	39.84	0.63	III.	3	33.246	26 36.3	6.8	6.3	39 51.28	1 39.4
73	8			3.5	22.0	40.8	0.0		41 22.17	39.85	0.54	IV.	3	23.551	36 44.6	6.4	8.5	42 2.56	11 49.5
74	9.10		22.2	40.7			18.1		45 40.74	39.89	0.50	IV.	3	21.344	39 3.1	5.5	9.0	46 21.13	14 7.6
75	8					18.0			47 18.05	39.90	0.36	IV.	3	6.389	54 42.0	5.1	12.3	47 58.31	29 49.4
76	9					19.0			47 41.26	39.90	0.38	IV.	2	9.188	51 46.7	5.1	11.7	48 31.54	26 53.5
77	8					35.5		13.0	53 16.63	39.94	0.57	IV.	3	31.740	28 10.8	3.6	6.6	53 57.14	3 11.2
78	9			6.0		44.0			54 6.23	39.95	0.54	IV.	3	29.034	31 0.6	3.7	7.2	54 46.72	6 1.5
79	7		30.0	48.5		7.5	26.1		55 48.61	39.96	0.46	IV.	3	20.038	40 24.8	3.4	9.2	56 29.03	15 7.4
80	8.9						56.0		56 18.38	39.96	0.51	VI.	3	25.182	35 2.1	3.2	8.1	56 55.85	35 10 3.4
81	7.8				14.0	32.5			56 55.07	39.96	0.60	V.	3	35.135	24 37.8	3.1	5.9	57 35.63	34 59 36.8
82	8							32.5	16 57 36.23	+39.97	+0.69	VII.	4	46.178	−13 1.5	−3.0	−3.4	16 58 16.39	−34 47 57.9

CORRECTIONS.

Date.	Corr. of Clock.	Hourly rate.	m	n	c	Zenith Point.	Mic. Co.
1846.	h.	s.	s.	s.	s.	° ′ ″	r.

INSTRUMENT READINGS.

Date.	CIRCLE.							Barom.	THERMOM.				
	A.	B.	C.	D.	E.	F.	Mean		At.	Ex.	U.	L.	I.
Zone 14	° ′ ″						″	in.	°	°	°	°	°
1846. May 20, 15 35											59.0		
16 3								29.930	62.8	57.5			
16 35											56.0		
16 57								29.926	61.2	55.0			
17 5	73 54 59.1	61.9	65.0	63.4	59.9	49.7	59.83				60.2	60.2	64.0

ZONE 15.   MAY 21.   P. $D_0 = -38°\ 20'\ 50''$.

No.	Mag.	I.	II.	III.	IV.	V.	VI.	VII.	T.	a_1	a_4	Micr.	n	r.	i	d_1	d_2	Mean Right Ascension, 1850.0	Mean Declination, 1850.0
									h. m. s.	s.	s.			r.	′ ″	″	″	h. m. s.	° ′ ″
1	5	15.0	35.0	55.0	14.5				13 30 14.58	+38.04	+0.93	IV.	3	22.930	−37 23.4	−38.3	−11.5	13 30 53.55	−38 59 3.2
2	7			10.0	30.0				31 29.92	38.05	0.94	IV.	3	24.560	35 41.4	38.3	11.0	32 8.91	57 20.7
3	8	39.0	59.0	19.0					33 38.48	38.08	0.99	IV.	3	32.110	27 47.7	38.2	8.2	34 17.55	49 24.1
4	8	3.5	23.5	43.0	2.5				36 2.66	38.10	1.04	III.	4	44.793	14 30.6	38.1	3.7	36 41.80	38 36 2.4
5	6		5.5	25.5	45.5			45.0	40 45.39	38.16	0.90	IV.	2	13.280	47 30.6	37.8	15.2	41 24.45	39 9 13.6
6	7	23.0	42.7	2.5	22.0				46 22.12	38.22	1.07	IV.	4	40.774	18 42.3	37.5	5.1	47 1.41	38 40 14.9
7	8			49.5	9.2	29.0			48 9.24	38.24	1.09	V.	4	44.845	14 26.2	37.4	3.7	48 48.57	35 57.3
8	7	39.0	58.5	18.0					51 37.84	38.28	1.11	III.	4	49.210	9 52.9	37.2	2.2	52 17.23	31 22.3
9	7			6.0	26.0				52 25.89	38.29	1.06	IV.	4	38.590	20 59.5	37.1	6.0	53 5.24	42 32.6
10	8				30.0		9.3		13 53 29.00	38.30	0.98	IV.	3	23.300	37 0.4	37.0	11.5	13 54 9.18	38 58 38.9
11	9	57.0	17.0		58.0				14 0 56.68	38.38	0.99	IV.	3	21.725	38 39.0	36.5	12.0	14 1 36.05	39 0 17.5
12	7	59.0	19.0	39.0					12 58.59	38.52	1.02	III.	3	25.620	34 34.6	35.6	10.6	13 38.13	38 51 10.8
13	4		30.0	49.5			48.5		13 9.26	38.52	1.06	VI.	3	32.950	27 57.2	35.6	8.3	13 48.84	49 31.1
14	7	43.0	3.0	22.5					16 42.31	38.56	1.06	III.	3	30.900	29 3.3	35.3	8.7	17 21.03	38 50 37.3
15	6					13.5	33.5		16 53.69	38.56	0.97	VI.	1	10.855	49 58.7	35.3	16.1	17 33.22	39 11 40.1
16	6	24.0	43.5	3.5	23.0			22.5	26 23.17	38.66	1.05	IV.	3	25.490	34 43.1	34.4	10.7	27 2.88	38 56 18.2
17	7	34.5	54.0	14.0	34.0				29 33.79	38.70	1.07	IV.	3	26.945	33 11.6	34.1	10.1	30 13.56	54 45.8
18	7	33.0	53.0						33 33.34	38.74	1.10	II.	3	32.070	27 49.6	33.7	8.3	34 13.18	38 49 21.6
19	9					53.0	13.0	33.0	33 33.38	38.74	1.05	VII.	3	21.620	38 44.8	33.7	12.1	34 13.17	39 0 20.6
20	8		1.0	21.0					40 40.62	38.82	1.13	III.	3	35.230	24 31.8	33.0	7.1	41 20.57	38 46 1.9
21	7					35.0			43 35.04	38.85	1.03	IV.	1	14.505	46 10.9	32.6	14.7	44 14.92	39 7 48.2
22	9					22.0			44 22.06	38.86	1.16	IV.	3	37.350	22 18.9	32.6	6.3	45 2.08	39 43 47.8
23	8					27.0			44 27.04	38.86	1.17	VII.	3	39.495	20 3.4	32.6	5.6	45 7.07	41 31.6
24	7				4.5	24.0			46 24.16	38.89	1.14	IV.	3	33.100	26 45.5	32.4	7.9	47 4.19	38 48 15.8
25	8							13.0	46 13.59	38.88	1.08	VII.	2	21.020	39 24.0	32.4	12.3	46 53.55	39 0 58.7
26	8	50.0	10.0	30.0	49.5				14 49 49.42	38.92	1.03	IV.	1	10.780	50 4.0	31.9	16.2	14 50 29.37	11 42.1
27	8	10.0	29.5	49.5	9.5				15 6 9.33	39.10	1.12	IV.	3	21.823	38 32.9	29.8	12.0	15 6 49.55	39 0 4.7
28	9					55.0			11 35.27	39.16	1.23	V.	4	40.165	19 20.3	29.1	5.3	12 15.66	39 10 44.7
29	4	18.3	38.5	58.3	18.0				14 18.07	39.19	1.08	IV.	1	12.120	48 40.2	28.7	15.6	14 58.34	39 10 14.5
30	6	51.5	11.5	30.7	50.5			50.0	23 50.69	39.28	1.20	IV.	3	31.090	28 51.7	27.3	8.6	24 31.17	38 50 17.6
31	8			45.0					27 4.71	39.32	1.28	III.	4	45.250	14 1.5	26.8	3.5	27 45.31	35 21.8
32	8					36.0			27 16.28	39.32	1.23	V.	3	35.170	24 35.6	26.7	7.1	27 56.83	45 59.4
33	6					21.0			28 1.28	39.33	1.26	V.	4	41.095	18 21.8	26.6	5.0	28 41.87	39 43.4
34	6					31.0			28 11.28	39.33	1.27	V.	4	42.850	16 31.5	26.6	6.7	28 51.88	37 52.5
35	8		35.0	55.0	15.0				33 14.80	39.38	1.18	IV.	3	23.130	37 11.0	25.0	11.5	33 55.36	38 58 38.3
36	9				40.0				41 40.04	39.47	1.17	VII.	2	18.530	42 0.2	24.4	13.2	42 20.68	39 3 27.8
37			57.0						44 37. .	39.50								45 (16.)	
38	8		33.5	54.0	13.5				48 13.38	39.53	1.34	IV.	4	47.180	12 0.2	23.3	2.9	48 54.25	38 33 16.4
39	8		0.0		43.0			42.0	49 42.95	39.55	1.34	IV.	4	46.600	12 36.5	23.0	3.1	50 23.84	33 52.6
40	7	8.0	27.0	47.0			46.0		50 6.71	39.55	1.32	VI.	4	41.370	19 4.1	23.0	4.9	50 47.58	38 50 37.9
41	7	2.0	22.0	42.0					53 1.59	39.58	1.21	III.	2	20.890	39 33.3	22.5	12.3	53 42.38	39 0 59.1
42	9	21.0				39.0		18.5	53 19.22	39.58	1.28	VII.	3	33.340	26 29.7	22.4	7.8	54 0.08	38 47 49.9
43	6					10.0	29.0		55 49.85	39.61	1.26	V.	3	30.665	29 18.2	22.0	8.8	56 30.72	50 39.0
44	7		12.0	31.0	51.0			50.0	57 51.01	39.63	1.33	IV.	4	38.990	20 34.3	21.6	5.8	58 31.97	41 51.7
45	7		12.0	31.5	51.5			50.5	15 57 51.37	39.63	1.33	VII.	4	39.650	19 51.2	21.6	5.5	15 58 32.33	41 8.3
46	8	58.5	18.0	38.0					16 3 57.62	39.68	1.31	III.	3	36.410	23 17.7	20.5	6.7	16 4 38.61	39 44 34.9
47	7	24.0	44.0	3.5	23.0				9 23.37	39.74	1.21	IV.	2	14.300	46 26.7	19.5	14.8	10 4.32	39 7 51.0
48	6	45.0	4.0	24.0		4.0			9 43.98	39.74	1.22	IV.	2	18.280	42 17.2	19.4	13.4	10 24.94	39 3 40.0
49	4	12.0	32.0	51.5	11.3			10.3	16 13 11.27	+39.77	+1.30	IV.	3	31.025	−28 55.7	−18.8	−8.6	16 13 52.34	−38 50 13.1

CORRECTIONS.

Date.	Corr. of Clock.	Hourly rate.	m	n	c	Zenith Point.	Mic. Co.
	h.	s.	s.	s.	s.	s.	° ′ ″	r.
1846, May 21,	16	+ 30.231	+ 0.021	+ 0.505	− 0.353	+ 0.207	0 0 2.18	30.000

REMARKS.

(15) 13. Mic. reading assumed as 31ʳ.950 instead of 32ʳ.950.

May 21. Very clear; observed all stars which would bear illumination.

INSTRUMENT READINGS.

	Date.	CIRCLE. A.	B.	C.	D.	E.	F.	Mean.	Barom.	At.	Ex.	U.	L.	I.
		° ′ ″						″	in.	°	°	°	°	°
Zone 15	1846, May 21, 13 30	77 39 68.0	68.3	73.7	69.7	68.5	58.3	67.75	30.104	65.3	60.7			
	14 29								30.140	64.8	60.9			
	15 14								30.148	65.0	60.3			
	16 3								30.152	64.8	59.8			
	17 1								30.150	64.4	58.5			
	17 38								30.158	64.0	57.5	65.0	62.5	

Zone 15. May 21. P. $D_0 = -38°\ 20'\ 50''$—Continued.

No.	Mag.	I.	II.	III.	IV.	V.	VI.	VII.	T. (h m s)	a_1	a_2	MICROMETER		r,	i (' ")	d_1 (")	d_2 (")	Mean Right Ascension, 1850.0 (h m s)	Mean Declination, 1850.0 (° ' ")
50	8			6.0	26.0				16 20 45.59	+39.84	+1.37	III.	4	40.635	−18 51.1	−17.4	−5.2	16 21 26.80	−38 40 3.7
51	9				50.0				24 50.05	39.88	1.31	IV.	3	28.890	31 9.6	16.5	9.4	25 31.24	52 25.5
52	7	39.0	58.5	18.3	38.0				27 38.08	39.90	1.33	IV.	3	30.554	29 23.4	16.0	8.8	28 19.31	50 38.2
53	8		24.0		3.0				34 3.24	39.96	1.41	IV.	4	42.180	17 14.1	14.7	4.6	34 44.61	38 23.4
54	7	23.0		2.0			1.0		34 21.79	39.96	1.40	VI.	4	41.455	17 58.7	14.6	4.9	35 3.15	38 39 8.2
55	7			32.0	52.0			51.0	35 51.79	39.97	1.27	IV.	2	16.195	44 27.8	14.3	14.1	36 33.03	39 5 46.2
56	8					25.5		4.0	36 4.99	39.98	1.23	VII.	1	7.095	53 53.7	14.3	17.6	36 46.20	15 15.6
57	8						22.0		16 57 42.37	40.16	1.31	VI.	2	14.130	46 36.6	9.8	14.9	16 58 23.84	39 7 51.3
58	7	18.5	38.0	57.5	17.0				17 1 17.32	40.18	1.47	IV.	4	42.677	16 42.8	9.0	4.4	17 1 58.97	38 37 46.2
59	8		19.3	39.3	59.0				3 58.94	40.20	1.45	IV.	3	40.050	19 29.3	8.4	3.4	4 40.59	38 40 33.1
60	8		22.5	42.0	1.5				6 1.89	40.22	1.29	IV.	1	7.000	54 0.7	8.0	17.6	6 43.40	39 15 16.3
61	9			57.0	16.5				20 16.67	40.33	1.42	IV.	3	27.440	32 40.8	4.8	9.9	20 58.43	38 53 45.5
62	10			16.					20 16.	40.33	1.37	VII.	2	19.020	41 0.9	4.8	13.1	20 (56.).	39 2 37.3
63	8		25.0	45.0	5.0				24 4.74	40.35	1.49	IV.	4	39.070	25 43.0	4.0	5.7	24 46.58	38 46 42.7
64	4		52.5	12.0	31.5			30.5	25 31.64	40.36	1.54	IV.	2	48.717	10 23.6	3.7	2.4	26 13.54	38 31 19.7
65	8	5.0	25.0					22.5	29 4.57	40.39	1.37	II.	2	15.495	45 11.5	2.9	14.4	29 46.33	39 6 18.8
66	9							22.5	28 22.90	40.38	1.33	VII.	1	7.142	53 50.8	3.0	17.6	29 4.61	39 15 1.4
67	3	26.0	45.7	5.5	25.2				31 25.27	40.40	1.42	IV.	3	24.530	35 43.3	2.3	11.0	32 7.09	38 56 46.6
68	7	4.0	23.0	43.0	3.0				33 2.86	40.41	1.49	IV.	4	37.020	22 38.0	2.0	6.5	33 44.76	38 43 36.5
69	8	25.5	45.0						35 24.90	40.43	1.36	II.	1	10.250	50 37.1	1.4	16.4	36 6.69	39 11 44.9
70	7	21.0	41.0	0.5	20.0				17 38 20.29	+40.45	+1.44	IV.	3	25.660	−34 32.3	−0.8	−10.6	17 39 2.18	−38 55 33.7

Zone 16. May 25. P. $D_0 = -35°\ 49'\ 40''$.

No.	Mag.	I.	II.	III.	IV.	V.	VI.	VII.	T. (h m s)	a_1	a_2	MICROMETER		r,	i (' ")	d_1 (")	d_2 (")	Mean Right Ascension, 1850.0 (h m s)	Mean Declination, 1850.0 (° ' ")
1	8	31.0			28.0				13 8 28.11	+41.20	+1.02	IV.	3	36.790	−22 53.9	−49.9	−5.2	13 9 10.33	−36 13 29.0
2	3	31.0	50.5	9.5	28.5				11 28.38	41.23	1.18	IV.	4	54.245	4 36.8	49.9	1.0	12 10.79	35 55 7.7
3	8	48.0	7.0		45.0				15 45.13	41.27	1.01	IV.	3	35.282	24 28.7	49.8	5.6	16 27.41	36 15 4.1
4	8		5.5	24.5	43.5	3.5			21 2.59	41.32	1.07	IV.	4	41.680	17 45.4	49.7	4.0	21 44.98	36 8 19.1
5	9							53.0	21 55.95	41.33	1.19	VII.	4	54.880	3 55.1	49.7	0.8	22 38.47	35 54 25.6
6	7						8.0	27.5	23 30.16	41.35	1.10	VI.	4	44.930	14 20.4	49.6	3.2	24 12.61	36 4 53.2
7	7	40.5		18.5	37.7				27 37.71	41.39	0.98	IV.	3	30.670	29 18.0	49.5	6.7	28 20.08	19 54.2
8	9	21.0		59.5					30 18.47	41.41	0.93	III.	3	25.395	34 48.9	49.4	8.0	31 0.81	25 26.3
9	4			41.5					33 0.64	41.44	0.84	V.	2	14.500	46 14.0	49.3	10.8	33 42.92	36 54.1
10	9		15.0		52.0				36 52.59	41.48	1.08	IV.	4	40.315	19 11.3	49.1	4.3	37 35.15	9 44.7
11	8				4.0	23.0			38 23.08	41.49	1.04	IV.	4	36.330	23 21.4	49.1	5.3	39 5.61	13 55.8
12	5				12.0	31.0	50.0	9.0	39 11.85	41.50	0.96	IV.	3	28.093	31 59.7	49.0	7.4	39 54.31	22 36.1
13	8	57.0	16.0	36.0					41 54.68	41.53	0.85	III.	2	12.740	48 4.2	48.9	11.2	42 37.06	38 44.3
14	8					17.0	36.0		42 57.06	41.54	1.12	VI.	4	44.360	14 56.4	48.9	3.3	43 40.62	5 28.6
15	8				38.0	57.0	15.5		44 37.80	41.55	1.09	VI.	4	42.615	16 45.8	48.8	3.8	45 20.44	7 18.4
16	8						25.0	44.0	47 46.70	41.59	0.95	VII.	3	25.080	35 8.0	48.6	8.1	48 29.24	25 44.7
17	7		52.0	11.0	30.0				51 30.23	41.62	0.81	IV.	1	7.330	53 40.2	48.4	12.6	52 12.66	44 21.2
18	8						23.0	42.0	51 44.60	41.63	0.87	VI.	2	15.200	45 29.7	48.4	10.6	52 27.10	36 8.7
19	9	28.0	48.0	7.0					54 26.07	41.65	0.81	III.	2	7.700	53 19.8	48.2	12.5	55 8.53	44 0.5
20	7	31.0	50.0	9.0			47.5	6.5	54 28.27	41.65	0.90	VI.	2	18.810	41 43.2	48.2	9.7	55 10.82	32 21.1
21	8							16.0	13 55 18.87	41.66	1.14	VII.	4	47.210	11 56.8	48.1	2.7	13 56 1.67	2 27.6
22	7	24.5		2.0	21.0				14 0 21.28	41.71	1.04	IV.	3	33.585	26 15.1	47.8	6.0	14 1 4.03	36 16 48.9
23	9			45.0					4 4.00	41.75	1.23	VI.	4	54.550	4 16.6	47.6	0.9	4 46.98	35 54 45.1
24	7	40.0	59.0	18.0	37.0				14 9 37.15	+41.80	+1.03	IV.	3	32.110	−27 47.7	−47.1	−6.3	14 10 19.98	−36 18 21.1

CORRECTIONS.

Date.	Corr. of Clock.	Hourly rate.	m	n	c	Zenith Point.	Mic. Co.
1846. May 25, 16h	+33.686 s	+0.044 s	+0.505 s	+0.353 s	+0.207 s	0° 0' 2.25"	r, 29.999

REMARKS.

(15) 63. Micrometer assumed as 34'.070 instead of 39'.070.
May 25, Readings of Bar. and Ther. at 15h 35m; no clouds apparent until 17h 15m.

INSTRUMENT READINGS.

	Date.	CIRCLE.							Barom.	THERMOM.				
		A.	B.	C.	D.	E.	F.	Mean.		At.	Ex.	U.	L.	I.
Zone 16	1846. May 25, 13 8								in. 30.060	78.0	76.5			
	14 26								30.056	76.0	74.5			
	15 51								30.046	75.7	72.0			
	18 17	75 9 60.0	55.4	64.6	57.3	55.2	47.0	56.58	30.014	73.0	69.4			7.3

ZONE 16.　MAY 25.　P. D. = −35° 49′ 40″—Continued.

No.	Mag.	I.	II.	III.	IV.	V.	VI.	VII.
25	9						36.0	
26	9						29.0	
27	7	40.0		18.3	37.0			
28	.		57.0					
29	8	18.0	37.0	56.0	15.3			
30	4	54.5	13.3	32.5	51.5			48.7
31	5	1.5	20.5	39.5	58.5			55.5
32	5	35.3	54.0	13.5	32.5			
33	7				48.0		26.7	46.0
34	4	4.0		42.0	1.0			
35	5	44.0	3.0		41.0			
36	6					19.0	38.0	57.0
37	7	46.0	5.0	24.0	43.3			
38	9				32.0			31.0
39	9	12.0	31.0	50.0				
40	9				0.0			
41	8				24.0	43.0	2.0	
42	8		43.5	2.0	21.5			
43	7	27.0		6.0				
44	8	28.0		7.0			4.0	23.0
45	8							37.5
46	8						49.0	8.0
47	7					21.0	40.0	59.8
48	7				54.0		32.0	
49	7	7.5	27.5	46.0	5.0			
50	7	55.0	15.0					
51	8					23.0		
52	7	45.0	4.0	23.5	42.0			
53	8	2.0		40.0				
54	8		12.0	31.0	50.0			
55	9	43.0	2.0	21.0	40.0			
56	8					11.0	30.5	50.0
57	7	58.5	17.0	36.5	55.5			
58	6			44.0	3.0	22.0		
59	7		56.0	15.0				
60	7	51.0	10.0	29.5	48.5			
61	7	39.0	58.0	17.0	36.0			
62	8				26.0			
63	6				14.0	33.3		
64	7	8.0	27.0	46.0	5.0			
65	7				17.0			
66	8							33.5
67	6.7			36.0	55.0			
68	8.9			57.5		35.5	54.5	
69	5	2.5		40.3				
70	4	34.0	52.5	11.5	30.7			
71	8			30.0	49.5			
72	7			8.0	27.5			
73	8		10.0	29.0				

No.	T.	a_1	a_2	MICROMETER		$r.$	i	d_1	d_2	Mean Right Ascension, 1850.0	Mean Declination, 1850.0
	h. m. s.	s.	s.			r.	′ ″	″	″	h. m. s.	° ′ ″
25	14 9 57.93	+41.81	+1.11	VII.	4	40.210	−19 16.3	−47.1	−4.3	14 10 40.85	−36 9 47.7
26	26 50.96	41.97	1.16	VI.	4	44.430	14 52.0	45.6	3.3	27 34.09	5 20.9
27	38 37.09	42.08	1.22	VII.	4	49.405	9 39.0	44.4	2.1	39 20.39	0 5.5
28	14 49 35. .	42.19	. .							14 50 (17.)	
29	15 9 15.30	42.39	0.99	IV.	2	18.675	41 52.3	40.7	9.7	15 9 58.68	32 22.7
30	12 51.56	42.42	1.09	IV.	3	31.435	28 30.1	40.2	6.5	13 35.07	18 56.8
31	16 58.55	42.46	1.13	IV.	3	35.955	23 46.3	39.6	5.4	17 42.14	14 11.3
32	51 32.48	42.78	1.13	IV.	3	31.265	28 40.8	34.1	6.6	52 16.39	19 1.5
33	52 48.28	42.79	0.94	VII.	1	8.723	52 11.8	33.9	12.3	53 32.01	42 38.0
34	56 1.16	42.82	1.09	IV.	3	27.175	32 57.3	33.4	7.6	56 45.07	23 18.3
35	56 41.17	42.82	1.12	IV.	3	29.760	30 15.0	33.3	6.9	57 25.11	20 35.2
36	15 56 59.79	42.82	1.13	VI.	3	31.613	28 18.5	33.2	6.5	15 57 43.74	18 38.2
37	16 7 43.17	42.92	1.22	IV.	3	38.363	21 15.3	31.2	4.8	16 8 27.31	36 11 31.3
38	9 32. .	42.93	1.36	VII.	4	54.300	−4 31.7	30.9	0.9	10 (16.)	35 54 43.5
39	13 9.08	42.96	1.26	IV.	4	43.925	15 24.4	30.2	3.4	13 53.30	36 5 38.0
40	28 0.05	43.08	1.07	IV.	2	18.100	42 28.4	27.2	9.9	28 44.20	32 45.5
41	29 23.96	43.10	1.24	VI.	3	38.990	20 35.5	27.0	4.6	30 8.30	10 47.1
42	32 21.46	43.12	1.16	IV.	F W	29.099	30 0.6	26.3	6.9	33 5.74	20 13.2
43	37 24.80	43.16	1.03	III.	2	14.450	46 17.3	25.3	10.8	38 8.99	36 33.4
44	37 25.70	43.16	1.04	VI.	2	14.133	46 36.5	25.3	10.9	38 9.90	36 52.7
45	38 40.29	43.17	1.27	VII.	4	41.410	18 1.0	25.0	4.0	39 24.73	8 10.0
46	40 10.65	43.18	1.10	VII.	2	21.445	38 57.7	24.7	9.1	40 54.93	29 11.5
47	42 1.58	43.20	0.96	V.	1	6.273	54 46.3	24.3	13.0	42 45.74	36 45 3.6
48	43 54.00	43.21	1.36	VI.	4	50.770	8 13.8	23.9	1.7	44 38.57	35 58 19.4
49	52 5.29	43.27	1.03	IV.	2	12.777	48 1.9	22.1	11.3	52 49.59	36 38 15.3
50	54 52.84	43.29	1.09	II.	2	19.160	41 21.8	21.5	9.6	55 37.22	31 32.9
51	55 3.84	43.29	1.17	V.	3	27.780	32 19.3	21.5	7.4	55 48.30	22 28.2
52	57 42.31	43.31	1.13	IV.	3	24.285	35 58.7	20.9	8.3	16 58 26.75	26 7.9
53	16 59 59.14	43.33	1.24	IV.	3	36.950	22 43.9	20.4	5.1	17 0 43.71	12 49.4
54	17 7 50.09	43.38	1.32	III.	4	43.843	15 29.7	18.6	3.4	8 34.78	55 1.6
55	11 40.16	43.41	1.19	IV.	3	28.583	31 29.0	17.7	7.2	12 24.76	21 33.9
56	13 52.29	43.43	1.21	VII.	3	31.230	28 42.3	17.2	6.6	14 36.93	18 46.1
57	16 55.56	43.45	1.17	IV.	3	26.837	33 18.4	16.5	7.7	17 40.18	23 22.6
58	18 2.97	43.46	1.05	IV.	2	12.173	48 39.8	16.3	11.5	18 47.48	38 47.6
59	24 34.18	43.50	1.18	IV.	3	26.390	33 46.7	14.7	7.8	25 18.86	23 49.2
60	40 48.43	43.60	1.19	IV.	3	25.100	35 7.4	10.8	8.1	41 33.22	25 6.3
61	42 36.21	43.61	1.16	IV.	3	22.400	37 56.9	10.4	8.8	43 20.98	27 56.1
62	43 26.06	43.61	1.23	IV.	3	29.900	30 6.2	10.2	6.9	44 10.90	20 3.3
63	44 14.09	43.62	1.18	IV.	3	23.860	36 25.1	10.0	8.4	44 58.89	36 26 23.5
64	47 5.03	43.63	1.42	IV.	4	50.000	9 3.1	9.3	1.9	47 50.08	35 58 54.3
65	48 16.98	43.64	1.41	IV.	4	48.300	10 50.0	9.0	2.3	49 2.03	36 0 41.3
66	48 36.40	43.64	1.42	VII.	4	48.935	10 8.3	8.9	2.2	49 21.46	35 59 59.4
67	50 55.09	43.66	1.23	IV.	3	28.850	32 2.3	8.4	7.4	51 39.98	36 21 58.1
68	51 16.43	43.66	1.23	VI.	3	29.025	31 0.9	8.3	7.1	52 1.32	36 20 56.3
69	53 59.35	43.67	1.46	III.	4	54.690	4 9.6	7.6	0.8	54 44.48	35 53 (57.)
70	55 30.73	43.68	1.40	IV.	4	47.490	11 40.7	7.2	2.5	56 15.81	36 1 30.4
71	56 49.33	43.69	1.29	IV.	3	35.750	23 59.2	6.9	5.4	57 34.31	13 51.5
72	17 58 27.34	43.70	1.08	IV.	1	9.570	51 19.9	6.5	12.2	17 59 12.12	41 18.6
73	18 1 48.21	+43.72	+1.17	III.	2	19.960	−40 31.7	−5.6	−9.5	18 2 33.10	−36 30 26.8

CORRECTIONS.

Date.	Corr. of Clock.	Hourly rate.	m	n	c	Zenith Point.	Mic. Co.
1846.	h.	s.	s.	s.	s.	° ′ ″	r.

INSTRUMENT READINGS.

Date.	CIRCLE.							Barom.	THERMOM.				
	A.	B.	C.	D.	E.	F.	Mean.		At.	Ex.	U.	L.	I.
1846. h. m.	° ′ ″						″	in.	°	°	°	°	°

REMARKS.

(16) 54. Assumed an error of 10^s, making micrometer reading $53^r.843$.

(16) 67. Micrometer reading assumed as $28^r.050$ instead of $28^r.850$.

ZONE 16. MAY 25. P. $D_o = -35° 49' 40''$—Continued.

No.	Mag.	I.	II.	III.	IV.	V.	VI.	VII.	T.	a_1	a_4	Micrometer	r.	i	d_1	d_2	Mean R.A. 1850.0	Mean Decl. 1850.0
74	6	59.0	18.0	37.3	56.5				h. m. s. 18 4 56.46	+43.73	+1.11	IV. 2	13.930	−46 50.3	−4.9	−11.0	h. m. s. 18 5 41.30	−36 36 46.2
75	8	29.3	48.0	7.0					9 26.36	43.76	1.18	III. 2	21.250	39 11.0	3.7	9.1	10 11.30	29 3.8
76	4	1.0	20.0						11 58.55	43.77	1.07	II. 1	6.960	54 2.8	3.1	12.9	12 43.30	43 58.8
77	4		58.0	17.0	36.3				12 36.22	43.77	1.27	IV. 3	31.445	28 29.5	2.9	6.5	13 21.26	18 18.9
78	6	34.0	52.7	11.7	30.5				14 30.79	43.78	1.39	IV. 4	45.060	14 13.2	2.5	3.1	15 15.96	3 55.8
79	7			13.0	32.0				16 32.04	43.79	1.38	IV. 4	43.300	16 3.9	2.0	3.5	17 17.21	5 49.4
80	8			16.5	35.0				18 17 35.28	+43.80	+1.40	IV. 4	45.650	−13 36.1	−1.7	−2.9	18 18 20.48	−36 3 20.7

ZONE 17. MAY 27. C. $D_o = -37° 5' 30''$.

No.	Mag.	I.	II.	III.	IV.	V.	VI.	VII.	T.	a_1	a_4	Micrometer	r.	i	d_1	d_2	Mean R.A. 1850.0	Mean Decl. 1850.0
1	9.10					48.0			13 33 28.54	+43.08	+0.99	V. 3	31.149	−28 48.0	−11.9	−8.0	13 34 12.61	−37 34 37.9
2	9.10						31.0		33 52.24	43.08	1.01	VI. 3	35.620	24 7.1	11.9	6.8	34 36.33	29 55.8
3	9		2.5		41.0				37 41.15	43.12	1.03	IV. 3	38.649	20 57.3	11.6	5.9	38 25.30	26 44.8
4	9		3.0	22.0	41.2	0.5	20.5		38 41.45	43.13	1.00	IV. 3	34.925	24 50.9	11.6	7.0	39 25.58	30 39.5
5	9		36.0	55.0	14.3				41 14.49	43.16	1.06	IV. 4	41.832	17 35.8	11.4	5.0	41 58.71	23 22.2
6	9.10				3.2	22.0			42 2.65	43.17	0.89	IV. 2	14.129	46 37.3	11.3	13.1	42 46.01	52 31.7
7	9		57.0	16.5					46 36.02	43.21	0.89	II. 2	11.249	49 37.5	10.9	14.0	47 20.12	55 32.4
8	8.9		52.0			50.0	9.5		47 11.25	43.22	0.98	IV. 3	26.351	33 49.1	10.9	9.4	47 55.45	39 39.4
9	8.9			3.5	43.0	2.0			47 3.82	43.22	1.01	IV. 3	30.898	29 3.6	10.9	8.1	47 48.05	34 52.6
10	9			45.2		43.0			51 4.45	43.26	1.08	IV. 3	41.631	17 50.0	10.6	5.0	51 48.79	23 35.6
11	9			55.0	14.0				51 14.17	43.26	1.12	IV. 3	47.884	11 17.3	10.6	3.3	51 58.55	17 1.2
12	9				18.7				54 18.75	43.29	0.96	IV. 3	22.082	38 16.7	10.3	10.7	55 3.00	44 7.7
13	9			53.0	12.0		51.0		55 12.22	43.30	1.02	IV. 3	32.280	27 37.1	10.2	7.7	55 56.54	33 25.0
14	9		22.0	41.0					59 0.60	43.34	1.06	III. 3	35.935	23 47.3	9.9	6.7	13 59 45.00	29 33.9
15	9			21.2	41.0	0.0			13 59 40.73	43.35	0.98	IV. 2	23.111	37 14.2	9.9	10.4	14 0 25.06	43 4.5
16	9			3.2	22.8	42.0			14 1 22.64	43.36	1.16	IV. 4	53.046	5 51.9	9.8	1.8	2 7.16	11 33.5
17	9					35.0			4 56.14	43.40	0.99	IV. 3	25.431	34 46.8	9.5	9.7	5 40.53	40 36.0
18	9		47.0		46.0	5.0			7 26.27	43.43	1.15	IV. 4	49.800	9 15.6	9.2	2.7	8 10.85	14 57.5
19	5			23.1	42.5	1.8	21.0	40.5	10 42.45	43.46	1.17	IV. 4	53.061	5 51.0	9.0	1.8	11 27.08	11 31.8
20	9			25.0	41.0				16 24.72	43.52	0.92	IV. 3	10.661	50 12.4	8.5	14.1	17 9.16	56 5.0
21	8.9			28.5	48.0	8.0			18 28.68	43.54	0.95	IV. 2	13.756	47 0.6	8.3	13.2	19 13.17	52 52.1
22	9			48.0		27.0			21 48.05	43.57	0.95	IV. 2	13.311	47 28.6	8.0	13.3	22 32.57	53 19.9
23	9		57.0	16.0	36.1		55.0		25 16.27	43.61	0.97	IV. 2	15.891	44 46.8	7.7	12.5	26 0.85	50 37.0
24	5		16.0	54.9	14.0	33.6	52.5		31 54.79	43.67	1.22	IV. 4	55.679	3 7.4	7.1	1.1	32 39.68	8 45.6
25	9			26.0		4.0			35 25.67	43.71	1.17	IV. 3	45.960	13 18.1	6.7	3.8	36 10.55	18 55.6
26	7				16.5	35.7	55.0		36 56.84	43.72	1.05	V. 2	26.748	33 25.9	6.6	9.4	37 41.61	39 11.9
27	9			11.0					41 11.05	43.77	1.03	IV. 2	21.360	39 4.1	6.1	10.9	41 55.85	44 51.1
28	8		37.0	56.0	15.7	35.0			42 56.22	43.78	1.07	IV. 3	27.681	32 25.5	6.0	9.0	43 41.07	38 10.5
29	9			18.5					48 37.94	43.84	1.05	IV. 3	23.551	36 44.6	5.3	10.3	49 22.83	42 30.2
30	7					40.0	50.9	7	49 1.51	43.85	1.20	V. 4	48.231	10 53.9	5.2	3.2	49 46.56	16 32.4
31	7			39.1	58.5	18.0	37.0	56.7	50 58.47	43.86	1.14	IV. 3	37.885	21 45.1	5.1	6.1	51 43.47	27 26.3
32	9				32.5	51.2			53 32.12	43.89	1.05	IV. 3	22.568	37 46.3	4.8	10.5	54 17.06	43 31.6
33	8.9		10.0		49.0	9.0		47.5	14 56 49.20	43.92	1.18	IV. 4	43.390	15 58.2	4.4	4.5	14 57 34.30	21 37.1
34	9		57.0		36.0				15 0 16.50	43.96	1.17	IV. 3	39.115	20 28.0	3.9	5.8	15 1 1.63	26 7.7
35	8			9.3	29.0	48.5	27.2		3 48.39	43.99	1.00	IV. 2	11.131	49 45.0	3.5	14.0	4 33.38	55 32.5
36	8		58.5		37.4	57.0	16.0		6 37.38	44.02	1.02	IV. 2	13.252	47 32.3	3.1	13.4	7 22.42	53 18.8
37	7.8		27.5	46.7	6.0	25.6	44.8	4.5	11 6.15	44.06	1.10	IV. 3	25.595	34 36.4	2.5	9.6	11 51.31	40 18.5
38	7.8			2.0	21.5	41.0	0.5	19.8	15 14 40.98	+44.10	+1.12	IV. 3	27.872	+32 13.5	−1.9	−9.0	15 15 26.20	−37 37 54.4

CORRECTIONS.

Date.		Corr. of Clock.	Hourly rate.	m	n	e	Zenith Point.	Mic. Co.
1846. May 27,	h. 16	s. + 35.269	s. + 0.038	s. + 0.505	s. + 0.353	s. + 0.207	° ' '' 0 0 2.73	r. 30.005

INSTRUMENT READINGS.

Date.		CIRCLE.							Barom.	THERMOM.				
		A.	B.	C.	D.	E.	F.	Mean.		At.	Ex.	U.	L.	I.
Zone 17	1846. May 27, 13 33	76 24 58.8	52.1	62.9	56.0	52.1	46.0	54.65	in. 29.739	78.0	75.5	78.0	77.0	77.5
	13 59								29.738	78.0	75.9			
	14 31	57.6	52.2	62.2	56.0	52.7	45.1	54.30	29.732	77.2	75.0	76.8	76.4	
	15 0								29.720		74.0			
	15 26									76.8	73.5			
	15 30	57.0	52.8	62.7	55.1	53.0	45.0	54.27				76.5	75.6	77.5
	19 20	60.9	58.0	67.0	61.1	57.9	49.1	59.00				74.0	74.4	77.5
	19 25								29.701	74.5	69.4			

REMARKS.

May 27. Night poor; hazy horizon.
14h 50m, cloud bank rising; magnitudes doubtful.
15h 27m, stopped by clouds.
19h 20m, resumed sweep.
19h 33m, again interrupted by clouds.

Zone 17. May 27. C. $D_0 = -37° 5' 30''$—Continued.

No.	Mag.	\	SECONDS OF TRANSIT	\	\	\	\	\	T.	a_1	a_2	MICROMETER	\	r	i	d_1	d_2	Mean Right Ascension, 1850.0	Mean Declination, 1850.0
		I.	II.	III.	IV.	V.	VI.	VII.	h. m. s.	s.	s.			r.	′ ″	″	″	h. m. s.	° ′ ″
39	9.10	..	..	..	..	55.0	14.8	14.8	15 15 35.98	+44.10	+1.10	V.	3	25.531	−34 40.4	− 1.8	− 9.7	15 16 21.18	−37 40 21.9
40	9	..	..	..	11.0	30.0	..	..	20 10.81	44.16	1.28	IV.	4	54.340	4 31.4	1.1	1.5	20 56.25	10 4.0
41	8.9	..	..	..	2.5	22.0	41.0	..	22 2.44	44.17	1.15	IV.	3	32.230	27 40.2	0.8	7.7	22 47.76	33 18.7
42	9	..	..	..	3.5	..	43.0	2.0	15 26 23.20	+44.21	+1.12	IV.	3	25.298	−34 55.1	− 0.1	− 9.8	15 27 8.53	−37 40 35.0

Zone 18. May 27. C. $D_0 = -37° 4' 30''$.

No.	Mag.	I.	II.	III.	IV.	V.	VI.	VII.	T.	a_1	a_2	MICROMETER		r	i	d_1	d_2	Mean Right Ascension, 1850.0	Mean Declination, 1850.0
1	8.9	..	..	..	..	28.0	..	..	19 25 10.68	+44.65	+1.66	V.	4	55.851	− 2 57.5	−12.3	− 1.0	19 25 56.99	−37 7 40.8
2	9	..	37.0	..	..	35.0	..	..	29 15.71	44.66	1.45	IV.	3	20.981	39 25.7	11.2	11.1	30 1.82	44 18.0
3	8 9	..	10.0	..	49.0	..	28.0	..	19 32 49.03	+44.66	+1.44	IV.	2	17.521	−43 4.8	−10.3	−12.1	19 33 36.13	−37 47 57.2

Zone 19. June 3. P. $D_0 = -30° 49' 0''$.

No.	Mag.	I.	II.	III.	IV.	V.	VI.	VII.	T.	a_1	a_2	MICROMETER		r	i	d_1	d_2	Mean Right Ascension, 1850.0	Mean Declination, 1850.0
1	7	..	..	..	..	..	27.0	45.0	12 51 9.00	+50.29	+1.37	VI.	3	35.573	−24 10.1	−43.3	− 4.8	12 52 0.66	−31 13 58.2
2	8	..	13.5	..	49.5	..	..	..	13 0 49.54	50.35	1.34	V.	3	32.095	27 48.6	43.2	5.3	13 1 41.23	17 37.1
3	5	..	2.0	20.0	38.0	..	..	32.0	3 38.01	50.37	1.38	IV.	4	45.340	13 55.8	43.1	3.3	4 29.76	3 42.2
4	.	..	..	..	24.0	..	..	..	13 6.02	50.43								13 (56.)	
5	7	50.0	..	26.0	44.0	..	..	..	20 44.04	50.48	1.27	IV.	3	25.360	34 51.3	42.9	6.4	21 35.79	24 40.6
6	6	..	..	16.5	34.5	..	..	..	22 16.50	50.49	1.27	IV.	3	28.035	32 3.3	42.7	6.0	23 8.26	21 52.0
7	7	..	..	..	24.0	32.0	..	..	22 55.94	50.49	1.29	VI.	3	32.703	27 10.2	42.6	5.2	23 57.72	16 58.0
8	6	58.7	16.5	34.5	53.0	..	..	..	25 52.70	50.49	1.26	IV.	3	23.650	36 38.4	42.6	6.7	26 44.45	26 27.7
9	7	..	..	..	..	..	..	19.5	26 25.32	50.51	1.22	VII.	2	14.340	46 23.3	42.5	8.1	27 17.05	36 13.9
10	7	..	..	..	..	1.0	19.0	..	27 24.82	50.52	1.21	VI.	2	12.335	48 29.3	42.4	8.5	28 16.55	38 20.2
11	8	..	..	..	..	..	11.0	..	28 16.82	50.53	1.20	VII.	2	14.965	45 43.9	42.4	8.0	29 8.55	35 34.3
12	8	52.0	..	28.0	..	4.0	..	..	34 45.94	50.57	1.29	VI.	4	45.480	13 46.4	42.1	3.2	35 37.80	31 3 31.7
13	.	49.0	..	..	..	..	..	..	38 42.82	50.59								39 (53.)	
14	4	..	..	16.0	34.0	..	..	..	42 33.95	50.62	1.32	IV.	4	55.170	2 35.9	41.7	1.5	43 25.89	30 52 18.1
15	3	..	..	..	..	..	..	..	44 ..	50.63	1.24	VII.	3	38.300	21 18.7	41.	4.3	45 ..	31 11 4.6
16	6	58.0	15.5	33.7	52.0	..	..	..	49 51.73	50.66	1.26	IV.	4	48.230	10 54.3	41.2	2.8	50 43.65	31 0 38.3
17	5	1.0	19.0	37.0	55.0	..	..	..	51 54.91	50.68	1.29	IV.	4	55.180	3 38.1	41.1	1.7	52 46.88	30 53 20.9
18	4	..	..	52.5	10.0	28.5	..	..	53 28.24	50.69	1.26	IV.	4	51.075	7 55.7	41.0	2.4	54 20.19	30 57 39.1
19	8	4.0	..	41.0	..	..	..	..	13 57 58.43	50.72	1.21	III.	4	39.830	19 41.7	40.6	4.1	13 58 50.36	31 9 26.4
20	4	20.5	39.0	57.0	..	..	..	..	14 1 14.87	50.74	1.16	III.	3	27.990	32 6.0	40.4	6.0	14 2 6.77	21 52.4
21	8	52.0	..	..	46.0	..	..	..	1 46.02	50.74	1.17	IV.	3	29.515	30 30.6	40.3	5.7	2 37.03	20 16.6
22	5	..	..	..	..	27.0	45.0	..	1 50.92	50.74	1.14	VI.	3	22.575	37 45.6	40.3	6.8	2 42.80	27 32.7
23	6	21.5	40.0	58.0	16.0	..	..	..	4 15.85	50.76	1.15	IV.	3	29.460	30 34.0	40.1	5.7	5 7.76	20 19.8
24	7	..	..	..	6.0	..	..	..	5 6.01	50.76	1.21	IV.	4	44.175	15 8.9	40.0	3.4	5 57.98	4 52.3
25	5	45.0	3.0	21.0	39.0	..	..	..	6 39.02	50.77	1.14	IV.	4	28.450	31 37.4	39.9	5.9	7 30.93	21 23.2
26	8	21.0	39.0	..	14.0	..	..	..	11 14.63	50.80	1.18	IV.	4	41.100	18 21.9	39.5	3.9	12 6.61	8 5.3
27	7	56.0	14.0	32.0	..	..	..	..	12 49.93	50.81	1.20	III.	4	47.450	11 43.4	39.4	2.9	13 41.94	31 1 25.7
28	8	..	..	..	..	10.0	..	..	12 34.15	50.81	1.21	VII.	4	49.790	9 14.8	39.4	2.5	13 26.17	30 58 56.7
29	7	3.5	21.5	39.5	57.0	..	..	..	17 57.34	50.84	1.14	IV.	3	38.083	21 32.8	38.9	4.4	18 49.32	31 11 16.1
30	8	59.0	..	36.0	..	..	..	..	21 13.52	50.87	1.10	III.	3	28.790	31 15.8	38.6	5.8	22 5.49	21 0.2
31	6	..	..	..	13.0	31.0	49.0	..	22 12.94	50.87	1.05	V.	2	14.205	46 28.8	38.5	8.2	23 4.86	36 15.5
32	5	..	42.0	0.0	18.0	..	..	..	24 18.03	50.88	1.11	IV.	3	32.060	27 50.8	38.2	5.3	25 10.02	17 34.3
33	7	49.0	..	..	42.0	..	..	..	28 42.48	50.91	1.10	IV.	3	33.725	26 6.3	37.8	5.0	29 34.49	15 49.1
34	7	41.0	59.0	17.0	35.5	..	..	..	14 36 35.07	+50.96	+1.12	IV.	4	46.070	−13 9.8	−36.9	− 3.1	14 37 27.15	−31 2 49.8

CORRECTIONS.

Date.	Corr. of Clock.	Hourly rate.	m	n	ε	Zenith Point.	Mic. Co.
	h.	s.	s.	s.	s.	° ′ ″	r.
1846. June 3.	16	+ 42.761	+ 0.008	+ 0.198	+ 0.396	+ 0.247	0 0 2.46	30.002

REMARKS.

(18) 1. Transit over T, V assumed as 30s.0, not 28s.0, to agree with Transit, 1846, August 12, and Mural, 1846, August 20.

(18) 3. Differs 5′ in d from Mural, Aug. 20.

(19) 7. Minutes assumed as 23 instead of 22.

(19) 14. Micrometer reading assumed as 56r.170 not 55r.170.

June 3. Lamp which illuminated the wires frequently extinguished by the wind.

INSTRUMENT READINGS.

Date.	CIRCLE							Barom.	THERMOM.				
	A.	B.	C.	D.	E.	F.	Mean.		At.	Ex.	U.	L.	I.
	° ′ ″						″	in.	°	°	°	°	°
Zone 18. 1846. May 27, 19 32										69.9			
Zone 19. June 3, 13 0	70 9 62.6	59.6	68.3	62.0	58.0	50.4	60.15						
13 20								30.062	75.0	71.5			
14 24								30.066	74.0	70.0			
16 0								30.066	72.0	68.5			
17 0								30.038	71.0	67.5	71.0		
17 21								30.032	71.0	66.8			

ZONE 19. JUNE 3. P. $D_0 = -30° 49' 0''$ — Continued.

No.	Mag.	I.	II.	III.	IV.	V.	VI.	VII.	T.	a_1	a_2	MICROMETER			i	d_1	d_2	Mean Right Ascension, 1850.0.	Mean Declination, 1850.0.
									h. m. s.	s.	s.			r.	' ''	''	''	h. m. s.	° ' ''
35	6		23.0	41.5	59.0				14 37 59.24	+50.97	+1.01	IV.	2	13.620	-47 9.2	-36.7	8.2	14 38 51.22	-31 36 54.1
36	7	41.0	59.5	17.5	35.0				42 35.29	51.00	1.03	IV.	3	26.515	33 38.8	36.2	6.2	43 27.32	23 21.2
37	8			16.0	34.0	52.0			43 34.00	51.01	1.02	V.	3	22.485	37 51.5	36.1	6.8	44 26.03	27 34.4
38	7						43.0	1.0	44 7.11	51.01	1.11	VI.	3	48.060	11 4.3	36.0	2.8	44 59.23	0 43.1
39	8		36.5		13.0	31.0			48 12.84	51.04	1.06	VI.	3	39.225	20 20.9	35.5	4.2	49 4.94	31 10 0.6
40	5				51.0	9.0			51 51.00	51.06	1.11	V.	4	51.950	7 0.3	35.0	2.2	52 43.17	30 56 37.5
41	8						53.0	10.5	52 16.88	51.06	1.10	V.	3	49.070	10 0.1	34.9	2.7	53 9.04	30 59 37.7
42	7				11.0	29.0	47.5		54 11.17	51.07	1.02	IV.	3	29.080	30 57.8	34.7	5.8	55 3.26	31 20 38.3
43	8			41.0		17.0		52.0	56 58.69	51.09	1.07	VII.	4	45.380	13 51.8	34.3	3.2	14 57 50.85	3 29.3
44	7		7.0	25.0	43.0				14 59 43.08	51.11	0.95	IV.	3	16.150	44 30.6	33.9	7.9	15 0 35.14	31 34 12.4
45	4	40.7	58.7	16.5	34.5			28.5	15 4 34.53	51.14	1.07	IV.	4	51.310	7 41.1	33.2	2.3	5 26.74	30 57 16.6
46	8				9.0				6 9.04	51.15	0.99	IV.	3	33.060	26 48.0	33.0	5.2	7 1.18	31 16 26.2
47	7	19.5	37.5		13.5				8 13.52	51.16	0.99	IV.	3	31.840	28 4.5	32.7	5.3	9 5.67	17 42.5
48	8						47.0		9 10.94	51.17	0.95	VI.	3	21.355	39 2.2	32.5	7.1	10 3.06	28 41.8
49	7	7.5	25.5	43.0	1.5				12 1.49	51.19	0.91	IV.	2	11.817	49 2.0	32.1	8.6	12 53.59	38 42.7
50	8			1.0			55.0		13 19.01	51.19	0.98	VI.	3	33.515	26 19.3	31.9	5.1	14 11.18	15 56.3
51	7				35.5		12.0		14 35.78	51.20	0.97	VI.	3	36.310	23 24.0	31.7	4.6	15 27.95	13 0.3
52	6											VII+	2	13.250	47 32.0	31.	8.4	(17) . .	31 37 (16.)
53	6	44.5	2.0	20.5	38.5				18 38.30	51.23	1.02	IV.	4	51.546	7 26.1	31.1	2.3	19 30.55	30 56 59.5
54	8					49.0			22 30.03	51.25	0.92	V.	3	25.920	34 15.9	30.5	6.3	23 23.10	31 23 52.7
55	8			59.0			54.0		25 17.50	51.27	0.92	IV.	3	26.770	33 22.6	30.0	6.2	26 9.69	22 58.8
56	7			47.0	4.5				27 4.79	51.28	0.88	IV.	2	16.920	43 42.2	29.7	7.8	27 56.95	33 19.7
57	7						52.0	10.0	27 16.10	51.28	0.98	VI.	4	47.280	11 53.4	29.7	2.9	28 8.30	1 26.0
58	8			7.0			0.0		29 24.50	51.29	0.99	VI.	3	27.070	33 3.6	29.3	6.1	30 16.69	22 39.0
59	7		55.5	13.5	31.5				31 31.54	51.31	0.90	IV.	3	28.190	31 53.7	29.0	5.9	32 23.75	21 28.6
60	7				26.0		1.5		32 25.70	51.31	0.83	IV.	1	8.530	52 25.0	28.8	9.1	33 17.84	42 2.9
61	4				51.0	9.0			33 51.01	51.32	0.95	IV.	4	41.850	17 34.7	28.6	3.7	34 43.28	7 7.0
62	8		38.5		14.5				38 14.59	51.35	0.84	IV.	2	13.290	47 30.0	27.8	8.3	39 6.78	37 6.1
63	8			41.5	0.0				41 0.24	51.36	0.93	IV.	4	45.887	13 21.2	27.3	3.2	41 52.53	2 51.7
64	8	18.0		54.0					43 11.93	51.37	0.89	IV.	3	38.300	21 19.3	26.9	4.3	44 4.19	10 50.5
65	4	1.7	19.8	38.0	55.8				45 55.86	51.39	0.87	IV.	3	29.050	30 59.6	26.5	5.8	46 48.12	20 31.9
66	8	45.0	5.5	24.0	42.0				47 41.89	51.40	0.87	IV.	3	32.100	27 48.3	26.2	5.3	48 34.16	17 19.8
67	4						10.0		47 33.92	51.40	0.82	VI.	2	18.490	42 3.5	26.2	7.5	48 26.14	31 37.2
68	4				31.5	49.5			49 31.49	51.41	0.84	IV.	3	25.660	34 32.3	25.8	6.3	50 23.74	24 4.4
69	4		24.0	42.0	0.0				51 0.06	51.42	0.83	IV.	3	22.260	38 5.6	25.5	6.9	51 52.31	27 35.0
70	4						56.0		51 2.03	51.42	0.90	VII.	4	41.825	17 34.8	25.5	3.8	51 54.35	7 4.1
71	4				14.3	32.0	50.5		53 14.21	51.43	0.80	IV.	2	15.360	45 20.3	25.1	8.0	54 6.44	34 53.4
72	7				54.0				54 54.01	51.44	0.90	IV.	4	46.290	12 56.1	24.8	3.0	55 46.35	2 23.9
73	8				5.0				15 55 5.00	51.44	0.90	IV.	4	46.290	12 56.1	24.8	3.0	15 55 57.34	2 23.9
74	5						46.0		16 0 51.91	51.48	0.81	VII.	3	26.290	33 52.4	23.7	6.2	16 1 44.20	23 22.3
75	6	57.0	14.5	33.0	51.0				3 50.87	51.49	0.83	IV.	3	33.410	26 26.2	23.1	5.1	4 43.19	15 54.4
76	7				1.0		36.0		7 42.47	51.51	0.82	IV.	3	32.716	27 9.6	22.3	5.0	6 34.80	31 10 36.9
77	7			17.0			53.0		11 59.10	51.54	0.91	V.	5	54.700	4 10.3	21.5	0.2	12 51.55	30 53 34.0
78	6		5.0	23.0					14 40.99	51.55	0.84	V.	5	44.565	14 44.5	20.9	3.3	15 33.38	31 4 8.7
79	7			32.0			8.0		14 32.04	51.55	0.81	III.	4	36.370	23 20.2	21.0	4.6	15 24.40	12 45.8
80	7						52.0	10.0	15 15.96	51.56	0.78	VI.	3	28.330	31 44.4	20.8	5.9	16 8.30	21 11.1
81	7	5.0		42.0					20 59.57	51.59	0.74	VII.	3	20.640	39 47.0	19.6	7.2	21 51.00	29 13.8
82	7					32.0			21 13.96	51.59	0.78	III.	3	30.002	30 0.0	19.6	5.6	22 6.33	19 25.2
83	7				17.5		54.0		16 22 35.72	+51.59	+0.79	VI.	F W	35.515	-24 14.1	-19.3	-4.8	16 23 28.10	-31 13 38.2

CORRECTIONS.

Date.	Corr. of Clock.	Hourly rate.	m	n	c	Zenith Point.	Mic. Co.
1846.	h.	s.	s.	s.	s.	s.	° ' ''	r.

INSTRUMENT READINGS.

Date.	CIRCLE.							Barom.	THERMOM.				
	A.	B.	C.	D.	E.	F.	Mean.		At.	Ex.	U.	L.	I.
1846. h. m.	° ' ''						''	in.	°				

REMARKS.

Zone 19. June 3. P. $D_0 = -30^\circ\ 49'\ 0''$—Continued.

No.	Mag.	I.	II.	III.	IV.	V.	VI.	VII.	T.	a_1	a_2	Mic.	n	r	i	d_1	d_2	Mean Right Ascension, 1850.0	Mean Declination, 1850.0
									h. m. s.	s.	s.			r.	′ ″	″	″	h. m. s.	° ′ ″
84	7						51.0	9.0	16 24 13.13	+51.60	+0.83	V.	3	50.340	− 8 41.4	−19.0	− 2.4	16 25 7.56	−30 58 2.8
85	7						21.0	29.0	24 45.42	51.61	0.83	VI.	4	50.340	8 41.4	18.8	2.4	25 37.86	30 58 2.6
86	8				8.0				26 8.03	51.61	0.78	IV.	3	38.400	21 13.0	18.6	4.3	27 0.42	31 10 35.9
87	8	6.5	25.0	43.0					29 0.87	51.63	0.72	III.	2	24.445	35 50.8	18.0	6.5	29 53.22	25 15.3
88	8			41.0	59.0				32 50.99	51.65	0.79	IV.	4	45.400	13 52.0	17.1	3.2	33 43.43	31 3 12.3
89	6						43.0		33 7.15	51.65	0.82	VI.	4	52.075	6 52.3	17.1	2.1	33 59.62	30 56 11.5
90	8					56.0	13.5	31.5	34 37.70	51.66	0.77	VII.	4	42.990	16 21.7	16.7	3.6	35 30.13	31 5 42.0
91	7				24.5		0.0		36 24.30	51.67	0.75	IV.	4	38.470	21 7.1	16.3	4.3	37 16.72	31 10 27.7
92	6			39.0	57.0	15.0			37 56.99	51.67	0.81	V.	4	52.470	6 27.8	16.0	2.1	38 49.47	30 55 45.9
93	6				3.5	21.5			39 3.49	51.68	0.70	IV.	3	26.595	33 33.7	15.8	6.2	39 55.87	31 22 55.7
94	8			52.0		27.7			40 9.83	51.69	0.69	VI.	3	27.250	32 52.4	15.5	6.1	41 2.21	22 14.0
95	8				49.8		25.0		41 48.97	51.69	0.66	V.	2	16.410	44 14.3	15.2	7.7	42 41.32	33 37.2
96	6					53.0		29.0	42 34.83	51.70	0.65	VI.	2	12.814	47 59.1	15.0	8.4	43 27.18	37 22.5
97	8			21.0		57.0			44 39.00	51.71	0.74	IV.	4	30.785	19 44.4	14.5	4.1	45 31.45	9 3.0
98	8					40.0			45 21.97	51.71	0.72	V.	4	35.750	23 57.3	14.4	4.7	46 14.40	13 16.4
99	7						24.0		45 48.06	51.71	0.71	VI.	4	39.875	14 24.4	14.3	3.3	46 40.48	31 3 42.0
100	8		11.0		47.0				48 46.99	51.73	0.76	IV.	4	50.960	8 2.8	13.6	2.3	49 39.48	30 57 18.7
101	8						55.0		49 18.91	51.73	0.63	VI.	2	16.225	44 25.5	13.5	7.9	50 11.27	31 33 46.9
102	8					41.0			50 22.89	51.74	0.64	V.	2	17.265	43 20.7	13.3	7.7	51 15.27	32 41.7
103	6		10.0	28.0	46.0				52 46.04	51.75	0.66	IV.	3	25.924	34 15.7	12.7	6.3	53 38.45	23 34.7
104	6			39.0	15.0				54 15.00	51.75	0.73	IV.	4	45.020	19 28.95	12.4	3.3	55 7.48	8 44.6
105	8	31.0			7.0		6.0		54 26.64	51.76	0.71	VI.	4	39.450	20 5.0	12.4	4.1	55 19.11	31 9 21.5
106	5				13.5				57 13.46	51.77	0.78	IV.	4	55.830	2 57.0	11.8	1.5	58 6.01	30 52 10.3
107	8				50.0				16 58 50.05	51.78	0.62	IV.	2	20.985	39 27.4	11.4	7.1	16 59 42.45	31 28 45.9
108	7				12.0	30.5			17 0 12.25	51.78	0.64	IV.	3	27.413	32 42.5	11.1	6.1	17 1 4.67	21 59.7
109	8	37.0	55.0	13.0					4 30.95	51.80	0.68	III.	4	39.907	19 36.8	10.1	4.1	5 23.43	8 51.0
110	6			26.0	43.3	1.5			8 43.61	51.82	0.66	IV.	4	37.160	22 29.3	9.2	4.5	9 36.09	11 43.0
111	7	57.0	15.0	33.0					10 51.04	51.83	0.60	III.	3	24.115	36 9.1	8.6	6.6	11 43.47	25 24.3
112	7			23.0					11 41.03	51.84	0.60	III.	3	23.680	36 36.2	8.5	6.7	12 33.47	25 51.4
113	8	3.0		39.5					12 57.35	51.84	0.58	III.	2	16.940	43 41.1	8.2	7.8	13 49.77	32 57.1
114	6	8.0	26.0	44.0					16 2.08	51.86	0.57	III.	2	21.473	38 57.1	7.5	7.1	16 54.51	28 11.7
115	7	44.5	2.5						17 38.41	51.86	0.66	II.	4	44.050	15 16.9	7.1	3.4	18 30.93	4 27.4
116	7			49.0					18 7.02	51.86	0.62	IV.	3	33.890	25 55.9	7.0	5.0	18 59.50	15 7.9
117	7	43.0					56.0	14.0	18 37.64	51.87	0.60	VI.	3	25.115	35 6.3	6.6	6.4	19 30.11	24 19.3
118	7	38.0		14.0					17 21 32.03	+51.88	+0.57	III.	3	23.687	−36 35.9	− 6.2	− 6.7	17 22 24.48	−31 25 48.8

Zone 20. June 4. C. $D_0 = -33^\circ\ 19'\ 50''$.

No.	Mag.	I.	II.	III.	IV.	V.	VI.	VII.	T.	a_1	a_2	Mic.	n	r	i	d_1	d_2	Mean Right Ascension, 1850.0	Mean Declination, 1850.0
1	8.9		29.5	48.3	6.8	26.1	44.5		14 32 7.06	+51.09	+1.01	IV.	3	39.392	−20 10.7	− 7.7	− 3.2	14 32 59.16	−33 40 11.6
2	8		0.0	18.6	37.0	55.8	14.5		37 37.18	51.13	0.66	IV.	2	14.819	45 54.0	7.0	8.1	38 28.97	34 5 59.1
3	8			14.5	33.0		44.0	3.0	39 25.74	51.14	1.18	IV.	4	55.368	3 26.5	6.8	0.1	40 18.06	33 23 23.2
4	9		14.5	33.0	52.0		3.0		41 51.71	51.16	0.82	IV.	3	28.638	31 25.5	6.5	5.3	42 43.69	51 27.3
5	8		44.4	3.0	21.9	39.8	58.2		44 21.48	51.18	1.09	IV.	4	47.647	11 30.8	6.1	1.6	45 13.75	33 31 28.5
6	8		48.0	6.5	25.0	44.0	2.5		46 25.18	51.19	0.69	IV.	2	19.431	41 5.1	5.8	7.1	47 17.06	34 1 8.0
7	9			49.7					47 49.76	51.20	0.85	IV.	3	30.903	29 3.3	5.6	4.8	48 41.81	33 49 3.7
8	6.7		13.8	32.0	50.0	9.0	27.6		51 50.49	51.23	0.90	IV.	2	34.191	25 37.1	5.1	4.2	52 42.62	33 45 36.4
9	9.10				10.5	29.5			14 53 10.69	51.24	0.61	IV.	2	13.786	46 58.7	4.9	8.2	14 53 2.54	34 7 1.8
10	9		0.0	19.1	36.0		15.0		15 1 37.11	+51.30	+0.54	IV.	2	9.587	−51 21.8	− 3.6	− 9.1	15 2 28.95	−34 11 24.5

CORRECTIONS.

Date.		Corr. of Clock.	Hourly rate.	m	n	c	Zenith Point.	Mic. Co.
	h.	s.	s.	s.	s.	s.	° ′ ″	r.
1846. June 4.	16	+ 43.204	+ 0.010	+ 0.198	+ 0.396	+ 0.247	0 0 2.90	29.997

INSTRUMENT READINGS.

	Date.		CIRCLE.							Barom.	THERMOM.				
			A.	B.	C.	D.	E.	F.	Mean.		At.	Ex.	U.	L.	I.
		h. m.	° ′ ″						″	in.	°				
Zone 19	1846. June 4.	14 30	72 39 61.8	61.4	66.9	60.2	58.1	50.0	59.73	29.815	75.0	71.5	73.5	73.5	74.2
		15 1								29.800	74.2	71.6			
		15 12		61.1	61.0	67.0	60.4	58.4	49.0	59.48	29.800	74.0	71.6	73.4	73.4
Zone 20	. 6.	13 29	71 24 66.0	62.5	76.4	65.0	62.2	53.6	63.45	30.010	73.5	67.0			70.5
		14 14								30.044	71.0	63.5			

REMARKS.

(19) 99. Micrometer reading assumed as 44ʳ.875 instead of 39ʳ.875.

(19) 104. Micrometer reading assumed as 40ʳ.020 instead of 45ʳ.020.

June 3, 17h 22m. Wind too fresh; lamp extinguished.

(19) 117. Minutes assumed as 18.

June 4. Hazy about horizon and above the belt; 15h, hazé increasing; mags. and transits doubtful.

ZONE 20. JUNE 4. C. $D_0 = -33°\ 19'\ 50''$—Continued.

No.	Mag.	I.	II.	III.	IV.	V.	VI.	VII.	T. (h m s)	a_1	a_2	Micr.	n	r.	i	d_1	d_2	Mean R.A. 1850.0	Mean Decl. 1850.0
11	8		19.0	37.0	55.6		33.0		15 6 55.81	+51.34	+0.67	IV.	3	19.369	−41 6.9	−2.8	−7.1	15 7 47.82	−34 1 6.8
12	8		32.0		8.2	26.7			9 8.47	51.35	1.10	IV.	4	50.177	8 52.1	2.5	1.1	10 0.92	33 28 45.7
13	8			54.6	13.4			8.0	15 12 13.02	+51.37	+0.98	IV.	3	42.447	−16 58.9	−2.0	−2.6	15 13 5.37	−33 36 53.5

ZONE 21. JUNE 6. P. $D_0 = -32°\ 4'\ 50''$.

No.	Mag.	I.	II.	III.	IV.	V.	VI.	VII.	T. (h m s)	a_1	a_2	Micr.	n	r.	i	d_1	d_2	Mean R.A. 1850.0	Mean Decl. 1850.0
1	7	31.5	50.0	8.0	26.0				13 29 26.19	+50.55	+2.23	IV.	4	43.647	−15 41.9	−8.2	−2.9	13 30 18.97	−32 20 43.0
2	8	24.5	42.5		19.0				32 19.20	50.57	−0.12	IV.	2	15.613	45 4.3	8.1	7.8	33 9.65	50 10.2
3	8	54.0	12.5	30.5					35 48.80	50.60	+1.36	III.	3	33.783	26 2.5	8.0	4.6	36 40.76	31 5.1
4	4			1.0	19.0			13.5	36 19.03	50.60	2.40	IV.	4	47.250	11 55.8	8.0	2.3	37 12.03	16 56.1
5	8	2.0	20.0	38.0	57.0				40 56.71	50.63	1.74	IV.	4	38.750	20 49.4	7.7	3.7	41 49.08	25 50.8
6	4	43.0	1.0	19.0	37.0				42 37.30	50.64	2.60	IV.	4	49.215	9 52.5	7.7	1.9	43 30.54	14 52.7
7	7	44.0	2.0	20.0	38.0				42 38.30	50.64	+2.60	VII.	4	49.375	9 47.3	7.7	1.9	43 31.54	14 46.9
8	8	12.0	30.5	49.3	7.3				51 7.28	50.70	−0.63	IV.	3	12.245	48 35.4	7.3	8.4	51 57.35	53 41.1
9	9		7.0		42.5				53 43.07	50.72	+0.19	IV.	3	22.363	37 59.2	7.1	6.6	54 33.98	43 2.9
10	6	48.0	6.3	24.5	43.0				13 58 42.02	50.75	1.97	IV.	4	44.150	15 10.4	6.9	2.8	13 59 34.74	20 10.1
11	7	59.0	17.0	35.3	53.5				14 0 53.56	50.77	+1.04	IV.	3	33.414	26 26.0	6.7	4.6	14 1 45.37	31 27.3
12	8	36.0					50.0		3 31.28	50.78	−0.44	IV.	2	14.830	45 53.3	6.6	7.9	4 21.61	50 57.8
13	7	39.0		17.0			50.0		3 34.76	50.78	−0.31	VII.	2	17.580	43 0.0	6.5	7.5	4 25.23	48 4.0
14	6		5.0	23.0			37.0		3 41.66	50.78	−0.36	VII.	2	16.960	43 39.1	6.5	7.6	4 32.08	48 43.2
15	4	40.0	59.3	16.3	34.0			29.3	6 34.79	50.80	+0.90	IV.	3	32.470	27 25.2	6.3	4.8	7 26.40	32 26.3
16	4	45.5	3.5	22.0	40.0				8 40.15	50.82	0.97	IV.	3	33.560	26 16.7	6.2	4.6	9 31.94	31 17.5
17	9	57.0		33.5	53.0				12 52.15	50.85	0.87	IV.	3	33.033	26 49.7	5.9	4.7	13 43.87	31 50.3
18	7	33.0	51.5	9.5	28.0				14 14 27.84	+50.86	+1.47	IV.	4	40.350	−19 9.1	−5.8	−3.5	14 15 20.17	−32 24 8.4

ZONE 22. JUNE 15. C. $D_0 = -33°\ 39'\ 10''$.

No.	Mag.	I.	II.	III.	IV.	V.	VI.	VII.	T. (h m s)	a_1	a_2	Micr.	n	r.	i	d_1	d_2	Mean R.A. 1850.0	Mean Decl. 1850.0
1	9.10		56.5	15.0	33.5				14 59 33.54	+55.63	+1.68	IV.	3	31.661	−28 15.8	−46.8	−5.1	15 0 30.85	−33 48 17.7
2	9.10					57.5	16.0		59 39.05	55.63	1.72	V.	4	43.461	15 53.5	46.8	2.6	0 36.40	35 52.9
3	9.10		43.5			34.0			15 4 18.00	55.65	1.65	IV.	3	24.448	35 48.5	46.1	6.4	5 15.30	33 55 51.0
4	8		14.1	32.5		9.4	28.0		6 50.99	55.67	1.63	IV.	3	19.406	41 4.6	45.8	7.5	7 48.29	34 1 7.9
5	8		26.5	45.5	4.0	22.0	40.3		9 3.69	55.68	1.74	IV.	4	50.198	8 50.8	45.5	1.2	10 1.11	33 28 47.5
6	9	5.7	24.5						12 1.54	55.70	1.60	II.	2	15.912	44 45.1	45.0	8.2	12 58.84	34 4 48.3
7	8				3.0	21.3	39.5		12 2.67	55.70	1.58	IV.	2	10.062	49 49.3	45.0	9.5	12 59.95	9 53.8
8	8.9					30.0	48.7	7.0	13 11.35	55.71	1.57	V.	2	8.968	52 0.3	44.9	9.7	14 8.63	12 4.9
9	9		15.0	24.0	43.0	1.7			15 42.71	55.72	1.59	IV.	2	15.478	45 12.9	44.5	8.3	16 40.02	34 5 15.7
10	8.9		50.0	8.2	28.0				18 27.28	55.74	1.65	IV.	3	31.720	28 12.1	44.1	4.9	19 24.67	33 48 11.1
11	8.9		30.9		7.5	26.0	44.0		23 7.48	55.77	1.64	IV.	3	29.210	30 49.7	43.4	5.5	24 4.89	50 48.6
12	9		6.1	24.0	43.0	1.5			27 42.67	55.79	1.64	IV.	3	32.710	27 10.0	42.7	4.7	28 40.10	47 7.4
13	10							33.0	27 37.47	55.79	1.64	VII.	3	33.567	26 15.9	42.7	4.6	28 34.90	46 13.2
14	6				19.0	36.7	55.0	13.5	29 17.99	55.80	1.61	IV.	3	25.121	35 6.1	42.4	6.3	30 15.40	33 55 4.8
15	7		34.1		11.2	30.0	49.0		32 11.43	55.82	1.54	IV.	2	7.621	53 24.8	41.9	10.0	33 8.79	34 13 26.7
16	9			9.0	28.0	46.0	6.0		33 27.93	55.82	1.53	IV.	2	8.361	52 38.6	41.6	9.8	34 25.28	34 12 40.0
17	9.10				32.0				35 32.01	55.84	1.65	IV.	4	39.	22 .	.	.	36 29.50	33 41 . .
18	7							8.0	36 12.21	55.84	1.53	VI.	2	6.481	52 30.7	41.3	9.8	37 9.58	34 12 31.8
19	9					21.0			38 2.50	55.85	1.60	V.	3	24.340	35 55.3	41.0	6.5	38 59.95	33 55 52.8
20	6		7.0	25.5	44.0	2.6	21.1		15 41 44.06	+55.87	+1.64	IV.	4	30.739	−19 47.3	−40.9	−3.3	15 42 41.57	−33 39 40.9

CORRECTIONS.

Date	Corr. of Clock	Hourly rate	m	n	c	Zenith Point	Mic. Co.
1846. June 6, 16ʰ	+43.146 s	+0.013 s	+0.198 s	+0.396 s	+0.247 s	0 0 2.46	r. 29.999
15, 16	+47.338	+0.020	+0.198	+0.396	+0.247	2.25	30.005

REMARKS.

June 6. 13ʰ 30ᵐ, very clear; 14ʰ 14ᵐ, thick clouds.

(22) 7. Micrometer reading assumed as 11ʳ.062 instead of 10ʳ.062.

June 15. Early part of evening unfavorable; after 14ʰ 30ᵐ beautifully clear.

INSTRUMENT READINGS.

Date	A.	B.	C.	D.	E.	F.	Mean	Barom.	At.	Ex.	U.	L.	I.
1846. h. m.	° ′ ″						″	in.	°	°	°	°	°

Zone 22. June 15. C. D. = −33° 19′ 10″—Continued.

No.	Mag.	Seconds of Transit (I.–VII.)	T. (h. m. s.)	a₁ (s.)	a₂ (s.)	Micrometer (r.)	i	d₁	d₂	Mean R.A. 1850.0	Mean Decl. 1850.0
21	9	19.0	15 44 0.50	+55.88	+1.64	V. 4 42.704	−16 40.8	−39.9	−2.7	15 44 58.02	−33 36 33.4
22	9	50.9 9.0	46 9.25	55.90	1.56	IV. 3 20.071	40 22.8	39.5	7.3	47 6.71	34 0 19.6
23	7	58.0 16.2	46 20.76	55.90	1.66	VI. 4 47.683	11 27.8	39.5	1.7	47 18.32	33 31 19.0
24	8	16.7	46 21.28	55.90	1.66	VII. 4 47.8	11 20.	39.5	1.7	47 18.84	33 31 (11.)
25	8	53.0 11.5 29.8	52 11.41	55.93	1.52	IV. 2 8.939	52 2.1	38.4	9.7	53 8.86	34 12 0.2
26	9	17.0 35.5 54.0 31.0	54 54.02	55.94	1.64	IV. 4 43.912	15 25.2	37.9	2.5	55 51.60	33 35 15.6
27	9.10	51.0	57 9.53	55.96	1.61	IV. 4 37.455	22 10.8	37.5	3.8	58 7.10	42 2.1
28	9	23.0 59.0 36.8	15 57 41.10	55.96	1.63	IV. 4 41.671	17 46.0	37.4	2.9	15 58 38.69	37 36.3
29	8	57.0 15.7 34.7 11.1	16 2 34.28	55.98	1.56	IV. 3 25.152	35 4.2	36.5	6.3	16 3 31.82	54 57.0
30	9	31.5 27.5	7 59.50	56.01	1.62	IV. 4 41.140	18 19.4	35.6	3.0	8 57.13	38 8.0
31	9	9.0	9 9.04	56.02	1.58	IV. 3 32.910	26 56.8	35.3	4.7	10 6.64	46 46.8
32	9.10	33.0	11 33.06	56.03	1.54	IV. 3 24.731	35 30.5	34.8	6.4	12 30.63	55 21.7
33	9.10	8.0 4.0	11 45.26	56.03	1.52	IV. 3 21.251	39 8.9	34.8	7.1	12 42.81	59 0.8
34	9	10.0 28.5 5.5	15 25.50	56.05	1.52	IV. 3 21.241	39 9.5	34.0	7.1	16 26.07	59 0.6
35	9	50.0 8.0 27.0	19 26.88	56.07	1.56	IV. 3 32.561	27 19.4	33.2	4.8	20 24.51	33 47 7.4
36	8	9.0 46.0 5.0	20 27.62	56.07	1.51	IV. 2 20.267	40 12.0	33.0	7.3	21 25.20	34 0 2.9
37	9	22.0 40.0 59.1	21 40.24	56.08	1.51	IV. 3 25.511	34 41.7	32.8	6.2	22 37.83	33 54 30.7
38	9	53.0 12.0	22 53.20	56.08	1.40	IV. 3 16.212	44 24.8	32.6	8.2	23 50.77	34 4 15.6
39	8.9	41.2	23 4.05	56.09	1.48	IV. 2 13.578	47 11.9	32.5	8.7	24 1.62	34 7 3.1
40	8.9	55.0 13.2 32.0	25 31.95	56.10	1.52	IV. 3 26.894	33 14.8	32.0	6.0	26 29.57	33 53 2.8
41	9	12.5 49.7	26 12.63	56.10	1.56	IV. 3 35.010	24 45.6	31.9	4.3	27 10.29	44 31.8
42	9	22.0 41.0	27 22.26	56.11	1.57	IV. 3 36.869	22 48.9	31.7	3.9	28 19.94	42 34.5
43	9	23.0 41.3	28 41.45	56.11	1.53	IV. 3 30.451	29 31.9	31.4	5.2	29 39.09	49 16.5
44	9	5.0 23.0	28 46.18	56.11	1.51	V. 3 25.825	34 21.9	31.4	6.2	29 43.80	33 54 9.5
45	9	5.0 24.0	29 46.65	56.12	1.49	V. 3 20.115	40 20.1	31.2	7.3	30 44.26	34 0 8.6
46	9.10	43.0 1.0 20.0	31 24.43	56.12	1.60	V. 4 50.435	8 35.7	30.8	1.2	32 22.15	33 28 17.7
47	7	13.8 32.1 50.7 9.4 27.5	34 50.72	56.14	1.58	IV. 4 45.171	14 6.3	30.1	2.2	35 48.44	33 48.6
48	8.9	52.0 29.0	36 52.68	56.15	1.60	IV. 4 53.319	5 34.9	29.7	0.6	37 49.83	25 15.2
49	8	15.0 10.7	38 33.62	56.16	1.54	IV. 3 34.861	24 54.9	29.4	4.3	39 31.32	44 38.6
50	9	6.0	38 10.51	56.16	1.56	VII. 3 39.439	20 7.4	29.4	3.4	39 8.23	33 39 50.2
51	4	7.0 15.7	39 29.96	56.16	1.47	VI. 1 19.358	41 6.4	29.2	7.5	40 27.50	34 0 53.1
52	9	11.4 30.0	45 30.00	56.19	1.50	IV. 3 28.539	31 31.8	27.9	5.6	46 27.69	33 51 15.3
53	9.10	52.0 28.5	45 33.22	56.19	1.53	V. 3 34.736	25 2.9	27.9	4.3	46 30.94	44 45.1
54	8	34.0 52.7 10.2	47 33.87	56.20	1.60	VI. 4 56.252	2 30.8	27.4	0.0	48 31.67	22 8.2
55	9	18.0	50 18.04	56.21	1.54	IV. 3 40.391	19 8.0	26.9	3.2	51 15.75	38 48.1
56	8.9	23.0	51 4.50	56.21	1.53	V. 3 38.840	20 45.2	26.7	3.5	52 2.24	40 25.4
57	7.8	23.0 41.5 0.7	54 0.29	56.23	1.57	IV. 3 25.548	34 39.4	25.8	6.2	54 58.09	54 21.4
58	9	33.0 10.0	54 33.05	56.23	1.55	IV. 4 45.684	13 21.4	25.9	2.1	55 30.83	32 59.4
59	9	1.2	56 19.69	56.23	1.55	III. 4 46.622	12 35.2	25.5	2.0	57 17.47	32 12.7
60	9	13.8 32.0	57 32.15	56.24	1.52	IV. 3 39.530	20 2.0	25.3	3.4	16 58 29.91	39 40.7
61	9	3.0 21.4 39.7	16 59 33.30	56.25	1.52	IV. 3 40.397	19 7.7	24.8	3.2	17 0 31.07	33 38 45.7
62	9	9.0 29.0	17 0 28.30	56.25	1.43	IV. 2 17.302	43 18.5	24.6	7.8	1 25.98	34 3 0.9
63	9	49.7	1 49.73	56.26	1.50	IV. 3 35.032	24 44.3	24.3	4.3	2 47.49	33 44 22.9
64	9	32.0	2 32.05	56.26	1.40	IV. 3 33.521	26 19.2	24.2	4.6	3 29.80	45 58.0
65	8.9	33.2	4 10.21	56.26	1.53	II. 4 45.000	14 16.9	23.8	2.3	5 8.00	33 53.0
66	8	24.7 43.0 2.0	5 1.73	56.27	1.53	IV. 4 45.339	13 55.8	23.6	2.2	5 59.53	33 31.6
67	8.9	7.0	4 48.50	56.27	1.51	V. −4 39.892	19 37.4	23.7	3.3	5 46.85	39 14.4
68	9	56.5	7 15.05	56.28	1.45	III. 3 24.441	35 48.7	23.1	6.4	8 12.78	33 55 28.2
69	9	8.0	17 7 6.05	+56.28	+1.42	IV. 3 17.050	−43 32.2	−23.1	−8.0	17 8 5.75	−34 3 13.3

CORRECTIONS.

Date.		Corr. of Clock.	Hourly rate.	m	n	c	Zenith Point.	Mic. Co.
1846. June 15.	h. 16	s. + 47.338	s. + 0.020	s. + 0.198	s. + 0.396	s. + 0.247	° ′ ″ 0 0 2.25	r. 30.005

REMARKS.

(22) 51. Transit over T. VII assumed as 25ˢ.7 instead of 15ˢ.7.

INSTRUMENT READINGS.

	Date.	A.	B.	C.	D.	E.	F.	Mean.	Barom. (in.)	At.	Ex.	U.	L.	l.
Zone 22	1846. June 15, 14 50	72 39 62.2	62.5	68.1	63.0	61.0	50.9	61.28				73.0	71.0	69.0
	14 50								29.914	73.0	70.7			
	15 38										69.6			
	15 50	62.5	63.1	68.9	62.0	62.1	50.0	61.43				72.1	70.9	
	15 57								29.902	72.2	69.4			
	16 39										68.6			
	18 6								29.888	70.7	67.7			
	18 10	61.9	62.9	69.1	62.7	62.0	49.0	61.27				69.7	69.4	69.2

ZONE 22. JUNE 15. C. $D_o = -33°\ 19'\ 10''$—Continued.

No.	Mag.	I.	II.	III.	IV.	V.	VI.	VII.	T. (h. m. s.)	a_1	a_2	MICROMETER.		r	i	d_1	d_2	Mean Right Ascension, 1850.0 (h. m. s.)	Mean Declination, 1850.0 (° ′ ″)
70	9					9.5			17 7 50.95	+56.28	+1.44	V.	3	21.979	−38 23.2	−23.0	−6.9	17 8 48.67	−33 58 3.1
71	9		25.0				0.5		13 12.78	56.30	1.50	IV.	4	39.242	20 18.6	21.7	3.4	14 10.58	39 53.7
72	9		50.2		27.0		4.5		13 27.25	56.30	1.50	IV.	4	39.059	20 30.0	21.7	3.4	14 25.05	33 40 5.1
73	9						3.0		14 25.87	56.30	1.41	VI.	2	14.118	46 37.6	21.5	8.6	15 23.58	34 6 17.7
74	8.9				49.0	7.8			15 49.14	56.31	1.45	IV.	3	22.802	37 31.5	21.1	6.8	16 46.99	33 57 9.4
75	9		13.0	32.8					17 50.63	56.32	1.52	III.	4	51.452	7 32.1	20.7	1.0	18 48.47	27 3.8
76	8			56.0	15.0		52.0		19 14.86	56.32	1.50	IV.	3	43.558	15 49.1	20.4	2.5	20 12.68	35 22.0
77	9			24.7					19 43.19	56.32	1.51	III.	3	47.090	12 10.8	20.2	1.9	20 41.02	31 42.9
78	9				58.0		35.0		20 58.09	56.33	1.52	IV.	3	49.490	8 34.4	20.0	1.2	20 55.93	28 5.6
79	8					15.0	33.7		20 56.65	56.33	1.50	V.	3	44.038	15 18.9	20.0	2.4	21 54.48	34 51.3
80	9						23.5		21 46.56	56.33	1.48	VI.	3	38.428	21 11.1	19.8	3.6	22 44.37	40 44.5
81	9				3.5	22.0			23 3.47	56.33	1.41	IV.	4	22.168	38 13.3	19.5	6.9	24 1.21	57 49.7
82	9				29.0	48.0			24 29.26	56.34	1.50	IV.	4	45.058	14 13.3	19.2	2.2	25 27.10	33 44.7
83	9					40.0			25 3.02	56.34	1.46	VI.	3	34.758	25 1.3	18.9	4.4	26 0.82	44 34.6
84	9.10				47.2	6.0			27 47.39	56.35	1.43	IV.	3	27.565	32 32.9	18.5	4.8	28 45.17	33 52 6.2
85	9.10				30.0				28 30.05	56.35	1.38	IV.	3	17.098	43 29.2	18.2	8.0	29 27.78	34 3 5.4
86	9			0.5	18.0		56.0	14.2	30 18.65	56.36	1.41	IV.	3	26.829	03 18.9	17.8	6.0	31 16.42	33 52 52.7
87	9		1.5	19.3		55.0			30 37.62	56.36	1.39	IV.	3	20.727	39 41.6	17.7	7.2	31 35.37	59 16.5
88	8					45.0			31 8.20	56.36	1.51	VI.	4	53.182	5 42.8	17.6	0.6	32 6.07	33 25 11.0
89	9				42.2				32 42.25	56.37	1.39	IV.	2	19.870	40 37.3	17.2	7.4	33 10.01	34 0 11.9
90	9				16.8				34 16.85	56.37	1.44	IV.	3	34.254	25 33.2	16.8	4.4	35 14.66	33 45 4.4
91	9.10				30.0	49.0			35 30.26	56.37	1.45	IV.	3	37.041	22 38.2	16.5	3.9	36 28.08	42 8.6
92	9.10			48.0	6.0		44.0		37 6.50	56.38	1.40	IV.	3	23.020	37 17.8	16.1	6.8	38 4.28	56 50.7
93	9			48.5	6.3	25.0	44.2		37 6.74	56.38	1.40	IV.	3	23.861	36 25.1	16.1	6.6	38 4.52	55 57.8
94	9			51.7		29.0		55.7	40 26.64	56.39	1.45	IV.	4	39.735	19 47.5	15.4	3.3	41 24.48	39 16.2
95	9				37.0				40 37.06	56.39	1.42	IV.	3	32.593	27 17.4	15.3	4.8	41 34.87	33 46 47.5
96	8			55.0		14.0	33.0		42 41.59	56.40	1.35	IV.	2	15.097	45 36.6	15.0	8.4	43 39.34	34 5 10.0
97	9			30.0	48.0		25.7		43 48.75	56.40	1.40	IV.	3	27.539	32 34.5	14.6	5.8	44 46.55	33 52 4.9
98	9						22.0		43 44.94	56.40	1.39	VI.	3	24.654	35 35.3	14.5	6.4	44 42.73	55 6.2
99	9		28.0	47.0	5.0	24.0			47 5.25	56.41	1.38	IV.	3	24.336	35 55.5	13.8	6.4	48 3.04	55 25.7
100	9			1.2	20.0				48 19.89	56.41	1.42	IV.	4	35.025	24 43.2	13.5	4.3	49 17.72	44 11.0
101	9					21.8			49 3.23	56.41	1.38	V.	3	27.258	32 52.2	13.3	5.9	50 1.02	52 2.4
102	9				4.0	22.8			50 4.13	56.42	1.36	IV.	3	20.460	39 58.5	13.0	7.3	51 1.91	59 28.8
103	9			6.3	25.0	43.5			51 24.95	56.42	1.41	IV.	3	33.892	25 55.7	12.7	4.5	52 22.78	45 22.9
104	9				49.2	8.0	26.7		51 49.44	56.42	1.37	IV.	3	26.819	33 19.5	12.6	6.0	52 47.23	33 52 48.1
105	9			56.2	15.0		52.0		54 14.91	56.43	1.34	IV.	3	17.110	43 28.4	12.0	8.0	55 12.68	34 2 58.4
106	9			57.0	15.7				58 15.60	56.44	1.44	IV.	4	44.098	15 13.7	11.0	2.4	17 59 13.48	33 34 37.1
107	8			44.0		21.0	39.0		60 2.32	56.44	1.38	IV.	3	30.100	29 53.8	10.7	5.3	18 1 0.14	49 19.7
108	9				48.0		25.0		17 59 47.99	56.44	1.36	IV.	3	23.459	36 50.5	10.6	6.6	0 45.79	33 56 17.8
109	8.9						49.0	8.0	18 1 12.07	56.41	1.33	VI.	2	14.566	46 9.6	10.3	8.5	2 9.84	34 5 38.4
110	9					43.0	1.3		2 24.45	56.45	1.44	V.	4	44.308	15 0.3	10.0	2.4	3 22.34	33 34 22.7
111	9			52.0	11.0				4 10.77	56.45	1.42	IV.	4	40.896	18 34.6	9.6	3.1	5 8.64	37 57.3
112	8.9				9.5	28.0	46.0		5 9.32	56.46	1.35	IV.	3	31.520	28 24.7	9.4	5.0	6 7.16	33 47 49.1
113	8			23.5	42.0				6 42.05	56.46	1.31	IV.	2	11.174	49 42.4	9.0	9.2	7 39.82	34 9 10.6
114	8.9						36.7		18 6 59.85	+56.46	+1.46	VI.	4	51.755	− 7 12.2	−8.9	−0.9	18 7 57.77	−33 26 32.0

CORRECTIONS.

Date.	Corr. of Clock.	Hourly rate.	m	n	c	Zenith Point.	Mic. Co.
1846.	h.	s.	s.	s.	s.	° ′ ″	r.
	s.	s.	s.	s.	s.		

REMARKS.

(22) 78. Minute assumed as 19′, not 20, and micrometer reading as 50′.490, not 49′.490, to agree with Transit, June 15.

INSTRUMENT READINGS.

Date.	CIRCLE.					Mean.	Barom.	THERMOM.				
	A.	B.	C.	D.	E.			At.	Ex.	U.	L.	I.
1846.	° ′ ″					″	in.	°	°	°	°	°
h. m.												

ZONE 23. JUNE 16. P. $D_o = -32°$ 4' 40".

No.	Mag.	I.	II.	III.	IV.	V.	VI.	VII.	T.	a_1	a_2	MICROMETER		r	i	d_1	d_2	Mean Right Ascension, 1850.0	Mean Declination, 1850.0
									h. m. s.	s.	s.			r.	' "	"	"	h. m. s.	° ' "
1	6	28.0	46.5	4.5	22.4				14 44 22.69	+56.31	+0.96	IV.	4	40.265	−19 14.4	−9.8	−3.2	14 15 19.99	−32 24 7.4
2	8			20.5	38.5				15 38.62	56.35	0.98	IV.	4	46.663	12 32.5	9.7	2.0	16 35.95	17 24.2
3	7				34.0	52.5	10.5		16 34.09	56.35	0.90	IV.	3	30.676	29 17.6	9.6	4.9	17 31.34	34 12.1
4	8				19.0				20 19.03	56.38	0.78	IV.	1	9.110	51 48.6	9.3	8.8	21 16.19	56 46.7
5	7	36.0	54.0	12.5	30.3				23 30.61	56.39	0.84	IV.	3	26.020	34 9.7	8.9	5.7	24 27.84	39 4.3
6	9	11.5			5.0				27 5.62	56.41	0.85	IV.	3	33.375	26 28.4	8.5	4.4	28 2.88	31 21.3
7	8	22.0	40.0	57.5	10.7				29 16.49	56.43	0.79	IV.	2	21.435	38 59.4	8.3	6.5	30 13.71	43 54.2
8	7					34.0	52.0		32 15.75	56.45	0.96	V.	4	56.400	2 21.2	8.0	0.3	33 13.16	7 9.5
9	5	37.0	55.3	13.3	32.0				44 31.82	56.52	0.73	IV.	3	24.070	37 14.8	6.5	6.2	45 29.07	42 7.4
10	7			56.0		34.0			47 14.99	56.53	0.84	V.	4	50.400	8 37.9	6.2	1.4	48 12.36	13 25.5
11	7		59.0		35.0				47 35.25	56.53	0.84	VI.	4	50.500	8 31.2	6.2	1.4	48 32.62	13 16.8
12	8	59.5	17.3	36.0					48 53.99	56.54	0.84	IV.	4	50.010	9 2.5	6.0	1.5	49 51.37	13 50.0
13	7	9.0	27.0	45.5	4.0				57 3.69	56.59	0.76	IV.	4	44.553	14 45.1	5.0	2.4	14 56 1.04	19 32.5
14	8			4.0					14 59 4.01	56.60	0.77	IV.	4	48.495	10 37.7	4.7	1.7	15 0 1.38	15 24.1
15	8		11.0	29.5			24.0		15 9 47.61	56.66	0.72	VI.	4	45.220	14 2.7	3.2	2.3	10 44.99	18 48.2
16	6	36.5	54.5	13.0	31.3				21 31.16	56.72	0.64	IV.	4	42.350	17 3.5	1.4	2.8	22 29.52	21 47.7
17	7	54.0	12.7	31.0	49.3				23 49.16	56.74	0.54	IV.	3	25.370	34 50.6	1.2	5.8	24 46.44	39 37.6
18	5	55.0	13.5	31.0	50.0				15 25 49.76	+56.75	+0.55	IV.	3	29.520	−30 30.2	−0.8	−5.1	15 26 47.06	−32 35 16.1

ZONE 24. JUNE 17. C. $D_o = -37°$ 5' 0".

No.	Mag.	I.	II.	III.	IV.	V.	VI.	VII.	T.	a_1	a_2	MICROMETER		r	i	d_1	d_2	Mean Right Ascension, 1850.0	Mean Declination, 1850.0
1	8		57.7	17.0	36.4	55.9	15.0		14 56 36.42	+56.90	+1.58	IV.	4	43.501	−15 51.2	−42.2	−3.9	14 57 34.90	−37 21 37.3
2	8.9		51.7	10.7	30.0	49.7	9.5		14 58 30.31	56.92	1.14	IV.	2	9.	52			14 59 28.37	57
3	9			12.0					15 1 10.78	56.94	1.67	II.	4	50.974	8 1.8	41.6	1.6	15 2 9.39	13 45.0
4	8.9		56.1	15.8	35.1	54.8	13.8		2 35.11	56.95	1.15	IV.	2	10.271	50 39.0	41.5	14.3	3 33.21	56 24.8
5	8.9		45.4	4.5	24.0	43.5			6 24.10	56.97	1.17	IV.	2	13.369	47 25.0	40.9	13.3	7 22.24	53 19.2
6	8		14.0		53.0	12.5	32.0		10 53.02	57.01	1.32	IV.	4	25.740	34 26.7	40.3	9.3	11 51.35	40 16.3
7	9.10					44.0	3.0		11 24.29	57.01	1.24	V.		19.001	41 29.9	40.2	11.5	12 22.54	47 21.6
8	8		49.0	8.4	28.0	47.4	6.6		14 27.89	57.03	1.33	IV.	3	27.971	32 7.3	39.8	8.0	15 26.25	37 55.7
9	9				57.7		36.0		19 57.53	57.07	1.66	IV.	4	54.489	4 21.4	39.0	0.6	20 56.26	10 1.0
10	8.9					9.0		47.5	21 49.39	57.08	1.36	IV.	3	32.	28			22 47.83	(33)
11	9				50.7	10.0			26 10.10	57.11	1.27	IV.	3	25.410	34 48.1	38.0	9.4	27 8.48	40 35.5
12	9			27.9	47.0	6.7	25.8		36 47.18	57.19	1.42	IV.	3	30.102	20 28.2	36.3	5.2	37 45.79	26 9.7
13	9.10							1.0	37 2.61	57.19	1.17	VI.	1	18.921	41 33.6	36.3	11.5	38 0.97	27 21.4
14	6		34.6	54.0	13.0		52.5	12.0	49 13.43	57.27	1.00	IV.	2	9.004	51 58.1	34.2	14.7	50 11.70	57 47.0
15	9.10		50.2						53 9.57	57.29	1.43	III.	4	44.462	14 50.9	33.5	3.6	54 8.29	20 28.0
16	7.8		25.0		4.5	23.7			53 44.83	57.29	1.37	IV.	4	38.809	20 45.6	33.4	5.3	54 43.49	26 24.3
17	9		30.0	49.1	8.7				15 53 49.27	57.30	1.39	IV.	4	41.269	18 11.4	33.4	4.5	15 54 47.96	23 49.3
18	9		29.0	48.5	8.0	27.7			16 6 45.62	57.37	1.37	IV.	4	42.529	16 52.2	31.0	4.2	16 7 47.36	22 27.4
19	6.7			14.0	33.0	52.7	12.0		13 33.25	57.41	1.49	IV.	4	51.874	7 5.4	29.8	1.4	14 32.15	12 36.6
20	9		42.0	1.7	21.1	40.7	0.0		19 21.10	57.45	1.15	IV.	3	27.499	32 37.1	28.7	8.8	20 19.70	38 14.6
21	9				19.7	39.2			29 19.76	57.50	1.34	IV.	4	44.498	14 48.6	26.7	3.6	30 18.60	20 18.9
22	7			2.0	21.8	41.0	1.0	20.5	32 41.57	57.52	0.94	IV.	2	14.471	46 15.0	26.1	12.9	33 40.03	51 54.0
23	9		57.0	16.4	36.0	55.7	15.0		37 36.02	57.55	0.98	IV.	3	18.241	42 17.6	25.1	11.7	38 34.55	47 54.4
24	7		16.7	35.6	55.0	14.7			39 55.18	57.56	1.38	IV.	3	49.589	9 29.3	24.7	2.0	40 54.12	14 56.0
25	6				44.5	4.0			40 44.52	57.56	0.99	IV.	2	19.062	41 28.0	24.5	11.5	41 43.07	47 4.0
26	7			53.0	12.2	32.0	51.0	11.0	41 12.39	57.57	1.00	IV.	3	20.699	39 43.4	24.4	10.9	42 10.95	45 18.7
27	9								16 41	+57.57	+1.29		4	44.4	−14 56.	−24.	−3.6	16 42	−37 20 (24.)

CORRECTIONS.

Date.	Corr. of Clock.	Hourly rate.	m	n	c	Zenith Point.	Mic. Co.
1846.	h. s.	s.	s.	s.	s.	° ' "	r.
June 16, 16	+ 48.384	+ 0.021	+ 0.198	+ 0.396	+ 0.247	0 0 3.07	30.006
17, 16	+ 48.420	+ 0.025	+ 0.198	+ 0.396	+ 0.247	0 0 2.52	30.006

INSTRUMENT READINGS.

Date.	CIRCLE.							Barom.	THERMOM.				
	A.	B.	C.	D.	E.	F.	Mean.		At.	Ex.	U.	L.	I.
	° ' "						"	In.	°	°	°	°	°
Zone 23 June 16, 14 14	71 24 64.6	61.4	71.2	60.5	63.3	51.0	62.00	29.968	77.8	73.3			73.0
15 25								29.976	75.5	71.0			
Zone 24 June 17, 14 56								30.076	74.0	70.8			
15 0	76 24 59.0	60.0	67.9	60.9	59.6	48.0	59.23				73.4	73.2	73.3
15 26										69.6			
16 0	59.0	59.2	67.9	60.6	59.9	47.0	58.93				73.0	72.9	
16 6								30.082	73.2	68.9			
16 29										68.6			

REMARKS.

June 16, 15h 25m. Stopped by clouds.
(23) 9. Mic. reading assumed as 23r.070 instead of 24r.070.
June 17. Smoky horizon; night unfavorable; first readings of barometer, &c., at 14h 50m; 18h 10m cloudy.

Zone 24. June 17. C. D_0 = −37° 5′ 0″—Continued.

Column groups: **SECONDS OF TRANSIT** = columns I–VII; **MICROMETER** = columns Micr. and r. Units: T and Mean R.A. in h m s; a_1, a_2 in s; i in ′ ″; d_1, d_2 in ″; Mean Decl. in ° ′ ″.

No.	Mag.	I	II	III	IV	V	VI	VII	T.	a_1	a_2	Micr.	r.	i	d_1	d_2	Mean R.A. 1850.0	Mean Decl. 1850.0
28	9.10		57.0				14.0		16 46 35.52	+57.59	+1.16	IV. 3	34.188	−25 37.3	−23.3	−6.7	16 47 34.27	−37 31 7.3
29	9			24.2	43.0		22.4		46 43.40	57.59	0.99	IV. 3	20.687	39 44.1	23.2	11.0	47 41.98	45 18.3
30	8						23.4	42.9	47 44.74	57.60	1.25	VI. 3	42.044	17 24.0	23.0	4.3	48 43.59	22 51.3
31	9					36.5	56.0	14.7	49 16.81	57.61	1.01	IV. 3	23.572	36 43.3	22.7	10.0	50 15.43	42 16.0
32	8.9		13.0	32.2	51.8	11.0	31.0		51 51.81	57.62	1.16	IV. 3	35.469	24 17.0	22.1	6.3	52 50.59	29 45.4
33	8.9			28.0	47.2	6.5	26.1		52 47.82	57.62	1.06	IV. 3	28.441	31 38.0	22.0	8.4	53 46.50	37 8.4
34	9					57.0	16.5		16 53 37.58	57.63	1.02	V. 3	25.482	34 43.6	21.8	9.4	16 54 36.23	40 14.8
35	8			38.1	56.9	16.5	35.6		17 1 57.04	57.67	0.94	IV. 3	20.071	40 22.8	20.0	11.1	17 2 55.65	37 45 53.9
36	8			28.0					4 7.13	57.67	0.74	II. 2	4.760	56 25.2	19.5	16.1	5 5.54	35 2 0.8
37	9			33.0	52.0				6 52.26	57.69	0.75	IV. 2	6.991	54 4.1	19.0	15.4	7 50.70	37 59 38.5
38	9				6.0				8 5.97	57.69	1.33	IV. 4	52.701	6 13.5	18.7	1.1	9 4.99	11 33.3
39	9						8.5		9 29.55	57.70	0.85	VI. 2	14.642	46 4.8	18.4	12.9	10 28.10	51 36.1
40	6		48.1	7.4	27.0	46.5	5.7		11 26.04	57.71	0.99	IV. 3	26.562	33 35.8	18.0	9.1	12 25.64	39 2.9
41	9		15.5	34.9		14.0			14 54.39	57.72	1.10	IV. 3	36.921	22 45.6	17.2	5.9	15 53.21	28 8.7
42	9					58.0	17.7		16 38.57	57.73	0.77	V. 2	10.910	49 58.6	16.8	14.1	17 37.07	55 29.5
43	8.9		59.0	17.5	36.8	56.0	15.0		19 36.88	57.74	1.22	IV. 4	45.801	13 20.0	16.2	3.1	20 35.84	18 40.2
44	7		56.1	16.0	35.1	54.5	13.5	33.0	19 35.08	57.74	1.32	IV. 4	53.989	4 52.7	16.2	0.7	20 34.14	10 9.6
45	9			57.0		36.1			24 16.52	57.76	0.90	IV. 2	21.508	38 54.8	15.2	10.7	25 15.18	44 20.7
46	8.9			12.0		50.5	9.8		24 31.20	57.76	1.13	IV. 3	39.722	19 49.9	15.1	5.0	25 30.00	25 10.0
47	9			16.0	35.5				26 35.50	57.77	0.93	IV. 2	24.741	35 31.0	14.7	0.7	27 34.20	40 56.3
48	9		18.0	37.0			6.0		26 56.82	57.77	0.87	IV. 2	20.482	39 59.1	14.6	11.0	27 55.46	45 24.7
49	9					11.0	30.5		27 51.58	57.77	0.92	V. 2	24.826	35 26.4	14.4	9.6	28 50.27	40 50.4
50	9			31.2	50.7				29 50.69	57.78	1.00	IV. 4	31.312	28 37.8	14.0	7.6	30 49.47	33 59.4
51	9			17.7	37.0	56.2	15.7		37 36.98	57.80	1.14	IV. 4	43.461	15 53.7	12.2	3.9	38 35.92	21 9.8
52	9		21.7	41.7	0.8	20.1	39.0		40 0.70	57.81	0.82	IV. 3	20.255	40 11.4	11.7	11.1	40 59.33	45 34.2
53	9.10				3.5		42.0		40 3.35	57.91	0.87	IV. 3	23.419	36 53.0	11.7	10.1	41 2.03	42 14.8
54	9		35.0	54.0	13.8		52.0		43 13.56	57.82	1.08	IV. 4	40.086	19 25.6	11.0	4.9	44 12.46	24 41.5
55	9		19.0	38.7	58.0		37.0		46 58.05	57.83	1.13	IV. 4	45.827	13 25.0	10.1	3.1	47 57.01	18 38.2
56	9.10						29.0		46 50.30	57.83	1.07	VI. 3	39.520	20 2.0	10.1	5.1	47 49.20	25 17.2
57	9		23.0	42.1	2.0				49 1.77	57.84	1.08	IV. 3	41.319	18 9.8	9.6	4.5	50 0.69	23 23.9
58	9.10						22.0	11.5	48 43.43	57.84	1.18	VI. 4	49.191	9 53.3	9.7	2.1	49 42.45	15 5.1
59	8		19.7	30.2	50.0				53 58.77	57.85	0.82	IV. 3	22.472	37 52.3	8.5	10.3	54 57.44	43 1.1
60	8			0.0	18.7	38.5			54 19.07	57.85	0.99	IV. 3	36.595	23 6.0	8.4	6.0	55 17.91	28 20.4
61	8					19.0			54 50.57	57.86	0.98	V. 3	35.119	24 38.8	8.3	6.4	55 58.41	20 53.5
62	8						50.0	9.0	55 11.07	57.86	1.05	IV. 3	40.	20 .			17 56 9.08	(25)
63	9				16.7				17 59 16.67	57.87	1.16	IV. 3	49.709	9 21.3	7.3	2.0	18 0 15.70	14 30.6
64	9				10.7	30.0	49.7		18 1 10.68	57.87	0.76	IV. 3	19.067	41 25.7	6.8	11.4	2 9.31	46 13.9
65	9		16.0			15.1		53.5	2 55.22	57.89	0.84	IV. 3	20.199	33 55.6	6.4	9.2	3 53.94	39 14.2
66	9				13.0				3 13.06	57.88	0.82	IV. 3	24.456	35 47.9	6.4	9.7	4 11.76	41 4.0
67	9		28.7	48.0	7.5	26.8	46.0		18 7 7.42	+57.89	+1.11	IV. 4	47.891	−11 15.4	−5.5	−2.5	18 8 6.42	−37 16 23.4

Zone 25. June 18. P. D_0 = −32° 3′ 20′.

No.	Mag.	I	II	III	IV	V	VI	VII	T.	a_1	a_2	Micr.	r.	i	d_1	d_2	Mean R.A. 1850.0	Mean Decl. 1850.0
1	5	54.0	12.5	30.5	49.3				15 25 48.96	+57.76	+1.13	IV. 3	29.540	−30 29.0	−82.7	−4.5	15 26 47.85	−32 35 16.2
2	7	29.5	48.0	6.0	24.5				37 24.42	57.82	1.08	IV. 3	25.203	35 1.1	80.8	5.4	38 23.32	39 47.3
3	8		40.0	57.0	16.5	35.0			39 16.25	57.82	1.29	V. 3	43.460	15 53.5	80.6	2.2	40 15.36	20 36.3
4	7		29.0	47.5	6.0				41 5.73	57.83	1.37	IV. 4	50.100	8 56.9	80.3	1.0	42 4.03	13 38.2
5	7	55.3	13.5	32.0	50.0				15 48 50.07	+57.87	+1.43	IV. 3	30.112	−29 53.1	−79.0	−4.5	15 49 49.07	−32 34 36.6

CORRECTIONS.

Date	Corr. of Clock	Hourly rate	m	n	c	Zenith Point	Mic. Co.
1846. June 18. 16 h	s. +49.390	s. +0.020	s. +0.198	s. +0.396	s. +0.247	0 0 2.66	r. 30.006

REMARKS.

INSTRUMENT READINGS.

Date	A.	B.	C.	D.	E.	F.	Mean.	Barom.	At.	Ex.	U.	L.	I.
Zone 24 1846. June 17, 17 1	76 24 59.2	59.1	68.1	60.9	59.0	47.5	58.97	in. 30.076	72.2	68.0	72.6	72.5	
17 29										67.2			
18 1	58.4	58.9	67.2	61.1	58.0	46.5	58.35	30.060	71.0	65.7	69.4	71.0	73.0
Zone 25 June 18, 15 25	71 24 65.0	62.6	71.8	64.0	63.6	53.0	63.33	29.996	74.7	72.3			
16 13								29.996	73.7	70.2			
17 27								29.980	73.0	70.0			
18 54								29.950	71.6	69.0			
19 18								29.950	71.5	68.0			

ZONE 25. JUNE 18. P. $D_0 = -32°\ 3'\ 20''$—Continued.

No.	Mag.	SECONDS OF TRANSIT. I. II. III. IV. V. VI. VII.	T.	m_1	m_2	MICROMETER.		$r.$	i	d_1	d_2	Mean Right Ascension, 1850.0.	Mean Declination, 1850.0.
			h. m. s.	s.	s.			r.	' "	"	"	h. m. s.	° ' "
6	8	..57.015.034.0	15 50 33.56	+57.88	+1.35	IV.	4	48.367	−10 45.8	−78.7	−1.3	15 51 32.79	−32 15 25.8
7	7	23.041.059.5	53 17.68	57.89	1.08	III.	3	25.980	34 12.0	78.2	5.3	54 16.65	38 55.5
8	6	....4.022.040.5	53 45.55	57.89	1.00	V.	2	17.710	42 52.7	78.1	6.8	54 44.44	47 37.6
9	9	...1.0..	56 37.59	57.91	1.03	VII.	2	20.790	39 39.1	77.6	6.2	57 36.53	44 22.9
10	7	...18.036.0	59 59.72	57.92	1.36	VII.	4	49.045	10 1.8	77.1	1.2	15 59 52.00	14 40.1
11	9	...19.037.0	15 59 18.89	57.92	1.36	VII.	4	49.045	10 1.8	77.1	1.2	16 0 18.17	14 40.1
12	6	53.011.529.547 7....42.5	10 3 47.82	57.94	1.09	IV.	3	27.400	32 43.3	76.3	5.0	4 46.85	37 24.6
13	8	....56.014.0	13 19.23	57.98	0.96	VII.	2	14.840	45 51.9	74.4	7.3	14 18.17	50 33.6
14	8	0.017.7..54.0	26 54.33	58.04	1.13	IV.	3	30.100	29 53.8	71.6	4.5	27 53.50	34 29.9
15	7	8.027.045.0	31 3.16	58.06	1.17	III.	3	32.970	26 53.4	70.8	4.0	32 2.39	31 28.2
16	8	...20.0..5.0	31 10.49	58.06	1.17	VII.	3	33.610	26 13.2	70.7	3.9	32 9.72	30 47.8
17	8	...43.0	32 6.59	58.06	1.25	VII.	3	40.520	18 59.5	70.5	2.7	33 5.90	23 32.7
18	9	...9.0	34 50.79	58.07	1.37	VII.	4	50.340	8 40.7	69.9	1.0	35 50.23	13 11.6
19	8	...54.0	35 59.17	58.08	1.07	VII.	3	24.700	35 32.1	69.7	5.5	36 58.32	40 7.3
20	8	38.057.015.034.0	44 33.34	58.11	1.20	IV.	4	41.150	18 18.5	67.8	2.6	45 32.71	22 49.2
21	7	..10.028.0....22.541.0	44 46.31	58.11	1.35	VII.	4	48.340	10 46.2	67.8	1.3	45 45.77	15 15.3
22	9	..9.0..45.0	47 45.32	58.12	1.03	IV.	2	21.960	38 26.3	67.1	6.0	48 44.47	42 59.4
23	9	...15.0	48 56.69	58.13	1.06	VII.+	3	23.920	36 21.1	66.9	5.6	49 55.88	40 53.6
24	8	...54.0	50 54.04	58.13	1.24	IV.	4	38.910	20 39.3	66.4	3.0	51 53.41	25 8.7
25		...19.0	50 58.79	58.13	1.38	VII.+	4	51.000	7 59.7	66.4	0.8	51 56.30	12 26.9
26	8	...22.0	52 27.17	58.14	1.06	VII.	3	26.210	33 57.5	66.1	5.3	53 26.39	38 28.9
27	8	...6.0	54 47.67	58.15	1.01	V.	2	19.820	40 40.4	65.6	6.4	55 46.83	45 12.4
28	9	...11.019.0	55 34.23	58.15	0.94	VII.	1	14.570	46 6.1	65.4	7.4	56 33.32	50 38.9
29	8	...43.0 1.0	57 24.67	58.16	1.27	VI.	4	41.980	17 25.9	65.0	2.4	16 58 24.10	21 53.3
30	9	...23.0..59.0	16 59 41.00	58.17	1.24	V.	4	38.550	21 1.8	64.4	3.0	17 0 40.41	25 29.2
31	4	...34.052.010.028.0	17 0 33.98	58.17	1.43	VII.	4	55.320	3 28.0	64.2	0.1	1 33.58	7 52.3
32	4	...14.033.0	2 14.39	58.17	1.35	IV.	4	48.515	10 36.4	63.9	1.3	3 13.91	15 1.6
33	7	...20.0	2 25.30	58.17	1.23	VII.	3	38.050	21 34.5	63.8	3.1	3 24.70	26 1.4
34	7	..11.530.049.0	4 48.43	58.18	1.17	IV.	3	33.615	26 13.2	63.3	3.9	5 47.78	30 40.4
35	4	24.543.0 1.0	6 19.30	58.19	1.19	III.	3	31.950	24 49.2	62.9	3.7	7 18.68	29 15.8
36	4	41.059.016.535.0	7 35.21	58.19	1.26	IV.	4	40.840	18 38.2	62.6	2.6	8 34.66	23 3.4
37	9	...12.030.0	7 35.55	58.19	1.42	VII.	4	53.810	5 2.6	62.6	0.4	8 35.10	9 25.6
38	8	...47.0	9 28.67	58.20	1.03	V.	2	22.300	38 5.1	62.2	6.0	10 27.90	42 33.3
39	8	...28.546.5 5.0	10 10.11	58.20	1.07	VII.	2	24.580	35 41.4	62.0	5.6	11 9.38	40 9.0
40	9	22.040.559.0	15 17.07	58.22	1.01	III.	2	20.065	40 25.1	60.8	6.4	16 16.30	44 52.3
41	8	...47.0 5.523.5	15 47.02	58.22	0.96	VI.	1	15.555	45 4.8	60.8	7.2	16 46.20	49 32.8
42	9	...30.0	16 35.30	58.22	1.24	VII.	4	39.440	20 4.9	60.6	2.9	17 34.76	24 28.4
43	8	..40.059.017.0	22 17.01	58.24	0.88	IV.	1	8.850	52 4.8	59.2	8.4	23 16.13	56 32.4
44	4	0.518.5..55.0	23 55.06	58.24	1.20	IV.	3	35.790	23 56.7	58.8	3.5	24 54.50	28 19.0
45	9	...46.0..22.0	27 27.37	58.25	0.99	VII.	2	18.420	42 7.7	58.0	6.7	28 26.61	46 32.4
46	8	...10.0	29 15.44	58.26	1.44	VII.	4	56.420	2 19.6	57.6	0.0	30 15.14	6 37.2
47	8	22.0	32 17.04	58.27	0.85	I.	1	7.130	53 51.8	56.8	8.8	33 16.16	58 17.4
48	5	...29.047.0	32 47.16	58.27	1.12	IV.	3	29.300	30 44.1	56.7	4.7	33 46.55	35 5.5
49	9	...12.0	33 35.62	58.27	1.32	VI.	4	45.650	13 35.5	56.5	1.8	34 35.21	17 53.8
50	8	..34.052.0	36 10.36	58.28	1.29	III.	4	42.787	16 35.9	55.9	2.3	37 9.93	20 54.1
51	5	..52.010.528.5	37 28.62	58.28	1.11	IV.	3	27.896	32 12.0	55.6	4.9	38 28.01	36 32.5
52	8	10.028.046.5	43 4.63	58.29	1.23	III.	3	37.670	21 58.5	54.3	3.2	44 4.15	26 16.0
53	4	33.552.010.0	45 28.30	58.30	1.23	III.	3	37.345	22 19.7	53.7	3.2	46 27.83	26 36.0
54	4	...43.0 1.0	17 46 1.16	+58.30	+1.07	IV.	3	24.995	−35 14.0	−53.6	−5.5	17 47 0.53	−32 39 33.1

CORRECTIONS.

Date.	Corr. of Clock.	Hourly rate.	m	n	c	Zenith Point.	Mic. Co.
1846.	h.	s.	s.	s.	s.	° ' "	r.

INSTRUMENT READINGS.

Date.		A.	B.	C.	D.	E.	F.	Mean.	Barom.	Al.	Ex.	U.	L.	I.
	1846. h. m.	° ' "							in.	°	°	°	°	°
Zone 25	June 18, 20 0								29.938	71.5	68.0			
	20 59								29.930	71.0	67.4			

REMARKS.

June 18. Examined the Readings of the Circle frequently without perceiving any change.

(25) 10. Transits over T.'s V and VI assumed as recorded over T.'s IV and V.

ZONE 25. JUNE 18. P. D.$_0$ = −32° 3′ 20″—Continued.

No.	Mag.	I.	II.	III.	IV.	V.	VI.	VII.	T.	a_1	a_2	MICROMETER		r.	i	d_1	d_2	Mean Right Ascension, 1850.0	Mean Declination, 1850.0
									h. m. s.	s.	s.			r.	′ ″	″	″	h. m. s.	° ′ ″
55	8	32.0	50.0						17 54 26.51	+58.32	+1.35	II.	4	47.765	−11 23.3	−51.5	1.4	17 55 26.18	−32 15 36.2
56	9				46.0		22.5	40.5	54 46.02	58.32	1.38	VII.	4	51.060	7 55.4	51.4	0.8	17 55 45.72	12 7.6
57	4	16.0	34.0	52.5					17 59 10.74	58.33	1.02	III.	3	20.765	39 39.0	50.4	6.3	18 0 10.09	43 55.7
58	8	56.0	14.0	32.0					18 0 50.46	58.34	1.23	III.	4	38.145	21 27.5	50.0	3.1	1 50.03	25 40.6
59	8					26.0		3.0	1 7.91	58.34	1.06	VII.	3	23.915	36 21.3	49.9	5.7	2 7.31	40 36.9
60	9				35.5				3 35.56	58.34	1.13	IV.	3	29.810	30 11.9	49.3	4.6	4 35.03	34 25.8
61	7			32.0	49.5	7.7			4 49.75	58.34	1.26	V.	4	40.850	18 37.2	49.0	2.6	5 49.35	22 48.8
62	9						41.0		7 4.64	58.35	1.33	VI.	.4	47.305	11 48.1	48.4	1.5	8 4.32	15 58.0
63	9		12.0	30.0					9 48.36	58.35	1.25	III.	4	39.700	19 49.8	47.8	2.8	10 47.96	24 0.4
64	9							14.0	9 19.30	58.35	1.25	VII.	4	39.870	19 37.8	47.9	2.8	10 18.90	23 48.5
65	6						10.0	28.0	10 33.50	58.35	1.36	VI.	4	48.770	10 19.6	47.6	1.2	11 33.21	14 28.4
66	8						14.0	33.0	11 37.98	58.36	1.33	VII.	4	46.660	12 31.4	47.4	1.6	12 37.67	16 40.4
67	5		13.5	31.5	50.0				13 49.92	58.36	1.27	IV.	4	41.820	17 36.6	46.8	2.4	14 49.55	21 45.8
68	8	51.0		28.0					15 46.12	58.36	0.94	III.	2	13.840	46 55.2	46.3	7.5	16 45.42	51 9.0
69	8		29.0		5.5				17 5.52	58.37	1.21	IV.	4	37.165	22 30.4	46.0	3.3	18 5.10	26 39.7
70	7					42.0	0.5	18.0	17 23.64	58.37	1.14	VII.	3	30.850	29 6.2	45.9	4.4	18 23.15	33 16.5
71	6	29.0	47.0						20 23.54	58.37	1.26	II.	4	40.610	18 52.7	45.2	2.6	21 23.17	23 0.5
72	8		55.0		31.0				21 31.30	58.37	1.05	IV.	3	23.120	37 11.6	44.9	5.8	22 30.72	32 41 22.3
73	7			19.0			14.0		24 37.32	58.38	0.83	VI.	1	5.160	55 56.	44.2	9.1	25 36.53	33 0 (9.)
74	8	37.0	55.0	13.5					27 31.83	58.38	0.91	III.	2	11.715	49 8.4	43.5	7.9	28 31.12	32 53 19.8
75	9					58.0			28 39.80	58.38	1.41	VII.	4	53.380	5 30.4	43.2	0.4	29 39.59	9 34.0
76	7			5.5	24.0				31 23.90	58.39	1.18	IV.	3	33.790	26 2.1	42.5	3.9	32 23.47	30 8.5
77	7	57.0	15.5	33.5					36 51.91	58.39	1.01	III.	4	27.510	38 51.2	41.2	6.1	37 51.31	42 58.5
78	6	21.5	39.5	58.0	16.3				38 16.33	58.40	0.90	IV.	1	12.677	48 5.2	40.0	7.8	39 15.63	52 13.9
79	4		21.0	39.0	57.5				42 57.40	58.40	1.40	IV.	4	52.880	6 2.3	39.7	0.4	43 57.20	10 2.4
80	9						43.0		46 6.50	58.40	1.14	VI.	3	31.555	28 22.5	38.9	4.3	47 6.04	32 25.7
81	7				52.0	10.0			47 33.67	58.41	1.25	VI.	4	41.460	17 58.7	38.6	2.5	48 33.33	21 59.8
82	7		44.0	2.0					49 20.37	58.41	1.19	III.	3	36.470	23 13.9	38.2	3.4	50 29.97	27 15.5
83	7						55.0		49 18.54	58.41	1.17	VI.	3	33.600	26 14.1	38.2	3.9	50 18.12	30 16.2
84	8							35.5	49 30.78	58.41	1.20	VII.	3	37.310	22 21.1	38.1	3.2	50 30.39	26 22.4
85	8				26.0	41.0			51 7.52	58.41	0.95	V.	1	16.440	44 9.6	37.7	7.1	52 6.88	48 14.4
86	7						53.5		52 16.85	58.41	0.86	VII.	1	7.730	53 14.3	37.4	8.7	53 16.12	57 20.4
87	9		3.0	21.5	39.5				54 39.62	58.41	1.08	IV.	3	26.635	33 31.2	36.9	5.2	55 39.11	37 33.3
88	8			5.0					18 57 5.04	58.41	0.95	IV.	2	16.417	44 14.0	36.3	7.1	18 58 4.40	48 17.4
89	8		9.0	27.5	45.5				19 4 45.60	58.42	1.19	IV.	3	36.380	23 19.8	34.5	3.4	19 5 45.21	27 17.7
90	8			43.0	1.0				6 1.07	58.42	1.42	IV.	4	54.280	4 34.6	34.2	0.2	7 0.91	8 29.0
91	9	45.5	4.0						11 40.42	58.42	1.04	II.	3	23.150	37 9.2	32.8	5.8	12 39.88	41 7.8
92	8			48.0	6.0				12 6.16	58.42	0.98	IV.	2	17.700	42 53.4	32.7	6.9	13 5.56	46 53.0
93	9	32.0	50.0	8.5					14 26.66	58.42	1.14	III.	3	32.240	27 39.6	32.2	4.2	15 26.22	31 36.0
94	8							40.5	18 45.57	58.42	0.95	VII.	2	15.840	44 49.2	31.2	7.2	19 44.94	48 47.6
95	4								19			VII.	4	39.750	19 45.5			19 (39)	(23)
96	8						1.0	19.5	20 0 24.53	58.41	0.99	VII.	2	18.750	41 46.8	21.3	6.7	20 1 23.93	45 34.8
97	9	5.0	23.7	42.0	0.0				9 0.12	58.40	0.99	IV.	2	19.370	41 8.9	19.3	6.5	9 59.51	44 54.7
98	7							7.3	9 12.69	58.40	1.37	VII.	4	51.100	7 52.9	19.3	0.7	10 12.46	11 32.9
99	7	5.5	24.0	42.0	0.5				16 0.47	58.39	0.95	IV.	2	15.650	45 2.0	17.8	7.2	16 59.81	48 47.0
100	8	52.5	10.5	28.7	47.0				31 47.06	58.37	1.10	IV.	3	29.163	30 52.6	14.4	4.7	32 46.53	34 31.7
101	6		10.0	28.0	46.3				33 46.37	58.37	1.17	IV.	3	35.550	24 11.8	14.0	3.6	34 45.91	27 49.4
102	4	37.0	55.0	13.5	31.5				40 31.66	58.36	1.07	IV.	3	27.380	32 44.6	12.0	5.0	41 31.09	36 22.2
103	6							18.0	20 40 23.35	+58.36	+1.30	VII.	4	46.185	−13 1.4	−12.6	−1.8	20 41 23.01	−32 16 35.8

CORRECTIONS.

Date.	Corr. of Clock.	Hourly rate.	m	n	e	Zenith Point.	Mic. Co.
1845.	h.	s.	s.	s.	s.	° ′ ″	r.

INSTRUMENT READINGS.

Date.	CIRCLE.							Barom.	THERMOM.				
	A.	B.	C.	D.	E.	F.	Mean.		At.	Ex.	U.	L.	I.
1846. h. m.	° ′ ″						″	in.	°	°	°	°	°

REMARKS.

Zone 25. June 18. P. $D_0 = -32°\ 3'\ 20''$—Continued.

No.	Mag.	I.	II.	III.	IV.	V.	VI.	VII.	T.	a_1	a_2
									h. m. s.	s.	s.
104	9				39.0			15.0	20 42 20.56	+58.35	+1.33
105	7		0.0	19.0	37.5				45 37.05	58.35	1.41
106	9	23.0	41.0		17.5				48 17.51	58.34	1.30
107	4	10.5	29.0	47.3	5.3				51 5.49	58.34	0.93
108	4	19.3	37.7	56.3	14.3				56 14.42	58.33	0.86
109	9			5.0					58 23.26	58.32	1.19
110	8							8.0	20 59 13.17	+58.32	+1.00

No.	Micrometer	i	d_1	d_2	Mean Right Ascension, 1850.0.	Mean Declination, 1850.0.
	r.	′ ″	″	″	h. m. s.	° ′ ″
104	VII. 4 47.657	−11 28.9	−12.2	−1.3	20 43 20.24	−32 15 2.4
105	IV. 4 55.220	3 35.5	11.5	0.0	46 36.81	7 7.0
106	IV. 4 46.080	13 9.2	11.0	1.6	49 17.15	16 41.8
107	IV. 2 13.970	46 47.2	10.4	7.5	52 4.76	50 25.1
108	IV. 1 8.337	52 37.1	9.4	8.6	57 13.61	56 15.1
109	VII. 3 37.010	22 39.7	9.0	3.3	20 59 22.77	26 12.0
110	VII. 3 26.130	−34 2.5	−8.8	−5.3	21 0 12.55	−32 37 36.6

Zone 26. June 22. C. $D_0 = -33°\ 19'\ 30''$.

No.	Mag.	I.	II.	III.	IV.	V.	VI.	VII.	T.	a_1	a_2
1	9		30.4	49.2					17 4 7.54	+58.98	+2.18
2	9				46.0			42.0	4 46.25	58.98	2.11
3	7			17.0	35.6	54.0			4 58.59	58.98	2.15
4	8		46.0	4.7	23.2				14 23.23	59.01	1.58
5	8			27.5	46.0	4.5	23.0		15 45.99	59.01	1.60
6	9			12.0	31.7				18 11.55	59.02	1.68
7	7.8		53.1	12.0	30.7	48.9			19 11.95	59.02	1.67
8	7	17.0	35.0	53.6	12.1	30.7			20 53.70	59.02	1.63
9	7				6.0	24.1			21 28.58	59.03	1.31
10	8.9			19.0	37.0				23 0.15	59.03	1.36
11	8.9		57.0	15.0	33.5	53.0			30 15.30	59.05	1.17
12	8.9			34.0	53.5	11.7			30 34.53	59.05	1.11
13	8.9		2.5	21.1	39.5				17 32 39.61	+59.05	+1.03

No.	Micrometer	i	d_1	d_2	Mean Right Ascension, 1850.0.	Mean Declination, 1850.0.
1	III. 4 45.112	−14 10.0	−7.7	−2.8	17 5 8.70	−33 33 50.5
2	IV. 4 39.970	19 32.8	7.6	3.8	5 47.34	39 14.2
3	IV. 4 45.451	13 48.8	7.5	2.7	5 59.72	33 33 29.0
4	IV. 2 14.198	46 33.0	5.5	9.3	15 23.82	34 6 17.8
5	IV. 3 22.888	37 26.1	5.2	7.4	16 46.60	33 57 8.7
6	IV. 4 41.434	18 1.0	4.6	3.5	19 32.25	37 39.1
7	IV. 4 43.631	15 43.0	4.4	3.4	20 12.64	35 20.5
8	IV. 4 44.076	15 15.0	4.1	3.0	21 54.35	33 34 52.1
9	VI. 2 11.041	49 50.3	4.0	10.0	22 28.92	34 9 34.3
10	V. 3 22.233	38 7.4	3.6	7.6	24 0.54	33 57 48.6
11	IV. 3 26.930	33 12.6	2.0	6.0	31 15.58	58 51.2
12	IV. 3 20.845	39 34.2	1.9	7.8	31 34.60	33 59 13.9
13	IV. 3 19.918	−40 32.3	−1.4	−8.1	17 33 39.60	−34 0 11.8

Zone 27. June 24. P. $D_0 = -28°\ 18'\ 20''$.

No.	Mag.	I.	II.	III.	IV.	V.	VI.	VII.	T.	a_1	a_2
1	9				18.0		53.5		14 30 35.75	+58.03	+1.55
2	9						29.0	47.0	31 54.01	58.03	1.40
3	7			47.5	5.0	22.5			40 4.98	58.06	1.63
4	8				5.0	22.0			45 22.30	58.08	1.44
5	6	25.3	42.5	0.3	17.7				47 17.73	58.09	1.56
6	7	22.0	39.3	57.0	14.5				57 14.58	58.12	1.43
7	8				6.0		40.5		58 5.75	58.13	1.53
8	7					35.0			14 58 42.31	58.13	1.47
9	9					15.0			15 4 22.40	58.15	1.57
10	8		0.0	17.5		52.0			6 52.55	58.16	1.52
11	6	47.0	4.5	22.0	39.5				12 39.59	58.18	1.45
12	8	30.0	58.0	16.0	34.0				18 33.15	58.20	1.37
13	7	20.0	37.5	55.0					25 12.54	58.22	1.53
14	6	12.0			4.5	22.0		57.0	26 4.45	58.22	1.55
15	8		36.0	53.0	11.0				28 10.95	58.23	1.34
16			21.0						29 56.	58.23	
17	7				4.0	22.0			31 21.81	58.24	1.45
18	7	35.0	52.0				2.0	19.5	31 27.12	58.24	1.48
19	7	45.5							38 38.	58.26	
20	8	24.5		0.5					45 17.57	58.26	1.46
21	4	45.7	3.3	21.0	38.3			31.0	15 46 38.40	+58.28	+1.45

No.	Micrometer	i	d_1	d_2	Mean Right Ascension, 1850.0.	Mean Declination, 1850.0.
1	V. 4 39.840	−19 40.6	−59.9	−4.2	14 31 35.33	−28 39 4.7
2	VII. 2 16.970	43 38.5	59.7	7.3	32 53.44	29 3 5.5
3	V. 4 53.750	5 7.3	58.7	2.4	41 4.67	28 24 28.3
4	IV. 3 24.413	35 50.6	57.9	6.3	46 21.82	55 14.8
5	IV. 4 45.750	13 29.8	57.7	3.4	48 17.38	32 50.9
6	IV. 3 24.460	35 47.7	56.2	6.3	58 14.13	55 10.2
7	VI. 4 41.540	17 53.6	56.1	4.0	59 5.41	37 13.7
8	VII. 3 32.150	27 44.9	56.1	5.2	14 59 41.91	47 6.2
9	VII. 4 47.800	11 20.0	55.1	3.2	15 5 22.12	30 39.3
10	IV. 4 38.750	20 49.4	54.6	4.3	9 52.26	40 8.3
11	IV. 3 31.280	28 39.9	53.8	5.3	13 39.22	28 47 59.3
12	IV. 2 17.425	43 10.8	52.8	7.2	19 32.72	29 2 30.8
13	III. 4 45.927	13 18.7	51.8	3.4	26 12.29	28 32 33.9
14	IV. 3 38.680	10 25.9	51.6	3.1	27 4.22	28 29 40.8
15	IV. 2 14.230	46 31.0	51.3	7.6	29 10.52	29 5 49.9
16		30 (57.)				
17	IV. 3 31.630	29 20.5	50.7	5.4	32 21.50	28 48 36.6
18	VI. 3 37.090	22 35.0	50.7	4.6	32 26.84	41 50.3
19		39 (39.)				
20	III. 3 34.390	25 24.5	48.3	4.9	46 17.31	44 37.7
21	IV. 3 32.820	−27 3.0	−48.1	−5.1	15 47 38.13	−28 46 16.2

CORRECTIONS.

Date.		Corr. of Clock.	Hourly rate.	m	n	c	Zenith Point.	Mic. Co.
1846.	h.	s.	s.	s.	s.	s.	° ′ ″	r.
June 22,	16	+ 50.529	+ 0.004	+ 0.198	+ 0.396	+ 0.247	0 0 2.43	30.004
24,	13	+ 50.453	+ 0.002	+ 0.198	+ 0.396	+ 0.247	0 0 2.46	30.008

INSTRUMENT READINGS.

	Date.		CIRCLE.							Barom.	THERMOM.				
			A.	B.	C.	D.	E.	F.	Mean.		At.	Ex.	U.	L.	I.
	1846.	h. m.	° ′ ″						″	in.	°	°	°	°	°
Zone 26	June 22,	16 55	72 39 60.0	63.9	60.0	65.0	59.0	48.9	60.97				62.0	63.0	70.0
		17 4								30.120	63.8	56.4			
		17 35		60.6	64.5	60.4	65.0	60.6	48.0	61.35	30.114	62.8	56.0	61.2	63.0	69.8
Zone 27	June 24,	14 30	67 39 60.8	60.0	69.0	62.3	59.3	48.6	60.00	30.126	70.6	67.5			70.0
		15 18								30.134	70.0	67.0			
		15 52								30.128	69.5	65.6			
		16 20								30.124	69.1	65.2			
		17 11								30.114	69.0	66.0			

REMARKS.

June 22. Night unfavorable; stars unsteady; indistinct as if through clouds.

(26) 2. 17h 3m, cloudy.

(26) 3. 1st reading of bar., &c., at 16h 55m.

(26) 4. 2d reading of bar., &c., at 17h 35m.

(27) 10. Minute assumed as 8 instead of 7.

(27) 17. Micrometer reading assumed as 30r.630, not 31r.630.

ZONE 27. JUNE 24. P. D_0 = −28° 18′ 20″—Continued.

No.	Mag.	I.	II.	III.	IV.	V.	VI.	VII.	T.	a_1	a_2
									h. m. s.	s.	s.
22	5	30.3	47.5		22.5			15.3	15 52 22.66	+58.30	+1.45
23	9			55.0		30.0			15 58 12.50	58.32	1.51
24	4	51.3		26.5		1.2			16 0 43.89	58.33	1.35
25	8		45.0			38.0			3 20.26	58.33	1.47
26	8			54.0					10 11.59	58.35	1.29
27	8			59.0	17.0	34.5			15 16.82	58.36	1.33
28	7	14.5	33.5	50.0	7.5				17 7.49	58.37	1.37
29	8			1.0					20 18.39	58.38	1.29
30	8			45.0		20.0			22 2.49	58.38	1.43
31	6	55.0		30.0	47.0				29 47.04	58.40	1.46
32	7	49.5	7.0	25.0					31 42.28	58.40	1.39
33	8	37.0	54.0	12.0	29.0	9.5			35 29.49	58.41	1.36
34	7	39.0		13.0	31.0				37 31.04	58.42	1.44
35	7			33.0	50.5				38 50.56	58.42	1.38
36	9			14.0		50.0			43 31.99	58.43	1.43
37	6			48.0		23.0			45 5.46	58.43	1.31
38	7				3.3	20.0			50 2.87	58.44	1.52
39	8			12.0	29.0		4.0		16 55 29.89	58.46	1.43
40	7	4.0	21.0	39.0					17 11 56.61	58.49	1.24
41	8		20.0	37.5	55.0				13 55.05	58.49	1.48
42	8	48.0		22.5	39.0				15 39.82	58.49	1.51
43	8				47.5	5.0			16 47.48	58.50	1.43
44	7				57.0	14.5	32.0		17 56.93	58.50	1.42
45					27 ?					58.51	1.29
46	7			35.5	53.0	11.0			29 53.17	58.52	1.36
47	9	30.0	47.0						41 22.30	58.53	1.43
48	8						37.0		41 44.44	58.53	1.48
49	8						52.5	10.5	43 17.70	58.54	1.43
50	4	15.5	33.0	50.5	8.0				48 8.07	58.54′	1.38
51	9							19.0	48 26.27	58.54	1.32
52	9		3.0	40.0					51 38.04	58.54	1.49
53	9		16.0		52.0				53 16.48	58.55	1.37
54	7	13.0	31.0	48.0					56 5.71	58.55	1.42
55	8					34.0			56 16.49	58.55	1.48
56	3			17.5	35.0				57 35.00	58.55	1.45
57	9			21.0					17 58 21.05	58.55	1.34
58	6	33.5	51.0	9.0	26.5				18 1 26.36	58.56	1.29
59	8	9.0	27.0	44.0					4 1.80	58.56	1.30
60	8			26.0	43.0	1.0			4 43.33	58.56	1.39
61	4	1.0	18.5	36.0	53.5				6 53.57	58.56	1.36
62	7			35.5	53.0				9 53.04	58.56	1.22
63	6			13.0	30.5	48.0			11 30.50	58.56	1.42
64	5	11.0	29.0	46.3	3.5				17 57 3.81	+58.58	+1.27

No.	MICROMETER.		r	i	d_1	d_2	Mean Right Ascension, 1850.0.	Mean Declination, 1850.0.
			r.	′ ″	″	″	h. m. s.	° ′ ″
22	IV.	3	36.234	−23 28.9	−47.0	−4.7	15 53 22.41	−28 42 40.6
23	V.	4	44.640	14 39.3	45.9	3.6	15 59 12.33	28 33 48.8
24	V.	2	18.853	41 40.9	45.4	7.0	16 1 43.57	29 0 53.3
25	V.	4	38.705	20 51.9	44.8	4.4	4 20.06	28 40 1.1
26	III.	1	11.170	49 39.6	43.5	8.0	11 11.23	29 8 51.1
27	IV.	2	16.815	43 48.8	42.4	7.3	16 16.51	29 2 58.5
28	IV.	2	22.880	37 28.6	42.0	6.5	18 7.23	28 56 37.1
29	III.	1	11.053	49 46.8	41.4	8.1	21 18.06	29 8 56.3
30	III.	3	35.930	23 47.7	41.0	4.7	23 2.30	28 42 53.4
31	IV.	4	40.280	19 13.5	39.3	4.1	30 46.90	35 16.9
32	III.	3	29.470	30 33.2	38.8	5.6	32 42.07	49 37.6
33	IV.	3	23.973	36 18.0	38.0	6.3	36 29.26	55 22.3
34	IV.	3	37.745	21 53.9	37.5	4.5	38 30.90	40 55.9
35	IV.	3	28.020	32 4.2	37.2	5.8	39 50.36	51 7.2
36	V.	4	36.750	22 54.6	36.1	4.6	44 31.85	28 41 55.3
37	V.	2	17.963	42 36.7	35.7	7.2	46 5.20	29 1 39.6
38	VII.	4	53.633	5 13.9	34.6	2.4	51 2.83	28 24 10.6
39	IV.	4	38.870	20 41.8	33.3	4.3	16 56 29.78	28 39 39.4
40	III.	1	7.735	53 14.5	29.4	8.6	17 10 56.34	29 12 12.5
41	IV.	4	47.630	11 31.9	28.9	3.1	14 55.02	29 30 23.9
42	III.	4	53.810	5 3.9	28.5	2.3	16 39.82	23 54.7
43	IV.	4	40.400	19 6.0	28.2	4.1	17 47.40	37 58.3
44	IV.	3	23.600	36 41.5	28.0	6.4	18 56.75	29 55 35.9
45	.	3	17.650	42 54.6	25.8	7.2	28 . .	29 1 47.6
46	IV.	3	28.840	31 12.8	25.1	5.7	30 53.05	28 50 3.6
47	III.	4	43.630	15 43.1	22.4	3.6	42 22.26	34 29.1
48	VII.	4	51.740	7 12.7	22.3	2.6	42 44.45	25 57.6
49	VI.	4	44.380	20 10.1	21.9	4.3	44 17.67	38 56.3
50	IV.	3	34.360	25 26.6	20.7	4.9	49 7.99	44 12.2
51	VII.	3	26.180	33 59.5	20.6	6.0	49 26.13	52 46.1
52	IV.	4	54.840	4 0.0	19.8	2.3	52 38.07	22 41.1
53	III.	3	34.680	25 6.2	19.4	4.9	54 16.40	43 50.5
54	III.	4	45.650	13 36.2	18.7	3.4	57 5.68	32 18.3
55	V.	4	55.350	3 27.7	18.7	2.2	57 16.52	22 8.6
56	IV.	4	49.700	9 21.9	18.4	2.8	58 35.00	29 3.1
57	IV.	3	32.470	27 25.2	18.2	5.2	17 59 20.94	46 8.6
58	IV.	3	23.370	36 56.1	17.4	6.4	18 2 26.21	55 39.9
59	III.	3	26.455	33 42.4	16.8	6.0	5 1.66	52 25.2
60	V.	4	39.177	20 22.4	16.6	4.3	5 41.28	30 3.3
61	IV.	3	36.520	23 11.0	16.0	4.6	7 53.49	28 41 51.6
62	IV.	1	12.135	48 39.3	15.3	8.0	10 52.82	29 7 22.6
63	IV.	4	47.230	10 54.5	14.9	3.2	12 30.48	28 29 32.6
64	IV.	3	26.880	−33 15.7	−3.8	−6.0	18 58 3.66	−28 51 45.5

CORRECTIONS.

Date.	Corr. of Clock.	Hourly rate.	m	n	c	Zenith Point.	Mic. Co.
1846.	h.	s.	s.	s.	s.	° ′	r.

REMARKS.

June 24. Microscope examined frequently without perceiving change in the readings.
After 15^h passing clouds occasionally.
At 19^h apparently very clear, yet only a few very faint stars passed the field in 17^m.
(27) 40. Min. assumed as 9 instead of 11.
(27) 49. Micrometer reading assumed as $39^r.380$, not $44^r.380$.
(27) 52. Transit over T. IV assumed as $38^s.0$, not $40^s.0$.
(27) 63. Mic. reading assumed as $48^r.230$ instead of $47^r.230$.

INSTRUMENT READINGS.

	Date.	CIRCLE.							Barom.	THERMOM.				
		A.	B.	C.	D.	E.	F.	Mean.		At.	Ex.	U.	L.	I.
		° ′ ″						″	in.	°	°	°	°	°
Zone 27	1846. June 24, 17 27								30.104	68.6	65.5			
	18 11								30.100	68.0	65.0			
	18 15		59.6	69.0	61.7	58.7	47.0	59.37						67.5
	18 57	60.2											64.5	
	19 0	67 39 60.0	59.0	69.2	62.3	58.8	47.4	59.45						

ZONE 28. JULY 1. C. $D_o = -29° 34' 0''$.

SECONDS OF TRANSIT

No.	Mag.	I.	II.	III.	IV.	V.	VI.	VII.
1	9.10				50.0?			
2	7.8		0.0	17.2	35.0	53.0	10.5	
3	8				5.0	23.0		
4	7.8			45.0	3.2			
5	7.8						0.1	
6	9			2.0	19.6			
7	8			34.5	52.0	10.0	27.5	
8	9				19.5	37.0		
9	8				8.7	26.5	44.5	
10	7		12.8	30.3	48.1	5.9	23.8	
11	9						56.0?	
12	9				51.0	10.0	27.5	
13	8				14.5	32.0	49.1	
14	8					11.7	28.7	
15	8.9				38.7	55.5	13.1	
16	8		1.3			54.5		
17	7.8		35.0	53.0	10.5	19.0		
18	9			3.5		39.0	56.5	
19	9			37.5	54.0		30.5	
20	8.9				45.0	13.0	30.7	
21	8				11.6	29.5		
22	7				22.5		58.0	
23	7.8		58.0	15.5	33.0	51.1	9.0	
24	8.9			6.0	23.7		0.5	
25	9		59.0		35.0		10.0	
26	8.9				28.0	56.0	3.5	
27	8	45.1	3.0		39.5			14.7
28	9			36.5			11.7	
29	9.10				9.0?			
30	8?				39.5	57.5		
31	8.9?							
32	8.9?							
33	9				55.0			
34	8						39.0	
35	7		10.0	28.0	46.0	3.5	21.5	
36	7.8			12.0	29.5	47.2		23.5
37	9						1.0	
38	9			7.2	25.0			
39	8.9			33.5		9.5		
40	8		57.5	15.5	33.3			
41	9					2.9	20.5	
42	8				30.0	47.0	5.0	
43	9				6.0		41.0	
44	7.8						51.0?	
45	8					59.6	17.5	35.0

No.	T. (h. m. s.)	a_1 (s.)	a_2 (s.)	MICROMETER		r.	i (′)	i (″)	d_1 (″)	d_4 (″)	Mean Right Ascension, 1850.0 (h. m. s.)	Mean Declination, 1850.0 (° ′ ″)
1	15 29 50.05	+63.28	+1.24	IV.	3	20.221	−40	13.5	−15.6	−5.0	15 30 54.57	−30 14 34.1
2	31 35.17	63.28	1.42	IV.	4	53.649	5	14.0	15.3	0.2	32 39.87	29 39 29.5
3	33 5.12	63.29	1.32	IV.	3	31.138	28	48.7	15.0	3.4	34 9.73	30 3 7.1
4	33 45.20	63.29	1.26	IV.	3	20.841	39	34.4	14.9	4.9	34 49.75	13 54.2
5	34 24.51	63.29	1.27	VI.	3	22.238	38	6.8	14.8	4.7	35 29.07	12 26.3
6	36 19.72	63.30	1.22	IV.	2	10.168	50	45.3	14.4	6.5	37 24.24	30 25 6.2
7	38 52.15	63.31	1.42	IV.	4	48.748	10	21.6	14.0	0.9	39 56.68	29 44 36.5
8	40 19.36	63.31	1.33	IV.	3	25.168	35	3.2	13.7	4.3	41 24.00	30 9 21.2
9	41 8.78	63.32	1.30	IV.	3	20.072	40	22.7	13.6	5.0	42 13.60	14 41.3
10	42 48.18	63.32	1.27	IV.	3	15.515	45	8.5	13.3	5.7	43 52.77	30 19 27.5
11	45 20.54	63.33	1.41	VI.	4	40.139	19	21.5	12.8	2.1	46 25.28	29 53 36.4
12	46 51.68	63.33	1.29	IV.	2	14.351	46	23.5	12.6	5.8	47 56.30	30 20 41.9
13	48 14.04	63.34	1.31	IV.	2	17.641	42	57.2	12.3	5.3	49 18.69	17 14.8
14	48 53.23	63.34	1.39	V.	3	30.821	29	8.4	12.2	3.4	49 58.96	3 24.0
15	50 37.98	63.35	1.36	IV.	3	25.727	34	28.1	11.8	4.8	51 42.69	30 8 44.1
16	52 36.79	63.35	1.47	IV.	4	43.206	16	9.7	11.5	1.7	53 41.61	29 50 22.9
17	56 10.77	63.36	1.38	IV.	3	25.192	35	1.7	10.8	4.3	57 15.51	30 9 16.8
18	56 21.12	63.36	1.37	IV.	3	22.466	37	52.7	10.8	4.7	15 57 25.85	12 8.2
19	15 59 54.76	63.38	1.42	IV.	3	26.576	33	34.9	10.1	4.0	16 0 59.56	7 49.0
20	16 0 45.07	63.38	1.56	IV.	2	14.524	46	12.6	9.9	−5.8	1 59.81	30 20 28.3
21	2 11.67	63.38	1.54	IV.	4	47.795	11	21.2	9.7	1.0	3 16.59	29 45 31.9
22	3 22.53	63.39	1.52	IV.	4	44.168	15	9.3	9.5	1.5	4 27.44	29 49 20.3
23	5 33.32	63.39	1.41	IV.	3	20.248	40	11.8	9.0	5.0	6 38.12	30 14 25.8
24	7 24.17	63.40	1.45	IV.	3	26.801	33	20.7	8.6	4.0	9 29.02	7 33.3
25	7 34.43	68.40	1.47	IV.	3	30.979	28	58.5	8.6	3.4	9 39.30	30 3 10.5
26	10 45.82	63.41	1.59	IV.	4	49.050	10	2.9	8.0	0.8	11 50.82	29 44 11.6
27	13 21.14	63.41	1.57	IV.	4	43.950	15	22.8	7.5	1.6	14 26.12	49 31.9
28	13 36.38	63.41	1.57	IV.	4	45.187	14	5.3	7.4	1.4	14 41.36	48 14.1
29	18 26.78	63.42	1.55	III.	3	37.528	22	7.6	6.5	2.5	19 31.75	56 16.6
30	20 39.62	63.43	1.64	IV.	4	53.152	5	45.3	6.1	0.3	21 44.69	30 51.7
31	22 ..	63.44	1.60	IV.	3	41.782	17	40.5	5.8	1.9	22 ..	51 48.2
32	22 ..	63.44	1.59	IV.	3	41.069	18	25.3	5.8	2.0	23 ..	52 33.1
33	24 55.04	63.44	1.57	IV.	3	36.766	22	55.4	5.3	2.6	26 0.05	29 57 3.3
34	26 2.41	63.45	1.50	VI.	3	18.548	41	58.1	5.0	5.2	27 7.36	30 16 8.3
35	28 45.80	63.45	1.54	IV.	3	24.731	35	30.5	4.5	4.3	29 50.79	9 39.3
36	31 29.69	63.46	1.53	IV.	3	20.526	39	54.4	3.9	4.9	32 34.68	14 3.2
37	31 25.41	63.46	1.54	VI.	3	21.591	38	47.3	3.9	4.8	32 30.41	30 12 56.0
38	33 25.01	63.47	1.62	IV.	4	35.549	24	10.4	3.5	2.8	34 30.10	29 58 16.7
39	37 51.48	63.48	1.60	IV.	3	29.629	31	26.2	2.6	5.8	38 56.56	30 5 32.6
40	40 33.28	63.49	1.53	IV.	2	10.549	50	21.6	2.1	6.4	41 38.30	30 24 30.1
41	40 45.11	63.49	1.70	V.	4	44.361	14	56.9	2.0	1.5	41 50.30	29 49 0.4
42	42 29.56	63.49	1.61	IV.	3	24.016	36	15.4	1.6	4.4	43 34.66	30 10 21.4
43	43 5.74	63.49	1.61	IV.	3	25.258	34	58.1	1.5	4.2	44 10.84	9 3.8
44	43 57.52	63.50	1.56	VII.	2	14.681	46	1.7	1.3	5.8	45 2.58	20 8.8
45	16 45 59.54	+63.50	+1.57	IV.	2	14.689	−46	2.2	−0.9	−5.8	16 47 4.61	−30 20 8.9

CORRECTIONS.

Date.	Corr. of Clock.	Hourly rate.	m	n	e	Zenith Point.	Mic. Co.
1846, July 1,	h. 13 + 55.312 s.	+ 0.034 s.	+ 0.213 s.	+ 0.298 s.	+ 0.330 s.	0° 0′ 2.44″	r. 30.001

INSTRUMENT READINGS.

Date.	CIRCLE. A.	B.	C.	D.	E.	F.	Mean.	Barom. (In.)	THERMOM. At.	Ex.	U.	L.	I.
Zone 28 1846, July 1, 15 25	68 54 60.2	58.1	68.8	59.2	58.1	45.0	58.23				77.5	76.0	74.6
15 29								29.846	77.0	74.9			
16 3										74.5			
16 29								29.944	76.2	73.5			
16 45	59.8	58.9	68.8	57.6	59.5	46.7	58.55	29.846	76.0	73.4	76.		74.6

REMARKS.

(28) 20. Transits over T.'s IV–VI assumed as 55s.0, 23s.0, and 40s.7; not 45s.0, 13s.0, and 30s.7.

(28) 24. Minutes assumed as 8; not 9.

(28) 25. Minutes assumed as 8; not 9.

(28) 27. Transits over T.'s II, III, and V assumed as recorded over T.'s I, II, and IV.

(28) 28. Transit over T. IV assumed as recorded over T. III.

After 16h interrupted by clouds, which rendered the mags. and transits doubtful.

ZONE 29. JULY 7. P. $D_a = -27°\ 2'\ 50''$.

No.	Mag.	I.	II.	III.	IV.	V.	VI.	VII.	T.	a_1	a_2	Micr.		r.	i	d_1	d_2	Mean Right Ascension, 1850.0	Mean Declination, 1850.0
									h. m. s.	s.	s.			r.	' ''	''	''	h. m. s.	° ' ''
1	9				59.0				15 33 59.05	+67.68	+2.61	IV.	3	27.555	−32 33.5	−73.7	3.3	15 35 9.34	−27 36 40.5
2	6	4.0	21.0	38.5					35 55.87	67.69	2.62	III.	3	28.960	31 5.2	73.4	3.1	37 6.18	35 11.7
3	9					28.0			36 10.61	67.69	2.61	V.	3	28.350	31 43.7	73.3	3.2	37 20.91	35 50.2
4	9			52.0	26.0				38 26.33	67.69	2.89	IV.	4	55.910	2 52.0	72.0	0.0	39 36.90	6 54.9
5	8	51.0	8.0	26.0	0.0				44 42.91	67.70	2.62	V.	3	36.490	23 12.9	71.7	2.2	45 53.23	27 16.8
6	8					45.0	3.0	20.0	45 27.97	67.70	2.58	V.	3	33.520	26 19.3	71.6	2.6	46 38.25	30 23.5
7	6					12.0	29.0	46.5	46 54.54	67.70	2.77	V.	4	51.100	7 53.8	71.3	0.5	48 5.01	11 55.6
8	9			24.0		59.0			50 41.49	67.71	2.54	III.	3	30.980	28 58.4	70.6	2.0	51 51.74	33 1.9
9	8	55.0	12.0	30.0					55 46.98	67.72	2.57	III.	4	38.930	20 38.2	69.7	1.0	56 57.27	24 39.5
10	7				19.0	36.0	54.0		56 36.37	67.72	2.63	IV.	4	44.840	14 26.9	69.6	1.2	57 46.72	18 27.7
11	7		28.0	45.0	2.5				57 45.16	67.72	2.61	IV.	4	43.940	15 23.5	69.3	1.3	15 58 55.49	19 24.1
12	6		43.0	1.0	18.0				15 59 18.03	67.72	2.50	IV.	3	34.390	25 24.7	69.0	2.5	16 0 28.25	20 26.2
13	4	2.5	20.0	37.3	55.0				16 1 54.74	67.72	2.46	IV.	3	31.993	27 54.9	68.5	2.8	3 4.02	31 56.2
14	8							18.0	2 25.85	67.72	2.33	VII.	2	20.060	40 24.6	68.4	4.2	3 35.90	44 27.2
15	8					51.0		25.0	3 33.16	67.72	2.25	VII.	1	12.940	47 48.0	68.1	5.1	4 43.13	51 51.2
16	7	59.0	16.0	34.0	51.0				7 51.05	67.72	2.35	IV.	3	24.290	35 58.4	67.3	3.7	9 1.12	39 50.4
17	7				42.0	50.0	16.0		8 41.58	67.72	2.19	IV.	1	10.200	50 40.5	67.1	5.4	9 51.49	54 43.0
18	7	47.0	4.0	21.5	39.0				12 38.91	67.73	2.42	IV.	3	32.560	27 19.5	66.3	2.7	13 49.06	31 18.5
19	8	54.5	11.5	29.0					14 46.30	67.73	2.52	III.	4	44.410	14 54.4	65.9	1.3	15 56.55	18 51.6
20	9					8.5	26.0	43.0	14 51.17	67.73	2.49	V.	4	41.200	18 15.4	65.9	1.7	16 1.39	22 13.0
21	8							55.0	16 2.99	67.73	2.50	VII.	4	42.890	16 28.0	65.6	1.5	17 13.22	20 25.1
22	6	56.3	13.5	31.0	48.0				19 48.24	67.74	2.30	IV.	3	29.147	30 53.6	64.9	3.1	20 58.28	31 51.6
23	7	52.5	10.0	27.5	44.0				22 44.60	67.74	2.15	IV.	2	17.180	43 26.1	64.3	4.5	23 54.40	47 24.9
24	2.3	31.3	48.5	6.0	23.0				25 23.32	67.74	2.07	IV.	1	10.885	49 57.5	63.7	5.3	26 33.13	53 56.5
25	8	44.0	1.0	15.5	35.5				28 35.82	67.74	2.18	IV.	3	23.655	36 38.0	63.8	3.8	29 45.74	40 34.8
26	6	16.5	33.5	51.0	8.5				31 8.41	67.74	2.27	IV.	3	33.063	26 47.8	62.5	2.0	32 18.42	30 42.9
27	5			31.0	49.3				33 48.79	67.74	2.44	IV.	4	52.710	6 12.9	61.0	0.3	34 58.97	10 5.1
28	8		22.0	39.0	56.0	13.5			34 21.65	67.74	2.43	V.	4	52.610	6 19.0	61.8	0.3	35 31.82	10 11.1
29	8			50.0		25.0			36 7.49	67.75	2.40	V.	4	50.775	8 14.1	61.4	0.5	37 17.64	12 6.0
30	9			4.5			14.0		38 39.29	67.75	2.32	VI.	4	45.020	14 14.9	61.0	1.2	39 49.36	18 7.1
31	8			16.0					40 16.05	67.75	2.11	IV.	3	25.950	34 14.1	60.5	3.5	41 25.97	38 38.1
32	7				52.0				40 34.58	67.75	2.06	V.	3	21.340	39 3.4	60.5	4.0	41 44.39	42 57.9
33	8				28.0	45.0			40 53.05	67.75	2.03	VI.	3	18.900	41 35.9	60.4	4.3	42 2.85	45 30.6
34	7	5.0	22.0	39.0					43 56.64	67.75	2.29	III.	3	44.160	15 10.0	59.7	1.3	45 6.67	19 1.0
35	7			18.5	36.0	53.0			44 18.50	67.75	2.18	IV.	3	33.845	25 58.7	59.6	2.0	45 28.43	29 50.9
36	8				18.0				45 43.23	67.75	1.95	VI.	2	13.470	47 18.2	59.4	5.0	46 52.93	51 12.6
37	7			6.0	23.0	40.5			47 23.17	67.75	2.22	IV.	4	41.130	18 20.0	59.0	1.7	48 33.14	22 10.7
38	8			32.0					48 49.37	67.75	2.07	III.	3	28.550	31 31.0	58.7	3.2	49 59.10	35 22.9
39	7			25.0				59.5	50 7.51	67.75	2.08	V.	3	30.000	29 51.4	58.4	3.0	51 17.34	33 45.8
40	7				24.0	41.0	55.5		51 23.70	67.75	1.97	IV.	2	21.540	38 52.8	58.1	4.0	52 33.51	42 44.9
41	8		40.0		10.0				54 15.32	67.75	2.21	IV.	4	46.505	12 55.2	57.5	1.0	55 25.28	16 43.7
42	7	12.0	29.0	47.0					57 4.03	67.75	2.05	III.	3	32.220	27 40.8	56.8	2.7	58 13.83	31 30.3
43	7	16.0	33.5	51.0				42.5	57 8.75	67.75	2.07	VII.	3	33.875	25 56.3	56.8	2.5	58 18.57	29 45.6
44	7				48.0	5.5			58 30.66	67.75	1.94	V.	3	22.620	37 43.0	56.5	3.9	16 59 40.35	41 33.4
45	7			36.0	53.5	11.0			16 59 36.16	67.75	2.00	IV.	3	29.430	30 35.9	56.3	3.1	17 0 45.91	34 25.3
46	4	0.0	17.5	34.5	52.0				17 1 52.03	67.75	2.00	IV.	3	20.573	30 26.9	55.3	3.1	3 1.78	34 15.7
47	4	36.5	53.5		28.5	46.0			3 28.47	67.75	1.95	IV.	3	27.160	32 58.3	55.4	3.3	4 38.17	36 47.0
48	8				48.0		22.5		4 47.89	67.75	1.84	IV.	2	17.060	43 33.5	55.1	4.6	5 57.48	47 23.2
49	7					15.0			17 5 57.65	+67.75	+2.07	V.	4	40.110	−19 23.7	−54.8	1.8	17 7 7.47	−27 23 10.3

CORRECTIONS.

Date.		Corr. of Clock.	Hourly rate.	m	n	c	Zenith Point.	Mic. Co.
1846,	h.	s.	s.	s.	s.	s.	° ' ''	r.
July 7,	12	+ 59.985	− 0.022	+ 0.213	+ 0.298	+ 0.330		

INSTRUMENT READINGS.

	Date.	A.	B.	C.	D.	E.	F.	Mean.	Barom.	At.	Ex.	U.	L.	I.
	1846,	° ' ''						''	in.	°	°			
Zone 29	July 7, 15 33	66 24	65.0	60.3	73.0	61.5	60.5	50.3	61.77	29.956	79.0	73.7		
	17 10									29.956	76.0	71.0		

REMARKS.

Zone 29. July 7. P. D = −27° 2′ 50″—Continued.

No.	Mag.	I.	II.	III.	IV.	V.	VI.	VII.	T. (h. m. s.)	a₁ (s.)	a₂ (s.)	Micrometer.		r.	i (′ ″)	d₁ (″)	d₂ (″)	Mean Right Ascension, 1850.0 (h. m. s.)	Mean Declination, 1850.0 (° ′ ″)
50	7					11.5	28.5		17 6 53.96	+67.75	+1.05	V.	3	28.135	−31 57.1	−54.6	−3.2	17 8 3.66	−27 35 44.9
51	8							12.0	7 19.89	67.75	1.04	VII.	3	27.830	32 15.6	54.5	3.3	8 29.58	36 3.4
52	8				34.0				9 34.05	67.75	1.00	IV.	3	27.270	33 51.4	54.0	3.3	10 43.70	36 38.7
53	8				22.0	37.0			10 21.97	67.75	2.14	IV.	4	51.690	7 17.2	53.8	0.4	11 31.86	11 1.4
54	7				33.0				33.00	67.75	2.12	VII.	4	47.290	11 52.0	53.8	0.9	11 42.87	15 36.7
55	7	10.0	57.0	15.0	32.0				17 15 32.01	+67.75	+1.96	IV.	3	36.020	−23 42.2	−52.6	−2.3	17 16 41.72	−27 27 27.1

Zone 30. July 7. P. D = −27° 2′ 50″.

No.	Mag.	I.	II.	III.	IV.	V.	VI.	VII.	T. (h. m. s.)	a₁ (s.)	a₂ (s.)	Micrometer.		r.	i (′ ″)	d₁ (″)	d₂ (″)	Mean Right Ascension, 1850.0 (h. m. s.)	Mean Declination, 1850.0 (° ′ ″)
1	9		48.0	5.0					19 40 22.58	+67.58	+1.23	III.	2	20.315	−40 9.7	−18.1	−4.2	19 41 31.39	−27 43 22.0
2	8			46.0	3.0				40 45.79	67.58	1.17	IV.	1	13.170	47 34.5	18.0	5.1	41 54.54	50 47.6
3	9					52.0	9.5		41 17.40	67.58	1.35	V.	3	35.450	24 16.2	17.0	2.3	42 26.33	27 28.4
4	9	53.5		28.0					44 45.42	67.57	1.35	III.	3	33.270	26 34.9	17.1	2.6	45 54.34	29 44.6
5	4	43.0	0.5	18.0	35.0			27.0	46 35.11	67.56	1.32	IV.	3	29.420	30 36.6	16.6	3.1	47 43.99	33 46.3
6	7				53.0	10.0	27.5		54 52.85	67.54	1.51	VI.	4	48.300	10 49.2	14.8	0.7	56 1.90	13 54.7
7	8			35.0	52.5	9.5			19 56 34.97	67.54	1.33	IV.	3	24.480	35 46.4	14.4	3.7	19 57 43.84	38 54.5
8	5	54.0	11.0	28.5	46.0				20 4 45.89	67.52	1.45	IV.	3	34.350	35 27.2	12.5	2.5	20 5 54.86	28 32.2
9	9	35.5	56.0	12.0	30.5				8 30.29	67.51	1.43	IV.	3	30.813	29 8.9	11.7	2.9	9 39.23	32 13.5
10	8			44.5	2.0	19.3			13 19.27	67.49	1.56	IV.	3	44.460	9 37.3	10.6	0.7	14 28.32	12 38.6
11	9	19.0	30.0		12.0				17 11.23	67.48	1.51	IV.	3	36.120	23 36.0	9.8	2.2	18 20.22	26 38.0
12	8	40.0		15.0	32.0				24 32.18	67.46	1.39	IV.	2	19.210	41 18.8	8.2	4.4	25 41.03	44 21.4
13	7			25.0	42.0	59.5			25 42.17	67.46	1.62	IV.	4	45.056	14 13.5	7.9	1.1	26 51.25	17 12.5
14	6	24.5	52.0		9.0	26.3			30 26.41	67.45	1.70	IV.	4	51.735	7 14.1	7.0	0.3	31 35.56	10 11.4
15	9	25.0	42.0	0.0					34 17.09	67.44	1.44	III.	2	18.650	41 54.0	6.1	4.5	35 25.97	44 54.6
16	5			46.0	3.0	20.5			35 3.15	67.43	1.41	IV.	2	16.460	44 11.3	6.0	4.7	36 11.99	47 12.0
17	8		56.0	13.5					36 30.85	67.43	1.45	III.	2	17.125	43 29.6	5.7	4.6	37 39.73	46 29.9
18	8				53.0	10.0	28.0		36 35.56	67.43	1.46	VI.	2	19.870	40 36.7	5.7	4.3	37 44.45	43 36.7
19	7	4.0	21.5	39.0					39 56.33	67.42	1.38	III.	1	8.830	52 6.0	5.0	5.7	41 5.13	55 6.7
20	5	33.5	51.0	8.0					41 25.62	67.42	1.44	III.	2	15.673	45 0.6	4.7	4.8	42 34.48	48 0.1
21	4					43.0	59.5	17.0	41 42.49	67.41	1.59	IV.	3	34.190	25 37.2	4.6	2.5	42 51.49	28 34.3
22	8	35.0	52.0	10.0	27.0				49 27.06	67.39	1.57	IV.	3	27.493	32 37.4	3.1	3.3	50 36.02	35 33.8
23	4	49.5	6.5	24.0	41.3				51 41.34	67.38	1.64	IV.	3	34.855	24 55.3	2.6	2.4	52 50.36	27 50.3
24	8	34.0		8.5					54 25.88	67.38	1.72	III.	4	42.690	16 42.2	2.1	1.4	55 34.98	19 35.7
25	8	27.0	44.5	1.7	19.0				57 19.18	67.37	1.46	IV.	1	10.473	50 23.4	1.5	5.5	20 58 28.01	53 20.4
26	8		29.0	47.0	5.0				20 59 4.40	+67.36	+1.56	IV.	2	20.770	−39 40.9	−1.2	−4.2	21 0 13.32	−27 42 36.3

Zone 31. July 9. P. D = −25° 48′ 0″.

No.	Mag.	I.	II.	III.	IV.	V.	VI.	VII.	T. (h. m. s.)	a₁ (s.)	a₂ (s.)	Micrometer.		r.	i (′ ″)	d₁ (″)	d₂ (″)	Mean Right Ascension, 1850.0 (h. m. s.)	Mean Declination, 1850.0 (° ′ ″)
1	7			13.0	30.5	48.0			15 50 47.72	+67.35	+1.65	IV.	2	12.690	−48 7.4	−48.7	−4.7	15 51 56.72	−26 37 0.8
2	7	8.5	25.0	43.0	0.0				52 59.82	67.35	1.74	IV.	3	31.520	28 24.7	48.3	2.6	54 8.91	17 15.6
3	9	3.0		37.0	54.0			46.0	52 54.48	67.35	1.76	VII.	3	36.120	23 35.5	48.3	2.1	54 3.39	12 25.9
4	7			27.0	44.0				54 44.21	67.35	1.67	IV.	2	17.610	42 59.1	48.0	4.1	55 53.23	31 51.2
5	8					12.0	29.0		55 11.89	67.36	1.66	V.	2	16.873	43 45.0	47.9	4.2	56 20.91	26 32 37.1
6	4	59.3		33.3	50.5				57 50.49	67.36	1.84	IV.	4	52.545	6 23.0	47.3	0.3	15 58 59.69	25 55 10.6
7	9		55.0	12.0					59 29.23	67.36	1.80	III.	4	45.720	13 31.9	47.0	1.0	16 0 38.39	26 2 19.9
8	6.7				48.0	15.0			15 59 57.90	67.36	1.66	IV.	2	18.905	41 37.8	47.0	4.0	1 6.92	30 28.8
9	8				37.0	54.0			16 14 19.70	+67.37	+1.65	VI.	2	21.960	−38 25.8	−44.1	−3.7	16 15 28.72	−26 27 13.6

CORRECTIONS.

Date.		Corr. of Clock. (s.)	Hourly rate. (s.)	m (s.)	n (s.)	c (s.)	Zenith Point.	Mic. Co.
1846. July 9,	12 h.	+ 59.630	− 0.004	+ 0.213	+ 0.298	+ 0.330		r.

INSTRUMENT READINGS.

Date.		CIRCLE. A.	B.	C.	D.	E.	F.	Mean.	Barom. (in.)	THERMOM. Al.	Ex.	U.	L.	I.
Zone 30	1846. July 7, 19 30 & 21 00	66 24 63.5	61.3	73.3	63.0	59.7	49.0	61.63						
	19 40								29.960	74.0	68.8			
	20 59								29.962	72.3	68.3			
Zone 31	July 9, 15 50	65 9 63.3	56.6	69.3	58.4	55.3	45.6	58.08	30.000	81.5	77.6			
	17 24								30.012	79.0	74.5			
	18 0	62.8	56.6		58.6		44.7		30.012	78.0	74.5			
	19 11								30.028	77.5	73.4			

REMARKS.

July 7, 17ʰ 20ᵐ. Stopped by moon-light.
19ʰ 30ᵐ. Helt resumed.
Reading of Bar., &c., at 19ʰ 30ᵐ.
(29) 54. Minutes assumed as 10.
(30) 10. Micrometer reading assumed as 49ʳ.460; not 44ʳ.460.
(31) 8. Transits over T.'s IV and V assumed as 58ˢ.0 and 25ˢ.0 instead of 48ˢ.0 and 15ˢ.0.

ZONE 31. JULY 9. P. D_o = −25° 48′ 0″—Continued.

No.	Mag.	I.	II.	III.	IV.	V.	VI.	VII.	T. (h. m. s.)	a_1	a_2	Mic.		r.	i	d_1	d_2	Mean Right Ascension, 1850.0	Mean Declination, 1850.0
10	7						4.5	22.0	16 15 30.37	+67.37	+1.72	VI.	3	35.395	−24 21.4	−43.8	− 2.2	16 16 39.46	−26 13 7.4
11	8						22.0	39.9	16 47.72	67.37	1.80	VII.	4	52.973	55.1	43.5	0.2	17 56.89	25 54 38.8
12	1	12.5	30.0	47.0	4.0				19 4.09	67.38	1.74	IV.	3	42.540	53.0	43.1	1.4	20 13.21	26 5 37.5
13	8					9.0			19 34.72	67.38	1.69	V.	3	33.380	28.0	42.9	2.4	20 43.79	15 13.3
14	6				2.0	19.0	36.5		21 2.04	67.38	1.71	IV.	3	36.120	36.0	42.6	2.1	22 11.13	12 20.7
15	7	2.0	19.0	36.5					24 53.44	67.38	1.71	III.	4	38.660	55.2	41.8	1.8	26 2.53	9 38.8
16	6	20.0	38.0		12.0				28 12.05	67.38	1.56	IV.	1	8.730	12.3	41.1	5.1	29 20.99	40 58.5
17	7			34.0	50.5				29 50.82	67.38	1.74	IV.	4	46.720	28.9	40.7	0.9	30 59.94	1 10.5
18	5						24.0	41.0	29 48.65	67.38	1.71	VII.	4	39.150	23.0	40.7	1.7	30 57.74	9 5.4
19	7	51.0	8.0	25.5	42.0				32 42.34	67.38	1.69	IV.	3	38.380	14.3	40.1	1.8	33 51.41	9 56.2
20	6					44.5	2.0		33 27.44	67.38	1.59	V.	2	18.317	14.7	40.0	4.0	34 36.41	30 58.7
21	6		50.0	7.0	24.5				35 24.35	67.39	1.62	IV.	3	26.857	17.1	39.5	3.1	36 33.36	21 59.7
22	7	54.0	11.0	28.5					39 45.54	67.39	1.59	III.	2	20.650	48.6	38.6	3.8	40 54.52	28 31.0
23	9				16.5		51.5		40 16.86	67.39	1.62	VI.	3	27.305	49.1	38.4	3.1	41 25.87	21 30.6
24	6					43.0	59.5		41 25.41	67.39	1.54	V.	2	12.790	0.9	38.2	4.7	42 34.34	36 43.8
25	9					48.0	5.0		42 30.70	67.39	1.58	V.	2	19.620	52.9	38.0	3.9	43 39.67	29 34.8
26	7			8.5	25.0				44 25.34	67.39	1.66	IV.	3	38.533	4.6	37.5	1.8	45 34.39	9 43.9
27	8	10.0	27.0	44.0					47 1.36	67.39	1.58	III.	3	22.485	51.5	36.9	3.6	48 10.33	26 32.0
28	7		28.0	45.0	2.0				49 2.16	67.39	1.66	IV.	4	39.830	41.5	36.5	1.7	50 11.21	8 19.7
29	8	6.5	24.0	41.3	58.3				50 58.29	67.39	1.58	IV.	3	24.005	16.1	36.0	3.4	52 7.26	24 55.5
30	7			31.0	48.0				53 48.11	67.39	1.50	IV.	1	7.183	49.3	35.4	5.4	54 57.00	42 30.1
31	7	47.0	5.0	21.5	38.5				55 38.77	67.39	1.58	IV.	3	26.623	31.9	35.0	3.1	56 47.74	22 10.0
32	5			10.0	26.5	44.0			56 26.84	67.39	1.60	IV.	3	30.655	18.9	34.8	2.7	57 35.83	17 56.4
33	9		6.0	23.0	40.0				16 58 40.17	67.39	1.61	IV.	3	34.994	46.6	34.3	2.2	16 59 49.17	13 23.1
34	8		32.5	49.5	6.5				17 0 0.66	67.39	1.66	IV.	4	45.020	15.7	33.9	1.1	17 1 15.71	2 50.7
35	9						59.5		0 25.21	67.39	1.60	VI.	3	33.060	47.8	33.9	2.4	1 34.20	18 24.1
36	7						44.0	1.0	1 9.52	67.39	1.53	VI.	2	18.595	57.0	33.7	4.0	2 18.44	30 34.7
37	7	54.0	12.0	28.0					4 45.67	67.39	1.57	III.	3	27.540	34.4	32.9	3.0	5 54.65	21 10.3
38	5.6	7.0				50.0	16.0		4 58.77	67.39	1.56	III.	3	26.213	57.7	32.8	3.2	6 7.72	22 33.7
39	7					9.0	25.5		5 51.49	67.39	1.58	V.	3	29.230	48.4	32.6	2.8	7 0.46	19 23.8
40	7				11.5	29.0	46.0		7 11.65	67.39	1.54	IV.	3	21.500	53.3	32.3	3.7	8 20.58	27 29.3
41	9	41.0	58.0	15.5					9 32.53	67.39	1.54	III.	3	22.150	12.4	31.8	3.6	10 41.46	26 47.8
42	7			3.0	20.0				10 2.91	67.39	1.55	IV.	3	25.440	46.2	31.6	3.3	11 11.85	23 21.1
43	9			58.5	15.5				10 58.42	67.39	1.56	V.	3	28.095	59.5	31.4	3.0	12 7.37	20 33.9
44	7		57.0	14.0		48.5			10 56.94	67.39	1.58	V.	4	31.810	5.9	31.4	2.6	12 5.91	16 39.9
45	7							47.0	11 55.58	67.39	1.64	VII.	3	44.320	58.4	31.3	1.2	13 4.61	3 30.9
46	7	32.0	49.0	6.0	23.0				16 23.23	67.39	1.59	IV.	3	36.575	7.5	30.1	2.0	17 32.21	11 39.6
47	7	29.0	46.0	3.0					18 20.41	67.39	1.47	III.	1	13.487	16.5	29.7	4.6	19 29.27	35 50.8
48	5	25.0	42.5	59.5	16.5				21 16.59	67.39	1.60	IV.	4	39.140	25.0	28.9	1.7	22 25.58	8 55.6
49	9	25.0	42.0	59.0					24 16.43	67.39	1.45	IV.	1	11.517	18.0	28.2	4.8	25 25.27	37 51.0
50	8		54.0	11.0	28.0				33 28.17	67.39	1.54	IV.	3	34.470	19.7	25.9	2.2	34 37.10	13 47.8
51	9					36.5		10.5	34 19.09	67.39	1.45	VII.	2	18.180	22.5	25.6	4.1	35 27.93	30 52.4
52	8				14.0	31.0	48.5		35 56.88	67.39	1.56	VII.	4	39.900	35.8	25.3	1.6	37 5.83	8 2.7
53	9						39.0		37 4.69	67.39	1.52	VI.	3	31.305	38.1	25.1	2.6	38 13.60	17 5.8
54	7	58.0	14.5	32.0	49.0				39 49.12	67.39	1.51	IV.	3	31.905	56.7	24.4	2.5	40 58.02	16 23.6
55	9				27.0	50.0			42 29.92	67.38	1.50	V.	3	30.930	1.6	23.8	2.6	43 38.80	17 28.0
56	8			39.0	56.0				43 56.10	67.38	1.53	IV.	3	36.340	22.3	23.3	2.1	45 5.01	11 47.7
57	8	7.0	24.0	41.0					47 58.26	67.38	1.56	III.	4	43.595	45.4	22.3	1.2	49 7.20	4 8.9
58	7	37.0	54.0	11.0					17 50 28.29	+67.38	+1.51	IV.	3	35.643	−24 6.0	−21.7	− 2.1	17 51 37.18	−26 12 29.8

CORRECTIONS.

Date.	Corr. of Clock.	Hourly rate.	m	n	c	Zenith Point.	Mic. Co.
1846.	h. s.	s.	s.	s.	s.	° ′ ″	r.

REMARKS.

INSTRUMENT READINGS.

Date.		CIRCLE.						Barom.	Thermom.				
		A.	B.	C.	D.	E.	F.	Mean.		At.	Ex.	U. L.	I.
	1846. h. m.	° ′ ″						″	In.	°	°	°	°
Zone 31	July 9. 19 15	65 9 61.7	56.0	69.3	58.7	54.4	44 0	57.35	..	..	..	..	77.0

ZONE 31. JULY 9. P. $D_0 = -25°\ 48'\ 0''$ — Continued.

No.	Mag.	I.	II.	III.	IV.	V.	VI.	VII.	T. (h m s)	a_1	a_2	Micr.		r	i	d_1	d_2	Mean Right Ascension, 1850.0	Mean Declination, 1850.0
59	6	3.0	20.5	37.5	54.5				17 52 54.63	+67.38	+1.48	IV.	3	29.560	−30 27.7	−21.1	−2.8	17 54 3.49	−26 18 51.6
60	9					58.0			53 40.86	67.38	1.55	VI.	4	45.860	13 22.1	21.0	1.0	54 49.79	1 44.1
61	9		16.0	33.0					55 50.25	67.38	1.48	III.	3	31.290	28 39.2	20.3	2.6	56 50.11	17 2.1
62	8				13.0	31.0			55 56.27	67.38	1.50	V.	3	35.920	23 48.4	20.3	2.1	57 5.15	12 10.8
63	9					4.0			56 29.75	67.38	1.53	VI.	3	41.410	18 3.9	20.2	1.5	57 38.66	6 25.6
64	7	56.0	13.0	30.0					17 58 47.28	67.38	1.52	III.	4	40.697	18 47.3	19.6	1.6	17 59 56.18	7 8.5
65	8	14.0	31.0	48.5	5.5				18 0 5.44	67.37	1.53	IV.	4	44.450	14 51.7	19.3	1.1	18 1 14.38	3 12.1
66	8		1.0	18.0	35.0				1 35.19	67.37	1.43	IV.	3	23.330	36 58.6	18.9	3.5	2 43.99	25 21.0
67	9	8.0	25.0	42.0					3 59.29	67.37	1.47	III.	3	34.115	25 41.8	18.3	2.3	5 8.13	14 2.4
68	8			24.7	41.5				4 41.71	67.37	1.44	IV.	3	27.460	32 39.5	18.1	3.0	5 50.52	21 0.6
69	8					27.5	44.5		5 10.23	67.37	1.43	VI.	3	26.490	33 40.2	18.0	3.1	6 19.03	26 22 1.3
70	8			57.0	14.5				8 14.29	67.37	1.56	IV.	4	53.300	5 36.1	17.2	0.2	9 23.22	25 53 53.5
71	7					13.5	30.5		8 56.23	67.37	1.42	V.	3	25.905	34 16.8	17.1	3.2	10 5.02	26 22 37.1
72	6		10.0	27.0	44.3				10 44.27	67.37	1.47	IV.	4	37.133	20 25.4	16.6	2.0	11 53.11	8 44.0
73	7			35.0	51.5	9.0			11 51.83	67.36	1.39	V.	2	19.970	40 30.9	16.3	3.9	13 0.58	28 51.1
74	7			19.0	5.0				13 5.36	67.36	1.46	IV.	3	33.820	26 0.3	16.0	2.3	14 14.18	14 18.6
75	7					58.0	15.0		13 40.68	67.36	1.37	V.	2	17.785	42 47.9	15.9	4.1	14 49.41	31 7.9
76	8						45.0	2.0	14 10.51	67.36	1.36	VII.	2	15.080	45 36.8	15.7	4.4	15 19.23	33 56.9
77	4	21.0	39.0	56.5					17 13.30	67.36	1.31	III.	1	6.370	54 40.3	15.0	5.4	18 21.97	43 0.7
78	4		53.3	10.5	27.7				18 27.73	67.36	1.32	IV.	1	9.090	51 49.9	14.7	5.1	19 36.41	40 9.7
79	7	53.3	10.5	28.0					21 45.03	67.36	1.34	III.	2	13.610	47 9.9	13.9	4.6	22 53.73	35 28.4
80	9				37.0				22 37.03	67.35	1.46	IV.	3	36.880	20 42.7	13.6	1.8	23 45.84	8 58.1
81	8	20.0	46.0	3.5	20.5				26 20.52	67.35	1.38	IV.	3	24.270	35 59.6	12.7	3.4	27 29.25	24 15.7
82	9	23.5		58.0	15.0				33 15.07	67.34	1.38	IV.	3	27.760	32 20.5	11.0	3.0	34 23.79	26 20 34.5
83	8			18.5	36.0	53.0			34 18.71	67.34	1.40	IV.	4	50.945	8 3.7	10.7	0.4	35 27.54	25 56 14.8
84	9			23.0			57.5		38 40.21	67.34	1.31	VI.	2	15.120	45 34.7	9.7	4.4	39 48.86	26 33 48.9
85	8			30.0				4.5	42 30.08	67.33	1.29	VI.	2	14.033	46 42.8	8.7	4.6	43 38.70	34 56.1
86	2.3	57.0		32.0	49.0	6.0	23.0	40.2	44 48.80	67.33	1.31	IV.	2	20.074	40 24.6	8.1	3.0	45 57.44	28 36.6
87	9		21.0	39.0					48 38.11	67.32	1.34	IV.	3	25.045	35 10.8	7.2	3.3	49 46.77	23 21.3
88	8		16.0	32.5					49 50.02	67.32	1.33	III.	3	25.400	34 48.7	6.9	3.3	50 58.67	22 58.9
89	8	25.0	42.0	59.0	16.0				51 16.23	67.32	1.38	IV.	3	35.300	24 27.6	6.5	2.7	52 24.93	26 12 36.3
90	9					17.0			51 59.88	67.32	1.47	V.	4	53.210	5 41.4	6.4	0.1	53 8.67	25 53 47.9
91	7	54.5		20.0	46.0				54 46.07	67.31	1.32	IV.	3	26.887	33 15.3	5.7	3.1	55 54.70	26 21 24.1
92	6		57.0	14.0	31.0				18 57 31.15	67.31	1.44	IV.	4	51.343	7 39.0	5.0	0.4	18 58 39.90	25 55 44.4
93	9			59.0					19 0 33.31	67.31	1.37	II.	4	38.790	20 47.1	4.3	1.8	19 1 41.99	26 8 53.2
94	9	59.0	16.0	33.0	50.0				2 50.22	67.30	1.37	IV.	3	38.340	21 16.8	3.8	1.8	3 58.89	26 9 22.4
95	7	58.0	14.7		49.0				5 49.10	67.30	1.43	IV.	4	51.740	7 13.8	3.0	0.3	6 57.83	25 55 17.1
96	9	27.0		1.5					8 18.57	67.29	1.30	III.	3	27.770	32 19.8	2.4	3.0	9 27.16	26 20 25.2
97	9				38.0		12.0		8 37.87	67.29	1.31	VI.	3	29.673	30 20.3	2.3	2.8	9 46.47	18 25.4
98	8	29.5	46.5	4.0	31.0				19 11 21.03	+67.29	+1.27	IV.	2	22.082	−38 18.7	−1.7	−3.6	19 12 29.59	−26 26 24.0

ZONE 32. JULY 10. C. $D_0 = -29°\ 33'\ 50''$.

No.	Mag.	I.	II.	III.	IV.	V.	VI.	VII.	T. (h m s)	a_1	a_2	Micr.		r	i	d_1	d_2	Mean Right Ascension, 1850.0	Mean Declination, 1850.0
1	9					36.7		8.0	16 20 36.65	+67.60	+1.16	IV.	4	53.092	− 5 49.0	−14.8	−0.3	16 21 45.41	−29 39 54.1
2	9					51.5			24 51.55	67.61	1.19	IV.	3	36.751	22 56.3	13.9	2.7	26 0.35	29 57 2.9
3	7			24.0	41.5	59.5			28 41.67	67.61	1.23	IV.	3	24.661	35 35.0	13.1	4.4	29 50.51	30 9 42.5
4	7						14.7	32.5	28 39.34	67.61	1.20	VI.	4	55.642	3 9.0	13.1	0.0	29 48.15	29 37 12.1
5	7.8			7.5	53.1		14.7	32.5	16 31 25.27	+67.62	+1.25	IV.	3	20.486	−39 56.9	−12.5	−5.0	16 32 34.14	−30 14 4.4

CORRECTIONS.

Date	Corr. of Clock	Hourly rate	m	n	c	Zenith Point	Mic. Co.
	h.	s.	s.	s.	s.	s.	° ′ ″	r.
1846. July 10,	17	+ 59.557	0.000	+ 0.213	+ 0.298	+ 0.330	0 0 2.87	30.002

REMARKS.

(31) 60. Transit over T. V assumed as recorded over T. VI.
(31) 72. Micrometer reading assumed as 39r.133; not 37r.133.
July 10, 16h 31m. Bright moon-light.

INSTRUMENT READINGS.

	Date	CIRCLE							Barom.	THERMOM.				
		A.	B.	C.	D.	E.	F.	Mean.		A¹.	Ex.	U.	L.	I.
	1846.	h. m.	° ′ ″	′	′	′	′	′	″	in.	°	°	°	°	°
Zone 32	July 10, 16 18	68 54 62.3	58.1	71.1	59.6	56.4	48.2	59.27	30.076	85.5	82.9	85.1	83.2	80.5
	16 31											83.3			
	16 50	62.1	57.9	71.9	59.5	56.5	48.1	59.33	30.084	85.0	82.3	85.0		83.0

Zone 32. July 10. C. $D_0 = -29° 33' 50''$—Continued.

No.	Mag.	I.	II.	III.	IV.	V.	VI.	VII.	T.	a_1	a_2
									h. m. s.	s.	s.
6	9		44.9	3.0	20.0	38.6			16 33 20.52	+67.62	+1.24
7	9				8.0	26.8			37 8.52	67.62	1.23
8	9						22.5	41.0	37 47.30	67.63	1.26
9	8		5.5	23.2	41.0	58.0			40 40.80	67.63	1.26
10	8		50.0	8.0	25.5				42 26.65	67.63	1.29
11	9					19.5			43 0.67	67.63	1.29
12	6.7					11.0	29.5	46.5	43 53.00	67.63	1.30
13	8			37.6	55.0	13.8			45 55.46	67.63	1.30
14	9			7.8	25.5				46 25.51	67.63	1.30
15	9			37.5		12.0	30.0		47 54.67	67.63	1.30
16	9			23.7					49 41.48	67.63	1.29
17	9					21.0			16 50 3.14	+67.63	+1.34

No.	Mag.	MICROMETER		r	i	d_1	d_2	Mean Right Ascension, 1850.0	Mean Declination, 1850.0
				r.	′ ″	″	″	h. m. s.	° ′ ″
6	9	IV.	3	35.544	-24 12.2	-12.1	-2.8	16 34 29.38	-29 58 17.1
7	9	IV.	4	53.171	5 44.1	11.3	0.4	38 17.37	29 39 45.8
8	9	VI.	2	28.606	31 29.1	11.1	3.8	38 56.19	30 5 34.0
9	8	IV.	3	44.352	14 59.3	10.5	2.1	41 49.69	29 49 1.9
10	8	IV.	3	23.984	36 17.4	10.1	4.5	43 35.57	30 10 22.0
11	9	V.	3	25.219	35 0.0	10.0	4.3	44 9.59	9 4.3
12	6.7	V.	2	14.645	46 4.8	9.8	5.8	45 1.93	20 10.4
13	8	IV.	2	14.689	46 2.2	9.4	5.8	47 4.39	30 20 7.4
14	9	IV.	3	35.249	24 30.8	9.3	2.9	47 34.44	29 58 33.0
15	9	IV.	3	40.659	18 51.1	9.0	2.1	49 3.60	29 52 52.2
16	9	IV.	3	33.429	26 25.0	8.5	3.1	50 50.40	30 0 26.6
17	9	V.	2	17.858	-42 43.3	-8.5	-5.4	16 51 12.11	-30 16 47.2

Zone 33. July 10. C. $D_0 = -34° 34' 10''$.

No.	Mag.	I.	II.	III.	IV.	V.	VI.	VII.	T.	a_1	a_2
									h. m. s.	s.	s.
1	8.9		33.0	51.4	10.0	29.0	47.5		17 3 10.19	+68.07	+1.66
2	9			20.7		58.5			4 39.50	68.07	1.63
3	8				11.0	30.0			6 11.04	68.07	1.70
4	8					36.0			6 17.06	68.07	1.70
5	8							33.1	6 36.68	68.07	1.67
6	6						12.0	31.0	7 34.64	68.08	1.64
7	9		0.0	19.0	37.6	56.2			10 37.61	68.08	1.67
8	9			5.2	24.0				11 24.04	68.08	1.68
9	7		23.8	42.8	1.5		39.0		14 1.50	68.08	1.60
10	9			21.0		58.5			23 39.75	68.09	1.60
11	9		42.0	1.5	20.0		57.0		26 19.85	68.09	1.65
12	9			38.0		14.0	32.0		29 55.45	68.09	1.62
13	8.9		28.5	47.2			43.2		30 5.91	68.09	1.61
14	9						11.7		30 34.18	68.09	1.60
15	7					33.2	52.0		32 14.33	68.09	1.63
16	8					8.5	27.0		33 49.36	68.09	1.64
17	6.7					36.0	56.0		35 17.89	68.09	1.57
18	7.8				30.2	49.0	8.0		36 30.25	68.09	1.61
19	8				36.2				37 36.25	68.09	1.59
20	8				57.0		34.5		38 56.98	68.09	1.59
21	8				10.0	29.0			39 51.30	68.09	1.58
22	7			26.5		4.0			41 45.25	68.09	1.58
23	8.9			54.3		31.5			42 12.90	68.09	1.57
24	6.7					32.0	51.0		42 13.37	68.09	1.55
25	8						50.0		43 12.56	68.09	1.55
26	9					8.0			44 49.18	68.09	1.57
27	8					15.5	34.5		44 56.82	68.09	1.57
28	9				59.5		37.0		49 59.42	68.09	1.60
29	9			58.7			36.0		52 17.36	68.09	1.53
30	9						3.0	21.0	52 2.60	68.09	1.53
31	9		36.5	55.0	14.2	33.0			56 14.03	68.09	1.54
32	9					2.0			56 43.17	68.09	1.55
33	9						53.0		17 57 15.56	+68.09	+1.53

No.	Mag.	MICROMETER		r	i	d_1	d_2	Mean Right Ascension, 1850.0	Mean Declination, 1850.0
				r.	′ ″	″	″	h. m. s.	° ′ ″
1	8.9	IV.	3	37.710	-21 56.2	-28.2	-3.9	17 4 19.92	-34 56 38.3
2	9	IV.	4	48.100	11 2.4	27.9	1.6	5 49.20	34 45 41.9
3	8	IV.	2	12.970	47 49.8	27.5	9.6	7 20.81	35 22 36.0
4	8	V.	2	13.660	47 5.9	27.5	9.4	7 26.83	21 52.8
5	8	VII.	3	31.421	28 30.3	27.5	5.3	7 46.42	35 3 13.1
6	6	VI.	4	44.995	14 16.4	27.3	2.3	8 44.36	34 48 56.0
7	9	IV.	3	23.579	36 42.9	26.6	7.1	11 47.36	35 11 26.6
8	9	IV.	3	21.589	38 47.7	26.4	7.6	12 33.80	35 13 31.7
9	7	IV.	4	54.891	3 56.0	25.9	0.1	15 11.18	34 38 32.0
10	9	IV.	4	45.889	13 21.1	23.8	2.1	24 49.44	34 47 57.0
11	9	IV.	3	21.074	39 19.9	23.2	7.7	27 29.59	35 14 0.8
12	9	IV.	3	25.242	34 55.6	22.3	6.8	31 5.16	9 37.7
13	8.9	IV.	4	31.060	28 52.0	22.3	5.4	31 15.61	35 3 29.7
14	9	VI.	4	37.801	21 48.0	22.2	3.9	31 43.87	34 56 24.1
15	7	V.	3	21.822	38 32.0	21.8	7.5	33 24.05	35 13 12.2
16	8	V.	3	8.170	52 48.4	21.5	10.7	34 59.11	35 27 30.6
17	6.7	V.	4	44.759	14 31.7	21.1	2.4	36 27.55	31 49 5.2
18	7.8	IV.	3	25.242	34 58.6	20.8	6.8	37 39.95	35 9 36.2
19	8	IV.	3	34.481	25 19.0	20.6	4.6	38 45.93	34 59 54.2
20	8	IV.	3	28.786	31 16.1	20.3	5.0	40 6.66	35 5 52.3
21	8	V.	3	33.249	26 36.2	20.1	4.9	41 0.97	35 1 11.2
22	7	IV.	3	35.782	23 57.1	19.6	4.4	42 54.92	34 58 31.1
23	8.9	IV.	3	35.782	23 57.1	19.5	4.4	43 22.56	58 31.0
24	6.7	V.	3	42.789	16 37.2	19.5	2.8	43 23.01	51 9.5
25	8	VI.	3	43.524	15 50.9	19.3	2.6	44 22.20	34 50 22.8
26	9	·	·	33.	26 23.	18.8	5.	45 58.84	35 0 (57.)
27	8	V.	3	33.410	26 26.1	18.9	4.9	46 6.48	0 59.9
28	9	IV.	2	16.319	44 20.1	17.7	8.8	51 9.11	35 18 56.6
29	9	IV.	4	43.411	15 56.9	17.1	2.7	53 26.98	34 50 26.7
30	9	V.	4	44.702	14 35.3	17.0	2.4	54 12.22	34 49 4.7
31	9	IV.	3	34.441	25 21.5	16.2	4.7	57 23.66	35 59 52.4
32	9	IV.	3	32.431	27 27.6	16.1	5.1	57 52.81	35 1 58.8
33	9	VI.	4	43.428	-15 54.9	-15.9	-2.7	17 58 25.18	-34 50 23.5

CORRECTIONS.

Date.	Corr. of Clock.	Hourly rate.	m	n	c	Zenith Point.	Mic. Co.
1846.	h.	s.	s.	s.	s.	° ″	r.

REMARKS.

(33) 29. Transit over T. V assumed as recorded over T. VI.

(33) 30. Transits over T.'s IV and V assumed as recorded over T.'s V and VI, and minutes as 53 instead of 54.

INSTRUMENT READINGS.

Date.	CIRCLE.							Barom.	THERMOM.				
	A.	B.	C.	D.	E.	F.	Mean.		At.	Ex.	U.	L.	I.
	° ′ ″						″	in.					
Zone 33 — 1846. July 10, 17 3	73 54 60.6	58.0	71.	59.0	56.2	45.1	58.32	30.084	85.0	82.3	85.0	83.0	
17 30										80.6			
18.15								30.074	83.0	80.0			
18.30	59.8	55.0	70.2	59.2	55.2	44.9	57.88				81.8	81.5	
18.50								30.080	82.2	80.3			

Zone 33. July 10. C. D = −34° 34' 10"—Continued.

No.	Mag.	I.	II.	III.	IV.	V.	VI.	VII.	T.	a_1	a_2	MICR.		r.	i	d_1	d_2	Mean Right Ascension, 1850.0	Mean Declination, 1850.0
									h. m. s.	s.	s.			r.	' "	"	"	h. m. s.	° ' "
34	7				41.5	59.0			17 58 40.87	+68.09	+1.52	IV.	4	47.659	−11 30.0	−15.6	−1.7	17 59 50.48	−34 45 57.3
35	7		52.5	10.5	29.8	48.0	7.5		18 0 29.67	68.09	1.55	IV.	3	31.440	28 29.8	15.1	5.4	18 1 39.31	35 3 0.3
36	7			38.4	57.0	15.7			2 57.01	68.09	1.50	IV.	4	55.430	3 22.3	14.6	0.0	4 6.60	34 37 46.9
37	8				41.0	59.5	19.5		3 41.19	68.09	1.55	IV.	3	27.619	32 29.5	14.4	6.2	4 50.83	35 7 0.1
38	8				16.0	34.4	53.5		4 15.84	68.09	1.54	IV.	4	29.950	30 3.1	14.2	5.7	5 25.47	4 33.0
39	8					20.0			5 1.12	68.09	1.56	V.	3	18.149	42 23.5	14.1	8.4	6 10.77	35 16 55.8
40	7.8		43.5	2.5	27.1	40.0			7 21.16	68.08	1.50	IV.	4	49.400	9 40.9	13.5	1.3	8 30.74	34 44 5.7
41	8.9		31.5	51.0	9.0		46.0		8 9.10	68.08	1.50	IV.	4	46.031	13 12.2	13.3	2.1	9 18.68	47 36.7
42	8.9					18.0	37.0		8 59.39	68.08	1.50	V.	3	43.954	15 24.0	13.1	2.5	10 8.37	34 49 49.6
43	9			21.0	30.5		17.3		10 39.69	68.07	1.53	IV.	3	28.037	32 3.2	12.7	6.1	11 49.29	35 6 32.0
44	8.9		17.7	36.0	54.8	13.8	32.5		12 54.37	68.07	1.52			30.	29 59.	12.1	6.	14 3.96	4(27.)
45	9				36.5				15 36.55	68.07	1.55	IV.	2	13.256	47 32.1	11.5	9.5	16 46.17	35 22 3.1
46	9			55.3		33.0	51.7		20 14.19	68.06	1.48	IV.	4	43.066	16 18.5	10.4	2.7	21 23.73	34 50 41.6
47	7		40.4	59.1	18.0	36.5	55.7		23 17.96	68.06	1.48	IV.	3	38.556	21 3.2	9.6	3.8	24 27.50	34 55 26.6
48	8			23.5	42.0	1.0	19.5		24 42.09	68.06	1.49	IV.	3	33.238	26 37.0	9.3	4.9	25 51.64	35 1 1.2
49	8		41.5	0.0	18.8	38.0	56.2		26 18.91	68.06	1.49	IV.	3	36.294	23 25.2	8.9	4.2	27 28.46	34 57 48.3
50	8							32.0	26 35.81	68.06	1.45	VII.	2	53.370	5 30.1	8.7	0.5	27 45.32	34 39 40.3
51	8			49.0	8.0	27.0	46.0		29 8.07	68.06	1.50	IV.	2	17.801	42 47.0	8.2	8.5	30 17.63	35 17 13.7
52	9			50.8	9.0	28.0	47.0		29 9.28	68.06	1.50	IV.	2	20.869	39 34.7	8.2	7.8	30 18.84	14 0.7
53	8		42.7	1.5	20.8	39.2	58.0		31 20.44	68.05	1.50	IV.	2	17.574	43 1.4	7.7	8.5	32 29.99	35 17 27.6
54	7		31.5	50.5	9.5		46.2		38 9.15	68.05	1.44	IV.	3	39.576	19 59.1	6.1	3.5	39 18.64	34 54 18.7
55	9					0.0	18.0		38 40.93	68.05	1.42	V.	4	51.648	7 19.3	5.9	0.8	39 50.40	34 41 36.0
56	9				21.0	40.2			40 21.10	68.05	1.47	IV.	3	27.120	33 0.7	5.5	6.3	41 30.71	35 7 22.5
57	9				40.0	58.0			41 39.58	68.05	1.48	IV.	3	21.764	38 36.6	5.2	7.5	42 49.11	12 59.3
58	9			33.0	52.0	11.0			43 51.99	68.04	1.48	IV.	2	16.831	43 47.8	4.7	8.7	45 11.51	18 11.2
59	9		43.2	2.0	20.7	40.0	58.4		47 20.87	68.04	1.44	IV.	3	32.515	27 22.3	3.0	5.1	48 30.35	35 1 41.3
60	9			20.7	39.2	58.0	17.0		48 39.39	68.03	1.40	IV.	4	48.096	15 40.0	3.5	1.6	49 48.82	34 40 4.4
61	9			3.7			0.0		50 22.52	68.03	1.39	IV.	4	50.823	8 11.4	3.1	1.0	51 31.94	42 25.5
62	8			27.2			4.7		18 51 27.23	+68.03	+1.41	IV.	3	43.289	−16 6.1	−2.9	−2.7	18 52 36.67	−34 50 21.7

Zone 34. July 11. P. D = −39° 35' 40".

No.	Mag.	I.	II.	III.	IV.	V.	VI.	VII.	T.	a_1	a_2	MICR.		r.	i	d_1	d_2	Mean Right Ascension, 1850.0	Mean Declination, 1850.0
1	7			14.0	34.0				16 8 34.11	+68.49	+2.06	IV.	2	15.720	−44 57.6	−29.2	−17.1	16 9 44.66	−40 21 13.0
2	8	12.0	32.0	52.0	12.0				11 12.07	68.50	1.39	IV.	4	44.590	14 42.8	27.7	4.6	12 21.96	39 50 55.1
3	8	14.0	34.0	54.0	14.5				20 14.19	68.53	1.48	IV.	4	41.980	17 26.6	25.9	5.7	21 24.20	39 53 38.2
4	8				47.5		28.0		22 7.69	68.53	2.23	V.	1	10.493	50 22.0	25.5	19.5	23 18.45	40 26 47.0
5	7	1.0	21.0	41.0					25 1.16	68.54	1.65	III.	3	36.650	23 2.6	25.0	8.0	26 11.33	39 50 15.6
6	6			41.0	1.0	21.0			31 21.15	68.56	1.64	IV.	3	36.168	23 33.0	23.7	8.2	32 31.35	39 50 44.9
7	6							51.0	33 10.54	68.57	2.37	VI.	1	4.365	56 46.8	23.3	22.3	34 21.48	40 33 12.4
8	8	29.5		9.5	29.0				36 29.31	68.57	1.26	IV.	4	53.680	5 12.1	22.6	0.9	37 39.14	39 41 15.6
9	8		31.0		11.0				38 11.14	68.58	1.76	IV.	3	31.875	28 2.3	22.3	10.0	39 21.48	40 4 14.6
10	8		21.0	41.0					40 1.16	68.58	1.75	IV.	3	32.983	26 52.8	21.9	9.5	41 11.49	3 4.2
11	8				32.0				40 32.04	68.58	2.24	IV.	1	12.250	48 32.1	21.9	18.7	41 42.86	24 52.7
12	7						14.0		40 53.70	68.58	2.28	V.	1	9.520	51 22.9	21.8	19.9	42 4.56	27 44.6
13	8				39.0				42 39.06	68.59	1.94	IV.	3	24.570	35 40.7	21.4	13.2	43 49.59	11 55.3
14	7				22.0				43 22.05	68.59	2.05	IV.	3	20.260	40 11.1	21.3	15.1	44 32.69	16 27.5
15	7			0.0	20.5				44 40.58	68.59	2.25	IV.	2	12.350	48 28.8	21.0	18.7	45 51.42	24 48.5
16	8			0.0	21.0				16 45 20.60	+68.60	+2.05	IV.	3	20.615	−39 48.7	−20.9	−14.9	16 46 31.25	−40 16 4.5

CORRECTIONS.

Date	Corr. of Clock	Hourly rate	m	n	c	Zenith Point	Mic. Co.
	h.	s.	s.	s.	s.	s.	° ' "	r.
1846 July 11	17	+ 59.647	− 0.005	+ 0.213	+ 0.298	+ 0.330		

REMARKS.

(33) 60. Micrometer reading assumed as 53r.096 instead of 48r.096.

July 11. Many very small stars, which could not be observed.

INSTRUMENT READINGS.

Date	CIRCLE. A.	B.	C.	D.	E.	F.	Mean.	Barom.	THERMOM. At.	Ex.	U.	L.	I.
	° ' "						"	in.	°	°	°	°	°
Zone 34 1846, July 11, 16 0	78 54 65.7	59.8	73.7	59.8	57.6	49.8	61.07						
16 8								30.030	87.5	85.6	84.0	..	84.5
16 51										85.0			
18 0	65.3	60.3	74.2	60.7	58.3	48.8	61.27	30.016	86.0	83.5			

Zone 34. July 11. P. D. = −39° 35′ 40″—Continued.

No.	Mag.	I.	II.	III.	IV.	V.	VI.	VII.	T. (h. m. s.)	a₁	a₂	Micr.	n	r.	i	d₁	d₂	Mean R. A. 1850.0 (h. m. s.)	Mean Decl. 1850.0 (° ′ ″)
17	8	. .	. .	33.0	. .	. .	33.5		16 46 33.09	+68.60	+1.84	IV.	3	29.400	−30 37.8	−20.6	−11.1	16 47 43.53	−40 6 49.5
18	7	49.0 9.5 29.0 49.0							51 49.19	68.61	1.53	IV.	4	43.590	15 45.0	19.5	5.0	52 39.33	39 51 50.1
19	8	7.5 . . 29.0							16 58 8.30	68.62	1.74	IV.	4	34.610	25 10.8	18.2	8.9	16 59 18.66	40 1 17.9
20	9	5.0							17 16 45.28	68.65	2.04	II.	3	24.070	36 11.5	14.3	13.4	17 17 55.97	12 19.2
21	7	42.0 . . 22.0							22 42.41	68.66	2.36	III.	1	11.810	48 59.4	13.1	18.9	23 53.43	40 25 11.4
22	9	58.0							23 17.89	68.66	1.73	VI.	3	38.000	21 37.6	12.9	7.4	24 28.28	39 57 37.9
23	8	20.0							25 39.73	68.66	2.08	VI.	3	23.210	37 5.7	12.4	13.8	26 50.47	40 13 11.9
24	8	31.0 . . 11.5							28 11.12	68.66	2.05	V.	3	25.100	35 7.4	11.9	13.0	29 22.13	11 12.3
25	8	8.0 28.0							29 28.08	68.66	1.81	IV.	3	35.513	24 14.2	11.6	8.5	30 38.55	0 14.3
26	8	15.0 . . 55.0							30 34.96	68.66	2.21	V.	2	14.140	46 36.6	11.4	17.8	31 45.83	40 22 45.8
27	9	24.0							32 3.95	69.66	1.47	V.	4	51.250	7 44.4	11.1	1.9	33 14.08	39 43 37.4
28	7	9.0 29.5 49.5							35 9.71	68.67	2.16	IV.	2	17.220	43 23.6	10.4	16.5	36 20.54	40 19 30.5
29	4	36.0 56.0							35 55.74	68.67	1.91	VI.	3	32.133	27 45.9	10.2	9.9	37 6.32	40 3 46.0
30	7	24.5 . . 4.0							37 4.13	68.67	1.61	VI.	4	44.840	14 26.0	10.0	4.5	38 14.41	39 50 20.5
31	7	52.0 12.0							38 31.86	68.67	1.86	V.	3	33.653	26 10.8	9.7	0.2	39 42.39	40 2 9.7
32	8	1.0 21.0 41.0							42 1.08	68.67	1.62	III.	4	44.985	14 18.0	8.9	4.5	43 11.37	39 50 11.4
33	8	26.6 46.0							45 6.29	68.67	2.23	III.	3	15.495	45 12.7	8.2	17.2	46 17.19	40 21 18.1
34	7	14.5 35.0							45 14.67	68.67	2.22	IV.	2	19.930	40 33.6	8.2	15.2	46 25.56	16 37.0
35	8	10.0 . . 10.0 30.0							49 30.25	68.67	2.27	IV.	2	17.305	43 12.7	7.3	16.4	50 41.10	19 16.4
36	9	35.0							55 15.23	68.67	1.98	II.	3	30.950	28 59.8	6.0	10.4	56 25.88	40 4 56.2
37	8	23.0 43.0 3.0							17 56 3.09	68.67	1.80	IV.	4	39.325	20 13.5	5.8	6.8	17 57 13.56	39 56 6.1
38	8	23.0 43.0 3.0							18 0 3.18	68.67	2.21	IV.	3	22.403	37 56.7	4.9	14.2	18 1 14.06	40 13 55.8
39	7	11.0 31.0							1 51.09	68.67	1.53	III.	4	50.770	8 14.8	4.5	2.1	3 1.29	39 44 1.4
40	7	13.0 34.0							2 33.58	68.67	1.87	IV.	3	36.625	23 4.3	4.4	8.0	3 44.12	39 58 56.7
41	8	46.5 6.5 27.0							18 8 47.03	+68.66	+2.35	III.	2	16.990	−43 38.1	−3.0	−16.5	18 9 58.04	−40 19 37.6

Zone 35. July 14. C. D. = −35° 12′ 0″.

No.	Mag.	I.	II.	III.	IV.	V.	VI.	VII.	T. (h. m. s.)	a₁	a₂	Micr.	n	r.	i	d₁	d₂	Mean R. A. 1850.0 (h. m. s.)	Mean Decl. 1850.0 (° ′ ″)
1	7.8	. .	. .	5.0 23.5 42.5 1.7					17 29 23.73	+67.47	+1.35	IV.	3	38.471	−21 8.5	−13.9	−3.9	17 30 32.55	−35 33 26.3
2	7	46.0 4.6 23.5 42.7							31 4.73	67.47	1.(x)	IV.	3	29.269	30 46.0	13.5	6.2	32 13.29	43 5.7
3	8	20.0 38.7 57.5							32 38.73	67.47	1.56	IV.	4	46.179	13 3.0	13.1	2.1	33 47.76	25 18.2
4	7	31.0 49.8 9.0 27.5							33 49.89	67.47	1.50	IV.	4	44.127	15 11.9	12.9	2.5	34 58.86	27 27.3
5	8	37.0 56.0 14.8							36 14.89	67.47	1.23	IV.	3	33.862	25 57.6	12.3	5.1	37 23.59	35 15.0
6	7	31.0 50.0							36 31.01	67.47	0.94	IV.	3	22.681	37 39.1	12.2	7.9	37 39.42	49 59.2
7	7	17.5 36.0							38 17.30	67.47	1.72	IV.	4	51.910	7 3.1	11.9	0.7	39 26.49	19 15.7
8	7	35.5 54.3							39 54.32	67.47	1.74	IV.	4	53.337	5 33.8	11.5	0.4	41 3.53	17 45.7
9	8	39.5							40 39.47	67.47	1.73	IV.	4	52.146	6 48.5	11.3	0.6	41 48.67	19 0.4
10	6.7	25.5 44.5 3.0 22.2							41 44.36	67.47	1.33	IV.	3	37.228	22 26.5	11.1	4.2	42 53.16	34 41.8
11	9	58.0 . . 35.7							17 42 57.90	+67.47	+0.94	IV.	4	22.079	−38 15.4	−10.8	−8.0	17 44 6.31	−35 50 34.2

CORRECTIONS.

Date	Corr. of Clock	Hourly rate	m	n	c	Zenith Point	Mic. Co.
1846. July 14. h. 17	s. +58.886	s. −0.011	s. +0.213	s. +0.298	s. +0.330	° ′ ″ 0 0 3.02	r. 30.005

INSTRUMENT READINGS.

Date		CIRCLE.						Barom.	THERMOM.				
		A.	B.	C.	D.	E.	F.	Mean.		At.	Ex.	U.	L.	I.
Zone 35	1846. July 14. 17 29	74 32 28.1	29.6	43.0	33.2	22.6	13.0	29.25	in. 30.044	75.0	69.0	73.0	74.8	80.3
	17 42	. .	. .	. .	. .	. .	. .	. .	. .	68.8				

REMARKS.

18ʰ 8ᵐ, interrupted by clouds.
(35) 6. Perhaps identical with No. 14, Transit Z., same night.

ZONE 36.　JULY 14.　C.　$D_s = -33°\ 18'\ 40''$.

SECONDS OF TRANSIT

No.	Mag.	I.	II.	III.	IV.	V.	VI.	VII.
1	8.9	.	.	46.1	4.4	22.7	41.4	.
2	7.8	.	.	18.7	37.0	56.0	.	.
3	6.7	.	.	33.0	51.0	.	28.2	.
4	8	.	.	.	.	19.7	38.1	.
5	9	.	.	.	33.0	.	.	.
6	9	.	.	.	58.0	.	.	.
7	8.9	.	.	.	58.5	16.0	35.5	.
8	7	.	53.7	13.0	31.0	.	17.7	.
9	9	.	58.0	.	34.0	.	23.0	.
10	7	.	17.2	35.5	54.0	12.6	.	.
11	7.8	.	.	.	32.0	50.5	9.0	.
12	6.7	.	.	32.0	50.1	9.0	27.6	.
13	7	.	53.0	11.5	30.0	48.0	7.0	.
14	9	.	.	.	30.0	48.0	.	.
15	9	.	.	.	22.0	41.0	.	.
16	9	.	.	.	42.0	.	.	37.0
17	9	.	.	.	.	.	.	.
18	9	.	.	.	51.9	10.0	.	.
19	9	.	.	.	14.0	32.0	49.7	.
20	7.9	.	53.0	11.5	29.5	48.0	.	.
21	9	.	.	.	.	.	.	5.8
22	7.8	.	.	.	14.6	33.0	51.4	.
23	9	.	.	.	.	.	.	37.7
24	8.9	.	.	.	18.0	36.0	54.6	.
25	8.9	.	.	12.8	32.0	50.5	9.0	.
26	8.9	.	51.0	10.0	28.0	47.0	5.7	.
27	8	.	35.0	54.0	12.5	31.1	49.6	.
28	9	.	.	.	22.2	40.8	59.0	.
29	9	.	.	.	9.0	.	.	45.5
30	9	.	.	.	12.0	30.0	48.7	.
31	8	.	23.0	41.0	0.0	18.5	.	.
32	9	.	44.0	.	21.0	.	58.0	.
33	7.8	.	.	58.0	17.0	.	.	.
34	9	.	12.5	31.2	.	.	.	.
35	7.8	.	.	.	2.0	.	39.0	.
36	7.8	.	.	.	39.3	58.1	16.7	.
37	9	.	.	27.0	45.2	14.0	.	.
38	8.9	.	.	5.0	23.5	42.5	.	.
39	9	.	.	26.1	.	3.1	.	.
40	8.9	.	.	27.1	.	.	.	.
41	8	.	.	31.7	51.0	.	.	.
42	9	.	.	.	53.0	11.0	29.0	.
43	9	.	.	.	.	.	14.0	.
44	7	.	49.7	8.6	27.0	.	.	.
45	7	.	27.5	.	4.5	.	.	.
46	7.8	.	.	11.5	.	.	.	.
47	8	.	.	47.2	6.4	.	43.1	.
48	9	.	.	.	48.7	7.2	.	.
49	9	.	.	50.0	.	27.5	46.1	.

No.	T. (h. m. s.)	a_1 (s.)	a_4 (s.)	MICROMETER		r	i	d_1	d_4	Mean Right Ascension, 1850.0 (h. m. s.)	Mean Declination, 1850.0 (° ' ")
1	17 58 4.42	+67.46	+1.57	IV.	4	44.056	−15 16.1	−40.2	−2.7	17 59 13.45	−33 34 39.0
2	58 37.24	67.46	1.43	IV.	3	23.448	36 51.2	40.1	6.9	17 59 46.13	56 18.2
3	17 58 51.25	67.46	1.47	IV.	3	30.462	29 31.1	40.1	5.4	18 0 0.18	33 48 56.6
4	18 1 1.02	67.28	1.36	V.	2	14.519	46 12.8	39.6	8.8	2 9.66	34 5 41.2
5	2 33.01	67.28	1.60	IV.	4	47.308	11 52.2	39.3	2.0	3 41.89	33 31 13.5
6	3 58.00	67.27	1.55	IV.	3	40.909	18 35.3	38.9	3.3	5 6.82	.37 57.5
7	4 58.46	67.27	1.48	IV.	3	31.506	28 25.6	38.7	5.2	6 7.21	33 47 49.5
8	6 31.01	67.27	1.32	IV.	2	11.171	49 42.6	38.4	9.4	7 39.60	34 9 10.4
9	6 35.03	67.27	1.33	VI.	2	12.208	48 37.1	38.4	9.2	7 43.63	34 8 4.7
10	9 54.08	67.27	1.63	IV.	4	54.699	−4 6.9	37.6	0.5	11 2.98	33 23 27.0
11	10 32.04	67.26	1.54	IV.	3	43.311	16 4.7	37.5	2.8	11 40.84	33 35 25.0
12	14 50.40	67.26	1.37	IV.	2	18.678	41 52.1	36.6	7.9	15 59.03	34 1 16.6
13	16 29.93	67.26	1.57	IV.	4	48.872	10 13.8	36.2	1.7	17 38.76	33 29 31.7
14	17 48.46	67.25	1.54	IV.	4	44.121	15 12.2	36.0	2.7	18 57.25	34 30.9
15	18 40.77	67.25	1.53	IV.	4	42.789	16 35.7	35.7	2.9	19 49.55	35 54.3
16	19 0.29	67.25	1.53	VI.	4	43.485	15 51.4	35.7	2.8	20 9.07	35 9.9
17	18 58 .	67.25	1.51	VII.	4	40.449	19 1.3	35.7	3.4	20 (6.)	38 20.4
18	22 10.20	67.25	1.56	IV.	4	46.659	12 32.8	35.0	2.1	23 19.01	31 49.9
19	22 31.91	67.25	1.47	IV.	3	35.552	24 11.7	34.9	4.4	23 40.63	43 31.0
20	27 29.76	67.24	1.51	IV.	3	42.659	16 45.5	33.8	3.0	28 38.51	33 36 2.3
21	27 28.63	67.24	1.29	VI.	2	12.977	47 48.8	33.8	9.1	28 37.16	34 7 11.7
22	29 33.00	67.23	1.36	IV.	3	20.958	39 27.1	33.3	7.4	30 41.59	33 58 47.8
23	30 0.61	67.23	1.36	VI.	3	18.781	41 43.3	33.2	7.9	31 9.20	34 1 4.4
24	31 36.15	67.23	1.44	IV.	3	32.996	26 52.0	32.9	4.9	32 44.82	33 46 9.8
25	33 50.33	67.22	1.53	IV.	4	46.850	12 20.7	32.4	2.1	34 59.08	33 31 35.2
26	35 28.34	67.22	1.31	IV.	2	16.495	44 9.1	32.0	8.3	36 36.87	34 3 29.4
27	37 12.44	67.22	1.30	IV.	2	16.162	44 29.9	31.7	8.4	38 20.96	34 3 50.0
28	38 40.48	67.22	1.43	IV.	3	33.651	26 11.0	31.3	4.8	39 49.13	33 45 27.1
29	39 8.78	67.21	1.43	IV.	3	33.516	26 19.5	31.2	4.8	40 17.42	45 35.5
30	39 11.74	67.21	1.45	IV.	4	37.671	21 58.6	31.2	4.0	40 20.40	41 13.8
31	44 59.88	67.20	1.55	IV.	4	51.638	7 20.3	29.9	1.2	46 8.63	26 31.4
32	45 21.05	67.20	1.54	IV.	4	51.035	7 58.1	29.9	1.3	46 29.79	27 9.3
33	45 58.20	67.20	1.52	IV.	4	47.374	11 48.1	29.7	2.0	47 6.98	33 30 59.8
34	48 49.75	67.19	1.25	III.	2	11.821	49 1.7	29.1	9.3	49 58.19	34 8 20.1
35	49 2.06	67.19	1.54	IV.	4	52.106	6 51.0	29.1	1.0	50 10.79	33 26 1.1
36	54 39.48	67.18	1.30	IV.	2	19.608	40 53.9	27.8	7.7	55 47.96	34 0 9.4
37	57 45.40	67.17	1.28	IV.	2	18.621	41 55.8	27.2	7.9	18 58 53.85	34 1 10.9
38	18 59 42.24	67.16	1.28	IV.	2	20.648	39 48.6	26.8	7.5	19 0 50.68	33 59 2.9
39	19 1 44.56	67.16	1.24	IV.	1	14.431	46 15.5	26.3	8.8	2 52.96	34 5 30.6
40	1 45.66	67.16	1.25	III.	1	14.586	46 5.7	26.3	8.7	2 54.07	34 5 20.7
41	4 50.65	67.15	1.36	IV.	1	32.049	27 51.5	25.6	5.1	5 59.16	33 47 2.2
42	4 52.49	67.15	1.34	IV.	3	29.636	30 22.9	25.6	5.6	6 0.98	49 34.1
43	5 37.10	67.15	1.45	VI.	2	44.055	14 18.9	25.5	2.5	6 45.70	33 26.9
44	7 26.91	67.14	1.51	IV.	4	53.122	5 47.2	25.1	0.8	8 35.56	24 53.1
45	8 4.51	67.14	1.46	VII.	3	46.130	13 6.0	25.0	2.2	9 13.11	32 14.1
46	8 11.48	67.14	1.51	IV.	4	52.598	6 20.0	25.0	0.9	9 20.13	25 25.9
47	13 6.09	67.13	1.33	IV.	3	29.718	30 17.7	23.9	5.6	14 14.55	33 49 27.2
48	19 48.66	67.11	1.23	IV.	2	16.211	44 26.8	22.5	8.4	20 57.00	34 3 37.7
49	19 21 27.53	+67.10	+1.21	IV.	2	15.765	−44 54.7	−22.1	−8.5	19 22 35.84	−34 4 5.3

CORRECTIONS.

Date	Corr. of Clock	Hourly rate	m	n	c	Zenith Point	Mic. Co.
1846. July 14.	h. 17　s. +58.886	s. −0.011	s. +0.213	s. +0.298	s. +0.330	° ' '' 0 0 3.02	r. 30.005

REMARKS.

July 14. Night clear; stars not very steady. (36) 14. Transits over threads III and IV assumed as recorded over IV and V, to agree with Transit Z., June 15.

INSTRUMENT READINGS.

Date	A.	B.	C.	D.	E.	F.	Mean.	Barom. in.	At.	Ex.	U.	L.	I.
Zone 36　1846. July 14, 17 50	72 39	62.9	64.4	76.0	66.0	59.9	47.1	62.72			72.5	74.0	80.5
17 58								30.041	74.5	68.7			
18 39										66.7			
18 50		63.1	65.0	75.9	66.0	60.1	47.0	62.85			71.0	74.0	
18 59								30.054	73.0	65.9			
19 30										64.7			
19 59								30.070	72.2	64.3			
20 0	62.8	66.0	76.3	66.6	61.0	46.4	63.18			69.0	71.0	

Zone 36. July 14. C. $D_0 = -33^\circ\,18'\,40''$—Continued.

No.	Mag.	I	II	III	IV	V	VI	VII	T. (h m s)	a_1	a_2	Micr.		r	i	d_1	d_2	Mean Right Ascension, 1850.0	Mean Declination, 1850.0
50	9		30.8	48.7		25.7			19 23 7.40	+67.10	+1.46	IV.	4	50.238	− 8 48.3	−21.8	− 1.4	19 24 15.96	−33 27 51.5
51	9							43.4	24 48.03	67.09	1.48	IV.	4	52.282	6 40.0	21.4	1.0	25 56.60	33 25 42.4
52	9		16.0		54.0	12.6			26 53.73	67.08	1.16	IV.	4	10.212	50 42.6	21.0	9.7	28 1.97	34 9 53.3
53	9				50.5				30 50.56	67.07	1.30	IV.	3	30.604	29 22.2	20.1	5.4	31 58.93	33 48 27.7
54	8			12.1	30.3	49.0	7.5		32 30.45	67.06	1.22	IV.	3	19.962	40 29.5	19.8	7.6	33 38.73	59 36.9
55	7		42.2		19.7	37.5	56.1		44 19.29	67.02	1.44	IV.	4	51.996	6 57.8	17.3	1.1	45 27.75	25 56.2
56	9		27.5			23.1	41.5		48 4.52	67.01	1.26	IV.	3	30.364	29 37.3	16.5	5.5	49 12.79	48 39.3
57	9				52.5				48 52.56	67.01	1.22	IV.	3	25.070	35 9.3	16.4	6.5	50 0.79	33 54 12.2
58	6					50.0	8.3	27.0	49 31.24	67.00	1.15	V.	2	14.102	46 38.9	16.2	8.8	50 39.39	34 5 43.9
59	9			58.0	16.5				54 16.55	66.98	1.17	IV.	2	16.898	41 38.9	15.2	7.8	55 24.70	34 0 41.9
60	7				49.0	7.6	25.8	44.5	54 49.05	66.98	1.43	IV.	4	52.710	6 12.9	15.1	0.9	55 57.46	33 25 8.9
61	8			36.5	55.2	13.6	32.2		56 55.14	66.97	1.27	IV.	3	33.320	26 31.9	14.7	4.8	58 3.38	45 31.4
62	8		55.0		32.0	50.5			58 32.01	66.97	1.25	IV.	3	31.101	28 51.0	14.3	5.3	19 59 40.23	47 50.6
63	8			29.7	48.0	6.8			19 59 48.16	66.96	1.17	IV.	2	20.611	39 51.0	14.1	7.5	20 0 56.29	58 52.6
64	9			3.1	21.3	38.5			20 5 20.98	66.94	1.27	IV.	3	36.165	23 33.2	13.0	−1.3	6 29.19	33 42 30.5
65	9			17.7	36.0	54.6	13.5		6 36.14	66.94	1.09	IV.	3	11.432	49 26.3	12.7	9.4	7 44.17	34 8 28.4
66	9			22.5		0.5			9 41.49	66.92	1.39	IV.	4	52.362	6 35.0	12.1	1.0	10 49.80	33 25 28.1
67	8		50.5	8.5		46.0	4.0		12 27.28	66.91	1.34	IV.	3	46.766	12 26.0	11.5	2.1	13 35.53	31 19.6
68	9					45.0	3.0		12 26.24	66.91	1.26	V.	3	34.909	24 51.9	11.5	4.5	13 34.41	33 43 47.9
69	8.9		40.7	59.0	17.6	36.3	54.2		15 17.56	66.90	1.08	IV.	2	12.715	49 5.8	10.9	9.1	16 25.54	34 7 5.8
70	9				26.0				18 26.04	66.89	1.27	IV.	4	40.531	18 57.7	10.3	3.4	19 34.20	33 37 51.4
71	9							2.5	19 7.06	66.88	1.32	V.	4	46.873	12 19.0	10.1	2.1	20 15.26	31 11.2
72	9			29.8		8.0			21 48.90	66.87	1.31	V.	4	45.941	13 17.8	9.6	2.3	22 57.08	32 9.7
73	8		42.3	0.9	19.0	37.5			27 19.21	66.84	1.13	IV.	2	21.721	38 39.3	8.5	7.2	28 27.18	33 57 35.0
74	7.8				12.0	30.6	49.0		28 11.93	66.84	1.02	IV.	2	8.122	52 53.4	8.4	10.1	29 19.79	34 11 51.9
75	6			28.0	46.5	5.0	23.0		20 29 46.35	+66.83	+1.12	IV.	3	21.828	−38 32.6	− 8.0	− 7.2	20 30 54.30	−33 57 27.8

Zone 37. July 15. P. $D_0 = -29^\circ\,33'\,30''$.

No.	Mag.	I	II	III	IV	V	VI	VII	T. (h m s)	a_1	a_2	Micr.		r	i	d_1	d_2	Mean Right Ascension, 1850.0	Mean Declination, 1850.0
1	9,8					30.0		56.0	16 43 2.41	+66.58	+1.55	VI.	3	25.467	−34 44.3	−44.1	− 4.4	16 44 10.54	−30 9 2.8
2	8		21.0	38.3	56.3				45 56.37	66.58	1.46	IV.	2	14.945	45 46.1	43.4	6.0	47 4.41	30 20 5.5
3	9			9.0	26.3				47 26.56	66.58	1.63	IV.	3	35.545	24 12.2	43.1	2.9	48 34.77	29 58 28.2
4	9						13.5	49.0	47 55.71	66.58	1.69	IV.	4	40.917	18 33.3	43.0	2.1	49 3.98	52 49.4
5	Neb.				6.0				50 48.23	66.58	1.69	V.	4	40.920	18 33.1	42.3	2.1	51 56.50	52 47.5
6	8				35.0			10.5	53 17.21	66.58	1.70	VII.	4	41.840	17 33.8	41.8	1.9	54 25.40	51 47.5
7	8				44.0	2.0			54 26.41	66.58	1.73	VI.	4	44.710	14 34.3	41.6	1.5	55 34.72?	48 47.4
8	7				48.0	6.0			55 49.12	66.58	1.67	V.	4	37.570	22 3.2	41.3	2.6	56 56.37	56 17.1
9	7	43.0	1.0	18.0					57 36.15	66.58	1.72	III.	4	42.780	16 36.4	40.8	1.8	58 44.45	50 49.0
10	7	57.0	15.0		8.0				58 50.30	66.58	1.74	V.	4	46.530	12 40.6	40.6	1.3	59 56.62	29 46 52.5
11	6							58.3	16 58 4.89	66.58	1.54	VII.	3	22.670	37 39.2	40.7	4.8	16 59 13.01	30 11 54.7
12	9	17.7	36.0						17 1 11.36	66.58	1.52	III.	2	19.903	40 29.6	40.0	5.3	17 1 19.46	14 44.9
13	9			36.0	54.0	12.0			1 36.18	66.58	1.50	VI.	2	16.875	43 44.6	39.9	5.7	2 44.26	18 0.2
14	9	53.0	11.5	29.0					4 46.71	66.58	1.59	III.	3	29.025	31 1.1	39.2	3.9	5 54.88	5 14.2
15	6				8.5	26.5			5 8.62	66.58	1.62	IV.	3	32.225	27 40.5	39.1	3.4	6 16.82	1 53.0
16	7			53.0	11.0				6 10.92	66.58	1.55	IV.	3	23.850	36 25.7	38.9	4.7	7 19.05	30 10 39.3
17	7				55.5	14.0			6 38.10	66.58	1.63	V.	3	34.490	25 18.4	38.8	3.0	7 46.31	29 59 30.2
18	7				17.0	24.5			7 41.46	66.58	1.78	VI.	4	50.040	8 3.2	38.5	0.6	8 49.82	42 12.3
19	7				29.0	48.0			17 13 11.93	+66.58	+1.80	V.	4	52.847	− 6 4.0	−37.3	− 0.3	17 14 20.31	−29 40 11.6

CORRECTIONS.

Date.		Corr. of Clock.	Hourly rate.	m	n	ϵ	Zenith Point.	Mic. Co.
1846. July 15,	17 h	+ 58.483 s	− 0.010 s	+ 0.213 s	+ 0.298 s	+ 0.330 s		r.

REMARKS.

(36) 75. Differs 13s.6 from Transit Z., Sept. 19.

(37) 8. Transits over T.'s IV and V assumed as recorded over T.'s V and VI.

(37) 12. Minute assumed as 0 instead of 1.

INSTRUMENT READINGS.

Date.			CIRCLE.						Barom.	THERMOM.				
		A.	B.	C.	D.	E.	F.	Mean.		At.	Ex.	U.	L.	I.
Zone 36	July 14, 20 29								30.074	72.0	63.9			
Zone 37	July 15, 16 43	68 54 67.0	67.6	79.5	70.2	64.3	49.7	66.38	30.232	69.6	61.3			
	17 28								30.230	68.4	60.3			
	18 45								30.228	66.0	58.0			
	19 20	66.0	68.2	79.6	71.3	62.7	48.3	66.02						
	19 30								30.230	65.0	57.2			63.0

ZONE 37. JULY 15. P. D.$_3$ = −29° 33′ 30″—Continued.

No.	Mag.	I.	II.	III.	IV.	V.	VI.	VII.	T.	a₁	a₂	MIC.		r.	i	d₁	d₂	Mean Right Ascension, 1850.0	Mean Declination, 1850.0
									h. m. s.	s.	s.			r.	′ ″	″	″	h. m. s.	° ′ ″
20	7						30.5		17 13 37.33	+66.58	+1.79	VII.	4	49.847	− 9 11.1	−37.1	− 0.8	17 14 45.69	−29 43 19.0
21	4	46.0	3.3	21.0	30.0				16 38.91	66.58	1.78	IV.	4	49.713	9 21.1	36.5	0.8	17 47.27	43 28.4
22	5							49.0	16 55.86	66.58	1.82	VII.	4	57.480	1 12.9	36.4	0.0	18 4.26	29 35 19.3
23	7			33.5	51.5				20 51.42	66.58	1.59	IV.	3	26.863	33 16.8	35.5	4.2	21 59.59	30 7 26.5
24	7					47.0			21 11.40	66.57	1.51	VI.	2	17.875	42 41.9	35.4	5.6	22 19.48	16 52.9
25	9							24.0	21 30.52	66.57	1.48	VII.	1	14.370	46 18.5	35.3	6.1	22 38.57	20 29.9
26	9							8.0	22 14.57	66.57	1.52	VI.	2	19.057	41 27.8	35.2	5.4	23 22.66	15 38.4
27	8						52.0	1.0	23 16.40	66.57	1.51	VI.	2	16.853	43 45.9	34.9	5.7	24 24.48	17 56.5
28	9						2.5		24 26.96	66.57	1.61	VI.	3	28.695	31 21.7	34.6	3.9	25 35.14	5 30.2
29	9		28.0	45.5					28 3.42	66.57	1.64	III.	3	31.923	27 59.2	33.8	3.4	29 11.63	30 2 6.4
30	7				43.0	0.5			28 42.87	66.57	1.72	IV.	4	41.547	17 53.8	33.7	2.0	29 51.16	29 51 59.5
31	9							30.0	29 36.61	66.57	1.59	VII.	3	26.415	33 44.5	33.4	4.3	30 44.77	30 7 52.2
32	10		49.0						32 24.33	66.57	1.74			42	18			33 32.64	29 51
33	7		51.0		25.5				32 26.02	66.57	1.74	IV.	4	41.970	17 27.2	32.8	1.9	33 34.33	29 51 31.9
34	8						20.5	38.5	32 44.90	66.57	1.60	VII.	4	28.290	31 46.8	32.7	4.0	33 53.07	30 5 53.5
35	8			33.0	51.0				34 33.12	66.57	1.76	IV.	4	46.587	12 37.4	32.3	1.2	35 41.45	29 46 40.9
36	10	27.5		3.0					37 20.81	66.56	1.58	III.	3	25.225	34 59.5	31.6	4.5	38 28.95	30 9 5.6
37	8				41.0		16.5		37 40.98	66.56	1.54	VI.	3	20.227	40 12.9	31.5	5.2	38 49.08	14 19.6
38	8	54.5	12.0	30.0					40 47.77	66.56	1.55	III.	2	20.307	40 10.1	30.8	5.2	41 55.88	14 16.1
39	7			25.0	44.0				41 43.42	66.56	1.56	IV.	3	24.000	36 16.4	30.6	4.6	42 51.54	10 21.6
40	9							20.0	41 26.64	66.56	1.61	VII.	3	27.880	32 12.4	30.7	4.0	42 34.81	30 6 17.1
41	9				57.0				43 57.00	66.56	1.76	IV.	4	44.455	14 51.3	30.1	1.6	45 5.32	29 48 53.0
42	8					0.0			44 24.59	66.56	1.77	V.	4	46.760	12 26.1	29.9	1.2	45 32.92	46 27.2
43	7							37.5	44 44.19	66.56	1.67	VII.	3	34.580	25 12.1	29.9	3.0	45 52.42	59 15.0
44	9						14.0		45 38.57	66.56	1.75	VI.	4	43.960	15 21.4	29.7	1.6	46 46.88	49 22.7
45	9							52.5	45 59.20	66.56	1.72	VII.	4	40.010	19 28.8	29.6	2.2	47 7.48	29 53 30.6
46	7				33.0	51.0			47 15.32	66.55	1.64	V.	3	31.580	28 21.0	29.3	3.5	48 23.51	30 2 24.8
47	5			19.5	37.0				48 19.35	66.55	1.55	IV.	2	20.647	39 48.7	29.1	5.1	49 27.45	30 13 52.9
48	6						19.0	36.5	49 43.41	66.55	1.76	VI.	4	44.790	14 29.3	28.7	1.5	50 51.72	29 48 29.5
49	7	59.0	16.5	34.5					52 52.15	66.55	1.74	III.	4	42.047	17 22.5	28.0	1.9	54 0.44	29 51 22.4
50	9			57.0					54 14.80	66.55	1.56	III.	2	20.905	39 32.4	27.7	5.1	55 22.91	30 13 35.2
51	2.3		2.5	20.5	38.5				55 2.75	66.55	1.47	N.	1	9.800	51 5.3	27.4	6.8	56 10.77	30 25 9.5
52	9	34.5		10.0					57 27.67	66.54	1.80	III.	4	48.740	10 22.2	26.9	0.9	58 36.01	29 44 20.0
53	6			52.0	10.0				17 58 9.92	66.54	1.67	IV.	3	33.425	26 25.3	26.7	3.2	17 59 18.13	30 0 25.2
54	7	26.5	44.5						18 0 19.83	66.54	1.78	III.	4	46.793	12 24.4	26.2	1.2	18 1 28.15	29 46 21.8
55	7	40.0		15.0		50.3			0 32.78	66.54	1.84	IV.	4	53.170	5 44.2	26.2	0.3	1 41.16	39 40.7
56	8					4.0			1 28.54	66.54	1.73	VI.	3	40.353	19 10.2	26.0	2.2	2 36.81	53 8.4
57	7	27.7	45.5	3.3					4 21.32	66.53	1.75	III.	4	41.840	17 35.5	25.3	1.9	5 29.60	51 32.7
58	9				5.0	23.0			6 5.12	66.53	1.73	IV.	4	39.347	20 12.1	24.9	2.3	7 13.38	54 9.3
59	9					0.0			7 24.57	66.53	1.79	VI.	4	47.420	11 44.4	24.5	1.1	8 32.89	45 40.0
60	9				16.5				8 58.76	66.53	1.84	V.	4	52.540	6 23.4	24.2	0.4	10 7.13	40 18.0
61	2.3			58.0	15.5	33.0			10 15.50	66.52	1.75	IV.	3	40.237	19 17.7	23.9	2.2	11 23.77	29 53 13.8
62	9						50.5		10 57.11	66.52	1.62	VII.	3	26.170	33 59.8	23.7	4.3	12 5.25	30 7 57.8
63	9					37.0			12 1.41	66.52	1.60	VI.	3	22.025	38 20.0	23.5	4.9	13 9.53	30 12 18.4
64	8				46.0	4.0			13 46.12	66.52	1.77	IV.	4	48.340	17 4.2	23.0	1.9	14 54.41	29 50 59.1
65	8					2.5			14 44.62	66.52	1.53	V.	2	15.020	45 41.3	22.8	6.0	15 52.67	30 19 40.1
66	9						45.0		14 51.54	66.52	1.56	VII.	2	17.150	3 27.0	22.6	5.7	15 59.62	30 17 25.5
67	6		30.0	48.0	6.0				17 5.77	66.51	1.74	IV.	4	39.420	20 7.5	22.3	2.3	18 14.02	29 54 2.1
68	9			21.0					18 18 21.04	+66.51	+1.69	IV.	3	33.637	−26 11.8	−22.0	− 3.2	18 19 29.24	−30 0 7.0

CORRECTIONS.

Date.	Corr. of Clock.	Hourly rate.	m	u ·	c	Zenith Point.	Mic. Co.
1846.	h. s.	s.	s.	s.	s.	° ′ ″	r.

REMARKS.

(37) 20. Transit over T. VII assumed as recorded over T. VI.

(37) 42. Transit over T. VI assumed as recorded over T. V.

(37) 51. Transits over T.'s IV–VI assumed as recorded over T.'s II–V.

INSTRUMENT READINGS.

Date.	CIRCLE.							Barom.	THERMOM.				
	A.	B.	C.	D.	E.	F.	Mean.		At.	Ex.	U.	L.	I.
1846. h. m.	° ′ ″						″	in.	°	°	°	°	°

Zone 37. July 15. P. D₀ = —29° 33′ 30″ —Continued.

No.	Mag.	I.	II.	III.	IV.	V.	VI.	VII.	T. (h. m. s.)	a_1 (s.)	a_2 (s.)	Micrometer		r.	i (′ ″)	d_1 (″)	d_2 (″)	Mean Right Ascension, 1850.0 (h. m. s.)	Mean Declination, 1850.0 (° ′ ″)
69	9	12.5	30.5	48.5					18 21 6.07	+66.51	+1.62	III.	3	24.160	−36 6.3	−21.3	− 4.6	18 22 14.20	−30 14 12.1
70	8	43.0		19.0					22 36.60	66.50	1.58	III.	3	20.180	40 15.0	21.0	5.2	23 44.68	10 2.2
71	7	6.5	24.5	43.0					25 0.21	66.50	1.67	III.	3	30.887	29 4.2	20.4	3.6	26 8.38	30 2 58.2
72	6				17.0	34.3	52.3		25 16.80	66.50	1.79	IV.	4	44.470	14 50.4	20.3	1.6	26 25.00	29 48 42.3
73	7	5.0	22.3	40.0					27 58.00	66.49	1.62	III.	3	25.090	35 7.9	19.7	4.5	29 6.11	30 9 2.1
74	8				23.5		59.0		28 5.71	66.49	1.80	V.	4	46.620	12 34.9	19.6	1.3	29 14.00	29 46 25.8
75	7				6.0				29 48.20	66.49	1.69	V.	3	33.080	26 46.8	19.3	3.3	30 56.38	30 0 39.4
76	8		13.0	30.0					31 30.36	66.49	1.82	III.	3	48.760	10 21.0	18.8	0.9	32 38.67	29 44 10.7
77	9				37.0				32 37.00	66.49	1.79	IV.	4	45.590	13 40.0	18.6	1.4	33 45.28	29 47 30.0
78	7			41.0	59.0				33 58.92	66.48	1.62	IV.	4	26.545	33 36.9	18.3	4.2	35 7.02	30 7 29.4
79	9		10.0		46.0				35 45.77	66.48	1.82	IV.	4	52.460	6 28.8	17.8	0.4	36 54.07	29 40 17.0
80	7	13.0	31.0	48.5			24.0		36 6.29	66.48	1.77	III.	4	46.170	13 3.7	17.8	1.3	37 14.54	46 52.8
81	9							56.0	36 2.83	66.48	1.84	VII.	4	53.880	4 57.9	17.8	0.2	37 11.15	29 38 45.9
82	9			11.0					39 11.06	66.47	1.62	IV.	3	23.970	36 18.3	17.0	4.6	40 19.15	30 10 9.9
83	9			14.5					40 32.30	66.47	1.61	III.	3	22.870	37 27.1	16.7	4.8	41 40.38	11 18.6
84	9						16.0		40 40.30	66.47	1.55	VI.	2	17.335	43 16.0	16.7	5.6	41 48.32	30 17 8.3
85	7		53.0	11.0	29.0				45 28.76	66.46	1.86	IV.	4	52.060	5 57.2	15.6	0.3	46 37.08	29 39 43.1
86	1.2	2.7	20.3	38.0	56.0				51 55.02	66.44	1.67	IV.	3	28.603	31 27.7	14.0	4.0	53 4.03	30 5 15.7
87	9	21.0	56.0						56 14.66	66.43	1.62	III.	3	23.457	36 50.5	13.0	4.7	57 22.11	10 38.2
88	9		56.0			40.0			56 31.37	66.43	1.64	V.	3	23.880	36 23.9	13.0	4.6	18 57 39.44	10 11.5
89	7	53.0	10.5	29.0					18 59 46.44	66.43	1.60	III.	2	19.900	40 35.4	12.2	5.3	19 0 54.47	14 22 9
90	8		28.0				30.0		19 0 3.50	66.42	1.60	VI.	3	30.940	29 0.7	12.1	3.6	1 11.61	30 2 46.4
91	6							33.5	0 40.28	66.42	1.84	VII.	4	48.443	10 39.4	12.0	1.0	1 48.51	29 14 22.4
92	9					29.0			2 29.02	66.42	1.77	IV.	4	40.200	19 12.9	11.6	2.2	3 37.21	29 52 56.7
93	7		21.5	39.0	57.0				3 56.96	66.41	1.67	IV.	3	28.940	31 6.5	11.2	3.0	5 5.03	30 4 54.6
94	7	8.0	25.0		0.5				11 0.74	66.40	1.78	IV.	4	40.420	19 4.7	9.6	2.1	12 8.92	29 52 46.4
95	7	32.0	50.0		26.0				11 25.55	66.40	1.82	IV.	4	45.060	14 13.2	9.4	1.5	12 33.77	29 47 54.1
96	6	16.5	34.0						15 9.87	66.39	1.53	II.	1	10.805	50 2.2	8.6	6.7	16 17.79	30 23 47.5
97	9		44.0	1.7	19.5				16 19.53	66.38	1.70	IV.	4	31.575	28 21.3	8.3	3.5	17 27.61	30 2 3.1
98	8			58.0	16.0				17 15.87	66.38	1.82	IV.	4	45.295	13 58.6	8.1	1.4	18 24.07	29 47 38.1
99	9				47.0		22.0		17 46.81	66.38	1.87	VI.	4	51.615	7 20.9	8.0	0.5	18 55.06	40 59.4
100	9							1.0	19 25.50	66.37	1.73	VI.	3	35.490	24 16.0	7.6	2.0	20 33.60	57 56.5
101	8					48.0			20 30.25	66.37	1.81	V.	4	45.000	14 16.6	7.3	1.5	21 38.43	47 55.4
102	9	33.0		9.0					26 26.47	66.35	1.78	III.	4	38.883	20 41.1	5.9	2.4	27 34.60	29 54 19.4
103	8	45.0		21.0					30 38.54	66.34	1.69	III.	3	28.783	31 16.2	5.0	3.9	31 46.57	30 4 55.1
104	9			48.0			42.0		19 51 6.10	+66.28	+1.65	VI.	2	22.313	−38 3.8	−2.3	−4.9	19 52 14.03	−30 11 41.0

Zone 38. July 24. C. D₀ = —30° 47′ 50″.

No.	Mag.	I.	II.	III.	IV.	V.	VI.	VII.	T. (h. m. s.)	a_1 (s.)	a_2 (s.)	Micrometer		r.	i (′ ″)	d_1 (″)	d_2 (″)	Mean Right Ascension, 1850.0 (h. m. s.)	Mean Declination, 1850.0 (° ′ ″)
1	7					52.8	11.2	29.0	21 30 10.99	+16.20	+1.40	IV.	4	48.611	−10 30.3	−19.7	− 0.9	21 30 28.59	−30 58 40.9
2	5.6		1.7	20.0		56.1		32.5	38 38.05	16.15	0.70	IV.	2	13.671	47 6.0	18.3	6.7	38 54.90	31 35 21.0
3	9		19.8	37.0	55.0	13.0	31.0		42 55.18	16.13	1.41	IV.	4	46.339	12 53.0	17.7	1.4	43 12.72	1 2.1
4	7		16.8		52.6	10.6	28.5		46 52.63	16.11	1.09	IV.	3	29.443	30 35.1	17.1	4.1	47 9.83	18 46.3
5	9							41.0	46 46.77	16.11	0.70	VII.	2	11.121	−19 44.7	17.1	7.1	47 3.55	37 58.9
6	9			6.5	24.7	43.5			52 42.96	16.07	0.97	IV.	3	22.650	37 41.1	16.2	5.2	53 0.00	25 52.5
7	9			6.0		42.0			55 42.09	16.06	0.84	IV.	3	15.421	45 14.5	15.6	6.4	55 58.99	33 26.7
8	8			18.0	37.0	55.0			21 56 36.67	16.06	1.00	IV.	3	22.482	37 51.7	15.7	5.2	21 56 53.73	26 2.6
9	9		34.0	53.0	11.7	29.7	47.5		22 5 11.19	+16.00	+1.31	IV.	3	34.900	−24 52.5	−14.5	− 3.2	22 5 28.50	−31 13 0.2

CORRECTIONS.

Date.		Corr. of Clock.	Hourly rate.	m	n	c	Zenith Point.	Mic. Co.
1846. July 24.	h. 17	s. + 8.856	s. + 0.003	s. + 0.079	s. + 0.300	s. + 0.230	° ′ ″ 0 0 2.16	r. 30.005

INSTRUMENT READINGS.

	Date.		CIRCLE.							Barom.	THERMOM.				
			A.	B.	C.	D.	E.	F.	Mean.		At.	Ex.	U.	L.	I.
	1846.	h. m.	° ′ ″						″	In.	°	°	°	°	°
Zone 38	July 24,	21 30	70 9 62.0	62.8	74.0	62.7	57.8	47.1	61.07	29.908	77.5	73.0	75.6	76.3	77.2
		21 56								29.916	76.7	73.0			
		22 30	62.2	62.2	74.0	61.6	57.0	47.0	60.70	29.922	76.3	72.6	74.8	75.2	
		22 50								29.924	75.8	71.5			
		23 10	61.9	61.9	73.8	61.8	57.1	46.4	60.48				74.0	75.0	77.3

Zone 38. July 24. C. $D_0 = -30° 47' 50''$—Continued.

No.	Mag.	I.	II.	III.	IV.	V.	VI.	VII.	T. (h. m. s.)	a_1 (s.)	a_2 (s.)	Micr.	r.	i (′ ″)	d_1 (″)	d_2 (″)	Mean Right Ascension, 1850.0 (h. m. s.)	Mean Declination, 1850.0 (° ′ ″)
10	8		18.0	36.0	54.0		30.1		22 7 54.05	+15.99	+1.31	IV. 3	33.900	−25 55.2	−14.2	− 3.4	22 8 11.35	−31 14 2.8
11	9			31.2	49.0	6.7			10 48.97	15.97	1.18	IV. 3	27.166	32 57.9	13.8	4.5	11 6.12	21 6.2
12	9			28.0	46.0	4.0			10 46.00	15.97	1.09	VII. 3	23.312	36 59.1	13.8	5.1	11 3.66	25 8.0
13	8.9		51.0	8.5	26.5	45.0	3.0		21 26.79	15.91	1.42	IV. 3	35.577	24 10.1	12.6	3.1	21 44.12	12 15.8
14	7			46.2	4.5	22.6	40.2		27 4.40	15.88	1.56	IV. 4	40.942	18 31.8	12.0	2.2	27 21.84	6 36.0
15	6		6.6	24.1	42.0	0.2	18.4		31 42.23	15.85	1.19	IV. 3	22.638	37 41.8	11.5	5.2	31 59.27	25 48.5
16	9		9.0	26.7	45.0	3.0	21.2		33 44.99	15.84	1.20	IV. 3	22.499	37 51.2	11.3	5.2	34 2.03	25 57.7
17	9					37.0	55.5		34 19.29	15.83	1.64	V. 4	43.518	15 49.8	11.2	1.9	34 36.76	3 52.9
18	9		45.7	3.8			57.7		44 21.76	15.77	1.76	IV. 4	46.210	13 1.1	10.3	1.4	44 39.29	1 2.8
19	9					55.7		32.0	46 37.77	15.76	1.37	V. 3	27.002	33 8.1	10.1	4.5	46 54.99	21 12.7
20	6.7		38.2	56.5	14.2	32.6	50.2		55 14.35	15.71	1.54	IV. 3	32.801	27 4.2	9.4	3.6	55 31.68	15 7.2
21	9							31.12	55 37.00	15.71	1.55	VII. 3	33.088	26 45.7	9.4	3.5	55 54.26	14 48.6
22	9		36.0	53.7	11.8	30.0	47.8		58 11.87	15.69	1.34	IV. 3	23.141	37 10.1	9.3	5.1	58 28.99	25 14.5
23	9				16.7		44.77		22 59 17.41	15.69	1.80	IV. 4	44.772	14 31.2	9.2	1.6	22 59 ..	31 2 32.0
24	8			36.0	54.0	11.7			23 4 53.88	+15.66	+2.04	IV. 4	54.659	− 4 11.4	− 8.9	− 0.1	23 5 11.58	−30 52 10.4

Zone 39. July 29. C. $D = -30° 44' 10''$.

No.	Mag.	I.	II.	III.	IV.	V.	VI.	VII.	T. (h. m. s.)	a_1 (s.)	a_2 (s.)	Micr.	r.	i (′ ″)	d_1 (″)	d_2 (″)	Mean Right Ascension, 1850.0 (h. m. s.)	Mean Declination, 1850.0 (° ′ ″)
1	7			59.2	17.5	35.0	53.7		18 0 17.32	+17.44	+0.41	IV. 2	16.520	−44 7.5	−44.9	− 6.1	18 0 35.17	−31 33 8.5
2	8.9		14.0	32.2	49.7	7.5	25.0		2 49.71	17.43	1.14	IV. 4	49.400	9 40.9	44.3	0.9	3 8.28	30 58 36.1
3	9				52.0	10.0	28.1		4 52.02	17.43	0.64	IV. 3	24.021	35 15.1	43.7	4.9	5 10.00	31 25 13.7
4	6.7		41.0	59.0	17.0	34.9			6 16.94	17.42	0.73	IV. 3	27.369	32 45.2	43.4	4.4	6 35.00	21 43.0
5	7						45.7		6 10.73	17.42	0.92	VI. 3	36.626	23 4.0	43.4	2.0	6 29.07	12 0.3
6	7						50.7	8.5	7 14.56	17.42	0.76	VI. 3	28.461	31 36.5	43.2	4.2	7 32.74	20 33.9
7	8				48.7	6.2			8 48.45	17.42	0.86	IV. 3	32.068	27 50.3	42.8	3.6	9 6.73	16 46.7
8	7			6.9	24.9	43.0			10 24.94	17.41	0.76	IV. 3	26.647	33 30.4	42.4	4.5	10 43.11	22 27.3
9	6.7				16.5	34.7	52.5		11 16.61	17.41	1.23	IV. 4	47.991	11 9.7	42.2	1.1	11 35.25	0 2.5
10	9			50.7	8.5	26.5			14 8.55	17.40	0.95	IV. 3	32.499	27 23.3	41.5	3.6	14 26.90	16 18.4
11	9		30.0			24.0			14 5.98	17.40	1.04	IV. 3	36.495	23 12.6	41.5	2.9	14 24.42	12 7.0
12	9			42.2					15 42.24	17.40	0.60	IV. 2	15.066	45 38.5	41.2	6.3	16 0.24	34 36.0
13	6			14.5	2.0	20.5	38.5		17 2.37	17.40	0.77	IV. 3	22.086	38 40.4	40.8	5.2	17 20.54	27 12.4
14	8.9						9.7		17 33.57	17.40	0.58	VI. 2	12.921	47 52.3	40.7	6.7	17 51.55	36 49.7
15	8.9			59.0		35.0	53.0		19 16.92	17.39	0.57	IV. 2	11.038	49 50.8	40.3	7.0	19 34.86	38 48.1
16	9						56.0		20 20.11	17.39	1.29	VI. 4	44.901	14 22.3	40.0	1.6	20 38.79	3 13.9
17	8			58.0	16.5	34.1		10.5	22 16.26	17.38	1.11	IV. 3	34.799	24 58.8	39.6	3.2	22 34.75	13 51.6
18	8		47.5	6.0					24 23.77	17.37	1.10	III. 3	32.896	26 58.2	39.0	3.5	24 42.24	15 50.7
19	7					50.7	8.0		24 32.30	17.37	0.97	V. 3	26.852	33 17.4	39.0	4.4	24 50.64	31 22 10.8
20	8.9			9.5	27.2	45.0			27 27.21	17.37	1.58	IV. 4	54.390	4 27.7	38.3	0.1	27 46.16	30 53 16.1
21	7.8				35.0	53.0			28 34.98	17.36	0.88	IV. 2	20.688	39 46.1	38.0	5.4	28 53.22	31 28 39.5
22	9			27.5	45.0	3.0			30 45.17	17.36	1.44	IV. 4	45.139	14 8.3	37.5	1.6	31 3.97	2 57.4
23	7.8				46.5	4.5			31 46.50	17.35	1.15	IV. 3	30.610	29 21.8	37.3	3.8	32 5.00	18 12.9
24	6.7						32.0	50.5	31 56.08	17.35	0.74	VI. 1	12.884	47 51.8	37.2	6.7	32 14.17	36 45.7
25	8			58.0				10.0	34 15.05	17.34	0.93	IV. 2	18.244	42 19.4	36.7	5.8	34 34.22	31 11.9
26	8		1.2			56.0	13.7		34 37.61	17.34	0.89	IV. 2	16.808	43 49.3	36.6	6.0	34 55.84	32 41.9
27	9		44.0		20.0	37.1	56.0		37 19.81	17.33	1.57	IV. 4	47.102	12 5.0	35.9	1.3	37 38.71	0 52.2
28	9		37.0		13.2		49.5		40 13.26	17.33	1.27	IV. 3	30.445	39 32.2	35.2	3.9	40 31.86	18 21.3
29	6.7			31.0	49.0	7.1	25.0		41 49.02	17.32	1.13	IV. 3	23.199	37 6.7	34.9	5.0	42 7.47	31 25 56.6
30	6					2.0	20.2	38.7	18 42 44.42	+17.32	+1.77	V. 4	53.262	− 5 38.1	−34.6	− 0.3	18 43 3.51	−30 54 23.0

CORRECTIONS.

Date.	Corr. of Clock.	Hourly rate.	m	n	c	Zenith Point.	Mic. Co.
	h.	s.	s.	s.	s.	s.	° ′ ″	r.
1846, July 29,	17	+ 9.228	+ 0.009	+ 0.117	+ 0.200	+ 0.330	0 0 2.58	30.001

REMARKS.

(38) 23. Observations in A. R. worthless.
July 29. A light haze, barely perceptible; clouds form and disappear rapidly.

INSTRUMENT READINGS.

	Date.	A.	B.	C.	D.	E.	F.	Mean.	Barom. (in.)	At.	Ex.	U.	L.	I.
Zone 39	1846, July 29, 18 0	70 9 61.4	61.0	74.0	63.4	55.0	46.1	60.30	29.960	76.0	70.8	75.5	76.2	78.5
	18 30								29.960	75.2	70.7			
	18 42									70.6				

ZONE 40. JULY 29. C. $D_s = -30°\,48'\,10''$.

No.	Mag.	I.	II.	III.	IV.	V.	VI.	VII.	T.	a_1	a_2	Mic.	n	r	i	d_1	d_2	Mean Right Ascension, 1850.0	Mean Declination, 1850.0
1	9			28.7	46.0	4.5	22.5		19 45 46.41	+17.07	+1.28	IV.	2	20.119	-40 21.8	-19.8	-5.5	19 46 4.76	-31 28 57.1
2	6.7					3.5	21.6		46 43.56	17.06	1.48	V.	4	49.838	9 12.8	19.6	0.8	47 22.10	30 57 43.2
3	7		35.0	53.0		29.0	47.0	4.7	49 10.09	17.05	1.48	IV.	4	51.379	7 36.7	19.0	0.6	49 28.62	30 56 6.3
4	7.8			14.6	32.8	50.5	8.8		54 32.70	17.03	1.40	IV.	3	40.121	19 24.9	17.8	2.5	54 51.13	31 7 55.1
5	8			4.3	22.8	40.7	58.7		56 22.64	17.02	1.36	IV.	3	34.642	25 8.8	17.4	3.2	56 41.02	13 39.4
6	8.9			43.2	2.0		36.7		58 0.99	17.01	1.34	IV.	3	31.602	28 19.6	17.0	3.7	58 19.34	16 50.3
7	9							3.5	19 58 9.48	17.01	1.35	VII.	3	33.516	26 18.9	17.0	3.4	58 27.64	14 49.3
8	9			10.7	28.0	46.0			20 0 28.22	17.00	1.22	IV.	2	13.401	47 23.0	16.5	6.6	20 0 46.44	31 35 56.1
9	9			55.0	14.0	32.0			4 13.67	16.98	1.32	IV.	3	27.689	32 25.0	15.7	4.3	4 31.97	20 55.0
10	9			54.7	12.5		48.7		6 12.67	16.97	1.40	IV.	3	39.630	19 55.7	15.2	2.4	6 31.04	31 8 23.3
11	9			58.7	16.5				8 16.57	16.96	1.46	IV.	4	48.786	10 19.2	14.8	1.0	8 34.99	30 56 45.0
12	8.9		13.2	31.0	49.1		25.7		10 49.28	16.95	1.27	IV.	3	20.968	39 26.5	14.2	5.4	11 7.50	31 27 56.1
13	7.8		57.0	15.5	33.3	51.0	9.2		14 33.22	16.93	1.46	IV.	4	49.511	9 33.9	13.4	0.9	14 51.61	30 57 58.2
14	9						33.0		14 57.12	16.93	1.45	VI.	4	48.552	10 33.2	13.3	1.0	15 15.50	30 56 57.5
15	8		26.1	44.4	2.0	20.7			17 2.31	16.91	1.37	IV.	3	39.444	21 10.3	12.9	2.6	17 20.59	31 9 35.8
16	6.7				7.0	25.0	42.8		18 6.93	16.91	1.31	IV.	3	28.512	31 33.5	12.6	4.2	18 25.15	20 0.3
17	9				33.7		5.7?		20 31.73	16.91	1.36	IV.	3	35.872	23 51.5	12.1	3.0	20 50.00	31 12 16.6
·18	6.7		37.5	55.0	13.5	30.8	49.1		25 13.20	16.88	1.44	IV.	2	48.600	10 31.0	11.2	1.0	25 31.62	30 58 53.2
19	9				2.0	21.0			26 2.51	16.88	1.37	IV.	3	39.317	20 15.5	11.0	2.5	26 20.76	31 8 39.0
20	9				22.5		58.5		26 22.56	16.88	1.41	IV.	3	44.679	15 16.3	10.9	1.8	26 40.85	3 39.0
21	8.9				35.6	54.0	11.8		27 35.81	16.87	1.40	IV.	3	43.166	16 13.7	10.6	1.9	28 54.08	4 36.2
22	7							37.0	27 42.87	16.87	1.24	VII.	1	20.638	39 45.3	10.6	5.5	28 0.98	28 11.4
23	8							58.0	30 3.87	16.86	1.25	VII.	2	21.986	38 23.7	10.1	5.2	30 21.98	26 49.0
24	8			26.7	45.0		20.2		32 44.67	16.84	1.39	IV.	4	42.416	16 59.4	9.6	2.0	33 2.99	5 21.0
25	9						26.0?		32 50.11	16.84	1.41	VI.	4	45.241	14 1.2	9.6	1.5	33 5.36	2 22.3
26	8.9				47.0?				35 47.05	16.83	1.23	IV.	2	19.428	41 5.3	9.0	5.0	36 5.11	29 29.9
27	6.7						29.5	47.4	35 53.54	16.83	1.42	VI.	4	46.581	12 36.9	9.0	1.3	36 11.79	0 57.2
28	7.8		9.0		45.2	3.5			42 45.24	16.79	1.31	IV.	3	32.950	26 54.9	7.6	3.5	43 3.34	15 16.0
29	7			38.5	56.0	14.6	32.0		43 56.28	16.78	1.31	IV.	3	31.493	28 26.5	7.4	3.7	44 14.37	16 47.6
30	9			34.0					46 10.00	16.77	1.34		3	35.	25			46 28.11	13
31	9				10.0	27.0			20 46 9.48	+16.77	+1.23	IV.	3	20.098	-40 21.7	-7.0	-5.5	20 46 27.48	-31 28 44.2

ZONE 41. AUGUST 5. C. $D_s = -27°\,3'\,20''$.

No.	Mag.	I.	II.	III.	IV.	V.	VI.	VII.	T.	a_1	a_2	Mic.	n	r	i	d_1	d_2	Mean Right Ascension, 1850.0	Mean Declination, 1850.0
1	7.8		48.5	6.0	23.0	41.0	58.0		17 16 23.31	+17.18	+2.23	IV.	3	35.872	-23 51.5	-14.4	-2.3	17 16 42.72	-27 27 28.2
2	6		52.0	9.0	26.7	44.5	1.7		28 26.77	17.15	1.20	IV.	2	7.624	53 24.6	11.7	5.6	28 45.12	57 1.0
3	8		23.7	41.0	58.0		33.0		30 58.29	17.14	1.52	IV.	2	16.961	44 42.4	11.2	4.6	31 16.95	48 18.2
4	6		58.0	15.5	33.0	50.0	7.7		33 32.64	17.14	1.48	IV.	2	15.879	44 47.5	10.6	4.6	33 51.46	48 22.7
5	8		13.0		47.7	5.0	22.0		36 47.61	17.13	2.37	IV.	3	40.679	18 49.8	9.8	1.8	37 7.11	22 21.4
6	5				49.2	6.7	23.5	41.0	37 49.03	17.13	1.56	IV.	2	18.064	42 30.6	9.6	4.3	38 7.72	46 4.5
7	8.9		50.0		25.0		0.0		41 25.03	17.12	1.58	IV.	2	17.346	43 35.8	8.8	4.4	41 43.67	47 9.0
8	6.7		16.6	33.5	51.1	8.4	25.7		17 43 51.07	+17.11	+2.63	IV.	4	48.082	-11 3.5	-8.2	-0.9	17 44 10.81	-27 14 32.6

CORRECTIONS.

Date.	Corr. of Clock.	Hourly rate.	m	n	c	Zenith Point.	Mic. Co.
1846.	h.	s.	s.	s.	s.	° ' ''	r.
Aug. 5,	17	+ 9.142	+ 0.005	+ 0.294	+ 0.300	+ 0.230		
Aug. 10,	18	+ 10.877	+ 0.004	+ 0.294	+ 0.300	+ 0.230		30.002

INSTRUMENT READINGS.

	Date.	A.	B.	C.	D.	E.	F.	Mean.	Barom.	At.	Ex.	U.	L.	I.
		° ' ''						''	in.	°	°	°	°	°
Zone 40	1846 July 29, 19 40	70 09 60.6	62.0	74.1	64.1	55.4	45.1	60.22	29.956	75.0	70.5	75.5	75.5	71.1
	20 20													
Zone 41	Aug. 5, 17 15	66 24 61.0	62.1	73.8	63.4	55.0	45.1	60.07	29.944	74.8	71.0	75.2	75.8	78.2
	20 45	59.2	55.8	70.9	56.6	50.2	41.0	55.62	30.076	81.0	78.3	81.0	78.8	
	17 43								30.078	80.6	76.1			
	17 50	59.0	56.0	71.1	56.9	50.2	41.1	55.72				79.8	78.4	76.5

REMARKS.

(40) 2. Minutes assumed as 47 instead of 46, and Transits over T.'s IV and V as recorded over T.'s V and VI.

(40) 21. Minutes assumed as 28 instead of 27.

August 5. Hazy; moon bright.

(41) 3. Micrometer reading assumed as 15^r.961 instead of 16^r.961.

ZONE 42. AUGUST 11. P. $D_0 = -24° 32′ 20″$.

No.	Mag.	I.	II.	III.	IV.	V.	VI.	VII.	T (h m s)	a_1	a_2	Micr.	n	r	i (′ ″)	d_1	d_2	Mean Right Ascension, 1850.0	Mean Declination, 1850.0
1	8	18.0	35.0	52.0	9.0				17 38 9.01	+16.53	+1.24	IV.	3	26.023	−34 9.5	−64.4	−3.7	17 38 28.78	−25 7 37.6
2	8		22.5	39.5	56.0				40 50.31	18.52	1.29	IV.	4	44.665	14 38.0	63.7	1.9	41 16.12	24 48 3.6
3	6	29.5	46.0	3.5	20.5				45 20.32	18.50	1.28	IV.	4	41.770	17 39.7	62.6	2.2	45 40.10	24 51 4.5
4	9			16.0	33.0				46 33.02	18.50	1.25	IV.	3	23.700	36 35.2	62.3	4.0	46 52.77	25 10 1.5
5	10					4.0		38.0	45 46.96	18.50	1.24	VII.	3	20.000	40 26.8	62.5	4.3	46 6.70	13 53.6
6	9					34.0			48 0.06	18.49	1.26	·	FW	30.006	29 59.6	62.0	3.3	48 19.81	3 24.9
7	9		51.5	8.5					50 25.48	18.49	1.26	III.	3	29.293	30 44.3	61.4	3.4	50 45.23	4 9.1
8	9					53.5			50 19.53	18.49	1.25	VI.	3	24.950	35 16.6	61.4	3.8	50 39.27	8 41.8
9	9		54.0	11.0					52 27.98	18.48	1.28	III.	3	32.910	26 57.2	60.8	3.1	52 47.74	25 0 21.1
10	9				47.0	4.0	20.0		52 46.72	18.48	1.29	VI.	4	41.167	18 17.1	60.8	2.2	53 6.49	24 51 40.1
11	7	34.3	51.0	8.0	25.0				55 24.99	18.47	1.31	IV.	4	51.450	7 32.2	60.1	1.2	55 44.77	24 40 53.5
12	8	1.5	18.5	36.0	52.5				57 52.62	18.46	1.26	IV.	3	26.630	33 31.5	59.5	3.7	58 12.34	25 6 54.7
13	9							43.0	57 52.00	18.46	1.27	VII.	3	26.640	33 30.5	59.5	3.6	58 11.73	6 53.6
14	8					52.0			17 59 17.93	18.46	1.23	VI.	1	5.170	55 56.6	59.2	5.8	17 59 37.62	29 21.6
15	8					55.0			18 0 20.98	18.45	1.25	VI.	2	15.750	44 55.3	58.9	4.7	18 0 40.68	18 18.9
16	6	50.5	13.7	30.5					3 47.57	18.44	1.27	III.	3	22.780	37 32.7	58.0	4.1	4 7.28	10 54.8
17	7			15.5		50.0			4 32.71	18.44	1.23	VI.	2	8.430	52 33.9	57.9	5.5	4 52.38	25 57.3
18	10		34.0	51.0					7 8.00	18.43	1.27	III.	3	23.830	36 26.8	57.2	3.9	7 27.70	9 47.9
19	9					33.0		6.5	7 15.75	18.43	1.28	VII.	3	30.345	29 38.2	57.2	3.3	7 35.46	25 2 58.7
20	5	6.5	23.5		57.5				11 57.45	18.41	1.30	IV.	3	34.504	25 17.5	56.0	2.9	12 17.16	24 58 36.4
21	10		33.0	40.0					12 40.02	18.41	1.31	IV.	3	34.960	24 48.8	55.8	2.8	12 59.74	58 7.4
22	9	42.0	59.0	15.0					18 32.54	18.39	1.35	III.	4	53.387	5 30.7	54.4	1.0	18 52.28	24 38 46.1
23	7			6.0		39.0			19 22.48	18.38	1.29	V.	3	25.680	34 31.0	54.2	3.8	19 42.15	25 7 49.0
24	6						21.0	38.3	19 47.09	18.38	1.27	VI.	2	13.280	47 30.2	54.1	5.0	20 6.74	25 20 49.3
25	7				29.0	46.0			21 29.02	18.37	1.32	IV.	3	33.813	26 0.7	53.7	2.9	21 48.71	24 59 17.3
26	9					35.0	9.0		22 35.07	18.37	1.34	VI.	4	42.880	16 29.3	53.4	2.1	22 54.78	24 49 44.8
27	8						53.0		23 19.63	18.36	1.30	VI.	3	26.175	38 10.9	53.2	3.6	23 39.29	25 11 28.1
28	9				39.0	56.0			26 56.02	18.35	1.32	IV.	3	34.300	25 30.4	52.3	2.9	27 15.69	24 58 45.6
29	9					32.5	49.5		27 15.54	18.35	1.32	VI.	3	36.860	22 49.3	52.2	2.7	27 35.21	56 4.2
30	8		50.0			23.5			29 23.74	18.34	1.35	IV.	2	42.705	16 44.6	51.7	2.1	29 43.43	24 49 58.4
31	8	13.0	30.0	47.0	3.5				32 3.87	18.33	1.31	IV.	3	26.070	34 6.6	51.1	3.7	32 23.51	25 7 21.4
32	8		46.0	3.0	20.0				33 20.01	18.32	1.31	IV.	3	23.255	37 3.2	50.8	4.0	33 39.64	10 18.0
33	4	25.5	42.5	59.5	17.0				35 16.62	18.32	1.31	IV.	3	24.122	36 8.8	50.3	3.0	35 36.25	25 9 23.0
34	9	47.0	4.0	21.0	38.0				38 37.96	18.31	1.34	IV.	3	37.050	22 37.6	49.5	2.6	38 57.61	24 55 49.7
35	8		6.0	23.0	40.0				40 39.98	18.30	1.36	IV.	2	44.223	15 9.4	49.0	1.9	40 59.64	48 20.3
36	8			47.0	3.3	20.7			42 20.97	18.30	1.36	III	2	43.040	16 23.5	48.6	2.0	42 40.63	49 34.1
37	8	0.0	17.3	31.3					44 51.14	18.29	1.35	III.	3	35.990	23 43.9	48.0	2.7	45 10.78	56 54.6
38	9					0.0	17.3		45 0.17	18.28	1.36	V.	3	39.280	20 17.8	47.9	2.4	45 19.81	24 53 28.1
39	7			11.0	28.0				46 28.02	18.28	1.32	IV.	2	19.690	40 48.7	47.6	4.3	46 47.62	25 14 0.6
40	9				55.0	12.3			47 12.13	18.27	1.37	IV.	2	43.983	15 24.3	47.4	2.0	47 31.77	24 48 33.7
41	5	58.0	15.0	32.0	49.0				48 48.98	18.27	1.34	IV.	3	28.967	31 4.8	47.0	3.4	49 8.59	25 4 15.2
42	5	2.0	19.0	36.0	53.0				50 52.90	18.26	1.33	IV.	3	24.686	35 33.4	46.5	3.9	51 12.58	8 43.8
43	4	6.0	23.3	40.0	57.0				52 57.05	18.25	1.34	IV.	3	30.253	29 44.3	46.0	3.3	53 16.64	2 54.6
44	5	22.5	39.5						55 13.65	18.24	1.30	II.	1	7.320	53 40.6	45.5	5.6	55 33.19	26 51.7
45	9					35.0			55 17.98	18.24	1.35	V.	3	31.080	28 52.3	45.4	3.2	55 37.57	25 2 0.9
46	9							20.0	55 29.08	18.24	1.37	VII.	4	39.540	19 58.6	45.4	2.4	55 48.69	24 53 6.4
47	5							58.5	56 7.58	18.23	1.37	VII.	4	38.933	20 36.6	45.2	2.5	56 27.18	53 44.3
48	8					2.5	19.3		57 45.49	18.23	1.39	VI.	4	47.307	11 51.6	44.9	1.6	58 5.11	44 58.1
49	7					2.0	19.0		18 58 45.06	+18.22	+1.37	V.	4	39.467	−20 4.2	−44.6	−2.4	18 59 4.65	−24 53 11.2

CORRECTIONS.

Date.	Corr. of Clock.	Hourly rate.	m	n	c	Zenith Point.	Mic. Co.
	h. s.	s.	s.	s.	s.	r.	
1846. Aug. 11.	18 + 10.685	− 0.003	+ 0.204	+ 0.300	+ 0.230		

REMARKS.

(42) 21. Transits over T.'s III and IV assumed as recorded over T.'s II and III.

(42) 27. Micrometer reading assumed as 22r.175, not 26r.175, to agree with Mer. Cir. Z. 1847, Aug. 30; Mural Z. 1848, Aug. 16; and Arg. Z. 220:127 and 309:57.

(42) 37. Transit over T. III assumed as 34s.3, not 31s.3.

INSTRUMENT READINGS.

Date.	CIRCLE.							Barom.	THERMOM.				
	A.	B.	C.	D.	E.	F.	Mean.		At.	Ex.	U.	L.	I.
Zone 42 1846. Aug. 11, 17 35	63 54 66.3	63.0	76.5	66.4	55.6	45.5	62.22	30.106	78.0	72.5		78.0	78.0
18 29								30.108	76.5	70.6			
19 30								30.110	75.2	68.0			
19 50	65.7	62.8	77.0	66.0	53.2	44.3	61.83	30.114	75.0	69.2			75.5

ZONE 42. AUGUST 11. P. D₀ = −24° 32′ 20″—Continued.

SECONDS OF TRANSIT

No.	Mag.	I.	II.	III.	IV.	V.	VI.	VII.
50	7							6.5
51	9	25.0		50.0				
52	7						50.0	7.0
53	7	43.0	0.0	17.0	34.0			
54	9							23.5
55	8			32.5	49.0	6.3		
56	5	58.0		32.0	49.0			
57	9	5.0	22.0	39.0	56.0			
58	9		5.5			56.0		
59	9						45.0	
60	9		47.5		17.0			
61	8				21.0	39.0		12.5
62	5	44.7	1.3	18.3				
63	4		42.0	59.0	15.0			
64	7		10.0					
65	8	19.0	36.0					
66	7		23.0	40.0	57.0			
67	8		45.0	2.0	19.0			
68	8	9.3	26.3	43.0				
69	8	59.3	16.0	33.5	50.5			
70	8					50.0		33.0
71	9			31.3				23.0
72	9							28.0

No.	Mag.	T.	a_1	a_2	Micr.	n	r.	i	d_1	d_2	Mean Right Ascension, 1850.0	Mean Declination, 1850.0
		h. m. s.	s.	s.			r.	′ ″	″	″	h. m. s.	° ′ ″
50	7	18 59 15.43	+18.22	+1.32	VII.	2	15.190	−45 30.1	−44.5	−4.8	18 59 34.97	−25 18 39.4
51	9	19 3 15.98	18.20	1.34	III.	3	24.255	36 0.4	43.5	3.9	19 3 35.82	25 9 7.8
52	7	3 16.15	18.20	1.39	VI.	4	48.297	10 49.5	43.5	1.6	3 35.74	24 43 54.6
53	7	6 33.96	18.19	1.36	IV.	3	34.480	25 19.1	42.7	2.9	6 53.51	24 58 24.7
54	9	8 32.43	18.18	1.33	VII.	2	13.730	47 1.5	42.3	4.9	8 41.94	25 20 8.7
55	8	10 49.28	18.17	1.39	IV.	4	38.500	21 5.2	41.8	2.5	11 8.84	24 54 9.5
56	5	15 48.92	18.14	1.40	IV.	4	44.680	14 37.0	40.6	1.9	16 8.46	47 39.5
57	9	15 55.91	18.14	1.41	VI.	4	50.060	8 58.7	40.5	1.4	16 15.46	42 0.6
58	9	20 39.23	18.12	1.38	V.	4	33.043	26 49.1	39.4	3.0	20 58.73	59 51.5
59	9	21 11.11	18.12	1.40	VI.	4	39.260	20 16.8	39.3	2.4	21 30.63	53 18.5
60	9	23 17.04	18.11	1.36	IV.	2	19.160	41 21.9	38.8	4.4	23 36.51	14 25.1
61	8	23 21.45	18.11	1.36	III.	2	18.240	42 18.9	38.8	4.5	23 40.92	24 15 22.2
62	5	26 35.30	18.09	1.38	III.	3	30.443	29 33.2	38.0	3.3	26 54.86	25 2 33.5
63	4	27 15.35	18.09	1.36	IV.	2	20.890	39 33.3	37.9	4.2	27 34.80	12 35.4
64	7	30 44.00	18.07	1.38	II.	3	23.623	36 39.7	37.0	4.0	31 3.45	9 41.7
65	8	32 10.01	18.06	1.37	III.	2	22.455	37 55.4	36.7	4.1	32 29.44	10 56.2
66	7	32 57.02	18.06	1.37	IV.	2	21.217	39 13.0	36.5	4.2	33 16.45	12 13.7
67	8	34 19.00	18.05	1.39	IV.	3	28.980	31 4.0	36.2	3.4	34 38.44	4 3.6
68	8	37 0.21	18.04	1.38	IV.	2	19.253	41 16.2	35.5	4.4	37 19.63	14 16.1
69	8	41 50.36	18.01	1.37	IV.	2	17.140	43 28.6	34.3	4.6	42 9.74	25 16 27.5
70	8	42 42.07	18.01	1.43	VII.	4	43.307	16 2.2	34.1	2.0	43 1.51	24 48 58.3
71	9	44 50.18	18.00	1.43	VI.	4	38.897	20 30.4	33.7	2.5	45 .	53 35.6
72	9	19 48 37.08	+17.98	+1.43	VII.	4	42.392	−16 59.6	−32.6	−2.1	19 48 56.19	−24 49 54.3

ZONE 43. AUGUST 11. P. D₀ = −24° 32′ 20″.

No.	Mag.	I.	II.	III.	IV.	V.	VI.	VII.
1	7			19.0	35.0			
2	8							32.0
3	8	48.5	5.7	22.3				
4	8	12.0	20.3	46.0	3.0			
5	9	14.0	31.5	48.0				
6	8	37.0	54.0	11.0	28.0			
7	8	29.0	45.5	2.5				
8	.		15.0					
9	9			38.0		11.5		
10	9			8.3				
11	8	1.0	18.5	36.0				
12	8					17.0	33.7	
13	7			47.5	4.5			
14	8				11.5			
15	.				33.0			
16	8	20.7		3.5				
17	8				17.0			
18	7						30.0	4.0
19	8	44.5			35.0			
20	6		28.0	45.0	2.2			

No.	Mag.	T.	a_1	a_2	Micr.	n	r.	i	d_1	d_2	Mean Right Ascension, 1850.0	Mean Declination, 1850.0
1	7	21 23 35.52	+17.46	+0.99	IV.	2	18.242	−40 19.6	−13.8	−4.5	21 23 53.97	−25 14 57.9
2	8	23 41.11	17.46	1.39	VII.	4	43.427	15 54.6	13.7	2.0	23 59.96	24 48 30.3
3	8	28 39.48	17.44	1.11	III.	3	25.545	34 39.4	12.9	3.8	28 58.03	25 7 16.1
4	8	30 3.07	17.43	1.11	IV.	3	25.523	34 41.0	12.7	3.8	30 21.61	7 17.5
5	9	33 5.21	17.41	0.92	III.	2	13.400	47 23.0	12.3	5.0	33 23.53	25 20 0.3
6	8	34 27.94	17.40	1.38	IV.	4	42.563	16 50.0	12.1	2.1	34 46.72	24 49 24.2
7	8	39 19.57	17.37	1.46	III.	4	46.873	12 19.3	11.4	1.6	39 38.40	44 52.3
8	.	44 49 .	17.35								45	
9	9	47 54.79	17.32	1.51	V.	4	48.713	10 23.5	10.2	1.4	48 13.62	43 55.1
10	9	50 25.25	17.31	1.62	III.	4	55.090	3 44.4	9.8	0.9	50 44.18	24 36 15.1
11	8	58 52.48	17.26	1.14	III.	3	25.490	34 42.0	8.7	3.8	59 10.88	25 7 15.4
12	8	21 58 59.83	17.26	1.04	VI.	2	18.510	42 2.4	8.7	4.5	21 59 18.13	25 14 35.6
13	7	22 6 4.49	17.22	1.51	IV.	4	46.913	12 16.8	7.8	1.6	22 6 23.22	24 44 46.2
14	8	11 11.51	17.10	1.42	III.	4	47.590	17 51.2	7.2	2.2	11 30.22	50 20.6
15	8	17 33 .	17.15								17 (52)	
16	8	20 20.50	17.14	1.39	III.	4	38.313	21 17.0	6.2	2.5	20 39.03	53 45.7
17	8	21 16.96	17.13	1.65	IV.	4	54.200	4 40.2	6.1	1.0	21 35.74	37 7.3
18	7	22 13.03	17.12	1.35	V.	3	36.115	23 36.3	6.0	2.7	22 31.50	24 56 5.0
19	8	25 35.24	17.11	1.19	IV.	3	26.600	33 33.1	5.7	3.7	25 53.54	25 6 2.8
20	6	22 27 2.06	+17.10	+1.51	IV.	4	45.820	−13 25.4	−5.5	−1.7	22 27 20.67	−24 45 52.6

CORRECTIONS.

Date.	Corr. of Clock.	Hourly rate.	m	n_0	e	Zenith Point.	Mic. Co.
1846.	h. s.	s.	s.	s.	s.	″	r.

REMARKS.

(42) 60. Transit over T. II rejected.
Aug. 11. 19h 50m, interrupted by clouds; 21h 23m, resumed sweep; wind fresh; the appearance of the stars indicate thin clouds, though none are visible; moon bright.

(43) 14. Transit over T. IV, assumed as recorded over T. III.

INSTRUMENT READINGS.

Date.	CIRCLE.							Barom.	THERMOM.				
	A.	B.	C.	D.	E.	F.	Mean.		At.	Ex.	U.	L.	I.
	° ′ ″						″	in.	°	°	°	°	°
Zone 43 1846, h. m. Aug. 11, 21 20	63 54 65.3	64.0	78.0	67.0	55.7	45.0	62.50	30.118	74.0	71.5			74.0
22 6								30.116	73.8	69.8			
22 27								30.120	74.0	69.0			

ZONE 44. AUGUST 12. C. $D_0 = -30° 48' 0''$.

No.	Mag.	I.	II.	III.	IV.	V.	VI.	VII.	T.	a_1	a_2	MICROMETER		r.	i	d_1	d_2	Mean Right Ascension, 1850.0	Mean Declination, 1850.0
									h. m. s.	s.	s.			r.	′ ″	″	″	h. m. s.	° ′ ″
1	8		28.2	46.5	4.0	22.5	40.2		17 22 4.29	+18.84	+1.78	IV.	3	23.573	−36 43.3	−59.4	−5.7	17 22 24.91	−31 25 48.4
2	8			44.5	2.1	20.5			34 2.57	18.81	1.67	IV.	3	36.581	23 7.1	56.4	3.7	34 23.05	12 7.2
3	7.8			50.0		32.2	49.5		39 13.91	18.80	1.67	IV.	3	36.781	22 54.4	55.2	3.7	30 34.38	11 53.3
4	8			14.0	32.5	50.5	8.5		41 32.38	18.79	1.73	IV.	3	27.238	32 53.4	54.6	5.1	41 52.80	21 53.1
5	7				14.5	32.6	50.0		42 14.39	18.79	1.70	IV.	3	31.989	27 55.2	54.4	4.4	42 34.88	16 54.0
6	8.7				13.0			7.2	44 13.12	18.78	1.67	IV.	3	35.384	24 22.3	53.9	3.9	44 33.57	31 13 20.1
7	8.9		54.2	12.1	30.5	48.0	6.0		47 30.18	18.77	1.54	IV.	4	48.768	10 20.4	53.1	1.8	47 50.49	30 59 15.3
8	8.9			53.7	11.7	29.5			49 11.63	18.76	1.74	IV.	3	23.923	36 21.2	52.7	5.7	49 32.13	31 25 19.6
9	9			16.0	34.0				50 34.00	18.76	1.58	IV.	5	43.551	15 49.8	52.4	2.7	50 54.34	31 4 44.9
10	8.9					48.0			52 45.03	18.75	1.52	V.	4	50.269	8 46.0	51.9	1.6	53 5.30	30 57 39.5
11	8.9								52 . .	18.75	1.52	V.	4	50.269	8 46.1	51.8	1.6	53 . .	30 57 39.5
12	7							4.7	54 10.47	18.75	1.86	VII.	2	11.290	49 34.4	51.5	7.7	54 31.08	31 38 33.6
13	8				4.5	23.2		58.5	56 4.64	18.74	1.82	IV.	2	16.151	44 30.6	51.0	6.9	56 25.20	33 28.5
14	7.8				0.7	18.2			58 0.46	18.73	1.53	IV.	4	47.259	11 55.3	50.6	2.1	58 20.72	0 48.0
15	8				56.5	14.3	32.5		17 58 56.47	18.73	1.61	IV.	3	38.061	21 34.2	50.3	3.5	17 59 16.81	10 28.0
16	8				15.7		52.5		18 0 16.07	18.72	1.80	IV.	3	16.446	44 10.1	50.0	6.9	18 0 36.59	33 7.0
17	9						29.5		4 52.47	18.71	1.73	VI.	3	23.971	36 18.0	49.0	5.7	5 12.91	25 12.7
18	7.8						51.5		6 15.47	18.70	1.70	VI.	3	27.289	32 50.1	48.6	5.2	6 35.87	21 43.9
19	7.8					31.0	49.5		7 12.22	18.70	1.68	V.	3	28.435	31 38.4	48.4	5.0	7 32.60	20 31.8
20	7		47.5	5.7	23.5	41.7			10 23.62	18.69	1.70	IV.	3	26.601	33 33.3	47.7	5.3	10 44.01	22 26.3
21	7			57.7	16.0	33.5			11 15.73	18.68	1.51	IV.	4	47.939	11 12.4	47.5	2.0	11 35.92	0 1.9
22	6.7		24.5	42.5	0.7		37.0		17 0.70	18.66	1.74	IV.	3	22.031	38 19.9	46.1	6.0	17 21.10	27 12.0
23	9					50.2	8.5		17 32.23	18.66	1.82	V.	2	12.819	47 59.1	46.0	7.4	17 52.71	36 52.5
24	8			42.5		18.5			20 18.50	18.64	1.53	IV.	3	44.846	14 20.6	45.4	2.4	20 38.67	31 3 14.4
25	8					54.2		28.0	20 35.17	18.64	1.47	V.	4	52.559	6 22.2	45.3	1.3	20 55.29	30 55 8.8
26	9							9.5	21 15.50	18.64	1.62	VII.	3	34.751	25 1.5	45.1	4.0	21 35.76	31 13 50.6
27	9			4.5	22.0				24 22.28	18.63	1.62	IV.	3	33.851	25 58.3	44.4	4.1	24 42.53	14 46.8
28	8					49.0	6.5	24.2	24 30.50	18.63	1.67	V.	3	26.802	33 20.6	44.4	5.2	24 50.80	22 10.2
29	8.9			15.5	34.0		10.0		29 33.84	18.61	1.73	IV.	3	20.605	39 49.3	43.4	6.2	28 54.18	28 38.9
30	8			27.5	45.2				31 45.39	18.59	1.64	IV.	3	30.546	29 25.8	42.6	4.7	32 5.62	19 13.1
31	7.8					12.8	31.0	49.0	31 54.79	18.59	1.80	V.	2	12.857	47 56.7	42.6	7.4	32 15.18	36 46.7
32	8		0.1	17.4	35.7	54.0	12.1		34 55.86	18.58	1.76	IV.	2	16.780	43 51.0	42.0	6.5	34 56.20	32 39.8
33	9					34.5			37 18.52	18.58	1.49	V.	4	46.996	12 11.3	41.3	2.1	37 38.59	0 54.7
34	8.9		22.5	40.7	58.0	16.5			40 58.43	18.55	1.55	IV.	3	40.539	18 58.7	40.4	3.1	41 18.53	7 42.2
35	9						6.5		41 30.61	18.55	1.50	V.	4	44.651	14 38.6	40.3	2.5	41 50.66	31 3 21.4
36	7					1.0	19.5	37.0	42 43.29	18.54	1.44	V.	4	53.202	5 41.9	40.0	1.2	43 3.27	30 54 23.1
37	9			22.0	39.5				44 39.79	18.53	1.63	IV.	3	30.220	29 46.3	39.6	4.7	44 59.95	31 18 30.6
38	7		32.5	50.5	8.7		45.5	3.5	48 8.97	18.51	1.49	IV.	4	46.888	12 18.3	38.7	2.2	46 28.97	0 59.2
39	6		47.0	5.0		42.5		16.0	48 23.62	18.51	1.58	IV.	3	34.849	24 55.7	38.7	4.0	48 43.71	13 38.4
40	8.9		48.5	6.5	24.3	42.1	0.5		52 24.40	18.50	1.53	IV.	3	39.521	20 2.6	37.7	3.3	52 44.43	8 43.6
41	6	33.0	50.7	8.7	27.0	45.0	2.8	21.0	54 26.88	18.49	1.60	IV.	3	32.885	26 58.9	37.1	4.3	54 46.97	15 40.3
42	8				3.0	21.0			58 2.99	18.47	1.56	IV.	3	36.346	33 49.4	36.5	5.3	58 23.02	22 31.2
43	8				44.0			28.0	58 44.02	18.47	1.56	IV.	3	36.399	23 18.6	36.2	3.8	59 4.05	11 58.6
44	8							30.0	18 58 35.96	18.47	1.61	VII.	3	29.252	30 46.7	36.2	4.8	18 58 56.04	19 27.7
45	8.9				35.7?		13.0		19 3 18.35	18.44	1.54	V.	3	37.062	21 40.3	35.2	3.5	19 3 38.33	10 19.0
46	7				12.0	30.0	48.0		4 54.05	18.44	1.50	IV.	4	42.681	16 42.6	34.7	2.8	5 13.99	5 20.1
47	9					14.5			8 38.58	18.41	1.49	VI.	4	42.524	16 51.8	33.9	2.8	8 58.48	5 28.5
48	8.9				6.6		43.0	0.7	11 6.62	18.40	1.85	IV.	2	5.424	55 43.9	33.3	8.6	11 26.87	44 25.8
49	8.9			37.0					19 14 13.00	+18.38	+1.45	II.	4	45.806	−13 26.4	−32.0	−2.3	19 17 32.83	−31 2 1.3

CORRECTIONS.

Date.	Corr. of Clock.	Hourly rate.	m	n	c	Zenith Point.	Mic. Co.
	s.	s.	s.	s.	s.	° ′ ″	r.
1846, Aug. 12.	h. 20 +10.387	−0.009	+0.294	+0.300	+0.230	0 0 2.45	30.002

REMARKS.

Aug. 12. Cloudy horizon except S. and SE.

(44) 10. Transit assumed as 45ˢ.0 instead of 48ˢ.0, and as over T. IV instead of T. V, as recorded, to agree with Transit Z., June 3, 1846, May 28, 1847; Mural Z., June 17, 1847.

(44) 33. Transit over T. V assumed as 36ˢ.5, to accord with Mural Z., July 29, and Transit Z., June 3.

INSTRUMENT READINGS.

	Date.	A.	B.	C.	D.	E.	F.	Mean.	Barom.	At.	Ex.	U.	L.	I.
	1846, Aug. 12,	° ′ ″						″	In.					
Zone 44	17 20	70 9 60.3	61.0	71.8	61.0	51.6	48.9	58.27	30.098	79.8	76.5	79.1	78.5	
	18 0											75.2		
	18 17								30.108	78.2	74.3			
	18 30		60.3	60.0	72.0	60.3	51.8	42.9	57.88		73.7	77.2	77.5		
	19 3								30.100	77.0	73.2			
	19 30		59.6	60.2	72.1	61.1	51.6	42.9	57.92		73.0	76.7	76.7		
	20 0		60.0	60.3	72.1	60.9	51.8	42.4	57.92	30.094	76.8	72.5	76.1	76.5	77.7
	20 30		59.7	60.0	72.5	60.9	51.6	42.4	57.85	30.098	76.5	72.1	75.8	76.5	

ZONE 44. AUGUST 12. C. $D_0 = -30°\ 48'\ 0''$—Continued.

No.	Mag.	I.	II.	III.	IV.	V.	VI.	VII.	T. (h. m. s.)	a_1 (s.)	a_2 (s.)	MICROMETER.	r.	i	d_1	d_2	Mean Right Ascension, 1850.0 (h. m. s.)	Mean Declination, 1850.0 (° ′ ″)
50	7	..	..	..	40.0	..	16.0	..	19 14 40.06	+18.38	+1.48	IV. 4	43.020	−16 21.3	−32.5	−2.7	19 14 59.92	−31 4 56.5
51	8	..	49.7	7.5	25.2	..	1.5	..	17 25.50	18.37	1.56	IV. 3	33.740	26 5.3	31.8	4.2	17 45.43	14 41.3
52	7	..	11.6	29.5	47.5	5.7	23.5	..	19 47.58	18.35	1.48	IV. 4	42.610	16 47.1	31.3	2.8	20 7.41	5 21.2
53	8	..	..	..	21.5	39.7	..	..	22 21.59	18.33	1.62	IV. 3	25.656	34 32.6	30.7	5.4	22 41.54	23 8.7
54	6	..	..	..	..	..	..	29.0	22 35.00	18.33	1.51	VII. 3	37.410	22 14.7	30.7	3.6	22 54.84	10 49.0
55	6.7	..	58.0	16.5	33.7	..	10.5	..	35 34.20	18.26	1.55	IV. 3	32.934	26 55.9	27.7	4.2	35 54.01	15 27.8
56	8	..	12.7	..	..	6.5	..	..	35 48.59	18.25	1.48	IV. 3	39.738	19 48.9	27.6	3.2	36 8.32	8 19.7
57	8	..	..	22.7	41.3	..	..	36.0	40 41.35	18.23	1.54	IV. 3	32.999	26 51.8	26.5	4.3	41 1.12	15 22.6
58	8	..	..	38.5	56.2	..	32.5	50.7	40 56.48	18.23	1.56	IV. 3	30.456	29 31.6	26.5	4.6	41 16.27	18 2.7
59	9	..	..	..	1.0	19.0	..	..	43 1.00	18.21	1.55	IV. 3	31.235	28 42.6	26.1	4.5	43 20.76	17 13.2
60	9	..	..	25.5	..	3.5	..	41.5	45 45.44	18.19	1.65	IV. 2	20.000	40 29.2	25.4	6.3	46 5.28	31 29 0.9
61	7	..	..	..	..	20.5	38.7	56.3	47 2.59	18.18	1.38	V. 4	49.786	0 16.1	25.2	1.7	47 22.15	30 57 43.0
62	7	..	33.6	51.8	9.5	28.0	46.0	..	49 9.80	18.17	1.37	IV. 4	51.319	7 40.5	24.7	1.4	49 29.34	30 56 6.6
63	8.9	..	55.5	13.7	31.5	49.5	..	..	54 31.55	18.13	1.46	IV. 3	40.050	19 29.3	23.6	3.2	54 51.14	31 7 56.1
64	8.9	..	..	3.5	21.2	39.5	57.3	..	56 21.39	18.12	1.50	IV. 3	34.602	25 11.3	23.2	4.0	56 41.01	13 38.5
65	8.9	..	7.3	25.1	42.8	..	19.0	..	19 58 43.07	18.11	1.38	IV. 4	47.527	11 58.4	22.7	2.0	19 59 2.56	0 3.1
66	9	..	51.5	9.2	..	..	3.5	..	20 0 27.43	18.10	1.68	IV. 2	13.528	47 15.0	22.3	7.3	20 0 47.21	35 44.6
67	9	..	..	..	..	..	..	..	32	17.87	1.40			42	17		32	5
68	7	..	..	..	52.5	..	28.6	46.1	35 52.00	17.85	1.35	IV. 4	46.512	12 42.1	15.1	2.2	36 11.26	0 59.4
69	8.9	..	8.0	26.0	44.0	2.0	..	..	42 43.74	17.80	1.47	IV. 3	32.892	26 58.5	13.8	4.3	43 3.21	15 16.6
70	7	..	19.2	37.0	55.0	12.9	31.0	..	43 55.03	17.79	1.48	IV. 3	31.466	28 28.2	13.6	4.5	44 14.30	16 46.3
71	8.9	..	32.5	50.5	9.2	26.7	44.6	..	46 8.71	17.77	1.56	IV. 3	21.018	39 23.4	13.2	6.1	46 28.04	27 42.7
72	8	..	22.7	40.6	58.2	16.5	34.5	..	49 58.52	17.75	1.38	IV. 3	42.411	16 59.7	12.4	2.8	50 17.65	5 14.9
73	9	..	..	54.0	..	31.2	58.5	..	53 12.54	17.73	1.51	IV. 3	26.381	33 47.2	11.8	5.3	53 31.78	22 4.3
74	7	..	41.0	58.3	17.0	35.2	53.0	..	20 58 16.90	17.69	1.64	IV. 2	9.671	51 16.4	10.9	8.0	20 58 36.23	39 35.3
75	7.8	..	9.1	27.3	45.0	..	11.6	..	21 2 45.27	17.67	1.41	IV. 3	36.072	23 39.0	10.1	3.8	21 3 4.35	11 52.9
76	8	..	33.6	..	9.5	27.7	..	..	5 9.61	17.64	1.49	IV. 3	26.119	34 3.6	9.7	5.3	5 28.74	22 18.6
77	8	..	..	..	..	58.6	16.3	34.3	5 40.26	17.64	1.61	V. 2	13.156	47 38.1	9.6	7.4	5 59.51	35 55.1
78	7	..	29.0	47.0	4.8	22.8	41.1	..	8 4.95	17.62	1.48	IV. 3	26.298	33 52.4	9.2	5.3	8 24.05	22 6.9
79	6.9	..	20.7	38.5	..	..	..	..	11 56.67	17.59	1.54	III. 3	20.402	40 2.1	8.6	6.2	12 15.80	28 16.9
80	9	..	..	..	32.5	..	9.5	..	11 32.96	17.59	1.60	V. 2	13.621	46 56.4	8.6	7.3	11 52.15	35 12.3
81	8	..	..	..	37.8	..	13.5	31.5	11 37.52	17.59	1.57	IV. 3	16.621	43 59.1	8.6	6.9	11 56.68	32 14.6
82	8	..	..	..	43.5	1.8	20.0	..	13 43.73	17.58	1.53	IV. 3	21.465	38 55.5	8.3	6.1	14 2.84	27 9.9
83	8	..	..	7.6	25.0	43.0	1.3	..	17 25.25	17.55	1.36	IV. 4	39.708	19 45.4	7.7	3.2	17 44.16	7 56.3
84	8	..	..	..	..	30.5	49.0	6.8	18 12.67	17.54	1.54	V. 3	19.132	41 21.7	7.6	6.4	18 31.75	29 35.7
85	8	..	33.5	51.5	9.4	27.6	..	..	20 9.50	17.53	1.33	IV. 3	43.772	15 35.5	7.3	2.7	20 28.36	3 45.5
86	8	..	..	16.0	34.0	52.2	..	..	27 34.07	17.47	1.48	IV. 3	24.915	35 19.0	6.1	5.5	27 53.02	23 30.6
87	8.9	..	..	..	11.2	..	..	..	28 13.13	17.46	1.50	V. 3	22.701	37 37.8	6.0	5.9	28 32.00	31 25 49.7
88	7.8	..	..	52.0	10.0	..	45.7	..	30 9.93	17.45	1.26	IV. 3	48.578	10 32.4	5.7	1.8	30 28.64	30 58 39.9
89	5.6	42.2	0.6	18.5	36.4	54.7	12.6	30.5	21 38 36.51	+17.38	+1.57	IV. 2	13.586	−47 11.4	−4.5	−7.3	21 38 55.46	−31 35 23.2

CORRECTIONS.

Date.	Corr. of Clock.	Hourly rate.	m	n	t	Zenith Point.	Mic. Co.
1846. h.	s.	s.	s.	s.	s.	° ′ ″	r.

INSTRUMENT READINGS.

Date.	CIRCLE.							Barom.	THERMOM.				
		A.	B.	C.	D.	E.	F.	Mean.		At.	Ex.	U.	L.	I.
Zone 44	1846, Aug. 12, 20 58	° ′ ″						″	in.	°	° 72.1	°	°	°
	21 30	70 9 59.5	60.0	71.9	61.2	51.8	42.1	57.78	30.088	76.0	71.5	75.2	75.6	77.4

ZONE 45. AUGUST 13. P. D_o = −27° 3′ 0″—Continued.

No.	Mag.	I.	II.	III.	IV.	V.	VI.	VII.	T. (h. m. s.)	a_1	a_2	Mic.	n	r.	i	d_1	d_2	Mean Right Ascension, 1850.0	Mean Declination, 1850.0
1	7			50.3	7.7				17 53 7.71	+18.18	+2.07	IV.	2	15.820	−44 51.2	−32.1	−4.9	17 53 27.96	−27 48 28.2
2	8			21.0	38.0				54 38.19	18.18	1.78	IV.	4	39.862	19 39.5	31.8	2.1	54 58.15	23 13.4
3	8				17.0	34.0			55 34.21	18.17	2.08	IV.	2	14.160	46 35.4	31.6	5.1	55 54.46	50 12.1
4	7			11.0		45.5			56 28.24	18.17	1.85	V.	3	33.600	26 14.2	31.3	2.8	56 48.26	29 48.3
5	8	48.0	5.0						58 40.17	18.16	1.95	II.	3	24.325	35 55.8	30.7	3.9	59 0.28	39 30.4
6	8				48.0				58 48.03	18.16	2.17	IV.	2	6.760	49 6.4	30.7	5.3	59 8.36	52 42.4
7	7					25.0			59 7.55	18.16	2.04	V.	2	16.240	44 24.9	30.6	4.8	59 27.75	48 0.3
8	8						5.0		17 59 30.26	18.16	2.00	VI.	2	19.020	41 30.3	30.5	4.5	17 59 50.42	45 5.3
9	9			18.0	35.0				18 3 35.15	18.14	1.62	IV.	4	47.875	11 16.4	29.5	1.2	18 3 54.91	14 47.1
10	7			8.5	25.7				4 25.81	18.14	1.84	IV.	3	31.293	28 39.0	29.3	3.1	4 45.79	32 11.4
11	7	46.5	3.7	21.0					6 38.41	18.13	1.77	III.	3	35.893	23 50.1	28.8	2.5	6 58.31	27 21.4
12	7				11.5				6 11.54	18.13	1.97	IV.	2	18.736	41 48.5	28.9	4.5	6 31.64	45 21.9
13	5			49.0					8 49.00	18.12	2.08	III.	1	9.730	51 9.6	28.4	5.6	9 9.20	54 43.6
14	8					42.0			8 7.38	18.12	1.72	VI.	4	38.893	20 39.7	28.4	2.2	8 27.22	24 10.3
15	9				58.0				9 58.05	18.12	1.83	IV.	3	29.935	30 4.0	28.0	3.2	10 18.00	33 35.2
16	7				36.5		11.0		10 36.44	18.12	1.76	IV.	3	35.420	24 20.1	27.8	2.6	10 56.32	27 50.5
17	8	49.3	6.3	24.0	41.3				13 41.26	18.10	1.82	IV.	3	29.300	30 44.1	27.0	3.3	14 1.18	34 14.4
18	8					50.0			22 32.66	18.06	1.60	V.	4	43.495	15 51.2	24.0	1.7	22 52.32	19 17.6
19	7		15.3	32.5					25 49.92	18.05	1.68	IV.	3	35.900	23 49.7	24.0	2.6	26 9.65	27 16.3
20	9						59.0		26 24.40	18.05	1.57	VI.	4	44.437	14 51.6	23.9	1.6	26 44.02	18 17.3
21	9				50.0				30 50.05	18.03	1.80	IV.	3	23.467	36 49.9	22.8	4.0	31 9.88	40 16.7
22	8				4.0				32 4.05	18.02	1.72	IV.	3	28.713	31 20.8	22.5	3.3	32 23.79	34 46.6
23	9					28.0			33 10.04	18.02	1.86	V.	2	16.845	43 46.8	22.2	4.7	33 29.92	47 13.7
24	4	5.5	23.0	40.0					35 57.47	18.01	1.41	III.	4	53.917	4 57.3	21.5	0.5	36 16.89	8 19.3
25	7						37.0		36 19.59	18.00	1.75	V.	3	24.503	35 39.3	21.4	3.8	36 39.34	39 4.5
26	8			56.0		30.3			38 13.15	17.99	1.45	V.	4	47.950	11 11.4	21.0	1.2	38 32.59	14 33.6
27	8			38.0	55.0				39 55.17	17.99	1.48	IV.	4	45.360	13 54.5	20.5	1.5	40 14.64	17 16.5
28	7	53.0	10.0	27.3	45.0				41 44.82	17.98	1.51	IV.	4	42.800	16 35.0	20.1	1.8	42 4.31	19 56.9
29	8		49.0	6.3	24.0				43 23.86	17.97	1.92	IV.	1	8.400	52 33.2	19.7	5.7	43 43.75	55 58.6
30	9						21.0		47 3.63	17.95	1.55	V.	4	36.943	22 44.3	18.8	2.4	47 23.13	25 5.5
31	9						21.0	38.5	47 40.34	17.95	1.69	VI.	3	24.880	35 21.0	18.6	3.8	48 5.98	38 43.4
32	9							29.0	49 36.97	17.94	1.50	VII.	4	40.345	19 8.1	18.2	2.0	49 56.41	22 28.3
33	9			2.0					53 19.37	17.92	1.60	III.	3	29.520	30 30.1	17.2	3.3	53 38.89	33 50.6
34	7.8	46.5	4.0	21.0	38.5				55 38.54	17.90	1.57	IV.	3	32.650	27 13.8	16.4	2.9	55 58.01	30 33.1
35	3.4						50.0	7.0	18 57 14.98	17.90	1.82	VI.	2	11.157	49 43.1	16.3	5.4	18 57 34.70	53 4.8
36	7			47.0	4.0				19 0 4.19	17.89	1.42	IV.	4	41.852	17 34.5	15.6	1.9	19 0 23.50	20 52.0
37	9			36.0		10.5			1 53.25	17.88	1.38	III.	4	43.670	15 40.6	15.1	1.6	2 12.51	18 57.3
38	8			41.0	58.0				3 58.21	17.87	1.61	IV.	3	25.000	35 13.7	14.6	3.8	4 17.69	38 32.1
39	8				49.0				4 49.05	17.86	1.60	IV.	3	25.707	34 29.3	14.4	3.7	5 8.51	37 47.4
40	8						34.5	52.0	4 59.57	17.86	1.56	VI.	3	29.042	31 0.0	14.4	3.3	5 19.29	34 17.7
41	8		27.0	44.0					8 1.54	17.84	1.51	III.	3	32.270	27 37.6	13.6	3.0	8 20.89	30 54.0
42	9						24.0		13 49.28	17.82	1.56	VI.	2	24.725	35 32.6	12.3	3.8	14 8.66	38 46.7
43	8	20.0	38.0						20 12.45	17.79	1.58	II.	2	19.460	41 3.1	10.7	4.4	20 31.81	44 18.2
44	8			6.5					20 23.87	17.78	1.52	III.	2	24.420	35 52.2	10.7	3.8	20 43.17	39 6.7
45	5						50.0	7.3	20 15.35	17.78	1.28	VI.	4	45.195	14 4.1	10.7	1.5	20 34.41	17 16.3
46	8	35.0	52.0	8.5					23 26.50	17.76	1.35	III.	3	36.995	22 40.9	10.0	2.9	23 45.61	25 53.3
47	8	14.5	32.0						25 49.28	17.75	1.38	III.	3	34.763	25 1.0	9.5	2.7	25 8.41	28 13.2
48	9					14.0	31.0		24 56.47	17.75	1.39	V.	3	34.260	25 32.9	9.6	2.7	25 15.61	28 45.2
49	9			3.0					19 27 20.38	+17.74	+1.62	III.	1	14.280	−46 25.0	−9.0	−5.0	19 27 39.74	−27 49 39.0

CORRECTIONS.

Date.		Corr. of Clock.	Hourly rate.	m	n	c	Zenith Point.	Mic. Co.
1846. Aug. 13,	h. 20	s. +10.132	s. −0.012	s. +0.294	s. +0.300	s. +0.230	° ′ ″	r.

INSTRUMENT READINGS.

	Date.	A.	B.	C.	D.	E.	F.	Mean.	Barom.	At.	Ex.	U.	L.	I.
	1846. h. m.	° ′ ″						″	in.	°	°	°	°	°
Zone 45	Aug. 13, 17 50	66 24 67.3	62.6	78.8	64.2	56.6	48.5	63.00	29.994	82.5	79.0			
	17 59								29.990	82.0	78.8			
	18 43								30.000	81.0	77.5			
	19 45								29.996	80.0	77.0			
	19 50	66.5	62.6	78.7	64.2	56.7	46.7	62.57				78.5		79.5

REMARKS.

(45) 3. Transits over T.'s III and IV assumed as recorded over T.'s IV and V.

(45) 6. Micrometer reading assumed as 4ʳ.760 instead of 0ʳ.760.

(45) 13. Transits over T. IV assumed as recorded over T. III, and minutes as 7 instead of 8.

(45) 47. Transits over T.'s II and III assumed as recorded over T.'s I and II, and minutes as 24, not 25.

ZONE 45. AUGUST 13. P. D_0 = −27° 3′ 0″ —Continued.

No.	Mag.	I.	II.	III.	IV.	V.	VI.	VII.	T.	a_1	a_2	MICROMETER			i	d_1	d_2	Mean Right Ascension, 1850.0.	Mean Declination, 1850.0.
									h. m. s.	s.	s.			r.	′ ″	″	″	h. m. s.	° ′ ″
50	8	28.0	45.5	3.0	20.0				19 29 20.20	+17.73	+1.55	IV.	2	21.346	−39 5.0	− 8.5	− 4.2	19 39 29.48	−27 42 17.7
51	9				56.0		30.0		30 55.66	17.72	1.48	VI.	3	25.203	35 0.9	8.1	3.8	31 14.86	38 12.8
52	9		45.0		19.3				35 19.49	17.69	1.12	IV.	4	52.510	6 25.6	7.1	0.7	35 38.30	9 33.4
53	8						15.0		35 40.26	17.69	1.53	VI.	2	18.620	41 55.4	7.1	4.5	35 59.48	45 7.0
54	7					2.0	19.0		36 44.44	17.69	1.44	V.	3	25.765	34 25.7	6.8	3.7	37 3.57	37 36.2
55	7		16.0	33.0					40 50.51	17.67	1.05	III.	4	56.587	2 10.6	5.8	0.2	41 9.23	5 16.6
56	7		33.0	50.0					42 7.52	17.65	1.29	III.	3	35.400	24 21.2	5.5	2.6	42 26.46	27 29.3
57	7							25.0	41 35.81	17.66	1.57	VII.	1	13.110	47 37.5	5.7	5.2	41 55.04	50 48.4
58	8			36.0		28.0			43 53.36	17.65	1.19	VI.	2	42.987	16 22.7	5.1	1.8	44 12.20	19 29.6
59	9				35.0				45 35.04	17.63	1.30	IV.	3	33.235	26 37.1	4.7	2.9	45 53.97	29 44.7
60	4.5		50.0	7.7	25.0				19 47 24.94	+17.62	+1.33	IV.	3	29.390	−30 38.5	− 4.3	− 3.3	19 47 43.89	−27 33 46.1

ZONE 46. AUGUST 13. P. D_0 = −23° 17′ 0″.

No.	Mag.	I.	II.	III.	IV.	V.	VI.	VII.	T.	a_1	a_2	MICROMETER			i	d_1	d_2	Mean Right Ascension, 1850.0.	Mean Declination, 1850.0.
									h. m. s.	s.	s.			r.	′ ″	″	″	h. m. s.	° ′ ″
1	8						59.0	16.0	20 3 25.43	+17.26	+1.51	VII.	3	24.913	−35 18.8	−37.2	+ 3.0	20 3 44.20	−23 52 59.0
2	7	7.0	25.0			14.0			6 57.77	17.24	1.47	VI.	3	20.280	40 9.7	36.4	3.5	7 16.48	57 49.6
3	7	27.0		1.0					12 17.66	17.21	1.49	III.	2	21.260	39 10.3	35.2	3.4	12 36.36	56 49.9
4	7	17.0	34.0		7.7				15 7.64	17.19	1.50	IV.	2	20.865	39 34.9	34.6	3.4	15 26.33	57 12.9
5	9	8.5	25.3	42.3	58.7				17 58.88	17.18	1.70	IV.	4	46.550	12 39.7	34.0	1.0	19 17.76	30 14.7
6	6			12.0	29.0				20 29.88	17.16	1.78	IV.	4	55.950	2 50.4	33.4	0.2	20 47.82	20 24.0
7	8		25.0	41.7	58.5				24 58.57	17.14	1.60	IV.	3	32.055	27 51.1	32.5	2.4	25 17.31	45 26.0
8	9					18.5			26 18.54	17.14	1.50	IV.	2	20.420	40 3.0	32.2	3.5	26 37.18	57 38.7
9	8		21.0	38.0					30 54.72	17.12	1.70	III.	4	43.525	15 49.8	31.3	1.3	31 13.54	33 22.4
10	7	55.0	11.5	28.3					32 45.19	17.10	1.65	III.	3	37.200	22 28.2	30.9	1.9	33 3.94	40 1.0
11	8						38.0		33 4.47	17.10	1.72	VI.	4	44.916	14 21.6	30.8	1.2	33 23.29	23 31 53.6
12	8						5.0	22.3	34 31.54	17.09	1.50	II.	2	17.837	42 44.5	30.5	3.7	34 50.13	24 0 18.7
13	8						6.0		35 32.41	17.09	1.63	VI.	3	33.850	25 55.3	30.3	2.2	35 51.13	23 43 30.8
14	8	52.0	9.0	26.0					38 43.69	17.07	1.49	III.	2	16.940	43 41.0	29.7	3.8	39 2.25	21 1 14.5
15	8		45.3						46 2.10	17.03	1.80	III.	4	51.460	7 31.7	28.2	0.6	46 20.03	23 25 0.5
16	7		17.0	33.0					57 50.23	16.96	1.63	III.	3	28.757	31 17.9	26.0	2.7	58 8.82	48 46.6
17	7	11.0		45.0		19.0			20 58 1.79	16.96	1.66	V.	3	32.513	27 22.4	26.0	2.3	20 58 20.41	44 50.7
18	8	49.0	6.0	23.0	39.7				21 1 39.68	16.94	1.58	IV.	3	22.060	37 24.3	25.3	3.2	21 1 58.20	54 52.8
19	6		52.1	10.5	27.5				4 26.83	16.92	1.84	IV.	4	53.835	5 2.3	24.8	0.4	4 45.59	22 27.5
20	8				34.0				5 34.01	16.92	1.78	IV.	4	47.003	12 11.2	24.6	1.0	5 52.71	29 36.8
21	6	23.3	40.0	57.0					15 13.65	16.86	1.84	III.	4	53.150	5 45.6	22.9	0.4	15 32.35	23 8.9
22	7						44.0	59.0	15 26.24	16.86	1.60	V.	2	22.995	38 24.0	22.8	3.2	15 44.70	55 50.0
23	8		26.0						20 59.66	16.83	1.63	II.	2	23.995	36 18.6	21.9	3.1	22 18.12	53 43.6
24	8	31.0	48.0	5.0					23 21.61	16.81	1.71	III.	3	34.100	25 37.1	21.5	2.2	23 40.13	43 0.8
25	8	40.0	57.0	13.5					26 30.46	16.80	1.68	IV.	3	30.383	29 36.1	21.0	2.5	26 48.94	46 59.6
26	8			33.0		6.5			29 6.57	16.78	1.71	IV.	3	33.023	26 50.3	20.6	2.3	29 25.06	44 13.2
27	9			32.0		6.0			31 5.65	16.77	1.65	IV.	3	25.173	35 2.9	20.3	3.0	31 24.27	52 26.2
28	4	19.0			52.5	9.5			33 9.46	16.76	1.63	IV.	2	21.523	36 53.9	19.9	3.4	33 27.85	56 17.2
29	9			50.3			26.3		34 9.28	16.75	1.67	V.	2	26.430	33 46.0	19.8	2.9	34 27.70	51 8.7
30	8	29.0	45.0		20.0				40 19.37	16.72	1.84	IV.	4	45.825	13 25.1	18.8	1.1	40 37.93	30 45.0
31	7	43.0	0.0	17.0	13.7				42 33.69	16.71	1.63	IV.	2	19.920	40 34.2	18.5	3.5	42 52.03	23 57 56.2
32	8		8.0		41.0				46 41.37	16.68	1.63	IV.	2	17.169	42 24.4	17.9	3.6	46 59.68	24 59 45.9
33	7							48.0	46 57.53	16.68	1.73	VII.	3	31.692	28 13.5	17.9	2.4	47 15.94	23 45 33.8
34	7				27.0				21 49 27.04	+16.67	+1.65	IV.	2	21.280	−39 9.1	−17.5	− 3.4	21 49 45.36	−23 50 30.0

CORRECTIONS.

Date.	Corr. of Clock.	Hourly rate.	m	n	ε	Zenith Point.	Mic. Co.
1846.	h.	s.	s.	s.	s.	′ ″	r.

INSTRUMENT READINGS.

Date.	A.	B.	C.	D.	E.	F.	Mean.	Barom.	At.	Ex.	U.	L.	I.
	° ′ ″						″	in.	°				
Zone 46 — 1846, Aug. 13, 20 0	62 39 61.5	58.7	71.3	59.0	50.0	42.3	57.13	29.996	50.0	76.7		78.5	79.5
20 57								29.992	79.0	76.5			
22 1								29.980	78.5	75.3			

REMARKS.

(46) 5. Min. assumed as 18 instead of 17.
(46) 15. Transit over T. III assumed as recorded over T. I.
(46) 15. Micrometer reading assumed as 21r.960 instead of 22r.960.
(46) 22. Micrometer reading assumed as 21r.995 instead of 22r.995.
(46) 23. Min. assumed as 21 instead of 20.
(46) 32. Micrometer reading assumed as 18 instead of 17.

ZONE 46. AUGUST 13. P. $D_0 = -23°\,17'\,0''$—Continued.

No.	Mag.	I.	II.	III.	IV.	V.	VI.	VII.
35	7				33.0	49.5		
36	7		24.0		57.0			
37	9			22.0				
38	9				11.0			

No.	T. (h. m. s.)	a_1	a_4	Micrometer		r	i (' ")	d_1	d_3	Mean Right Ascension, 1850.0	Mean Declination, 1850.0
35	21 50 32.85	+16.66	+1.81	IV.	4	41.537	−17 54.5	−17.4	−1.5	21 50 51.32	−24 35 13.4
36	51 57.37	16.65	1.62	IV.	2	17.304	43 18.4	17.2	3.7	52 15.64	24 0 39.3
37	21 57 38.83	16.62	1.71	III.	3	27.710	32 23.6	16.4	2.8	21 57 57.16	23 49 42.8
38	22 1 11.04	+16.60	+1.75	IV.	3	31.363	−28 34.7	−15.9	−2.4	22 1 29.39	−23 45 53.0

ZONE 47. AUGUST 18. C. $D_0 = -28°\,17'\,50''$.

SECONDS OF TRANSIT.

No.	Mag.	I.	II.	III.	IV.	V.	VI.	VII.
1	7.8		28.1	45.7	3.5	21.1	38.6	
2	6.7		33.5	51.0	8.5	26.4	43.7	
3	8		9.0	26.5	44.5	1.5		
4	7.8			25.1	43.5	0.5		
5	7		0.7	18.7	35.5	53.5	10.6	
6	8			18.0	35.1	54.2	10.7	
7	6			55.5	12.8	30.4	47.9	
8	8.9			0.7	18.7		53.5	
9	8						15.7	32.5
10	7.8			25.5	42.5	0.6	18.0	
11	7.8			48.5	5.1	22.8		
12	8			8.7	26.2	43.8		
13	8				52.0	8.3		
14	6.7			58.7	16.3	34.4	51.5	
15	8.9		53.0		27.6		2.0	
16	8		44.7	2.2	19.7			
17	8						5.5	
18	8		59.0	16.2	33.0	51.3		
19	8.9		17.7					
20	7.8		17.0		52.0	9.8	26.8	
21	7.8		0.6	18.3	35.5	53.5	10.6	
22	8.9		14.0		48.5	7.0		
23	9			10.5	29.7		3.0	
24	9				23.0			15.0
25	9			3.4		38.5		
26	8.9						3.5	
27	8.9		29.5	17.0		23.0		
28	6.7		28.6	46.3	4.1	21.5		
29	8.9			53.5	10.7		46.6	
30	8.9		53.2	11.0	28.5			
31	7.8			48.0	5.5	23.1	40.5	
32	8					28.5		
33	8						32.5	50.0
34	8			47.5	5.5			57.7
35	8							40.0
36	8		57.0	14.7	32.0			
37	7		49.0			41.5	50.2	
38	8				52.0			
39	8					19.2	36.0	
40	8		48.0	6.0	23.0	41.0		
41	8			28.0	45.8	4.0	21.0	

No.	T. (h. m. s.)	a_1	a_4	Micrometer		r	i (' ")	d_1	d_3	Mean Right Ascension, 1850.0	Mean Declination, 1850.0
1	17 59 3.41	+16.15	+1.35	IV.	3	32.386	−27 30.5	−46.2	−3.4	17 59 20.91	−28 46 10.1
2	18 2 8.62	16.14	1.16	IV.	3	23.289	37 1.1	45.5	4.5	18 2 25.92	55 41.1
3	4 44.16	16.13	1.22	IV.	3	26.338	33 49.9	44.8	4.2	5 1.51	52 28.9
4	5 25.51	16.13	1.51	IV.	4	39.121	20 26.2	44.7	2.5	5 43.15	39 3.4
5	7 35.81	16.12	1.44	IV.	3	36.451	23 15.3	44.2	2.8	7 53.37	28 41 52.3
6	10 35.68	16.10	0.89	IV.	2	11.049	49 50.1	43.5	6.1	10 52.67	29 8 29.7
7	12 12.90	16.10	1.72	IV.	4	48.154	10 59.0	43.1	1.4	12 30.72	28 29 33.5
8	18 18.47	16.07	1.75	IV.	4	49.580	9 29.5	41.6	1.2	18 36.29	28 2.3
9	18 40.17	16.07	1.23	VI.	3	26.736	33 24.5	41.6	4.1	18 57.47	52 0.2
10	20 42.87	16.06	1.21	IV.	3	25.462	34 44.8	41.1	4.3	21 0.14	53 20.2
11	22 5.48	16.04	1.56	IV.	4	41.478	17 58.2	40.8	2.2	22 23.08	36 31.2
12	24 26.22	16.03	1.76	IV.	4	50.374	8 39.6	40.2	1.1	24 44.01	27 11.1
13	25 51.37	16.02	1.78	IV.	4	51.231	7 46.0	39.8	1.0	26 9.17	26 16.8
14	27 16.48	16.02	1.54	IV.	3	40.542	18 58.5	39.5	2.4	27 34.04	37 30.4
15	29 27.56	16.01	1.52	IV.	3	39.722	19 49.9	39.0	2.4	29 45.09	38 21.3
16	31 19.73	16.00	1.85	IV.	4	54.121	4 45.2	38.6	0.6	31 37.58	23 24.4
17	31 30.35	16.00	1.12	VI.	2	21.459	38 57.5	38.5	4.8	31 47.47	57 30.8
18	34 33.65	15.98	1.58	IV.	3	42.574	16 50.9	37.9	2.1	34 51.21	35 20.9
19	35 52.87	15.98	1.16	II.	3	23.262	37 2.4	37.5	4.6	36 10.01	55 34.5
20	37 52.04	15.97	1.79	IV.	4	51.353	7 38.3	37.1	1.0	38 9.80	26 6.4
21	40 35.71	15.95	1.35	IV.	3	31.995	27 54.8	36.4	3.4	40 53.01	46 24.6
22	44 49.03	15.93	1.21	IV.	3	25.630	34 34.2	35.4	4.3	45 6.17	53 3.9
23	48 28.56	15.91	1.13	IV.	3	22.071	38 17.4	34.6	4.7	48 45.60	56 46.7
24	49 22.58	15.91	1.33	IV.	3	31.078	28 52.4	34.4	3.5	49 39.82	47 20.3
25	51 30.93	15.89	1.18	IV.	3	23.913	36 21.8	33.9	4.5	51 38.00	54 50.2
26	52 25.37	15.89	1.25	VI.	3	27.320	32 48.2	33.6	4.0	52 15.51	51 15.8
27	52 47.33	15.89	1.25	IV.	3	27.620	32 29.4	33.6	4.0	53 4.47	50 57.0
28	57 46.34	15.86	1.22	IV.	3	26.821	33 19.4	32.4	4.1	58 3.42	51 45.9
29	18 59 11.09	15.85	1.10	IV.	3	20.721	39 42.0	32.1	4.9	18 59 28.04	58 9.0
30	19 1 28.48	15.84	1.35	IV.	3	31.951	27 57.6	31.5	3.4	19 1 45.67	46 22.5
31	7 5.49	15.80	1.16	IV.	3	23.182	37 7.8	30.2	4.6	7 22.45	55 32.6
32	9 10.96	15.80	1.59	IV.	4	47.746	11 24.5	29.7	1.4	9 28.35	29 45.6
33	13 57.29	15.78	1.12	IV.	2	21.694	38 43.0	28.6	4.8	14 14.19	57 6.4
34	14 5.18	15.77	1.11	VI.	2	21.203	39 13.6	28.6	4.8	14 22.06	57 37.0
35	14 51.26	15.77	1.19	VII.	2	24.622	35 38.6	28.5	4.4	15 0.22	54 1.5
36	21 32.13	15.72	1.52	IV.	3	39.361	20 12.7	26.9	2.5	21 49.37	38 32.1
37	22 24.08	15.72	1.66	IV.	2	46.172	13 6.9	26.7	1.6	22 41.46	31 25.2
38	22 34.42	15.72	1.46	V.	3	36.912	22 46.2	26.7	2.8	22 51.60	41 5.7
39	24 1.24	15.71	1.25	V.	3	27.446	32 40.4	26.4	4.0	24 18.20	51 0.8
40	26 23.29	15.69	1.07	IV.	3	19.272	41 13.0	25.8	5.1	26 40.05	28 59 33.9
41	26 45.91	15.69	1.06	IV.	3	18.659	−41 51.3	−25.6	−5.2	19 27 2.66	−29 0 12.1

CORRECTIONS.

Date		Corr. of Clock	Hourly rate	m	n	c	Zenith Point	Mic. Co.
1846. Aug. 18	20h	+7.043 s	−0.017 s	+0.294 s	+0.300 s	+0.230 s	0° 0′ 2.22″	r 30.016

INSTRUMENT READINGS.

Date	CIRCLE							Barom.	THERMOM.				
	A.	B.	C.	D.	E.	F.	Mean.	In.	At.	Ex.	U.	L.	I.
Zone 47, 1846, Aug. 18, 18 2	67 39 60.0	60.0	74.1	62.0	49.8	42.6	58.08	30.108	75.7	70.0	74.0	76.0	80.0
18 20										69.5			
18 40										68.8			
19 1		60.2	60.2	75.2	62.0	51.0	42.4	58.50	30.126	74.1	68.4		
19 21										68.0			
19 43										67.0			
20 1	59.8	60.9	75.2	62.5	51.7	42.1	58.70	30.130	73.8	67.2	72.8	73.7	
20 18										67.1			

REMARKS.

Aug. 18. 18h.20, clouds near horizon; 19h.1, clear.

(47) 35. Doubtless 4s in error; transit assumed at 44s.0.

Zone 47. August 18. C. D_0 = −28° 17′ 50″—Continued.

No.	Mag.	I.	II.	III.	IV.	V.	VI.	VII.	T. (h. m. s.)	a_1 (s.)	a_2 (s.)
42	7	·	41.7	59.2	16.8	34.8	52.6	·	19 29 17.02	+15.67	+1.13
43	9	·	·	14.0	·	49.0	·	·	33 31.47	15.65	1.07
44	6.7	·	36.5	53.4	11.6	29.0	46.5	·	38 11.41	15.62	1.24
45	9	·	·	·	·	·	28.0	·	38 52.82	15.62	0.99
46	7	·	·	·	·	·	7.5	25.5	39 32.46	15.61	0.87
47	8.9	·	14.7	32.2	50.0	·	·	·	41 49.88	15.60	1.27
48	8	·	·	·	14.5	32.0	·	·	42 14.45	15.59	1.14
49	8	·	·	·	·	40.0	57.1	·	42 22.17	15.59	1.22
50	9	·	·	·	·	·	·	3.4	43 10.82	15.59	1.66
51	9	·	·	6.5	·	·	·	·	48 24.08	15.55	1.08
52	8.9	·	·	56.5	14.0	31.5	49.0	·	49 13.94	15.55	1.00
53	7.8	·	26.5	43.5	1.7	18.8	36.8	·	51 1.46	15.54	1.08
54	8	·	·	16.5	33.5	·	9.0	·	52 33.85	15.53	1.81
55	8	·	·	49.2	7.2	24.3	42.1	·	57 6.93	15.49	1.32
56	7.8	·	·	29.0	46.1	4.0	21.8	·	19 59 46.44	15.48	1.22
57	8.9	·	19.5	·	54.5	12.5	·	·	20 1 54.70	15.46	0.89
58	8.9	·	·	·	·	13.2	·	·	5 55.56	15.44	1.14
59	9	·	·	·	·	·	·	20.0	8 27.37	15.42	1.57
60	9	·	·	·	50.5	·	·	·	14 50 ·	15.38	·
61	6.7	·	·	·	·	·	34.0	·	15 58.79	15.37	0.88
62	8	·	11.7	28.9	46.0	4.3	·	·	18 29.18	15.35	1.37
63	7.8	·	3.7	21.5	38.2	56.2	·	·	22 21.15	15.32	1.53
64	8.9	·	·	16.0	·	·	51.5	·	23 16.18	15.31	0.93
65	8	·	3.3	20.7	38.5	56.1	13.6	·	29 38.44	15.26	1.12
66	7	·	53.7	11.7	28.5	46.6	4.2	·	31 28.84	15.25	0.07
67	8	·	·	·	·	29.0	46.6	4.5	32 11.65	15.24	1.56
68	8	·	59.7	16.7	34.5	·	·	·	34 34.50	15.23	1.76
69	7.8	·	·	13.6	31.3	48.8	·	·	35 13.69	15.22	1.38
70	8	·	·	50.0	·	·	42.5	·	40 7.47	15.19	1.19
71	6.7	42.5	59.7	17.6	35.0	52.5	·	·	42 17.48	15.17	1.62
72	8.9	26.0	44.2	1.5	·	·	·	·	44 1.46	15.16	1.58
73	7.8	43.5	·	·	·	36.1	53.5	·	45 18.55	15.15	1.59
74	7	·	·	·	49.5	7.2	24.5	·	44 49.55	15.15	1.60
75	9	28.0	46.0	3.7	·	·	·	·	48 3.49	15.13	1.16
76	8	·	1.5	18.3	·	·	·	10.5	52 18.43	15.10	1.83
77	7	9.2	26.1	44.0	1.7	19.7	·	·	20 59 47.17	15.04	0.96
78	8	·	58.3	·	33.5	51.0	·	·	21 1 15.84	15.03	0.94
79	8	31.5	48.7	·	23.5	41.2	·	·	21 3 6.25	+15.02	+1.57

No.	MICROMETER		r.	i (′ ″)	d_1 (″)	d_2 (″)	Mean Right Ascension, 1850.0 (h. m. s.)	Mean Declination, 1850.0 (° ′ ″)
42	IV.	3	22.188	−38 10.1	−25.2	−4.7	19 29 33.82	−28 56 30.0
43	IV.	3	19.059	41 26.2	24.3	5.1	33 48.19	59 45.6
44	IV.	3	27.118	33 0.9	23.2	4.1	38 28.27	28 51 18.2
45	VI.	2	15.332	45 21.6	23.1	5.6	39 9.43	29 3 40.3
46	VI.	2	10.041	50 52.9	22.9	6.3	39 48.94	29 9 12.1
47	IV.	3	28.222	31 51.7	22.4	3.9	42 6.75	28 50 8.0
48	IV.	3	22.611	37 43.5	22.4	4.6	42 31.18	56 0.5
49	V.	3	25.926	34 15.5	22.3	4.2	42 38.98	52 32.0
50	VII.	4	46.147	13 3.7	22.2	1.6	43 28.07	31 17.5
51	III.	2	19.416	41 6.0	21.0	5.0	48 40.71	28 59 22.0
52	IV.	2	15.829	44 50.7	20.8	5.5	49 30.49	29 3 7.0
53	IV.	2	19.308	41 12.7	20.4	5.1	51 18.08	28 59 28.2
54	IV.	4	52.748	6 10.5	20.1	0.8	52 51.19	24 21.4
55	IV.	3	30.484	29 29.8	19.1	3.6	19 57 23.74	47 42.5
56	IV.	3	26.126	34 3.1	18.5	4.1	20 0 3.14	28 52 15.7
57	IV.	2	11.178	49 42.1	18.1	6.1	2 11.05	29 7 56.3
58	V.	3	22.622	37 42.8	17.2	4.6	6 12.14	28 55 54.6
59	VII.	5	41.918	17 32.3	16.6	2.2	8 44.36	28 35 41.1
60	·	·	·	·	·	·	15 (6)	·
61	VII.	2	10.342	50 33.8	15.1	6.2	16 15.04	29 8 45.1
62	IV.	3	32.936	26 55.7	14.6	3.3	18 45.90	28 45 3.6
63	IV.	4	43.071	16 18.1	13.8	2.0	22 38.00	28 34 23.9
64	IV.	2	13.056	47 44.5	13.6	5.9	23 32.42	29 5 54.0
65	IV.	3	21.649	38 43.9	12.4	4.7	29 54.82	28 56 51.0
66	IV.	2	14.296	46 27.0	12.0	5.7	31 45.06	29 4 34.7
67	V.	4	45.948	13 17.5	11.9	1.6	32 28.45	28 31 21.0
68	V.	4	50.008	8 57.0	11.4	1.1	34 51.49	26 59.5
69	IV.	3	33.461	26 23.0	11.3	3.2	35 30.29	44 27.5
70	IV.	3	24.411	35 50.8	10.4	4.4	40 23.85	53 55.6
71	IV.	4	44.248	15 4.3	9.9	1.9	42 34.27	33 6.1
72	IV.	4	42.341	17 4.1	9.6	2.1	44 18.20	35 5.8
73	IV.	4	47.472	11 41.9	9.4	1.5	45 35.29	29 42.8
74	IV.	4	47.882	11 15.9	9.5	1.4	45 6.30	29 16.8
75	IV.	3	23.545	36 45.0	8.9	4.5	48 19.78	54 46.4
76	IV.	4	53.649	5 14.0	8.2	0.7	20 52 35.36	28 23 12.9
77	IV.	2	14.285	46 27.6	6.9	5.7	21 0 0.17	29 4 30.2
78	IV.	2	13.008	47 47.4	6.6	5.9	1 31.81	29 5 49.9
79	IV.	4	46.299	−12 55.5	−6.3	−1.6	21 3 22.84	−28 30 53.4

CORRECTIONS.

Date.	Corr. of Clock.	Hourly rate.	m	n	c	Zenith Point.	Mic. Co.
1846.	h. s.	s.	s.	s.	s.	° ′ ″	r.

INSTRUMENT READINGS.

Date.	CIRCLE.							Barom.	THERMOM.				
		A.	B.	C.	D.	E.	F.	Mean.		At.	Ex.	U.	L.	I.
Zone 47	1846. Aug. 18, 21 0 h. m.	67 39 59.7	61.8	75.1	62.7	52.0	42.0	58.89	in. 30.138	72.0	66.5	72.6	73.6	79.3

REMARKS.

ZONE 48. AUGUST 20. P. $D_0 = -37°\ 4'\ 40''$.

No.	Mag.	I.	II.	III.	IV.	V.	VI.	VII.
1	9			53.0				
2	8				37.0		15.5	
3	9							33.0
4	8	10.3	30.0	49.3	8.5			
5	7	25.0	44.3	4.0	23.3			
6	9				57.0			55.0
7	8	2.5	21.7	41.0	0.5			
8	8				42.0	20.5		
9	8	38.0	57.0	16.7	36.0			
10	9			42.0				
11	7				33.0	52.0	11.5	
12	8	52.0	11.0	31.0				
13	9	10.0	30.0					
14	8				26.0	46.0		
15	8			33.0	52.5			
16	9							33.0
17	8	50.5	10.0	29.5	49.0			
18	7			31.0	54.0	13.0		
19	9				30.0			
20	8			18.0	57.0			
21	8		17.3	37.3	57.0			
22	7	57.0		30.0				
23	6	14.0	34.0	53.5	12.5			
24	8	49.0	9.0					
25	5		40.0		19.0			
26	7	39.0	59.0	18.0		57.0		35.2
27	7	40.5	0.0	19.0		58.0		36.5
28	3	1.0	20.5	40.0	59.2			
29	5						6.0	
30	7	45.0	4.0		43.0			
31	7	11.5	30.0		28.0			
32	9			54.0	33.5			
33	7						32.0	51.3
34	7		23.0	42.5	2.0			
35	8	50.0		29.0	48.0			
36	8			45.0	4.0	23.0		
37	7		1.0		40.0			
38	7	48.0		27.0	46.0			
39	7		54.3	14.0	33.0			
40	6			17.0	37.0			
41	7				19.0	38.5	58.0	
42	7	32.7	52.0	11.3	31.0			

No.	T. (h. m. s.)	a_1 (s.)	a_2 (s.)	Micr.		r.	i (′ ″)	d_1 (″)	d_2 (″)	Mean Right Ascension, 1850.0 (h. m. s.)	Mean Declination, 1850.0 (° ′ ″)
1	18 3 12.37	+16.25	+1.24	III.	4	47.280	-11 54.0	-22.9	-2.6	18 3 29.86	-37 16 59.5
2	3 36.85	16.25	0.99	IV.	3	26.083	34 5.8	22.8	8.9	3 54.09	39 17.5
3	3 54.14	16.24	0.97	VI.	3	24.373	35 52.9	22.8	9.4	4 11.35	41 5.1
4	10 8.53	16.21	1.26	IV.	4	47.865	11 17.0	21.3	2.3	10 26.00	16 20.6
5	10 23.27	16.21	1.07	IV.	3	32.295	27 36.2	21.2	7.0	10 40.55	32 44.4
6	10 56.96	16.21	1.24	IV.	4	45.883	13 21.4	21.1	2.9	11 14.41	18 25.4
7	14 0.21	16.19	1.24	IV.	4	46.437	12 46.9	20.3	2.8	14 17.64	17 50.0
8	15 1.24	16.18	1.30	V.	4	50.633	8 23.1	20.1	1.6	15 18.72	13 24.8
9	18 35.98	16.17	1.19	IV.	4	41.283	18 10.5	19.2	4.3	18 53.34	23 14.0
10	20 1.44	16.16	1.02	III.	3	26.735	33 24.6	18.9	8.7	20 18.62	38 22.2
11	20 52.17	16.16	0.99	IV.	3	24.117	36 9.1	18.7	9.5	21 9.32	41 17.3
12	22 50.07	16.15	1.17	III.	4	38.955	20 36.6	18.2	5.0	23 7.39	25 39.8
13	26 8.66	16.13	0.94	II.	2	19.166	41 21.3	17.4	11.1	26 25.73	46 29.8
14	26 26.30	16.13	1.11	IV.	3	33.120	46 44.3	17.4	6.7	26 43.54	31 48.4
15	28 52.46	16.12	1.19	IV.	3	39.875	19 40.2	16.8	4.7	29 9.77	24 41.7
16	29 34.68	16.11	1.03	VII.	3	27.250	32 52.5	16.6	8.5	29 51.62	37 57.6
17	36 18.93	16.07	0.99	IV.	3	23.330	36 58.6	14.9	9.7	37 5.99	42 3.2
18	37 53.63	16.07	1.36	IV.	4	53.653	5 13.8	14.7	0.7	38 11.06	10 9.2
19	39 10.57	16.06	1.15	V.	3	36.343	23 22.1	14.4	5.8	39 27.78	28 22.3
20	40 37.50	16.05	1.20	III.	4	39.617	19 55.1	14.0	4.8	40 54.75	24 53.9
21	42 56.61	16.04	1.18	IV.	3	37.723	21 55.3	13.5	5.4	43 13.83	26 54.2
22	44 55.31	16.03	1.09	III.	3	30.853	29 6.2	13.0	7.5	45 12.43	34 6.7
23	46 12.61	16.02	1.13	IV.	3	33.112	26 44.8	12.7	6.8	46 29.76	31 44.3
24	47 47.46	16.01	1.14	II.	3	34.280	25 31.1	12.4	6.4	48 4.61	30 29.9
25	48 18.89	16.00	1.28	IV.	4	46.333	12 53.4	12.2	5.8	48 36.17	17 51.4
26	50 37.37	15.99	1.31	III	4	48.332	10 48.0	11.7	2.2	50 54.67	15 41.9
27	50 38.53	15.99	1.31	V.	4	48.276	10 51.2	11.7	2.2	50 55.83	15 45.6
28	55 59.20	15.96	1.31	IV.	4	47.710	11 26.8	10.5	2.4	56 16.47	37 16 19.7
29	18 56 26.95	15.95	0.80	VI.	1	5.102	56 0.7	10.4	15.4	18 56 43.70	38 1 6.5
30	19 1 43.16	15.92	0.93	III.	2	16.203	44 27.3	9.1	12.0	19 2 0.01	37 49 28.4
31	2 9.10	15.92	0.97	V.	2	19.525	40 59.0	9.1	10.9	2 25.99	45 59.0
32	4 33.21	15.90	1.06	IV.	3	26.950	33 11.4	8.5	6.6	4 50.17	38 8.5
33	5 12.66	15.89	1.36	V.	4	51.720	7 14.8	8.3	1.3	5 29.91	12 4.4
34	9 1.86	15.87	1.39	IV.	4	54.093	4 46.2	7.5	0.6	9 19.12	9 34.3
35	11 48.19	15.85	1.17	IV.	3	34.862	24 54.9	6.8	6.2	12 5.21	29 47.9
36	13 23.40	15.84	1.26	IV.	4	42.933	16 26.7	6.5	3.8	13 40.50	21 17.0
37	25 39.87	15.74	1.42	IV.	4	55.870	2 55.4	3.6	0.0	25 57.03	7 39.0
38	29 46.18	15.71	1.01	IV.	2	21.028	39 24.7	2.7	10.5	30 2.90	44 17.9
39	31 33.13	15.70	1.36	IV.	4	50.000	9 3.1	2.4	1.7	31 50.19	13 47.2
40	32 36.75	15.69	0.98	IV.	2	18.300	42 16.0	2.1	11.3	32 53.42	47 9.4
41	33 19.00	15.68	0.91	IV.	1	12.493	48 16.9	2.0	13.1	33 35.59	53 12.0
42	19 41 30.95	+15.62	+1.04	IV.	3	22.620	-37 43.0	-0.1	-10.0	19 41 47.61	-37 42 33.1

CORRECTIONS.

Date	Corr. of Clock	Hourly rate	m	n	c	Zenith Point	Mic. Co.
1846.	h.	s.	s.	s.	s.	° ′ ″	r.

REMARKS.

Aug. 20. 19h 20m, hazy; 19h.30, cloudy.

(48) 41. Differs 5′ in d from Mural, May 27.

INSTRUMENT READINGS.

Date		A.	B.	C.	D.	E.	F.	Mean.	Barom.	At.	Ex.	U.	L.	I.
					CIRCLE.				in.			THERMOM.		
Zone 48	1846. Aug. 20, 18 3	76 24 65.5	62.5	80.3	67.0	55.0	45.0	62.55	30.092	76.5	73.0	76.0		75.0
	18 29								30.076	76.0	72.5			
	19 1								30.076	75.0	72.0			
	19 25								30.070	73.3				
	19 40	64.5	63.6	80.6	67.8	55.6	44.0	62.68	30.066	74.7	71.7			74.0

Zone 49. August 29. C. $D_s = -35°\ 49'\ 0''$.

Seconds of Transit and times:

No.	Mag.	I.	II.	III.	IV.	V.	VI.	VII.	T. (h. m. s.)	a_1 (s.)	a_2 (s.)
1	7.8	..	..	39.7	58.5	17.7	36.2	..	18 16 58.52	+16.88	+1.41
2	7.8	..	..	..	43.5	2.5	21.5	..	17 43.47	16.88	1.41
3	8	..	51.5	10.6	30.0	49.0	8.5	..	23 29.92	16.85	1.36
4	8.9	..	..	..	..	6.7	25.5	..	26 47.51	16.83	1.40
5	8	..	..	35.6	54.4	13.7	33.0	..	28 54.64	16.82	1.38
6	7	..	13.7	33.0	51.7	11.0	30.5	..	30 51.98	16.81	1.37
7	8	..	59.6	18.7	37.7	56.8	16.0	..	32 37.77	16.80	1.38
8	6.7	..	18.5	37.4	56.5	15.5	34.3	..	34 56.46	16.79	1.42
9	7.8	..	..	..	13.4	32.4	51.2	..	41 13.16	16.75	1.35
10	7	..	45.0	4.5	23.0	42.5	1.8	..	43 23.36	16.74	1.37
11	8.9	..	..	51.0	..	..	..	..	48 10.06	16.71	1.41
12	7.8	..	4.5	23.5	12.0	1.5	20.7	..	48 32.48	16.71	1.40
13	8.9	..	..	..	..	34.5	..	0.5	48 .	16.71	1.41
14	7	..	48.0	7.0	26.0	45.0	..	..	51 26.04	16.68	1.41
15	7	..	..	2.0	21.0	40.4	59.5	..	51 21.19	16.68	1.38
16	8.9	..	..	44.5	3.5	22.7	..	..	55 3.57	16.66	1.37
17	8.9	..	..	..	..	54.5	13.4	..	55 35.26	16.66	1.37
18	7	..	37.5	56.5	15.7	35.0	54.2	..	18 59 15.80	16.63	1.37
19	9	..	..	..	..	36.5?	..	13.5	19 2 16.73	16.61	1.37
20	8.9	..	10.0	..	48.0	..	27.0	..	5 48.37	16.59	1.34
21	7.8	..	16.2	35.5	54.2	13.8	32.8	..	9 54.50	16.56	1.36
22	8.9	..	7.5	..	45.5	..	23.2	..	11 45.44	16.54	1.40
23	8	..	7.5	..	45.5	4.7	23.4	..	13 45.52	16.53	1.39
24	7.8	..	..	12.5	31.0	50.5	10.0	..	18 31.46	16.49	1.39
25	8	..	..	27.5	..	5.7	24.5	..	18 46.55	16.49	1.41
26	8	..	54.5	13.5	32.3	51.5	10.6	..	21 32.50	16.47	1.40
27	9	..	..	..	11.3	..	..	..	28 11.35	16.42	1.38
28	8	..	17.7	..	55.7	15.0	34.5	..	30 55.94	16.40	1.34
29	7.8	..	9.5	28.5	47.5	6.4	25.6	..	32 47.51	16.38	1.39
30	9	..	..	41.0	0.0	19.0	38.5	..	44 0.08	16.28	1.34
31	7	..	..	..	52.5	12.0	30.9	..	44 52.65	16.27	1.35
32	7.8	..	57.6	16.7	35.8	55.0	13.8	..	53 35.78	16.19	1.36
33	8.9	..	..	..	34.0	53.2	12.5	..	54 34.12	16.18	1.37
34	7.8	..	38.7	57.5	17.0	36.0	55.0	..	57 16.86	16.16	1.43
35	7.8	..	..	13.0	32.0	51.0	9.8	..	57 31.94	16.16	1.42
36	7.8	..	14.4	33.4	52.5	11.5	30.5	..	19 59 52.50	16.14	1.42
37	6.7	..	..	..	2.5	21.5	40.6	59.7	20 1 2.37	16.13	1.36
38	9	..	8.5	27.6	46.7	6.0	..	..	3 46.77	16.10	1.36
39	9	..	..	7.8	..	44.7	3.5	..	4 25.94	16.10	1.39
40	7	..	14.5	33.6	52.0	11.0	50.0	..	10 52.24	16.04	1.41
41	8	..	..	..	..	29.7	48.5	..	11 10.41	16.03	1.38
42	8	..	29.5	48.0	7.7	26.9	..	..	17 7.58	15.98	1.40
43	7	..	..	31.5	50.9	10.0	48.8	..	18 50.77	15.96	1.42
44	8	..	..	54.7	13.5	32.6	52.3	11.1	23 13.72	15.92	1.38
45	9	..	..	..	54.0	..	32.2	..	27 53.97	15.87	1.35
46	8	..	21.0	39.7	59.0	18.4	37.5	..	29 59.12	15.86	1.35
47	8	..	..	..	..	45.5	4.5	..	30 26.34	15.85	1.39
48	8.9	..	..	..	45.8	..	..	..	33 45.81	15.82	1.42
49	7.8	..	..	..	..	9.7	28.7	47.6	20 34 50.08	+15.82	+1.39

Micrometer, corrections and positions:

No.	MICROMETER		r	i (' ")	d_1 (")	d_2 (")	Mean Right Ascension, 1850.0 (h. m. s.)	Mean Declination, 1850.0 (° ' ")
1	IV.	4	43.291	−16 4.4	−41.7	−3.4	18 17 16.81	−36 5 49.5
2	IV.	5	45.678	13 36.4	41.5	2.9	18 1.76	3 20.8
3	IV.	3	21.417	38 58.5	40.1	9.1	23 48.13	28 47.7
4	V.	4	38.868	20 41.6	39.3	4.6	27 5.74	10 25.5
5	IV.	3	28.701	31 21.5	38.8	7.2	29 12.84	21 7.5
6	IV.	3	23.671	36 37.0	38.3	8.5	31 10.16	26 23.8
7	IV.	3	30.467	29 29.6	37.9	6.7	32 55.95	19 14.2
8	IV.	4	48.740	10 22.1	37.3	2.1	35 14.67	0 1.5
9	IV.	2	12.701	48 6.7	35.8	11.4	41 31.26	37 53.9
10	IV.	3	22.249	38 6.3	35.2	8.9	43 41.47	27 50.4
11	III.	4	44.027	15 18.1	34.1	3.3	48 28.18	4 55.5
12	IV.	4	39.571	19 59.4	34.0	4.4	48 50.59	9 37.8
13	VI.	4	42.478	16 54.6	34.1	3.6	49 .	6 32.3
14	IV.	4	44.540	14 46.0	33.3	3.1	51 44.13	4 22.4
15	IV.	3	31.534	28 23.9	33.3	6.5	51 39.25	18 3.7
16	IV.	3	26.501	33 39.7	32.5	7.7	55 21.60	23 19.9
17	V.	3	24.998	35 13.8	32.3	8.1	55 53.29	24 54.2
18	IV.	3	26.014	34 10.1	31.4	7.9	18 59 33.80	23 49.4
19	V.	3	25.761	34 25.9	30.7	6.0	19 2 34.71	24 4.6
20	IV.	2	10.338	50 34.8	29.0	12.0	6 6.30	40 16.7
21	IV.	3	20.248	40 11.8	29.0	9.4	10 12.42	29 50.2
22	IV.	4	40.448	19 2.9	28.5	4.2	12 3.38	8 35.6
23	IV.	3	35.872	23 51.5	27.0	6.0	14 3.44	13 24.9
24	IV.	3	31.520	28 21.8	27.0	6.4	18 49.34	17 58.2
25	IV.	4	42.099	17 19.2	26.9	3.8	19 4.45	6 49.9
26	IV.	3	33.289	26 33.8	26.3	6.0	21 50.37	16 6.1
27	IV.	3	27.536	32 34.7	24.7	7.5	28 29.15	22 6.9
28	IV.	3	10.145	50 46.8	24.1	12.1	31 13.68	40 23.0
29	IV.	3	29.771	30 14.3	24.1	6.9	33 5.28	19 44.9
30	IV.	3	27.440	32 40.8	21.2	7.5	41 17.74	22 9.5
31	IV.	3	14.902	45 45.0	21.0	10.8	45 10.27	35 16.8
32	IV.	3	27.441	38 57.0	21.0	9.1	53 53.33	28 25.2
33	IV.	3	24.342	35 55.1	18.9	8.3	54 51.67	36 25 22.3
34	IV.	3	51.011	6 59.6	18.4	1.5	57 34.45	35 56 19.5
35	IV.	4	43.817	15 31.2	18.3	3.3	19 57 49.52	36 4 52.8
36	IV.	4	40.220	13 0.5	17.8	2.7	20 0 10.06	2 21.0
37	IV.	3	21.508	38 52.8	17.6	9.0	1 19.86	28 19.4
38	IV.	3	20.559	39 50.4	17.0	6.8	4 4.23	29 16.7
39	IV.	3	32.261	27 38.3	16.0	6.2	4 43.43	17 1.4
40	IV.	3	40.323	19 12.3	15.6	4.2	11 9.69	8 32.1
41	V.	3	26.453	33 42.7	15.5	7.8	11 27.82	23 6.0
42	IV.	3	35.031	24 44.3	14.4	5.5	17 24.06	14 4.2
43	IV.	3	43.504	15 52.5	14.0	3.4	19 8.15	5 9.9
44	IV.	3	26.786	33 21.6	13.2	7.6	23 31.02	22 42.4
45	IV.	2	14.089	46 39.8	12.3	11.0	28 11.19	36 3.1
46	IV.	2	16.718	43 55.0	11.9	10.3	30 16.33	33 17.2
47	V.	3	29.960	30 2.5	11.8	6.6	30 43.58	19 21.1
48	IV.	3	44.706	14 35.4	11.2	3.1	34 3.05	3 49.7
49	V.	3	27.511	−32 36.3	−11.0	−7.5	20 35 7.29	−36 21 54.8

CORRECTIONS.

Date.		Corr. of Clock.	Hourly rate.	m	n	c	Zenith Point.	Mic. Co.
1846. Aug. 29,	h. 21	s. + 7.935	s. + 0.010	s. + 0.273	s. + 0.347	s. + 0.230	° ' " 0 0 1.97	r. 30.010

REMARKS.

(49) 12. Transits over T.'s II–VII assumed as 10ˢ too large, to agree with Transit Z., July 10, and Lacaille 7939.

Aug. 29, 21ʰ 2ᵐ, interrupted by clouds.

INSTRUMENT READINGS.

	Date.	CIRCLE.							Barom.	THERMOM.				
		A.	B.	C.	D.	E.	F.	Mean.		At.	Ex.	U.	L.	I.
Zone 49	1846. Aug. 29, 18 23	° ' "						"	In. 30.072	76.5	75.5			
	18 30	75 9 65.1	65.0	80.1	68.2	58.1	46.1	63.77	..	..	..	76.6	75.9	
	18 48	..	..	..	..	..	..	..	..	..	75.0			
	19 2	..	..	..	..	..	..	..	..	..	75.0			
	19 18	..	..	..	..	..	..	..	30.070	76.5	74.7			
	19 30	65.1	65.0	80.0	68.9	58.1	46.0	63.85	..	..	..	76.1	75.7	
	19 44	..	..	..	..	..	..	..	30.075	76.0	74.8			
	19 59	..	..	..	..	..	..	..	..	..	74.5			

Zone 49. August 29. C. $D_0 = -35° 49' 0''$—Continued.

No.	Mag.	SECONDS OF TRANSIT. I.	II.	III.	IV.	V.	VI.	VII.	T. (h. m. s.)	a_1 (s.)	a_2 (s.)	MICROMETER.		r_1 ('')	i (' '')	d_1 ('')	d_2 ('')	Mean Right Ascension, 1850.0 (h. m. s.)	Mean Declination, 1850.0 (° ' '')
50	7.8	...	58.	...	46.5	5.8	24.8		20 36 27.32	+15.79	+1.35	V.	2	10.682	−50 13.0	−10.7	−11.9	20 36 44.46	−36 39 35.6
51	9	...	58.7	17.7	...	...	15.0		41 17.77	15.74	1.41	IV.	4	42.011	17 24.7	9.8	3.8	41 34.92	6 38.3
52	9	...	1.0	...	...	58.3	17.5		43 20.11	15.72	1.38	IV.	3	23.853	36 25.6	9.5	8.4	43 37.21	25 43.5
53	7	... 35.0	54.5	13.5	33.0	52.0	...		50 13.60	15.65	1.35	IV.	2	7.985	53 1.9	8.3	12.7	50 30.60	42 22.9
54	8	...	49.5	8.7	27.9	...	...		51 8.67	15.64	1.35	IV.	2	11.895	48 56.9	8.2	11.6	51 25.66	36 38 16.7
55	9	... 22.7	...	...	...	39.0	...		53 0.94	15.62	1.44	IV.	4	53.034	5 52.7	7.9	1.0	53 18.00	35 55 1.6
56	9	... 45.5	4.7	23.5	...	2.0	...		20 57 23.75	15.58	1.37	IV.	3	21.594	38 47.4	7.2	9.0	20 57 40.70	36 28 3.6
57	9	...	46.5	5.0	...	43.7	...		21 2 5.39	+15.53	+1.37	IV.	3	19.309	−41 10.7	−6.5	−9.6	21 2 22.29	−36 30 26.8

Zone 50. August 31. P. $D_0 = -25° 48' 0''$.

No.	Mag.	SECONDS OF TRANSIT. I.	II.	III.	IV.	V.	VI.	VII.	T. (h. m. s.)	a_1 (s.)	a_2	MICROMETER.		r_1 ('')	i (' '')	d_1 ('')	d_2 ('')	Mean Right Ascension, 1850.0	Mean Declination, 1850.0 (° ' '')
1	8	20.0	...	54.0	11.0	...	...		19 12 11.07	+17.11		IV.	2	21.070	−38 19.5	−4.4	−3.1	...	−26 26 27.0
2	8	...	...	29.0	47.0	...	...		21 46.57	17.05		IV.	4	44.733	14 33.7	2.1	0.7	...	2 36.5
3	8	...	...	22.5	...	...	...		19 23 22.54	+17.04		IV.	3	27.620	−32 29.4	−1.7	−2.6	...	−26 20 33.7

Zone 51. September 9. C. $D_0 = -32° 3' 10''$.

No.	Mag.	SECONDS OF TRANSIT. I.	II.	III.	IV.	V.	VI.	VII.	T. (h. m. s.)	a_1 (s.)	a_2 (s.)	MICROMETER.		r_1 ('')	i (' '')	d_1 ('')	d_2 ('')	Mean Right Ascension, 1850.0 (h. m. s.)	Mean Declination, 1850.0 (° ' '')
1	9	...	...	11.5	29.2	48.0	...	23.7	19 26 29.45	+13.15	+0.49	IV.	4	53.251	−5 39.2	−36.6	−0.6	19 26 43.09	−32 9 26.4
2	8	... 7.7	26.0	44.5	3.0	21.2	...		29 44.48	13.12	1.11	IV.	2	16.056	44 36.5	35.9	7.1	29 58.71	48 29.5
3	9	...	26.5	...	3.6	22.0	...		32 45.19	13.10	0.92	IV.	3	28.809	31 14.7	35.2	4.9	32 59.21	35 4.8
4	8	41.0	59.1	17.3	35.5	53.5	...		35 17.31	13.07	0.56	IV.	4	54.254	4 36.8	34.7	0.4	35 30.94	8 21.9
5	7	...	54.5	12.8	30.8	50.0	...		36 12.94	13.07	0.67	IV.	4	47.068	12 7.2	34.5	1.6	36 26.68	15 53.3
6	8	...	28.0	47.8	...	23.5			36 47.06	13.06	0.71	IV.	4	45.388	13 52.7	34.4	1.9	37 0.83	17 39.0
7	7	20.7	38.7	57.4	15.8	33.8	...		42 57.30	13.00	0.82	IV.	3	41.876	17 34.5	33.0	2.6	43 11.12	21 20.1
8	8	6.5	25.0	43.2	...	20.0	...		48 43.26	12.95	1.30	IV.	3	15.122	45 35.1	31.7	7.3	48 57.51	49 24.1
9	7	16.3	34.4	53.0	11.5	29.5	...		50 52.95	12.93	1.06	IV.	3	29.056	30 59.2	31.2	4.8	51 6.94	34 45.2
10	6.7	58.6	6.5	34.4	53.1	11.5	...		54 34.83	12.90	1.02	IV.	3	35.161	24 36.3	30.3	3.7	54 48.75	28 20.3
11	9	...	43.0	1.0	...				19 59 42.89	12.85	1.09	IV.	3	33.981	25 50.2	29.2	3.9	19 59 56.83	29 33.3
12	7	...	53.0	11.2	29.0	47.0	...		20 1 10.91	12.83	1.34	IV.	2	18.743	41 48.0	28.8	6.7	20 1 25.08	45 33.5
13	9	...	...	30.5	...				1 54.12	12.83	0.93	VI.	4	45.647	13 35.5	28.7	1.9	2 7.88	17 16.1
14	8	22.9	41.0	59.5	17.5	35.5	...		20 9 59.31	+12.75	+0.91	IV.	4	51.053	−7 57.0	−26.9	−1.0	20 10 12.97	−32 11 34.9

CORRECTIONS.

Date.		Corr. of Clock. (s.)	Hourly rate. (s.)	m (s.)	u (s.)	c (s.)	Zenith Point. (° ' '')	Mic. Co. (r)
1846.	h.							
Aug. 31,	21	+ 7.367	+ 0.006	+ 0.167	+ 0.294	+ 0.115	0 0 1.72	30.011
Sept. 9,	22	+ 4.777	− 0.021	− 0.356	+ 0.527	+ 0.022		

REMARKS.

Aug. 31. Haze and moon-light.
(50) 1. Micrometer reading assumed as 22ʳ.070 instead of 21ʳ.070.

INSTRUMENT READINGS.

	Date.		CIRCLE. A.	B.	C.	D.	E.	F.	Mean.	Barom. (in.)	THERMOM. At.	Ex.	U.	L.	I.
	1846.	h. m.													
Zone 49	Aug. 29,	20 11	...	...	...	...	...	...	...	30.084	76.0	74.3			
		20 30	75 9 65.1	65.0	79.9	69.1	58.1	45.8	63.83	...	...	74.0	75.6	75.3	
		20 43	...	...	...	...	...	...	...	30.086	...	74.0			
		21 2	65.1	65.8	80.0	69.0	58.4	46.1	64.07	30.088	75.5	73.5	75.5	75.3	74.7
Zone 50	Aug. 31,	19 20	65 9 65.0	59.2	76.2	61.6	53.8	43.5	59.88	30.132	81.0	76.5	77.0	...	81.0
Zone 51	Sept. 9,	19 20	71 24 63.0	64.0	78.0	65.9	53.1	45.1	61.52	30.228	74.0	66.0	72.4	73.0	78.6
		19 42	...	...	...	...	...	...	...	...	...	64.7			
		20 1	...	...	...	...	...	...	...	0.230	72.6	64.6			
		20 10	71 24 62.0	65.1	77.0	65.5	53.9	64.2	61.43	...	...	...	...	70.2	71.5

ZONE 52. SEPTEMBER 9. C. $D_0 = -32° 3' 10''$.

No.	Mag.	I.	II.	III.	IV.	V.	VI.	VII.	T. (h. m. s.)	a_1 (s.)	a_2 (s.)	MICROMETER		r.	i (' '')	d_1 ('')	d_2 ('')	Mean Right Ascension, 1850.0 (h. m. s.)	Mean Declination, 1850.0 (° ' '')
1	8		10.2		46.0	5.2	23.5		20 55 46.65	+12.26	+0.56	IV.	2	8.338	−52 40.0	−17.5	−8.5	20 55 59.47	−32 56 16.0
2	6				1.0	19.5	37.8	56.0	57 1.06	12.25	0.56	IV.	2	8.338	52 40.0	17.3	8.5	57 13.89	56 15.8
3	8.9					27.5	45.7	4.0	20 59 5.25	12.22	0.82	V.	3	37.036	22 38.5	16.6	3.4	20 59 18.29	26 8.7
4	8							55.0	21 0 0.17	12.22	0.73	VII.	3	26.061	34 6.5	16.7	5.4	21 0 13.12	37 38.6
5	7		14.0	32.2	50.5	8.6	26.7		6 50.41	12.14	0.82	IV.	3	37.118	22 33.4	15.5	3.4	7 3.37	26 2.3
6	6			18.8	36.7	55.0	13.6		8 36.86	12.12	0.66	IV.	2	16.458	44 11.4	52.2	7.1	8 49.64	47 43.7
7	9				55.0	14.2			10 55.47	12.10	0.75	IV.	3	26.283	33 53.4	14.8	5.3	11 8.32	37 23.5
8	9				22.8				16 22.81	12.04	0.94	IV.	4	48.979	10 7.2	14.0	1.3	16 35.79	13 32.5
9	7.8			8.5	26.8	45.0	3.5		18 26.85	12.01	0.85	IV.	3	36.539	23 9.8	13.7	3.5	18 39.71	26 37.0
10	8.9					31.5			19 13.10	11.99	0.63	V.	2	12.110	48 43.6	13.5	7.9	19 25.72	52 15.0
11	8.9					32.2			20 13.89	11.99	0.75	V.	3	24.964	35 15.9	13.4	5.5	20 26.63	38 44.8
12	8			20.2	38.7	56.5	15.0		22 38.51	11.97	0.96	IV.	4	50.202	8 50.6	13.0	1.1	22 51.44	12 14.7
13	9				56.5	14.8	32.3		24 56.34	11.94	0.90	IV.	4	43.228	16 8.4	12.6	2.3	25 9.18	19 33.3
14	8			41.5	0.0				28 59.89	11.89	0.86	IV.	4	38.721	20 51.2	12.0	3.1	29 12.64	21 16.3
15	8				45.5				29 45.56	11.89	0.77	IV.	3	28.621	31 26.6	11.9	4.9	29 58.22	34 53.4
16	8			33.6			28.0	46.1	31 51.54	11.86	0.78	IV.	3	27.529	32 35.2	11.6	5.1	32 4.18	36 1.9
17	9		42.0		18.7	37.0			34 18.67	11.83	0.64	IV.	2	12.162	48 40.5	11.3	7.8	34 31.14	52 9.6
18	8		15.8		52.2	10.5		47.0	37 52.21	11.79	0.76	IV.	3	25.585	34 37.0	10.8	5.4	38 4.76	38 3.2
19	9			54.0	12.0	30.2			50 12.07	11.65	0.95	IV.	4	46.882	12 18.7	9.2	1.7	50 24.67	15 39.6
20	6.7				57.5	16.0	34.0	52.1	50 57.60	11.65	0.96	IV.	4	48.129	11 0.6	9.1	1.5	51 10.21	14 21.2
21	7		59.0	16.8	35.0	53.5	12.4		53 35.34	11.61	0.66	IV.	2	12.951	47 51.0	8.8	7.7	53 47.61	51 17.5
22	7.8						56.2	14.8	54 20.04	11.60	1.00	VI.	4	52.309	6 37.5	8.7	0.8	54 32.64	9 57.0
23	8		3.3	22.0	40.5	58.0	16.6		21 57 40.10	11.57	0.94	IV.	4	44.821	14 28.1	8.4	2.0	21 57 52.61	17 48.5
24	9		48.2	6.9	25.2	44.0	2.0		22 3 25.26	11.50	0.69	IV.	2	16.068	44 35.7	7.8	7.1	22 3 37.45	48 0.6
25	9				44.0			58.7	22 5 2.79	+11.48	+0.97	IV.	4	47.968	−11 10.6	−7.6	−1.5	22 5 15.24	−32 14 29.7

ZONE 53. SEPTEMBER 13. P. $D_0 = -34° 33' 30''$.

No.	Mag.	I.	II.	III.	IV.	V.	VI.	VII.	T. (h. m. s.)	a_1 (s.)	a_2 (s.)	MICROMETER		r.	i (' '')	d_1 ('')	d_2 ('')	Mean Right Ascension, 1850.0 (h. m. s.)	Mean Declination, 1850.0 (° ' '')
1	8	49.0	7.3	26.5					19 25 45.12	+12.12	+0.34	III.	4	43.523	−15 49.9	−39.6	−2.6	19 25 57.58	−34 50 2.1
2	9					32.5			26 13.69	12.11	0.34	V.	3	35.077	24 41.5	39.5	4.4	26 26.14	58 55.4
3	7						51.0		27 13.64	12.10	0.34	VI.	4	55.808	2 58.4	39.2	0.0	27 26.08	37 7.7
4	7					52.0	40.7		19 28 33.22	12.09	0.34	V.	4	41.113	18 23.9	39.0	3.1	19 28 45.65	34 52 32.9
5	7	39.0	47.5	6.3	25.0				20 10 25.14	11.67	0.31	IV.	3	31.100	28 51.0	30.6	5.3	20 10 37.12	35 2 56.9
6	9			31.0	49.0			45.7	11 49.39	11.66	0.30	IV.	3	35.827	23 54.3	30.3	4.2	12 1.35	34 57 58.8
7	9	25.0	44.0	2.5	21.0				14 21.30	11.63	0.30	IV.	3	36.726	22 57.9	29.8	4.0	14 33.23	34 57 1.7
8	9							39.0	14 42.50	11.62	0.29	VII.	3	23.100	37 12.2	29.7	7.0	14 51.41	35 11 18.9
9	7		9.5	28.5	47.0				17 47.13	11.59	0.30	IV.	4	30.590	19 56.7	29.0	3.4	17 59.02	34 53 59.1
10	8			51.0	10.0				22 9.03	11.54	0.29	IV.	3	34.077	25 41.2	28.1	4.6	22 21.76	50 46.9
11	8	4.0	23.0						25 0.35	11.51	0.29	III.	4	45.107	14 10.4	27.5	2.2	25 12.15	34 48 10.1
12	8					36.0			25 17.12	11.51	0.28	V.	2	20.195	40 16.9	27.5	7.7	25 28.91	35 14 22.1
13	9						35.0		25 57.64	11.50	0.30	VI.	4	54.430	4 24.9	27.4	0.2	26 9.44	34 38 22.5
14	9				36.0				27 35.99	11.48	0.30	IV.	4	52.480	6 27.5	27.0	0.6	27 47.76	40 25.1
15	9.10		48.0						30 25.56	11.45	0.30	II.	4	49.270	9 49.2	26.4	1.3	30 37.31	43 16.9
16	9		11.0		40.0				31 48.76	11.43	0.29	IV.	4	55.010	3 49.4	26.2	0.1	32 0.48	37 45.7
17	9							7.0	32 10.71	11.43	0.29	VII.	4	43.670	15 38.9	26.1	2.5	32 22.43	34 49 37.5
18	9.10						19.0		34 41.11	11.40	0.28	VI.	3	30.650	29 18.9	25.6	5.4	34 53.09	35 3 19.9
19	9.10					45.0			38 26.12	11.35	0.27	V.	2	16.950	43 40.2	24.8	8.5	38 37.74	17 43.5
20	9						18.0		20 43 40.34	+11.29	+0.27	VI.		21.285	−39 8.2	−23.8	−7.5	20 43 51.99	−35 13 9.5

CORRECTIONS.

Date.	Corr. of Clock.	Hourly rate.	m	n	c	Zenith Point.	Mic. Co.
1846. Sept. 13.	h. 22 s. +3.459	s. −0.020	s. −0.356	s. +0.527	s. +0.022	° ' ''	r.

REMARKS.

Sept. 9. Very clear; reading of Barometer, &c., at 19h 20m; 20h 15m, moved the circle for other observations.

Sept. 13. 19h 29m, found the Micrometer and fixed wires connected by a small fiber; suspended sweeping until it could be removed; previous observations probably impaired by it. Readings of Barometer, &c., at 19h 50m, 22h 59m, hazy; few stars visible.

INSTRUMENT READINGS.

	Date.	A.	B.	C.	D.	E.	F.	Mean.	Barom. (in.)	At.	Ex.	U.	L.	I.
Zone 52	1846. Sept. 9, 21 0	71 24	61.9	64.2	76.9	65.9	52.6	44.1 60.93	30.242	70.0	64.3	69.9	71.0	78.0
	21 20										64.0			
	21 50										64.0			
	22 0		61.0	65.1	76.6	66.7	53.1	44.3 61.13	30.250	69.5	63.5	68.0	69.4	
Zone 53	Sept. 13, 19 20	73 54	67.3	64.4	81.5	68.7	56.6	46.4 64.15	30.038	78.8	74.8	79.5	77.5	75.0
	20 0		67.5	65.5	82.6	69.3	58.6	46.6 65.02						
	20 10								30.040	78.1	74.0			
	20 43								30.042	77.3	73.7			
	20 58								30.038	77.0	73.7			

Zone 53. September 13. P. D. = −34° 33′ 30″—Continued.

No.	Mag.	I.	II.	III.	IV.	V.	VI.	VII.	T.	a_1	a_2	Mic.		r	i	d_1	d_2	Mean Right Ascension, 1850.0	Mean Declination, 1850.0
									h. m. s.	s.	s.			r.	′ ″	″	″	h. m. s.	° ′ ″
21	7	..	3.0	22.0	40.0	..	..	..	20 50 40.44	+11.21	+0.27	IV.	4	44.430	−14 52.9	−22.5	− 2.3	20 50 51.92	−34 48 47.7
22	8	..	0.0	..	37.5	..	..	..	52 37.51	11.18	0.28	IV.	4	54.640	3 9.8	22.1	0.2	52 48.97	34 37 2.1
23	6	56.5	15.0	34.0	52.7	..	..	..	56 52.82	11.13	0.26	IV.	2	20.975	39 28.0	21.4	7.5	57 4.21	35 13 26.9
24	7	..	43.0	1.3	20.0	..	..	..	20 58 20.22	11.12	0.27	IV.	4	45.365	13 54.2	21.1	2.1	20 58 31.61	34 47 47.4
25	8	..	..	..	..	36.0	..	..	21 8 17.27	11.00	0.27	V.	4	55.400	3 24.6	19.3	0.1	21 8 28.54	37 14.0
26	7	..	..	..	..	..	31.0	..	8 53.64	10.99	0.27	VI.	4	55.280	3 31.6	19.2	0.1	9 4.90	34 37 20.9
27	8	..	..	..	42.0	0.0	..	..	10 41.58	10.97	0.25	IV.	2	19.990	40 29.8	18.9	7.8	10 52.80	35 14 26.6
28	5.6	..	21.0	39.0	58.0	..	..	..	22 58.08	10.82	0.25	IV.	4	56.402	2 22.0	17.0	0.0	23 9.15	34 36 9.0
29	9	..	..	..	..	56.0	..	..	23 18.44	10.82	0.24	VI.	3	33.637	26 11.5	16.9	4.7	23 29.50	35 0 3.1
30	6	1.0	19.5	38.0	57.0	..	..	..	25 57.05	10.78	0.24	IV.	3	34.280	25 31.6	16.5	4.6	26 6.07	34 59 22.7
31	8	..	..	..	..	2.0	..	..	28 43.07	10.75	0.24	VI.	2	13.710	47 2.9	16.1	9.2	28 54.06	35 20 58.2
32	7	17.0	36.0	55.0	14.0	..	..	..	31 13.76	10.71	0.24	IV.	2	21.905	38 29.7	15.7	7.4	31 25.71	12 22.8
33	9	..	..	..	42.0	0.0	19.0	..	31 41.50	10.71	0.23	IV.	2	22.463	37 54.9	15.7	7.2	31 52.44	35 11 47.8
34	8	..	..	59.5	18.0	37.3	..	..	45 37.06	10.53	0.23	IV.	4	42.683	16 42.5	13.8	2.7	45 47.82	34 50 29.0
35	8.9	..	..	..	..	51.0	..	..	46 13.30	10.52	0.22	VI.	2	13.527	47 14.5	13.7	9.2	46 24.04	35 21 7.4
36	8	11.0	29.5	49.0	7.7	..	..	..	51 7.58	10.46	0.22	IV.	2	18.453	42 6.4	13.1	8.1	51 18.26	15 57.6
37	8	5.7	24.0	42.7	1.3	..	..	..	53 1.65	10.43	0.22	IV.	3	27.820	32 16.7	12.9	6.0	53 12.30	6 5.6
38	9	4.5	..	42.0	10.0	..	..	..	57 0.69	10.38	0.22	IV.	3	26.400	33 46.0	12.4	6.3	57 11.29	7 34.7
39	8	..	42.0	1.0	..	..	..	..	59 19.78	10.35	0.21	III.	2	17.410	43 11.7	12.1	8.4	59 30.34	35 17 2.2
40	4	..	..	..	..	46.5	5.0	..	21 59 27.64	10.35	0.23	V.	4	46.580	12 37.5	12.1	1.9	21 59 38.22	34 46 21.5
41	3.4	..	..	..	58.5	..	30.0	..	22 1 58.55	10.32	0.23	IV.	4	47.870	11 16.7	11.8	1.6	22 2 9.10	34 45 0.1
42	7	..	..	..	..	..	59.0	18.0	2 40.23	10.31	0.21	V.	3	22.110	38 15.0	11.6	7.3	2 50.75	35 12 3.9
43	9	..	..	..	..	10.0	..	..	8 10.05	10.24	0.22	IV.	2	35.870	23 51.6	11.2	4.2	8 20.51	34 57 37.0
44	7	56.0	15.0	31.0	53.0	..	..	..	11 52.78	10.19	0.21	IV.	2	18.347	42 13.0	10.8	8.1	12 3.18	35 16 1.9
45	7	..	..	47.0	5.5	..	..	..	13 5.69	10.17	0.20	IV.	2	17.890	42 41.3	10.6	8.2	13 16.06	16 30.1
46	7	..	..	13.0	..	..	..	9.0	13 12.76	10.17	0.20	VI.	2	19.645	40 51.0	10.6	7.8	13 23.13	35 14 39.4
47	7	..	..	27.0	40.0	..	..	..	20 45.84	10.07	0.21	IV.	4	55.463	3 20.9	9.8	0.0	20 56.12	34 37 0.7
48	7	..	4.5	..	42.5	..	..	..	25 42.44	10.01	0.19	IV.	1	7.927	53 2.6	9.3	10.5	25 52.64	35 26 52.4
49	8	38.0	57.5	16.0	31.5	..	..	..	33 34.70	9.90	0.19	IV.	3	30.110	29 53.2	8.6	5.5	33 44.79	3 37.3
50	8	..	..	..	46.0	5.0	23.7	..	34 46.04	9.89	0.18	V.	2	17.948	42 37.7	8.5	8.2	34 56.11	35 16 24.4
51	6	46.7	5.7	24.3	43.0	..	..	..	38 43.10	9.84	0.19	IV.	3	36.280	23 26.1	8.2	4.1	38 53.13	34 57 8.4
52	7	..	58.5	17.0	35.7	..	..	..	43 35.97	9.78	0.18	IV.	1	8.970	51 57.3	7.8	10.3	43 45.93	35 25 45.4
53	5	..	..	42.0	0.5	..	..	..	22 59 0.69	9.58	0.17	IV.	3	32.330	27 34.0	6.8	5.0	22 59 10.44	1 15.8
54	8	..	..	..	..	..	5.0	..	23 15 46.14	9.36	0.16	V.	3	26.550	33 36.5	6.0	6.3	23 15 55.66	35 7 18.8
55	9	..	..	..	35.0	..	..	..	44 35.05	9.00	0.14	IV.	3	37.290	22 22.7	5.4	3.9	44 44.19	34 56 2.0
56	9	..	..	17.0	36.0	..	..	..	50 35.94	8.93	0.13	IV.	3	26.650	33 30.2	5.4	6.3	50 45.00	35 7 11.9
57	9	1	..	46.0	5.0	..	..	..	23 56 23.76	+ 8.86	+0.12	V.	2	19.260	−41 15.6	− 5.4	− 7.9	23 56 32.74	−35 14 58.9

Zone 54. September 14. C. D. = −34° 33′ 30″.

No.	Mag.	I.	II.	III.	IV.	V.	VI.	VII.	T.	a_1	a_2	Mic.		r	i	d_1	d_2	Mean Right Ascension, 1850.0	Mean Declination, 1850.0
1	9	..	..	..	36.2	..	..	37.0	18 49 35.99	+12.26	+0.62	IV.	4	53.141	− 5 46.0	−40.5	− 0.4	18 49 48.87	−34 39 56.9
2	9	..	0.5	19.1	37.6	..	..	..	51 19.06	12.25	0.61	IV.	4	50.741	8 16.6	40.1	0.9	51 31.92	42 27.6
3	8	..	5.2	24.1	42.5	1.3	..	..	52 23.92	12.24	0.59	IV.	3	43.205	16 11.3	39.9	2.5	52 36.75	34 50 23.7
4	8.9	..	..	..	47.4	..	25.1	..	53 28.58	12.23	0.55	V.	3	27.608	32 30.2	39.6	5.9	53 41.36	35 6 45.7
5	9	..	..	37.0	..	14.6	..	..	57 55.79	12.20	0.64	IV.	4	50.938	8 4.1	38.6	0.9	58 8.63	34 42 13.6
6	8.9	..	..	..	14.6	33.5	52.0	..	18 59 14.64	12.19	0.65	IV.	4	49.921	9 8.0	38.3	1.1	18 59 27.48	34 43 17.4
7	8.9	..	56.6	15.2	34.1	..	..	..	19 1 15.30	12.17	0.56	IV.	3	25.806	34 23.1	37.8	6.3	19 1 28.03	35 8 37.2
8	9	..	..	42.0	..	20.0	..	..	19 2 42.29	+12.16	+0.66	IV.	4	52.344	− 6 36.1	−37.4	− 0.6	19 2 55.11	−34 40 44.1

CORRECTIONS.

Date.	Corr. of Clock.	Hourly rate.	m	n	c	Zenith Point.	Mic. Co.
	s.	s.	s.	s.	s.	° ′ ″	r.
1846, Sept. 14, 22h	+ 3.248	− 0.024	− 0.356	+ 0.527	+ 0.022		

INSTRUMENT READINGS.

Date.	A.	B.	C.	D.	E.	F.	Mean.	Barom.	At.	Ex.	U.	L.	I.
	° ′ ″						″	in.	°	°	°	°	°
Zone 53, Sept. 13, 21 45	..	..	..	..	..	..	..	30.038	76.8	73.5			
22 8	..	..	..	..	..	..	..	30.038	76.5	72.6			
22 59	..	..	..	..	..	..	..	30.032	75.8	72.5			
23 56	..	..	..	..	..	..	..	30.008	75.3	72.0	..	..	75.5
0 0	66.7	65.5	82.6	69.3	58.6	..	64.67						
Zone 54, Sept. 14, 1 40	73 54 61.2	58.0	75.0	62.5	48.5	..	57.92	29.942	82.0	79.9	83.0	80.0	77.0
18 49	..	..	..	..	..	..	..		..	78.5			
19 1	..	..	..	..	..	..	..						
19 19								29.934	81.7	78.7			

REMARKS.

(53) 22. Micrometer reading assumed as 55ˢ.640 instead of 54ˢ.640.

(53) 35. Differs 21ˢ from Transit Z., Sept. 19.

Zone 54. September 14. C. D₀=−34° 33' 30"—Continued.

No.	Mag.	I.	II.	III.	IV.	V.	VI.	VII.	T.	a₁	a₂	Micrometer (r.)	i	d₁	d₂	Mean Right Ascension, 1850.0	Mean Declination, 1850.0
									h. m. s.	s.	s.	r.	° ′ ″	″	″	h. m. s.	° ′ ″
9	9	· ·	· ·	52.1	· ·	30.0	48.2	· ·	19 5 10.89	+12.14	+0.59	IV. 3 30.408	−29 34.6	−36.7	−5.3	19 5 23.62	−35 3 46.6
10	7.8	· ·	44.2	3.0	21.5	40.4	59.6	· ·	11 21.74	12.08	0.58	IV. 2 19.479	41 2.0	35.3	7.7	11 34.40	15 15.0
11	8	· ·	6.0	25.0	43.1	· ·	21.1	· ·	13 43.52	12.06	0.58	IV. * 19.775	40 43.3	34.6	7.7	13 56.14	14 55.6
12	9	· ·	54.0	13.4	32.0	51.0	10.0	· ·	19 32.09	12.01	0.57	IV. 3 11.953	48 51.5	33.1	9.4	19 44.67	35 23 4.0
13	9	· ·	· ·	· ·	46.0	4.2	22.5	· ·	25 44.50	11.95	0.70	IV. 4 43.466	15 53.4	31.7	2.5	25 57.15	34 49 57.6
14	9	· ·	· ·	· ·	· ·	· ·	51.0	· ·	26 13.46	11.95	0.67	VI. 3 34.981	24 47.1	31.7	4.3	26 26.08	58 53.1
15	7.8	· ·	· ·	14.5	33.2	52.0	10.5	· ·	28 33.19	11.93	0.70	IV. 3 41.011	18 29.0	31.1	3.0	28 45.82	52 33.1
16	9	· ·	35.0	54.0	12.5	31.1	50.1	· ·	47 12.55	11.74	0.75	IV. 3 36.379	23 19.9	26.9	4.0	47 25.04	34 57 20.8
17	6.7	57.7	16.6	35.2	54.0	12.8	31.6	50.5	49 54.73	11.71	0.73	IV. 3 28.279	31 48.1	26.3	5.8	50 7.17	35 5 50.2
18	8.9	· ·	6.5	25.6	44.5	3.2	22.1	· ·	51 44.39	11.69	0.76	IV. 3 34.291	25 30.9	25.8	4.5	51 56.84	34 59 31.2
19	8	· ·	53.5	12.6	· ·	50.2	9.0	· ·	55 31.32	11.65	0.75	IV. 3 28.911	31 8.3	24.9	5.6	55 43.72	35 5 8.8
20	9	· ·	· ·	· ·	· ·	· ·	53.0	· ·	57 15.34	11.63	0.74	IV. 3 22.774	37 33.2	24.5	7.0	57 27.71	11 34.7
21	8	· ·	48.0	· ·	25.6	45.0	3.5	· ·	58 25.85	11.62	0.77	IV. 3 30.521	29 27.4	24.2	5.3	58 38.22	35 3 26.9
22	8	· ·	· ·	· ·	· ·	· ·	· ·	34.0	19 58 37.65	11.62	0.79	VII. 3 37.109	22 33.3	24.1	3.8	19 58 50.06	34 56 31.2
23	9	· ·	· ·	· ·	18.7	· ·	· ·	· ·	20 4 18.75	11.56	0.77	IV. 3 26.666	33 29.2	22.7	6.1	20 4 31.08	35 7 25.0
24	7.8	· ·	47.5	6.0	24.5	43.4	2.5	· ·	10 24.78	11.50	0.80	IV. 3 30.961	28 59.7	21.0	5.2	10 37.08	35 2 55.9
25	9	· ·	· ·	· ·	49.7	8.0	27.0	· ·	11 49.46	11.48	0.83	IV. 3 36.691	23 0.1	20.7	3.9	12 1.77	34 56 54.7
26	9	· ·	5.8	24.7	43.5	· ·	21.0	· ·	20 14 43.47	+11.45	+0.79	IV. 3 23.958	−36 19.0	−20.9	−6.7	20 14 55.71	−35 10 16.6

Zone 55. September 14. C. D.=−35° 48' 40".

No.	Mag.	I.	II.	III.	IV.	V.	VI.	VII.	T.	a₁	a₂	Micrometer (r.)	i	d₁	d₂	Mean Right Ascension, 1850.0	Mean Declination, 1850.0
1	9	· ·	· ·	· ·	29.6	· ·	8.0	· ·	20 57 29.69	+11.07	+1.54	IV. 3 21.451	−38 56.4	−16.4	−9.4	20 57 42.30	−36 28 2.2
2	9	· ·	· ·	0.8?	· ·	· ·	· ·	· ·	21 2 19.93	10.08	1.60	III. 3 19.088	41 24.3	15.6	10.0	21 2 32.51	30 29.9
3	7.8	· ·	· ·	· ·	45.5	· ·	53.0	11.2	3 14.72	10.97	1.45	IV. 3 26.639	33 30.9	15.4	8.1	3 27.14	36 22 34.4
4	9	· ·	· ·	· ·	55.5	3.0	22.0	41.0	4 44.33	10.95	1.03	IV. 4 48.671	10 26.5	15.1	2.4	4 56.31	35 59 24.0
5	9	· ·	· ·	· ·	· ·	16.5	35.0	· ·	5 57.09	10.93	1.39	V. 3 29.037	31 0.5	14.9	7.4	6 9.41	36 20 2.8
6	9	· ·	· ·	· ·	· ·	· ·	9.0	28.1	6 30.91	10.93	1.16	VI. 4 41.036	18 25.0	14.8	4.4	6 43.00	7 24.2
7	8	· ·	25.0	44.5	4.1	23.0	42.0	· ·	11 3.73	10.87	1.36	IV. 3 29.011	31 2.0	14.1	7.4	11 15.96	20 3.5
8	9	· ·	· ·	5.0	23.8	43.0	· ·	· ·	16 23.93	10.80	1.52	IV. 3 20.685	39 44.3	13.2	9.6	16 35.25	28 47.1
9	9, 10	· ·	· ·	· ·	· ·	24.5	· ·	· ·	16 46.37	10.79	1.20	VI. 4 37.491	22 7.7	13.1	5.2	16 58.36	11 6.0
10	9	· ·	28.0	47.0	6.0	25.2	· ·	· ·	21 6.12	10.74	1.68	IV. 2 10.814	50 4.8	12.4	12.2	21 18.54	39 9.4
11	9	· ·	· ·	7.0	26.0	· ·	· ·	22.2	22 25.70	10.72	1.20	IV. 4 35.021	24 43.4	12.2	5.9	22 37.62	13 41.5
12	8	· ·	58.2	17.5	36.2	55.7	14.9	· ·	27 36.50	10.65	1.55	IV. 2 16.540	44 6.2	11.4	10.7	27 48.70	33 8.3
13	9	· ·	59.0	· ·	36.5	· ·	15.2	· ·	30 36.92	10.61	1.50	IV. 2 18.558	41 59.7	11.0	10.2	30 49.03	31 0.9
14	7	· ·	· ·	42.0	1.5	20.8	40.0	· ·	32 1.55	10.59	1.22	IV. 3 33.018	26 50.6	10.8	6.4	32 13.36	15 47.8
15	9	· ·	· ·	· ·	27.5	47.0	6.0	· ·	33 27.77	10.57	1.21	IV. 3 33.069	26 47.5	10.5	6.4	33 39.55	15 44.4
16	8.9	· ·	45.5	4.6	23.5	42.5	2.0	· ·	35 23.63	10.55	1.24	IV. 3 31.064	28 53.3	10.2	6.9	35 35.48	17 50.4
17	9	· ·	55.3	· ·	33.5	· ·	11.7	· ·	37 33.52	10.52	1.35	IV. 3 25.388	34 49.5	9.9	8.4	37 45.39	23 47.8
18	9	· ·	20.8	40.0	59.0	18.0	· ·	· ·	39 59.01	10.48	1.27	IV. 3 29.304	30 50.1	9.6	7.4	40 10.70	19 47.1
19	9	· ·	26.0	· ·	1.5	23.5	· ·	· ·	40 4.37	10.48	1.00	IV. 3 37.726	21 55.2	9.6	8.2	40 15.04	10 50.0
20	9	· ·	· ·	12.0	· ·	50.6	10.0	· ·	43 31.37	10.44	1.53	IV. 2 7.922	53 5.8	9.2	13.0	43 43.31	8 0.0
21	9	· ·	· ·	· ·	26.0	45.0	4.0	· ·	44 25.86	10.42	1.34	IV. 3 17.445	43 7.5	9.0	10.5	44 37.62	32 7.0
22	7.8	· ·	9.0	27.8	47.0	6.1	25.0	· ·	47 47.00	10.38	0.95	IV. 3 44.036	15 17.5	8.6	3.6	48 58.33	4 9.7
23	8.9	· ·	15.5	· ·	· ·	12.7	31.8	· ·	51 53.60	10.32	1.05	IV. 3 38.028	21 36.2	8.1	5.1	52 4.97	10 29.4
24	7.8	· ·	· ·	· ·	59.0	18.4	37.0	· ·	52 59.05	10.31	1.13	IV. 3 32.841	27 1.7	8.0	6.4	53 10.49	15 56.1
25	8	· ·	· ·	· ·	· ·	· ·	58.0	17.1	53 19.65	10.31	1.44	VI. 4 16.423	44 12.5	7.9	10.5	53 31.40	33 11.2
26	8	· ·	· ·	18.0	37.1	56.1	15.4	· ·	55 37.10	10.28	1.29	IV. 3 23.955	36 19.2	7.6	8.8	55 48.67	25 15.6
27	8.9	· ·	24.0	43.0	2.1	21.0	10.0	· ·	21 58 2.04	+10.25	+0.77	IV. 4 51.802	−7 9.9	−7.4	−1.6	21 58 13.06	−35 55 58.9

CORRECTIONS.

Date.		Corr. of Clock.	Hourly rate.	m	n	c	Zenith Point.	Mic. Co.
1846.	h.	s.	s.	s.	s.	s.	°	r.
Sept. 14,	22	+ 3.248	− 0.024	− 0.356	+ 0.527	+ 0.022		

REMARKS.

Sept. 14. 18ʰ 49ᵐ, clear; stars unsteady.

INSTRUMENT READINGS.

	Date.	A.	B.	C.	D.	E.	F.	Mean.	Barom.	At.	Ex.	U.	L.	L.
	1846.	° ′ ″						″	in.	°	°	°	°	°
Zone 54	Sept. 14, 19 28	73 54										77.7		
	19 47											77.5		
	20 4								29.926	80.5		77.9		
	20 15	60.8	59.0	75.0	52.0	49.0	41.0	57.80	29.928	80.5	77.8	80.0	79.0	
Zone 55	Sept. 14, 21 2	75 9 60.9	58.6	75.1	61.9	49.1	41.0	57.77	29.926	80.0	77.2	79.6	78.6	77.8
	21 21											77.0		
	21 40											76.6		
	21 58								29.920	79.0		75.9		
	22 0	75 9 60.5	58.1	75.1	61.3	48.4	40.9	57.42					78.8	78.0

Zone 55. September 14. C. $D_o = -35° 48' 40'$—Continued.

No.	Mag.	I.	II.	III.	IV.	V.	VI.	VII.	T.	a_1	a_2	Mic.		r.	i	d_1	d_2	Mean Right Ascension, 1850.0.	Mean Declination, 1850.0.
									h. m. s.	s.	s.			r.	′ ″	″	″	h. m. s.	° ′ ″
28	8.9			21.5	40.5				22 12 40.59	+10.05	+1.54	IV.	2	8.566	−52 25.7	− 5.6	−12.8	22 12 52.18	−36 41 24.3
29	8.9		23.6		1.8		39.8	59.2	15 1.76	10.01	1.29	IV.	3	20.841	39 34.4	5.5	9.6	15 13.06	28 29.5
30	8		24.8		3.0			50.6	17 3.10	9.99	1.22	IV.	3	24.142	36 7.5	5.4	8.7	17 14.31	25 1.6
31	8					15.8	35.2		17 56.81	9.98	1.24	V.	3	23.088	37 13.6	5.3	9.0	18 8.03	26 7.9
32	7		18.5	37.1	56.1		34.4		22 56.32	9.91	0.81	IV.	4	44.588	14 42.9	4.8	3.5	23 7.04	36 3 31.2
33	8			42.0	1.1	20.0			24 1.02	9.89	0.64	IV.	4	53.181	5 43.5	4.8	1.3	24 11.55	35 54 29.6
34	6					48.0	7.0		24 28.88	9.89	0.97	V.	3	35.989	23 44.2	4.7	5.6	24 39.74	36 12 34.5
35	8					33.5	52.5		25 14.31	9.88	1.15	V.	3	26.468	33 41.7	4.6	8.1	25 25.34	22 34.4
36	9					56.5			27 37.43	9.84	0.85	V.	2	42.576	16 48.9	4.4	4.0	27 48.10	36 5 37.3
37	7,8		36.5	55.1	14.4	33.5	52.0		31 14.44	9.79	0.68	IV.	4	50.601	8 25.4	4.1	2.0	31 24.91	35 57 11.5
38	8		30.1	49.1	8.0		46.7		43 6.29	9.63	1.42	IV.	2	8.940	52 2.1	3.3	12.7	43 19.34	36 40 58.1
39	6,7	5.5	24.5	44.0	3.0	22.2	41.3	0.3	22 50 2.96	9.53	1.00	IV.	3	29.641	30 22.6	2.8	7.2	22 50 13.49	19 12.6
40	8		14.0	33.0	52.0	11.1	30.2		23 1 52.08	+9.37	+0.85	IV.	3	35.858	−23 52.3	− 2.2	− 5.7	23 2 2.30	−36 12 40.2

Zone 56. September 15. P. $D_o = -25° 47' 20''$.

No.	Mag.	I.	II.	III.	IV.	V.	VI.	VII.	T.	a_1	a_2	Mic.		r.	i	d_1	d_2	Mean Right Ascension, 1850.0.	Mean Declination, 1850.0.
1	7	27.0	44.5	2.0	19.0				19 12 18.91	+10.53	+0.75	IV.	2	22.115	−38 16.6	−45.4	− 4.4	19 12 30.19	−26 26 26.4
2	8		52.0				46.0		12 27.59	10.53	0.74	V.	2	21.328	39 6.0	45.3	4.5	12 38.86	27 15.8
3	7	25.0	42.3	59.5	16.5				17 16.65	10.49	0.71	IV.	2	12.285	48 29.9	44.1	5.5	17 27.85	36 39.5
4	8	34.5	51.5	9.0					19 25.96	10.47	0.80	III.	3	35.830	23 54.0	43.6	2.9	19 37.93	12 0.5
5	8				49.0				19 48.02	10.47	0.84	IV.	4	43.810	15 31.6	43.5	2.1	19 59.33	3 37.2
6	9					49.0			20 14.75	10.47	0.83	VI.	1	41.300	−18 8.7	43.4	2.3	20 26.05	6 14.4
7	7		19.5	37.0					21 53.98	10.46	0.84	III.	4	44.820	14 28.3	42.9	2.0	22 5.28	26 2 33.2
8	8							27.0	21 35.64	10.46	0.88	VII.	4	56.340	2 24.6	43.0	0.8	21 46.98	25 50 28.4
9	7		13.0	30.0					23 30.11	10.44	0.76	III.	3	27.690	32 24.9	42.6	3.8	23 41.31	26 20 31.3
10	8		55.0	12.0					26 29.33	10.42	0.70	III.	2	11.500	49 22.1	41.8	5.5	26 40.44	37 29.4
11	8					58.0	16.0		26 41.27	10.42	0.79	V.	3	34.400	25 24.1	41.8	3.1	26 52.48	13 29.0
12	8	37.0		11.0					29 28.28	10.39	0.79	III.	3	39.963	23 45.7	41.1	2.9	29 39.46	11 49.7
13	9					53.0			36 53.05	10.33	0.77	IV.	3	31.397	28 32.5	39.3	3.4	37 4.15	26 16 35.2
14	7		46.0	3.0	20.5				38 20.32	10.32	0.84	IV.	4	47.785	11 22.0	38.9	1.7	38 31.48	25 59 22.6
15	8						5.0		38 47.80	10.32	0.77	V.	2	32.300	27 35.9	38.8	3.3	39 58.80	26 15 38.0
16	8					38.0			41 20.74	10.29	0.70	V.	2	16.135	44 31.4	38.3	5.0	41 31.73	32 34.7
17	8		51.5					17.5	43 25.66	10.28	0.70	VII.	2	15.245	45 26.6	37.8	5.1	43 36.64	33 29.5
18	6						2.2	19.5	46 27.80	10.25	0.67	VI.	1	7.434	53 33.2	37.1	6.0	46 38.72	41 36.3
19	8					13.0	30.5		47 55.90	10.24	0.69	V.	2	12.050	48 47.3	36.8	5.5	48 6.83	36 49.6
20	7		4.0	21.0					49 38.30	10.22	0.70	III.	2	14.003	17 47.8	36.4	5.2	49 49.22	35 49.4
21	9		23.0				15.0		50 40.38	10.22	0.67	VI.	1	7.300	53 41.7	36.1	6.0	50 51.27	41 43.8
22	8		1.5	19.0					51 36.08	10.20	0.68	III.	2	11.040	49 50.7	35.9	5.6	51 46.96	37 52.2
23	8						55.0		51 20.67	10.20	0.75	VI.	3	27.303	32 49.2	36.0	3.8	51 31.62	20 49.0
24	8			9.0	26.0				53 43.28	10.19	0.72	III.	2	21.210	39 13.4	35.5	4.5	53 54.19	27 13.4
25	8	29.0			4.0	20.5			57 20.65	10.15	0.82	IV.	4	47.100	12 5.2	34.7	1.7	57 31.62	0 1.6
26	9			19.0					59 36.18	10.13	0.73	III.	3	26.005	34 10.5	34.2	4.0	59 47.04	22 8.7
27	7					5.0	22.0		19 59 47.65	10.13	0.66	V.	2	9.785	51 12.9	34.2	5.7	19 59 58.44	30 12.8
28	9						2.5	19.5	20 0 44.74	10.13	0.75	V.	3	29.510	30 30.9	34.0	3.6	20 0 55.62	18 28.5
29	9			13.0					2 55.84	10.12	0.79	IV.	4	40.570	18 55.2	33.7	2.4	2 6.75	6 51.3
30	9			23.0					3 40.19	10.11	0.66	III.	2	10.730	50 10.1	33.4	5.6	3 50.96	38 9.1
31	9							44.0	3 52.43	10.11	0.70	VII.	2	18.690	41 50.6	33.3	4.7	4 3.24	29 48.6
32	9	39.0		13.5					20 8 30.61	+10.06	+0.72	III.	2	22.690	−37 40.6	−32.3	− 4.3	20 8 41.39	−26 25 37.2

CORRECTIONS.

Date.	Corr. of Clock.	Hourly rate.	m	n	c	Zenith Point.	Mic. Co.
	h.	s.	s.	s.	s.	s.	° ′ ″	r.
1846. Sept. 15.	22	+ 2.484	− 0.021	− 0.356	+ 0.527	+ 0.022		

REMARKS.

(56) 20. Micrometer reading assumed as 13r.003 instead of 14r.003.

(56) 26. Declination apparently about 30″ too large by Mural and Meridian Circle in 1847.

(56) 29. Transit over T. V assumed as recorded over T. IV, and minutes as 1, not 2.

INSTRUMENT READINGS.

	Date.		A.	B.	C.	D.	E.	F.	Mean.	Barom.	At.	Ex.	U.	L.	I.
			° ′	″					″	in.					
Zone 55	1846. Sept. 14.	22 17													75.6
		22 43													75.2
		23 0	60.0	58.2	75.5	61.5	48.6	40.9	57.45	29.900	78.2	74.8	77.5	77.4	78.0
Zone 56	Sept. 15.	19 10	65 9	66.6	61.5	79.0	65.2	52.4	45.7	61.73					
		19 43								30.048	76.7	67.7	79.0		78.0
		20 18								30.051	75.8	65.5			
		20 40								30.052	75.0	64.5			
		20 50	65.5	62.4	79.7	64.8	54.5	43.6	61.75						
		21 15								30.086	74.0	63.8			

ZONE 56. SEPTEMBER 15. P. D$_0$ = −25° 47′ 20″.—Continued.

No.	Mag.	I.	II.	III.	IV.	V.	VI.	VII.	T. (h. m. s.)	a_1 (s.)	a_2 (s.)	MICROMETER		r	i	d_1	d_2	Mean R.A. 1850.0 (h. m. s.)	Mean Decl. 1850.0 (° ′ ″)
33	8					44.0	1.0		20 11 26.65	+10.04	+0.66	V.	2	11.833	−49 0.8	−31.7	5.5	20 11 37.35	−26 36 58.0
34	9	11.0							14 2.49	10.01	0.72	IV.	3	26.175	34 0.1	31.2	3.9	14 13.22	21 55.2
35	6			7.7	24.7			16.0	15 24.70	10.00	0.74	IV.	3	29.243	30 47.6	20.9	3.6	15 35.44	18 42.1
36	5.6			33.5	50.5	8.0			18 50.67	9.97	0.78	IV.	4	41.510	17 56.2	30.2	2.3	19 1.42	5 48.7
37	9				24.0				23 24.04	9.93	0.73	IV.	3	27.193	32 56.2	29.2	3.9	23 34.70	20 49.3
38	9		8.5	26.0					27 42.99	9.89	0.77	III.	3	38.420	21 11.7	28.4	2.6	27 53.65	9 2.7
39	9	39.0		13.0					29 30.28	9.87	0.75	III.	4	36.480	23 12.7	28.0	2.0	29 40.00	11 3.0
40	5				16.0	33.5	50.5		32 16.13	9.84	0.67	IV.	2	16.912	43 42.7	27.5	4.9	32 26.64	31 35.1
41	8	53.0	10.0	27.0	44.3				34 44.31	9.82	0.71	IV.	3	26.377	33 47.5	27.0	3.9	34 54.84	21 38.4
42	5.6	21.0	38.0	55.3	12.3				40 12.40	9.77	0.71	IV.	3	28.104	31 59.0	25.9	3.7	40 22.88	19 48.6
43	7	16.0	33.0		7.0				42 7.23	9.76	0.70	IV.	4	39.086	20 28.3	25.5	2.6	42 17.75	8 16.4
44	8	29.5	46.5	3.7	20.7				45 20.81	9.73	0.76	IV.	4	39.083	20 28.5	24.9	2.6	45 31.30	8 16.0
45	9						12.5		45 38.12	9.73	0.65	VI.	2	13.755	47 0.2	24.8	5.3	45 48.50	34 50.3
46	9	50.0	7.0	24.0					49 41.42	9.68	0.65	III.	2	13.655	47 7.0	24.1	5.3	49 51.75	26 34 56.4
47	9						53.0		50 1.61	9.68	0.80	VI.	4	50.000	9 2.3	24.0	1.4	50 12.00	25 56 47.7
48	7		20.3	37.3	54.0				20 57 54.37	9.61	0.73	IV.	3	37.813	21 49.7	22.7	2.7	20 58 4.71	26 9 35.1
49	7	56.0	13.0	30.0	47.5				21 5 47.44	9.53	0.65	IV.	2	16.770	43 51.7	21.0	5.0	21 5 57.62	31 37.7
50	8	31.0	47.5	5.0			56.0		9 22.05	9.49	0.68	IV.	3	27.760	32 20.5	20.4	3.8	9 32.22	26 20 4.7
51	6		28.0	45.0					15 2.23	9.44	0.79	III.	4	56.070	2 43.0	19.4	0.8	15 12.16	25 50 23.2
52	7					38.0	55.0		15 20.77	9.43	0.71	V.	4	35.470	24 16.9	19.4	3.0	15 30.91	26 11 59.3
53	7.8				55.7	12.5			16 55.53	9.42	0.79	IV.	4	53.713	5 10.0	19.2	1.0	17 5.74	25 52 50.2
54	7	57.0	14.0		48.5				19 48.44	9.39	0.69	IV.	3	30.100	29 53.8	18.7	3.5	19 58.52	26 17 36.0
55	7	1.0	18.0	35.3					21 52.42	9.37	0.67	III.	3	26.030	34 8.9	18.4	4.0	22 2.36	26 21 51.3
56	7						9.0	26.5	21 34.99	9.37	0.80	V.	4	55.713	3 4.9	18.4	0.8	21 45.16	25 50 44.1
57	7					6.0			22 48.86	9.36	0.76	VI.	4	49.370	9 42.5	18.2	1.5	22 58.98	25 57 22.2
58	7						35.0		23 0.78	9.36	0.75	VI.	4	47.885	10 28.7	18.2	2.1	23 10.89	26 4 9.0
59	8							9.0	23 17.63	9.36	0.77	VII.	4	53.499	5 22.8	18.2	1.0	23 27.76	25 53 2.0
60	8	36.0	53.0	10.3					26 27.36	9.33	0.79	III.	4	47.840	11 18.7	17.7	1.6	26 37.48	25 58 58.0
61	7	30.5	47.7	4.7	21.3				29 21.76	9.30	0.72	IV.	4	40.255	19 15.1	17.3	2.4	29 31.78	26 6 54.8
62	8	16.0	33.0	50.0					31 7.24	9.28	0.77	III.	4	52.850	6 4.3	17.0	1.1	31 17.29	25 53 42.4
63	8		38.0	55.0					32 12.30	9.27	0.63	III.	2	17.015	43 36.3	16.9	5.0	32 22.20	26 31 18.2
64	8		42.0	59.0	15.5				33 16.05	9.26	0.62	IV.	2	16.053	44 36.7	16.7	5.1	33 25.93	32 18.5
65	8					18.5			34 1.20	9.26	0.59	V.	1	7.900	53 4.2	16.7	5.9	34 11.05	40 46.8
66	7							15.0	39 23.40	9.20	0.61	VII.	2	14.263	46 28.2	16.0	5.2	39 33.21	26 34 9.4
67	8					26.0			41 8.90	9.18	0.77	V.	4	55.725	3 4.2	15.8	0.8	41 18.85	25 50 40.8
68	8	48.5	6.0	23.0					43 40.11	9.16	0.72	III.	4	42.780	16 36.4	15.4	2.2	43 49.99	26 4 14.0
69	8	20.3	38.0	54.0					45 11.81	9.14	0.63	III.	2	19.353	41 10.0	15.2	4.7	45 21.58	28 49.9
70	7.8	55.5	12.3	29.5	46.7				47 46.73	9.12	0.69	IV.	3	34.910	24 51.9	14.9	3.0	47 56.54	12 29.8
71	9		27.0						50 1.33	9.09	0.67	II.	3	30.600	29 22.1	14.7	3.5	50 11.00	17 0.3
72	8			8.7		43.0			50 25.85	9.09	0.72	IV.	4	43.007	16 22.1	14.6	2.2	50 35.66	3 58.9
73	9							47.0	50 55.43	9.00	0.64	VII.	3	22.203	38 8.7	11.6	4.4	51 5.16	25 47.7
74	6.7					49.0	6.0		21 55 31.66	9.04	0.59	V.	2	12.060	48 46.7	11.6	5.5	21 55 41.20	36 26.2
75	7			50.3		24.5			22 0 7.37	9.00	0.61	V.	2	18.220	42 20.8	13.5	4.8	22 0 16.98	29 59.1
76	8	43.0		17.7					2 34.61	8.98	0.70	IV.	4	40.790	18 41.3	13.2	2.4	2 44.29	26 6 16.9
77	4.5				8.5	25.5			5 8.42	8.95	0.74	IV.	4	51.322	7 40.3	12.9	1.3	5 18.11	25 55 14.5
78	7						6.5		6 32.17	8.94	0.64	VI.	3	24.472	35 46.7	12.8	4.1	6 41.75	26 23 23.6
79	4			44.5	2.0	19.0			8 1.81	8.92	0.57	IV.	2	10.000	50 55.8	12.6	5.7	8 11.30	38 34.1
80	7	31.0	48.5	5.5	22.7				13 22.64	8.87	0.69	IV.	4	39.994	19 31.3	12.0	2.5	13 32.20	7 5.8
81	8				38.0	55.0			22 14 37.84	+8.86	+0.58	V.	2	12.795	−48 0.6	−11.9	5.4	22 14 47.28	− 35 37.9

CORRECTIONS.

Date.	Corr. of Clock.	Hourly rate.	m	u	c	Zenith Point.	Mic. Co.
1846.	h.	s.	s.	s.	s.		
	s.					° ′	r.

REMARKS.

(56) 47. Transit over T. VII assumed as recorded over T. VI.

(56) 58. Micrometer reading assumed as 42^r.885 instead of 47^r.885.

INSTRUMENT READINGS.

Date.		CIRCLE.							Barom.	THERMOM.				
		A.	B.	C.	D.	E.	F.	Mean		At.	Ex.	U.	L.	I.
	1846. Sept. 15, h. m.	°			″			″	in.	°				
Zone 56	21 40	64.2	63.4	80.2	65.0	55.3	42.5	61.77						
	22 0								30.096	72.0	60.5			
	22 29								30.098	71.0	59.0			
	23 0	65	9	66.6					30.104	69.5	57.9			
	23 30								30.103	68.3	57.5			
	23 59								30.110	67.7	56.5			
	0 0	62.4	64.5	79.2	66.0	54.8	41.0	61.32				68.5	66.5	77.0

ZONE 56. SEPTEMBER 15. P. D$_0$ = −25° 47' 20"—Continued.

No.	Mag.	I.	II.	III.	IV.	V.	VI.	VII.	T.	a_1	a_2	Mic.		r.	i	d_1	d_2	Mean Right Ascension, 1850.0	Mean Declination, 1850.0
									h. m. s.	s.	s.			r.	' "	"	"	h. m. s.	° ' "
82	9				57.5				22 16 57.53	+8.84	+0.69	IV.	4	40.450	−19 2.8	−11.7	−2.4	22 17 7.06	−26 6 36.9
83	9				5.0				24 5.03	8.76	0.56	IV.	1	10.640	50 12.8	10.9	5.7	24 14.35	37 49.4
84	7	54.0	11.0	28.0	45.0				29 45.28	8.71	0.61	IV.	2	22.120	38 16.3	10.4	4.4	29 54.60	25 51.1
85	7.8			33.0	50.0	7.0			30 50.01	8.70	0.65	IV.	3	31.885	28 1.7	10.3	3.3	30 59.36	15 35.3
86	7		5.0	22.0	39.0	56.5			32 56.34	8.68	0.68	IV.	4	39.223	20 19.9	10.1	2.5	33 5.70	7 52.5
87	7		0.7		35.3	52.0			34 52.25	8.66	0.60	IV.	4	21.067	39 20.3	10.0	4.5	35 1.51	26 54.8
88	7	17.3	34.5	51.7	8.7				37 8.76	8.63	0.68	IV.	4	40.410	13 51.5	9.8	2.4	37 18.07	1 23.7
89	8		47.0	4.0	21.0				38 21.17	8.62	0.65	IV.	3	36.170	23 32.9	9.6	2.9	38 30.44	11 5.4
90	6		58.0	15.5	32.3				39 32.51	8.61	0.54	IV.	1	6.770	54 16.5	9.6	6.0	39 41.66	41 52.1
91	8	37.0	54.0	11.0					44 28.32	8.56	0.63	III.	3	29.155	30 53.0	9.2	3.6	44 37.51	18 25.8
92	8							23.0	44 31.58	8.56	0.70	VII.	4	46.685	12 29.8	9.2	1.7	44 40.84	26 0 0.7
93	8						22.0		44 47.81	8.56	0.71	VII.	4	50.050	8 59.2	9.1	0.9	44 57.07	25 56 29.2
94	9		44.5		19.0				49 19.94	8.51	0.64	IV.	3	32.610	27 16.3	8.8	3.3	49 28.00	26 14 48.4
95	4	57.3	14.7	31.7					51 46.81	8.49	0.71	III.	3	48.855	10 15.0	8.6	1.5	51 58.01	25 57 45.1
96	4.5					24.0	41.0		52 6.70	8.46	0.60	V.	2	22.265	38 7.2	8.6	4.4	52 15.78	26 25 40.2
97	8	48.0	4.7	22.0					55 49.30	8.45	0.56	III.	2	14.535	46 12.0	8.4	5.2	55 58.31	33 45.6
98	7.8			1.5	18.0	36.0			22 56 18.49	8.44	0.58	IV.	4	18.610	41 56.5	8.3	4.8	22 56 27.51	29 29.6
99	6	48.0	55.0	23.0	40.0				23 0 39.83	8.40	0.54	IV.	1	10.013	50 52.1	8.0	5.8	23 0 48.77	38 25.9
100	9		23.0						3 57.31	8.37	0.64	II.	3	34.230	25 34.4	7.8	3.1	4 6.32	13 5.3
101	8	42.5	59.3	16.7	34.0				6 33.88	8.35	0.60	IV.	3	25.113	35 6.6	7.7	4.1	6 42.83	22 38.4
102	9		3.0						9 37.33	8.32	0.61	II.	3	31.095	28 51.1	7.5	3.4	9 46.26	16 22.0
103	9				55.0				10 55.05	8.31	0.61	IV.	3	29.767	30 14.6	7.4	3.6	11 3.97	17 45.6
104	6	6.0	23.0	40.0	57.0				12 57.21	8.29	0.66	IV.	4	42.500	16 54.0	7.4	2.2	13 6.16	4 23.6
105	6.7	29.0	47.0	3.3	20.3				20 20.65	8.21	0.62	IV.	3	32.710	27 10.0	7.0	3.2	20 29.48	14 40.2
106	7			35.5		10.0			23 52.71	8.18	0.54	V.	2	13.930	46 49.5	6.9	5.3	24 1.43	34 21.7
107	6.7	48.3	5.0	22.3	39.3				28 39.49	8.14	0.65	IV.	4	42.750	16 35.2	6.7	2.2	28 48.28	4 7.1
108	9					25.0			30 7.84	8.12	0.66	V.	4	43.860	15 28.2	6.6	2.0	30 16.62	2 56.8
109	8				22.0		57.0		35 22.38	8.07	0.62	IV.	3	35.716	24 1.3	6.5	2.9	35 31.07	11 30.7
110	9				52.0	10.0			36 52.40	8.06	0.56	IV.	2	18.760	41 47.0	6.4	4.6	37 1.02	29 18.2
111	5	3.0	20.0	37.0	54.0				41 54.23	8.02	0.62	IV.	3	37.330	22 20.2	6.4	2.7	42 2.87	26 9 49.3
112	5			29.0			3.3	21.0	44 46.37	7.99	0.70	V.	4	57.053	1 40.9	6.3	0.7	44 55.06	25 49 7.9
113	9	49.5	7.0	24.0					52 41.20	7.92	0.55	III.	2	20.587	39 52.5	6.3	4.6	52 49.67	26 27 23.4
114	9			44.0					54 1.19	7.91	0.49	III.	1	11.240	49 35.3	6.3	5.6	54 9.59	37 7.2
115	9			46.0					55 3.17	7.90	0.58	III.	3	33.530	26 18.5	6.3	3.2	55 11.65	13 48.0
116	9					34.0		8.0	55 16.69	7.90	0.61	V.	3	41.250	18 12.3	6.3	2.3	55 25.20	5 40.9
117	6.7	41.0	58.0	15.0	32.0				23 59 32.23	+7.87	+0.59	IV.	3	36.080	−23 38.5	−6.3	−2.9	23 59 40.69	−26 11 7.7

ZONE 57. SEPTEMBER 16. C. D$_0$ = −38° 19' 30".

No.	Mag.	I.	II.	III.	IV.	V.	VI.	VII.	T.	a_1	a_2	Mic.		r.	i	d_1	d_2	Mean Right Ascension, 1850.0	Mean Declination, 1850.0
1	7.8			16.0	37.2	57.5	17.1	37.0	20 24 57.35	+10.07	+1.12	IV.	4	43.523	−15 49.8	−27.1	−4.9	20 25 8.57	−38 35 51.8
2	9.10					20.0		19.8	32 20.15	9.97	0.91	IV.	2	14.089	46 39.8	25.7	15.9	32 31.03	39 6 51.4
3	9.10		42.1		21.4		1.2		40 21.59	9.86	1.00	IV.	3	32.389	27 30.3	24.3	9.0	40 32.45	38 47 33.6
4	8.9				23.0	42.0		22.0	41 22.65	9.85	0.98	IV.	3	30.711	29 15.4	24.1	9.7	41 33.48	49 19.2
5	8.9				13.0		53.0		42 13.31	9.83	1.01	IV.	3	36.544	23 9.5	24.0	7.5	42 25.15	43 11.0
6	9.10					43.0			46 3.69	9.78	1.07	VI.	4	47.106	12 3.9	23.3	3.7	46 14.54	38 32 0.9
7	7	58.6	18.5	38.2	58.2		38.0		52 38.33	9.70	0.84	IV.	2	14.324	46 25.2	22.2	15.9	52 48.87	39 6 33.3
8	7		32.1		11.8	31.2		11.5	53 11.72	9.69	0.80	IV.	2	8.333	52 40.3	22.1	18.2	53 22.21	39 12 50.6
9	8.9			52.7	12.0	32.0	51.4		20 57 12.20	+9.63	+1.00	IV.	4	40.683	−18 48.1	−21.5	−6.0	20 57 22.83	−38 38 45.6

CORRECTIONS.

Date.		Corr. of Clock.	Hourly rate.	m	n	c	Zenith Point.	Mic. Co.
		s.	s.	s.	s.	s.	° ' "	r.
1846. Sept. 16,	h. 22	+ 1.622	− 0.027	− 0.356	+ 0.527	+ 0.022		

REMARKS.

(56) 88. Micrometer assumed as 45^r.410 instead of 40^r.410.

INSTRUMENT READINGS.

	Date.	CIRCLE.							Barom.	THERMOM.				
		A.	B.	C.	D.	E.	F.	Mean.		At.	Ex.	U.	L.	I.
	1846. h. m.	° ' "						"	in.	°	°	°	°	°
Zone 57	Sept. 16, 20 20	77 39 63.0	65.7	80.0	70.0	53.1	45.0	62.80			60.1	66.0	67.0	72.0
	20 32								30.150	66.5	59.9			
	20 42										59.9			
	20 54								30.142	65.8	59.0			
	21 30	63.0	66.9	79.6	70.6	54.9	43.0	63.15	30.138	65.1	57.8	64.0	65.5	
	21 45										58.0			
	22 1								30.138	64.0	56.4			
	22 30								30.128	63.5	54.2			
	22 40	62.1	67.0	80.1	70.5	55.9	43.6	63.35			55.0	61.2	63.2	

ZONE 57. SEPTEMBER 16. C. $D_a = -38°\ 19'\ 30''$—Continued.

No.	Mag.	I.	II.	III.	IV.	V.	VI.	VII.	T.	a_1	a_2	MICROMETER.			i	d_1	d_2	Mean Right Ascension, 1850.0	Mean Declination, 1850.0
									h. m. s.	s.	s.			r.	' "	"	"	h. m. s.	° ' "
10	7.8	..	57.8	17.7	37.5	57.0	16.7	..	20 59 37.36	+ 9.60	+ 1.02	IV.	4	46.941	−12 15.0	−21.1	− 3.7	20 59 47.98	−38 32 9.8
11	9	..	55.5	..	35.1	..	15.7	..	21 4 35.47	9.53	0.78	IV.	2	9.508	51 26.7	20.4	17.7	21 4 45.78	39 11 34.8
12	9.10	..	..	6.2	..	..	6.2	..	8 26.31	9.48	0.82	IV.	2	18.931	41 36.2	19.8	14.1	8 36.61	39 1 40.1
13	9	..	6.4	26.0	45.8	6.0	25.5	..	11 45.95	9.44	0.90	IV.	3	31.348	28 35.6	19.3	9.4	11 56.29	38 48 34.3
14	8	..	..	41.1	1.0	20.8	..	..	14 0.93	9.40	1.05	IV.	4	56.692	2 3.8	19.0	0.7	14 11.38	21 53.5
15	6.7	..	9.7	29.3	49.0	8.6	28.1	..	16 48.98	9.37	1.00	IV.	4	50.508	8 31.3	18.6	2.5	16 59.35	28 22.4
16	9.10	..	..	0.0	..	..	..	..	18 19.79	9.34	0.83	III.	2	24.569	35 42.9	18.4	11.9	18 29.06	53 43.2
17	9	..	..	..	..	32.5	..	..	18 12.68	9.34	0.83	V.	2	25.181	35 2.4	18.4	11.7	18 22.85	55 2.5
18	8	..	..	..	..	19.7	39.3	..	19 59.90	9.32	0.90	V.	2	35.561	24 11.1	18.2	7.8	20 10.12	44 7.1
19	8	..	26.0	46.7	..	25.7	45.1	..	33 5.90	9.13	0.92	IV.	3	42.512	16 54.8	16.4	5.3	33 15.05	38 36 46.5
20	7	..	24.5	..	..	25.0	..	5.0	35 4.91	9.10	0.66	IV.	2	7.289	53 46.9	16.2	18.6	35 14.67	39 13 51.7
21	7.8	..	55.0	..	34.0	53.8	..	..	35 34.18	9.10	0.70	IV.	2	13.271	47 31.6	16.1	16.3	35 43.98	39 7 34.0
22	7.8	..	35.7	55.4	15.0	34.8	..	..	38 15.10	9.05	0.89	IV.	4	40.834	18 38.5	15.8	5.9	38 25.14	38 38 30.2
23	9.10	..	..	..	..	..	41.0	..	45 17.32	8.95	0.66	VI.	2	10.540	50 21.5	14.9	17.3	45 10.93	39 10 23.7
24	7	..	8.2	28.5	48.2	8.0	27.7	..	46 48.17	8.92	0.92	IV.	4	51.371	7 37.2	14.7	2.2	47 58.01	38 27 24.1
25	8	..	26.0	15.2	..	25.0	..	3.8	47 5.09	8.91	0.92	IV.	4	50.681	8 20.3	14.7	2.4	47 14.92	38 28 7.4
26	7	..	..	..	..	..	43.0	2.8	50 3.34	8.87	0.67	VI.	2	14.209	46 31.7	14.3	15.0	50 12.88	39 6 31.9
27	8	..	..	19.2	39.0	59.0	..	..	59 5.90	8.73	0.75	IV.	3	31.158	28 47.4	13.8	9.5	59 48.55	38 48 40.7
28	8.9	..	..	..	43.0	3.0	..	..	21 59 43.15	8.73	0.86	IV.	4	48.247	10 53.3	13.8	3.3	21 59 52.74	30 40.4
29	8	..	49.0	9.0	28.7	..	8.0	..	22 1 28.63	8.70	0.87	IV.	4	49.989	9 3.8	13.7	2.6	22 1 38.20	28 50.1
30	8	..	..	1.8	21.1	41.0	..	..	2 21.96	8.69	0.76	IV.	3	32.749	27 7.5	13.6	8.9	2 31.41	38 47 0.0
31	7.8	..	..	..	..	..	..	56.0	2 56.55	8.68	0.66	VII.	2	18.085	42 28.1	13.5	14.4	3 5.89	39 2 26.0
32	9	..	28.0	..	..	..	28.7	..	9 49.02	8.58	0.58	IV.	2	9.979	50 57.1	13.0	17.5	9 58.18	39 10 57.6
33	8	..	3.0	22.8	42.4	..	..	..	15 42.54	8.50	0.64	IV.	3	22.157	38 12.0	12.7	12.8	15 51.68	38 58 7.5
34	7.8	..	..	..	9.5	29.4	49.0	..	16 9.66	8.48	0.70	IV.	4	43.946	15 23.1	12.6	4.8	16 18.93	35 10.4
35	8.9	..	..	37.4	57.0	16.7	36.0	..	24 56.89	8.35	0.64	IV.	3	25.449	34 45.7	12.1	11.6	25 5.88	38 54 39.5
36	7	..	27.5	47.5	7.0	27.2	47.0	..	30 7.16	8.27	0.48	IV.	2	5.810	55 19.7	11.7	19.1	30 15.91	39 15 20.7
37	8	..	..	58.5	18.7	38.0	57.8	..	34 18.42	8.20	0.78	IV.	4	51.481	7 30.2	11.4	2.1	34 27.40	38 27 13.6
38	7.8	..	..	..	5.7	25.7	45.7	..	39 5.90	8.12	0.55	IV.	2	19.891	40 36.0	10.9	13.7	39 14.57	39 0 30.4
39	7.8	..	..	..	..	..	..	28.0	39 23.89	8.12	0.72	VII.	4	46.144	13 3.5	10.9	4.0	39 32.73	38 32 48.6
40	8	..	..	..	..	26.0	45.7	5.7	41 6.38	8.10	0.68	V.	4	41.068	18 23.5	10.8	5.8	41 15.16	38 10.1
41	8	..	..	15.5	35.0	..	14.5	..	47 35.10	8.00	0.58	IV.	3	27.401	32 43.2	10.7	10.9	47 43.58	52 34.8
42	8	..	..	57.8	17.7	37.1	56.9	..	49 17.53	7.98	0.63	IV.	3	35.444	24 18.6	10.7	7.9	49 26.14	44 7.2
43	9	..	..	24.5	44.0	3.5	23.2	..	52 43.97	7.93	0.72	IV.	4	51.576	7 24.2	10.7	2.1	52 52.62	38 27 7.0
44	7	..	18.7	38.6	58.0	18.5	38.2	..	22 54 58.39	7.89	0.45	IV.	1	11.612	54 25.8	10.7	16.9	22 55 6.73	39 14 23.4
45	9	..	..	20.0	..	58.2	18.2	..	23 12 39.03	7.62	0.67	IV.	4	48.289	10 50.7	9.9	3.2	23 12 47.32	38 30 33.8
46	9	..	32.5	52.0	11.8	..	51.4	11.0	20 11.88	7.51	0.60	IV.	4	44.181	15 8.5	9.4	4.7	20 19.99	38 34 52.6
47	9	..	..	..	..	47.0	6.8	26.2	22 26.94	7.48	0.36	V.	2	11.475	49 23.2	9.3	17.0	22 34.78	39 9 19.5
48	6.7	..	..	26.8	46.5	6.2	25.8	45.6	24 46.45	7.44	0.55	IV.	4	40.410	19 5.3	9.3	6.1	24 54.44	38 38 50.7
49	9	..	..	..	29.5	..	..	..	26 29.54	7.42	0.38	IV.	2	14.928	45 47.1	9.2	15.6	26 37.34	39 5 41.9
50	9	..	..	..	..	..	..	..	29 ..	7.38	0.50	IV.	4	48.903	10 11.9	9.1	3.0	29 ..	38 29 54.0
51	8	..	..	36.0	55.8	15.7	35.3	..	32 55.85	7.33	0.50	IV.	3	37.571	22 5.0	9.1	7.1	33 3.68	38 41 51.2
52	8	..	..	30.8	50.3	10.4	30.3	..	36 50.51	7.27	0.31	IV.	2	10.911	49 58.7	9.0	17.2	36 58.09	39 9 54.9
53	8.9	..	..	..	..	18.0	37.8	57.2	37 58.15	7.25	0.44	V.	3	31.221	28 43.5	9.0	9.4	38 5.84	38 48 31.9
54	8	..	..	..	..	49.1	8.9	28.7	39 29.28	7.23	0.38	V.	3	20.901	39 30.6	8.9	13.3	39 36.89	59 22.6
55	8.9	..	6.0	25.8	45.6	5.3	25.0	..	47 45.54	7.11	0.39	IV.	3	25.935	34 15.0	8.9	11.4	47 53.03	38 54 5.3
56	8	..	9.0	..	48.5	8.1	28.0	..	50 48.45	7.06	0.32	IV.	2	16.891	43 44.0	8.9	14.9	50 55.83	39 3 37.8
57	7	..	..	48.5	8.2	28.0	48.0	..	55 8.33	7.00	0.42	IV.	1	35.381	24 22.5	8.9	7.9	55 15.75	38 44 9.3
58	8	..	42.3	2.3	21.8	41.8	1.7	..	23 59 22.00	6.94	0.40	IV.	3	33.746	26 4.9	8.9	8.5	23 59 29.34	45 52.3
59	7	32.4	52.1	11.9	31.8	51.5	11.1	30.8	0 5 31.66	+ 6.85	+ 0.42	IV.	3	39.822	−19 43.5	−9.0	−6.3	0 5 38.03	−38 39 28.8

<table>
<tr><td colspan="8" align="center">CORRECTIONS.</td><td colspan="4" rowspan="6">REMARKS.

(57) 24. Minutes assumed as 47 instead of 46.
(57) 32. Transit over T. III rejected.
(57) 39. Transit assumed at 23ˢ.0, to agree with Transit 1846 and Lacaille 9253.
(57) 44. Micrometer reading assumed as 6ʳ.612 instead of 11ʳ.612.</td></tr>
</table>

Date.	Corr. of Clock.	Hourly rate.	m	n	c	Zenith Point.	Mic. Co.
1846.	h.	s.	s.	s.	s.	s.	° ' "	r.

INSTRUMENT READINGS.

	Date.	CIRCLE.							Barom.	THERMOM.				
		A.	B.	C.	D.	E.	F.	Mean.		At.	Ex.	U.	L.	I.
	1846.	° ' "						"	in.	°	°	°	°	°
Zone 57	Sept. 16, 23 12	.	.	.	.	.	.	.	30.118	61.8	52.4			
	23 20	.	.	.	.	.	.	.			53.0			
	23 29	.	.	.	.	.	.	.	30.112	60.2	53.5			
	23 50	61.5	68.6	79.7	71.0	55.6	43.0	63.23	.	52.3	60.0	63.0	71.0	
	23 59	.	.	.	.	.	.	.	30.108	59.5	53.5			

ZONE 58. SEPTEMBER 19. P. D₀ = −29° 33′ 10″.

No.	Mag.	I.	II.	III.	IV.	V.	VI.	VII.	T. (h. m. s.)	a₁ (s.)	a₂ (s.)
1	8	44.0	1.5	19.5	37.0				19 31 37.18	+7.22	+1.00
2	5.6			9.5	27.0	45.0			46 27.16	7.09	1.24
3	7				6.0				48 56.03	7.06	0.91
4	8.7	11.5	29.0		5.0				52 4.86	7.03	1.03
5	7		51.0		26.5				57 26.52	6.98	1.18
6	6				55.0	13.0			19 57 55.11	6.98	1.07
7	8	10.0	28.0	46.0					20 0 3.51	6.96	1.15
8	8			23.5					0 23.56	6.96	1.10
9	7	52.0	10.0	28.0					2 45.53	6.94	1.13
10	5	29.3	47.0	5.0	23.0				6 22.87	6.90	0.98
11	8		36.0		11.0				8 11.27	6.88	1.20
12	7	5.0	23.0	40.5	58.5				9 58.42	6.86	1.13
13	6				4.5				11 4.49	6.86	1.29
14	8			34.0					11 3.61	6.86	1.30
15	8						39.0		13 33.97	6.83	1.31
16	8		53.0	10.5		46.0			15 28.34	6.81	1.17
17	7							4.5	16 11.20	6.80	1.21
18	7			9.0	26.0	44.3			18 44.92	6.78	1.24
19	7	29.0	47.0	5.0					20 21 24.09	+6.05	+1.12

No.	MICROMETER.		r.	i (′ ″)	d₁ (″)	d₂ (″)	Mean Right Ascension, 1850.0 (h. m. s.)	Mean Declination, 1850.0 (° ′ ″)
1	IV.	3	28.643	−31 25.2	−15.6	−4.8	19 31 45.40	−30 4 55.6
2	IV.	4	57.325	1 24.1	12.2	0.8	46 35.49	29 34 47.1
3	IV.	1	6.273	54 47.7	11.6	8.0	49 4.00	30 28 17.3
4	IV.	2	22.122	38 16.2	11.0	5.7	52 12.92	30 11 42.9
5	IV.	4	42.493	16 54.4	9.8	2.8	57 34.68	29 50 17.0
6	IV.	3	24.752	35 29.2	9.7	5.3	19 58 3.16	30 8 54.2
7	III.	3	36.660	23 2.0	9.2	3.6	20 0 11.62	29 56 24.8
8	V.	3	29.317	30 43.0	9.1	4.7	0 31.62	30 4 6.8
9	III.	3	33.570	26 16.0	8.6	4.1	2 53.60	29 59 38.7
10	IV.	1	6.956	54 4.8	7.8	7.9	6 30.75	30 27 30.5
11	IV.	4	41.633	17 48.4	7.4	3.0	8 19.35	29 51 8.8
12	IV.	3	28.182	31 54.3	7.1	4.8	10 6.41	30 5 16.2
13	V.	4	52.447	6 29.3	6.8	1.5	11 12.64	29 39 47.6
14	VII.	4	52.740	6 10.3	6.8	1.5	11 11.77	39 28.6
15	IV.	4	54.630	4 13.2	6.3	1.2	13 42.11	29 37 30.7
16	V.	3	31.685	28 14.2	5.9	4.4	15 36.32	30 1 34.5
17	VII.	3	37.735	21 54.0	5.8	3.5	16 19.21	29 55 13.3
18	IV.	4	41.003	18 27.9	5.2	3.1	18 52.04	29 51 46.2
19	III.	2	22.420	−37 57.6	−4.7	−5.7	20 21 31.26	−30 11 18.0

ZONE 59. SEPTEMBER 19. P. D₀ = −33° 18′ 20″.

No.	Mag.	I.	II.	III.	IV.	V.	VI.	VII.	T. (h. m. s.)	a₁ (s.)	a₂ (s.)
1	7			18.0	36.0				20 29 36.29	+7.95	+0.63
2	5.6			28.0	46.5	4.5			30 46.33	7.94	0.78
3	8			50.0		35.0			39 35.50	7.84	0.56
4	5.6	35.3	53.5	12.3		49.3			42 30.72	7.80	0.65
5	7				2.0	20.0			50 1.68	7.71	0.92
6	8			12.0	31.0				51 30.74	7.70	0.54
7	6.7				3.0		39.5		52 2.81	7.69	0.51
8	8		6.0						56 24.55	7.64	0.80
9	8						14.0		56 37.15	7.63	0.49
10	8		33.0		10.0	28.0			20 59 9.89	7.60	0.88
11	7		24.0	43.0	1.0				21 1 1.19	7.58	0.50
12	8	3.0	22.0	47.0					5 59.03	7.52	0.70
13	9					6.0			8 47.53	7.48	0.51
14	8					5.0			9 46.47	7.47	0.63
15	6.7	44.5	2.5	21.5					27 39.84	7.25	0.65
16	9						7.0		27 29.59	7.25	0.67
17	9		20.0		57.0				33 57.09	7.17	0.77
18	4	57.0	15.0	34.0	52.3				35 52.33	7.14	0.64
19	7		44.0	2.5	21.0				37 20.97	7.13	0.47
20	9					32.0			38 13.50	7.11	0.60
21	9	0.0	18.0	37.5					43 35.57	7.04	0.76
22	9		11.5		49.0				45 48.75	7.02	0.61
23	7					41.0	59.0		46 22.24	7.01	0.64
24	5	34.3	53.0	11.0					59 29.76	6.84	0.65
25	9			13.0		9.0			59 31.00	6.84	0.62
26	7							45.5	21 59 49.87	+6.83	+0.73

No.	MICROMETER.		r.	i (′ ″)	d₁ (″)	d₂ (″)	Mean Right Ascension, 1850.0 (h. m. s.)	Mean Declination, 1850.0 (° ′ ″)
1	IV.	3	36.705	−22 59.3	−26.0	−4.3	20 29 48.87	−33 41 49.6
2	IV.	2	21.815	38 35.4	25.8	7.3	30 55.05	57 28.5
3	IV.	4	44.245	15 4.5	24.2	2.7	39 43.90	33 51.4
4	IV.	3	34.510	25 17.2	23.6	4.7	42 39.17	33 44 5.5
5	IV.	1	8.530	52 25.0	22.3	10.0	50 10.31	34 11 17.3
6	IV.	4	45.633	13 37.2	22.0	2.5	51 38.98	33 32 21.7
7	IV.	4	49.157	9 56.1	21.0	1.8	52 11.01	28 39.6
8	III.	2	20.110	40 22.3	21.2	7.6	56 32.99	59 11.1
9	VI.	4	51.386	7 35.4	21.1	1.3	56 45.27	33 26 17.8
10	V.	1	11.680	49 7.5	20.7	9.3	20 59 18.37	34 7 57.5
11	IV.	4	50.427	8 36.4	20.4	1.5	21 1 9.27	33 27 18.3
12	III.	3	30.455	29 31.5	19.5	5.5	6 7.25	48 16.5
13	VI.	4	48.590	10 30.7	19.0	1.9	8 55.52	29 11.6
14	V.	3	36.710	22 58.9	18.8	4.3	9 54.57	41 42.0
15	III.	3	35.480	24 16.2	15.9	4.5	27 47.74	42 56.6
16	VI.	3	32.785	27 4.9	16.0	5.0	27 37.51	45 45.9
17	IV.	2	22.770	37 35.5	15.0	7.1	34 5.03	56 17.6
18	IV.	3	35.957	23 46.2	14.7	4.4	36 0.11	42 25.3
19	IV.	4	53.383	5 30.9	14.5	0.9	37 28.57	24 6.3
20	V.	4	39.970	19 32.4	14.4	3.6	38 21.21	38 10.4
21	III.	3	23.910	36 21.8	13.6	6.8	43 43.37	55 2.2
22	IV.	4	39.230	20 19.4	13.3	3.7	45 56.38	38 56.4
23	V.	3	35.610	24 8.0	13.2	4.5	46 29.89	42 45.7
24	III.	3	35.295	24 27.8	11.6	4.5	59 37.25	43 3.9
25	V.	3	37.683	21 57.8	11.6	4.0	59 38.46	40 33.4
26	VII.	3	27.265	−32 51.1	−11.5	−6.2	21 59 57.43	−33 51 28.8

CORRECTIONS.

Date.	Corr. of Clock.	Hourly rate.	m	n	c	Zenith Point.	Mic. Co.
	h.	s.	s.	s.	s.	° ′ ″	r.
1846. Sept. 19	18	+ 0.090	− 0.019	− 0.415	+ 0.429	+ 0.022		

INSTRUMENT READINGS.

	Date.		CIRCLE.							Barom.	THERMOM.				
			A.	B.	C.	D.	E.	F.	Mean.		At.	Ex.	U.	L.	I.
	1846,	h. m.	° ′ ″						″	in.					
Zone 58	Sept. 19,	19 30	68 54 64.0	63.6	79.0	68.0	53.3	44.3	62.03	30.208	71.8	63.7	72.0	71.5	71.0
		20 21								30.216	70.0	61.8			
Zone 59	Sept. 19,	20 30	72 39 65.2	67.0	80.0	68.8	55.5	43.3	63.30	30.216	70.0	61.8			
		21 1								30.216	69.0	60.6			
		21 43								30.216	68.0	60.0			
		22 9								30.216	67.0	59.5			
		22 30	64.6	67.0	79.0	66.8	55.4	42.5	62.98						
		22 44								30.222	66.5	58.7			
		23 31								30.216	65.7	58.2			

REMARKS.

Sept. 19, 20ʰ 21ᵐ. Perfectly clear.

(58) 3. Transit over T. IV assumed as at 56″.0 instead of 6″.0, to agree with Transit Z., 1847, and Arg. Z. 235.68.

ZONE 59. SEPTEMBER 19. P. D₀ = −33° 18′ 20″—Continued.

No.	Mag.	I.	II.	III.	IV.	V.	VI.	VII.	T. (h. m. s.)	a₁ (s.)	a₄ (s.)
27	8				47.0	5.0			22 9 46.71	+6.70	+0.86
28	9	56.0	14.0	32.5	51.0				13 51.10	6.65	0.61
29	9	59.5	18.0	36.4	55.0				15 55.12	6.62	0.82
30	9			46.0	4.3				17 4.45	6.61	0.88
31	6	20.0	39.3	56.5	15.0				30 15.26	6.44	0.73
32	9		11.0	29.0	48.0				31 47.82	6.42	0.48
33	9					0.0			37 41.50	6.34	0.57
34	7				40.0				38 21.40	6.33	0.79
35	5.6	34.7	53.0	12.0	30.0				41 30.14	6.29	0.58
36	4	8.3	27.0	45.3	3.7				44 3.83	6.26	0.63
37	9				20.0	39.0			49 20.22	6.19	0.81
38	9	58.0	16.5	35.0					55 53.55	6.10	0.72
39	9				18.0		55.0		22 56 18.05	6.10	0.59
40	3.4			18.0	36.5	54.7			23 10 36.52	5.91	0.44
41	7	53.5	12.0	30.0	48.7				31 48.76	5.64	0.56
42	7	28.3	46.7	5.0	23.5				35 23.69	5.59	0.76
43	8	59.7	18.0	37.0	55.0				37 55.21	5.56	0.67
44	7	5.0	23.3	42.0	0.7				44 0.59	5.49	0.78
45	7				47.0	5.0			49 46.71	5.42	0.82
46	7	33.0	51.3	10.3	28.7				23 58 28.56	5.31	0.60
47	9	38.0		15.5	33.5				0 0 33.61	+5.29	+0.54

No.	MICROMETER	n	r.	i (′ ″)	d₁ (″)	d₂ (″)	Mean Right Ascension, 1850.0 (h. m. s.)	Mean Declination, 1850.0 (° ′ ″)
27	V.	2	14.060	−46 41.4	−10.4	−8.9	22 9 54.27	−34 5 20.7
28	IV.	4	39.105	20 27.1	10.0	3.8	13 58.36	33 39 0.9
29	IV.	2	17.697	42 53.6	9.8	8.1	16 2.56	34 1 31.5
30	IV.	1	11.690	49 7.0	9.7	9.4	17 11.94	34 7 46.1
31	IV.	3	27.125	33 0.4	8.5	6.2	30 22.43	33 51 35.1
32	IV.	4	52.343	6 36.2	8.3	1.2	31 54.72	25 5.7
33	V.	4	42.700	16 41.0	7.9	3.0	37 48.41	35 11.9
34	V.	3	20.770	39 38.9	7.8	7.5	38 28.52	58 14.2
35	IV.	4	42.155	17 15.7	7.6	3.2	41 37.01	35 46.2
36	IV.	3	37.000	21 38.0	7.4	4.0	44 10.72	40 9.4
37	IV.	2	19.267	41 15.3	7.0	7.8	49 27.22	59 50.1
38	III.	3	27.780	32 19.1	6.7	6.0	56 0.37	50 51.8
39	IV.	4	40.565	18 55.5	6.7	3.5	22 56 24.74	37 25.7
40	IV.	4	56.340	2 25.9	5.9	0.4	23 10 42.87	20 52.2
41	IV.	4	44.153	15 10.3	5.4	2.7	31 54.96	33 38.4
42	IV.	3	23.980	36 17.6	5.4	6.6	35 30.04	54 49.8
43	IV.	3	32.780	27 5.5	5.3	5.1	38 1.44	45 35.9
44	IV.	2	21.595	38 49.3	5.4	7.3	44 6.86	33 57 22.0
45	V.	2	17.647	42 56.6	5.4	8.2	49 52.95	34 1 30.2
46	IV.	4	40.093	19 25.1	5.6	3.6	23 58 34.47	33 37 54.3
47	IV.	4	45.675	−13 34.6	−5.7	−2.4	0 0 39.44	−33 32 2.7

ZONE 60. SEPTEMBER 21. C. D₀ = −37° 4′ 10″.

No.	Mag.	I.	II.	III.	IV.	V.	VI.	VII.	T. (h. m. s.)	a₁ (s.)
1	8.9			24.5	44.5	3.6	23.0	42.3	19 41 3.62	+8.42
2	7.8							37.0?	41 38.61	8.42
3	8		0.7	19.8	38.5	58.5	17.7		19 46 39.05	8.36
4	7.8	58.1	17.8	37.0	56.7	16.0			49 37.12	8.33
5	9		12.2	31.6	51.0	10.2			51 31.61	8.31
6	8		15.8		54.0	14.4	33.6		53 54.64	8.29
7	7.8								19 54	8.29
8	9				31.0	50.5			20 3 31.66	8.17
9	9			31.6	50.8	10.0	29.2		10 50.76	8.09
10	9			33.0	52.2	30.8			11 52.24	8.07
11	8	15.8	35.0	54.3	13.8	33.4			14 54.47	8.04
12	7	21.8	41.0	1.0	20.1	39.2			17 0.62	8.00
13	6.9	19.0	37.7	57.3	17.0	36.2			18 57.46	7.99
14	9			34.0			32.2		22 34.06	7.94
15	9					10.??			26 34.16	7.89
16	7.5						2.6		27 4.10	7.88
17	9		51.0		30.0	49.2	8.2		29 29.79	7.85
18	9						35.1		38 36.59	7.73
19	8.9				56.0	15.7			39 17.48	7.72
20	8.9				43.2	2.6			40 4.17	7.71
21	9			54.0		32.0			44 53.64	7.65
22	9	5.0	25.2	44.0	3.8				46 44.25	7.63
23	7	34.4	54.1	13.2	32.8	51.5			52 13.24	7.55
24	7	51.0	10.5	29.7	49.5	8.8			55 29.91	+7.51

No.	MICROMETER	n	r.	i (′ ″)	d₁ (″)	d₂ (″)	Mean Right Ascension, 1850.0	Mean Declination, 1850.0 (° ′ ″)
1	IV.	4	47.681	−11 28.6	−25.8	−2.3	19 . . .	−37 16 6.7
2	VII.	3	22.541	37 47.2	25.0	9.9	. . . .	42 32.7
3	IV.	3	34.638	25 9.0	24.5	6.2	. . . .	29 49.7
4	IV.	2	18.754	41 47.3	23.9	11.1	. . . .	46 30.3
5	IV.	3	48.222	10 54.8	23.5	2.2	. . . .	15 30.5
6	IV.	4	44.548	14 45.4	23.0	3.3	. . . .	19 21.7
7	VII.	2	9.419	51 32.1	23.1	14.0	. . . .	56 17.
8	IV.	4	46.614	12 35.6	21.2	2.6	. . . .	17 9.4
9	IV.	4	44.691	14 36.3	19.9	3.2	. . . .	19 9.4
10	IV.	3	41.719	17 43.9	19.7	4.1	. . . .	22 17.7
11	IV.	3	35.858	23 52.4	19.2	5.8	. . . .	28 27.4
12	IV.	2	17.506	48 19.5	18.8	11.5	. . . .	52 59.8
13	IV.	4	43.922	15 24.6	18.5	3.4	. . . .	19 56.5
14	IV.	4	43.568	15 46.9	17.9	3.6	. . . .	20 18.4
15	VI.	3	27.471	32 38.8	17.2	8.4	. . . .	37 14.4
16	VII.	2	11.394	49 27.3	17.5	13.4	. . . .	54 7.9
17	IV.	4	46.758	12 26.2	16.7	2.6	. . . .	16 55.8
18	VII.	2	10.938	49 55.9	15.2	13.5	. . . .	54 34.6
19	VI.	4	44.176	15 8.6	15.1	3.3	. . . .	19 36.4
20	VI.	4	39.664	19 51.2	14.9	4.7	. . . .	24 20.8
21	IV.	3	36.787	22 54.1	14.1	5.5	. . . .	27 23.7
22	IV.	2	11.281	49 35.8	13.8	13.4	. . . .	54 13.0
23	IV.	4	53.799	5 4.5	12.9	0.5	. . . .	9 27.9
24	IV.	2	16.085	−44 34.7	−12.3	−11.9	. . . .	−37 49 8.9

CORRECTIONS.

Date.	Corr. of Clock. (s.)	Hourly rate. (s.)	m (s.)	n (s.)	c (s.)	Zenith Point. (° ′ ″)	Mic. Co. (r.)
1846, Sept. 21,	18h −0.419	−0.020	−0.415	+0.429	+0.022		

REMARKS.

(59) 36. } Piscis Australis. Micrometer reading assumed as 38r.0 instead of 37r.0.

Sept. 21, Apparently clear; stars unsteady, variable, as if through clouds.

(60) 12. Micrometer reading assumed as 12r.506 instead of 17r.506.

INSTRUMENT READINGS.

Date.	CIRCLE. A.	B.	C.	D.	E.	F.	Mean.	Barom. (in.)	THERMOM. At.	Ex.	U.	L.	I.
Zone 59 Sept. 19, 0 0	72 39 63.7	67.5	79.1	69.5	55.4	42.5	63.03	30.216	65.7	58.2	65.0	65.0	70.5
Zone 60 Sept. 21, 19 30	76 24 62.1	60.5	75.2	65.0	49.8	42.7	59.22				73.2	72.1	71.0
19 41								30.108			73.8	69.0	
20 3											68.3		
20 22								30.122			72.5	66.3	
20 40	62.2	61.0	75.7	65.0	49.9	41.4	59.20				64.8	70.2	70.5
20 59								30.130			71.5	64.2	
21 21											65.2		
21 40											64.9		

ZONE 60. SEPTEMBER 21. C. $D_0 = -37° 4' 10''$—Continued.

No.	Mag.	Seconds of Transit (I.–VII.)	T. (h. m. s.)	a_1	a_2	Mic.	r	i	d_1	d_2	Mean R.A. 1850.0	Mean Decl. 1850.0
25	9	. . 33.5	20 58 12.53	+ 7.47	. .	II. 2	13.521	−47 15.3	−11.8	−12.7	. . . .	−37 51 49.8
26	8.9	. . . . . . 51.3	58 31.82	7.47	. .	V. 3	25.054	34 11.9	11.8	8.8	. . . .	38 42.5
27	7.8	. . 26.0 . . 5.0 . . 43.5 3.0	59 4.78	7.46	. .	VI. 2	14.702	46 0.8	11.6	12.4	. . . .	50 34.8
28	7	. . . . 45.5	20 59 47.42	7.45	. .	VII. 4	45.456	13 46.8	11.5	3.0	. . . .	18 11.3
29	9	. . . . 53.0 . . . . 51.0 . .	21 5 12.27	7.37	. .	IV. 2	19.156	41 22.2	10.5	11.0	. . . .	45 53.7
30	9	. . . . 25.0	9 26.98	7.32	. .	VII. 4	50.151	8 52.1	9.7	1.6	. . . .	13 13.4
31	9	. . . . 29.8? . .	10 51.07	7.30	. .	VI. 3	38.856	20 43.9	9.4	4.9	. . . .	25 8.2
32	9	. . . . 3.0? . .	11 24.35	7.29	. .	VI. 4	46.359	12 50.9	9.3	2.7	. . . .	17 12.9
33	9	. . 31.0 50.2	15 9.79	7.23	. .	III. 3	20.082	40 22.0	8.6	10.7	. . . .	44 51.3
34	9	. . . . 36.7 56.5 15.6	17 56.26	7.20	. .	IV. 3	19.754	40 42.6	8.0	10.8	. . . .	45 11.4
35	9	. . . . 40.0 59.7	18 1.26	7.19	. .	VI. 4	25.080	35 6.3	8.0	9.1	. . . .	30 33.4
36	7.8	. . 56.3 15.9 35.0 54.5 13.8 . .	21 35.12	7.15	. .	IV. 4	51.186	7 48.8	7.4	1.3	. . . .	12 7.5
37	6.7	. . 40.2 59.7 18.7 35.0 58.0 17.0	25 18.94	7.09	. .	IV. 4	45.061	14 13.1	6.9	3.1	. . . .	18 33.1
38	9	. . . . 29.5? . .	25 50.83	7.09	. .	VI. 4	44.358	14 56.5	6.8	3.3	. . . .	19 16.6
39	8.9	. . 5.0 24.6 43.2 3.8 23.0 . .	28 43.92	7.05	. .	IV. 2	15.112	45 29.5	6.4	12.2	. . . .	49 58.1
40	8	. . . . 39.5 59.0 18.7 38.5 . .	29 59.18	7.03	. .	IV. 2	16.447	44 12.1	6.2	11.8	. . . .	48 40.1
41	9	. . . . 16.3?	30 18.19	7.02	. .	VII. 4	43.771	15 32.4	6.1	3.5	. . . .	19 52.0
42	9	. . 8.3 28.1 47.2 6.0 26.3 . .	32 47.34	6.99	. .	IV. 3	21.208	39 11.6	5.8	10.3	. . . .	43 37.7
43	9	. . . . 20.0 . . 59.2 . . 38.7	36 39.78	6.93	. .	IV. 2	13.286	47 30.2	5.2	12.8	. . . .	51 58.2
44	8	. . 44.0 3.3 22.7 42.0 1.2 . .	40 22.66	6.88	. .	IV. 4	40.386	19 6.9	4.7	4.5	. . . .	23 26.1
45	7.8	. . . . 44.1 3.4 23.0	44 3.51	6.82	. .	IV. 3	28.642	31 25.3	4.2	8.0	. . . .	35 47.5
46	8	. . 33.1 . . . . 10.1	47 11.88	6.79	. .	IV. 3	33.058	26 48.1	3.8	6.7	. . . .	31 8.6
47	6	. . 33.4 53.1 12.8 32.0 51.8 11.0	47 12.59	6.78	. .	IV. 2	7.776	53 15.0	3.8	14.5	. . . .	57 43.3
48	8	. . . . 33.0	48 34.88	6.76	. .	VII. 4	42.741	16 37.1	3.6	3.8	. . . .	20 54.5
49	7	. . 14.0 33.0 52.7 12.0 31.5 . .	51 52.66	6.71	. .	IV. 3	47.161	12 2.9	3.1	2.5	. . . .	16 18.5
50	8.9	. . . . 9.8 . . 48.7	52 50.20	6.70	. .	V. 2	11.618	49 14.4	3.0	13.3	. . . .	53 40.7
51	8.9	. . . . 6.2 25.1	53 26.94	6.68	. .	VI. 2	15.921	44 44.3	2.9	12.0	. . . .	49 9.2
52	8	. . 11.7 . . 51.0 10.1 29.2 . .	21 5 50.64	+ 6.50	. .	IV. 4	45.953	−13 17.1	−1.2	−2.9	. . . .	−37 17 31.2

ZONE 61. SEPTEMBER 23. C. $D_0 = -29° 32' 50''$.

No.	Mag.	Seconds of Transit (I.–VII.)	T. (h. m. s.)	a_1	a_2	Mic.	r	i	d_1	d_2	Mean R.A. 1850.0	Mean Decl. 1850.0
1	7.8	. . 29.5 47.0 4.5 . . 40.0 58.0	20 0 4.70	+ 6.50	+0.76	IV. 3	36.599	−23 6.0	−29.0	− 3.0	20 0 11.96	−29 56 28.0
2	8	. . . . . . 25.0 43.0 0.5 . .	0 25.08	6.50	0.84	IV. 3	29.349	30 44.0	28.9	4.1	0 32.42	30 4 4.0
3	8	. . 11.1 28.5 46.2 4.3 22.2 . .	2 46.53	6.48	0.79	IV. 3	33.551	26 17.3	28.4	3.4	2 53.60	29 59 39.1
4	6.7	48.5 5.8 23.8 41.8 59.7 17.3	5 23.87	6.45	1.10	IV. 2	6.964	54 7.3	27.8	7.3	6 31.42	30 27 32.4
5	8	. . . . 54.8 12.5 . . . . 5.7	9 12.49	6.42	0.69	IV. 4	41.648	17 47.5	27.2	2.3	8 19.60	29 51 7.0
6	7.8	12.0 59.5 17.0 34.5	9 59.37	6.41	0.83	IV. 3	28.171	31 54.9	26.8	4.2	10 6.61	30 5 15.9
7	8	. . . . 4.0 22.0 30.0 57.0	11 3.92	6.38	0.54	VI. 4	52.731	6 10.5	26.6	0.8	11 10.84	29 39 28.2
8	7.8	. . . . 6.0 23.8 41.0 59.0	11 5.87	6.38	0.56	IV. 4	52.334	6 33.6	26.6	0.8	11 12.81	29 39 51.0
9	9	. . 35.1 52.8 . . 28.3 . .	11 52.80	6.36	0.98	IV. 2	14.092	45 48.8	25.8	6.1	15 0.14	30 19 10.7
10	9	. . . . 22.5	15 29.15	6.35	0.78	IV. 5	31.608	28 15.4	25.7	3.7	15 36.28	30 1 54.8
11	8.9	. . . . 5.7	16 12.39	6.34	0.74	VII. 3	37.721	21 54.9	25.5	2.9	16 19.45	29 55 13.3
12	7	9.8 27.6 45.3 2.9 20.8 . .	18 45.29	6.32	0.68	VII. 3	41.002	18 28.9	25.0	2.4	18 52.29	29 51 46.3
13	7.8	. . 5.7 23.3 41.5 50.0 . .	21 23.47	6.29	0.89	IV. 3	22.383	37 57.9	24.4	5.1	21 30.65	30 11 17.4
14	6.7	. . . . 12.7 30.8	21 37.49	6.29	0.50	VI. 4	55.421	3 22.7	24.4	0.4	21 44.28	29 36 37.5
15	7	. . 54.7 12.7 30.5 48.1 5.7 . .	24 30.59	6.26	0.62	IV. 4	44.607	14 41.7	23.8	1.9	24 37.47	47 57.4
16	9	. . . . . . 37.5 . . 4.0 21.8	29 38.20	6.20	0.61	IV. 4	45.558	13 42.0	22.7	1.8	29 45.01	46 56.5
17	8	. . . . 51.0 8.9 26.8 44.8 . .	20 31 9.02	+ 6.18	+0.56	IV. 4	48.849	−10 15.2	−22.3	− 1.3	20 31 15.76	−29 43 29.0

CORRECTIONS.

Date		Corr. of Clock	Hourly rate	m	n	c	Zenith Point	Mic. Co.
		s.	s.	s.	s.	s.	° ' ''	r.
1846. Sept. 23	18 h.	− 1.513	0.011	− 0.415	+ 0.429	+ 0.022		

REMARKS.

(61) 4. Minutes assumed as 6 instead of 5.

INSTRUMENT READINGS.

Date		CIRCLE. A.	B.	C.	D.	E.	F.	Mean.	Barom. (in.)	Thermom. At.	Ex.	U.	L.	I.
Zone 60	Sept. 21, 22 5	76 24 62.0	61.0	75.2	65.0	49.9	41.6	59.12	30.135	70.2	65.3	68.5	68.8	
Zone 61	Sept. 23, 20 0	68 54 64.1	63.1	77.1	68.9	53.2	44.9	61.88	30.140	71.2	66.6	71.5	70.3	69.0
	20 21											65.7		
	21 0	63.1	64.1	75.0	68.9	53.1	43.9	61.85	30.138	70.0	64.7	69.0	68.9	
	21 24											64.2		
	21 40								30.138	69.0	63.4			
	22 0	63.0	64.1	78.0	68.5	53.0	43.1	61.62			63.2	67.0	68.0	
	22 20											63.3		
	22 31								30.136	68.3	63.0			

ZONE 61. SEPTEMBER 23. C. $D_e = -29°\ 32'\ 50''$—Continued.

No.	Mag.	— SECONDS OF TRANSIT. I.	II.	III.	IV.	V.	VI.	VII.	T. (h. m. s.)	a_1 (s.)	a_2 (s.)	MICROMETER		r.	i (° ' ")	d_1 ('')	d_2 ('')	Mean Right Ascension, 1850.0 (h. m. s.)	Mean Declination, 1850.0 (° ' '')
18	9	..	..	..	..	..	51.2	..	20 31 15.61	+ 6.18	+0.53	VI.	4	52.361	− 6 34.2	−22.5	− 0.8	20 31 22.32	− 29 39 47.5
19	7	..	24.8	42.8	0.5	18.3	35.7	..	34 0.43	6.15	0.71	IV.	3	36.032	23 41.5	21.9	3.1	34 7.29	56 56.5
20	8.9	..	..	5.7	..	40.8	58.7	..	35 23.25	6.14	0.61	IV.	4	43.752	15 35.3	21.6	2.0	35 30.08	48 49.9
21	8.9	..	57.2	14.8	32.7	50.7	8.0	..	37 32.69	6.12	0.67	IV.	3	39.164	20 25.0	21.2	2.7	37 39.48	53 38.9
22	9	..	23.0	..	57.8	16.7	..	50.5	39 58.12	6.09	0.63	IV.	3	42.458	16 58.2	20.7	2.2	40 4.84	29 50 11.1
23	7.8	..	50.6	8.1	25.6	43.5	..	..	42 25.86	6.06	0.94	IV.	2	13.799	46 57.9	20.2	6.3	42 32.86	30 20 14.4
24	7.8	..	..	..	..	44.5	2.0	20.2	42 26.69	6.06	0.72	V.	3	33.399	26 26.8	20.2	3.5	42 33.67	29 59 40.5
25	8.9	..	..	15.0	32.8	50.2	8.2	26.1	45 32.69	6.03	0.70	IV.	3	34.531	25 15.8	19.6	3.3	45 39.42	58 28.7
26	9	..	..	32.0	49.7	7.7	25.6	..	45 49.88	6.02	0.67	IV.	3	37.187	22 29.1	19.6	2.9	45 56.57	55 41.6
27	8.9	..	..	..	..	..	37.2	55.0	47 1.82	6.01	0.47	VI.	4	53.768	5 5.7	19.3	0.7	47 8.30	29 38 15.7
28	9	..	..	..	53.8	..	29.8	46.8	50 53.86	5.97	0.75	IV.	3	29.911	30 5.5	18.6	4.0	51 0.58	30 3 18.1
29	8	..	..	..	..	10.0	27.5	46.0	51 52.87	5.96	0.92	V.	2	14.391	45 18.0	18.4	6.2	51 59.75	18 32.6
30	8.9	..	..	..	..	13.5	31.5	49.0	51 55.67	5.96	0.92	V.	2	14.738	46 36.6	18.4	6.2	52 2.55	30 19 51.2
31	7	..	..	..	47.6	5.7	23.4	40.7	53 47.76	5.94	0.51	IV.	4	50.368	8 40.1	18.1	1.1	53 54.21	29 41 49.3
32	8	..	..	..	..	21.5	39.5	56.8	55 3.82	5.92	0.53	V.	4	48.181	10 57.0	17.8	1.4	55 10.27	29 44 6.2
33	8	..	14.5	32.8	50.7	8.1	25.7	..	57 50.36	5.89	0.82	IV.	3	22.645	37 41.4	17.3	5.0	57 57.07	30 10 53.7
34	8	..	0.7	17.8	35.7	..	11.5	..	20 59 35.89	5.87	0.79	IV.	3	25.327	34 53.3	17.0	4.6	20 59 42.55	8 4.9
35	6.7	..	..	40.7	..	16.5	33.9	51.7	21 0 58.40	5.86	0.92	IV.	2	14.389	46 21.1	16.8	6.2	21 1 5.18	19 34.1
36	7	..	17.7	35.7	53.0	10.8	28.7	..	4 53.18	5.82	0.88	IV.	2	17.200	43 24.9	16.0	5.8	4 59.68	30 16 36.7
37	9	..	..	..	49.2	..	24.8	..	5 49.27	5.80	0.67	IV.	3	34.478	25 19.2	15.9	3.3	5 55.74	29 58 28.4
38	8	..	..	42.6	0.7	18.7	36.5	..	9 0.73	5.76	0.77	IV.	3	25.419	34 47.6	15.3	4.6	9 7.26	30 7 57.5
39	8	..	..	..	..	..	9.8	27.5	9 34.27	5.76	0.60	VI.	4	39.698	19 49.0	15.2	2.6	9 40.63	29 52 56.8
40	8	..	..	..	56.7	14.6	31.0	59.7	10 56.35	5.75	0.67	IV.	3	34.129	25 41.8	15.0	3.3	11 2.77	58 49.3
41	6.7	..	..	..	47.5	..	22.8	40.7	12 47.44	5.72	0.55	IV.	4	44.461	14 51.0	14.7	1.9	12 53.71	29 47 57.6
42	7.8	..	..	..	..	..	14.6	32.1	13 38.90	5.71	0.72	VI.	3	28.918	31 7.6	14.6	4.1	13 45.33	30 4 16.3
43	8	..	8.1	..	..	1.7	19.0	..	17 43.73	5.67	0.44	IV.	4	52.698	6 13.7	13.9	0.8	17 49.84	29 39 18.4
44	9	..	..	..	..	35.7	..	..	18 17.95	5.66	0.53	V.	4	45.308	13 57.4	13.8	1.8	18 24.14	29 47 3.0
45	8	..	16.0	33.7	52.0	10.0	..	..	24 51.82	5.60	0.75	IV.	3	25.598	34 36.3	12.7	4.6	24 58.17	30 7 43.6
46	6	..	..	37.2	55.1	13.1	30.8	48.6	25 55.11	5.60	0.91	IV.	2	12.400	48 25.7	12.6	6.5	26 1.62	21 34.6
47	7.8	..	51.8	9.8	27.7	45.6	3.6	..	29 27.70	5.53	0.86	IV.	2	15.062	45 38.6	12.0	6.1	29 34.09	18 46.9
48	8.9	..	..	..	33.5	51.4	9.7	..	30 33.75	5.52	0.74	IV.	3	24.828	35 24.4	11.9	4.7	30 40.01	8 31.0
49	9	..	..	..	52.3	..	29.?	..	31 52.83	5.50	0.94	IV.	2	8.041	52 58.5	11.7	7.1	31 59.27	26 7.3
50	9	..	..	..	..	..	..	1.0?	33 6.60	5.49	0.88	VII.	2	12.831	47 57.5	11.5	6.4	33 12.97	30 21 5.4
51	9	..	12.8	..	..	..	25.0	..	39 48.92	5.41	0.61	IV.	3	34.758	25 1.4	10.6	3.3	39 54.94	29 58 5.3
52	7	..	23.5	..	69.0	..	36.7	54.5	40 0.10	5.40	0.66	IV.	3	29.522	30 30.1	10.5	4.0	40 6.16	30 3 34.6
53	8	..	17.0	..	52.8	10.8	28.2	..	46 52.74	5.32	0.89	IV.	2	9.691	51 15.2	9.5	6.9	46 58.95	30 24 21.6
54	9	..	..	..	..	2.0	19.7	..	49 1.97	5.30	0.50	IV.	4	43.061	16 18.8	9.2	2.1	49 7.77	29 49 20.1
55	6.7	..	9.5	27.1	44.9	2.5	20.7	..	50 44.96	5.28	0.47	IV.	4	46.018	13 13.0	8.9	1.7	50 50.71	46 13.6
56	9	..	..	..	..	..	53.5	..	51 18.12	5.27	0.41	VI.	4	50.867	8 7.8	8.9	1.0	51 24.10	41 7.7
57	9	..	..	..	21.0	49.0	..	22.0	53 21.13	5.25	0.42	IV.	4	48.700	10 24.7	8.6	1.3	53 26.80	43 24.6
58	9	..	54.5	..	..	..	19.1	37.5	53 42.92	5.25	0.53	IV.	4	39.908	19 36.6	8.5	2.6	53 48.70	29 52 37.7
59	7.8	..	..	..	..	..	..	..	53 . .	5.25	0.65	VII.	3	28.911	31 7.6	8.5	4.1	55 . .	30 4 10.2
60	7.8	..	..	..	..	48.0	6.0	..	57 30.41	5.20	0.47	V.	4	44.422	14 53.0	8.0	1.9	57 36.08	29 47 52.9
61	7.8	..	..	..	..	..	..	0.?	21 58 8.52	5.19	0.83	VII.	2	13.046	47 44.1	7.9	6.4	21 58 14.54	30 20 48.4
62	9	..	..	..	25.7	43.2	1.1	..	22 4 25.51	5.12	0.79	IV.	2	17.039	43 34.8	7.1	5.8	22 4 31.42	16 37.7
63	9	..	..	..	..	12.5	..	47.2	5 54.23	5.10	0.69	V.	3	24.801	35 26.0	6.9	4.7	6 0.02	8 27.6
64	9	..	..	35.7	56.7	..	..	51.0	7 56.95	5.09	0.65	IV.	3	27.965	32 7.7	6.7	4.2	8 2.69	5 8.6
65	9	..	41.0	..	16.5	34.0	..	9.7	8 16.41	5.08	0.64	IV.	3	29.102	30 56.4	6.6	4.1	8 22.13	3 57.1
66	8.9	..	29.7	48.0	5.7	23.6	41.6	..	22 14 5.71	+ 5.01	+0.83	IV.	2	11.706	−49 9.0	− 5.9	− 6.6	22 14 11.54	−30 22 11.5

CORRECTIONS.

Date	Corr. of Clock	Hourly rate	m	n	c	Zenith Point	Mic. Co.
1846.	h. s.	s.	s.	s.	s.	° ' ''	r.

INSTRUMENT READINGS.

Date	CIRCLE A	B	C	D	E	F	Mean	Barom. (In.)	THERMOM. At.	Ex.	U.	L.	I.
Zone 61	1846. Sept. 23, 22 40 ; 23 0 — 68 54 62.8	64.1	77.3	69.1	53.0	44.1	61.73	30.138	68.2	62.4	67.0	67.8	69.0

(THERMOM. header also prints the value 62.8.)

REMARKS.

(61) 29. Micrometer reading assumed as 15^r.391 instead of 14^r.391.

(61) 52. Transits discordant. Those over T.'s II and IV assumed to be 2^s too small.

(61) 56. Transit over T. VI assumed to have been recorded as over T. VII.

(61) 61. Transit assumed as at 2^s, to agree with Mural Z., 1847, and Arg. Z. 245.83.

ZONE 61. SEPTEMBER 23. C. $D_0 = -29°\,32'\,50''$—Continued.

No.	Mag.	I.	II.	III.	IV.	V.	VI.	VII.	T.	a_1	a_2	Mic.	n	r.	i	d_1	d_2	Mean Right Ascension, 1850.0	Mean Declination, 1850.0
67	8	..	0.0	17.7	35.0	53.0	11.0	..	22 17 35.35	+4.97	+0.47	IV.	4	41.906	-17 31.2	-5.5	-2.3	22 17 40.79	-29 50 29.0
68	8.9	..	23.0	..	58.7	16.4	34.1	..	20 58.63	4.93	0.47	IV.	4	41.708	17 43.6	5.2	2.3	21 4.03	50 41.1
69	8	..	..	11.8	..	47.0	5.0	..	24 29.45	4.89	0.40	IV.	4	46.992	12 11.9	4.8	1.6	24 34.74	29 45 8.3
70	7.8	..	..	..	..	20.0	37.5	55.5	25 1.95	4.88	0.85	V.	2	7.869	53 9.0	4.8	7.1	25 7.68	30 26 10.9
71	7.8	..	38.0	55.7	13.5	31.1	49.0	..	29 13.47	4.83	0.43	IV.	4	43.016	16 21.6	4.4	2.1	29 18.73	29 49 18.1
72	8	..	..	24.5	42.1	0.1	17.8	..	31 42.24	4.80	0.61	IV.	3	27.581	32 31.9	4.2	4.3	31 47.65	30 5 30.4
73	8	..	..	..	..	29.0	47.0	4.8	32 11.20	4.80	0.86	V.	2	6.808	54 17.0	4.2	7.3	32 16.80	27 18.5
74	7	..	..	37.5	55.0	13.1	31.0	..	33 55.24	4.78	0.63	IV.	3	24.631	35 36.9	4.0	4.7	34 0.65	30 8 35.6
75	-9	..	4.0	21.8	39.8	57.5	..	..	35 39.65	4.77	0.35	IV.	4	49.149	9 56.6	3.8	1.3	35 44.77	29 42 51.7
76	8	..	16.2	34.2	..	..	..	46.0	40 52.13	4.70	0.75	IV.	2	13.741	47 1.5	3.5	6.3	41 57.58	30 20 1.3
77	8	..	..	..	..	8.2	26.2	44.2	40 50.66	4.70	0.52	V.	3	34.023	25 47.5	3.5	3.4	41 55.88	29 58 44.4
78	7	..	..	..	..	..	34.0	52.0	42 58.44	4.67	0.75	VI.	1	13.911	46 47.5	3.3	6.2	43 3.86	30 19 47.0
79	8	..	..	..	20.5	38.5	55.8	..	44 20.51	4.65	0.52	IV.	3	34.151	25 39.6	3.2	3.4	44 25.68	29 58 36.2
80	9	..	45.0	..	20.2	..	..	13.6	46 20.35	4.63	0.61	IV.	3	26.310	33 51.6	3.1	4.5	46 25.59	30 6 49.2
81	8.9	..	..	..	..	..	34.0	52.3	46 58.56	4.62	0.80	VI.	2	9.360	51 35.6	3.0	6.9	47 3.93	24 35.5
82	1.2	..	57.2	15.2	33.5	51.5	9.2	..	49 15.49	4.59	0.80	IV.	2	9.013	51 57.6	2.8	7.0	49 20.87	24 56.4
83	7.8	..	..	..	17.2	35.5	53.6	..	51 17.61	4.57	0.69	IV.	3	17.612	42 57.0	2.7	5.7	51 22.87	30 15 55.4
84	7.8	..	..	45.0	..	19.5	37.2	55.0	53 2.03	4.55	0.29	IV.	4	52.370	6 34.5	2.6	0.8	53 6.87	29 39 27.9
85	8.9	..	..	51.0	10.0	..	..	2.0	22 53 9.17	4.55	0.47	IV.	4	37.181	22 28.0	2.6	2.9	22 53 14.19	55 23.5
86	6.7	..	32.2	50.2	8.0	..	43.5	1.5	23 0 8.03	4.46	0.26	IV.	4	53.770	5 6.4	2.2	0.6	23 0 12.75	37 59.2
87	8	..	18.8	36.5	54.5	12.3	29.4	..	1 54.32	4.45	0.35	IV.	4	46.604	12 36.3	2.1	1.6	1 59.12	29 45 30.0
88	7.8	..	..	..	..	52.0	9.8	27.6	2 34.12	4.44	0.73	V.	2	13.595	47 10.6	2.1	6.3	2 39.29	30 20 9.0
89	9	..	..	..	11.8	..	..	..	23 4 53.89	+4.41	+0.76	V.	2	10.229	-50 41.4	-2.0	-6.8	23 4 59.06	-30 23 40.2

ZONE 62. SEPTEMBER 24. P. $D_0 = -38°\,19'\,40'$.

No.	Mag.	I.	II.	III.	IV.	V.	VI.	VII.	T.	a_1	a_2	Mic.	n	r.	i	d_1	d_2	Mean Right Ascension, 1850.0	Mean Declination, 1850.0
1	9	..	2.5	..	42.0	..	..	..	19 19 42.03	+7.67	..	IV.	3	28.050	-32 2.4	-18.2	-10.7	19 19 .	-38 52 11.3
2	8	50.0	..	..	..	..	..	48.5	27 49.24	7.59	..	VII.	2	15.697	44 57.9	16.8	15.2	27 .	39 5 9.9
3	7	47.5	6.5	26.7	46.7	..	..	..	41 46.47	7.44	..	IV.	3	33.197	26 39.5	13.6	8.9	41 .	38 46 42.0
4	9	..	17.0	..	..	..	..	..	41 56.44	7.44	..	IV.	4	45.290	13 58.9	13.6	4.7	42 .	33 57.2
5	7	..	..	..	0.5	20.0	..	..	46 0.41	7.39	..	IV.	4	41.730	17 42.2	12.7	5.9	46 .	37 40.9
6	6.7	..	52.0	12.5	32.0	..	..	..	47 31.87	7.38	..	IV.	4	51.940	7 1.3	12.4	2.4	47 .	38 26 56.1
7	9	4.0	24.0	..	..	..	..	..	51 3.57	7.33	..	II.	2	16.017	44 38.7	11.6	15.1	51 .	39 4 45.4
8	9	..	..	..	3.0	..	..	..	51 3.05	7.33	..	IV.	2	26.087	34 7.5	11.6	11.4	51 .	38 54 10.5
9	6.7	..	..	7.5	27.0	..	..	..	53 27.05	7.30	..	IV.	4	57.585	1 8.4	11.1	0.5	53 .	21 0.0
10	7	7.0	27.0	46.3	..	..	..	..	19 59 6.22	7.23	..	III.	3	35.640	24 6.1	9.9	8.0	19 59 .	44 4.0
11	8.9	..	43.0	..	..	22.0	..	..	20 0 2.38	7.22	..	II.	2	20.570	39 53.3	9.7	13.4	20 0 .	50 56.4
12	7	30.0	49.7	9.5	29.3	..	..	..	3 29.29	7.18	..	IV.	3	26.995	33 8.5	9.0	11.1	3 .	53 8.6
13	7	2.0	21.7	41.3	1.0	..	..	..	20 25 1.05	+6.91	..	IV.	4	43.290	-16 4.5	-4.5	-5.3	20 25 .	-38 35 54.3

CORRECTIONS.

Date.	Corr. of Clock.	Hourly rate.	m	n	c	Zenith Point.	Mic. Co.
	h. s.	s.	s.	s.	s.	° ' "	r.
1846. Sept. 24.	20 -1.620	-0.015	-0.415	+0.429	+0.022		

REMARKS.

(61) 82. Transit over T.'s III–VII assumed as recorded over T.'s II–VI.

INSTRUMENT READINGS.

Date.	CIRCLE.							Barom.	THERMOM.				
	A.	B.	C.	D.	E.	F.	Mean.		At.	Ex.	U.	L.	I.
	° ' "						"	in.	°	°	°	°	°
Zone 62 Sept. 24, 19 19	77 39 61.3	59.0	75.4	62.8	49.4	40.6	58.08	30.088	74.5	73.0	73.0	71.0	70.0
19 46	..	..	..	..	..	..	..	30.093	74.2	70.8	.		
20 25	..	..	..	..	..	..	..	30.100	73.4	69.9			

Zone 63. September 24. P. $D_0 = -28°\,17'\,30''$.

No.	Mag.	I.	II.	III.	IV.	V.	VI.	VII.
1	7	33.5	50.5	8.0	26.0	..	..	..
2	7	..	42.0	59.0	16.3	..	..	..
3	9	..	..	..	..	..	36.0	..
4	9	..	51.0	..	..	..	..	..
5	9	..	..	..	..	..	..	14.0
6	9	..	..	..	6.0	..	..	..
7	9	..	15.0	..	51.0	..	..	..
8	7	..	0.5	18.0	35.7	..	..	..
9	8	..	..	..	16.0	33.5	..	..
10	7	..	5.0	23.0	40.3	..	..	..
11	8	..	..	..	15.3	..	50.7	..
12	7	..	5.0	22.3	40.0	57.0	..	..
13	7	2.0	19.0	36.7	54.3	..	..	..
14	8	..	..	..	..	..	59.0	17.0
15	7	..	..	..	0.0	..	35.0	..
16	8	..	..	..	14.0	31.0	..	..
17	7	..	..	..	52.5	10.0	..	..
18	5.6	..	..	..	..	25.0	42.0	..
19	9	..	..	47.5	4.5	..	..	..
20	7	..	..	..	58.0	15.5	..	..
21	9	..	..	..	..	..	5.0	..
22	9	..	..	..	..	4.0	..	..
23	8	..	..	44.0	..	..	..	..
24	7	..	..	..	..	..	40.0	57.5
25	7	..	46.0	3.0	21.0	..	..	..
26	9	..	..	..	..	..	..	24.0
27	9	..	56.0	..	..	50.0	..	..
28	5.6	..	..	..	42.5	0.0	17.3	..
29	8	7.0	25.0	42.0	..	..	..	..
30	7	..	..	28.0	45.0	3.0	..	..
31	9	..	..	..	..	25.0	..	..
32	8	5.7	23.3	41.0	..	..	..	..
33	7.8	46.5	4.0	21.7	30.0	..	..	..
34	9	..	..	33.0	..	..	..	..
35	8	35.0	52.5	10.0	27.5	..	..	..
36	9	..	..	..	..	..	..	39.0
37	6.7	..	32.0	..	7.2	..	..	..
38	8	51.0	8.7	26.3	..	..	..	..
39	7	32.7	50.5	8.0	25.3	..	..	..
40	9	..	..	..	23.0	..	..	..
41	9	..	..	39.0	..	..	..	..
42	8.9	..	33.0	..	8.0	..	..	..
43	9	0.0	17.5	35.5	..	..	..	..
44	6	10.5	58.0	15.3	33.0	..	..	..
45	9	..	..	..	40.0	..	..	..
46	5.6	..	21.0	38.5	56.0	..	..	..
47	9	..	..	..	..	5.5	..	..
48	8	..	41.5	59.0	16.0	..	..	..
49	7	11.5	29.5	47.0	..	..	..	..

No.	T. (h. m. s.)	a_1	a_2	MICR. wire	n	r.	i (' ")	d_1	d_2	Mean Right Ascension, 1850.0 (h. m. s.)	Mean Declination, 1850.0 (° ' ")
1	21 1 25.92	+5.70	+1.13	IV.	2	12.933	-47 52.1	-20.7	-6.4	21 1 32.75	-29 5 49.2
2	3 16.65	5.68	0.65	IV.	4	46.253	12 58.4	20.4	1.1	3 22.98	28 30 49.9
3	5 0.85	5.66	1.00	VI.	2	21.290	39 8.1	20.1	5.3	5 7.51	28 57 3.5
4	7 26.28	5.63	1.16	II.	1	10.925	49 54.8	19.7	6.6	7 33.07	29 7 51.1
5	7 21.27	5.63	0.95	VII.	3	24.660	35 34.5	19.7	4.9	7 27.85	28 53 29.1
6	14 6.04	5.55	0.84	IV.	3	33.565	26 16.4	18.6	3.7	14 12.43	44 8.7
7	17 50.56	5.51	0.75	IV.	3	40.333	19 11.7	17.9	2.8	17 56.82	37 2.4
8	24 35.62	5.44	0.69	IV.	4	44.475	14 50.1	16.8	2.3	24 41.75	32 39.2
9	25 15.48	5.43	0.71	IV.	4	43.545	15 48.4	16.7	2.4	25 21.62	33 37.5
10	29 40.31	5.38	0.72	IV.	4	43.253	16 6.8	16.0	2.5	29 46.41	33 55.3
11	33 15.51	5.34	0.54	IV.	4	54.697	4 9.0	15.4	1.0	33 21.39	21 55.4
12	36 39.86	5.30	0.91	IV.	3	29.083	30 57.6	14.9	4.3	36 46.07	48 46.8
13	38 54.27	5.28	0.61	IV.	4	50.350	8 41.3	14.6	1.5	39 0.16	26 27.4
14	39 24.07	5.27	1.01	VI.	3	23.947	36 19.5	14.5	4.9	39 30.35	54 8.9
15	42 0.00	5.24	0.77	IV.	4	39.503	20 2.3	14.1	2.9	42 6.01	37 49.3
16	48 13.70	5.17	1.01	IV.	3	22.900	37 25.3	13.1	5.1	48 19.88	55 13.5
17	50 52.47	5.14	0.54	V.	4	55.850	2 56.4	12.7	0.9	50 58.15	28 20 40.0
18	52 7.05	5.12	1.23	V.	1	8.485	52 27.7	12.6	7.0	52 13.40	29 10 17.3
19	55 4.81	5.09	0.90	IV.	3	31.355	25 35.2	12.1	4.0	55 10.80	28 46 21.3
20	55 57.92	5.08	1.22	IV.	1	9.120	51 48.0	12.0	6.9	56 4.22	29 9 36.9
21	56 29.87	5.07	1.02	VI.	3	23.667	36 37.1	11.9	5.0	56 35.96	28 54 24.0
22	57 28.93	5.06	0.89	V.	3	32.545	27 1.4	11.8	3.8	57 34.88	44 47.0
23	59 1.58	5.04	0.92	III.	3	30.590	29 22.9	11.6	4.1	59 7.54	47 8.6
24	21 59 4.82	5.04	1.00	VI.	3	25.350	34 51.7	11.6	4.7	21 59 10.86	28 52 38.0
25	22 1 20.94	5.02	1.12	IV.	2	16.790	43 50.4	11.3	5.9	22 1 27.08	29 1 37.6
26	1 31.46	5.02	0.61	VII.	4	52.450	6 28.0	11.3	1.3	1 37.09	28 24 11.6
27	4 31.78	4.98	1.11	V.	2	16.805	43 49.3	10.9	5.9	4 37.87	29 1 36.1
28	5 42.42	4.97	0.69	V.	4	46.455	12 45.4	10.8	2.0	5 48.08	28 30 28.2
29	9 50.80	4.92	1.00	III.	3	26.015	34 9.8	10.3	4.7	10 5.72	51 54.6
30	10 45.33	4.91	1.07	IV.	3	20.690	39 43.9	10.2	5.4	10 51.31	57 29.5
31	12 7.36	4.89	1.09	V.	2	19.360	51 9.4	10.0	5.5	12 13.34	58 54.9
32	14 58.41	4.86	0.82	III.	4	38.760	20 48.9	9.7	3.0	15 4.69	38 31.6
33	17 39.14	4.83	0.93	IV.	3	31.343	28 35.9	9.5	4.0	17 44.90	46 19.4
34	18 50.58	4.82	0.94	III.	3	30.060	29 56.1	9.4	4.1	18 56.34	47 39.6
35	34 27.57	4.74	0.85	IV.	3	37.290	22 22.7	7.8	3.2	34 33.16	40 3.7
36	34 46.23	4.74	1.06	VII.	2	21.920	38 27.9	7.8	5.2	34 52.03	28 56 10.9
37	45 7.28	4.51	1.30	IV.	1	6.093	54 59.0	6.9	7.3	45 13.09	29 12 43.2
38	47 43.78	4.49	0.98	III.	3	28.455	31 37.0	6.7	4.4	47 49.25	28 49 18.1
39	49 25.47	4.47	0.94	IV.	3	31.587	28 20.5	6.6	4.0	49 30.88	46 1.1
40	50 23.05	4.46	1.09	IV.	2	21.073	39 22.0	6.5	5.3	50 28.60	57 3.8
41	51 56.57	4.44	0.90	III.	3	33.970	25 50.7	6.4	3.7	52 7.91	43 30.8
42	53 8.08	4.42	0.99	IV.	3	28.973	31 4.5	6.3	4.3	53 13.41	28 48 45.1
43	22 55 52.83	4.40	1.11	III.	2	20.690	44 59.7	6.1	6.0	22 55 58.34	29 2 41.8
44	23 1 33.07	4.33	1.06	IV.	3	23.910	36 22.0	5.8	4.9	23 1 38.46	28 54 2.7
45	2 40.05	4.31	1.02	IV.	3	26.820	33 19.5	5.7	4.6	2 45.38	28 50 59.8
46	10 56.15	4.22	1.32	IV.	1	6.253	54 48.9	5.2	7.3	11 1.69	29 12 31.4
47	12 47.96	4.20	0.74	V.	4	46.955	18 13.8	5.2	2.0	12 52.90	28 29 51.0
48	19 16.42	4.12	1.05	IV.	3	25.643	34 33.4	4.8	4.7	19 21.50	28 52 12.9
49	23 21 4.56	+4.10	+1.23	III.	2	13.163	-47 37.8	-4.8	-6.4	23 21 9.89	-29 5 19.0

CORRECTIONS.

Date.	Corr. of Clock.	Hourly rate.	m	n	c	Zenith Point.	Mic. Co.
	h.	s.	s.	s.	s.	° ' "	r.
1846. Sept. 24,	20	- 1.620	- 0.015	- 0.415	+ 0.429	+ 0.022		

REMARKS.

(63) 22. Transit over T. VI assumed as recorded over T. V.

Sept. 24. Readings of Barometer, &c., at 20h 35m.

(63) 43. Micrometer reading assumed as 15r.690, not 20r.690.

INSTRUMENT READINGS.

	Date.	A.	B.	C.	D.	E.	F.	Mean.	Barom. (in.)	At.	Ex.	U.	L.	I.
Zone 63	1846. Sept. 24, 21 1	67 39 60.2	58.7	75.0	61.6	48.6	40.0	57.35	30.104	73.0	69.0	75.0	71.0	70.0
	21 29	..	..	..	..	..	..	..	30.108	72.5	68.0			
	21 59	..	..	..	..	..	..	..	30.114	73.2	68.3			
	22 34	..	..	..	..	..	..	..	30.110	72.0	67.0			
	23 1	59.5	59.0	75.0	62.0	49.2	39.0	57.12	30.110	71.7	67.0			
	0 1	..	..	..	..	..	..	..	30.100	70.8	66.0			
	0 30	59.0	58.8	75.0	62.2	47.5	38.6	56.85	30.100	70.3	66.0	70.0	70.0	70.0

Zone 63. September 24. P. D.$_0$ = −28° 17′ 30″—Continued.

No.	Mag.	I.	II.	III.	IV.	V.	VI.	VII.	T.	a_1	a_2	Mic.		r.	i	d_1	d_2	Mean Right Ascension, 1850.0	Mean Declination, 1850.0
									h. m. s.	s.	s.			r.	′ ″	″	″	h. m. s.	° ′ ″
50	9	..	..	..	..	..	50.0	..	23 21 15.03	+4.10	+0.69	VI.	4	51.270	−7 42.8	−4.8	−1.4	23 21 19.82	−28 25 19.0
51	9	59.0	16.5	34.0	51.5	..	..	..	26 51.54	4.04	0.77	IV.	4	44.415	14 53.8	4.6	2.3	26 56.35	28 32 30.7
52	9	..	17.0	..	52.0	..	..	..	30 52.15	4.00	1.24	IV.	2	12.655	48 9.6	4.5	6.4	30 57.39	29 5 50.5
53	6.7	..	42.7	0.0	17.5	..	..	..	32 17.72	3.98	1.32	IV.	1	7.450	53 32.7	4.4	7.1	32 23.02	29 11 14.2
54	8	..	45.0	3.0	..	..	..	..	34 20.31	3.96	0.73	III.	4	48.580	10 32.4	4.4	1.8	34 25.00	28 28 8.6
55	9	..	..	..	..	58.0	15.0	..	34 40.08	3.96	1.18	V.	2	17.460	43 8.5	4.4	5.8	34 45.22	29 0 48.7
56	7	..	..	27.0	..	..	..	..	37 44.51	3.92	0.66	III.	4	55.287	3 32.1	4.3	0.9	37 49.09	29 21 7.3
57	9	34.0	52.0	..	..	..	..	..	40 26.86	3.89	0.96	II.	3	33.790	26 1.8	4.3	3.7	40 31.71	43 39.8
58	5	..	27.0	44.3	2.0	..	..	..	41 2.04	3.89	1.14	IV.	2	20.530	39 56.1	4.3	5.4	41 7.07	57 35.8
59	7	..	..	..	28.0	45.5	..	..	41 27.98	3.88	0.92	IV.	3	36.205	23 30.7	4.2	3.4	41 32.78	28 41 8.3
60	8	10.3	28.0	45.5	..	..	..	..	44 3.17	3.85	1.30	III.	1	8.940	51 59.1	4.2	0.9	44 8.32	29 9 40.2
61	8	48.5	..	24.0	..	..	..	..	49 41.38	3.80	1.08	III.	3	25.213	35 0.3	4.1	4.8	49 46.26	28 52 39.2
62	9	..	..	..	14.0	..	..	..	50 14.05	3.79	1.05	IV.	3	27.640	32 28.1	4.1	4.5	50 18.89	50 6.7
63	8	..	..	..	2.5	..	37.5	..	51 2.50	3.78	0.86	VI.	4	40.540	18 56.4	4.1	2.8	51 7.14	36 33.3
64	7.8	..	22.3	40.0	..	..	..	..	23 52 57.48	3.76	0.98	III.	3	32.955	26 54.4	4.2	3.8	23 53 2.22	44 32.4
65	6.7	45.0	..	..	37.5	55.0	..	..	0 1 37.54	3.67	1.05	IV.	3	28.357	31 43.3	4.2	4.3	0 1 42.26	49 21.8
66	5.6	0.3	17.7	35.3	52.7	..	..	..	3 52.81	3.65	0.89	IV.	4	39.053	20 30.4	4.2	3.0	3 57.35	38 7.6
67	9	..	..	..	..	46.0	..	..	4 30.44	3.64	0.88	V.	4	39.960	19 33.1	4.2	2.9	4 34.96	37 10.2
68	9	..	..	..	28.5	..	3.5	..	5 28.50	3.63	0.91	IV.	4	38.335	21 15.6	4.2	3.1	5 33.04	38 52.9
69	9	57.0	..	32.0	..	..	..	..	11 49.61	3.57	1.02	III.	3	31.453	28 28.8	4.3	4.0	10 54.20	46 7.1
70	9	1.0	..	..	..	11.0	..	..	11 53.52	3.57	1.02	V.	3	30.514	29 27.9	4.3	4.1	10 58.11	47 6.3
71	7	17.5	35.0	52.5	10.0	..	..	..	19 10.03	3.50	0.84	IV.	4	44.515	14 47.5	4.5	2.3	18 14.37	28 32 24.3
72	7	56.0	13.5	31.0	..	..	..	..	19 49.72	3.49	1.28	III.	2	13.982	46 46.4	4.5	6.2	19 53.49	29 4 27.1
73	8.9	..	31.5	..	6.0	..	..	..	23 6.34	3.46	1.02	IV.	3	31.643	28 17.0	4.6	3.9	23 10.82	28 45 55.5
74	9	..	31.0	50.0	..	..	..	..	25 6.85	3.44	1.05	III.	3	29.036	31 0.4	4.6	4.3	25 11.34	28 48 39.3
75	7	45.3	2.5	20.5	37.5	..	..	..	0 30 37.73	+3.38	+0.77	IV.	4	49.840	−9 13.1	−4.8	−1.6	0 30 41.88	−28 26 49.5

Zone 64. September 28. P. D.$_0$ = −24° 32′ 40″.

No.	Mag.	I.	II.	III.	IV.	V.	VI.	VII.	T.	a_1	a_2	Mic.		r.	i	d_1	d_2	Mean Right Ascension, 1850.0	Mean Declination, 1850.0
1	9	30.0	47.5	4.0	..	..	..	..	20 1 21.23	+2.36	+0.76	III.	2	12.237	−48 35.9	−15.8	−4.5	20 1 24.35	−25 21 36.2
2	8	..	..	..	25.0	..	58.5	..	2 24.83	2.35	2.36	IV.	4	52.052	6 54.3	15.6	0.5	2 29.54	24 39 50.4
3	8	..	..	..	59.0	..	..	..	3 41.94	2.34	1.04	IV.	2	18.656	41 53.5	15.2	3.9	3 45.32	25 14 52.6
4	9	..	..	16.0	..	..	..	..	6 32.95	2.31	2.44	III.	4	52.710	6 13.1	14.7	0.5	6 37.70	24 39 8.3
5	8	13.0	..	47.0	..	..	..	..	9 3.90	2.29	2.07	III.	4	42.540	10 51.6	14.1	1.5	9 8.26	49 47.2
6	9	..	..	..	..	..	..	55.5	9 4.64	2.29	2.31	VII.	4	48.456	10 38.8	14.1	0.9	9 9.24	24 43 33.8
7	8	50.5	7.5	25.0	42.5	..	..	..	11 42.91	2.26	1.10	IV.	2	17.664	42 55.7	13.5	4.0	11 46.27	25 15 53.2
8	8	..	..	..	..	..	45.0	..	12 11.13	2.26	2.18	IV.	4	44.342	14 57.7	13.4	1.3	12 15.57	24 47 52.4
9	9	..	..	..	..	..	27.0	..	13 52.96	2.24	0.82	VI.	1	9.780	51 6.2	13.0	4.8	13 56.02	25 24 4.0
10	8	..	38.0	55.5	..	..	..	..	17 12.30	2.21	0.79	III.	1	8.133	52 49.8	12.2	5.0	17 15.30	25 25 47.0
11	8	..	..	59.0	..	..	..	..	19 15.99	2.19	2.18	III.	4	41.975	17 27.0	11.8	1.5	18 20.36	24 50 20.3
12	6.7	..	..	55.0	12.5	29.0	..	..	19 39.13	2.19	2.62	IV.	4	52.940	5 58.5	11.7	0.4	19 33.94	24 38 50.6
13	7	..	..	..	18.0	..	..	..	23 18.03	2.15	0.99	IV.	1	11.397	49 25.6	10.9	4.6	23 21.17	25 22 21.1
14	6.7	..	..	..	..	8.5	26.0	..	23 51.65	2.15	0.84	V.	1	7.210	53 47.6	10.8	5.0	23 54.64	26 43.4
15	8	..	..	..	..	7.5	..	..	24 50.47	2.14	1.50	V.	3	23.240	37 4.2	10.6	3.4	24 54.11	25 9 58.2
16	7	..	16.0	33.5	50.0	..	..	..	26 50.16	2.12	2.17	IV.	4	39.350	20 11.9	10.1	1.8	26 54.45	24 53 3.8
17	8	..	8.5	..	42.5	..	..	..	28 42.49	2.10	2.18	IV.	4	39.060	20 30.0	9.7	1.8	28 46.77	53 21.5
18	7	..	..	..	..	23.5	40.5	..	29 6.59	2.09	2.52	V.	4	47.320	11 51.2	9.6	1.0	29 11.20	44 41.8
19	7	33.0	50.0	6.5	24.0	..	..	..	20 31 23.77	+2.07	+2.81	IV.	4	53.980	−4 54.0	−9.1	−0.3	20 31 28.65	−24 37 43.4

CORRECTIONS.

Date.	Corr. of Clock.	Hourly rate.	m	n	c	Zenith Point.	Mic. Co.
	h.	s.	s.	s.	s.	° ′ ″	r.
1846.	h.	s.	s.	s.	s.		

INSTRUMENT READINGS.

Date.	A.	B.	C.	D.	E.	F.	Mean.	Barom.	At.	Ex.	U.	L.	I.
	° ′ ″						″	in.	°	°	°	°	°
Zone 64 1846, Sept. 28, 20 0	63 54 07.3	68.4	81.2	73.4	53.4	45.0	64.78	30.250	62.0	56.7	64.0	64.5	68.0
20 19	..	..	..	..	..	..	..	30.262	62.0	55.5			
20 46	..	..	..	..	..	..	..	30.272	62.0	55.2			

REMARKS.

Sept. 28. 20h 19m, hazy; stars unsteady.

(63) 69. Minutes assumed as 10 instead of 11.

(63) 70. Minutes assumed as 10 instead of 11.

(63) 71. Minutes assumed as 18 instead of 19.

(64) 11. Minutes assumed as 18 instead of 19.

(64) 2. Transit over T. V assumed as recorded over T. IV.

Zone 64. September 24. P. D_0 = −24° 34′ 4″—Continued.

Seconds of Transit are columns I.–VII.

No.	Mag.	I.	II.	III.	IV.	V.	VI.	VII.	T.	a_1	a_2	Micr.		r	i	d_1	d_2	Mean Right Ascension, 1850.0	Mean Declination, 1850.0
									h. m. s.	s.	s.			r	′ ″	″	″	h. m. s.	° ′ ″
20	9	45.0	2.5						20 34 36.26	+ 2.04	+1.48	II.	2	19.853	−40 38.3	− 8.5	− 3.7	20 34 39.78	−25 13 30.5
21	9			34.0					36 51.00	2.02	1.98	III.	3	31.333	28 36.4	8.0	2.6	36 55.00	1 27.0
22	9			2.0					38 19.00	2.00	2.01	III.	3	31.665	28 15.4	7.9	2.6	38 23.01	25 1 5.9
23	8				44.0	1.0			44 0.99	1.95	2.64	IV.	4	45.620	13 38.0	6.5	1.2	44 5.58	24 46 25.7
24	6.7		33.0	50.5	7.0				45 7.15	1.93	2.51	IV.	4	41.730	17 42.2	6.2	1.6	45 11.59	50 30.0
25	8			52.0	9.0				20 46 25.97	+ 1.92	+2.61	III.	4	44.090	−15 14.3	− 6.0	− 1.3	20 46 30.50	−24 48 1.6

Zone 65. September 28. P. D_0 = −27° 2′ 50″.

No.	Mag.	I.	II.	III.	IV.	V.	VI.	VII.	T.	a_1	a_2	Micr.		r	i	d_1	d_2	Mean Right Ascension, 1850.0	Mean Declination, 1850.0
1	8				9.0		1.5		21 0 9.19	+ 3.94	+0.59	IV.	2	20.955	−39 29.3	− 9.0	− 4.4	21 0 13.72	−27 42 32.7
2	8	1.0	18.0	35.0					3 52.64	3.91	0.92	III.	4	43.563	15 47.4	8.3	1.6	3 57.47	18 47.3
3	9	32.0	50.0	7.0	24.0				6 24.29	3.88	0.70	IV.	3	29.755	30 15.3	7.9	3.3	6 28.87	33 16.5
4	7		11.0	28.5	44.5	3.0			8 45.41	3.88	1.10	V.	4	55.463	3 20.6	7.4	0.2	8 50.39	6 18.2
5	9				55.0				9 55.00	3.84	0.97	IV.	4	47.712	11 26.7	7.2	1.1	9 59.81	14 25.0
6	7				57.5				10 57.54	3.83	0.42	IV.	1	13.510	47 13.2	7.0	5.3	11 1.79	50 15.5
7	9							42.0	11 7.17	3.82	0.33	VI.	1	7.862	53 6.3	7.0	5.9	11 11.32	56 9.2
8	9							35.5	12 0.90	3.81	0.96	VI.	4	47.450	11 42.5	6.9	1.2	12 5.67	14 40.6
9	9							54.0	13 1.85	3.80	0.49	VII.	2	18.055	42 30.3	6.7	4.7	13 6.14	45 31.7
10	9	40.0	57.0	14.5					18 31.84	3.74	0.72	III.	4	34.270	25 32.1	5.8	2.7	18 36.30	28 30.6
11	7.8				12.5	29.5			19 29.64	3.73	0.97	IV.	4	50.826	8 11.2	5.6	0.8	19 34.34	11 7.6
12	9		36.0	54.0					22 11.08	3.70	0.51	VII.	2	21.017	44 48.2	5.1	5.0	22 15.29	47 49.3
13	8				57.5		32.5		24 14.98	3.68	0.55	V.	3	25.080	35 8.7	4.9	3.9	24 19.21	38 7.5
14	5.6				1.0	18.5	36.0		21 30 18.47	+ 3.61	0.21	IV.	1	5.510	−55 34.0	− 3.8	− 6.3	21 30 22.29	−27 58 34.1

Zone 66. September 30. P. D_0 = −27° 2′ 30″.

No.	Mag.	I.	II.	III.	IV.	V.	VI.	VII.	T.	a_1	a_2	Micr.		r	i	d_1	d_2	Mean Right Ascension, 1850.0	Mean Declination, 1850.0
1	6.7		45.0	2.5	20.0				21 30 19.94	+ 2.67	+0.07	IV.	1	5.373	−55 42.7	−14.2	− 6.3	21 30 22.68	−27 58 33.2
2	9			31.0					34 48.34	2.62	0.29	III.	4	43.445	21 8.6	13.6	2.3	34 51.25	23 54.5
3	8				17.0				35 16.97	2.61	0.32	IV.	4	49.770	9 17.5	13.5	1.0	35 19.90	12 2.0
4	7			1.0	18.3				36 18.30	2.60	0.32	IV.	4	51.140	7 51.9	13.3	0.8	36 21.22	10 35.8
5	8						17.5	52.0	37 0.07	2.59	0.32	V.	4	51.275	7 42.9	13.2	0.8	37 2.98	10 26.9
6	9						35.0		39 17.52	2.57	0.12	V.	1	10.055	50 49.4	12.9	5.7	39 20.21	53 35.0
7	7	33.0	50.3	7.5					48 24.89	2.46	0.32	III.	4	50.550	8 28.8	11.5	0.9	48 27.67	11 11.2
8	8			59.3	16.7	34.0			52 16.66	2.42	0.30	V.	4	47.480	11 41.1	11.0	1.2	52 19.38	14 23.3
9	7	40.5	55.0	15.3	33.0				54 32.80	2.39	0.15	IV.	2	16.890	43 44.1	10.6	4.9	54 35.34	46 29.6
10	5		27.0	44.3	1.5			53.5	21 56 1.58	2.37	0.22	IV.	4	29.947	30 5.3	10.4	3.3	21 56 4.17	32 47.0
11	9	35.0	52.0	9.5					22 0 26.84	2.32	0.26	III.	4	37.840	21 46.6	9.8	2.4	22 0 29.42	24 28.8
12	7						12.0		2 54.52	2.30	0.12	I.	1	10.383	50 29.0	9.5	5.7	2 56.94	53 14.2
13	7			48.0	5.0				4 5.21	2.28	0.14	IV.	2	14.130	46 37.2	9.4	5.2	4 7.63	49 21.8
14	6							2.5	4 27.95	2.28	0.35	VI.	1	57.470	1 14.2	9.3	0.1	4 30.58	3 53.6
15	7								5 ..	2.28	0.31	VII.	4	47.760	11 22.8	9.2	1.2	5 ..	14 3.2
16	6.7			22.0	39.5				15 39.41	2.15	0.34	IV.	4	53.737	5 8.5	7.9	0.5	15 41.00	7 46.9
17	6				19.5	37.0			16 19.57	2.14	0.20	V.	3	25.880	34 18.4	7.8	3.8	16 21.91	37 0.0
18	6	22.3	39.5	57.0	14.3				19 14.24	2.10	0.33	IV.	4	50.820	8 11.5	7.5	0.9	19 16.67	10 49.9
19	6							20.0	19 45.17	2.10	0.08	VI.	1	5.515	55 34.8	7.4	6.3	19 47.35	58 18.5
20	6				2.5	19.5			21 19.70	2.08	0.13	IV.	2	11.230	49 38.9	7.2	5.6	21 21.91	52 21.7
21	9			45.0					22 24 19.70	+ 2.04	+0.32	II.	4	47.797	−11 21.0	− 6.9	− 1.2	22 24 22.66	−27 13 59.7

CORRECTIONS.

Date.	Corr. of Clock.	Hourly rate.	m	n	c	Zenith Point.	Mic. Co.
1846. h.	s.	s.	s.	s.	s.	° ′ ″	r

INSTRUMENT READINGS.

	Date.	CIRCLE.							Barom.	THERMOM.				
		A.	B.	C.	D.	E.	F.	Mean.		At.	Ex.	U.	L.	I.
	1846. h. m.	° ′ ″						″	In.	°	°	°	°	°
Zone 65	Sept. 28, 21 0	66 24 68.4	70.5	85.0	74.6	59.8	46.4	67.45	30.274	62.0	55.5	63.5	62.5	67.0
	21 30								30.284	62.8	54.5			
Zone 66	Sept. 30, 21 25	66 24 65.8	64.0	78.7	67.6	51.3	43.7	61.85	29.922	66.0	60.6	65.5		64.0
	22 0								29.918	65.7	60.3			
	22 38								29.914	65.0	60.7			
	23 19								29.918	64.6	62.0			
	23 51								29.914	64.0	58.5			
	0 28								29.914	63.3	57.0			

REMARKS.

(65) 12. Micrometer reading assumed as 16ʳ.017, not 21ʳ.017.

(66) 2. Micrometer reading assumed as 38ʳ.445, not 43ʳ.445.

ZONE 66. SEPTEMBER 30. P. $D_o = -27^\circ\ 2'\ 30''$—Continued.

No.	Mag.	I.	II.	III.	IV.	V.	VI.	VII.	T. (h. m. s.)	a_1	a_2	Micrometer		r.	i	d_1	d_2	Mean Right Ascension, 1850.0	Mean Declination, 1850.0
22	9	46.0	3.3	20.5	38.0				22 27 38.03	+ 2.01	+0.18	IV.	2	20.840	−39 36.5	− 6.5	− 4.4	22 27 40.22	−27 42 17.4
23	7.8	9.0	26.5	43.7	1.0				30 1.10	1.98	0.19	IV.	3	24.067	36 12.2	6.3	4.0	30 3.27	38 52.5
24	3.4	26.7	44.0	1.5	18.7				32 18.83	1.95	0.15	IV.	2	14.003	46 45.1	6.0	5.2	32 20.93	49 26.3
25	8	32.5	49.5	7.3	24.5				35 24.52	1.92	0.20	IV.	3	23.530	36 46.0	5.7	4.1	35 26.64	39 25.8
26	7		49.5	6.7	24.0				37 24.14	1.89	0.17	IV.	2	17.395	43 12.7	5.5	4.8	37 26.20	45 53.0
27	7			21.0	38.5	55.7			38 38.38	1.88	0.36	V.	4	56.047	2 43.9	5.4	0.3	38 40.62	5 19.6
28	9			27.0					42 44.34	1.83	0.32	III.	4	47.623	11 32.4	5.0	1.3	42 46.49	14 8.7
29	9				5.0				45 5.04	1.80	0.16	IV.	2	16.600	44 2.5	4.8	4.0	45 7.00	46 42.2
30	8		50.5	8.0	25.5				46 25.40	1.79	0.17	IV.	2	18.907	41 37.7	4.7	4.6	46 27.36	44 17.0
31	7.8				38.0				47 38.04	1.77	0.27	IV.	3	35.403	24 21.1	4.6	2.7	47 40.08	26 58.4
32	9			40.0	57.5				51 57.45	1.72	0.26	IV.	3	34.325	25 28.6	4.2	2.8	51 59.43	28 5.8
33	8							55.5	52 3.27	1.72	0.14	IV.	1	9.580	51 19.2	4.2	5.8	52 5.13	53 59.2
34	6.7	36.0	53.3	10.7	28.0			20.3	55 28.08	1.68	0.22	IV.	3	25.617	34 35.0	3.9	3.8	55 29.98	37 12.7
35	6					58.5		33.3	22 56 41.01	1.67	0.13	V.	1	7.020	53 59.4	3.8	6.1	22 56 42.81	56 39.3
36	7.8	13.5	31.0		6.0		41.0		23 3 5.92	1.59	0.19	IV.	2	19.540	40 58.2	3.3	4.6	23 3 7.70	43 36.1
37	8.9		32.5		7.5		42.5		3 7.52	1.59	0.19	VI.	2	20.885	39 33.2	3.3	4.4	3 9.30	42 10.9
38	8				9.0				5 8.97	1.57	0.33	IV.	4	48.820	10 17.1	3.2	1.1	5 10.87	12 51.4
39	8						44.0	17.7	5 26.16	1.57	0.29	V.	4	40.683	18 47.7	3.2	2.0	5 28.02	21 22.9
40	7	34.0	51.3	8.7	26.0				8 26.13	1.53	0.14	IV.	1	9.640	51 15.4	3.0	5.7	8 27.80	53 54.1
41	9		54.0	11.0	28.5				11 28.51	1.50	0.32	IV.	4	45.495	13 46.0	2.8	1.5	11 30.33	16 20.3
42	5.6	21.5	39.0	50.5	13.7				13 13.75	1.48	0.19	IV.	2	19.923	45 47.7	2.7	5.1	13 15.42	48 25.5
43	9	29.0		3.5					15 20.83	1.45	0.33	III.	4	48.824	10 17.0	2.5	1.1	15 22.61	12 50.6
44	8	54.0	11.0	28.7					19 45.93	1.40	0.25	III.	3	32.275	27 37.3	2.3	3.0	19 47.58	30 12.6
45	7.8				57.0		32.5		19 57.45	1.40	0.32	V.	4	45.187	14 5.0	2.3	1.5	19 59.17	16 38.8
46	9					34.0			24 16.61	1.35	0.24	V.	3	29.765	30 14.7	2.2	3.3	24 18.20	32 50.2
47	9	5.0	22.5	39.7					26 57.17	1.32	0.18	III.	2	18.323	42 14.5	2.1	4.7	26 58.67	44 51.3
48	7		40.3	58.0	15.0				28 15.16	1.31	0.19	IV.	2	20.726	39 43.7	2.1	4.4	28 16.66	42 20.2
49	7	34.3	51.7	9.2	26.5				32 26.50	1.26	0.20	IV.	2	19.913	40 34.6	2.1	4.5	32 27.96	43 11.2
50	9	50.0	7.5	25.0					36 42.14	1.21	0.32	III.	4	43.520	15 50.1	2.0	1.7	36 43.67	18 23.8
51	9			54.5	12.0				38 11.96	1.20	0.22	IV.	3	23.855	36 25.4	2.0	4.1	38 13.38	39 1.5
52	7			17.0	35.0	52.5	9.5	27.0	46 34.78	1.11	0.15	IV.	1	10.805	50 2.4	2.1	5.6	46 36.04	52 40.1
53	5.6							14.0	49 21.95	1.07	0.27	VII.	3	31.805	24 58.0	2.1	2.7	49 23.29	27 32.8
54	7					3.0			51 45.65	1.05	0.30	V.	4	40.343	19 9.2	2.2	2.1	51 47.00	21 43.5
55	7							37.0	23 51 44.07	1.05	0.30	VII.	4	40.463	19 59.3	2.2	2.1	23 51 46.32	21 33.6
56	9		48.5	6.0					0 4 23.33	0.91	0.20	III.	2	19.753	40 44.7	2.5	4.5	0 4 24.44	43 21.7
57	7				58.0	15.0			4 57.81	0.91	0.20	IV.	2	21.473	38 57.0	2.5	4.3	4 58.92	41 33.8
58	7					52.5			5 35.17	0.90	0.36	V.	4	51.953	7 0.2	2.5	0.7	5 36.43	9 33.4
59	4.5						41.0	58.3	6 6.41	0.89	0.37	VI.	4	54.227	4 37.7	2.5	0.5	6 7.67	7 10.7
60	8.9	34.0	51.0	9.5	26.0				14 26.17	0.81	0.25	IV.	3	29.957	30 2.7	2.8	3.3	14 27.23	32 38.8
61	9						22.0	39.3	14 47.13	0.81	0.16	VI.	2	12.560	48 15.2	2.8	5.4	14 48.10	50 53.4
62	8			29.0	45.0				16 45.70	0.79	0.16	IV.	1	11.667	49 8.5	2.9	5.5	16 46.65	51 46.9
63	8.9					15.0	32.0		16 57.42	0.79	0.19	V.	2	18.293	42 16.3	2.9	4.7	16 58.40	44 53.9
64	7.8	45.0	2.3	19.7	37.0				21 37.12	0.74	0.17	IV.	1	13.015	47 44.1	3.0	5.3	21 38.03	50 22.4
65	8.9	18.0	36.0	53.5					28 10.59	0.67	0.22	III.	3	21.930	38 26.0	3.3	4.3	28 11.48	41 3.6
66	8				45.0	2.0			0 28 44.82	+ 0.67	+0.25	IV.	3	27.545	−32 34.1	− 3.4	− 3.6	0 28 45.74	−27 35 11.1

CORRECTIONS.

Date. 1846.	Corr. of Clock.	Hourly rate.	m	n	c	Zenith Point.	Mic. Co.
h.	s.	s.	s.	s.	s.	° ' "	r.

REMARKS.

(66) 42. Micrometer reading assumed as $14^{s}.923$, not $19^{s}.923$.

INSTRUMENT READINGS.

Date. 1846, h. m.	CIRCLE							Barom.	THERMOM.				
	A.	B.	C.	D.	E.	F.	Mean.	At.	Ex.	U.	L.	I.	
	° ' "						"	in.	°	°	°	°	°

ZONE 67. OCTOBER 6. P. $D_0 = -32°\ 3'\ 10''$.

No.	Mag.	I.	II.	III.	IV.	V.	VI.	VII.	T.	a_1	a_2	MICROMETER.		r	i	d_1	d_2	Mean Right Ascension, 1850.0.	Mean Declination, 1850.0.
1	8			34.0	53.0				22 41 52.21	+ 1.69	+1.19	IV.	3	26.337	−33 50.0	−9.6	−5.6	22 41 55.09	−32 37 15.2
2	8		28.0		5.0				44 4.80	1.66	1.16	IV.	3	25.943	34 14.5	9.4	5.7	44 7.62	37 39.6
3	5.6	36.5	55.0	13.5	31.2				47 31.41	1.61	1.24	IV.	3	37.123	22 33.1	9.1	3.7	47 34.26	25 55.9
4	5.6	5.0			59.5	18.3			47 59.73	1.61	1.27	IV.	4	41.320	18 8.2	9.1	3.0	48 2.61	21 30.3
5	8	43.0	0.5	18.5	37.0				51 37.12	1.56	1.19	IV.	3	34.080	25 44.0	8.8	4.3	51 39.87	29 7.1
6	8.9					32.5			52 14.26	1.55	1.23	V.	3	39.160	20 25.3	8.8	3.3	52 17.04	23 47.4
7	8	40.0	58.3	16.5					55 34.93	1.50	0.95	III.	1	9.330	51 34.9	8.5	8.8	55 37.38	55 2.2
8	8	20.0				33.5			22 58 14.99	1.46	1.08	V.	3	26.445	33 43.3	8.4	5.6	22 58 17.53	37 7.3
9	8		12.5		49.0				23 20 49.00	1.16	1.11	IV.	4	49.640	9 25.7	7.1	1.5	23 20 51.27	12 44.3
10	8		37.0	55.0					23 13.35	1.12	1.03	III.	4	43.933	15 23.9	7.0	2.5	23 15.50	18 43.4
11	6.7				26.0				25 25.97	1.09	1.12	IV.	4	55.070	3 45.6	6.9	0.6	25 28.18	7 3.1
12	5.6			49.0	7.0	25.5			23 29 7.17	+ 1.04	+0.81	IV.	3	21.718	−38 39.5	−6.8	−6.5	23 29 9.02	−32 42 2.8

ZONE 68. OCTOBER 7. C. $D_0 = -32°\ 3'\ 10''$.

No.	Mag.	I.	II.	III.	IV.	V.	VI.	VII.	T.	a_1	a_2	MICROMETER.		r	i	d_1	d_2	Mean Right Ascension, 1850.0.	Mean Declination, 1850.0.
1	7.8		57.1	15.8	34.0	52.0	10.6		22 3 33.90	+ 2.21	+1.25	IV.	2	16.112	−44 33.0	−11.0	−7.5	22 3 37.36	−32 48 1.5
2	9					11.5		15.0	5 10.93	2.19	1.54	IV.	4	47.990	11 9.3	10.8	1.8	5 14.66	14 31.9
3	8.9					32.5	50.7	9.3	7 14.29	2.16	1.35	V.	3	27.236	32 53.6	10.6	5.5	7 17.80	36 19.7
4	7.8			38.0	56.5	14.7	32.5		8 56.31	2.14	1.40	IV.	3	32.484	27 24.3	10.4	4.5	8 59.85	30 49.2
5	7.8			6.4	24.1	42.3			15 24.26	2.05	1.55	IV.	4	48.376	10 45.2	9.6	1.7	15 27.86	14 6.5
6	7.8	18.3	36.8	55.2	13.5			50.2	18 55.17	2.00	1.52	IV.	4	43.797	15 32.5	9.2	2.5	18 58.69	18 54.2
7	8							50.2	18 55.64	2.00	1.61	VII.	4	54.211	4 38.2	9.2	0.7	18 59.25	7 58.1
8	8.9	39.1	57.2	15.3	33.4	51.8			22 15.38	1.95	1.53	IV.	4	44.071	15 15.3	8.8	2.5	22 18.86	18 36.6
9	7	55.3	13.7	31.5	50.6	8.6			25 31.94	1.91	1.22	IV.	2	9.597	51 21.1	8.4	8.7	25 35.07	54 48.2
10	7.8	27.5	46.5		23.4	41.2	59.7		28 4.71	1.87	1.46	IV.	3	36.789	22 53.9	8.2	3.8	28 8.04	26 15.9
11	8.9	31.2	50.3	8.2		44.8			28 8.21	1.87	1.47	IV.	3	37.979	21 39.3	8.1	3.6	28 11.55	25 1.0
12	7.8	45.2	3.2	21.5	40.3	58.2			32 21.68	1.81	1.30	IV.	2	17.705	42 53.1	7.7	7.2	32 24.79	46 18.0
13	9						31.5		32 55.07	1.81	1.48	VI.	3	38.359	21 15.5	7.7	3.5	32 58.36	24 36.7
14	8				24.5	43.4	1.3		34 24.85	1.78	1.48	IV.	3	38.149	21 28.7	7.5	3.5	34 28.11	24 49.7
15	8			3.5	21.5		57.2		38 21.33	1.73	1.36	IV.	3	24.408	35 51.0	7.1	6.0	38 24.42	39 14.1
16	8.9	16.1		52.5	10.7	29.1			41 52.54	1.68	1.37	IV.	3	26.342	33 49.7	6.8	5.7	41 55.59	37 12.2
17	8.9			6.3	24.5	42.3			43 6.08	1.66	1.32	IV.	3	18.607	41 54.6	6.8	7.0	43 9.06	45 18.4
18	8.9					22.5		58.6	44 3.98	1.65	1.38	V.	3	25.899	34 17.3	6.7	5.7	44 7.01	37 39.7
19	6.7	54.2	12.7	31.0	49.1	7.1	25.4		47 30.80	1.60	1.48	IV.	3	37.112	22 33.8	6.5	3.7	47 33.88	25 54.0
20	6.7	23.1	41.2	59.5	18.0	36.0	54.4		47 59.60	1.60	1.52	IV.	3	41.327	18 9.3	6.4	3.0	48 2.72	21 28.7
21	9	0.3	19.0			55.7		31.1	51 36.96	1.55	1.46	IV.	3	34.032	25 47.0	6.2	4.3	51 39.97	29 7.5
22	9	37.1		13.1	31.1	50.5	8.2		52 13.43	1.54	1.51	IV.	2	39.141	20 26.4	6.2	3.4	52 16.48	23 46.0
23	8.9	57.6	16.0	34.6	52.9	11.1			55 34.55	1.50	1.24	IV.	2	9.364	51 35.8	6.0	8.8	55 37.29	55 0.6
24	9	38.0		14.5	33.0	51.0			22 59 14.56	1.45	1.40	IV.	3	26.716	33 26.1	5.8	5.6	22 59 17.41	36 47.5
25	9				1.2		37.2		23 8 0.01	+ 1.32	+1.55	IV.	3	42.836	−16 34.3	−5.4	−7.7	23 8 2.88	−32 19 52.4

CORRECTIONS.

Date.	Corr. of Clock.	Hourly rate.	m	n	ε	Zenith Point.	Mic. Co.
	h.	s.	s.	s.	s.	° ′ ″	r.
1846. Oct. 7. 21	− 4.757	+ 0.013	− 0.261	+ 0.273	+ 0.022		

REMARKS.

Oct. 7, 22h 3m. Hazy about horizon.
Oct. 7, 23h 0m. Clear; moon-light.

INSTRUMENT READINGS.

Date.	A.	B.	C.	D.	E.	F.	Mean.	Barom.	At.	Ex.	U.	L.	I.
	° ′ ″						″	in.	°	°	°	°	°
Zone 67 1846. Oct. 6, . .	71 24 65.3	66.5	81.0	69.8	55.3	44.7	63.77						
22 41								30.300	63.3	59.6			
23 20								30.306	63.5	59.6			
23 29								30.306	63.5	60.0			
Zone 68 Oct. 7, 22 3	71 24 63.9	65.7	77.9	68.8	52.9	44.3	62.25	30.302	67.1	62.6	66.1	65.7	64.2
22 22										62.6			
22 41								30.302		62.8			
23 0	63.7	65.0	69.0	68.9	53.1	44.3	62.17	30.316	66.0	61.7	65.2	65.0	

ZONE 69.　OCTOBER 8.　P.　$D_0 = -37° 4' 10''$.

No.	Mag.	I.	II.	III.	IV.	V.	VI.	VII.	T.	a_1	a_2
									h. m. s.	s.	s.
1	8.9	56.5	16.0	35.0	54.5	··	··	··	22 5 54.53	+ 2.77	··
2	7	26.5	46.0	5.3	24.3	··	··	··	9 24.57	2.71	··
3	8	22.3	41.7	1.0	20.3	··	··	··	20 20.52	2.53	··
4	8.9	31.3	51.0	··	29.3	··	··	··	25 29.52	2.45	··
5	9	··	45.0	4.5	··	··	··	··	30 23.98	2.37	··
6	9.10	··	··	··	··	··	··	39.0	40.49	2.36	··
7	7	48.0	··	26.5	45.7	··	··	··	46 45.81	2.11	··
8	8.9	··	··	··	43.3	··	··	··	47 43.34	2.09	··
9	9	10.0	29.5	49.0	··	··	··	··	53 8.32	2.00	··
10	6.7	··	··	50.0	9.7	··	··	··	54 9.50	1.98	··
11	9	··	··	··	··	50.0	··	··	54 30.63	1.98	··
12	9	··	··	··	··	··	··	11.0	55 12.74	1.97	··
13	9	··	··	··	8.0	··	··	··	59 8.04	1.90	··
14	9	··	··	··	··	··	··	21.0	22 59 22.92	1.90	··
15	7	30.0	49.5	9.0	28.3	··	··	··	23 22 28.44	1.52	··
16	7	57.0	··	36.0	··	··	··	··	28 55.36	1.42	··
17	7	11.7	31.0	50.5	9.7	··	··	··	35 9.88	1.31	··
18	6.7	43.0	2.5	21.5	41.3	··	··	··	23 49 41.20	1.09	··
19	7	47.0	6.5	25.5	··	··	··	··	0 10 45.07	+ 0.76	··

No.	MICROMETER		r.	i	d_1	d_2	Mean Right Ascension, 1850.0	Mean Declination, 1850.0
			r.	′ ″	″	″	h. m. s.	° ′ ″
1	IV.	4	46.005	−13 13.8	− 5.7	− 3.6	22 5 · ·	−37 17 33.1
2	IV.	4	43.123	16 14.9	5.3	4.5	· · ·	20 34.7
3	IV.	2	20.750	39 42.2	4.2	11.4	· · ·	44 7.8
4	IV.	3	37.433	22 13.7	3.8	6.2	· · ·	26 33.7
5	III.	2	15.817	44 51.3	3.3	13.0	· · ·	49 17.6
6	VII.	1	11.025	49 48.9	3.	14.6	· · ·	54 (15.)
7	IV.	4	51.970	6 59.4	1.9	1.8	· · ·	11 13.1
8	IV.	3	35.440	24 18.8	1.9	6.8	· · ·	28 37.5
9	III.	3	30.683	29 16.9	1.5	8.3	· · ·	33 36.7
10	IV.	4	49.770	9 17.5	1.4	2.5	· · ·	13 31.4
11	V.	4	46.137	13 5.3	1.4	3.6	· · ·	17 20.3
12	VII.	3	31.430	26 29.9	1.4	8.1	· · ·	32 49.4
13	IV.	1	12.520	48 15.2	1.1	14.1	· · ·	52 40.4
14	VII.	2	45.923	13 17.6	1.1	3.6	· · ·	17 32.3
15	IV.	2	17.865	42 13.0	0.1	12.4	· · ·	47 5.5
16	III.	3	26.655	33 29.6	0.0	9.6	· · ·	37 49.2
17	IV.	3	27.387	32 44.1	0.0	9.3	· · ·	37 3.4
18	IV.	3	31.773	28 8.7	0.1	8.0	· · ·	32 26.8
19	III.	4	42.973	−16 24.2	− 0.6	− 4.5	· · ·	−37 20 39.3

ZONE 70.　OCTOBER 9.　C.　$D_0 = -25° 47' 20''$.

No.	Mag.	I.	II.	III.	IV.	V.	VI.	VII.	T.	a_1	a_2
1	7	··	2.7	19.7	··	55.1	11.7	··	23 59 37.30	+ 1.06	+1.05
2	7	··	46.5	3.7	21.0	37.8	55.2	··	0 12 20.86	0.93	0.92
3	8.9	··	··	··	··	··	42.2	59.1	13 7.74	0.92	1.12
4	8.9	··	··	··	··	54.5	11.7	··	14 37.41	0.91	0.97
5	6	··	6.7	23.6	41.0	58.3	15.3	32.4	19 40.98	0.85	1.18
6	9	··	··	··	··	··	52.0	··	20 17.75	0.85	1.01
7	8.9	··	··	··	40.2	56.2	··	··	23 56.75	0.81	0.89
8	7	··	34.0	51.0	7.5	25.3	42.5	··	25 8.07	0.80	1.05
9	8	··	28.7	45.4	3.4	20.3	37.0	··	28 2.97	0.77	1.06
10	8	··	··	··	··	28.0	··	1.2	30 10.22	0.75	1.18
11	8	··	··	44.2	1.5	19.0	36.0	··	30 1.54	0.75	1.30
12	8	··	··	··	··	42.0	59.1	··	31 24.76	0.73	1.20
13	9	··	··	··	··	··	··	··	31 · ·	0.73	1.20
14	7	··	32.0	50.0	7.1	24.0	40.9	··	34 6.94	0.71	0.95
15	8	··	··	2.6	19.4	37.0	··	28.1	38 36.78	0.66	1.07
16	8.9	··	··	33.0	··	··	24.0	··	38 49.92	0.66	1.16
17	9	··	··	··	30.0	37.1	44.1	··	39 9.92	0.65	1.07
18	6	··	··	9.5	26.7	··	··	··	46 26.64	0.59	0.86
19	8	··	··	40.3	··	··	22.3	··	48 57.72	0.56	1.18
20	7	··	··	··	27.3	··	··	19.4	49 27.63	0.56	1.05
21	8	··	··	··	··	10.0	27.0	43.7	50 52.43	0.55	1.37
22	8	··	··	··	31.0	48.5	··	··	52 31.12	0.53	1.36
23	7.8	··	··	··	··	31.5	47.8	5.7	53 13.92	0.52	1.29
24	9	··	··	··	34.2	··	9.1	··	0 58 34.52	0.47	1.12
25	9	··	55.0	12.7	30.0	··	··	··	1 1 29.80	0.45	1.36
26	9	··	··	··	··	3.7	··	38.5	1 1 46.72	+ 0.44	+1.15

No.	MICROMETER		r.	i	d_1	d_2	Mean Right Ascension, 1850.0	Mean Declination, 1850.0
1	IV.	3	36.002	−23 43.4	− 3.9	− 2.9	23 59 39.41	−26 11 10.2
2	IV.	4	49.471	9 36.4	4.2	1.5	0 12 22.71	25 57 2.1
3	VI.	3	29.534	30 29.4	4.2	3.6	13 9.78	26 17 57.2
4	V.	4	43.918	15 24.6	4.3	2.0	14 39.29	2 50.9
5	IV.	3	25.049	35 10.6	4.4	4.1	19 43.01	22 39.1
6	VI.	4	40.162	19 20.3	4.4	2.5	20 19.61	26 6 47.2
7	IV.	4	51.514	7 28.2	4.6	1.2	23 58.45	25 54 54.0
8	IV.	3	35.995	23 43.8	4.6	2.9	25 9.92	26 11 11.3
9	IV.	3	33.729	26 6.0	4.7	3.2	26 4.82	13 33.9
10	V.	3	24.590	35 39.1	4.8	4.2	30 12.15	23 8.1
11	IV.	2	13.719	47 2.9	4.8	5.4	30 3.50	34 33.1
12	IV.	3	22.579	37 45.6	4.9	4.4	31 26.69	25 14.9
13	VII.	3	22.329	38 1.2	4.9	4.4	31 ·	25 30.5
14	IV.	4	45.571	13 41.1	5.0	1.9	34 8.60	1 8.0
15	IV.	3	35.140	24 37.5	5.3	3.0	38 38.51	12 5.8
16	IV.	3	26.216	33 57.5	5.3	4.0	38 51.74	21 26.8
17	IV.	3	34.355	25 26.9	5.3	3.1	40 11.64	26 12 55.3
18	IV.	4	54.831	4 0.6	5.7	0.9	46 28.09	25 51 27.2
19	IV.	2	24.728	35 32.7	5.9	4.2	48 59.46	26 23 2.8
20	IV.	3	36.588	23 6.7	5.9	2.8	49 29.24	10 35.4
21	V.	2	7.244	53 48.4	6.0	6.1	50 54.35	41 20.5
22	IV.	2	8.069	52 56.7	6.1	6.0	52 33.01	40 28.8
23	IV.	3	14.812	45 54.4	6.1	5.3	53 15.73	33 25.8
24	IV.	3	30.182	29 48.7	6.5	3.5	0 58 36.11	17 16.7
25	IV.	2	8.619	52 22.3	6.7	6.0	1 1 31.61	39 55.0
26	V.	3	27.431	−32 41.4	− 6.7	− 3.9	1 1 48.31	−26 20 12.0

CORRECTIONS.

Date.		Corr. of Clock.	Hourly rate.	m	n	c	Zenith Point.	Mic. Co.
1846.	h.	s.	s.	s.	s.	s. .	° ′ ″	r.
Oct. 8,	21	− 4.427	+ 0.010	− 0.261	+ 0.273	+ 0.022		
Oct. 9,	21	− 4.283	− 0.004	− 0.261	+ 0.273	+ 0.022		

INSTRUMENT READINGS.

	Date.		CIRCLE.							Barom.	THERMOM.				
			A.	B.	C.	D.	E.	F.	Mean.		At.	Ex.	U.	L.	I.
	1846.	h. m.	° ′ ″						″	in.	°	°	°	°	°
Zone 69	Oct. 8,	· ·	76 24 61.0	60.0	75.7	63.5	48.6	39.0	57.97	· ·	· ·	· ·	67.5	66.5	66.0
		· ·	60.2	60.4	76.	63.5	49.0	37.7	57.80	· ·	· ·	· ·	66.5	65.0	
		22 5	· ·	· ·	· ·	· ·	· ·	· ·	· ·	30.364	68.0	62.7	· ·		
		22 30	· ·	· ·	· ·	· ·	· ·	· ·	· ·	30.364	67.2	61.6			
		22 59	· ·	· ·	· ·	· ·	· ·	· ·	· ·	30.364	67.0	61.7			
		23 49	· ·	· ·	· ·	· ·	· ·	· ·	· ·	30.364	66.8	60.3			
Zone 70	Oct. 9,	23 59	· ·	· ·	· ·	· ·	· ·	· ·	· ·	30.182	67.7	64.2			
		0 0	65 9 60.0	59.1	73.9	63.1	46.4	38.9	56.90	· ·	· ·	· ·	66.5	66.8	67.7
		0 20	· ·	· ·	· ·	· ·	· ·	· ·	· ·	· ·	· ·	64.1			

REMARKS.

Oct. 9, $0^h 0^m$. Clear; moon bright.

(70) 10. Declination apparently 40″ too large; perhaps micrometer should have been 25ʳ.196.

(70) 13. Precedes 12.3ˢ.

(70) 17. Transits over T.'s IV and V assumed at 10ˢ.0 and 27ˢ.1 instead of 30ˢ.0 and 37ˢ.1; and minutes as 40ᵐ, not 39ᵐ.

(70) 18. Transits assumed to have been 10ˢ later than recorded, to agree with Mural Z., 1847, December 18, and Arg. Z. 315.89.

Zone 70. October 9. C. $D_0 = -25°$ 47′ 20″—Continued.

SECONDS OF TRANSIT / T / a_1 / a_2

No.	Mag.	I.	II.	III.	IV.	V.	VI.	VII.	T. (h. m. s.)	a_1 (s.)	a_2 (s.)
27	8.9					+1.2	1.2		1 9 26.91	+ 0.37	+1.23
28	9						31.0		9 36.64	0.36	1.23
29	8			0.7	18.0	35.0	52.0	26.0	13 34.53	0.33	0.87
30	9			5.6			56.5		17 22.50	0.29	1.00
31	9				27.5	44.3	1.4		20 27.37	0.27	1.01
32	9					15.0			21 57.74	0.26	1.27
33	6.7				35.2	52.2	9.7	27.0	22 35.26	0.25	1.19
34	9			59.2			49.6		25 15.85	0.23	0.98
35	9						41.0	1.2	26 9.64	0.22	1.21
36	9		49.1				58.2		28 23.66	0.20	1.06
37	9		3.0	20.1		55.7		29.0	30 37.64	0.18	1.14
38	9		36.2		12.0		45.0		40 11.09	0.11	1.21
39	9			36.3	53.2		28.1		45 53.43	0.07	1.28
40	8.9		43.3	0.7	18.0	34.7	52.2		48 17.79	0.05	1.00
41	8.9				19.2	36.1	53.3		49 19.07	0.04	0.95
42	8					37.7	55.0		50 20.58	0.03	1.15
43	9						11.0	28.2	50 36.72	0.03	1.00
44	9					59.5	16.3	33.2	53 42.07	0.01	0.96
45	9					57.8			1 54 40.59	+ 0.00	1.15
46	9					5.5	22.2		2 1 48.05	− 0.05	1.21
47	8.9		33.0	50.3	7.5	24.2			4 7.33	0.07	1.03
48	9					29.3		4.5	9 12.57	0.10	1.07
49	7		39.6	56.4	13.8	31.4	48.3		12 13.89	0.12	1.34
50	8.9		49.0	5.7	23.3	40.8	57.2		15 23.23	0.14	0.86
51	7		59.7	17.5	34.2	51.3	8.7		17 34.28	0.15	1.25
52	7		53.2	10.4	27.3	44.5	1.4		23 27.38	0.19	0.84
53	9					53.7			2 24 19.51	− 0.20	+0.89

MICROMETER / i / d_1 / d_2 / Mean Right Ascension, 1850.0 / Mean Declination, 1850.0

No.	MICROMETER		r.	i (′ ″)	d_1 (″)	d_2 (″)	Mean R.A. 1850.0 (h. m. s.)	Mean Decl. 1850.0 (° ′ ″)
27	V.	3	19.981	−40 28.4	− 7.3	− 4.7	1 9 28.51	−26 28 0.4
28	VI.	3	19.981	40 28.4	7.3	4.7	9 38.23	26 28 0.4
29	IV.	4	52.948	5 58.0	7.6	1.1	13 35.73	25 53 26.7
30	IV.	3	40.764	18 44.4	8.0	2.4	17 23.79	26 6 14.8
31	IV.	3	40.301	19 13.7	8.2	2.4	20 28.55	6 44.3
32	V.	2	16.116	44 32.7	8.4	5.1	21 59.27	32 6.2
33	IV.	3	24.071	36 12.0	8.4	4.3	22 36.70	23 44.7
34	IV.	4	42.387	17 1.2	8.7	2.2	25 17.06	4 32.1
35	VI.	3	21.629	38 45.1	8.8	4.5	26 11.07	26 18.4
36	IV.	3	35.180	24 35.1	9.0	3.0	28 24.92	12 7.1
37	IV.	3	27.689	32 25.0	9.2	3.9	30 38.96	19 58.1
38	IV.	2	21.241	39 11.5	10.2	4.6	40 12.41	26 46.3
39	IV.	2	14.241	46 30.4	10.9	5.4	45 54.78	34 6.7
40	IV.	4	40.698	18 47.1	11.2	2.4	48 18.84	6 20.7
41	IV.	4	45.842	13 24.0	11.4	1.8	49 20.06	0 57.2
42	V.	3	26.401	33 46.0	11.5	4.0	50 21.76	21 21.5
43	VI.	3	33.020	26 50.5	11.5	3.3	50 37.84	14 25.3
44	IV.	3	44.231	15 6.9	11.9	2.0	53 43.04	2 40.8
45	V.	2	26.209	33 59.9	12.1	4.0	1 54 41.74	21 36.0
46	V.	2	20.786	39 39.9	13.1	4.6	2 1 49.21	27 17.6
47	IV.	3	37.430	22 13.9	13.4	2.8	4 8.29	9 50.1
48	IV.	3	34.058	25 45.4	14.2	3.2	9 13.54	13 22.8
49	IV.	2	9.154	51 48.9	14.7	5.9	12 15.11	26 39 29.5
50	IV.	4	53.461	5 26.0	15.2	1.0	15 23.95	25 53 2.2
51	IV.	2	16.499	44 8.8	15.6	5.1	17 35.38	26 31 49.5
52	IV.	4	55.008	3 49.5	16.6	0.8	23 29.03	25 51 26.9
53	V.	4	51.037	− 7 57.6	−16.3	− 1.3	2 24 20.20	−25 55 35.9

Zone 71. October 10. P. $D_0 = -35°$ 49′ 0″.

SECONDS OF TRANSIT / T / a_1 / a_2

No.	Mag.	I.	II.	III.	IV.	V.	VI.	VII.	T. (h. m. s.)	a_1 (s.)	a_2 (s.)
1	7.8		21.0	40.0	59.3				23 1 59.21	+ 1.98	+1.52
2	9			5.0					7 24.13	1.89	1.88
3	9				45.0				7 45.05	1.89	1.89
4	7					28.5			7 50.24	1.89	1.84
5	9						23.5		8 26.27	1.87	1.45
6	9	45.0		23.0					19 42.25	1.69	1.72
7	6.7				13.5	33.0			19 50.65	1.69	1.41
8	8						22.0		20 23.82	1.68	1.26
9	8		14.0	33.5	52.5				22 52.35	1.64	1.07
10	8.9	46.0	5.0	24.5					25 43.36	1.59	1.53
11	7			33.0	52.0				26 51.99	1.55	1.02
12	9			0.5	19.0	38.5			28 38.44	1.58	1.35
13	9				40.0				29 40.04	1.53	1.99
14	9				49.0				33 49.00	1.46	1.15
15	9							8.0	23 55 48.83	1.12	1.54
16	7			4.5	3.5	22.5			0 1 22.55	1.03	0.66
17	6				45.0	4.0	23.0		4 3.99	0.98	0.90
18	8	39.0	58.0	17.5					0 6 36.53	+ 0.95	+1.74

MICROMETER / i / d_1 / d_2 / Mean Right Ascension, 1850.0 / Mean Declination, 1850.0

No.	MICROMETER		r.	i (′ ″)	d_1 (″)	d_2 (″)	Mean R.A. 1850.0 (h. m. s.)	Mean Decl. 1850.0 (° ′ ″)
1	IV.	3	36.260	−23 27.3	− 7.9	− 6.2	23 2 2.71	−36 12 41.4
2	III.	2	18.140	42 25.9	7.6	11.3	7 27.90	31 44.8
3	IV.	2	17.760	42 49.6	7.6	11.4	7 48.83	32 8.6
4	VI.	3	19.780	40 42.6	7.6	10.8	7 53.97	30 1.0
5	VII.	3	38.170	21 26.9	7.6	5.7	8 29.59	10 40.2
6	III.	3	22.873	37 26.8	7.2	9.9	19 45.66	26 43.9
7	V.	3	37.220	22 27.1	7.2	5.9	19 53.75	11 40.2
8	VII.	4	43.700	15 37.2	7.2	4.2	20 26.76	36 4 48.6
9	IV.	4	52.140	6 48.9	7.1	1.9	22 55.06	35 55 57.9
10	III.	4	29.003	31 2.4	7.0	8.2	25 46.18	36 20 17.0
11	IV.	4	53.396	5 30.1	7.0	1.6	26 54.59	35 54 38.7
12	IV.	3	37.667	21 46.3	7.0	5.7	28 47.37	36 10 59.0
13	IV.	1	7.795	53 10.8	7.0	14.2	29 43.56	42 32.0
14	IV.	4	45.600	13 39.3	6.9	3.7	33 51.61	3 49.9
15	V.	3	23.335	36 58.3	7.0	9.8	23 55 57.49	36 26 15.1
16	V.	4	52.530	6 24.4	7.1	1.8	0 1 24.44	35 55 33.3
17	IV.	4	49.864	9 11.6	7.2	2.5	4 5.88	35 58 21.3
18	III.	1	11.660	−49 8.8	− 7.3	−13.1	0 6 39.22	−36 38 29.2

CORRECTIONS.

Date.	Corr. of Clock.	Hourly rate.	m	n	c	Zenith Point.	Mic. Co.
1846.	h. s.	s.	s.	s.	s.	° ′ ″	r.

REMARKS.

(70) 53. Transit over T. VI assumed as recorded over T. V.

(71) 2. Differs in R. A. 3s.9 from Transit Z., September 21.

INSTRUMENT READINGS.

Date.		CIRCLE.							Barom.	THERMOM.				
		A.	B.	C.	D.	E.	F.	Mean.		At.	Ex.	U.	L.	I.
	1846. h. m.	° ′ ″						″	In.	°	°	°	°	°
Zone 70	Oct. 9, 0 39								30.180	67.2	63.6			
	1 1	65 0 59.9	59.6	74.2	63.6	46.9	38.5	57.12			63.8	65.4	66.0	
	1 20								30.170	67.0	63.8			
	1 40										64.2			
	2 1	59.6	59.6	74.7	63.1	46.2	38.4	56.93			63.7	65.7	66.0	67.8
	2 23								30.164	66.8	63.0			
Zone 71	Oct. 10, 23 0	75 9 66.6	73.0	86.3	78.0	59.6	16.7	68.37	30.410	55.8	49.0	55.0	57.5	
	23 29								30.414	55.5	48.5			
	0 1								30.422	55.5	48.0			

ZONE 71. OCTOBER 10. C. $D_0 = -35°\ 49'\ 0''$—Continued.

No.	Mag.	I.	II.	III.	IV.	V.	VI.	VII.	T.	a_t	a_2	Micr.	n	r.	i	d_1	d_2	Mean Right Ascension, 1850.0	Mean Declination, 1850.0
									h. m. s.	s.	s.			r.	′ ″	″	″	h. m. s.	° ′ ″
19	9			30.5	49.0				0 8 8.34	+ 0.92	+ 0.89	III.	4	49.230	− 9 51.6	− 7.4	− 2.7	0 8 10.15	− 35 59 1.7
20	7		59.5		38.0				12 38.00	0.85	1.83	IV.	1	6.240	54 49.8	7.6	14.6	12 40.68	36 44 12.0
21	6.7			24.5	43.5				13 43.59	0.84	1.77	IV.	2	12.355	45 28.5	7.7	12.9	13 46.20	37 49.1
22	7	17.0	36.0	55.0					15 14.15	0.82	1.15	III.	3	35.790	23 56.4	7.8	6.4	15 16.12	13 10.6
23	8.9	52.5	12.0	31.0					16 50.09	0.79	1.47	III.	2	21.460	38 57.8	7.8	10.3	16 52.35	28 15.9
24	9	4.0	23.0	42.0					21 1.29	0.72	1.56	III.	2	16.362	44 17.4	8.2	11.7	21 3.57	33 37.3
25	8			37.0					21 56.14	0.71	1.54	III.	2	16.745	43 53.2	8.3	11.6	21 58.39	33 13.1
26	9						47.0		22 8.66	0.71	1.67	VI.	1	10.900	49 56.1	8.3	13.3	22 11.04	39 17.7
27	9	18.5	37.5	56.0					25 16.11	0.66	1.14	III.	3	33.875	25 56.6	8.6	6.8	25 17.91	36 15 12.0
28	8.9				13.0				26 13.00	0.65	1.04	IV.	4	48.585	10 32.0	8.6	2.9	26 14.60	35 59 43.5
29	8	59.5	18.5	37.5					0 29 57.27	+ 0.59	+ 1.12	III.	3	34.270	− 25 32.0	− 9.0	− 6.8	0 29 58.98	− 36 14 47.8

ZONE 72. OCTOBER 16. C. $D_0 = -39°\ 35'\ 0''$.

No.	Mag.	I.	II.	III.	IV.	V.	VI.	VII.	T.	a_t	a_2	Micr.	n	r.	i	d_1	d_2	Mean Right Ascension, 1850.0	Mean Declination, 1850.0
1	7.8		59.2	19.0	39.1	59.5	20.0		21 29 39.13	+ 2.39		IV.	3	23.615	− 36 40.6	− 10.2	− 15.7		− 40 12 6.5
2	8.9			37.5		17.7			32 37.60	2.34		IV.	4	52.081	6 52.5	9.6	3.3		39 42 5.4
3	8			11.3	31.0	51.2			31.16	2.24		IV.	2	23.544	36 47.1	8.4	15.8		40 12 11.3
4	8				42.3	2.2	22.1	42.2	46 2.14	2.10		IV.	4	52.106	6 51.0	7.0	3.3		39 42 1.3
5	8						30.2	50.0	46 50.03	2.08		VI.	3	33.680	26 8.9	6.8	11.3		40 1 27.0
6	7.8				18.0		58.7	19.1	53 38.45	1.97		IV.	2	13.602	47 10.4	5.6	20.3		22 36.3
7	8.9							43.0	53 42.43	1.97		VII.	2	15.939	44 42.8	5.6	19.3		20 7.7
8	8	0.0	20.2	40.0	0.3	20.4	40.7	0.8	57 0.52	1.90		IV.	3	19.934	40 31.3	5.0	17.4		15 53.7
9	8			0.8	21.0	41.0	1.3	21.1	21 59 41.05	1.86		IV.	3	23.871	36 24.4	4.6	15.6		11 44.6
10	8			17.5	38.0	57.8	18.5	38.0	22 1 58.06	+ 1.82		IV.	2	19.137	− 41 23.4	− 4.2	− 17.8		− 40 16 45.4

ZONE 73. OCTOBER 16. C. $D_0 = -32°\ 3'\ 10''$.

No.	Mag.	I.	II.	III.	IV.	V.	VI.	VII.	T.	a_t	a_2	Micr.	n	r.	i	d_1	d_2	Mean Right Ascension, 1850.0	Mean Declination, 1850.0
1	9				19.0		50.7	12.2	23 11 35.15	+ 0.36	+ 1.95	IV.	4	51.771	− 7 11.9	− 1.9	− 1.3	23 11 37.46	− 32 10 25.1
2	9						47.0	24.0	19 28.99	0.24	2.26	IV.	3	35.249	24 30.8	1.6	4.2	19 31.49	27 46.6
3	9					25.5	43.7		20 49.12	0.22	1.93	VI.	4	49.518	9 32.8	1.6	1.7	20 51.27	12 46.1
4	8		36.4		13.5			7.5	23 13.08	0.10	2.04	IV.	4	43.866	15 28.1	1.5	2.7	23 15.31	18 42.3
5	9			4.2				35.0	23 40.54	0.18	1.87	IV.	4	52.408	6 32.1	1.5	1.2	23 42.59	9 44.8
6	7.8						3.0	21.5	25 26.82	0.15	1.79	VI.	4	54.953	3 52.3	1.5	0.7	25 28.76	7 4.5
7	7		31.2	49.2	7.4	26.2	44.2		29 7.64	0.10	2.50	IV.	3	21.622	38 45.5	1.4	6.6	29 10.24	42 3.5
8	9							7.2	29 12.42	0.10	2.27	VII.	3	32.272	27 37.2	1.4	4.7	29 14.79	30 53.3
9	9						7.0		30 30.47	0.08	2.48	VI.	3	26.869	33 16.3	1.3	5.7	30 33.03	36 33.3
10	6.7			26.0	44.2	2.2	20.5	39.0	32 44.04	0.04	2.76	IV.	2	9.131	50 47.6	1.3	8.4	32 46.84	54 7.3
11	7.8					31.0	49.0	7.0	23 33 12.33	+ 0.03	+ 2.75	IV.	2	9.002	− 51 58.2	− 1.3	− 8.9	23 33 15.11	− 32 55 18.4

CORRECTIONS.

Date.		Corr. of Clock.	Hourly rate.	m	n	c	Zenith Point.	Mic. Co.
	h.	s.	s.	s.	s.	s.	° ′ ″	r.
1846. Oct. 16,	22	− 5.709	− 0.010	− 0.530	+ 0.507	+ 0.022		

REMARKS.

Oct. 16. Night unfavorable, not perfectly clear ; stars, at times, lost sight of entirely, lamp flaring.

(72) 3. Probably 38ᵐ.
(73) 10. Micrometer reading assumed as 10ʳ.131, not 9ʳ.131.

INSTRUMENT READINGS.

Date.		CIRCLE.							Barom.	THERMOM.				
		A.	B.	C.	D.	E.	F.	Mean.		At.	Ex.	U.	L.	I.
	1846. h. m.	° ′ ″						″	in.	°	°	°	°	°
Zone 71	Oct. 10, 0 29								30.412	53.5	45.2			
Zone 72	Oct. 16, 21 0	78 54 64.3	67.4	78.6	69.9	54.4	45.2	63.30				63.5	64.0	
	21 29								30.134	63.3	62.0			
	21 46										63.0			
	22 1								30.144	63.7	64.1			
Zone 73	Oct. 16, 23 0	71 24 63.2	65.1	76.2	67.6	53.3	44.2	61.60				64.2	62.5	57.0
	23 11								30.154	64.8	62.2			
	23 33								30.144	64.5	61.4			

ZONE 74. OCTOBER 17. C. $D_0 = -39° 34' 50''$.

No.	Mag.	I.	II.	III.	IV.	V.	VI.	VII.	T.	a_1	a_2	Micr.	n	r.	i	d_1	d_2	Mean Right Ascension, 1850.0	Mean Declination, 1850.0
1	8					23.0			21 9 42.86	+2.85	+0.39	VI.	3	36.560	−23 8.3	−23.0	−9.0	21 9 46.10	−39 58 30.3
2	7.8		26.0	46.0	6.0				14 6.23	2.78	0.13	IV.	1	11.450	49 22.2	22.3	20.2	14 9.14	40 24 54.7
3	8	12.0	32.0	52.0					16 12.08	2.74	0.54	III.	4	43.250	16 7.0	22.0	6.1	16 15.36	39 51 25.1
4	8			55.0			55.0		25 14.95	2.59	0.40	III.	3	24.360	35 53.7	20.5	14.4	25 17.94	40 11 18.6
5	7	39.0	59.0	19.0	39.0				29 39.24	2.51	0.44	IV.	3	23.610	36 40.9	19.7	14.7	29 42.19	40 12 5.3
6	7.8					37.5		17.0	30 17.20	2.50	0.66	VII.	4	41.890	17 30.7	19.7	6.7	30 20.36	39 52 47.1
7	7	31.0	51.0	11.0	31.0				38 31.22	2.35	0.53	IV.	3	23.460	36 50.4	18.3	14.8	38 34.10	40 12 13.5
8	8				32.0		12.0		39 32.02	2.34	0.84	VI.	4	49.010	11 7.2	18.2	4.1	39 35.20	39 46 19.5
9	7.8	2.0	22.5	42.3					46 2.32	2.22	0.95	III.	4	52.103	6 51.1	17.2	2.5	46 5.49	39 42 0.8
10	7.8				50.0	9.5			46 49.71	2.21	0.74	V.	3	34.237	25 34.3	17.0	10.0	46 52.66	40 0 51.3
11	8			25.0					49 45.16	2.15	0.63	III.	2	21.690	38 43.1	16.6	15.6	49 47.94	14 5.3
12	8	38.0	58.0	18.0					53 38.39	2.09	0.56	III.	2	13.565	47 12.6	16.0	19.2	53 41.03	22 37.8
13	3.4	0.0	20.0	40.3	0.5				57 0.45	2.02	0.67	IV.	2	19.970	40 31.0	15.6	16.3	57 3.14	15 52.9
14	8.7			21.0					21 59 41.15	1.97	0.74	III.	3	23.850	36 25.5	15.2	14.6	21 59 43.86	11 45.3
15	8		18.0	38.0					22 1 58.25	1.93	0.70	III.	2	19.147	41 22.6	14.9	16.7	22 2 0.88	16 44.2
16	7.8	43.0	3.0	23.0					9 43.38	1.79	0.76	III.	2	17.963	42 36.7	13.9	17.3	9 45.93	40 17 57.9
17	8.9					29.0			14 7.97	1.71	1.25	V.	4	54.325	4 32.1	13.3	1.5	14 10.93	39 39 36.9
18	6.7					2.0	22.5		15 42.16	1.68	1.12	V.	4	41.520	17 55.3	13.1	6.9	15 44.96	53 5.3
19	6.7	22.0	42.0	1.5					19 21.91	1.61	1.16	III.	4	43.385	15 58.5	12.7	6.1	19 24.68	51 7.3
20	3.4				48.0	8.0		49.0	19 48.06	1.61	1.15	IV.	4	41.267	18 11.5	12.7	7.0	19 50.82	53 21.2
21	6	12.5	32.5	52.5	12.5				30 12.60	1.41	1.21	IV.	4	38.858	20 42.5	11.6	8.0	30 15.22	39 55 52.1
22	7	36.5	56.5	16.5					38 36.82	1.25	1.10	III.	2	21.053	39 23.1	10.8	15.7	38 39.17	40 14 39.6
23	3.4	26.5		6.5	26.5				42 26.62	1.18	1.32	IV.	3	37.543	22 6.7	10.5	8.6	42 29.12	39 57 15.8
24	7				34.5				43 34.48	1.16	1.49	IV.	4	49.340	9 44.7	10.4	3.6	43 37.13	39 44 49.7
25	7						31.5		43 41.29	1.16	1.25	VI.	3	29.505	30 31.0	10.3	12.1	43 43.70	40 5 43.4
26	7						36.0		44 55.70	1.13	1.17	VI.	3	22.580	37 45.3	10.3	15.1	44 58.00	40 13 0.7
27	8	43.0	3.0	23.0					49 43.12	1.04	1.43	III.	4	39.930	19 35.3	9.9	7.6	49 45.59	39 54 42.8
28	8		28.0						52 48.00	0.98	1.65	III.	4	54.970	3 51.9	9.7	1.3	52 50.63	38 52.9
29	7			10.0	31.0				57 30.61	0.89	1.29	IV.	2	22.017	38 22.7	9.5	15.4	57 32.79	13 37.6
30	4.5			28.0	40.0	9.5			22 58 28.84	0.87	1.66	IV.	4	51.870	7 5.6	9.4	2.6	22 58 31.37	42 7.6
31	7			17.0					23 6 37.11	0.72	1.54	III.	3	35.255	24 30.1	9.0	9.6	23 6 39.37	59 38.7
32	6	10.0	30.0	50.0	10.5				11 10.21	0.64	1.59	IV.	3	36.207	23 30.6	8.8	9.2	11 12.44	58 38.6
33	7	45.0	5.0	25.0					23 27 45.08	+0.32	+1.89	III.	4	47.263	−11 55.1	−8.2	−4.5	23 27 47.29	−39 46 57.8

ZONE 75. OCTOBER 19. C. $D_0 = -30° 47' 50''$.

No.	Mag.	I.	II.	III.	IV.	V.	VI.	VII.	T.	a_1	a_2	Micr.	n	r.	i	d_1	d_2	Mean Right Ascension, 1850.0	Mean Declination, 1850.0
1	8.9			37.5	55.6	12.7	31.0		23 0 55.28	−0.08	+1.33	IV.	4	50.358	−8 40.8	−9.9	−1.4	23 0 56.53	−30 56 42.1
2	8		34.0	52.0	9.8	27.5	45.7		5 9.83	0.14	1.41	IV.	4	54.689	4 9.5	9.7	0.6	5 11.10	30 52 9.8
3	7.8	12.3	30.8	48.8	7.0	24.4			10 48.66	0.22	0.76	IV.	3	26.032	34 8.9	9.4	5.4	10 49.20	31 22 13.7
4	9		38.3	56.2	14.7	32.7	50.4		13 14.46	0.26	0.71	IV.	3	24.365	35 53.7	9.2	5.6	13 14.91	23 58.5
5	9		24.0	42.0					15 0.04	0.29	0.69	III.	3	23.162	37 8.8	9.2	5.8	15 0.44	25 13.8
6	9				9.0			47.0	15 10.04	0.29	1.02	IV.	3	37.525	22 7.0	9.2	3.4	15 10.77	10 10.5
7	9				24.5	42.0			20 6.11	0.36	0.35	V.	2	9.371	51 35.3	9.0	8.2	20 6.10	39 44.5
8	7.8		28.0	46.1	4.0		40.2		28 4.19	0.48	0.56	IV.	3	20.110	40 20.4	8.9	6.4	28 4.27	28 25.7
9	9							50.0	35 56.00	0.60	0.89	V.	3	35.529	24 13.3	8.8	3.8	35 56.29	12 15.9
10	9					18.0			37 59.93	0.63	0.69	V.	3	27.298	32 49.7	8.8	5.2	37 59.90	20 53.7
11	9					46.0		18.5	39 25.75	0.65	0.79	V.	3	31.669	28 15.4	8.8	4.4	39 25.69	16 18.6
12	7.8		35.0	52.4	10.3	29.2	47.0		23 46 10.79	−0.74	+0.88	IV.	3	36.356	−23 21.3	−8.9	−3.6	23 46 10.93	−31 11 23.8

CORRECTIONS.

Date.	Corr. of Clock.	Hourly rate.	m	n	c	Zenith Point.	Mic. Co.
	h.	s.	s.	s.	s.	° ' "	r.
1846. Oct. 19,	22	s. −6.303	−0.018	−0.530	+0.507	+0.022		

REMARKS.

Oct. 17, 23h 30m. Interrupted by clouds; very clear.

Oct. 19. Night unfavorable; stars unsteady.

(74) 17. Differs 2s.36 from Transit Z., 1846, October 16.

INSTRUMENT READINGS.

	Date.	A.	B.	C.	D.	E.	F.	Mean.	Barom.	At.	Ex.	U.	L.	I.
	1846. h. m.	° ' "						"	in.					
Zone 74	Oct. 17, 21 10	78 54 67.6	69.2	82.0	71.2	59.2	47.8	66.00	29.916	66.0	65.5			66.5
	21 30								29.912	66.2	65.0			
	22 9								29.904	66.3	65.0			
	22 38								29.912	67.0	65.2			
	23 11								29.918	66.8	64.8			
	23 27								29.912	66.8	64.7			
Zone 75	Oct. 19, 23 0	70 9 50.0	58.7	70.0	60.1	42.3	31.9	52.13	30.244	48.3	38.0	50.4	50.4	57.2
	23 20											37.6		
	23 39								30.240	47.8	36.0			

ZONE 75. OCTOBER 19. C. $D_0 = -30°\ 47'\ 50'$—Continued.

No.	Mag.	I.	II.	III.	IV.	V.	VI.	VII.	T. (h. m. s.)	m_1	m_2	MICROMETER (r.)	i (′ ″)	d_1 (″)	d_2 (″)	Mean Right Ascension, 1850.0 (h. m. s.)	Mean Declination, 1850.0 (° ′ ″)
13	9			48.3	6.?			5.7	23 50 6.19	− 0.80	+ 0.76	IV. 3 31.448	−25 29.3	− 8.9	− 4.5	23 50 6.15	−31 16 32.7
14	8.9		38.2	54.5		30.0			53 12.34	0.85	1.24	IV. 4 52.991	5 55.3	8.9	1.0	53 12.73	30 53 55.2
15	9				40.0	57.1			54 21.45	0.86	0.45	V. 1 17.430	43 7.6	8.9	6.8	54 21.04	31 31 13.3
16	7				48.1	6.2			56 30.24	0.89	1.15	V. 2 48.951	10 8.6	8.9	1.6	56 30.50	30 58 4.1
17	8					49.0	6.2		57 12.65	0.90	0.98	VI. 4 41.911	17 30.2	9.0	2.7	57 12.73	31 5 31.9
18	8					51.0	8.1		23 58 14.57	0.92	0.83	VI. 3 35.965	23 45.6	9.0	3.7	23 58 14.48	31 11 48.3
19	9		46.0		22.2		58.0		0 5 22.17	1.02	1.20	IV. 4 53.372	5 31.6	9.0	0.9	0 5 22.35	30 53 31.5
20	9		14.3		49.3				7 49.80	1.06	1.07	IV. 4 47.046	12 8.6	9.0	1.9	7 49.81	31 0 9.5
21	8.9			6.0	24.0			0.5	9 6.15	1.07	0.71	IV. 3 31.927	27 59.0	9.1	4.4	9 5.79	16 2.5
22	9			38.0			32.2		12 56.10	1.13	0.55	IV. 2 25.011	35 13.0	9.1	5.5	12 55.52	23 17.6
23	8		57.2	15.7	33.5	52.0			17 33.62	1.19	0.30	IV. 2 17.671	42 55.3	9.2	6.8	17 32.79	31 1.3
24	8		51.0	8.7	26.8	45.0		21.0	18 26.49	1.20	0.28	IV. 2 14.111	46 38.4	9.2	7.4	18 25.57	34 45.0
25	9				20.7		55.7		24 20.24	1.28	0.71	IV. 3 33.610	26 13.5	9.5	4.1	24 19.67	14 17.1
26	8		58.0	17.2	35.2	53.2	11.2		26 34.98	1.31	0.87	IV. 4 38.750	20 49.3	9.6	3.3	26 34.54	8 52.2
27	9		29.0	47.0	4.2	23.0	40.5		0 29 4.73	− 1.35	+ 0.35	IV. 3 18.041	−42 30.0	− 9.8	− 6.7	0 29 3.73	−31 30 36.5

ZONE 76. OCTOBER 26. C. $D_0 = -29°\ 32'\ 50'$.

No.	Mag.	I.	II.	III.	IV.	V.	VI.	VII.	T. (h. m. s.)	m_1	m_2	MICROMETER (r.)	i (′ ″)	d_1 (″)	d_2 (″)	Mean Right Ascension, 1850.0 (h. m. s.)	Mean Declination, 1850.0 (° ′ ″)
1	6.7				25.0	42.8	0.7	18.6	22 51 25.02	− 1.47	− 0.67	IV. 2 17.802	−42 47.0	−10.8	− 6.8	22 51 22.88	−30 15 54.6
2	6.7		51.8	8.3	27.2	44.6	2.4		22 53 9.14	1.50	0.86	IV. 4 53.535	5 21.3	10.7	1.5	22 53 6.78	29 38 23.5
3	7	40.6	58.0	15.2	33.2	51.0			23 0 15.83	1.60	0.88	IV. 4 53.920	4 57.0	10.2	1.4	23 0 13.35	37 58.6
4	8.9			44.5	2.2	19.8	37.5		2 2.14	1.63	0.84	IV. 2 46.750	12 26.4	10.1	2.5	0 59.67	29 45 29.0
5	7				59.8	17.3	35.4		2 41.84	1.64	0.67	V. 2 13.742	47 1.4	10.0	7.4	2 39.53	30 20 8.8
6	9.10							30.0	17 36.48	1.86	0.70	VII. 2 11.530	49 18.9	9.1	7.7	17 33.92	22 25.7
7	9				47.4	5.5	23.5		19 47.64	1.89	0.72	IV. 2 13.232	47 53.5	9.0	7.5	19 45.03	30 20 40.0
8	9			18.2		54.5	11.2		23 36.22	1.95	0.90	IV. 4 46.045	13 11.3	8.8	2.6	23 33.37	29 46 12.7
9	9.10			24.8?					27 42.53	2.01	0.93	III. 4 50.919?	8 5.4	8.6	1.9	27 39.59	29 41 5.9
10	9		55.7			48.2	5.7		31 30.59	2.06	0.79	IV. 3 22.039	38 19.4	8.5	6.1	31 27.74	30 11 24.0
11	8					23.8	41.2		32 5.91	2.07	0.92	V. 4 45.869	13 22.1	8.4	2.6	32 2.92	29 46 23.1
12	9						0.2	22.0	32 .	2.07	0.93	VI. 4 47.521	11 38.2	8.4	2.4	32 . .	44 39.0
13	7.8		38.2	55.7	13.4		49.0		35 13.54	2.12	0.90	IV. 3 40.058	19 28.8	8.3	3.5	35 10.52	29 52 30.6
14	8		52.1	9.5	27.2	45.5			37 27.45	2.15	0.79	IV. 2 19.411	41 6.3	8.3	6.5	37 24.51	30 14 11.1
15	8			42.4	0.3		36.0		46 0.32	2.27	0.81	IV. 2 19.688	40 48.8	8.1	6.5	45 57.24	13 53.4
16	8			31.5	49.3	7.7	25.2		48 49.51	2.31	0.79	IV. 2 13.218	47 34.4	8.1	7.4	48 46.41	20 39.9
17	6		12.2	30.1	47.5	5.7	23.4		51 47.78	2.35	0.80	IV. 2 14.597	46 8.1	8.1	7.2	51 44.63	19 13.4
18	9.10					41.0?			52 5.44	2.36	0.86	VI. 3 25.000?	35 13.6	8.0	5.7	52 2.22	8 17.3
19	8			24.6	42.2		17.5		56 42.19	2.42	0.89	IV. 3 26.931	33 12.5	8.0	5.4	56 38.88	6 15.9
20	8.9		27.3	45.7	3.0	20.5	38.5		56 45.21	2.42	0.85	IV. 3 20.460	39 58.5	8.0	6.4	56 41.94	30 13 2.9
21	8					49.5	7.3	25.2	23 58 31.89	2.45	0.93	V. 3 33.642	26 11.6	8.0	4.4	23 58 28.51	29 59 14.0
22	9.10			43.8	1.5		40.0		0 6 1.49	2.56	0.81	IV. 2 9.449	51 30.5	8.0	5.0	0 5 58.12	30 24 36.5
23	9.10				35.3				7 35.32	2.58	0.99	IV. 4 41.955	17 28.1	8.0	3.2	7 31.75	29 50 29.3
24	6.7	8.5	26.2	44.0	1.3	19.4	37.0	55.0	14 1.63	2.67	1.01	IV. 4 43.669	15 40.6	8.0	2.9	13 57.95	48 41.5
25	9		15.4	33.2	50.7	8.2	26.0	44.0	16 50.72	2.71	1.02	IV. 4 43.601	15 44.9	8.0	2.9	16 46.99	29 48 45.8
26	9		12.3			47.3	5.8		19 47.72	2.75	0.85	IV. 2 9.311	51 39.1	8.0	8.1	19 44.12	30 24 45.2
27	7				49.7	6.8	24.3	42.0	20 49.07	2.76	1.01	IV. 4 40.308	19 11.8	8.0	3.4	20 45.30	29 52 13.2
28	6.7		43.3	1.0	19.0	36.0	54.8		26 18.99	2.86	0.86	IV. 2 10.836	50 3.4	8.0	7.8	26 15.27	30 23 9.2
29	9					23.0	41.5	0.2	27 6.12	2.86	1.08	V. 4 50.785	8 13.5	8.0	1.9	27 2.18	29 41 13.4
30	9						53.4	11.8	0 28 11.46	− 2.67	− 1.08	V. 4 51.232	− 7 45.7	− 8.0	− 1.8	0 29 7.51	−29 40 45.5

CORRECTIONS.

Date	Corr. of Clock	Hourly rate	m	n	c	Zenith Point	Mic. Co.
1846. Oct. 26, h. 22	s. . .	s. − 0.012	s. − 0.168	s. + 0.103	s. + 0.351	° ′ ″	r.

REMARKS.

(76) 30. Minute assumed as 29 instead of 28, and Transits over T.'s III and IV as recorded over T.'s V and VI.

INSTRUMENT READINGS.

Date	CIRCLE A.	B.	C.	D.	E.	F.	Mean.	Barom. (In.)	THERMOM. At.	Ex.	U.	L.	I.
Zone 75 — 1846. Oct. 19, 23 58								30.235	47.1	35.1			
0 18										35.4			
0 29	70 9 49.6	50.4	69.9	60.7	42.9	31.1	52.27	30.236	46.5	34.8	48.5	47.8	
Zone 76 — Oct. 26, 22 50	68 54 64.2	68.5	80.6	71.6	57.5	45.4	64.63	30.282	54.5	50.3	53.5	52.5	51.3
23 10											50.0		
23 27								30.270	54.0	49.8			
23 50	64.4	68.6	80.2	72.1	56.9	45.2	64.57				49.4	53.0	52.0
0 14								30.264	53.7	49.3			
0 28								30.250	53.7	51.0			
0 40										51.4			

Zone 76. October 26. C. $D_0 = -29°\ 32'\ 50''$—Continued.

No.	Mag.	I.	II.	III.	IV.	V.	VI.	VII.	T. (h. m. s.)	a_1 (s.)	a_2 (s.)
31	7.8	..	38.2	56.2	14.0	32.0	49.8	..	0 33 14.04	− 2.93	−0.92
32	8	..	5.0	23.0	40.8	..	16.2	..	40 40.72	3.03	0.97
33	6	..	50.6	8.2	26.0	44.1	1.7	19.5	51 26.12	3.18	1.00
34	7	..	36.1	53.7	11.5	29.4	47.0	..	0 56 11.54	3.24	0.96
35	8	..	16.7	4.6	22.4	40.3	58.0	..	1 13 22.42	3.45	1.17
36	9	..	..	..	..	..	..	19.5	13 25.98	3.45	0.98
37	9	..	..	35.5	53.0	..	28.3	..	19 53.02	3.53	1.05
38	9	..	..	..	52.0	11.2	..	44.7	20 52.32	3.54	1.22
39	8.9	..	42.2	0.4	17.4	35.6	53.1	..	23 17.76	3.57	1.24
40	9	..	..	..	14.0	..	..	..	26 12.02	3.61	1.17
41	9	..	44.0	1.0	19.3	..	..	..	29 19.24	3.64	1.09
42	9	..	..	56.3	14.4	32.0	49.7	..	30 14.22	3.65	1.10
43	8	..	49.9	7.3	25.0	43.1	0.8	..	32 25.24	3.68	1.21
44	8	..	35.9	53.5	11.3	29.0	46.6	..	43 11.28	3.80	1.24
45	8	..	30.3	48.5	5.8	21.0	42.0	..	49 6.22	3.87	1.24
46	9	..	..	20.9?	..	..	..	..	54 38.70	3.92	1.13
47	6.7	..	..	32.2	19.2	7.3	25.2	43.0	55 49.91	3.94	1.09
48	6.7	..	..	32.5	50.3	8.2	26.0	43.7	1 57 50.38	3.96	1.21
49	8	..	..	28.3	47.0	4.2	22.2	..	2 0 46.59	3.99	1.34
50	8	..	30.0	47.3	5.4	23.1	40.8	..	3 5.35	4.01	1.31
51	8.9	..	52.2	10.0	27.3	45.2	3.2	..	15 27.58	4.13	1.25
52	9	..	..	..	37.7	..	..	32.0	17 38.26	4.15	1.34
53	9	..	13.5	..	50.8	..	24.0	42.2	2 19 49.34	− 4.18	−1.33

No.	Micrometer (r.)	i (′ ″)	d_1 (″)	d_2 (″)	Mean Right Ascension, 1850.0 (h. m. s.)	Mean Declination, 1850.0 (° ′ ″)
31	IV. 2 18.874	−41 39.7	− 8.1	− 6.6	0 33 10.19	−30 14 44.4
32	IV. 3 23.487	36 48.7	8.3	5.9	40 36.72	9 52.9
33	IV. 3 23.231	37 4.8	9.0	5.9	51 21.94	10 9.7
34	IV. 2 13.962	46 47.6	9.3	7.4	0 56 7.34	30 19 54.3
35	IV. 4 45.771	13 28.5	10.9	2.6	1 13 17.80	29 46 32.0
36	VII. 1 10.659	50 11.0	10.9	7.9	13 21.55	30 23 19.8
37	IV. 2 18.811	41 43.7	11.7	6.6	19 48.44	30 14 52.0
38	IV. 4 51.589	7 23.4	11.8	1.8	20 47.56	29 40 27.0
39	IV. 4 53.479	5 24.8	12.2	1.5	23 12.95	39 28.5
40	IV. 4 40.749	18 43.9	12.7	3.4	26 7.24	29 51 50.0
41	IV. 3 23.752	36 31.9	13.1	5.9	29 14.51	30 9 40.9
42	IV. 3 24.989	36 17.1	13.2	5.8	30 9.47	30 9 26.1
43	IV. 4 45.176	14 6.0	13.5	2.7	32 20.35	29 47 12.2
44	IV. 4 45.176	14 6.0	14.4	2.7	43 6.24	47 13.1
45	IV. 4 41.520	17 55.6	15.0	3.2	49 1.11	29 51 3.8
46	III. 2 19.822	40 40.3	15.7	6.4	54 33.65	30 13 52.4
47	IV. 2 10.645	50 15.5	15.8	7.9	55 44.88	23 29.2
48	IV. 4 31.970	27 56.4	16.1	4.7	1 57 45.21	30 1 7.2
49	IV. 4 55.240	3 34.6	16.5	1.3	2 0 41.26	29 36 42.4
50	IV. 4 48.134	9 57.5	16.8	2.3	3 0.03	29 43 6.6
51	IV. 3 31.246	28 42.0	18.9	4.7	15 22.20	30 1 55.6
52	IV. 4 48.741	10 22.1	19.4	2.2	16 32.77	29 43 33.7
53	IV. 4 43.424	−15 56.1	−19.0	−3.0	2 19 43.83	−29 49 9.0

Zone 77. October 28. C. $D_0 = -32°\ 3'\ 10''$.

No.	Mag.	I.	II.	III.	IV.	V.	VI.	VII.	T. (h. m. s.)	a_1 (s.)	a_2 (s.)
1	9	..	..	1.3	19.1	38.0	55.1	..	22 59 19.24	− 1.25	−0.39
2	9.10	..	..	48.2	6.0	24.2	..	0.7	23 8 6.11	1.39	0.23
3	9.10	..	..	..	6.5	24.5	..	..	10 6.66	1.42	0.61
4	9	..	..	..	..	47.2	..	..	11 38.99	1.44	0.15
5	9	..	..	..	45.0	..	21.8	39.0	13 44.93	1.48	0.20
6	9	..	35.7	52.0	..	28.1	..	..	16 10.96	1.51	0.15
7	9.10	..	..	..	..	29.0	46.7	..	18 10.40	1.54	0.50
8	9.10	..	..	..	..	..	8.9	27.5	19 32.60	1.57	0.35
9	9.10	..	..	..	..	..	29.0	46.0	20 52.02	1.58	0.20
10	8.9	..	..	59.0	17.4	35.2	53.2	..	23 17.16	1.63	0.27
11	9	..	..	..	..	2.8	21.4	39.7	23 44.90	1.63	0.18
12	7.8	..	..	..	30.3	48.7	6.5	..	25 30.32	1.66	0.16
13	7	..	34.7	53.2	11.2	29.8	47.7	..	29 11.32	1.72	0.53
14	9	..	..	..	..	..	..	11.0	29 16.26	1.73	0.41
15	9	..	..	..	..	52.2	10.7	28.7	30 33.91	1.74	0.40
16	6.7	..	10.8	29.2	47.3	6.4	24.2	42.4	32 47.55	1.78	0.69
17	8	..	39.2	..	16.2	34.4	52.5	10.6	33 15.92	1.79	0.69
18	9.10	..	..	29.5	47.0	5.3	24.0	..	35 47.32	1.82	0.56
19	9.10	..	..	57.0	..	..	1.2	28.0	40 33.44	1.89	0.26
20	9	..	9.7	27.3	45.7	4.0	22.4	..	41 45.85	1.92	0.29
21	9.10	..	..	..	16.2	..	..	..	46 16.25	1.99	0.60
22	7	..	..	15.0	33.2	51.3	10.0	28.1	23 47 33.23	− 2.01	−0.61

No.	Micrometer (r.)	i (′ ″)	d_1 (″)	d_2 (″)	Mean Right Ascension, 1850.0 (h. m. s.)	Mean Declination, 1850.0 (° ′ ″)
1	IV. 3 26.771	−33 22.6	− 6.0	− 6.2	22 59 17.60	−32 36 44.8
2	IV. 4 42.889	16 29.4	5.6	3.2	23 8 4.40	19 48.2
3	IV. 2 11.188	49 41.5	5.5	9.0	10 4.63	53 6.0
4	V. 2 51.504	7 9.5	5.4	1.6	11 37.40	10 26.5
5	IV. 4 46.738	12 27.6	5.3	2.5	13 43.25	15 45.6
6	IV. 4 53.396	5 30.1	5.2	1.3	16 9.30	8 46.6
7	V. 2 21.886	38 30.8	5.1	7.0	18 8.36	41 52.9
8	VI. 4 35.384	24 22.3	5.0	4.6	19 30.68	27 41.9
9	VI. 4 49.627	9 25.9	4.9	2.0	20 50.24	12 42.8
10	IV. 4 43.961	15 22.2	4.8	3.0	23 15.26	18 40.0
11	V. 4 52.519	6 24.8	4.8	1.5	23 43.09	9 41.1
12	IV. 4 55.114	3 42.8	4.8	1.0	25 28.50	6 58.6
13	IV. 3 22.710	37 37.3	4.6	6.9	29 9.07	40 55.8
14	VII. 3 33.402	26 20.6	4.6	4.9	29 14.12	29 40.1
15	V. 3 26.952	33 11.3	4.5	6.1	30 31.68	36 31.9
16	IV. 2 10.211	50 42.7	4.4	9.3	32 45.08	54 6.4
17	IV. 2 10.121	50 48.3	4.4	9.3	33 13.44	54 12.0
18	IV. 3 21.651	38 43.7	4.4	7.1	35 44.94	42 5.2
19	IV. 4 51.209	7 17.3	4.2	1.7	40 35.59	11 3.2
20	IV. 4 48.271	10 51.8	4.2	2.2	41 43.64	14 8.2
21	IV. 3 25.882	34 18.3	4.1	6.3	46 13.66	37 38.7
22	IV. 3 20.662	−39 45.7	− 4.0	− 7.3	23 47 30.61	−32 43 7.0

CORRECTIONS.

Date	Corr. of Clock	Hourly rate	m	n	c	Zenith Point	Mic. Co.
1846 Oct. 28, 22h	− 10.649 s.	0.012 s.	− 0.168 s.	+ 0.103 s.	+ 0.351 s.		r.

REMARKS.

Oct. 26. Clear; stars steady.

(76) 42. Micrometer reading assumed as 23r.989, not 24r.989.
(76) 50. Micrometer reading assumed as 49r.134 instead of 48r.134.
(76) 52. Minutes assumed as 16 instead of 17.
(77) 4. Transit over T. V assumed as 57s.2 instead of 47s.2.
(77) 19. Transits discordant; T. II assumed as recorded over T. III, and T. VI rejected.

INSTRUMENT READINGS.

	Date	A. (° ′ ″)	B.	C.	D.	E.	F.	Mean.	Barom. (In.)	At.	Ex.	U.	L.	l.
Zone 76	1846 Oct. 26, 0 50	68 54 64.0	68.9	80.1	72.1	56.9	44.9	64.48	..	..	51.0	52.8	52.0	
	0 56								..	..	50.8			
	1 13								30.242	53.2	50.7			
	1 30										47.7			
	1 43										48.2			
	1 49										49.6			
	2 0								30.230	53.2	49.4			
	2 10	63.9	69.0	80.2	72.3	57.1	43.5	64.33			49.7	53.2	52.0	
	2 19								30.218	53.1	47.5			
Zone 77	Oct. 28, 22 59								30.072	53.0	42.9			

Zone 77. October 28. C. $D_o = -32°\ 3'\ 10''$—Continued.

No.	Mag.	I.	II.	III.	IV.	V.	VI.	VII.	T.	a_1	a_2	MICROMETER.		i	d_1	d_2	Mean Right Ascension, 1850.0	Mean Declination, 1850.0
									h. m. s.	s.	s.			r.	′ ″	″	″	h. m. s.	° ′ ″
23	7			15.0	33.2	51.3	10.0	28.2	23 47 33.24	−2.01	−0.64	IV.	3	18.529	−41 59.6	−4.0	−7.7	23 47 30.59	−32 45 21.3
24	9		29.3	49.3	8.0	26.2			51 7.32	2.07	0.36	IV.	4	43.808	15 31.6	4.0	3.0	51 4.89	18 48.8
25	7.8		17.3	35.5	53.7	12.0	40.0		51 53.71	2.08	0.50	IV.	3	31.772	28 8.8	4.0	5.2	51 51.13	31 28.0
26	9.10		37.7				32.0	50.4	55 14.01	2.13	0.30	IV.	4	50.792	8 13.3	4.0	1.8	55 11.58	11 29.1
27	8		39.5	57.5	16.3	34.6	53.0		57 16.18	2.16	0.73	IV.	2	14.288	46 27.4	4.0	8.5	57 13.29	49 49.9
28	9		7.0			2.0	20.6		23 59 43.75	2.20	0.77	IV.	2	11.054	49 49.8	4.0	9.1	23 59 40.78	53 12.9
29	7		26.6	44.7	2.7	21.2	39.2		0 3 2.92	2.25	0.28	IV.	4	55.338	3 26.8	4.0	1.0	0 2 0.39	6 43.8
30	9		38.5		15.2	33.5			5 15.17	2.29	0.69	IV.	2	19.831	40 39.8	4.1	7.4	5 12.19	44 1.3
31	6.7		59.2	17.3	36.2	54.2	12.3	30.3	8 35.83	2.35	0.41	IV.	2	45.789	13 27.3	4.2	2.7	8 33.07	16 44.2
32	9		40.8	58.8	17.0	35.2	53.7		0 15 17.11	−2.45	−0.60	IV.	3	31.049	−28 54.2	−4.4	−5.4	0 15 14.06	−32 32 14.0

Zone 78. October 28. C. $D_o = -32°\ 3'\ 10''$.

No.	Mag.	I.	II.	III.	IV.	V.	VI.	VII.	T.	a_1	a_2	MICROMETER.		i	d_1	d_2	Mean Right Ascension, 1850.0	Mean Declination, 1850.0
1	7			22.0	40.3	58.3	17.1	35.4	1 49 58.62	−3.76	−0.65	IV.	2	12.034	−48 48.4	−18.5	−9.0	1 49 54.21	−32 52 25.9
2	9			21.2	40.8		17.0		51 40.26	3.78	0.60	IV.	3	20.721	39 42.0	18.8	7.3	51 35.88	43 19.1
3	8.9				6.2	24.5			53 6.24	3.79	0.52	IV.	3	34.561	25 12.6	19.0	4.7	53 1.93	28 40.3
4	9						29.8	47.7	1 53 53.11	3.80	0.54	VI.	3	29.819	30 11.2	19.1	5.6	1 53 48.77	33 45.9
5	7.8		49.0	7.7	25.8			21.0	2 2 25.89	3.90	0.52	IV.	3	35.851	23 52.8	20.4	4.5	2 2 21.47	27 27.7
6	7.8		23.7	42.0		18.5	36.6		2 41.96	3.91	0.54	IV.	3	32.189	27 42.8	20.4	5.1	2 37.51	31 18.3
7	8					44.5	2.3	20.9	4 26.03	3.94	0.63	V.	2	18.006	42 34.1	20.7	7.8	4 21.46	46 12.6
8	9			56.0	13.7	32.8	50.3		19 14.09	4.10	0.55	IV.	3	34.796	24 59.0	23.0	4.7	19 9.44	28 36.7
9	9				43.0	1.5	19.2		20 24.84	4.11	0.46	V.	4	49.832	9 13.3	23.2	1.9	20 20.27	12 43.4
10	9		35.8	54.2	12.3	30.5	49.3		25 12.49	4.16	0.63	IV.	2	21.446	38 58.7	24.1	7.2	25 7.70	42 40.0
11	9		20.7	37.8			32.8		26 56.54	4.18	0.52	IV.	3	40.319	19 12.6	24.4	3.6	26 51.84	22 50.6
12	8		14.8		50.8	8.7	27.3		27 50.88	4.19	0.45	IV.	4	51.621	7 21.4	24.5	1.6	27 46.24	10 57.5
13	9		41.0	59.2	17.2	35.5	53.7		30 17.33	4.21	0.57	IV.	3	33.152	26 42.3	25.0	5.0	30 12.55	30 22.3
14	9.10				26.0				32 26.05	4.23	0.64	IV.	3	21.287	39 6.7	25.4	7.2	32 21.18	42 49.3
15	7.8		38.0	56.0	14.0	32.0	50.2		34 14.07	4.25	0.45	IV.	4	55.649	3 9.3	25.8	0.9	34 9.37	6 46.0
16	9				49.0	8.2	26.0		41 49.40	4.32	0.72	IV.	2	9.770	51 10.2	27.2	9.4	41 44.36	54 56.8
17	9		50.3	8.0	26.7	45.1	3.3		46 26.71	4.37	0.48	IV.	4	51.669	7 18.3	28.1	1.5	46 21.86	10 57.9
18	9		27.5			22.0			2 54 3.88	4.43	0.51	IV.	4	48.551	10 34.1	29.6	2.1	2 53 58.94	14 15.8
19	8		32.7	51.2	9.5	28.2	46.2		3 1 9.56	4.50	0.76	IV.	2	8.966	52 0.4	31.0	9.6	3 1 4.30	55 51.0
20	9						32.0	50.0	1 55.51	4.51	0.51	VI.	4	49.650	9 24.4	31.2	1.9	1 50.49	13 7.5
21	9.10					14.6		49.7	3 55.64	4.53	0.59	V.	3	36.159	23 33.6	31.6	4.4	3 50.52	27 19.6
22	9						42.7	0.7	5 6.01	4.54	0.67	VI.	2	24.769	35 29.8	31.8	6.5	5 0.80	39 18.1
23	9					35.1	43.4	12.0	6 17.08	4.55	0.54	V.	4	46.634	12 34.1	32.0	2.5	6 11.99	16 18.6
24	9.10				49.5		25.2		17 49.13	4.63	0.66	IV.	3	28.000	32 5.5	34.4	5.9	17 43.84	35 55.8
25	9.10		5.7		41.2		18.7		20 41.88	4.66	0.66	IV.	3	27.899	32 11.8	35.0	5.1	20 36.56	36 2.7
26	9		44.0	2.5			57.2		23 20.68	4.67	0.54	IV.	4	51.342	7 39.0	35.6	1.6	23 15.47	11 26.2
27	9.10			27.2	46.0	3.7		41.0	24 45.75	4.68	0.73	IV.	2	18.761	41 45.6	35.9	7.7	24 40.34	45 39.2
28	9					37.2	55.1	13.7	26 18.70	4.69	0.75	V.	1	15.482	45 9.7	36.2	8.3	26 13.26	49 4.2
29	9				15.0				3 28 15.02	4.71	0.57	IV.	4	46.292	12 56.0	36.6	8.5	28 9.74	16 45.1
30	7.8			19.0		56.2		33.0	28 37.83	4.71	0.61	IV.	3	40.650	18 51.6	36.7	3.6	28 32.51	22 41.9
31	8		26.8	44.8	3.0	21.2			35 3.08	4.75	0.61	IV.	3	42.072	17 22.4	38.2	3.3	34 57.72	21 13.9
32	6.7		45.5	4.2	22.2	40.7	58.2		36 22.72	4.76	0.63	IV.	3	38.282	21 20.4	38.5	4.0	36 17.33	25 12.9
33	9						3.2		36 26.69	4.76	0.69	VI.	3	28.469	31 36.2	38.5	5.8	36 21.24	35 30.5
34	9		13.1		49.5	8.0			40 49.63	4.78	0.72	IV.	3	23.485	36 48.8	39.6	6.8	40 44.13	40 45.42
35	8.9		5.5	22.5	41.0	59.5			3 42 41.24	−4.79	−0.57	IV.	4	48.574	−10 32.6	−40.1	−2.1	3 42 35.88	−32 14 24.8

CORRECTIONS.

Date.		Corr. of Clock.	Hourly rate.	m	n	c	Zenith Point.	Mic. Co.
1846, Oct. 28,	h. 22	s. −10.649	s. −0.012	s. −0.168	s. +0.103	s. +0.351	° ′ ″	r.

REMARKS.

Oct. 28. Night clear. $0^h\ 16^m$, suspended sweep for other observations. Reading of Barometer, &c., at $1^h\ 40^m$.

INSTRUMENT READINGS.

	Date.		CIRCLE.							Barom.	THERMOM.				
			A.	B.	C.	D.	E.	F.	Mean.		At.	Ex.	U.	L.	I.
	1846,	h. m.	° ′ ″						″	in.	°	°	°	°	°
Zone 77	Oct. 28,	23 0	71 24 58.5	64.6	75.1	65.9	50.9	40.9	59.32				50.0	52.3	56.5
		23 30								30.064	51.7	42.1			
		0 0	58.0	65.4	75.1	66.8	50.8	40.5	59.45	30.058		42.5	46.5	48.7	
		0 15										41.5			
Zone 78	Oct. 28,	1 40	71 24 62.1	72.0	80.4	73.7	56.4	45.0	64.93	30.077	47.5	39.5	45.2	47.7	55.8
		2 2										38.4			
		2 20								30.078	46.8	38.3			
		2 40	61.5	72.2	80.0	73.0	57.1	44.0	64.63			37.8	45.8	46.8	
		3 1								30.088	46.0	37.5			

11—Z

ZONE 78. OCTOBER 28. C. $D_0 = -32°\ 3'\ 10''$—Continued.

No.	Mag.	I.	II.	III.	IV.	V.	VI.	VII.	T.	a_1	a_2	Mic.		r	i	d_1	d_2	Mean Right Ascension, 1850.0	Mean Declination, 1850.0
									h. m. s.	s.	s.			r.	' "	"	"	h. m. s.	° ' "
36	8	..	51.2	9.8	27.8	46.0	4.4	..	3 44 27.84	−4.80	−0.75	IV.	2	19.933	−40 33.4	−40.6	−7.4	3 44 22.29	−32 44 31.4
37	9	..	..	21.0	39.1	57.2	..	..	3 50 39?.09	4.84	0.55	IV.	4	54.720	4 7.6	42.2	1.7	3 50 33?.70	8 0.9
38	9	..	40.5	..	17.3	35.0	53.3	..	4 2 17.03	−4.89	−0.56	IV.	4	54.208	−4 39.7	−45.2	−1.2	4 1 11.58	−32 8 36.1

ZONE 79. NOVEMBER 16. P. $D_0 = -27°\ 57'\ 40''$.

No.	Mag.	I.	II.	III.	IV.	V.	VI.	VII.	T.	a_1	a_2	Mic.		r	i	d_1	d_2	Mean Right Ascension, 1850.0	Mean Declination, 1850.0
1	7	..	..	13.	30.3	..	..	..	1 42 30.81	−0.93	−0.54	IV.	3	26.633	−33 31.3	−6.3	−4.7	1 42 29.34	−28 31 22.3
2	8	30.0	47.7	5.	22.3	..	..	..	45 23.65	0.96	0.53	IV.	3	27.977	32 6.9	6.7	4.5	45 22.16	29 58.1
3	7.8	51.0	8.7	26.3	43.7	..	..	..	48 43.74	1.01	0.48	IV.	3	30.833	29 7.7	7.1	4.1	48 42.25	26 58.9
4	9.10	..	..	14.0	32.0	..	..	..	50 31.81	1.03	0.52	IV.	3	29.130	30 54.6	7.3	4.4	50 30.26	28 46.3
5	8	49.0	6.5	23.7	..	..	..	..	52 41.57	1.05	0.74	III.	2	18.283	42 17.0	7.6	5.0	52 39.78	40 10.5
6	8	..	..	..	..	..	20.0	..	52 44.97	1.05	0.30	VI.	4	42.300	17 6.1	7.6	2.5	52 43.62	14 56.2
7	8	..	..	..	..	..	..	..	1 52 ..	1.05	0.25	VII.	4	45.040	14 13.8	8.	2.2	1 53 ..	12 (2)
8	8	35.0	52.3	10.0	27.0	..	..	..	2 0 27.44	1.15	0.61	IV.	4	26.090	34 5.4	8.7	4.8	2 0 25.68	31 58.9
9	7	..	..	..	..	41.0	..	16.0	1 23.41	1.17	0.36	V.	4	40.210	19 17.6	8.9	2.8	1 21.88	17 9.3
10	8	..	9.0	27.0	..	..	..	..	3 44.37	1.19	0.61	III.	3	26.520	33 38.3	9.2	4.7	3 42.57	31 32.2
11	7	35.0	52.5	10.3	27.5	..	..	..	5 27.62	1.21	0.31	IV.	4	44.073	15 15.2	9.4	2.3	5 26.10	13 6.9
12	7	45.3	2.7	20.5	37.7	..	..	..	7 37.94	1.24	0.70	IV.	2	21.953	38 26.7	9.6	5.4	7 36.00	30 21.9
13	7	..	..	7.0	24.7	..	..	..	15 24.66	1.33	0.69	IV.	3	25.220	35 0.0	11.0	4.9	15 22.64	32 55.9
14	8	..	..	35.0	53.0	..	..	..	20 52.79	1.40	0.45	IV.	4	39.390	20 9.4	11.9	2.9	20 50.94	18 4.2
15	7	5.5	23.0	40.0	..	..	..	..	24 57.87	1.44	0.29	III.	4	46.820	12 22.7	12.6	1.9	24 56.15	10 17.2
16	7	..	..	21.5	39.0	..	..	..	25 39.06	1.46	0.62	IV.	3	30.585	29 23.4	12.7	4.2	25 36.98	27 20.3
17	8	..	..	32.0	..	6.5	..	..	28 49.21	1.49	0.88	IV.	2	16.812	43 49.0	13.3	6.1	28 46.84	41 48.4
18	6	41.0	58.5	16.0	33.5	..	..	..	32 33.59	1.53	0.66	IV.	4	29.850	30 9.3	14.0	4.3	32 31.40	28 7.6
19	8	..	..	..	..	45.5	..	..	33 27.84	1.54	0.92	IV.	2	15.850	44 49.3	14.1	6.2	33 25.38	42 49.6
20	8	..	..	43.0	..	..	..	..	35 0.54	1.56	0.37	III.	4	47.520	11 38.9	14.4	1.8	34 58.61	9 35.1
21	8	..	..	..	..	45.0	..	..	35 27.36	1.56	0.81	V.	3	22.755	37 34.4	14.5	5.3	35 24.99	35 34.2
22	7	..	40.0	58.0	15.0	..	..	..	37 15.26	1.58	0.75	IV.	3	25.852	34 20.2	14.8	4.8	37 12.93	32 19.8
23	4.5	34.0	51.5	9.0	20.5	..	..	..	43 26.62	1.65	0.81	IV.	3	24.260	36 0.2	16.0	5.1	43 24.16	34 1.3
24	6	13.0	30.3	47.7	5.5	..	..	..	46 5.49	1.67	0.84	IV.	3	23.784	36 29.9	16.5	5.1	46 2.98	34 31.5
25	9	..	49.0	..	24.0	..	..	..	48 24.10	1.70	0.77	IV.	3	27.790	32 18.6	17.0	4.5	48 21.63	30 20.1
26	8.9	..	40.0	57.0	..	..	..	..	51 14.82	1.73	0.54	III.	4	41.170	18 17.6	17.6	2.7	51 12.55	16 17.9
27	9	..	..	..	..	..	2.0	..	51 26.97	1.73	0.56	VI.	4	39.115	20 25.9	17.6	3.0	51 24.68	18 20.5
28	8	..	..	29.0	..	..	..	..	53 46.58	1.75	0.97	III.	2	17.043	42 38.0	18.1	5.9	53 43.80	40 42.0
29	8	..	..	..	19.0	..	..	..	54 19.02	1.76	0.51	V.	4	43.363	15 59.7	18.1	2.4	54 16.75	14 0.2
30	4	..	..	12.0	29.0	46.0	..	..	55 11.42	1.77	0.96	IV.	2	18.550	42 0.3	18.3	5.8	55 8.69	40 4.4
31	9	59.0	17.0	35.0	..	..	..	..	2 58 52.74	1.80	0.84	III.	3	26.107	34 4.1	19.1	4.8	2 58 49.50	32 8.0
32	8	36.0	53.7	11.3	28.5	..	..	..	3 1 26.70	1.83	0.71	IV.	4	33.393	26 27.3	19.6	3.8	3 1 26.16	24 30.7
33	6	8.5	26.0	43.5	1.0	..	..	..	7 1.01	1.88	0.45	IV.	4	48.824	10 16.8	20.8	1.7	6 58.68	8 19.3
34	5	31.0	48.5	6.0	23.5	..	..	..	17 23.59	1.97	0.84	IV.	3	30.180	29 48.8	23.1	4.2	17 20.78	27 56.1
35	7	33.0	50.5	8.0	25.7	..	..	..	24 25.66	2.03	0.83	IV.	3	31.553	28 22.7	24.7	4.0	24 22.80	26 31.4
36	8	..	..	30.0	..	..	..	..	30 47.58	2.06	1.04	III.	2	21.530	38 53.4	26.2	5.4	30 44.46	37 5.0
37	4	43.0	0.7	18.3	..	..	..	..	32 35.78	2.09	0.85	III.	3	31.003	28 0.3	26.6	4.0	32 32.84	26 10.9
38	8.9	..	..	..	10.0	..	..	..	32 52.38	2.10	0.94	V.	3	27.615	32 29.8	26.7	4.6	32 49.34	30 41.1
39	6.7	..	4.0	21.3	30.0	..	..	..	34 39.01	2.11	0.89	IV.	3	30.883	29 4.6	27.1	4.1	34 36.01	27 15.8
40	8	..	..	..	1.0	..	..	..	37 1.05	2.13	1.06	IV.	2	21.523	38 53.8	27.7	5.4	36 57.86	37 6.9
41	7	18.0	35.5	53.0	..	..	..	..	39 10.58	2.14	0.79	III.	3	37.383	22 16.7	28.2	3.2	39 7.65	20 28.1
42	8	..	..	..	..	..	..	52.5	3 38 59.89	−2.14	−0.69	VII.	4	42.983	−16 22.5	−28.2	−2.4	3 38 57.00	−28 14 33.1

CORRECTIONS.

Date.		Corr. of Clock.	Hourly rate.	m	n	c	Zenith Point.	Mic. Co.
1846. Nov. 16	h. 0	s. − 7.609	s. − 0.032	s. − 0.168	s. + 0.103	s. + 0.351	° ' "	r.

REMARKS.

Nov. 16. After $3^h\ 30^m$ stars very unsteady.

(79) 29. Transit over T. IV assumed as recorded over T. V.

INSTRUMENT READINGS.

Date.			CIRCLE.							Barom.	THERMOM.				
			A.	B.	C.	D.	E.	F.	Mean.		At.	Ex.	U.	L.	I.
	1846.	h. m.	° ' "						"	In.	°	°	°	°	°
Zone 78	Oct. 28,	3 20	..	..	..	..	..	..	..	..	..	38.4			
		3 40	..	..	..	..	..	..	..	30.086	45.5	38.4			
		3 50	71 24 60.9	72.0	80.1	72.5	56.9	43.9	64.38	30.090	45.0	37.0	43.8	46.0	
Zone 79	Nov. 16,	1 40	67 39 61.5	66.8	82.4	69.3	54.0	42.3	62.72	30.190	51.5	45.5	50.0		
		2 15	..	..	..	..	..	..	..	..	..	44.7			
		3 1	..	..	..	..	..	..	..	30.190	50.0	43.0			
		3 40	60.8	67.5	82.3	70.0	54.5	41.3	62.73	30.196	49.7	42.6	48.0	..	55.0

ZONE 80. NOVEMBER 20. P. $D_0 = -35° 48' 50''$.

No.	Mag.	I.	II.	III.	IV.	V.	VI.	VII.	T. (h. m. s.)	a_1	a_2	Micr.		r.	i (' '')	d_1 ('')	d_2 ('')	Mean R.A. 1850.0 (h. m. s.)	Mean Decl. 1850.0 (° ' '')
1	9							58.0	0 45 0.51	−2.53	−2.41	VII.	2	15.880	−44 46.6	−2.2	−10.8	0 44 55.57	−36 33 49.6
2	6	31.0	51.0	10.0	29.0				0 59 28.96	2.81	2.19	IV.	2	21.663	38 45.0	3.0	9.2	0 59 23.96	27 47.2
3	7	56.0	14.5	33.5					1 5 52.72	2.92	0.93	III.	4	48.020	11 7.4	3.5	1.9	1 5 48.87	0 2.8
4	8					41.0			6 2.70	2.92	2.41	VI.	2	17.147	43 27.8	3.5	10.4	5 57.37	32 31.7
5	8		25.5	44.0	3.5				28 3.42	3.32	1.26	IV.	4	41.580	17 51.8	5.5	3.6	27 58.84	6 50.9
6	8	31.0	50.0	10.0					1 43 28.52	−3.59	−1.74	III.	3	31.960	−27 56.8	−7.3	−6.3	1 43 23.19	−36 17 0.4

ZONE 81. NOVEMBER 20. P. $D_0 = -30° 48' 0''$.

No.	Mag.	I.	II.	III.	IV.	V.	VI.	VII.	T. (h. m. s.)	a_1	a_2	Micr.		r.	i (' '')	d_1 ('')	d_2 ('')	Mean R.A. 1850.0 (h. m. s.)	Mean Decl. 1850.0 (° ' '')
1	8					35.0			2 3 56.74	4.65	−0.77	VI.	2	18.513	−42 2.3	−4.6	−6.8	2 3 51.32	−31 30 13.7
2	3.4			47.0	5.5	23.3			6 23.33	4.68	0.71	IV.	2	22.850	37 30.4	5.0	6.1	6 17.94	25 41.5
3	7	4.0	22.0	40.0					10 58.04	4.74	0.69	III.	3	23.520	36 46.4	5.7	6.0	10 52.61	24 58.1
4	8			23.5					11 46.54	4.75	0.72	III.	3	19.670	40 49.9	5.8	6.6	11 41.07	29 2.3
5	8							19.0	11 25.00	4.75	0.52	VII.	3	37.920	21 42.6	5.8	3.5	11 19.73	9 51.9
6	9		15.0						14 51.20	4.80	0.80	II.	1	11.470	49 20.6	6.3	8.0	14 45.60	37 34.9
7	7	39.5	58.0	16.0	34.0				21 33.84		0.46	IV.	4	40.750	18 43.8	7.5	3.1	21 (38)	6 54.4
8	8		21.0	39.0					23 56.99	4.93	0.39	III.	4	46.240	12 59.3	7.9	2.2	23 51.67	1 9.4
9	7	32.5	50.0	8.0	26.0				32 26.13	5.02	0.53	IV.	3	33.120	26 44.3	9.4	4.3	32 20.58	14 58.0
10	6			7.0	25.0	43.5			33 43.20	5.04	0.53	IV.	3	31.470	28 27.9	9.7	4.6	33 37.63	16 42.2
11	7	38.0	56.0	14.0					35 31.93	5.06	0.37	III.	4	44.665	14 38.1	10.0	2.4	35 26.50	2 50.5
12	7		10.5	29.0					36 46.89	5.08	0.78	III.	1	6.840	54 12.0	10.2	9.4	36 41.03	42 31.6
13	7	43.5	1.5	19.0					39 37.28	5.11	0.39	III.	4	40.950	18 31.3	10.8	3.0	39 31.78	6 45.1
14	7			35.0	52.5	10.3			43 10.06	5.15	0.58	IV.	2	22.350	38 2.0	11.4	6.2	43 4.93	26 19.6
15	7	12.0	30.0	48.0					45 5.95	5.18	0.34	III.	4	44.220	15 6.1	11.8	2.5	45 0.43	3 20.4
16	6			23.0	40.5	59.0			45 40.84	5.18	0.57	IV.	2	22.450	37 55.8	11.9	6.1	45 35.09	26 13.8
17	6	30.5	48.5	6.5	24.0				48 24.45	5.21	0.60	IV.	2	18.717	41 49.7	12.4	6.8	48 18.64	31 30 8.9
18	7	51.0	9.0	27.5	45.3				2 59 45.14	5.34	0.22	IV.	4	50.070	8 58.7	14.7	1.6	2 59 39.58	30 57 15.0
19	7			11.0	29.0	47.0			3 1 46.97	5.36	0.18	IV.	4	53.745	5 8.0	15.1	1.0	3 1 41.43	30 53 24.1
20	6	12.5	30.5	48.5	6.0				10 6.42	5.45	0.46	IV.	3	25.610	34 35.5	16.9	5.6	10 0.51	31 22 58.0
21	7				4.5				18 22.55	5.54	0.60	III.	1	9.500	51 24.2	18.6	8.3	18 16.41	39 51.1
22	7			31.0		6.0			20 6.51	5.55	0.28	IV.	4	38.650	20 55.7	19.0	3.4	20 0.68	9 18.1
23	7	0.5	18.5	36.0	54.0				3 27 54.22	−5.63	−0.24	IV.	4	39.950	−19 34.0	−20.6	−3.2	3 27 48.35	−31 7 57.8

ZONE 82. NOVEMBER 21. C. $D_r = -33° 28' 10''$.

No.	Mag.	I.	II.	III.	IV.	V.	VI.	VII.	T. (h. m. s.)	a_1	a_2	Micr.		r.	i (' '')	d_1 ('')	d_2 ('')	Mean R.A. 1850.0 (h. m. s.)	Mean Decl. 1850.0 (° ' '')
1	8			6.0	24.5	43.0	1.5	20.0	0 0 43.02	−0.03	−4.00	IV.	4	45.505	−13 45.3	−0.1	−6.0	0 0 38.99	−33 32 1.4
2	8			28.0	46.3		23.0		3 46.30	0.10	3.30	IV.	4	39.748	19 46.7	0.1	7.1	3 42.90	38 3.9
3	8.9			50.8	9.3	27.9	46.3		7 9.32	0.16	1.62	IV.	3	25.732	34 27.7	0.0	10.1	7 7.54	52 47.8
4	8.9			25.0	43.5		39.0	57.8	9 2.09	0.20	3.59	IV.	4	42.072	17 20.8	0.0	6.7	8 58.30	35 37.5
5	7.8			12.3	31.0	49.5	8.0		9 12.49	0.21	−4.08	IV.	4	46.221	13 0.4	0.0	5.8	9 8.20	33 31 16.2
6	9					7.2		42.8	11 24.96	0.24	+0.28	IV.	2	9.812	51 7.5	0.0	13.4	11 25.00	34 9 30.9
7	9					47.5	5.8	23.8	0 12 47.22	−0.26	−3.56	IV.	4	41.796	−17 38.1	−0.0	−6.7	0 12 43.40	−33 35 54.8

CORRECTIONS.

Date.	Corr. of Clock.	Hourly rate.	m	n	c	Zenith Point.	Mic. Co.
1846. Nov. 21, 0h	s. −11.589	s. −0.032	s. −0.168	s. +0.103	s. +0.351	(° ' '')	r.

INSTRUMENT READINGS.

	Date.	A. (° ' '')	B.	C.	D.	E.	F.	Mean. ('')	Barom. (in.)	At.	Ex.	U.	L.	I.
Zone 80	1846, Nov. 20, 0 45	75 9 68.0	73.2	87.0	76.0	60.0	47.0	68.53	29.988	52.5	40.5	52.0		
	1 28								29.988	51.5	40.6			
	1 43								29.984	51.0	40.0			
Zone 81	Nov. 20, 1 55	70 9 65.8	74.2	84.3	74.0	61.3	45.7	67.55				54.0		
	2 3								29.984	51.0	40.0			
	3 1								29.996	50.0	38.5			
	3 27								29.996	50.0	38.6			
Zone 82	Nov. 21, 0 0	72 39 58.8	69.2	78.0	71.2	53.9	41.2	62.05	29.954	49.0	38.0	51.0	50.5	53.3
	0 12										37.9			

REMARKS.

Nov. 20. Night unfavorable. Stars appear and disappear. Reading of Barometer, &c., at 1h 20m. 1h 45m, moved to another belt.

Nov. 21. Stars very unsteady and poorly defined; appear and disappear.

(81) 6. T. II perhaps 13'.

Zone 83. December 3. P. $D_0 = -34°\ 33'\ 30''$.

No.	Mag.	I.	II.	III.	IV.	V.	VI.	VII.	T.	a_1	a_2	Mic.		r.	i	d_1	d_2	Mean Right Ascension, 1850.0.	Mean Declination, 1850.0.
									h. m. s.	s.	s.			r.	′ ″	″	″	h. m. s.	° ′ ″
1	9						45.0		0 2 7.46	−11.86	−2.45	VI.	3	36.610	−23 5.3	0.0	−6.5	0 1 53.15	−34 56 41.8
2	8					28.0			4 9.09	11.90	2.74	V.	2	16.663	43 58.4	0.0	11.1	4 54.45	35 17 39.5
3	8					12.0			7 53.09	11.97	2.75	V.	2	14.553	46 10.8	0.0	11.6	7 38.37	19 52.4
4	8.9					18.5			10 59.69	12.03	2.40	V.	3	33.003	26 51.6	0.0	7.3	10 45.20	35 0 28.9
5	9							53.0	11 56.78	12.05	2.13	VII.	2	48.207	10 57.0	0.0	3.8	11 42.60	34 44 30.8
6	8			56.5	16.0				14 5.98	12.09	2.36	IV.	3	33.423	26 25.4	0.0	7.2	13 51.53	35 0 2.6
7	8	9.0	27.0	46.0	4.0				20 4.57	12.20	2.00	IV.	4	49.850	9 12.4	0.1	3.5	19 50.37	34 42 46.0
8	9			6.0				21.5	21 25.00	12.23	2.08	III.	4	44.910	14 21.4	0.1	4.6	21 10.69	47 56.1
9	9		5.0						25 42.57	12.31	2.22	II.	3	33.470	26 21.7	0.2	7.2	25 28.04	59 59.1
10	9		28.0						29 5.56	12.37	1.91	II.	4	49.205	9 53.0	0.3	3.6	29 51.28	43 26.9
11	6	52.5	11.5	30.0	49.0				32 48.87	12.44	1.92	IV.	4	45.960	13 16.6	0.4	4.5	32 34.51	46 51.5
12	8.9		29.0		6.0				42 6.26	12.62	1.68	IV.	4	53.680	5 12.1	0.7	2.6	41 51.96	38 45.4
13	8	20.0	39.0	58.0	17.0				44 16.65	12.66	1.91	IV.	4	39.030	20 31.8	0.8	6.0	44 2.08	54 8.6
14	8.9	46.0	5.0		43.0				47 42.57	12.73	1.72	IV.	4	46.500	12 42.9	1.0	4.2	47 28.12	46 18.1
15	8.9						48.0		50 10.60	12.78	1.62	VI.	4	51.630	7 20.2	1.1	3.1	49 56.20	34 40 54.4
16	7		55.0	14.0					0 52 32.86	12.82	2.25	III.	1	7.830	53 8.4	1.3	13.2	0 52 17.79	35 26 52.9
17	8	27.5	46.5	5.0					1 9 23.88	13.13	1.63	III.	3	36.910	22 46.1	2.5	6.4	1 9 9.12	34 56 25.0
18	8			19.0					10 37.86	13.15	2.21	III.	1	7.535	53 27.1	2.5	13.3	10 22.50	35 27 12.9
19	7				21.0				11 21.05	13.17	1.59	IV.	3	37.635	22 0.9	2.6	6.3	11 6.29	34 55 30.8
20	8			19.0	38.0				12 37.94	13.19	1.92	IV.	2	17.450	43 9.2	2.7	11.0	12 22.83	35 16 52.9
21	7		12.0	31.0					15 49.83	13.25	2.06	III.	1	7.700	53 16.6	3.0	13.3	15 34.52	35 27 2.9
22	6.7	5.5	24.0	43.0	2.0				18 1.80	13.29	1.50	IV.	3	37.810	21 49.8	3.2	6.2	17 47.01	34 55 29.2
23	8	52.0		30.0					33 48.66	13.57	1.62	III.	2	19.920	40 34.0	4.9	10.4	33 33.47	35 14 19.3
24	7			52.5	11.0				38 11.19	13.65	1.50	IV.	3	24.430	35 49.6	5.4	9.3	37 56.04	9 34.3
25	8		35.0				53.0		43 14.01	13.73	1.48	VI.	2	21.810	38 35.5	6.0	9.9	42 58.80	35 12 21.4
26	7.8	17.0	35.5	54.0					46 13.05	13.78	1.16	III.	3	37.260	22 24.3	6.4	6.3	45 58.11	34 56 7.0
27	8			6.0	25.0	44.0			1 50 43.76	−13.86	−0.89	IV.	4	52.145	−6 48.5	7.0	−3.0	1 50 29.01	−34 40 28.5

Zone 84. December 4. C. $D_0 = -33°\ 18'\ 20''$.

No.	Mag.	I.	II.	III.	IV.	V.	VI.	VII.	T.	a_1	a_2	Mic.		r.	i	d_1	d_2	Mean Right Ascension, 1850.0.	Mean Declination, 1850.0.
1	7			29.5	48.0	7.1	25.6	44.1	23 50 6.85	−13.42	−0.24	IV.	3	17.598	−42 57.9	−0.1	−9.0	23 49 53.19	−34 1 27.0
2	9			32.3	51.0		26.0		23 58 50.90	13.58	0.58	IV.	4	39.000	19 37.2	0.0	4.5	23 58 36.74	33 38 1.7
3	8			34.0	53.8	11.0	30.5	49.0	0 0 53.17	13.62	0.67	IV.	4	45.647	13 36.3	0.0	3.3	0 0 39.68	31 59.6
4	9			19.5		58.0			3 57.26	13.68	0.58	IV.	4	39.838	19 41.0	0.0	4.5	3 43.00	33 38 5.5
5	9					42.0	1.8	21.7	4 24.66	13.69	0.20	V.	2	15.255	45 26.7	0.0	9.6	4 10.77	34 3 56.3
6	9						55.0	13.7	5 17.87	13.70	0.15	VI.	2	12.012	48 49.5	0.0	10.3	5 4.02	34 7 19.8
7	9						52.0		5 56.22	13.71	0.30	VII.	3	21.061	39 20.5	0.0	8.3	5 42.21	33 57 48.8
8	8.9					48.1	57.1		7 29.78	13.74	0.37	V.	3	25.891	34 17.8	0.0	7.3	7 15.67	52 45.1
9	8					31.5	41.0		9 13.55	13.79	0.61	V.	4	42.191	17 13.2	0.0	4.0	8 59.15	35 37.2
10	7					41.5	59.1		10 22.60	13.80	0.68	V.	4	46.369	12 50.9	0.0	3.2	9 8.12	33 31 14.1
11	9						53.1	31.0	11 34.82	13.81	0.12	V.	2	9.922	51 0.5	0.0	10.7	11 20.89	34 9 31.2
12	8						35.0	53.5	12 58.06	13.84	0.61	VI.	4	41.916	17 30.0	0.0	4.1	12 43.61	33 35 54.1
13	9					38.5	57.0		14 19.93	13.87	0.33	V.	3	23.178	37 8.1	0.0	7.9	14 5.73	55 36.0
14	5	48.0	6.7	25.0	43.8	2.6	20.8	39.1	20 43.71	13.99	0.41	IV.	3	28.411	31 39.9	0.1	6.8	20 29.31	50 6.8
15	9				4.5	22.0	40.5	59.0	0 22 22.29	−13.02	−0.79	IV.	4	52.952	−5 57.7	−0.1	−1.9	0 22 8.48	−33 24 19.7

CORRECTIONS.

Date.	Corr. of Clock.	Hourly rate.	m	n	c	Zenith Point.	Mic. Co.
	h. s.	s.	s.	s.	s.	° ′ ″	r.
1846. Dec. 4.	0 − 22.074	− 0.024	− 0.425	+ 0.089	+ 0.192		

INSTRUMENT READINGS.

	Date.	A.	B.	C.	D.	E.	F.	Mean.	Barom.	At.	Ex.	U.	L.	I.
	1846. h. m.	° ′ ″						″	In.	°				
Zone 83	Dec. 3, 0 2	73 54 66.4	75.0	86.3	76.2	63.4	46.2	68.92	29.986	53.5	48.0	52.0		
	1 9								29.986	53.0	46.2			
	1 50								29.994	52.0	44.0			
Zone 84	Dec. 4, 23 45	72 39 62.9	74.0	83.3	73.1	60.8	43.9	66.33	30.306	47.5	38.8	48.0	47.5	50.1
	0 14								30.322	46.5	37.4			
	0 22								30.326	46.0	36.5			
	0 30	62.6	74.0	82.8	73.0	60.4	42.9	65.95					42.8	44.2

REMARKS.

Dec. 3. Readings at 1h 0m and 2h 0m.

Dec. 4. Readings of Barometer, &c., at 23h 45m; foggy about horizon; stars unsteady. 0h 30m, interrupted by fog. Readings of Barometer, &c., at 0h 30m.

(84) 2. Transit over T. III discordant and rejected; discordant 1m in R. A. and 2′ in Declination from Transit, October 15th.

(84) 9. Minutes assumed as 9 instead of 10. See Zone 84.

(84) 10. Minutes assumed as 9 instead of 10. See Zone 84.

ZONE 85. DECEMBER 23. C. $D_0 = -33° 18' 20''$.

No.	Mag.	I.	II.	III.	IV.	V.	VI.	VII.	T. (h m s)	a_1	a_2
1	9.10			48.1				58.5	0 4 4.81	−25.14	−0.56
2	9	36.3	54.3	12.8		50.0	9.0	27.0	7 31.56	25.20	0.88
3	8			6.0	24.2		1.2	20.0	9 24.58	25.24	0.52
4	7.8		58.0		34.3	53.2		30.0	9 34.65	25.24	0.43
5	9				11.5	28.5	47.0	5.4	13 10.39	25.31	0.53
6	9		35.7	54.0		32.0	50.5	9.0	16 13.10	25.37	1.06
7	6.7		18.2	36.8	55.8	13.8	32.7	50.7	20 55.41	25.46	0.86
8	8.9			15.5	33.3		10.7	29.3	22 33.75	25.48	0.30
9	9.10			4.8				20.0	36 23.88	25.75	0.79
10	9.10			22.0	40.2	58.9	17.2		39 40.30	25.81	1.06
11	9.10						49.7		48 12.85	25.97	0.38
12	8		4.7	23.3	41.9	0.8	19.1		54 41.96	26.09	1.35
13	9.10			12.8			8.0		0 56 31.19	26.13	0.55
14	8		25.3	44.3	2.7		39.7	58.2	1 1 2.66	26.21	0.65
15	9.10					11.0	30.0		6 53.78	26.32	0.66
16	9				47.3			42.0	9 46.93	26.37	0.54
17	8			25.2	43.3	3.1	21.6		11 44.04	26.41	1.08
18	9							5?	12 9.32	26.42	1.15
19	7.8		32.5	51.3	9.8	28.0	47.0		15 9.73	26.48	1.20
20	9.10						39.2		23 2.07	26.62	1.32
21	8.9			41.8			37.3		30 0.24	26.74	1.40
22	8	58.0	16.8	36.0	54.5	13.2	31.3	50.2	34 54.31	26.84	1.44
23	8.9			19.3		55.5	14.0	32.5	38 37.22	26.90	0.68
24	9			42.3			39.0		41 1.95	26.95	0.51
25	9		54.0		31.5				46 31.34	27.05	1.22
26	8					11.0		48.3	46 52.47	27.06	1.30
27	8.9		51.0	9.3		46.2	4.9		50 27.81	27.11	0.86
28	7			59.1	17.5	36.0	54.3	13.2	52 17.51	27.15	0.99
29	9				36.0	55.0	13.2		1 58 36.26	27.26	1.02
30	7.8			52.8	11.0	29.5	48.4	6.7	2 7 29.68	−27.40	−1.33

No.	Micrometer		r	i (′ ″)	d_1 (″)	d_2 (″)	Mean Right Ascension, 1850.0	Mean Declination, 1850.0
1	VI	3	39.981	−19 33.6	−3.9	−3.6	0 3 39.11	−33 38 1.2
2	IV	3	25.671	34 29.0	3.8	6.6	7 5.48	52 49.4
3	IV	4	42.236	17 10.7	3.8	3.1	8 58.82	35 37.6
4	IV	4	46.394	12 49.6	3.7	2.3	9 8.98	31 15.6
5	IV	4	41.906	17 31.2	3.7	3.2	12 44.55	33 35 58.1
6	IV	2	18.787	41 45.2	3.7	8.1	15 46.67	34 0 17.0
7	IV	3	28.428	31 38.8	3.6	6.0	20 29.09	33 50 8.4
8	IV	4	52.941	5 58.4	3.7	0.9	22 7.97	24 23.0
9	IV	3	32.395	27 29.9	3.8	5.2	35 57.34	45 58.9
10	IV	3	21.018	39 23.4	3.9	7.6	39 13.43	57 54.9
11	VI	4	52.188	6 45.3	4.2	1.1	47 46.50	33 25 10.6
12	IV	2	9.377	51 35.0	4.4	10.1	54 14.52	34 10 9.5
13	IV	4	44.700	14 35.8	4.4	2.6	0 56 4.51	33 33 2.8
14	IV	4	41.011	18 27.4	4.6	3.4	1 0 35.80	36 55.4
15	V	4	40.941	18 31.6	4.9	3.4	6 26.80	36 59.4
16	IV	4	47.096	12 5.4	5.1	2.1	9 20.02	30 32.6
17	IV	3	23.108	37 12.4	5.2	7.2	11 16.55	55 44.8
18	VII	3	20.205	40 14.2	5.3	7.8	11 41.75	33 58 47.3
19	IV	2	17.923	42 39.4	5.4	8.3	14 42.05	34 1 13.1
20	VI	2	13.451	47 19.6	6.0	9.3	22 34.13	5 54.9
21	IV	2	10.475	50 26.2	6.6	9.9	28 32.10	9 2.7
22	IV	2	9.075	51 53.7	7.1	10.2	34 26.03	31 10 31.0
23	IV	4	42.949	16 25.7	7.4	3.0	38 9.64	33 34 56.1
24	IV	4	50.800	8 12.4	7.6	1.4	40 34.40	26 41.4
25	V	2	20.100	40 20.4	8.2	7.8	46 3.07	33 58 56.4
26	V	2	16.338	44 18.9	8.2	8.6	46 24.11	34 2 55.7
27	IV	3	36.021	23 42.2	8.6	4.4	49 59.84	33 42 15.2
28	IV	3	30.668	29 18.1	8.8	5.5	51 49.37	47 52.4
29	IV	3	30.293	29 41.8	9.5	5.6	1 58 7.98	33 48 16.9
30	IV	2	16.898	−43 43.6	−10.4	−8.5	2 7 0.95	−34 2 22.5

CORRECTIONS.

Date.	Corr. of Clock.	Hourly rate.	m	n	ε	Zenith Point.	Mic. Co.
1846.	h. s.	s.	s.	s.	s.	° ′ ″	r.

REMARKS.

Dec. 23. Stars unsteady; at 2h very much so. Readings of Barometer, &c., at 0h 0m, 0h 30m, 0h 45m.

(85) 21. Differs 1m in a from Transit Z., 1846, October 24th.

INSTRUMENT READINGS.

Date.	Circle A.	B.	C.	D.	E.	F.	Mean.	Barom.	Therm. At.	Ex.	U.	L.	I.
1846. h. m.	° ′ ″						″	in.	°	°	°	°	°
Zone 85 Dec. 23, 0 0	72 39 59.7	72.0	62.2	68.4	62.1	63.2	64.60	30.526	38.3	30.1	32.4	35.9	40.0
0 16										29.9			
0 22								30.520	37.2	29.5			
0 48										29.0			
1 1	59.5	72.1	63.9	67.5	63.8	61.4	64.70	30.520	36.0	28.7	37.7	33.5	
1 15										28.3			
1 29								30.525	35.0	27.8			
1 40										27.1			
2 0	58.0	72.3	63.2	67.6	63.4	61.2	64.28				30.5	32.4	
2 7								30.528	33.2	26.9			

Zone 86. January 6, C. $D_o = -30°\ 10'\ 0''$.

No.	Mag.	I.	II.	III.	IV.	V.	VI.	VII.	T. (h. m. s.)	a_1 (s.)	a_2 (s.)	MICROMETER.		(r.)	i (' '')	d_1 ('')	d_2 ('')	Mean Right Ascension, 1850.0. (h. m. s.)	Mean Declination, 1850.0. (° ' '')
1	9	..	..	..	52.	8.2	35.	52.9	2 3 0.18	−33.24	−0.75	IV.	3	28.149	−31 56.26	−19.01	−4.28	2 3 26.21	−30 42 19.55
2	9	..	55.7	13.8	32.	49.	7.3	..	12 31.58	33.38	0.65	IV.	4	47.660	11 29.69	20.16	1.37	11 57.55	21 51.22
3	9	..	..	10.3	..	47.	..	24.1	13 29.20	33.39	0.86	IV.	2	19.492	41 0.36	20.31	5.58	13 54.95	51 26.25
4	9	..	25.	..	0.2	..	..	..	17 0.48	33.45	0.65	IV.	4	51.141	7 51.52	20.78	0.88	16 26.38	18 13.18
5	8	..	..	..	15.7	33.9	51.7	9.3	17 15.80	33.45	0.83	IV.	3	27.092	33 2.52	20.82	4.45	16 41.52	43 27.79
6	9	..	..	..	49.1	7.	24.7	..	18 49.04	33.48	0.84	IV.	3	27.408	32 42.81	21.03	4.39	18 14.72	43 8.23
7	9	..	..	35.3	52.8	..	28.8	..	21 53.04	33.53	0.71	IV.	4	46.468	12 44.56	21.48	1.54	21 18.80	30 23 7.58
8	8.9	..	49.8	8.	26.3	44.1	..	..	24 26.02	33.56	1.01	IV.	2	10.184	50 44.58	21.88	7.02	23 51.45	31 1 13.48
9	8	..	17.8	35.7	53.	11.5	29.5	47.2	27 53.52	33.62	0.84	IV.	3	34.379	25 25.46	22.38	3.34	27 19.06	30 35 51.16
10	9	..	..	..	37.	55.2	12.8	..	28 37.12	33.63	0.84	IV.	3	33.701	26 7.81	22.49	3.45	28 2.65	36 33.75
11	6.7	..	..	57.8	15.7	33.8	51.9	9.6	30 15.86	33.66	0.89	IV.	3	28.479	31 35.61	22.74	4.23	29 41.31	42 2.58
12	6.7	..	49.3	7.6	24.9	43.5	1.4	..	32 25.35	33.69	0.97	IV.	3	20.388	40 3.32	23.09	5.45	31 50.68	50 31.86
13	9	..	5.	23.	40.7	58.5	16.3	..	34 40.71	33.72	0.95	IV.	3	23.669	36 37.30	23.44	4.96	34 6.04	47 5.70
14	7.8	..	..	..	48.	6.	24.	..	35 48.12	33.73	0.93	IV.	3	28.291	31 47.41	23.63	4.26	35 13.46	30 42 15.30
15	8	..	59.8	17.7	35.2	53.8	11.5	..	45 35.60	33.89	1.14	IV.	2	8.194	52 49.51	25.20	7.34	45 0.57	31 3 22.05
16	9	..	50.3	..	26.2	44.2	..	..	47 26.20	33.92	0.89	IV.	4	42.852	16 31.17	25.49	2.08	46 51.39	30 26 58.74
17	8.9	..	..	32.2	50.	6.	25.9	..	48 50.11	33.94	0.89	IV.	4	42.553	16 50.11	25.71	2.12	48 15.28	27 17.94
18	7	..	51.4	9.3	27.3	45.	3.5	..	51 27.32	33.98	0.91	IV.	4	42.220	17 10.99	26.15	2.17	50 52.43	27 39.31
19	9	..	28.	46.2	4.3	22.4	40.4	..	54 4.27	34.02	1.06	IV.	3	24.582	35 40.01	26.57	4.81	53 29.19	46 11.39
20	8	..	..	14.7	33.1	50.8	..	..	2 55 14.91	34.03	1.15	IV.	2	13.954	46 47.74	26.78	6.47	2 54 39.73	57 20.99
21	8	..	40.3	57.3	15.8	34.	..	..	3 0 57.93	34.10	1.00	IV.	3	36.151	23 34.25	27.74	3.08	3 0 22.63	34 5.07
22	8	..	..	..	34.3	52.7	..	..	2 16.59	34.13	1.16	V.	2	17.681	42 53.84	27.97	5.88	1 41.30	53 27.69
23	9.10	..	54.2	..	31.	..	..	..	6 12.58	34.19	1.16	IV.	2	20.384	40 4.45	28.68	5.45	5 37.23	51 38.58
24	8.9	..	..	..	15.	32.3	51.	..	6 56.95	34.20	1.10	V.	3	27.406	32 43.06	28.80	4.39	6 21.65	43 16.25
25	9.10	..	..	..	..	36.3	..	..	8 0.49	34.21	1.14	VI.	3	23.728	36 33.60	28.99	4.96	7 25.14	47 7.55
26	9	..	59.3	..	35.5	53.	..	..	14 17.32	34.30	1.17	IV.	4	24.479	35 46.54	30.16	4.84	13 41.85	46 21.54
27	9	..	25.	42.5	..	18.	..	..	15 42.57	34.32	1.07	IV.	4	38.521	21 3.00	30.43	2.72	15 7.18	31 36.15
28	8.9	..	..	17.6	..	53.1	..	..	19 35.35	34.38	1.02	IV.	4	47. ..	12 ..	..	..	18 59.95	22 ..
29	9	..	27.	45.3	2.8	21.	38.9	..	25 3.01	34.45	1.27	IV.	2	20.070	40 23.46	32.28	5.51	24 27.29	51 1.25
30	8.9	..	20.	37.	55.	12.6	..	..	31 37.24	34.54	1.06	IV.	4	50.079	8 58.06	33.62	1.02	31 1.64	19 32.70
31	9	..	..	..	..	..	..	43.0	31 49.30	34.54	1.23	VII.	3	29.838	30 10.04	33.66	4.02	31 13.53	40 47.72
32	9	..	2.	..	37.3	..	..	..	36 37.59	34.61	1.28	IV.	3	26.331	33 50.30	34.09	4.56	36 1.70	44 29.64
33	9	..	38.7	56.	14.7	32.	50.	..	40 14.29	34.65	1.23	IV.	3	36.841	22 50.77	35.40	2.97	39 38.41	33 29.20
34	8	..	..	14.7	32.7	..	9.	26.5	41 32.68	34.66	1.20	IV.	3	39.992	19 33.18	35.76	2.51	40 57.02	30 11.45
35	7.8	..	..	..	..	7.	25.	..	41 49.25	34.66	1.16	V.	4	47.848	11 17.59	35.81	1.34	41 13.43	21 54.74
36	7.8	..	..	..	..	4.	22.	..	42 28.29	34.67	1.27	VI.	3	33.151	26 42.51	35.96	3.53	41 52.35	37 22.00
37	9	..	..	..	..	4.	22.	..	42 28.33	34.67	1.24	VI.	3	36.619	23 4.95	35.96	3.01	41 52.42	33 43.92
38	9	..	21.7	39.7	57.	15.7	..	..	45 57.47	34.72	1.24	IV.	3	38.451	21 10.02	36.73	2.73	45 21.51	31 49.48
39	9	..	..	48.2	..	..	42.1	..	51 6.25	34.78	1.24	IV.	4	43.038	15 16.62	37.91	1.92	50 30.23	25 56.45
40	7	..	..	..	17.3	..	53.8	11.5	55 17.65	34.83	1.45	IV.	2	16.461	44 10.65	38.90	6.06	54 41.37	54 55.61
41	9	..	55.	12.	30.	48.	6.	..	59 30.21	34.88	1.37	IV.	3	32.559	27 19.57	39.88	3.62	58 53.96	38 3.07
42	9	..	..	19.2	..	..	13.2	..	3 59 37.29	34.88	1.35	IV.	3	35.028	24 44.56	39.91	3.25	3 59 1.06	35 27.72
43	9	..	..	32.3	..	..	..	44.2	4 6 50.32	34.96	1.49	IV.	2	21.679	38 42.99	41.60	5.26	4 6 13.87	49 29.85
44	9	..	..	12.5	30.7	48.5	6.	..	7 30.49	34.97	1.43	IV.	3	28.787	31 16.04	41.76	4.19	6 54.09	42 1.99
45	8	..	..	..	0.4	18.2	..	..	8 42.52	34.99	1.36	V.	4	40.510	18 57.99	42.04	2.43	8 6.17	29 42.47
46	8	..	..	45.	..	3.	21.	..	9 45.15	35.00	1.34	IV.	4	43.071	16 17.50	42.28	2.04	9 8.81	27 1.82
47	9	..	19.2	36.5	54.6	12.8	..	..	20 54.73	35.12	1.51	IV.	4	30.351	29 38.17	44.93	3.95	20 18.10	40 27.05
48	9	..	..	..	6.	..	..	..	21 48.15	35.13	1.35	V.	4	49.401	9 40.44	45.15	1.12	21 11.67	20 26.71
49	9	..	..	..	43.	..	..	..	4 22 25.16	−35.13	−1.37	V.	4	51.791	−7 10.33	−45.30	−0.77	4 21 48.66	−30 17 56.40

CORRECTIONS.

Date.	Corr. of Clock.	Hourly rate.	m	n	c	Zenith Point.	Mic. Co.
1847.	h. s.	s.	s.	s.	s.	° ' ''	r.

REMARKS.

Jan. 6. Clear; stars tolerably steady.

(86) 1. Transits over T.'s IV and V assumed as 2ˢ and 18ˢ.2 instead of 52ˢ and 8ˢ.2; and minutes as 4, not 3.

(86) 3. Minutes assumed as 14 instead of 13.

(86) 39. Micrometer reading assumed as 44ʳ.038 instead of 43ʳ.038.

INSTRUMENT READINGS.

Date.		CIRCLE.							Barom.	THERMOM.				
		A.	B.	C.	D.	E.	F.	Mean.		At.	Ex.	U.	L.	I.
	1847.	h. m.							in.	°	°	°	°	°
Zone 86	Jan. 6,	2	69 32 31.7	41.3	32.0	42.8	26.3	37.9	35.33	29.870	49.5	46.3	49.9	48.9	48.0
		2 30								29.864	49.5	44.0			
		3 0	32.2	40.9	31.3	43.2	26.4	37.8	35.30	29.856	49.0	43.2	47.5	47.5	
		3 31	..	..	..	..	..	..	..	29.852	48.5	42.7			
		3 59								29.844	..	41.5			
		4 0	31.8	41.4	31.6	43.2	26.5	37.6	35.35		..	..	47.9	47.3	
		4 30								29.838	48.0	41.2			
		5	31.4	41.5	31.8	42.6	26.7	37.1	35.17		..	..	46.8	47.0	48.0
		5 6	..	..	..	..	..	..	..	29.830	47.5	40.0			

Zone 86. January 6. C. $D_0 = -30° 10' 0''$—Continued.

No.	Mag.	I.	II.	III.	IV.	V.	VI.	VII.	T.	a_1	a_2	MIC.		r.	i	d_1	d_2	Mean Declination, 1850.0	Mean Right Ascension, 1850.0
									h. m. s.	s.	s.			r.	′ ″	″	″	° ′ ″	h. m. s.
50	8	..	30.7	48.7	6.3	24.7	42.2	..	4 25 6.53	−35.16	−1.57	IV.	3	24.697	−35 32.73	−45.96	−4.79	−30 46 23.48	4 24 29.80
51	9	..	26.5	..	..	19.2	..	..	27 1.80	35.18	1.42	IV.	4	44.356	14 57.09	46.44	1.86	25 45.39	26 25.20
52	9	..	..	35.	52.7	11.	28.5	..	28 52.83	35.20	1.63	IV.	2	18.161	42 23.91	46.90	5.81	53 16.62	28 16.00
53	4	..	..	1.5	19.5	37.3	55.3	13.6	30 19.52	35.21	1.64	IV.	2	19.061	41 27.35	47.26	5.66	52 20.27	29 42.67
54	8	..	..	..	..	..	27.	45.	31 51.25	35.23	1.59	VI.	3	26.857	33 17.27	47.64	4.47	44 9.38	31 14.43
55	9	..	..	51.	..	8.5	26.5	..	34 8.67	35.25	1.62	IV.	3	25.775	34 25.03	48.24	4.63	30 45 17.90	33 31.80
56	7	..	22.5	40.	58.	..	34.1	..	58.15	35.30	1.74	IV.	2	9.049	51 55.76	48.40	7.21	31 2 51.37	37 21.11
57	7	..	59.5	16.8	34.5	52.7	10.3	..	42 34.79	35.33	1.45	IV.	4	52.211	6 44.42	50.42	0.70	30 17 35.54	41 58.01
58	9	..	19.7	37.	55.3	13.3	31.	..	44 55.28	35.35	1.56	IV.	3	39.204	20 22.73	51.04	2.63	31 16.40	44 18.37
59	9	..	51.7	9.8	27.3	45.6	..	..	47 27.57	35.37	1.75	IV.	2	16.881	43 44.04	51.72	6.00	54 41.76	46 50.45
60	8.9	..	..	38.2	..	14.2	32.1	..	49 56.27	35.39	1.60	IV.	3	38.701	20 54.15	52.37	2.70	31 49.22	49 19.28
61	9	..	41.	59.	16.7	34.4	52.	..	4 56 16.64	35.44	1.61	IV.	4	42.988	16 22.70	54.11	2.06	27 18.87	4 55 39.59
62	8	..	44.	2.	19.8	37.5	55.7	..	5 6 19.82	−35.52	−1.64	IV.	4	45.540	−13 42.76	−56.94	−1.68	−30 24 41.38	5 5 42.66

Zone 87. January 22. C. $D_0 = -30° 48' 0''$.

No.	Mag.	I.	II.	III.	IV.	V.	VI.	VII.	T.	a_1	a_2	MIC.		r.	i	d_1	d_2	Mean Declination, 1850.0	Mean Right Ascension, 1850.0
1	5	..	46.2	4.	22.	40.	58.3	16.7	3 55 22.24	−39.88	−0.65	IV.	4	52.369	−6 34.58	−17.97	−1.06	−30 54 53.61	3 54 41.71
2	9	..	..	18.	36.	53.7	11.7	..	57 35.80	39.90	0.64	IV.	2	9.736	51 12.57	18.43	8.19	31 39 39.19	56 55.26
3	9	..	15.	..	51.2	9.7	..	..	3 59 51.32	39.94	0.64	IV.	2	14.379	46 21.32	18.93	7.38	34 47.63	59 10.74
4	7.8	..	..	..	21.7	39.3	58.3	..	4 0 21.74	39.94	0.64	IV.	3	21.289	39 6.77	19.04	6.19	27 32.00	3 59 41.16
5	9	..	..	..	..	7.	24.7	..	1 48.82	39.94	0.64	IV.	3	26.053	32 2.34	19.37	5.04	20 26.75	4 1 8.24
6	8.9	..	26.2	44.7	2.8	21.3	39.	..	8 2.80	40.03	0.62	V.	2	9.378	51 35.23	20.78	8.25	40 4.26	7 22.15
7	9.10	..	57.5	16.2	..	..	..	..	13 33.92	40.10	0.61	III.	3	20.445	39 59.42	22.09	6.34	28 27.85	12 53.21
8	8	..	..	..	..	13.	31.1	..	13 54.91	40.10	0.61	V.	2	7.813	53 13.16	22.17	8.55	41 43.88	13 14.20
9	9	..	..	41.	59.2	..	..	..	15 59.14	40.13	0.60	IV.	3	15.109	45 34.51	22.67	7.25	34 4.43	15 18.41
10	9	..	20.7	..	56.7	15.	32.2	..	18 56.66	40.17	0.59	IV.	3	36.327	23 23.26	23.38	3.67	11 50.31	18 15.90
11	9	..	..	..	8.	25.9	44.3	..	22 8.06	40.20	0.58	IV.	3	26.655	33 29.94	24.18	5.28	21 59.40	21 27.28
12	9	..	..	56.	14.	31.7	..	..	27 55.88	40.26	0.57	IV.	3	22.236	38 7.29	25.66	6.03	31 26 38.98	27 15.05
13	5	..	47.3	6.	24.	42.	59.7	..	30 23.83	40.29	0.56	IV.	4	54.952	3 52.37	26.30	0.61	30 52 19.28	29 42.08
14	7.8	..	..	24.	42.5	0.7	18.7	..	4 31 42.51	−40.30	−0.56	IV.	4	46.311	−12 54.48	−26.65	−2.02	−31 1 23.15	4 31 1.65

Zone 88. January 27. P. $D_0 = -29° 33' 0''$.

No.	Mag.	I.	II.	III.	IV.	V.	VI.	VII.	T.	a_1	a_2	MIC.		r.	i	d_1	d_2	Mean Declination, 1850.0	Mean Right Ascension, 1850.0
1	7	..	..	14.5	32.5	50.	..	..	4 9 50.19	−39.62	−1.41	IV.	1	7.195	−53 51.02	−8.34	−7.46	−30 27 6.82	4 9 9.16
2	8	46.	..	21.	..	56.	..	..	17 38.76	39.71	1.48	IV.	3	26.970	33 10.11	10.11	4.45	30 6 24.67	16 57.57
3	8	..	..	..	5.	..	..	..	20 5.00	39.74	1.55	IV.	4	46.480	12 43.81	10.68	1.58	29 45 56.07	19 23.71
4	7	..	..	..	36.	..	..	..	21 36.03	39.75	1.43	IV.	2	8.660	52 20.18	11.01	7.21	30 25 38.40	20 54.85
5	8	..	..	..	..	30.	..	..	22 12.09	39.75	1.44	IV.	2	11.030	49 51.25	11.15	6.67	23 9.30	21 30.90
6	7	..	..	..	20.5	38.5	57.	..	23 20.90	39.77	1.50	IV.	3	27.863	32 14.01	11.43	4.32	5 29.76	22 39.63
7	7	..	..	..	15.	33.	..	..	26 15.12	39.80	1.50	IV.	3	27.425	32 41.75	12.09	4.39	5 58.23	25 33.82
8	3	25.3	43.5	1.3	19.	37.	54.5	12.3	28 18.99	39.82	1.51	IV.	3	49.016	31 1.74	12.57	4.15	30 4 18.46	27 37.66
9	8	..	..	..	..	18.	..	..	30 0.27	39.84	1.58	V.	4	52.010	6 56.66	12.98	0.76	29 40 10.40	29 18.85
10	8	..	25.	42.	1.	..	..	..	32 0.49	39.86	1.48	IV.	2	18.595	41 56.60	13.46	5.71	30 15 15.77	31 19.15
11	7	..	..	..	..	45.	2.	..	32 26.79	39.87	1.48	V.	2	21.550	38 51.15	13.56	5.27	30 12 9.98	31 45.44
12	8	..	..	34.	..	10.	..	..	36 52.00	39.91	1.54	III.	3	37.620	22 1.78	14.63	2.87	29 55 19.28	36 10.55
13	7	58.	15.	33.	..	..	..	..	41 50.88	39.96	1.52	III.	3	30.220	29 46.07	15.84	3.97	30 3 5.88	41 9.40
14	6	..	..	..	..	4.5	..	..	4 41 46.77	−39.96	−1.58	V.	4	51.520	−7 27.57	−15.82	−0.83	−29 40 44.22	4 41 5.23

CORRECTIONS.

Date.	Corr. of Clock.	Hourly rate.	m	n	c	Zenith Point.	Mic. Co.
1847.	h.	s.	s.	s.	s.	° ′ ″	r.

REMARKS.

Jan. 22, 4ʰ 13ᵐ, clouds forming. Too cold for good transits.

Jan. 27. Moon very bright; magnitudes of the smaller stars doubtful.

(86) 56. Minute assumed as 37.
(88) 6. Transit over T. IV assumed as 20ˢ.5, not 26ˢ.5.

INSTRUMENT READINGS.

	Date.		CIRCLE.							Barom.	THERMOM.				
			A.	B.	C.	D.	E.	F.	Mean.		At.	Ex.	U.	L.	I.
	1847.	h. m.	° ′ ″						″	in.	°	°	°	°	°
Zone 87	Jan. 22,	3 50	70 9 52.3	73.5	63.6	63.0	63.7	56.8	62.15	30.218	26.0	21.5	26.8	26.9	30.7
		4 13	..	..	..	..	..	..	..	..	..	21.2			
		4 30	..	..	..	..	..	..	..	30.206	25.0	20.0			
Zone 88	Jan. 27,	4 0	68 54 53.0	71.3	62.7	61.0	63.7	56.0	61.28	..	..	..			
		4 9	..	..	..	..	..	..	..	30.338	38.0	28.0			
		4 41	..	..	..	..	..	..	..	30.352	36.2	27.8			
		5 22	..	..	..	..	..	..	..	30.378	36.0	27.6			
		6 25	..	..	..	..	..	..	..	30.412	35.0	26.8			
		8 0	..	..	..	..	..	..	..	30.460	34.0	26.0			

ZONE 88. JANUARY 27. P. $D_0 = -29°\ 33'\ 0''$—Continued.

No.	Mag.	I.	II.	III.	IV.	V.	VI.	VII.	T. (h. m. s.)	a_1 (s.)	a_2 (s.)	MICROMETER		r.	i (′ ″)	d_1 (″)	d_2 (″)	Mean Right Ascension, 1850.0 (h. m. s.)	Mean Declination, 1850.0 (° ′ ″)
15	5				40.	58.	16.		4 42 40.19	−39.97	−1.49	V.	1	16.466	−44 9.21	−16.03	−6.05	4 41 58.73	−30 17 31.29
16	8	39.		15.	32.				45 32.37	40.00	1.53	IV.	3	31.380	28 33.61	16.75	3.79	44 50.84	30 1 54.15
17	8				8.				47 7.99	40.02	1.60	IV.	4	51.160	7 50.27	17.14	0.87	46 26.37	29 41 8.28
18	8	46.		22.					49 39.44	40.04	1.58	III.	4	44.400	14 54.39	17.77	1.86	48 57.82	48 14.02
19	8		23.		56.	5.			50 57.27	40.05	1.60	IV.	4	50.140	8 54.23	18.09	1.05	50 15.62	42 13.37
20	7	54.		29.5	47.	5.			54 47.16	40.09	1.58	V.	4	44.460	14 50.32	19.07	1.86	54 5.49	29 48 11.25
21	7			5.		40.			56 22.45	40.10	1.47	V.	1	7.240	53 48.32	19.46	7.46	55 40.88	30 27 15.24
22	8					4.			57 46.20	40.12	1.55	V.	3	32.265	27 38.14	19.82	3.66	57 4.53	1 1.62
23	8			26.					4 59 50.48	40.13	1.55	IV.	3	31.817	28 5.94	20.36	3.73	4 58 8.80	30 1 30.03
24	8			27.					5 5 44.78	40.19	1.58	III.	3	36.980	22 41.80	21.87	2.96	5 5 3.01	29 56 6.63
25	7				22.	40.			6 4.41	40.19	1.61	V.	4	45.790	13 26.65	21.97	1.65	5 22.61	46 50.27
26	8							20.	6 26.78	40.20	1.61	VII.	4	47.780	11 20.97	22.07	1.35	5 44.97	44 44.39
27	8							45.	7 51.75	40.21	1.61	VII.	4	45.150	14 6.03	22.43	1.75	7 9.93	47 30.21
28	6	21.	39.	56.					10 14.18	40.23	1.59	III.	4	37.190	22 26.55	23.05	2.93	9 32.36	55 52.53
29	8						59.	17.	10 23.71	40.23	1.63	VII.	4	51.330	7 38.60	23.10	0.83	9 41.85	29 41 2.53
30	7				58.				12 58.05	40.25	1.55	IV.	2	23.940	36 21.05	23.77	4.90	12 16.25	30 9 49.72
31	7	40.		16.					15 33.55	40.27	1.57	III.	3	29.330	30 41.91	24.45	4.10	14 51.71	4 10.46
32	6				6.	24.	42.		16 6.20	40.28	1.54	VI.	2	20.580	39 51.77	24.60	5.43	15 24.38	30 13 21.80
33	7	52.	10.	28.	45.				22 45.34	40.33	1.64	IV.	4	50.473	8 33.41	26.37	0.96	22 3.37	29 42 0.74
34	5			46.		21.3			24 3.63	40.34	1.55	IV.	2	19.690	40 47.82	26.72	5.55	23 21.74	30 14 20.09
35	8	34.5	52.	10.					26 27.63	40.35	1.63	III.	4	46.540	12 40.11	27.38	1.53	25 45.65	29 46 9.02
36	8	52.		28.5					28 45.79	40.37	1.59	III.	3	30.705	29 15.52	27.99	3.90	28 3.83	30 2 47.41
37	5.6	54.	12.	30.		5.3			28 47.51	40.37	1.61	V.	3	36.007	23 43.28	28.00	3.10	28 5.53	29 57 14.38
38	8	16.5	34.5	52.					34 9.80	40.41	1.64	III.	4	44.955	14 19.33	29.48	1.77	33 27.75	47 50.58
39	6		12.	30.	47.5			40.7	35 47.56	40.42	1.64	IV.	4	44.772	14 30.75	29.90	1.80	35 5.50	48 2.15
40	7	42.7		18.	35.5				39 35.75	40.45	1.62	IV.	3	34.874	24 54.16	30.98	3.27	38 53.68	58 28.41
41	8.9		55.5					24.0	45 30.86	40.48	1.64	VII.	4	39.525	19 58.90	32.62	2.56	44 48.74	29 53 32.08
42	8		20.		56.				48 55.8	40.51	1.63	IV.	3	32.017	27 53.45	33.58	3.70	48 13.6	30 1 30.73
43	8	59.	17.						50 52.39	40.52	1.63	III.	3	33.850	25 58.15	34.13	3.42	50 10.24	29 59 35.70
44	6	58.				51.	9.		50 51.15	40.52	1.64	V.	3	36.595	23 6.45	34.12	3.01	50 8.99	29 56 43.58
45	8						30.		51 54.46	40.53	1.61	VI.	3	28.167	31 55.19	34.42	4.29	51 12.32	30 5 33.90
46	8	39.		15.					55 32.79	40.54	1.61	III.	3	28.245	31 49.98	35.30	4.27	54 50.64	30 5 29.55
47	8				38.				56 38.02	40.55	1.65	IV.	4	40.340	19 8.98	35.76	2.44	55 55.82	29 52 47.18
48	8							37.	5 57 43.68	40.56	1.64	VII.	3	33.695	26 8.13	36.08	3.45	5 57 1.48	59 47.66
49	4.5	8.3	26.	43.5	1.	18.5	36.5	54.	6 1 1.16	40.58	1.68	IV.	4	48.135	10 59.96	37.00	1.28	6 0 18.90	44 38.24
50	7	10.5	46.	3.	21.	30.			5 3.44	40.60	1.68	IV.	4	45.435	13 49.35	38.15	1.69	4 21.16	29 47 29.19
51	7		46.	4.					7 21.78	40.61	1.57	III.	1	7.910	53 5.69	38.81	7.39	6 39.60	30 26 51.89
52	7			53.5	11.	29.			8 11.18	40.61	1.64	IV.	3	30.780	29 11.00	39.05	3.88	7 28.93	30 2 53.93
53	7	0.	17.	35.	53.				10 52.85	40.63	1.70	IV.	4	48.390	10 44.09	39.82	1.25	10 10.52	29 44 25.16
54	8.9			35.					11 52.75	40.63	1.69	III.	4	43.760	15 34.28	40.11	1.93	11 10.43	49 16.32
55	8			37.	53.				12 53.88	40.64	1.69	IV.	4	45.295	13 58.20	40.41	1.71	12 11.55	47 40.32
56	8	17.	34.	52.					15 9.85	40.65	1.67	III.	3	36.195	23 31.23	41.06	3.07	14 27.53	57 15.36
57	2.3	22.5	40.	58.		33.5	51.	9.	15 15.66	40.65	1.66	V.	3	33.620	26 13.08	41.08	3.46	14 33.35	59 57.62
58	8			57.					17 14.75	40.65	1.70	III.	4	45.690	13 33.29	41.66	1.65	16 32.40	47 16.60
59	8	32.	50.						18 25.33	40.66	1.70	II.	4	45.890	13 20.62	42.00	1.62	17 42.97	47 4.24
60	8			22.					18 22.03	40.66	1.68	IV.	3	36.977	22 42.30	41.99	2.95	17 39.69	56 27.24
61	7			0.	18.				20 35.63	40.67	1.73	III.	4	55.387	3 25.42	42.63	0.22	19 53.23	37 8.27
62	8		14.	32.					22 49.66	40.68	1.67	III.	3	35.430	24 19.28	43.28	3.19	22 7.31	58 5.75
63	8				51.				6 25 33.22	−40.69	−1.69	V.	3	37.900	−21 44.47	−44.05	−2.81	6 24 50.84	−29 55 31.33

CORRECTIONS.

Date.	Corr. of Clock.	Hourly rate.	m	n	c	Zenith Point.	Mic. Co.
1847.	h.	s.	s.	s.	s.	° ′ ″	r.
	s.	s.	s.	s.	s.		

INSTRUMENT READINGS.

Date.	CIRCLE.							Barom.	THERMOM.				
	A.	B.	C.	D.	E.	F.	Mean.		At.	Ex.	U.	L.	I.
1847. h. m.	° ′ ″						″	In.	°	°	°	°	°

REMARKS.

(88) 23. Transit over T. VI assumed as recorded over T. IV; and minutes as 58, not 59.

(88) 44. T. II assumed to have been recorded as T. I. If T.'s IV and V were recorded as T.'s V and VI, T=35^s.43.

(88) 46. Transit over T. I rejected.

(88) 50. T.'s III–VI are assumed to have been recorded as T.'s II–V.

Zone 88. January 27. P. $D_e = -29°\ 33'\ 0''$—Continued.

Seconds of Transit.

No.	Mag.	I.	II.	III.	IV.	V.	VI.	VII.
64	7	16.	33.	51.				
65	8			43.	1.			
66	6				33.	50.	8.5	
67	9				25.			
68	5.6	47.	5.	23.	40.5			
69	8					36.		
70	7	39.	56.5	14.	32.			
71	6						20.	
72	8				17.			
73	7	12.5	30.	48.				
74	8	55.						
75	8				48.			
76	8					27.		3.
77	8		59.5	17.	35.			
78	8				15.	32.		
79	7			52.	10.5			
80	8			19.				
81	7		16.					
82	7		1.	55.				
83	9				33.			
84	9							31.
85	7				11.			
86	8							59.
87	8			50.	7.			1.
88	7	29.	47.	5.				
89	7		48.5	6.				
90	7			52.5	10.			4.
91	7		53.	10.5	28.5			
92	7	18.	36.	54.	12.			
93	6			48.5	6.	24.5		
94	5.6			6.	24.	41.3		
95	8	39.	57.	15.				
96	8			23.				15.3
97	8				19.5			13.
98	8			18.				12.
99	9				8.5			
100	8	26.	44.	1.5				

No.	T. (h m s)	m_1	a_2	Mic.	n	r	i (' ")	d_1	d_2	Mean Right Ascension, 1850.0 (h m s)	Mean Declination, 1850.0 (° ' ")
64	6 28 8.77	−40.70	−1.74	III.	4	53.720	− 5 9.75	−44.81	−0.45	6 27 26.33	−29 38 55.01
65	29 0.93	40.70	1.64	IV.	2	20.925	39 30.24	45.06	5.39	28 18.59	30 13 20.69
66	29 50.51	40.70	1.68	IV.	3	35.060	24 42.62	45.21	3.24	29 8.13	29 58 31.07
67	32 25.03	40.71	1.70	IV.	3	38.090	21 32.55	46.05	2.78	31 42.62	29 55 21.38
68	6 34 40.59	40.72	1.65	IV.	2	19.925	45 46.63	46.70	6.24	6 33 58.22	30 19 39.57
69	7 16 18.16	40.79	1.71	V.	3	21.987	38 22.91	58.75	5.23	7 15 35.66	12 26.89
70	18 32.07	40.79	1.72	IV.	3	24.625	35 37.32	59.39	4.83	17 49.56	30 9 41.54
71	18 44.52	40.79	1.76	VI.	4	37.980	21 36.19	59.45	2.79	18 1.97	29 55 38.43
72	20 59.21	40.79	1.75	V.	3	35.090	24 40.86	60.11	3.23	20 16.67	29 58 44.20
73	24 5.81	40.79	1.69	III.	2	14.650	46 4.07	61.00	6.35	23 23.33	30 20 11.42
74	25 48.39	40.79	1.71	I.	2	20.985	39 25.85	61.49	5.38	25 5.89	13 32.72
75	25 48.05	40.79	1.72	IV.	2	22.250	38 7.20	61.49	5.21	25 5.54	12 13.99
76	26 9.42	40.79	1.74	V.	3	28.855	31 11.90	61.59	4.18	25 26.89	5 17.67
77	28 34.96	40.79	1.75	IV.	3	30.480	29 30.01	62.28	3.93	27 52.42	30 3 36.22
78	30 32.36	40.79	1.81	IV.	4	49.460	9 36.93	62.84	1.06	29 49.76	29 43 40.83
79	32 10.17	40.79	1.68	IV.	1	7.765	53 15.04	63.31	7.44	31 27.70	30 27 25.79
80	33 36.79	40.79	1.74	III.	3	26.920	33 12.93	63.72	4.48	32 54.26	30 7 21.13
81	34 51.53	40.78	1.80	II.	4	43.920	15 24.78	64.06	1.89	34 8.95	29 49 30.13
82	35 12.73	40.78	1.82	III.	4	49.110	9 58.89	64.28	1.11	34 30.13	44 4.28
83	35 15.26	40.78	1.82	V.	4	50.905	8 5.88	64.18	0.84	34 32.66	42 10.90
84	35 37.83	40.78	1.83	VII.	4	53.220	5 40.03	64.29	0.49	34 55.22	33 44.81
85	36 53.23	40.78	1.80	V.	4	43.330	16 1.19	64.66	1.97	36 10.68	50 7.82
86	36 5.75	40.78	1.80	VII.	4	45.165	14 5.15	64.43	1.70	35 23.17	48 11.28
87	39 7.50	40.78	1.70	IV.	4	40.980	18 28.64	65.30	2.33	38 24.93	29 52 36.27
88	42 22.59	40.77	1.74	III.	3	23.690	36 35.67	66.21	4.98	41 40.05	30 10 16.86
89	43 24.01	40.77	1.71	III.	2	12.000	48 50.30	66.51	6.70	42 41.52	23 3.69
90	44 10.31	40.77	1.75	IV.	3	23.490	36 48.60	66.72	5.02	43 27.70	30 11 0.34
91	46 28.45	40.77	1.79	IV.	3	37.515	22 8.68	67.36	2.85	45 45.89	29 56 18.89
92	50 11.64	40.76	1.80	IV.	3	36.480	23 13.60	68.42	3.02	49 29.08	57 25.04
93	51 6.33	40.76	1.81	IV.	4	40.520	18 57.62	68.67	2.39	50 23.76	53 8.68
94	52 23.78	40.76	1.80	IV.	4	37.803	21 47.86	69.03	2.80	51 41.22	29 55 59.69
95	54 32.51	40.75	1.79	IV.	3	33.765	26 3.73	69.63	3.44	53 49.97	30 0 16.80
96	54 40.30	40.75	1.80	VI.	3	35.910	23 49.30	69.67	3.10	53 57.75	29 58 2.07
97	54 19.57	40.75	1.76	IV.	2	22.235	38 8.23	69.57	5.21	53 37.06	30 12 23.01
98	56 18.33	40.74	1.76	VII.	2	23.860	36 25.44	70.12	4.96	55 35.83	10 40.52
99	7 58 8.54	40.74	1.74	IV.	1	16.140	44 29.49	70.64	6.16	57 26.06	30 18 46.29
100	8 0 19.33	−40.74	−1.81	III.	3	37.903	−21 43.90	−71.25	−2.79	7 59 36.78	−29 55 57.94

Zone 89. February 1. C. $D_e = -30°\ 48'\ 0''$.

No.	Mag.	I.	II.	III.	IV.	V.	VI.	VII.
1	8.9		46.5	4.6	22.		58.6	
2	7.8		13.3	31.9	49.4	8.1	25.8	
3	9.10		43.2	6.				
4	9					40.7	59.	
5	9				44.	1.8	19.8	
6	8		39.5		15.7	33.8	51.4	
7	9				20.5	1.	56.2	
8	7.8			4.7	22.	40.9		

No.	T. (h m s)	m_1	a_2	Mic.	n	r	i (' ")	d_1	d_2	Mean Right Ascension, 1850.0 (h m s)	Mean Declination, 1850.0 (° ' ")
1	3 30 22.45	−40.08	−0.62	IV.	3	33.591	−26 14.77	−4.79	−3.92	3 29 41.75	−31 14 23.48
2	37 49.71	40.18	0.74	IV.	2	18.882	41 38.46	6.27	6.32	37 8.79	29 51.05
3	40 24.14	40.22	0.68	III.	3	25.560	34 38.40	6.79	5.23	39 43.24	22 50.42
4	40 22.81	40.22	0.69	V.	3	24.243	36 1.46	6.78	5.46	39 41.90	24 13.70
5	41 25.84	40.23	0.65	V.	3	28.957	31 5.56	7.01	4.68	40 44.96	19 17.[illegible]
6	45 15.62	40.28	0.59	IV.	3	39.048	20 32.39	7.81	3.06	44 34.75	8 43.26
7	46 2.31	40.29	0.66	V.	3	28.671	31 23.51	7.98	4.73	45 21.36	31 19 36.22
8	3 55 22.52	−40.41	−0.48	IV.	4	52.208	− 6 44.62	−8.99	−0.96	3 54 41.63	−30 54 54.57

CORRECTIONS.

Date.	Corr. of Clock.	Hourly rate.	m	n	c	Zenith Point.	Mic. Co.
1847.	h.	s.	s.	s.	s.	° ' "	r.

REMARKS.

(88) 66. Transits over T.'s III, IV, and V assumed as recorded over T.'s IV, V, and VI.

(88) 68. Micrometer reading assumed as 14r.925, not 19r.925.

(88) 82. Transit over T. II rejected.

Feb. 1, Moon up at 4h 20m.

(89) 3. Transit over T. II assumed to have been at 48s.2.

INSTRUMENT READINGS.

Date.	A.	B.	C.	D.	E.	F.	Mean.	Barom. in.	At.	Ex.	U.	L.	I.
Zone 89, 1847, Feb. 1, 3 30	70 9 52.9	70.1	61.2	58.9	62.9	56.5	60.42	30.036	43.5	37.9	43.5	46.9	41.7
3 55										36.9			
4 10								30.040	42.8	35.6			
4 30	52.4	70.7	61.3	58.9	63.2	55.9	60.40			34.6	43.7	39.7	
4 49										34.1			
5 11										32.9			
5 30	51.1	70.8	60.6	58.9	63.4	54.9	59.95	30.060	41.0	32.8	39.7	38.0	41.7

ZONE 89. FEBRUARY 1. C. $D_o = -30°\,48'\,0''$—Continued.

No.	Mag.	I.	II.	III.	IV.	V.	VI.	VII.	T.	a_1	a_2	Mic.	n	r	i	d_1	d_2	Mean Right Ascension, 1850.0.	Mean Declination, 1850.0.
9	9.10	..	..	26.3	44.	..	20.	..	3 56 44.12	−40.43	−0.47	IV.	4	53.620	− 5 16.02	−10.27	−0.73	3 56 3.22	−30 53 27.02
10	9	..	..	..	..	..	..	30.7	3 57 36.47	40.43	0.84	VII.	2	9.568	51 22.55	10.47	7.86	56 55.20	31 39 40.88
11	7.8	..	46.7	4.5	22.8	40.8	58.8	..	4 0 22.73	40.47	0.74	IV.	3	21.136	39 16.25	11.08	5.95	3 59 41.52	27 33.28
12	9	..	..	..	..	49.	7.2	..	1 31.08	40.49	0.68	V.	3	28.842	31 12.72	11.34	4.69	4 0 49.91	19 28.75
13	9.10	..	27.	45.5	3.5	..	39.8	..	8 3.49	40.57	0.86	IV.	2	9.252	51 43.08	12.63	7.93	7 22.06	31 40 3.84
14	9	..	..	..	27.	..	3.	..	10 27.05	40.60	0.50	IV.	4	51.248	7 44.80	13.39	1.12	9 45.95	30 55 59.31
15	9.10	..	21.	39.	..	15.	..	..	17 57.00	40.69	0.63	IV.	3	36.201	23 31.11	15.16	3.51	17 15.68	31 11 49.78
16	9	..	..	..	26.2	..	..	..	21 26.24	40.72	0.66	IV.	3	34.167	25 38.70	15.94	3.84	20 44.86	13 58.48
17	9	..	..	..	..	25.	40.3	..	22 5.62	40.73	0.71	V.	3	27.519	32 35.91	16.04	4.91	21 24.18	20 56.86
18	9	..	..	..	..	..	..	3.2	22 9.13	40.73	0.72	VII.	3	26.582	33 34.46	16.06	5.05	21 27.68	31 21 55.57
19	8	..	22.4	39.2	..	16.2	34.	..	28 57.99	40.82	0.49	IV.	4	53.926	4 56.70	17.81	0.68	28 16.68	30 53 15.19
20	4	..	..	6.7	24.5	42.4	0.7	..	30 24.61	40.83	0.49	IV.	4	54.784	4 2.91	18.16	0.55	29 43.29	30 52 21.62
21	7.8	..	..	25.8	43.2	1.	15.8	..	31 43.33	40.84	0.57	IV.	4	46.171	13 3.12	18.48	1.91	31 1.90	31 1 23.51
22	9.10	..	44.	..	..	..	..	..	35 20.19	40.88	0.86	II.	2	11.192	49 41.01	19.37	7.60	34 38.45	38 7.98
23	7	..	27.	45.	3.2	21.	39.5	..	38 3.16	40.91	0.58	IV.	4	44.834	14 26.85	20.04	2.12	37 21.67	2 49.01
24	9	..	33.5	51.7	9.7	27.7	46.	..	44 9.72	40.97	0.90	IV.	2	8.100	52 55.34	21.57	8.12	43 27.85	41 25.93
25	8	..	..	..	..	..	28.	46.5	44 52.27	40.98	0.68	VI.	4	34.261	25 29.66	21.75	3.81	44 10.61	31 13 55.22
26	8	..	57.	..	32.8	..	8.2	..	47 32.71	41.01	0.52	IV.	4	52.591	6 20.55	22.41	0.88	46 51.18	30 54 43.64
27	8.9	..	5.5	23.	41.1	59.7	17.8	..	49 41.40	41.03	0.88	IV.	2	9.422	51 32.46	22.96	7.90	48 59.49	31 40 3.32
28	9	..	35.	53.2	..	29.7	47.	..	53 11.24	41.07	0.66	IV.	3	36.592	23 6.51	23.86	3.44	52 29.51	11 33.81
29	8	..	44.5	2.	20.3	..	..	..	56 20.35	41.09	0.87	IV.	2	12.406	48 25.17	24.66	7.40	55 38.39	36 57.23
30	7.8	..	..	48.7	7.	25.1	43.	..	4 57 6.92	41.10	0.84	IV.	2	15.266	45 25.65	24.86	6.94	4 56 24.98	33 57.45
31	9.10	..	..	..	17.	..	..	..	5 2 17.05	41.15	0.82	IV.	2	18.489	42 3.31	26.19	6.38	5 1 35.08	30 35.88
32	8.9	..	33.7	51.3	..	27.8	46.	..	5 9.70	41.18	0.83	IV.	2	16.849	43 46.05	26.93	6.67	4 27.69	32 19.65
33	9.10	..	4.5	..	..	..	..	34.5	6 40.49	41.20	0.81	IV.	2	19.786	40 41.72	27.32	6.17	5 58.46	28 15.21
34	9	..	37.4	..	13.2	31.3	..	..	11 13.31	41.24	0.66	IV.	4	40.853	18 36.55	28.49	2.75	10 31.41	7 7.79
35	6	..	..	..	..	20.	..	55.	12 1.41	41.24	0.79	V.	3	21.992	38 22.59	28.70	5.82	11 19.38	26 57.11
36	9.10	..	..	10.	..	46.3	..	22.2	17 28.08	41.29	0.87	IV.	2	13.467	47 18.49	30.12	7.23	16 45.92	35 55.84
37	9	..	..	..	7.	..	43.6	..	20 7.26	41.31	0.89	IV.	2	12.154	48 40.86	30.80	7.46	19 25.06	37 19.12
38	8	..	..	53.	11.	29.	47.2	..	22 11.00	41.33	0.93	IV.	2	7.811	53 13.34	31.33	8.19	21 28.74	41 52.86
39	8.9	..	49.	6.8	25.	43.	1.4	..	24 25.06	41.35	0.63	IV.	4	43.268	16 5.27	31.90	2.36	23 43.08	31 4 30.53
40	9	..	0.8	..	35.7	54.	..	..	26 36.18	41.36	0.59	IV.	4	48.329	10 47.93	32.46	1.55	25 54.23	30 59 21.94
41	9	..	..	5.2	22.7	42.	..	..	28 23.28	41.40	0.53	IV.	4	54.941	3 53.06	32.91	0.50	27 41.35	30 52 26.47
42	8	..	56.2	14.7	32.7	50.7	8.6	..	32 32.60	41.41	0.68	IV.	3	38.978	20 36.78	33.97	3.04	31 50.51	31 9 13.79
43	8.9	..	..	51.1	9.	27.1	45.	..	35 9.06	41.43	0.76	IV.	3	28.972	31 4.49	34.64	4.66	34 26.87	19 43.79
44	9	..	20.	..	..	13.	32.	..	5 35 55.66	−41.44	−0.80	IV.	3	23.981	−36 17.66	−34.84	−5.48	5 35 13.42	−31 24 57.98

ZONE 90. FEBRUARY 5. P. $D_o = -28°\,56'\,30''$.

No.	Mag.	I.	II.	III.	IV.	V.	VI.	VII.	T.	a_1	a_2	Mic.	n	r	i	d_1	d_2	Mean Right Ascension, 1850.0.	Mean Declination, 1850.0.
1	7	..	..	14.	32.	49.5	..	..	7 29 31.82	−41.03	−0.82	IV.	4	50.570	− 6 27.27	0.12	−1.10	7 28 49.97	−29 4 56.49
2	9	..	10.	..	46.	..	..	..	33 45.76	41.03	0.98	IV.	1	9.650	51 16.84	1.31	6.93	33 3.75	47 55.08
3	8	..	..	51.	..	..	..	..	34 51.03	41.03	0.99	IV.	1	8.110	52 53.52	1.61	7.16	34 9.01	49 32.29
4	7	..	..	..	30.	..	..	..	35 12.22	41.03	0.97	V.	2	13.230	47 33.31	1.71	6.42	34 30.22	44 11.44
5	9	..	..	..	..	..	..	30.5	35 37.37	41.03	0.95	VII.	2	17.320	43 16.05	1.83	5.83	34 55.39	39 53.71
6	7	..	..	..	..	28.	46.	..	36 52.68	41.03	0.99	VI.	1	7.476	53 33.43	2.19	7.26	36 10.66	50 12.58
7	8	..	..	..	..	..	..	46.	37 53.07	41.03	0.85	VII.	4	43.265	16 4.33	2.47	2.13	37 11.19	12 38.93
8	8	..	59.	..	34.	..	..	..	41 34.22	41.03	0.93	IV.	3	21.985	38 22.91	3.45	5.14	40 52.26	35 1.50
9	8	..	..	..	..	..	..	4.	7 42 11.03	−41.03	−0.67	VII.	3	36.790	−22 53.91	3.66	−3.04	7 41 29.13	−29 19 30.61

CORRECTIONS.

Date.	Corr. of Clock.	Hourly rate.	u	n	c	Zenith Point.	Mic. Co.
1847.	h. s.	s.	s.	s.	s.	° ′ ″	$r.$

INSTRUMENT READINGS.

Date.		CIRCLE.							Barom.	THERMOM.					REMARKS.
		A.	B.	C.	D.	E.	F.	Mean.		At.	Ex.	U.	L.	I.	
Zone 90	1847 Feb. 5 h. m. 7 30	68 17 29.0	48.0	38.7	41.0	35.4	31.7	[a]37.30	In. 29.880	34.0	27.0	36.0	35.0	41.0	[a] Corr. for runs, 0″.48.
	8 14	..	..	..	..	..	..	..	29.888	33.3	26.7				
	9 1	..	..	..	..	..	..	..	29.888	33.0	26.8				
	9 44	..	..	..	..	..	..	..	29.878	33.0	26.0				
	10 46	27.4	48.7	39.7	39.7	36.6	30.5	[b]37.10	29.884	32.0	26.0	33.3			[b] Corr. for runs, 0″.48.
	11 42	..	..	..	..	..	..	..	29.884	31.8	25.0				

Zone 90. February 5. P. $D_0 = -28°\ 56'\ 30''.00$—Continued.

No.	Mag.	I.	II.	III.	IV.	V.	VI.	VII.	T. (h. m. s.)	a_1 (s.)	a_4 (s.)	Micrometer	r.	i (' '')	d_1 ('')	d_2 ('')	Mean Right Ascension, 1850.0 (h. m. s.)	Mean Declination, 1850.0 (° ' '')
10	8	33.	8.	26.					7 46 25.85	−41.02	−0.86	III 4	39.187	−20 21.26	−4.91	−2.70	7 45 43.97	−29 16 58.89
11	8	17.	35.	52.5					48 10.16	41.02	0.00	III 3	30.470	29 30.38	5.33	3.93	47 28.24	26 9.64
12	7.8	53.		28.	43.5				54 44.98	41.02	0.83	IV 4	49.383	9 41.82	7.10	1.26	54 3.13	6 20.18
13	8				51.				55 50.99	41.02	0.84	IV 4	46.983	12 12.14	7.42	1.60	55 9.13	29 8 51.16
14	8		45.	7.					58 19.48	41.01	0.81	III 4	55.530	3 16.38	8.10	0.39	57 37.66	28 59 54.87
15	7			1.	18.				59 18.36	41.01	0.93	IV 4	24.340	35 55.32	8.36	4.86	58 36.42	29 32 38.48
16	8					58.			7 59 40.27	41.01	0.93	V 3	25.567	34 38.39	8.46	4.64	58 58.33	31 21.49
17	8					37.			8 0 19.26	41.01	0.94	V 3	23.050	37 16.27	8.64	5.00	7 59 37.31	33 59.91
18	7	52.		27.5	45.				3 45.06	41.01	0.91	IV 3	30.595	29 22.73	9.56	3.92	8 3 3.14	26 6.21
19	8				43.				5 0.69	41.00	0.95	III 2	21.310	39 6.21	9.90	5.26	4 18.74	35 51.37
20	8				23.				5 23.04	41.00	0.97	IV 2	15.055	45 38.71	10.00	6.17	4 41.07	42 24.88
21	8			16.					6 33.70	41.00	0.98	III 1	11.625	49 12.62	10.32	6.66	5 51.72	45 59.60
22	6			6.	24.	[4]			7 23.87	41.00	0.91	IV 3	28.970	31 4.62	10.55	4.13	6 41.96	27 49.30
23	8		40.5		15.				12 15.41	40.99	0.87	IV 4	42.340	17 3.54	11.85	2.24	11 33.55	13 47.63
24	6.7					52.	9.5		13 34.21	40.98	0.94	IV 3	24.643	35 36.32	12.20	4.75	11 52.29	32 23.27
25	7		17.	35.	52.				14 52.31	40.98	0.83	IV 4	51.494	7 30.02	12.54	0.96	14 10.50	4 13.52
26	7		31.5	48.5	7.				17 6.65	40.98	0.85	IV 4	43.250	16 6.39	13.13	2.11	16 24.80	12 51.63
27	7.8			18.	36.				18 35.86	40.97	0.91	IV 3	33.970	25 50.03	13.53	3.44	17 53.98	22 37.90
28	8.9							37.	18 44.01	40.97	0.91	VII 3	34.418	25 22.95	13.57	3.39	18 2.13	22 9.91
29	8				21.	39.			20 21.17	40.97	0.92	IV 3	30.900	29 3.47	13.99	3.87	19 39.28	25 51.33
30	7.8		50.	7.5	25.				23 25.19	40.96	0.92	IV 3	29.543	30 28.80	14.79	4.05	22 43.31	27 17.64
31	8.9				32.				25 32.04	40.95	0.94	IV 3	24.987	35 14.53	15.34	4.73	24 50.15	32 4.60
32	9				31.				27 36.05	40.95	0.92	IV 3	28.970	31 4.62	15.85	4.15	26 54.18	27 54.62
33	8						23.		27 47.68	40.95	0.92	VI 3	29.960	30 2.57	15.93	4.01	27 5.81	26 52.51
34	7		24.	41.	59.				29 58.96	40.94	0.82	IV 4	55.117	3 12.15	16.49	0.44	29 17.20	0 29.08
35	8					14.			30 56.27	40.94	0.95	V 3	25.737	34 27.59	16.74	4.63	30 14.38	31 18.96
36	8		17.	35.					32 52.51	40.92	0.93	III 3	29.225	30 48.50	17.22	4.10	32 10.66	27 39.82
37	3.4		35.5	53.	11.	28.5			34 10.82	40.92	0.83	IV 4	53.920	4 57.08	17.56	0.59	33 29.07	29 1 45.23
38	7.8				31.				37 30.94	40.91	0.83	IV 4	56.325	2 26.55	18.42	0.27	36 49.20	28 59 15.24
39	8					49.			38 31.23	40.91	0.99	V 2	15.575	45 6.07	18.68	6.10	37 49.33	29 42 0.85
40	7.8	8.	26.	44.					41 1.26	40.90	0.88	III 4	43.470	15 52.72	19.31	2.08	40 19.48	12 44.11
41	7	10.	28.	46.		20.			41 3.03	40.90	0.87	IV 4	45.240	14 1.32	19.32	1.82	40 21.26	10 52.46
42	9		56.						43 31.44	40.89	0.98	II 2	17.655	42 55.20	19.94	5.78	42 49.57	39 51.01
43	8		24.	42.					46 59.49	40.87	0.90	III 3	37.630	22 1.16	20.81	2.92	46 17.72	18 54.89
44	9		52.						8 51 27.31	40.85	0.90	IV 4	40.220	19 16.43	21.92	3.54	8 50 45.56	16 10.89
45	7	55.5	13.5	32.	49.5				9 1 49.14	40.80	0.95	IV 3	28.090	31 59.90	24.45	4.27	9 1 7.39	28 58.62
46	6.7	0.5	17.7	35.5	53.3				3 53.20	40.79	0.89	IV 4	43.635	15 42.18	24.94	2.04	3 11.52	12 39.16
47	3.4						52.3	10.	4 16.85	40.79	1.01	VI 2	12.	48	25.03	6.63	3 35.05	45
48	7.8	10.			45.5				9 3.10	40.76	0.96	III 3	25.060	35 9.70	26.17	4.73	8 21.38	32 10.60
49	9.8				22.				9 22.04	40.76	1.01	IV 2	13.020	−47 16.43	26.25	6.49	8 40.27	44 49.17
50	9	56.		32.					13 49.23	40.73	0.89	III 4	44.907	14 22.34	27.29	1.85	13 7.61	11 21.48
51	9	31.	48.7	6.3	24.	41.3			20 23.91	40.69	0.94	IV 3	33.615	26 13.27	28.82	3.50	19 42.28	23 15.59
52	8	29.	40.5	4.					24 21.83	40.66	0.96	III 3	27.835	32 15.52	29.71	4.31	23 40.21	29 19.54
53	7.8	30.	48.	5.5					31 23.19	40.61	0.98	III 3	25.010	35 12.64	31.29	4.73	30 41.60	32 18.86
54	7.8						12.		31 36.81	40.61	0.89	VII 4	48.300	10 42.96	31.34	1.36	30 55.31	7 45.66
55	8						2.		33 44.35	40.59	0.90	V 4	44.660	14 37.64	31.80	1.89	33 2.86	11 41.33
56	7	7.	25.	42.	0.3				36 0.13	40.58	1.00	IV 2	20.287	40 10.53	32.29	5.43	35 18.55	37 18.25
57	7	34.5	52.5	10.	28.				39 27.77	40.55	0.97	IV 3	26.460	33 42.29	33.05	4.52	38 46.25	30 49.86
58	7.8	44.5	2.5	20.5					9 42 37.89	−40.53	−1.00	III 2	19.993	−40 28.73	−33.70	−5.47	9 41 56.36	−29 37 37.90

CORRECTIONS.

Date.	Corr. of Clock.	Hourly rate.	m	n	c	Zenith Point.	Mic. Co.
1847.	h.	s.	s.	s.	s.	° ' ''	r.
	s.	s.	s.	s.	s.		

INSTRUMENT READINGS.

Date	CIRCLE							Barom.	THERMOM.				
	A.	B.	C.	D.	E.	F.	Mean.		At.	Ex.	U.	L.	I.
1847. h. m.	° ' ''						''	in.	°	°	°	°	°

REMARKS.

(90) 10. Transits over T.'s III and IV assumed as recorded over T.'s II and III.

(90) 24. Minutes assumed as 12 instead of 13.

(90) 32. Time of transit assumed as 36ˢ instead of 31ˢ, to agree with Mer. Circle, 1847, March 18, and Arg. Z., 275, 44.

Zone 90. February 5. P. $D_o = -28° 56' 30'$.—Continued.

No.	Mag.	I.	II.	III.	IV.	V.	VI.	VII.	T.	a_1	a_4	MIC.		r.	i	d_1	d_4	Mean Right Ascension, 1850.0	Mean Declination, 1850.0
									h. m. s.	s.	s.				' "	"	"	h. m. s.	° ' "
59	8			32.		7.			9 44 7.16	−40.52	−0.90	IV.	4	44.175	−15 8.31	−34.00	−1.95	9 43 25.74	−29 12 14.26
60	8.9						8.		10 46 50.35	39.92	0.93	V.	4	43.940	20 36.21	45.00	2.64	10 46 9.50	17 43.85
61	9.9	45.			20.				56 37.79	39.82	0.97	III.	3	34.695	25 5.20	46.42	3.33	55 57.00	22 24.95
62	8.7	48.	6.	24.					10 58 41.50	39.79	1.04	III.	2	20.190	40 16.44	46.71	5.46	58 0.73	37 38.61
63	7	28.	45.5	3.	21.				11 0 20.96	39.77	1.07	IV.	2	13.620	47 8.84	46.94	6.44	10 59 40.12	44 32.22
64	7				10.	27.5			1 27.61	39.76	0.98	IV.	3	35.600	24 8.74	47.09	3.19	11 0 46.87	21 29.02
65	7					59.5	17.		1 41.83	39.76	0.93	V.	4	46.865	12 19.23	47.12	1.54	1 1.14	9 37.89
66	8							54.	2 1.04	39.75	0.97	VII.	3	38.060	21 34.37	47.17	2.82	1 20.32	18 54.36
67	9.8				30.				12 47.68	39.63	1.02	III.	3	27.370	32 44.88	48.57	4.38	12 7.03	30 7.83
68	8						36.		13 18.25	39.62	1.05	V.	2	20.260	40 12.11	48.64	5.45	12 37.58	37 36.20
69	9				50.				21 7.69	39.53	1.06	III.	2	17.435	43 9.40	49.57	5.87	20 27.10	40 34.84
70	7							57.5	28 22.28	39.44	0.95	VI.	4	44.510	14 46.80	50.39	1.67	27 41.89	12 9.06
71	7.8				56.	13.			33 13.37	39.37	1.06	IV.	2	19.035	41 28.92	50.90	5.64	32 32.94	38 55.46
72	7						49.		37 48.96	39.31	0.93	IV.	4	52.870	6 2.92	51.37	0.66	37 8.72	3 24.95
73	8.9	16.5	34.5	52.					40 9.74	39.28	1.07	III.	2	17.963	42 36.07	51.61	5.79	39 29.39	40 3.47
74	6					26.	44.		40 26.17	39.28	1.02	IV.	3	30.785	29 10.68	51.64	3.89	39 45.47	26 36.21
75	8				4.				11 42 21.70	−39.26	−1.11	III.	1	8.430	−52 33.29	−51.83	−7.24	11 41 41.31	−29 50 2.36

Zone 91. February 6. C. $D_o = -28° 55' 30''$.

No.	Mag.	I.	II.	III.	IV.	V.	VI.	VII.	T.	a_1	a_4	MIC.		r.	i	d_1	d_4	Mean Right Ascension, 1850.0	Mean Declination, 1850.0
1	9				23.3	40.7		16.2	4 1 40.88	−39.49	−1.07	IV.	4	42.003	−17 24.48	−0.45	−2.17	4 1 0.32	−29 12 57.10
2	9			59.2	17.2	35.	52.7		3 34.86	39.50	1.07	IV.	3	36.892	22 47.58	0.92	2.65	2 54.29	18 21.35
3	9					12.	29.3	47.2	3 54.22	39.51	1.07	V.	4	43.758	15 34.14	1.00	1.93	3 13.64	11 7.07
4	9			33.7		9.		2.	7 9.02	39.55	1.06	IV.	3	26.495	33 40.04	1.79	4.28	6 28.41	29 16.11
5	9			17.1	34.7	52.	10.2	27.3	9 52.27	39.58	1.06	IV.	3	37.337	22 19.91	2.45	2.79	9 11.63	17 55.15
6	9				17.7	35.5	53.	11.	11 35.49	39.60	1.06	IV.	3	39.230	20 21.09	2.86	2.55	10 54.83	15 56.50
7	9				55.7	12.	30.	6.	14 12.70	39.64	1.05	IV.	4	45.681	13 33.79	3.50	1.68	13 32.01	9 8.97
8	9.10						47.		16 11.74	39.66	1.05	VI.	3	38.586	21 1.56	3.98	2.62	15 31.03	16 38.16
9	9			38.5		13.7		49.1	19 13.79	39.69	1.05	IV.	3	22.266	38 5.47	4.71	4.85	18 33.05	33 45.03
10	9			44.3	2.7		37.5	55.1	21 19.91	39.71	1.05	IV.	4	37.831	21 46.10	5.22	2.71	20 39.15	17 24.03
11	8.9					27.	44.7	2.	22 9.17	39.72	1.05	IV.	3	23.613	36 40.82	5.43	4.69	21 28.40	32 20.94
12	8.9			51.	9.	26.2		19.7	24 26.48	39.75	1.04	IV.	3	33.958	25 51.62	5.96	3.25	23 45.69	21 30.83
13	8.9					15.			24 39.76	39.75	1.04	VI.	4	42.441	16 56.57	6.02	2.09	23 58.97	12 34.68
14	8.9					20.		55.7	26 2.56	39.77	1.04	V.	4	42.629	16 45.03	6.36	2.06	25 21.75	12 23.45
15	8.9						22.5	40.7	26 47.55	39.78	1.04	VI.	4	47.367	11 47.62	6.54	1.45	26 6.73	7 25.61
16	9.10					3.5		39.	31 45.97	39.84	1.03	V.	4	44.708	14 34.56	7.73	1.79	31 5.10	10 14.08
17	9.10			9.2		43.7	19.7	47.	35 44.14	39.88	1.03	IV.	2	15.824	44 50.38	8.68	5.77	35 3.23	10 34.85
18	9				31.7	50.7		35.5	40 50.11	39.93	1.02	IV.	3	35.151	24 36.98	9.88	3.10	40 9.10	20 19.96
19	7.8					4.7	22.	40.	41 46.79	39.94	1.02	V.	2	15.650	45 1.37	10.11	5.78	41 5.83	40 47.26
20	9				50.		25.6	1.2	47 7.86	39.99	1.02	IV.	2	15.384	45 18.18	11.33	5.82	46 26.85	41 5.33
21	8.9				9.				50 26.64	40.03	1.01	III.	4	47.212	11 57.96	12.11	1.45	48 45.60	7 41.52
22	9					32.	49.3		50 31.83	40.03	1.01	VII.	3	39.320	20 15.46	12.13	2.53	48 50.79	16 0.12
23	8.9			45.		20.		55.3	53 20.13	40.05	1.01	IV.	4	47.754	11 23.73	12.79	1.38	52 39.07	7 7.90
24	8.9				29.2	46.8	4.7	22.5	54 46.92	40.07	1.01	IV.	2	8.616	52 22.94	13.11	6.77	54 5.84	48 12.82
25	9.10				20.	39.5			4 58 20.62	40.10	1.00	IV.	4	47.509	11 39.28	14.01	1.41	4 57 39.52	7 24.70
26	9				8.7	27.	44.7	2.	5 2 26.79	40.14	1.00	IV.	4	44.532	14 45.99	14.95	1.80	5 1 45.65	10 32.74
27	9.10					24.			4 24.05	40.16	1.00	IV.	3	31.074	28 52.68	15.46	3.65	3 42.89	24 41.79
28	9					8.7		44.1	5 6 26.36	−40.18	−0.99	IV.	2	11.939	−48 54.22	−15.98	−6.32	5 5 45.19	−29 44 46.42

CORRECTIONS.

Date.	Corr. of Clock.	Hourly rate.	m	n	c	Zenith Point.	Mic. Co.
1847.	h. s.	s.	s.	s.	s.	° '	r.

INSTRUMENT READINGS.

Date.	A.	B.	C.	D.	E.	F.	Mean.	Barom.	At.	Ex.	U.	L.	I.
	° ' "	"					"	In.					
Zone 91 1847, Feb. 6, h. m. 4 0	66 17 25.7	44.8	34.2	35.7	33.0	30.4	33.97	29.972	39.8	36.0	39.0	38.9	39.5
4 31										33.2			
4 40										32.6			
5 2								29.968	38.5	32.8			
5 15		25.5	44.9	34.5	35.7	33.5	29.5	33.93				36.8	36.2
5 52								29.956					
6 20		24.8	45.1	34.0	36.0	33.3	29.2	33.73	29.946	35.8	29.6	33.8	34.0	39.8
6 41										29.4			
7 0								29.946	34.6	29.2			

REMARKS.

(90) 60. Micrometer reading assumed as 38ʳ.940, not 43ʳ.940.

Feb. 6. Night fine; stars steady.

(91) 17. Transit over T. VII assumed as 37ˢ instead of 47ˢ.

(91) 21. Minutes assumed as 49, not 50.

(91) 22. Minutes assumed as 49, not 50.

(91) 25. Transits discordant; observations over T.'s IV and V assumed as recorded over T.'s III and IV.

ZONE 91.   FEBRUARY 6.   C. $D_0 = -28°\ 55'\ 30.''$—Continued.

No.	Mag.	I.	II.	III.	IV.	V.	VI.	VII.	T.	a_1	a_2	MICR.		r.	i	d_1	d_2	Mean Right Ascension, 1850.0	Mean Declination, 1850.0
									h. m. s.	s.	s.			r.	′ ″	″	″	h. m. s.	° ′ ″
29	8.9		48.2	6.		41.7			5 6	−40.18	−0.99	VII.	2	9.892	−51 2.09	−15.87	−6.60	5	−29 46 54.56
30	9		48.2	6.		41.7			10 23.76	40.22	0.99	IV.	2	15.475	45 12.47	17.01	5.83	9 42.55	41 5.31
31	9						44.5	2.7	11 9.36	40.23	0.99	VI.	2	20.220	40 14.43	17.21	5.16	10 28.14	36 6.80
32	9		59.7		35.	52.7			13 35.02	40.25	0.99	IV.	4	52.830	6 5.42	17.87	0.71	12 53.76	1 54.00
33	8		59.8	18.	35.7	53.	10.7		15 35.45	40.26	0.98	IV.	3	34.119	25 41.65	18.40	3.25	14 54.21	21 33.30
34	9		9.6	27.	44.7	3.2			22 44.98	40.33	0.98	IV.	2	14.582	46 8.46	20.32	5.05	22 3.67	42 4.73
35	9					41.2		16.2	23 23.22	40.33	0.97	V.	3	27.407	32 39.23	20.50	4.16	23 41.92	28 33.89
36	9		52.1	9.5	27.2	45.	2.8		26 27.32	40.35	0.97	IV.	2	10.639	50 15.95	21.33	6.53	25 46.00	46 13.81
37	9.10		42.7		18.1				28 18.16	40.37	0.97	IV.	2	11.602	49 2.83	21.83	6.30	27 36.82	45 1.02
38	8	49.2	6.	23.5	41.3	59.	16.8		5 32 41.28	40.41	0.96	IV.	3	53.106	5 50.82	23.01	0.66	5 31 59.91	1 44.49
39	8		13.2	30.7	48.3	6.	23.4	41.	6 26 48.29	40.74	0.90	IV.	4	43.388	15 57.60	37.79	1.95	6 26 6.65	12 7.54
40	9				20.	36.8		12.8	28 19.68	40.75	0.90	IV.	4	49.336	9 44.78	38.22	1.12	27 38.03	5 54.12
41	9						8.7		28 33.49	40.75	0.90	VI.	4	45.782	13 26.84	38.28	1.62	27 51.84	9 36.74
42	9				57.5	15.	33.		33 57.56	40.78	0.89	IV.	4	53.394	5 30.31	39.80	0.58	33 15.89	1 40.69
43	8		21.9	39.	57.	14.7			37 56.97	40.79	0.89	IV.	4	49.788	9 16.19	40.90	1.07	37 15.29	5 28.16
44	8.9					41.	58.7		39 23.32	40.79	0.89	V.	3	27.126	33 0.52	41.03	4.35	37 41.64	39 15.90
45	8		33.2	50.7	8.7	26.2			41 8.54	40.80	0.88	IV.	3	31.962	27 56.90	41.80	3.53	40 26.86	24 12.23
46	9			30.	47.	5.			41 47.34	40.81	0.89	IV.	3	29.380	30 39.09	41.98	3.88	41 5.65	26 54.95
47	8		8.	25.5	43.	1.3	18.7		43 43.30	40.82	0.88	IV.	3	22.027	38 20.28	42.52	4.93	43 1.60	34 37.73
48	9			1.5	19.	36.5			45 36.67	40.82	0.88	IV.	4	39.371	20 9.74	43.05	2.48	44 54.97	16 25.27
49	9				23.5	41.5			46 23.68	40.82	0.88	IV.	4	43.640	15 41.87	43.28	1.90	45 41.98	11 57.05
50	9						33.5		46 58.32	40.82	0.88	IV.	4	50.232	8 48.53	43.43	1.03	46 16.62	5 2.99
51	9		32.5	50.5	8.	25.5			51 7.96	40.84	0.87	VI.	3	33.150	26 42.57	44.60	3.36	50 26.25	23 0.53
52	9.10					49.7	7.7		51 32.16	40.84	0.87	V.	3	24.060	36 12.89	44.72	4.64	50 50.45	32 32.25
53	9.10							57.	52 4.04	40.84	0.87	VII.	4	38.060	21 30.73	44.87	2.67	51 22.33	17 48.27
54	9		59.	17.		52.4	10.		54 34.59	40.85	0.87	IV.	3	26.651	33 30.19	45.57	4.28	53 52.87	29 50.04
55	9		38.7		14.	31.7			6 56 14.03	40.86	0.87	IV.	3	25.527	34 40.78	46.05	4.44	55 32.30	30 1.27
56	9.10		59.	17.	34.7	52.			7 0 34.53	40.87	0.86	IV.	2	15.268	45 25.47	47.26	5.90	6 59 52.80	41 48.63
57	9		23.5		59.				1 58.95	40.67	0.86	IV.	3	27.498	32 37.10	47.65	4.16	7 1 17.22	28 58.91
58	9				40.	57.5	15.		2 39.88	40.87	0.86	IV.	3	43.802	15 34.16	47.84	1.89	1 58.15	11 53.89
59	9.10			26.2					4 43.89	40.88	0.85	III.	2	19.111	41 24.15	48.42	5.35	4 2.16	37 47.92
60	8					33.5	51.2	0.	5 15.75	40.88	0.85	V.	2	8.602	52 23.75	48.58	6.87	4 34.02	48 49.20
61	8.9					49.5	7.		6 31.70	40.88	0.85	V.	3	23.035	37 17.15	48.91	4.70	5 49.37	33 40.85
62	9					58.7			7 40.94	40.88	0.85	V.	3	17.438	43 8.50	49.24	5.59	6 59.21	39 33.42
63	9				58.	16.			8 58.14	40.98	0.85	IV.	3	16.650	43 57.70	49.61	5.70	8 16.41	40 23.10
64	9			31.	48.				10 48.34	40.89	0.85	IV.	4	41.940	17 28.37	50.11	2.12	10 6.60	13 50.60
65	8				47.5		23.7		11 47.96	40.89	0.85	IV.	3	28.638	31 25.52	50.30	4.00	11 6.22	27 49.91
66	9					49.3			12 31.58	40.89	0.85	V.	3	26.591	33 34.08	50.50	4.29	11 49.84	29 58.96
67	8						41.3	59.4	13 6.11	40.89	0.85	VI.	3	19.998	40 27.73	50.75	5.22	12 24.37	36 53.70
68	8.9		3.5	21.1	39.	56.7			15 38.97	40.90	0.84	IV.	3	21.758	39 37.15	51.40	4.97	14 57.23	35 3.58
69	9.10				23.	41.			16 23.11	40.90	0.84	IV.	2	8.087	52 56.15	51.67	6.95	15 41.37	49 24.77
70	9.10				34.	42.5?			16 24.37	40.90	0.84	VII.	3	11.7	49 8.	51.67	6.42	15 42.63	45 36.
71	5			51.3		26.	44.4		20 8.85	40.90	0.84	IV.	4	54.437	4 24.85	52.71	0.41	19 27.11	0 47.97
72	9.10			8.					22 25.65	40.90	0.84	III.	3	42.259	17 10.87	53.36	2.09	21 43.91	13 36.32
73	9.10				55.7			49.5	22 55.64	40.91	0.83	IV.	3	36.893	22 47.51	53.50	2.83	22 13.90	19 13.84
74	9							26.5	23 33.58	40.91	0.83	III.	3	43.617	15 45.64	53.65	1.91	22 51.84	12 11.23
75	9.10		3.5		38.				26 38.40	40.91	0.83	IV.	4	46.800	12 23.56	54.57	1.44	25 56.66	8 49.57
76	9					11.5	29.	46.7	26 53.76	40.91	0.83	V.	3	37.049	22 37.91	54.65	2.72	26 12.02	19 5.28
77	9		56.9	14.2	32.				7 29 32.01	−40.91	−0.83	IV.	4	50.482	−8 32.85	−55.31	−0.94	7 28 50.27	−29 4 59.10

CORRECTIONS.

Date.	Corr. of Clock.	Hourly rate.	m	n	c	Zenith Point.	Mic. Co.
1847.	h. s.	s.	s.	s.	s.	° ′ ″	r.

REMARKS.

(91) 70. Transit over middle thread assumed to have been at 24ˢ instead of 34ˢ.

(91) 71. Transit of Arg. Z. 282, 60, suspected to have been recorded with declination of η Canis Majoris.

INSTRUMENT READINGS.

	Date.		CIRCLE.							Barom.	THERMOM.				
			A.	B.	C.	D.	E.	F.	Mean.		At.	Ex.	U.	L.	l.
Zone 91	1847. Feb. 6,	h. m. 7 20	° ′ ″						″	in.		29.2			
		7 40	68 17 24.5	45.9	34.6	36.1	33.1	28.5	33.78d	29.946	33.5	28.3	32.6	33.0	38.8

ZONE 91. FEBRUARY 6. C. $D_0 = -28^\circ\,55'\,30''$—Continued.

No.	Mag.	I	II	III	IV	V	VI	VII	T.	m_1	a_1	Micr.	n	r	i	d_1	d_2	Mean Right Ascension, 1850.0	Mean Declination, 1850.0
									h. m. s.	s.	s.			r.	′ ″	″	″	h. m. s.	° ′ ″
78	9	..	46.	2.5	31.	..	..	14.	7 30 20.88	−40.91	−0.82	IV.	2	16.864	−43 45.11	−55.64	−5.69	7 29 39.15	−29 40 16.44
79	9	..	..	32.	49.2	..	..	25.2	30 31.83	40.91	0.82	IV.	2	13.520	47 15.18	55.69	6.17	29 50.10	43 47.04
80	9.10	..	..	..	..	..	..	17.5	31 24.48	40.91	0.82	VII.	3	29.512	30 30.68	55.95	3.92	30 42.75	27 0.55
81	9.10	..	19.5	37.	..	..	..	..	33 54.73	40.91	0.82	III.	4	47.580	11 34.99	56.68	1.34	33 13.00	8 2.92
82	8.9	..	15.7	33.	..	..	..	..	34 50.96	40.91	0.82	III.	2	8.038	52 59.10	56.95	6.95	34 9.23	49 33.00
83	8.9	..	..	..	12.5	30.5	..	5.	35 12.36	40.91	0.82	IV.	2	13.186	47 36.15	57.06	6.21	34 30.63	44 9.42
84	9	..	..	..	..	33.	..	7.6	36 14.84	40.91	0.82	VI.	2	15.010	45 41.28	57.37	5.95	35 33.11	42 14.60
85	8	..	..	..	..	11.	28.2	46.	36 52.91	40.91	0.82	V.	2	7.432	53 37.26	57.56	7.05	36 11.18	50 11.87
86	9.10	..	..	..	..	..	29.	46.	37 53.43	40.91	0.82	VI.	4	43.691	15 38.04	57.85	1.87	37 11.70	12 7.76
87	9.10	..	..	..	2.5	..	..	..	40 2.51	40.91	0.81	IV.	2	25.350	34 51.95	58.48	4.50	39 20.82	31 24.93
88	9.10	..	..	..	..	48.5	7.3	..	40 31.34	40.92	0.81	V.	3	21.695	38 41.24	58.62	4.99	39 49.61	35 14.85
89	9	..	..	..	..	52.	..	27.5	41 34.34	40.92	0.81	V.	3	22.021	38 20.78	58.94	4.95	40 52.61	34 54.67
90	9	..	..	..	..	..	..	26.	7 41 32.94	−40.92	−0.81	VII.	3	25.021	−35 12.34	−58.93	−4.55	7 40 51.21	−29 31 45.82

ZONE 92. FEBRUARY 12. C. $D_0 = -29^\circ\,33'\,40''$.

No.	Mag.	I	II	III	IV	V	VI	VII	T.	m_1	a_1	Micr.	n	r	i	d_1	d_2	Mean Right Ascension, 1850.0	Mean Declination, 1850.0
1	9	..	..	33.2	50.7	8.7	26.	..	6 22 50.78	−43.10	−0.75	IV.	3	35.342	−24 25.05	−1.67	−3.21	6 22 6.93	−29 58 9.93
2	9	59.6	17.6	34.3	53.	..	..	..	25 35.01	43.11	0.93	IV.	3	37.844	21 47.86	2.39	2.84	24 50.97	29 55 33.09
3	9	6.2	25.	38.	..	..	..	..	27 42.35	43.13	1.10	IV.	2	12.025	48 46.89	2.95	6.69	26 58.12	30 22 38.53
4	8.9	27.	45.1	3.	..	..	..	..	29 2.86	43.13	1.04	IV.	3	20.847	39 34.26	3.31	5.35	28 18.69	30 13 22.92
5	8	..	35.	52.	10.	23.	..	..	29 52.38	43.13	0.93	IV.	4	34.974	24 45.32	3.53	3.26	29 8.32	29 58 32.11
6	9.10	59.	..	34.7	52.2	..	..	..	33 34.57	43.15	1.14	IV.	2	12.572	48 14.68	4.51	6.61	31 50.28	30 22 5.80
7	9	11.7	29.2	..	..	..	..	..	34 47.10	43.16	0.95	IV.	4	38.972	20 34.52	4.83	2.69	34 2.99	29 54 22.04
8	6	..	..	..	..	..	18.	35.7	34 42.30	43.16	0.15	VI.	2	14.854	45 51.19	4.81	6.26	33 57.99	30 19 42.26
9	9	44.2	..	..	38.	55.7	..	..	39 20.04	43.18	1.07	IV.	3	32.533	27 21.21	6.04	3.62	35 35.79	1 10.87
10	7	..	..	..	20.7	38.	56.3	..	40 2.63	43.18	1.27	V.	2	8.856	52 7.81	6.23	7.17	39 18.18	26 1.21
11	9	23.7	41.8	..	18.	..	..	..	6 42 59.70	−43.19	−1.34	IV.	2	18.168	−42 23.47	−7.02	−5.74	6 42 15.17	−30 16 16.23

ZONE 93. FEBRUARY 12. C. $D_0 = -29^\circ\,33'\,40''$.

No.	Mag.	I	II	III	IV	V	VI	VII	T.	m_1	a_1	Micr.	n	r	i	d_1	d_2	Mean Right Ascension, 1850.0	Mean Declination, 1850.0
1	9	..	16.7	34.2	52.1	..	..	..	8 38 34.33	−43.25	−1.03	IV.	4	51.266	−7 43.69	−33.63	−0.85	8 37 50.05	−29 41 58.17
2	9	..	36.	53.8	10.3	..	..	..	39 35.63	43.25	1.14	IV.	3	39.716	19 50.49	33.91	2.55	38 51.24	54 6.95
3	9	..	41.7	2.	..	..	..	..	41 44.48	43.24	1.16	IV.	3	38.348	21 16.49	34.49	2.74	41 0.08	55 33.72
4	9	58.2	..	51.3	..	..	..	..	43 33.66	43.23	1.01	IV.	4	53.319	5 35.01	34.98	0.56	42 49.42	29 30 50.55
5	8.9	..	..	18.7	36.6	..	..	..	44 0.89	43.23	1.41	V.	2	12.529	48 17.45	35.11	6.66	43 16.25	30 22 39.22
6	8.9	..	..	..	20.7	38.6	..	..	44 45.29	43.23	1.12	VI.	4	42.124	17 16.58	35.31	2.18	44 0.04	29 51 34.07
7	9	17.	34.8	52.2	..	..	..	..	49 52.52	43.21	1.46	IV.	2	8.415	52 35.69	36.71	7.30	49 7.85	30 26 50.70
8	9	..	..	24.5	41.3	..	..	..	50 6.27	43.21	1.17	V.	4	36.859	22 46.94	36.77	2.96	49 21.89	29 57 6.67
9	9	..	17.8	36.2	53.5	..	..	..	51 18.06	43.21	1.27	IV.	3	26.682	33 28.19	37.09	4.50	50 33.55	30 7 49.78
10	9	..	43.3	1.4	18.8	..	..	..	52 43.33	43.20	1.42	IV.	2	11.809	49 2.39	37.46	6.78	51 58.71	23 26.63
11	9	..	15.7	33.	51.	..	..	..	54 33.24	43.19	1.27	IV.	3	27.012	33 7.49	37.94	4.45	53 48.78	7 29.87
12	8.9	..	34.1	52.	9.7	27.3	..	..	55 51.89	43.19	1.27	IV.	3	27.299	32 49.66	38.30	4.41	55 7.43	7 12.37
13	8.9	..	46.7	2.8	20.7	..	..	..	8 57 3.14	43.18	1.44	IV.	2	9.695	51 15.15	38.61	7.09	56 18.52	25 10.85
14	9.10	..	..	29.2	..	..	..	..	9 0 29.25	43.16	1.36	IV.	3	15.281	42 15.55	39.53	5.78	59 44.73	16 40.86
15	9.10	..	..	36.2?	..	15.2	..	..	0 38.	43.17	1.42	IV.	2	12.231	48 36.08	39.53	6.72	8 59 53.	30 23 2.33
16	9	..	..	0.7	18.7	..	..	..	3 0.83	43.16	1.16	IV.	3	37.607	22 2.85	40.18	2.84	9 2 16.51	29 56 25.87
17	5	..	44.	1.3	19.3	37.	55.	..	9 4 19.34	−43.15	−1.06	IV.	4	48.188	−10 56.04	−40.53	−1.28	9 3 35.13	−29 45 18.45

CORRECTIONS.

Date.	Corr. of Clock.	Hourly rate.	m	n	c	Zenith Point.	Mic. Co.
1847.	h.	s.	s.	s.	s.	° ′ ″	r.

REMARKS.

(92) 3. Transit over T. IV rejected.
(92) 6. Minutes assumed as 32, not 33, and 18 discordant from Mural Z., 1849, January 23.
(93) 15. Transits discordant.

INSTRUMENT READINGS.

	Date.	CIRCLE.							Barom.	THERMOM.				
		A.	B.	C.	D.	E.	F.	Mean.		At.	Ex.	U.	L.	I.
		° ′ ″						″	in.	°	°	°	°	°
Zone 92	1847. Feb. 12, 6 20	68 54 54.6	75.0	65.0	64.4	66.5	57.9	63.90	30.128	34.8	29.5	33.0	33.8	39.5
	6 42										29.9			
	8 40	51.1	70.1	61.7	60.4	61.8	53.8	59.82	30.102	35.5	30.0	37.0	36.9	39.0
	9 0										28.5			
	9 24								30.112	35.0	27.0			
	9 40	51.0	70.1	62.0	60.0	62.6	53.5	59.87	30.106	34.8	27.0	35.5	34.8	

ZONE 93.　FEBRUARY 12.　C.　$D_0 = -29°\ 33'\ 40''$—Continued.

No.	Mag.	I.	II.	III.	IV.	V.	VI.	VII.	T.	a_1	a_2	MICROMETER		r	i	d_1	d_2	Mean Right Ascension, 1850.0.	Mean Declination, 1850.0.
									h. m. s.	s.	s.			r.	' ''	''	''	h. m. s.	° ' ''
18	7		45.3	3.	20.7		56.2		9 7 20.78	−43.14	−1.46	IV.	2	8.430	−52 34.73	−41.30	−7.30	9 6 36.18	−30 27 3.33
19	9			8.2	25.7		1.6		7 25.92	43.14	1.36	VI.	2	17.913	42 39.21	41.33	5.83	6 41.42	30 17 6.37
20	8			7.2	24.7	42.6			9 24.83	43.13	1.05	IV.	4	48.704	10 24.22	41.84	1.21	8 40.65	29 44 47.27
21	9.10		28.2	47.3			41.2		15 5.38	43.09	1.24	IV.	3	29.521	30 30.18	43.29	4.08	14 21.05	30 4 57.55
22	8		10.7	28.2	46.2		21.3	39.3	15 46.04	43.09	1.30	IV.	3	24.	36	43.46	4.91	15 1.65	30 10
23	8.9							59.	17 5.71	43.08	1.13	VII.	4	40.772	18 40.88	43.78	2.38	16 21.50	29 53 7.04
24	8.9							25.	17 31.73	43.08	1.11	VII.	4	42.922	16 26.02	43.90	2.05	16 47.54	50 51.97
25	9		15.8			9.			24 51.30	43.04	1.04	IV.	4	49.982	9 4.08	45.63	1.00	24 7.22	43 30.71
26	9.10			6.	23.5	44.8	59.2		26 23.67	43.03	1.17	IV.	3	37.458	22 12.31	45.96	2.87	25 39.47	29 56 41.16
27	9			6.	23.6	44.5			28 23.82	43.02	1.30	IV.	2	23.870	36 25.44	46.44	4.94	27 39.50	30 10 56.82
28	7.8			13.5	31.0		6.8	24.5	31 31.18	43.00	1.38	IV.	2	17.289	43 18.68	47.11	5.94	30 46.80	17 51.73
29	8.9			41.7	59.7		35.3		31 59.67	43.00	1.21	IV.	3	33.975	25 50.61	47.21	3.39	31 15.46	30 0 21.21
30	8.9			56.2		31.6	49.3		34 13.89	42.98	1.11	IV.	4	44.451	14 50.88	47.66	1.83	33 29.80	29 49 20.37
31	8							23.7	34 30.27	42.98	1.35	VII.	2	20.406	40 2.75	47.71	5.46	33 45.94	30 14 35.92
32	8						37.3	56.	36 2.39	42.97	0.99	VI.	4	55.932	2 50.55	48.05	0.12	35 18.43	29 37 18.72
33	9			36.2	53.7	12.8	30.7		41 12.11	42.94	1.37	IV.	2	18.326	42 13.61	49.10	5.78	40 27.80	30 16 48.49
34	9			34.	52.	9.7	27.3		9 45 9.66	−42.91	−1.34	IV.	2	20.857	−39 34.51	−49.84	−5.40	9 44 25.41	−30 14 9.75

ZONE 94.　FEBRUARY 14.　P.　$D_0 = -27°\ 3'\ 0''$.

No.	Mag.	I.	II.	III.	IV.	V.	VI.	VII.	T.	a_1	a_2	MICROMETER		r	i	d_1	d_2	Mean Right Ascension, 1850.0.	Mean Declination, 1850.0.
1	7	21.	38.	55.5	13.				4 45 12.87	−42.44	−1.51	IV.	4	40.847	−18 36.93	−1.18	−2.71	4 44 28.92	−27 21 40.82
2	9				42.				48 42.00	42.48	1.47	IV.	4	44.180	15 8.00	1.92	2.34	47 58.05	18 12.26
3	8	33.	50.5		25.				4 53 25.14	42.52	1.72	IV.	3	23.280	37 1.84	2.95	4.80	4 52 40.90	40 9.59
4	7	44.	1.5	19.			11.		5 7 36.21	42.66	1.51	III.	4	41.088	18 21.87	6.08	2.68	5 6 52.04	21 30.63
5	7	48.	5.5	23.				15.	7 40.21	42.66	1.49	VI.	4	42.137	17 15.76	6.09	2.56	6 56.06	20 24.41
6	7					38.			9 20.69	42.67	1.36	V.	4	53.070	5 12.74	6.47	1.23	8 36.66	8 20.44
7	4					25.	42.		10 7.58	42.68	1.34	V.	4	55.100	3 43.10	6.64	1.06	9 23.56	6 50.80
8	8			43.					12 0.35	42.69	1.54	III.	3	39.167	21 27.41	7.09	3.04	11 16.12	24 37.54
9	8					38.5			12 21.17	42.69	1.47	V.	4	44.635	14 39.34	7.17	2.28	11 37.01	17 48.79
10	5.6		35.			9.5		44.	13 9.53	42.70	1.62	IV.	3	31.550	28 22.88	7.37	3.81	13 25.21	31 34.06
11	9		13.	30.					16 47.55	42.74	1.64	III.	3	30.435	29 33.52	3.23	3.95	16 3.17	32 44.70
12	9		4.						26 38.70	42.82	1.41	II.	4	48.910	15 24.75	10.63	2.32	25 54.47	18 37.70
13	9						45.		27 10.38	42.82	1.51	VI.	4	41.280	18 9.64	10.75	2.66	26 36.05	21 23.05
14	8	18.	35.	53.					30 9.97	42.84	1.45	III.	4	46.360	12 51.34	11.49	2.06	29 25.68	16 4.89
15	8						46.		30 28.57	42.85	1.76	V.	2	21.070	39 21.27	11.57	5.08	29 43.96	42 37.92
16	9							34.	30 41.85	42.85	1.78	VII.	2	19.100	41 24.60	11.61	5.31	29 57.22	44 41.58
17	7					23.			32 5.52	42.86	1.90	V.	1	9.080	51 52.81	11.97	6.53	31 20.76	55 11.31
18	8							13.	32 20.87	42.86	1.73	VII.	3	22.970	37 21.41	12.03	4.85	31 36.28	40 38.29
19	4								34	42.88	1.48	VII.	4	44.450	14 50.44	12.46	2.29	32	18 5.19
20	8						12.		34 37.32	42.88	1.63	VI.	3	32.180	27 43.73	12.61	3.74	33 52.81	31 0.08
21	8							3.	35 10.79	42.89	1.85	VII.	2	13.410	47 21.83	12.75	6.01	34 26.05	50 40.59
22	8					9.	26.		37 8.80	42.90	1.81	IV.	2	17.010	43 36.01	13.25	5.57	36 24.09	46 54.83
23	7		26.	43.	0.5				39 0.56	42.92	1.69	IV.	3	26.635	33 31.20	13.72	4.40	38 15.95	36 49.32
24	7		44.	1.					40 18.55	42.93	1.66	III.	3	29.355	29 37.54	14.05	3.96	39 33.96	32 55.55
25	8			38.					40 38.04	42.93	1.59	IV.	3	35.450	24 18.27	14.13	3.36	39 53.52	27 35.76
26	7		33.	50.5	8.				42 7.83	42.94	1.40	IV.	4	50.850	8 9.59	14.52	1.54	41 23.49	11 25.65
27	8.9				46.				44 46.05	42.96	1.69	IV.	3	27.203	32 55.61	15.19	4.34	44 1.40	36 15.14
28	8	14.	31.5	49.					5 52 6.15	−43.01	−1.51	III.	4	41.720	−17 42.16	−17.00	−2.60	5 51 21.63	−27 21 1.85

CORRECTIONS.

Date.	Corr. of Clock.	Hourly rate.	m	n	c	Zenith Point.	Nic. Co.
1847.	h.	s.	s.	s.	s.	° ' ''	r.

INSTRUMENT READINGS.

Date.		A.	B.	C.	D.	E.	F.	Mean.	Barom.	At.	Ex.	U.	L.	I.
	1847. Feb. 14,	h. m. ° ' ''						''	in.	°	°	°	°	°
Zone 94	4 40	66 25 1.6	17.3	9.0	5.3	9.3	2.0	7.42	30.000	41.0	34.0			
	5 26								30.008	40.0	36.0			
	6 0								30.070	40.0	36.0			
	8 0								30.058	38.5	32.0			
	9 15								30.042	38.0	31.5			

REMARKS.

(94) 6. Micrometer reading assumed as 53r.670 instead of 53r.070, to agree with Arg. Z. 350, 92, and 357, 19.

(94) 10. Minutes assumed as 14 instead of 13.

(94) 12. Micrometer reading assumed as 43r.910 instead of 48r.910, to agree with Arg. Z., 350, 114, and 357, 45.

(94) 17. Declination discordant by 2r.5 (= 2' 36".8) from Meridian Circle, 1848, December 16, and Arg. Z. 350, 120, and 357, 58.

(94) 24. Micrometer reading assumed as 30r.355, not 29r.355, to agree with Mural Circle, 1848, and Meridian Circle, 1847.

ZONE 94. FEBRUARY 14. P. $D_o = -27°\ 3'\ 0''$—Continued.

No.	Mag.	I.	II.	III.	IV.	V.	VI.	VII.	T.	a_1	a_2	MICROMETER		r_o	i	d_1	d_2	Mean Right Ascension, 1850.0	Mean Declination, 1850.0
									h. m. s.	s.	s.				′ ″	″	″	h. m. s.	° ′ ″
29	8					35.			5 52 17.56	−43.01	−1.81	V.	2	16.920	−43 41.65	−17.14	−5.58	5 51 32.74	−27 47 4.37
30	8	3.	21.						54 55.41	43.03	1.70	II.	3	25.620	34 34.01	17.83	4.52	54 10.68	37 56.36
31	7			2.					55 19.38	43.03	1.88	III.	4	10.490	50 25.18	17.93	6.37	54 34.47	53 49.48
32	7		6.	23.	41.				56 40.69	43.05	1.52	IV.	2	41.140	18 16.67	18.28	2.67	55 56.12	21 39.62
33	7					29.			5 56 54.36	43.05	1.56	V.	4	37.465	22 9.31	18.35	3.11	56 9.75	25 30.77
34	9	25.							6 0 16.83	43.07	1.39	I.	4	51.360	7 37.35	19.22	1.47	5 59 32.37	10 58.04
35	9			32.					2 49.37	43.08	1.73	III.	3	23.470	36 49.48	19.91	4.79	6 3 4.56	40 14.18
36	4		46.5	4.	21.				5 21.16	43.10	1.35	IV.	4	54.760	4 4.42	20.59	1.08	4 36.71	7 26.09
37	7.8			11.					6 28.32	43.10	1.41	III.	4	50.565	8 27.59	20.89	1.57	5 43.81	11 50.05
38	8							19.	6 26.77	43.10	1.89	VII.	1	10.400	50 30.14	20.88	6.38	5 41.78	53 57.40
39	8.7			33.				25.	10 50.35	43.13	1.58	V.	3	35.540	24 12.83	22.06	3.33	10 5.64	27 38.22
40	8							50.	11 57.98	43.14	1.52	VII.	3	41.315	18 7.07	22.36	2.65	11 13.32	21 32.08
41	7		57.		31.5				16 31.61	43.17	1.57	IV.	3	36.895	22 47.39	23.58	3.17	15 46.87	26 14.14
42	8					33.			17 15.59	43.17	1.70	V.	3	26.115	34 4.07	23.80	4.48	16 30.72	37 32.35
43	6.7			54.	11.				19 11.16	43.18	1.43	IV.	2	48.045	11 5.54	24.31	1.85	18 26.55	14 31.70
44	9		45.		21.				23 20.41	43.20	1.75	IV.	2	21.450	38 57.54	25.45	5.04	22 35.46	42 28.03
45	9					18.			25 0.63	43.21	1.59	V.	3	34.970	24 48.45	25.92	3.41	24 15.63	28 17.78
46	4.5					52.		27.	25 34.74	43.21	1.72	V.	2	23.753	36 32.84	26.08	4.77	24 49.81	40 3.69
47	7			14.					27 31.34	43.22	1.47	III.	4	44.788	14 29.69	26.61	2.24	26 46.65	17 58.54
48	8.7				49.				27 49.04	43.22	1.60	IV.	3	34.130	25 40.96	26.70	3.51	27 4.22	29 11.17
49	7	4.	21.	39.					30 56.02	43.24	1.60	III.	3	33.955	25 51.43	27.56	3.53	30 11.18	29 22.52
50	7	55.	12.5	30.					32 47.24	43.25	1.73	III.	3	23.620	36 40.00	28.08	4.78	32 2.26	40 12.86
51	8			19.		54.			33 36.49	43.25	1.69	V.	3	27.020	33 7.23	28.31	4.37	32 51.55	36 39.91
52	9					8.			34 50.59	43.26	1.73	V.	3	24.540	35 42.96	28.65	4.67	34 5.60	39 16.28
53	8				30.				36 12.63	43.26	1.57	IV.	3	36.345	23 19.56	29.12	3.23	35 27.80	26 51.91
54	8						7.		36 32.33	43.26	1.61	VI.	4	33.740	26 2.41	29.13	3.54	35 47.46	29 35.08
55	7			23.	40.5				38 40.44	43.27	1.57	III.	3	36.680	23 0.93	29.73	3.21	37 55.60	26 33.87
56	6.7				37.5				39 37.47	43.28	1.40	IV.	3	50.460	8 34.22	30.00	1.55	38 52.79	12 5.77
57	7			3.					43 20.32	43.29	1.41	III.	4	49.670	9 33.64	31.04	1.66	42 35.62	12 56.34
58	6.7	59.	16.5	34.					44 51.11	43.30	1.38	III.	4	52.700	6 13.57	31.46	1.32	44 6.43	9 46.35
59	9					23.			45 5.70	43.30	1.36	V.	4	54.255	4 36.14	31.53	7.12	44 21.04	8 8.70
60	9				52.				46 52.04	43.31	1.82	IV.	2	15.930	44 43.72	32.03	5.72	46 6.91	48 21.47
61	9					43.			47 25.56	43.31	1.80	V.	2	17.710	42 52.15	32.18	5.51	46 40.45	46 29.84
62	8					33.			48 15.59	43.31	1.72	V.	2	24.030	36 15.53	32.43	4.73	47 30.56	39 52.69
63	8							40.	48 47.02	43.32	1.66	VII.	3	29.110	30 56.28	32.58	4.11	48 2.94	34 32.97
64	6.7		53.	10.	27.5				52 27.52	43.33	1.50	IV.	4	42.613	16 46.28	33.62	2.48	51 42.69	20 22.38
65	7	30.	47.	5.					54 22.08	43.34	1.74	III.	3	22.817	37 30.26	31.15	4.88	53 37.00	41 9.29
66	8				58.				54 58.05	43.34	1.67	IV.	3	28.190	31 53.69	34.33	4.22	54 13.04	35 32.24
67	9						46.		55 11.31	43.34	1.64	VI.	3	30.620	29 21.54	34.39	3.93	54 26.33	32 59.86
68	9							26.	55 33.98	43.34	1.65	VII.	3	29.770	30 14.74	34.49	4.03	54 48.93	33 53.26
69	2.3						5.		56 30.26	43.35	1.76	VI.	3	20.700	39 43.93	34.76	5.14	55 45.15	43 23.83
70	8				42.5				58 42.49	43.36	1.46	IV.	4	45.760	13 26.79	35.39	2.11	57 57.67	17 6.29
71	7				38.				6 59 37.97	43.36	1.42	IV.	4	49.160	9 55.69	35.65	1.72	6 58 53.19	13 33.06
72	8	50.		24.					7 2 41.69	43.37	1.62	III.	3	32.445	27 26.41	36.50	3.71	7 1 56.70	31 6.62
73	8	55.	12.			22.			2 47.02	43.37	1.63	VI.	3	32.097	27 48.87	36.54	3.75	2 2.02	31 29.16
74	7			11.	28.5				4 28.46	43.37	1.71	IV.	3	25.400	34 48.81	37.01	4.56	3 43.38	38 30.38
75	3				3.				5 2.98	43.37	1.44	IV.	4	47.620	11 32.27	37.17	1.89	4 18.17	15 11.33
76	7			54.					6 11.36	43.38	1.61	III.	3	33.340	25 27.53	37.49	3.48	5 26.37	29 8.50
77	6		33.						7 7 7.70	−43.38	−1.42	II.	4	49.245	− 9 50.22	−37.75	−1.70	7 6 22.90	−27 13 29.67

CORRECTIONS.

Date.	Corr. of Clock.	Hourly rate.	m	n	c	Zenith Point.	Mic. Co.
1847.	h. s.	s.	s.	s.	s.	° ′ ″	r.

REMARKS.

(94) 35. Minutes assumed as 3 instead of 2.

(94) 39. Transit over T. VI assumed to have been recorded as over T. VII.

(94) 53. Transit over T. V assumed as recorded over T. IV.

(94) 76. Micrometer reading assumed as 34ʳ.340 instead of 33ʳ.340.

INSTRUMENT READINGS.

Date.	CIRCLE.							Barom.	THERMOM.				
	A.	B.	C.	D.	E.	F.	Mean.		At.	Ex.	U.	L.	I.
1847.	h. m. ° ′ ″			°			″	in.	°	°	°	°	°

ZONE 94. FEBRUARY 14. P. D₀ = −27° 3′ 0″—Continued.

No.	Mag.	I.	II.	III.	IV.	V.	VI.	VII.	T.	a₁	a₂	Mic.		r.	i	d₁	d₂	Mean Right Ascension, 1850.0	Mean Declination, 1850.0
									h. m. s.	s.	s.			r.	′ ″	″	″	h. m. s.	° ′ ″
78	7						22.		7 6 47.45	−43.38	−1.32	VI.	4	57.185	− 1 32.18	−37.67	−0.77	7 6 2.75	−27 5 10.62
79	6				19.				8 18.95	43.39	1.33	IV.	4	56.340	2 25.60	38.09	0.86	7 34.23	6 4.55
80	7					17.			8 59.63	43.39	1.59	V.	3	35.370	24 23.55	38.29	3.36	8 14.65	28 5.20
81	7							54.	9 1.77	43.39	1.90	VII.	1	9.257	51 4.18	38.30	4.93	8 16.48	54 47.41
82	7					53.			10 35.69	43.39	1.39	V.	4	51.590	7 23.25	38.74	1.42	9 50.91	11 3.41
83	5					36.5			11 19.10	43.39	1.69	V.	3	26.753	33 23.91	38.94	4.40	10 34.02	37 7.25
84	9							21.	11 28.92	43.39	1.64	VII.	3	30.690	29 17.09	38.99	3.92	10 43.89	33 0.00
85	9				39.				13 39.05	43.40	1.69	IV.	3	26.605	33 33.08	39.61	4.42	12 53.96	37 17.11
86	9			20.					14 37.37	43.40	1.73	III.	3	23.370	36 55.82	39.87	4.82	13 52.24	40 40.51
87	9						2.		14 27.31	43.40	1.67	VI.	3	28.670	31 23.82	39.82	4.16	13 42.24	35 7.80
88	9			56.		31.			16 13.45	43.40	1.89	V.	1	10.000	50 55.00	40.31	6.46	15 28.16	54 41.77
89	5.6		37.	54.5	12.				18 11.88	43.41	1.64	IV.	3	30.930	29 1.59	40.89	3.89	17 26.83	32 46.37
90	8			3.					19 20.38	43.41	1.83	III.	2	14.890	45 48.81	41.18	5.84	18 35.14	49 35.83
91	8			43.					20 0.38	43.41	1.88	III.	1	11.090	49 46.08	41.37	6.33	19 15.09	53 33.78
92	8			43.					21 0.38	43.41	1.86	III.	1	12.680	48 6.27	41.65	6.14	20 15.11	51 54.06
93	8		50.		24.				23 24.39	43.42	1.67	IV.	3	28.145	31 56.45	42.32	4.23	22 39.30	35 43.00
94	7.8	36.5		12.					25 29.03	43.42	1.80	III.	2	17.355	43 14.36	42.91	5.56	24 43.81	47 2.83
95	7.8	37.				46.5			25 29.11	42.42	1.82	V.	2	15.925	44 44.10	42.91	5.73	24 43.87	48 32.74
96	9				55.				26 55.05	43.42	1.67	IV.	3	28.313	31 46.03	43.29	4.21	26 9.96	35 33.53
97	9		41.	59.					28 16.06	43.43	1.71	III.	3	24.675	35 33.74	43.67	4.65	27 30.92	39 22.06
98	7	55.5	13.	30.5					30 47.62	43.43	1.38	III.	4	52.345	6 36.03	44.38	1.32	30 2.81	10 21.73
99	6.7			43.					31 42.95	43.43	1.32	IV.	4	57.230	1 29.74	44.63	0.74	30 58.20	5 15.11
100	10							55.	32 2.85	43.43	1.80	VII.	3	18.760	41 45.62	44.72	5.39	31 17.62	45 35.73
101	8	19.	37.						35 11.54	43.43	1.86	II.	2	12.185	48 38.48	45.60	6.20	34 26.25	52 30.28
102	6.7			24.	41.				35 23.83	43.43	1.67	IV.	3	27.950	32 8.55	45.65	4.26	34 38.73	35 58.46
103	7		30.5	48.					37 5.27	43.44	1.52	III.	4	40.596	18 52.79	46.12	2.71	36 20.31	22 41.62
104	7			25.			59.5		37 42.26	43.44	1.48	V.	4	44.215	15 5.75	46.28	2.29	36 57.34	18 54.32
105	9			50.					38 50.02	43.44	1.51	IV.	4	41.770	17 39.04	46.60	2.57	38 5.07	21 28.21
106	7.8			38.5					39 55.84	43.44	1.46	III.	4	46.285	12 56.04	46.90	2.04	39 10.94	16 44.98
107	9			25.					42 24.99	43.44	1.44	IV.	4	47.785	11 21.80	47.57	1.86	41 40.11	15 11.23
108	9	15.		50.					44 7.17	43.44	1.58	III.	3	36.050	23 40.08	48.04	3.27	43 22.15	27 31.39
109	8		23.	40.5					44 57.80	43.44	1.67	III.	3	28.265	31 48.66	48.27	4.22	44 12.69	35 41.15
110	8	30.	47.	4.5					46 21.88	43.44	1.67	III.	3	28.420	31 38.94	49.20	4.20	47 36.77	35 32.34
111	8.9						56.		48 21.28	43.44	1.70	VI.	3	26.010	34 10.72	49.19	4.49	47 36.14	38 4.40
112	7						56.		49 3.85	43.44	1.75	VII.	3	21.380	39 1.38	49.38	5.07	48 18.66	42 55.83
113	8							36.	49 1.21	43.44	1.87	VII.	2	11.380	49 29.32	49.57	6.31	49 15.90	53 25.20
114	7					26.5			50 51.75	43.44	1.81	VI.	2	17.375	43 13.23	49.86	5.56	50 6.50	47 8.65
115	8			35.					52 35.03	43.44	1.56	IV.	3	37.500	22 9.61	50.34	3.10	51 50.03	26 3.05
116	7		12.		47.				53 29.50	43.44	1.61	V.	3	33.600	26 14.21	50.57	3.57	52 44.45	30 8.35
117	8				41.				54 23.58	43.44	1.74	IV.	3	22.370	37 59.20	50.81	4.95	53 38.40	41 54.96
118	9			7.					56 6.98	43.44	1.45	IV.	4	46.710	12 29.26	51.27	1.98	55 22.09	16 22.51
119	9						49.		56 14.42	43.44	1.44	VI.	4	47.260	11 54.59	51.30	1.91	55 29.54	15 47.80
120	7						36.		7 57 11.45	43.44	1.35	VI.	4	55.060	3 45.35	51.52	0.99	56 26.66	7 37.86
121	9		28.						8 0 2.75	43.44	1.70	II.	3	26.330	33 49.58	52.33	4.46	59 17.61	37 46.37
122	8			27.					0 44.38	43.44	1.82	III.	2	15.895	44 45.74	52.52	5.74	7 59 59.12	48 44.00
123	9		12.	29.					7 46.52	43.44	1.53	III.	4	39.960	19 32.56	54.36	2.79	8 7 1.55	23 29.71
124	9	24.		59.					11 16.15	43.43	1.54	III.	4	39.245	20 17.58	55.28	2.87	10 31.18	24 15.73
125	7	11.	28.5	45.5	3.0				18 2.98	43.43	1.48	IV.	4	42.953	16 24.83	57.01	2.42	17 18.07	20 24.26
126	7		24.5	42.					8 21 59.34	−43.42	−1.79	III.	2	17.090	−43 30.87	−58.02	−5.60	8 21 14.13	−27 47 34.49

CORRECTIONS.

Date.	Corr. of Clock.	Hourly rate.	m	n	ε	Zenith Point.	Mic. Co.
1847.	h. s.	s.	s.	s.	s.	° ′ ″	r.

INSTRUMENT READINGS.

Date.	CIRCLE.							Barom.	THERMOM.				
	A.	B.	C.	D.	E.	F.	Mean.		At.	Ex.	U.	L.	I.
1847. h. m.	° ′ ″						″	in.	°	°	°	°	°

REMARKS.

(94) 81. Micrometer reading assumed as 9r.857 instead of 9r.257.

(94) 113. Transit over T. VI assumed to have been recorded as over T. VII; and minutes as 50, not 49.

(94) 120. Transit over T. VI assumed as 46s instead of 36s, to agree with Arg. Z. 352, 66 and 396, 132.

ZONE 94. FEBRUARY 14. P. $D_0 = -27°\ 3'\ 0''$—Continued.

No.	Mag.	I.	II.	III.	IV.	V.	VI.	VII.	T.	m_1	a_2	MICROMETER.			i	d_1	d_2	Mean Right Ascension, 1850.0.	Mean Declination, 1850.0.
									h. m. s.	s.	s.			r.	' "	"	"	h. m. s.	° ' "
127	9		4.						8 23 29.42	−43.42	−1.45	II.	4	46.745	−12 26.82	−58.44	−1.97	8 22 44.55	−27 16 27.23
128	7	13.	30.5	48.	5.				25 5.11	43.42	1.49	IV.	4	43.480	15 51.97	58.80	2.36	24 20.20	19 53.13
129	9							44.	30 51.92	43.41	1.65	VII.	3	30.187	29 48.71	60 25	3.98	30 6.86	33 52.94
130	8							33.	31 58.28	43.40	1.72	VII.	3	25.050	35 10.96	60.45	4.77	31 13.16	39 16.18
131	8				51.				33 51.04	43.40	1.85	IV.	2	13.790	46 58.03	61.00	6.00	33 5.79	51 5.12
132	9				39.		13.		34 38.62	43.39	1.87	VI.	2	11.800	49 2.95	61.10	6.26	33 53.36	53 10.40
133	8.9				14.				40 14.00	43.38	1.48	IV.	4	44.640	14 39.15	62.57	2.23	39 29.14	18 43.95
134	8.9			45.					42 2.38	43.38	1.83	III.	2	15.460	45 13.28	63.00	5.80	41 17.17	49 22.08
135	7			49.	6.5				44 6.47	43.37	1.75	IV.	3	22.475	37 52.29	63.49	4.94	43 21.35	42 0.72
136	9						32.		44 57.31	43.37	1.65	VI.	3	31.145	28 48.61	63.70	3.86	44 12.29	32 56.17
137	8			13.					47 30.38	43.36	1.81	III.	2	17.193	43 24.47	64.32	5.59	46 45.21	47 34.38
138	7	32.0		7.					48 24.36	43.36	1.62	III.	3	33.265	26 34.91	64.53	3.61	48 39.38	30 43.05
139	4.5						25.	42.	49 50.27	43.35	1.34	VI.	4	56.550	2 11.99	64.88	0.79	49 5.58	6 17.66
140	7				52.				51 51.95	43.35	−1.37	IV.	4	54.560	4 17.14	65.35	1.03	51 7.23	8 23.52
141	7	10.	28.	45.					54 2.29	43.34	1.43	III.	4	49.270	9 48.85	65.87	1.66	53 17.52	13 56.38
142	8	18.	35.	53.					57 10.05	43.33	1.60	III.	3	27.790	32 18.21	66.61	4.28	56 25.03	36 29.10
143	8.9			30.		5.			8 57 47.49	43.33	1.65	IV.	3	31.225	28 43.27	66.76	3.86	57 2.51	32 53.89
144	8.9	10.			2.				9 0 2.01	43.32	1.60	IV.	3	34.830	24 56.93	67.29	3.41	8 59 17.09	29 7.63
145	8.9							37.5	0 45.48	43.31	1.52	VII.	4	41.285	18 8.95	67.45	2.62	9 0 0.65	22 19 02
146	8						41.		2 6.31	43.31	1.68	VI.	3	28.560	31 30.85	67.76	4.18	1 21.32	35 42.79
147	8							50.	2 57.95	43.31	1.61	VII.	3	34.325	25 29.16	67.96	3.47	2 13.03	29 40.59
148	8							19.	3 26.92	43.30	1.65	VII.	3	30.640	29 20.23	68.06	3.92	2 41.97	33 32.21
149	7.8		14.						5 48.82	43.29	1.83	II.	2	15.920	44 43.85	68.61	5.77	5 3.70	45 58.23
150	7			51.		26.			6 8.48	43.29	1.75	III.	2	22.395	37 58.07	68.69	4.95	5 23.44	42 11.71
151	7	6.	24.						7 58.43	43.28	1.74	II.	2	23.290	37 1.59	69.12	4.84	7 13.41	41 15.55
152	7				3.				8 3.04	43.28	1.59	IV.	3	35.585	24 9.69	69.13	3.32	7 18.17	28 22.14
153	7					41.	58.		8 23.49	43.28	1.61	V.	3	34.117	25 42.03	69.21	3.50	7 38.60	29 54.74
154	8			51.5	9.				10 8.96	43.28	1.67	IV.	3	29.330	30 42.23	69.61	3.08	9 24.01	34 54.92
155	8				5.				11 5.04	43.27	1.83	IV.	2	15.995	44 39.71	69.82	5.74	10 19.94	48 55.27
156	9				59.				11 58.97	43.27	1.43	IV.	4	49.080	10 0.71	70.03	1.69	11 14.27	14 12.43
157	9			8.					13 25.36	43.26	1.62	III.	3	33.495	26 20.48	70.35	3.57	12 40.48	30 34.40
158	7				10.				14 9.95	43.25	1.37	IV.	4	54.510	4 20.28	70.52	1.03	13 25.33	8 31.83
159	8		8.						9 15 42.71	−43.25	−1.39	II.	4	52.845	− 6 4.30	−70.86	−1.23	9 14 58.07	−27 10 16.39

ZONE 95. FEBRUARY 23. C. $D_0 = -30°\ 11'\ 0''$.

No.	Mag.	I.	II.	III.	IV.	V.	VI.	VII.	T.	m_1	a_2	MICROMETER.			i	d_1	d_2	Mean Right Ascension, 1850.0.	Mean Declination, 1850.0.
1	9		10.8	28.2					5 30 46.42	−43.39	−0.97	III.	2	16.261	−44 22.96	− 0.47	−6.17	5 30 2.06	−30 55 29.60
2	7.8				34.2	15.2	33.		30 57.26	43.40	0.79	IV.	3	32.952	26 54.73	0.53	3.54	30 13.07	37 58.80
3	8.9		24.2	42.4	0.2		36.5		32 0.32	43.41	0.74	IV.	3	34.466	25 20.00	0.79	3.32	31 16.17	36 24.11
4	9			11.8	39.2			12.7	34 19.14	43.42	0.62	IV.	4	47.332	11 50.45	1.35	1.32	33 35.10	22 53.12
5	8				12.8			52.8	34 59.08	43.43	0.84	VII.	3	27.074	33 3.90	1.55	1.46	34 14.81	44 9.91
6	7.8		37.		12.5	31.	48.7	6.7	37 12.88	43.45	0.76	IV.	3	34.279	25 31.73	2.11	3.33	36 28.67	36 37.17
7	7			46.2	4.	22.			39 4.08	43.47	0.81	IV.	3	30.376	29 36.60	2.60	3.94	38 19.80	40 43.44
8	9		17.1		53.	11.3	29.7		5 57 53.34	43.61	0.60	IV.	4	46.		7.45	1.52	5 57 9.13	
9	8.9		42.0		17.8	35.8	53.8		6 2 17.89	43.65	0.73	IV.	3	34.396	25 24.40	8.60	3.23	6 1 33.51	36 36.32
10	8.9		58.	16.3	34.				4 34.06	43.66	0.98	IV.	2	12.116	48 43.25	9.20	6.85	3 49.42	59 59.30
11	9			10.3	38.2		12.		5 10.29	43.67	0.91	IV.	2	18.788	41 44.36	9.35	5.77	4 25.71	52 59.48
12	9						8.2	26.	6 6 32.33	−43.68	−0.82	VI.	3	25.153	−35 4.56	− 9.71	−4.77	6 4 47.83	−30 46 19.04

CORRECTIONS.

Date.	Corr. of Clock.	Hourly rate.	m	n	c	Zenith Point.	Mic. Co.
1847.	h. s.	s.	s.	s.	s.	° ' "	r.

INSTRUMENT READINGS.

Date.	CIRCLE.							Barom.	THERMOM.				
	A.	B.	C.	D.	E.	F.	Mean.		At.	Ex.	U.	L.	I.
1847. h. m.	° ' "						"	in.	°	°	°	°	°

REMARKS.

(94) 127. Transit over T. VI assumed as recorded over T. II, to agree with Arg. Z. 352, 107.

(94) 130. Transit over T. VI assumed as recorded over T. VII.

(94) 138. Minutes assumed as 49 instead of 48.

(95) 3. Differs 3' 30" in d from Arg. Z. 353, 7.

(95) 4. Transits discordant; those over T.'s IV and V rejected.

(95) 11. Transits discordant.

(95) 12. Minutes assumed as 5 instead of 6.

ZONE 95. FEBRUARY 23. C. $D_o = -30°\ 11'\ 0''$—Continued.

No.	Mag.	I.	II.	III.	IV.	V.	VI.	VII.	T. (h. m. s.)	a_1	a_2	Mic.	r	i	d_1	d_2	Mean Declination 1850.0	Mean Right Ascension 1850.0
13	9				24.	42.	59.2		6 7 23.89	-43.69	-0.62	IV. 4	43.706	-15 37.66	-9.93	-1.85	6 6 39.58	-30 26 49.44
14	9						42.3	0.1	8 6.54	43.69	0.68	VI. 4	38.734	20 49.14	10.13	2.64	7 22.17	32 1.91
15	8			40.5	58.2	16.3	34.2		9 58.36	43.70	0.84	IV. 3	23.998	36 16.59	10.61	4.95	9 13.82	47 32.15
16	8		19.5	37.2	55.3	13.3			12 55.29	43.72	0.93	IV. 2	14.751	45 57.79	11.40	6.42	12 10.64	57 15.61
17	9			43.5					15 1.30	43.74	0.57	III. 3	46.921	12 18.16	11.94	1.38	14 17.05	23 31.48
18	8			33.8	52.	9.5			15 51.78	43.74	0.60	IV. 3	36.705	22 59.36	12.16	2.95	15 7.35	34 14.47
19	8			46.5	4.2	22.			17 4.24	43.76	0.62	IV. 3	42.802	16 36.88	12.49	2.00	16 19.86	27 51.37
20	9.10					45.2	3.2		17 27.44	43.76	0.61	V. 3	44.048	15 19.04	12.59	1.83	16 43.07	26 33.46
21	9			5.	23.	41.2			20 23.07	43.77	0.83	IV. 2	23.670	36 38.06	13.30	5.01	19 38.47	47 56.43
22	9					39.		16.1	22 21.73	43.78	0.78	V. 3	28.752	31 18.49	13.88	4.20	21 37.17	30 42 36.57
23	9		28.2		4.7		40.3		4.43			IV. 2	7.825	53 12.48	14.62	7.57	(25)	31 4 34.67
24	9			42.8	0.7				28 0.74	43.82	0.78	IV. 3	26.262	33 54.72	15.40	4.59	27 16.14	30 45 14.71
25	9					4.3		40.	28 46.42	43.82	0.60	V. 4	42.425	16 56.06	15.60	2.05	28 2.00	28 15.71
26	9				7.	25.			30 7.05	43.83	0.62	V. 3	22.500	37 50.72	15.96	5.19	29 22.40	49 11.87
27	9				58.	16.			30 58.06	43.84	0.78	IV. 3	26.441	33 43.49	16.19	4.56	30 13.44	45 4.24
28	9			17.			10.		32 34.62	43.85	0.54	IV. 4	48.379	10 44.78	16.63	1.14	31 50.23	22 2.55
29	9			36.2		12.	30.		32 54.17	43.85	0.63	IV. 4	40.398	19 5.33	16.70	2.37	32 9.69	30 24.40
30	5			24.2	42.	0.	18.		34 42.14	43.85	0.50	IV. 4	50.619	8 24.20	17.19	0.80	33 57.79	19 42.19
31	8			50.	8.5	26.2	44.		36 8.26	43.86	0.62	IV. 4	40.419	19 4.01	17.57	2.37	35 23.78	30 23.95
32	9					3.2		39.2	36 45.43	43.87	0.65	V. 4	37.092	22 32.46	17.74	2.88	36 0.91	33 53.08
33	6		55.	13.	31.	48.5	6.5		39 30.81	43.88	0.87	IV. 2	16.858	43 45.49	18.48	6.10	38 46.06	55 10.07
34	6		39.		15.	32.5			40 32.72	43.88	0.80	IV. 3	24.017	36 15.40	18.68	4.94	39 48.04	47 39.02
35	9				21.	39.2	57.0		40 21.24	43.88	0.51	IV. 3	49.951	9 5.96	18.70	0.90	39 36.85	20 25.56
36	9						46.3		42 10.50	43.90	0.79	VI. 3	23.852	36 26.01	19.19	4.98	41 25.81	47 50.18
37	9		42.7		18.	36.2			45 18.27	43.91	0.71	IV. 3	30.788	29 10.50	20.03	3.87	44 33.65	40 34.40
38	9		10.3	28.					45 45.97	43.91	0.54	III. 3	46.331	12 53.16	20.15	1.45	45 1.52	24 14.76
39	8			50.	8.		43.2		47 7.80	43.92	0.44	IV. 4	55.468	3 20.21	20.52	0.06	46 23.44	14 40.79
40	8			52.5		28.			49 10.25	43.93	0.54	IV. 3	45.039	14 16.63	21.07	1.65	48 25.78	25 39.35
41	8.9				50.		7.7	25.5	49 49.79	43.93	0.88	IV. 2	14.624	46 5.82	21.25	6.64	49 4.98	57 33.71
42	9			42.2	0.2				52 0.18	43.94	0.71	IV. 3	29.580	30 26.48	21.83	4.06	51 15.53	41 52.37
43	7			49.5	7.3	25.2			53 7.34	43.95	0.62	IV. 3	38.375	21 14.79	22.13	2.69	52 22.77	52 39.61
44	6.7					2.	20.	37.3	53 43.93	43.95	0.78	V. 2	23.975	36 18.91	22.29	4.95	52 59.20	47 40.15
45	8					28.	46.2		54 10.17	43.95	0.86	V. 2	15.985	44 40.34	22.41	6.22	53 25.36	56 8.97
46	9							2.5	56 8.91	43.96	0.56	VII. 4	43.423	15 54.79	22.95	1.88	55 24.39	27 19.62
47	9		7.4	25.5	43.4				58 43.31	43.97	0.50	IV. 4	48.066	11 4.23	23.64	1.17	57 58.84	22 29.04
48	8.9				18.8	37.	55.		6 59 19.08	43.97	0.61	IV. 3	37.869	21 46.29	23.81	2.74	6 58 34.50	33 12.84
49	7			40.2	58.	16.2	33.5		7 0 58.06	43.98	0.53	IV. 3	45.054	-14 15.75	24.25	1.65	7 0 13.55	25 41.65
50	9				9.5	27.3	45.		7 2 9.41	-43.99	-0.62	IV. 3	37.		-24.58	-2.90	7 1 24.81	-30

ZONE 96. FEBRUARY 23. C. $D_o = -30°\ 11'\ 0''$.

No.	Mag.	I.	II.	III.	IV.	V.	VI.	VII.	T. (h. m. s.)	a_1	a_2	Mic.	r	i	d_1	d_2	Mean Declination 1850.0	Mean Right Ascension 1850.0
1	9					8.	25.7	43.	7 56 49.76	-44.10	-1.15	V. 3	28.499	-31 34.55	-39.28	-4.24	7 55 4.51	-30 43 18.07
2	8.9							30.2	7 57 36.45	44.10	1.20	VII. 3	24.006	36 10.76	39.48	4.94	55 51.15	47 55.18
3	9			59.6	17.9	35.6			8 0 17.74	44.10	0.89	IV. 4	48.275	10 51.25	40.41	1.13	7 59 32.75	22 32.79
4	9		59.1	16.8	34.5	52.7			1 34.73	44.10	1.16	IV. 3	27.551	32 33.78	40.74	4.38	8 0 49.47	30 44 18.90
5	9		11.	28.8	16.7				2 46.80	44.10	1.36	IV. 2	11.511	49 21.28	41.03	6.98	2 1.34	31 1 9.29
6	9							46.8	2 53.26	44.10	0.87	VII. 4	48.568?	10 32.07	40.79	1.08	1 8.29	30 22 13.94
7	9							50.	8 2 56.47	-44.10	-0.86	VII. 4	49.389	- 9 40.63	-41.08	-0.97	8 2 11.51	-30 21 22.68

CORRECTIONS.

Date	Corr. of Clock	Hourly rate	m	n	c	Zenith Point	Mic. Co.
1847. h.	s.	s.	s.	s.	s.	° ' ''	r.

INSTRUMENT READINGS.

	Date	CIRCLE A	B	C	D	E	F	Mean	Barom.	THERMOM. At.	Ex.	U.	L.	I.
	1847. (h. m.)								in.					
Zone 96	Feb. 23, 5 34								30.314	35.0	28.6			
	6 0	69 32 21.1	42.9	29.5	35.1	28.0	27.3	30.65	30.314	35.0	28.1	33.5	34.3	41.8
	6 40										27.9			
	7 0								30.337	33.7	27.8			
	8 0								30.362	32.5	26.7			
	8 20										26.2			
	8 30	20.4	43.7	29.5	35.9	28.1	26.8	30.73				31.9	32.0	41.0
	8 39										25.7			
	9 0								30.370	32.0	25.0			

REMARKS.

(95) 34. Time of transit over T. V assumed as 32s.5 instead of 52s.5, and transits over T.'s I, III, and IV as recorded over T.'s II, IV, and V.

Feb. 23. Night favorable but cold; 5h 40m to 5h 57m, suspended observations; 6h 52m to 7h, many small stars missed; observations suspended from 7h 2m to 7h 57m and from 9h 7m to 10h 20m.

(96) 1. Minutes assumed as 55 instead of 56.

(96) 2. Minutes assumed as 56 instead of 57.

(96) 6. Minutes assumed as 1 instead of 2.

ZONE 96. FEBRUARY 23. C. $D_s = -30°\ 11'\ 0''$—Continued.

No.	Mag.	I.	II.	III.	IV.	V.	VI.	VII.	T.	a_1	a_2
									h. m. s.	s.	s.
8	9.10		42.7	5.			36.		8 5 18.32	−44.10	−0.93
9	9			8.7	26.2	44.7			7 26.54	44.10	1.04
10	8.9			26.2	44.1	2.2			9 44.10	44.10	0.88
11	8		1.	18.3	36.5	54.6		30.	10 36.51	44.10	0.92
12	9							32.5	10 38.96	44.10	0.85
13	8		12.1	30.1	48.2	6.	24.		14 48.09	44.10	1.03
14	9.10						28.2	47.	14 52.96	44.10	0.92
15	9.10		52.	0.					17 27.95	44.10	1.22
16	9				42.5	0.7	18.2		17 42.52	44.10	1.26
17	8							5.	8 18 11.48	44.10	0.76
18	9					26.7	44.7		20 8.81	44.10	1.16
19	9			26.7	44.	2.1			21 26.32	44.10	1.27
20	8			18.7	36.5	54.6	12.1		23 36.57	44.10	0.77
21	8		53.	11.1	28.3	40.5	4.6		25 28.71	44.10	0.98
22	8			20.7	38.2		14.		26 38.37	44.09	0.91
23	7.8					3.5	21.5	39.3	27 45.50	44.09	1.26
24	8		18.3	36.3	54.2	12.			29 54.16	44.09	1.08
25	8		20.	37.7	55.7	13.8			30 55.76	44.08	1.11
26	9					51.2	9.7		31 33.73	44.08	0.72
27	9.10			41.2	59.2				35 59.19	44.07	1.13
28	9				41.2		16.5		37 41.07	44.07	1.25
29	9					47.	4.7		38 29.06	44.07	0.85
30	8				35.	53.3	10.5		39 35.06	44.07	0.79
31	9					10.	27.8		40 51.99	44.07	1.15
32	9		59.2	17.	35.				42 34.98	44.06	0.77
33	9			51.	9.	27.			43 9.00	44.06	1.09
34	8.9				1.	18.8		54.5	44 0.96	44.05	0.73
35	9			59.	17.	35.			46 17.01	44.05	0.87
36	9				5.	22.8			47 4.97	44.05	0.88
37	9				42.8	0.7	18.5		47 42.79	44.05	0.92
38	9					56.2	14.3		48 38.41	44.04	0.93
39	9		32.	49.2			43.	0.7	50 7.28	44.04	0.92
40	9			49.3		25.	43.2	1.0	50 7.28	44.04	0.87
41	8.9		7.5	25.		0.			52 42.76	44.03	0.70
42	8.9			58.5	16.2	34.2			53 16.31	44.03	0.90
43	8					27.3	45.3		54 9.43	44.03	0.99
44	8.9			45.	3.	20.7			57 2.90	44.02	0.71
45	9							41.7	57 47.38	44.02	0.78
46	9		41.	58.8	16.8				9 0 16.78	44.01	0.87
47	9					55.2			0 37.23	44.01	1.02
48	9							40.2	0 46.35	44.01	1.12
49	9			46.			21.5		6 45.84	44.01	1.08
50	9		29.	47.		23.	40.7		7 4.92	44.01	1.03
51	8							14.7	9 7 21.12	−44.01	−0.69

No.	MICROMETER		r.	i	d₁	d₂	Mean Right Ascension, 1850.0.	Mean Declination, 1850.0.
			r.	′ ″	″	″	h. m. s.	° ′ ″
8	IV.	4	43.118	−16 14.61	−41.68	−1.93	8 3 33.29	−30 27 58.22
9	IV.	3	33.818	26 0.41	42.22	3.39	6 41.40	37 46.02
10	IV.	4	46.816	12 22.56	42.81	1.37	8 59.12	24 6.74
11	IV.	4	43.088	16 16.49	43.03	1.93	9 51.49	28 1.45
12	VII.	4	48.689	10 24.34	43.05	1.05	9 54.01	22 8.44
13	IV.	3	33.002	26 51.66	44.11	3.52	14 2.96	38 39.29
14	VI.	3	41.539	17 56.59	44.13	2.18	14 7.94	29 42.90
15	III.	2	17.660	42 55.04	44.79	5.98	16 42.63	54 45.81
16	IV.	2	14.851	45 51.45	44.84	6.47	16 57.16	57 42.76
17	VII.	4	51.495	7 28.51	44.97	0.62	17 26.62	19 14.10
18	IV.	2	21.482	38 55.48	45.46	5.38	19 23.55	50 46.32
19	IV.	2	13.376	47 24.28	45.82	6.72	20 40.95	59 16.82
20	IV.	4	49.736	9 19.44	46.41	0.88	22 51.70	21 6.73
21	IV.	3	33.754	26 4.48	46.92	3.41	24 43.63	37 54.81
22	IV.	3	38.915	20 40.67	47.23	2.59	25 53.37	30 32 30.49
23	V.	3	11.339	49 32.14	47.53	7.04	27 0.15	31 1 26.71
24	IV.	3	25.661	34 19.63	48.12	4.66	29 9.01	30 46 12.41
25	IV.	3	23.013	37 18.40	48.40	5.14	30 10.57	49 11.94
26	V.	4	52.101	6 51.14	48.57	0.53	30 48.93	18 40.24
27	IV.	2	19.031	41 29.17	49.78	5.78	35 13.99	30 53 24.73
28	IV.	3	9.450	51 29.83	50.23	7.34	36 55.75	31 3 27.40
29	V.	4	40.487	18 59.56	50.45	2.32	37 44.14	30 30 52.33
30	IV.	4	45.012	14 15.75	50.75	1.64	38 50.20	26 8.14
31	V.	2	16.988	43 37.39	51.08	6.11	40 6.77	55 34.58
32	IV.	3	30.452	29 31.83	51.52	3.93	41 49.95	41 27.28
33	IV.	3	21.045	39 21.90	51.67	5.45	42 23.65	51 19.02
34	IV.	4	48.351	10 46.55	51.89	1.11	43 16.18	22 39.55
35	IV.	3	36.601	23 5.90	52.49	2.95	45 32.09	35 1.40
36	IV.	3	35.349	24 24.61	52.69	3.16	46 20.04	36 20.46
37	IV.	3	32.228	27 40.34	52.85	3.64	46 57.82	39 36.83
38	V.	3	31.270	28 40.69	53.09	3.80	47 53.44	40 37.58
39	IV.	3	28.935	31 6.75	53.47	4.17	49 22.32	43 4.39
40	IV.	3	34.647	25 8.53	53.47	3.25	49 22.37	37 5.25
41	IV.	4	47.600	11 33.52	54.11	1.20	51 58.03	23 28.83
42	IV.	3	31.982	27 55.65	54.25	3.68	52 31.38	39 53.58
43	V.	3	24.786	35 27.33	54.46	4.84	53 24.41	47 26.63
44	IV.	4	45.557	13 41.63	55.19	1.56	56 18.17	25 38.38
45	VII.	4	39.651	19 51.25	55.37	2.46	57 2.58	31 49.08
46	IV.	3	32.242	27 39.46	55.98	3.64	8 59 31.90	39 39.08
47	V.	3	21.312	39 5.58	56.06	5.41	8 59 52.20	51 7.05
48	VII.	2	13.160	47 37.40	56.10	6.76	9 0 1.22	59 40.26
49	IV.	2	15.510	45 10.27	57.50	6.36	6 0.75	57 14.13
50	IV.	2	17.757	42 49.06	57.58	6.00	6 19.88	54 52.64
51	VII.	4	44.262	−15 2.17	−57.64	−1.73	9 6 36.42	−30 27 1.54

CORRECTIONS.

Date.	Corr. of Clock.	Hourly rate.	m	n	ε	Zenith Point.	Mic. Co.
1847.	h.	s.	s.	s.	s.	° ′ ″	r.
	s.	s.	s.	s.,	s.		

REMARKS.

(96) 8. Minutes assumed as 4 instead of 5.
(96) 15. Observation of transit over T, III assumed as 10ˢ instead of 0ˢ.

INSTRUMENT READINGS.

	Date.	CIRCLE.							Barom.	THERMOM.				
		A.	B.	C.	D.	E.	F.	Mean.		At.	Ex.	U.	L.	I.
Zone 96	1847, Feb. 23, 10 24	° ′ ″						″	In. 30.386	31.0	24.9			
	11 2								30.382	30.5	24.5			
	11 21	69 32 19.9	44.5	30.4	35.9	28.4	26.1	30.87	30.384	30.1	24.3	29.0	30.5	40.0

ZONE 97. FEBRUARY 23. C. $D_0 = -30° 11' 0''$.

No.	Mag.	I	II	III	IV	V	VI	VII	T	a_1	a_2	MICROMETER		r	i	d_1	d_2	Mean Right Ascension, 1850.0.	Mean Declination, 1850.0.
									h. m. s.	s.	s.			r.	° ' ''	''	''	h. m. s.	° ' ''
1	6	8.2	25.7	43.7	1.3	19.5	37.	55.1	10 21 1.50	−43.54	−0.08	IV.	4	52.835	− 6 5.11	−72.84	−0.36	10 20 17.88	−30 18 18.31
2	9		22.5		59.3				25 58.90	43.50	0.51	IV.	2	9.105	51 52.24	73.71	7.44	25 14.89	31 4 13.39
3	9		1.	18.8	36.5	54.7	12.6		28 36.74	43.48	0.25	IV.	3	37.812	21 49.86	74.17	2.74	27 53.01	30 34 6.77
4	9			45.2	3.1		39.		31 3.17	43.46	0.26	IV.	3	37.732	21 54.94	74.58	2.75	30 19.45	34 12.27
5	9						8.		30 32.17	43.47	0.44	VI.	2	19.272	41 14.11	74.50	5.77	29 48.26	53 34.38
6	8.9						37.1	55.	31 1.19	43.46	0.48	VI.	2	13.938	46 48.68	74.57	6.64	30 17.25	59 9.89
7	9						11.3	29.	32 35.31	43.44	0.48	VI.	2	15.984	44 40.34	74.84	6.31	31 51.39	30 57 1.49
8	9		30.	47.8	5.7				35 5.81	43.42	0.54	IV.	2	10.002	50 55.87	75.25	7.31	34 21.85	31 3 18.43
9	8		27.	45.	3.				37 2.06	43.41	0.51	IV.	2	14.691	46 1.56	75.57	6.52	36 19.04	30 58 23.65
10	9				23.		58.3		37 22.84	43.41	0.15	IV.	4	52.900	6 1.03	75.63	0.35	36 39.28	18 17.01
11	9				23.4		59.	17.	37 23.40	43.41	0.21	IV.	4	46.418	12 47.76	75.63	1.36	36 39.78	25 4.75
12	9					8.2	26.5	44.1	38 50.53	43.39	0.29	V.	3	38.022	20 40.48	75.87	2.56	38 6.85	32 58.91
13	8		40.7	58.	16.2				41 16.23	43.37	0.44	IV.	3	23.870	36 24.57	76.26	5.00	40 32.42	48 45.83
14	8			39.5	57.	15.2			41 57.23	43.36	0.49	IV.	3	19.067	41 26.10	76.36	5.80	41 13.38	53 48.26
15	9				59.7	17.6	35.2		42 59.62	43.36	0.38	IV.	3	29.755	30 15.37	76.53	4.04	42 15.88	42 35.94
16	9						4.7	22.	43 28.66	43.36	0.34	VI.	3	34.782	25 0.30	76.60	3.22	42 44.96	37 20.12
17	9.10				33.	50.7			45 32.92	43.34	0.27	IV.	4	46.012	13 13.03	76.92	1.42	44 49.31	25 31.37
18	9		16.4	34.5	52.1				47 52.20	43.32	0.23	IV.	4	50.528	8 29.97	77.29	0.71	47 8.65	30 20 47.97
19	9			32.			26.		48 50.03	43.30	0.57	IV.	2	13.061	47 43.86	77.44	6.82	48 6.16	31 0 8.12
20	8				30.5	48.3	6.		49 30.32	43.29	0.56	IV.	2	13.939	46 48.68	77.54	6.65	48 46.47	30 59 12.87
21	8					47.4	5.7	23.3	50 29.78	43.28	0.27	V.	4	47.383	11 47.12	77.65	1.20	49 46.23	24 6.01
22	8.9				51.8	9.7	27.4		51 51.74	43.27	0.46	IV.	3	26.900	33 14.44	77.89	4.52	51 8.01	30 45 36.85
23	7.8		42.3	0.1	18.	36.	54.		54 18.08	43.25	0.61	IV.	2	10.933	49 57.37	78.25	7.14	53 34.22	31 2 22.76
24	9.10				37.	54.7	13.		54 36.95	43.25	0.59	IV.	2	13.361	47 25.22	78.30	6.74	53 53.11	30 59 50.26
25	9		54.3	12.4	29.8	48.			10 57 30.08	43.22	0.47	IV.	3	27.481	32 38.16	78.73	4.78	10 56 46.39	45 1.67
26	9.10			11.3		46.8			11 2 29.05	43.17	0.38	IV.	4	40.961	18 29.77	79.44	2.22	11 1 45.50	30 51.43
27	9.10		20.7		57.				4 56.75	43.15	0.43	IV.	4	37.455	22 9.86	79.79	2.79	4 13.17	34 32.44
28	9			41.8		17.3			5 59.55	43.14	0.28	IV.	4	52.258	6 41.48	79.93	0.43	5 16.13	19 1.84
29	9		1.		37.	54.7			7 36.87	43.13	0.43	IV.	3	38.581	21 1.80	80.15	2.61	6 53.31	30 33 24.56
30	9.10		27.			20.7			9 2.81	43.11	0.67	IV.	2	12.214	48 37.16	86.36	6.96	8 19.03	31 1 4.48
31	9		0.2	18.	36.1				11 35.99	43.08	0.41	IV.	4	42.271	17 7.80	80.70	2.01	10 52.50	30 29 30.51
32	8				54.	12.			11 36.09	43.08	0.64	V.	3	17.168	43 25.54	80.70	6.14	10 52.37	55 52.38
33	9					48.2	6.2		12 12.55	43.08	0.43	VI.	4	39.658	19 51.19	80.78	2.43	11 29.04	32 14.40
34	9		21.	39.		14.2			14 56.65	43.05	0.42	IV.	4	42.411	16 59.01	81.14	1.97	14 13.18	29 22.12
35	9		24.3	42.4		18.5	36.		15 0.30	43.05	0.54	IV.	3	30.366	29 37.23	81.15	3.95	14 16.71	42 2.33
36	9.10			57.7		33.			17 15.33	43.02	0.60	IV.	3	23.297	37 0.77	81.44	5.12	16 31.71	49 27.33
37	9.10				36.5		12.8		17 36.74	43.02	0.68	IV.	2	16.270	44 22.58	81.49	6.29	16 53.04	56 50.36
38	9		55.		30.7	49.			21 30.87	42.77	0.40	IV.	4	46.932	12 15.28	81.99	1.26	20 47.70	30 24 38.53
39	8.9					27.6	45.7		11 21 51.77	−42.97	−0.73	VI.	2	11.472	−49 23.53	−82.04	−7.10	11 21 8.07	−31 1 52.67

CORRECTIONS.

Date.	Corr. of Clock.	Hourly rate.	m	n	c	Zenith Point.	Mic. Co.
1847.	h.	s.	s.	s.	s.	° ' ''	r.

INSTRUMENT READINGS.

Date.	CIRCLE.							Barom.	THERMOM.				
	A.	B.	C.	D.	E.	F.	Mean.		At.	Ex.	U.	L.	I.
1847. h. m.	° ' ''						''	in.	°	°	°	°	°

REMARKS.

ZONE 98.   MARCH 5.   P. $D_0 = -27° 40' 50''$.

No.	Mag.	I.	II.	III.	IV.	V.	VI.	VII.	T. (h. m. s.)	a_1 (s.)	a_2 (s.)
1	8					10.5			6 9 53.00	−44.91	−1.17
2	9					26.			11 8.53	44.92	1.14
3	8	52.	10.	27.					13 44.54	44.94	1.12
4	8	20.5	38.	55.	12.5				19 12.63	44.98	1.07
5	8	16.		51.	8.				22 8.32	44.99	1.30
6	8			17.					23 34.47	45.00	1.19
7	7.8							28.5	23 36.21	45.00	1.05
8	7						35.		25 59.99	45.02	1.43
9	7				51.				26 51.00	45.02	1.07
10	6				45.				27 44.98	45.03	1.02
11	9			31.					31 48.47	45.05	1.25
12	7						32.5		31 57.48	45.06	1.46
13	8						27.		32 52.06	45.06	1.34
14	7				19.				34 19.04	45.06	1.30
15	7			8.	26.				35 25.75	45.07	1.20
16	8			12.					36 29.47	45.08	1.22
17	7						1.5		36 26.76	45.08	0.99
18	7				1.	19.			38 1.27	45.09	1.25
19	7.8		34.	51.					41 8.68	45.11	1.16
20	7				19.				42 19.04	45.11	1.37
21	9							13.	42 20.52	45.11	1.38
22	8						4.		43 29.10	45.12	1.26
23	7						4.5		44 19.52	45.12	1.42
24	7				51.				45 51.03	45.13	1.45
25	8			53.					47 10.48	45.14	1.41
26	6.7			4.5	22.				49 22.01	45.14	1.35
27	8.9			21.					49 38.47	45.15	1.26
28	9				47.				51 47.03	45.16	1.44
29	7	42.	0.	17.5					54 34.74	45.17	1.27
30	9					12.			54 54.55	45.17	1.15
31	6.7					51.			55 33.49	45.18	1.32
32	8					27.			57 9.54	45.19	1.21
33	9							2.	6 57 9.64	45.19	1.25
34	9	45.		20.					7 0 37.42	45.20	1.32
35	8		24.		59.				1 58.95	45.21	1.15
36	8					39.			2 21.55	45.21	1.19
37	9						30.		2 55.20	45.21	1.15
38	8					6.			3 48.56	45.22	1.13
39	8						57.		4 22.10	45.22	1.29
40	7							44.	4 51.47	45.22	1.47
41	8				44.				6 44.04	45.23	1.27
42	8			41.					7 58.47	45.24	1.33
43	8				32.				8 32.04	45.24	1.39
44	9						32.		8 57.08	45.24	1.34
45	8					25.			10 7.53	45.24	1.25
46	8.7		21.	38.5					11 55.98	45.25	1.38
47	8.9				36.				12 36.01	45.25	1.20
48	8.9		12.5		47.5				14 42.49	45.26	1.33
49	9.10			42.					7 15 41.99	−45.26	−1.13

No.	MICROMETER		(r.)	i (′ ″)	d_1 (″)	d_2 (″)	Mean Right Ascension, 1850.0 (h. m. s.)	Mean Declination, 1850.0 (° ′ ″)
1	V	3	31.003	−28 57.32	−6.11	−3.87	6 9 6.92	−28 9 57.30
2	V	3	33.980	25 50.55	6.44	3.50	10 22.47	6 50.49
3	III	3	36.570	23 7.58	7.13	3.17	12 58.48	28 4 7.88
4	IV	4	43.570	15 46.26	8.56	2.31	18 26.58	27 56 47.13
5	IV	2	19.015	41 30.18	9.33	5.39	21 22.03	28 22 34.90
6	III	3	32.380	27 30.49	9.72	3.69	22 48.28	28 8 33.90
7	VII	4	45.950	13 16.17	9.73	2.02	22 50.16	27 54 17.92
8	VI	1	8.643	52 20.30	10.37	6.72	25 13.54	28 33 27.39
9	IV	4	44.785	14 29.94	10.59	2.16	26 4.91	27 55 32.69
10	IV	4	50.233	8 48.46	10.84	1.50	26 58.93	27 49 50.80
11	III	3	28.193	31 53.12	11.91	4.23	31 2.17	28 12 59.26
12	VI	1	7.270	53 46.61	11.95	6.91	31 10.97	34 55.47
13	VI	2	19.425	41 4.57	12.20	5.35	32 5.66	22 12.12
14	IV	2	22.995	37 24.11	12.59	4.89	33 32.68	18 31.59
15	IV	3	33.293	26 33.59	12.88	3.59	34 39.48	7 40.06
16	III	3	32.033	27 52.07	13.16	3.73	35 43.17	28 8 58.96
17	VI	4	55.475	3 19.46	13.15	0.85	35 40.69	27 44 23.46
18	V	3	28.825	31 13.91	13.57	4.16	37 14.93	28 12 21.64
19	III	4	38.483	21 5.39	14.41	2.94	40 22.41	2 12.74
20	IV	2	17.890	42 40.72	14.72	5.54	41 32.56	28 23 50.98
21	VII	2	17.035	43 34.19	14.73	5.65	41 34.03	24 44.57
22	VI	3	28.980	31 4.37	15.04	4.14	42 42.72	12 13.55
23	VI	2	12.883	47 54.97	15.31	6.18	43 32.98	29 6.46
24	IV	1	10.095	50 52.61	15.66	6.54	45 4.45	32 4.81
25	III	2	14.523	46 12.03	16.03	5.98	46 23.93	27 24.04
26	IV	2	21.315	39 6.02	16.53	5.10	47 35.52	20 17.65
27	III	3	29.807	30 11.67	16.70	4.03	48 52.06	11 22.40
28	IV	2	11.720	49 8.05	17.27	6.34	51 0.43	30 21.64
29	III	3	29.533	30 29.08	18.02	4.06	53 48.30	28 11 41.13
30	V	3	42.425	16 58.07	18.11	2.43	54 8.23	27 58 8.61
31	V	3	24.693	35 33.24	18.29	4.67	54 46.99	28 16 46.20
32	V	3	36.905	22 47.01	18.72	3.12	56 23.14	3 58.85
33	VII	3	32.575	27 18.88	18.72	3.67	56 23.20	8 31.27
34	III	3	25.610	34 35.13	19.65	4.55	6 59 50.90	28 15 49.33
35	IV	4	43.040	16 19.44	20.03	2.35	7 1 12.59	27 57 31.82
36	V	4	38.965	20 34.90	20.12	2.84	1 35.15	28 1 47.86
37	VI	4	42.663	16 42.77	20.27	2.39	2 8.84	27 57 55.43
38	V	4	45.230	14 2.08	20.52	2.09	3 2.21	27 55 14.69
39	VI	3	28.975	31 4.68	20.67	4.14	3 35.59	28 12 19.49
40	VII	2	11.675	49 10.61	20.80	6.35	4 4.78	30 27.76
41	IV	2	31.875	28 2.30	21.32	3.75	5 57.54	9 17.37
42	III	3	25.877	34 18.25	21.65	4.52	7 11.90	15 34.42
43	IV	2	20.370	40 5.32	21.80	5.23	7 45.41	21 22.35
44	VI	3	25.620	34 35.25	21.92	4.55	8 10.50	15 51.72
45	V	3	34.783	25 0.12	22.23	3.39	9 21.04	6 15.74
46	III	2	21.630	38 45.94	22.72	5.07	11 9.35	20 3.73
47	IV	3	39.760	19 47.74	22.90	2.77	11 49.56	1 3.41
48	IV	3	27.930	32 9.51	23.51	4.27	14 0.00	28 13 27.59
49	IV	4	48.070	−11 3.98	−23.74	−1.75	7 14 55.60	−27 52 19.47

CORRECTIONS.

Date.	Corr. of Clock.	Hourly rate.	m	n	c	Zenith Point.	Mic. Co.
1847.	h.	s.	s.	s.	s.	° ′ ″	r.

INSTRUMENT READINGS.

Date.	CIRCLE.							Barom.	THERMOM.				
	A.	B.	C.	D.	E.	F.	Mean.	(in.)	At.	Ex.	U.	L.	I.
Zone 98 1847. Mar. 5, 6 10	67 2 32.3	47.0	38.0	40.2	34.5	36.0	38.37 [a]	30.372	43.0	38.0	42.0	..	42.0
7 49								30.390	40.5	34.0			
8 20	41.7	58.0	48.5	50.0	47.4	44.6	48.74 [b]	30.390	39.5	32.0			
10 26								30.402	38.5	30.5			
11 0								30.420	38.0	30.0			

REMARKS.

March 5, 6h 18m, instrument disturbed by a blow from the observer's head, occasioning a change in the reading and in the nadir point. Observations suspended from 8h 25m to 10h 25m. Readings of barometer, &c., at 10h 20m; at 11h, interrupted by clouds.

(98) 23. Transit over T. VI assumed as 54'.5, not 4'.5.

(98) 26. Transits over T.'s III and IV assumed as 4s.5 and 22s, not 45s and 2s.2, and minutes as 48, not 49, to agree with Arg. Z. 349, 6, and Brisbane 1390.

(a) Corr. for runs = 0″.37.

(b) Corr. for runs = 0″.37.

ZONE 98. MARCH 5. P. $D_o = -27°\,40'\,50''$—Continued.

No.	Mag.	I.	II.	III.	IV.	V.	VI.	VII.	T. (h. m. s.)	a_1 (s.)	a_2 (s.)	MICROMETER		r.	i (′ ″)	d_1 (″)	d_2 (″)	Mean Right Ascension, 1850.0 (h. m. s.)	Mean Declination, 1850.0 (° ′ ″)
50	7				15.			7.	7 16 14.86	−45.27	−1.15	IV,	4	45.857	−13 22.70	−23.90	−2.01	7 15 26.44	−27 54 38.61
51	7.8					44.			17 26.49	45.27	1.37	V,	3	23.583	36 42.95	24.21	4.82	16 39.85	28 18 1.98
52	7						5.		18 30.13	45.27	1.27	VI,	3	33.800	26 1.91	24.50	3.51	17 43.59	7 19.92
53	7							49.5	18 56.96	45.27	1.51	VII,	1	9.980	50 56.25	24.62	6.57	18 10.18	28 32 17.44
54	8.9							54.	20 1.72	45.28	1.14	VII,	4	46.835	12 20.62	24.92	1.89	19 15.30	27 53 37.43
55	8						36.		21 1.22	45.28	1.14	VI,	4	48.437	10 40.77	25.18	1.71	20 14.80	27 51 57.66
56	7				35.5				22 35.52	45.28	1.25	IV,	3	36.873	22 48.77	25.61	3.12	21 48.99	28 4 7.50
57	9						21.5		22 46.60	45.28	1.31	VI,	3	30.790	29 10.75	25.66	3.90	22 0.01	10 30.31
58	8		38.						25 13.07	45.29	1.53	II,	1	9.860	51 2.71	26.32	6.58	24 26.25	32 25.61
59	9			17.					25 17.03	45.29	1.52	III,	1	10.755	50 7.04	26.42	6.47	24 30.22	31 29.93
60	9						12.		25 37.03	45.29	1.47	VI,	2	15.935	44 43.41	26.43	5.81	24 50.27	26 5.65
61	9.10			14.					27 31.46	45.30	1.27	III,	3	35.540	24 12.19	26.95	3.30	26 44.89	5 32.44
62	8.9					4.			27 46.55	45.30	1.22	V,	3	40.510	19 1.07	27.01	2.68	27 0.03	0 20.76
63	9					56.			28 38.49	45.30	1.36	V,	3	26.790	33 21.59	27.25	4.40	27 51.83	14 43.24
64	9				49.5				29 49.55	45.31	1.32	IV,	3	31.095	28 51.36	27.57	3.86	29 2.92	10 12.79
65	5.6				26.			0.5	30	45.31									
66	9.10							51.	30 58.66	45.31	1.27	VII,	3	36.610	23 5.77	27.89	3.15	30 12.08	4 26.81
67	8				53.				32 53.04	45.32	1.46	IV,	2	18.035	42 31.68	28.40	5.54	32 6.26	28 23 55.62
68	7.8	21.	38.5	56.					35 13.33	45.32	1.15	III,	4	48.980	10 6.85	29.04	1.60	34 26.86	27 51 27.49
69	8	46.		21.					37 35.47	45.33	1.48	III,	4	17.440	43 9.02	29.70	5.62	36 51.66	28 24 34.34
70	4.5					14.5			38 14.52	45.33	1.27	IV,	3	37.640	22 0.77	29.86	3.02	37 27.92	3 23.65
71	5						9.		38 33.98	45.33	1.58	VI,	1	6.513	54 34.14	29.93	7.03	37 47.07	36 1.10
72	7	12.	29.5	47.					41 4.54	45.34	1.55	III,	1	9.515	51 25.07	30.62	6.64	40 17.65	28 32 52.33
73	9	8.5	26.	44.					43 1.02	45.34	1.24	III,	4	41.530	17 54.21	31.14	2.54	42 14.44	27 59 17.89
74	6					5.	22.		49 4.77	45.36	1.10	IV,	4	57.215	1 30.67	32.77	0.64	48 18.31	42 54.06
75	7						19.		50 1.57	45.36	1.20	V,	4	47.120	12 3.49	33.29	1.83	49 15.01	53 28.61
76	7						10.5		50 53.08	45.36	1.14	V,	4	53.180	5 43.54	33.26	1.13	50 6.58	47 7.93
77	7.8					12.			52 12.00	45.36	1.23	IV,	4	44.015	15 18.29	33.60	2.22	51 25.41	27 56 44.11
78	7	18.	35.	52.5					54 10.02	45.36	1.29	III,	4	39.455	20 4.41	34.13	2.80	53 23.37	28 1 31.34
79	8		53.5	11.					56 28.42	45.37	1.27	III,	4	41.270	18 10.58	34.75	2.56	55 41.78	27 59 37.89
80	9					2.5			57 2.49	45.37	1.20	IV,	4	48.110	11 1.53	34.90	1.75	56 15.92	52 28.18
81	8.9					12.			58 12.00	45.37	1.26	IV,	4	43.015	16 21.01	35.21	2.35	57 25.37	27 57 48.57
82	9.10						2.		7 59 27.13	45.37	1.35	VI,	3	33.907	25 55.20	35.55	3.49	7 58 40.41	28 7 24.24
83	9.10			23.					8 1 40.47	45.37	1.39	III,	3	29.700	30 18.44	36.13	4.04	8 0 53.71	28 11 48.61
84	8				20.				2 19.99	45.38	1.22	IV,	4	47.267	11 54.46	36.31	1.82	1 33.39	27 53 22.59
85	9			54.5	30.				5 29.71	45.38	1.33	IV,	3	37.270	22 24.11	37.14	2.97	4 43.00	28 3 54.22
86	7				41.5				6 41.53	45.38	1.61	IV,	1	9.082	51 52.49	37.45	6.71	5 54.54	28 33 26.65
87	8			3.	20.7				9 38.02	45.38	1.30	III,	4	41.165	18 17.10	38.24	2.57	8 51.34	27 59 47.91
88	9.10				49.				13 6.45	45.38	1.29	III,	4	42.157	17 14.88	38.62	2.44	10 19.78	58 45.94
89	9.10				59.				14 16.43	45.39	1.25	III,	4	47.183	11 59.67	39.45	1.84	13 29.79	53 30.96
90	8							45.	14 27.56	45.39	1.27	V,	4	44.580	14 42.85	39.50	2.15	13 40.90	27 56 14.50
91	8.9				42.				15 59.46	45.39	1.36	III,	3	36.083	23 38.07	39.90	3.22	15 12.71	28 5 11.19
92	7				24.	40.			16 40.75	45.39	1.39	IV,	3	32.590	27 17.57	40.07	3.66	15 53.97	8 51.30
93	8					27.			17 9.44	45.39	1.59	V,	1	12.730	48 3.70	40.20	6.23	16 22.46	29 40.13
94	7				8.	25.			18 25.26	−45.39	−1.59	IV,	1	13.150	47 37.21	−40.53	−6.19	8 17 38.28	−28 29 13.93
95	9							23.	8 25 48.21			VI,	4	45.830	−13 24.02				

CORRECTIONS.

Date.	Corr. of Clock.	Hourly rate.	m	n	c	Zenith Point.	Mic. Co.
1847.	h.　　s.	s.	s.	s.	s.	°　′　″	r.

REMARKS.

(98) 59. Transit over T, IV assumed as recorded over T, III.

INSTRUMENT READINGS.

Date.	CIRCLE.							Barom.	THERMOM.				
	A.	B.	C.	D.	E.	F.	Mean.		At.	Ex.	U.	L.	I.
1847. h. m.	°　′　″						″	in.	°	°	°	°	°

Zone 99. March 5. P. $D_0 = -27° 40' 50''$.

No.	Mag.	I.	II.	III.	IV.	V.	VI.	VII.	T.	a_1	a_2	Micrometer	r.	i	d_1	d_2	Mean Right Ascension, 1850.0	Mean Declination, 1850.0
									h. m. s.	s.	s.			′ ″	″	″	h. m. s.	° ′ ′
1	8.9	27.	. .	2.	. .	. .	. .	. .	10 26 19.42	. .	. .	III. 3	25.930	−34 14.02	−69.71	−4.54	. . .	−28 16 19.17
2	9	47.	. .	23.	. .	. .	. .	. .	29 39.95	. .	. .	III. 2	21.395	39 0.82	70.30	5.15	. . .	28 21 6.27
3	7	. .	. .	. .	21.	38.5	. .	. .	30 21.03	. .	. .	V. 4	41.870	17 32.62	70.42	2.44	. . .	27 59 35.48
4	8	. .	. .	. .	31.	. .	. .	. .	31 31.04	. .	. .	IV. 3	23.337	36 58.26	70.61	4.87	. . .	28 19 3.74
5	7	21.3	38.5	56.3	13.5	. .	. .	. .	37 13.61	. .	. .	IV. 3	25.827	34 21.77	71.58	4.55	. . .	16 27.90
6	9	. .	. .	. .	. .	39.	. .	. .	41 21.50	. .	. .	V. F.W.			72.26	4.00	. . .	
7	8	. .	. .	. .	. .	56.5	. .	. .	42 38.99	. .	. .	V. 3	23.970	36 18.60	72.48	4.80	. . .	18 25.88
8	8	. .	. .	1.	. .	. .	. .	. .	51 1.03	. .	. .	IV. 2	14.275	46 27.79	73.80	6.10	. . .	28 37.69
9	7	. .	. .	. .	47.	5.	. .	. .	10 51 47.24	. .	. .	V. 2	16.723	43 54.15	73.92	5.79	. . .	28 26 3.86
10	6.7	. .	36.	54.	11.	28.3	. .	. .	11 0 11.05	. .	. .	V. 4	46.517	−12 41.37	−75.18	−1.84	. . .	−27 54 48.39

Zone 100. March 10. C. $D_0 = -30° 11' 0''$.

No.	Mag.	I.	II.	III.	IV.	V.	VI.	VII.	T.	a_1	a_2	Micrometer	r.	i	d_1	d_2	Mean R. A.	Mean Dec.
1	9	. .	. .	. .	. .	37.2	55.	. .	6 58 19.30	+15.45	. .	V. 4	37.688	−22 0.09	−16.44	−2.85	. . .	−30 33 19.38
2	8	. .	. .	41.	59.1	16.8	. .	. .	6 59 55.97	15.45	. .	IV. 4	44.861	14 25.16	16.89	1.79	. . .	35 43.84
3	9	. .	. .	52.1	. .	. .	. .	3.7	7 1 10.03	15.45	. .	IV. 3	37.196	22 28.69	17.22	2.92	. . .	33 48.83
4	9.10	. .	. .	51.	. .	25.	. .	. .	3 7.99	15.45	. .	IV. 2	28.387	31 41.39	17.75	4.24	. . .	43 3.38
5	9	. .	. .	4.7	21.2	39.5	57.1	. .	4 21.67	15.45	. .	IV. 2	19.122	41 23.53	18.09	5.65	. . .	52 47.27
6	8	. .	. .	23.8	41.7	59.3	17.1	. .	5 1.49	15.46	. .	IV. 3	36.622	23 4.64	18.45	3.01	. . .	34 26.10
7	9	. .	. .	. .	12.	29.	. .	. .	7 11.56	15.46	. .	IV. 3	28.649	31 24.83	18.87	4.20	. . .	42 47.90
8	8.9	. .	. .	. .	. .	4.5	22.3	39.3	7 46.18	15.46	. .	V. 3	21.980	38 23.47	19.03	5.21	. . .	49 47.71
9	7	. .	. .	. .	18.2	. .	53.8	11.7	7 9 18.16	+15.46	. .	IV. 2	44.971	−14 18.26	−19.45	−1.77	. . .	−30 25 39.48

Zone 101. March 18. C. $D_0 = -30° 11' 0''$.

No.	Mag.	I.	II.	III.	IV.	V.	VI.	VII.	T.	a_1	a_2	Micrometer	r.	i	d_1	d_2	Mean R. A.	Mean Dec.
1	8	. .	24.	41.3	59.3	17.2	. .	. .	7 10 59.40	+9.38	+0.57	IV. 3	33.510	−26 19.92	−27.70	−3.47	7 11 9.35	−30 37 51.09
2	9	. .	29.2	. .	5.2	23.7	. .	. .	12 5.34	9.38	0.56	IV. 3	31.291	28 39.19	27.97	3.82	12 15.28	40 20.98
3	8	. .	. .	17.7	. .	53.2	10.4	. .	12 35.21	9.38	0.62	IV. 4	44.385	20 8.97	28.05	2.59	12 45.21	31 29.61
4	9	. .	. .	13.7	31.3	. .	. .	. .	13 13.57	9.34	0.65	IV. 3	50.321	8 43.01	30.73	0.99	23 23.56	20 14.73
5	7	. .	. .	. .	42.5	0.3	18.7	36.4	24 42.65	9.33	0.56	IV. 3	32.441	27 27.04	31.10	3.63	24 52.54	39 1.77
6	9	. .	58.2	16.4	34.	. .	. .	. .	30 34.17	9.31	0.47	IV. 2	13.094	47 41.85	32.56	6.59	30 43.95	59 21.00
7	8.9	. .	. .	. .	. .	. .	53.2	11.5	31 17.72	9.31	0.62	VI. 4	43.479	15 55.48	32.74	1.99	31 27.65	27 30.21
8	9	. .	. .	46.2	4.	. .	. .	. .	38 4.09	9.29	0.46	IV. 2	13.823	46 55.96	34.42	6.48	38 13.84	58 36.86
9	9	. .	. .	. .	. .	. .	40.	. .	38 4.17	9.29	0.49	VI. 2	20.489	39 57.73	34.42	5.44	38 13.95	51 37.59
10	8	. .	56.1	13.8	32.	49.8	7.1	. .	42 31.79	9.27	0.63	IV. 4	47.672	11 28.93	35.52	1.37	42 41.69	23 5.82
11	7.8	. .	33.1	50.7	8.3	26.4	44.2	. .	49 8.56	9.26	0.59	IV. 4	39.662	19 53.94	37.17	2.56	49 18.41	31 33.67
12	9	. .	. .	. .	30.2	. .	. .	. .	50 12.33	9.25	0.61	V. 4	44.721	14 33.87	37.44	1.81	50 22.19	26 13.12
13	8.9	. .	. .	. .	7.8	25.5	44.2	. .	53 7.99	9.25	0.62	IV. 4	45.855	13 22.82	38.16	1.64	53 17.86	25 2.62
14	9	. .	. .	. .	8.3	. .	44.5	. .	54 8.53	9.25	0.51	IV. 3	24.622	35 37.51	38.41	4.81	54 18.29	47 20.73
15	9	. .	. .	. .	39.2	55.	13.7	. .	55 55.34	9.24	0.53	IV. 3	28.478	31 35.67	38.87	4.23	55 5.11	43 18.77
16	8.9	. .	. .	. .	3.5	3.18	. .	36.2	56 42.01	9.24	0.51	V. 3	24.072	36 12.20	39.07	4.90	55 51.76	47 56.17
17	9	. .	. .	. .	22.7	40.7	. .	26.	7 59 22.66	9.24	0.63	IV. 4	48.234	10 53.82	39.74	1.28	7 59 32.53	22 34.84
18	9	. .	. .	. .	3.3	. .	. .	56.2	8 3 20.83	9.23	0.55	IV. 3	32.744	27 7.84	40.72	3.59	8 2 30.61	38 52.15
19	8.9	. .	14.	31.3	49.2	. .	. .	. .	8 49.37	9.22	0.62	IV. 4	46.791	12 24.13	42.10	1.49	8 59.21	24 7.72
20	8	. .	. .	6.2	24.2	42.1	. .	17.2	9 42.33	9.22	0.61	IV. 4	43.038	16 19.56	42.32	2.05	9 52.16	28 3.93
21	9	. .	. .	. .	45.	. .	. .	. .	9 44.99	9.22	0.63	IV. 4	48.657	10 27.22	42.33	1.23	9 54.84	22 10.78
22	8	. .	31.3	50.4	. .	. .	44.2	. .	8 56 7.96	9.21	0.61	IV. 4	45.413	13 50.79	53.96	1.70	8 56 17.78	25 46.45
23	9	. .	. .	52.1	. .	28.	. .	4.2	9 6 10.14	+9.23	+0.47	IV. 2	17.586	−42 59.93	−56.47	−5.90	9 6 19.84	−30 55 2.30

CORRECTIONS.

Date.	Corr. of Clock.	Hourly rate.	m	n	c	Zenith Point.	Mie. Co.
1847.	h. s.	s.	s.	s.	s.	° ′ ″	r.

INSTRUMENT READINGS.

	Date.	CIRCLE.							Barom.	THERMOM.				
		A.	B.	C.	D.	E.	F.	Mean.		At.	Ex.	U.	L.	l.
	1847. h. m.	° ′ ″						″	in.	°	°	°	°	°
Zone 100	Mar. 10, 7 0	69 32 26.1	41.1	28.9	37.7	26.5	33.2	32.25	30.100	50.2	46.6	49.0	48.5	50.0
	7 9										45.9			
Zone 101	Mar. 18, 7 10	69 32 35.0	50.1	37.5	45.1	35.0	40.1	40.47			46.4	48.5	45.0	42.5
	7 23	. .	. .	. .	. .	. .	. .	. .	30.152	46.6	46.1			
	7 42	. .	. .	. .	. .	. .	. .	. .			46.3			
	7 59	. .	. .	. .	. .	. .	. .	. .	30.160	46.5	45.9			

REMARKS.

Mar. 10, $7^h 10^m$. Interrupted by clouds.
Mar. 18. Hazy; night unfavorable; many stars doubtless obscured by the haze.

(100) 6. Transits over T.'s III, V, and VI assumed as 43ˢ.8, 19ˢ.3, and 37ˢ.8, respectively, and minutes as 6.

(101) 3. Micrometer reading assumed as 39ʳ.385, not 44ʳ.385.

(101) 15. Transit observation of T. III assumed as 37ˢ.2 instead of 39ˢ.2; and minutes as 54 instead of 55.

(101) 16. Minutes assumed as 55 instead of 56.

(101) 17. Transit across T. VII assumed at 16ˢ instead of 26ˢ.

(101) 18. Minutes assumed at 2 instead of 3.

ZONE 102. MARCH 22. P. $D_o = -28°\,18'\,40''$.

No.	Mag.	I.	II.	III.	IV.	V.	VI.	VII.	T. (h m s)	a_1	a_2	Mic.		r	i	d_1	d_2	Mean Right Ascension, 1850.0	Mean Declination, 1850.0
1	8		23.	41.					7 31 58.32	+7.77	+1.08	III.	4	53.580	−5 18.53	+0.60	−1.06	7 32 7.17	−28 24 0.19
2	7	38.3	56.	13.5					33 31.06	7.76	1.03	III.	3	27.830	32 15.71	0.98	4.27	33 39.85	51 0.96
3	9				47.3				33 47.35	7.76	1.02	IV.	3	23.833	36 26.89	1.06	4.79	33 56.13	55 12.74
4	9	51.	8.	25.5					36 43.18	7.75	1.08	III.	4	53.030	5 52.88	1.79	1.12	36 52.01	24 35.79
5	3		3.3	21.	38.3				37 38.43	7.74	1.05	IV.	4	42.173	17 13.87	2.02	2.45	37 47.22	35 58.34
6	9					18.			38 0.46	7.74	1.07	V.	4	47.930	11 12.57	2.11	1.75	38 9.27	29 56.43
7	8		34.	51.5	9.				40 9.05	7.74	1.06	IV.	4	45.190	14 4.72	2.64	2.08	40 17.85	28 32 49.44
8	9		20.						41 55.20	7.73	1.01	II.	2	18.730	41 47.49	3.08	5.46	42 3.94	29 0 36.03
9	9		9.						43 44.10	7.72	1.06	II.	4	44.197	15 6.74	3.53	2.20	43 52.88	28 33 52.47
10	7			55.	12.5				44 12.55	7.72	1.03	IV.	3	37.007	22 40.42	3.65	3.10	44 21.30	41 27.17
11	8	29.	46.3	4.					47 21.55	7.71	1.02	III.	3	28.615	31 26.59	4.44	4.18	47 30.28	50 15.21
12	9		34.		9.				49 9.06	7.70	1.06	IV.	4	48.165	10 58.08	4.87	1.70	49 17.82	29 44.65
13	9				53.				50 53.05	7.70	1.02	IV.	3	28.225	31 51.49	5.31	4.23	51 1.77	50 41.03
14	9							47.	50 54.27	7.70	1.01	VII.	3	26.065	34 7.21	5.31	4.50	51 2.98	52 57.02
15	8			54.	11.5				53 11.56	7.70	1.00	IV.	3	22.540	37 48.22	5.88	4.96	53 20.26	28 56 39.06
16	7.8				55.3	13.			53 55.34	7.69	0.99	V.	2	13.310	47 28.35	6.05	6.16	54 4.02	29 6 20.56
17	7					16.5			54 58.91	7.69	1.02	V.	3	33.700	26 8.13	6.32	3.53	55 7.62	28 44 57.98
18	8			48.7					56 6.26	7.68	1.02	III.	3	33.030	26 49.53	6.60	3.62	56 14.96	45 39.75
19	9				35.				56 35.05	7.68	1.01	IV.	3	29.190	30 50.95	6.73	4.10	56 43.74	28 49 41.78
20	8		12.						57 29.58	7.68	0.98	III.	2	14.410	41 5.49	6.95	5.37	57 38.24	59 57.81
21	9				11.5			4.4	7 57 51.34	7.68	1.02	IV.	3	33.557	26 16.97	7.05	3.55	7 58 0.04	28 45 7.57
22	6	50.3	8.	25.7	43.				8 0 43.16	7.67	0.98	IV.	2	16.810	43 48.49	7.74	5.71	8 0 51.81	29 2 41.94
23	9.10	52.		27.					2 44.61	7.67	1.01	III.	3	30.553	29 25.05	8.25	3.93	2 53.29	29 48 17.23
24	9				26.				3 26.05	7.67	1.00	IV.	3	27.450	32 40.17	8.41	4.32	3 34.72	29 51 32.90
25	9					32.			4 14.36	7.67	0.99	V.	2	18.910	41 36.77	8.62	5.43	4 23.02	29 0 30.82
26	7				46.3	3.5			5 46.13	7.66	1.05	IV.	4	49.737	9 19.37	8.99	1.50	5 54.84	29 28 9.86
27	9					54.			7 54.02	7.66	1.04	V.	4	43.006	16 21.45	9.49	2.33	8 2.72	35 13.27
28	9					2.			8 44.44	7.66	1.03	V.	4	41.477	17 57.47	9.73	2.53	8 53.13	36 50.73
29	9							1.	9 25.95	7.65	1.02	VI.	3	36.405	23 18.68	9.90	3.18	9 34.62	42 11.76
30	7			34.3	51.7	9.2			11 9.30	7.65	1.02	IV.	3	38.350	21 16.36	10.31	2.94	11 17.97	28 40 9.61
31	6							1.	11 25.76	7.65	0.95	VI.	1	6.160	54 56.25	10.38	7.10	11 34.36	29 13 53.73
32	7					54.	12.		12 36.59	7.65	0.97	V.	2	17.290	43 18.63	10.68	5.65	12 45.21	29 2 14.96
33	7					37.5			13 39.89	7.65	0.99	V.	3	26.420	33 45.05	10.93	4.46	13 48.53	28 52 40.44
34	7						37.7		14 2.52	7.64	0.97	VI.	2	15.407	45 16.74	11.03	5.89	14 11.13	29 4 13.66
35	7		39.5	57.					16 14.58	7.64	1.04	III.	4	48.393	10 43.84	11.57	1.66	16 23.26	28 29 37.07
36	6					35.			16 17.31	7.64	0.95	V.	1	7.110	53 56.54	11.58	6.99	16 25.90	29 12 55.11
37	6			12.	30.		4.5		17 29.68	7.64	1.04	IV.	4	48.670	10 26.35	11.88	1.63	17 38.36	28 29 19.86
38	8			26.5		2.			18 44.25	7.63	1.04	V.	4	49.703	9 21.44	12.19	1.50	18 52.92	28 15.13
39	6	39.	56.3	14.	31.5				20 31.52	7.63	1.00	IV.	3	35.173	24 35.60	12.61	3.34	20 40.15	43 31.55
40	9					40.			21 22.37	7.63	0.98	V.	2	23.370	36 57.06	12.82	4.85	21 30.98	55 54.73
41	8.9	48.7		24.	41.3				25 41.43	7.62	0.98	IV.	3	27.530	32 35.09	13.87	4.31	25 50.03	51 33.27
42	8.9		16.	34.					26 51.37	7.62	0.98	III.	3	25.933	34 14.73	14.15	4.52	26 59.97	53 13.40
43	8		30.5		5.5				28 5.56	7.62	1.02	IV.	4	43.797	15 31.90	14.45	2.24	28 14.20	34 28.59
44	7				42.5				28 42.47	7.62	1.04	IV.	4	54.583	4 15.64	14.61	0.90	28 51.13	28 23 11.15
45	7							44.3	29 9.11	7.62	0.96	VI.	2	13.995	41 31.40	14.71	5.46	29 17.69	29 0 31.57
46	7	45.	2.3	20.3					32 37.65	7.62	0.98	III.	3	29.960	30 2.07	15.56	4.00	32 46.25	28 49 1.63
47	7				0.	17.			32 59.73	7.62	0.98	IV.	3	32.450	27 26.47	15.64	3.68	33 8.33	28 46 25.79
48	3				39.	56.			33 21.10	7.62	0.96	VI.	2	17.793	42 46.74	15.72	5.50	33 29.68	29 1 48.05
49	9					8.3			8 34 33.32	+7.61	+1.01	VI.	4	47.060	−12 7.00	−15.99	−1.84	8 34 41.94	−28 31 4.83

CORRECTIONS.

Date.	Corr. of Clock.	Hourly rate.	m	n	c	Zenith Point.	Mic. Co.
1847.	h.	s.	s.	s.	s.	s.	° ' "	r.

INSTRUMENT READINGS.

Date.		A.	B.	C.	D.	E.	F.	Mean.	Barom.	At.	Ex.	U.	L.	I.
	1847. h. m.	° ' "						"	in.	°	°	°	°	°
Zone 102	Mar. 22, 7 30	67 39 59.3	73.0	59.6	68.5	58.2	66.4	64.17	29.867	52.0	48.7	52.0	50.5	
	8 0								29.868	51.1	47.9			
	9 8								29.888	49.7	45.0	50.5	49.5	52.0

REMARKS.

March 22. $9^h\,9^m$, cloudy.

(102) 20. Micrometer reading assumed as $19^r.410$, not $14^r.410$.
(102) 21. Transit over T. IV rejected.
(102) 33. Transit over T. V assumed as $57^s.5$ instead of $37^s.5$.
(102) 45. Micrometer reading assumed as $18^r.995$, not $13^r.995$.

ZONE 102. MARCH 22. P. $D_s = -28° 18' 40''$—Continued.

No.	Mag.	I.	II.	III.	IV.	V.	VI.	VII.	T. (h. m. s.)	a_1 (s.)	a_4 (s.)	MICROMETER		r.	i	d_1	d_2	Mean Right Ascension, 1850.0. (h. m. s.)	Mean Declination, 1850.0. (° ' ")
50	8			5.7	23.	40.7			8 36 40.75	+ 7.61	+0.95	IV.	2	15.233	−40 13.96	−16.52	−5.31	8 36 49.31	−28 59 15.79
51	9					48.			37 30.47	7.61	1.02	V.	4	49.075	10 0.89	16.72	1.58	37 39.10	28 59.19
52	8.9						49.7		38 14.69	7.61	1.01	VI.	4	43.583	15 45.13	16.90	2.26	38 23.31	28 34 44.29
53	7			54.					40 11.60	7.61	0.93	III.	1	7.390	53 38.46	17.36	6.95	40 20.14	29 12 42.77
54	7					30.5	48.		40 12.81	7.61	0.94	V.	1	9.090	51 52.18	17.37	6.72	40 21.36	29 10 56.27
55	5.6	44.	1.5	19.	36.5				43 36.62	7.61	0.97	IV.	3	24.840	35 23.70	18.17	4.66	43 45.20	28 54 26.53
56	9					14.			43 56.42	7.61	0.98	V.	3	35.970	23 45.72	18.25	3.24	44 5.01	42 47.21
57	8				21.3	39.			45 21.37	7.61	0.96	IV.	3	25.160	35 3.81	18.58	4.62	45 29.94	54 7.01
58	8.9						39.		46 4.05	7.61	1.02	VI.	4	53.265	5 38.03	18.75	1.09	46 12.68	24 37.87
59	7.8	58.5	16.	33.3					49 51.07	7.61	0.96	III.	3	26.497	33 39.53	19.65	4.41	49 59.64	52 43.62
60	7					18.			50 0.41	7.61	0.98	V.	3	32.624	27 15.69	19.69	3.66	50 9.00	28 46 19.04
61	9		50.	7.5					52 25.15	7.61	0.94	III.	2	17.085	43 31.18	20.26	5.68	52 33.70	29 2 37.12
62	9					44.			52 26.43	7.61	0.98	V.	3	36.960	22 43.55	20.26	3.09	52 35.02	28 41 46.90
63	6.7			0.5	17.	34.5			8 58 34.87	7.61	1.03	IV.	4	52.650	6 16.84	21.69	1.16	8 58 43.51	25 19.69
64	8.9	25.5	43.	0.3					9 0 18.01	7.61	0.97	III.	3	37.273	22 23.48	22.09	3.05	9 0 26.59	28 41 28.62
65	6.7		28.3	16.	3.5				3 3.57	7.61	0.92	IV.	1	7.503	53 31.67	22.71	6.95	3 12.10	29 12 41.33
66	8.9		54.5	12.					6 29.59	7.61	0.97	III.	3	33.207	26 38.55	23.50	3.58	6 38.17	28 45 45.63
67	6				48.5	6.			6 48.45	7.61	0.93	IV.	2	16.845	43 46.30	23.57	5.72	6 56.99	29 2 55.50
68	9					52.			9 8 16.91	+ 7.61	+0.96	VI.	3	29.137	−30 54.59	−23.90	−4.12	9 8 25.48	−28 50 2.61

ZONE 103. MARCH 24. C. $D_s = -29° 33' 50''$.

No.	Mag.	I.	II.	III.	IV.	V.	VI.	VII.	T. (h. m. s.)	a_1 (s.)	a_4 (s.)	MICROMETER		r.	i	d_1	d_2	Mean Right Ascension, 1850.0. (h. m. s.)	Mean Declination, 1850.0. (° ' ")
1	9		5.3		41.3	59.	17.		7 53 41.22	+ 8.09	+0.83	IV.	3	33.477	−26 21.98	−4.76	−3.52	7 53 50.14	−30 0 20.26
2	9		13.3	31.		6.7	24.		53 48.76	8.09	0.84	IV.	3	35.618	24 7.61	4.80	3.22	53 57.69	29 58 5.63
3	9				15.	3.	21.		55 27.40	8.08	0.78	V.	1	23.529	36 46.03	5.23	4.93	55 36.26	30 10 46.19
4	9			28.2	46.	4.2	22.		55 28.40	8.08	0.77	IV.	1	21.922	38 26.48	5.15	5.15	55 37.25	30 12 26.86
5	9	52.2	10.			3.5			7 59 27.84	8.07	0.85	IV.	3	37.534	22 7.48	6.27	2.94	7 59 36.76	29 56 6.69
6	8	20.	37.5	55.5	13.6	31.2			8 2 55.58	8.06	0.86	IV.	3	40.391	19 8.35	7.14	2.53	8 3 4.50	53 8.02
7	9	56.2	14.	32.	49.4				4 31.78	8.05	0.91	IV.	4	50.606	8 25.01	7.55	1.11	4 40.74	42 23.67
8	9		7.	24.5	42.8	1.1	18.0		5 42.70	8.05	0.90	IV.	4	47.155	12 1.42	7.87	1.59	5 51.65	46 0.88
9	9.10				16.2				5 40.74	8.05	0.86	IV.	3	40.756	18 45.58	7.86	2.49	5 49.65	29 52 45.93
10	9			33.	50.7				5 50.77	8.04	0.71	IV.	2	10.814	50 4.84	8.66	6.80	5 59.52	30 24 10.30
11	9				6.2	24.	41.5		8 48.36	8.04	0.84	V.	4	35.854	23 49.99	8.65	3.17	8 57.24	29 57 51.81
12	9				10.				9 34.45	8.04	0.70	VI.	3	26.852	33 17.77	8.85	4.44	9 43.28	30 7 21.06
13	9					13.7	32.		9 38.38	8.04	0.79	VI.	3	25.621	34 35.14	8.87	4.62	9 47.21	30 8 38.63
14	9					17.7			11 42.20	8.04	0.83	VI.	3	31.231	25 34.99	9.39	3.41	11 51.07	29 59 37.79
15	9.10					34.		50.8	11 58.04	8.04	0.87	VI.	3	41.728	17 44.61	9.45	2.35	12 6.95	29 51 46.41
16	8		42.2	0.0	18.				17 17.90	8.03	0.74	IV.	2	15.518	45 9.78	10.78	6.09	17 26.67	30 19 16.65
17	8		51.3		27.2	45.5	3.		17 27.33	8.03	0.86	IV.	4	38.941	20 36.46	10.82	2.73	17 36.22	29 54 40.01
18	9.10			1.3	19.2				21 19.17	8.02	0.80	IV.	3	25.412	34 48.05	11.78	4.65	21 27.99	30 8 54.48
19	9			7.6	25.3	43.			22 43.14	8.02	0.74	IV.	2	13.699	47 3.83	12.11	6.36	22 51.99	30 21 12.30
20	9				1.	19.3			23 1.27	8.02	0.87	IV.	4	41.308	18 8.26	12.19	2.40	23 10.16	29 52 12.85
21	8.9					53.	10.6		23 35.20	8.02	0.89	IV.	4	43.792	15 32.09	12.33	2.03	23 44.11	49 36.45
22	9.10			59.	17.		52.		27 16.78	8.01	0.86	IV.	3	37.753	21 53.62	13.22	2.93	27 25.65	29 55 59.76
23	10			13.8			7.2		28 31.64	8.01	0.82	IV.	3	31.131	28 49.11	13.53	3.84	28 40.47	30 2 56.48
24	8.9				56.2	14.8	31.5		29 56.40	8.01	0.82	IV.	3	29.352	30 40.85	13.87	4.10	30 5.23	48.82
25	8.9					9.2	27.		30 51.42	8.01	0.80	V.	3	25.762	34 26.10	14.09	4.61	31 0.23	30 8 34.80
26	8.9							7.	8 31 13.68	+ 8.00	+0.85	VII.	3	35.212	−24 33.39	−14.18	−3.26	8 31 22.53	−29 58 40.83

CORRECTIONS.

Date.	Corr. of Clock.	Hourly rate.	m	n	c	Zenith Point.	Mic. Co.
1847.	h. s.	s.	s.	s.	s.	° ' "	r.

REMARKS.

(102) 50. Micrometer reading assumed as 20r.233, not 15r.233.

March 24. Moon bright; a light mist over the river and in the valley.

INSTRUMENT READINGS.

	Date.	CIRCLE.							Barom.	THERMOM.				
		A.	B.	C.	D.	E.	F.	Mean.	In.	At.	Ex.	U.	L.	I.
Zone 103	1847. Mar. 24, 7 50	68 54 59.2	72.1	60.5	69.8	57.5	66.8	64.32				52.7	51.5	52.5
	8 2								30.002	52.4	46.9			
	8 21										45.1			
	8 40										44.2			
	9 0	59.0	72.1	60.0	69.1	58.0	65.9	64.02				51.3	49.7	
	9 3								30.004	50.5	43.1			
	9 40								30.008	49.9	42.2			
	10 0	58.1	72.4	60.1	70.0	57.4	65.9	63.98			41.2	49.5	46.5	
	10 19								30.008	49.5	40.5			

ZONE 103. MARCH 24. C. $D = -29°\ 33'\ 50''$—Continued.

SECONDS OF TRANSIT.

No.	Mag.	I.	II.	III.	IV.	V.	VI.	VII.
27	9	. .	. .	. .	. .	51.	9.5	25.3
28	8,9	. .	5.7	23.1	41.5	59.	16.5	. .
29	8	. .	. .	. .	. .	59.7	17.3	. .
30	9,10	. .	15.6	33.4	51.	. .	. .	. .
31	9,10	. .	. .	57.	. .	. .	. .	. .
32	9	. .	. .	. .	40.1	58.	15.8	. .
33	8,9	. .	. .	. .	52.5	9.8	27.8	. .
34	9	. .	37.8	55.6	13.	. .	43.2	. .
35	9	. .	. .	6.5	. .	42.5	. .	. .
36	9	. .	. .	32.	49.3	. .	25.	. .
37	9	. .	. .	40.7	59.3	16.5	. .	. .
38	9	. .	. .	. .	10.	27.2	45.2	3.5
39	7	. .	50.3	8.2	26.	43.5	1.4	. .
40	8,9	. .	. .	49.	6.2	24.4	42.2	. .
41	9	. .	45.3	3.	20.7	. .	. .	. .
42	8,9	. .	. .	. .	. .	54.2	12.1	30.
43	8,9	. .	. .	. .	9.5	27.2	44.6	. .
44	10	. .	. .	58.7	. .	35.5	. .	. .
45	9,10	. .	42.	. .	19.3	. .	55.	. .
46	9	. .	. .	. .	47.	. .	22.7	. .
47	9,10	. .	41.3	58.3	16.5	. .	. .	. .
48	8,9	. .	53.	10.7	28.	46.	. .	. .
49	9	. .	. .	. .	40.2	58.	15.5	. .
50	8,9	. .	51.8	9.5	27.2	45.	3.	. .
51	9	. .	. .	39.	56.2	14.1	. .	. .
52	9	. .	. .	. .	47.	. .	23.	. .
53	7	. .	. .	40.2	58.1	15.9	33.6	. .
54	9,10	. .	. .	46.	. .	. .	. .	. .
55	9,10	. .	. .	. .	. .	52.5	. .	28.
56	9	. .	9.	. .	44.7	. .	20.5	. .
57	8,9	. .	43.	1.	18.7	36.	. .	. .
58	9	. .	55.2	13.	. .	48.7	. .	. .
59	9	. .	11.0	. .	46.3	4.6	. .	. .
60	9	. .	. .	30.	48.	6.3	. .	. .
61	9	. .	. .	3.	20.3	38.	. .	. .
62	9	. .	5.8	23.2	41.8	59.5	. .	. .
63	9	. .	. .	40.1	. .	15.5	33.2	. .
64	9	. .	16.5	34.2	52.	9.6	. .	. .
65	9	. .	. .	. .	53.2	11.	. .	. .
66	9	. .	43.6	1.3	10.5	. .	. .	. .
67	4	. .	33.	51.	8.6	26.4	44.2	. .
68	9	. .	. .	58.	. .	50.	. .	. .
69	7	. .	56.5	. .	51.	. .	25.4	. .
70	9	. .	. .	59.	. .	34.	. .	. .
71	9	. .	. .	. .	. .	59.2	17.	. .
72	8,9	. .	. .	10.1	46.	. .	22.	. .
73	9	. .	. .	12.	. .	47.5	. .	23.2
74	9	. .	. .	. .	43.	1.	19.	. .
75	8,9	. .	10.8	28.6	40.6	2.	. .	. .

No.	Mag.	T. (h. m. s.)	n_1 (s.)	a_1 (s.)	MICROMETER.		r.	i (′ ″)	d_1 (″)	d_2 (″)	Mean Right Ascension, 1850.0 (h. m. s.)	Mean Declination, 1850.0 (° ′ ″)
27	9	8 32 33.10	+8.00	+0.88	V.	4	41.761	−17 39.47	−14.50	−2.34	8 32 41.98	−29 51 46.31
28	8,9	37 41.19	8.00	0.93	IV.	4	51.051	7 57.04	15.72	1.03	37 50.12	29 42 3.79
29	8	38 41.72	8.00	0.71	V.	2	8.985	51 59.77	15.94	7.05	38 50.43	30 26 12.76
30	9,10	40 51.11	8.00	0.86	IV.	4	38.161	21 25.52	16.46	2.83	40 59.97	29 55 34.81
31	9,10	42 14.73	8.00	0.92	III.	4	49.706	10 24.03	16.79	1.35	42 23.65	44 32.17
32	9	42 40.26	8.00	0.94	IV.	4	53.192	5 42.92	16.89	0.72	42 49.20	39 50.53
33	8,9	43 52.30	8.00	0.88	IV.	3	42.032	17 25.23	17.18	2.30	44 1.18	51 34.71
34	9	49 13.12	7.99	0.86	IV.	3	36.699	22 59.75	18.44	3.05	49 21.97	29 57 11.24
35	9	50 24.49	7.99	0.81	IV.	3	26.495	33 40.04	18.72	4.50	50 33.29	30 7 53.26
36	9	51 49.50	7.99	0.73	IV.	2	11.579	49 16.94	19.06	6.69	51 58.22	23 32.69
37	9	54 58.84	7.99	0.82	IV.	3	27.127	33 0.32	19.80	4.40	55 7.65	7 14.52
38	9	8 56 9.71	7.99	0.72	IV.	2	9.478	51 28.89	19.84	6.99	8 56 18.42	30 25 45.72
39	7	9 3 25.90	7.99	0.92	IV.	4	48.061	10 55.33	21.79	1.41	9 3 34.81	29 45 11.53
40	8,9	31 6.58	8.03	0.84	IV.	3	32.754	26 4.47	27.66	3.44	31 15.45	30 0 25.57
41	9	33 20.76	8.03	0.91	IV.	4	44.226	15 5.18	28.12	1.95	33 29.70	29 49 25.25
42	8,9	33 36.48	8.03	0.79	V.	3	20.165	40 17.45	28.17	5.44	33 45.30	30 14 41.06
43	8,9	35 9.40	8.03	0.97	IV.	4	55.760	3 1.72	28.47	0.33	35 18.40	29 37 20.52
44	10	37 17.10	8.04	0.96	IV.	4	54.347	4 30.56	28.91	0.52	37 26.10	29 38 49.99
45	9,10	40 19.38	8.04	0.78	IV.	2	18.145	42 24.85	29.57	5.74	40 28.20	30 16 50.16
46	9	41 47.16	8.05	0.97	IV.	4	55.522	3 16.82	29.86	0.35	41 56.18	29 37 37.03
47	9,10	44 16.53	8.05	0.80	IV.	2	20.688	39 45.18	30.38	5.37	44 25.38	30 14 10.93
48	8,9	49 28.34	8.07	0.76	IV.	2	12.371	48 27.36	31.44	6.59	49 37.17	22 55.39
49	9	49 40.12	8.07	0.82	IV.	3	24.816	35 25.20	31.46	4.76	49 49.01	30 9 51.44
50	8,9	52 27.31	8.08	0.88	IV.	3	35.708	24 1.91	32.05	3.20	52 36.27	29 58 27.16
51	9	53 56.44	8.08	0.85	IV.	3	30.631	29 20.48	32.34	3.91	53 5.37	30 3 46.73
52	9	47.26	8.08	0.84	IV.	3	29.511	30 30.81	32.31	4.07	53 56.18	30 4 57.19
53	7	55 58.09	8.09	0.91	IV.	4	42.420	16 58.45	32.74	2.22	56 7.09	29 51 23.41
54	9,10	58 3.75	8.09	0.92	III.	4	44.410	14 53.64	33.16	1.96	58 12.76	49 18.76
55	9,10	9 58 34.73	8.10	0.92	V.	4	43.319	16 2.01	33.26	2.12	9 58 43.75	29 50 27.39
56	9	10 1 44.77	8.10	0.77	IV.	2	13.087	47 42.29	33.88	6.49	10 1 53.64	30 22 12.65
57	8,9	3 18.58	8.11	0.82	IV.	3	24.975	35 15.28	34.17	4.73	3 27.51	30 9 44.18
58	9	6 30.81	8.12	0.96	IV.	4	52.038	6 55.15	34.77	0.84	6 39.89	29 41 20.76
59	9	7 46.57	8.13		IV.	.	F.W.	. . .	35.01	4.00	7	30
60	9	8 48.07	8.13	0.74	IV.	2	8.128	52 53.58	35.19	7.24	8 56.94	27 26.01
61	9	10 2.65	8.14	0.82	IV.	3	24.219	36 2.85	35.43	4.85	10 11.61	10 33.13
62	9	12 41.33	8.15	0.80	IV.	3	20.244	40 12.29	35.90	5.43	12 50.28	30 14 43.62
63	9	14 57.77	8.15	0.90	IV.	4	38.269	21 18.81	36.30	2.80	15 6.82	29 55 47.91
64	9	15 34.21	8.16	0.91	IV.	4	39.006	19 35.94	36.40	2.56	15 43.28	29 54 4.90
65	9	16 35.41	8.16	0.83	V.	4	24.640	35 36.63	36.59	4.78	16 44.40	30 10 8.00
66	9	19 19.23	8.17	0.91	IV.	4	41.728	17 41.72	37.08	2.32	19 28.31	29 52 11.12
67	4	21 8.65	8.18	0.79	IV.	4	16.831	43 46.30	37.39	5.94	20 17.61	30 18 19.63
68	9	22 15.17	8.18	0.94	IV.	4	47.228	11 56.91	37.58	1.52	22 24.20	29 46 26.01
69	7	22 32.46	8.18	0.92	IV.	4	43.404	15 56.73	37.63	2.09	22 41.56	50 26.45
70	9	33 16.50	8.24	0.95	IV.	3	48.536	10 34.87	39.41	1.35	34 25.60	45 5.63
71	9	34 23.70	8.24	0.89	VI.	3	36.191	23 32.05	39.59	3.11	34 32.83	29 58 4.75
72	8,9	36 28.24	8.25	0.86	IV.	3	29.681	30 20.02	39.91	4.05	36 37.35	30 4 53.98
73	9	36 29.73	8.25	0.79	VI.	2	16.828	43 47.31	39.92	5.95	36 38.77	18 23.18
74	9	38 43.24	8.26	0.86	IV.	3	30.491	29 29.32	40.27	3.93	38 52.36	4 3.52
75	8,9	10 41 46.36	+8.28	+0.81	IV.	2	19.270	−41 14.30	−40.74	−5.59	10 41 55.45	−30 15 50.67

CORRECTIONS.

Date.	Corr. of Clock.	Hourly rate.	m	n	ε	Zenith Point.	Mic. Co.
1847.	h.	s.	s.	s.	s.	″	r.

REMARKS.

(103) 40. Micrometer reading assumed as 33ʳ.754, not 32ʳ.754.

(103) 51. 53ᵈ assumed to belong to next star; this assumed the same as preceding. Differs 1″ in d from Arg. Z. 363, 79.

(103) 67. Minutes assumed as 20 instead of 21.

(103) 70. Minutes assumed as 34 instead of 33.

INSTRUMENT READINGS.

Date.	A.	B.	C.	D.	E.	F.	Mean.	Barom. (in.)	At.	Ex.	U.	L.	I.
Zone 103　1847. Mar. 24. 10 41 (h. m.)										39.9			
11 0	68 54 57.5	72.4	50.0	70.6	56.9	65.1	63.75	30.016	49.0	39.5	49.0	48.5	
11 20										39.9			
11 30								30.008	48.0	39.7			
12 0	57.2	72.5	59.8	70.1	57.0	65.5	63.68	30.008	48.0	39.1	47.0	46.5	

ZONE 103. MARCH 24. C. $D_0 = -29°\ 33'\ 50''$—Continued.

No.	Mag.	I.	II.	III.	IV.	V.	VI.	VII.	T.	a_1	a_2	MICROMETER		r	i	d_1	d_2	Mean Right Ascension, 1850.0	Mean Declination, 1850.0
									h. m. s.	s.	s.			r.	′ ″	″	″	h. m. s.	° ′ ″
76	8.9				9.5	27.2			10 42 51.72 +	+8.28	+0.89	IV.	3	36.770	−22 55.23	−40.80	−3.03	10 42 0.89	−29 57 29.06
77	9					35.2			42 17.43	8.28	0.92	V.	4	42.967	16 23.89	40.83	2.14	42 26.63	29 50 56.86
78	9		23.	41.1	59.	16.9			46 58.91	8.30	0.79	IV.	2	14.461	46 16.11	41.53	6.30	47 8.00	30 20 53.94
79	10				59.?				47 59.00	8.31	0.94	IV.	2	44.658	14 41.47	41.68	1.88	48 8.25	29 49 15.03
80	8.9			19.	37.		12.8		49 36.99	8.32	0.77	IV.	2	11.338	49 32.20	41.92	6.77	49 46.08	30 24 10.89
81	9		37.	54.5	12.5	30.2			57 12.45	8.36	0.88	IV.	3	32.452	27 26.35	42.98	3.66	57 21.69	30 2 2.99
82	8.9				51.5	9.	27.		57 51.46	8.37	1.00	IV.	4	55.665	3 7.73	43.06	0.33	58 0.83	29 37 41.12
83	8			13.	30.9	48.2	6.		10 59 30.67	8.37	0.97	IV.	4	49.122	0 58.07	43.29	1.26	10 59 40.01	44 32.62
84	9.10					39.2			11 1 21.41	8.38	0.90	V.	3	36.772	22 55.35	43.52	3.03	11 1 30.69	29 57 31.90
85	9				36.7			0.5	5 36.87	8.41	0.80	IV.	2	16.198	44 27.11	44.03	6.06	5 46.06	30 19 7.20
86	9.10				38.?				7 38.05	8.43	0.83	IV.	3	21.735	38 38.50	44.28	5.24	7 47.31	13 18.11
87	9				27.	45.	2.6		8 27.11	8.43	0.88	IV.	3	32.679	27 11.92	44.37	3.62	8 36.42	1 49.91
88	9		2.5	20.3	38.3		13.8		11 38.19	8.45	0.84	IV.	3	23.576	36 43.21	44.74	4.96	11 47.48	11 22.91
89	9		27.3	44.7	2.5		38.2		15 2.64	8.47	0.87	IV.	3	29.871	30 8.03	45.12	4.02	15 11.08	4 47.17
90	9		55.2	13.	30.7				15 30.76	8.47	0.68	IV.	3	30.306	29 40.99	45.17	3.96	15 40.11	30 4 20.12
91	9.10			1.1?					20 18.82	8.51	0.99	III.	4	53.185	5 43.28	45.71	0.65	20 28.32	29 40 19.64
92	9						13.5		20 37.84	8.51	0.78	VI.	2	10.850	50 2.52	45.74	6.78	20 47.13	30 24 45.04
93	9.10		43.	1.2					23 18.73	8.53	0.99	III.	4	52.152	6 48.07	46.03	0.77	23 28.25	29 41 24.87
94	9.10				58.?		33.5		23 58.05	8.53	0.97	IV.	4	49.754	9 18.31	46.11	1.11	24 7.55	29 43 55.53
95	5			2.	20.1	38.	55.4		25 19.98	8.54	0.83	IV.	2	19.611	40 52.84	46.26	5.56	25 29.35	30 15 34.66
96	8.9		53.	10.2	28.	46.			27 28.19	8.56	0.93	IV.	4	40.384	19 6.21	46.49	2.47	27 37.68	29 53 45.17
97	8.9		34.9	52.6	10.7	28.	46.3		30 10.54	8.58	0.79	IV.	2	12.378	48 26.92	46.79	6.65	30 19.91	30 23 10.36
98	9				9.	26.2			31 26.52	8.58	0.89	IV.	3	31.733	28 11.27	46.93	3.76	31 35.99	30 2 51.96
99	8.9					41.	58.5	16.2	32 23.15	8.59	1.00	V.	4	54.559	4 17.08	47.04	0.47	32 32.74	29 38 54.59
100	9			32.		7.8			35 49.88	8.62	0.85	IV.	3	23.540	30 45.47	47.41	4.97	35 59.35	30 11 27.85
101	9			23.	41.1	58.8			37 58.77	8.63	0.87	IV.	3	27.436	32 41.05	47.65	4.37	38 8.27	7 23.07
102	9			17.	35.	52.2	10.3	28.1	38 52.53	8.64	0.88	IV.	3	29.035	31 0.54	47.74	4.15	39 2.05	5 42.43
103	8.9						19.7	37.	39 43.76	8.65	0.78	VI.	2	10.362	50 33.40	47.64	6.95	39 53.19	30 25 18.19
104	9				32.	49.2	7.		42 32.00	8.67	0.95	IV.	4	43.927	15 23.74	48.14	1.95	42 41.62	29 50 3.83
105	7			39.6	57.2	15.3	33.	50.5	43 57.36	8.68	0.91	IV.	3	35.192	24 34.40	48.25	3.23	44 6.95	29 59 15.88
106	9			49.2		25.2		1.	46 25.16	8.70	0.89	IV.	3	30.332	29 39.36	48.49	3.95	46 34.75	30 4 21.80
107	9			1.	18.7				48 36.59	8.71	0.81	III.	2	14.241	46 29.73	48.69	6.37	48 46.11	21 14.79
108	9.10					4.?			49 46.16	8.72	0.84	V.	3	21.638	38 45.01	48.71	5.25	48 55.72	30 13 28.97
109	9.10				39.7				51 57.44	8.74	0.98	III.	4	48.006	11 7.93	49.01	1.39	52 7.16	29 45 48.33
110	9		0.	17.5	35.2	53.2	10.8		52 35.36	8.75	0.98	IV.	4	47.821	11 19.53	49.06	1.40	52 45.09	45 59.99
111	9		47.5	5.7	23.			59.	54 23.27	8.76	0.98	IV.	4	47.601	11 33.46	49.22	1.41	54 33.01	29 46 14.09
112	9			7.2	25.2	43.2	0.7	18.6	56 42.98	8.78	0.81	IV.	2	14.428	46 18.24	49.43	6.35	56 52.57	30 21 4.02
113	9.10				0.	18.		54.	58 18.09	8.79	0.86	IV.	3	23.532	36 45.97	49.58	4.97	58 27.74	11 30.52
114	9.10					46.		22.?	11 58 28.39	8.79	0.86	V.	3	24.600	35 39.14	49.59	4.81	11 58 38.04	10 23.54
115	9							1.3	12 0 7.84	8.81	0.83	VII.	2	17.009	43 35.76	49.74	5.95	12 0 17.48	30 18 21.45
116	9			12.	29.5	47.4		40.7	12 3 47.42 +	+8.84	+0.98	IV.	4	47.742	−11 24.48	−50.05	−1.39	12 3 57.24	−29 46 5.92

CORRECTIONS.

Date.	Corr. of Clock.	Hourly rate.	m	n	c	Zenith Point.	Mic. Co.
1847.	h. s.	s.	s.	s.	s.		r.

INSTRUMENT READINGS.

Date.	CIRCLE.							Barom.	THERMOM.				
	A.	B.	C.	D.	E.	F.	Mean.		At.	Ex.	U.	L.	I.
1847. h. m.	° ′ ″						″	in.	°	°	°	°	°

REMARKS.

(103) 76. Minutes assumed as 41 instead of 42, and transits over T.'s V and VI as recorded over T.'s IV and V, to agree with Arg. Z. 375, 14.

(103) 85. Observed transit over T. VII supposed to be 30s.5 instead of 0s.5.

(103) 104. Transits over T.'s IV, V, and VI assumed as recorded over T.'s III, IV, and V, and minutes as 41, not 42, to agree with Arg. Z. 401, 67, and W. Mer. Cir., April 18.

(103) 113. Transit over T. VI assumed to have been recorded as over T. V.

ZONE 104.　APRIL 3.　C.　$D_0 = -27° 41' 0''$.

No.	Mag.	SECONDS OF TRANSIT.							T.	a_1	a_2	MICROMETER.			i		d_1	d_2	Mean Right Ascension, 1850.0.	Mean Declination, 1850.0.
		I.	II.	III.	IV.	V.	VI.	VII.	h. m. s.	s.	s.			r.	' ''	''	''	h. m. s.	° ' ''
1	8.9	..	..	.. 34.	51.3	9.1	26.6	..	8 15 51.54	+ 2.13	+0.86	IV.	3	32.278	−27 37.20	−11.68	−3.73	8 15 54.53	−28 8 52.67
2	8.9	..	..	.. 18.	35.	53.	10.6	..	17 35.39	2.12	0.70	IV.	2	12.680	48 7.78	12.11	6.11	17 38.30	29 26.00
3	9	..	.13.2	31.	..	6.	23.2	..	22 48.35	2.11	0.84	IV.	3	29.682	30 19.96	13.35	4.04	22 51.30	11 37.35
4	8	..	20.7	37.	54.	11.5	..	..	22 54.54	2.11	0.84	IV.	3	31.081	28 52.24	13.37	3.87	22 57.49	10 9.48
5	9	..	..	29.5	48.	..	..	41.2	28 47.91	2.10	0.80	IV.	2	18.672	41 51.71	14.76	5.36	28 50.81	28 23 11.83
6	8	..	..	..	..	..	..	19.3	29 27.00	2.10	0.87	VII.	4	42.937	16 25.08	14.91	2.45	29 29.07	27 57 42.44
7	9.10	..	28.	..	..	20.	..	..	33 2.74	2.09	0.88	IV.	4	49.218	9 52.11	15.74	1.73	33 5.71	51 9.58
8	9	..	..	51.	..	26.1	..	..	34 8.55	2.09	0.87	IV.	4	47.306	11 52.05	15.99	1.95	34 11.51	27 53 10.02
9	8	..	17.5	35.	52.3	9.6	27.1	..	41 52.35	2.08	0.83	IV.	3	35.816	23 55.07	17.77	3.30	41 55.26	28 5 16.14
10	8	..	23.7	41.1	58.3	16.	..	..	43 58.50	2.07	0.82	IV.	3	37.364	22 18.21	18.25	3.12	44 1.30	3 39.58
11	9	..	..	..	..	..	32.2	50.3	43 57.57	2.07	0.78	VI.	2	23.449	36 52.05	18.24	4.79	44 0.42	28 18 15.08
12	9	..	..	25.	42.2	..	17.3	..	46 42.38	2.07	0.87	IV.	4	52.605	6 19.67	18.87	1.32	46 45.32	27 47 39.86
13	7.8	..	16.	33.4	51.	8.4	26.	..	52 50.97	2.06	0.78	IV.	3	27.889	32 12.38	20.23	4.25	52 53.81	28 13 36.86
14	9	..	14.7	32.	47.2	..	..	..	54 49.45	2.06	0.78	IV.	3	26.608	33 32.88	20.67	4.41	54 52.29	14 57.96
15	9.10	..	..	..	..	..	..	..	54	2.06	0.79	VI.	3	30.867	29 5.92	20.70	3.90	54	10 30.52
16	8	..	..	22.3	39.8	57.3	15.4	..	8 58 39.95	2.06	0.74	IV.	2	16.714	43 54.59	21.52	5.62	8 58 42.75	28 25 21.73
17	9	..	..	..	19.7	..	..	..	9 1 19.71	2.06	0.81	IV.	4	41.354	18 5.35	22.09	2.64	9 1 22.58	27 59 30.11
18	9.10	..	..	..	..	1.	..	..	1 43.57	2.06	0.83	V.	4	47.579	11 34.78	22.17	1.91	1 46.46	52 58.86
19	9	..	..	..	50.2	..	35.	..	4 50.70	2.06	0.84	IV.	4	51.398	7 35.47	22.88	1.46	5 2.60	27 48 59.81
20	8	..	..	..	..	10.	27.8	45.	5 52.63	2.06	0.75	V.	2	21.771	38 37.22	23.06	5.00	5 55.44	28 20 5.28
21	8.9	..	1.8	..	37.	54.7	11.4	..	9 36.86	2.05	0.76	IV.	3	25.817	34 22.39	23.86	4.50	9 39.67	15 50.75
22	9	..	19.7	37.	54.2	..	..	..	13 54.49	2.05	0.31	IV.	2	12.728	48 4.76	24.76	6.12	13 57.25	29 35.04
23	9	..	..	..	14.7	32.2	50.	..	14 14.85	2.05	0.76	IV.	3	31.202	28 44.71	24.83	3.86	14 17.66	10 13.40
24	7	47.5	5.	22.6	39.8	57.6	14.8	32.3	16 39.94	2.05	0.76	IV.	3	29.780	30 13.74	25.34	4.02	16 42.75	11 43.10
25	9	..	10.	..	44.	2.5	19.7	..	18 44.69	2.05	0.73	IV.	3	21.792	38 34.97	25.77	4.99	18 47.47	20 5.73
26	7.8	..	..	52.2	9.8	27.3	45.	..	20 9.86	2.05	0.76	IV.	3	32.937	26 52.60	26.00	3.64	20 12.07	28 8 22.30
27	9	..	53.	10.2	..	..	2.5	..	23 27.75	2.06	0.79	IV.	4	44.462	14 50.44	26.72	2.27	23 30.60	27 56 19.43
28	8	..	29.	46.5	3.8	21.3	..	..	24 3.88	2.06	0.75	IV.	3	34.768	25 0.80	26.84	3.43	24 6.69	28 6 31.07
29	8	..	..	24.2	42.	59.	16.7	..	25 41.78	2.06	0.78	IV.	4	42.709	16 40.19	27.16	2.47	25 44.62	27 58 9.84
30	9.10	..	..	52.2	9.7	27.	..	..	33 9.64	2.06	0.73	IV.	3	27.494	32 37.35	28.67	4.30	33 12.43	28 14 10.32
31	9	..	44.1	1.7	19.	37.	54.5	..	43 19.27	2.07	0.71	IV.	3	30.368	29 37.10	30.64	3.96	43 22.05	28 11 11.70
32	9	..	..	25.2	42.2	0.8	..	..	48 25.33	2.08	0.78	IV.	4	51.835	7 7.82	31.60	1.38	48 28.19	27 49 40.80
33	9	..	..	54.5	..	29.2	..	..	50 11.80	2.08	0.65	IV.	2	9.221	51 45.02	31.94	6.56	50 14.53	28 33 23.52
34	8	..	22.2	40.	57.3	15.3	32.5	..	51 57.46	2.09	0.63	IV.	2	7.282	53 46.80	32.26	6.81	52 0.18	28 35 25.87
35	9	..	..	45.5	..	20.2	..	..	55 2.85	2.09	0.75	IV.	4	43.491	15 51.28	32.82	2.37	55 5.69	27 57 26.47
36	9	..	16.2	..	51.3	..	..	..	56 51.25	2.09	0.68	IV.	3	22.724	37 36.54	33.15	4.89	56 54.02	28 19 14.58
37	9	..	..	..	..	..	41.	58.2	57 6.10	2.09	0.77	VI.	4	53.874	4 59.59	33.20	1.15	57 8.96	27 46 33.94
38	9	..	0.5	..	..	..	1.	18.	59 35.40	2.10	0.74	II.	4	45.635	13 36.49	33.66	2.12	59 38.24	27 55 12.27
39	9	..	..	..	..	..	..	..	59 25.79	2.10	0.66	VI.	3	18.639	41 53.34	33.63	5.38	9 59 28.55	28 23 32.35
40	9	..	..	..	..	34.6	..	..	9 59 59.65	2.10	0.65	VI.	3	17.824	42 44.36	33.73	5.50	10 0 2.40	24 23.59
41	9	..	..	..	..	..	..	..	10 1	2.10	0.70	IV.	3	33.211	26 38.67	33.91	3.62	1	28 8 16.20
42	8	..	34.7	52.1	9.3	27.1	44.2	..	5 9.50	2.11	0.74	IV.	4	48.659	10 27.04	34.64	1.77	5 12.35	27 52 3.45
43	9	..	..	53.4	..	28.7	46.2	..	9 11.17	2.12	0.73	IV.	4	48.460	10 39.64	35.35	1.79	9 14.02	27 52 16.78
44	9	..	49.8	..	24.5	..	..	..	9 24.64	2.12	0.67	IV.	3	27.823	32 16.52	35.39	4.87	9 27.43	28 13 56.18
45	7	..	37.	55.	12.2	29.8	47.4	..	11 12.29	2.12	0.66	IV.	3	27.178	32 57.19	35.71	4.35	11 15.07	14 37.25
46	9.10	..	..	..	29.	..	..	3.5	12 11.30	2.13	0.67	V.	3	29.075	30 58.35	35.88	4.11	12 14.10	12 38.34
47	9.10	..	..	..	..	9.5	..	43.7	12 51.66	2.13	0.67	V.	3	29.047	31 0.04	36.00	4.12	12 54.46	12 40.16
48	9.10	..	2.2	19.7	37.	..	..	..	16 37.14	2.14	0.64	IV.	3	19.342	41 9.84	36.67	5.30	16 39.92	22 51.81
49	8	..	51.4	9.	20.3	43.4	1.5	..	10 18 26.32	+ 2.14	+0.62	IV.	2	16.293	−44 21.20	−36.99	−5.68	10 18 29.08	−28 26 3.67

CORRECTIONS.										REMARKS.
Date.	Corr. of Clock.	Hourly rate.	m	n	c		Zenith Point.	Mic. Co.		April 3. Hazy about the horizon; probably many stars obscured.
	h.	s.	s.	s.	s.	s.		° ' ''	r.	(104) 15. Precedes the last 4 or 5 seconds.
1847.										

INSTRUMENT READINGS.

Date.			CIRCLE.						Barom.	THERMOM.				
			A.	B.	C.	D.	E.	F.	Mean.		At.	Ex.	U.	L.	I.
	1847.	h. m.	° ' ''						''	in.					
Zone 104	April 3.	8 15	67 2 28.8	39.0	26.5	36.8	21.7	35.4	31.37	29.892	57.3	53.0	56.6	55.0	51.0
		8 41											52.0		
		9 1								29.898	56.0	51.8			
		9 20	28.8	39.0	26.5	37.4	21.8	34.5	31.33				51.2	55.8	53.5
		9 33								29.904	56.1	51.1			
		9 59											50.6		
		10 20	29.8	39.0	26.6	37.2	21.5	34.4	31.42	29.902	55.2	50.0	54.5	52.8	
		10 30											49.9		

Zone 104. April 3. C. $D_0 = -27° 41′ 0″$—Continued.

Seconds of Transit

No.	Mag.	I.	II.	III.	IV.	V.	VI.	VII.
50	9.10		55.	13.	30.7			
51	8		57.	14.7	32.	49.6	6.8	
52	9				42.	59.7	17.	

No.	T.	a_1	a_2	Micrometer		r	i	d_1	d_2	Mean Right Ascension, 1850.0	Mean Declination, 1850.0
	h. m. s.	s.	s.			r	′ ″	″	″	h. m. s.	° ′ ″
50	10 25 30.39	+ 2.16	+0.64	IV.	3	25.413	−34 47.99	−38.11	−4.56	10 25 33.19	−28 16 30.66
51	29 32.04	2.18	0.68	IV.	4	41.329	18 6.95	38.77	2.64	29 34.90	27 59 48.36
52	10 30 42.10	+ 2.18	+0.62	IV.	3	22.818	−37 30.58	−38.95	−4.88	10 30 44.90	−28 19 14.41

Zone 105. April 7. P. $D_0 = -27° 3′ 40″$.

Seconds of Transit

No.	Mag.	I.	II.	III.	IV.	V.	VI.	VII.
1	7					30.		
2	7							29.5
3	8.9			5.				
4	9			2.3				
5	9		4.					
6	8			7.3				
7	7	5.	22.3	39.5				
8	7		4.5					
9	7.8			41.				
10	8				25.			
11	7			48.				
12	8			36.				
13	8					7.5		
14	6				5.3	22.3		
15	6					56.		
16	8				12.			
17	7.8				23.			
18	5						19.	
19	9							8.5
20	8		4.					
21	8					10.		
22	7.8					7.7		
23	7		55.	21.7				
24	9				45.7			
25	5.6					47.		22.
26	8							39.
27	7			41.7	58.7			
28	9						55.5	
29	8					51.3		
30	7		49.2		24.			
31	9					31.		
32	6.7	27.7	45.		2.2			
33	8					55		
34	7					27.7		
35	9					37.		
36	8					27.		
37	7.8			42.3	59.5			
38	7		13.	30.2	47.7			
39	7	16.3	34.		8.			
40	7	37.5	55.				4.5	
41	7						34.	
42	7							15.

No.	T.	a_1	a_2	Micrometer		r	i	d_1	d_2	Mean Right Ascension, 1850.0	Mean Declination, 1850.0
	h. m. s.	s.	s.			r	′ ″	″	″	h. m. s.	° ′ ″
1	9 7 12.58	− 0.97	+1.84	V.	3	22.860	−37 28.19	− 7.37	−4.02	9 7 13.45	−27 41 19.58
2	7 37.44	0.98	1.90	VII.	3	33.697	26 8.44	7.46	2.79	7 38.36	29 58.69
3	9 22.37	0.98	1.87	III.	3	29.913	31 7.76	7.84	3.33	9 23.26	34 58.93
4	10 19.68	0.98	1.78	III.	2	15.632	45 2.38	8.05	4.86	10 20.48	45 55.29
5	12 38.71	0.98	1.88	II.	3	33.093	26 45.14	8.54	2.84	12 39.61	30 36.52
6	13 24.61	0.98	2.01	III.	4	54.012	4 51.31	8.70	0.50	13 25.64	8 40.51
7	14 56.88	0.98	1.99	III.	4	52.440	6 30.06	9.03	0.68	14 57.89	10 19.77
8	16 39.39	0.98	1.72	II.	1	6.322	54 45.01	9.39	5.05	16 40.13	58 40.35
9	17 58.35	0.98	1.93	III.	4	41.612	17 49.07	9.67	1.86	17 59.30	21 40.60
10	18 25.03	0.98	1.90	IV.	4	38.045	21 32.73	9.76	2.29	18 25.95	25 24.78
11	20 5.38	0.98	1.79	III.	2	20.707	39 43.81	10.12	4.28	20 6.19	43 38.21
12	20 53.38	0.98	1.79	III.	2	19.593	40 53.78	10.29	4.41	20 54.19	44 48.48
13	21 50.17	0.99	1.93	V.	4	43.992	15 19.60	10.48	1.61	21 51.09	19 11.69
14	23 22.51	0.99	1.83	IV.	3	28.690	31 22.19	10.79	3.36	23 23.35	35 16.34
15	23 38.62	0.99	1.85	V.	3	31.910	28 0.35	10.86	2.97	23 39.48	31 54.18
16	24 42.04	0.99	1.87	IV.	3	34.524	25 16.30	11.07	2.68	24 42.92	29 10.05
17	25 23.05	0.99	1.84	IV.	3	29.345	29 38.54	11.22	3.14	25 23.90	33 32.90
18	25 44.19	0.99	1.70	VI.	1	6.820	54 14.68	11.29	5.90	25 44.90	58 11.87
19	28 16.36	0.99	1.78	VII.	2	21.625	38 46.19	11.81	4.18	28 17.15	42 42.18
20	30 38.83	0.99	1.72	II.	1	13.920	46 47.86	12.36	5.04	30 39.56	50 45.20
21	30 52.51	0.99	1.69	V.	1	7.790	53 13.73	12.36	5.78	30 53.21	57 11.87
22	31 50.37	0.99	1.91	V.	4	44.525	14 46.30	12.54	1.54	31 51.29	18 40.38
23	35 39.07	0.99	1.81	III.	3	30.690	29 16.34	13.30	3.12	35 39.89	33 12.76
24	36 45.74	0.99	1.75	IV.	3	18.490	42 3.25	13.51	4.51	36 46.50	46 1.27
25	37 29.89	0.99	1.97	V.	4	57.522	1 11.31	13.66	0.12	37 30.87	5 5.09
26	38 46.85	0.99	1.75	VII.	2	21.390	39 4.07	13.92	4.19	38 47.61	42 59.18
27	40 58.91	0.99	1.76	IV.	3	23.112	37 13.13	14.35	4.00	40 59.68	41 11.48
28	41 20.81	0.98	1.80	VI.	3	29.422	30 36.82	14.41	3.27	41 21.63	34 34.50
29	42 33.84	0.98	1.69	V.	2	14.330	46 24.52	14.66	5.02	42 34.55	50 24.20
30	44 24.02	0.98	1.71	IV.	2	17.488	43 6.13	14.63	4.66	44 24.75	47 5.42
31	45 13.59	0.98	1.75	V.	3	26.442	33 43.67	15.16	3.61	45 14.36	37 42.44
32	47 19.60	0.98	1.87	III.	4	45.607	13 38.44	15.57	1.42	47 20.49	17 35.43
33	47 37.55	0.98	1.70	V.	2	17.090	43 31.12	15.62	4.70	47 38.27	47 31.44
34	48 27.74	0.98	1.69	IV.	2	14.972	45 43.91	15.79	4.95	48 28.45	49 44.65
35	49 19.55	0.98	1.70	V.	2	17.052	43 33.44	15.96	4.70	49 20.27	47 34.20
36	50 9.54	0.98	1.68	V.	2	14.973	45 43.91	16.12	4.96	50 10.24	49 44.99
37	52 59.61	0.98	1.75	IV.	3	26.972	33 9.98	16.65	3.55	53 0.38	37 10.18
38	54 5.13	0.98	1.63	IV.	1	7.575	53 27.16	16.98	5.80	55 5.78	57 29.94
39	57 8.43	0.97	1.69	IV.	2	18.120	42 26.42	17.42	4.56	57 9.15	46 28.40
40	57 29.70	0.97	1.73	VI.	3	25.105	35 7.57	17.49	3.77	57 30.46	39 5.83
41	57 59.34	0.97	1.70	VI.	4	35.905	23 46.52	17.58	2.52	58 0.16	27 46.62
42	9 58 22.95	− 0.97	+1.75	VII.	4	35.487	−24 12.63	−17.64	−2.56	9 58 23.76	−27 28 12.83

CORRECTIONS.

Date.	Corr. of Clock.	Hourly rate.	m	n	c	Zenith Point.	Mic. Co.
1847.	h.	s.	s.	s.	s.	s.	° ′ ″	r.

REMARKS.

(105) 17. Micrometer reading assumed as 30ʳ.345, not 29ʳ.345.

(105) 30. Minutes assumed as 44 instead of 42.

(105) 38. Transits over T.'s I, II, and III assumed as recorded over T.'s II, III, and IV, and minutes as 55, not 54.

INSTRUMENT READINGS.

Date.	CIRCLE.							Barom.	THERMOM.				
		A.	B.	C.	D.	E.	F.	Mean.		At.	Ex.	U.	L.	I.
	1847. h. m.	° ′ ″						″	in.	°	°	°	°	°
Zone 105	April 7, 9 0	66 24 59.6	65.3	57.2	63.8	49.4	64.8	60.07	30.074	62.2	60.0	63.0	59.5	57.0
	10 25	59.0	65.3	56.8	63.8	49.4	63.0	59.55						
	11 0								30.076	58.4	52.5			
	12 37	57.8	66.3	55.6	63.8	48.5	62.3	59.05	30.090	55.0	49.0	53.5		
	15 0	59.3	70.4	59.5	69.7	53.5	65.7	63.02	30.072	52.0	46.7	51.5	51.5	
	16 3								30.064	51.4	44.2			

ZONE 105. APRIL 7. P. $D_0 = -27°\ 3'\ 40''$—Continued.

No.	Mag.	I.	II.	III.	IV.	V.	VI.	VII.	T.	a_1	a_4	MICROMETER		i	d_1	d_4	Mean Right Ascension, 1850.0	Mean Declination, 1850.0
									h. m. s.	s.	s.		r.	′ ″	″	″	h. m. s.	° ′ ″
43	7						12.7		9 59 37.90	0.97	+1.63	VI 1	9.754	−51 10.56	−17.88	−5.57	9 59 38.56	−27 55 14.01
44	8						56.5		10 0 21.80	0.97	1.74	VI 3	28.777	31 17.04	18.01	3.35	10 0 22.57	35 18.40
45	9						2.		2 27.44	0.97	1.88	VI 4	52.982	5 55.58	18.39	0.59	2 28.35	9 54.56
46	7						57.7		3 23.04	0.97	1.77	VI 3	35.800	23 56.45	18.56	2.53	3 23.84	27 57.54
47	4.5				12.			4.	5 11.92	0.96	1.64	IV 2	12.793	48 0.62	18.89	5.20	5 12.60	62 4.71
48	9						36.		6 1.25	0.96	1.66	VI 2	18.290	42 15.80	19.03	4.58	6 1.95	46 19.41
49	8						23.7		6 49.13	0.96	1.85	VI 4	49.807	9 14.62	19.18	0.94	6 50.02	13 14.74
50	9			38.					8 55.38	0.96	1.66	III 2	18.535	36 46.54	19.55	3.95	8 56.08	40 50.03
51	6					31.			9 13.53	0.96	1.63	V 1	12.608	48 11.42	19.61	5.24	9 14.20	52 16.27
52	8	59.		34.					11 51.19	0.95	1.74	III 3	32.627	27 2.20	20.07	2.86	11 51.98	31 5.13
53	7					16.			11 58.55	0.95	1.65	V 2	18.152	37 10.77	20.09	3.98	11 59.25	41 14.84
54	7				14.				13 14.03	0.95	1.60	IV 1	9.967	50 56.87	20.31	5.55	13 14.68	55 2.73
55	7			22.	39.5				14 39.45	0.95	1.72	IV 3	32.525	27 21.71	20.55	2.90	14 40.22	31 25.16
56	8			38.	55.				15 55.16	0.95	1.82	IV 4	47.664	11 29.44	20.76	1.17	15 56.03	15 31.37
57	9	7.	24.						17 53.78	0.94	1.81	II 4	46.550	12 39.18	21.13	1.29	17 59.65	16 41.60
58	9		5.5						21 40.33	0.94	1.60	II 2	13.595	47 9.91	21.75	5.13	21 40.99	51 16.79
59	8				7.7				22 7.74	0.94	1.64	IV 2	21.670	38 43.57	21.83	4.17	22 8.44	42 49.57
60	4.5	56.7	14.2	31.5	48.8				24 48.82	0.93	1.72	IV 3	35.790	23 56.69	22.27	2.53	24 49.61	28 1.49
61	9	52.		27.					26 44.24	0.92	1.64	III 2	22.723	37 37.30	22.59	4.05	26 44.96	41 43.94
62	8			49.		24.			36 6.48	0.90	1.59	III 2	19.120	41 23.47	24.14	4.48	36 7.17	45 32.09
63	9	13.		47.					38 4.69	0.90	1.66	III 3	31.990	27 54.77	24.40	2.96	38 5.45	32 2.13
64	7			5.3					39 22.65	0.89	1.72	III 4	42.372	17 1.46	24.60	1.76	39 23.48	21 7.82
65	8						57.		39 22.38	0.89	1.72	VI 4	41.965	18 29.23	24.60	1.94	39 23.21	22 35.77
66	6			32.	49.5				41 49.38	0.89	1.80	IV 4	55.290	3 31.42	24.98	0.30	41 50.89	7 36.70
67	8					17.			45 59.61	0.88	1.64	V 3	29.315	30 43.42	25.60	3.28	46 0.37	34 52.30
68	7.8	1.	18.	35.3	52.7				49 52.82	0.86	1.59	IV 3	23.912	36 21.92	26.18	3.92	49 53.55	40 32.02
69	7				48.				50 48.04	0.86	1.64	IV 3	33.150	26 42.45	26.31	2.82	50 48.82	30 51.58
70	8				56.3				51 56.35	0.86	1.59	IV 3	25.280	34 56.34	26.47	3.76	51 57.08	39 6.57
71	9					32.5			53 15.14	0.85	1.67	V 4	38.133	21 27.15	26.66	2.26	53 15.96	25 36.07
72	9						49.		54 14.38	0.85	1.68	VI 3	42.080	17 19.28	26.79	1.78	54 15.21	21 27.85
73	8					55.3			55 37.82	0.85	1.49	V 2	10.060	50 52.30	26.98	5.53	55 38.46	55 4.81
74	6.7					45.			10 59 23.52	0.85	1.48	V 1	10.070	50 50.67	27.52	5.53	10 59 24.17	55 3.72
75	6					29.3			11 0 11.88	0.83	1.56	V 3	23.622	36 40.50	27.63	3.96	11 0 12.61	40 52.09
76	4						2.3		1 27.72	0.83	1.70	VI 4	47.260	11 54.59	27.70	1.21	1 28.59	16 3.59
77	8						45.		2 10.34	0.82	1.62	VI 4	35.082	24 41.61	27.88	2.61	2 11.14	28 52.10
78	7						35.3		3 0.65	0.82	1.63	VI 3	36.540	23 10.21	28.00	2.43	3 1.46	27 20.64
79	7	34.7		9.					7 26.52	0.81	1.61	III 3	34.540	25 14.92	28.59	2.67	7 27.32	29 26.18
80	7				47.3				7 29.88	0.81	1.54	V 3	23.347	36 57.89	28.60	3.99	7 30.61	41 10.48
81	7			12.5					9 12.50	0.80	1.67	IV 4	44.720	14 34.07	28.82	1.49	9 13.37	16 14.38
82							6.		9 31.31	0.80	1.58	VI 3	30.830	29 8.24	28.86	3.10	9 32.06	33 20.20
83	7				22.3				12 4.89	0.79	1.54	V 3	25.153	35 4.44	29.18	3.77	12 5.64	39 17.39
84	6				1.				12 26.38	0.79	1.64	VI 4	41.630	17 47.56	29.22	1.84	12 27.23	21 58.62
85	6				34.				12 59.33	0.79	1.59	VI 4	33.360	26 26.44	29.29	2.81	13 0.13	30 38.54
86	8			21.					16 21.05	0.77	1.52	IV 2	23.435	36 52.99	29.69	3.95	16 21.80	41 6.66
87	8							15.	16 22.87	0.77	1.52	VII 2	23.340	36 58.71	29.70	3.90	16 23.62	41 12.40
88	8	39.		14.					20 31.23	0.75	1.52	III 3	24.487	35 45.66	30.21	3.85	20 32.00	39 59.72
89	8					55.5			20 38.11	0.75	1.55	III 3	30.520	29 27.12	30.22	3.13	20 38.91	33 40.48
90	5.6			54.	11.				22 11.15	0.75	1.67	IV 2	50.910	8 9.27	30.40	0.78	22 12.07	12 20.45
91	7		2.	20.					11 23 37.39	−0.74	+1.40	III 2	7.188	−53 52.46	−30.56	−5.92	11 23 39.05	−27 58 8.94

CORRECTIONS.

Date.	Corr. of Clock.	Hourly rate.	m	n	c	Zenith Point.	Mic. Co.
1847.	h. s.	s.	s.	s.	s.	° ′ ″	r.

INSTRUMENT READINGS.

Date.	CIRCLE.						Barom.	THERMOM.				
	A.	B.	C.	D.	E.	F.	Mean.		At.	Ex.	U.	L.	I.
1847. h. m.	° ′ ″							in.				

REMARKS.

April 7. 12h 38m, moved the circle for other observations. 16h, somewhat hazy; moon-light.

(105) 50. Micrometer reading assumed as 21r.535, not 18r.535.

(105) 53. Micrometer reading assumed as 21r.152, not 18r.152.

(105) 65. Micrometer reading assumed as 40r.965, not 41r.965.

ZONE 105. APRIL 7. P. D₀ = −27° 3′ 40″—Continued.

No.	Mag.	I.	II.	III.	IV.	V.	VI.	VII.	T. (h m s)	a₁ (s)	a₂ (s)
92	8					29.5			11 25 12.10	− 0.73	
93	7			8.3					30 25.65	0.71	+1.57
94	7					0.3			30 42.94	0.71	1.57
95	6.7	53.3	11.2	28.5					32 45.73	0.70	1.48
96	9.					18.			33 43.43	0.69	1.64
97	9		28.5		3.5				36 3.36	0.68	1.59
98	7	0.7	17.7	35.					37 52.50	0.67	1.52
99	6			30.3					38 47.61	0.67	1.65
100	6.7	27.	44.	1.					40 18.68	0.66	1.53
101	9						58.		40 23.31	0.66	1.51
102	8							52.	45 59.97	0.63	1.53
103	5.6			44.5	1.7			53.7	48 1.74	0.62	1.46
104	7	28.3	45.5	3.	20.				55 20.20	0.59	1.51
105	9			53.					57 10.38	0.58	1.37
106	7				28.		3.		11 57 28.13	0.57	1.36
107	7		11.5		46.3				12 0 46.23	0.56	1.58
108	8						3.1		0 28.53	0.56	1.56
109	6			32.2	49.5				3 6.86	0.54	1.56
110	8					11.			3 53.59	0.54	1.40
111	8				27.3				6 27.33	0.52	1.48
112	8				31.				8 30.95	0.51	1.59
113	7		23.7	41.2	58.3				9 58.43	0.50	1.48
114	7	18.3	35.7	53.3		28.			12 10.53	0.49	1.38
115	9			19.					16 19.04	0.47	1.36
116	7			30.	47.				17 47.21	0.46	1.41
117	7	41.7	50.	16.5					19 33.88	0.44	1.29
118	9						16.5		23 41.77	0.42	1.35
119	8		12.						25 29.37	0.41	1.37
120	7.8					10.5			25 53.06	0.41	1.32
121	9			22.3					27 39.68	0.39	1.30
122	8	42.	59.	16.7					29 33.95	0.33	1.37
123	7.8	30.5		14.3					35 31.53	0.35	1.42
124	4					0.	17.3	35.	35 0.10	0.35	1.38
125	4						33.		12 37 15.52	− 0.38	+1.23

No.	MICROMETER	r	i	d₁	d₂	Mean Right Ascension, 1850.0 (h m s)	Mean Declination, 1850.0 (° ′ ″)
92	[illegible]	[illegible]	[illegible]	[illegible]	[illegible]	11 25 [illegible]	−27 [illegible]
93	4	39.192	−21 23.57	−31.33	−2.24	30 26.51	25 37.14
94	V. 3	36.402	23 18.81	31.35	2.45	30 43.80	27 32.61
95	III. 2	24.630	35 37.70	31.58	3.84	32 46.51	39 53.12
96	VI. 4	49.735	9 19.19	31.68	0.90	33 44.38	13 31.77
97	IV. 4	42.745	16 37.87	31.93	1.69	36 4.27	20 51.49
98	III. 3	31.817	28 5.56	32.12	2.98	37 53.35	32 20.66
99	III. 4	55.180	3 38.21	32.21	0.27	38 48.55	7 50.69
100	III. 3	34.655	25 7.66	32.37	2.66	40 19.55	29 22.69
101	III. 3	30.910	29 3.22	32.38	3.09	40 24.16	33 18.69
102	VII. 3	37.273	−22 24.23	32.90	2.34	46 0.87	26 39.47
103	IV. 3	26.023	34 9.53	33.09	3.68	48 2.58	38 26.30
104	IV. 4	38.495	21 4.63	33.73	2.20	55 21.12	25 20.56
105	III. 2	15.580	45 5.63	33.89	4.92	57 11.17	49 24.44
106	IV. 2	13.230	47 33.38	33.92	5.21	11 57 28.92	51 52.51
107	IV. 4	52.037	6 55.15	34.19	0.63	12 0 47.25	11 9.97
108	VI. 4	49.173	9 54.62	34.17	0.95	0 29.53	14 9.74
109	III. 4	49.477	9 35.88	34.36	0.92	3 7.88	13 51.16
110	IV. 3	23.913	36 22.11	34.42	3.93	3 54.45	40 30.46
111	IV. 3	38.830	20 46.01	34.60	2.17	6 28.29	25 2.78
112	IV. 4	56.023	2 45.28	34.77	0.16	8 32.03	7 0.21
113	IV. 3	37.784	21 51.62	34.87	2.27	9 59.41	26 8.76
114	IV. 3	23.204	37 6.55	35.00	4.02	12 11.42	41 25.57
115	IV. 2	21.337	39 4.65	35.27	4.23	16 19.93	43 24.15
116	IV. 3	29.220	30 49.06	35.46	3.30	17 48.16	35 7.82
117	III. 2	12.053	48 46.94	35.51	5.35	19 34.73	53 7.80
118	VI. 2	23.630	36 40.58	35.70	3.96	23 42.70	41 0.24
119	III. 3	27.203	32 51.47	35.79	3.54	25 30.33	37 10.80
120	V. 2	17.933	42 38.08	35.81	3.63	25 53.97	46 57.52
121	III. 2	16.003	44 35.32	35.91	3.86	27 40.59	48 55.09
122	III. 3	28.985	31 3.30	36.01	3.32	29 34.99	35 22.63
123	III. 4	41.930	17 28.99	36.26	2.79	35 38.60	21 48.04
124	IV. 3	34.164	25 38.69	36.28	2.70	36 1.13	29 57.87
125	III. 1	8.700	−52 16.09	−36.34	−5.76	12 37 16.37	−27 56 38.19

ZONE 106. APRIL 7. P. D₀ = −27° 3′ 40″.

No.	Mag.	I.	II.	III.	IV.	V.	VI.	VII.	T. (h m s)	a₁ (s)	a₂ (s)
1	7						31.	5.5	15 6 13.59	+ 2.86	+0.05
2	7	35.3	53.	10.	27.3				11 27.48	2.91	0.25
3	8				6.				12 31.37	2.92	0.10
4	7	43.7	1.	18.3	35.5				16 35.67	2.95	0.20
5	7			27.	44.	1.3			17 44.11	2.97	0.15
6	8		40.7						20 15.40	2.97	0.05
7	8	43.3	18.7						22 35.80	3.00	0.34
8	8				0.			33.	23 0.17	3.01	0.23
9	5	37.5	55.	12.	29.3	47.			25 23.51	3.03	0.19
10	3.4	0.7	18.	35.5	52.7	10.3			27 52.81	3.05	0.23
11	6				6.			41.	15 29 6.16	+ 3.07	+0.27

No.	MICROMETER	r	i	d₁	d₂	Mean Right Ascension, 1850.0 (h m s)	Mean Declination, 1850.0 (° ′ ″)
1	V. 4	45.880	−13 21.12	−35.24	−1.28	15 6 16.51	−27 17 37.64
2	IV. 2	30.510	39 56.47	34.71	4.38	11 30.64	44 15.56
3	VI. 4	41.043	18 24.39	31.61	1.86	12 34.30	22 40.85
4	IV. 3	30.547	27 25.81	34.17	3.14	16 38.82	33 43.12
5	IV. 3	37.377	22 17.40	34.05	2.31	17 47.23	26 33.76
6	II. 4	52.390	6 33.01	33.79	0.52	20 18.44	10 47.32
7	III. 1	11.740	49 5.21	33.55	5.18	22 39.14	53 24.20
8	IV. 3	25.450	31 45.67	33.47	3.77	23 3.41	30 2.91
9	V. 3	31.970	27 56.65	33.18	2.06	25 32.73	32 12.79
10	IV. 3	26.435	33 43.86	32.91	3.65	27 56.10	38 0.42
11	IV. 3	22.165	−38 11.76	−32.78	−4.18	15 29 9.50	−27 42 28.72

CORRECTIONS.

Date.	Corr. of Clock.	Hourly rate.	m	n	c	Zenith Point.	Mic. Co.
1847.	h.	s.	s.	s.	s.	° ′ ″	r.

INSTRUMENT READINGS.

Date.	CIRCLE							Barom.	THERMOM.				
	A.	B.	C.	D.	E.	F.	Mean.		At.	Ex.	U.	L.	I.
1847. h. m.	° ′ ″						″	in.	°	°	°	°	°

REMARKS.

(105) 124. Minutes assumed as 36 instead of 35.

Zone 106. April 7. P. $D_0 = -27°\ 3'\ 40''$—Continued.

No.	Mag.	I.	II.	III.	IV.	V.	VI.	VII.	T.	a_1	a_2	Mic.		r.	i	d_1	d_2	Mean Right Ascension, 1850.0	Mean Declination, 1850.0
									h. m. s.	s.	s.			r.	′ ″	″	″	h. m. s.	° ′ ″
12	7					45.5			15 30 28.20	+3.08	+0.06	V.	4	54.130	−4 43.91	−32.61	−0.33	15 30 31.34	−27 8 56.85
13	8		27.						34 1.75	3.11	0.26	II.	3	24.590	35 38.63	32.19	3.89	34 5.12	39 54.71
14	7						29.		33 54.34	3.11	0.20	VI.	3	34.537	25 15.86	32.20	2.65	33 57.65	29 30.71
15	8						40.		35 5.29	3.12	0.26	VI.	3	27.715	32 23.74	32.06	3.50	35 8.67	36 39.30
16	6		28.		8.5				37 2.64	3.14	0.17	IV.	3	29.135	30 54.34	31.82	3.33	37 5.95	35 9.49
17	7			15.3					39 32.61	3.16	0.06	III.	4	56.035	2 44.53	31.52	0.07	39 35.83	6 56.12
18	8				40.				40 40.03	3.17	0.19	IV.	4	38.873	20 40.73	31.38	2.13	40 43.39	24 54.24
19	8.9	24.3		59.					44 16.23	3.20	0.11	III.	4	49.010	10 4.97	30.91	0.94	44 19.54	14 16.82
20	8		15.						45 49.70	3.21	0.20	II.	3	36.595	23 5.45	30.71	2.40	45 53.11	27 18.56
21	8.9			35.					46 35.04	3.23	0.23	IV.	3	33.640	26 11.70	30.63	2.77	46 38.50	30 25.10
22	9						46.		47 11.30	3.23	0.26	VI.	3	27.780	32 19.60	30.53	3.49	47 14.79	36 33.62
23	7							53.	48 1.05	3.23	0.09	VII.	4	51.205	7 46.76	30.43	0.65	48 4.37	11 57.84
24	9	56.		31.					51 48.20	3.27	0.25	III.	3	31.140	28 48.17	29.92	3.07	51 51.72	33 1.16
25	8	50.3		25.5		0.3			57 42.65	3.32	0.13	V.	4	49.975	9 4.39	29.13	0.78	57 46.10	18 28.00
26	7					9.			58 51.67	3.33	0.16	V.	4	44.050	15 16.03	28.96	1.50	15 58 55.16	19 26.49
27	8				24.3		59.3		16 0 24.49	3.34	0.24	IV.	3	34.550	25 14.67	28.75	2.65	16 0 28.07	29 26.07
28	4	9.3		44.	1.5				16 3 1.41	+3.36	+0.26	IV.	3	32.180	−27 43.36	−28.39	−2.94	16 3 5.03	−27 31 54.69

Zone 107. April 9. C. $D_0 = -30°\ 49'\ 0''$.

No.	Mag.	I.	II.	III.	IV.	V.	VI.	VII.	T.	a_1	a_2	Mic.		r.	i	d_1	d_2	Mean Right Ascension, 1850.0	Mean Declination, 1850.0
1	8			38.2	56.2		32.8	50.7	8 36 56.52	+0.64	−0.70	IV.	3	44.932	−14 23.28	−5.41	−1.71	8 36 56.46	−31 3 30.40
2	7.8				22.	40.2	58.7	16.6	38 22.32	0.63	0.99	IV.	3	20.741	39 40.97	5.78	5.44	38 21.96	31 28 52.19
3	9				7.	24.7			40 6.86	0.63	0.62	IV.	4	52.445	6 29.75	6.19	0.60	40 6.87	30 55 36.54
4	9		28.7	47.	5.	23.	40.7		47 4.89	0.62	0.97	IV.	3	25.392	34 49.32	7.86	4.72	47 4.54	31 24 1.90
5	9				11.				47 52.93	0.62	1.00	VII.	3	22.849	37 28.88	8.06	5.10	47 52.55	26 42.04
6	7				19.7	37.2			48 1.35	0.62	1.09	V.	2	14.591	46 7.95	8.08	6.40	48 0.88	35 22.43
7	9				52.	9.2			49 33.49	0.62	1.11	V.	2	13.474	47 18.12	8.45	6.57	49 33.00	36 33.14
8	7.8		4.7	22.7	40.5	58.7		30.	51 40.65	0.62	0.79	IV.	4	42.954	16 24.77	8.96	1.99	51 40.48	5 35.72
9	7			36.	54.			30.	52 35.89	0.62	1.15	IV.	2	11.241	49 38.22	9.17	6.94	52 35.36	38 54.33
10	7							14.	52 19.93	0.62	0.97	V.	3	26.438	33 43.93	9.10	4.56	52 19.58	22 57.59
11	9	30.2	48.						56 6.08	0.61	0.65	III.	4	53.138	5 46.18	9.98	0.50	56 6.04	30 54 56.66
12	9				57.2	15.	33.		56 39.04	0.61	0.92	V.	3	30.659	29 18.91	10.10	3.90	56 38.73	31 18 32.91
13	9				23.				8 57 47.00	0.61	0.93	VI.	3	30.117	29 53.04	10.38	3.98	8 57 46.68	31 19 7.40
14	8	25.7	43.9	2.	20.				9 0 1.89	0.61	0.73	IV.	4	48.631	10 28.87	10.89	1.15	9 0 1.77	30 59 40.91
15	9								0	0.61	0.89	IV.	3	35.039	24 43.87	10.89	3.23	0	31 13 57.99
16	7.8					21.	39.		1 2.98	0.61	0.95	V.	3	30.413	29 34.52	11.12	3.94	1 2.64	18 49.58
17	7.8					12.	30.5		1 36.18	0.61	1.04	VI.	3	23.471	36 50.16	11.25	5.01	1 35.75	26 6.42
18	8.9			45.7	22.	40.			6 3.90	0.60	0.95	IV.	3	31.351	28 35.43	12.25	3.79	6 3.55	17 51.47
19	8.9		16.2	34.					6 34.13	0.60	0.89	IV.	3	36.405	23 18.36	12.40	3.01	6 33.84	12 33.77
20	9				59.7				7 59.75	0.60	1.11	IV.	2	18.542	41 59.99	12.70	5.80	7 59.21	31 18.49
21	8	57.4	15.3	33.2	51.6				9 33.41	0.60	1.17	IV.	2	13.653	47 6.77	13.04	6.58	9 32.84	36 26.39
22	9.10	31.3		8.					12 7.69	0.60	0.97	IV.	3	30.710	29 15.45	13.62	3.89	12 7.32	18 32.96
23	9		43.				37.2		13 1.07	0.60	1.16	IV.	3	14.518	46 11.66	13.82	6.44	13 0.51	35 31.92
24	8				59.3	17.7	35.2		13 59.39	0.60	1.05	IV.	3	24.286	35 58.71	14.04	4.89	13 58.94	25 17.64
25	6						59.2	17.6	14 23.46	0.60	0.86	VI.	4	41.133	18 16.73	14.13	2.27	14 23.20	7 35.13
26	8					7.3		43.4	15 49.37	0.60	0.88	V.	4	39.123	20 25.05	14.44	2.59	15 49.09	9 42.08
27	9	34.7	53.2		29.2				19 11.06	0.60	1.20	IV.	2	13.332	47 27.04	15.19	6.63	19 10.46	36 48.86
28	9	54.7	12.1	30.2					9 19 30.40	+0.60	−1.15	IV.	2	17.530	−43 3.49	−15.26	−5.96	9 19 29.85	−31 32 24.71

CORRECTIONS.

Date.	Corr. of Clock.	Hourly rate.	m	n	c	Zenith Point.	Mic. Co.
1847.	h.	s.	s.	s.	s.	° ′ ″	r.

INSTRUMENT READINGS.

Date.	A.	B.	C.	D.	E.	F.	Mean	Barom.	At.	Ex.	U.	L.	I.
							″	in.					
Zone 107　1847. April 9.　8 40	70 9 56.2	66.4	54.1	64.1	46.8	63.9	58.58	29.998	62.5	56.3	61.5	60.0	60.5
8 57										55.1			
9 20										54.1			
9 40								29.996	60.0	52.5			

REMARKS.

(106) 21. Transit over T. IV assumed as recorded over T. III, to agree with Arg. Z. 373, 106; and 388, 13.

(106) 25. Micrometer reading assumed as 44ʳ.975, not 49ʳ.975.

Zone 107. April 9. C. $D_0 = -30°\ 49'\ 0''$—Continued.

No.	Mag.	I.	II.	III.	IV.	V.	VI.	VII.
29	9.10					37.		
30	9.10				34.		10.	
31	9			3.		39.1		
32	7.8			3.2	21.	39.5		
33	7.8				8.	25.7	43.8	
34	9							16.8
35	8		57.2	16.	33.7		9.7	
36	8		59.2	18.	35.7	54.	12.	
37	9			54.				
38	7			25.3	43.	1.	20.	
39	9.10							46.
40	9.10					41.3		
41	9		45.8	3.5	21.4			
42	9		39.		15.2	32.8		
43	9				48.	6.2		
44	9.10			8.	26.2	44.2	1.2	
45	9.10							
46	9.10		17.2	35.	53.			
47	9.10				9.5			
48	8			49.	7.	25.3	43.	
49	9			32.7	50.	8.7	26.7	
50	9			1.	19.2	37.	55.	
51	9				20.3		56.3	
52	9.10					13.		
53	9		15.7	34.	52.			
54	8			48.	6.	23.7	42.	
55	9.10							25.
56	9			12.8	30.7	48.8		
57	9.10						39.7	
58	8				21.5	39.4	57.4	
59	9.10			15.7	33.2	51.5		
60	9.10						30.7	48.5
61	9.10							
62	8.9		30.5	48.7			43.	
63	9		21.3		57.9			
64	9			24.7	43.			
65	7		12.	30.	48.	6.3	24.1	
66	9.10		55.			49.		
67	9.10			19.				
68	9.10				48.	7.		
69	8.9		10.2	28.5		5.		41.
70	8.9			40.7		10.2	34.2	
71	9		34.7	53.	11.			
72	9		39.	57.2	15.7			
73	9		40.7	57.8	15.2			
74	9				43.	1.	19.	
75	8.9			10.7	29.8			
76	7			59.	17.3	35.2	53.5	
77	9			33.5	51.7	9.6		

No.	T. (h. m. s.)	a_1 (s.)	a_2 (s.)	Micrometer		r.	i (' '')	d_1 ('')	d_2 ('')	Mean Right Ascension, 1850.0 (h. m. s.)	Mean Declination, 1850.0 (° ' '')
29	9 20 1.14	+ 0.60	− 0.76	VI.	4	49.672	− 9 23.14	−15.37	−0.99	9 20 0.98	−30 58 39.50
30	22 34.06	0.60	0.81	IV.	4	46.831	12 21.62	15.93	1.42	22 33.85	31 1 38.97
31	24 21.05	0.60	0.95	IV.	3	35.138	24 37.73	16.33	3.21	24 20.70	13 57.27
32	24 21.25	0.60	0.95	IV.	3	35.246	24 31.01	16.33	3.20	24 20.90	13 50.54
33	25 7.85	0.60	0.94	IV.	3	36.278	23 26.33	16.50	3.03	25 7.51	12 45.86
34	25 22.84	0.60	0.88	VII.	3	40.552	18 58.43	16.57	2.37	25 22.56	8 17.37
35	27 33.68	0.61	1.00	IV.	3	32.362	27 32.00	17.06	3.63	27 33.29	16 52.69
36	27 35.79	0.61	1.04	IV.	3	27.910	32 11.06	17.06	4.32	27 35.36	21 32.44
37	30 12.04	0.61	1.21	III.	2	15.543	45 8.02	17.63	6.28	30 11.44	34 31.93
38	30 43.31	0.61	1.15	IV.	2	19.505	40 59.55	17.74	5.40	30 42.77	30 22.78
39	30 51.87	0.61	1.15	VII.	2	19.5		17.76	5.49	30 51.33	
40	32 23.16	0.61	1.26	V.	2	11.136	49 44.83	18.11	6.98	32 22.51	39 9.92
41	35 21.63	0.61	1.17	IV.	2	19.281	41 13.68	18.73	5.68	35 21.07	30 38.09
42	36 15.01	0.61	0.84	IV.	4	46.615	12 35.04	18.95	1.45	36 14.78	1 55.44
43	36 48.12	0.61	0.89	IV.	4	42.726	16 39.13	19.07	2.02	36 47.84	6 0.22
44	38 25.88	0.61	1.21	IV.	2	16.186	43 48.11	19.41	6.07	38 25.28	33 13.60
45	38	0.61	1.12	IV.	3	23.758	36 31.65	19.33	4.97	38	25 55.95
46	40 53.14	0.62	1.22	IV.	3	16.291	44 20.44	19.95	6.15	40 52.54	31 33 46.54
47	41 9.47	0.62	0.79	IV.	3	52.012	6 56.78	19.09	0.64	41 9.30	30 56 17.41
48	47 7.07	0.62	1.12	IV.	3	25.862	34 19.57	21.20	4.65	47 6.57	31 23 45.42
49	49 50.49	0.63	1.27	IV.	3	13.037	47 44.49	21.75	6.68	49 49.85	37 12.92
50	51 19.08	0.63	0.92	IV.	4	43.852	15 28.45	22.04	1.83	51 18.79	4 52.32
51	52 20.31	0.63	1.13	IV.	3	25.726	34 28.16	22.24	4.67	52 19.81	23 55.07
52	53 54.93	0.63	1.17	V.	3	22.531	37 40.03	22.56	5.17	53 54.39	27 16.76
53	55 51.92	0.64	1.00	IV.	3	37.248	22 25.42	22.92	2.88	55 51.56	11 51.22
54	56 5.94	0.64	1.04	IV.	3	34.330	25 27.97	22.97	3.31	56 5.54	14 54.25
55	56 30.97	0.64	1.08	VII.	2	30.971	28 50.33	23.05	3.84	56 30.53	18 26.22
56	9 58 30.77	0.64	1.18	IV.	3	24.055	36 13.08	23.44	4.94	9 58 30.23	25 41.46
57	10 0 3.82	0.64	0.91	IV.	3	46.679	12 31.21	23.74	1.30	10 0 3.55	1 56.34
58	1 21.44	0.65	1.11	IV.	3	29.845	30 0.66	23.98	4.02	1 20.98	19 37.66
59	4 51.50	0.65	1.11	IV.	3	30.008	29 2.07	24.65	3.86	4 51.04	31 18 31.48
60	4 54.73	0.65	0.88	VI.	4	49.855	0 11.60	24.66	0.92	4 54.50	30 58 37.18
61	7	0.66	0.94	IV.	3	46.919	12 16.09	25.07	1.39	7	31 1 42.54
62	9 6.76	0.66	1.20	IV.	3	23.875	36 24.25	25.47	4.97	9 6.22	25 54.69
63	11 57.60	0.67	0.92	IV.	4	47.905	11 10.50	26.01	1.21	11 57.35	0 37.72
64	12 42.87	0.67	1.01	IV.	3	40.671	18 50.66	26.14	2.34	12 42.53	8 19.14
65	13 48.10	0.68	0.96	IV.	4	44.952	14 19.45	26.34	1.66	13 47.82	3 47.45
66	15 31.03	0.68	1.38	IV.	2	10.768	50 7.72	26.64	7.08	15 30.33	39 41.44
67	15 37.04	0.68	1.35	III.	2	13.		26.66	6.72	15 36.37	
68	15 48.46	0.68	1.35	IV.	2	13.113	47 40.66	26.70	6.70	15 47.79	37 14.06
69	19 46.66	0.69	1.28	IV.	2	20.202	40 15.81	27.43	5.55	19 46.07	29 48.79
70	19 58.38	0.69	1.09	IV.	3	35.850	23 52.38	27.46	3.09	19 57.98	13 22.93
71	22 10.97	0.70	1.31	IV.	2	19.610	41 55.66	27.79	5.81	22 10.36	31 29.26
72	23 15.35	0.70	1.25	IV.	3	23.399	36 54.38	27.96	5.04	23 14.80	26 27.38
73	25 15.89	0.71	1.00	IV.	4	44.536	14 45.73	28.27	1.73	25 15.60	31 4 15.73
74	25 43.05	0.71	0.92	IV.	4	50.915	8 5.50	28.33	0.76	25 42.84	30 57 34.59
75	29 29.95	0.72	1.00	IV.	4	45.345	13 55.06	28.92	1.61	29 28.97	31 3 25.59
76	30 17.28	0.72	0.95	IV.	4	48.392	10 43.97	29.03	1.15	30 17.05	31 0 14.15
77	10 31 51.59	+ 0.73	− 0.92	IV.	4	51.468	− 7 31.01	−29.25	−0.68	10 31 51.40	−30 57 0.94

CORRECTIONS.

Date.	Corr. of Clock.	Hourly rate.	m	n	c	Zenith Point.	Mic. Co.	Remarks.
1847.	h. s.	s.	s.	s.	s.	° ' ''	r.	(107) 59. Transit over middle thread assumed to be recorded against T. V.

INSTRUMENT READINGS.

Date	A.	B.	C.	D.	E.	F.	Mean.	Barom.	At.	Ex.	U.	L.	I.
Zone 107 April 9, 9 50	70 9 56.9	66.3	55.9	64.7	46.9	63.1	58.97						
10 20								29.990	58.1	50.2			
11 0		55.9	66.9	55.9	65.2	46.8	63.0	58.95	29.988	58.0	49.6	56.4	56.0

ZONE 107. APRIL 9. C. $D_0 = -30° 49' 0''$—Continued.

No.	Mag.	I	II	III	IV	V	VI	VII	T. (h. m. s.)	a_1 (s.)	a_2 (s.)
78	9	. .	10.	28.	46.5	. .	. .	. .	10 33 46.18	+ 0.73	− 1.07
79	9	. .	. .	. .	22.2	39.7	58.	. .	34 22.09	0.73	1.02
80	7	. .	43.2	0.7	19.	. .	. .	12.7	36 18.91	0.74	0.96
81	7	. .	. .	. .	. .	42.2	0.7	18.6	36 24.46	0.74	1.22
82	7	. .	37.	54.5	12.7	31.	49.	. .	40 12.87	0.75	0.92
83	9.10	. .	. .	. .	. .	. .	. .	59.	40 5.00	0.75	1.16
84	9	. .	. .	. .	. .	. .	59.7	17.5	43 23.46	0.77	1.41
85	9	. .	. .	. .	6.2	25.	. .	. .	43 48.63	0.77	1.10
86	9	. .	21.	38.2	50.2	. .	. .	. .	45 56.46	0.78	1.04
87	8.9	. .	. .	27.	44.	3.	21.	. .	46 44.73	0.78	1.36
88	9	. .	58.2	. .	10.	. .	. .	. .	48 34.17	0.79	1.01
89	7	. .	. .	. .	46.2	4.5	22.	. .	48 46.28	0.79	0.99
90	9	. .	. .	. .	6.2	24.6	42.1	. .	50 6.32	0.79	1.18
91	9	. .	. .	. .	. .	. .	11.	29.	50 35.06	0.79	1.10
92	9	. .	. .	36.	. .	54.	12.	. .	52 35.98	0.80	1.32
93	9	. .	. .	. .	. .	30.2	48.	. .	52 53.99	0.80	1.38
94	7	. .	. .	. .	. .	. .	. .	. .	54	0.81	1.05
95	7.8	. .	31.5	50.	. .	7.5	25.3	43.4	56 7.56	0.82	1.13
96	9	. .	. .	15.	. .	51.2	. .	. .	57 33.09	0.82	1.21
97	9	. .	28.2	46.2	4.7	. .	. .	. .	10 58	0.83	1.29
98	9	. .	. .	. .	. .	. .	57.	15.	11 1 4.39	0.84	1.22
99	9	. .	. .	. .	. .	57.	15.	. .	1 39.01	0.84	1.20
100	7	. .	. .	. .	. .	0.	17.7	36.	11 2 41.79	+ 0.84	− 1.41

No.	MICROMETER		r.	i	d_1	d_2	Mean Right Ascension, 1850.0 (h. m. s.)	Mean Declination, 1850.0 (° ′ ″)
78	III.	3	40.368	−19 9.42	−29.54	−2.39	10 33 45.84	−31 8 41.35
79	IV.	4	45.472	13 47.03	29.61	1.59	34 21.73	31 3 18.23
80	IV.	3	50.149	8 56.24	29.91	0.88	36 18.69	30 58 27.03
81	V.	3	28.498	31 34.61	29.92	4.23	36 23.98	31 21 8.76
82	IV.	4	54.533	4 18.83	30.48	0.21	41 12.70	30 53 49.52
83	VII.	3	34.		30.46	3.36	40 4.59	
84	VI.	2	14.169	46 34.32	30.96	6.54	43 22.82	31 36 11.82
85	V.	3	40.340	19 11.80	31.02	2.39	43 48.30	8 44.21
86	IV.	3	45.176	14 8.17	31.34	1.63	45 56.20	3 41.14
87	IV.	2	18.399	42 9.03	31.46	5.85	46 44.15	31 46.34
88	IV.	4	48.494	10 37.51	31.75	1.14	48 33.95	31 0 10.40
89	IV.	4	49.381	9 41.95	31.78	0.99	48 46.08	30 59 14.72
90	IV.	3	35.418	24 20.28	31.97	3.16	50 5.93	31 13 55.41
91	VI.	3	42.127	17 19.65	32.04	2.10	50 34.75	6 53.79
92	IV.	3	23.619	36 40.45	32.34	5.00	52 35.46	26 17.79
93	VI.	2	18.621	41 54.91	32.39	5.81	52 53.41	31 33.11
94	VII.	4	46.379	12 49.39	32.55	1.45	54	2 23.39
95	IV.	4	39.897	19 36.50	32.86	2.45	56 7.25	9 11.81
96	IV.	3	33.361	26 29.33	33.06	3.47	57 32.70	16 5.86
97		3	27.533	32 34.91	33.14	4.39	58	22 12.44
98	IV.	3	32.950	26 54.86	33.57	3.52	11 1 4.01	16 31.95
99	V.	3	34.825	24 57.49	33.65	3.24	1 38.65	14 34.38
100	V.	2	17.040	−43 34.18	−33.79	−6.09	11 2 41.22	−31 33 14.06

ZONE 108. APRIL 9. C. $D_0 = -30° 49' 0''$.

No.	Mag.	I	II	III	IV	V	VI	VII	T. (h. m. s.)	a_1 (s.)	a_2 (s.)
1	8	. .	. .	32.	50.	8.	26.2	. .	12 22 8.06	+ 1.32	− 1.03
2	8	. .	32.1	50.2	8.	26.2	. .	. .	24 8.16	1.34	1.13
3	8	. .	. .	38.2	56.3	15.	. .	. .	24 38.43	1.34	1.13
4	8	. .	. .	. .	50.	8.	. .	. .	25 31.89	1.35	1.14
5	8	. .	. .	. .	26.	44.	. .	. .	26 7.87	1.35	1.14
6	8	. .	. .	. .	. .	. .	. .	9.	26 14.99	1.35	1.05
7	9	. .	. .	51.2	. .	27.8	45.7	. .	28 9.59	1.37	1.03
8	8.9	. .	. .	54.	12.	30.2	. .	. .	28 54.07	1.37	1.06
9	9	. .	. .	52.7	. .	28.3	. .	. .	29 52.47	1.38	1.14
10	8.9	. .	24.3	42.	0.	17.8	36.1	. .	33 0.07	1.41	0.98
11	9	. .	. .	51.	9.	25.	. .	. .	34 8.32	1.42	0.99
12	9.10	. .	. .	33.7	52.	10.	. .	. .	37 51.90	1.44	1.02
13	8.9	. .	25.	43.	. .	18.7	36.6	. .	38 0.86	1.44	1.01
14	9	. .	. .	. .	. .	. .	15.7	6.8	39 21.81	1.45	1.00
15	8	. .	. .	. .	31.2	49.1	. .	. .	40 12.94	1.46	1.11
16	9	. .	. .	0.	18.1	36.1	. .	. .	43 36.09	1.50	1.06
17	9	. .	. .	34.2	52.6	10.	. .	. .	44 52.27	1.50	1.03
18	8	. .	. .	50.7	9.	26.5	. .	3.	49 26.83	1.54	1.12
19	8.9	. .	24.	42.	0.	17.8	36.	. .	52 59.97	1.57	1.08
20	8.9	. .	42.	0.	. .	36.	. .	. .	52 18.00	1.57	1.06
21	9	. .	48.9	. .	25.	42.5	. .	. .	54 24.80	1.58	1.03
22	9.10	. .	. .	. .	. .	38.5	. .	. .	12 59 20.38	+ 1.62	− 1.17

No.	MICROMETER		r.	i	d_1	d_2	Mean Right Ascension, 1850.0 (h. m. s.)	Mean Declination, 1850.0 (° ′ ″)
1	IV.	3	35.708	−24 1.91	−42.07	−3.09	12 22 8.35	−31 13 47.07
2	IV.	2	8.561	52 26.45	42.19	7.52	24 8.37	42 16.16
3	IV.	2	12.518	48 18.07	42.22	6.86	24 38.64	38 7.15
4	V.	2	13.052	47 44.49	42.27	6.77	25 32.10	37 33.53
5	IV.	2	10.110	50 49.22	42.31	7.24	26 8.08	40 38.77
6	VII.	3	33.709	26 7.56	42.32	3.41	26 15.29	15 53.29
7	IV.	3	40.968	18 31.96	42.43	2.24	28 9.93	8 16.63
8	IV.	3	28.910	31 8.32	42.48	4.19	28 54.38	20 54.99
9	IV.	2	13.118	47 40.35	42.53	6.76	29 52.71	31 37 29.64
10	IV.	4	53.895	4 58.65	42.69	0.26	33 0.50	30 54 41.60
11	IV.	4	49.779	9 54.49	42.74	1.00	34 8.75	30 59 38.23
12	IV.	4	45.025	14 14.94	42.92	1.62	37 52.32	31 3 59.48
13	IV.	4	52.186	6 46.00	42.93	0.51	38 1.29	30 56 29.44
14	VII.	4	56.098	8 56.05	42.95	0.84	39 22.26	30 58 39.84
15	V.	2	20.012	40 27.66	43.04	5.62	40 13.29	31 30 16.32
16	IV.	3	35.879	23 51.12	43.19	3.07	43 36.53	13 37.38
17	IV.	4	46.482	12 43.68	43.25	1.40	44 52.74	2 28.33
18	IV	2	21.038	39 23.21	43.47	5.46	49 27.25	29 12.14
19	IV.	3	35.571	24 10.62	43.59	3.11	52 0.46	13 57.32
20	IV.	2	42.162	17 17.21	43.57	2.06	52 18.51	31 7 2.84
21	IV.	4	50.530	8 29.84	43.65	0.76	54 25.35	30 58 14.25
22	V.	2	13.124	−47 40.04	−43.84	−6.76	12 59 20.83	−31 37 30.64

CORRECTIONS.

Date.	Corr. of Clock.	Hourly rate.	m	n	c	Zenith Point.	Mic. Co.
1847.	h.	s.	s.	s.	s.	° ′ ″	r.

REMARKS.

(107) 82. Minutes assumed as 41 instead of 40.

(108) 19. Minutes assumed as 51, not 52.

INSTRUMENT READINGS.

Date.	CIRCLE.							Barom.	THERMOM.				
		A.	B.	C.	D.	E.	F.	Mean.		At.	Ex.	U.	L.	I.
Zone 108 April 9, 12 20									29.982	53.5	46.2			
12 40											45.9			
13 0		70 9 54.4	67.5	55.4	66.3	46.9	62.1	58.82	29.986	53.0	45.0	53.0	53.0	
13 30											44.7			
13 40									29.982		44.7			
14 0		53.8	68.5	55.5	67.0	46.7	62.0	58.92	29.872	52.0	44.2	53.0	53.0	60.0

ZONE 108. APRIL 9. C. $D_0 = -30°\ 49'\ 0''$—Continued.

No.	Mag.	I.	II.	III.	IV.	V.	VI.	VII.	T. (h. m. s.)	a_1	a_0	Micrometer	n	r.	i	d_1	d_2	Mean Right Ascension, 1850.0	Mean Declination, 1850.0
23	9			45.5	3.2	21.5	39.5		13 1 3.44	+1.63	−1.08	IV.	3	36.420	−23 17.42	−43.88	−2.97	13 1 3.99	−31 13 4.27
24	8.9				58.1	16.	34.		1 58.04	1.64	1.10	IV.	3	32.098	27 48.43	43.90	3.67	1 58.58	17 36.00
25	.			37.2					3 55.25	1.66	1.18	III.	3	11.444	49 24.22	43.94	7.07	3 55.73	39 15.23
26	8				28.7	46.6	4.5	22.8	4 28.70	1.67	1.05	IV.	4	45.296	13 58.14	43.95	1.55	4 29.32	3 43.64
27	9.10						22.	40.7	5 46.28	1.67	1.13	VI.	3	22.762	37 34.46	43.98	5.19	5 46.82	27 23.63
28	9		34.		10.				10 10.04	1.71	1.11	IV.	3	30.972	28 59.01	44.07	3.84	10 10.64	18 46.92
29	9.10						47.8		10 11.80	1.71	1.11	VI.	3	29.560	30 28.04	44.07	4.06	10 12.40	20 16.17
30	9.10		31.3						13 7.42	1.73	1.15	II.	2	18.058	42 29.74	44.09	5.98	13 8.00	32 19.81
31	9.10			0.					13 18.04	1.73	1.15	III.	2	19.581	40 54.53	44.09	5.73	13 18.62	30 44.35
32	9.10			2.					13 20.04	1.74	1.16	III.	2	17.788	42 46.93	44.09	6.02	13 20.62	32 37.04
33	9								15	1.75	1.18	VII.	2	15.860	44 47.74	44.07	6.33	15	34 38.14
34	9.10		59.		34.7		10.6		21 34.86	1.80	1.15	IV.	3	25.381	34 50.01	44.12	4.76	21 35.51	24 38.89
35	8.9			49.2	7.	25.5			23 7.24	1.82	1.14	IV.	3	26.038	32 3.10	44.12	4.34	22 7.92	21 51.56
36	8.9				56.5	14.5	32.9		23 56.64	1.83	1.12	IV.	3	32.732	27 8.59	44.11	3.57	23 57.35	16 56.27
37	9					12.			24 53.97	1.84	1.12	V.	3	32.537	27 21.21	44.11	3.60	24 54.69	17 8.92
38	9							44.	24 50.05	1.84	1.09	VII.	4	42.518	16 51.49	44.11	1.99	24 50.80	6 37.59
39	8				43.		19.3		26 43.16	1.84	1.16	IV.	3	23.671	36 37.13	44.10	5.04	26 43.84	26 26.27
40	8				16.	33.7	52.2		27 15.91	1.85	1.20	IV.	2	14.379	46 21.32	44.10	6.60	27 16.56	36 12.02
41	8.9					33.4	51.6	10.	28 15.59	1.86	1.22	V.	2	12.549	48 16.13	44.09	6.90	28 16.23	38 7.12
42	8.9				8.	26.	43.7		29 7.84	1.88	1.20	IV.	2	14.900	45 42.78	44.09	6.46	29 8.52	35 33.33
43	9							33.7	29 39.58	1.88	1.18	VII.	3	21.889	38 29.12	44.08	5.33	29 40.28	28 18.53
44	8.9		0.7	19.		55.			35 36.90	1.93	1.09	IV.	4	45.483	13 46.34	44.01	1.52	35 37.74	3 31.87
45	9.10			24.	42.	0.2			36 42.06	1.94	1.20	IV.	2	16.325	44 19.19	43.99	6.25	36 42.80	34 9.43
46	9			46.5	4.8	23.			39 4.75	1.96	1.23	IV.	2	10.151	50 46.65	43.96	7.28	39 5.48	40 37.89
47	9.10					51.			39 32.92	1.97	1.19	V.	3	21.021	39 23.65	43.96	5.47	39 33.70	29 13.08
48	9.10						46.		40 9.95	1.97	1.18	VI.	3	22.588	37 45.52	43.95	−5.22	40 10.74	31 27 34.69
49	5				24.2	42.	0.7		43 24.36	2.02	1.06	IV.	4	56.168	2 36.26	43.90	+0.15	43 25.32	30 52 20.01
50	6					52.	10.	28.2	45 34.09	2.03	1.13	V.	3	38.338	21 17.37	43.86	−2.66	44 34.99	31 11 3.89
51	8							35.7	45 41.65	2.03	1.16	VII.	3	28.582	31 29.28	43.86	4.25	45 42.52	21 17.39
52	8.9								47	2.04	1.16	VII.	3	28.320	31 45.84	43.84	4.29	46	21 33.97
53	8.9		6.2		42.	59.8	18.		50 59.94	2.07	1.09	IV.	4	48.244	10 53.19	43.77	1.11	51 0.92	31 0 38.07
54	6.7		43.	1.	19.		54.7		54 18.94	2.10	1.11	IV.	4	51.066	7 56.10	43.69	0.64	54 19.93	30 57 40.43
55	9.10		26.7	44.7			39.		56 2.82	2.12	1.20	IV.	3	26.658	33 29.75	43.65	4.56	56 3.74	31 23 17.96
56	9.10		13.	31.3	49.7				13 58 49.34	2.15	1.15	IV.	3	39.906	19 38.51	43.59	2.39	13 58 50.34	9 24.49
57	8		29.2	47.		23.2	41.		14 2 5.10	2.18	1.19	IV.	3	29.559	32 3.72	43.49	4.34	14 2 6.09	21 51.55
58	9				18.	36.			2 18.01	2.18	1.18	IV.	3	29.028	30 27.79	43.48	4.10	2 19.01	20 15.37
59	8.9						17.8	35.7	2 41.67	2.18	1.21	VI.	3	22.636	37 42.51	43.46	5.23	2 42.64	27 31.20
60	8.9		30.3	48.2	6.8				5 6.47	2.20	1.18	IV.	3	29.468	30 33.56	43.38	4.11	5 7.49	20 21.05
61	9			39.	56.8				5 56.90	2.21	1.13	IV.	4	44.191	15 7.37	43.35	1.70	5 57.98	4 52.42
62	9					23.2	42.		6 5.50	2.22	1.24	V.	2	14.539	46 11.28	43.34	6.61	6 6.48	36 1.23
63	7.8							23.5	14 7 29.45	+2.23	−1.19	VII.	3	28.491	−31 35.05	−43.29	−4.26	14 7 30.49	−31 21 22.60

CORRECTIONS.

Date.	Corr. of Clock.	Hourly rate.	m	n	c	Zenith Point.	Mic. Co.
1847.	h.	s.	s.	s.	s.	° ′ ″	r.

INSTRUMENT READINGS.

Date.	Circle A.	B.	C.	D.	E.	F.	Mean.	Barom.	Thermom. At.	Ex.	U.	L.	I.
1847. h. m.	° ′ ″						″	In.	°	°	°	°	°

REMARKS.

(108) 35. Minutes assumed as 22 instead of 23.

(108) 50. Minutes assumed as 44 instead of 45.

(108) 53. Transit across T. I assumed to be recorded as over T. II.

Zone 109. April 13. C. $D_e = -28° 56' 30''$.

No.	Mag.	I.	II.	III.	IV.	V.	VI.	VII.	T. (h. m. s.)	a_1	a_2	MICROMETER		r	i (′ ″)	d_1	d_2	Mean Declination, 1850.0	Mean Right Ascension, 1850.0
1	7.8						35.	52.4	9 41 59.46			VI.	2	19.561	−40 55.97	5.67	5.41		−29 37 37.05
2	8				29.	46.7	4.	21.7	43 28.90			IV.	4	43.724	15 36.53	5.93	2.18		12 14.64
3	9.10				4.	21.7			47 4.03			IV.	3	38.759	20 50.52	6.55	2.85		17 29.92
4	9		23.7	41.		15.3			49 58.43			IV.	3	31.873	28 2.43	7.06	3.76		24 43.25
5	9		22.5	40.		14.			49 57.27			IV.	4	42.440	16 57.19	7.06	2.35		13 36.60
6	9		14.7	32.	50.	7.6	24.		51 49.66			IV.	3	26.610	33 32.77	7.39	4.46		30 14.62
7	9.10				15.2				53 15.24			IV.	3	24.054	36 13.14	7.63	4.80		32 25.57
8	9						57.		54 21.75			VI.	4	40.342	19 8.47	7.83	2.62		15 48.92
9	8							15.5	56 22.43			VI.	3	24.058	36 13.21	8.19	4.80		32 56.20
10	8							43.	56 49.94			VII.	3	25.356	34 51.83	8.27	4.63		31 34.73
11	9				27.	45.	2.7		58 27.22			IV.	3	25.982	34 12.10	8.57	4.54		30 55.21
12	9				45.7				9 50 45.74			IV.	3	33.071	26 47.40	8.80	3.60		23 29.80
13	9			48.7		23.7	41.5		10 1 6.17			IV.	3	26.208	33 58.04	9.02	4.52		30 41.58
14	9				4.		35.		2 0.4			IV.	4	42.048	17 21.66	9.18	2.40	10 1 57.8	14 3.24
15	8				43.	1.3	18.5		6 43.22			IV.	2	16.106	44 32.87	10.00	5.89		41 18.76
16	8.9		8.	26.	43.7				13 43.64			IV.	2	12.079	48 45.56	11.22	6.44		45 33.22
17	8			26.	43.3	1.3			14 43.53			IV.	4	44.951	14 19.52	11.39	2.00		11 2.91
18	7		48.	5.3	23.7		59.2		16 23.48			IV.	3	32.361	27 32.06	11.68	3.70		24 17.44
19	9			25.		1.2			16 43.09			IV.	3	35.708	24 1.91	11.73	3.24		20 46.88
20	8							52.7	16 59.64			VII.	3	25.485	34 43.73	11.77	4.62		31 30.12
21	9		46.2	4.7	22.				19 2.98			IV.	3	32.762	27 6.71	12.13	3.64		23 52.48
22	9				34.	52.			19 34.18			IV.	3	41.222	18 16.16	12.22	2.50		15 0.88
23	9					16.2	34.	52.3	19 58.86			V.	3	37.778	21 52.23	12.30	2.97		18 37.50
24	9		53.	10.5	28.2				10 22 28.31			IV.	2	11.252	−49 31.32	−12.73	−6.54		−29 46 20.59

Zone 110. April 16. C. $D_e = -27° 4' 0''$.

No.	Mag.	I.	II.	III.	IV.	V.	VI.	VII.	T. (h. m. s.)	a_1	a_2	MICROMETER		r	i (′ ″)	d_1	d_2	Mean Declination, 1850.0	Mean Right Ascension, 1850.0
1	7.8				17.2	34.	51.1		10 5 16.27	− 2.50	−1.37	IV.	2	12.889	−47 54.60	−0.99	−6.04	10 5 12.40	−27 52 1.63
2	9				53.5	11.2	28.3		6 53.61	2.50	0.96	IV.	4	49.891	9 9.72	1.27	1.69	6 50.15	13 12.68
3	9		24.7						8 59.71	2.50	1.25	II.	3	23.501	36 47.03	1.63	4.76	8 55.96	40 53.42
4	7.8			19.2	35.7	52.9	10.2		9 18.00	2.50	1.37	IV.	3	12.690	48 7.15	1.68	6.06	9 14.13	52 14.89
5	8		19.7	38.	56.				11 55.08	2.50	1.14	IV.	3	32.924	26 56.48	2.12	3.64	11 51.44	31 2.24
6	8				20.5	38.	55.2		12 3.04	2.50	1.25	V.	3	23.169	37 9.00	2.13	4.80	11 59.29	41 15.93
7	8.9		8.2	26.8	44.7	1.4			14 43.80	2.50	1.13	IV.	3	33.560	26 16.22	2.57	3.57	14 40.17	30 22.36
8	8.9		23.2	42.	0.				16 59.99	2.49	0.97	IV.	4	47.721	11 25.86	2.95	1.95	16 55.53	15 30.76
9	8.9		55.2	12.8		47.3	4.3		22 12.23	2.49	1.35	IV.	3	21.708	38 40.29	3.79	4.95	22 8.49	42 49.06
10	6	1.6	17.7	36.6	53.8		28.2	45.6	24 53.38	2.48	1.09	IV.	3	35.826	23 54.45	4.21	3.31	24 49.81	28 1.97
11	9		12.7	30.7		6.2			26 48.15	2.48	1.23	IV.	3	22.782	37 32.84	4.51	4.85	26 44.44	41 42.20
12	8.9			21.	38.2	55.2			30 37.90	2.47	0.97	IV.	4	45.891	13 20.56	5.11	2.15	30 34.52	17 27.82
13	9			12.	29.5		3.4		31 29.02	2.47	0.99	IV.	4	43.478	15 52.09	5.24	2.41	31 25.56	19 59.74
14	9				48.	6.			31 30.97	2.47	1.05	V.	4	38.216	21 22.00	5.24	3.03	31 27.45	25 30.27
15	9		41.3	0.7	18.5	35.2			34 17.47	2.47	1.00	IV.	4	42.448	16 56.68	5.60	2.54	34 14.00	21 4.88
16	9		35.		12.	28.2			36 10.62	2.46	1.26	IV.	2	19.172	41 20.46	5.95	5.26	36 6.90	45 31.67
17	9		46.3	4.8		39.5			37 21.82	2.46	1.24	IV.	2	20.029	40 26.54	6.13	5.18	37 18.12	44 37.85
18	9		51.		27.4		1.1		39 26.39	2.46	1.01	IV.	4	41.008	18 26.89	6.44	2.71	39 22.92	22 36.04
19	8.9		51.2		27.7		1.6	19.	39 26.79	2.46	0.99	IV.	4	42.402	16 59.64	6.44	2.54	39 23.34	21 8.62
20	9				21.2		56.3		46 3.93	2.44	1.13	V.	3	29.371	30 39.90	7.38	4.07	46 0.36	34 51.35
21	9		51.3	28.					10 48 26.85	− 2.44	−0.91	IV.	4	49.329	− 9 45.22	−7.72	−1.76	10 48 23.50	−27 13 54.70

CORRECTIONS.

Date.	Corr. of Clock.	Hourly rate.	m	n	c	Zenith Point.	Mic. Co.
1847.	h.	s.	s.	s.	s.	° ′ ″	r.

REMARKS.

INSTRUMENT READINGS.

	Date.	A.	B.	C.	D.	E.	F.	Mean.	Barom.	At.	Ex.	U.	L.	I.
	1847. (h. m.)	° ′ ″						″	In.	°	°	°	°	°
Zone 109	April 13, 9 40								30.132	55.8	50.5			
	10 20	{68 17 26.2	36.1	25.0	36.2	15.8	32.2}	28.39	30.138	54.5	49.8	53.7	53.5	59.8
		24.8	34.8	25.6	36.7	15.8	31.5}				50.7			
Zone 110	April 16, 10 5	66 24 56.3	70.1	56.9	69.0	49.9	63.6	61.12				45.7		56.7 53.5
	10 20								30.038	54.0	45.5		53.7	
											45.3			
	10 40													
	10 50	56.1	70.9	57.7	69.9	50.3	63.6	61.42	30.035	52.5	45.2		52.6	51.4

Zone 110. April 16. C. $D_o = -27° 4' 0''$ — Continued.

No.	Mag.	I.	II.	III.	IV.	V.	VI.	VII.	T.	a_1	a_2	Mic.	n	r	i	d_1	d_2	Mean Right Ascension, 1850.0	Mean Declination, 1850.0
									h. m. s.	s.	s.			r.	' "	"	"	h. m. s.	° ' "
22	8.9	..	22.	40.2	58.2	14.8	..	..	10 49 57.30	− 2.43	−1.18	IV.	3	23.942	−36 20.04	− 7.96	−4.70	10 49 53.69	−27 40 32.70
23	8.9	..	..	35.	52.8	9.7	..	..	50 52.23	2.43	1.08	IV.	3	33.201	26 39.31	8.07	3.62	50 48.72	30 51.00
24	9	..	..	43.5	1.5	18.7	35.7	..	10 52 0.90	− 2.43	−1.16	IV.	3	25.317	−34 54.02	− 8.24	−4.55	10 51 57.31	−27 39 6.81

Zone 111. April 21. C. $D_n = -26° 26' 20''$.

No.	Mag.	I.	II.	III.	IV.	V.	VI.	VII.	T.	a_1	a_2	Mic.	n	r	i	d_1	d_2	Mean Right Ascension, 1850.0	Mean Declination, 1850.0
1	6	..	20.5	37.3	55.	12.	29.7	..	10 26 54.85	− 5.01	−0.59	IV.	4	50.846	− 8 9.84	− 3.08	−0.80	10 26 49.25	−26 34 33.72
2	5	54.	10.8	26.2	46.	..	22.5	37.7	29 45.90	5.01	0.58	IV.	3	33.431	26 24.93	3.51	2.62	29 40.37	52 51.06
3	4	..	42.6	..	17.5	34.	51.7	..	30 17.09	5.01	0.60	IV.	4	47.329	11 50.64	3.58	1.17	30 11.48	38 15.39
4	8	..	9.7	27.	44.7	..	..	..	38 44.23	5.00	0.60	IV.	4	42.255	17 8.80	4.77	1.68	38 38.63	26 43 35.25
5	7	..	21.5	39.5	37.	13.8	31.	..	10 41 56.35	− 5.00	−0.60	IV.	2	19.381	−41 7.39	− 5.23	−4.14	10 41 50.78	−27 7 30.76

Zone 112. May 4. Γ. $D_o = -26° 26' 40''$.

No.	Mag.	I.	II.	III.	IV.	V.	VI.	VII.	T.	a_1	a_2	Mic.	n	r	i	d_1	d_2	Mean Right Ascension, 1850.0	Mean Declination, 1850.0
1	8	..	15.	32.5	50.3	..	..	..	11 47 49.68	−11.72	−0.75	IV.	3	32.534	−27 21.14	− 0.75	−2.72	11 47 37.21	−26 54 4.61
2	8	..	..	..	..	..	..	59.	48 6.82	11.72	0.66	VII.	1	9.153	51 48.42	0.78	5.37	47 54.44	27 18 34.57
3	6.7	..	8.	25.5	43.3	..	..	..	50 42.69	11.71	0.53	IV.	3	35.730	24 0.53	1.04	2.36	50 30.23	26 50 43.93
4	8.9	..	..	..	..	..	..	10.	51 18.38	11.71	0.81	VII.	4	49.630	9 25.53	1.10	0.82	51 5.86	36 7.45
5	8	..	..	..	18.5	..	..	..	53 18.26	11.70	0.82	IV.	4	52.615	6 19.04	1.29	0.48	53 5.74	33 0.81
6	8	..	..	..	46.	..	..	..	54 45.47	11.70	0.76	IV.	3	37.704	21 56.69	1.42	2.14	54 33.01	48 40.25
7	8	..	..	..	59.	..	..	..	11 59 58.58	11.69	0.77	IV.	4	43.465	15 52.91	1.92	1.50	11 59 46.12	26 42 36.33
8	7.8	..	..	..	..	..	52.	..	12 1 59.93	11.68	0.66	VII.	2	16.170	44 29.61	2.09	4.58	12 1 47.59	27 11 15.28
9	8	..	..	..	..	..	43.	..	2 50.96	11.68	0.67	VII.	2	18.410	42 8.08	2.16	4.34	2 38.61	8 54.58
10	7	..	..	..	22.	38.	..	..	3 20.78	11.68	0.65	IV.	2	13.640	47 7.58	2.20	4.85	3 8.45	27 13 54.63
11	6.7	..	33.	50.5	8.	..	..	..	6 7.62	11.67	0.81	IV.	4	56.305	2 27.79	2.43	0.08	5 55.14	26 29 10.30
12	8	..	20.	..	55.3	..	..	..	7 54.72	11.66	0.74	IV.	4	38.580	20 59.24	2.58	2.05	7 42.32	26 47 43.87
13	8	..	..	..	1.3	..	..	..	8 43.91	11.66	0.67	V.	2	20.170	40 17.82	2.65	4.12	8 31.58	27 7 4.59
14	7.8	..	25.	42.5	17.	..	..	..	13 59.70	11.65	0.69	V.	3	28.016	32 4.73	3.04	3.24	13 47.36	26 58 51.01
15	8	..	31.	48.	6.	..	..	..	15 5.41	11.64	0.70	IV.	3	30.950	29 0.33	3.11	2.89	14 53.07	55 46.33
16	5.6	48.3	5.3	..	40.5	..	..	..	17 39.96	11.63	0.71	IV.	3	31.662	28 15.79	3.29	2.82	17 27.62	55 1.90
17	7	..	54.	..	29.	..	..	..	19 28.55	11.63	0.70	IV.	3	34.380	25 25.40	3.42	2.52	19 16.22	26 52 11.34
18	8	.41.	..	16.3	34.	..	..	..	23 33.16	11.62	0.67	IV.	3	26.096	34 5.01	3.62	3.45	23 20.87	27 0 52.08
19	6	..	..	..	46.	3.	..	..	24 28.64	11.62	0.74	V.	4	41.905	17 30.44	3.66	1.67	24 16.28	26 44 15.77
20	8.9	..	..	..	..	..	..	59.5	26 7.44	11.61	0.64	VII.	2	16.825	43 47.31	3.74	4.51	25 55.19	27 10 35.56
21	8	..	..	..	34.	..	..	..	28 33.71	11.60	0.76	IV.	4	49.770	9 17.32	3.86	0.80	28 21.35	26 36 1.98
22	7	15.	32.	49.	..	..	..	..	33 6.52	11.58	0.69	III.	3	33.333	26 31.34	4.02	2.63	32 54.25	26 53 17.99
23	6.7	..	..	..	29.5	..	..	3.3	33 28.66	11.58	0.65	IV.	2	22.153	38 13.32	4.03	3.90	33 16.43	27 5 1.25
24	8	..	..	..	..	..	..	20.	35 28.41	11.58	0.76	VII.	4	52.897	6 0.53	4.09	0.46	35 16.07	26 32 45.08
25	7.8	16.	32.5	50.3	..	..	..	..	40 7.37	11.56	0.72	III.	4	41.665	17 45.67	4.22	1.70	39 55.09	44 31.59
26	5	..	..	..	40.	56.7	..	..	40 39.47	11.56	0.71	IV.	4	39.770	19 41.48	4.23	1.91	40 27.20	46 30.61
27	8	..	..	..	7.5	..	..	..	42 6.82	11.55	0.66	IV.	3	30.447	29 32.14	4.24	2.95	41 54.61	26 56 19.33
28	7	..	..	..	53.	..	..	..	42 52.21	11.55	0.64	IV.	3	25.093	35 7.95	4.25	3.56	42 40.02	27 1 55.76
29	7	..	17.7	35.	52.3	..	..	..	45 52.11	11.54	0.74	IV.	4	50.614	8 24.51	4.27	0.70	45 39.83	26 35 9.48
30	8.9	..	..	..	36.	..	..	..	46 18.73	11.54	0.70	V.	4	41.320	18 7.39	4.27	1.74	46 6.49	26 44 53.40
31	8	..	..	..	..	..	..	15.	47 22.91	11.53	0.60	VII.	2	14.635	46 4.89	4.28	4.75	47 10.78	27 12 53.91
32	7	..	..	..	11.	28.	..	..	48 53.72	11.53	0.75	V.	4	51.610	7 21.93	4.30	0.59	48 41.44	26 31 6.82
33	7	..	3.	..	38.	..	..	..	53 37.63	11.51	0.74	IV.	4	52.333	6 36.85	4.32	0.52	53 25.38	33 21.69
34	7.8	..	..	..	7.	23.5	..	..	12 55 6.43	−11.50	−0.71	IV.	4	44.333	−14 58.54	− 4.32	−1.40	12 54 54.22	−26 41 44.26

CORRECTIONS.

Date.	Corr. of Clock.	Hourly rate.	m	n	c	Zenith Point.	Mic. Co.
1847. h.	s.	s.	s.	s.	s.	° ' "	r.

REMARKS.

INSTRUMENT READINGS.

	Date.	A.	B.	C.	D.	E.	F.	Mean.	Barom.	At.	Ex.	U.	L.	I.
	1847. h. m.	° ' "						"	In.	°	°	°	°	°
Zone 111	April 21, 10 26	{65 47 28.1 / 28.1	38.8 / 38.3	22.9 / 23.9	35.9 / 38.2	20.1 / 20.7	35.4 / 36.0}	30.53		..	..	..	74.6	
	30	.	.	.	.	.	.	.	30.092	70.6	70.6			
	40	.	.	.	.	.	.	.		..	70.4	..	69.5	59.5
Zone 112	May 4, 11 47	.	.	.	.	.	.	.	30.064	51.4	44.2			
		{65 47 34.3 / 34.0	43.4 / 42.0	30.6 / 31.0	44.5 / 45.6	19.4 / 19.6	37.8 / 37.4}	34.96	30.218	60.4	54.0	60.0	60.0	
	12 30	.	.	.	.	.	.	.	30.224	59.0	51.4			
	13 00	.	.	.	.	.	.	.	30.228	58.0	53.0			

ZONE 112. MAY 4. P. D_a = −26° 26′ 40″—Continued.

No.	Mag.	I.	II.	III.	IV.	V.	VI.	VII.	T.	a_1	a_2	Mic.		r.	i	d_1	d_2	Mean Right Ascension, 1850.0.	Mean Declination, 1850.0.
									h. m. s.	s.	s.			r.	′ ″	″	″	h. m. s.	° ′ ″
35	8		43.	1.					12 58 17.98	−11.49	−0.63	III.	3	27.400	−32 42.93	−4.33	−3.29	12 58 5.86	−26 59 30.55
36	8		1.	18.5					13 0 35.80	11.48	0.59	III.	2	17.243	43 21.33	4.33	4.47	13 0 23.73	27 10 10.13
37	7				23.2			14.3	1 22.48	11.48	0.64	IV.	3	31.190	28 45.47	4.34	2.87	1 10.36	26 55 32.68
38	7.8		13.5	31.					5 48.16	11.46	0.66	III.	3	36.577	23 7.08	4.39	2.27	5 36.04	49 53.74
39	8				6.		40.		6 5.41	11.46	0.64	V.	3	31.693	28 14.04	4.40	2.82	5 53.31	55 1.26
40	8				31.				7 30.65	11.45	0.70	IV.	4	46.930	12 15.40	4.41	1.10	7 18.50	26 39 0.91
41	8						1.		8 26.25	11.45	0.55	VI.	1	11.403	49 27.24	4.42	5.12	8 14.25	27 16 16.78
42	7	36.	53.3	10.3					12 27.58	11.43	0.70	III.	4	48.716	10 23.40	4.47	0.92	12 15.45	26 37 8.79
43	9		56.						17 30.72	11.41	0.63	II.	3	32.010	27 53.01	4.54	2.78	17 18.66	54 40.33
44	7.8				55.		29.5		17 54.85	11.41	0.68	VI.	4	44.925	14 20.83	4.54	1.32	17 42.74	41 6.69
45	6.7		52.7	10.3	28.				20 27.44	11.40	0.68	IV.	4	48.628	10 29.05	4.58	0.92	20 15.36	37 14.55
46	7				25.	42.			21 24.74	11.39	0.69	IV.	4	49.217	9 52.18	4.59	0.86	21 12.66	36 37.63
47	7				43.5				22 42.93	11.38	0.63	IV.	3	36.465	23 14.60	4.61	2.28	22 30.92	26 50 1.49
48	5.6					43.5	0.5		23 25.89	11.38	0.52	V.	1	7.623	53 24.34	4.63	5.56	23 13.98	27 20 14.53
49	9					8.			24 50.79	11.38	0.69	V.	4	51.113	7 53.09	4.65	0.65	24 38.72	26 34 38.39
50	7	5.5	22.3	40.	57.7				28 57.11	11.36	0.61	IV.	3	33.733	26 5.80	4.72	2.60	28 45.14	52 53.12
51	7					52.			30 34.81	11.35	0.70	V.	4	55.895	2 53.12	4.75	0.12	30 22.76	29 37.99
52	8					2.			31 44.73	11.34	0.65	V.	3	41.670	17 48.25	4.77	1.70	31 32.74	44 34.72
53	5.6							50.3	32 58.52	11.34	0.63	VII.	3	37.627	22 1.98	4.80	2.15	32 46.55	48 48.93
54	8.9							15.	33 23.19	11.34	0.62	VII.	3	35.550	24 12.31	4.80	2.38	33 11.23	26 50 59.49
55	9			24.					35 41.19	11.32	0.58	III.	3	26.707	33 26.23	4.85	3.39	35 29.29	27 0 14.47
56	8				56.				36 38.68	11.32	0.60	V.	3	33.315	26 32.47	4.86	2.64	36 26.76	26 53 19.97
57	7						56.3		37 21.65	11.32	0.56	VI.	2	21.345	39 4.08	4.88	3.99	37 9.77	27 5 52.95
58	7.8	47.7	4.5	22.	40.				42 39.29	11.29	0.59	IV.	3	29.240	30 47.81	4.93	3.10	42 27.41	26 57 35.84
59	8					27.			43 9.68	11.29	0.59	V.	3	33.427	26 25.43	4.93	2.61	42 57.80	53 12.98
60	6		38.5	56.					48 13.19	11.26	0.59	III.	3	32.627	27 14.87	4.94	2.71	48 1.34	54 2.52
61	7				36.5				48 35.83	11.26	0.59	IV.	3	31.400	28 32.35	4.95	2.85	48 23.98	55 20.15
62	7.8					7.5	1.	42.5	48 50.48	11.26	0.62	V.	3	39.293	20 17.45	4.95	1.97	48 38.60	26 47 4.37
63	8			41.					50 58.22	11.25	0.52	III.	2	18.333	42 12.98	4.94	4.34	50 46.45	27 9 2.26
64	7					36.3			51 18.91	11.25	0.53	V.	2	21.140	39 16.94	4.94	4.02	51 7.13	6 5.90
65	9							22.5	51 30.55	11.25	0.55	VII.	2	25.480	34 44.42	4.94	3.52	51 18.75	27 1 32.68
66	5					4.	20.7		54 3.45	11.24	0.61	IV.	3	38.985	15 22.64	4.91	1.21	53 51.60	26 42 8.76
67	6.7	49.	5.5	23.3	40.7				58 40.34	11.21	0.63	IV.	4	47.837	11 18.52	4.87	1.02	58 28.50	38 4.41
68	8			34.5					13 59 34.17	11.21	0.63	IV.	4	48.345	10 46.92	4.86	0.95	13 59 22.33	37 32.73
69	7		52.	10.	28.				14 1 27.11	11.20	0.62	IV.	4	45.983	13 14.85	4.82	1.21	14 1 15.29	40 0.88
70	5			23.	40.	57.3			4 22.84	11.18	0.65	IV.	4	52.593	6 20.42	4.75	0.49	4 11.01	26 33 5.66
71	7		43.3	1.	19.				6 18.17	11.18	0.52	IV.	2	23.723	36 34.73	4.70	3.73	6 6.47	27 3 23.16
72	8						29.		7 54.32	11.17	0.50	VI.	2	18.323	42 13.73	4.66	4.35	7 42.65	27 9 2.74
73	8				21.				9 46.50	11.16	0.58	VI.	3	37.050	22 38.10	4.62	2.22	9 34.76	26 49 24.94
74	6			24.		58.3			11 41.05	11.14	0.46	III.	1	6.560	54 30.50	4.55	5.68	11 29.45	27 21 20.73
75	7			58.	15.				13 14.89	11.14	0.61	IV.	4	48.075	11 3.67	4.50	0.98	13 3.14	26 37 49.15
76	4.5		5.	22.8	40.7				14 39.90	11.13	0.51	IV.	3	23.396	36 54.57	4.44	3.77	14 28.26	27 3 42.78
77	7.8					32.0			15 57.34	11.12	0.51	VI.	3	19.783	40 41.41	4.40	4.19	15 45.72	7 30.00
78	7							22.	15 30.03	11.12	0.56	VII.	3	23.530	36 46.47	4.41	3.75	15 18.40	3 34.63
79	8.9					22.			17 4.63	11.12	0.52	V.	3	25.340	34 52.83	4.36	3.53	16 52.99	27 1 40.72
80	7							26.	17 34.42	11.11	0.63	VII.	4	53.080	5 49.13	4.34	0.43	17 22.68	26 32 33.90
81	7			14.					19 31.11	11.10	0.60	III.	4	48.083	11 3.16	4.27	0.98	19 19.41	26 39 48.41
82	7						4.5		20 3.47	11.10	0.46	IV.	2	12.987	47 48.50	4.25	4.93	19 51.91	27 14 37.68
83	6.7			19.5	56.				21 54.67	11.09	0.44	IV.	1	7.317	53 43.42	4.16	4.59	21 43.14	20 32.17
84	6.7	43.	0.5	17.5	36.				14 23 34.99	−11.08	−0.51	IV.	3	24.790	−35 26.83	−4.07	−3.59	23 23.40	−27 2 14.49

CORRECTIONS.

Date.	Corr. of Clock.	Hourly rate.	m	n	c	Zenith Point.	Mic. Co.
1847.	h.	s.	s.	s.	s.	° ′ ″	r.

INSTRUMENT READINGS.

Date.	CIRCLE.							Barom.	THERMOM.				
		A.	B.	C.	D.	E.	F.	Mean.		At.	Ex.	U.	L.	l.
Zone 112	1847 May 4, 14 00								In.	°	°	°	°	°
	14 23	65 47 31.5	41.7	32.0	46.2	20.5	34.7	34.93*	30.230 / 30.236	56.5 / 55.0	47.5 / 46.0	60.	57.5	55.5

REMARKS.

(112) 35. Minutes assumed as 59 instead of 58.

(112) 66. Micrometer reading assumed as 43r.985 instead of 38r.985.

(112) 80. Transit time is evidently 1s in error.

*Corr. for runs, +0″.11.

ZONE 113. MAY 6. P. $D_e = -25°\ 48'\ 30''$.

No.	Mag.	I.	II.	III.	IV.	V.	VI.	VII.	T. (h. m. s.)	a_1 (s.)	a_2 (s.)	MICROMETER.		r.	i (' ")	d_1 (")	d_2 (")	Mean Right Ascension, 1850.0. (h. m. s.)	Mean Declination, 1850.0. (° ' ")
1	7				1.5	18.			11 32 1.01	−12.77	−0.57	IV.	4	47.403	−11 45.99	−33.83	−1.21	11 31 47.67	−26 0 51.03
2	8.9			21.	39.				33 38.35	12.77	0.57	IV.	4	49.433	9 38.69	33.97	1.01	33 25.01	25 58 43.67
3	9							25.5	33 34.14	12.77	0.57	VII.	4	48.613	10 29.30	33.96	1.09	33 20.80	25 59 34.35
4	8					33.5			35 16.15	12.76	0.64	V.	1	9.273	51 40.81	34.11	5.20	35 2.75	26 40 50.12
5	8				45.5			35.5	36 44.60	12.76	0.57	IV.	4	45.297	13 58.07	34.24	1.42	36 31.27	3 3.73
6	9	8.3		42.7				51.3	38 59.73	12.76	0.59	III.	3	34.973	24 47.63	34.43	2.48	38 46.38	26 13 54.54
7	4.5	32.7	49.7	7.					41 23.96	12.75	0.54	III.	4	53.033	5 52.76	34.63	0.64	41 10.67	25 54 58.03
8	8					53.3			41 35.95	12.75	0.63	V.	1	9.475	51 28.14	34.64	5.16	41 22.57	26 40 37.94
9	6.7		41.3	59.					43 16.02	12.75	0.61	III.	3	22.800	37 31.33	34.77	3.75	43 2.66	26 39.85
10	7				44.	0.7			43 43.44	12.75	0.59	IV.	3	34.178	25 38.01	34.81	2.54	43 30.10	14 45.36
11	9	53.	10.	27.3	45.3				45 44.51	12.75	0.60	IV.	2	21.170	39 15.06	34.96	3.92	45 31.16	28 23.94
12	8						45.		46 10.79	12.75	0.54	VI.	1	47.733	11 24.74	35.00	1.18	45 57.50	0 30.92
13	6.7	15.	32.	49.5	7.	23.8	40.7	58.	50 6.47	12.74	0.56	IV.	3	35.752	23 59.15	35.31	2.41	49 53.17	13 6.87
14	8		8.3	26.	43.7				52 42.98	12.73	0.56	IV.	3	32.983	26 52.85	35.49	2.67	52 29.69	16 1.01
15	8						53.		53 18.50	12.73	0.59	VI.	2	16.750	43 52.26	35.53	4.39	53 5.18	33 2.18
16	8.9			32.		6.5			54 49.17	12.73	0.56	IV.	3	30.740	29 13.57	35.64	2.92	54 35.88	18 22.13
17	9	34.3	51.	9.					58 25.86	12.72	0.57	III.	3	22.325	38 1.39	35.90	3.80	58 12.57	27 11.09
18	8.9	59.	16.	33.3					11 59 50.56	12.72	0.58	III.	2	16.487	44 8.77	36.00	4.42	11 59 37.26	33 19.19
19	8	0.0	17.	34.7					12 2 51.48	12.71	0.52	III.	4	42.587	16 47.02	36.19	1.69	12 2 38.25	5 55.80
20	7.8		27.5	45.	3.				4 2.15	12.71	0.54	IV.	3	34.730	25 3.26	36.27	2.48	3 48.90	14 12.01
21	7	16.7	34.	51.5	9.7	25.5			6 8.51	12.70	0.56	IV.	2	20.410	40 2.82	36.40	4.03	5 55.25	29 13.25
22	7		10.7	28.					8 45.14	12.70	0.53	III.	3	32.893	26 58.05	36.57	2.69	8 31.91	16 7.31
23	7						15.		8 40.47	12.70	0.57	VI.	2	13.930	46 49.24	36.56	4.67	8 27.20	36 0.47
24	8							24.	9 32.39	12.69	0.53	VII.	3	29.910	30 6.02	36.62	3.01	9 19.17	26 19 15.65
25	6	29.7	46.7	3.8	21.				12 20.86	12.69	0.48	IV.	4	53.810	5 3.99	36.78	0.53	12 7.69	25 54 11.30
26	7			24.					13 40.99	12.68	0.48	III.	4	54.020	4 50.87	36.86	0.51	13 27.83	25 53 58.24
27	7				3.7	21.			14 3.30	12.68	0.54	IV.	3	23.067	37 15.08	36.88	3.73	13 50.08	26 26 25.69
28	9			27.5					15 44.52	12.68	0.49	III.	4	46.943	12 14.59	36.98	1.21	15 31.35	26 1 22.78
29	9		26.	43.					18 0.18	12.67	0.47	IV.	4	49.337	9 44.65	37.11	0.95	17 47.04	25 58 52.71
30	7		26.	43.3	1.7				19 0.64	12.67	0.52	IV.	3	28.214	31 52.16	37.16	3.18	18 47.45	26 21 2.52
31	8.9		34.3		9.5				21 8.85	12.66	0.50	IV.	3	33.064	26 47.84	37.28	2.66	20 55.69	15 57.78
32	7.8			27.	44.3				22 43.88	12.66	0.49	IV.	3	33.613	26 13.40	37.36	2.60	22 30.73	15 23.36
33	5.6		54.5	12.3	30.7				24 29.44	12.65	0.55	IV.	1	6.027	55 4.21	37.45	5.58	24 16.24	44 17.24
34	7	40.5		15.3					26 32.17	12.65	0.51	III.	3	28.043	32 2.41	37.56	3.20	26 19.01	21 13.17
35	8				48.3		22.3		26 47.86	12.65	0.49	IV.	3	36.103	23 31.61	37.57	2.35	26 34.72	26 12 41.53
36	7							11.	27 19.72	12.64	0.45	VII.	4	54.887	3 55.76	37.60	0.42	27 6.63	25 53 3.78
37	8					6.5			28 49.38	12.64	0.45	V.	4	52.040	6 54.97	37.68	0.71	28 36.29	25 56 3.36
38	4.5				59.3	15.5	32.7		29 58.41	12.64	0.49	IV.	3	30.633	29 20.35	37.74	2.93	29 45.28	26 18 31.02
39	9				30.5				31 30.05	12.63	0.46	IV.	4	42.250	17 9.12	37.81	1.73	31 16.96	6 18.66
40	9					20.5			32 3.33	12.63	0.46	V.	4	43.243	16 6.71	37.84	1.63	31 50.24	5 16.18
41	8						34.		33 59.79	12.62	0.45	VI.	4	47.940	11 11.75	37.89	1.14	33 46.72	0 20.78
42	8							32.	33 40.11	12.62	0.53	VII.	1	8.853	52 7.05	37.91	5.27	33 26.96	41 20.23
43	9				30.				35 29.15	12.62	0.50	IV.	2	21.075	38 24.41	38.01	3.85	35 16.03	27 36.27
44	8				50.	6.5			36 49.46	12.61	0.45	IV.	4	43.675	15 39.62	38.06	1.58	36 36.40	4 49.26
45	9						20.7		38 46.23	12.61	0.50	VI.	2	20.293	40 10.10	38.15	4.04	38 33.12	26 29 22.28
46	5.6	19.	36.2	53.3	10.5				44 10.32	12.59	0.41	IV.	4	52.742	6 10.94	38.37	0.64	43 57.33	25 55 19.95
47	9.10							0.0	44 8.66	12.59	0.42	VII.	4	49.720	9 19.82	38.37	0.96	43 55.65	25 58 29.15
48	7				53.3	10.3			45 52.65	12.59	0.49	IV.	2	14.727	45 59.38	38.44	4.62	45 39.57	26 35 12.34
49	9		18.	36.					12 47 52.94	−12.58	−0.48	III.	2	13.673	−47 5.33	−38.52	−4.74	12 47 39.88	−26 36 18.59

CORRECTIONS.

Date.	Corr. of Clock.	Hourly rate.	m	n	c	Zenith Point.	Mic. Co.
1847.	h. s.	, s.	s.	s.	s.	° ' "	r.

REMARKS.

(113) 41. Minutes assumed as 32 instead of 33.

INSTRUMENT READINGS.

Date.	CIRCLE.							Barom.	THERMOM.				
	A.	B.	C.	D.	E.	F.	Mean.		At.	Ex.	U.	L.	I.
Zone 113 1847. May 6. 11 31	65 9 62.5	72.2	60.8	73.5	48.8	67.5	64.22	30.074	63.0	59.5	62.5	61.	
12 14								30.070	61.8	58.8			
13 00								30.058	61.0	55.5			
13 10										54.0			
13 27								30.050	60.5				
15 00	61.4	72.2	60.8	73.5	49.5	64.6	63.67	30.014	57.0	47.6			
16 00								29.992	55.0	45.2	56.	53.5	60.
18 20								29.956	52.0	44.0			

ZONE 113. MAY 6. P. D.=−25° 48′ 30″—Continued.

No.	Mag.	SECONDS OF TRANSIT. I.	II.	III.	IV.	V.	VI.	VII.	T.	a_1	a_2	MICROMETER.			i	d_1	d_2	Mean Right Ascension, 1850.0.	Mean Declination, 1850.0.
									h. m. s.	s.	s.			r.	′ ″	″	″	h. m. s.	° ′ ″
50	8.9	..	8.	..	..	..	..	..	12 48 42.70	−12.58	−0.48	II.	2	16.482	−44 8.77	−38.55	−4.44	12 48 29.64	−26 33 21.76
51	6.7	..	..	..	55.5	..	29.	..	48 54.51	12.58	0.48	IV.	2	15.713	44 57.41	38.56	4.52	48 41.45	34 10.49
52	8.9	..	..	..	..	28.	..	..	50 10.76	12.57	0.45	V.	3	31.370	28 34.49	38.61	2.85	49 57.74	17 45.95
53	9	..	..	..	28.5	..	..	..	52 27.81	12.56	0.45	IV.	3	30.200	29 47.58	38.67	2.98	52 14.80	18 59.23
54	8	..	..	..	39.5	..	12.7	..	53 38.36	12.56	0.47	IV.	2	16.443	44 11.78	38.70	4.44	53 25.33	26 33 24.92
55	7.8	..	..	..	..	..	3.3	..	54 29.11	12.56	0.40	VI.	4	49.998	9 2.76	38.73	0.91	54 16.15	25 58 12.40
56	7	..	..	..	..	45.5	..	..	56 28.39	12.55	0.38	V.	4	55.290	3 31.31	38.78	0.36	56 15.46	25 52 40.45
57	8	..	..	..	..	..	56.	..	12 57 21.63	12.55	0.43	VII.	3	31.335	28 36.81	38.81	2.86	12 57 8.65	26 17 45.48
58	9	..	..	..	..	..	50.	..	13 10 15.76	12.50	0.38	VI.	4	45.450	13 48.16	39.02	1.36	13 10 2.88	2 58.54
59	7	..	..	..	29.	..	..	..	12 27.97	12.49	0.44	IV.	2	12.880	47 55.16	39.04	4.85	12 15.04	37 9.05
60	9	..	..	..	..	..	..	17.5	12 25.79	12.49	0.42	VII.	3	22.285	38 4.65	39.04	3.83	12 12.88	27 17.52
61	9	32.	47.7	6.	23.5	..	..	..	15 22.88	12.48	0.39	IV.	3	37.403	22 15.76	39.07	2.21	15 10.01	11 27.04
62	9	..	..	..	..	11.3	..	..	16 54.05	12.47	0.41	V.	3	27.300	32 49.84	39.06	3.29	16 41.17	22 2.21
63	8	..	..	..	..	13.5	..	..	17 56.15	12.47	0.43	V.	1	9.017	51 56.76	39.09	5.28	17 43.25	41 11.13
64	6.7	36.5	53.5	10.7	29.3	..	..	..	20 28.12	12.46	0.42	IV.	2	12.773	48 1.87	39.11	4.87	20 15.24	37 15.85
65	7.8	..	..	9.	27.	43.	..	..	21 25.93	12.45	0.42	IV.	2	13.370	47 24.65	39.11	4.80	21 13.06	36 38.56
66	9	..	58.5	..	34.	..	..	..	24 33.22	12.44	0.37	IV.	3	38.733	20 52.14	39.11	2.06	23 20.41	10 3.31
67	7.8	..	..	..	..	15.	32.	..	24 57.73	12.44	0.37	V.	3	35.160	24 36.66	39.11	2.45	24 44.92	13 48.22
68	9	..	..	24.3	..	..	..	..	26 41.41	12.43	0.41	III.	2	18.550	41 59.30	39.10	4.23	26 28.57	31 12.63
69	8	..	..	29.5	..	..	20.7	..	27 46.47	12.43	0.37	IV.	3	36.597	23 6.20	39.10	2.30	27 33.67	12 17.60
70	8	..	..	9.7	27.	..	..	..	29 26.54	12.42	0.37	IV.	3	31.660	28 15.92	39.10	2.82	29 13.75	17 27.84
71	7.8	..	..	..	..	23.	..	..	30 5.81	12.42	0.35	V.	4	40.310	19 10.73	39.10	1.91	29 53.04	8 21.74
72	7	..	..	..	..	..	10.	..	30 35.53	12.41	0.39	VI.	2	20.000	40 28.35	39.10	4.08	30 22.70	29 41.53
73	8.9	..	..	..	..	1.5	..	..	31 44.23	12.41	0.38	V.	3	26.150	34 1.88	39.08	3.42	31 31.44	23 14.38
74	7	..	45.	2.3	20.3	..	..	..	33 19.50	12.40	0.38	IV.	3	21.340	39 3.58	39.06	3.95	33 6.72	28 16.59
75	9	..	..	..	..	55.5	..	..	33 38.20	12.40	0.38	V.	3	19.055	41 27.10	39.06	4.18	33 25.42	30 40.34
76	8	..	53.	10.3	27.7	..	..	..	36 27.34	12.39	0.33	IV.	4	46.983	12 12.14	39.03	1.19	36 14.62	1 22.36
77	9	..	..	..	..	..	..	40.5	36 48.77	12.39	0.38	VII.	2	21.035	39 23.21	39.03	3.97	36 36.00	28 36.21
78	9	..	..	39.	..	..	..	..	41 56.11	12.37	0.37	III.	2	19.410	41 5.39	38.96	4.14	41 43.37	26 30 18.49
79	6.7	36.7	53.7	11.	28.	..	..	..	45 27.92	12.35	0.30	IV.	4	50.313	8 43.51	38.89	0.85	45 15.27	25 57 53.25
80	8.9	..	..	..	37.	..	..	..	48 36.20	12.34	0.34	IV.	3	24.367	35 52.38	38.84	3.60	48 23.52	26 25 4.82
81	8	..	..	11.	..	..	..	..	50 28.00	12.33	0.29	III.	4	51.910	7 3.12	38.80	0.69	50 15.38	25 56 12.61
82	8.9	..	42.3	..	..	..	..	..	53 16.77	12.32	0.31	II.	3	36.633	23 3.06	38.73	2.29	53 4.14	26 12 14.08
83	7	..	46.5	..	21.3	..	..	..	54 20.88	12.32	0.30	IV.	4	41.382	18 3.62	38.70	1.79	54 8.26	26 57 14.11
84	8	..	47.	..	..	..	..	..	57 21.27	12.30	0.26	II.	4	54.570	4 16.26	38.63	0.42	57 8.71	25 53 25.31
85	3.4	..	29.	46.	2.3	..	..	..	58 2.78	12.30	0.27	IV.	4	50.773	8 14.41	38.61	0.80	57 50.21	57 23.82
86	8	..	..	..	..	..	34.5	51.5	58 0.30	12.30	0.26	VI.	4	56.453	2 18.13	38.61	0.22	7 47.74	25 51 26.96
87	8	..	..	..	..	52.5	..	..	13 59 35.16	12.29	0.34	V.	1	12.320	48 29.56	38.57	4.92	13 59 22.53	26 37 43.05
88	7	..	..	..	..	0.0	..	..	14 0 42.70	12.27	0.33	V.	2	20.825	39 36.58	38.54	4.00	14 0 30.10	28 49.12
89	8.9	..	..	..	..	3.5	..	..	0 46.20	12.27	0.33	V.	2	20.625	39 36.58	38.54	4.00	0 33.60	28 49.12
90	7	..	..	..	..	..	..	57.	2 5.51	12.27	0.30	VII.	3	38.644	20 58.17	38.49	2.06	1 52.94	10 8.72
91	5.6	..	49.	6.7	25.	..	..	..	4 23.85	12.26	0.33	IV.	2	16.742	43 52.82	38.41	4.45	4 11.26	33 5.68
92	6.7	..	..	..	..	9.3	26.5	..	4 52.26	12.26	0.25	V.	4	53.760	5 7.05	38.39	0.47	4 39.75	54 15.91
93	8	..	..	..	45.5	..	..	..	6 44.57	12.26	0.33	IV.	2	18.130	42 25.79	38.33	4.30	6 31.98	31 38.42
94	8	..	..	..	..	45.5	..	..	7 28.15	12.25	0.34	IV.	1	11.297	49 33.77	38.31	5.06	7 15.56	38 47.14
95	7	..	..	54.	11.8	28.3	..	..	9 11.10	12.24	0.28	IV.	3	33.420	26 25.62	38.25	2.63	10 58.58	15 36.50
96	6.7	..	8.3	25.5	44.	..	..	..	10 42.90	12.23	0.30	IV.	3	22.762	37 34.10	38.19	3.79	10 30.37	26 46.08
97	8.9	..	..	..	..	..	..	33.	10 41.53	12.23	0.27	VII.	4	40.177	19 18.44	38.19	1.91	10 29.03	8 28.54
98	7	..	41.	57.7	17.	..	..	..	14 13 15.51	−12.22	−0.32	IV.	1	12.183	−48 37.91	−38.08	−4.96	14 13 2.97	−26 37 50.95

CORRECTIONS.

Date.		Corr. of Clock.	Hourly rate.	m	n	c	Zenith Point.	Mic. Co.
1847.	h.	s.	s.	s.	s.	s.	° ′ ″	r.

REMARKS.

INSTRUMENT READINGS.

	Date.		CIRCLE. A.	B.	C.	D.	E.	F.	Mean.	Barom.	THERMOM. At.	Ex.	U.	L.	I.
	1847.	h. m.	° ′ ″						″	In.	°	°	°	°	°

ZONE 113.   MAY 6.   P.' D_0=−25° 48′ 30″—Continued.

No.	Mag.	I.	II.	III.	IV.	V.	VI.	VII.	T.	a_1	a_2	MIC.		r.	i	d_1	d_2	Mean Right Ascension, 1850.0	Mean Declination 1850.0
									h. m. s.	s.	s.			r.	′ ″	″	″	h. m. s.	° ′ ″
99	7.8			17.	33.5	50.5			14 14 16.39	−12.21	−0.25	IV.	4	42.585	−16 48.04	−38.03	−1.65	14 14 3.93	−26 5 57.72
100	7.8			41.	57.	14.3			15 57.25	12.21	0.25	IV.	4	44.043	15 16.53	37.97	1.49	15 44.79	4 25.99
101	7			3.5					17 20.52	12.20	0.24	III.	4	45.273	13 59.52	37.91	1.36	.17 8.08	3 8.79
102	7					39.	56.		17 21.76	12.20	0.26	V.	3	38.640	20 58.29	37.91	2.06	17 9.30	10 8.26
103	8					29.			18 11.80	12.20	0.26	V.	3	38.080	21 33.42	37.88	2.12	17 59.34	10 43.42
104	9							16.	18 24.27	12.20	0.29	VII.	2	20.930	39 29.74	37.87	3.99	18 11.78	28 41.60
105	7.8						7.		19 32.46	12.19	0.30	VI.	1	12.110	48 42.75	37.83	4.97	19 19.97	37 55.55
106	7		42.3	0.	17.5				22 16.93	12.18	0.26	IV.	3	38.850	20 44.75	37.69	2.04	22 4.49	9 54.43
107	8						57.		22 22.58	12.18	0.28	VI.	3	26.350	33 49.58	37.68	3.40	22 10.12	23 0.66
108	7.8					1.	18.		23 43.78	12.17	0.24	V.	4	41.660	17 45.93	37.62	1.75	23 31.37	6 55.30
109	7	18.3		52.3					31 9.45	12.13	0.22	III.	4	44.170	15 8.62	37.24	1.47	30 57.10	4 17.33
110	7						0.5		31 26.03	12.13	0.27	VI.	3	20.788	39 38.33	37.23	4.01	31 13.63	28 49.56
111	9	56.							36 47.59	12.10	0.27	I.	2	15.624	45 2.12	36.90	4.57	36 35.22	34 13.89
112	7.8				0.5		33.7		36 59.58	12.10	0.24	IV.	4	30.845	29 6.92	36.89	2.91	36 47.24	18 16.72
113	8			20.					38 18.98	12.09	0.27	III.	2	13.320	47 27.61	36.79	4.84	38 6.52	36 39.24
114	5.6					41.	58.		39 23.82	12.09	0.20	V.	4	47.460	11 42.30	36.75	1.12	39 11.53	0 50.17
115	7.8		4.	21.3					43 38.33	12.07	0.20	III.	1	48.155	10 58.71	36.49	1.04	43 26.06	0 6.24
116	9			31.					44 48.14	12.06	0.25	III.	1	12.185	48 37.41	36.39	4.96	44 35.83	37 49.76
117	8.9					10.			44 52.65	12.06	0.26	V.	1	10.973	49 53.91	36.39	5.09	44 40.33	39 5.39
118	8.9							13.	45 21.55	12.06	0.20	VII.	4	41.720	17 41.53	36.36	1.74	45 9.29	6 49.63
119	8.9				19.5				47 18.59	12.05	0.24	IV.	2	18.503	41 43.41	36.22	4.22	47 6.30	30 53.85
120	8				23.				48 22.45	12.04	0.20	IV.	3	37.383	22 17.02	36.15	2.20	48 10.21	11 25.37
121	9						38.5		49 4.07	12.04	0.22	VI.	3	24.330	35 53.20	36.11	3.61	48 51.81	25 2.92
122	8	8.		42.5					55 59.58	12.00	0.22	III.	2	20.902	39 31.50	35.59	3.99	55 47.36	28 41.08
123	7.8				44.2		18.		56 43.61	12.00	0.19	IV.	3	33.280	26 34.41	35.53	2.64	56 31.42	15 42.58
124	7			54.	11.				58 10.74	11.99	0.18	IV.	3	34.525	25 16.24	35.42	2.50	57 58.57	14 24.16
125	7		8.	25.5	43.				14 59 42.50	−11.98	−0.17	IV.	3	40.570	−18 57.05	−35.30	−1.87	14 59 30.35	−26 8 4.22

ZONE 114.   MAY 6.   P. D_0=−25° 48′ 30″.

No.	Mag.	I.	II.	III.	IV.	V.	VI.	VII.	T.	a_1	a_2	MIC.		r.	i	d_1	d_2	Mean Right Ascension, 1850.0	Mean Declination 1850.0
1	8				33.				16 0 50.02	−11.64	−0.32	III.	4	45.890	−13 20.56	−28.68	−1.24	16 0 38.06	−26 2 20.48
2	7					19.	35.7	10.	1 18.25	11.64	0.27	IV.	2	19.090	41 25.53	28.61	4.24	1 6.34	30 28.38
3	9						6.5		2 32.11	11.63	0.29	VI.	3	28.750	31 18.80	28.44	3.15	2 20.19	26 20 20.39
4	9				15.				4 57.89	11.62	0.34	V.	4	53.857	5 0.91	28.10	0.38	4 45.93	25 53 59.39
5	8			23.5					15 40.60	11.56	0.28	III.	2	22.210	38 9.61	26.57	3.88	15 28.76	26 27 10.06
6	7.8		16.7	34.	51.7				16 51.12	11.55	0.31	IV.	3	35.588	24 9.49	26.40	2.38	16 39.26	26 13 8.27
7	8			51.7					18 8.70	11.54	0.34	III.	4	53.135	5 46.42	26.22	0.46	17 56.82	25 54 43.10
8	1	33.5	50.7	7.3	25.5	42.			20 24.83	11.53	0.32	IV.	4	42.712	16 40.00	25.88	1.59	20 12.98	26 5 37.47
9	6		48.3	5.3	23.				22 22.52	11.52	0.31	IV.	3	36.328	23 23.20	25.58	2.30	22 10.69	12 21.08
10	7.8		40.	57.					26 14.25	11.50	0.32	III.	4	38.843	20 42.47	25.00	2.02	26 2.43	9 39.49
11	7		58.						29 32.78	11.48	0.27	II.	1	8.843	52 6.56	24.50	5.40	29 21.03	41 6.46
12	8	18.3		53.					31 9.84	11.47	0.33	III.	4	39.360	20 10.37	24.26	1.98	30 58.04	9 6.61
13	7						46.		31 11.78	11.47	0.34	VI.	4	46.890	12 17.60	24.26	1.13	30 59.97	1 12.99
14	7.8	12.	29.	46.3					34 3.38	11.45	0.33	III.	3	38.570	21 2.12	23.79	2.05	33 51.60	9 57.96
15	6.7			31.	49.				34 48.10	11.45	0.29	IV.	2	18.543	41 59.93	23.67	4.30	34 36.36	30 57.90
16	8						36.5		35 19.34	11.44	0.34	V.	4	45.910	13 19.24	23.59	1.24	35 7.56	2 14.07
17	7			28.	46.				36 45.17	11.44	0.31	IV.	3	27.087	33 2.83	23.37	3.33	36 33.42	21 59 53
18	7	14.7	31.5	49.3	7.				16 41 6.23	−11.41	−0.29	IV.	2	20.917	−39 30.74	−22.67	−4.02	16 40 54.53	−26 28 27.43

CORRECTIONS.

Date.	Corr. of Clock.	Hourly rate.	m	n	e	Zenith Point.	Mic. Co.
1847.	h.	s.	s.	s.	s.	° ′ ″	r.
	s.	s.					

REMARKS.

(113) 99. Transits over T.'s IV, V, and VI assumed as recorded over T.'s III, IV, and V.

(113) 113. Transit over T. IV assumed as recorded over T. III.

INSTRUMENT READINGS.

Date.	CIRCLE.							Barom.	THERMOM.				
	A.	B.	C.	D.	E.	F.	Mean.		At.	Ex.	U.	L.	I.
1847. h. m.	° ′ ″						″	In.	°	°	°	°	°

ZONE 114. MAY 6. P. $D_0 = -25^\circ\,48'\,30''$—Continued.

No.	Mag.	I.	II.	III.	IV.	V.	VI.	VII.	T.	a_1	a_2	Mic.	n	r.	i	d_1	d_2	Mean Right Ascension, 1850.0	Mean Declination, 1850.0
									h. m. s.	s.	s.			r.	′ ″	″	″	h. m. s.	° ′ ″
19	7	54.2	11.5	29.2	47.2				16 42 46.15	−11.40	−0.28	IV.	2	13.010	−47 47.06	−22.39	−4.92	16 42 34.47	−26 36 44.37
20	8						42.		43 7.44	11.40	0.28	VI.	1	10.310	50 35.85	22.34	5.22	42 55.70	39 33.41
21	9						25.		43 50.53	11.40	0.29	VI.	2	19.804	40 34.95	22.23	4.11	43 38.84	29 31.29
22	7.8			29.	46.5	3.5			45 46.11	11.38	0.33	IV.	4	38.733	20 49.50	21.90	2.03	45 34.40	9 43.43
23	9	30.7		5.					48 22.16	11.37	0.30	III.	2	22.720	37 37.48	21.48	3.82	48 10.49	26 32.78
24	9				24.				49 23.53	11.36	0.33	IV.	4	41.243	18 12.27	21.31	1.76	49 11.84	7 5.34
25	8					40.3			50 23.11	11.36	0.33	V.	4	40.073	19 25.47	21.14	1.68	50 11.42	8 18.49
26	8			2.	20.				52 19.14	11.35	0.30	IV.	3	24.285	35 58.77	20.82	3.65	52 7.49	24 53.24
27	8	39.3		13.7					55 30.65	11.33	0.35	III.	4	45.172	14 5.79	20.28	1.32	55 18.97	2 57.38
28	7.8		25.	42.3	0.5				56 59.57	11.32	0.31	IV.	3	26.860	33 16.95	20.02	3.36	56 47.94	22 10.33
29	6.7				48.2	4.7			57 47.50	11.32	0.32	IV.	3	30.610	29 21.80	19.88	2.94	57 35.86	18 14.62
30	9				30.5				16 59 29.45	11.31	0.29	IV.	1	11.683	49 9.17	19.60	5.07	16 59 17.85	38 3.84
31	8		53.						17 1 27.38	11.29	0.35	II.	4	45.273	13 59.33	19.25	1.28	17 1 15.74	2 49.86
32	8				46.5				1 45.87	11.29	0.33	IV.	3	33.248	26 30.35	19.20	2.65	1 34.25	15 28.20
33	7.8				31.	47	4.3		2 29.87	11.29	0.30	IV.	2	18.863	41 39.65	19.07	4.29	2 16.28	30 33.01
34	8.9		32.						6 6.57	11.27	0.32	II.	3	27.790	32 17.72	18.44	3.26	5 54.98	21 9.42
35	7			2.5	20.				6 19.41	11.27	0.31	IV.	3	26.462	33 42.17	18.41	3.40	6 7.83	22 33.98
36	7						54.		6 19.59	11.27	0.31	VI.	3	26.547	33 37.15	18.41	3.39	6 8.01	22 28.95
37	7					29.3			7 12.06	11.26	0.32	V.	3	29.490	30 32.37	18.25	3.07	7 0.48	19 23.69
38	7			15.	33.		6.5		8 32.10	11.26	0.30	IV.	3	21.800	38 34.47	18.02	3.94	8 20.54	27 26.43
39	8		19.						10 53.63	11.24	0.31	II.	3	22.530	37 47.96	17.60	3.86	10 42.08	26 39.42
40	7				6.5	24.5			11 23.66	11.24	0.32	IV.	3	25.677	34 31.30	17.51	3.49	11 12.10	23 22.30
41	7					36.			12 18.75	11.24	0.32	V.	3	28.350	31 43.96	17.35	3.19	12 7.19	20 34.50
42	7.8							9.	12 17.42	11.24	0.33	VII.	3	32.080	27 49.94	17.35	2.77	12 5.85	16 40.06
43	8						50.5		13 16.26	11.23	0.36	VI.	4	44.514	14 46.80	17.17	1.37	13 4.67	3 35.34
44	7	52.	9.	26.5	44.			35.	17 43.46	11.20	0.35	IV.	3	36.855	22 49.90	16.37	2.24	17 31.91	11 38.51
45	9			24.					19 41.13	11.20	0.30	IV.	2	13.770	46 59.28	16.00	4.87	19 29.63	35 50.15
46	6.7	46.		2.5	20.	37.7		28.5	22 37.11	11.18	0.35	IV.	4	39.353	20 10.88	15.48	1.96	22 25.58	8 58.32
47	7.8				38.0				25 36.95	11.16	0.30	IV.	2	11.817	49 1.88	14.93	5.08	25 25.49	37 51.89
48	8.9		14.0	31.0					34 48.28	11.11	0.35	III.	3	34.730	25 2.87	13.20	2.48	34 36.82	13 48.55
49	9					56.0			35 55.07	11.11	0.32	V.	2	18.438	42 6.57	13.01	4.33	35 43.64	30 53.91
50	9					34.3			37 33.81	11.10	0.36	V.	3	40.313	19 13.49	12.69	1.84	37 22.35	7 58.02
51	7.8	18.3	35.		52.5	10.2			41 9.59	11.08	0.34	IV.	3	32.265	27 38.08	12.02	2.75	40 58.17	16 22.85
52	9						27.0		43 52.63	11.06	0.34	VI.	3	31.230	28 43.33	11.49	2.87	43 41.13	17 27.69
53	9					33.3			45 16.09	11.06	0.35	V.	3	36.600	23 6.27	11.22	2.26	45 4.68	11 49.75
54	9						35.5		46 1.15	11.05	0.35	VI.	3	32.550	27 20.51	11.09	2.72	45 49.75	16 4.32
55	6.7							5.5	47 13.57	11.04	0.30	VII.	1	5.483	55 38.80	10.86	5.80	47 2.23	44 25.46
56	7.8					36.3	53.		49 18.94	11.03	0.37	VI.	4	43.816	15 30.40	10.45	1.45	49 7.54	4 12.30
57	7.8		14.		49.				51 48.46	11.02	0.34	IV.	3	35.912	23 49.04	9.97	2.31	51 37.10	12 31.35
58	7	23.5	40.5	58.	15.7				54 15.02	11.01	0.35	IV.	3	29.870	30 8.10	9.49	3.04	54 3.66	26 18 50.63
59	8							6.0	54 14.69	11.01	0.40	VII.	4	53.013	5 53.32	9.49	0.41	54 3.28	25 54 33.25
60	9				11.5				17 57 10.83	10.99	0.35	IV.	3	31.330	28 36.50	9.92	2.86	56 59.49	26 17 19.28
61	7.8			33.	50.	7.7			18 0 7.23	10.98	0.37	IV.	4	40.983	18 28.45	8.36	1.75	17 59 55.88	7 8.56
62	7			51.3	8.5	26.			1 25.60	10.97	0.38	IV.	4	44.715	14 34.38	8.10	1.34	18 1 14.25	3 13.82
63	8			38.5					2 55.59	10.96	0.34	III.	3	23.610	36 40.64	7.84	3.72	2 44.20	25 22.20
64	8			2.7					5 19.76	10.95	0.36	III.	3	34.435	25 21.57	7.34	2.51	5 8.45	14 1.42
65	7				2.5				6 1.77	10.95	0.34	IV.	3	27.767	32 20.03	7.20	3.27	5 50.48	21 0.50
66	9						5.0		6 30.59	10.94	0.34	VI.	3	26.877	33 16.26	7.11	3.37	6 19.31	21 56.74
67	7.8	24.7	42.	59.3					18 10 16.39	−10.92	−0.34	III.	3	26.213	−33 57.35	−6.35	−3.44	18 10 5.13	−26 22 37.14

CORRECTIONS.

Date.	Corr. of Clock.	Hourly rate.	m	n	c	Zenith Point.	Mic. Co.
1847.	h.　　　s.	s.	s.	s.	s.	°　′　″	r.

REMARKS.

(114) 45. Transit over T. III assumed as recorded over T. IV.

(114) 49. Transit evidently noted 15ˢ too late.

INSTRUMENT READINGS.

Date.	CIRCLE.							Barom.	THERMOM.				
	A.	B.	C.	D.	E.	F.	Mean.		At.	Ex.	U.	L.	I.
1847.	h. m.	°　′　″					″	in.	°	°	°	°	°

Zone 114. May 6. P. D₀ = −25° 48′ 30″—Continued.

No.	Mag.	I.	II.	III.	IV.	V.	VI.	VII.	T.	a_1	a_4	Micr.	n	r.	i	d_1	d_4	Mean Right Ascension, 1850.0	Mean Declination, 1850.0
									h. m. s.	s.	s.			r.	′ ″	″	′	h. m. s.	° ′ ″
68	9				57.				18 10 56.41	−10.92	−0.36	IV.	3	34.710	−25 4.50	−6.22	−2.48	18 10 45.13	−26 13 43.20
69	7			47.5	5.				12 4.52	10.92	0.38	IV.	3	39.455	20 7.05	6.01	1.94	11 53.22	8 45.00
70	7				12.3				13 11.41	10.91	0.34	IV.	2	20.270	40 11.54	5.77	4.12	13 0.16	28 51.43
71	9				25.7				14 25.09	10.91	0.37	IV.	3	34.138	25 40.46	5.53	2.55	14 13.81	14 18.54
72	7					18.			15 0.69	10.90	0.34	V.	2	18.100	42 27.73	5.41	4.36	14 49.45	31 7.50
73	8						5.		15 30.48	10.90	0.33	VI.	2	15.430	45 15.29	5.31	4.68	15 19.25	26 33 55.28
74	8.9			15					17 32.01	10.89	0.40	III.	4	48.040	11 5.86	4.90	0.97	17 20.72	25 59 41.73
75	9		25.		1.				18 18 59.94	−10.88	−0.36	IV.	3	32.553	−27 19.95	−4.60	−2.72	18 18 48.70	−26 15 57.27
									Zone 115. May 17. P. D₀ = −28° 41′ 50″.										
1	7				30.		4.7		12 8 29.78			IV.	4	53.353	−5 32.88	+0.00	−0.87		−28 47 23.66
2	7		37.7	55.5	13.3				17 12.98			IV.	3	34.174	25 38.26	−0.08	3.34		29 7 31.68
3	7		12.	30.	48.				13 47.46			IV.	4	47.574	11 35.15	0.24	1.61		28 53 27.00
4	6	17.2	34.5	52.5	11., 28,	45.5	3.		16 10.05			IV.	2	12.634	48 10.73	0.39	6.18		29 30 7.30
5	8						22.5		17 47.20			VI.	3	30.265	29 43.87	0.49	3.85		11 38.21
6	7		14.	32.3	50.5				19 49.68			IV.	3	26.830	33 18.84	0.61	4.30		29 15 13.75
7	8					41.			19 48.23			VII.	4	44.003	15 14.53	0.61	2.05		28 57 7.19
8	6	15.2	32.7	50.5	8.7	26.		1.	25 8.10			IV.	3	29.040	31 0.23	0.91	2.01		29 12 53.15
9	8	58.7	16.	34.	52.3				27 51.52			IV.	3	26.685	33 28.00	1.06	4.31		15 23.37
10	4.5	25.3	42.7	1.	19.5	36.3	54.	11.5	31 18.40			IV.	1	7.247	53 47.74	1.24	6.90		29 35 45.88
11	8.9		57.2		33.				37 32.56			IV.	4	43.645	15 41.56	1.53	2.11		28 57 35.20
12	8	0.	17.3	35.	53.				39 52.59			IV.	3	42.825	16 32.87	1.61	2.22		28 58 26.70
13	8	32.	49.5	7.7					45 25.00			IV.	3	30.010	29 59.37	1.85	3.88		29 11 55.10
14	7			21.3	39.7	56.5			47 38.85			IV.	3	26.790	33 21.34	1.94	4.31		15 17.59
15	7	9.7	27.	45.	3.				51 2.44			IV.	3	30.674	29 17.72	2.06	3.79		29 11 15.57
16	8			27.					12 55 26.71			IV.	4	49.560	9 30.61	2.19	1.35		28 57 24.15
17	7		26.	44.		19.3			13 7 1.55			V.	2	19.377	41 7.66	2.48	5.28	13 6 48	29 23 3.42
18	7.8				32.				11 37.88			IV.	1	10.377	50 31.33	2.56	6.47	11 25.	32 30.36
19	5.6	17.5	34.7	53.	11.				13 30 10.32			IV.	3	36.590	−23 6.64	−2.67	−3.05	13 29 57.	−29 5 2.34

CORRECTIONS.

Date.	Corr. of Clock.	Hourly rate.	m	n	c	Zenith Point.	Mic. Co.
1847.	h.	s.	s.	s.	s.	° ′ ″	r.

INSTRUMENT READINGS.

Date.	A.	B.	C.	D.	E.	F.	Mean.	Barom.	At.	Ex.	U.	L.	I.
	° ′ ″							In.	°	°	°	°	°
Zone 115 1847. May 17, 12	68 2 31.2	39.4	30.3	43.8	15.7	36.6	32.85°					66.0	
12 8								29.936	65.0	57.5			
13 7								29.936	63.5	55.0			
13 30								29.936	63.0	53.7			

REMARKS.

May 17, 12ʰ. Night poor; only slight illumination possible; circle reading noted at 67°, but evidently should have been 68°.

(115) 19. Declination about 38″ too large by Mer. C., 1846; Trans., 1849; and Arg. Z. 383 and 404.

*Corr. for runs, +0″.07.

Zone 116. May 29. P. $D_0 = -27^\circ\ 4'\ 0''$.

No.	Mag.	I.	II.	III.	IV.	V.	VI.	VII.	T. (h. m. s.)	a_1	a_4	Mic.	n	r.	i	d_1	d_4	Mean Right Ascension, 1850.0 (h. m. s.)	Mean Declination, 1850.0 (° ′ ″)
1	7.8						52.	8.	13 0 16.65	−15.28	−0.82	VI.	4	39.575	− 19 56.52	− 6.93	−1.94	13 0 0.55	−27 24 5.39
2	8	45.	2.	19.5	38.	54.3			6 36.98	15.26	0.92	IV.	2	20.315	40 8.78	7.00	4.10	6 20.80	44 19.88
3	9.10			13.					8 30.20	15.26	0.78	III.	4	47.115	12 3.87	7.01	1.11	8 14.16	16 11.99
4	6.7		50.7	8.3	26.2	43.			10 25.57	15.26	0.87	IV.	3	31.857	28 3.43	7.03	2.80	10 9.44	32 13.26
5	10							38.	10 45.57	15.25	0.97	VII.	1	12.153	48 39.98	7.03	5.03	10 29.35	52 52.04
6	9.10			41.					12 58.23	15.25	0.83	III.	4	40.665	18 48.39	7.03	1.82	12 42.15	22 57.24
7	9.10			7.5					14 24.78	15.25	0.87	III.	3	28.383	31 41.26	7.03	3.19	14 8.66	35 51.48
8	7	4.	21.	38.5		13.			15 55.82	15.24	0.88	V.	3	29.083	30 57.85	7.03	3.11	15 39.70	35 7.99
9	8					21.			17 3.47	15.24	0.96	V.	2	13.430	47 20.88	7.03	4.90	16 47.27	51 32.81
10	8							8.	17 15.68	15.24	0.93	VII.	2	19.620	40 52.03	7.03	4.20	16 59.51	45 3.26
11	6		55.2	12.5	30.3	47.2	4.3		23 29.82	15.22	0.81	IV.	4	43.244	16 6.77	7.00	1.54	23 13.79	20 15.31
12	5.6					48.	6.5		24 31.00	15.22	0.98	V.	1	10.036	50 52.80	6.99	5.27	24 14.80	55 5.06
13	8.9	48.	5.2	22.7	41.	57.5			26 40.10	15.21	0.93	IV.	2	20.090	40 22.77	6.98	4.12	26 23.96	44 33.87
14	7	16.3	33.3	51.3	9.7	26.			29 8.54	15.21	0.98	IV.	1	9.660	51 16.21	6.96	5.31	28 52.35	55 28.48
15	7	47.5	5.		40.2	56.8			32 39.58	15.20	0.86	IV.	3	35.168	24 35.91	6.91	2.42	32 23.52	28 45.24
16	8.9					53.7	11.		33 36.32	15.20	0.85	VI.	4	38.650	20 54.47	6.89	2.04	33 20.27	25 3.40
17	7				47.5		20.		35 45.74	15.19	0.99	I.	1	10.607	50 17.02	6.86	5.20	35 29.56	54 29.08
18	9					47.			37 29.47	15.19	0.97	V.	2	13.845	46 54.65	6.83	4.85	37 13.31	51 6.33
19	7	58.5	15.7	33.3	51.2				40 50.50	15.18	0.90	IV.	3	27.362	32 45.71	6.77	3.30	40 34.48	36 55.78
20	7				42.5				41 41.96	15.18	0.85	IV.	3	37.587	22 4.16	6.75	2.16	41 25.93	26 13.07
21	9						23.5		41 48.82	15.18	0.85	VI.	3	37.716	21 56.32	6.75	2.14	41 32.79	26 5.21
22	8						8.		42 33.25	15.17	0.89	VI.	3	30.513	29 28.32	6.73	2.95	42 17.19	33 38.00
23	8							39.	42 46.85	15.17	0.87	VII.	3	33.230	26 37.86	6.72	2.65	42 30.81	30 47.23
24	8							26.5	43 34.32	15.16	0.89	VII.	3	30.015	29 59.37	6.65	3.00	43 18.27	34 9.02
25	8				30.				45 29.48	15.16	0.85	IV.	4	39.035	20 30.64	6.65	2.00	45 13.47	24 39.29
26	8					5.			45 47.62	15.16	0.84	V.	4	39.600	19 55.20	6.65	1.93	45 31.62	24 3.78
27	6							56.5	46 4.18	15.16	0.94	VII.	2	20.340	45 19.77	6.64	4.67	45 48.08	49 31.08
28	7			44.3	3.	19.2			49 1.74	15.09	0.99	IV.	1	11.117	49 44.76	6.56	5.15	48 45.60	53 56.47
29	8.9			26.	44.	0.5			50 43.24	15.15	0.88	IV.	3	34.095	25 43.15	6.52	2.55	50 27.21	29 52.22
30	7.8	11.	28.2	46.	4.2				56 3.25	15.13	0.97	IV.	2	17.423	48 23.97	6.34	5.04	55 47.15	52 35.35
31	7.8				47.3		21.2		56 46.53	15.13	0.96	V.	2	17.070	43 32.31	6.32	4.47	56 30.24	47 43.10
32	8.9		0.5	18.	35.5				13 59 35.18	15.12	0.86	IV.	3	38.584	21 1.62	6.21	2.05	13 59 19.20	25 9.88
33	8	45.5	2.3	20.	38.2	55.	12.2		14 2 37.41	15.11	0.92	IV.	3	25.973	34 16.99	6.09	3.46	14 2 21.38	38 26.54
34	9		46.	3.2	21.5				7 20.71	15.10	0.98	IV.	2	14.495	46 13.97	5.90	4.78	7 4.63	50 24.65
35	8					16.			7 58.71	15.10	0.78	V.	4	53.920	4 56.95	5.68	0.36	7 42.83	9 3.19
36	9					11.			8 53.71	15.09	0.78	V.	4	53.680	5 12.07	5.84	0.39	8 37.84	9 18.30
37	9							3.	9 11.16	15.09	0.78	VII.	4	55.070	3 44.35	5.82	0.24	8 55.29	7 50.41
38	7	53.	10.	27.5	45.2	2.3	19.3		10 44.79	15.09	0.85	IV.	4	42.210	17 11.63	5.76	1.65	10 28.85	21 19.04
39	6.7		2.2	20.	38.3	55.			13 37.38	15.08	0.92	IV.	3	27.137	32 59.70	5.61	3.33	13 21.38	37 8.64
40	8	33.5	51.	8.5	26.	43.			15 25.62	15.08	0.88	IV.	3	35.952	23 46.53	5.53	2.34	15 9.66	27 54.40
41	7		12.	30.	47.8	4.3			16 47.06	15.07	0.87	IV.	3	36.943	22 44.37	5.46	2.23	16 31.12	26 52.06
42	9	2.	19.		54.				18 53.73	15.06	0.82	IV.	4	48.710	10 23.84	5.34	0.94	18 37.85	14 30.12
43	7.8		28.	45.5			37.2		19 2.68	15.06	0.81	VI.	4	49.613	9 26.97	5.35	0.83	18 46.81	13 33.15
44	7					25.3			20 7.97	15.06	0.82	V.	4	48.580	10 32.00	5.30	0.95	19 52.09	14 38.25
45	9					23.			21 5.61	15.06	0.87	V.	3	38.135	21 29.98	5.24	2.10	20 49.68	25 37.32
46	7.8				59.		33.2		21 58.51	15.05	0.84	IV.	4	43.140	16 13.23	5.19	1.55	21 42.68	20 20.97
47	9				39.5				23 39.02	15.05	0.85	IV.	4	41.417	18 1.42	5.10	1.74	23 23.12	22 8.26
48	9							41.	23 49.11	15.05	0.80	VII.	4	52.055	6 53.40	5.08	0.57	23 33.26	10 59.05
49	8	12.5	30.	47.2	5.2	22.			14 27 4.59	−15.04	−0.84	IV.	4	41.673	− 17 45.18	− 4.90	−1.71	14 26 48.71	−27 21 51.79

CORRECTIONS.

Date.	Corr. of Clock.	Hourly rate.	m	n	c	Zenith Point.	Mic. Co.
1847.	h. s.	s.	s.	s.	s.	° ′ ″	r.

REMARKS.

(116) 24. Minutes assumed as 43 instead of 45.

(116) 27. Micrometer reading assumed as 15ʳ.340 instead of 20ʳ.340.

(116) 30. Micrometer reading assumed as 12ʳ.423 instead of 17ʳ.423, to agree with Arg. Z. 302, 67.

INSTRUMENT READINGS.

Date.		CIRCLE.							Barom.	THERMOM.				
		A.	B.	C.	D.	E.	F.	Mean.		At.	Ex.	U.	L.	I.
Zone 116	1847. May 29, 13 0 (h. m.)	66 24 66.7	67.0	63.2	72.2	43.3	69.0	63.57	in. 29.936	72.5	74.0	67.0	63.0	62.0
	13 59								29.940	74.0	72.5			
	15 0								29.944	73.2	71.0			

ZONE 116. MAY 29. P. $D_a = -27°\ 4'\ 0''$—Continued.

No.	Mag.	I.	II.	III.	IV.	V.	VI.	VII.	T.	a_1	a_2	MIC.	n	r.	i	d_1	d_2	Mean Right Ascension, 1850.0.	Mean Declination, 1850.0.
									h. m. s.	s.	s.			r.	′ ″	″	″	h. m. s.	° ′ ″
50	7				0.7		35.2		14 28 0.20	−15.03	−0.92	IV.	3	28.350	−31 43.71	−4.84	−3.19	14 27 44.25	−27 35 51.74
51	9							37.	28 44.76	15.03	0.94	VII.	3	25.633	34 34.30	4.81	3.49	28 28.79	38 42.69
52	9					10.			31 52.59	15.02	0.90	V.	3	34.510	25 17.43	4.62	2.51	31 36.67	29 24.56
53	7		50.2	8.	25.5	42.3			33 25.04	15.02	0.88	IV.	3	38.522	21 5.51	4.51	2.05	33 9.14	25 12.07
54	7						29.		33 54.48	15.02	0.80	VI.	4	54.410	4 26.23	4.48	0.31	33 38.66	8 31.02
55	7.8			17.	35.	51.5			35 34.15	15.01	0.95	IV.	3	21.822	38 33.08	4.38	2.93	35 18.19	42 40.39
56	8						0.7	17.5	36 25.74	15.01	0.87	VI.	4	39.045	20 29.69	4.32	2.00	36 9.86	24 36.01
57	8.9				39.				38 38.17	15.00	0.95	IV.	3	23.495	36 48.29	4.18	3.75	38 22.22	40 56.22
58	8	56.		30.5	48.3				40 47.81	14.99	0.89	IV.	3	35.923	23 48.35	4.03	2.34	40 31.93	27 54.72
59	4				45.5	3.			41 45.36	14.99	0.85	IV.	4	43.520	15 49.46	3.96	1.51	41 29.52	19 54.93
60	7.8					36.	54.		42 18.85	14.99	0.96	V.	3	22.540	37 48.47	3.93	3.85	42 2.90	41 56.25
61	7	17.	35.	52.5					45 9.69	14.98	0.98	III.	2	17.460	43 7.70	3.72	3.43	44 53.73	47 14.85
62	6.7			27.	44.7	1.3			45 44.15	14.98	0.97	III.	2	20.672	39 46.00	3.68	4.06	45 28.20	43 53.74
63	9							51.5	46 59.25	14.97	0.95	VII.	3	24.850	35 23.45	3.59	3.60	46 43.33	39 30.64
64	8	59.		31.					48 51.09	14.96	0.89	III.	3	36.950	22 43.55	3.46	2.23	48 35.24	26 49.24
65	9	32.		6.					53 23.64	14.95	0.92	III.	3	31.435	28 29.78	3.11	2.85	53 7.77	32 35.74
66	6.7	35.	51.7			44.			53 26.70	14.95	0.90	V.	3	36.083	23 38.70	3.11	2.32	53 10.85	27 44.13
67	7.8		47.3	4.5	22.5				55 21.95	14.94	0.90	IV.	3	35.670	24 4.30	2.95	2.37	55 6.11	28 9.62
68	7					4.5	27.		55 52.16	14.94	0.97	V.	2	22.052	38 19.65	2.93	3.91	55 36.25	42 26.49
69	9				27.				14 57 26.16	14.94	0.97	IV.	2	22.590	37 45.89	2.78	3.85	14 57 10.25	41 52.52
70	7	30.	47.	5.	23.	39.5			15 0 22.12	−14.93	−0.99	IV.	2	17.093	−42 53.15	−2.54	−4.41	15 0 6.20	−27 47 0.10

ZONE 117. JUNE 11. P. $D_a = -27°\ 41'\ 0''$.

No.	Mag.	I.	II.	III.	IV.	V.	VI.	VII.	T.	a_1	a_2	MIC.	n	r.	i	d_1	d_2	Mean Right Ascension, 1850.0.	Mean Declination, 1850.0.
1	7	9.	26.5	44.	2.	19.			14 17 1.42	−17.50	−0.57	IV.	3	29.057	−30 59.23	−36.16	−4.09	14 16 43.35	−28 12 39.48
2	7		6.7	24.5	43.	59.7			20 42.02	17.50	0.63	V.	2	20.900	39 31.87	35.96	5.05	20 23.89	28 21 12.88
3	8.0			31.5	49.				23 6.40	17.49	0.46	III.	4	43.567	15 46.45	35.81	2.42	22 48.45	27 57 24.68
4	8						17.		23 41.82	17.49	0.75	VI.	1	8.000	53 0.67	35.77	6.57	23 23.58	28 34 43.01
5	9		28.5		4.			24.5	28 3.47	17.48	0.59	IV.	3	29.270	30 45.99	35.50	4.06	27 45.40	12 25.55
6	7.8				49.			24.5	28 31.82	17.48	0.53	V.	3	37.430	22 19.97	35.47	3.15	28 13.81	28 3 58.59
7	8				14.5				31 14.06	17.48	0.49	IV.	4	42.923	16 26.71	35.30	2.50	30 56.09	27 58 4.51
8	7	36.3	53.3	11.	40.5				33 28.47	17.47	0.59	III.	3	30.665	29 17.07	35.17	3.92	33 10.41	28 10 57.06
9	8				40.5				33 39.77	17.47	0.61	IV.	3	28.610	31 27.28	35.16	4.14	33 21.69	13 6.58
10	8.0							27.	33 34.46	17.47	0.61	VII.	3	25.655	34 20.32	35.17	4.47	33 16.38	15 59.96
11	8.9							47.5	35 54.87	17.47	0.68	VII.	2	19.700	40 46.94	35.00	5.18	35 36.72	22 27.12
12	8	1″.	17.	34.7		40.5			40 52.13	17.46	0.64	III.	3	27.495	32 36.91	34.69	4.27	40 34.03	14 15.87
13	7				24.	40.5			41 22.98	17.46	0.70	IV.	2	17.718	42 51.58	34.66	5.41	41 4.82	24 31.65
14	7.8	22.	39.	56.7	15.				44 14.21	17.45	0.66	IV.	3	24.333	35 55.77	34.48	4.64	43 56.10	28 17 34.89
15	6.7				12.	29.5			45 11.93	17.44	0.45	IV.	4	53.200	5 42.41	34.42	1.35	44 54.04	27 47 18.18
16	6					3.7	21.		45 46.30	17.44	0.42	IV.	4	56.423	2 20.27	34.39	0.99	45 28.44	27 43 55.65
17	5	42.7	59.8	18.3	37.				48 35.52	17.44	0.80	IV.	1	9.728	51 11.88	34.22	6.37	48 17.28	28 32 52.47
18	7			37.	55.	11.5			49 54.25	17.44	0.58	IV.	3	35.387	24 22.23	34.14	3.39	49 36.23	5 59.76
19	8	9.3	26.	44.5					54 1.05	17.43	0.75	III.	2	17.660	42 55.73	33.87	5.43	53 43.47	24 35.03
20	8			47.5	4.				55 46.44	17.43	0.77	IV.	2	15.057	45 35.58	33.81	5.74	54 28.24	27 18.13
21	9					25.			56 7.39	17.42	0.75	V.	2	16.783	43 54.09	33.74	5.54	55 49.22	25 33.37
22	8.9				18.				57 0.49	17.42	0.64	V.	3	33.763	26 4.11	33.68	3.55	56 42.43	7 41.34
23	7.8			9.	26.5				58 26.06	17.42	0.69	IV.	3	27.427	32 41.61	33.59	4.28	58 7.95	14 19.48
24	8							18.	14 58 42.98	−17.42	−0.72	VI.	3	23.673	−36 37.38	−33.57	−4.72	14 58 24.84	−28 18 15.67

CORRECTIONS.

Date.	Corr. of Clock.	Hourly rate.	m	n	c	Zenith Point.	Mic. Co.
1847.	h.	s.	s.	s.	s.	° ′ ″	r.

INSTRUMENT READINGS.

Date.	CIRCLE.							Barom.	THERMOM.				
		A.	B.	C.	D.	E.	F.	Mean.		At.	Ex.	U.	L.	I.
Zone 117	1847. June 11. h. m. 14 15	67 2 34.3	36.0	30.5	44.0	10.5	36.7	32.00ᵃ	in. 29.756	74.7	71.5	75.0	..	75.0
	14 40								29.762	74.2	71.4			
	15 18								29.774	74.0	69.0			
	16 24								29.800	73.0	67.7			
	16 47								29.808	72.6	67.5			
	17 29								29.820	72.5	66.5			
	18 14								29.826	72.0	64.2			

REMARKS.

(116) 63. Right ascension 1ᵐ discordant from Arg. 373, 24.

(116) 68. Transits discordant; that over T. V rejected.

(117) 8. Declination 30′ discordant from Arg. Z. 383, 126; and Mural, 1848, May 3.

(117) 20. Transits over T.'s IV and V assumed as recorded over T.'s III and IV; and minutes as 54, not 55.

ᵃ Corr. for runs, +0″.06.

ZONE 117. JUNE 11. P. $D_0 = -27°\ 41'\ 0''$—Continued.

No.	Mag.	I.	II.	III.	IV.	V.	VI.	VII.	T. (h m s)	a_1	a_2	Micr.		r	i	d_1	d_2	Mean Right Ascension, 1850.0.	Mean Declination, 1850.0.
25	7						59.	16.	15 1 24.06	−17.41	−0.49	VI.	4	53.450	− 5 26.42	−33.38	−1.28	15 1 6.16	−27 47 1.08
26	9						4.		4 29.04	17.41	0.67	VI.	3	29.982	30 1.50	33.15	4.00	4 10.96	28 11 38.65
27	8							50.5	5 57.75	17.40	0.82	VII.	2	11.820	49 1.44	33.04	6.15	5 39.53	30 40.63
28	7		59.5	17.3	35.5	52.3			10 34.69	17.39	0.79	IV.	2	16.880	43 44.11	32.68	5.55	10 16.51	28 25 22.34
29	6				48.5		23.		11 48.30	17.39	0.45	IV.	4	56.055	2 43.28	32.58	1.00	11 30.43	27 44 16.86
30	8						22.		12 47.07	17.39	0.66	VI.	3	33.317	26 32.40	32.49	3.60	12 29.02	28 8 8.49
31	9				54.				18 53.22	17.37	0.72	IV.	3	25.720	34 28.54	31.97	4.50	18 35.13	16 5.01
32	6			54.	12.	29.			20 11.32	17.37	0.76	IV.	3	21.577	38 48.64	31.86	4.98	19 53.19	20 25.48
33	8						57.		20 39.43	17.37	0.75	V.	3	22.590	37 45.27	31.82	4.86	20 21.31	28 19 21.95
34	7		22.	39.5	57.3	14.3			22 56.89	17.36	0.57	IV.	4	47.345	11 49.63	31.60	1.98	22 38.96	27 53 23.21
35	7	33.	50.	7.5					26 24.99	17.36	0.60	·3·	4	43.025	16 20.32	31.27	2.48	26 7.03	27 57 54.07
36	7					48.3			26 30.65	17.35	0.86	V.	2	9.920	51 1.01	31.26	6.38	26 12.44	28 32 38.65
37	6					40.	57.7		27 22.47	17.35	0.84	V.	2	12.705	48 6.27	31.17	6.05	27 4.28	28 29 43.49
38	6.7				27.		2.		29 27.09	17.35	0.48	IV.	4	57.750	0 56.96	30.97	0.70	29 9.26	27 42 28.72
39	9	25.		0.					33 17.44	17.34	0.80	III.	2	18.115	42 26.54	30.57	5.40	34 59.30	28 24 2.51
40	7			28.5	46.5	4.			34 46.09	17.33	0.66	IV.	3	36.105	23 37.07	30.42	3.29	34 28.10	5 10.78
41	7	29.5	46.7	4.5				14.	36 21.73	17.33	0.64	III.	3	37.885	21 44.91	30.26	3.08	35 3.76	3 18.25
42	7	37.5	54.	12.3	30.5				39 29.62	17.32	0.77	IV.	3	22.688	37 38.81	29.92	4.85	39 11.53	19 13.58
43	8			17.5					40 34.93	17.32	0.84	III.	2	15.653	45 1.06	29.81	5.70	40 16.77	26 36.57
44	8					7.			40 49.38	17.32	0.83	V.	2	15.678	44 59.68	29.78	5.70	40 31.23	26 35.16
45	8							10.5	41 17.98	17.32	0.75	VII.	3	27.175	32 57.69	29.73	4.32	40 59.91	14 31.74
46	7.8		56.		32.5				44 31.39	17.31	0.88	IV.	4	10.417	50 28.82	29.37	6.32	44 13.20	28 32 4.51
47	7.8	59.	16.3	34.	51.5				46 51.20	17.31	0.59	IV.	4	45.867	13 22.07	29.11	2.16	46 33.30	27 54 53.34
48	8			54.3		29.			48 11.57	17.30	0.75	V.	3	27.403	32 43.38	28.95	4.29	47 53.52	28 14 16.62
49	8				40.				49 39.68	17.30	0.57	IV.	4	48.772	10 19.89	28.79	1.81	49 21.81	27 51 50.49
50	7.8					55.			50 37.35	17.30	0.90	V.	1	9.190	51 45.97	28.68	6.47	50 19.15	28 33 21.12
51	8						34.		52 16.56	17.29	0.60	V.	4	46.446	12 45.87	28.48	2.09	51 58.67	27 54 16.44
52	8.9						31.5		52 56.68	17.29	0.62	VI.	4	43.980	15 20.11	28.41	2.36	52 38.77	27 56 50.88
53	8						33.5		53 58.62	17.29	0.66	VI.	4	38.135	21 26.84	28.28	3.05	53 40.67	28 2 58.17
54	9							24.5	54 32.12	17.29	0.68	VII.	4	36.590	23 3.38	28.21	3.23	54 14.15	4 34.82
55	7							25.	55 32.25	17.29	0.88	VII.	2	11.617	49 14.31	28.09	6.18	55 14.08	30 48.58
56	8							14.	56 39.06	17.28	0.72	VI.	3	31.820	28 6.13	27.96	3.78	56 21.06	9 37.87
57	9						43.		58 25.38	17.28	0.86	V.	2	14.780	45 55.97	27.75	5.80	58 7.24	27 29.52
58	8							23.	15 59 30.21	17.28	0.91	VII.	1	8.630	52 21.13	27.62	6.54	15 59 12.02	33 55.29
59	5	26.	42.3	1.	19.				16 3 18.00	17.27	0.66	IV.	4	39.667	19 50.98	27.15	2.85	16 3 0.16	28 1 20.98
60	7				18.	35.5			5 0.65	17.27	0.59	V.	4	48.753	10 21.02	26.93	1.79	4 42.79	27 51 49.74
61	4	26.	43.3	1.	19.	30.			9 18.38	17.26	0.77	IV.	3	27.453	32 39.99	26.39	4.30	9 0.35	28 14 10.68
62	8					9.3	26.5		10 8.99	17.25	0.61	V.	4	45.960	13 16.17	26.29	2.12	9 51.13	27 54 44.58
63	9					50.			11 14.94	17.25	0.82	VI.	2	20.070	39 21.23	26.14	5.18	10 56.87	28 20 52.55
64	7.8		37.5		12.5				24 12.32	17.22	0.56	IV.	4	52.935	5 58.84	24.40	1.32	23 54.54	27 47 24.56
65	3	59.	16.	33.8	51.5				26 51.07	17.21	0.61	IV.	4	46.640	12 33.72	24.04	2.05	26 33.25	27 53 59.81
66	8					35.			27 0.12	17.21	0.67	VI.	4	38.395	21 10.58	24.01	3.00	26 42.24	28 2 37.59
67	9						9.		28 33.97	17.21	0.79	VI.	3	23.450	36 51.48	23.81	4.78	28 15.97	18 20.07
68	8.9			14.		49.			32 31.42	17.20	0.78	V.	3	24.335	35 55.89	23.25	4.67	32 13.44	17 23.81
69	8			5.	23.5				34 22.67	17.20	0.66	IV.	4	39.715	19 47.09	22.98	2.85	34 4.81	1 13.82
70	6		20.7	38.2	56.5		31.		35 55.81	17.19	0.76	IV.	3	28.043	32 2.78	22.76	4.23	35 37.86	13 29.77
71	7						3.5		36 28.33	17.19	0.90	VI.	1	8.975	51 59.45	22.68	6.53	36 10.24	33 28.66
72	7	0.5	17.7	35.5	53.3				38 52.77	17.18	0.69	IV.	3	34.880	24 53.79	22.34	3.42	38 34.90	28 6 19.55
73	7			44.5					16 42 1.78	−17.18	−0.53	III.	4	57.140	− 1 35.32	−21.89	−0.83	16 41 44.07	−27 42 58.04

CORRECTIONS.

Date.	Corr. of Clock.	Hourly rate.	m	n	c	Zenith Point.	Mic. Co.
1847. h.	s.	s.	s.	s.	s.	° ' "	r.

REMARKS.

(117) 41. Minutes assumed as 35 instead of 36.

(117) 63. Micrometer reading assumed as $21''.070$ instead of $20''.070$.

INSTRUMENT READINGS.

Date.	CIRCLE.							Barom.	THERMOM.				
	A.	B.	C.	D.	E.	F.	Mean.		At.	Ex.	U.	L.	I.
1847. h. m.	° ' "						"	in.	°	°	°	°	°

ZONE 117. JUNE 11. P. $D_s = -27° 41' 0''$—Continued.

SECONDS OF TRANSIT.

No.	Mag.	I.	II.	III.	IV.	V.	VI.	VII.
74	7					38.		
75	8				56.			
76	7.8							59.5
77	9							16.
78	8							3.5
79	8			24.				
80	7.8					13.		
81	7.8						46.5	
82	7					39.		
83	7					13.5		
84	9						5.	
85	7				53.			
86	6					36.		11.5
87	8.9	49.	6.	24.				
88	8					30.		
89	8						17.	
90	8	35.	52.	10.	28.3			
91	9			59.				
92	8				4.5		38.5	
93	8.9		33.5	51.5	9.5			
94	4			56.	13.3	30.5		
95	8					30.5		
96	9			23.				
97	7				59.			
98	7						41.	58.5
99	7.8					54.		
100	8							33.
101	8		26.	43.5	1.5			
102	7.6	41.5	58.	16.5	35.			
103	7		15.5	33.	51.5	8.5		
104	7.8			17.	34.5			
105	8	30.	47.3	5.3				
106	6				9.	26.3	44.	
107	8				27.			
108	8					44.		
109	4.5				7.3	42.3		
110	8					58.		33.
111	9		24.					
112	8			20.				
113	7.8				11.5			
114	5.6	39.3	56.7	14.	32.			
115	8		41.					
116	8				17.			
117	8	3.5	21.	38.5				
118	6						34.	
119	7						19.5	37.5
120	8				32.3			
121	8				12.		46.5	
122	8				24.5			

No.	T.	a_1	a_2	MICROMETER.		r.	i	d_1	d_2	Mean Right Ascension, 1850.0.	Mean Declination, 1850.0.
74	16 42 20.60	−17.18	−0.53	V.	4	54.727	− 4 6.42	−21.84	−1.10	16 42 2.89	−27 45 29.36
75	43 55.53	17.17	0.64	IV.	4	41.510	17 55.53	21.61	2.64	43 37.72	27 59 19.78
76	44 7.02	17.17	0.73	VII.	3	29.905	30 2.51	21.58	4.00	43 49.12	28 11 28.09
77	45 23.41	17.17	0.79	VII.	3	23.113	37 12.51	21.39	4.82	45 5.45	28 18 38.72
78	47 11.21	17.17	0.61	VII.	4	44.127	9 56.87	21.12	1.76	46 53.43	27 51 19.75
79	49 41.34	17.16	0.66	III.	3	37.830	21 48.36	20.75	3.07	49 23.52	28 3 12.18
80	49 55.42	17.16	0.80	V.	2	22.230	38 7.91	20.72	4.93	49 37.46	19 33.56
81	50 11.52	17.16	0.74	VI.	3	27.983	32 6.86	20.68	4.33	49 53.62	13 31.67
82	51 21.40	17.16	0.82	V.	2	17.865	42 42.35	20.51	5.45	51 3.42	24 8.31
83	51 55.92	17.15	0.80	V.	2	22.403	37 57.75	20.41	4.90	51 37.97	19 23.06
84	53 30.04	17.15	0.73	VI.	3	30.312	29 40.93	20.18	3.96	53 12.16	11 5.07
85	54 52.48	17.15	0.66	IV.	3	38.743	20 51.52	19.97	2.96	54 34.67	2 14.45
86	55 18.65	17.15	0.80	V.	2	20.580	39 52.08	19.91	5.12	55 0.70	21 17.11
87	58 41.37	17.14	0.81	III.	2	19.430	41 4.13	19.40	5.23	58 23.42	28 22 28.76
88	59 12.56	17.14	0.60	V.	4	46.585	12 37.11	19.32	2.05	58 54.82	27 53 58.45
89	16 59 42.14	17.13	0.65	VI.	4	39.920	19 34.68	19.24	2.83	16 59 24.36	28 0 56.75
90	17 5 27.36	17.12	0.73	IV.	3	27.780	32 19.22	18.36	4.27	17 5 9.51	13 41.85
91	10 16.41	17.11	0.80	III.	2	20.760	39 40.40	17.64	5.12	9 58.50	21 3.16
92	11 3.82	17.11	0.64	VI.	4	39.660	19 51.11	17.52	2.84	10 46.07	28 1 11.47
93	13 8.80	17.10	0.55	IV.	4	49.485	9 39.81	17.21	1.69	12 51.15	27 50 58.71
94	14 13.06	17.10	0.62	IV.	4	41.273	18 10.40	17.04	2.65	13 55.34	27 59 30.09
95	15 12.86	17.10	0.83	V.	2	11.830	49 1.13	16.88	6.22	14 54.93	28 30 24.23
96	16 40.44	17.09	0.85	III.	2	11.605	49 15.13	16.66	6.24	16 22.50	30 38.03
97	16 58.06	17.09	0.79	IV.	2	18.003	42 33.69	16.61	5.45	16 40.18	23 55.75
98	17 5.97	17.09	0.74	VI.	3	25.070	35 9.70	16.60	4.59	16 48.14	16 30.89
99	18 36.46	17.09	0.71	V.	3	28.003	32 5.54	16.36	4.24	18 18.66	28 13 26.14
100	22 58.15	17.08	0.60	VI.	4	40.940	18 30.77	15.69	2.60	22 40.47	27 59 49.15
101	26 0.04	17.07	0.65	IV.	3	35.345	24 24.86	15.19	3.36	25 43.22	28 5 43.41
102	28 33.80	17.07	0.76	IV.	2	21.415	38 59.75	14.81	5.04	28 15.97	24 19.73
103	29 50.68	17.07	0.75	IV.	2	22.712	37 38.17	14.62	4.89	29 32.86	28 18 57.68
104	31 34.27	17.06	0.51	IV.	4	51.955	7 0.29	14.34	1.39	31 16.70	27 48 16.02
105	33 22.44	17.06	0.70	IV.	3	27.488	32 37.79	14.06	4.30	33 4.68	28 13 56.15
106	34 8.96	17.06	0.50	V.	4	51.880	7 4.67	13.95	1.41	33 51.40	27 49 20.23
107	35 26.40	17.05	0.64	IV.	3	34.780	25 0.06	13.74	3.42	35 8.71	29 6 17.22
108	36 26.42	17.05	0.75	V.	2	21.563	39 50.40	13.58	5.02	36 8.62	28 20 9.00
109	38 24.74	17.05	0.48	III.	4	54.020	4 50.81	13.27	1.15	38 7.21	27 46 5.23
110	39 40.50	17.04	0.67	VII.	3	29.976	30 1.82	13.07	4.00	39 22.79	28 11 18.89
111	42 59.28	17.04	0.77	II.	2	17.550	43 1.68	12.54	5.51	42 41.47	24 19.73
112	43 2.38	17.04	0.78	V.	2	15.915	44 44.73	12.54	5.70	42 44.56	26 2.97
113	44 11.00	17.03	0.59	IV.	3	39.840	19 42.66	12.35	2.82	43 53.38	0 57.83
114	47 31.51	17.03	0.59	IV.	3	38.707	20 53.77	11.83	2.96	47 13.89	2 8.56
115	48 58.36	17.02	0.64	III.	3	32.810	27 3.26	11.59	3.66	48 40.70	8 18.51
116	48 59.50	17.02	0.63	V.	3	34.000	25 49.30	11.59	3.52	48 41.85	7 4.41
117	52 56.04	17.01	0.74	III.	2	18.960	41 33.37	10.96	5.31	52 38.29	28 22 49.64
118	52 41.77	17.01	0.50	VII.	4	48.320	10 47.74	11.00	1.82	52 24.26	27 52 0.56
119	53 45.03	17.01	0.48	VI.	4	50.983	8 0.93	10.83	1.51	53 27.54	49 13.27
120	55 31.97	17.01	0.48	IV.	4	48.465	10 39.33	10.54	1.81	55 49.48	51 51.68
121	56 11.72	17.01	0.49	IV.	4	50.083	8 57.74	10.43	1.62	55 54.22	27 50 9.79
122	17 57 23.40	−17.00	−0.80	IV.	1	9.880	−51 2.27	−10.24	−6.44	17 57 5.60	−28 32 18.95

CORRECTIONS.

Date.	Corr. of Clock.	Hourly rate.	m	n	ϵ	Zenith Point.	Mic. Co.
	h.	s.	s.	s.	s.	° ' ''	r.
1847.							

REMARKS.

(117) 78. Micrometer reading assumed as 49r.127, not 44r.127.

INSTRUMENT READINGS.

Date.	CIRCLE.							Barom.	THERMOM.				
	A.	B.	C.	D.	E.	F.	Mean.		At.	Ex.	U.	L.	I.
1847.	° ' ''						''	in.	°	°	°	°	°
h. m.													

Zone 117. June 11. P. $D_0 = -27°\ 41'\ 0''$.—Continued.

No.	Mag.	I.	II.	III.	IV.	V.	VI.	VII.	T. (h m s)	a_1	a_2	Micrometer	r	i	d_1	d_4	Mean Right Ascension, 1850.0	Mean Declination, 1850.0
123	7						9.3		17 57 34.24	−17.00	−0.72	VI. 2	19.503	−40 59.67	−10.21	−5.27	17 57 16.52	−28 22 15.15
124	4				54.	10.5			58 52.93	17.00	0.77	IV. 2	13.928	46 49.37	10.01	5.96	58 35.16	28 28 5.34
125	7						0.0		59 25.22	17.00	0.50	V. 4	47.690	11 27.68	9.92	1.90	59 7.72	27 52 38.50
126	9							37.	17 59 44.83	17.00	0.46	VII. 4	52.170	6 46.25	9.87	1.37	59 27.37	47 57.49
127	7							1.5	18 0 9.37	17.00	0.44	VII. 4	54.970	3 50.56	9.80	1.00	17 59 51.93	27 45 1.36
128	7							14.	1 21.53	17.00	0.63	VII. 3	30.730	29 14.51	9.61	3.92	18 1 3.90	28 10 28.04
129	7					52.			2 34.51	16.99	0.57	V. 3	37.482	22 10.99	9.40	3.09	2 16.95	3 23.48
130	7				27.5				3 26.70	16.99	0.67	IV. 3	25.340	34 52.58	9.27	4.57	3 9.04	16 6.42
131	8	34.5	51.7	9.3					5 26.68	16.99	0.54	III. 4	39.750	19 45.73	8.95	2.83	5 9.15	0 57.51
132	7.8			11.5	29.3				6 28.77	16.98	0.59	IV. 3	33.847	25 58.59	8.78	3.54	6 11.20	7 10.91
133	9				19.				7 18.12	16.98	0.69	IV. 2	20.603	39 37.89	8.65	5.12	7 0.45	20 51.66
134	6				12.	28.3			8 10.93	16.98	0.69	IV. 2	21.905	38 28.12	8.50	5.00	7 53.26	19 41.62
135	8							19.3	8 26.85	16.98	0.60	VII. 3	32.715	27 9.97	8.47	3.68	8 9.27	8 22.12
136	9						27.7		9 52.69	16.98	0.65	VI. 3	25.423	34 47.68	8.23	4.56	9 35.06	16 0.47
137	8		10.5	28.					11 45.50	16.97	0.60	III. 3	30.517	29 27.31	7.93	3.94	11 27.93	10 39.18
138	5.6		13.	31.3					12 48.54	16.97	0.79	III. 2	12.485	48 19.95	7.76	6.17	12 30.82	29 33.68
139	8.9		28.	46.					18 14 3.39	−16.97	−0.74	III. 2	13.330	−47 26.98	−7.56	−6.07	18 13 45.68	−28 28 40.61

Zone 118. June 14. P. $D_0 = -27°\ 3'\ 0''$.

No.	Mag.	I.	II.	III.	IV.	V.	VI.	VII.	T. (h m s)	a_1	a_2	Micrometer	r	i	d_1	d_4	Mean Right Ascension, 1850.0	Mean Declination, 1850.0
1	7			30.5	48.2	5.			16 0 47.64	−18.88	−1.06	IV. 3	34.344	−25 27.66	−54.97	−2.48	16 0 27.70	−27 29 25.11
2	7	7.	23.7	41.					2 58.43	18.88	0.97	III. 4	53.434	5 27.74	54.71	0.31	2 38.58	9 22.76
3	4				25.	41.8	59.		3 24.32	18.88	1.08	IV. 3	31.940	27 58.22	54.65	2.77	3 4.36	31 55.64
4	8						31.5		3 56.64	18.87	1.15	VI. 2	19.995	40 28.61	54.59	4.16	3 36.62	44 27.36
5	7					20.3	37.8		5 2.82	18.87	1.20	V. 2	12.910	47 53.34	54.45	4.99	4 42.75	51 52.78
6	8.9			9.	27.5				7 26.44	18.87	1.17	IV. 2	17.567	43 1.18	54.14	4.44	7 6.40	46 59.76
7	6.7	28.5	45.3	3.3	21.5	38.			9 20.54	18.87	1.15	IV. 3	24.207	36 3.61	53.91	3.66	9 0.52	40 1.18
8	7					28.7	45.7		10 10.94	18.86	1.22	IV. 1	10.110	50 47.97	53.80	5.33	9 50.86	54 47.10
9	8	48.5	5.5	23.3	41.				12 40.46	18.86	1.12	IV. 3	29.924	30 4.70	53.49	3.00	12 20.48	34 1.19
10	7			51.3	9.				14 8.46	18.86	1.12	IV. 3	32.515	27 22.33	53.30	2.70	13 48.48	31 18.33
11	7.8	24.2	41.	58.7					16 15.91	18.85	1.06	III. 4	44.359	14 57.22	53.02	1.33	15 56.00	18 51.57
12	7.8					38.3			16 20.93	18.85	1.10	V. 4	47.170	18 16.72	53.02	1.72	16 0.98	22 11.46
13	8						28.		16 53.29	18.85	1.12	VI. 3	35.505	24 15.13	52.93	2.36	16 33.32	28 10.42
14	7.8						8.3		17 33.67	18.85	1.07	VI. 4	42.807	16 33.61	52.86	1.51	17 13.75	20 27.98
15	6	26.	43.3	1.	19.	35.7	53.	10.3	21 18.21	18.84	1.15	IV. 3	29.104	30 56.28	52.37	3.09	20 58.22	34 51.74
16	7	22.3		57.3			49.		24 14.40	18.84	1.23	VI. 2	17.105	43 30.05	51.98	4.50	23 54.33	47 26.53
17	3	1.	18.	36.	54.3	10.7	27.8		26 53.16	18.83	1.28	V. 1	10.838	50 2.33	51.62	5.24	26 33.05	53 59.19
18	7			48.		23.			30 5.41	18.83	1.22	V. 3	23.615	36 40.95	51.19	3.73	29 45.36	40 35.87
19	7						13.		32 38.27	18.82	1.16	VI. 3	33.020	26 50.91	50.84	2.64	32 18.27	30 44.39
20	6		44.5	2.					35 19.18	18.82	1.09	III. 4	52.643	6 17.22	50.46	0.41	34 59.27	10 8.09
21	7				52.		26.3		35 51.76	18.82	1.09	IV. 4	52.564	6 22.24	50.38	0.41	35 31.85	10 13.03
22	7				37.5		12.		37 37.33	18.81	1.10	V. 4	50.740	8 16.41	50.13	0.63	37 17.42	12 7.17
23	7	17.	34.	52.					40 8.98	18.81	1.16	III. 4	40.045	19 27.28	49.80	1.85	39 49.01	23 18.93
24	8		10.						41 44.87	18.81	1.19	II. 3	35.890	34 16.95	49.57	2.79	41 24.87	38 9.31
25	6.7				5.	22.			42 4.32	18.80	1.26	IV. 3	21.340	39 3.58	49.52	4.00	41 44.26	42 57.10
26	7.8						37.5		42 22.62	18.80	1.28	VI. 2	18.920	41 36.07	49.52	4.28	42 2.54	45 29.87
27	8		22.						44 56.80	18.80	1.16	II. 4	42.080	17 19.46	49.09	1.60	44 36.84	21 10.15
28	7				27.				16 45 26.58	−18.80	−1.16	IV. 4	44.177	−15 8.18	−49.02	−1.35	16 45 6.62	−27 18 58.55

CORRECTIONS.

Date.	Corr. of Clock.	Hourly rate.	m	n	c	Zenith Point.	Mic. Co.
1847.	h.	s.	s.	s.	s.	° ' "	r.

INSTRUMENT READINGS.

	Date.	A.	B.	C.	D.	E.	F.	Mean.	Barom.	At.	Ex.	U.	L.	I.
	1847. h. m.	° ' "						"	in.					
Zone 118	June 14, 16 0	*66 24 62.0	65.5	62.3	72.5	38.0	64.8	60.85	29.804	68.0	59.0	69.0	69.0	72.5
	17 24								29.804	67.0	57.0			
	18 0	60.2	67.0	62.5	72.3	40.0	63.0	60.83						
	18 10								29.798	66.0	56.0			
	19 14								29.796	65.0	55.0			
	19 59								29.790	64.0	53.5			
	20 58								29.782	64.0	56.0			

REMARKS.

(117) 127. a 1s.4 in error by Arg. Z. 223, 46, and Mural Circle, 1846, Aug. 13.

(118) 8. Transits over T.'s V and VI assumed as recorded over T.'s IV and V.

(118) 24. Micrometer reading assumed as 25s.890, not 35s.890.

(118) 26. Transit over T. VI assumed as 57s.5, not 37s.5, to agree with Mural Circle, 1846, July 7, and Arg. Z. 214, 46.

*This reading has been assumed as too small by 1°, the intervals of the transit threads affording sufficient evidence of the fact. The reading 66° 25' is adopted, and the correction made in all the subsidiary computations. [Observing book has 66° 24'.]

17—z

ZONE 118. JUNE 14. P. $D_0 = -27° 3' 0''$—Continued.

No.	Mag.	I	II	III	IV	V	VI	VII	T.	a_1	a_2	Mic.		r.	i	d_1	d_2	Mean Right Ascension 1850.0	Mean Declination 1850.0
									h. m. s.	s.	s.			r.	' ''	''	''	h. m. s.	° ' ''
29	6.7						6.	23.	16 45 48.43	−18.80	−1.21	V.	3	33.803	−26 1.60	−48.98	−2.54	16 45 28.42	−27 29 53.12
30	7				14.5				47 13.47	18.70	1.33	IV.	1	13.465	47 17.50	45.77	4.93	46 53.35	51 11.20
31	6			54.					48 53.52	18.79	1.18	IV.	4	41.170	16 16.78	48.53	1.71	48 33.55	22 7.02
32	7					53.			50 18.23	18.79	1.25	VI.	3	28.580	31 29.53	48.33	3.15	49 58.19	35 21.01
33	7				41.				51 6.09	18.79	1.33	VI.	2	15.230	45 27.85	48.21	4.73	50 45.97	49 20.79
34	6			11.					52 53.52	18.78	1.30	V.	2	21.545	38 51.66	47.95	3.98	52 33.44	42 43.59
35	8			3.					55 45.66	18.78	1.18	VI.	4	46.310	12 54.16	47.56	1.12	55 25.70	16 42.84
36	8							44.	55 52.13	18.78	1.15	VII.	4	52.770	6 8.50	47.50	0.39	55 32.20	9 56.30
37	7		58.5		34.4				56 33.58	18.77	1.27	IV.	3	32.260	27 38.39	47.10	2.73	58 13.54	31 28.22
38	8							30.	16 58 37.87	18.77	1.27	VII.	3	33.940	25 53.12	47.10	2.53	58 17.83	29 42.75
39	7					17.5			17 0 0.02	18.77	1.34	V.	3	22.628	37 42.89	46.89	3.87	16 59 39.91	41 33.65
40	7					23.			1 5.56	18.77	1.29	V.	3	29.423	30 36.64	46.72	3.07	17 0 45.50	34 26.43
41	6			46.5	4.3	22.5			3 21.60	18.76	1.30	IV.	3	29.597	30 25.35	46.39	3.05	3 1.54	34 14.79
42	6.7		23.2	40.6	58.7				4 55.00	18.76	1.31	IV.	3	27.185	32 56.75	46.13	3.32	4 37.93	36 46.20
43	7.8	42.			18.5				6 17.33	18.76	1.36	IV.	2	22.040	43 33.04	45.93	4.50	5 57.21	47 24.47
44	8					45.			7 27.62	18.76	1.25	V.	4	40.160	19 20.07	45.75	1.81	7 7.61	23 7.03
45	6				24.5	41.3			8 23.80	18.75	1.33	IV.	3	28.153	31 56.01	45.61	3.20	8 3.72	35 44.82
46	8						24.		8 49.22	18.75	1.33	VI.	3	27.890	32 12.70	45.54	3.23	8 29.14	36 1.47
47	7.8	11.	28.5	46.					11 3.26	18.75	1.35	III.	3	27.315	32 48.28	45.20	3.30	10 43.16	36 36.78
48	6				41.				11 6.03	18.75	1.44	VI.	1	8.860	52 6.62	45.19	5.51	10 45.84	55 57.32
49	8		36.	54.					13 11.22	18.75	1.42	III.	2	13.820	46 55.96	44.86	4.91	12 51.05	50 45.73
50	7.8					59.			13 41.57	18.74	1.32	V.	3	32.340	27 33.63	44.79	2.72	13 21.51	31 21.14
51	3					50.7	8.		14 15.59	18.74	1.47	VI.	1	5.495	55 38.05	44.69	5.91	13 55.38	59 28.65
52	6	9.7	27.	44.	2.3			53.7	17 1.61	18.74	1.32	IV.	3	36.075	23 38.95	44.27	2.29	16 41.35	27 25.51
53	7				15.				17 24 14.54	−18.73	−1.31	IV.	4	41.970	−17 26.49	−43.13	−1.59	17 23 54.50	−27 21 11.21

ZONE 119. JUNE 14. P. $D_0 = -27° 3' 0''$.

No.	Mag.	I	II	III	IV	V	VI	VII	T.	a_1	a_2	Mic.		r.	i	d_1	d_2	Mean Right Ascension 1850.0	Mean Declination 1850.0
1	7							30.	18 10 37.82	−18.64	−1.30	VII.	3	30.093	−29 54.54	−35.38	−2.99	18 10 17.88	−27 33 32.91
2	7							8.	11 15.89	18.64	1.30	VII.	3	35.597	24 9.30	35.26	2.34	10 55.95	− 27 46.90
3	7	29.	46.		3.5	38.5			14 20.95	18.64	1.30	IV.	3	29.463	30 33.88	34.74	3.06	14 1.01	34 11.68
4	8				57.3				16 32.19	18.63	1.29	II.	3	34.090	25 42.59	34.36	2.52	16 12.27	29 19.47
5	7					40.3			16 39.65	18.63	1.20	IV.	3	32.475	27 24.90	34.32	2.71	16 19.73	31 1.93
6	8							20.5	16 54.83	18.63	1.29	VI.	3	35.700	20 54.59	34.29	1.97	16 34.91	24 30.85
7	8						7.5		19 50.13	18.63	1.29	V.	4	42.060	17 20.85	33.77	1.57	19 30.21	20 56.19
8	7	20.	37.	54.5					23 11.79	18.62	1.29	III.	4	43.453	15 53.66	33.19	1.41	22 51.88	19 28.26
9	8.9				35.				23 34.61	18.62	1.29	IV.	4	45.427	13 49.91	33.13	1.19	23 14.70	17 24.23
10	8					49.5			24 32.05	18.62	1.29	V.	3	28.160	31 55.76	32.97	3.21	24 12.14	35 31.94
11	8				33.				25 32.17	18.62	1.28	IV.	3	23.385	36 55.26	32.79	3.79	25 12.27	40 31.84
12	7			12.	28.				26 28.34	18.62	1.28	IV.	3	36.114	23 36.50	32.62	2.28	26 8.44	27 11.40
13	8				22.				27 4.65	18.62	1.28	V.	4	44.670	14 37.06	32.53	1.30	26 44.75	18 10.91
14	7.8	37.			12.				31 29.19	18.61	1.28	III.	3	23.637	36 38.94	31.75	3.76	31 9.30	40 14.45
15	7				25.5	44.			32 43.03	18.61	1.28	IV.	3	28.970	31 4.62	31.54	3.11	32 23.14	34 39.27
16	8							35.3	32 43.45	18.61	1.28	VII	4	54.160	4 41.47	31.54	0.16	32 23.56	8 13.17
17	8							41.5	33 49.21	18.61	1.28	VII.	2	22.013	43 35.48	31.34	4.52	33 29.32	47 11.34
18	3.4		2.	19.7					36 36.77	18.60	1.27	III.	4	54.030	4 50.25	30.86	0.18	36 16.90	8 21.29
19	6.7						59.5	16.5	36 58.86	18.60	1.27	VI.	1	24.810	35 25.96	30.79	3.61	36 38.99	39 0.36
20	7.8							5.	18 37 12.86	−18.60	−1.27	VII.	3	33.760	−26 4.42	−30.75	−2.45	18 36 52.99	−27 29 37.62

CORRECTIONS.

Date.	Corr. of Clock.	Hourly rate.	m	n	c	Zenith Point.	Mic.Co.
1847.	h.	s.	s.	s.	s.	° ' ''	r.

REMARKS.

(118) 35. Transit over T. V assumed as recorded over T. VI, to agree with Mural Z., 1846, July 7, and Arg. Z.

(118) 43. Micrometer reading assumed as 17r.040 instead of 22r.040.

(119) 17. Micrometer reading assumed as 17r.013 instead of 22r.013.

INSTRUMENT READINGS.

Date.	CIRCLE.							Barom.	THERMOM.				
	A.	B.	C.	D.	E.	F.	Mean.		At.	Ex.	U.	L.	I.
1847. h. m.	° ' ''						''	in.	°				

ZONE 119. JUNE 14. P. D₀ = −27° 3′ 0″—Continued.

No.	Mag.	I.	II.	III.	IV.	V.	VI.	VII.	T. (h. m. s.)	a_1 (s.)	a_2 (s.)	MICROMETER (r)	i	d_1	d_2	Mean Right Ascension, 1850.0 (h. m. s.)	Mean Declination, 1850.0 (° ′ ″)
21	7					52.5			18 38 52.16	−18.60	−1.27	IV. 4 48.195	−10 56.27	−30.46	−0.60	18 38 32.29	−27 14 27.59
22	8						27.		40 9.66	18.60	1.27	V. 4 46.685	12 30.71	30.24	1.04	39 49.79	16 1.99
23	7							9.	40 34.39	18.60	1.27	VI. 4 45.520	13 43.64	30.16	1.18	40 14.52	17 14.98
24	7			49.5	6.3	24.5			42 23.96	18.59	1.27	IV. 4 42.957	16 24.58	29.84	1.46	42 4.10	19 55.88
25	7		28.	45.5					44 3.02	18.59	1.27	III. 1 8.620	52 21.18	29.55	5.58	43 43.16	55 56.31
26	9							54.	44 19.40	18.59	1.27	VI. 4 45.550	13 41.76	29.50	1.17	43 59.54	17 12.43
27	9							53.5	45 18.70	18.59	1.27	VI. 3 25.905	34 17.24	29.33	3.48	44 58.84	37 50.05
28	8.9			7.					47 24.30	18.59	1.26	III. 3 22.320	38 1.71	28.96	3.91	47 4.45	41 34.58
29	7			8.5	26.5				48 25.75	18.59	1.26	IV. 3 25.070	35 9.39	28.78	3.58	48 5.90	38 41.75
30	8							19.5	48 27.56	18.59	1.26	VII. 4 47.890	11 14.45	28.78	0.89	48 7.71	14 44.12
31	8				17.5				50 17.01	18.58	1.26	IV. 4 40.560	18 55.11	28.45	1.76	49 57.17	22 25.32
32	8			11.5					51 28.84	18.58	1.26	III. 2 13.535	47 14.04	28.24	4.98	51 9.00	50 47.26
33	8			13.5					52 12.58	18.58	1.26	IV. 1 18.782	41 44.73	28.12	4.34	51 52.74	45 17.19
34	8			41.	59.				53 55.26	18.58	1.26	IV. 3 29.707	30 18.38	27.80	3.03	53 38.45	33 49.21
35	8.9			20.					55 37.22	18.57	1.26	III. 4 42.140	17 15.05	27.52	1.57	55 17.39	20 45.04
36	8					17.5			56 0.01	18.57	1.26	V. 2 19.807	40 40.47	27.45	4.22	55 40.18	44 12.14
37	7			0.	18.5				57 17.56	18.57	1.25	IV. 3 32.877	26 59.45	27.22	2.66	56 57.74	30 29.33
38	3			55.3			29.		18 57 54.14	18.57	1.25	IV. 1 11.363	49 29.44	27.12	5.24	57 34.32	52 51.80
39	9	28.							19 0 2.87	18.57	1.25	II. 3 35.760	23 57.70	26.75	2.31	18 59 43.05	27 26.76
40	7		8.5	2.34	1.				0 43.50	18.57	1.25	IV. 4 42.050	17 21.53	26.63	1.57	19 0 23.68	20 49.73
41	6			50.3					2 7.51	18.56	1.25	III. 4 45.430	13 49.66	26.38	1.17	1 47.70	17 17.21
42	7.8				33.	49.7			2 32.46	18.56	1.25	V. 4 43.840	15 29.08	26.31	1.35	2 12.65	18 56.74
43	8				59.5				3 59.16	18.56	1.25	IV. 4 47.883	11 15.64	26.06	0.88	3 39.35	14 42.58
44	7				57.7				4 57.50	18.56	1.25	IV. 4 54.987	3 50.24	25.88	0.04	4 37.69	7 16.16
45	8						46.		5 28.53	18.56	1.25	V. 3 19.807	34 16.17	25.80	3.49	5 8.72	37 45.46
46	7.8							31.	5 38.81	18.56	1.25	VII. 3 29.265	30 46.61	25.77	3.08	5 19.00	34 15.46
47	9			31.5					7 48.73	18.56	1.24	III. 4 39.920	19 35.06	25.39	1.81	7 28.93	23 2.26
48	8				41.5				8 40.85	18.56	1.24	IV. 3 32.527	27 21.58	25.24	2.70	8 21.05	30 49.52
49	8	36.	53.	10.5					14 27.05	18.55	1.24	III. 3 24.910	35 18.92	24.23	3.61	14 8.16	38 46.76
50	8.9			17.3					15 34.51	18.55	1.24	IV. 4 44.825	14 27.36	24.04	1.24	15 14.72	17 52.64
51	8	59.5	16.7						20 51.70	18.54	1.24	II. 4 19.500	40 59.36	23.13	4.26	20 31.92	44 26.75
52	8.9			46.					21 3.29	18.54	1.23	III. 2 24.670	35 35.13	23.09	3.64	20 43.52	39 1.86
53	8.6						29.		20 54.39	18.54	1.23	VI. 4 45.415	13 50.29	23.12	1.17	20 34.62	17 14.58
54	8.9	13.5	31.	48.5					24 5.68	18.54	1.23	III. 3 37.210	22 27.43	22.57	2.14	23 45.91	25 52.14
55	9		25.						24 59.89	18.54	1.23	II. 3 34.483	25 17.90	22.41	2.46	24 40.12	28 42.86
56	8			11.					25 28.25	18.53	1.23	III. 3 34.065	24 48.07	22.33	2.40	25 8.49	28 12.60
57	9						53.3		25 35.89	18.53	1.23	V. 3 34.525	25 16.49	22.31	2.46	25 16.13	28 41.26
58	9							45.5	26 10.67	18.53	1.23	VI. 2 22.785	37 33.53	22.21	3.87	25 50.91	40 59.61
59	8			42.3					27 59.63	18.53	1.23	III. 2 14.580	46 8.46	21.90	4.86	27 39.87	49 35.22
60	8.9	34.	51.						29 26.06	18.53	1.23	II. 2 22.365	37 59.64	21.65	3.92	29 6.30	41 25.21
61	8		24.3	41.7					29 39.17	18.53	1.23	III. 2 21.590	38 48.46	21.56	4.01	29 39.41	42 14.03
62	8		26.3	44.					31 1.39	18.53	1.22	III. 1 11.933	48 53.09	21.38	5.20	30 41.64	52 19.67
63	8				35.5		9.3		31 34.60	18.53	1.22	IV. 3 25.483	34 43.54	21.29	3.54	31 14.85	38 8.37
64	8			54.	29.				35 28.68	18.52	1.22	II. 4 44.940	14 20.02	20.62	1.23	35 8.94	17 41.87
65	8				19.7				36 18.78	18.52	1.22	IV. 2 18.880	41 38.59	20.49	4.34	35 59.04	45 3.42
66	7.8				24.5	41.			37 23.63	18.52	1.22	IV. 3 26.045	34 8.15	20.30	3.48	37 3.89	37 31.93
67	8.9							29.	37 36.96	18.52	1.22	VII. 4 41.180	18 15.47	20.27	1.67	37 17.22	21 37.41
68	8							21.	38 29.17	18.52	1.22	VII. 4 56.120	7 52.28	20.11	0.50	38 9.43	11 12.89
69	8.9							24.5	19 39 32.39	−18.52	−1.22	VII. 3 35.703	−24 2.59	−19.94	−2.32	19 39 12.65	−27 27 24.85

CORRECTIONS.

Date.	Corr. of Clock.	Hourly rate.	m	n	c	Zenith Point.	Mic. Co.
1847.	h.	s.	s.	s.	s.	° ′ ″	r.

REMARKS.

(119) 37. Transits over T.'s III and IV assumed as recorded over T.'s IV and V.

(119) 68. Micrometer reading assumed as 51ʳ.120 instead of 56ʳ.120.

INSTRUMENT READINGS.

Date.	A.	B.	C.	D.	E.	F.	Mean.	Barom.	At.	Ex.	U.	L.	I.
1847. h. m.	° ′ ″						″	in.	°	°	°	°	°

ZONE 119. JUNE 14. P. $D_s = -27°\ 3'\ 0''$—Continued.

No.	Mag.	I.	II.	III.	IV.	V.	VI.	VII.	T. (h. m. s.)	a_1	a_2	MICR.		r	i (' ")	d_1	d_2	Mean Right Ascension, 1850.0 (h. m. s.)	Mean Declination, 1850.0 (° ' ")
70	9				36.5				19 41 35.68	−18.52	−1.22	IV.	3	24.205	−36 3.73	−19.59	−3.70	19 41 15.94	−27 39 27.02
71	8					9.			41 51.51	18.51	1.22	V.	3	20.410	40 2.15	19.55	4.15	41 31.78	43 25.88
72	7						49.5		42 14.57	18.51	1.22	VI.	2	13.415	47 21.77	19.49	5.02	41 54.84	50 46.28
73	7							38.5	42 46.39	18.51	1.22	VII.	3	35.635	24 6.86	19.39	2.33	42 26.66	27 28.58
74	9							43.	43 51.08	18.51	1.22	VII.	4	49.330	9 44.40	19.22	0.71	43 31.35	13 4.33
75	7			57.	15.				46 14.31	18.51	1.21	IV.	3	33.430	26 25.00	18.81	2.59	45 54.59	29 46.40
76	4.5	11.7		46.7	4.5	21.3			48 3.84	18.51	1.21	IV.	3	29.626	30 23.53	18.50	3.05	47 44.12	33 45.08
77	7				1.5				52 0.76	18.50	1.21	IV.	3	28.260	31 49.35	17.83	3.21	51 41.05	35 10.39
78	7	30.3	48.3	5.	22.5	39.3			56 22.29	18.50	1.20	IV.	4	48.460	10 39.64	17.08	0.80	56 2.59	13 57.52
79	7.8			46.7	5.				58 4.09	18.50	1.20	IV.	3	24.605	35 38.58	16.80	3.65	57 44.39	38 59.03
80	8			0.5	18.3	36.3			19 59 35.55	18.50	1.20	IV.	3	36.873	22 48.77	16.54	2.18	19 59 15.85	26 7.49
81	8			31.	48.7	5.5			20 4 48.13	18.49	1.20	IV.	3	33.225	26 37.80	15.63	2.62	20 4 28.44	29 56.05
82	4.5			57.5	15.3	32.3			6 14.78	18.49	1.19	IV.	3	34.565	25 13.73	15.38	2.45	5 55.10	28 31.56
83	7	7.3		42.0	0.				10 59.30	18.48	1.19	IV.	3	31.043	28 54.56	14.71	2.88	9 39.63	32 12.15
84	8.9	6.	22.3	40.3					10 57.73	18.48	1.19	III.	2	15.710	44 57.42	14.37	4.75	11 38.06	48 16.54
85	7	56.3	13.7	31.	48.5				14 48.22	18.48	1.19	IV.	4	49.670	9 23.64	13.86	0.64	14 29.55	12 38.14
86	8			22.					18 39.25	18.48	1.18	III.	3	36.137	23 34.68	13.18	2.27	18 19.59	26 50.13
87	8			21.3					19 38.62	18.48	1.18	III.	2	17.695	42 52.84	12.99	4.51	19 18.06	46 10.34
88	8			36.	54.3				20 53.32	18.47	1.18	IV.	2	15.535	45 8.71	12.76	4.77	20 33.67	48 26.24
89	7			43.7	1.7	18.5			26 0.94	18.47	1.17	IV.	2	19.413	41 5.39	11.86	4.29	25 41.30	44 21.54
90	7				11.5	28.3	45.5		27 10.98	18.47	1.17	IV.	4	45.260	14 0.33	11.65	1.17	26 51.34	17 13.15
91	7	3.3	20.3	38.	55.	12.5			31 55.03	18.47	1.17	IV.	4	51.910	7 3.12	10.81	0.37	31 35.39	10 14.30
92	7	54.	10.7	28.7					35 45.97	18.46	1.17	III.	2	18.820	41 42.16	10.13	4.37	35 26.34	44 56.66
93	9					4.5			35 47.05	18.46	1.17	V.	3	28.090	32 0.15	10.13	3.23	35 27.42	35 13.51
94	7					49.5	6.7		36 31.90	18.46	1.16	V.	2	16.670	43 57.42	9.98	4.63	36 12.28	47 12.03
95	7.8			42.	1.				37 59.58	18.46	1.16	IV.	2	17.297	43 18.19	9.73	4.56	37 39.96	46 32.48
96	7.8						39.	56.7	38 4.26	18.46	1.16	VI.	2	20.050	40 25.22	9.72	4.22	37 44.64	43 39.16
97	8						29.		39 54.25	18.46	1.16	VI.	3	30.753	29 13.07	9.30	2.91	39 34.63	32 25.37
98	8							5.	40 12.62	18.46	1.16	VII.	3	29.845	32 9.98	9.34	3.02	39 53.20	33 22.34
99	8							38.	40 45.87	18.46	1.16	VII.	3	34.120	25 41.96	9.24	2.51	40 26.25	28 53.71
100	7		19.	37.					42 54.21	18.46	1.16	III.	2	15.895	44 45.74	8.85	4.73	42 34.59	47 59.32
101	4				11.7	28.5	46.		43 11.15	18.46	1.16	IV.	3	34.435	25 21.04	8.80	2.47	42 51.53	28 33.21
102	8					40.5		15.3	44 23.00	18.46	1.16	V.	2	20.003	40 28.23	8.59	4.22	44 3.38	43 41.04
103	9	3.5			56.				47 55.38	18.46	1.15	IV.	3	25.550	34 39.33	7.96	3.53	47 35.77	37 50.82
104	8	4.	27.	39.	55.5				50 55.76	18.45	1.15	IV.	3	27.765	32 20.16	7.43	2.27	50 36.16	35 29.86
105	6	18.	35.3	52.8	10.5	27.5			53 10.04	18.45	1.15	IV.	3	35.105	24 39.80	7.02	2.39	52 50.44	27 49.21
106	8		20.		55,				55 54.67	18.45	1.14	IV.	4	42.950	16 25.02	6.54	1.44	55 35.08	19 33.00
107	7	57.	13.	30.5			22.5		20 58 48.20	−18.45	−1.14	IV.	1	10.790	−50 5.15	−6.02	−5.37	20 58 28.61	−27 53 16.54

CORRECTIONS.

Date.	Corr. of Clock.	Hourly rate.	m	n	c	Zenith Point.	Mic. Co.
1847.	h.	s.	s.	s.	s.	° ' "	r.

REMARKS.

(119) 83. Minutes assumed as 9 instead of 10.

(119) 84. Minutes assumed as 11 instead of 10.

(119) 95. The observed time of transit over T. IV is assumed to have been at 0s.7, not 7s.
[Observing book has 1s.]

INSTRUMENT READINGS.

Date.	CIRCLE.							Barom.	THERMOM.				
	A.	B.	C.	D.	E.	F.	Mean.		At.	Ex.	U.	L.	I.
1847.	h. m.	° ' "					"	In.	°		°	°	°

ZONE 120. JUNE 17. P. $D_0 = -30° 10' 50''$.

No.	Mag.	I.	II.	III.	IV.	V.	VI.	VII.	T. (h. m. s.)	a_1 (s.)	a_2 (s.)	MICR.		r.	i (' ")	d_1 ('')	d_4 ('')	Mean Right Ascension, 1850.0 (h. m. s.)	Mean Declination, 1850.0 (° ' '')
1	8	29.7	47.5	5.5	23.3	41.2			15 3 23.18	−20.75	−0.75	IV.	4	52.097	−6 52.15	−59.99	−0.84	15 3 1.68	−30 18 42.98
2	9							37.	3 43.60	20.75	0.76	VII.	4	55.225	3 34.63	59.97	0.39	3 22.09	15 24.99
3	6			31.	50.	16.3		42.5	5 48.64	20.75	0.69	IV.	2	15.308	45 23.01	59.81	6.18	5 27.20	57 19.00
4	8.9	56.	13.2	31.3					8 49.43	20.74	0.70	III.	2	18.330	42 13.17	59.57	5.72	8 27.99	54 8.46
5	6.7		16.3	34.3	52.5	10.			9 52.07	20.74	0.71	IV.	3	32.413	27 28.79	59.50	3.64	9 30.62	39 21.93
6	8.9				24.				11 23.77	20.73	0.76	IV.	3	53.425	5 28.37	59.38	0.65	11 2.28	17 18.40
7	8						48.		13 11.98	20.73	0.69	VI.	2	13.215	47 34.25	59.23	6.48	12 50.56	59 29.96
8	7	41.2	58.7	16.7	35.	53.			17 34.67	20.72	0.71	IV.	3	24.908	35 19.43	58.87	4.74	17 13.24	47 13.04
9	7	58.7	16.2	34.7					19 52.49	20.71	0.69	III.	2	15.593	45 4.82	58.68	6.13	19 31.09	56 59.63
10	9					26.			19 50.12	20.71	0.71	VI.	3	25.803	34 17.94	58.69	4.61	19 28.70	46 11.24
11	8		50.5	8.7	44.3				23 26.43	20.71	0.72	V.	3	34.070	25 44.97	58.37	3.39	23 5.00	37 36.73
12	8		44.3	1.5			55.5		25 1.65	20.70	0.73	IV.	4	40.943	18 30.90	58.23	2.40	24 40.22	30 21.53
13	8	37.	54.3	12.3					28 30.54	20.70	0.63	III.	2	11.293	49 34.83	57.92	6.77	28 9.16	51 29.52
14	7			57.	14.	32.			28 56.12	20.70	0.71	IV.	3	26.874	33 16.07	57.88	4.46	28 34.71	45 8.41
15	6			45.					31 2.85	20.69	0.70	III.	2	18.883	41 38.21	57.69	5.64	30 41.46	53 31.54
16	7			20.3	37.5				31 19.55	20.69	0.70	IV.	3	28.708	31 21.06	57.67	4.19	30 58.16	43 12.92
17	8.9			30.3	47.				32 20.31	20.69	0.72	IV.	3	29.635	30 22.97	57.56	4.06	32 7.90	42 14.59
18	9		27.		4.				35 3.18	20.68	0.73	IV.	3	37.023	22 39.42	57.31	2.97	34 41.77	30 34 29.70
19	6						59.		35 4.84	20.68	0.68	VII.	1	5.850	55 15.45	57.31	7.59	34 43.48	31 7 10.35
20	8			28.3		4.			37 46.09	20.67	0.75	V.	4	45.960	13 16.11	57.04	1.68	37 24.67	30 25 4.83
21	8	37.5	55.3	13.3					40 31.13	20.67	0.74	III.	3	35.088	24 40.49	56.79	3.26	40 9.72	36 30.54
22	7.8						11.		42 35.45	20.66	0.77	VI.	4	55.920	2 51.30	56.58	0.25	42 14.02	14 38.13
23	7			14.5	32.				44 14.19	20.66	0.76	IV.	4	51.312	7 40.86	56.42	0.95	43 52.77	19 28.23
24	7	36.	53.6	11.7	30.	47.3			46 29.47	20.66	0.73	IV.	3	33.364	26 29.14	56.18	3.50	46 8.08	38 18.82
25	9			0.					48 59.51	20.65	0.74	IV.	4	40.765	18 42.07	55.94	2.44	47 38.12	30 30.45
26	8				54.				48 18.38	20.65	0.76	VI.	4	50.135	8 54.18	56.00	1.11	47 56.97	20 41.29
27	8			40.7	58.3				49 40.47	20.65	0.77	VI.	4	53.430	5 27.68	55.86	0.65	49 19.05	17 14.19
28	7				8.5	20.3			50 50.48	20.65	0.72	V.	3	27.863	32 14.27	55.74	4.31	50 29.11	44 4.32
29	7.8			51.3		26.5			53 50.78	20.64	0.74	IV.	4	40.220	19 16.44	55.42	2.52	53 29.40	30 31 4.38
30	6.7	26.	43.3	1.3					56 19.54	20.63	0.69	IV.	1	10.360	50 32.40	55.15	6.91	55 58.22	31 2 24.46
31	9						2.		56 7.90	20.63	0.69	VII.	1	10.343	50 33.65	55.17	6.91	55 46.58	31 2 25.73
32	9			31.					15 58 48.71	20.63	0.76	III.	4	52.384	5 30.83	54.88	0.80	15 58 27.32	30 17 16.51
33	7	30.	47.5	5.7	24.3	11.3			16 0 23.51	20.62	0.72	IV.	3	32.830	27 2.39	54.71	3.58	16 0 2.17	38 50.68
34	8			4.	21.5				2 21.46	20.62	0.76	IV.	4	50.337	8 42.00	54.48	1.05	2 0.08	20 27.53
35	7			59.5					6 59.32	20.62	0.77	IV.	4	56.135	2 38.33	53.94	0.23	6 37.93	14 22.50
36	9					15.5			7 39.78	20.61	0.74	VI.	3	41.090	18 24.69	53.86	2.37	7 18.43	30 10.92
37	7.8	31.	48.3	6.3					10 24.25	20.60	0.74	III.	3	39.393	20 10.57	53.54	2.62	10 2.91	31 56.73
38	6.7	32.	49.3	7.3	44.3	1.3			10 25.54	20.60	0.74	V.	3	39.140	20 26.93	53.54	2.66	10 4.20	32 13.13
39	8	19.5	37.						13 13.21	20.60	0.70	II.	2	18.940	41 34.25	53.19	5.64	12 51.91	53 23.08
40	7.8		20.	37.3					13 19.21	20.60	0.71	IV.	3	22.840	37 29.20	53.17	5.07	12 57.90	49 17.44
41	9						39.		13 45.48	20.59	0.75	VII.	4	46.695	12 29.39	53.13	1.57	13 24.14	30 24 14.09
42	7		37.3	56.5					15 55.27	20.59	0.69	IV.	1	8.635	52 20.55	52.86	7.21	15 33.99	31 4 10.62
43	8		34.	52.3	9.3				16 51.49	20.59	0.70	IV.	2	19.370	41 8.08	52.75	5.58	16 30.20	30 52 56.41
44	9	59.	33.						18 51.71	20.58	0.72	III.	3	30.703	29 15.52	52.50	3.90	18 30.41	41 1.92
45	8		13.5				46.7		19 12.75	20.58	0.71	IV.	3	25.055	35 10.33	52.45	4.74	18 51.46	46 57.52
46	8.9		49.						20 48.30	20.58	0.72	IV.	3	31.003	28 57.07	52.25	3.85	20 27.00	40 43.17
47	9	20.							22 56.16	20.57	0.70	II.	2	16.830	43 46.66	51.99	5.97	22 34.89	55 34.64
48	9			24.					23 41.77	20.57	0.73	III.	3	38.410	21 12.21	51.87	2.76	23 20.47	32 56.84
49	8			31.					16 24 29.97	−20.57	−0.69	IV.	2	14.670	−46 2.88	−51.77	−6.29	16 24 8.71	−30 57 50.94

CORRECTIONS.

Date.	Corr. of Clock.	Hourly rate.	m	n	c	Zenith Point.	Mic. Co.
	h. s.	s.	s.	s.	s.	° ' ''	r.
1847.							

REMARKS.

(120) 3. Time of transit over T. V assumed to have been at 6s.3 instead of 16s.3.

(120) 25. Minutes assumed as 47 instead of 48.

(120) 32. Micrometer reading assumed as 53r.384 instead of 52r.384.

INSTRUMENT READINGS.

	Date.	CIRCLE.							Barom.	THERMOM.				
		A.	B.	C.	D.	E.	F.	Mean.		At.	Ex.	U.	L.	I.
	1847. (h. m.)	°						''	in.	°	°	°	°	°
Zone 120	June 17, 15 0	69 32	30.3	32.5	29.4	39.6	7.7	31.9 28.57*	30.208	71.5	64.5	71.0	70.0	70.0
	15 35								30.210	70.2	63.0			
	16 0								30.210	69.0	61.5			
	16 10								30.214	69.0	61.4			
	16 57								30.220	67.8	60.0			
	17 33								30.230	67.0	59.3			
	18 0								30.228	67.0	58.0			
	19 1								30.230	66.5	58.2			
	19 47								30.226	65.0	57.7			

* Corr. for runs +0''.07.

ZONE 120. JUNE 17. P. $D_o = -30°\ 10'\ 50''$—Continued.

No.	Mag.	I.	II.	III.	IV.	V.	VI.	VII.	T. (h. m. s.)	a_1 (s.)	a_2 (s.)	Mic.		r.	i (' '')	d_1 ('')	d_2 ('')	Mean Right Ascension, 1850.0 (h. m. s.)	Mean Declination, 1850.0 (° ' '')
50	8					18.			16 24 59.93	−20.57	−0.69	V.	2	14.786	−45 55.59	−51.71	−6.27	16 24 38.67	−30 57 43.57
51	8.9		34.	52.	11.				27 10.03	20.57	0.71	IV.	3	25.647	34 33.18	51.42	4.65	26 48.75	30 46 19.25
52	8					48.			29 29.90	20.56	0.69	V.	2	10.773	50 7.48	51.12	6.88	29 8.65	31 1 55.48
53	7.8		56.7	14.7	33.				31 32.51	20.56	0.75	IV.	4	39.375	20 9.49	50.86	2.62	31 11.20	30 31 52.97
54	7			38.					32 55.70	20.55	0.78	III.	4	56.410	2 21.15	50.68	0.18	32 34.37	30 14 2.01
55	7.8			37.7					33 55.59	20.55	0.69	III.	1	9.460	51 28.51	50.55	7.07	33 34.35	31 3 16.13
56	8				22.3		57.		34 21.15	20.55	0.70	IV.	2	16.217	44 25.91	50.49	6.06	33 59.90	30 56 12.46
57	7.8						34.3		34 58.45	20.55	0.73	VI.	3	28.623	31 26.77	50.40	4.20	34 37.17	43 11.37
58	7				8.7		43.5		36 7.98	20.54	0.75	IV.	4	39.820	19 41.34	50.25	2.56	35 46.69	31 24.15
59	8			28.					37 45.80	20.54	0.73	III.	3	28.725	31 19.62	50.03	4.18	37 24.53	43 3.83
60	7	17.3	35.	53.3	12.3			5.2	39 11.10	20.54	0.70	IV.	2	16.627	44 0.12	49.83	6.00	38 49.95	55 45.95
61	8.9							53.	39 59.38	20.54	0.75	VII.	4	40.565	18 53.98	49.73	2.45	39 38.09	30 36.16
62	7			42.		17.3			41 59.59	20.54	0.76	IV.	4	46.107	12 48.45	49.46	1.61	41 38.29	24 29.52
63	8			56.					43 13.74	20.53	0.76	III.	4	44.830	14 27.05	49.28	1.84	42 52.45	26 8.17
64	8	20.	38.7						45 14.00	20.53	0.76	II.	4	43.047	16 18.75	49.02	2.08	44 52.71	27 59.85
65	7				24.	41.5			45 23.69	20.53	0.77	IV.	4	50.580	8 26.65	49.00	1.02	45 2.39	20 6.67
66	7						8.3		45 32.45	20.53	0.73	VI.	3	28.215	31 52.43	48.98	4.26	45 11.19	30 43 35.67
67	8							12.	46 17.87	20.52	0.69	VII.	1	7.890	53 7.40	48.57	7.32	45 56.66	31 4 53.59
68	7							56.	47 1.89	20.52	0.69	VII.	1	9.090	51 52.18	48.78	7.14	46 40.68	31 3 38.10
69	7.8		44.3	3.7	22.				49 21.04	20.52	0.74	IV.	3	35.050	24 43.18	48.46	3.27	48 59.78	30 36 24.91
70	9		57.						51 32.73	20.51	0.78	II.	4	53.760	5 6.86	48.16	0.58	51 11.44	16 45.60
71	8				20.				52 19.40	20.51	0.75	IV.	3	40.190	19 20.89	48.05	2.50	51 58.23	31 1.44
72	7					53.	10.5	28.7	52 34.96	20.51	0.75	V.	3	38.190	21 26.59	48.01	2.79	52 13.70	33 7.39
73	7.8							28.	53 34.00	20.50	0.71	VII.	2	21.920	38 27.49	47.87	5.20	53 12.88	50 10.56
74	8.9			42.					57 59.86	20.50	0.70	III.	2	17.010	43 35.82	47.25	5.94	57 38.66	55 19.01
75	7				28.7	45.7			16 58 27.72	20.50	0.71	IV.	2	19.983	40 29.42	47.18	5.49	16 58 6.51	52 12.09
76	7		14.5		51.				17 0 50.42	20.49	0.74	IV.	3	33.168	26 41.39	46.85	3.53	17 0 29.19	38 21.76
77	9						42.		1 6.12	20.49	0.72	VI.	3	25.515	34 41.84	46.82	4.68	0 44.91	46 23.34
78	8			36.					2 53.78	20.49	0.74	III.	3	36.463	23 14.29	46.55	3.04	2 32.55	34 53.88
79	9						42.		3 6.41	20.48	0.78	VI.	4	52.545	6 23.11	46.53	0.72	2 45.15	18 0.36
80	8	7.2	25.	43.	1.		36.5		6 0.72	20.48	0.77	IV.	4	49.255	9 49.79	46.09	1.20	5 39.47	21 27.06
81	8		14.3						7 50.24	20.48	0.74	II.	3	35.773	23 56.94	45.83	3.14	7 29.02	35 35.91
82	9		14.						8 31.76	20.48	0.75	III.	2	38.600	21 0.19	45.73	2.72	8 10.53	32 38.64
83	8						4.		8 28.23	20.48	0.74	VI.	3	35.543	24 12.69	45.73	3.18	8 7.01	30 35 51.60
84	8					0.5			9 42.40	20.48	0.69	V.	1	11.345	49 30.76	45.55	6.62	9 21.23	31 1 13.13
85	8							36.	9 41.99	20.48	0.70	VII.	2	15.577	45 5.70	45.55	6.18	9 20.81	30 56 47.43
86	7	0.5	18.	35.7	54.				12 53.69	20.47	0.77	IV.	4	49.683	9 10.22	45.08	1.08	12 32.45	20 46.38
87	8		3.5						14 21.36	20.47	0.70	III.	2	17.463	43 7.51	44.86	5.89	14 0.19	54 48.26
88	8			12.5					15 12.16	20.46	0.77	IV.	4	47.820	11 19.59	44.73	1.40	14 50.93	22 55.72
89	8				42.5				16 24.57	20.46	0.74	V.	3	36.520	23 11.34	44.55	3.04	16 3.37	30 31 48.93
90	7	59.	16.5	35.					18 52.86	20.46	0.69	III.	1	8.285	52 12.28	44.18	7.29	18 31.71	31 4 23.75
91	7			28.5			3.5		19 27.63	20.46	0.72	IV.	3	23.950	36 19.54	44.09	4.90	19 6.45	30 47 58.53
92	8		5.	22.7					22 40.57	20.45	0.78	III.	4	53.585	5 18.21	43.61	0.57	22 19.34	16 52.39
93	8				1.3				23 1.00	20.45	0.77	IV.	4	50.155	8 53.29	43.56	1.05	22 39.78	20 27.90
94	7				44.5				23 44.30	20.45	0.78	IV.	4	54.760	4 4.42	43.46	0.41	23 23.07	15 39.29
95	7			28.	46.		3.7		24 45.78	20.45	0.78	IV.	4	52.560	6 22.55	43.30	0.71	24 24.55	17 56.56
96	8.9			38.5					26 56.24	20.44	0.76	III.	4	44.605	14 41.28	42.98	1.85	26 35.04	26 16.11
97	7.8		56.5	14.5	33.5	50.3			28 32.47	20.44	0.72	IV.	3	23.343	36 57.89	42.73	5.00	28 11.31	48 35.62
98	8				21.5				17 33 20.85	−20.43	−0.74	IV.	3	33.305	−26 32.84	−42.01	−3.51	17 32 59.68	−30 38 8.36

CORRECTIONS.

Date.	Corr. of Clock.	Hourly rate.	m	n	c	Zenith Point.	Mic. Co.
1847.	h.	s.	s.	s.	s.	° ' ''	r.

REMARKS.

INSTRUMENT READINGS.

Date.	A.	B.	C.	D.	E.	F.	Mean.	Barom.	At.	Ex.	U.	L.	I.
Zone 120	1847. June 17, 21 1 h. m.	° ' ''						''	In. 30.228	° 64.0	° 56.0	°	°	°

ZONE 120.   JUNE 17.   P. $D_0 = -30°\ 10'\ 50''$—Continued.

SECONDS OF TRANSIT

No.	Mag.	I.	II.	III.	IV.	V.	VI.	VII.
99	7.8		1.		38.			
100	8						28.	
101	7				17.			
102	7.8					7.5		
103	7				55.			
104	6.9							48.5
105	8				50.			
106	8							46.
107	8							51.
108	5.6					6.5		42.5
109	8	32.5						
110	8			21.				
111	7.6					4.7		
112	7				32.			
113	4.5			14.	32.	49.5		
114	8							29.
115	8.9							27.
116	7.8						18.5	
117	6.7		11.	29.	47.5	4.5	22.5	
118	8.9	36.3		12.				
119	8.7							7.
120	8							57.7
121	6.7	3.		39.3				
122	7.8				7.			
123	6.7					2.5	20.3	
124	7				42.	59.5		
125	7	6.		42.7				
126	7.8						34.	10.
127	7	3.7	21.3	39.7				
128	8				38.			
129	8	14.	31.5	50.				
130	7	42.	59.	17.3	36.	53.3		
131	7	50.2	8.	26.	44.3	2.		
132	9						54.	
133	8						14.	
134	8	1.5	19.3	37.5	55.7	13.	31.	
135	8				6.3			
136	8.9			24.		0.3		
137	7			49.	7.	26.		
138	7	56.3		32.	51.	8.		
139	9							17.
140	9			6.				
141	9		25.					
142	7.8	0.	17.3	35.7	54.7			
143	6.7		40.	57.5	15.5	33.3		

No.	Mag.	T. (h. m. s.)	σ1 (s.)	σ2 (s.)	Micrometer		r.	i (' ")	d1 (")	d2 (")	Mean Declination, 1850.0 (h. m. s.)	Mean Right Ascension, 1850.0 (° ' ")
99	7.8	17 38 37.12	—20.42	—0.71	IV.	2	21.830	—38 33.45	—41.21	—5.23	17 38 15.99	—30 50 9.89
100	8	38 10.20	20.42	0.78	VI.	4	55.910	2 51.93	41.17	0.22	38 49.05	14 23.32
101	7	39 59.08	20.42	0.75	V.	3	38.840	20 45.63	41.00	2.69	39 37.91	32 19.32
102	7.8	40 49.45	20.42	0.71	V.	2	17.760	42 48.94	40.86	5.85	40 28.32	54 25.67
103	7	41 54.51	20.41	0.75	IV.	4	40.610	18 51.91	40.71	2.43	41 33.35	30 25.05
104	6.9	41 54.87	20.41	0.75	VII.	4	40.403	19 4.20	40.71	2.46	41 33.71	30 37.37
105	8	44 49.08	20.41	0.71	IV.	3	20.223	38 8.1	40.27	5.47	44 27.96	49 43.9
106	8	44 52.11	20.41	0.71	VII.	3	22.610	37 44.02	40.27	5.11	44 30.99	49 19.40
107	8	45 57.33	20.41	0.74	VII.	4	37.200	22 25.05	40.10	2.93	45 36.18	33 55.06
108	5.6	49 48.90	20.40	0.78	V.	4	56.340	2 25.48	39.50	0.07	49 27.72	13 55.05
109	8	53 26.31	20.39	0.71	I.	2	14.560	46 8.83	38.93	6.32	53 5.21	57 44.08
110	8	53 38.87	20.39	0.71	III.	2	14.663	46 3.13	38.89	6.31	53 17.77	57 38.33
111	7.6	53 46.70	20.39	0.73	V.	3	25.193	35 1.87	38.87	4.72	53 25.58	46 35.46
112	7	55 31.44	20.39	0.75	IV.	3	37.450	22 12.81	38.59	2.90	55 10.30	33 44.30
113	4.5	56 31.66	20.39	0.77	IV.	4	45.540	13 42.76	38.43	1.72	56 10.50	25 12.91
114	8	56 35.24	20.39	0.74	VII.	3	31.687	28 14.41	38.42	3.75	56 14.11	30 46.58
115	8.9	57 33.17	20.38	0.73	VII.	3	27.367	32 45.64	38.27	4.39	57 12.06	30 44 18.30
116	7.8	17 58 42.47	20.38	0.70	VI.	2	11.575	49 17.20	38.08	0.78	17 58 21.30	31 0 52.06
117	6.7	18 0 46.75	20.38	0.73	IV.	3	26.877	33 15.89	37.75	4.48	18 0 25.64	30 44 48.12
118	8.9	3 30.00	20.37	0.71	III.	2	13.700	47 3.57	37.30	6.50	3 8.92	58 37.37
119	8.7	7 13.43	20.37	0.77	VII.	4	43.960	15 20.92	36.69	1.91	6 52.29	26 49.52
120	8	9 3.85	20.36	0.73	VII.	3	25.963	34 13.54	36.38	4.61	8 42.76	30 45 44.53
121	6.7	11 57.02	20.36	0.70	III.	2	12.317	48 30.56	35.89	6.71	11 35.96	31 0 3.16
122	7.8	15 6.20	20.36	0.73	IV.	3	26.086	34 5.64	35.34	4.60	14 45.11	30 45 35.58
123	6.7	15 44.43	20.35	0.72	V.	3	22.225	38 8.23	35.23	5.18	15 23.36	49 38.64
124	7	17 23.96	20.35	0.76	V.	4	42.587	16 47.79	34.95	2 12	17 2.85	30 28 14.86
125	7	21 0.25	20.35	0.70	III.	1	9.250	51 41.69	34.31	7.18	20 30.20	31 3 13.18
126	7.8	21 15.98	20.35	0.71	V.	2	16.920	43 41.65	34.27	6.00	20 54.92	30 55 11.92
127	7	24 57.55	20.34	0.71	III.	2	12.910	47 53.08	33.62	6.62	24 36.50	59 23.32
128	8	25 37.10	20.34	0.72	IV.	2	21.460	38 56.92	33.51	5.29	25 16.04	50 25.72
129	8	28 7.75	20.34	0.72	III.	2	18.712	41 49.00	33.07	5.73	27 46.69	53 17.80
130	7	29 35.27	20.33	0.75	IV.	3	32.790	27 4.90	32.81	3.56	29 14.19	38 31.27
131	7	31 43.85	20.33	0.74	IV.	3	31.677	28 14.79	32.45	3.75	31 22.78	39 40.99
132	9	33 36.09	20.33	0.76	V.	4	39.830	19 40.59	32.12	2.54	33 15.00	31 5.25
133	8	35 13.46	20.32	0.76	IV.	4	38.420	21 9.33	31.84	2.74	34 52.38	32 33.91
134	8	38 55.17	20.32	0.76	IV.	4	40.063	19 26.16	31.20	2.51	38 34.09	30 49.87
135	8	40 5.64	20.32	0.75	IV.	3	33.330	26 31.28	31.00	3.50	39 44.57	37 55.78
136	8.9	41 42.05	20.32	0.71	V.	2	14.365	46 22.20	30.71	6.40	41 21.02	37 49.31
137	7	43 25.02	20.31	0.72	IV.	2	17.615	42 58.11	30.42	5.89	43 3.99	30 54 24.42
138	7	48 49.96	20.30	0.70	IV.	1	11.270	49 35.27	29.48	6.86	48 28.96	31 1 1.61
139	9	49 22.94	20.30	0.71	VII.	2	12.943	47 52.77	29.37	6.62	49 1.93	30 59 18.76
140	9	53 45.02	20.30	0.76	II.	3	37.680	21 57.26	28.62	2.85	53 20.80	33 18.73
141	9	58 0.80	20.29	0.77	II.	4	47.395	11 46.24	27.87	1.44	57 39.74	23 5.55
142	7.8	18 59 53.63	20.29	0.72	IV.	2	20.383	40 4.51	27.54	5.45	18 59 32.62	51 27.50
143	6.7	19 1 15.43	—20.29	—0.79	IV.	4	55.640	— 3 9.37	—27.30	—0.20	19 0 54.35	—30 14 26.87

CORRECTIONS.

Date.	Corr. of Clock.	Hourly rate.	m	n	ε	Zenith Point.	Mic. Co.
1847.	h. s.	s.	s.	s.	s.	° ' "	r.

REMARKS.

June 17, 19h 1m to 19h 45m, stopped to rest.

(120) 100. Transit over T. V assumed as recorded over T. VI.

(120) 105. Micrometer reading assumed as 22r.223 instead of 20r.223.

INSTRUMENT READINGS.

Date.	CIRCLE.							Barom.	THERMOM.				
	A.	B.	C.	D.	E.	F.	Mean.		At.	Ex.	U.	L.	I.
1847. h. m.	° ' "						"	in.	°	°	°		

ZONE 121. JUNE 17. P. D_a = −30° 10′ 50″.

No.	Mag.	Seconds of Transit (I. II. III. IV. V. VI. VII.)	T. (h. m. s.)	a_1 (s.)	a_2 (s.)	Micrometer	r.	i (° ′ ″)	d_1 (″)	d_2 (″)	Mean Right Ascension, 1850.0 (h. m. s.)	Mean Declination, 1850.0 (° ′ ″)
1	7	.. 7.3 25.7 44.5 1.3	19 47 43.44	−20.24	−0.96	IV. 2	14.275	−46 27.79	−19.38	−0.44	19 47 22.24	−30 57 43.61
2	6,7	57. 14.3 33. 51.7 9.	49 50.76	20.24	0.94	IV. 2	15.810	44 51.25	19.02	6.18	49 29.58	56 6.45
3	7	29. 46. 4.5 .. 40.5 58.3 ..	55 22.37	20.24	0.66	IV. 3	35.970	23 45.47	18.10	3.10	55 1.47	30 34 56.67
4	8,9	30.3 47.7 6.3 25.3	19 59 24.12	20.23	.97	IV. 1	11.960	48 51.77	17.43	6.78	19 59 2.92	31 0 5.98
5	6,7	58.3 .. 34.3 52.5 9.7 27.5 ..	20 6 51.89	20.23	0.52	IV. 4	43.010	16 21.32	16.23	2.03	20 0 31.14	30 27 29.58
6	8,9	27.5 45. 3.3 21.	10 20.88	20.23	0.68	IV. 3	30.810	29 9.12	15.66	3.88	0 59.97	40 18.66
7	8,9	.. 21. 39. 57.	12 56.92	20.23	0.82	IV. 2	20.585	39 51.74	15.25	5.45	12 35.87	51 2.41
8	8,9	19.3 37. 55.3 13.5	15 12.09	20.22	0.89	IV. 1	13.910	46 49.31	14.89	6.40	14 51.86	58 0.69
9	8	.. .. 25.3 .. 1.	16 25.08	20.22	0.51	V. 4	42.540	16 50.80	14.70	2.10	16 4.35	27 57.60
10	8	50. 7.5 26. 44.3	24 43.65	20.22	0.66	IV. 3	29.807	30 12.05	13.40	4.03	24 22.75	41 19.18
11	7	.. 16.3 35. 54. III.	25 52.82	20.22	0.88	IV. 2	13.083	47 42.54	13.22	6.64	25 31.72	30 58 52.40
12	7,8	.. 39. .. 16.3	29 15.21	20.22	0.94	IV. 1	7.553	53 28.54	12.69	7.50	28 54.05	31 4 38.73
13	7,8	53. 10.3 29. 47.3 4.3	34 46.53	20.22	0.69	IV. 3	25.545	34 39.64	11.85	4.69	34 25.62	30 45 46.15
14	7	.. 56.7 15.3 34.3 51.3 .. 26.7	36 33.03	20.22	0.87	IV. 1	11.003	49 51.85	11.59	6.95	36 11.94	31 1 0.39
15	7	34.5 52. 10.3 29.3 46.3 4.3 ..	40 28.26	20.22	0.65	IV. 3	26.800	33 20.72	10.99	4.50	40 7.39	30 44 26.21
16	7	0.3 18. 35.7 54.	42 53.64	20.22	0.34	IV. 4	49.870	9 11.04	10.63	1.00	42 33.08	20 12.67
17	8	33.3 51. 9.3 28.	46 27.08	20.21	0.61	IV. 3	28.830	31 13.35	10.10	4.20	46 6.26	30 42 17.65
18	7	.. .. 57. 14.5 ..	50 38.65	20.21	0.87	V. 1	6.900	54 9.52	9.49	7.60	50 17.77	31 5 16.61
19	7	.. .. .. 20. 37.7	52 19.79	20.21	0.29	V. 4	51.490	7 29.52	9.25	1.78	51 59.20	30 18 30.55
20	6	.. 42. 0.3 18.7 .. .. 11.7	20 57 17.99	20.21	0.59	IV. 3	28.113	31 58.46	8.53	4.31	20 56 57.19	43 1.30
21	7	32.3 50. 8. 26.3 43.5 1.3 19.2	21 1 25.74	−20.21	−0.29	IV. 4	50.457	− 8 34.41	− 7.94	−0.92	21 1 5.24	−30 19 33.27

ZONE 122. JUNE 24. P. D_a = −25° 11′ 0″.

No.	Mag.	Seconds of Transit (I. II. III. IV. V. VI. VII.)	T. (h. m. s.)	a_1 (s.)	a_2 (s.)	Micrometer	r.	i (° ′ ″)	d_1 (″)	d_2 (″)	Mean Right Ascension, 1850.0 (h. m. s.)	Mean Declination, 1850.0 (° ′ ″)
1	6	30. 47.3 4.7 22.5 39.	15 59 21.64	−19.30	−2.55	IV. 2	16.690	−43 56.10	−10.92	−3.76	15 58 59.79	−25 55 10.78
2	8,9	.. .. 1.5	16 1 18.56	19.30	2.49	IV. 1	9.813	51 6.48	10.70	4.46	16 0 56.77	26 2 21.64
3	9	.. .. 10.	1 35.65	19.30	2.52	IV. 2	13.660	41 52.63	10.66	3.56	1 13.83	25 53 6.85
4	8	.. .. .. 9. 26.	3 8.73	19.30	2.78	IV. 4	41.430	18 0.54	10.48	1.30	2 46.65	29 12.32
5	9	.. .. 51. 9.	5 8.06	19.30	2.56	IV. 2	17.790	42 47.00	10.24	3.65	4 46.20	54 0.89
6	7,8	15. 31.7 49. 6.3	8 5.95	19.29	2.78	IV. 4	41.614	17 48.94	9.89	1.28	7 43.88	29 0.11
7	7	.. .. 21.5 38.7 55.5	10 38.41	19.29	2.83	IV. 4	47.017	12 10.01	9.58	−0.75	10 10.29	23 20.34
8	4	.. 52.5 9.5 27. 44.	12 26.70	19.29	2.97	IV. 4	56.260	2 30.55	9.36	+0.16	12 4.50	13 39.75
9	9	.. 25. 42.5	14 59.52	19.29	2.54	III. 2	16.970	43 38.33	9.04	−3.73	14 37.69	54 51.10
10	8	28.3 45. 2.5 20.3 .. 53.3 ..	18 19.39	19.28	2.53	VI. 2	17.070	43 32.31	8.62	3.73	17 57.58	25 54 44.66
11	1	.. 0.5 18. 36.5 52.5	20 35.19	19.28	2.47	IV. 1	6.630	54 26.43	8.34	4.79	20 13.44	26 5 39.56
12	7,8	.. 32. 49.3 7. 23.	23 6.21	19.28	2.69	IV. 3	30.235	29 45.38	8.00	2.41	22 44.24	25 40 55.79
13	9	.. .. 53.	27 18.94	19.27	2.83	VI. 4	44.190	15 7.12	7.45	1.03	26 56.84	26 15.60
14	7	25. 41.7 59. 16.7 32.3	31 15.86	19.27	2.66	IV. 3	25.800	34 23.46	6.91	2.85	30 53.95	25 45 33.22
15	6	.. .. 13.3	31 21.72	19.27	2.52	VII. 2	10.805	50 5.22	6.90	4.36	30 59.03	26 1 16.48
16	9	.. .. .. 2.	35 1.54	19.26	2.80	IV. 4	41.213	18 14.15	6.39	1.32	34 39.48	25 29 21.86
17	8	.. .. 21.	35 29.41	19.26	2.51	VII. 1	9.820	51 6.35	6.32	−4.46	35 7.64	26 2 17.13
18	7	.. 28.7 .. 2.7 19.5	38 2.60	19.26	2.94	IV. 4	54.930	3 53.75	5.96	+0.02	37 40.40	25 14 59.69
19	8,9	.. .. .. 12.	39 54.82	19.26	2.66	V. 3	23.700	36 35.55	5.69	−3.06	39 32.90	47 44.30
20	8	.. .. 38.	40 4.04	19.26	2.96	VI. 4	55.740	3 2.65	5.67	+0.10	39 41.82	14 8.22
21	8	.. .. .. 8.	41 50.81	19.26	2.66	V. 3	22.210	38 9.17	5.41	−3.21	41 28.89	49 17.79
22	8,9	.. .. 49.5	41 56.14	19.26	2.71	VII. 3	28.390	31 41.58	5.39	2.59	41 36.17	42 49.56
23	8	.. 56. .. 52.	43 0.98	19.25	2.94	VII. 4	53.580	5 17.90	5.24	0.10	42 38.79	16 23.24
24	7	.. 56. 13. 31.	16 45 30.23	−19.25	−2.77	IV. 3	36.303	−23 24.77	− 4.87	−1.80	16 45 8.21	−25 34 31.44

CORRECTIONS.

Date.	Corr. of Clock.	Hourly rate.	m	n	c	Zenith Point.	Mic. Co.
1847.	h.	s.	s.	s.	s.	° ′ ″	r.

REMARKS.

(121) 7. Transit over middle thread assumed to have been at 57s.7 instead of 5s.7.

(122) 3. Micrometer reading assumed as 18r.660 instead of 13r.660.

INSTRUMENT READINGS.

Date.	Circle A.	B.	C.	D.	E.	F.	Mean.	Barom.	Thermom. At.	Ex.	U.	L.	I.	
Zone 122. 1847. June 24, 16 0	64 32 31.6	31.2	29.0	40.2	6.3	30.9	28.20″	In. 30.210	75.0	70.0	75.0	74.0	74.0	*Corr. for runs +0″.07
16 35	.	.	.	.	.	.	.	30.208	74.0	68.0				
17 4	.	.	.	.	.	.	.	30.208	73.2	67.8				

ZONE 122. JUNE 24. P. $D_o = -25°\ 11'\ 0''$—Continued.

No.	Mag.	I.	II.	III.	IV.	V.	VI.	VII.	T. (h. m. s.)	a_1 (s.)	a_4 (s.)	MICROMETER.		r.	i (' ")	d_1 (")	d_4 (")	Mean Right Ascension, 1850.0 (h. m. s.)	Mean Declination, 1850.0 (° ' ")
25	8					58.3		33.	16 45 41.48	−19.25	−2.75	V.	3	37.163	−22 31.01	−4.84	−1.71	16 45 19.45	−25 33 37.56
26	8						51.5		47 17.27	19.25	2.68	VI.	3	25.840	34 21.32	4.60	2.85	46 55.34	45 28.77
27	7		49.7	7.	25.	47.3			49 24.11	19.25	2.64	IV.	2	22.287	38 5.03	4.28	3.21	49 2.22	49 12.52
28	9				1.3				53 0.64	19.24	2.72	IV.	3	31.010	28 56.63	3.74	2.33	52 38.68	40 2.70
29	6.7	18.	35.	52.	9.				55 8.95	19.24	2.84	IV.	4	41.793	17 37.59	3.41	1.26	54 46.87	28 42.26
30	7				52.5	9.3			55 52.18	19.24	2.87	IV.	4	44.820	14 27.74	3.31	0.97	55 30.07	25 32.02
31	8					46.5			56 31.49	19.24	2.95	V.	3	54.127	4 47.05	3.20	0.05	56 9.30	15 50.30
32	8							37.	56 45.73	19.24	2.77	VII.	3	34.745	25 2.69	3.17	1.96	56 23.72	30 7.82
33	7			43.		17.2			16 59 0.05	19.24	2.96	III.	4	54.720	4 6.92	2.81	0.00	16 58 37.85	15 9.73
34	6		11.		15.5				17 0 45.18	19.24	2.91	IV.	4	49.597	9 28.29	2.55	0.50	17 0 23.03	20 31.34
35	8	47.		21.3					2 38.28	19.23	2.66	III.	3	23.110	37 12.01	2.25	3.12	2 16.39	48 17.38
36	7				9.				3 8.54	19.23	2.83	IV.	4	41.173	18 16.59	2.17	1.32	2 46.48	29 20.08
37	8						1.5		3 27.43	19.23	2.85	VI.	4	42.665	16 42.65	2.12	1.17	3 5.35	27 45.94
38	7.8					45.			17 4 27.80	−19.23	−2.64	V.	3	20.980	−39 26.22	−1.95	−3.33	17 4 5.93	−25 50 31.50

ZONE 123. JULY 17. P. $D_o = -25°\ 10'\ 20''$.

No.	Mag.	I.	II.	III.	IV.	V.	VI.	VII.	T. (h. m. s.)	a_1 (s.)	a_4 (s.)	MICROMETER.		r.	i (' ")	d_1 (")	d_4 (")	Mean Right Ascension, 1850.0 (h. m. s.)	Mean Declination, 1850.0 (° ' ")
1	7.8				15.	49.			17 3 14.72	−27.07	−1.01	IV.	4	41.053	−18 24.06	−43.35	−1.41	17 2 46.64	−25 29 28.85
2	8.9		27.5		3.				11 2.06	27.08	1.02	IV.	3	24.564	40 54.90	42.14	3.55	10 33.96	25 52 0.59
3	7	42.	58.5	16.5	34.5				13 31.36	27.08	1.05	IV.	1	8.467	52 31.22	41.75	4.60	13 5.23	26 3 37.57
4	4	15.3	32.	49.5	7.5			57.	18 6.35	27.09	1.01	IV.	3	23.023	37 17.78	41.02	3.17	17 38.25	25 48 21.97
5	6					8.7	25.5	42.7	19 51.57	27.09	0.97	V.	4	47.137	11 43.73	40.74	0.82	19 23.51	22 45.29
6	8	55.		29.5					31 46.27	27.11	0.96	III.	4	38.400	21 10.58	38.82	1.67	31 18.20	32 11.07
7	8		20.		55.				37 54.34	27.12	0.98	IV.	3	29.640	30 22.65	37.82	2.54	37 26.24	41 23.01
8	7.8	20.	37.	54.3	12.				40 11.28	27.12	0.97	IV.	3	29.456	30 34.31	37.15	2.56	39 43.19	41 34.02
9	7	14.3	31.	48.5	6.3	22.5			43 5.45	27.13	0.97	IV.	3	27.523	32 35.53	36.97	2.74	42 37.35	43 35.24
10	8			29.					45 28.04	27.13	1.00	IV.	2	16.130	44 31.31	36.57	3.85	44 59.91	55 31.73
11	7	34.3	51.5	9.	26.5	43.			47 25.80	27.13	0.96	IV.	3	32.330	27 34.01	36.25	2.27	46 57.71	38 32.53
12	7	14.	31.3	48.3					50 5.42	27.14	0.97	V.	3	24.060	36 13.02	35.81	3.06	49 37.31	47 11.89
13	7							18.	50 26.57	27.14	0.97	VII.	3	23.320	36 59.71	35.75	3.14	49 58.46	47 58.60
14	7	40.8	57.	15.					54 31.88	27.14	0.96	III.	2	17.003	43 36.26	35.07	3.76	54 3.78	54 35.09
15	8					9.3			55 8.64	27.14	0.95	IV.	3	31.150	28 47.92	34.97	2.39	54 40.55	39 45.28
16	7					17.	34.		55 59.86	27.15	0.94	V.	3	34.363	25 26.72	34.82	2.06	55 31.77	36 23.60
17	8		27.3						57 44.26	27.15	0.92	III.	4	41.410	18 1.80	34.53	1.40	57 16.19	28 57.73
18	8		11.						58 45.20	27.15	0.93	II.	4	35.820	23 53.94	34.37	1.93	58 17.21	34 50.24
19	7					6.			58 48.88	27.15	0.93	V.	3	34.415	25 23.45	34.36	2.06	58 20.80	36 19.87
20	8					53.			17 59 18.97	27.15	0.90	VI.	4	48.307	10 48.99	34.26	0.73	58 50.92	21 43.98
21	6						40.	57.	18 0 5.86	27.15	0.92	VI.	4	41.060	18 23.31	34.13	1.41	17 59 37.79	25 29 16.85
22	7			44.					1 42.90	27.15	0.98	IV.	1	8.633	52 20.69	33.86	4.63	18 1 14.77	20 3 19.18
23	6.7					33.	50.		2 15.79	27.16	0.95	V.	3	24.020	36 15.47	33.76	3.09	1 47.68	25 47 12.32
24	8	17.7	5.	23.					6 22.11	27.16	0.95	IV.	3	21.660	38 44.26	33.03	3.32	5 54.00	49 40.61
25	8				25.5				7 7.28	27.16	0.95	V.	3	25.987	34 12.03	32.90	2.89	6 39.17	45 7.82
26	7.8			31.	48.5				8 48.05	27.17	0.91	IV.	4	46.720	12 28.63	32.66	0.87	8 19.97	23 22.16
27	6.7			36.	54.	10.3			9 53.17	27.17	0.94	IV.	3	31.533	28 23.95	32.48	2.35	9 25.06	39 18.78
28	8.9							11.	10 19.74	27.17	0.91	VII.	3	36.124	23 36.25	32.41	1.90	9 51.66	34 30.56
29	8				12.				11 54.91	27.17	0.91	V.	3	38.680	20 55.72	32.14	1.64	11 26.83	31 49.50
30	7.8					59.			12 41.93	27.17	0.90	V.	4	44.995	14 16.70	32.00	1.04	12 13.86	25 9.74
31	8						3.		18 13 28.98	−27.17	−0.89	VI.	4	49.325	−9 45.15	−31.87	−0.61	18 13 0.92	−25 20 37.63

CORRECTIONS.

Date.	Corr. of Clock.	Hourly rate.	m	n	c	Zenith Point.	Mic. Co.
1847.	h. s.	s.	s.	s.	s.	° ' "	r.

INSTRUMENT READINGS.

Date.	CIRCLE.							Barom.	THERMOM.				
		A.	B.	C.	D.	E.	F.	Mean.	in.	At.	Ex.	U.	L.	I.
	1847. h. m.	° ' "						"		°	°	°	°	°
Zone 123	July 17, 17 0	64 32 35.4	32.2	30.7	43.6	5.6	34.6	30.35*	30.238	80.0	76.5	79.5	
	18 0								30.230	79.0	75.3		
	19 14								30.226	77.3	74.3		
	20 1								30.226	77.0	73.0		
	21 24								30.226	76.5	72.5		

REMARKS.

July 17. Work interrupted by lamp going out at 21h 30m.

(123) 2. Micrometer reading assumed as 19ʳ.564 instead of 24ʳ.564.

(123) 24. Transits over T.'s II, III, and IV assumed to have been recorded as over T.'s I, II, and III.

(123) 25. Transit over T. V assumed to have been recorded as over T. IV.

* Corr. for runs + 0ʳ.07.

ZONE 123. JULY 17. P. D₀=−25° 10′ 20″—Continued.

No.	Mag.	I.	II.	III.	IV.	V.	VI.	VII.
32	7		37.		13.			
33	8					26.		
34	3.4		36.5	53.7	11.	28.		
35	6			17.7		52.		
36	8							46.
37	7							23.
38	7.8					8.7		
39	8				18.			
40	7					14.5		
41	6			32.				
42	7				23.5	39.7		
43	7				28.		2.	
44	8			44.				
45	8					31.3		56.
46	8		31.3		6.			
47	7	5.	21.3	39.				
48	7.8					11.		
49	8				32.			
50	8	1.		35.5	53.			
51	8.9				35.5			
52	7				16.	32.		
53	8				23.		57.3	
54	8				54.3			
55	7.8					52.5		
56	7.8		3.		38.3	55.		
57	8						52.	
58	8.9				28.3			
59	7					18.3	35.5	
60	7		34.	51.3	9.3			
61	6				4.		37.5	
62	9						24.	
63	9				39.5			
64	9				50.			
65	4	57.	14.2	31.5	49.3		22.7	
66	7						41.	0.7
67	9				55.			
68	9						54.	
69	7.8	23.	40.	57.				
70	7			52.	9.7	27.		
71	8				2.			
72	7.8	42.	59.	16.	34.			
73	7				31.			
74	8						21.	
75	7						25.	
76	8.9						22.	
77	3.4					19.5		53.3
78	7					1.		35.5
79	9				12.			
80	8						6.	

No.	T. (h m s)	a₁ (s)	a₂ (s)	Micrometer	r.	i (′ ″)	d₁ (″)	d₂ (″)	Mean Right Ascension, 1850.0 (h m s)	Mean Declination, 1850.0 (° ′ ″)
32	18 16 11.76	−27.18	−0.07	IV. 1	10.935	−49 56.05	−31.41	−4.39	18 15 43.61	−26 0 51.85
33	17 8.79	27.18	0.95	V. 2	18.150	42 24.60	31.25	3.67	16 40.66	25 53 19.52
34	19 10.71	27.18	0.91	IV. 4	40.415	19 4.26	30.90	1.48	18 42.62	29 56.64
35	20 34.79	27.18	0.89	IV. 4	49.136	9 57.19	30.66	0.63	20 6.72	20 48.48
36	20 54.70	27.19	0.93	VII. 3	32.330	27 34.38	30.61	2.27	20 26.58	38 27.26
37	21 31.70	27.19	0.93	VII. 3	32.162	27 44.86	30.51	2.28	21 3.58	38 37.65
38	22 51.52	27.19	0.94	V. 3	23.837	36 26.89	30.28	3.11	22 23.39	47 20.28
39	24 17.78	27.19	0.88	IV. 4	52.630	6 18.10	30.03	0.31	23 49.71	17 8.44
40	24 57.39	27.19	0.91	V. 3	37.280	22 23.73	29.92	1.78	24 29.29	33 15.43
41	27 48.94	27.20	0.89	III. 4	44.367	14 56.33	29.43	1.08	27 20.85	25 46.84
42	28 22.62	27.20	0.93	IV. 3	24.460	35 47.79	29.33	3.04	27 54.49	46 40.16
43	29 27.66	27.20	0.91	IV. 4	37.800	31 48.04	29.15	1.73	28 59.57	32 38.92
44	31 0.98	27.20	0.91	III. 3	32.970	26 53.29	28.89	2.20	30 32.87	37 44.38
45	31 4.44	27.20	0.91	V. 3	32.757	27 7.27	28.88	2.23	30 36.33	37 58.38
46	34 5.50	27.21	0.91	IV. 3	32.545	27 20.45	28.36	2.25	33 37.39	38 11.06
47	35 56.06	27.21	0.95	III. 2	15.243	45 26.85	28.05	3.96	35 27.90	56 18.86
48	35 53.91	27.21	0.90	V. 4	39.480	20 2.70	28.05	1.57	35 25.80	30 52.41
49	38 31.68	27.21	0.89	IV. 4	47.695	11 27.49	27.61	0.77	39 3.58	22 15.87
50	40 52.32	27.22	0.92	IV. 4	24.490	35 45.91	27.20	3.04	40 24.18	46 36.15
51	42 35.18	27.22	0.87	IV. 4	48.163	10 58.21	26.92	0.72	42 7.09	21 45.85
52	47 15.41	27.23	0.86	IV. 4	55.480	3 19.46	26.12	0.04	46 47.32	14 5.62
53	48 22.73	27.23	0.91	IV. 3	31.460	28 28.58	25.94	2.35	47 54.50	30 16.87
54	50 11.22	27.23	0.87	III. 4	50.055	8 59.50	25.63	0.57	49 43.12	19 45.70
55	50 51.88	27.23	0.90	IV. 3	32.993	26 52.23	25.52	2.20	50 23.75	37 39.95
56	53 37.55	27.24	0.94	IV. 2	17.530	43 3.50	25.05	3.73	53 9.37	53 52.28
57	54 0.91	27.24	0.86	VII. 4	50.863	8 8.08	24.98	0.48	53 32.84	18 53.54
58	55 28.02	27.24	0.86	IV. 4	49.955	9 5.70	24.73	0.57	54 59.92	19 51.00
59	56 1.33	27.24	0.89	V. 4	43.275	16 4.77	24.65	1.19	55 33.20	26 50.61
60	18 59 8.40	27.25	0.93	IV. 2	15.650	45 1.43	24.12	3.92	58 40.22	55 49.47
61	19 0 3.62	27.25	0.86	IV. 4	51.107	7 53.50	23.90	0.43	18 59 35.51	18 37.98
62	0 32.91	27.25	0.86	VII. 4	48.897	10 11.30	23.69	0.63	19 0 4.80	20 55.88
63	2 38.74	27.25	0.91	IV. 3	26.340	33 49.83	23.52	2.87	2 10.58	44 36.22
64	3 58.05	27.26	0.93	IV. 2	16.567	44 3.94	23.30	3.84	3 29.86	54 51.08
65	6 48.48	27.26	0.88	IV. 4	39.633	19 53.19	22.83	1.55	6 20.34	30 37.57
66	7 26.57	27.26	0.93	V. 2	16.070	44 35.07	22.73	3.89	6 58.38	55 21.69
67	8 54.14	27.26	0.92	IV. 2	21.100	39 19.39	22.48	3.39	8 25.96	50 5.26
68	9 19.99	27.27	0.86	VI. 4	49.765	9 17.32	22.41	0.56	8 51.86	20 0.29
69	12 14.23	27.27	0.91	III. 3	22.533	37 29.46	21.92	3.25	11 46.05	48 14.63
70	14 26.45	27.27	0.91	IV. 3	25.785	31 24.39	21.56	2.92	13 58.27	45 8.87
71	18 1.09	27.28	0.92	IV. 2	18.723	41 48.51	20.96	3.63	17 32.89	52 33.10
72	20 33.22	27.28	0.91	IV. 3	24.807	35 25.77	20.54	3.02	20 5.03	46 9.33
73	21 30.24	27.29	0.91	IV. 3	26.360	33 48.57	20.38	2.86	21 2.04	44 31.81
74	21 29.56	27.29	0.92	VII. 3	21.797	35 35.02	20.38	3.32	21 1.35	49 18.72
75	22 33.67	27.29					20.22		22 (5)	
76	26 30.83	27.30	0.87	VII. 4	43.260	16 5.15	19.56	−1.18	26 2.66	26 45.89
77	28 2.41	27.30	0.85	V. 4	56.830	1 54.51	19.32	+0.12	27 34.26	12 33.71
78	33 44.27	27.31	0.86	V. 4	57.207	1 31.06	18.39	+0.16	33 16.10	12 9.29
79	36 11.34	27.31	0.91	IV. 3	30.800	29 4.10	17.99	−2.41	35 43.12	39 44.50
80	19 36 31.78	−27.31	−0.92	VI. 3	26.920	−33 13.56	−17.94	−2.81	19 36 3.55	−25 43 54.31

CORRECTIONS.

Date.	Corr. of Clock.	Hourly rate.	m	n	c	Zenith Point.	Mic. Co.
			s.	s.	s.	° ′ ″	r.
1847.	h.	s.	s.				

REMARKS.

(123) 69. Micrometer reading assumed as 22ʳ.833 instead of 22ʳ.533.

INSTRUMENT READINGS.

Date.	CIRCLE.						Barom.	THERMOM.				
	A.	B.	C.	D.	E.	F.	Mean.		At.	Ex.	U.	L.	I.
1847. h. m.	° ′ ″					″	In.	°	°	°	°	°

Zone 123. July 17. P. $D_0 = -25°\ 10'\ 20''$—Continued.

No.	Mag.	I.	II.	III.	IV.	V.	VI.	VII.	T. (h m s)	a_1 (s)	a_2 (s)
81	9.9				43.				19 39 0.05	−27.32	−0.95
82	7.8	10.3	27.	44.5	2.3				42 1.48	27.32	0.91
83	7					55.		29.	42 37.98	27.32	0.86
84	7.8				31.	47.3			44 30.12	27.33	0.93
85	8	39.	55.5						48 29.91	27.33	0.89
86	8			25.					48 41.95	27.33	0.89
87	7.8					8.5			48 51.38	27.33	0.90
88	9				10.				50 9.70	27.34	0.87
89	9							17.	50 25.81	27.34	0.89
90	9			23.					19 56 39.96	27.35	0.89
91	7	41.	58.	15.					20 1 32.19	27.36	0.92
92	8.9					50.		24.	20 1 32.78	27.36	0.90
93	7						56.		21 24 22.03	27.50	0.88
94	7.8		31.7	49.					27 6.15	27.50	0.97
95	7.8	55.		29.	47.				31 46.13	27.51	0.99
96	7	47.	4.	21.5	20.5				21 33 38.46	−27.51	−0.96

No.	Micrometer		r.	i	d_1	d_2	Mean Right Ascension, 1850.0 (h m s)	Mean Declination, 1850.0 (° ' ")
81	IV.	2	12.090	−48 44.87	−17.58	−4.30	19 38 31.78	−25 59 26.75
82	IV.	3	29.930	30 4.33	17.05	2.51	41 33.25	40 43.89
83	V.	4	53.033	5 52.63	16.96	0.24	42 9.80	16 29.83
84	IV.	2	20.630	39 48.90	16.66	3.44	44 1.86	50 29.00
85	II.	4	41.160	18 17.29	16.02	1.39	48 1.69	28 54.70
86	III.	4	42.880	16 29.35	15.99	1.22	48 13.73	27 6.56
87	V.	4	35.920	23 45.84	15.97	1.91	48 23.15	34 23.72
88	IV.	4	49.330	9 45.15	15.76	0.61	49 41.49	20 21.52
89	VII.	4	40.560	18 54.42	15.72	1.45	49 57.58	29 31.59
90	III.	4	41.315	18 7.76	14.74	1.38	19 56 11.72	28 43.88
91	III.	3	27.530	32 34.72	13.99	2.76	20 1 3.91	43 11.47
92	V.	3	32.767	27 6.58	13.99	2.22	20 1 4.52	37 42.79
93	VI.	4	54.188	4 40.14	2.13	0.06	21 23 53.65	15 2.33
94	III.	2	12.187	48 38.67	1.76	4.35	26 37.68	59 4.80
95	IV.	2	17.190	43 24.85	1.19	3.82	31 17.63	53 49.86
96	IV.	3	23.780	−36 30.22	−0.97	−3.15	21 33 9.99	−25 46 54.34

Zone 124. July 19. P. $D_0 = -28°\ 18'\ 30''$.

No.	Mag.	I.	II.	III.	IV.	V.	VI.	VII.	T. (h m s)	a_1 (s)	a_2 (s)
1	7						19.5		17 28 41.60	−28.06	−0.52
2	7	29.	46.	4.3	22.5			14.3	31 21.60	28.07	0.64
3	8		35.2	11.					39 10.45	28.08	0.63
4	8					58.3			39 40.72	28.08	0.62
5	8			44.3					42 1.72	28.09	0.62
6	8			34.					42 51.41	28.09	0.61
7	8					31.5			43 13.99	28.08	0.58
8	8				10.				44 39.11	28.09	0.71
9	7.8						30.		44 46.34	28.09	0.62
10	9			25.					48 42.41	28.09	0.61
11	9						24.		48 48.94	28.09	0.62
12	7					54.5	29.5		49 36.83	28.09	0.66
13	8.9				42.				51 41.43	28.10	0.67
14	9			49.3					53 6.67	28.10	0.59
15	7.8		9.7	27.5	45.5				54 44.05	28.10	0.67
16	9			34.5					57 52.03	28.11	0.76
17	7			46.5	4.				59 3.80	28.11	0.61
18	9				50.				17 59 49.35	28.11	0.69
19	7	2.5	19.5	38.	56.				18 2 55.20	28.12	0.73
20	8	38.	55.	13.3					18 5 30.62	−28.12	−0.72

No.	Micrometer		r.	i	d_1	d_2	Mean Right Ascension, 1850.0 (h m s)	Mean Declination, 1850.0 (° ' ")
1	VI.	4	57.080	−1 38.71	−13.03	+0.23	17 28 16.02	−28 20 21.51
2	IV.	3	28.743	31 18.86	12.61	−3.17	30 52.89	50 4.64
3	IV.	3	36.245	23 28.34	11.31	2.29	38 41.74	42 11.90
4	V.	4	41.345	18 5.82	11.23	1.64	39 12.02	36 48.69
5	III.	4	41.650	17 46.62	10.81	1.61	41 33.02	36 29.08
6	III.	4	43.507	15 50.21	10.72	1.38	43 22.72	34 32.31
7	V.	4	51.660	7 18.80	10.65	0.41	42 45.33	35 59.86
8	IV.	2	20.850	39 34.95	10.42	4.12	44 10.31	58 19.49
9	VII.	3	39.443	20 8.11	10.30	1.87	44 17.63	38 50.37
10	III.	4	45.275	14 3.08	9.75	1.18	48 13.71	32 44.01
11	VI.	4	41.295	18 8.70	9.74	1.66	48 20.83	36 50.10
12	V.	3	34.270	25 32.48	9.59	2.49	49 8.08	44 14.56
13	IV.	3	36.605	23 5.70	9.25	2.21	51 12.66	41 47.16
14	III.	4	54.650	4 11.37	9.02	0.05	52 37.98	22 50.44
15	IV.	3	34.635	25 9.28	8.75	2.45	54 16.18	26 43 50.48
16	III.	2	14.455	46 16.29	8.22	4.91	57 23.16	29 4 59.42
17	IV.	4	49.620	9 26.85	8.03	0.66	58 35.08	28 28 5.54
18	IV.	3	32.407	27 29.17	7.90	2.71	17 59 20.55	46 9.78
19	IV.	3	23.320	36 59.33	7.39	3.82	18 2 26.35	55 40.54
20	III.	3	26.354	−33 48.57	−6.95	−3.45	18 5 1.78	−28 52 28.97

CORRECTIONS.

Date.	Corr. of Clock.	Hourly rate.	m	n	c	Zenith Point.	Mic. Co.
1847.	h.	s.	s.	s.	s.	° ' "	r.

REMARKS.

(123) 81. Minutes assumed as 39 instead of 38, and transit over T. III as recorded over T. IV.

(123) 96. Transit over middle thread assumed as at $39^s.5$ instead of $29^s.5$.

INSTRUMENT READINGS.

Date.		CIRCLE.							Barom.		THERMOM.				
		A.	B.	C.	D.	E.	F.	Mean.		in.	At.	Ex.	U.	L.	I.
Zone 124	1847. July 19, 17 28 / 18 5	67 39	65.7	60.0	62.3	70.6	31.7	66.2	59.42	30.282 / 30.186	83.5 / 83.0	81.5 / 81.5	83.0	82.5	81.0

Zone 125. August 2. C. $D_0 = -5°\ 20'\ 0''$.

No.	Mag.	I.	II.	III.	IV.	V.	VI.	VII.	T.	a_1	a_2	MICROMETER		$r.$	i	d_1	d_2	Mean Right Ascension, 1850.0	Mean Declination, 1850.0
									h. m. s.	s.	s.				′ ″	″	″	h. m. s.	° ′ ″
1	7	51.	6.5	22.	38.	·	8.3	23.7	16 32 37.39	−35.00	·	IV.	3	33.325	−26 31.59	− 8.75	−0.87	·	− 5 46 41.21
2	8	·	·	43.	59.7	·	·	·	39 58.69	35.03	·	IV.	3	23.412	36 53.55	7.58	1.24	·	5 57 2.37
3	8	·	·	·	3.	·	·	46.7	40 1.07	35.03	·	VII.	2	11.934	48 54.78	7.58	1.69	·	6 9 4.05
4	9	·	·	·	2.	18.	31.	·	44 1.25	35.05	·	IV.	3	25.415	34 47.87	6.93	1.17	·	5 54 55.97
5	7	·	·	·	·	·	·	37.	44 50.62	35.05	·	VII.	4	47.437	11 43.60	6.70	0.32	·	5 31 50.62
6	7	·	·	55.	11.	25.8	41.5	·	47 10.36	35.06	·	IV.	3	26.068	31 6.77	6.42	1.15	·	5 54 14.34
7	8	·	·	·	·	39.	·	9.6	16 48 23.27	−35.07	·	V.	3	27.034	−32 28.82	− 6.22	−1.09	·	− 5 52 36.13

Zone 126. August 5. C. $D_0 = -4°\ 2'\ 30''$.

No.	Mag.	I.	II.	III.	IV.	V.	VI.	VII.	T.	a_1	a_2	MICROMETER		$r.$	i	d_1	d_2	Mean Right Ascension, 1850.0	Mean Declination, 1850.0
1	7	·	39.2	54.3	·	24.3	40.7	·	16 45 9.37	−36.68	·	IV.	2	9.998	−50 56.12	− 8.20	−1.77	·	− 4 53 36.09
2	7	·	·	46.	1.5	·	·	·	51 1.33	36.70	·	IV.	4	55.088	3 43.97	7.21	0.04	·	4 6 21.22
3	8.9	·	33.2	·	5.5	19.8	35.3	·	55 4.20	36.72	·	IV.	3	35.845	20 45.06	6.51	0.65	·	4 23 22.22
4	7	·	21.4	·	53.	7.7	·	·	16 57 52.27	36.73	·	IV.	2	14.946	45 45.48	6.03	1.57	·	4 48 23.05
5	9.10	·	33.	·	·	·	·	·	17 0 4.03	36.74	·	II.	3	37.970	21 39.32	5.66	0.68	·	4 24 15.66
6	8	·	·	·	59.	15.2	·	·	0 43.98	36.75	·	V.	4	53.882	4 59.40	5.55	0.08	·	4 7 35.03
7	7	·	53.5	8.8	24.4	·	55.	·	4 23.02	36.76	·	IV.	3	35.242	24 31.26	4.90	0.79	·	4 27 6.95
8	9	·	·	·	3.2	18.2	33.2	·	5 2.70	36.76	·	VII.	4	48.52?	10 35.69	4.79	0.28	·	4 13 10.76
9	8	·	·	·	·	·	·	49.?	7 18.03	36.77	·	IV.	4	43.622	15 43.00	4.39	0.47	·	4 18 17.86
10	7.8	·	8.3	23.8	39.2	·	·	·	11 39.12	36.79	·	IV.	4	52.822	6 5.93	3.62	0.12	·	4 8 39.67
11	8.9	·	19.7	35.5	51.7	·	·	·	13 50.72	36 80	·	IV.	3	23.132	37 11.01	3.24	1.26	·	4 39 45.51
12	8	·	·	51.	6.3	·	·	·	17 15 6.00	−36.81	·	IV.	3	27.431	−32 41.36	− 3.01	−1.09	·	− 4 35 15.40

Zone 127. August 20. P. $D_0 = -25°\ 48'\ 0''$.

No.	Mag.	Seconds of transit	T.	a_1	a_2	MICROMETER		$r.$	i	d_1	d_2	Mean Right Ascension, 1850.0	Mean Declination, 1850.0
1	7	50.	18 15 32.69	−42.41	−1.38	V.	2	17.910	−42 39.53	−23.50	−4.27	18 14 48.90	−26 31 7.39
2	9	37.	16 2.48	42.41	1.38	VI.	2	15.263	45 25.78	23.41	4.53	15 18.69	26 33 53.72
3	9	22.	18 4.86	42.42	1.21	V.	4	47.830	11 18.85	23.07	1.18	17 21.23	25 59 43.10
4	6	7.	19 7.84	42.42	1.44	IV.	1	6.504	54 34.39	22.90	5.46	18 21.98	26 43 2.75
5	7	45. 3. 21.	20 19.94	42.43	1.41	IV.	1	9.220	51 43.89	22.70	5.16	19 36.10	40 11.75
6	9	54.	20 19.43	42.43	1.42	VI.	1	8.510	52 28.78	22.70	5.24	19 35.58	40 56.72
7	9	7.	21 15.54	42.43	1.24	VII.	4	41.003	18 20.93	22.55	1.86	20 31.87	6 45.34
8	8	2. 20. 38.3	23 37.05	42.44	1.37	IV.	2	13.730	47 1.87	22.15	4.68	22 53.24	35 28.70
9	9	12. 30.	24 29.20	42.45	1.29	IV.	3	31.004	28 57.01	22.00	2.00	23 45.46	17 21.91
10	7	21. 38.3 55.7 13.5 47.	28 12.69	42.47	1.32	IV.	3	24.440	35 49.05	21.39	3.60	27 28.90	24 14.04
11	8.9	21.3 38.3 55.5	33 12.78	42.49	1.32	III.	3	22.933	37 22.98	20.56	3.75	32 28.97	25 47.29
12	9.10	39.	33 38.19	42.49	1.31	IV.	3	23.760	36 31.46	20.49	3.66	32 54.30	24 55.61
13	7.8	33. 50.3 8.	35 7.40	42.50	1.30	IV.	3	26.887	33 15.26	20.24	3.33	34 23.60	26 21 38.83
14	7	11.3 28.	36 10.95	42.50	1.17	V.	4	51.087	7 54.72	20.06	0.85	35 27.28	25 56 15.63
15	9	49.	37 31.66	42.51	1.38	V.	1	11.800	49 2.01	19.84	4.89	36 47.77	26 37 20.74
16	9	37.	38 36.24	42.52	1.30	IV.	1	26.487	33 40.54	19.66	3.37	37 52.42	22 3.57
17	8	51.	39 16.72	42.52	1.22	VI.	4	40.323	19 9.67	19.55	1.94	38 32.98	7 31.16
18	9	37.	40 19.78	42.52	1.24	V.	3	35.707	24 2.27	19.38	2.41	39 36.02	12 24.01
19	8	24.	40 32.20	42.53	1.35	VII.	2	15.220	45 28.29	19.35	4.54	39 48.32	33 52.18
20	8	16.	41 24.54	42.53	1.21	VII.	4	41.140	18 17.98	19.20	1.86	40 40.80	6 39.04
21	9	55.	42 37.79	42.54	1.24	V.	4	36.803	22 50.46	19.00	2.30	41 54.01	11 11.76
22	7	5.5 23. 40.	18 44 22.44	−42.55	−1.35	IV.	2	15.400	−45 17.24	−18.71	−4.52	18 43 38.54	−26 33 40.47

CORRECTIONS.

Date.	Corr. of Clock.	Hourly rate.	m	n	c	Zenith Point.	Mic. Co.
1847.	h.	s.	s.	s.	s.	° ′ ″	$r.$

REMARKS. — Aug. 2. Sweeping for Iris.

INSTRUMENT READINGS.

Date.	CIRCLE.							Barom.	THERMOM.				
	A.	B.	C.	D.	E.	F.	Mean.		At.	Ex.	U.	L.	I.
	° ′ ″						″	In.	°	°	°	°	°
Zone 125 Aug. 2, 16 30	44 41 91.2	87.3	84.7	99.5	59.4	90.6	85.50*	30.146	78.5	75.0	76.5	75.8	75.5
16 48	·	·	·	·	·	·	·	30.144	78.0	72.8			
Zone 126 Aug. 5, 16 40	43 24 66.1	62.1	62.0	48.1	50.3	65.9	59.08	29.744	·	·	73.8	72.7	74.0
16 45	·	·	·	·	·	·	·	·	75.7	71.0			
17 15	·	·	·	·	·	·	·	29.748	74.8	68.8			
Zone 127 Aug. 20, 18 15	65 9 66.3	62.2	63.7	50.5	52.6	65.4	60.12	30.054	70.2	63.5	71.5	71.0	72.0
19 29	·	·	·	·	·	·	·	30.056	68.4	60.2			

*Corr. for runs +0."08.

ZONE 127. AUGUST 20. P. $D_0 = -25°\ 48'\ 0''$—Continued.

No.	Mag.	SECONDS OF TRANSIT.							T.	a_1	a_2	MICROMETER.			i	d_1	d_2	Mean Right Ascension, 1850.0.	Mean Declination, 1850.0.
		I.	II.	III.	IV.	V.	VI.	VII.	h. m. s.	s.	s.			r.	′ ″	b.	′	h. m. s.	° ′ ″
23	2.3	..	6.7	24.3	42.	58.5	..	..	18 46 41.27	−42.56	−1.32	IV.	2	20.212	−40 15.19	−18.33	−4.02	18 45 57.39	−26 28 37.54
24	9	..	..	..	..	..	49.	..	47 14.72	42.56	1.21	VI.	4	40.580	18 53.48	18.24	1.91	46 30.95	7 13.63
25	8	38.7	55.5	13.	..	..	..	..	50 30.13	42.58	1.29	III.	3	25.260	34 57.15	17.70	3.49	49 46.26	23 18.34
26	8	..	..	..	..	9.	..	..	50 51.64	42.58	1.38	V.	1	7.705	53 19.12	17.64	5.32	50 7.68	41 42.08
27	8	..	..	..	..	59.5	16.	..	51 41.91	42.58	1.28	V.	3	25.647	34 33.43	17.50	3.46	50 58.05	22 54.39
28	9.8	..	..	..	9.	..	43.3	..	53 8.69	42.59	1.23	IV.	3	35.435	24 19.21	17.27	2.44	52 24.87	26 12 38.92
29	7.8	..	..	..	..	..	27.	..	53 52.83	42.59	1.13	VI.	4	53.475	5 28.62	17.14	0.62	53 9.11	25 53 46.38
30	9	..	..	..	..	..	..	44.	54 52.49	42.60	1.22	VII.	3	37.350	22 19.47	16.98	2.25	54 8.67	26 10 38.70
31	7	..	..	..	39.5	..	12.7	..	56 38.52	42.61	1.28	IV.	3	27.080	33 3.27	16.70	3.31	55 54.63	21 23.28
32	8	..	..	..	..	..	5.7	..	57 31.23	42.61	1.29	VI.	2	20.670	39 46.32	16.55	3.97	56 47.33	28 6.84
33	8	..	..	49.	6.5	23.	..	..	59 5.92	42.62	1.22	IV.	3	34.523	25 16.36	16.29	2.53	58 22.08	26 13 35.18
34	7	..	..	..	..	..	..	14.7	18 59 23.38	42.62	1.13	VII.	4	51.470	7 30.27	16.24	0.81	18 58 39.63	25 55 47.32
35	8	..	..	26.5	..	..	..	..	19 1 43.65	42.63	1.38	III.	1	8.515	52 27.84	15.86	5.24	19 0 59.64	26 40 46.94
36	8	..	..	..	26.	..	..	..	2 25.49	42.64	1.19	IV.	3	39.000	20 35.40	15.75	2.06	1 41.66	8 53.23
37	8	..	..	..	..	..	5.	..	2 30.76	42.64	1.16	VI.	3	44.850	14 25.54	15.74	1.48	1 46.96	26 2 42.76
38	8	..	..	55.5	..	..	..	..	4 12.50	42.64	1.12	III.	4	52.400	6 32.58	15.46	0.72	3 28.74	25 54 46.76
39	5.6	..	..	26.	43.	0.	..	..	4 42.78	42.65	1.20	IV.	3	38.745	20 51.39	15.38	2.11	3 58.93	26 9 8.88
40	7	..	7.5	24.7	12.	..	..	..	7 41.75	42.66	1.11	IV.	4	51.013	7 2.93	14.89	0.77	6 57.98	25 55 18.59
41	8	30.5	47.	4.7	..	..	..	..	9 21.70	42.67	1.20	III.	3	36.620	23 4.39	14.63	2.32	8 37.83	26 11 21.34
42	7.	..	..	54.	..	..	..	..	10 11.08	42.68	1.25	III.	3	28.060	32 1.40	14.49	3.21	9 27.15	20 19.10
43	8	..	..	..	30.5	..	4.	..	10 29.72	42.68	1.24	IV.	3	29.870	30 8.10	14.44	3.01	9 45.80	18 25.55
44	7	22.	39.	56.3	..	..	..	..	13 13.52	42.69	1.28	III.	2	22.260	38 6.47	14.01	3.81	12 29.55	26 24.29
45	9	..	..	..	..	40.5	..	..	13 23.21	42.69	1.28	V.	2	21.493	38 54.85	13.98	3.89	12 39.24	27 12.72
46	9	..	4.	..	..	..	..	..	16 38.44	42.71	1.17	II.	4	39.696	19 48.99	13.46	2.00	15 54.50	8 4.45
47	7	20.	36.7	54.3	..	..	..	..	18 11.50	42.72	1.33	III.	2	12.470	48 20.89	13.21	4.82	17 27.45	26 36 38.92
48	7.8	..	..	..	..	..	51.	..	18 16.85	42.72	1.08	VI.	4	54.630	4 12.38	13.20	0.50	17 33.05	25 52 26.08
49	7	..	46.	..	3.5	21.	..	..	20 20.49	42.73	1.19	IV.	3	36.080	23 38.63	12.87	2.37	19 36.57	26 11 53.87
50	8	..	..	..	..	..	..	12.	20 20.48	42.73	1.19	VII.	3	36.110	23 37.13	12.87	2.37	19 36.56	11 52.37
51	8.9	..	..	..	..	..	..	0.5	21 9.05	42.73	1.16	VII.	3	41.487	17 59.91	12.74	1.82	20 25.10	6 14.47
52	7	..	..	..	49.5	..	23.	..	22 48.94	42.74	1.14	IV.	4	44.940	14 20.21	12.48	1.47	22 5.06	2 34.76
53	7	..	..	7.5	25.	41.5	..	..	24 24.37	42.75	1.23	IV.	3	27.863	32 14.01	12.23	3.23	23 40.39	20 29.47
54	7	45.	2.	19.	36.8	..	..	..	27 36.29	42.77	1.19	IV.	3	34.447	25 21.19	11.73	2.56	26 52.33	13 35.48
55	7	..	..	..	..	..	..	10.	19 29 18.61	−42.78	−1.13	VII.	3	46.473	−12 47.19	−11.45	−1.31	19 28 34.70	−26 0 59.95

CORRECTIONS.

Date.	Corr. of Clock.	Hourly rate.	m	n	c	Zenith Point.	Mic. Co.
1847.	h.	s.	. s.	s.	s.	s.	° ′ ″	r.

INSTRUMENT READINGS.

Date.	CIRCLE.							Barom.	THERMOM.				
	A.	B.	C.	D.	E.	F.	Mean.		At.	Ex.	U.	L.	I.
1847. h. m.	° ′ ″						″	in.	°	°	°	°	°

REMARKS.

ZONE 128, AUGUST 26. P. $D_0 = -27° 40' 30''$.

No.	Mag.	I.	II.	III.	IV.	V.	VI.	VII.	T. (h m s)	a_1 (s)	a_2 (s)
1	8	32.3	49.2	7.3	25.5				18 19 24.64	−47.52	−0.88
2	9			28.					20 45.35	47.53	0.68
3	7		40.	57.3	15.3	32.5			22 14.86	47.54	0.66
4	8			15.5	33.3	51.2			24 50.60	47.55	0.74
5	7.8				33.3				25 32.30	47.56	0.87
6	8					23.			26 5.17	47.56	0.72
7	7					15.5			26 57.88	47.56	0.85
8	8				21.				28 20.68	47.57	0.56
9	8.9					19.			29 1.50	47.57	0.68
10	7		59.5		35.5			27.	30 34.60	47.58	0.79
11	7		50.7	7.2	27.				32 25.55	47.59	0.83
12	8						21.		33 46.09	47.59	0.68
13	8				18.				34 17.76	47.60	0.52
14	8						42.		35 6.93	47.60	0.81
15	7				31.				36 30.09	47.61	0.80
16	8							30.5	36 39.96	47.61	0.75
17	7			40.	59.3	16.			38 58.08	47.63	0.80
18	7.8		5.	22.7	40.5				40 40.03	47.63	0.56
19	8				59.	17.			43 16.25	47.65	0.79
20	7.8				21.5	38.			44 20.53	47.65	0.77
21	6.7							23.5	44 31.22	47.65	0.58
22	8						25.3		45 50.44	47.66	0.62
23	7				21.5	39.			47 21.03	47.67	0.77
24	8				30.	46.5			48 29.04	47.68	0.76
25	8.9		49.		6.2				50 23.71	47.69	0.53
26	9				51.3				50 50.88	47.69	0.57
27	7.8				41.	58.			51 23.22	47.69	0.73
28	7.8					50.			51 57.78	47.70	0.53
29	9			37.	54.7				55 11.99	47.71	0.57
30	8			22.					56 39.40	47.72	0.77
31	9					17.			56 59.41	47.72	0.78
32	4.5			23.	40.	57.5			18 59 22.61	47.73	0.55
33	9			32.			8.		19 0 7.28	47.74	0.58
34	8	26.2	43.	1.2	19.2				2 18.44	47.75	0.76
35	8		11.		47.3				3 46.32	47.76	0.80
36	9						3.		4 28.01	47.77	0.71
37	8.9			1.					6 18.29	47.78	0.49
38	8				7.				7 6.38	47.78	0.65
39	7.8				0.	35.			10 17.40	47.80	0.86
40	8			28.	45.7	4.			12 3.16	47.81	0.74
41	8	6.	23.3	41.					14 58.30	47.83	0.63
42	6	5.	22.3	40.3	58.3	15.			15 57.50	47.83	0.68
43	9				32.				17 14.58	47.84	0.53
44	7				21.		55.3		21 20.70	47.86	0.51
45	8					56.3			22 38.82	47.87	0.63
46	7.8				43.				23 42.44	47.88	0.66
47	7						23.		23 30.23	47.88	0.89
48	7						0.		24 7.41	47.88	0.77
49	9							52.	19 24 59.38	−47.89	−0.80

No.	Mag.	MICROMETER		r_1	i (' ")	d_1 (")	d_2 (")	Mean Right Ascension, 1850.0 (h m s)	Mean Declination, 1850.0 (° ' ")
1	8	IV.	2	13.763	−46 59.72	−30.64	−4.88	18 18 36.24	−28 28 5.24
2	9	III.	3	36.480	23 13.22	30.42	2.25	19 57.14	4 15.89
3	7	V.	3	37.863	21 46.92	30.16	2.09	21 26.66	2 49.17
4	8	IV.	3	28.610	31 27.28	29.70	3.14	24 2.31	12 30.12
5	7.8	IV.	2	14.560	46 9.90	29.58	4.78	24 43.87	27 14.26
6	8	V.	3	30.307	29 35.53	29.48	2.95	25 17.19	10 37.96
7	7	V.	2	15.442	45 14.60	29.33	4.69	26 9.47	28 26 18.62
8	8	IV.	4	49.252	9 49.98	29.10	0.75	27 32.55	27 50 49.86
9	8.9	V.	3	34.490	25 18.68	28.97	2.49	28 13.25	28 6 20.14
10	7	IV.	3	22.987	37 20.03	28.70	3.80	29 46.23	18 22.53
11	7	IV.	2	18.340	42 12.73	28.39	4.34	31 37.13	23 15.46
12	8	VI.	3	35.280	24 29.25	28.33	2.40	31 57.82	28 5 29.98
13	8	IV.	4	52.674	6 15.27	28.07	0.41	33 29.64	27 47 13.75
14	8	VI.	2	19.140	41 22.40	27.94	4.24	34 18.52	28 22 24.58
15	7	IV.	2	19.475	41 1.43	27.70	4.20	35 41.68	22 3.33
16	8	VII.	3	25.710	34 20.48	27.67	3.49	35 51.60	15 30.64
17	7	IV.	2	20.590	45 5.00	27.28	4.60	38 9.65	28 26 7.06
18	7.8	IV.	4	46.875	12 18.85	27.00	1.07	39 51.84	27 53 16.92
19	8	IV.	2	19.430	41 4.31	26.58	4.21	42 27.81	28 22 5.10
20	7.8	IV.	3	22.207	38 9.99	26.40	3.90	43 32.11	28 19 10.29
21	6.7	VII.	3	44.325	15 1.92	26.37	1.33	43 42.99	27 55 59.62
22	8	VI.	4	39.673	19 50.31	26.15	1.89	45 2.16	28 0 48.35
23	7	IV.	3	22.397	37 57.35	25.94	3.87	46 32.59	18 57.03
24	8	IV.	3	23.047	37 16.27	25.71	3.80	47 40.60	28 18 15.78
25	8.9	IV.	4	49.287	9 47.79	25.40	0.81	49 35.49	27 50 44.00
26	9	IV.	4	44.217	15 5.75	25.33	1.39	50 2.02	27 56 2.47
27	7.8	V.	3	26.143	31 2.32	25.23	3.44	50 34.80	28 15 0.99
28	7.8	VII.	4	49.220	9 51.24	25.14	0.79	51 9.55	27 50 47.17
29	9	III.	2	44.415	11 53.33	24.62	1.36	54 23.71	27 55 49.30
30	8	III.	2	21.607	38 47.39	24.39	3.97	55 50.91	28 19 45.75
31	9	V.	2	19.493	41 0.36	24.33	4.22	56 10.91	28 21 58.91
32	4.5	IV.	4	47.010	12 8.57	24.10	1.05	57 34.36	27 53 3.72
33	9	IV.	4	43.815	15 30.77	23.82	1.38	18 59 18.96	27 56 25.97
34	8	IV.	2	21.910	38 26.55	23.48	3.92	19 1 29.93	28 19 23.95
35	8	IV.	2	18.373	42 9.40	23.24	4.37	2 57.70	23 7.01
36	9	VI.	3	27.199	32 56.82	23.13	3.32	3 39.53	28 13 53.27
37	8.9	III.	4	53.047	5 51.88	22.85	0.33	5 30.02	27 46 45.06
38	8	IV.	3	34.074	25 44.47	22.72	2.51	6 17.95	28 6 39.70
39	7.8	III.	1	11.900	48 51.40	22.24	5.13	9 28.74	29 48.77
40	8	IV.	3	21.905	35 19.61	21.94	3.59	11 14.61	16 15.14
41	8	III.	3	37.120	22 33.02	21.48	2.17	14 9.83	3 26.67
42	6	IV.	3	31.770	28 8.89	21.33	2.79	15 8.99	28 9 3.01
43	9	V.	4	49.543	9 31.61	21.14	0.75	16 26.21	27 50 23.50
44	7	IV.	4	55.347	3 27.87	20.50	0.08	20 32.33	27 44 18.45
45	8	V.	4	39.700	19 48.80	20.30	1.88	21 50.32	28 0 40.98
46	7.8	IV.	3	36.910	22 46.44	20.13	2.19	22 53.90	3 38.76
47	7	VII.	1	10.377	50 31.52	20.16	5.33	22 41.46	31 27.01
48	7	VII.	3	23.133	37 11.26	20.07	3.80	23 18.76	18 5.13
49	9	VII.	3	20.535	−39 54.34	−19.93	−4.11	19 24 10.69	−28 20 45.38

CORRECTIONS.

Date.	Corr. of Clock.	Hourly rate.	m	n	c	Zenith Point.	Mic. Co.
1847.	h.	s.	s.	s.	s.	° ' "	r.

REMARKS.

Aug. 26, 21h 44m. Moon too bright.

(128) 17. Micrometer reading assumed as 15r.590 instead of 20r.590.

INSTRUMENT READINGS.

Date.		CIRCLE.							Barom.	THERMOM.				
		A.	B.	C.	D.	E.	F.	Mean.		At.	Ex.	U.	L.	I.
Zone 128	1847. Aug. 26, h. m. 18 15	67 2 33.0	28.5	29.5	17.3	23.0	31.6	27.15"	in. 30.132	72.0	68.0			
	18 50								30.142	72.0	67.5			
	19 35								30.146	71.0	64.5			
	20 0								30.140	70.8	64.2			
	20 59								30.136	70.2	63.4			
	21 29								30.134	69.5	62.5			
	21 44										61.5			

*Corr. for runs = −0".31.

ZONE 128. AUGUST 26. P. $D_s = -27°\ 40'\ 30''$—Continued.

No.	Mag.	I.	II.	III.	IV.	V.	VI.	VII.	T. (h. m. s.)	a1 (s.)	a2 (s.)	Micr.	n	r.	i (' '')	d1 ('')	d2 ('')	Mean Right Ascension, 1850.0 (h. m. s.)	Mean Declination, 1850.0 (° ' '')
50	8			46.		20.3			19 27 3.08	−47.90	−0.60	V.	4	43.010	−16 21.19	−19.62	−1.48	19 26 14.58	−27 57 12.29
51	7.8			11.	28.5				28 28.25	47.91	0.54	IV.	4	50.255	8 47.08	19.41	0.66	27 39.80	27 49 37.15
52	9			37.					29 54.35	47.92	0.68	III.	3	33.495	26 20.48	19.17	2.58	29 5.75	28 7 12.23
53	8.9					20.			30 2.52	47.92	0.63	V.	3	40.235	19 17.18	19.16	1.81	29 13.97	28 0 8.15
54	8			13.					31 30.30	47.92	0.56	III.	4	47.615	11 32.52	18.93	0.95	30 41.62	27 52 22.40
55	7			2.3	20.3			12.	32 19.68	47.93	0.66	IV.	3	38.360	21 15.73	18.81	2.02	31 31.09	28 2 6.56
56	7	1.3	18.7	36.3	54.	11.3			35 53.63	47.95	0.63	IV.	4	40.707	18 45.76	18.26	1.76	35 5.05	27 59 35.78
57	7.8			42.					35 59.35	47.96	0.67	III.	3	36.407	23 17.86	18.10	2.25	36 10.72	28 4 8.21
58	7							40.	36 47.86	47.96	0.50	VII.	4	54.503	4 19.96	18.13	0.18	35 59.40	27 45 8.27
59	8	32.	49.5	7.3	25.	42.			37 24.48	47.96	0.60	IV.	3	34.895	24 52.84	18.04	2.43	36 35.83	28 5 43.31
60	9			13.					41 0.33	47.98	0.64	III.	3	39.785	19 45.73	17.49	−1.86	40 11.71	28 0 35.08
61	7		46.	3.					42 20.56	47.99	0.53	III.	4	56.133	2 38.46	17.29	+0.01	41 32.04	27 43 25.74
62	7				14.	1.	18.5		42 43.60	47.99	0.55	IV.	4	49.085	10 0.39	17.22	−0.76	41 55.12	27 50 48.37
63	7				18.				44 16.90	48.00	0.91	IV.	1	10.340	50 33.65	16.98	5.33	43 27.99	28 31 25.96
64	8.9				35.				45 34.65	48.01	0.58	IV.	4	47.520	11 38.60	16.78	0.96	44 46.06	27 52 26.34
65	8		35.	52.3					48 9.83	48.02	0.65	III.	4	39.493	20 2.03	16.39	1.00	47 21.16	28 0 50.32
66	9	19.		54.					50 11.32	48.04	0.70	III.	3	32.910	26 56.98	16.07	2.65	49 22.58	7 45.70
67	8	56.		30.7					51 48.13	48.05	0.67	III.	3	37.730	21 54.69	15.82	2.09	50 59.41	2 42.60
68	7	47.7	5.	23.					53 40.29	48.06	0.85	III.	2	17.040	43 33.94	15.53	4.53	52 51.38	24 24.00
69	4			57.	15.3	32.3			54 14.60	48.06	0.71	IV.	3	33.300	26 33.15	15.45	2.60	53 25.83	7 21.20
70	7		16.3	44.					56 1.40	48.07	0.73	III.	3	30.960	28 59.33	15.17	2.83	55 12.60	9 47.38
71	7		18.	35.7	54.	10.5			19 56 53.11	48.08	0.77	IV.	3	27.020	33 6.98	15.02	3.34	56 4.26	13 55.34
72	7	49.	6.	23.3					20 0 41.15	48.10	0.84	III.	2	18.390	42 9.40	14.45	4.35	19 59 52.21	22 58.23
73	7				57.5	14.			0 56.48	48.10	0.85	IV.	2	18.090	42 28.20	14.41	4.43	20 0 7.53	23 17.13
74	8							2.	1 9.55	48.11	0.72	VII.	3	32.000	27 54.83	14.38	2.76	0 20.72	8 41.97
75	8							34.	1 41.56	48.11	0.72	VII.	3	32.725	27 9.35	14.29	2.68	0 52.73	7 56.32
76	9		45.5		21.7				4 20.78	48.13	0.84	IV.	2	19.540	40 57.35	13.93	4.25	3 31.81	21 45.50
77	7.8	21.	38.	55.3	13.7				8 13.02	48.15	0.70	IV.	2	36.895	22 47.39	13.30	2.19	7 24.17	28 3 32.88
78	8		54.						11 28.89	48.17	0.58	II.	4	51.003	7 56.10	12.81	0.53	10 40.14	27 48 39.44
79	7		52.	9.7					12 26.91	48.17	0.58	III.	4	51.430	7 33.40	12.64	0.49	11 38.19	27 51 56.29
80	7.8	12.	29.5	47.3					14 4.55	48.18	0.78	III.	3	28.855	31 11.40	12.43	3.13	13 15.59	28 11 56.96
81	8		13.5						15 48.84	48.20	0.93	II.	2	12.690	48 10.48	12.17	5.09	14 59.71	28 57.74
82	8				59.				16 57.96	48.20	0.94	IV.	2	12.890	47 54.53	11.99	5.05	16 8.82	26 28 41.57
83	7						43.		19 8.27	48.22	0.58	VI.	4	53.435	5 27.36	11.66	0.25	19 19.47	27 46 9.27
84	7				23.		57.		21 22.40	48.23	0.60	IV.	4	51.210	7 45.31	11.31	0.51	20 33.66	27 48 27.16
85	7			50.	8.				23 7.31	48.24	0.84	IV.	3	26.055	34 7.58	11.09	3.46	22 18.23	28 14 52.13
86	6.7					45.3			23 27.64	48.24	1.01	V.	1	7.360	53 40.91	11.04	5.73	22 38.30	28 34 27.68
87	6						5.		26 30.29	48.26	0.57	VI.	4	55.100	3 42.85	10.60	0.07	25 41.46	27 44 23.52
88	8.9							5.	27 12.78	48.27	0.65	VII.	2	47.853	11 14.89	10.50	0.90	26 23.86	27 51 56.29
89	8.9			31.					29 48.40	48.28	0.89	III.	2	21.820	38 33.59	10.13	3.97	28 59.23	28 19 17.99
90	6.7	49.3	5.7	23.5					31 40.80	48.30	0.86	III.	3	26.443	33 42.95	9.86	3.42	30 51.64	14 26.26
91	6			4.	22.	39.			32 21.41	48.30	0.79	IV.	3	33.745	26 5.05	9.78	2.55	31 32.32	47.38
92	6				19.	35.5			33 17.68	48.31	1.00	IV.	1	10.233	50 40.30	9.64	5.38	32 28.57	28 31 25.32
93	7.8							32.	33 39.87	48.31	0.60	VII.	4	54.804	4 0.91	9.59	0.10	32 50.96	27 44 40.60
94	7				41.5				35 40.50	48.32	0.97	IV.	2	14.450	46 14.93	9.31	4.85	34 51.21	28 26 59.07
95	7					42.			36 24.53	48.33	0.75	V.	4	41.673	17 45.05	9.20	1.62	35 35.45	27 58 25.87
96	5.6					19.	36.		37 1.43	48.33	0.62	V.	4	52.375	6 34.07	9.12	0.37	36 12.48	47 13.58
97	7			11.	28.5				38 28.29	48.31	0.63	IV.	4	53.013	5 54.01	8.91	−0.30	37 39.31	46 33.22
98	6						8.3		20 38 33.60	−48.31	−0.61	VI.	4	55.800	−2 58.84	−8.90	+0.02	20 37 44.65	−27 43 37.72

CORRECTIONS.

Date.	Corr. of Clock.	Hourly rate.	m	n	c	Zenith Point.	Mic. Co.
1847.	h.	s.	s.	s.	s.	s.	° ' ''	r.

REMARKS.

(128) 83. Minutes of transit assumed as 20 instead of 19.

INSTRUMENT READINGS.

Date.		CIRCLE.						Barom.	THERMOM.				
	A.	B.	C.	D.	E.	F.	Mean.		At.	Ex.	U.	L.	I.
1847. h. m.	° ' ''						'	in.	°	°	°	°	°

ZONE 128. AUGUST 26. P. $D_o = -27°\,40'\,30''$—Continued.

No.	Mag.	I.	II.	III.	IV.	V.	VI.	VII.	T.	a_1	a_2	MICROMETER.		r	i	d_1	d_2	Mean Right Ascension, 1850.0	Mean Declination 1850.0
									h. m. s.	s.	s.			r.	′ ″	″	″	h. m. s.	° ′ ″
99	7						14.3		20 30 39.27	−48.35	−0.90	VI.	3	23.137	−37 11.07	−5.75	−3.82	20 30 50.02	−28 17 53.64
100	7			37.	55.				41 54.46	48.36	0.72	IV.	4	44.783	14 30.06	8.44	1.27	41 5.38	27 55 9.77
101	9						30.7		41 55.85	48.36	0.75	VI.	4	40.903	18 33.03	8.44	1.71	41 6.74	59 13.18
102	6				24.	41.3			43 23.81	48.37	0.65	IV.	4	51.580	7 23.94	8.24	0.47	42 34.79	27 48 2.65
103	6							16.	43 23.21	48.37	1.04	VII.	1	8.513	52 28.53	8.24	5.59	42 33.80	28 33 12.36
104	6	3.3		36.3					45 55.79	48.38	1.02	III.	2	12.225	48 36.14	7.00	5.14	45 6.39	29 19.18
105	8			7.5	26.				46 24.94	48.39	1.02	IV.	2	11.777	49 4.39	7.84	5.19	45 35.53	29 47.42
106	8	38.5		13.3					49 30.81	48.41	0.94	III.	2	21.990	38 23.28	7.42	3.95	48 41.36	28 19 4.65
107	7.8	19.	36.		11.7				52 11.13	48.43	0.74	IV.	4	44.693	14 35.77	7.07	1.28	51 21.96	27 55 14.12
108	7.8				13.7				53 12.87	48.43	0.94	IV.	3	23.560	36 44.21	6.94	3.76	52 23.50	28 17 24.91
109	7						59.3		53 24.22	48.43	0.99	VI.	2	17.997	42 34.00	6.91	4.13	52 34.80	23 15.34
110	6			45.	3.	20.			55 2.32	48.44	0.95	IV.	2	21.990	38 23.47	6.71	3.95	54 12.03	19 4.13
111	7					31.			56 13.49	48.45	0.85	V.	3	33.153	26 42.51	6.56	2.63	55 24.19	7 21.70
112	7.8	52.3	9.7	27.5					58 44.82	48.47	0.93	III.	3	25.263	34 57.03	6.24	3.56	57 55.42	28 15 36.83
113	6.7					35.	52.3		20 59 17.53	48.47	0.75	V.	4	46.483	12 43.56	6.16	1.05	20 58 28.31	27 53 20.77
114	7		37.	55.	13.5				21 4 12.41	48.50	1.10	IV.	1	10.615	50 16.27	5.56	5.36	21 3 22.81	28 30 57.19
115	5.6			55.3	13.3	30.			5 12.56	48.51	0.94	IV.	3	27.115	33 1.07	5.44	3.35	4 23.11	28 13 39.86
116	7.8	52.5		27.5					9 44.69	48.54	0.75	III.	4	48.600	10 30.81	4.88	0.79	8 55.40	27 51 6.48
117	6 7	59.	16.	33.7					11 51.00	48.55	0.76	III.	4	49.340	9 44.46	4.64	0.70	11 1.69	50 19.80
118	7					18.3	36.		12 1.01	48.55	0.80	V.	4	43.933	15 23.24	4.62	1.33	11 11.66	27 55 59.19
119	7					25.			13 7.41	48.56	1.03	V.	2	19.323	41 11.03	4.50	4.29	12 17.82	28 21 49.82
120	6.7	41.	58.	16.	34.3				19 33.37	48.60	1.05	IV.	2	18.730	41 48.06	3.76	4.37	18 43.72	22 26.19
121	7.8			32.					20 49.42	48.61	1.06	III.	2	17.950	42 36.76	3.63	4.45	19 59.75	28 23 14.84
122	7					27.5			21 10.04	48.61	0.83	V.	4	43.863	15 27.63	3.58	1.34	20 20.60	27 56 2.55
123	7.8							27.	21 34.83	48.61	0.75	VII.	4	51.980	6 58.04	3.55	0.30	20 45.47	47 31.98
124	7						39.		23 4.26	48.62	0.76	VI.	4	51.850	7 7.77	3.34	0.41	22 14.88	27 47 41.56
125	7		56.	14.					25 31.42	48.64	1.15	III.	1	8.623	52 20.99	3.12	5.62	24 41.63	28 32 59.73
126	7				13.				26 11.86	48.64	1.16	IV.	1	7.960	53 2.86	3.05	5.67	25 22.06	33 41.60
127	7.8					26.			27 8.44	48.65	1.05	V.	3	24.300	35 58.09	2.95	3.69	26 18.74	16 34.73
128	7.8			10.					29 27.40	48.66	1.10	III.	3	23.173	37 8.12	2.69	3.83	28 37.64	28 17 44.64
129	6		37.	54.5	12.	29.5			31 11.85	48.67	0.93	IV.	4	41.143	17 59.79	2.52	1.63	30 22.85	27 58 33.94
130	6	18.5	36.	54.					34 11.20	48.69	1.15	III.	2	19.970	41 20.3	2.23	4.31	33 31.36	28 21 56.93
131	7.8					36.			34 18.48	48.69	1.04	V.	3	31.560	28 22.50	2.22	2.81	33 28.75	8 57.53
132	6	57.3		32.2	51.			42.3	39 40.75	48.73	1.23	IV.	2	14.820	45 53.39	1.68	4.83	38 59.79	26 29.90
133	6.7		28.5	45.3	4.2	21.			42 5.33	48.74	1.05	IV.	3	34.420	25 22.88	1.48	2.47	41 13.54	5 56.83
134	7					3.			42 45.51	48.75	1.03	V.	3	38.370	21 15.36	1.41	1.96	41 55.73	1 48.73
135	7				43.				43 42.39	48.75	1.05	IV.	3	34.480	25 19.06	1.33	2.46	42 52.59	5 52.85
136	7			23.		15.5			21 44 40.48	−48.76	−1.02	IV.	3	39.160	−20 25.50	−1.21	−1.00	21 43 50.70	−28 0 58.61

CORRECTIONS.

Date.	Corr. of Clock.	Hourly rate.	m	n	c	Zenith Point.	Mic. Co.
1847.	h.	s.	s.	s.	s.	° ′ ″	r.

REMARKS.

(128) 136. Transit over T. VI assumed to have been recorded as over T. V.

INSTRUMENT READINGS.

Date.	CIRCLE.							Barom.	THERMOM.				
	A.	B.	C.	D.	E.	F.	Mean.		At.	Ex.	U.	L.	I.
1847. h. m.	° ′ ″						″	in.					

Zone 129. August 30. C. $D_0 = -25^\circ\,47'\,40''.$

SECONDS OF TRANSIT.

No.	Mag.	I.	II.	III.	IV.	V.	VI.	VII.
1	9				2.	18.6	35.6	
2	9			10.	27.6	44.2		
3	9					33.5	50.4	
4	8			38.6	56.2	12.6	30.0	
5	8		57.	14.3	32.2	48.4	5.5	
6	9.10				40.3			
7	8.9		8.7		43.5	0.3	17.4	
8	9.10		51.1		26.0			
9	9.10			2.	19.5	36.		
10	9.10					14.2		
11	9					24.5		
12	9					12.5		
13	8.9						56.8	13.6
14	8					39.7	56.1	13.3
15	9					39.5	57.	
16	9			10.7	28.5	44.5		
17	9.10	57.	14.	32.				
18	5			12.2	30.7	47.	3.8	
19	8				58.7	14.7	31.7	49.
20	6			22.	40.5	56.6	13.8	
21	9			3.7	21.4	38.	55.2	
22	9		10.	27.7	45.5	1?		36.
23	9			5.		39.	56.5	
24	8				50.7	6.7	23.8	
25	9					4.	20.7	38.2
26	9.10		19.2		51.			45.3
27	9.10			8.7				
28	8		53.7	11.	29.5		3.1	
29	8.9		51.3	8.7	27.	43.5	0.7	
30	8		18.	35.		9.	26.	
31	9.10			13.7		5.		
32	9				38.2		12.2	
33	9					42.		
34	9			46.5	4.	21.	38.	
35	8				45.	1.5		35.7
36	6	25.7	42.9	0.7	18.7	35.	52.	9.
37	9	54.2	11.	28.7	46.2			
38	9.10					18.7	35.	
39	9.10					39.2	56.5	
40	6.7	22.5	39.	56.2	14.6	31.	48.2	
41	9.10				38.7			29.6
42	7			51.2	9.	26.	43.5	
43	9	31.	47.5	5.	22.8			
44	9				4.2	21.	38.	
45	8.9			38.7	56.	12.6	30.	
46	9	32.5				40.7	57.5	
47	7.8						40.	

No.	T. (h m s)	a_1	a_2	MICROMETER.	r	i	d_1	d_2	Mean Right Ascension, 1850.0. (h m s)	Mean Declination, 1850.0.
1	19 19 1.34	−50.56	−0.28	IV. 3	34.046	−25 46.16	−24.68	−2.60	19 18 10.50	−26 13 55.44
2	20 27.02	50.57	0.27	IV. 3	35.928	23 48.04	24.46	2.40	19 36.18	11 54.90
3	21 16.22	50.57	0.23	V. 4	41.274	18 10.26	24.34	1.85	20 25.42	6 16.45
4	22 55.66	50.58	0.22	IV. 4	44.762	14 31.38	24.10	1.49	22 4.86	2 36.97
5	24 31.33	50.59	0.34	IV. 3	27.682	32 25.44	23.86	3.24	23 40.40	20 32.54
6	25 39.93	50.60	0.21	IV. 4	46.089	13 8.27	23.69	1.36	24 49.12	1 13.32
7	27 43.06	50.61	0.29	IV. 3	34.395	25 24.46	23.38	2.56	26 52.16	13 30.40
8	29 25.63	50.62	0.21	IV. 4	46.291	12 55.67	23.13	1.34	28 34.80	1 0.14
9	34 18.99	50.65	0.21	IV. 4	45.495	13 45.59	22.37	1.42	33 28.13	26 1 49.38
10	34 40.05	50.65	0.15	VI. 4	54.010	4 51.19	22.31	0.57	33 49.25	25 52 54.07
11	37 7.34	50.66	0.22	V. 4	45.056	14 12.93	21.93	1.47	36 16.46	26 2 16.33
12	37 55.26	50.67	0.32	V. 3	31.382	28 33.73	21.81	2.86	37 4.27	16 38.40
13	38 22.10	50.67	0.46	VI. 2	11.188	49 41.56	21.72	4.95	37 30.97	26 37 48.23
14	39 22.13	50.68	0.21	V. 4	47.784	11 21.73	21.58	1.19	38 31.24	25 59 24.50
15	42 22.31	50.70	0.43	V. 2	16.166	44 29.11	21.10	4.43	41 31.21	26 32 34.64
16	44 27.51	50.71	0.43	IV. 2	15.303	45 23.32	20.76	4.52	43 36.37	33 28.60
17	46 48.73	50.72	0.36	III. 3	25.256	34 57.41	20.39	3.49	45 57.65	23 1.29
18	47 29.45	50.73	0.49	IV. 2	7.525	53 31.50	20.27	5.32	46 38.23	41 37.09
19	48 57.33	50.73	0.47	V. 2	12.044	48 47.76	20.03	4.87	48 6.13	36 52.66
20	50 39.28	50.74	0.46	IV. 3	13.012	47 46.06	19.77	4.77	49 48.08	35 50.60
21	52 20.85	50.76	0.27	IV. 2	40.092	19 27.85	19.50	1.98	51 29.82	7 29.33
22	54 44.59	50.77	0.40	IV. 3	21.169	39 14.25	19.12	3.91	53 53.42	27 17.28
23	19 56 22.05	50.79	0.22	IV. 4	47.126	12 3.11	18.55	1.26	57 31.04	0 2.92
24	20 0 49.40	50.81	0.48	IV. 2	9.787	51 9.30	18.16	5.09	19 59 58.11	39 12.55
25	1 40.56	50.81	0.34	V. 3	29.497	30 31.93	18.01	3.05	20 0 55.41	18 32.99
26	4 53.72	50.83	0.42	IV. 2	18.666	41 52.09	17.55	4.18	4 2.47	29 53.82
27	8 25.79	50.85	0.38	III. 3	26.142	34 1.75	17.02	3.40	7 34.56	22 2.17
28	12 28.40	50.88	0.48	IV. 2	11.850	18 59.81	16.42	4.89	11 37.04	37 1.12
29	16 26.10	50.90	0.36	IV. 3	29.255	30 46.86	15.85	3.09	15 34.84	18 45.80
30	19 52.00	50.92	0.27	IV. 4	41.524	17 54.65	15.34	1.83	19 0.81	5 51.82
31	19 30.74	50.92	0.26	IV. 4	43.349	16 0.25	15.39	1.65	18 39.56	3 57.29
32	21 37.90	50.94	0.24	IV. 4	45.712	13 31.85	15.07	1.40	20 46.72	1 28.32
33	24 24.74	50.95	0.38	V. 3	27.234	32 53.91	14.67	3.29	23 33.41	20 51.87
34	27 3.71	50.97	0.24	IV. 4	47.540	11 37.34	14.29	1.22	26 12.50	59 32.85
35	28 44.32	50.98	0.30	IV. 3	38.442	21 10.58	14.04	2.15	27 53.04	9 6.77
36	33 17.55	51.01	0.45	IV. 2	16.938	47 40.46	13.38	4.36	32 26.09	31 38.20
37	35 45.62	51.02	0.39	IV. 3	26.436	33 43.80	13.03	3.37	34 54.21	21 40.20
38	35 43.96	51.02	0.30	VI. 4	38.379	21 11.65	13.03	2.15	34 52.64	9 6.83
39	37 21.96	51.03	0.44	V. 3	16.866	41 38.84	12.79	4.16	36 30.49	29 35.79
40	41 13.71	51.06	0.37	IV. 3	28.163	31 55.38	12.24	3.19	40 22.28	19 50.81
41	41 37.95	51.06	0.38	IV. 3	26.602	33 33.27	12.18	3.35	40 46.51	21 28.60
42	43 8.69	51.07	0.31	IV. 4	39.130	20 24.74	11.97	2.08	42 17.31	8 18.79
43	46 22.15	51.09	0.31	IV. 3	39.113	20 25.80	11.51	2.08	45 30.75	26 8 19.39
44	51 3.86	51.12	0.23	IV. 4	50.041	9 0.38	10.85	0.97	50 12.51	25 56 52.20
45	20 58 55.58	51.17	0.33	IV. 3	37.894	21 44.72	9.76	2.20	20 59 4.08	26 9 36.68
46	21 6 23.54	51.21	0.23	IV. 4	52.211	6 44.42	8.77	0.75	21 5 32.10	25 54 33.94
47	21 6 48.22	−51.21	−0.49	VII. 2	16.779	−43 50.25	−8.72	−4.37	21 5 56.52	−26 31 43.34

CORRECTIONS.

Date.	Corr. of Clock.	Hourly rate.	m	n	c	Zenith Point.	Mic. Co.
1847.	h.	s.	s.	s.	s.	° ′ ″	r.

REMARKS.

(129) 28. Transit over T. VI assumed to have been at 3ˢ.1, not 31ˢ.

August 30, 21ʰ 0ᵐ. Became very hazy.

INSTRUMENT READINGS.

Date.	CIRCLE.							Barom.	THERMOM.				
		A.	B.	C.	D.	E.	F.	Mean		At.	Ex.	U.	L.	I.
Zone 129	1847. Aug. 30, 19 20	65 9 61.3	55.3	55.1	44.2	45.4	62.1	53.90ᵃ	in. 30.156	75.0	72.4	75.5	73.8	73.0
	19 39											71.2		
	20 0								30.154	75.0	71.0			
	20 20	61.9	54.9	56.1	43.9	46.2	61.1	54.02	30.144			70.3	73.5	73.0
	20 41									72.8	70.0			
	21 0	61.4	55.0	56.0	43.9	46.2	61.2	53.95	30.142	73.5	69.9	73.0	72.8	

ᵃ Corr. for runs +0″.01.

ZONE 130. SEPTEMBER 6. C. $D_o = -28°\,18'\,0''$.

No.	Mag.	Seconds of Transit (I. II. III. IV. V. VI. VII.)	T. (h. m. s.)	a_1 (s.)	a_2 (s.)	Micrometer		(r.)	i	d_1	d_2	Mean R.A. 1850.0 (h. m. s.)	Mean Decl. 1850.0 (° ' ")
1	9	...12.7...47.7 42	19 2 29.78	+26.37	+1.34	IV.	4	54.121	−4 44.24	−19.54	−1.91	19 2 57.49	−28 23 5.69
2	9.10	34.	5 9.13	26.35	1.26	II.	4	48.972	10 7.16	19.11	2.53	5 30.74	28 28.80
3	8	20.3 38. 56.3 13.4	6 55.60	26.34	0.84	IV.	3	23.182	37 7.93	18.82	5.68	7 22.78	55 32.43
4	9	2. 19. 36.3	9 1.48	26.32	1.22	IV.	4	47.736	11 24.93	18.47	2.67	9 29.02	29 46.07
5	9	31.	9 38.19	26.32	0.93	VII.	3	29.139	30 54.40	18.37	4.95	10 5.44	49 17.72
6	9	12. .. 15. 30.7	13 47.38	26.29	0.79	IV.	2	21.669	38 43.63	17.66	5.86	14 14.46	57 7.17
7	9	37.7 .. 13.	13 55.26	26.29	0.79	IV.	2	21.151	39 16.19	17.64	5.93	14 22.34	57 39.76
8	9	59.8	14 6.86	26.29	0.76	VII.	2	19.674	40 48.57	17.63	6.10	14 33.01	59 12.30
9	8.9	33.7	14 40.83	26.29	0.84	VII.	2	24.675	35 34.74	17.53	5.48	15 7.96	53 57.75
10	9.10 15.1 31.3 50. 8.5		18 7.66	26.26	0.83	IV.	2	24.708	35 32.92	16.06	5.48	18 34.75	53 55.36
11	9.10	46. 3.5	18 28.35	26.26	0.91	V.	3	30.236	29 45.57	16.89	4.60	18 55.52	48 7.26
12	9	46.6 5. 22.7	21 22.16	26.24	1.13	IV.	4	44.354	14 57.22	16.41	3.08	21 49.53	33 16.71
13	8	57. 14.7 31.7	22 14.30	26.24	1.16	IV.	4	46.182	13 2.44	16.27	2.86	22 41.70	31 21.57
14	9	58.5 17.	22 23.86	26.23	1.01	VI.	3	36.932	22 45.44	16.24	3.98	22 51.10	41 5.66
15	9	19. 26.8 44.2	24 51.44	26.22	0.85	V.	3	27.458	32 39.86	15.83	5.15	25 18.51	28 51 0.84
16	9	23.	26 5.29	26.21	0.68	V.	2	17.465	43 7.64	15.62	6.39	26 32.18	29 1 29.65
17	8.9	48.7 6.2	26 13.33	26.21	0.71	VI.	2	19.331	41 10.47	15.60	6.14	26 40.25	28 59 32.21
18	8.9	11.5 28.5	26 35.88	26.21	0.71	VI.	2	18.896	41 37.52	15.53	6.22	27 2.80	59 59.27
19	7.8	8.2 24.5 42.	29 6.97	26.21	0.74	IV.	3	22.241	38 6.97	15.10	5.80	29 33.92	28 56 27.87
20	9.10	58.7	31 57.73	26.17	0.67	IV.	2	17.340	43 15.49	14.64	6.40	32 24.57	29 1 36.53
21	9.10	14.2 32.7	33 14.14	26.16	0.69	IV.	2	19.163	41 20.96	14.43	6.18	33 40.99	28 59 41.57
22	9	2. 19. 37.2 55.5	35 54.63	26.14	0.73	IV.	3	22.539	37 48.28	13.98	5.76	36 21.50	56 6.02
23	7	26.3 44. 2.5 19.5 36.4	38 1.59	26.13	0.79	IV.	3	27.161	32 58.26	13.63	5.18	38 28.51	28 51 17.07
24	8.9	0.5	38 42.77	26.12	0.60	V.	2	15.366	45 19.38	13.52	6.64	39 9.49	29 3 39.54
25	7	40.5 58. 15.7	39 22.66	26.12	0.52	V.	2	10.079	50 51.10	13.37	7.31	39 49.30	29 9 11.78
26	8.9	23. 40.5 57.7	41 40.10	26.10	0.80	IV.	3	28.253	31 49.73	13.03	5.05	42 7.00	28 50 7.81
27	8.9	13. 30. 47.2	42 12.18	26.10	0.77	IV.	3	25.975	34 12.66	12.94	5.32	42 39.05	52 30.92
28	8	57.	42 4.09	26.10	0.70	VII.	3	22.048	37 47.90	12.97	5.82	42 30.89	56 6.69
29	9	39.2 56.3	48 14.24	26.05	0.64	III.	2	19.424	41 4.50	11.96	6.13	48 40.93	28 59 22.59
30	8.9	46.2 22.2 39.3	49 4.06	26.05	0.50	IV.	2	15.842	44 49.25	11.82	6.58	49 30.70	29 3 7.65
31	7.8	16.3 34. 52.7 9.5	50 51.71	26.03	0.63	IV.	2	19.321	41 11.16	11.54	6.14	51 18.37	28 59 28.84
32	9	7. 24.7 59.5	52 24.47	26.02	1.16	IV.	4	52.748	6 10.56	11.30	2.07	52 51.65	24 23.93
33	9	1.2 18.5	52 26.00	26.02	0.98	VI.	3	41.095	18 24.38	11.30	3.47	52 53.00	36 39.15
34	9.10	27.	53 26.82	26.01	1.13	VI.	4	51.131	7 51.72	11.07	2.27	54 53.96	26 5.06
35	8	58. 14.7 32.7	56 57.30	25.99	0.78	IV.	3	30.535	29 26.56	10.58	4.76	19 57 24.07	47 41.90
36	8	1.3 19.3 37.6 12.	59 36.77	25.97	0.71	IV.	2	26.170	34 0.43	10.17	5.30	20 0 3.45	52 15.00
37	9	33.	19 59 40.54	25.97	1.15	VII.	4	53.792	5 4.36	10.16	1.95	0 7.66	28 23 16.47
38	8	27.2 46. 2.7 20.7	20 1 44.98	25.96	0.45	IV.	3	10.227	49 39.12	9.86	7.28	2 11.39	29 7 56.26
39	9	10.3 28.3 16.3 4.	5 45.82	25.93	0.65	IV.	3	22.714	37 37.16	9.28	5.74	6 12.40	28 55 52.18
40	9	45.3	6 10.21	25.92	0.90	VI.	4	38.274	21 18.18	9.21	3.82	6 37.03	39 31.21
41	9	2. 19.3	8 19.13	25.91	0.96	IV.	4	42.126	17 16.70	8.90	3.35	8 46.00	35 28.95
42	9	13.7 32. 48.5 6.	14 31.01	25.86	0.70	IV.	3	26.591	33 33.95	8.03	5.25	14 57.57	28 51 47.23
43	6	31. 49.7 6.6 24.1 41.8	15 48.69	25.85	0.44	IV.	2	10.446	50 26.19	7.86	7.26	16 14.98	29 8 43.31
44	8.9	44.1 2. 20. 37. 54.4	18 19.38	25.83	0.31	IV.	3	33.030	26 49.91	7.51	4.46	18 46.02	28 45 1.88
45	8.9	54.2 12. 29.	22 11.54	25.81	0.97	IV.	4	43.149	16 12.67	6.98	3.23	22 38.32	28 34 22.88
46	8.9	7. 41.5	23 6.06	25.80	0.49	IV.	2	13.135	47 39.20	6.86	6.91	23 32.35	29 5 53.06
47	10	1.3 55.	25 19.25	25.78	0.48	IV.	2	12.908	47 53.40	6.56	6.93	25 45.51	29 6 6.89
48	8	12.2 30.2 47. 4.7 21.7	29 29.32	25.76	0.62	IV.	3	21.754	38 37.40	5.65	5.85	29 55.09	28 56 49.24
49	7.8	2. 20.7 36.8 54.6	20 31 19.39	+25.74	+0.50	IV.	2	14.417	−46 18.93	−5.75	−6.76	20 31 45.63	−29 4 31.44

CORRECTIONS.

Date.	Corr. of Clock. (h. s.)	Hourly rate. (s.)	m (s.)	n (s.)	c (s.)	Zenith Point. (° ' ")	Mic. Co. (r.)
1847.							

INSTRUMENT READINGS.

Date.		Circle.							Barom. (In.)	Thermom.				
	(h. m.)	A.	B.	C.	D.	E.	F.	Mean.		At.	Ex.	U.	L.	I.
Zone 130 Sept. 6,	19 0	67 39 61.7	56.5	59.9	44.4	45.6	62.1	55.03*	30.130	77.0	70.0	74.5	..	79.5
	19 29										68.4			
	19 45								30.142	76.0	68.1			
	20 0	61.2	55.8	59.5	44.9	45.1	62.5	54.83			68.5	73.0	75.5	
	20 22								30.152	75.0	67.5			
	20 45										66.5			
	21 0	60.9	56.4	59.1	45.8	44.9	62.6	54.95	30.148	74.0	65.6	71.0	75.0	
	21 7										65.4			

REMARKS.

(130) 6. Transit observations very discordant; that of T. V assumed as 5s instead of 15s.

(130) 10. Transit over T. II rejected.

(130) 15. Time of transit over T. V assumed as 9s instead of 19s.

(130) 21. Right ascension 8s smaller than by Mural Circle, 1846, August 18, and Arg. Z. 235, 49.

(130) 28. Micrometer reading assumed as 22r.548 instead of 22r.048.

(130) 34. Transit over T. IV assumed as recorded over T. VI, and minutes at 54, not 53, to agree with Transit Z., 1847, September 4; Arg. Z. 394, 67, 8.

(130) 38. Micrometer reading assumed as 11r.227 instead of 10r.227.

* Corr. for runs, +0".01.

ZONE 130. SEPTEMBER 6. C. $D_o = -28° 18' 0''$—Continued.

Seconds of transit and time:

No.	Mag.	I	II	III	IV	V	VI	VII	T. (h. m. s.)	a_1 (s.)	a_2 (s.)
50	8						37.	54.5	20 32 1.96	+25.73	+1.01
51	9		49.7	7.	25.	42.			34 24.60	25.71	1.07
52	7.8				4.3	21.4	39.		35 3.78	25.71	0.80
53	9.10			27.		2.7	20.		36 44.75	25.70	0.59
54	9.10				9.7		45.		39 9.58	25.68	0.90
55	9			43.2	59.		33.2	51.2	40 58.99	25.67	0.96
56	9		35.2			39.			41 10.92	25.67	0.96
57	8							0.5	42 7.91	25.66	0.93
58	9					9.6			43 52.03	25.64	0.92
59	8				40.	57.1	14.7		44 39.65	25.64	1.02
60	7.8					26.2	14.	1.7	45 8.95	25.63	1.03
61	9.10				54.		29.7		47 53.32	25.61	0.64
62	9						35.		50 59.77	25.59	0.65
63	9							25.7	51 32.90	25.58	0.74
64	8							0.7	52 8.24	25.58	1.11
65	7.8		0.	18.7	35.7	52.			20 59 35.18	25.52	0.49
66	8				7.	23.7	41.		21 1 5.86	25.51	0.46
67	8		21.6	38.8	57.	14.3	31.6		2 56.59	25.50	0.90
68	8.9		25.7		2.	18.7			21 7 1.11	+25.46	+0.65

Micrometer and places:

No.	Mic.		r	i (' '')	d_1 ('')	d_2 ('')	Mean Right Ascension, 1850.0 (h. m. s.)	Mean Declination, 1850.0 (° ' '')
50	VI.	4	46.006	-13 13.03	-5.66	-2.88	20 32 28.70	-26 31 21.57
51	IV.	4	50.176	8 51.98	5.35	2.38	34 51.38	26 59.71
52	IV.	3	33.558	26 16.91	5.27	4.39	35 30.29	44 26.57
53	IV.	2	19.756	40 43.60	5.06	6.09	37 11.04	58 54.75
54	IV.	3	40.580	18 56.43	4.73	3.53	39 36.16	37 4.69
55	IV.	4	47.746	15 35.10	4.51	3.15	41 25.62	33 42.76
56	IV.	4	44.646	13 35.86	4.51	2.91	41 37.55	31 43.28
57	VII.	4	44.304	14 59.60	4.37	3.08	42 34.53	33 7.05
58	V.	4	42.431	16 57.70	4.16	3.31	44 18.60	35 5.17
59	IV.	4	47.972	11 10.06	4.06	2.64	45 6.31	29 16.76
60	V.	4	47.545	11 36.90	4.01	2.70	45 35.61	29 43.61
61	IV.	3	23.660	36 37.87	3.67	5.62	48 19.57	54 47.16
62	VI.	3	24.329	35 56.33	3.29	5.52	51 26.01	54 5.14
63	VII.	3	29.592	30 25.97	3.23	4.87	51 59.22	48 34.07
64	VII.	4	53.722	5 8.80	3.16	1.96	20 52 34.93	28 23 13.92
65	IV.	2	14.408	46 19.50	2.28	6.76	21 0 1.18	29 4 28.54
66	IV.	2	13.129	47 39.66	2.12	6.01	1 31.83	29 5 48.69
67	IV.	4	46.412	12 48.13	1.91	2.83	3 23.08	28 30 52.87
68	IV.	3	24.864	-35 22.19	-1.44	-5.46	21 7 27.22	-28 53 29.09

ZONE 131. SEPTEMBER 14. P. $D_o = -29° 33' 0''$.

Seconds of transit and time:

No.	Mag.	I	II	III	IV	V	VI	VII	T. (h. m. s.)	a_1 (s.)	a_2 (s.)
1	8.9			53.					18 38 52.06	+19.15	+1.05
2	9					16.5			39 58.60	19.15	1.02
3	8			2.5					41 20.22	19.14	1.02
4	8					46.			41 28.06	19.14	1.06
5	9	49.	6.	24.5					44 42.24	19.11	1.07
6	7		41.	58.5	16.5				46 16.20	19.10	0.83
7	8.9						5.		46 29.51	19.10	0.92
8	8.9					13.			47 55.21	19.09	0.92
9	3.4	50.3	8.	26.	44.2	1.5		37.3	52 43.67	19.06	0.67
10	9					59.3			53 41.53	19.05	0.68
11	9					16.			54 58.19	19.04	0.94
12	8		26.3						57 2.17	19.03	1.00
13	8			2.					57 19.72	19.03	0.99
14	7				17.5				57 19.53	19.03	1.07
15	8.9			35.					57 50.30	19.02	1.02
16	8.9				23.				18 58 29.53	19.02	0.97
17	7		58.3	16.					19 0 33.98	19.00	1.02
18	8				51.				0 50.31	19.00	0.96
19	4.5				28.	46.			1 27.96	19.00	0.85
20	8			59.	17.				3 16.58	18.98	0.90
21	7	51.5	9.2	27.3	45.5	3.			4 44.90	18.97	0.96
22	7	55.5	13.	30.	49.2				11 48.42	18.92	0.89
23	7				14.	31.5			12 13.67	18.92	0.86
24	9		25.						12 59.51	18.91	0.89
25	6		41.3	59.	17.	34.5			15 16.75	18.90	0.79
26	6	14.	31.5	49.7	8.3	25.			19 17 7.34	+18.88	+0.94

Micrometer and places:

No.	Mic.		r	i (' '')	d_1 ('')	d_2 ('')	Mean Right Ascension, 1850.0 (h. m. s.)	Mean Declination, 1850.0 (° ' '')
1	IV.	2	19.370	-41 8.08	-43.15	-5.34	18 39 12.26	-30 14 56.57
2	V.	3	23.822	36 27.83	42.95	4.72	40 18.77	10 15.50
3	III.	3	22.820	37 30.08	42.72	4.86	41 40.38	11 17.66
4	V.	3	17.240	43 21.77	42.69	5.63	41 48.26	17 10.09
5	III.	3	14.505	46 13.16	42.17	6.01	45 2.42	30 20 1.29
6	IV.	4	52.880	6 2.29	41.84	0.79	46 36.22	29 39 44.92
7	VI.	4	40.670	18 47.71	41.81	2.42	46 49.53	52 31.94
8	IV.	4	39.645	19 52.31	41.56	2.53	48 15.22	29 53 36.40
9	IV.	3	28.510	31 33.61	40.72	4.07	53 3.70	30 5 18.40
10	V.	4	43.525	15 49.02	40.54	2.02	54 1.46	29 49 31.58
11	V.	4	36.910	22 46.69	40.32	2.91	55 18.17	29 56 29.92
12	II.	3	23.375	36 54.93	39.96	4.78	57 22.20	30 10 39.67
13	III.	3	23.813	36 27.77	39.91	4.72	57 39.74	10 12.40
14	V.	2	11.513	49 21.22	39.88	6.43	57 39.63	23 7.53
15	VI.	3	20.020	39 30.05	39.79	5.12	58 19.34	13 15.96
16	VII.	3	28.843	31 12.78	39.70	4.02	18 58 49.52	4 56.50
17	III.	3	19.807	40 40.21	39.35	5.20	19 0 54.00	30 2 48.22
18	IV.	3	30.873	29 5.17	39.30	3.75	1 10.27	30 2 48.22
19	IV.	4	48.372	10 45.22	39.18	1.36	1 47.81	29 44 25.76
20	IV.	4	40.200	19 17.68	38.97	2.47	3 36.46	29 52 59.12
21	IV.	4	28.853	31 11.90	38.63	4.04	5 4.87	30 4 54.57
22	IV.	4	40.323	19 10.04	37.41	2.46	12 8.93	29 52 49.91
23	IV.	4	44.990	14 17.14	37.34	1.83	12 33.45	47 56.31
24	VI.	4	41.020	18 25.76	37.20	2.36	13 19.31	52 5.32
25	IV.	4	56.750	1 59.64	36.62	0.25	15 36.44	29 35 36.71
26	IV.	3	31.552	-28 22.75	-36.51	-3.65	19 17 27.16	-30 2 2.91

CORRECTIONS.

Date.	Corr. of Clock.	Hourly rate.	m	n	c	Zenith Point.	Mic. Co.
	h.	s.	s.	s.	s.	' ''	r. ''
1847.	h.	s.	s.	s.	s.		30.052

REMARKS.

(130) 56. Transit over T. V assumed as 29', not 39', and micrometer reading as 45'.646.

(131) 14. Transit over T. V assumed as 37s.5, not 47s.5, to agree with Arg. Z. 221, 147, and Mural Z. June 17.

INSTRUMENT READINGS.

	Date.	CIRCLE. A.	B.	C.	D.	E.	F.	Mean.	Barom. (in.)	THERMOM. At.	Ex.	U.	L.	I.
Zone 131	1847, Sept. 14, 18 40	68 54 64.2	63.8	63.0	52.0	50.4	64.3	59.62	30.180	63.2	56.3	64.0	64.0	66.0
	20 30	.	.	.	.	.	.	.	30.204	61.0	54.0			
	20 59							.	30.212	61.0	53.0			
	22 2							.	30.230	61.0	52.0			
	22 59							.	30.236	60.0	50.0			
	23 58							.	30.244	59.0	48.8			59.0

ZONE 131. SEPTEMBER 14. P. $D_o = -29° 33' 0''$—Continued.

No.	Mag.	SECONDS OF TRANSIT. I.	II.	III.	IV.	V.	VI.	VII.	T. (h. m. s.)	a_1 (s.)	a_2 (s.)
27	7.8				4.				19 18 3.60	+18.88	+0.86
28	9						40.		18 4.50	18.88	0.89
29	8							28.	18 34.87	18.88	0.82
30	8						12.		19 36.43	18.87	0.93
31	8						49.		20 13.46	18.86	0.91
32	7					37.			21 19.24	18.85	0.85
33	9		32.			26.			30 7.99	18.79	1.01
34	8				27.	44.			31 26.19	18.78	0.95
35	8					27.			35 9.12	18.75	0.95
36	8				23.				38 22.56	18.72	0.86
37	9					34.			39 16.15	18.71	0.92
38	8		58.	16.					42 33.76	18.69	0.94
39	8					39.			45 21.24	18.67	0.84
40	8	0.5		36.5					51 54.06	18.61	0.97
41	8	42.		17.3					54 35.05	18.59	0.86
42	6.7		8.	26.3	44.5				57 43.85	18.57	0.94
43	9			50.5					59 8.26	18.56	1.00
44	8		37.		14.				60 13.04	18.55	0.91
45	8							45.5	19 59 52.16	18.55	0.87
46	8							30.	20 0 36.39	18.55	0.97
47	7							27.	2 33.60	18.53	0.89
48	5.6		35.3	53.7	13.	29.7			6 11.59	18.50	1.05
49	8		25.	42.5	1.				8 0.44	18.48	0.84
50	9		54.						9 29.86	18.47	0.94
51	7.6				48.		22.7		9 47.17	18.47	0.91
52	6.7						29.		10 53.04	18.46	0.76
53	7.8					41.			13 23.30	18.44	0.75
54	7		9.						15 45.07	18.42	1.05
55	8.9						52.5		15 16.92	18.42	0.89
56	7						35.5		15 59.98	18.42	0.85
57	7	40.	57.3	15.3	33.5		8.7		18 33.05	18.40	0.84
58	7.8		35.5	53.5	12.3				21 11.35	18.38	0.95
59	6						1.	18.5	21 25.56	18.37	0.75
60	7	25.	42.3	0.5	18.5				24 18.06	18.35	0.80
61	7		21.3	39.3	57.				30 56.82	18.29	0.77
62	6.7		12.5	30.3	48.7				33 48.10	18.27	0.86
63	8			54.					35 11.63	18.25	0.81
64	8	27.5		3.					37 20.66	18.24	0.83
65	6.7		39.	57.					42 14.71	18.20	0.86
66	6				31.5	40.			42 13.40	18.19	0.97
67	8	27.	45.	3.					45 20.54	18.17	0.85
68	7		15.	32.					46 50.05	18.16	0.72
69	8		5.5	23.5					50 41.24	18.12	0.88
70	7.6				41.	58.		33.	51 39.79	18.12	0.97
71	8							36.	51 42.31	18.12	0.97
72	7				36.	53.5			53 35.75	18.10	0.75
73	8			44.			9.		54 51.44	18.08	0.76
74	8	45.	2.	20.	39.				57 38.03	18.06	0.91
75	8	30.		6.					20 59 23.44	+18.04	+0.84

No.	MICROMETER. (Tel.)		r.	i (' '')	d_1 ('')	d_2 ('')	Mean Declination, 1850.0. (h. m. s.)	Mean Right Ascension, 1850.0. (° ' '')
27	IV.	4	45.240	−14 1.58	−36.35	−1.80	19 18 23.34	−29 47 39.73
28	VI.	4	39.870	19 37.82	36.35	2.52	18 24.27	52 16.69
29	VII.	4	51.480	7 29.52	36.27	0.95	18 54.57	29 41 6.74
30	VI.	3	32.980	26 53.34	36.08	3.45	19 56.23	30 0 32.87
31	VI.	3	35.510	24 14.76	35.99	3.11	20 33.23	29 57 53.86
32	V.	4	44.935	14 20.39	35.80	1.84	21 38.94	29 47 58.03
33	V.	2	18.783	41 44.73	34.34	5.43	30 27.79	30 15 24.50
34	IV.	3	28.790	31 15.85	34.13	4.03	31 45.92	4 54.01
35	V.	3	27.223	32 54.61	33.53	4.25	35 28.82	30 6 32.39
36	IV.	4	42.830	16 32.55	32.99	2.11	38 42.14	29 50 7.65
37	V.	3	31.425	28 31.03	32.84	3.67	39 35.78	30 2 7.54
38	III.	3	27.973	32 6.79	32.33	4.14	42 53.39	30 5 43.26
39	V.	4	45.625	13 37.25	31.89	1.75	45 40.75	29 47 10.89
40	III.	2	22.040	38 20.15	30.84	4.98	52 13.64	30 11 55.97
41	III.	4	40.273	19 13.12	30.42	2.46	54 54.50	29 52 46.00
42	IV.	3	24.940	35 17.42	29.94	4.57	58 3.36	30 8 51.93
43	III.	2	14.920	45 46.92	29.71	5.07	19 59 27.82	19 22.60
44	IV.	3	29.500	30 31.49	29.56	3.94	20 0 32.50	30 4 4.99
45	VII.	3	36.840	22 51.09	29.60	2.93	0 11.58	29 56 23.62
46	VII.	2	19.513	40 58.74	29.49	5.34	0 55.91	30 14 33.57
47	VII.	3	33.750	26 4.98	29.19	3.35	2 53.02	29 59 37.52
48	IV.	1	7.137	53 54.60	28.64	7.10	6 31.14	30 27 30.34
49	IV.	4	41.866	17 33.00	28.37	2.23	8 19.76	29 51 3.60
50	II.	3	24.120	36 8.07	28.14	4.70	9 49.27	30 9 40.91
51	IV.	3	28.417	31 39.50	28.10	4.09	10 6.55	30 5 11.69
52	VI.	4	52.590	6 20.23	27.93	0.78	11 12.86	29 30 48.94
53	V.	4	54.705	4 7.80	27.57	0.51	13 42.49	29 37 35.88
54	II.	1	6.650	54 24.29	27.23	7.17	16 4.54	30 27 58.69
55	VI.	3	31.900	28 1.05	27.29	3.60	15 36.23	30 1 31.94
56	VI.	3	37.905	21 44.34	27.19	2.73	16 19.25	29 55 14.26
57	IV.	4	40.730	18 44.33	26.82	2.39	18 52.29	29 52 13.54
58	IV.	3	22.590	37 45.08	26.43	4.91	21 30.68	30 11 16.42
59	VI.	4	55.635	3 9.31	26.40	0.39	21 44.68	29 36 36.10
60	IV.	4	44.820	14 27.74	25.99	1.65	24 37.21	47 55.58
61	IV.	4	49.070	10 1.33	25.05	1.27	31 15.88	43 27.65
62	IV.	3	36.263	23 27.28	24.66	3.00	34 7.23	56 54.94
63	III.	4	43.965	15 21.36	24.46	1.93	35 30.69	48 47.75
64	III.	4	39.350	20 11.01	24.17	2.56	37 39.73	53 37.74
65	III.	3	33.610	26 13.21	23.51	3.37	42 33.77	29 50 40.09
66	V.	2	14.023	46 43.54	23.47	6.13	42 32.56	30 20 13.14
67	III.	3	34.790	24 59.05	23.10	3.20	45 39.56	29 58 25.35
68	III.	4	53.940	4 55.76	22.90	0.59	47 8.03	29 38 19.25
69	III.	3	30.137	20 51.09	22.40	3.86	51 0.24	30 3 17.35
70	IV.	2	15.630	45 2.69	22.27	5.75	51 58.88	18 30.71
71	VII.	2	14.390	46 20.32	22.27	6.09	52 1.40	30 19 48.68
72	IV.	4	50.590	8 26.02	22.03	1.00	53 54.60	29 41 49.11
73	V.	4	48.437	10 41.02	21.88	0.34	55 10.28	29 44 3.24
74	IV.	3	22.940	37 22.92	21.53	4.86	57 57.03	30 10 49.31
75	III.	3	35.593	−24 8.80	−21.30	−3.09	20 59 42.32	−29 57 33.19

CORRECTIONS.

Date.	Corr. of Clock.	Hourly rate.	m	u	c	Zenith Point.	Mic. Co.
1847.	h.	s.	s.	s.	s.	° ' ''	r.

REMARKS.

(131) 66. Transits over T.'s III and IV assumed as recorded over T.'s IV and V, to agree with Mural Z. June 17, and Arg. Z. 245, 15.

(131) 73. Transit over T. III assumed as 34ˢ instead of 44ˢ.

INSTRUMENT READINGS.

Date.	CIRCLE. A.	B.	C.	D.	E.	F.	Mean.	Barom.	THERMOM. At.	Ex.	U.	L.	I.
1847. h. m.	° ' ''						''	In.					

ZONE 131. SEPTEMBER 14. P. $D_0 = -29°\ 33'\ 0''$—Continued.

No.	Mag.	I.	II.	III.	IV.	V.	VI.	VII.	T. (h. m. s.)	a_1 (s.)	a_4 (s.)
76	6		10.	28.3	46.7		21.7		21 0 45.91	+18.03	+0.96
77	7					59.	16.		4 40.67	18.00	0.95
78	7						20.		10 44.45	17.95	0.84
79	6			17.5	35.5	53.			12 35.16	17.93	0.78
80	7				27.	44.5			13 26.46	17.92	0.87
81	8			43.5					15 1.13	17.91	0.78
82	8.9						46.5		15 11.05	17.91	0.77
83	7	38.3	56.	14.					17 31.47	17.89	0.72
84	8		4.	22.	40.3				24 39.69	17.82	0.69
85	6.7				44.	0.7			25 42.87	17.82	0.95
86	7	22.	39.3	57.7					29 15.40	17.78	0.95
87	8			31.	49.				39 48.49	17.69	0.86
88	7				41.				46 39.88	17.63	0.99
89	8					39.			47 21.14	17.62	0.85
90	8.9				50.				48 49.56	17.61	0.77
91	6.7		57.	15.3	33.3				50 32.82	17.60	0.75
92	8.9			6.5					51 6.22	17.59	0.72
93	8.9			4.					54 21.65	17.56	0.79
94	6.7					59.3	17.5		54 41.67	17.56	0.85
95	6.7	25.	42.3	0.3	18.			10.7	57 17.80	17.54	0.76
96	7							49.7	21 57 55.09	17.53	0.96
97	8				57.				22 2 56.04	17.49	0.92
98	8					31.3			4 13.37	17.48	0.93
99	8			24.3	42.3				5 41.75	17.46	0.88
100	8				18.5				7 17.47	17.45	0.94
101	8				21.3				8 3.44	17.44	0.85
102	8			14.5					11 13.98	17.42	0.79
103	7.8	0.		35.5					13 53.39	17.39	0.96
104	7		5.3	23.5	41.				17 23.07	17.36	0.79
105	8		28.3				21.5		20 45.93	17.33	0.79
106	8.9				41.				22 23.14	17.32	0.86
107	8			59.3	34.7				24 16.94	17.30	0.76
108	7					25.3			24 49.46	17.30	1.00
109	7	25.3	43.	1.3					29 0.81	17.26	0.78
110	7				26.				31 8.30	17.23	0.71
111	7							23.	31 29.52	17.23	0.87
112	6.7			25.	43.	0.3			33 42.44	17.22	0.89
113	8		52.	9.5					35 27.33	17.20	0.74
114	8	45.	2.5		38.7				40 39.18	17.16	0.83
115	7.8							33.	40 39.37	17.16	0.96
116	6			28.3	47.	3.7			42 45.92	17.14	0.96
117	7			50.	8.3	25.5			44 7.68	17.13	0.83
118	7.8							39.5	46 45.74	17.11	1.00
119	7			45.	4.	21.3			49 2.99	17.09	1.01
120	6	11.3	29.	47.2	5.7	22.7			51 4.83	17.07	0.95
121	6		13.5	31.3	54.?				52 48.89	17.06	0.73
122	8						31.3		52 55.78	17.06	0.83
123	5						30.7		22 59 55.35	16.99	0.73
124	8			42.					23 1 41.64	+16.98	+0.77

No.	MICROMETER		r.	i (′ ″)	d_1 (″)	d_2 (″)	Mean Right Ascension, 1850.0 (h. m. s.)	Mean Declination, 1850.0 (° ′ ″)
76	IV.	2	14.627	−46 5.64	−21.14	−6.04	21 1 4.90	−30 19 32.82
77	V.	2	17.437	43 9.40	20.67	5.65	4 59.62	30 16 35.72
78	VI.	3	34.443	25 21.75	19.95	3.25	11 3.24	29 58 44.95
79	IV.	4	44.755	14 31.81	19.74	1.84	12 53.87	29 47 53.39
80	IV.	3	29.240	30 47.81	19.64	3.98	13 45.25	30 4 11.43
81	III.	4	44.050	15 16.09	19.46	1.94	15 19.82	29 48 37.49
82	VI.	4	45.165	14 5.84	19.44	1.78	15 29.73	47 27.06
83	III.	4	52.983	5 55.83	19.17	0.70	17 50.08	29 39 15.70
84	IV.	3	25.865	34 19.38	18.39	4.45	24 58.40	30 7 42.22
85	IV.	2	14.670	48 8.36	18.28	6.27	26 1.64	21 32.91
86	III.	2	15.310	45 22.71	17.88	5.95	29 34.13	18 46.54
87	IV.	3	29.835	30 10.29	16.82	3.90	40 7.04	3 31.01
88	IV.	1	9.915	51 0.07	16.17	6.72	46 58.50	24 22.96
89	V.	3	29.995	30 0.56	16.11	3.87	47 39.61	30 3 20.54
90	IV.	4	43.340	16 0.82	15.96	2.02	49 7.94	29 49 18.80
91	IV.	4	46.340	12 52.66	15.81	0.62	50 51.17	46 9.09
92	III.	4	51.200	7 47.82	15.73	0.95	51 24.53	41 4.50
93	III.	4	40.255	19 14.24	15.47	2.45	54 40.00	29 52 32.16
94	V.	3	29.290	30 44.98	15.44	3.97	55 0.08	30 4 4.39
95	IV.	4	44.740	14 32.76	15.21	1.84	57 36.10	29 47 49.81
96	VII.	2	13.410	47 21.85	15.15	6.23	21 58 14.48	30 20 43.21
97	IV.	2	18.050	48 30.74	14.74	5.59	22 3 14.45	15 51.07
98	V.	2	17.384	43 12.73	14.63	5.68	4 31.78	16 33.04
99	IV.	3	25.150	35 4.38	14.52	4.55	6 0.09	8 23.45
100	IV.	2	14.590	46 8.02	14.39	6.07	7 35.86	19 28.48
101	V.	3	29.450	30 34.88	14.33	3.95	8 21.73	30 3 53.16
102	IV.	3	39.000	20 35.40	14.08	2.61	11 32.19	29 53 52.09
103	III.	2	11.995	48 50.58	13.90	6.45	14 11.74	30 22 10.93
104	IV.	4	42.193	17 12.68	13.64	2.16	17 41.22	29 50 28.48
105	IV.	4	42.010	17 24.04	13.40	2.19	21 4.10	29 50 39.63
106	V.	3	29.950	30 3.32	13.30	3.87	22 41.32	30 3 20.49
107	V.	4	47.313	11 51.51	13.17	1.46	24 35.00	29 45 6.14
108	VI.	1	8.170	52 50.06	13.14	7.04	25 7.76	30 26 10.24
109	IV.	4	43.360	15 59.56	12.86	2.00	29 18.85	29 49 14.42
110	IV.	4	54.520	4 19.52	12.74	0.48	31 26.24	29 37 32.74
111	VII.	3	28.020	32 4.54	12.72	4.15	31 47.62	30 5 21.41
112	IV.	3	24.990	35 14.34	12.59	4.57	34 0.55	30 8 31.50
113	III.	4	49.510	9 33.74	12.49	1.17	35 45.27	29 42 47.40
114	IV.	3	34.380	25 25.40	12.20	3.26	40 56.17	29 58 40.66
115	VII.	2	14.040	46 42.10	12.20	6.15	40 57.42	30 20 0.45
116	IV.	2	14.305	46 25.97	12.11	6.13	43 4.02	30 19 44.21
117	IV.	3	34.500	25 17.80	12.03	3.24	44 25.64	29 58 33.07
118	VII.	1	9.645	51 17.34	11.91	6.78	47 3.85	30 24 36.03
119	IV.	1	9.317	51 37.87	11.79	6.83	49 21.09	24 56.49
120	IV.	2	17.970	42 35.76	11.71	5.59	51 22.85	30 15 53.06
121	IV.	4	52.710	6 13.01	11.65	0.72	53 6.68	29 39 25.38
122	VI.	3	37.530	22 8.06	11.64	2.82	22 53 13.67	55 22.52
123	VI.	4	54.140	4 43.04	11.39	0.53	23 0 13.07	37 54.96
124	IV.	4	47.015	−12 10.14	−11.33	−1.49	23 1 59.39	−29 45 22.96

CORRECTIONS.

Date.	Corr. of Clock.	Hourly rate.	m	n	c	Zenith Point.	Mic. Co.
			s.	s.	s.	° ′ ″	r.
1847.	h.	s.	s.	s.	s.		

INSTRUMENT READINGS.

Date.	CIRCLE.							Barom.	THERMOM.				
	A.	B.	C.	D.	E.	F.	Mean.		At.	Ex.	U.	L.	I.
1847.	h. m.	° ′ ″					″	in.	°				

REMARKS.

(131) 85. Micrometer reading assumed as 12ʳ.670, not 14ʳ.670, to agree with Arg. Z. 228, 19; 245, 52; and Mural Z., 1846, September 23.

(131) 92. Transit over T. IV assumed as recorded over T. III.

(131) 100. Transit over T. V. probably recorded over T. IV, to agree with Transit Z., 1846, September 23.

(131) 121. The time of transit over T. IV is assumed as 49ˢ instead of 54ˢ.

ZONE 131. SEPTEMBER 14. P. $D_0 = -29°\ 33'\ 0''$ —Continued.

No.	Mag.	I.	II.	III.	IV.	V.	VI.	VII.	T. (h. m. s.)	a_1	a_2	MICROMETER	r	i	d_1	d_2	Mean R.A. 1850.0 (h. m. s.)	Mean Decl. 1850.0 (° ′ ″)
125	7					39.5	57.3		23 2 21.54	+16.98	+0.98	V. 2	13.963	−46 47.24	−11.31	−6.19	23 2 39.50	−30 20 4.74
126	8.9	22.5			16.				14 15.58	16.88	0.79	IV. 4	43.240	16 7.02	10.96	2.00	15 33.25	29 49 19.98
127	8				46.				19 28.04	16.84	0.99	V. 2	13.515	47 15.55	10.83	6.26	19 45.87	30 20 32.64
128	8			56.					20 55.60	16.83	0.79	IV. 4	44.605	14 41.35	10.81	1.82	21 13.22	29 47 53.98
129	8			5.					27 22.61	16.77	0.75	III. 4	51.190	7 48.39	10.70	0.91	27 40.13	29 41 0.00
130	8		34.	52.					30 9.81	16.75	0.94	III. 3	22.235	38 6.97	10.66	4.99	30 27.50	30 11 22.62
131	7	53.	9.3	27.5	46.5				31 45.56	16.74	0.78	IV. 4	46.080	13 8.77	10.65	1.62	32 3.08	29 46 21.04
132	8.9						43.		32 7.59	16.74	0.77	VI. 4	48.102	11 1.66	10.64	1.34	32 25.10	29 44 13.64
133	7				53.5				33 52.32	16.72	1.03	IV. 1	7.003	54 2.94	10.63	7.20	34 10.07	30 27 20.77
134	7			35.3	53.3	11.			34 52.99	16.72	0.82	IV. 4	40.255	19 14.24	10.62	2.43	35 10.53	29 52 27.29
135	7.8				49.	8.			42 6.91	16.66	0.95	IV. 2	19.635	40 51.34	10.56	5.37	42 24.52	30 14 7.27
136	7		3.5	22.3	40.7			33.5	45 39.78	16.63	0.95	IV. 2	19.890	40 35.20	10.55	5.32	45 57.36	13 51.07
137	7	35.	53.3	11.3	30.				48 28.95	16.61	1.00	IV. 2	13.405	47 22.46	10.51	6.27	48 46.56	20 39.27
138	8	39.	56.	14.3	32.7				50 32.01	16.60	0.90	IV. 3	30.490	29 29.38	10.53	3.60	50 49.51	2 43.71
139	5.6				28.3	45.	3.		51 27.19	16.59	0.99	IV. 2	14.810	45 54.01	10.53	6.05	51 44.77	19 10.59
140	8			16.5					55 34.24	16.56	0.96	III. 3	20.675	39 44.75	10.55	5.21	55 51.76	13 0.51
141	6					39.5		15.3	56 21.71	16.56	0.92	V. 3	27.170	32 57.88	10.55	4.28	56 39.19	30 6 12.71
142	7.8			54.	12.			5.	23 58 11.55	+16.54	+0.88	IV. 3	33.940	−25 52.75	−10.55	−3.32	23 58 28.97	−29 50 6.62

ZONE 132. SEPTEMBER 16. P. $D_0 = -28°\ 55'\ 30''$.

No.	Mag.	I.	II.	III.	IV.	V.	VI.	VII.	T. (h. m. s.)	a_1	a_2	MICROMETER	r	i	d_1	d_2	Mean R.A. 1850.0 (h. m. s.)	Mean Decl. 1850.0 (° ′ ″)
1	7					17.	35.		18 55 59.50	+16.61	+1.95	V. 3	37.640	−22 1.03	−30.77	−3.00	18 56 18.06	−29 18 4.80
2	8.9						54.		57 18.65	16.60	1.88	VI. 3	32.813	27 3.77	30.52	3.62	57 37.13	23 7.91
3	9							57.	58 4.00	16.60	1.96	VII. 4	39.230	20 17.78	30.38	2.79	58 22.56	29 16 20.95
4	7							3.	18 59 56.59	16.59	2.18	VII. 4	56.595	2 8.74	30.15	0.66	18 59 29.03	28 48 9.55
5	8			49.	6.3				19 1 6.24	16.57	2.09	IV. 4	49.270	0 48.86	29.80	1.57	19 1 24.90	29 5 50.23
6	6.7				50.	5.5			1 31.03	16.57	1.61	V. 2	12.445	48 22.71	29.72	5.27	1 49.21	44 27.70
7	8		46.	3.	21.5				4 38.91	16.55	1.78	III. 3	24.835	35 23.63	29.14	4.66	4 57.24	31 27.43
8	7	0.			53.7	10.5			4 52.89	16.55	1.79	IV. 4	26.630	33 31.51	29.09	4.43	5 11.23	29 35.03
9	9.10						36.		5 42.61	16.54	1.61	VII. 2	12.920	47 52.39	28.93	5.20	6 0.76	43 56.52
10	7		49.	6.5	24.	42.3	59.5		9 41.78	16.51	1.92	IV. 3	38.295	21 19.81	28.18	2.91	10 0.21	17 20.90
11	9.10			19.					11 36.66	16.50	1.58	III. 1	12.030	48 47.07	27.84	5.32	11 54.74	44 50.23
12	7				16.7	34.			12 15.85	16.50	1.54	IV. 1	9.045	51 54.75	27.72	6.69	12 33.89	47 59.16
13	6.7				12.	29.3			13 11.47	16.49	1.88	IV. 3	35.133	24 38.04	27.55	3.33	13 20.86	29 20 38.92
14	7					21.7			14 4.11	16.48	2.14	V. 4	57.065	1 39.90	27.40	0.59	14 22.73	28 57 37.89
15	6				1.	19.5	30.5		15 18.64	16.47	1.67	IV. 2	20.825	30 36.52	27.17	5.17	15 36.78	29 35 38.86
16	8	29.	46.3		4.3	22.3			17 21.85	16.46	1.67	IV. 2	20.470	39 58.98	26.79	5.21	17 39.98	36 0.98
17	7					23.7			18 5.83	16.45	1.53	V. 1	9.260	51 41.63	26.66	6.66	18 23.81	47 44.95
18	7.8					55.	12.5		18 37.00	16.45	1.61	IV. 2	15.550	45 7.77	26.56	5.86	18 55.12	41 10.19
19	7							3.3	19 10.31	16.45	1.92	VII. 3	39.353	20 13.77	26.45	2.78	19 28.68	16 13.70
20	8			48.					21 5.65	16.43	1.61	III. 2	15.415	45 16.11	26.12	5.88	21 23.60	41 18.11
21	7				23.			15.	21 21.71	16.43	1.52	IV. 1	8.025	52 2.22	26.08	6.70	21 39.66	48 5.00
22	9					30.			21 54.46	16.43	1.61	IV. 3	15.773	44 53.51	25.93	5.83	22 12.50	40 55.32
23	9					34.			24 58.73	16.40	1.92	VI. 4	40.600	18 52.16	25.44	2.63	25 17.05	29 14 50.23
24	8.7		22.						26 21.80	16.39	2.11	III. 4	55.190	3 37.58	25.15	0.82	26 40.30	28 59 33.55
25	7						2.		26 44.40	16.39	2.11	VI. 4	54.703	4 7.67	25.19	0.90	27 2.90	29 0 3.76
26	7.8		54.		29.				28 11.43	16.37	1.99	IV. 4	46.460	12 45.06	24.82	1.91	28 29.79	8 41.79
27	7.8		54.			29.			19 28 53.84	+16.37	+2.05	VI. 4	50.550	−8 28.21	−24.75	−1.40	19 29 12.26	−29 4 24.36

CORRECTIONS.

Date	Corr. of Clock	Hourly rate	m	n	c	Zenith Point	Mic. Co.
1847.	h.	s.	s.	s.	s.	° ′ ″	r.
			.				

INSTRUMENT READINGS.

Date		CIRCLE							Barom.	THERMOM.				
	Date	A.	B.	C.	D.	E.	F.	Mean		At.	Ex.	U.	L.	I.
	1847, Sept. 16, h. m.	° ′ ″						″	in.					
Zone 132	18 55								30.090	67.0	63.0		67.0	63.0
	19 0	68 17 31.9	30.5	26.1	19.5	19.8	33.4	26.87						
	19 15								30.096	67.0	63.7			
	20 1								30.097	66.7	62.5			
	21 14								30.098	65.5	60.0			
	22 1								30.102	65.0	59.0			
	22 30								30.094	65.0	58.6			
	23 59								30.088	64.1	57.0			
	1 49								30.070	63.8	56.2			

REMARKS.

(131) 126. Minutes assumed as 15 instead of 14.

(132) 6. Transit observations very discordant.

(132) 24. Transit over T. IV assumed as recorded over T. III, to agree with Arg. Z. 235, 38 ; 241, 31 ; and Mer. Cir. Z., 1846.

(132) 25. Transit over T. V assumed as recorded over T. VI, to agree with Arg. Z. 235, 39 ; 241, 32 ; and Mer. Cir. Z., 1846.

(132) 26. Transits over T.'s III and V assumed as recorded over T.'s II. and IV, to agree with Arg. Z. 235. 40, and Mer. Cir. Z., 1846.

* Corr. for runs +0″.08.

ZONE 132. SEPTEMBER 16. P. $D_o = -28° 55' 30''$—Continued.

No.	Mag.	SECONDS OF TRANSIT.							T.	a_1	a_2	MICROMETER.			i	d_1	d_2	Mean Right Ascension, 1850.0.	Mean Declination, 1850.0.
		I.	II.	III.	IV.	V.	VI.	VII.	h. m. s.	s.	s.			r.	' "	"	"	h. m. s.	° ' "
28	7.8	17.5	35.	53.					19 32 10.40	+16.35	+1.94	III.	4	43.550	-15 47.51	-24.20	-2.25	19 32 28.69	-29 11 43.96
29	7	19.	36.	54.					38 11.75	16.30	1.70	III.	3	24.750	35 28.96	23.18	4.66	38 29.75	31 26.80
30	8				52.				38 51.72	16.30	2.03	IV.	4	51.220	7 46.57	23.08	1.32	39 10.05	3 40.97
31	6.7				32.	49.5			39 31.73	16.29	1.96	IV.	4	45.953	13 16.67	22.96	1.96	39 49.98	9 11.59
32	7.8	59.	16.3	35.					45 52.16	16.24	1.70	III.	3	26.970	33 9.73	21.94	4.37	46 10.10	29 6.04
33	8				6.5				46 5.60	16.24	1.62	IV.	2	20.500	39 57.10	21.90	5.21	46 23.46	35 54.21
34	7					36.	53.5		46 18.11	16.24	1.63	V.	2	21.550	38 51.22	21.87	5.07	46 35.98	29 34 48.16
35	8						58.5		48 23.39	16.22	2.07	VI.	4	55.360	3 26.67	21.54	0.80	48 41.68	28 59 19.01
36	7					30.			49 12.38	16.22	2.02	V.	4	51.720	7 14.97	21.41	1.26	49 30.62	29 3 7.64
37	7						10.7		49 35.42	16.21	1.87	VI.	3	40.355	19 10.92	21.35	2.67	49 53.50	29 15 4.94
38	6.7			43.	1.				51 0.64	16.20	2.06	IV.	4	55.180	3 38.21	21.13	0.82	51 18.90	28 59 30.16
39	8.9	17.	34.	52.					53 9.47	16.19	2.02	III.	4	53.485	5 24.54	20.80	1.04	53 27.66	29 1 16.38
40	7	49.7	7.	25.5	44.				55 42.91	16.17	1.67	IV.	3	26.393	33 46.50	20.41	4.45	56 0.75	29 41.36
41	8			24.3	43.				56 42.03	16.16	1.62	IV.	3	22.200	38 9.55	20.26	4.98	56 59.81	34 4.79
42	7					35.5	53.		57 17.49	16.15	1.41	V.	2	6.680	54 24.47	20.16	7.02	57 35.05	50 21.65
43	9				51.				19 58 50.42	16.14	1.78	IV.	3	30.173	23 32.87	19.95	3.19	19 59 8.34	19 26.01
44	7	1.	18.3	36.					20 1 53.63	16.12	1.92	III.	4	47.097	12 5.00	19.46	1.70	20 2 11.67	7 56.25
45	9.10						23.		1 47.84	16.12	1.97	VI.	4	50.855	8 8.89	19.48	1.32	2 5.93	3 59.69
46	9		46.						10 21.74	16.05	1.51	II.	2	15.900	44 45.05	18.18	5.83	10 39.30	40 39.06
47	7.8			25.					10 42.63	16.05	1.56	III.	2	20.510	39 56.16	18.13	5.23	11 0.24	35 49.52
48	8				55.	12.		47.	10 54.03	16.04	1.59	IV.*	2	22.000	43 36.54	18.10	5.69	11 11.66	39 30.33
49	6.7				56.	13.		48.	10 55.03	16.04	1.58	IV.	2	21.678	43 56.75	18.10	5.77	11 12.65	39 50.62
50	9						1.		12 25.54	16.03	1.59	VI.	2	22.475	37 53.17	17.87	4.97	12 43.16	33 46.01
51	8						0.		13 24.49	16.02	1.54	VI.	2	18.825	41 41.97	17.72	5.46	13 42.05	37 35.15
52	7		36.	54.	12.5				15 11.64	16.01	1.59	IV.	2	22.900	37 26.31	17.45	4.91	15 29.24	33 18.67
53	8					56.			15 38.28	16.00	1.75	V.	3	35.000	24 46.57	17.35	3.34	15 56.83	20 37.29
54	6						33.		15 57.79	16.00	1.89	VI.	4	46.330	12 52.91	17.33	1.89	16 15.68	8 42.13
55	7						38.		17 2.54	15.99	1.60	VI.	3	22.753	37 35.03	17.17	4.93	17 20.13	33 27.13
56	7.8						34.5	52.	17 59.09	15.99	1.77	VI.	3	37.302	22 16.77	17.02	3.03	18 16.85	18 6.82
57	8.9		38.	56.					20 13.62	15.97	1.61	III	3	24.857	35 22.25	16.69	4.66	20 31.20	31 13.60
58	6.7	34.	52.	9.7	28.3	44.7			21 27.38	15.96	1.49	IV.	2	14.712	40 46.53	16.51	5.38	21 44.73	36 38.42
59	8.9			37.					22 54.51	15.94	1.92	III.	4	48.460	10 39.64	16.30	1.61	23 12.37	6 27.55
60	7				14.3	32.5		7.7	23 14.57	15.94	1.93	IV.	4	49.003	10 5.47	16.25	1.54	23 32.41	5 53.26
61	7					38.	55.3		24 19.91	15.93	1.41	V.	1	8.863	52 6.31	16.10	6.75	24 37.25	47 59.16
62	8.9						3.		25 27.82	15.92	1.92	VI.	4	48.790	10 18.40	15.93	1.57	25 45.66	6 5.90
63	7	57.	14.	31.7		7.		42.5	27 49.46	15.90	1.82	III.	4	41.500	17 56.09	15.59	2.50	28 7.18	13 44.18
64	7.8	50.	7.5	25.3					30 42.95	15.88	1.70	III.	3	31.940	27 57.84	15.17	3.72	31 0.53	23 46.73
65	7		46.	4.	22.				32 21.49	15.87	1.77	IV.	3	37.885	21 45.28	14.95	3.97	32 39.13	17 33.20
66	7					56.			33 38.29	15.86	1.76	V.	3	37.300	22 22.48	14.77	3.04	33 55.91	18 10.29
67	8			55.					35 12.68	15.84	1.38	III.	1	8.007	52 59.54	14.55	6.87	35 29.90	48 50.96
68	8.9					55.			35 37.19	15.84	1.54	V.	3	20.970	39 26.79	14.49	5.16	35 54.57	35 16.44
69	7.8							10.	36 17.09	15.83	1.86	VII.	4	45.405	13 50.48	14.40	2.01	36 34.78	9 36.89
70	8.9							5.	37 11.92	15.82	1.71	VII.	3	33.965	25 51.49	14.27	3.46	37 29.45	21 39.22
71	7.8			2.	20.1	39.			39 37.91	15.80	1.54	IV.	2	21.320	39 5.71	13.93	5.12	39 55.25	34 54.76
72	7.8	15.3	33.						41 8.51	15.79	1.56	II.	2	21.960	38 24.79	13.73	5.03	41 25.86	34 13.55
73	8					10.3	27.5		41 9.72	15.79	1.70	IV.	3	32.860	27 0.51	13.73	3.61	41 27.21	22 47.85
74	8	56.	13.	31.3					45 48.50	15.75	1.94	III.	4	51.363	7 37.60	13.11	1.25	46 6.23	3 21.96
75	8						9.5	27.	46 51.58	15.74	1.49	V.	2	18.090	42 28.35	12.98	5.55	47 8.81	38 16.88
76	9		58.						20 50 33.66	+15.71	+1.56	II.	3	23.100	-37 12.07	-12.48	-4.89	20 50 50.93	-29 32 59.44

CORRECTIONS.

Date.	Corr. of Clock.	Hourly rate.	m	n	c	Zenith Point.	Mic. Co.
1847.	h.	s.	s.	s.	s.	s.	° ' "	r.

INSTRUMENT READINGS.

Date.	CIRCLE.							Barom.	THERMOM.				
		A.	B.	C.	D.	E.	F.	Mean.		At.	Ex.	U.	L.	I.
Zone 132	1847. h. m. Sept. 16, 2 59	° ' "						"	in. 30.062	63.2	54.7			63.0

REMARKS.

(132) 48. Micrometer reading assumed as 17r.000, not 22r.000, to agree with Mural Z., 1846, September 19, and Arg. Z. 235, 94.

(132) 49. Micrometer reading assumed as 16r.678, not 21r.678, to agree with Mural Z., 1846, September 19, and Arg. Z. 235, 95.

(132) 58. Micrometer reading assumed as 19r.712, not 14r.712.

ZONE 132. SEPTEMBER 16. P. $D_o = -28°\,55'\,30''$—Continued.

No.	Mag.	Seconds of Transit (I.–VII.)	T. (h. m. s.)	a_1	a_2	Micrometer (r)	i	d_1	d_2	Mean Right Ascension, 1850.0	Mean Declination, 1850.0
77	8	47. 5. · 46.3 · · 21.3	20 51 22.55	+15.71	+1.69	III. 3 33.635	−26 11.64	−12.37	−3.51	20 51 39.95	−29 21 57.52
78	8.9	46.3 · · 21.3	51 45.73	15.71	1.63	IV. 3 28.440	31 38.06	12.33	4.19	52 3.07	27 24.58
79	6.7	20. 38.7 55.3	53 37.60	15.69	1.45	IV. 2 14.695	46 1.31	12.09	6.00	53 54.74	41 49.40
80	8	36. 54.3	54 53.45	15.67	1.42	IV. 2 12.502	48 19.07	11.92	6.29	55 10.54	44 7.28
81	9	8.	56 6.95	15.66	1.42	IV. 2 13.300	47 29.04	11.77	6.18	56 23.05	43 16.99
82	8.9	15.	57 39.85	15.65	1.93	VI. 4 51.910	7 2.74	11.57	1.18	57 57.43	2 45.49
83	8	59.	20 58 58.11	15.64	1.52	IV. 2 21.073	39 21.08	11.40	5.15	20 59 15.27	35 7.63
84	8.9	51.	21 0 50.00	15.63	1.45	IV. 2 15.477	45 12.34	11.17	5.91	21 0 7.08	40 59.42
85	6.7	36.	0 43.17	15.63	1.90	VII. 4 50.270	6 45.39	11.19	1.37	0 0.70	4 27.95
86	7.8	15. 32.	1 14.52	15.62	1.89	IV. 4 48.075	10 7.16	11.12	1.52	1 32.03	5 49.80
87	8	7.	1 31.73	15.62	1.76	VI. 4 41.062	18 23.19	11.09	2.54	1 49.11	14 6.82
88	8	53.3	2 0.11	15.61	1.60	VII. 3 26.445	33 43.49	11.03	4.46	2 17.32	29 28.98
89	8	32.3 50.	4 7.71	15.60	1.66	III. 3 31.890	28 0.98	10.77	3.74	4 24.97	23 45.49
90	8.9	59.	4 23.59	15.60	1.60	VI. 3 27.005	33 8.23	10.74	4.38	4 40.79	28 53.35
91	9	59.	5 41.15	15.59	1.43	V. 2 13.760	46 59.98	10.58	6.15	5 58.17	42 46.71
92	9	2.	6 44.30	15.58	1.75	V. 4 38.383	21 11.59	10.46	2.89	7 1.63	16 54.94
93	8	50.3	7 15.10	15.57	1.86	VI. 4 47.087	12 5.31	10.39	1.77	7 32.53	7 47.47
94	7.8	36. 54.5	8 53.74	15.55	1.73	IV. 3 36.325	23 23.39	10.19	3.16	9 11.02	19 6.74
95	6.7	27. 45.5 37.5	9 44.60	15.55	1.67	IV. 3 32.220	27 40.84	10.09	3.69	10 1.82	23 24.62
96	7	44. 1.3 19.3 38.3	12 37.12	15.53	1.36	IV. 1 8.753	52 13.08	9.76	6.80	12 54.01	47 59.64
97	9	46.	14 3.65	15.51	1.43	III. 2 14.113	46 37.71	9.59	6.11	14 20.59	42 23.41
98	8	57.2 34.	17 32.98	15.48	1.47	IV. 2 17.025	43 35.07	9.19	5.71	17 49.93	39 19.97
99	9	24.	17 48.40	15.48	1.38	VI. 1 9.630	51 18.35	9.16	6.68	18 5.26	47 4.19
100	7.8	22.3 39.7 58.	21 15.40	15.45	1.59	III. 3 26.313	33 51.15	8.75	4.47	21 32.44	29 34.40
101	8	11.3	21 53.57	15.44	1.67	V. 3 32.562	27 19.64	8.73	3.65	22 10.68	29 23 2.02
102	8	26.	22 50.89	15.43	1.95	VI. 4 54.700	4 7.86	8.61	0.79	23 8.27	28 59 47.26
103	7.6	40. 57.5 16.	25 33.27	15.41	1.55	III. 3 23.013	37 18.03	8.31	4.91	25 50.23	29 33 1.25
104	9	52.	25 34.22	15.41	1.59	V. 3 26.320	33 51.33	8.31	4.47	25 51.22	29 34.11
105	8.9	3.3 20.5	27 56.10	15.39	1.69	II. 3 34.270	25 31.36	8.06	3.43	28 13.18	21 12.85
106	7	56. 13.3	27 55.54	15.39	1.75	IV. 3 38.625	20 58.99	8.06	2.86	28 12.68	16 39.91
107	9	42. 35.5	31 34.91	15.36	1.78	IV. 3 40.255	19 16.80	7.68	2.65	31 52.05	11 57.13
108	9	26.	34 1.53	15.34	1.70	II. 3 33.740	26 4.42	7.44	3.49	34 18.57	21 45.35
109	8.9	41. 59.	35 16.39	15.33	1.95	III. 4 53.400	5 29.87	7.32	0.96	35 33.67	1 8.15
110	6.7	55.3 13. 31.5	36 30.75	15.31	1.66	IV. 3 31.015	28 56.32	7.19	3.85	36 47.72	24 37.36
111	9	52.5	37 34.75	15.30	1.66	V. 3 30.740	29 13.82	7.09	3.89	37 51.71	24 54.80
112	9	51.5	38 16.06	15.30	1.59	VI. 3 25.445	34 46.30	7.02	4.58	38 32.95	30 27.90
113	8	54.3 29.3	39 53.98	15.28	1.83	IV. 4 44.205	15 6.49	6.86	2.13	40 11.09	10 45.48
114	8.9	23.	41 5.31	15.27	1.79	V. 4 40.990	18 27.89	6.75	2.55	41 22.37	14 7.19
115	8.9	49.	42 48.44	15.26	1.74	IV. 3 36.863	22 49.39	6.60	3.09	43 5.44	18 29.08
116	9	43.	43 42.10	15.25	1.52	IV. 2 20.490	39 57.73	6.50	5.24	43 58.87	35 39.47
117	8.9	33.	43 57.60	15.25	1.62	VI. 3 27.710	32 23.99	6.48	4.29	44 14.47	28 4.76
118	7	17.3 35.	44 41.94	15.24	1.70	VI. 3 33.643	26 11.83	6.42	3.51	44 58.88	21 51.76
119	8	30.	45 36.77	15.24	1.57	VII. 3 23.500	36 48.29	6.34	4.85	45 53.58	32 29.48
120	7	33. 51.	47 50.39	15.22	1.57	IV. 3 24.295	35 58.15	6.13	4.74	48 7.18	31 39.02
121	7	41.3 59. 17.3	50 34.76	15.19	1.39	III. 1 10.350	50 32.65	5.88	6.60	50 51.34	46 15.13
122	7	54. 11.	50 53.34	15.19	1.72	IV. 3 35.395	24 21.73	5.86	3.28	51 10.25	20 0.87
123	6	56. 13.	51 55.47	15.18	1.84	IV. 4 44.670	14 37.21	5.77	2.07	52 12.49	10 15.05
124	8.9	57.	53 32.53	15.17	1.70	II. 3 33.640	26 10.76	5.63	3.51	53 49.40	21 49.90
125	8.9	29.3	21 54 26.74	+15.16	+1.74	IV. 3 36.820	−22 52.09	−5.55	−3.10	21 54 43.64	−29 18 30.74

CORRECTIONS.

Date.	Corr. of Clock.	Hourly rate.	m	n	c	Zenith Point.	Mic. Co.
1847.	h. s.	s.	s.	s.	s.	° ' "	r.

INSTRUMENT READINGS.

Date.	CIRCLE.							Barom.	THERMOM.				
	A.	B.	C.	D.	E.	F.	Mean.		At.	Ex.	U.	L.	I.
1847. h. m.	° ' "						"	in.	° '		° '		

REMARKS.

(132) 84. Minutes assumed as 59 instead of 0, to agree with Transit Z., 1846, August 18.

(132) 85. Minutes assumed as 59 instead of 0, to agree with Arg. Z. 228, 1; and 245, 30.

(132) 111. Differs from Transit Z., 1846, September 22, by 2s.17 in right ascension and 1' 32".5 in declination.

(132) 125. T. IV assumed as 27s.3 instead of 29s.3, to agree with Transit Z., 1846, September 24.

ZONE 132. SEPTEMBER 16. P. $D_0 = -28° 55′ 30″$—Continued.

No.	Mag.	I.	II.	III.	IV.	V.	VI.	VII.	T. (h. m. s.)	a_1 (s.)	a_2 (s.)
126	7			29.	47.	4.			21 55 46.49	+15.15	+1.85
127	7	28.5	46.	4.3	22.3				57 21.63	15.14	1.65
128	7							13.	21 57 19.55	15.14	1.37
129	6.7	16.7	34.	52.	9.5				22 1 9.35	15.10	1.95
130	9							13.	4 20.21	15.07	1.96
131	8.9					27.			5 51.50	15.06	1.52
132	6						9.	26.5	10 33.84	15.02	2.02
133	8			34.	52.3	9.3			12 51.53	15.00	1.59
134	7.8	34.5	52.3	10.	28.3				15 27.63	14.98	1.67
135	8	18.	35.	53.					17 10.72	14.96	1.64
136	8				42.3				17 41.96	14.96	1.91
137	9			41.5					19 59.10	14.91	1.63
138	8				42.5				20 41.73	14.93	1.63
139	7						19.	36.3	20 43.40	14.93	1.68
140	9		6.						23 41.55	14.91	1.71
141	7				20.	37.			24 19.02	14.90	1.44
142	8		11.3	59.2	17.7				26 16.87	14.89	1.59
143	7				5.				27 4.50	14.88	1.83
144	9					51.			27 15.68	14.88	1.77
145	7				4.				29 2.84	14.86	1.40
146	6			49.5	7.				30 6.64	14.85	1.62
147	6.7			53.7	12.				31 11.20	14.85	1.55
148	7							59.	31 6.14	14.85	1.94
149	7							1.	31 8.13	14.85	1.92
150	7				35.				34 24.31	14.82	1.70
151	8	35.		10.	28.3				39 27.72	14.77	1.70
152	7.8				16.3				40 15.58	14.77	1.70
153	8		20.	38.	56.				44 55.50	14.73	1.87
154	7	5.	22.	40.	58.5	15.3			47 57.69	14.70	1.73
155	7.6	18.	35.	53.					50 10.52	14.68	1.95
156	8					29.			50 11.42	14.68	2.07
157	7	58.	15.3	33.5	52.		26.3		52 51.02	14.66	1.56
158	5.6	48.7	6.	23.5					55 41.22	14.64	2.02
159	7.8					57.			56 39.30	14.63	1.83
160	8.9	18.		54.					59 11.25	14.61	1.77
161	8.9				58.5		32.7		22 59 57.37	14.60	1.58
162	5.6			26.		1.5			23 1 43.65	14.59	1.49
163	7						43.		2 7.72	14.58	1.88
164	8	3.	21.	38.3	56.3				4 55.98	14.56	1.89
165	8		36.	54.					6 11.50	14.55	1.87
166	7.8	59.	16.						7 51.60	14.54	1.93
167	9			1.5	20.				8 19.16	14.54	1.71
168	7					6.	24.		8 48.56	14.53	1.95
169	6.7			52.	10.3				10 9.65	14.52	1.86
170	7.8				45.	2.			11 44.44	14.51	1.93
171	6.7	18.	36.	53.5					15 11.24	14.48	1.73
172	7.8				27.	44.			15 26.28	14.48	1.79
173	7.6	0.	17.3	35.3	53.3				20 52.78	14.44	2.04
174	7		42.			19.			23 23 17.85	+14.42	+1.55

No.	MICROMETER		r.	i (′ ″)	d_1 (″)	d_2 (″)	Mean Right Ascension, 1850.0 (h. m. s.)	Mean Declination, 1850.0 (° ′ ″)
126	IV.	4	45.280	−13 59.08	−5.44	−2.01	21 56 3.49	−29 9 36.53
127	IV.	3	29.737	30 16.50	5.30	4.03	57 38.42	25 55.83
128	VII.	1	8.725	52 15.03	5.30	6.80	21 57 36.06	47 57.13
129	IV.	4	52.850	6 2.29	4.98	1.00	22 1 26.40	1 38.27
130	VII.	4	52.875	6 1.85	4.72	1.00	4 37.24	1 37.57
131	VI.	2	19.300	41 12.42	4.59	5.30	6 8.08	29 36 52.40
132	VI.	4	56.815	1 55.20	4.21	0.51	10 50.88	28 57 29.92
133	IV.	3	24.350	35 54.70	4.03	4.75	13 8.12	29 31 33.48
134	IV.	3	29.800	30 12.49	3.82	4.01	15 44.28	25 50.32
135	III.	3	27.007	33 7.41	3.69	4.39	17 27.32	28 45.49
136	IV.	4	48.095	11 2.47	3.64	1.62	17 58.83	6 37.73
137	III.	3	25.720	34 25.16	3.46	4.56	20 15.67	30 6.18
138	IV.	3	26.450	33 42.92	3.41	4.46	20 58.29	29 20.79
139	VI.	3	30.195	29 48.02	3.41	3.96	21 0.01	25 25.39
140	II.	3	31.740	28 9.89	3.20	3.76	23 58.17	23 46.85
141	IV.	1	11.340	49 30.88	3.15	6.49	24 35.36	45 10.52
142	IV.	3	21.925	38 26.61	3.01	5.06	26 33.35	34 4.68
143	IV.	3	40.010	19 32.05	2.95	2.67	27 21.21	15 7.67
144	VI.	3	35.880	23 51.37	2.94	3.21	27 32.33	19 27.52
145	IV.	1	7.385	53 39.15	2.81	7.02	29 19.10	49 16.98
146	IV.	3	24.340	35 55.33	2.73	4.75	30 23.11	31 32.81
147	IV.	2	18.580	41 57.54	2.67	5.53	31 27.60	37 35.74
148	VII.	4	48.460	10 38.89	2.68	1.57	31 22.93	6 13.14
149	VII.	4	47.105	12 3.80	2.68	1.75	31 24.90	7 38.23
150	IV.	3	30.580	29 23.67	2.46	3.91	34 40.83	25 0.04
151	IV.	3	36.743	22 56.98	2.15	3.10	39 44.28	18 32.23
152	IV.	3	28.830	31 13.35	2.10	4.16	40 32.05	26 49.61
153	IV.	4	42.300	17 0.05	1.86	2.37	45 12.10	12 40.28
154	IV.	3	31.225	28 43.27	1.70	3.82	48 14.12	24 18.79
155	III.	4	48.320	10 48.43	1.58	1.59	50 27.15	29 6 21.60
156	V.	4	57.200	1 31.50	1.58	0.45	50 28.17	28 57 3.53
157	IV.	2	16.795	43 49.44	1.47	5.74	53 7.24	29 39 26.65
158	III.	4	51.833	7 7.89	1.35	1.14	55 57.88	2 40.38
159	V.	3	38.020	21 37.13	1.30	2.93	56 55.76	17 11.36
160	III.	3	31.813	28 5.82	1.19	3.75	22 59 27.63	23 40.76
161	IV.	2	18.213	42 20.64	1.16	5.54	23 0 13.55	37 57.34
162	IV.	1	10.980	49 53.29	1.10	6.56	1 59.73	45 30.95
163	VI.	4	40.613	18 51.35	1.07	2.57	2 24.18	14 24.99
164	IV.	4	41.377	18 3.93	0.99	2.48	5 12.43	13 37.40
165	III.	4	38.703	20 51.40	0.94	2.84	6 27.92	16 25.18
166	II.	4	43.313	16 2.25	0.89	2.22	8 8.07	11 35.36
167	IV.	3	25.720	34 28.54	0.87	4.56	8 35.41	30 3.97
168	V.	4	44.930	19 34.41	0.85	2.00	9 5.04	15 7.26
169	IV.	4	37.495	22 7.37	0.81	3.00	10 26.03	17 41.18
170	IV.	4	42.475	16 55.00	0.76	2.33	11 0.88	12 28.09
171	III.	3	26.110	34 3.76	0.67	4.51	15 27.45	29 38.94
172	IV.	3	31.182	28 45.97	0.66	3.83	15 42.55	24 20.46
173	IV.	4	47.304	9 46.78	0.51	1.44	21 9.26	5 18.73
174	IV.	1	10.270	−50 38.01	−0.46	−6.67	23 23 33.82	−29 46 15.17

CORRECTIONS.

Date.	Corr. of Clock.	Hourly rate.	m	n	c	Zenith Point.	Mic. Co.
	h. s.	s.	s.	s.	s.	° ′ ″	r.
1847.	h. s.	s.	s.	s.	s.	° ′ ″	r.

REMARKS.

(132) 137. Differs in right ascension 1s.88 from Transit Z., 1846, September 22.

(132) 163. Transit over T. V assumed as 43s, not 4s.3.

(132) 168. Micrometer reading assumed as 30r.930 instead of 44r.930.

(132) 170. Time of transit across middle thread assumed as 45s, not 4s.5; and minutes assumed as 10 instead of 11, to agree with Arg. Z. 259, 69; and 265, 82.

INSTRUMENT READINGS.

Date.	CIRCLE.							Barom.	THERMOM.				
	A.	B.	C.	D.	E.	F.	Mean.		At.	Ex.	U.	L.	I.
1847. h. m.	° ′ ″							in.					

Zone 132. September 16. P. D. = −28° 55′ 30″—Continued.

No.	Mag.	I.	II.	III.	IV.	V.	VI.	VII.	T. (h. m. s.)	a_1 (s.)	a_2 (s.)	MICROMETER		r.	i	d_1	d_2	Mean Right Ascension, 1850.0 (h. m. s.)	Mean Declination, 1850.0 (° ′ ″)
175	8.9	10.		45.3	4.				23 25 3.04	+14.41	+1.75	IV.	3	25.680	−34 34.88	−0.43	−4.57	23 25 19.20	−29 30 9.88
176	7.8	17.	35.	52.5					27 10.28	14.39	1.72	III.	3	22.025	38 20.03	0.38	5.05	27 26.39	33 55.46
177	8.9				42.				27 24.16	14.39	1.62	V.	2	15.175	45 31.31	0.38	5.99	27 40.17	41 7.68
178	8.9	0.	18.	36.					29 53.46	14.37	1.70	III.	2	20.630	39 48.70	0.32	5.25	30 9.53	35 24.27
179	8			23.					30 40.50	14.36	2.06	III.	4	48.777	10 19.53	0.31	1.51	30 56.92	5 51.35
180	8			30.					31 47.67	14.35	1.57	III.	1	10.110	50 47.60	0.29	6.69	32 3.59	46 24.58
181	7				6.		41.5		32 5.92	14.35	2.00	IV.	4	43.665	15 40.24	0.29	2.18	32 22.27	11 12.71
182	6	36.	53.	11.					34 28.47	14.33	2.14	III.	4	53.590	5 17.00	0.25	0.88	34 44.94	0 49.03
183	8	40.	57.	15.3					36 32.89	14.32	1.72	III.	2	21.250	39 9.85	0.22	5.16	36 48.93	34 45.23
184	8	49.5	6.	24.					38 41.97	14.30	1.70	III.	2	18.935	41 34.94	0.19	5.46	38 57.97	29 37 10.59
185	3.4			32.5		8.			40 50.19	14.28	2.21	IV.	4	56.713	2 2.03	0.16	0.48	41 6.68	28 57 32.67
186	7.6					58.			41 40.34	14.28	2.04	V.	4	44.330	14 58.60	6.16	2.09	41 56.66	29 10 30.85
187	7.8	58.	15.7	33.3					43 50.89	14.26	2.05	III.	4	45.120	14 8.98	0.14	1.99	44 7.20	9 41.11
188	8		22.	39.5					44 57.22	14.25	2.03	III.	4	43.560	15 46.89	0.13	2.19	45 13.50	11 19.21
189	8.9			44.		19.			46 1.42	14.24	1.95	V.	3	35.933	23 47.96	0.12	3.20	46 17.61	19 21.30
190	8.9		27.	45.					51 2.60	14.21	1.83	IV.	3	26.540	33 37.22	0.08	4.45	51 18.64	29 11.75
191	7	30.5	48.	6.	24.5				53 23.62	14.19	1.79	IV.	3	22.340	38 0.83	0.08	5.01	53 39.60	33 35.92
192	8			8.					54 25.58	14.18	1.90	III.	3	31.275	28 39.75	0.07	3.82	54 41.66	24 13.64
193	8		4.						55 39.45	14.17	2.02	II.	4	39.910	19 35.44	0.07	2.68	55 55.64	15 8.19
194	8					59.			55 41.31	14.17	2.05	V.	4	41.430	18 0.48	0.07	2.47	55 57.53	13 33.02
195	7.8						31.	48.	55 55.39	14.17	2.06	VI.	4	41.260	18 10.84	0.07	2.49	56 11.62	13 43.40
196	8							37.5	56 44.14	14.16	1.69	VII.	2	15.095	45 35.95	0.07	6.00	23 56 59.99	41 12.02
197	8.9	3.		38.5					23 59 55.89	14.14	2.10	III.	4	45.250	14 0.89	0.06	1.97	0 0 12.13	9 32.92
198	9			51.5					0 1 9.02	+14.13	+2.10	III.	4	44.950	−14 19.58	−0.06	−1.98	0 0 25.25	−29 9 51.62

Zone 133. September 16. P. D. = −28° 55′ 30″.

No.	Mag.	I.	II.	III.	IV.	V.	VI.	VII.	T. (h. m. s.)	a_1 (s.)	a_2 (s.)	MICROMETER		r.	i	d_1	d_2	Mean Right Ascension, 1850.0 (h. m. s.)	Mean Declination, 1850.0 (° ′ ″)
1	8	38.	55.	13.	31.5	48.5			1 49 30.74	+13.51	+1.56	IV.	2	19.710	−40 46.57	−5.32	−5.44	1 49 45.81	−29 36 27.33
2	8			30.5					50 48.13	13.51	1.55	III.	2	21.195	39 13.37	5.45	5.21	51 3.19	34 54.03
3	8					19.			51 1.21	13.51	1.57	V.	2	23.180	37 8.93	5.47	4.95	51 16.29	32 49.35
4	7.8	27.	44.5	2.					55 19.67	13.49	1.76	III.	4	50.840	8 10.15	5.00	1.19	55 34.93	3 47.24
5	7	1.5	19.						57 54.26	13.48	1.73	II.	4	49.883	9 9.97	6.15	1.32	58 9.47	4 47.44
6	7			58.					58 15.50	13.48	1.71	III.	4	48.840	10 15.57	6.19	1.46	58 30.69	5 53.22
7	7						51.3	9.	1 58 16.00	13.48	1.64	VI.	3	38.645	20 58.05	6.19	2.83	1 58 31.12	16 37.07
8	8			9.3		45.			2 0 27.06	13.47	1.46	V.	2	19.490	41 0.55	6.41	5.49	2 0 41.09	36 42.45
9	8.9					49.			2 13.60	13.46	1.52	VI.	3	28.663	31 24.26	6.60	4.19	1 28.58	27 5.05
10	7				4.	21.			2 45.79	13.46	1.39	V.	2	13.373	47 24.47	6.65	6.35	3 0.64	43 7.47
11	7.8	13.	30.	48.3					5 5.93	13.45	1.39	III.	2	16.565	44 3.88	6.90	5.87	5 20.77	39 46.65
12	8.9	36.	53.7	11.5					6 29.08	13.45	1.51	III.	3	31.990	27 54.77	7.05	3.62	6 44.04	23 35.44
13	9						4.5		6 28.96	13.45	1.37	VI.	2	15.830	44 49.94	7.05	5.97	6 43.78	40 32.96
14	7.8	19.	36.5	54.3					9 11.89	13.44	1.53	III.	3	38.233	21 23.26	7.33	2.68	9 26.86	17 3.47
15	7.8	11.3	28.5	46.3	4.				11 3.83	13.43	1.62	IV.	4	50.580	8 26.65	7.53	1.19	11 18.88	4 5.37
16	8			52.		27.5			12 9.66	13.43	1.35	IV.	2	19.200	41 18.70	7.65	5.53	12 24.44	37 1.88
17	8	25.3	42.5	0.5					16 18.30	13.41	1.28	III.	2	12.960	47 49.94	8.13	6.39	16 32.99	43 34.46
18	7	59.5	16.7	34.5	10.				17 52.23	13.41	1.45	III.	3	35.560	24 10.93	8.31	3.23	18 7.09	19 52.47
19	7.8	12.5	30.	48.	6.				21 5.48	13.40	1.35	IV.	3	27.580	32 31.89	8.68	4.34	21 20.23	26 14.91
20	8	48.7	6.	24.					23 41.53	13.39	1.41	III.	3	37.020	22 39.23	8.99	3.04	23 56.33	18 21.26
21	8			58.3					2 24 15.88	+13.39	+1.33	III.	3	28.620	−31 26.27	−9.06	−4.21	2 24 30.60	−29 27 9.54

CORRECTIONS.

Date.	Corr. of Clock.	Hourly rate.	m	n	c	Zenith Point.	Mic. Co.
1847.	h.	s.	s.	s.	s.	° ′ ″	r.

REMARKS.

(132) 198. Minutes assumed as 0 instead of 1.

(133) 9. Minutes assumed as 1 instead of 2.

INSTRUMENT READINGS.

Date.	CIRCLE.							Barom.	THERMOM.				
	A.	B.	C.	D.	E.	F.	Mean.		At.	Ex.	U.	L.	I.
1847. h. m.	° ′ ″						″	in.	°	°	°	°	°

ZONE 133.   SEPTEMBER 16.   P. $D_0 = -28° 55' 30''$—Continued.

Seconds of Transit

No.	Mag.	I.	II.	III.	IV.	V.	VI.	VII.
22	7	30.5	48.	6.	24.	41.	.	.
23	8.9	.	.	.	21.	.	.	.
24	7	.	.	1.	19.3	36.3	.	.
25	9	18.3	35.5	.	.	.	.	.
26	8	.	.	.	36.3	.	11.5	.
27	7	.	.	.	4.7	.	.	.
28	8	.	.	.	.	47.	.	.
29	8	.	.	.	10.5	.	.	.
30	8.9	.	16.5	.	.	.	.	.
31	9	.	.	.	39.	.	.	.
32	8	.	44.	.	.	.	.	.
33	8.9	49.	.	.	24.3	.	.	.
34	7	47.7	5.	23.3	41.3	58.3	.	.
35	6.7	35.3	52.5	10.7	29.	46.	.	.
36	7.8	54.7	.	30.	47.5	.	.	.
37	7.8	39.5	57.	14.7	.	.	.	.

No.	T. (h m s)	a_1	a_2	Mic.		r.	l (′ ″)	d_1 (″)	d_2 (″)	Mean Right Ascension, 1850.0	Mean Declination, 1850.0
22	2 28 23.43	+13.38	+1.28	IV.	3	34.160	−25 39.14	−9.55	−3.44	2 28 38.09	−29 21 22.13
23	29 20.01	13.37	1.18	IV.	2	16.130	44 31.31	9.66	5.93	29 34.56	40 16.92
24	30 18.48	13.37	1.19	IV.	2	17.340	43 15.49	9.78	5.77	30 33.04	39 1.04
25	35 10.99	13.36	1.38	II.	4	43.697	15 37.97	10.39	2.13	35 25.73	11 20.49
26	35 36.04	13.36	1.37	IV.	4	42.120	17 17.21	10.44	2.34	35 50.77	12 59.99
27	37 3.98	13.35	1.22	IV.	3	29.040	31 0.23	10.62	4.15	37 18.55	26 45.00
28	37 11.83	13.35	1.40	VI.	4	50.233	8 48.09	10.64	1.23	36 26.58	4 29.96
29	39 9.94	13.35	1.28	IV.	3	37.330	22 20.35	10.88	3.00	39 24.57	18 4.23
30	41 51.89	13.34	1.32	II.	4	44.780	14 30.00	11.23	1.99	42 6.55	10 13.22
31	42 38.00	13.34	1.05	IV.	2	15.420	45 15.98	11.33	6.02	42 52.39	41 3.33
32	44 19.71	13.34	1.08	II.	2	18.887	41 37.58	11.55	5.56	44 34.13	37 24.69
33	47 41.93	13.33	1.13	III.	3	28.065	32 1.03	12.00	4.27	47 56.39	27 47.30
34	49 40.66	13.32	1.07	IV.	3	22.580	37 45.70	12.26	5.04	49 55.05	33 33.00
35	52 28.23	13.32	1.00	IV.	3	25.623	34 34.69	12.64	4.59	52 42.61	30 21.92
36	54 47.37	13.31	1.28	IV.	4	52.770	6 9.20	12.96	0.90	55 1.96	1 53.06
37	2 59 32.42	+13.30	+1.06	III.	3	32.113	−27 47.12	−13.62	−3.71	2 59 46.78	−29 23 34.45

ZONE 134.   SEPTEMBER 21.   P. $D_0 = -24° 32' 30''$.

Seconds of Transit

No.	Mag.	I.	II.	III.	IV.	V.	VI.	VII.
1	8	.	.	.	12.	.	.	2.
2	8	.	.	.	32.	.	.	.
3	8.9	.	.	.	.	21.	.	.
4	8	.	.	.	.	.	22.5	.
5	9	.	40.	.	31.	.	.	.
6	8	3.	19.5	36.5	.	.	.	.
7	8.9	.	.	11.	.	.	.	.
8	8.9	.	9.	.	43.3	.	.	.
9	8	.	.	32.	.	.	.	.
10	9	.	.	.	.	18.	.	.
11	8	.	26.	.	.	.	.	.
12	7.8	.	.	.	5.	.	.	.
13	8	.	.	.	59.5	.	.	.
14	8	.	.	49.	.	.	.	.
15	8.9	.	.	55.5	.	.	.	.
16	7	.	.	.	37.	.	.	.
17	8	.	.	.	28.	.	.	.
18	8	.	19.	.	10.	.	.	.
19	7	.	.	.	41.3	.	.	.
20	6	.	.	.	32.	.	.	.
21	8	.	.	.	31.	.	.	.
22	7	.	.	23.	40.5	.	.	.
23	7.8	58.	15.	.	.	.	.	.
24	7.6	.	.	.	57.	.	47.3	.
25	6.7	23.	39.5	56.7	.	.	.	.
26	8.9	.	.	.	59.	.	.	.
27	8	.	52.	.	27.	.	.	.
28	8	50.5	7.	24.3	.	.	.	.
29	7	.	.	.	85.	.	.	.

No.	T. (h m s)	a_1	a_2	Mic.		r.	l (′ ″)	d_1 (″)	d_2 (″)	Mean Right Ascension, 1850.0	Mean Declination, 1850.0
1	20 1 10.83	+14.71	+0.22	IV.	2	12.123	−48 42.80	−23.73	−4.68	20 1 25.76	−25 21 41.21
2	2 15.06	14.70	0.45	V.	4	51.963	6 59.73	23.55	0.97	2 30.21	24 39 54.25
3	2 47.15	14.70	0.43	VI.	4	48.913	10 10.74	23.46	1.26	3 2.28	24 43 5.46
4	3 31.29	14.69	0.26	VII.	2	18.600	41 56.10	23.34	4.06	3 46.24	25 14 53.50
5	5 56.97	14.67	0.38	VI.	−3	38.610	21 0.37	22.94	2.17	6 12.02	24 53 55.48
6	8 53.56	14.65	0.40	III.	4	42.503	10 53.24	22.45	1.84	9 8.61	49 47.53
7	8 54.01	14.65	0.43	V.	4	48.290	10 50.25	22.45	1.31	9 9.12	24 43 44.01
8	10 26.07	14.64	0.30	IV.	3	25.375	34 50.35	22.20	3.43	10 41.01	25 7 46.01
9	11 31.07	14.63	0.25	IV.	2	17.560	43 1.62	22.03	4.16	11 45.95	15 57.81
10	11 26.78	14.63	0.26	VII.	2	17.990	42 34.31	22.04	4.12	11 41.67	15 30.47
11	13 42.97	14.62	0.21	III.	1	9.760	51 9.50	21.67	4.90	13 57.80	24 6.07
12	13 47.80	14.62	0.19	V.	1	6.220	54 52.47	21.66	5.26	14 2.61	25 27 49.39
13	14 42.56	14.61	0.44	V.	4	53.360	5 32.32	21.51	0.85	14 57.61	24 38 24.68
14	15 32.04	14.60	0.43	V.	4	47.880	11 15.70	21.38	1.35	15 47.07	24 44 8.43
15	16 54.50	14.59	0.23	IV.	2	13.925	46 49.57	21.16	4.51	17 9.32	25 19 45.24
16	17 2.79	14.59	0.20	VI.	1	9.075	51 53.25	21.14	4.97	17 17.58	24 49.36
17	17 53.94	14.58	0.31	VI.	3	26.330	33 50.83	21.01	3.34	18 8.83	25 6 45.18
18	19 19.00	14.57	0.46	IV.	4	52.805	6 7.00	20.77	0.90	19 34.03	24 38 58.67
19	23 7.11	14.54	0.22	VI.	2	11.410	49 27.69	20.18	4.76	23 21.87	25 22 22.63
20	23 40.65	14.54	0.18	VII.	1	7.165	53 53.22	20.09	5.16	23 55.37	26 48.47
21	24 39.84	14.53	0.28	VII.	3	23.270	37 2.84	19.93	3.62	24 54.65	25 9 56.39
22	26 39.94	14.51	0.38	IV.	4	39.250	20 17.28	19.62	2.11	26 54.83	24 53 9.01
23	28 31.98	14.50	0.38	III.	3	39.080	20 30.07	19.32	2.12	28 46.86	53 21.51
24	28 56.56	14.49	0.41	IV.	4	47.230	11 56.78	19.26	1.41	29 11.46	44 47.45
25	31 13.53	14.48	0.44	III.	4	53.850	5 1.42	18.92	0.80	31 28.45	24 37 51.14
26	31 58.34	14.47	0.32	IV.	3	30.930	29 1.59	18.80	2.91	32 13.13	25 1 53.30
27	34 26.21	14.45	0.25	IV.	2	19.810	40 40.21	18.44	3.94	34 40.91	13 32.59
28	36 41.26	14.43	0.32	III.	3	31.360	28 34.49	18.10	2.86	36 56.01	1 25.45
29	20 37 23.85	+14.43	+0.17	IV.	1	6.535	−54 32.45	−17.99	−5.23	20 37 38.45	−25 27 25.67

CORRECTIONS.

Date.	Corr. of Clock.	Hourly rate.	m	n	c	Zenith Point.	Mic. Co.
	h.	s.	s.	s.	s.	° ′ ″	r.
1847. Sept. 21, 20	. .	. .	. .	. .	. .	. . .	30.051

REMARKS.

(133) 23. Declination 5′ 12″ discordant from Arg. Z. 336, 113; micrometer reading probably 21r.130, not 16r.130.

(133) 28. Minutes assumed as 36 instead of 37.

Sept. 21. Stars very unsteady and faint; night unfavorable.

INSTRUMENT READINGS.

Date.	A.	B.	C.	D.	E.	F.	Mean.	Barom.	At.	Ex.	U.	L.	I.
	h. m.	° ′ ″					″	in.	°	°	°	°	°
Zone 134 1847. Sept. 21, 20 0	63 54 62.0	59.5	57.8	47.6	46.3	60.3	55.58	30.030	64.0	58.0	64.0	64.0	65.0
20 26	.	.	.	.	.	.	.	30.034	63.7	57.8			
21 12	.	.	.	.	.	.	.	30.044	63.8	57.0			
21 21	.	.	.	.	.	.	.	30.054	63.5	57.0			
21 59	.	.	.	.	.	.	.	30.059	63.5	56.0			
22 17	.	.	.	.	.	.	.	30.058	63.2	56.2			
22 45	.	.	.	.	.	.	.	30.064	63.2	56.5			
23 2	.	.	.	.	.	.	.	30.064	63.2	56.0			
23 29	.	.	.	.	.	.	.	30.066	63.2	55.4			

ZONE 134. SEPTEMBER 21. P. $D_0 = -24°\ 32'\ 30''$—Continued.

No.	Mag.	I.	II.	III.	IV.	V.	VI.	VII.	T. (h m s)	a_1	a_2
30	8				19.				20 38 9.35	+14.42	+0.32
31	8	24.		57.5					43 14.52	14.38	0.41
32	7.8			33.5		7.5			43 50.44	14.36	0.40
33	6.7			40.	57.5				44 56.96	14.37	0.37
34	7.8		41.3	58.5					46 15.35	14.36	0.39
35	8	10.	26.5	43.5					48 0.54	14.34	0.40
36	7.8			19.	37.				48 36.10	14.34	0.29
37	8					8.			48 50.91	14.34	0.27
38	8	18.		52.					52 8.64	14.31	0.34
39	7.8				29.				53 27.84	14.30	0.16
40	6.7				48.		21.		54 47.27	14.29	0.34
41	7.8	0.7	17.	34.5					57 51.49	14.26	0.22
42	6.7	42.	59.	16.	33.				20 59 32.81	14.25	0.37
43	7		18.		52.5				21 0 52.02	14.24	0.30
44	8							57.	1 5.66	14.24	0.16
45	7							53.	2 1.66	14.23	0.17
46	7						38.3		3 4.44	14.22	0.40
47	6				20.3			10.5	4 19.14	14.21	0.16
48	7.8	46.		21.					8 37.24	14.18	0.43
49	8				16.		7.		12 32.88	14.15	0.20
50	8						28.		13 53.90	14.14	0.23
51	6			8.5	26.	42.			15 25.21	14.13	0.27
52	8				27.				16 26.72	14.12	0.40
53	7				14.				17 13.22	14.11	0.25
54	8						48.		17 13.99	14.11	0.29
55	8			41.5					19 58.32	14.09	0.42
56	7.8	39.5	55.7	13.5					21 30.25	14.08	0.27
57	6	48.7	5.3	23.					23 39.76	14.06	0.20
58	7.8					2.5	19.		23 45.31	14.06	0.35
59	6.7	52.5	9.3	26.5	44.				28 43.41	14.02	0.24
60	7	16.5	33.	50.5	8.3				30 7.41	14.01	0.24
61	8			3.					31 19.97	14.00	0.17
62	8	18.	35.3	53.					33 9.56	13.98	0.18
63	8			39.					33 55.97	13.97	0.16
64	6				33.	49.3			34 32.44	13.97	0.35
65	7		50.		7.				39 23.93	13.93	0.36
66	7.8			43.					39 59.92	13.93	0.22
67	8		47.5			39.5			43 22.07	13.90	0.24
68	8					53.			44 36.02	13.89	0.37
69	7.8		25.5	42.			33.		47 59.16	13.86	0.37
70	7.8	40.	6.	23.					50 40.06	13.84	0.19
71	8					4.			50 46.84	13.84	0.15
72	8	38.5		12.5					56 29.36	13.79	0.29
73	7	6.3	23.	40.3					58 57.23	13.77	0.23
74	7				5.		38.		21 59 3.99	13.77	0.19
75	7.8	32.	48.7	6.					22 5 23.04	13.72	0.15
76	6.7			52.	2.				6 8.76	13.72	0.35
77	8				16.5			7.	11 16.07	13.68	0.29
78	8	46.5		21.					22 17 37.72	+13.63	+0.19

No.	MICROMETER.		r.	i	d_1	d_2	Mean Right Ascension, 1850.0. (h m s)	Mean Declination, 1850.0. (° ′ ″)
30	IV.	3	31.680	−28 14.60	−17.89	−2.83	20 38 24.09	−25 1 5.32
31	III.	4	49.015	10 4.65	17.13	1.25	43 20.31	24 42 53.03
32	IV.	4	45.615	13 38.00	17.05	1.56	44 5.22	46 26.61
33	IV.	4	41.670	17 45.37	16.89	1.91	45 11.70	50 34.17
34	III.	4	44.075	15 14.53	16.70	1.70	46 30.10	48 2.93
35	III.	4	46.020	13 12.53	16.44	1.52	48 15.28	24 46 0.49
36	IV.	3	29.197	30 50.51	16.35	3.05	48 50.73	25 3 39.91
37	V.	3	24.770	35 28.34	16.32	3.37	49 5.52	25 6 18.03
38	III.	4	38.800	20 45.25	15.86	2.15	52 23.49	24 53 33.26
39	IV.	1	6.345	54 44.43	15.67	5.25	53 42.30	25 27 35.35
40	IV.	3	37.847	21 47.67	15.48	2.25	55 1.90	24 54 35.40
41	III.	2	18.530	42 0.55	15.06	4.07	58 5.97	25 14 49.68
42	IV.	4	43.825	15 30.15	14.82	1.72	20 59 47.43	24 48 16.69
43	IV.	3	32.310	27 35.26	14.65	2.77	21 1 6.56	25 0 22.68
44	VII.	1	8.175	52 49.61	14.61	5.09	1 20.06	25 39.51
45	VII.	1	7.725	53 17.93	14.49	5.14	2 16.06	25 26 7.56
46	VI.	4	48.060	11 4.29	14.35	1.32	3 19.06	24 43 49.96
47	I.		6.375	54 42.56	14.19	5.27	4 33.51	25 27 32.02
48	III.	4	52.510	6 25.69	13.62	0.90	8 51.85	24 39 10.21
49	IV.	2	13.110	47 40.85	13.11	4.62	12 47.23	25 20 28.58
50	VI.	3	21.370	39 2.07	12.94	3.82	14 8.27	11 48.83
51	IV.	3	29.153	30 53.27	12.75	3.06	15 39.61	25 3 39.08
52	IV.	4	49.690	9 22.39	12.62	1.17	16 41.24	24 42 6.18
53	IV.	3	25.363	34 51.14	12.52	3.43	17 27.58	25 7 37.09
54	VI.	3	31.470	28 28.33	12.52	3.85	17 28.39	25 1 14.70
55	III.	4	54.255	4 36.26	12.17	0.74	20 12.83	24 37 19.17
56	III.	3	28.005	32 4.85	11.99	3.17	21 44.60	25 4 50.01
57	III.	2	18.335	42 12.85	11.73	4.11	23 54.02	25 14 58.69
58	V.	4	43.550	15 47.45	11.72	1.73	23 59.72	24 48 30.90
59	IV.	3	25.680	34 31.05	11.13	3.40	28 57.67	25 7 15.58
60	IV.	3	25.680	34 31.05	10.97	3.40	30 21.66	7 15.42
61	III.	2	11.340	49 31.89	10.84	4.80	31 34.14	22 17.53
62	III.	2	13.550	47 25.66	10.63	4.58	33 23.72	20 10.87
63	III.	1	10.520	50 21.97	10.55	4.88	34 10.10	25 23 7.40
64	IV.	4	42.713	16 39.05	10.48	1.81	34 46.76	24 49 22.24
65	III.	4	47.010	12 10.39	9.94	1.41	39 38.22	24 44 51.74
66	III.	3	23.673	36 36.69	9.87	3.59	40 14.07	25 9 20.14
67	V.	3	27.363	32 45.89	9.52	3.23	43 36.21	25 5 28.64
68	V.	4	46.255	12 57.86	9.40	1.48	44 50.28	24 45 38.74
69	III.	4	48.875	10 13.37	9.05	1.24	48 13.39	24 42 53.66
70	III.	2	21.670	38 43.37	8.77	3.79	50 54.09	25 11 25.93
71	V.	1	12.317	48 29.75	8.76	4.70	51 0.83	25 21 13.21
72	III.	3	36.370	23 20.19	8.20	2.37	56 43.44	24 56 0.76
73	III.	3	25.670	34 31.30	7.96	3.40	59 11.23	25 7 12.66
74	IV.	2	18.667	41 52.02	7.94	4.07	21 59 17.95	14 34.03
75	III.	1	17.635	49 12.05	7.33	4.77	22 5 36.91	25 21 54.17
76	IV.	4	47.090	12 5.50	7.26	1.38	6 22.83	24 44 44.14
77	IV.	4	41.760	17 39.67	6.78	1.88	11 30.04	24 50 18.33
78	III.	2	21.060	−39 21.71	−6.19	−3.86	22 17 51.54	−25 12 1.76

CORRECTIONS.

Date.	Corr. of Clock.	Hourly rate.	m	n	c	Zenith Point.	Mic. Co.
1847	h.	s.	s.	s.	s.	° ′ ″	r.
	s.	s.					

REMARKS.

(134) 49. Transit over T. III assumed to have been recorded as over T. IV.

INSTRUMENT READINGS.

Date.	CIRCLE.							Barom.	THERMOM.				
		A.	B.	C.	D.	E.	F.	Mean.		At.	Ex.	U.	L.	I.
Zone 134	1847. Sept. 21.	h. m. 0 0							in. 30.068	63.2	55.0			

ZONE 134. SEPTEMBER 21. P. $D_c = -24° 32' 30''$—Continued.

No.	Mag.	I.	II.	III.	IV.	V.	VI.	VII.	T. (h. m. s.)	a_1 (s.)	a_2 (s.)
79	8			29.5					22 18 46.32	+13.62	+0.38
80	7	34.3	51.		25.5				20 25.07	13.61	0.29
81	7				32.				21 21.80	13.60	0.39
82	7			0.5	18.3				22 17.57	13.59	0.28
83	7.8	19.	35.5		11.3				24 10.08	13.58	0.13
84	7		5.5	23.	40.5				25 39.80	13.57	0.23
85	6				7.	24.			27 6.83	13.55	0.33
86	8							30.	27 39.12	13.55	0.32
87	8	48.		22.					32 38.90	13.51	0.24
88	7.8			44.	1.5				35 0.81	13.49	0.20
89	8	34.	51.5	8.5					39 25.27	13.46	0.27
90	8			35.					43 34.58	13.43	0.30
91	8						41.5		44 7.31	13.42	0.12
92	7						34.7		45 0.84	13.42	0.33
93	7.8		14.3	31.5					46 48.34	13.40	0.31
94	7		19.	36.					47 53.01	13.39	0.25
95	8			11.					48 44.06	13.39	0.36
96	8.9	25.	42.	59.					51 15.93	13.37	0.27
97	8.9						19.5		51 45.32	13.36	0.12
98	8	14.		48.					56 4.86	13.33	0.26
99	9	17.	33.				42.		56 7.66	13.33	0.25
100	6						31.		22 56 56.91	13.33	0.18
101	8.9	16.	33.	50.					23 2 7.00	13.29	0.21
102	7		40.5	57.5					4 14.39	13.27	0.35
103	7			49.			22.3		4 47.90	13.27	0.26
104	8			16.					6 32.82	13.26	0.35
105	7.8		48.3						8 22.71	13.25	0.09
106	8			53.					8 52.60	13.24	0.29
107	9	3.5	21.						10 54.82	13.22	0.19
108	7.8	17.7	34.5	51.5		9.3	25.5		14 8.55	13.20	0.25
109	9	33.	49.5						19 23.81	13.16	0.20
110	8					39.5			19 22.36	13.16	0.12
111	7				17.3	34.5			21 17.16	13.15	0.26
112	7			14.5	32.	49.			22 31.56	13.14	0.22
113	9			16.					29 59.05	13.09	0.31
114	6	12.	29.	46.3	3.7	20.3			33 3.11	13.07	0.22
115	7.8	59.	16.	33.3	51.				38 50.16	13.03	0.16
116	8			41.					41 57.89	13.01	0.21
117	8	59.		33.3					43 50.01	13.00	0.23
118	6	31.	47.5	4	22.3				45 21.65	12.99	0.18
119	8	50.		42.					47 41.11	12.97	0.18
120	8				30.5				47 56.39	12.97	0.13
121	7.8	43.5	0.	17.3	35.3	51.3			50 34.33	12.95	0.20
122	6	21.5	38.5	55.3	13.3	29.5		3.3	55 12.44	12.92	0.20
123	8			47.5					58 21.87	12.90	0.08
124	8	45.		19.					23 59 35.75	12.89	0.31
125	7			0.5	17.5 35.	51.5			0 0 34.48	+12.89	+0.22

No.		MICROMETER. $r.$		i (' ")		d_1 (")	d_4 (")	Mean Right Ascension, 1850.0 (h. m. s.)	Mean Declination, 1850.0 (° ' ")
79	III.	4	53.250	−5	39.28	−6.08	−0.81	22 19 0.32	−24 38 16.17
80	IV.	3	38.500	21	6.88	5.93	2.17	20 35.97	53 44.98
81	IV.	4	54.353	4	30.37	5.85	0.71	21 35.79	37 6.93
82	IV.	4	36.305	23	24.65	5.77	2.39	22 31.44	24 56 2.81
83	IV.	1	10.370	50	31.77	5.61	4.91	24 23.79	25 23 12.29
84	IV.	3	26.750	33	23.91	5.46	3.31	25 53.60	25 6 2.68
85	IV.	4	46.030	13	11.91	5.36	1.48	27 20.71	24 45 48.75
86	VII.	4	45.285	13	58.14	5.31	−1.55	27 52.99	24 46 35.00
87	III.	3	31.413	28	31.16	4.92	−2.86	32 52.65	25 1 8.94
88	IV.	4	23.100	37	13.01	4.74	3.66	35 14.50	25 9 51.41
89	III.	3	37.575	22	4.54	4.41	2.26	39 39.00	24 54 41.21
90	IV.	4	42.690	16	41.40	4.15	1.80	43 48.31	24 49 17.35
91	VI.	2	11.880	48	57.93	4.12	4.76	44 20.85	25 21 36.81
92	VI.	4	48.340	10	46.92	4.06	1.27	45 14.59	24 43 22.25
93	III.	3	45.850	13	23.08	3.95	1.50	47 2.05	45 58.53
94	III.	4	35.455	24	17.58	3.88	2.48	48 6.65	56 53.94
95	IV.	4	52.600	6	19.98	3.86	0.87	48 7.81	38 54.71
96	III.	3	38.273	21	20.81	3.68	2.19	51 29.57	24 53 56.68
97	VI.	3	12.625	48	10.41	3.66	4.69	51 58.80	25 20 48.76
98	III.	3	36.985	22	43.30	3.44	2.33	56 18.45	24 55 19.07
99	VI.	3	36.600	23	6.45	3.44	2.36	56 21.24	24 55 42.25
100	VI.	3	23.430	36	52.80	3.40	3.63	22 57 10.42	25 9 29.83
101	III.	3	28.883	31	9.64	3.15	3.10	23 2 20.50	25 3 45.89
102	III.	1	52.995	5	23.70	3.06	0.81	4 28.01	24 37 57.57
103	IV.	4	37.083	22	35.72	3.03	2.30	5 1.43	55 11.05
104	III.	4	52.680	6	14.89	2.96	0.84	6 46.43	24 38 48.69
105	II.	1	8.634	52	19.75	2.88	5.11	8 36.05	25 24 57.74
106	IV.	4	44.250	15	3.68	2.86	1.66	9 6.13	24 47 38.19
107	II.	3	26.770	33	21.78	2.78	3.31	11 8.23	25 5 57.87
108	IV.	3	38.420	31	39.31	2.67	3.18	14 22.00	4 15.06
109	II.	3	28.900	31	5.07	2.49	3.10	19 37.17	3 43.66
110	V.	2	15.490	45	11.59	2.49	4.43	19 35.64	25 17 48.51
111	IV.	3	40.172	19	19.38	2.44	2.02	21 30.57	24 51 53.84
112	IV.	3	31.110	28	31.72	2.40	2.86	22 44.92	25 1 6.98
113	V.	4	50.075	8	58.18	2.19	1.08	30 12.45	24 41 31.45
114	IV.	3	33.000	26	51.79	2.13	2.70	33 16.40	24 59 26.62
115	IV.	3	25.250	34	58.16	2.00	3.47	39 3.35	25 7 33.63
116	III.	3	32.570	27	18.52	1.96	2.74	42 11.11	24 59 53.22
117	III.	3	37.220	22	26.80	1.93	2.29	44 3.24	24 55 1.02
118	IV.	3	28.857	31	11.65	1.91	3.11	45 34.82	25 3 46.67
119	IV.	3	28.785	31	16.16	1.88	3.11	47 54.26	3 51.15
120	VI.	3	20.155	40	18.70	1.89	3.97	48 9.49	12 54.55
121	IV.	2	32.230	27	40.21	1.85	2.78	50 47.48	25 0 14.84
122	IV.	3	33.595	26	14.52	1.83	2.64	55 25.56	24 58 48.99
123	II.	2	13.130	47	39.10	1.81	4.66	58 34.85	25 20 15.57
124	III.	4	52.070	6	53.15	1.80	0.89	23 59 48.95	24 39 25.84
125	IV.	3	36.580	−23	7.34	−1.80	−2.35	0 0 47.59	−24 55 41.49

CORRECTIONS.

Date.	Corr. of Clock.	Hourly rate.	m	n	c	Zenith Point.	Mic. Co.
1847.	h.	s.	s.	s.	s.	° ' "	r.
	s.	s.					

INSTRUMENT READINGS.

Date.	CIRCLE.							Barom.	THERMOM.				
	A.	B.	C.	D.	E.	F.	Mean.		At.	Ex.	U.	L.	I.
1847. h. m.	° ' "					"		In.	°				

REMARKS.

(134) 95. Transit over T. V assumed as recorded over T. IV, and as 1^s, not 11^s; minutes as 47, not 48.

(134) 102. Micrometer reading assumed as $53^r.495$ instead of $52^r.995$.

(134) 108. Micrometer reading assumed as $28^r.420$, not $38^r.420$.

ZONE 135. SEPTEMBER 27. C. $D_o = -14°\ 2'\ 0''$.

No.	Mag.	I.	II.	III.	IV.	V.	VI.	VII.	T.	a_1	a_1	MICROMETER.	i	d_1	d_2	Mean Right Ascension, 1850.0	Mean Declination, 1850.0
									h. m. s.	s.	s.	r.	' "	"	"	h. m. s.	° ' "
1	8.9	..	17.	32.7	49.	4.6	20.7	..	19 41 48.73	.	..	IV. 4 43.861	−15 27.85	−20.22	−0.79	..	−14 17 48.89
2	9	..	32.	48.2	4.7	..	..	..	45 4.02	.	..	IV. 3 28.918	31 7.82	19.65	1.57	..	33 29.04
3	9	..	..	..	24.7	41.	56.5	..	45 24.74	.	..	IV. 4 47.335	11 50.07	19.60	0.60	..	14 10.27
4	9	..	..	..	..	44.2	0.0	..	46 28.31	.	..	V. 4 51.026	7 58.54	19.40	0.41	..	10 18.35
5	10	..	..	32.7	..	..	20.	..	49 48.36	.	..	IV. 3 37.455	22 12.50	18.81	1.12	..	24 32.43
6	8	..	57.3	13.7	29.	46.	..	..	52 29.34	.	..	IV. 4 40.901	18 33.53	18.35	0.94	..	20 52.82
7	10	..	31.5	..	..	..	..	..	57 3.59	.	..	II. 2 17.556	43 1.49	17.55	2.16	..	45 21.20
8	8.9	..	26.3	42.3	59.	14.2	30.	..	19 59 58.20	.	..	IV. 3 21.586	38 48.08	17.03	1.95	..	41 7.06
9	9	..	..	38.6	54.7	10.3	26.1	..	20 2 54.39	.	..	IV. 4 48.176	10 57.40	16.53	0.56	..	13 24.49
10	9	..	..	..	12.2	28.	44.	..	20 4 12.0	.	..	IV. 4 47.356	−11 48.91	−16.30	−0.60	..	−14 14 5.84

ZONE 136. SEPTEMBER 27. C. $D_o = -26°\ 25'\ 20''$.

No.	Mag.	I.	II.	III.	IV.	V.	VI.	VII.	T.	a_1	a_1	MICROMETER.	i	d_1	d_2	Mean Right Ascension, 1850.0	Mean Declination, 1850.0
1	7.8	..	48.8	6.2	24.5	41.4	58.5	..	20 31 23.69	+11.06	+0.89	IV. 2 16.043	−44 36.70	−11.46	−4.47	20 31 35.64	−27 10 12.63
2	7	..	..	..	31.7	48.	5.7		32 14.09	11.05	0.87	V. 4 52.808	6 6.75	11.33	0.66	32 26.01	26 31 38.74
3	9.10	..	..	53.5	12.	..			36 11.09	11.01	0.90	IV. 3 41.912	17 32.69	10.70	1.77	36 23.00	43 5.16
4	7.8	..	14.	31.5	49.5	6.	23.	..	44 48.68	10.94	0.96	IV. 3 32.700	27 10.60	9.37	2.73	45 0.58	52 42.70
5	9	..	..	57.2	..	33.7			45 15.04	10.94	0.95	IV. 4 44.086	15 13.90	9.31	1.55	46 26.93	40 44.76
6	6.7	..	..	23.	40.7	57.6	14.8	..	47 40.20	10.92	0.97	IV. 3 33.513	26 19.73	8.93	2.65	47 52.09	51 51.31
7	9	..	..	..	41.5	58.5	15.8	..	48 41.14	10.90	0.97	IV. 3 36.506	23 11.97	8.78	2.33	48 53.01	26 48 43.08
8	9	..	..	..	9.5	27.4	..		59 26.56	10.81	1.05	IV. 2 13.818	46 56.28	7.24	4.69	59 38.42	27 12 28.21
9	9	..	..	..	..	58.7			20 59 23.34	+10.81	+1.04	VI. 3 19.930	−40 32.13	−7.24	−4.05	20 59 35.19	−27 6 3.47

ZONE 137. SEPTEMBER 29. C. $D_o = -14°\ 2'\ 0''$.

No.	Mag.	I.	II.	III.	IV.	V.	VI.	VII.	T.	a_1	a_1	MICROMETER.	i	d_1	d_2	Mean Right Ascension, 1850.0	Mean Declination, 1850.0
1	8.9	..	34.3	50.	6.3	..	..		19 45 5.99	.	..	IV. 3 28.765	−31 17.42	−8.59	−1.57	..	−14 33 27.58
2	8.9	..	..	..	42.5	58.3	..		45 20.59	.	..	V. 4 47.169	12 0.47	8.53	0.61	..	14 9.61
3	8.9	..	..	46.	..	18.2			46 30.36	.	..	V. 4 50.861	8 8.83	8.34	0.42	..	10 17.59
4	9	..	26.	42.	..	..			49 41.50	.	..	IV. 2 19.646	40 50.65	7.76	2.06	..	43 0.47
5	7.8	..	59.6	15.8	32.	46.9	3.6		52 31.50	.	..	IV. 3 40.758	18 45.14	7.27	0.94	..	20 53.35
6	9.10	..	..	..	49.5	..	..		19 57 5.35	.	..	III. 2 17.378	43 12.91	6.45	2.17	..	45 21.53
7	8	..	28.6	44.5	1.2	16.7	..		20 0 0.52	.	..	IV. 3 21.402	38 59.69	5.94	1.06	..	41 7.59
8	9.10	..	..	56.	..	28.	..	59.6	1 11.85	.	..	IV. 3 19.842	40 37.33	5.73	2.05	..	42 45.11
9	9	..	..	40.7	57.	..	28.3	..	2 56.58	.	..	IV. 4 47.991	11 8.93	5.43	0.57	..	13 14.93
10	8	..	..	..	14.7	..	45.8		4 14.93	.	..	IV. 4 47.175	12 0.16	5.21	0.61	..	14 5.98
11	8	..	..	20.5	37.	52.7	8.		20 5 36.47	.	..	IV. 4 41.050	−18 22.44	−4.97	−0.93	..	−14 20 28.34

CORRECTIONS.

Date.	Corr. of Clock.	Hourly rate.	m	n	c	Zenith Point.	Mic. Co.
1847. h.	s.	s.	s.	s.	s.	° ' "	r.

INSTRUMENT READINGS.

	Date.	CIRCLE.							Barom.	THERMOM.				
		A.	B.	C.	D.	E.	F.	Mean.		At.	Ex.	U.	L.	I.
	1847, h. m.	° ' "						"	In.	°	°	°	°	°
Zone 135	Sept. 27, 19 41	. . .	. .	. .	. .	. .	. .	. .	29.828	67.0	64.2			
	20 0	53 24 60.8	57.1	55.1	47.1	45.7	61.5	54.55*	29.820	66.5	63.3	65.7	65.6	65.7
Zone 136	Sept. 27, 20 30	65 47 35.8	32.9	31.3	23.5	24.2	36.2	30.65	29.814	66.5	63.1	65.5	64.8	65.7
	20 44	. .	. .	. .	. .	. .	. .	. .	. .		63.5			
	20 59	. .	. .	. .	. .	. .	. .	. .	29.814	66.0	63.4			
Zone 137	Sept. 29, 19 45	. .	. .	. .	. .	. .	. .	. .			56.0			
	19 57	. .	. .	. .	. .	. .	. .	. .	29.868	65.0				
	20 0	53 24 48.2	45.3	43.2	33.2	34.9	48.3	42.18*	. .			63.4	64.3	65.8
	20 5	. .	. .	. .	. .	. .	. .	. .			55.4			

REMARKS.

(136) 5. Minutes assumed as 46, not 45.
(136) 9. Right ascension 2ˢ small by Arg. Z. 232, 42, and Mer. Circle Z. 1846.

September 27, 21ʰ. Clouds forming.
September 29. Reading of external thermometer at 19ʰ 40ᵐ.

* Corr. for runs +0".07.

* Corr. for runs +0".04.

ZONE 138. OCTOBER 15. C. $D_0 = -26° 25' 20''$.

No.	Mag.	Seconds of Transit (I. II. III. IV. V. VI. VII.)	T. (h. m. s.)	a_1 (s.)	a_2 (s.)	Micrometer	i	d_1	d_2	Mean Right Ascension 1850.0 (h. m. s.)	Mean Declination 1850.0 (° ' '')
1	8.9	. . 57.3 . . . . 51.7	22 58 33.21	− 5.37	−1.21	IV. 3 26.837	−33 18.40	5.62	−3.37	22 58 26.63	−26 58 47.39
2	8.9	. . . . 46.5 2.8 . .	22 59 28.66	5.38	1.22	V. 3 24.980	35 15.22	5.57	3.57	22 59 22.06	27 0 44.36
3	6	. . . . 12.5 29.5 . .	23 0 55.17	5.39	0.99	V. 4 46.231	12 59.30	5.51	1.16	23 0 48.79	26 38 25.97
4	9	. . 43. 1. 19.5 35.5	5 16.18	5.44	1.34	IV. 2 13.389	47 23.46	5.30	4.92	5 11.40	27 12 53.68
5	9	. . 29. 46.1 3.2	8 3.20	5.47	1.01	IV. 4 41.023	18 25.94	5.16	1.75	7 56.72	26 43 52.85
6	8	. . 23. 39.5 57.3	10 57.03	5.50	1.02	IV. 4 39.288	20 14.96	5.03	1.96	10 50.51	26 45 41.95
7	9	. . . . 29.5 . .	10 54.87	5.50	1.19	VI. 3 23.186	37 7.93	5.03	3.77	10 48.18	27 2 36.73
8	9	. . . . 29.2	11 37.04	5.50	1.37	VII. 2 10.072	50 51.29	5.01	5.31	11 30.20	27 16 21.61
9	9.10	. . . . 23.2?	13 5.96	5.52	0.92	V. 4 47.151	12 1.61	4.95	1.05	12 59.52	26 37 27.61
10	8.9	. . . . 12. 30.3 . . 4. . . .	15 29.26	5.54	1.29	IV. 2 13.405	47 22.46	4.85	4.91	15 22.43	27 12 52.22
11	9.10	. . . . . . 59.2 16.	16 56.65	5.56	1.02	IV. 3 35.355	24 24.24	4.79	2.39	16 52.07	26 49 51.42
12	8	. . 30. 47.8 6.3 23. 40.2 . .	20 5.24	5.59	1.30	IV. 2 9.793	51 8.93	4.67	5.34	19 58.35	27 16 38.94
13	6	. . . . 50.7 7.8 25. . . 59. .	24 7.62	5.61	0.82	IV. 4 50.128	8 54.98	4.54	0.72	24 1.16	26 34 20.24
14	9	. . . . 50. . . 24.2 . . 58.3	24 6.90	5.61	0.88	IV. 4 45.328	13 56.13	4.54	1.26	24 0.38	39 21.93
15	9	. . . . . . 5.8 22.8 40. . .	26 5.55	5.66	0.83	IV. 4 48.471	10 38.06	4.48	0.91	25 59.06	36 4.35
16	9	. . . . 6.8 . . 41. 58.2 . .	29 23.81	5.69	0.87	IV. 4 43.142	16 13.11	4.38	1.52	29 17.25	26 41 39.01
17	7	. . 6.2 23.2 41.2 58. 15.2 . .	32 40.60	5.73	1.07	IV. 3 24.132	36 8.26	4.30	3.66	32 33.80	27 1 36.22
18	7	. . 12. 29.5 47.5 4. 21.1 . .	36 46.65	5.77	1.00	IV. 3 21.201	39 12.24	4.20	4.01	36 39.79	27 4 40.45
19	9.10	. . . . . . 28. 45.	41 27.49	5.81	0.94	V. 3 29.866	30 8.60	4.10	3.04	41 20.74	26 55 35.74
20	8	. . . . . . 3. 19. 36.8 . .	43 2.19	5.83	0.85	IV. 4 40.451	19 2.01	4.07	1.81	42 55.51	44 27.89
21	9	. . 58. 15.2 32.	45 32.15	5.86	0.93	IV. 3 31.725	28 11.77	4.02	2.81	45 25.36	53 38.60
22	9	. . 54.6 11.7 29.7 . . 2.8 . .	48 28.90	5.88	0.82	IV. 4 40.348	19 8.46	3.97	1.82	48 22.20	44 34.26
23	8.9	. . 5.4 23. 41.1 57.4	51 40.20	5.92	0.89	IV. 3 32.278	27 37.26	3.95	2.75	51 33.39	26 53 3.94
24	9	. . . . . . 48. 5.7 . .	52 30.86	5.93	0.96	V. 3 24.828	35 24.70	3.92	3.57	52 23.97	27 0 52.19
25	9	. . . . 15.8 33.2 50.3 . .	54 15.77	5.94	0.70	IV. 4 47.419	11 44.92	3.90	1.03	54 9.13	26 37 9.85
26	9	. . . . 52. . . 25.7 . .	55 50.94	5.96	1.11	IV. 2 11.318	49 33.46	3.88	5.16	55 43.87	27 15 2.50
27	9	. . . . . . 6. . .	56 31.54	5.97	0.77	VI. 4 41.300	18 8.39	3.88	1.72	56 24.80	26 43 33.99
28	9	. . . . 33.?	23 56 41.25	5.97	0.78	VII. 4 40.297	19 10.92	3.87	1.83	23 56 34.50	44 36.62
29	9	. . 39.7 57.2 14.7 . . 59.2	0 0 56.96	6.01	0.79	IV. 3 36.322	23 23.58	3.84	2.29	0 0 50.16	48 49.71
30	9	. . . . . . 59.2 . .	1 24.80	6.02	0.66	VI. 4 46.606	12 35.54	3.84	1.11	1 18.12	38 0.49
31	7	. . 27.2 44.2 1.3 18.5	2 26.83	6.03	0.72	IV. 3 42.261	17 11.05	3.84	1.61	2 20.08	26 42 36.50
32	8	10.3 28.7 46.7 . . . 37.7	5 45.62	6.06	0.99	IV. 2 16.518	44 7.02	3.83	4.55	5 38.57	27 9 35.40
33	7	40.2 . 15.7 32.3 49.4 . .	0 6 14.87	− 6.06	−0.95	IV. 2 18.793	−41 44.04	−3.83	−4.26	0 6 7.86	−27 7 12.15

CORRECTIONS.

Date.	Corr. of Clock.	Hourly rate.	m	n	c	Zenith Point.	Mic. Co.
1847. h.	s.	s.	s.	s.	s.	° ' ''	r.

INSTRUMENT READINGS.

	Date.		CIRCLE.							Barom.	THERMOM.				
			A.	B.	C.	D.	E.	F.	Mean.		At.	Ex.	U.	L.	I.
Zone 138	1847. Oct. 15,	22 50	65 47 34.0	38.0	35.7	24.1	29.5	32.3	32.27ª	In.			43.8	45.8	53.3
		22 59								30.288	46.0	36.2			
		23 20										36.1			
		23 41								30.292	45.2	35.6			
		0 0	34.3	37.8	36.3	24.0	29.2	31.9	32.25	30.290	45.0	35.9	43.0	44.4	

REMARKS.

(138) 12. Transits across T.'s IV and V assumed as at 6ˢ.3 and 23ˢ instead of 3ˢ and 2ˢ.3.

Oct 15. Stars very unsteady; of many only glimpses would be obtained, and no observations could be made of them; mist over the river.

ª Corr. for runs +0''.07.

ZONE 139. OCTOBER 16. P. $D_0 = -30° 10' 40''$.

No.	Mag.	I.	II.	III.	IV.	V.	VI.	VII.	T. (h. m. s.)
1	8		44.3	3.					22 1 20.65
2	9				13.				2 12.30
3	9						56.5		3 20.92
4	9		16.						5 52.11
5	8.9		26.	43.3		20.5			8 1.82
6	8		58.3	16.5					9 34.15
7	7.8	1.7	19.	37.5					11 55.09
8	9							55.	12 0.93
9	9						15.		13 39.37
10	7						54.		14 18.36
11	8						45.		15 9.30
12	8				39.5		14.7		16 39.05
13	8.9					24.			19 5.91
14	7		15.	33.5	52.				20 51.19
15	8		39.3	58.					22 15.66
16	9		33.			27.			25 8.99
17	7		39.	57.				8.	25 14.67
18	6.7					47.			27 28.87
19	8			52.	11.				29 10.02
20	8	41.	58.3						31 34.36
21	7			33.	51.3				31 50.67
22	7				24.				32 23.55
23	7			21.3	40.				33 39.13
24	8							22.	33 46.38
25	8				3.				35 2.55
26	9						59.		35 23.29
27	8.9		16.5						40 52.51
28	7.8				12.				41 11.31
29	7.8							53.	41 4.52
30	5.6		36.3	53.3	11.3				43 11.36
31	8.9		1.5						44 37.52
32	8				18.				44 46.89
33	8						22.		45 46.26
34	7				11.5	29.3			47 11.27
35	1	34.5	52.3	10.5	28.5			21.7	49 28.11
36	7		54.	12.	30.				51 29.73
37	8.9		55.						53 30.96
38	9					46.			53 28.17
39	9							25.	53 31.58
40	8.9						25.		54 49.18
41	8					34.			56 15.87
42	6.7	1.	18.5	37.	56.				58 54.83
43	9				41.				22 59 39.85
44	7		28.	46.					23 1 4.04
45	8	49.3	7.						2 43.00
46	7					5.			2 47.16
47	8						46.		3 10.08
48	8.9			42.					5 6.74
49	7.8			18.					5 35.75
50	7						12.5		23 5 18.55

No.	a_1 (s.)	a_2 (s.)	MICROMETER		r	i	d_1	d_2	Mean Right Ascension 1850.0 (h. m. s.)	Mean Declination 1850.0 (° ' ")
1	−5.76	−0.77	II.	2	19.230	−41 16.25	−11.52	−5.64	22 1 14.10	−30 52 13.41
2	5.79	0.78	IV.	3	30.940	29 0.96	11.44	3.86	2 5.73	39 56.26
3	5.80	0.79	VI.	4	53.805	5 3.92	11.33	0.49	3 14.33	15 55.74
4	5.84	0.77	II.	3	22.920	37 23.23	11.07	5.08	5 45.50	48 19.38
5	5.86	0.79	III.	4	50.230	8 48.59	10.87	1.03	7 55.17	19 40.49
6	5.88	0.79	III.	4	48.860	10 14.31	10.71	1.20	9 27.48	21 6.22
7	5.91	0.79	III.	4	42.015	17 23.66	10.50	2.21	11 48.39	30 28 16.37
8	5.91	0.78	VII.	2	11.580	49 16.57	10.49	6.79	11 54.24	31 0 13.85
9	5.93	0.80	VI.	4	48.790	10 18.40	10.34	1.21	13 32.64	30 21 9.93
10	5.94	0.80	VI.	4	47.830	11 18.60	10.29	1.36	14 11.62	22 10.25
11	5.95	0.80	VI.	4	43.255	16 5.41	10.22	2.02	15 2.55	26 57.65
12	5.96	0.80	IV.	4	44.185	15 7.74	10.09	1.89	16 32.29	25 59.72
13	5.99	0.79	V.	2	12.115	48 43.37	9.87	6.70	18 59.13	59 39.94
14	6.01	0.80	IV.	3	26.153	34 1.50	9.73	4.58	20 44.38	44 55.81
15	6.03	0.79	III.	2	17.662	42 54.97	9.61	5.87	22 8.84	53 50.45
16	6.07	0.80	V.	4	40.305	19 11.05	9.30	2.47	25 2.12	30 2.92
17	6.07	0.81	VII.	4	44.000	15 18.41	9.38	1.91	25 7.79	30 26 9.70
18	6.09	0.80	V.	1	5.453	55 40.62	9.20	7.74	27 21.98	31 6 37.56
19	6.11	0.81	IV.	3	26.650	33 30.26	9.04	4.51	29 3.10	30 44 23.81
20	6.14	0.81	II.	3	37.890	21 44.02	8.89	2.83	31 27.41	32 35.74
21	6.14	0.81	IV.	3	27.460	32 39.54	8.87	4.38	31 43.72	43 32.79
22	6.15	0.81	IV.	4	42.955	16 24.70	8.84	2.08	32 16.59	27 15.64
23	6.16	0.80	IV.	3	22.593	37 44.83	8.75	5.12	33 32.17	48 38.70
24	6.16	0.82	VII	4	50.305	8 37.54	8.70	1.00	33 39.40	19 27.30
25	6.18	0.82	IV.	4	43.205	16 9.22	8.65	2.03	34 55.55	26 59.90
26	6.19	0.82	VI.	4	41.593	17 49.88	8.62	2.27	35 16.28	29 40.77
27	6.25	0.82	II.	3	30.850	29 5.67	8.25	3.88	40 45.44	39 57.80
28	6.26	0.82	IV.	4	31.550	28 22.98	8.23	3.77	41 4.23	39 14.88
29	6.26	0.83	VII.	4	49.850	9 11.47	8.24	1.09	40 57.43	20 0.80
30	6.28	0.83	IV.	4	50.110	8 56.12	8.12	1.04	43 4.25	19 45.28
31	6.30	0.82	II.	1	29.495	30 30.87	8.03	4.08	44 30.40	30 41 22.98
32	6.30	0.81	IV.	1	10.670	50 12.75	8.02	0.94	44 39.78	31 1 7.71
33	6.31	0.82	VI.	3	38.850	20 45.06	7.97	2.69	45 30.13	30 31 35.72
34	6.33	0.83	IV.	4	45.500	13 45.27	7.58	1.71	47 4.11	24 34.86
35	6.36	0.84	IV.	4	50.187	14 4.72	7.75	1.66	49 20.91	24 54.13
36	6.38	0.84	IV.	3	53.770	5 6.50	7.05	0.49	51 22.51	15 54.64
37	6.40	0.83	II.	3	35.150	24 36.10	7.55	3.24	53 23.73	35 26.89
38	6.40	0.84	V.	4	52.200	6 41.99	7.55	0.73	53 20.93	17 33.27
39	6.40	0.84	VII.	1	53.680	5 11.38	7.55	0.51	53 24.34	15 59.44
40	6.42	0.83	VI.	3	31.343	28 36.24	7.49	3.80	54 41.93	30 39 27.53
41	6.43	0.83	V.	1	6.270	54 49.33	7.42	7.01	56 8.61	31 5 44.36
42	6.47	0.83	IV.	4	19.900	40 34.57	7.30	5.52	58 47.53	30 57 27.39
43	6.48	0.83	IV.	1	9.200	51 39.56	7.26	7.13	22 59 32.54	31 2 33.95
44	6.49	0.83	III.	2	14.870	45 50.07	7.20	6.30	23 0 56.72	30 36 43.57
45	6.51	0.84	II.	3	27.193	32 55.29	7.14	4.43	2 35.65	43 46.86
46	6.51	0.85	V.	3	49.763	9 17.63	7.13	1.05	2 39.80	20 5.81
47	6.52	0.85	VI.	3	22.350	38 0.51	7.12	5.17	3 2.73	48 52.80
48	6.54	0.85	III.	4	46.410	12 48.20	7.05	1.55	4 59.35	23 36.80
49	6.54	0.85	III.	4	42.855	16 30.92	7.03	2.07	5 28.30	27 20.02
50	−6.54	−0.83	VII.	2	19.210	−41 17.76	−7.04	−5.60	23 5 11.18	−30 52 10.46

CORRECTIONS.

Date.	Corr. of Clock.	Hourly rate.	M	H	ϵ	Zenith Point.	Mic. Co.
1847.	h.	s.	s.	s.	s.	° ' "	r.
1847.							

REMARKS.

(139) 24. Transit over T, VI assumed as recorded over T, VII, to agree with Arg. Z. 259, 34.

(139) 35. Micrometer reading assumed as $45^v.187$, not $30^v.187$.

INSTRUMENT READINGS.

Date.	CIRCLE							Barom.	THERMOM.				
		A.	B.	C.	D.	E.	F.	Mean.		At.	Ex.	U.	L.	I.
Zone 139	1847. Oct. 16, 22 0 (h. m.)	69 32 34.0	35.3	34.8	24.8	26.2	35.1	31.70*	In. 30.262	53.3	45.5	53.5		
	22 40								30.260		45.0			
	23 11								30.260	52.2	43.9			
	23 28								30.258	52.1	43.5			
	0 19								30.242	51.5	42.7			

*Corr. for runs $+0''.07$.

ZONE 139. OCTOBER 16. P. D_o=−30° 10′ 40″—Continued.

No.	Mag.	I.	II.	III.	IV.	V.	VI.	VII.	T.	a_1	a_2	MIC.		r,	i	d_1	J_1	Mean Right Ascension, 1850.0.	Mean Declination, 1850.0.
									h. m. s.	s.	s.			r,	′ ″	″	″	h. m. s.	° ′ ″
51	7	51.	9.	27.	45.5	3.			23 7 44.85	6.57	−0.84	IV.	3	30.990	−28 57.88	−6.05	−3.85	23 7 37.44	−30 39 48.68
52	8.9			34.	53.				8 52.02	6.58	0.84	IV.	3	27.470	32 38.93	6.91	4.39	8 44.60	43 30.23
53	9						13.		11 37.05	6.61	0.83	VI.	2	18.900	41 37.27	6.61	5.71	11 29.61	52 29.79
54	8						5.7		12 29.73	6.62	0.83	VI.	2	17.450	43 6.52	6.78	5.93	12 22.26	54 1.23
55	7		57.	16.					17 33.48	6.69	0.83	III.	2	21.460	33 56.73	6.63	5.30	17 25.96	49 48.66
56	8	59.5	17.	35.3					19 52.89	6.71	0.85	III.	4	49.210	9 52.55	6.50	1.13	19 45.33	20 40.24
57	7.8				23.5				22 22.49	6.74	0.93	IV.	2	15.710	44 57.61	6.49	6.19	22 14.97	55 50.29
58	8					18.			23 0.03	6.75	0.84	V.	3	30.196	29 48.03	6.48	3.97	22 52.44	40 38.53
59	8.9		25.	43.					28 0.95	6.81	0.84	III.	3	25.420	34 47.18	6.36	4.70	27 53.30	45 38.24
60	8.9			54.					29 11.80	6.82	0.84	III.	3	28.667	31 23.26	6.33	4.21	28 4.14	42 13.80
61	8					2.			29 43.94	6.83	0.83	V.	2	16.620	44 0.62	6.32	6.05	29 36.28	54 52.99
62	8	8.7	26.5	44.3					32 2.13	6.85	0.85	III.	4	45.290	10 50.31	6.28	1.27	31 54.43	21 37.86
63	7	24.5	42.	0.	18.3				34 17.85	6.88	0.84	IV.	4	42.855	16 30.98	6.24	2.07	34 10.13	27 19.29
64	8	22.		57.5					39 15.47	6.04	0.83	III.	3	28.700	31 21.18	6.16	4.21	38 7.70	42 11.55
65	8.9							59.	40 5.49	6.95	0.85	VII.	4	47.195	11 58.16	6.15	1.43	39 57.69	22 45.74
66	8			45.7	4.5				42 21.99	6.97	0.83	III.	3	32.093	27 48.37	6.14	3.69	42 14.19	38 38.20
67	8			47.					43 4.82	6.98	0.83	III.	3	26.060	34 6.83	6.13	4.60	42 57.01	44 57.56
68	8							26.	42 32.60	6.97	0.85	VII.	4	55.360	3 26.23	6.13	0.25	42 24.78	14 12.61
69	8						16.		43 40.09	6.99	0.83	VI.	3	23.123	37 11.88	6.13	5.05	43 32.27	46 3.06
70	7		29.3	47.5	5.3				46 5.10	7.02	0.85	IV.	4	55.680	3 6.79	6.11	0.20	45 57.23	13 53.10
71	9			34.					49 51.79	7.06	0.83	III.	3	33.250	26 35.85	6.08	3.52	49 43.90	37 25.45
72	9		24.						49 59.92	7.06	0.84	II.	3	38.147	21 28.10	6.08	2.76	49 52.02	32 16.96
73	8		30.						51 5.77	7.07	0.85	II.	4	49.663	9 23.89	6.08	1.06	50 57.85	20 11.03
74	8.9			23.					51 22.20	7.07	0.93	IV.	3	26.230	33 56.06	6.08	4.58	51 14.30	44 47.32
75	6.7					10.5	28.		51 52.53	7.08	0.85	V.	4	50.580	8 26.58	6.08	0.94	51 44.60	19 13.60
76	8				21.3				53 20.32	7.10	0.83	IV.	2	17.475	43 6.95	6.08	5.02	53 12.39	53 58.05
77	8		10.	28.	46.5				54 45.88	7.11	0.84	IV.	3	37.115	22 33.71	6.08	2.04	54 37.93	33 22.73
78	8					39.7			55 21.64	7.12	0.63	V.	2	17.330	48 29.66	6.08	6.68	55 13.69	59 22.42
79	7		21.	40.3					56 39.06	7.13	0.82	IV.	2	13.420	47 21.50	6.09	6.53	56 31.11	58 14.12
80	7					25.			56 49.45	7.13	0.85	VI.	4	56.500	2 15.13	6.09	0.08	56 41.47	13 1.30
81	7							11.3	23 57 17.70	7.14	0.84	VII.	4	42.050	17 20.75	6.09	2.20	23 57 9.72	28 9.07
82	9		35.						0 0 55.86	7.18	0.83	III.	2	17.205	43 23.72	6.10	5.98	0 0 47.85	54 15.80
83	8	54.5	12.	30.					3 47.86	7.22	0.84	III.	4	41.700	17 43.42	6.13	2.24	3 39.80	28 31.79
84	7.8	37.	54.5	12.5					5 30.60	7.23	0.82	III.	2	17.830	42 44.30	6.14	5.89	5 22.55	53 36.33
85	8.9					5.			5 39.40	7.23	0.84	VI.	4	51.620	7 21.05	6.14	0.76	5 21.33	18 7.95
86	7.8							0.	6 6.46	7.24	0.63	VII.	4	45.470	13 46.40	6.15	1.67	5 58.39	30 24 34.22
87	7.8				0.				7 58.90	7.26	0.61	IV.	1	11.515	49 19.83	6.17	0.86	7 50.83	31 0 6.86
88	8.9					35.			9 17.06	7.27	0.83	V.	3	35.720	24 1.41	6.18	3.14	9 8.96	30 34 50.73
89	9						35.		9 59.19	7.28	0.82	VI.	3	31.450	28 29.52	6.19	3.79	9 51.09	39 19.50
90	8				16.	33.5			11 15.33	7.29	0.82	IV.	3	23.670	36 37.18	6.21	4.95	11 7.22	47 26.37
91	7	38.	56.	13.	31.5				13 31.28	7.32	0.82	IV.	4	39.183	20 21.41	6.26	2.61	13 23.14	31 10.28
92	7	5.5	23.	41.5					15 59.15	7.34	0.61	III.	3	30.150	29 50.28	6.31	3.98	15 51.00	40 40.57
93	8.9				31.7				16 13.86	7.34	0.83	V.	4	50.620	8 24.01	6.31	0.91	16 5.69	19 11.23
94	9			15.5					18 33.28	7.35	0.61	III.	3	33.930	25 53.00	6.32	3.41	16 25.12	36 42.73
95	7				53.				19 52.60	7.39	0.81	IV.	4	45.323	13 56.44	6.37	1.69	19 44.40	24 44.52
96	8			33.					20 32.76	7.40	0.82	IV.	4	52.703	6 13.45	6.40	0.60	20 24.54	17 0.45
97	9					4.			21 46.03	7.41	0.80	V.	3	30.323	29 40.18	6.44	3.95	21 37.82	40 30.57
98	6	30.5	48.	6.	24.				26 23.76	7.46	0.82	IV.	4	46.835	12 21.37	6.57	1.47	26 15.48	23 9.41
99	7.8	50.	8.5	26.3					29 44.00	7.49	0.80	III.	3	36.037	31 35.43	6.66	2.79	29 35.71	32 24.88
100	8			28.5		4.3			0 30 40.34	−7.50	−0.61	V.	4	49.560	−9 30.55	−6.69	−1.05	0 30 38.03	−30 20 18.30

CORRECTIONS.

Date.	Corr. of Clock.	Hourly rate.	m	n	c	Zenith Point.	Mic. Co.
1847. h.	s.	s.	s.	s.	s.	°, ′ ″	r.

REMARKS.

(139) 78. Micrometer reading assumed as 12ʳ.313, not 17ʳ.313.

INSTRUMENT READINGS.

Date.	CIRCLE.							Barom.	THERMOM.				
	A.	B.	C.	D.	E.	F.	Mean.		At.	Ex.	U.	L.	I.
1847. h. m.	° ′ ″						″	In.	°	°		°	°

ZONE 140. OCTOBER 18. C. $D_0 = -27° 40′ 20″$.

No.	Mag.	Seconds of Transit (I. II. III. IV. V. VI. VII.)	T. (h. m. s.)	a_1 (s.)	a_2 (s.)	Micrometer		r.	i (′ ″)	d_1 (″)	d_2 (″)	Mean Right Ascension, 1850.0 (h. m. s.)	Mean Declination, 1850.0 (° ′ ″)
1	8	.. 16.7 34.5 53.2 9.5 26.3 44.	22 56 51.91	− 8.14	−0.55	IV.	4	43.178	−16 10.84	− 5.42	−1.84	22 56 43.22	−27 56 38.10
2	9.10	.. .. 44. 3.2	23 1 2.03	8.18	0.56	IV.	4	41.992	17 25.17	5.28	1.97	23 0 53.29	57 52.42
3	9.10	.. .. .. 27. 43. 1.7 ..	1 26.35	8.19	0.55	IV.	4	45.114	14 9.42	5.27	1.61	1 17.61	27 54 36.30
4	9	.. .. 35. 53.7 ..	2 18.14	8.20	0.62	V.	3	34.251	25 33.68	5.24	2.89	2 9.32	28 6 1.81
5	8.9	.. .. 51.3 ..	3 16.59	8.21	0.47	VI.	4	55.610	3 10.94	5.21	0.39	3 7.91	27 43 36.54
6	9	.. .. 14.9 32.3 49.7	6 32.14	8.24	0.53	IV.	4	47.822	11 19.46	5.11	1.28	6 23.37	51 45.85
7	8.9	.. .. .. 49.5 6.	7 48.76	8.26	0.59	IV.	3	40.256	19 16.74	5.07	2.18	7 39.91	59 43.99
8	8	.. .. .. 36.8 54.2 11.6 ..	8 36.66	8.27	0.56	IV.	4	45.761	13 28.72	5.04	1.53	8 27.83	53 55.29
9	7	32.3 .. 7.2 24.3 42. 59.4 16.5	13 24.40	8.32	0.54	IV.	4	50.961	8 2.62	4.91	0.92	13 15.54	27 48 28.45
10	6.9	.. 36.5 53.5 12. 29.	16 11.33	8.35	0.65	IV.	3	34.014	25 48.17	4.83	2.92	16 2.33	28 6 15.92
11	8.9	.. ?. 35. 53.5 10.	16 52.55	8.36	0.69	IV.	3	30.012	29 59.25	4.82	3.40	16 43.50	10 27.47
12	7	.. 47. 4.8 23. 39.7 57. ..	18 22.15	8.37	0.74	IV.	3	25.686	34 30.67	4.76	3.92	18 13.04	14 59.37
13	8	.. .. 26.3 44.5 1.6 18.7 ..	19 43.85	8.39	0.66	IV.	3	34.062	25 45.22	4.74	2.91	19 34.80	6 12.87
14	9	.. 25.5 43.8 1.7 19.3	23 1.15	8.42	0.69	IV.	3	33.028	26 50.03	4.66	3.04	22 52.04	7 17.73
15	9	.. 30.2 48.2 7.	27 5.71	8.46	0.87	IV.	2	8.025	52 3.41	4.56	6.02	26 56.38	32 33.99
16	7.8	.. .. .. 55.2 11.7 29.3 ..	27 54.24	8.47	0.76	IV.	3	22.034	38 19.84	4.54	4.36	27 45.01	18 48.74
17	9	.. 59.3 17.7 35.3 52.5	34 34.73	8.54	0.86	IV.	2	13.074	47 43.11	4.40	5.42	34 25.33	28 12.93
18	9.10	.. 51. 9.2 27.2	36 26.42	8.56	0.67	IV.	3	38.328	21 17.74	4.36	2.40	36 17.19	1 44.50
19	9	.. .. 41.3 .. 16.3 33.5 ..	37 58.62	8.58	0.80	IV.	2	19.771	40 42.66	4.32	4.61	37 49.24	28 21 11.59
20	9.10	.. .. .. 49.2 7.5	42 32.20	8.62	0.64	V.	4	42.066	17 23.41	4.24	1.96	42 22.94	27 57 49.61
21	10	.. .. .. 43.2 1.5 .. 35.	44 43.20	8.64	0.64	IV.	4	45.900	13 19.99	4.20	1.51	44 33.96	53 45.70
22	8.9	.. 27.3 45.2 2.5 19.8	46 44.88	8.66	0.64	IV.	4	46.919	12 16.09	4.17	1.39	46 35.58	52 41.65
23	8.9	.. 27.7 45.7 2.8 20.	46 45.23	8.66	0.64	IV.	4	46.919	12 16.09	4.17	1.39	46 35.93	52 41.65
24	9	.. 25.3 43.3 0.8	54 42.93	8.75	0.67	IV.	4	41.579	17 51.14	4.07	2.02	54 33.51	27 58 17.23
25	8.9	8. 25.7 43.7	57 43.08	8.78	0.74	IV.	3	33.915	25 54.32	4.04	2.03	57 33.56	28 6 21.29
26	9	.. 11.9 29.3 47.5	23 59 46.83	8.80	0.79	IV.	3	26.659	33 29.69	4.01	3.80	23 59 37.24	28 13 57.50
27	9.10	.. .. 28.7	0 3 53.93	8.84	0.63	V.	4	48.671	10 26.16	4.01	1.16	0 3 44.46	27 50 51.33
28	7.8	18.7 36.7 55. 11.3	6 53.97	8.87	0.85	IV.	2	19.394	41 6.58	4.00	4.66	6 44.25	28 21 35.24
29	9	.. .. 34.5 51.7 ..	6 59.50	8.87	0.70	VI.	4	39.851	19 42.34	4.00	2.22	6 49.93	28 0 8.56
30	10	.. .. .. 56.2 13.5	8 55.86	8.89	0.69	IV.	3	41.212	18 16.78	4.00	2.06	8 46.28	27 58 42.84
31	9	.. 40.9 58. 15.7 32.8	14 58.05	8.95	0.63	IV.	4	48.621	10 29.49	4.05	1.18	14 48.47	50 54.72
32	8	21.5 39. 56.8 13.7	16 56.36	8.97	0.64	IV.	4	47.795	11 21.17	4.07	1.20	16 46.75	51 46.50
33	8	.. .. 51. .. 25.7 43.2 ..	17 8.35	8.97	0.59	IV.	4	54.334	4 31.37	4.07	0.49	16 58.79	27 44 55.93
34	7	.. .. 17.5	18 24.72	8.98	0.94	VII.	4	9.007	51 58.07	4.08	5.04	18 14.80	28 32 28.09
35	8.9	.. 30.2 48.1 5.7 22.5	21 47.82	9.01	0.64	IV.	4	49.111	9 58.70	4.14	1.11	21 38.17	27 50 24.01
36	8	.. 7.5 25.3 .. 50.3	29 24.64	9.08	0.76	IV.	3	34.128	25 41.09	4.30	2.91	29 14.80	28 6 8.30
37	8	.. .. 28.5 .. .. 19.7 ..	29 27.44	9.08	0.82	VI.	3	25.856	34 20.33	4.30	3.91	29 17.54	14 48.54
38	8	.. .. 27. ..	30 51.88	9.10	0.91	VI.	2	14.367	46 22.01	4.33	5.28	30 41.87	26 51.62
39	8.9	.. .. 1. 18.7	33 18.23	9.12	0.76	IV.	3	34.636	25 9.21	4.41	2.85	33 8.35	5 36.47
40	8.9	.. .. .. 51.3 8.6	33 33.70	9.12	0.80	V.	3	28.628	31 26.40	4.42	3.58	33 23.78	28 11 54.40
41	9.10	.. .. 43.8 .. 18.8 35.7 ..	38 1.11	9.17	0.70	IV.	2	42.522	16 52.05	4.56	1.90	37 51.24	27 57 18.51
42	9	.. 37.7 55.5 14.5	42 13.15	9.20	0.89	IV.	2	15.744	44 55.46	4.71	5.14	42 3.06	28 25 25.31
43	9.10	.. .. .. 50.7 7.7	44 49.89	9.23	0.90	IV.	2	14.746	45 58.00	4.82	5.24	44 39.76	26 28.15
44	6	.. 13.2 31.5 49.8 6.5 24. ..	49 48.77	9.26	0.97	IV.	4	6.222	54 53.28	4.99	6.30	48 38.54	28 35 24.57
45	8	.. 35.2 53. 10.8 27.9	51 10.33	9.28	0.68	IV.	4	45.456	13 48.03	5.10	1.55	51 0.37	27 54 14.68
46	9.10	.. .. .. 7.7 26.2	54 25.25	9.31	0.83	IV.	3	25.102	35 7.39	5.26	4.00	54 15.11	28 15 36.65
47	9.10	.. .. 14.7 ..	54 39.71	9.31	0.82	VI.	3	27.178	32 57.51	5.28	3.75	54 29.58	28 13 26.54
48	9	.. 56.3 .. 32.8 50.	0 58 32.11	9.35	0.62	IV.	4	53.792	5 5.12	5.47	0.55	0 58 22.14	27 45 31.14
49	9.10	.. 9.3 27.7	1 0 44.59	9.36	−0.64	III.	4	51.988	− 6 58.23	− 5.59	−0.75	1 0 34.59	−27 47 24.57

CORRECTIONS.

Date.	Corr. of Clock.	Hourly rate.	m	n	c	Zenith Point.	Mic. Co.
1847.	h.	s.	s.	s.	s.		r.

REMARKS.

October 18. Stars remarkably steady and well defined; 1^h, apparently light mist; 2^h 30^m, moved the circle for other observations; 5^h, a mist barely perceptible; fog-bank near the horizon.

INSTRUMENT READINGS.

	Date.		CIRCLE.							Barom.	THERMOM.					
		h. m.	A.	B.	C.	D.	E.	F.	Mean.		At.	Ex.	U.	L.	I.	
Zone 140	1847. Oct. 18,	23 9	67 2 35.0	34.0	32.1	22.6	26.3	36.0	31.00ᵃ	30.140	59.5	55.9	58.3	56.8	54.7	*Corr. for runs +0″.07
		23 19										54.0				
		23 42								30.142	59.5	53.5				
		23 59										53.3				
		0 30	34.5	34.0	32.1	22.8	26.3	35.4	30.90	30.132	59.0	53.4	57.5	56.5		
		0 42										53.0				
		1 0								30.125	58.8	52.5				
		1 21										52.1				
		2 0	35.1	34.4	32.4	22.8	26.1	35.5	31.05	30.110	57.5	52.0	55.6	55.4	55.0	

ZONE 140. OCTOBER 18. C. $D_0 = -27° 40' 20''$—Continued.

No.	Mag.	I.	II.	III.	IV.	V.	VI.	VII.	T. (h. m. s.)	a_1 (s.)	a_2 (s.)	Mic.	n	r.	i (' ")	d_1 (")	d_2 (")	Mean Right Ascension, 1850.0 (h. m. s.)	Mean Declination, 1850.0 (° ' ")
50	9.10			22.		56.2			1 10 39.04	−9.45	−0.63	IV.	4	51.114	−7 53.16	6.19	−0.86	1 10 26.96	−27 48 20.21
51	9.10			22.7			15.4		11 40.23	9.46	0.85	IV.	2	22.434	37 55.80	6.27	4.34	11 29.92	28 18 26.41
52	8		32.1	49.5	7.5	24.1	41.6		15 6.86	9.49	0.72	IV.	3	38.820	20 46.63	6.50	2.33	14 56.65	28 1 15.46
53	8		33.	50.7	8.2	25.2			21 7.88	9.54	0.67	IV.	4	46.192	13 1.88	6.91	1.44	20 57.67	27 53 30.23
54	9		34.	51.		26.3			23 8.67	9.55	0.60	IV.	4	54.428	4 25.48	7.07	0.46	22 58.52	27 44 53.01
55	8		27.6	45.5	4.4	21.			25 3.15	9.57	0.91	IV.	2	12.709	48 5.96	7.21	5.53	24 52.67	28 28 36.70
56	8		53.2	10.5	28.7	45.8			27 28.13	9.58	0.77	IV.	3	32.315	27 34.95	7.40	3.12	27 17.78	28 8 5.47
57	8.9		35.	52.8	10.6	27.5		2.5	31 10.09	9.61	0.70	IV.	4	40.707	18 46.14	7.68	2.10	30 59.78	27 59 15.92
58	9.10								33		0.70	VI.	4	39.002	20 32.33	7.84	2.31	33	28 1 2.48
59	9		12.7		49.			40.5	38 48.06	9.67	0.77	IV.	3	30.635	29 20.23	8.33	3.33	38 37.62	9 51.89
60	7.8		40.	57.7	15.7	32.5	49.6		39 14.98	9.67	0.74	IV.	3	34.306	25 30.04	8.37	2.88	39 4.57	6 1.29
61	9						46.5		40 11.40	9.66	0.88	VI.	2	15.946	44 42.72	8.45	5.13	40 0.84	28 25 16.30
62	9.10			14.	32.				42 31.51	9.69	0.62	IV.	4	50.559	8 27.96	8.60	0.92	42 21.20	27 48 57.54
63	8						32.		42 39.23	9.69	0.92	VII.	2	10.077	50 50.98	8.67	5.86	42 28.62	28 31 25.51
64	9			0.1					45 17.40	9.72	0.62	III.	4	48.250	10 52.82	8.92	1.19	45 7.06	27 51 22.93
65	9			43.	0.7				46 0.28	9.72	0.69	IV.	4	40.740	18 43.64	8.98	2.09	45 49.87	27 59 14.71
66	9							20.?	45 27.25	9.72	0.90	VII.	2	11.408	49 27.56	8.93	5.71	45 16.63	28 30 2.20
67	9		17.6	35.8	53.8				48 52.98	9.74	0.89	IV.	2	14.303	46 26.08	9.24	5.31	48 42.35	27 0.63
68	9		22.2	39.8	58.3	15.3			49 57.45	9.75	0.81	IV.	3	22.923	37 23.98	9.35	4.28	49 46.89	17 57.61
69	9.10		18.6	36.1	54.7	11.7			52 53.84	9.77	0.79	IV.	3	25.734	34 27.66	9.64	3.93	52 43.28	15 1.23
70	9			51.		25.5	43.2		53 8.19	9.77	0.76	IV.	3	31.60	31 31.60	9.66	3.59	52 57.66	12 4.85
71	9					45.	2.5		1 54 27.43	9.78	0.83	V.	3	20.796	39 37.71	9.80	4.54	1 54 16.82	20 12.05
72	9					54.?			2 0 36.35	9.82	0.90	V.	2	9.505	51 27.26	10.42	5.97	2 0 25.63	32 3.65
73	7					50.	7.6	25.2	1 32.55	9.83	0.80	V.	3	23.677	36 37.00	10.52	4.20	1 21.92	17 11.72
74	9				54.2				3 53.10	9.84	0.89	IV.	2	9.932	51 0.20	10.78	5.91	3 42.37	28 31 36.89
75	8.9					41.3	59.		4 24.02	9.85	0.64	V.	4	44.025	15 17.53	10.84	1.68	4 13.53	27 55 50.05
76	8			37.5	54.3	11.7			5 36.75	9.85	0.76	IV.	3	27.523	32 35.53	10.97	3.72	5 26.14	28 13 10.22
77	8.9		15.7	33.3	50.8	8.1			13 50.57	9.90	0.64	IV.	4	42.119	17 17.27	11.90	1.92	13 40.03	27 57 51.09
78	9					31.7			13 56.62	9.90	0.82	VII.	3	17.569	43 0.49	11.91	4.04	13 45.90	28 23 37.34
79	7.8				51.3	8.8			15 33.64	9.91	0.86	V.	2	8.598	52 24.14	12.09	6.07	15 22.87	28 33 2.30
80	8.9		37.6	55.2	12.8	30.1			19 12.55	9.94	0.56	IV.	4	50.162	8 52.86	12.54	0.94	19 2.05	27 49 26.34
81	9.10		26.2		2.5		36.7		21 1.58	9.95	0.76	IV.	3	22.601	37 44.32	12.76	4.33	20 50.87	28 18 21.41
82	9			21.3	10.	13.2			22 38.70	9.96	0.74	IV.	3	25.601	24 8.7	12.90	3.95	22 28.00	28 4 45.6
83	9						21.3	38.5	22 46.29	9.96	0.63	VI.	4	39.051	15 15.5	12.98	2.30	22 35.70	27 55 50.8
84	8.9			49.5	7.5	24.6			25 6.91	9.97	0.69	IV.	3	30.256	29 44.06	13.28	3.37	24 56.25	28 10 20.71
85	9					5.3	22.8		2 25 47.68	−9.98	−0.81	V.	2	14.008	−46 44.48	−13.37	−5.40	2 25 36.89	−28 27 23.25

CORRECTIONS.

Date.	Corr. of Clock.	Hourly rate.	m	n	c	Zenith Point.	Mic. Co.
1847.	h.	s.	s.	s.	s.	° ' "	r.

REMARKS.

(140) 82. Micrometer reading assumed as 35r.601 instead of 25r.601.

(140) 83. Micrometer reading assumed as 44r.051 instead of 39r.051.

INSTRUMENT READINGS.

	Date.	A.	B.	C.	D.	E.	F.	Mean.	Barom. (in.)	At.	Ex.	U.	L.	I.	
	1847. (h. m.)	° ' "						"							
Zone 140	Oct. 18, 2 19								30.109	57.5	51.9				
	3 59								30.088	57.5	51.3				
	4 19										51.2				
	4 40	67 2 33.0	33.7	31.1	21.6	25.1	33.6	29.68ᵃ	30.080	58.0	51.0	58.5	56.0	55.3	ᵃCorr. for runs +0".07.
	4 58								30.078	57.5	50.6				

ZONE 141. OCTOBER 18. C. $D_e = -27°\ 40'\ 20''$—Continued.

No.	Mag.	I.	II.	III.	IV.	V.	VI.	VII.	T. (h. m. s.)	a_1 (s.)	a_2 (s.)	MICROMETER		$r.$	i (′ ″)	d_1 (″)	d_2 (″)	Mean Right Ascension, 1850.0 (h. m. s.)	Mean Declination, 1850.0 (° ′ ″)
1	8		8.1	25.	43.1	0.5			3 56 42.78	− 9.31	−1.46	IV.	4	45.679	−13 33.92	−25.54	−1.46	3 56 42.01	−27 54 20.92
2	9			7.5	25.5		59.7		58 24.86	9.31	1.76	IV.	3	36.565	23 8.27	25.84	2.50	58 13.79	28 3 56.70
3	7.8			38.	55.3	12.3			3 59 37.55	9.32	1.76	IV.	3	36.584	23 7.09	26.05	2.59	3 59 26.47	28 3 55.73
4	9.10				23.5		58.		4 1 23.23	9.32	1.35	IV.	4	50.661	8 21.90	26.37	0.84	4 1 12.56	27 49 8.71
5	9.10				3.2				6 2.77	9.33	1.48	IV.	4	43.619	15 43.19	27.23	1.71	5 51.96	27 56 32.13
6	9.10							31.5	6 35.86	9.33	1.89	VI.	2	19.132	41 22.90	27.31	4.77	6 27.64	28 22 14.98
7	9		0.	17.2	35.2				17 34.75	9.34	1.58	IV.	4	39.892	19 36.82	29.32	2.21	17 23.83	0 28.35
8	9				48.2		22.5		17 47.52	9.34	1.74	IV.	3	29.995	30 0.31	29.36	3.40	17 36.44	10 53.07
9	9			2.	18.7	35.4			19 0.72	9.34	2.10	IV.	2	8.569	52 25.94	29.59	6.14	18 49.28	33 21.67
10	9			5.7	23.7	40.5			25 23.02	9.34	1.74	IV.	3	30.624	29 20.92	30.79	3.33	25 11.94	28 10 15.04
11	9.10		9.	26.3	44.7				27 43.96	9.34	1.43	IV.	4	49.256	9 49.73	31.23	1.01	27 33.19	27 50 41.97
12	9			23.5					28 40.94	9.34	2.05	III.	2	13.271	47 30.67	31.42	5.53	28 29.55	28 28 27.62
13	9			29.5		3.7			28 46.50	9.34	2.10	IV.	2	10.267	50 39.36	31.44	5.92	28 35.06	31 36.72
14	9.10				55.1	12.	29.3		34 54.20	9.34	2.06	IV.	2	12.753	48 3.12	32.62	5.59	34 42.80	29 1.33
15	9		4.5	23.	40.7				38 40.00	9.34	1.73	IV.	3	27.300	32 49.58	33.35	3.75	36 28.93	28 13 46.68
16	8							15.7	38 23.48	9.34	1.47	VII.	4	48.525	10 34.82	33.30	1.10	38 12.67	27 51 29.22
17	8				38.6	55.5	12.8		40 37.78	9.34	1.95	IV.	2	19.749	40 44.11	33.73	4.70	40 26.49	28 21 42.54
18	9.10					25.7			4 58 8.27	9.33	1.62	V.	4	47.851	11 17.53	37.22	1.18	4 57 57.32	27 52 15.93
19	9.10				12.	30.7			5 6 12.07	− 9.32	−2.05	IV.	2	17.075	−43 32.00	−38.86	−5.04	5 6 0.70	−28 24 35.90

ZONE 142. OCTOBER 26. P. $D_e = -23°\ 17'\ 40''$.

No.	Mag.	I.	II.	III.	IV.	V.	VI.	VII.	T. (h. m. s.)	a_1	a_2	MICROMETER		$r.$	i (′ ″)	d_1 (″)	d_2 (″)	Mean R.A.	Mean Declination (° ′ ″)
1	7						17.3		21 0 43.41			VI.	1	5.210	−55 56.00	− 9.49	−4.76		−24 13 50.25
2	8				20.5				2 12.57			V.	3	23.340	36 58.33	9.27	3.10		23 54 50.70
3	8			24.					3 7.13			V.	3	34.533	25 16.00	9.13	2.09		43 7.22
4	7			17.					4 0.23			V.	4	54.240	4 37.14	9.00	0.34		22 26.48
5	8				7.			57.	6 6.66			IV.	4	47.420	11 44.86	8.69	0.94		29 34.49
6	8							8.5	8 18.19			VII.	4	51.040	7 57.10	8.36	0.63		23 25 40.09
7	8					7.5			13 50.53			V.	2	15.200	45 29.80	7.57	3.84		24 3 21.21
8	7	9.2	26.	42.5	0.3	16.			16 59.48			IV.	2	22.360	38 0.45	7.12	3.19		23 55 50.70
9	8	4.		38.					21 23 54.54			III.	3	34.575	−25 12.72	− 6.16	−2.09		−23 43 0.97

CORRECTIONS.

Date.	Corr. of Clock.	Hourly rate.	m	n	c	Zenith Point.	Mic. Co.
	h.	s.	s.	s.	s.	° ′ ″	r.
1847.							

REMARKS.

October 18. Unable to observe stars of the 9th magnitude; can observe those of the 8th magnitude only with great difficulty.

INSTRUMENT READINGS.

	Date.	CIRCLE.							Barom.	THERMOM.				
		A.	B.	C.	D.	E.	F.	Mean.		At.	Ex.	U.	L.	I.
	1847.	° ′ ″						″	in.	°	°	°	°	°
Zone 142	Oct. 26, 21 0	62 39 65.5	67.2	66.2	51.6	55.3	62.6	61.40	30.435	52.5	41.5	52.0		
	21 23								30.454	52.0	41.3		52.0	

ZONE 143.　OCTOBER 27.　C.　$D_0 = -23° 17' 40''$.

No.	Mag.	I.	II.	III.	IV.	V.	VI.	VII.	T.	a_1	a_2	Mic.		r	i	d_1	d_2	Mean Right Ascension, 1850.0	Mean Declination, 1850.0
									h. m. s.	s.	s.			r.	' ''	''	''	h. m. s.	° ' ''
1	9.10				43.?			57.7	1 58 42.14	−16.84	−0.45	IV.	3	19.921	−40 32.37	−6.13	−3.49	1 58 24.85	−23 58 21.99
2	9.10								1 59 23.85	16.85	0.34	VI.	2	11.304	49 34.33	6.06	4.35	1 59 6.6	24 7 24.74
3	6.7			52.5	9.6	26.3	43.5	0.0	2 2 26.27	16.67	0.02	IV.	4	35.112	24 39.36	5.86	2.00	2 2 8.78	23 42 27.22
4	7			3.3	20.	37.3	53.8	10.4	6 36.88	16.89	0.71	IV.	4	42.314	17 5.10	5.59	1.32	6 19.28	23 34 52.01
5	8			6.3	23.2	41.3			8 40.21	16.91	0.47	IV.	2	19.112	41 24.15	5.46	3.57	8 22.83	23 59 13.18
6	8			44.	1.3	17.5	34.		9 0.46	16.91	0.40	IV.	2	14.164	46 34.70	5.43	4.66	8 43.15	24 4 24.19
7	8							27.3	9 36.77	16.92	0.62	VII.	3	33.001	26 52.15	5.39	2.20	9 19.23	23 44 39.74
8	9					20.3	36.5		11 3.18	16.93	0.70	V.	3	39.188	20 23.99	5.31	1.59	10 45.55	38 10.89
9	8.9		8.2	23.7	42.				19 41.30	16.98	0.74	IV.	3	41.248	18 14.52	4.82	1.42	19 23.58	36 0.76
10	8.9			13.3	29.6	46.5			20 12.81	16.98	0.71	IV.	3	38.226	21 23.95	4.79	1.69	19 55.12	39 10.43
11	8.9		57.3	13.5	32.	48.			22 31.02	16.99	0.57	IV.	3	25.076	35 9.01	4.68	2.98	22 13.40	52 56.67
12	7					38.3	55.4		23 21.74	17.00	0.87	V.	4	55.145	3 40.33	4.64	0.07	23 3.87	21 25.04
13	8		55.5	12.8	29.5				25 29.24	17.01	0.65	IV.	4	32.416	27 28.60	4.53	2.26	25 11.58	45 15.39
14	8.9			56.9		29.5			25 55.87	17.02	0.52	IV.	2	18.502	42 2.49	4.51	3.63	25 38.35	59 50.63
15	9		35.3	52.5	9.0				28 9.11	17.03	0.65	IV.	3	29.422	30 36.45	4.40	2.55	27 51.43	23 48 23.40
16	8.9		57.5	15.	32.8	49.			29 31.77	17.04	0.41	IV.	2	7.908	53 7.26	4.33	4.60	29 14.32	24 10 56.28
17	7		42.2	59.3	17.2	34.	51.	8.	31 16.79	17.05	0.74	IV.	3	38.335	21 14.54	4.26	1.68	30 59.0	23 39 0.48
18	9.10						35.5	52.2	31 1.86	17.05	0.78	VI.	4	42.230	17 10.06	4.27	1.33	30 44.03	34 55.66
19	9.10				20.2?				34 19.75	17.06	0.77	IV.	4	40.940	18 31.09	4.13	1.45	34 1.92	36 16.67
20	10						36.?		40 19.08	17.10	0.64	V.	3	26.050	34 8.15	3.97	2.89	40 1.34	51 54.91
21	9			44.5	2.	18.5			42 1.42	17.11	0.72	IV.	3	34.214	25 35.75	3.81	2.08	41 43.59	43 21.64
22	7.8		50.6	7.	25.	41.	57.3		44 24.08	17.12	0.78	IV.	3	38.237	21 23.38	3.72	1.68	44 6.16	39 8.78
23	6			41.2	58.5				45 24.56	17.12	0.70	IV.	3	29.882	30 7.34	3.67	2.51	45 6.74	23 47 53.52
24	9							2.5	46 11.73	17.13	0.51	VII.	2	13.708	47 3.12	3.65	4.11	45 54.00	24 4 50.88
25	8						53.8	10.3	47 19.95	17.13	0.72	VI.	3	31.918	28 0.04	3.61	2.31	47 2.10	23 45 45.96
26	8.9		58.3	15.2	32.7				49 32.03	17.14	0.70	IV.	3	27.956	32 8.21	3.53	2.70	49 14.19	49 54.47
27	9			10.8	28.3	44.8		17.8	50 27.67	17.15	0.85	IV.	4	41.402	16 2.30	3.50	1.40	50 9.67	35 47.20
28	9		47.2		22.5	38.2			53 21.34	17.16	0.59	IV.	3	19.234	41 15.65	3.41	3.56	53 3.59	59 2.65
29	9			19.8	37.8				54 36.06	17.17	0.90	IV.	4	44.608	14 41.16	3.38	1.12	54 18.89	32 25.66
30	9				1.5		31.4		56 1.09	17.18	0.98	IV.	4	52.438	6 30.10	3.34	0.34	55 42.93	24 13.87
31	9			52.8		25.5			2 57 52.02	17.18	0.78	IV.	3	33.555	26 17.00	3.28	2.15	2 57 34.06	23 44 2.52
32	9.10			19.5		51.5			3 1 18.12	17.20	0.58	IV.	2	14.751	45 57.73	3.21	4.01	3 1 0.34	24 5 44.95
33	9.10				10.2				6 9.79	17.22	0.88	IV.	3	42.668	16 42.75	3.09	1.29	5 51.69	23 34 27.16
34	9				10.3		44.5		7 10.40	17.22	0.89	IV.	4	41.603	17 49.63	3.06	1.39	6 52.29	35 34.08
35	9	17.8	35.						10 51.62	17.24	0.91	III.	4	42.368	17 1.71	2.99	1.32	10 33.47	23 34 46.02
36	7			1.3		34.	51.5		11 0.41	17.24	0.59	IV.	4	13.989	46 45.60	2.99	4.08	10 42.58	24 4 32.67
37	9.10			50.3		26.3			13 9.48	17.25	0.93	IV.	4	44.738	14 32.88	2.95	1.11	12 51.30	23 32 16.94
38	9					42.5			14 25.59	17.26	0.74	V.	3	26.492	33 40.47	2.93	2.84	14 7.59	23 51 26.24
39	6				26.3	43.	59.7		15 9.10	17.26	0.54	V.	2	8.145	52 52.38	2.92	4.67	14 51.30	24 10 39.97
40	9.10						59.2		16 25.67	17.27	0.96	VI.	4	47.137	12 2.30	2.90	0.85	16 7.44	23 29 46.05
41	7	46.6	3.5	21.3	37.4	54.			23 20.38	17.29	0.71	IV.	2	18.484	42 3.62	2.83	3.63	23 2.38	59 50.08
42	9.10		21.3		57.			46.5	24 55.85	17.29	0.86	IV.	3	35.695	24 7.17	2.81	1.95	24 37.70	41 51.93
43	9			6.8	23.5	39.6		28.3	27 23.23	17.30	1.02	IV.	4	49.330	9 45.15	2.79	0.65	27 4.91	27 28.59
44	9.10			20.2			28.3		28 37.36	17.31	0.86	IV.	3	35.383	24 22.48	2.78	1.97	28 19.17	42 7.23
45	9			32.3		6.3		39.2	28 49.07	17.31	0.91	IV.	3	38.130	21 30.04	2.76	1.70	28 30.85	23 39 14.52
46	9						38.3		29 47.58	17.31	0.69	VII.	2	17.316	43 16.81	2.77	3.75	29 29.58	24 1 3.33
47	9.10				16.	32.3			32 15.52	17.32	0.96	IV.	3	42.355	17 5.17	2.77	1.32	31 57.24	23 34 49.26
48	9.10						54.2		33 37.28	17.32	0.67	VII.	2	23.991	36 17.47	2.77	3.08	33 19.29	54 3.32
49	8			37.3	54.6	10.8			3 35 53.99	−17.33	−0.87	IV.	3	33.805	−26 1.22	−2.76	−2.12	3 35 35.79	−23 43 46.10

CORRECTIONS.

Date.	Corr. of Clock.	Hourly rate.	m	n	c	Zenith Point.	Mic. Co.
	h.	s.	s.	s.	s.	° ' ''	r.
1847.							

INSTRUMENT READINGS.

Date.		CIRCLE.							Barom.	THERMOM.				
		A.	B.	C.	D.	E.	F.	Mean.		At.	Ex.	U.	L.	1.
	1847.	° ' ''						''	in.	°	°	°	°	°
Zone 143	Oct. 27, 2 0	62 39 67.7	72.4	72.9	56.2	60.9	64.8	65.82	30.586	38.7	31.4	37.3	39.3	49.0
	2 20										31.3			
	2 40								30.604	38.5	31.3			
	3 1										31.8			
	3 23								30.610	38.8	31.2			
	3 50	49.3	54.4	56.1	36.3	43.8	45.8	47.62				37.0	39.5	

REMARKS.

Oct. 27. Stars unsteady; night unfavorable; a very great change in the reading of the circle, which had been left without the usual pressure of the clamp.

(143) 1. Declination 1' discordant from Arg. Z. 324, 114.

(143) 17. Transits discordant.

(143) 23. Transits over T.'s V and VI assumed as recorded over T.'s IV and V.

(143) 37. Transits discordant; that over T. III probably 2ˢ in error, (see Transit Z., 1847, October 18,) and rejected.

ZONE 143. OCTOBER 27. C. $D_0 = -23° 17' 40''$—Continued.

No.	Mag.	Seconds of Transit (I–VII)	T	$'a_1$	a_1	Micrometer	i	d_1	d_2	Mean Right Ascension, 1850.0	Mean Declination, 1850.0
			h. m. s.	s.	s.	r.	′ ″	″	″	h. m. s.	° ′ ″
50	8	53.2	3 36 36.42	−17.33	−1.08	V. 4 53.206	− 5 41.91	−2.76	−0.27	3 36 18.01	−23 23 24.94
51	8	8.2 42.8 56.3 15.4	38 41.81	17.34	0.82	IV. 3 26.687	33 27.87	2.76	2.82	38 23.65	51 13.45
52	9	42.8	40 59.49	17.34	1.01	III. 4 43.938	15 23.05	2.76	1.18	40 41.14	33 6.99
53	4	43.3 59. 15.7	40 42.32	17.34	0.93	IV. 3 35.751	23 59.21	2.76	1.94	40 24.05	41 43.91
54	9	8.3 25.	40 51.42	17.34	0.95	V. 3 37.652	22 0.28	2.76	1.75	40 33.13	39 44.79
55	9	57.8 14.7 31.8	45 31.45	17.35	1.13	IV. 4 53.576	5 18.78	2.78	0.24	45 12.97	23 1.80
56	9.10	55.7	46 38.07	17.36	1.12	V. 4 53.106	5 48.13	2.78	0.28	46 20.44	23 31.19
57	7	29.2 45.7 2.8	47 45.72	17.36	1.02	IV. 4 42.882	16 31.86	2.79	1.27	47 27.34	34 15.92
58	9	14.2 30.7	49 47.81	17.37	0.78	III. 2 18.931	41 35.19	2.80	3.59	49 29.66	59 21.58
59	8.9	20. 53.5	3 50 2.99	−17.37	−0.85	V. 3 26.102	−34 4.88	−2.80	−2.88	3 49 44.77	−23 51 50.56

ZONE 144. OCTOBER 28. P. $D_0 = -23° 17' 30''$.

No.	Mag.	Seconds of Transit (I–VII)	T	$'a_1$	a_1	Micrometer	i	d_1	d_2	Mean Right Ascension, 1850.0	Mean Declination, 1850.0
1	7.8	6. 22.5 40. 57.	21 23 56.45	−16.11	−0.21	IV. 3 34.635	−25 9.28	−18.36	−2.54	21 23 40.13	−23 43 0.18
2	6.7	6.3 23. 40.3	26 57.00	16.14	0.31	III. 1 11.613	49 13.31	17.96	4.81	26 40.55	24 7 6.11
3	7.8	6. 39.	27 5.34	16.14	0.23	IV. 3 30.845	29 6.92	17.94	2.92	26 48.97	23 46 57.78
4	8	29.	27 55.47	16.15	0.15	VI. 4 47.670	11 28.81	17.83	1.26	27 39.17	29 17.90
5	8	42.	29 41.40	16.17	0.22	IV. 3 33.490	26 21.23	17.60	2.65	29 25.01	44 11.48
6	7	41.5	31 40.75	16.19	0.24	IV. 3 25.577	34 37.64	17.36	3.44	31 24.32	52 28.44
7	Neb.	59.	32 8.40	16.19	0.24	VII. 3 26.810	33 20.53	17.30	3.32	31 51.07	51 11.15
8	6	1. 34.5	33 43.95	16.21	0.26	V. 3 21.025	38 26.86	17.10	3.81	33 27.48	50 17.77
9	7	18.	34 44.29	16.22	0.24	VI. 3 26.887	33 15.70	16.98	3.31	34 27.83	51 5.99
10	7.8	3.3 21. 55.	40 54.29	16.28	0.14	IV. 4 46.240	12 58.86	16.22	1.41	40 37.87	30 46.49
11	7	18. 34.5 51.5 9.3	43 8.42	16.30	0.27	IV. 2 20.365	40 5.64	15.95	3.96	42 51.85	57 55.55
12	8	26.	43 52.49	16.31	0.12	VI. 4 49.340	9 44.21	15.87	1.10	43 36.06	27 31.18
13	8	12.5	44 22.22	16.32	0.10	VII. 4 53.785	5 4.93	15.80	0.66	44 5.80	22 51.39
14	8	23.5	46 6.65	16.33	0.18	V. 3 37.407	22 15.76	15.60	2.27	45 50.14	40 3.63
15	7	17.	47 16.11	16.35	0.27	IV. 2 18.570	41 58.23	15.46	4.14	46 59.49	59 47.83
16	7	6. 22.7	47 32.25	16.35	0.20	VI. 4 32.165	27 44.61	15.43	2.78	47 15.70	45 32.82
17	8	16.5	49 16.28	16.37	0.11	IV. 4 52.843	6 4.62	15.23	0.76	48 59.80	23 50.61
18	7	18.3	50 1.36	16.38	0.25	V. 3 21.690	38 41.67	15.14	3.83	49 44.73	56 30.64
19	6.7	8. 41.9	51 7.95	16.39	0.15	IV. 4 42.000	17 24.67	15.02	1.82	50 51.41	23 35 11.51
20	7	15.7 49.3	52 32.47	16.40	0.27	V. 2 17.743	42 50.00	14.86	4.23	52 15.74	24 0 39.15
21	8.9	25.	53 34.17	16.40	0.31	VII. 1 8.720	52 15.47	14.86	5.14	52 17.46	24 10 5.47
22	7	28.	21 59 54.55	16.48	0.07	VI. 4 55.920	2 51.37	14.04	0.45	21 59 38.00	23 20 35.86
23	7.8	46.3	22 1 45.67	16.50	0.19	IV. 3 31.780	28 8.20	13.85	2.82	22 1 28.98	45 54.93
24	8	58. 15.	7 48.43	16.56	0.10	II. 4 49.660	9 24.15	13.22	1.07	7 31.77	27 8.44
25	6.7	46.3 4. 20.	8 3.18	16.56	0.19	IV. 3 32.450	27 26.47	13.19	3.77	7 46.43	45 13.43
26	5.6	56. 12.5	8 55.41	16.57	0.22	IV. 3 25.023	35 12.28	13.10	3.50	8 38.62	52 58.88
27	7.8	45.	9 28.08	16.58	0.21	V. 3 26.347	33 49.64	13.04	3.37	9 11.29	23 51 36.05
28	7	26. 59.	10 25.12	16.59	0.26	IV. 2 14.925	46 49.55	12.95	4.53	10 8.27	24 4 37.03
29	7	47.	10 56.62	16.59	0.12	VII. 4 44.470	14 49.25	12.90	1.56	10 39.91	23 32 33.71
30	7.8	49.5	12 49.20	16.61	0.09	IV. 4 48.020	10 10.61	12.72	1.13	12 32.50	27 54.46
31	8	36.	13 35.56	16.62	0.13	IV. 4 42.680	16 42.02	12.64	1.74	13 18.83	23 34 26.40
32	7	42.3 58.5 16.	16 32.74	16.65	0.27	III. 1 11.154	49 42.13	12.36	4.91	16 15.82	24 7 29.40
33	8	13. 46.5	18 3.27	16.67	0.15	III. 3 36.445	23 15.48	12.21	2.37	17 46.45	23 41 0.06
34	8	58.5	18 8.23	16.67	0.06	VII. 4 53.845	5 1.16	12.20	0.64	17 51.50	22 44.00
35	7.8	7.	22 19 50.23	−16.69	−0.06	V. 4 54.673	− 4 9.87	−12.04	−0.55	22 19 33.48	−23 21 52.46

CORRECTIONS.

Date.	Corr. of Clock.	Hourly rate.	m	n	c	Zenith Point.	Mic. Co.
1847.	h.	s.	s.	s.	s.	° ′ ″	r.

REMARKS.

(144) 28. Micrometer reading assumed as 13′.928 instead of 14′.928.

INSTRUMENT READINGS.

Date.		CIRCLE.							Barom.	THERMOM.				
		A.	B.	C.	D.	E.	F.	Mean.		At.	Ex.	U.	L.	I.
	1847. h. m.	° ′ ″						″	in.	°	°	°	°	°
Zone 144	Oct. 28, 21 20	62 39 65.0	68.0	68.3	47.8	58.5	58.8	61.07				43.5		
	21 26								30.714	45.8	35.8			
	21 50								30.712	44.8	34.7			
	22 39								30.704	43.1	33.2			
	23 1								30.708	42.5	33.2			
	23 59								30.702	41.0	32.0			
	1 33								30.686	39.5	31.0			38.5

ZONE 144. OCTOBER 28. P. $D_a = -23°\ 17'\ 30''$—Continued.

No.	Mag.	Seconds of Transit (I. II. III. IV. | V. VI. VII.)	T. (h. m. s.)	a₁ (s.)	a₂ (s.)	Micrometer	r.	i (′ ″)	d₁ (″)	d₂ (″)	Mean Declination, 1850.0 (h. m. s.)	Mean Right Ascension, 1850.0 (° ′ ″)
36	8	. . . . . 36.5	22 21 19.60	−16.70	−0.18	V. 3	29.905	−30 6.15	−11.90	−3.01	22 21 2.72	−23 47 51.06
37	7	25. 41.5 58.5	23 15.31	16.72	0.17	III. 3	31.900	28 0.35	11.73	2.81	22 58.42	45 44.89
38	7,8	. . . . . 54. . . .	23 37.21	16.73	0.08	V. 4	50.340	8 41.69	11.70	0.99	23 20.40	23 26 24.38
39	8	21. . . 55. . . .	26 11.67	16.76	0.25	III. 1	14.620	46 4.57	11.47	4.46	25 54.66	24 3 50.60
40	8	. . . . 15. . . .	26 58.03	16.76	0.25	V. 2	16.155	44 29.80	11.40	4.40	26 41.02	2 15.60
41	8	. . . . 42.5 . . .	29 41.56	16.79	0.25	IV. 2	16.083	44 34.25	11.16	4.40	29 24.52	24 2 19.81
42	7	. . . . . . 2.5 . . .	30 28.96	16.80	0.10	VI. 4	46.030	13 11.59	11.09	1.42	30 12.06	23 30 54.10
43	7	. . . . . . 44.3 . . .	31 10.61	16.81	0.08	VI. 4	51.870	7 5.31	11.03	0.85	30 53.92	24 47.17
44	7	. . . . 27.	31 36.60	16.81	0.11	VII. 4	43.625	15 42.18	11.00	1.65	31 19.68	33 24.83
45	8	19.3 . . 52.5	36 9.52	16.86	0.21	III. 2	23.125	37 12.13	10.63	3.70	35 52.45	54 56.46
46	7,8	. . . 52.	37 8.74	16.87	0.17	III. 3	31.370	28 33.86	10 55	2.86	36 51.70	46 17.27
47	8	. . . . . 33. . . .	37 16.08	16.87	0.20	V. 3	24.773	35 28.15	10.54	3.53	36 59.01	53 12.22
48	8	54.3 . . 28.	39 44.78	16.90	0.22	III. 2	20.545	39 54.09	10.33	3.96	39 27.66	57 38.36
49	7,9	. . 32. 49.	41 5.66	16.91	0.07	III. 4	50.100	6 56.68	10.23	1.01	40 48.68	26 37.92
50	7	. . . . 26.3 . 59. . . .	41 25.41	16.92	0.20	IV. 3	24.970	35 15.60	10.21	3.50	41 8.29	52 59.31
51	8	. . . . . 6.5 . . .	42 49.69	16.93	0.08	V. 4	46.710	12 29.14	10.10	1.35	42 32.68	30 10.59
52	8	34.5 . . 8.	45 24.68	16.96	0.06	III. 4	50.605	8 25.08	9.91	0.96	45 7.66	26 5.95
53	7,8	9.5 26. 43.	47 59.87	16.99	0.19	III. 3	23.667	36 37.05	9.72	3.64	47 42.69	54 20.41
54	8	. . . 34.5	47 51.16	16.99	0.05	III. 4	52.930	5 59.15	9.73	0.73	47 34.12	23 39.61
55	7	8. 24.3 41.	49 57.92	17.01	0.05	III. 4	52.017	6 56.47	9.57	0.82	49 40.86	24 36.86
56	8	. . . . . 22. . .	50 5.16	17.01	0.11	V. 3	39.013	20 34.84	9.56	2.11	49 48.04	38 16.51
57	7,8	. . . . 15.3 . 49.3 . .	51 32.23	17.02	0.11	IV. 3	39.380	20 11.76	9.47	2.07	51 15.10	37 53.30
58	8	. . . 30.	52 46.72	17.04	0.13	III. 3	35.997	23 43.40	9.39	2.41	52 29.55	41 25.20
59	5,6	. . . . . 36.3 53. 9.5 . .	53 35.99	17.04	0.10	IV. 4	41.510	17 55.53	9.33	1.86	53 18.85	35 36.72
60	8	. . . 53.5	55 10.16	17.06	0.04	III. 4	51.507	7 28.57	9.23	0.87	54 53.06	25 8.67
61	7	. . . 1. 17.5 34.3 . .	56 17.44	17.07	0.07	IV. 4	45.895	13 20.31	9.16	1.43	56 0.30	31 0.90
62	8,9	. . . . 42. . . .	22 57 8.23	17.08	0.20	VI. 2	20.380	40 4.70	9.10	3.97	22 56 50.95	57 47.77
63	7	. . . . 39.	23 1 55.76	17.13	0.18	III. 3	23.270	37 2.00	8.80	3.68	23 1 38.45	54 44.57
64	7,8	. . . . . 31. 48. . . .	2 14.17	17.13	0.18	V. 3	23.003	37 19.28	8.78	3.71	1 56.86	55 1.77
65	8	1.3 18.	4 51.80	17.16	0.16	II. 3	28.413	31 38.87	8.63	3.17	4 34.45	49 20.67
66	8	. . . 3.5	6 20.27	17.18	0.20	III. 2	19.045	41 28.17	8.54	4.12	6 2.89	59 10.83
67	7	. . . . . 48. 4.5	9 47.58	17.21	0.10	IV. 3	39.290	20 17.40	8.33	2.07	9 30.27	23 37 57.80
68	7	10.7 27.3 44.	12 1.11	17.24	0.20	III. 2	15.710	44 57.42	8.22	4.45	11 43.67	24 2 40.09
69	7	. . . . . 22.5 38.5 . . .	12 21.83	17.24	0.10	IV. 4	38.720	20 50.39	8.19	2.13	12 4.49	23 38 30.71
70	7	27. 43.5 0.5 17.5	15 17.21	17.27	0.16	IV. 3	27.103	33 1.83	8.06	3.30	14 59.78	50 43.19
71	7,8	. . . . . 5.7 23.	16 5.82	17.28	0.04	IV. 4	50.783	8 13.79	8.02	0.93	15 48.50	25 52.74
72	7	. . . 3. 20.5	17 20.00	17.30	0.01	IV. 4	56.880	1 51.49	7.96	0.32	17 2.69	19 29.77
73	7,8	. . . 6.	18 22.65	17.31	0.01	III. 4	55.900	2 52.93	7.90	0.42	18 5.33	20 31.25
74	8	. . . . . 43.5	18 42.72	17.31	0.16	IV. 3	24.255	36 0.59	7.89	3.59	18 25.75	53 42.07
75	7	. . . . . 24. . . 57. . .	19 23.67	17.31	0.01	IV. 4	54.135	15 11.13	7.85	1.59	19 6.35	23 32 50.57
76	8,9	. . 0.5	21 34.51	17.34	0.20	II. 2	14.310	46 25.15	7.76	4.66	21 16.97	24 4 7.51
77	8	. . . . 56.	21 55.24	17.34	0.16	IV. 3	24.965	35 15.91	7.74	3.51	21 37.71	23 52 57.16
78	7	. . . . . 44.7 . . .	22 27.90	17.35	0.04	V. 4	47.750	11 23.92	7.72	1.24	22 10.51	29 2.88
79	7	33. 49.5 6.5 23.7 40.	26 23.22	17.39	0.12	IV. 3	31.480	28 27.27	7.56	2.85	26 5.71	46 7.68
80	8,9	. . 44.	28 0.67	17.41	0.03	II. 4	50.320	8 42.88	7.48	0.95	27 43.23	26 21.34
81	7	. . . 52. 9.	32 8.74	17.45	0.00	IV. 4	54.715	4 7.30	7.34	0.54	31 51.29	21 45.78
82	8	. . . . 1.	33 0.57	17.45	0.09	IV. 4	40.990	17 19.09	7.31	1.80	32 43.03	34 58.20
83	8	39.5	35 29.03	17.48	0.16	I. 2	21.910	38 27.55	7.23	3.82	35 12.34	56 8.60
84	7	. . 29. 46. 3. 19.3	23 36 2.59	−17.48	−0.10	IV. 3	33.643	−26 11.51	−7.21	−2.64	23 35 45.01	−23 43 51.36

CORRECTIONS.

Date.	Corr. of Clock.	Hourly rate.	m	f	c	Zenith Point.	Mic. Co.
1847.	h.	s.	s.	s.	s.	s.	° ′ ″	r.

REMARKS.

(144) 75. Micrometer reading assumed as 44ʳ.135, not 54ʳ.135.

(144) 80. Transit over T. III assumed as recorded over T. II.

INSTRUMENT READINGS.

Date.	CIRCLE.							Barom.	THERMOM.				
	A.	B.	C.	D.	E.	F.	Mean.		At.	Ex.	U.	L.	I.
1847. h. m.	° ′ ″						″	in.	°	°			

Zone 144. October 28. P. D₀ = −23° 17′ 30″—Continued.

No.	Mag.	I.	II.	III.	IV.	V.	VI.	VII.	T.	a₁	a₂	Mic.	n	r.	i	d₁	d₂	Mean Right Ascension, 1850.0	Mean Declination, 1850.0
									h. m. s.	s.	s.			r.	′ ″	″	″	h. m. s.	° ′ ″
85	8			2.					23 37 18.78	−17.50	−0.18	III.	2	17.627	−42 57.17	−7.17	−4.26	23 37 1.10	−24 0 38.60
86	7					54.5			37 37.71	17.50	0.02	V.	4	49.103	9 59.14	7.16	1.10	37 20.19	23 27 37.40
87	8				59.				38 58.22	17.52	0.15	IV.	3	24.375	35 53.13	7.11	3.57	38 40.55	53 33.81
88	8		47.3	4.5	22.				40 21.23	17.53	0.14	IV.	3	26.350	33 49.20	7.07	3.38	40 3.50	51 29.65
89	7.8							13.5	40 23.18	17.53	0.02	VII.	4	50.190	8 50.47	7.07	0.99	40 5.63	23 26 28.53
90	7						14.		41 40.19	17.54	0.19	VI.	2	14.997	45 42.34	7.04	4.52	41 22.40	24 3 23.90
91	8	22.			13.				47 12.35	17.60	0.13	IV.	3	25.870	31 19.07	6.99	3.42	46 54.62	23 51 59.41
92	7.8			28.5					52 45.17	17.65	0.01	III.	4	50.950	8 3.31	6.81	0.92	52 27.51	25 41.04
93	7.8				17.3				53 16.97	17.66	0.02	IV.	4	46.725	12 28.32	6.80	1.34	52 59.29	30 6.46
94	7.8					54.			53 37.16	17.66	0.05	V.	4	40.520	18 57.40	6.80	1.06	53 19.45	36 36.25
95	5.6		53.	10.3	28.				59 27.06	17.72	0.13	IV.	2	21.673	38 43.37	6.72	3.84	59 9.21	23 56 23.93
96	9					7.			23 59 50.05	−17.72	−0.14	V.	2	21.230	−39 11.35	−6.70	−3.80	23 59 32.19	−23 56 51.94

Zone 145. October 28. P. D₀ = −23° 17′ 30″.

No.	Mag.	I.	II.	III.	IV.	V.	VI.	VII.	T.	a₁	a₂	Mic.	n	r.	i	d₁	d₂	Mean Right Ascension, 1850.0	Mean Declination, 1850.0
1	7					40.			1 33 6.38	−18.55		VI.	3	36.950	−22 44.37	−9.63	−2.31		−23 40 26.31
2	8		4.	21.					43 37.69	18.62		III.	4	46.150	13 4.44	10.42	1.38		30 46.24
3	8	22.	38.5	55.5					45 12.37	18.64		III.	3	24.465	35 47.10	10.55	3.58		53 31.23
4	9		29.						47 2.89	18.65		II.	3	25.695	34 29.80	10.70	3.44		23 52 13.43
5	8			14.					49 30.80	18.67		III.	1	9.250	51 41.60	10.90	5.14		24 9 27.73
6	7	28.	45.3	1.5					52 18.53	18.69		III.	3	38.277	21 20.56	11.14	2.17		23 39 3.87
7	7	29.			36.				1 52 19.23	−18.69		V.	3	38.247	−21 23.01	−11.14	−2.18		−23 39 6.33

Zone 146. November 2. P. D₀ = −22° 40′ 0″.

No.	Mag.	I.	II.	III.	IV.	V.	VI.	VII.	T.	a₁	a₂	Mic.	n	r.	i	d₁	d₂	Mean Right Ascension, 1850.0	Mean Declination, 1850.0
1	8				44.				21 31 43.70	−17.26	−0.37	IV.	4	49.320	−9 45.78	−10.81	0.00	21 31 26.07	−22 49 56.59
2	7	4.	20.3	37.3	54.5				36 54.11	17.32	0.71	IV.	3	25.446	34 45.92	10.15	−1.42	36 36.08	23 14 57.49
3	9			1.	35.			25.	38 34.54	17.33	0.64	IV.	3	29.830	30 10.61	9.92	−1.02	38 16.57	23 10 21.55
4	9			0.	34.				40 33.69	17.35	0.38	IV.	4	50.012	9 2.19	9.69	+0.83	40 15.96	22 49 11.05
5	8						30.		40 56.15	17.36	0.92	VI.	1	10.205	50 42.43	9.64	−2.84	40 37.67	23 30 54.91
6	8		20.						43 54.02	17.39	0.88	II.	2	13.360	47 24.84	9.28	2.52	43 35.75	27 36.64
7	8				7.5				44 24.28	17.39	0.81	III.	2	17.823	42 44.73	9.22	2.14	44 6.08	22 56.09
8	8.9	17.			50.5				47 7.38	17.42	0.78	III.	2	21.445	38 57.66	8.90	−1.79	46 49.18	23 19 8.37
9	9				7.				48 23.67	17.43	0.39	III.	4	50.523	8 30.28	8.74	+0.85	48 5.85	22 48 38.14
10	8				19.				49 18.08	17.44	0.83	IV.	2	16.866	43 44.08	8.62	−2.22	48 59.81	23 23 55.82
11	9				44.5				53 1.28	17.48	0.82	III.	2	17.705	48 52.21	8.20	2.15	52 42.98	23 2.56
12	9				46.				53 45.25	17.49	0.72	IV.	3	25.540	34 39.07	8.12	−1.41	53 27.04	23 14 49.50
13	9						59.		53 8.68	17.48	0.39	VII.	4	49.030	9 6.71	8.10	0.82	52 50.81	22 40 14.08
14	8		16.		50.5				56 49.90	17.52	0.52	IV.*	4	41.397	18 2.67	7.79	+0.05	56 31.86	22 58 10.39
15	9						37.		57 46.54	17.52	0.55	VII.	4	38.935	20 36.27	7.78	−0.18	56 28.47	23 0 44.23
16	7	21.3			12.3				21 59 11.72	17.54	0.52	IV.	4	41.320	18 7.51	7.48	+0.05	58 53.66	22 58 14.94
17	9					13.			22 0 56.05	17.58	0.81	V.	2	19.990	40 29.04	7.41	−1.93	21 59 37.67	23 20 38.38
18	8.9	18.	35.						3 6.65	17.59	0.70	II.	2	28.210	31 52.87	7.08	−1.17	22 2 50.36	23 12 1.12
19	8				21.			10.5	3 20.34	17.59	0.50	IV.	4	42.780	16 35.68	7.06	+0.18	3 2.25	22 56 42.56
20	8	2.		35.					5 52.00	17.61	0.53	III.	4	39.550	19 58.39	6.79	−0.12	5 33.86	23 0 5.30
21	8	0.3	16.3	34.					7 50.65	17.63	0.90	III.	2	13.715	47 2.62	6.58	2.51	7 32.12	27 11.71
22	7	21.3	37.5	54.7	11.5	28.3	45.		22 10 11.35	−17.66	−0.58	IV.	3	37.060	−22 37.16	−6.33	−0.35	22 9 53.11	−23 2 43.84

CORRECTIONS.

Date.	Corr. of Clock.	Hourly rate.	m	n	c	Zenith Point.	Mic. Co.
1847.	h.	s.	s.	s.	s.	s.	° ′ ″	r.

INSTRUMENT READINGS.

Date.	CIRCLE							Barom.	THERMOM.				
		A.	B.	C.	D.	E.	F.	Mean.		At.	Ex.	U.	L.	I.
Zone 146	1847, Nov. 2, 21 30	62 2 36.8	35.0	34.2	22.3	28.3	37.2	32.30*	in. 30.052	61.0	56.2	60.0	58.0	

REMARKS.

(144) 87. Declination 2′ discordant from Arg. Z. 270, 8; and 6′ from Transit Z., 1847, October 18.

(146) 15. Minutes assumed as 56 instead of 57.

(146) 17. Minutes assumed as 59 instead of 0.

* Corr. for runs +0.″07.

ZONE 146. NOVEMBER 2. P. $D_0 = -22°\ 40'\ 0''$—Continued.

No.	Mag.	I.	II.	III.	IV.	V.	VI.	VII.	T. (h. m. s.)	a_1 (s.)	a_2 (s.)	MICROMETER		r.	i (' ")	d_1 (")	d_2 (")	Mean Right Ascension, 1850.0 (h. m. s.)	Mean Declination, 1850.0 (° ' ")
23	8.9		28.5	45.3	2.				22 12 1.95	−17.08	−0.37	IV.	4	52.920	− 5 59.78	− 6.15	+1.11	22 11 43.90	−22 46 4.82
24	8	34.	50.	7.3					16 24.02	17.72	0.59	III.	4	38.770	20 47.20	5.72	−0.19	16 5.71	23 0 53.11
25	8.9	19.5		53.3					18 10.05	17.74	0.80	III.	2	17.900	42 36.20	5.55	2.13	17 51.51	22 43.58
26	8		55.		29.5				19 28.80	17.75	0.79	IV.	3	22.743	37 35.34	5.41	1.69	19 10.26	17 42.44
27	9					9.			19 52.05	17.76	0.82	V.	2	18.813	41 42.85	5.38	−2.06	19 33.48	23 21 50.29
28	7					8.7	25.3		20 51.85	17.77	0.43	V.	4	49.053	10 2.27	5.30	+0.75	20 33.65	22 50 6.82
29	9	48.5		22.5					23 39.17	17.80	0.91	III.	2	14.416	46 18.81	5.04	−2.44	23 20.46	23 26 26.29
30	8.9		26.5		0.				26 59.93	17.83	0.48	IV.	4	46.785	12 24.51	4.74	+0.55	26 41.62	22 52 28.70
31	8					44.	0.		26 26.63	17.82	0.87	V.	2	18.170	42 23.40	4.78	−2.12	26 7.94	23 22 30.30
32	9			46.					29 2.79	17.85	0.90	III.	2	15.680	44 59.30	4.56	2.34	28 44.04	25 6.20
33	7						5.		30 31.15	17.87	0.98	VI.	1	10.070	50 50.79	4.43	2.88	30 12.30	30 58.10
34	7.8						16.		31 12.19	17.88	0.89	VI.	2	15.907	44 45.17	4.37	2.32	30 53.42	24 51.86
35	9			52.					33 8.75	17.90	0.77	III.	3	26.430	33 43.80	4.22	1.33	32 50.08	13 49.35
36	9					46.			33 29.05	17.90	0.85	V.	3	20.410	40 2.18	4.18	1.89	33 10.30	20 8.25
37	9	42.		15.5					37 32.42	17.94	0.90	III.	2	16.185	44 27.73	3.85	−2.30	37 13.58	23 24 33.86
38	9	6.5		40.					40 56.73	17.98	0.55	III.	4	43.395	15 57.92	3.58	+0.23	40 38.20	22 56 1.27
39	8			50.5		24.5			41 7.41	17.98	0.94	III.	2	14.715	46 37.58	3.57	−2.47	40 48.49	23 26 43.62
40	8			35.					42 51.60	18.00	0.99	III.	1	10.745	50 7.66	3.44	2.81	42 32.81	30 13.91
41	8	36.3		10.					45 26.82	18.03	0.93	III.	2	14.633	46 5.06	3.25	2.42	45 7.86	26 10.73
42	6			9.					47 25.75	18.05	0.79	III.	3	24.956	35 16.10	3.11	1.46	47 6.91	15 20.67
43	7			50.5	7.5	24.			47 7.00	18.04	0.73	IV.	3	30.577	29 23.92	3.13	0.95	46 48.23	9 28.00
44	9					9.			47 52.04	18.05	0.90	IV.	2	16.997	43 36.89	3.08	2.22	47 33.09	23 44.19
45	9		9.5	26.	43.3	0.7			50 59.97	18.07	0.92	IV.	2	16.047	44 36.45	2.94	−2.31	49 40.96	23 24 41.70
46	8						47.7		50 14.18	18.08	0.47	V.	4	48.980	10 6.60	2.92	+0.75	49 55.63	22 50 8.77
47	9					0.5			51 43.67	18.09	0.57	V.	4	42.217	17 11.06	2.81	+0.13	51 25.01	22 57 13.74
48	7.8				41.5				52 40.66	18.10	0.86	IV.	3	20.697	39 43.74	2.75	−1.87	52 21.70	23 19 48.36
49	7				49.5	5.			53 48.44	18.11	0.76	IV.	3	26.903	33 14.25	2.67	1.29	53 29.57	13 18.21
50	9			55.					54 11.79	18.13	0.92	III.	2	15.630	45 2.50	2.59	2.35	54 52.70	25 7.44
51	7		45.3	2.5	20.5				56 19.36	18.14	1.00	IV.	1	9.930	50 59.13	2.51	2.58	56 0.22	31 4.52
52	7		8.	25.3	42.5				57 41.89	18.15	0.83	IV.	3	22.715	37 37.10	2.43	1.69	57 22.91	17 41.22
53	9				19.3				22 59 18.79	18.17	0.63	IV.	3	38.105	21 31.74	2.31	0.25	22 58 59.99	1 34.30
54	5	22.5	39.	56.5	13.7	29.7	46.5		23 2 12.93	18.20	0.81	IV.	3	24.167	36 6.12	2.15	−1.56	23 1 53.92	23 16 9.83
55	8					23.			5 6.23	18.23	0.43	V.	4	53.620	5 15.89	1.99	+1.17	4 47.57	22 45 16.71
56	9					0.			7 43.10	18.26	0.78	V.	3	28.650	31 25.02	1.90	−1.14	6 24.66	23 11 28.06
57	9			46.					7 2.72	18.25	0.68	III.	3	35.090	24 40.36	1.82	−0.52	7 43.79	23 4 42.70
58	9		38.						11 11.73	18.29	0.58	II.	3	42.323	17 4.41	1.65	+0.14	10 52.86	22 57 5.92
59	8		34.	51.					16 7.90	18.35	0.06	III.	2	14.820	45 53.20	1.42	−2.40	15 48.59	23 25 57.02
60	8					38.5			16 21.60	18.35	0.75	V.	3	30.963	28 59.83	1.41	0.91	16 2.50	9 2.15
61	8				22.7				17 21.86	16.36	0.88	IV.	2	20.970	39 27.48	1.36	1.84	17 2.62	19 30.68
62	8.9			7.			57.		18 23.50	18.37	0.89	VI.	2	19.903	40 34.38	1.31	1.94	18 4.24	20 37.63
63	7						59.		19 25.14	18.38	1.06	VI.	1	8.125	52 52.95	1.25	−3.05	19 5.70	23 32 57.25
64	7		4.7	39.					21 38.50	18.40	0.61	IV.	4	41.075	18 22.69	1.17	+0.03	21 19.49	22 58 23.53
65	7.8		23.	39.5					22 56.42	18.42	0.51	III.	4	49.030	10 3.78	1.12	+0.75	22 37.49	22 50 4.15
66	7							20.	22 29.21	18.41	1.01	VII.	1	11.760	49 4.64	1.13	−2.71	22 9.79	23 29 8.48
67	7.8				28.5				31 45.15	18.50	0.46	IV.	4	53.590	5 17.90	0.80	+1.17	31 26.19	22 45 17.53
68	7						27.5	44.	32 10.38	18.51	0.93	V.	2	18.785	41 44.61	0.75	−2.06	31 50.94	23 21 47.42
69	8		5.3		40.5				37 39.40	18.57	1.01	IV.	2	13.163	47 37.59	0.61	2.56	37 19.82	27 40.76
70	8			41.7		15.5			39 58.52	18.59	0.74	IV.	2	33.584	26 15.28	0.54	0.68	39 39.10	6 16.50
71	8	9.3	26.	43.					23 43 59.72	−18.63	−0.72	III.	3	35.200	−24 33.52	0.46	−0.51	23 43 40.37	−23 4 31.49

CORRECTIONS.

Date.	Corr. of Clock.	Hourly rate.	m	n	c	Zenith Point.	Mic. Co.
	h.	s.	s.	s.	s.	° ' "	r.
1847.							

INSTRUMENT READINGS.

	Date.	CIRCLE.							Barom.	THERMOM.				
		A.	B.	C.	D.	E.	F.	Mean.		At.	Ex.	U.	L.	I.
	1847. h. m.	° ' "						"	in.	°	°	°	°	°

REMARKS.

(146) 45. Minutes of transit assumed as 49, not 50.

(146) 50. Minutes of transit assumed as 55, not 54.

(146) 56. Minutes of transit assumed as 6, not 7.

(146) 57. Minutes of transit assumed as 8, not 7.

(146) 67. Transit over T. III assumed as recorded over T. IV.

(146) 68. Transits over T.'s V and VI assumed as recorded over T.'s VI and VII.

ZONE 146. NOVEMBER 2. P. $D_o = -22°\ 40'\ 0''$—Continued.

No.	Mag.	I.	II.	III.	IV.	V.	VI.	VII.	T.	a_1	a_2	MICROMETER.	i	d_1	d_2	Mean Right Ascension, 1850.0.	Mean Declination, 1850.0.
									h. m. s.	s.	s.	r.	' ''	''	''	h. m. s.	° ' ''
72	7	52.5	9.	26.3	43.	59.5	16.	32.7	23 48 42.66	−18.68	−0.53	IV. 4 49.426	− 9 39.06	− 0.36	+0.79	23 48 23.45	−22 49 38.63
73	8	..	11.	..	..	..	..	..	50 44.60	18.70	0.47	II. 4 54.650	4 11.26	0.32	+1.27	50 25.43	22 44 10.31
74	8	38.	55.5	12.5	..	..	..	..	52 29.03	18.72	0.88	III. 3 24.420	35 49.93	0.30	−1.53	52 9.43	23 15 51.76
75	8	..	..	..	4.	..	..	..	52 47.03	18.72	1.00	V. 2 14.970	45 44.10	0.30	2.40	52 27.31	25 46.80
76	8	..	..	..	..	..	52.	..	23 53 18.15	18.73	1.06	VI. 1 10.763	50 7.22	0.30	2.81	23 52 58.36	30 10.33
77	5	36.	52.	9.3	27.3	43.5	0.	16.5	24 1 26.22	−18.81	−0.94	IV. 2 19.983	−40 39.42	− 0.22	−1.95	0 1 6.47	−23 20 31.59

ZONE 147. NOVEMBER 15. C. $D_o = -23°\ 55'\ 0''$.

No.	Mag.	I.	II.	III.	IV.	V.	VI.	VII.	T.	a_1	a_2	MICROMETER.	i	d_1	d_2	Mean Right Ascension, 1850.0.	Mean Declination, 1850.0.
1	8	..	..	50.6	7.8	25.	41.5	..	23 34 24.52	−28.17	−1.37	IV. 3 28.757	−31 17.98	− 6.15	−3.13	23 33 54.98	−24 26 27.26
2	8	..	..	34.7	52.3	8.6	25.6	..	35 51.59	28.18	1.55	IV. 3 25.008	35 13.22	6.07	3.50	35 21.66	30 22.79
3	7.8	..	..	0.5	18.5	35.2	51.8	..	37 34.8?	28.21	1.49	IV. 3 34.734	25 3.01	5.97	2.53	37 5.11	20 11.51
4	9	..	..	..	..	..	..	21.2	37 30.68	28.21	1.28	VII. 4 53.332	5 33.57	5.97	0.70	37 1.19	0 40.24
5	8.9	..	..	36.	53.	9.6	26.	..	41 52.63	28.26	1.36	IV. 4 50.710	8 18.42	5.75	0.96	41 23.01	3 25.13
6	9.10	..	..	..	..	36.	52.6	..	43 19.02	28.27	1.42	V. 4 47.589	11 34.15	5.69	1.26	42 49.33	6 41.10
7	9.10	..	..	..	50.?	..	..	..	45 49.36	28.30	1.62	IV. 3 31.601	28 19.62	5.58	2.84	45 19.44	23 28.04
8	9.10	..	..	19.3	36.3	..	..	..	48 35.86	28.31	1.68	IV. 3 28.758	31 17.92	5.46	3.13	48 5.87	26 26.51
9	9	..	..	47.6	5.2	21.8	..	..	53 4.64	28.39	1.67	IV. 3 37.452	22 12.69	5.31	2.26	52 34.58	17 20.26
10	9.10	..	..	..	47.2	..	21.2	..	53 47.05	28.40	1.67	IV. 3 38.198	21 25.84	5.29	2.18	53 16.98	16 33.31
11	9.10	..	..	..	..	..	25.5	42.5	53 51.76	28.40	1.66	V. 3 38.648	20 57.79	5.29	2.14	53 21.70	16 5.22
12	9	..	..	49.	6.6	..	..	..	56 5.86	28.43	1.83	IV. 3 28.266	31 48.98	5.23	3.17	55 35.60	26 57.38
13	9	..	..	52.3	..	..	42.	..	57 8.68	28.44	1.59	IV. 4 48.856	10 14.63	5.20	1.14	56 38.65	5 20.97
14	9.10	..	..	..	26.2	..	0.	..	23 59 25.98	28.47	1.72	IV. 3 40.289	19 14.80	5.12	1.98	23 58 55.79	14 21.90
15	9	..	22.	..	56.7	..	29.2	..	24 4 55.79	28.53	1.92	IV. 3 29.216	30 49.31	5.04	3.08	0 4 25.34	25 57.43
16	8	..	..	..	29.	45.5	2.3	..	4 29.40	28.52	1.94	IV. 3 27.258	32 52.16	5.04	3.28	3 57.94	28 0.48
17	9	..	..	36.2	53.5	..	..	..	24 6 10.32	−28.54	−2.13	III. 3 21.500	−38 53.10	− 5.02	−3.85	0 5 39.65	−24 34 1.97

CORRECTIONS.

Date.	Corr. of Clock.	Hourly rate.	m	n	c	Zenith Point.	Mic. Co.
1847.	h.	s.	s.	s.	s.	° ' ''	r.

INSTRUMENT READINGS.

	Date.	A.	B.	C.	D.	E.	F.	Mean.	Barom.	At.	Ex.	U.	L.	I.
	1847. h. m.	° ' ''					''	''	in.	°	°	°	°	°
Zone 147	Nov. 15, 23 30	63.17 {37.1 35.9}	37.9 38.1	34.9 36.8	22.9 24.2	30.1 30.2	34.4 35.	33.12*	30.152	54.	43.4	51.5	51.5	53.
	23 40										44.1			
	0 0								30.152	54.2	44.5			
	0 10	{37.1 36.}	37.9 38.2	35.6 37.4	22.5 23.8	30.7 30.4	33.1 34.2	33.07			44.1	49.7	50.2	

*Corr. for runs +0''.07.

ZONE 148. NOVEMBER 20. C. $D_0 = -23°\ 17'\ 30''$.

No.	Mag.	I.	II.	III.	IV.	V.	VI.	VII.	T.	a_1	a_2	Micr.	r	i	d_1	d_2	Mean Right Ascension 1850.0	Mean Declination 1850.0
									h. m. s.	s.	s.		r.	' "	"	"	h. m. s.	° ' "
1	9					18.?			23 52 1.21	−34.69	−0.39	IV. 4	50.812	− 8 11.97	− 1.01	+0.03	23 52 26.	−23 25 42.95
2	9						50.?		53 33.19	34.70	0.39	V. 4	46.618	12 34.97	0.99	−0.37	52 58.	30 6.33
3	8.9							27.5	53 53.91	34.71	0.39	VI.	40.459	19 1.20	0.98	0.98	53 18.81	36 33.16
4	7			10.6 27.6 45.5			18.1		23 59 44.48	34.77	0.37	IV. 3	21.540	38 50.96	0.87	2.84	59 9.34	56 24.67
5	9					7.8			0 0 6.96	34.77	0.37	IV. 3	21.041	39 22.15	0.87	−2.89	23 59 31.82	56 55.91
6	7							32.	1 41.75	34.79	0.39	VII. 4	55.765	3 0.77	0.86	+0.50	0 1 6.57	20 31.13
7	8.9			36. 53.	8.5?			42.2	5 52.15	34.82	0.39	IV. 3	38.129	21 30.10	0.84	−1.20	4 16.93	23 39 2.14
8	8		8.5 25.5	43.2	59.2	16.2			6 42.33	34.84	0.37	IV. 2	15.488	45 11.65	0.82	−3.44	6 7.12	24 2 45.91
9	9		48.5 5.3	22.3	39.1				9 22.12	34.89	0.39	IV. 4	51.281	7 42.75	0.81	+0.08	8 46.84	23 25 13.48
10	10					23.5		57.	12 6.55	34.91	0.38	V. 3	32.741	27 8.29	0.80	−1.73	11 31.26	44 40.82
11	8		18.1 35.2	53.					14 52.07	34.94	0.38	III. 3	27.510	32 35.97	0.80	2.24	14 16.75	50 9.01
12	9							43.	15 52.66	34.94	0.39	V. 4	48.270	10 51.50	0.80	0.20	14 17.33	28 22.50
13	9			10.1 26.5	42.8				21 26.23	35.02	0.40	IV. 3	36.187	23 31.99	0.83	1.39	20 50.81	41 4.22
14	7		40.6 57.2			34.5	48.1		29 14.35	35.11	0.40	IV. 3	37.202	22 28.31	0.92	1.29	28 38.84	40 0.52
15	10			55.			45.6		34 11.80	35.17	0.39	IV. 2	19.728	40 45.42	1.00	3.02	33 36.24	58 19.44
16	10				38.2	55.			36 38.06	35.20	0.41	IV. 4	49.125	9 57.86	1.05	0.12	36 2.45	23 27 29.05
17	8			17.	34.2		7.2		42 33.48	35.26	0.39	IV. 2	16.077	44 34.63	1.17	3.39	41 57.83	24 2 9.19
18	9				35.		7.5		42 33.78	35.26	0.39	VI. 2	8.698	52 17.74	1.17	4.13	41 58.13	9 53.04
19	7							36.5	43 45.67	35.26	0.39	VII. 3	7.841	53 11.03	1.18	−4.22	42 10.02	24 10 40.43
20	8.9						43.5	17.	45 26.70	35.29	0.42	V. 3	51.022	7 58.73	1.25	+0.05	44 50.99	23 25 29.93
21	10		41.5 58.2	15.7					51 15.15	35.36	0.42	IV. 4	52.135	6 49.13	1.39	+0.16	50 39.37	24 20.36
22	9		55.8 13.5	31.					0 56 30.05	−35.41	−0.40	IV. 2	18.894	−41 37.71	−1.55	−3.10	0 55 54.24	−23 59 12.36

ZONE 149. DECEMBER 18. C. $D_0 = -25°\ 10'\ 0''$.

No.	Mag.	I.	II.	III.	IV.	V.	VI.	VII.	T.	a_1	a_2	Micr.	r	i	d_1	d_2	Mean Right Ascension 1850.0	Mean Declination 1850.0
1	7	46.9	3.7	21.1	38.1	54.0	12.4	29.4	23 49 37.97	−50.94	−1.12	IV. 3	35.469	−24 17.08	− 4.06	−2.43	23 48 45.91	−25 34 23.57
2	8.9		19.2	36.4	53.4				52 53.25	50.98	1.14	IV. 4	40.822	18 41.38	3.88	1.89	51 1.13	28 47.15
3	8.9	30.3		4.4	21.	38.1			56 21.07	51.03	1.15	IV. 4	44.008	15 21.61	3.68	1.57	55 28.89	25 26.86
4	9			10.5	27.2	44.2			59 27.16	51.07	1.16	IV. 4	48.928	10 12.99	3.45	1.07	58 34.93	20 17.54
5	9					9.2	26.5	43.5	23 59 52.89	51.07	1.13	V. 4	42.332	17 6.67	3.47	1.74	23 59 0.09	27 11.88
6	10				58.2	17.			0 15.70	51.15	1.03	IV. 3	23.155	37 9.62	3.14	3.73	0 5 23.52	47 16.49
7	9				29.	45.5		20.3	8 28.80	51.18	1.14	IV. 4	50.007	9 1.69	3.01	0.95	7 36.48	19 5.65
8	9		43.5	0.7	17.5	35.1			12 17.64	51.23	1.14	IV. 4	52.498	6 29.38	2.83	0.70	11 25.27	16 32.91
9	7.8			16.3		50.5	7.5		13 15.80	51.24	0.96	IV. 3	13.869	46 58.03	2.80	4.67	12 23.60	57 5.50
10	8.9							29.5	13 38.27	51.24	1.08	VII. 3	37.598	22 2.91	2.78	2.22	12 45.95	32 7.91
11	8.9					9.5	27.		14 52.47	51.27	0.97	V. 3	16.358	44 22.58	2.73	4.43	14 0.23	54 29.74
12	8.9						29.5	36.3	15 45.04	51.28	0.99	VI. 3	21.413	39 5.65	2.68	3.90	14 52.77	49 12.23
13	9		18.6	35.3	52.5		26.8		18 52.39	51.32	0.98	IV. 3	22.341	38 0.77	2.56	3.81	18 0.09	48 7.14
14	9		40.2	57.1	14.2				21 14.05	51.35	1.02	IV. 3	29.302	30 43.08	2.48	3.09	20 21.68	40 49.55
15	7		37.5	55.4	12.	29.5	46.	3.5	22 12.05	51.36	1.08	IV. 4	41.505	17 58.77	2.45	1.82	21 19.61	28 3.04
16	9							28.1	22 36.70	51.37	0.97	VII. 3	24.988	35 13.97	2.44	3.52	21 44.34	45 19.93
17	8.9		27.5		52.1		26.3		24 51.80	51.40	0.94	IV. 2	15.958	44 46.99	2.38	4.46	23 59.46	54 53.83
18	8				0.8	18.1			25 43.86	51.41	1.00	V. 3	41.024	18 28.52	2.36	1.87	24 51.39	28 32.75
19	8		15.5	32.5	49.3	6.5			28 49.33	51.45	0.99	IV. 3	28.661	31 24.08	2.27	3.15	27 56.89	41 29.50
20	8						32.5	49.	29 15.06	51.45	0.97	IV. 3	27.894	32 12.07	2.26	3.23	28 22.62	42 17.56
21	5		13.3	30.	47.5	4.6	21.5		30 30.14	51.47	1.02	IV. 3	34.295	25 30.73	2.23	2.57	29 37.65	35 35.53
22	8.9				50.2	7.5	24.5		31 50.17	51.49	1.05	IV. 3	40.272	19 15.81	2.21	1.94	30 57.63	29 19.96
23	6.7							5.5	0 32 13.97	−51.49	−0.92	VII. 2	14.984	−45 49.06	−2.21	−4.56	0 31 21.56	−25 55 55.83

CORRECTIONS.

Date.	Corr. of Clock.	Hourly rate.	m	n	c	Zenith Point.	Mic. Co.
1847.	h.	s.	s.	s.	s.	s.	° ' " r.

INSTRUMENT READINGS.

Date.		CIRCLE.							Barom.	THERMOM.				
		A.	B.	C.	D.	E.	F.	Mean.		At.	Ex.	U.	L.	I.
	1847. h. m.	° ' "						"	in.	°	°	°	°	°
Zone 148	Nov. 20, 23 50	62 39 02.7	66.4	66.1	49.8	54.7	59.1	59.80				35.4	46.5	45.5 54.
	0 0								30.390	44.		35.		
	0 20												34.7	
	0 40								30.406	43.0	33.5			
	0 50	62.0	67.4	65.9	50.7	54.7	58.2	59.82	30.400	43.0	33.0	44.5	43.3	
Zone 149	Dec. 18, 23 45	64 32 30.2	31.0	35.5	25.0	29.5	22.6	28.97*	30.150	42.5	34.6	43.8	43.4	44.0
	23 59												34.6	
	0 28												35.5	
	0 41								30.148	41.2	35.6			

REMARKS.

(148) 1. Minutes of transit assumed as 53, not 52.

(148) 7. Minutes of transit assumed as 4, not 5.

(148) 12. Minutes of transit assumed as 14, to agree with Arg. Z. 270, 47.

(148) 18. Declination 1' larger than in Oeltzen.

(148) 19. Minutes of transit assumed as 42, to agree with Arg. Z. 338, 14.

(149) 4. Transits over T.'s III, IV, and V assumed to have been recorded as over T.'s II, III, and IV.

(149) 12. Transit over T. VI assumed to have been at 19ˢ.5 instead of 29ˢ.5.

(149) 17. Transit over T. I assumed to have been at 17ˢ.5 instead of 27ˢ.5.

*Corr. for runs +0''.07.

ZONE 149. DECEMBER 18. C. $D_0 = -25°\ 10'\ 0''$—Continued.

Seconds of transit, T, a_1, a_2:

No.	Mag.	I.	II.	III.	IV.	V.	VI.	VII.	T. (h m s)	a_1 (s)	a_2 (s)
24	7		28.	45.2	2.5				0 35 2.10	−51.53	−0.94
25	8					27.	44.		35 9.87	51.53	1.01
26	9		53.2	10.	27.5	44.5			37 27.18	51.56	0.97
27	9.10			14.8	32.	49.2			41 31.63	51.61	0.91
28	9.10			12.1	29.2				42 28.94	51.62	1.05
29	7			26.4	42.5	0.5	17.8		46 43.07	51.67	0.98
30	9				31.	49.	5.1	23.1	47 31.08	51.68	0.91
31	9					49.8	5.9	23.8	47 32.17	51.68	0.91
32	7.8						29.	46.2	48 54.96	51.71	1.01
33	9.10			25.2	42.6				52 42.01	51.76	0.92
34	9						49.	16.	53 14.93	51.76	1.03
35	9						15.8	33.	0 54 41.70	51.78	0.97
36	9				0.	17.5			1 0 16.78	51.85	0.85
37	7.8					5.7	23.7	40.3	0 49.04	51.86	0.93
38	9							23.5	11 32.36	51.87	1.00
39	8			55.5	12.	29.5	46.6		13 12.11	52.02	0.88
40	8			12.8	30.7	47.5			14 29.95	52.03	0.84
41	9		40.3		14.?	32.5	49.5		19 14.72	52.09	0.93
42	9.10				6.?				21 5.38	52.12	0.89
43	7.8		0.5	17.6	34.5		8.9		22 34.51	52.14	0.91
44	9.10			4.5	21.				24 20.88	52.16	0.85
45	9.10		47.5		23.5		57.8		30 22.00	52.23	0.97
46	9					59.6	17.6	34.	30 59.65	52.24	0.83
47	7.8			24.5	40.8	58.	14.		32 40.51	52.26	0.83
48	9							46.7	33 55.20	52.28	0.78
49	6	39.4	56.	13.3	30.5	47.9	5.1	22.2	39 30.48	52.35	0.80
50	9		32.3	49.5	56.	13.1			43 56.16	52.40	0.94
51	9		42.		16.4	33.5			46 16.11	52.43	0.79
52	7.8		27.	44.6	1.5	18.6			49 1.31	52.46	0.82
53	9							6.	49 14.95	52.46	0.92
54	9							6.3	50 14.71	52.48	0.71
55	9.10				56.8				54 50.61	52.53	0.92
56	9		36.5	53.8	10.8				57 10.61	52.56	0.87
57	9						59.8	16.7	1 57 25.38	52.56	0.75
58	9			10.6	26.8	44.7			2 0 27.20	52.60	0.87
59	9			17.5	34.2	51.7			1 51.40	52.62	0.91
60	9					31.5			2 2 14.43	−52.62	−0.86

Micrometer, i, d_1, d_2, Mean Right Ascension 1850.0, Mean Declination 1850.0:

No.	Micrometer		r	i (' '')	d_1 ('')	d_2 ('')	Mean R.A. 1850.0 (h m s)	Mean Decl. 1850.0 (° ' '')
24	IV.	2	19.022	−41 34.69	−2.17	−4.16	0 34 9.63	−25 51 41.02
25	VI.	3	34.812	24 57.87	2.17	2.52	34 17.33	35 2.56
26	IV.	3	28.541	31 31.66	2.14	3.17	36 34.65	47 36.97
27	IV.	2	16.987	43 42.41	2.10	4.36	40 39.11	54 48.87
28	IV.	4	46.032	13 14.73	2.10	1.36	41 36.27	23 18.19
29	IV.	3	34.206	25 36.25	2.09	2.58	45 50.42	35 40.92
30	IV.	2	19.296	41 17.69	2.09	4.13	46 38.49	51 23.91
31	VI.	2	19.202	41 24.34	2.09	4.14	46 39.58	51 30.57
32	VII.	3	47.115	18 22.31	2.08	1.86	48 2.24	28 26.25
33	IV.	3	24.474	35 46.92	2.11	3.59	51 49.33	45 52.62
34	VII.	4	47.492	11 42.11	2.11	1.21	52 22.14	21 45.43
35	VI.	3	36.371	23 20.25	2.13	2.34	53 48.95	33 24.72
36	IV.	2	14.566	46 14.48	2.16	4.59	59 24.08	56 21.25
37	V.	3	30.555	29 25.24	2.20	2.95	0 59 56.22	39 30.39
38	VII.	4	44.884	14 25.48	2.21	1.48	1 0 39.40	24 29.17
39	IV.	3	26.124	34 3.26	2.50	3.41	12 19.21	44 9.17
40	IV.	3	17.252	43 20.07	2.54	4.34	13 37.08	53 26.95
41	IV.	3	39.744	19 48.74	2.71	2.01	18 21.70	29 53.46
42	IV.	3	32.855	27 0.83	2.79	2.72	20 12.37	37 6.34
43	IV.	3	35.274	24 29.32	2.88	2.45	21 41.46	34 34.65
44	IV.	3	26.582	33 34.58	2.97	3.36	23 27.87	43 40.91
45	IV.	4	52.668	6 18.60	3.33	0.68	29 29.70	16 22.61
46	IV.	3	23.486	36 48.91	3.37	3.69	30 6.58	46 55.97
47	IV.	3	23.246	37 3.90	3.50	3.72	31 47.42	47 11.12
48	VII.	2	16.550	44 11.03	3.59	4.41	33 2.14	54 19.03
49	IV.	3	22.260	38 5.78	4.01	3.81	38 37.33	48 13.60
50	IV.	4	51.915	7 5.75	4.22	0.76	43 2.82	17 10.73
51	IV.	3	23.152	37 9.81	4.32	3.73	45 22.89	47 17.86
52	IV.	3	32.280	27 37.14	4.44	2.77	48 8.03	37 44.35
53	VII.	4	51.354	7 39.97	4.45	0.82	48 21.57	25 17 45.24
54	VII.	2	10.234	50 47.47	4.48	5.07	49 21.52	26 0 57.02
55	IV.	4	54.644	4 14.70	4.50	0.49	54 3.16	25 14 19.69
56	IV.	3	44.068	15 17.60	4.51	1.56	56 17.16	25 23.67
57	VI.	2	19.683	40 54.09	4.51	4.09	56 32.07	51 2.69
58	IV.	4	45.697	13 35.69	4.52	1.39	1 59 33.73	23 41.60
59	IV.	4	53.068	5 53.51	4.52	0.64	2 0 57.87	15 58.67
60	V.	4	44.962	−14 21.52	−4.53	−1.46	2 1 20.95	−25 24 27.51

CORRECTIONS.

Date	Corr. of Clock	Hourly rate	m	n	c	Zenith Point	Mic. Co.
1847.	h.	s.	s.	s.	s.	° ' ''	r.
	s.	s.					

REMARKS.

(149) 34. One of the transits erroneous by 10^s; if T. VII is correct, T $= 24^s.93$.

(149) 50. Either the transits over T.'s II and III or those over T.'s IV and V are erroneous by 10^s; in the latter case, T $= 6^s.16$.

INSTRUMENT READINGS.

Date	Circle A	B	C	D	E	F	Mean	Barom.	Therm. At.	Ex.	U.	L.	I.
Zone 149 Dec. 18	1847. h. m.						''	in.	°	°	°	°	°
1 0	64 32 30.3	30.9	35.3	24.7	28.7	21.9	28.63a				35.5	38.5	40.3
1 19								30.148	40.5	35.1			
1 39										33.3			
2 0	30.5	30.7	35.1	24.0	28.7	21.6	28.58	30.144	39.2	32.5	37.5	38.7	43.8

a Corr. for runs $+0''.07$.

ZONE 150. JANUARY 3. C. $D_o = -23°\ 17'\ 20''$.

No.	Mag.	\multicolumn{7}{SECONDS OF TRANSIT} I.	II.	III.	IV.	V.	VI.	VII.	T. (h m s)	a_1 (s.)	a_2 (s.)	Micrometer	r.	i	d_1	d_2	Mean Right Ascension, 1850.0	Mean Declination, 1850.0
1	9	..	..	..	34.5	51.5	..	..	1 50 34.43	−64.86	−0.25	IV. 2	9.182	−51 51.64 −	2.56	−9.19	1 49 29.32	−24 9 23.30
2	9	..	32.	49.	..	21.3	38.5	..	52 5.28	64.90	0.73	III. 3	30.019	29 58.75	2.65	7.00	50 59.65	23 47 28.40
3	9	..	32.3	49.7	..	22.	39.	..	1 52 5.84	64.90	0.89	V. 3	37.956	21 40.71	2.65	6.18	1 51 0.05	39 9.54
4	8	24.5	..	57.	..	31.7	..	..	2 3 14.56	65.00	0.83	IV. 3	35.090	24 40.70	3.33	6.48	2 2 8.73	42 10.51
5	8	..	51.5	8.5	..	..	59.	..	7 25.40	65.06	0.09	IV. 4	42.375	17 3.95	3.59	5.73	6 19.35	34 33.27
6	9	..	54.3	10.5	28.	..	..	..	9 27.84	65.09	0.45	IV. 3	19.069	41 25.75	3.72	8.16	8 22.30	23 58 57.63
7	9	..	..	..	..	..	22.5	39.5	2 9 48.73	−65.09	−0.33	VI. 2	14.274	−46 33.23 −	3.74	−8.64	2 8 43.31	−24 4 5.61

ZONE 151. JANUARY 4. P. $D_o = -27°\ 2'\ 40''$.

No.	Mag.	I.	II.	III.	IV.	V.	VI.	VII.	T. (h m s)	a_1 (s.)	a_2 (s.)	Micrometer	r.	i	d_1	d_2	Mean Right Ascension, 1850.0	Mean Declination, 1850.0
1	7	..	..	..	..	..	..	52.3	2 10 0.15	−66.20	−1.27	. 4	58.557	−10 34.98 −	4.84	−1.64	2 8 52.68	−27 13 21.46
2	7	19.	36.3	53.5	11.	28.3	45.5	2.7	13 10.90	66.24	1.27	IV. 4	53.60	5 19.22	5.11	0.84	12 3.39	8 5.17
3	7	..	..	..	..	..	22.5	..	14 47.68	66.26	1.29	I. 1	6.13	54 55.09	5.24	7.30	13 40.13	57 47.63
4	6.7	57.5	14.5	32.	49.5	7.	24.3	41.3	17 49.44	66.30	1.28	IV. 3	22.53	37 48.73	5.49	5.02	16 41.86	40 39.24
5	8.9	..	..	52.7	9.	..	..	..	20 9.58	66.33	1.28	IV. 2	14.28	46 32.04	5.69	6.17	19 1.97	49 23.90
6	9	..	4.	21.5	..	..	..	..	21 38.93	66.35	1.27	III. 3	32.95	26 54.79	5.82	3.58	20 31 31	29 44.19
7	7	..	..	24.7	41.7	59.	..	..	22 41.93	66.36	1.26	IV. 4	55.255	3 35.38	5.93	0.61	21 34.26	6 21.92
8	7	..	..	..	..	1.	..	..	23 43.33	66.38	1.28	. 1	8.053	52 55.03	6.02	7.03	22 35.67	55 48.08
9	9	..	..	..	14.	..	..	..	24 56.63	66.39	1.27	. 3	37.29	22 22.69	6.13	3.01	23 48.97	25 11.83
10	6.7	7.3	24.5	42.	59.3	..	34.3	51.8	26 59.39	66.41	1.27	IV. 3	23.11	37 12.29	6.33	4.94	25 51.71	40 3.56
11	9	..	56.	13.5	31.	..	..	..	29 30.91	66.45	1.27	IV. 3	37.275	22 23.70	6.50	3.01	28 23.19	25 13.27
12	9	..	..	..	14.	..	..	..	30 13.87	66.45	1.26	. 3	41.14	18 21.40	6.63	2.51	29 6.16	21 10.54
13	9	..	..	..	54.5	..	..	..	31 54.37	66.48	1.26	. 3	25.163	35 3.58	6.80	4.66	30 46.63	37 55.04
14	9	18.5	35.3	..	10.	..	..	..	47 10.16	66.66	1.24	IV. 4	41.983	17 28.36	8.41	2.39	46 2.26	20 19.16
15	7.8	28.	..	3.	20.5	..	55.	..	53 20.30	66.73	1.25	IV. 3	31.063	28 53.37	9.11	3.85	52 12.32	31 46.33
16	8.9	56.	..	31.	..	..	..	..	55 48.23	66.76	1.25	III. 3	34.387	25 24.87	9.39	3.51	54 40.22	28 17.77
17	8	19.	6.	24.	..	58.5	..	..	2 57 41.13	66.79	1.24	V. 3	28.57	31 29.78	9.61	4.19	2 56 33.10	34 23.58
18	7	..	..	54.7	..	29.3	..	..	3 3 54.62	66.83	1.23	IV. 4	44.718	14 36.76	10.37	2.02	3 2 46.53	17 29.15
19	9	..	..	17.	..	..	..	..	7 16.85	66.89	1.24	. 3	31.66	28 15.92	10.79	3.78	6 8.72	31 10.49
20	7	46.3	3.	30.7	38.	55.3	13.	30.5	10 38.11	66.94	1.23	IV. 4	22.163	38 11.76	11.21	5.07	9 29.94	41 8.04
21	6	..	54.	11.7	29.	46.7	3.7	..	15 29.10	66.99	1.22	IV. 4	52.773	6 11.03	11.85	0.94	14 20.89	9 3.82
22	8	..	57.	14.5	..	..	..	..	17 32.00	67.02	1.24	III. 2	17.065	43 36.64	12.11	5.77	16 23.74	46 34.52
23	7	..	..	..	59.3	16.	..	..	17 41.46	67.02	1.24	V. 2	13.465	47 23.59	12.14	5.26	16 33.20	50 20.99
24	8.9	..	..	..	16.3	..	..	..	18 58.80	67.03	1.23	. 2	22.85	37 28.54	12.31	4.95	17 50.54	40 25.83
25	8	..	..	..	59.	..	..	..	19 58.91	67.04	1.23	. 2	17.115	43 34.13	12.44	5.77	18 50.64	46 32.34
26	7	..	..	..	..	41.5	..	..	20 23.92	67.04	1.23	. 2	15.577	45 11.08	12.49	5.99	19 15.65	48 9.56
27	6	..	..	11.	28.5	46.	..	..	21 11.02	67.05	1.23	IV. 2	13.003	47 51.93	12.61	6.33	20 2.74	50 50.87
28	8.9	..	..	..	..	..	..	53.	21 0.79	67.05	1.22	. 3	36.51	23 11.08	12.58	3.12	19 52.52	26 6.78
29	9	..	..	15.	32.	49.3	..	47.	23 12.30	67.07	1.21	. 4	53.745	5 9.30	12.88	0.80	22 4.02	8 2.98
30	8	..	..	..	..	..	..	..	25 49.55	67.09	1.21	IV. 4	53.78	5 7.79	13.23	0.80	24 41.25	8 1.82
31	8	..	..	22.3	39.5	57.	..	..	30 39.63	67.15	1.21	IV. 4	45.027	14 17.29	13.88	1.98	29 31.27	17 13.15
32	8	1.	18.	35.5	52.7	..	..	..	33 52.84	67.19	1.20	IV. 4	43.98	15 23.00	14.36	2.13	32 44.45	18 19.40
33	8	..	..	..	..	..	..	18.5	34 25.94	67.20	1.22	. 2	12.695	48 12.25	14.43	6.37	33 17.52	51 13.05
34	9	25.	..	0.	..	..	..	..	37 17.18	67.22	1.20	III 4	43.71	15 40.15	14.84	2.17	36 8.76	18 37.16
35	9	..	57.	14.3	31.7	..	..	..	41 31.77	67.28	1.21*	IV. 3	24.26	36 0.23	15.60	4.77	41 23.28	39 0.60
36	8.9	..	..	..	..	21.5	..	..	43 4.23	67.28	1.19	. 3	49.50	9 36.37	15.69	1.39	41 55.76	12 33.45
37	7.8	..	..	10.	27.	44.3	..	..	44 27.05	67.29	1.20	IV. 3	29.02	31 1.49	15.90	4.14	43 18.56	34 1.53
38	8.9	..	..	..	..	..	27.	44.	3 51 52.08	−67.37	−1.19	VII. 4	50.867	− 8 9.43 −	17.03	−1.20	3 50 43.52	−27 11 7.66

CORRECTIONS.

Date.	Corr. of Clock.	Hourly rate.	m	n	c	Zenith Point.	Mic. Co.
1848. (h.)	(s.)	(s.)	(s.)	(s.)	(s.)	(° ′ ″)	(r.)
Jan. 3, 0	..	..	..	..	..	359 59 60.20	29.9876
Jan. 4, 0	..	..	..	..	..	58.51	29.9930

INSTRUMENT READINGS.

	Date.		\multicolumn{7}{CIRCLE} A.	B.	C.	D.	E.	F.	Mean.	Barom. (in.)	\multicolumn{5}{THERMOM} At.	Ex.	U.	L.	I.
Zone 150	Jan. 3,	1 50	72 39 63.6	66.5	65.9	58.8	61.3	57.9	62.33	30.144	45.	37.2	50.	45.7	47.2
		2 0	..	..	..	..	..	..	..	..	..	36.9			
		2 20	..	..	..	..	..	..	..	30.130	43.5	37.			
Zone 151	Jan. 4,	2 10	76 24 61.0	63.7	65.3	54.8	59.0	53.5	59.55	30.212	46.	39.7	..	47.5	46.5
		3 10	..	..	..	..	..	..	..	30.236	44.8	37.8			
		4 0	..	..	..	..	..	..	..	30.240	43.1	37.	..	43.	

REMARKS.

(151) 1. Micrometer reading assumed as $48^r.557$, not $58^r.557$,

(151) 37. Differs 2′ in declination from Arg. Z. 322, 94.

ZONE 151. JANUARY 4. P. $D_0 = -27° 2' 40''$—Continued.

No.	Mag.	I.	II.	III.	IV.	V.	VI.	VII.	T.	a_1	a_2	Mic.	n	r	i	d_1	d_4	Mean Right Ascension, 1850.0	Mean Declination, 1850.0
									h. m. s.	s.	s.			r.	′ ″	″	″	h. m. s.	° ′ ″
39	8					48.5			3 53 31.12	−67.39	−1.20	.	3	35.25	−24 30.72	−17.28	−3.29	3 52 22.53	−27 27 31.29
40	8.9				59.				54 58.89	67.40	1.20	.	2	21.895	38 34.22	17.52	5.10	53 50.29	41 36.84
41	9				52.				55 51.91	67.40	1.20	.	2	16.695	44 0.41	17.60	5.82	54 43.31	47 3.89
42	9							0.	56 7.46	67.42	1.20	.	2	13.985	46 51.36	17.69	6.19	54 58.84	49 55.24
43	7				40.5	58.	15.5		3 57 40.50	67.43	1.20	IV.	1	9.66	51 14.65	17.93	6.79	3 56 31.87	54 19.37
44	8	7.5	24.3	42.	59.				4 1 59.26	−67.46	−1.19	IV.	3	30.675	−29 17.65	−18.02	−3.01	4 0 50.61	−27 32 20.18

ZONE 152.* JANUARY 4. P. $D_0 = -26° 25' 50''$.

No.	Mag.	I.	II.	III.	IV.	V.	VI.	VII.	T.	a_1	a_2	Mic.	n	r	i	d_1	d_4	Mean Right Ascension, 1850.0	Mean Declination, 1850.0
1	8					36.5			6 35 2.03	−68.32	−0.65	.	4	46.047	−13 12.64	−5.36	−7.95	6 31 53.06	−26 39 15.92
2	7	10.5	27.7	45.	2.3	19.7	37.		40 2.40	68.33	1.06	IV.	2	14.863	45 55.24	6.41	11.98	38 54.01	27 12 3.63
3	7.8	53.	10.	27.5					43 44.96	68.33	1.09	III.	2	14.025	46 47.28	7.21	12.09	42 35.54	12 56.58
4	7		41.	58.5					45 15.86	68.34	1.07	III.	2	17.00	43 40.72	7.53	11.72	44 6.45	27 9 49.97
5	8				41.				45 40.85	68.34	0.95	.	3	28.795	31 15.54	7.62	10.16	44 31.56	26 57 23.32
6	8				20.				46 19.89	68.34	1.03	.	2	21.335	30 3.76	7.76	11.15	45 10.52	27 5 12.67
7	9					14.			46 56.77	68.34	0.78	.	4	42.333	17 0.33	7.89	8.42	45 47.65	26 43 13.26
8	7.8			51.	8.			59.5	48 7.92	68.34	0.83	IV.	4	39.27	20 18.82	8.15	8.80	46 58.75	46 25.77
9	9		4.5	22.					50 39.26	68.34	0.98	III.	3	29.303	30 43.80	8.69	10.09	49 29.94	56 52.58
10	9		58.7	16.					51 33.39	68.34	1.01	.	3	26.84	33 18.12	8.89	10.42	51 24.03	59 27.43
11	7.8			58.5	15.5	33.			53 15.02	68.34	1.02	IV.	3	28.33	31 44.97	9.26	10.22	52 6.26	57 54.45
12	9							34.7	53 42.84	68.34	0.72	.	3	54.183	4 41.43	9.36	6.87	52 33.78	30 47.66
13	9			36.					55 53.32	68.34	1.01	.	3	30.814	29 8.81	9.84	9.90	54 43.97	55 18.55
14	9					15.			55 57.79	68.35	0.84	.	3	45.05	13 38.01	9.85	7.99	54 48.60	30 45.85
15	9					52.			56 34.79	68.35	0.83	.	3	45.647	13 38.20	9.95	7.99	55 25.61	39 46.17
16	9				5.5				6 59 5.37	68.35	0.94	.	3	37.82	21 49.25	10.54	8.90	57 56.08	47 58.78
17	8			50.	7.				7 0 7.10	68.35	1.04	IV.	3	32.567	27 19.07	10.76	9.67	6 58 57.71	26 53 29.50
18	8	35.5		10.					7 5 27.58	−68.35	−1.35	III.	2	10.173	−48 46.94	−11.93	−12.35	7 4 17.88	−27 15 1.20

ZONE 153. JANUARY 18. S. $D_0 = -25° 47' 50''$.

No.	Mag.	I.	II.	III.	IV.	V.	VI.	VII.	T.	a_1	a_2	Mic.	n	r	i	d_1	d_4	Mean Right Ascension, 1850.0	Mean Declination, 1850.0
1	8			13.					4 21 30.33	−76.65	−1.49	III.	2	11.508	−49 25.24	−0.92	−12.32	4 20 12.10	−26 37 28.48
2	7				10.				23 9.86	76.67	1.31	IV.	3	28.280	31 48.10	1.20	10.24	21 51.88	19 49.54
3	7		28.						26 2.52	76.69	1.16	II.	4	42.592	16 50.39	1.67	8.44	24 44.67	4 50.50
4	8							13.	26 21.31	76.69	1.32	VII.	3	28.148	31 55.76	1.75	10.26	25 3.30	19 57.77
5	9				53.				30 10.22	76.73	1.30	III.	3	30.892	29 3.91	2.39	9.90	28 52.19	17 6.20
6	9			16.			50.		33 32.96	76.76	1.45	III.	2	16.250	42 22.45	2.92	11.45	32 14.75	30 26.82
7	10			3.			36.5		35 45.38	76.77	1.18	V.	4	43.338	16 3.25	3.29	8.35	34 27.43	4 4.89
8	8	20.		54.				20.	39 11.34	76.81	1.27	III.	3	35.808	23 55.44	3.68	9.27	37 53.26	11 58.59
9	8			11.5			52.		40 28.53	76.81	1.35	III.	3	29.078	30 57.85	4.11	10.11	39 10.37	19 2.07
10	8				18.		52.		41 0.64	76.82	1.19	V.	2	44.412	15 2.04	4.19	8.22	39 42.63	3 4.45
11	9				48.				46 5.25	76.87	1.41	III.	3	25.182	35 2.33	5.05	10.60	44 46.97	23 8.00
12	8				34.	8.			47 51.10	76.88	1.19	III.	4	45.780	13 30.16	5.37	8.04	46 33.03	1 33.57
13	7			23.		57.			50 40.12	76.90	1.17	III.	5	48.818	10 19.45	5.90	7.66	49 22.05	58 23.01
14	6				40.				4 57 22.67	76.95	1.51	IV.	2	19.165	41 25.63	7.15	11.38	56 4.21	29 34.16
15	6			12.					5 0 29.24	76.97	1.43	III.	3	26.802	33 20.51	7.67	10.40	4 59 10.84	21 28.58
16	7		23.			14.			5 5 57.20	77.01	1.29	II.	4	41.375	18 6.89	8.69	8.60	5 4 38.90	6 14.17
17	10				34.				5 7 51.22	−77.05	−1.41	IV.	3	30.758	−29 12.38	−8.82	−9.91	5 6 32.78	−26 17 21.11

CORRECTIONS.

Date.	Corr. of Clock.	Hourly rate.	m	n	ε	Zenith Point.	Mic. Co.
	h.	s.	s.	s.	s.	s.	° ′ ″	r.
1848, Jan. 18, 0	. .	. .	. .	. .	. .	359 59 57.07	29.9820

INSTRUMENT READINGS.

	Date.	CIRCLE.							Barom.	THERMOM.				
		A.	B.	C.	D.	E.	F.	Mean.		At.	Ex.	U.	L.	I.
	1848, h. m.	° ′ ″						″	In.	°	°	°	°	°
Zone 152	Jan. 4, 6 55	75 47 {35.3 / 33.7}	40.4 / 40.	40.6 / 41.5	31.6 / 32.6	36.0 / 36.8	27.7 / 27.7	35.32	30.234	42.	33.2	. .	40.5	
Zone 153	Jan. 18, 7 5								30.228	41.3	33.2			
	4 21	75 9 60.	68.0	67.4	54.2	64.9	51.9	61.07	30.380	39.5	28.8			
	5 36	.	.	.	.	.	.	.	30.386	39.0	27.5			
	5 38	.	.	.	.	.	.	.	30.398	38.2	28.2			
	6 38	.	.	.	.	.	.	.	30.404	37.8	27.2			

REMARKS.

(152) 10. Minutes assumed as 52, not 51.

(152) 18. Micrometer reading assumed as 12ʳ.038.

(153) 4. Right ascension 9ˢ discordant from Arg. Z. 325, 129.

(153) 8. Minutes assumed as 35, not 39.

(153) 14. Transit over T. V assumed to have been recorded as over T. IV.

ZONE 153. JANUARY 18. S. $D_o = -25° 47' 50''$—Continued.

No.	Mag.	SECONDS OF TRANSIT. I.	II.	III.	IV.	V.	VI.	VII.	T.	a_1	a_2	MICROMETER.			i	d_1	d_2	Mean Right Ascension, 1850.0.	Mean Declination, 1850.0.
									h. m. s.	s.	s.			r.	' "	"	"	h. m. s.	° ' "
18	9	..	..	..	..	..	55.	..	5 8 20.74	−77.03	−1.35	VI.	3	36.352	−23 21.37	− 9.12	− 9.22	5 7 2.36	−26 11 29.71
19	7	..	..	..	..	..	18.	..	9 43.72	77.04	1.48	VI.	2	25.600	34 42.68	9.37	10.55	8 25.20	22 52.60
20	7	..	25.	..	59.5	..	..	..	14 59.45	77.08	1.31	IV.	4	42.330	17 6.77	10.37	8.48	13 41.06	5 15.62
21	10	..	44.5	..	..	..	..	..	21 19.04	77.12	1.44	II.	3	31.545	28 22.88	11.56	9.82	20 0.48	16 34.26
22	10	..	43.	..	17.	..	..	..	23 17.20	74.13	1.47	II.	3	30.179	29 48.59	11.95	9.98	21 58.60	17 0.52
23	9	..	..	13.	..	..	..	..	25 12.85	77.14	1.47	III.	3	30.330	29 39.42	12.37	9.96	23 54.24	17 51.75
24	8	..	33.	..	..	..	..	..	28 7.56	77.17	1.52	II.	3	26.024	34 9.18	12.87	10.50	26 48.87	22 22.55
25	7	43.	..	19.	..	..	..	..	5 36 36.45	−77.21	−1.57	III.	3	23.039	−37 16.62	−14.55	−10.86	5 35 17.67	−26 25 32.03

ZONE 154. JANUARY 18. S. $D_o = -25° 47' 50''$.

No.	Mag.	I.	II.	III.	IV.	V.	VI.	VII.	T.	a_1	a_2	MICROMETER.			i	d_1	d_2	Mean Right Ascension, 1850.0.	Mean Declination, 1850.0.
1	8	..	9.	..	..	..	..	34.	5 38 42.95	−76.23	−1.08	II.	4	35.068	−24 42.56	−14.95	− 9.37	5 37 25.64	−26 12 56.90
2	9	..	..	..	..	14.5	..	..	39 57.32	76.24	1.12	V.	4	35.030	24 44.46	15.21	9.38	38 39.96	12 59.05
3	9	..	..	45.4	..	..	..	..	43 2.62	76.26	1.00	III.	3	29.395	30 38.09	15.83	10.10	41 45.36	18 54.02
4	8	..	..	36.	..	..	27.5	..	44 53.24	76.26	0.90	III.	3	24.810	35 25.48	16.21	10.66	43 36.08	23 42.35
5	8	49.	..	23.	40.2	..	..	..	47 40.26	76.28	1.13	IV.	3	28.519	31 33.04	16.76	10.20	46 22.85	19 50.00
6	10	59.	..	33.	50.	..	..	..	51 50.34	76.30	0.79	III.	2	16.150	44 34.08	17.62	11.72	50 33.25	32 53.42
7	10	..	..	..	35.	..	..	..	5 53 34.86	76.31	1.53	IV.	3	34.735	25 2.90	17.96	9.41	5 52 17.02	13 20.27
8	7	39.	..	..	30.5	..	..	..	6 6 30.53	76.37	1.43	V.	2	21.715	38 46.07	20.62	11.05	6 5 12.73	27 7.74
9	9	42.	..	..	34.	..	..	..	7 33.62	76.37	2.16	IV.	4	40.490	19 2.25	20.84	8.69	6 15.09	7 21.78
10	10	..	..	..	..	0.	..	..	10 51.60	76.39	2.17	V.	4	38.338	21 17.06	21.50	8.97	8 33.04	9 37.53
11	10	..	10.	..	..	..	..	..	12 44.51	76.40	2.62	II.	5	49.142	9 58.55	21.90	7.63	11 25.49	58 18.08
12	9	..	58.	..	..	..	..	..	16 32.58	76.41	1.80	II.	3	23.260	37 2.69	22.71	10.84	15 14.37	25 26.24
13	8	..	..	..	..	32.	..	..	17 14.79	76.41	2.07	.	3	30.325	29 39.74	22.86	9.96	15 56.31	18 2.56
14	8	..	..	42.	..	..	..	..	19 59.22	76.42	2.14	.	3	30.076	29 55.23	23.44	9.99	18 40.66	18 18.66
15	8	..	..	..	..	..	6.	..	19 31.73	76.42	2.00	.	3	26.323	33 50.62	23.33	10.47	18 13.31	22 14.42
16	9	..	..	..	48.	..	..	..	21 47.88	76.42	2.80	.	4	46.398	12 51.42	23.82	7.96	20 28.66	1 13.20
17	9	..	..	..	..	..	4.	..	22 29.71	76.42	2.88	.	5	48.098	11 4.02	23.96	7.72	21 10.41	59 25.70
18	9	..	..	..	..	..	1.	..	24 26.72	76.43	2.86	.	4	46.180	13 4.41	24.37	7.98	23 7.43	1 26.76
19	8	..	..	..	4.	..	39.	..	26 4.30	76.44	2.52	.	3	34.838	24 56.38	24.71	9.39	24 45.34	13 20.48
20	7	..	21.	..	55.	..	..	..	28 55.20	76.45	2.59	IV.	3	35.055	24 42.89	25.32	9.38	27 36.16	13 7.59
21	7	..	0.1	..	35.5	..	..	..	31 35.48	76.46	2.26	IV.	2	23.998	36 22.36	25.88	10.77	30 16.76	24 49.01
22	8	..	54.	..	..	..	..	..	34 28.59	76.47	2.29	.	2	22.426	37 59.85	26.50	10.96	33 9.83	26 27.32
23	7	..	..	..	44.	..	18.	..	35 43.80	76.48	2.89	.	3	37.660	21 59.42	26.76	9.02	34 24.43	10 25.20
24	8	..	0.1	..	35.	..	..	..	38 35.20	76.49	2.66	.	3	29.072	30 58.29	27.37	10.14	37 16.05	19 25.80
25	7	..	..	35.5	..	..	..	..	46 52.74	76.50	2.80	III.	3	26.065	34 6.80	29.14	10.50	45 33.44	22 36.44
26	7	..	..	..	..	22.	..	..	47 4.72	76.50	2.74	V.	3	24.398	35 51.57	29.18	10.72	45 45.48	24 21.47
27	9	15.	..	49.5	..	..	..	..	53 6.58	76.52	3.27	III.	3	33.512	26 19.71	30.46	9.54	51 46.79	14 49.71
28	6	..	..	58.	..	..	49.5	..	54 15.24	76.52	3.26	III.	3	32.050	27 51.32	30.71	9.76	52 55.46	16 21.79
29	8	..	..	..	..	54.	..	..	55 36.77	76.53	3.16	V.	3	28.202	31 52.87	31.00	10.25	54 17.08	20 24.12
30	7	..	..	..	12.	..	..	..	57 11.90	76.53	2.92	IV.	2	20.239	40 18.33	31.34	11.23	55 52.45	28 50.90
31	6	..	39.5	..	13.	..	..	..	6 59 13.48	76.53	3.10	IV.	3	23.265	37 2.69	31.77	10.86	6 57 53.85	25 35.32
32	4	..	..	19.	..	53.	..	..	7 3 36.06	−76.53	−3.81	III.	4	38.632	−20 58.93	−32.71	− 8.93	7 2 15.72	−26 9 30.57

CORRECTIONS.

Date.	Corr. of Clock.	Hourly rate.	m	n	c	Zenith Point.	Mic. Co.
1848. h.	s.	s.	s.	s.	s.	° ' "	r.

INSTRUMENT READINGS.

Date.	CIRCLE. A.	B.	C.	D.	E.	F.	Mean.	Barom.	THERMOM. At.	Ex.	U.	L.	I.
1848. h. m.	° ' "						"	in.	°	°	°	°	°

REMARKS.

(153) 23. Transit over T. IV assumed to have been recorded as over T. III.

(154) 3. Differs 38ˢ.5 in right ascension from Arg. Z. 323, 94, and Mer. Circle, 1849, February 16.

(154) 10. Transit over T. I assumed as recorded over T. V.

(154) 31. Differs 8ˢ in right ascension from Arg. Z. 287, 51, and 1848, January 22, and Transit Inst., 1848, January 20.

ZONE 155. JANUARY 19. C. $D_0 = -23° 17' 30''$.

No.	Mag.	I.	II.	III.	IV.	V.	VI.	VII.	T.	a_1	a_2
									h. m. s.	s.	s.
1	8		32.	48.9	5.5	22.7	39.6		2 2 5.78	+2.07	+0.98
2	8	26.	42.6	59.5	16.2	32.9	49.6		6 16.23	2.02	1.02
3	9		45.5	2.8	19.5		52.5?		8 19.36	1.99	0.91
4	9		6.	23.6			13.5	30.5	8 39.98	1.99	0.88
5	9			4.6	21.5				19 21.46	1.88	1.02
6	9				52.4	9.5		42.4	19 52.26	1.87	1.00
7	8			54.	10.8	27.6			22 10.75	1.85	0.94
8	8.9		35.1	42.	8.3	25.7	42.5		25 8.76	1.82	0.97
9	9							26.2?	25 35.40	1.81	0.90
10	9			31.6	48.7	5.8	22.		27 48.60	1.79	0.96
11	9				10.8	27.8	44.6	1.6	29 10.74	1.77	0.85
12	7.8				54.8	11.2	28.	45.2	30 54.52	1.75	1.01
13	9		8.8	25.5					41 42.52	1.64	0.99
14	7.8	13.5	29.6	47.1	3.5	20.5	37.4	53.6	44 3.63	1.61	1.01
15	9						38.2	55.	45 4.52	1.60	0.97
16	9			43.2	59.3	16.6			46 59.67	1.58	0.98
17	9				46.	3.2	19.7		47 46.13	1.57	1.04
18	8.9				11.5	28.5			49 11.50	1.56	0.96
19	8.9					23.7	40.7		50 7.01	1.55	1.03
20	6				22.5		56.6		51 22.68	1.54	0.85
21	9	25.5			15.7	32.8			54 15.79	1.51	1.01
22	5		10.5	27.5	43.7	1.5			2 54 41.25	1.51	0.85
23	7		6.8	24.2		57.5	14.5		3 10 40.79	1.31	0.88
24	9			48.5	5.				14 5.14	1.30	0.95
25	6.7					5.3	23.	39.5	14 48.66	1.29	0.86
26	7.8	9.5	26.5	43.5	0.1				23 0.35	1.21	0.91
27	.9	12.5	28.8	45.7	3.				27 2.73	1.16	1.07
28	9		55.5				2.8		28 29.28	1.15	1.01
29	9						18.6		29 27.77	1.14	0.91
30	9	39.5	55.8	13.4	29.5				35 29.98	1.09	0.88
31	8.9						49.5	6.2	36 15.74	1.09	1.09
32	9			21.3	38.5		12.		38 21.37	1.07	0.96
33	4			5.2	21.5	38.7	55.4	12.2	40 21.76	1.05	1.01
34	9						5.2	22.2	41 31.62	1.01	1.02
35	9		37.4	55.	11.6				45 11.58	1.01	1.10
36	9.10			18.					46 17.90	1.00	1.09
37	8			9.2	25.5	43.	59.5		47 25.92	0.99	1.04
38	9			10.5	27.5				49 27.43	0.97	0.92
39	9					59.2	16.8		49 42.76	0.96	0.96
40	9			11.8	28.2				52 28.42	0.94	1.01
41	9				26.5			17.	53 26.40	0.93	1.03
42	9				18.5			39.5	53 48.64	0.92	1.01
43	9		12.2	29.5			19.5	35.	59 45.68	0.87	0.95
44	9						18.2	36.5	3 59 45.27	+0.87	+1.01

No.	Mag.	MICROMETER.	r.	i	d_1	d_2	Mean Right Ascension, 1850.0	Mean Declination, 1850.0
				' ''	''	''	h. m. s.	° ' ''
1	8	IV. 3	35.149	−24 37.06	−2.77	−2.11	2 2 8.83	−23 42 11.94
2	8	IV. 4	42.405	17 2.06	3.04	1.36	6 19.27	34 36.46
3	9	IV. 2	19.249	41 20.42	3.16	3.75	8 22.26	23 58 57.33
4	9	V. 2	14.338	46 28.91	3.18	4.28	8 42.85	24 4 6.37
5	9	III. 4	41.319	18 10.34	3.80	1.47	19 24.36	23 35 45.70
6	9	IV. 4	38.295	21 20.01	3.95	1.79	19 55.13	38 55.75
7	8	V. 3	25.166	35 3.33	4.10	3.14	22 13.54	52 40.57
8	8.9	IV. 3	32.469	27 25.28	4.31	2.39	25 11.55	45 1.98
9	9	IV. 2	18.639	41 58.56	4.34	3.82	25 38.11	54 36.72
10	9	IV. 3	29.483	30 32.56	4.51	2.71	27 51.35	23 46 9.78
11	9	V. 2	8.030	53 3.75	4.61	4.96	29 13.36	24 10 43.32
12	7.8	V. 4	39.488	21 7.64	4.74	1.77	30 57.28	23 38 44.15
13	9	III. 3	34.269	25 32.20	5.64	2.21	41 45.15	43 10.05
14	7.8	III. 3	38.278	21 20.75	5.85	1.79	44 6.25	38 58.39
15	9	VI. 3	29.945	30 3.26	5.95	2.64	45 7.09	47 41.85
16	9	IV. 3	31.952	27 57.46	6.13	2.44	47 2.23	45 36.03
17	9	V. 4	43.245	16 9.08	6.20	1.28	47 48.74	33 46.56
18	8.9	V. 3	28.008	32 4.91	6.33	2.86	49 14.02	49 44.10
19	8.9	V. 4	41.497	17 58.80	6.41	1.45	50 9.59	23 35 36.66
20	6	V. 2	6.175	55 0.60	6.54	5.16	51 25.07	24 12 42.30
21	9	V. 4	44.705	14 37.26	6.83	1.13	54 18.34	23 32 15.22
22	5	IV. 2	6.015	55 10.07	6.87	5.18	2 54 46.61	24 12 52.12
23	7	V. 2	13.116	47 45.41	8.58	4.45	3 10 43.01	24 5 28.44
24	9	III. 2	26.556	33 36.12	8.98	3.00	14 7.39	23 51 18.10
25	6.7	V. 2	8.284	52 48.52	9.06	4.94	14 50.81	24 10 32.52
26	7.8	III. 2	18.582	42 1.56	10.06	3.83	23 2.47	23 59 45.45
27	.9	III. 4	49.371	9 44.99	10.57	0.64	27 4.96	27 26.20
28	9	IV. 3	38.112	21 31.06	10.76	1.78	28 31.44	23 39 13.60
29	9	VII. 4	17.483	43 12.94	10.88	3.97	29 29.82	24 0 57.79
30	9	III. 3	11.087	49 51.58	11.70	4.65	35 31.95	24 7 37.93
31	8.9	IV. 4	53.218	5 43.26	11.80	0.24	36 17.92	23 23 25.30
32	9	V. 3	26.711	33 26.28	12.09	2.99	38 23.40	51 11.36
33	4	IV. 3	35.745	23 59.53	12.36	2.05	40 23.82	41 43.94
34	9	VI. 3	37.659	21 59.23	12.53	1.86	41 33.68	39 43.62
35	9	III. 3	53.610	5 18.72	13.07	0.20	45 13.69	23 1.99
36	9.10	IV. 3	53.145	5 47.80	13.23	0.25	46 19.99	23 31.28
37	8	III. 3	42.861	16 32.68	13.39	1.30	47 27.95	34 17.57
38	9	III. 3	18.882	41 37.30	13.69	3.83	49 29.32	59 24.82
39	9	V. 3	26.108	34 4.24	13.72	3.05	49 44.68	51 51.01
40	9	III. 4	42.724	16 42.04	14.15	1.32	52 30.40	34 27.51
41	9	V. 3	40.992	18 30.30	14.30	1.49	53 28.36	36 16.09
42	9	V. 4	41.374	18 6.52	14.36	1.45	53 50.60	35 52.33
43	9	II. 3	24.752	35 28.98	15.28	3.18	59 47.50	53 17.44
44	9	VI. 3	36.172	−23 32.61	−15.28	−2.00	3 59 47.15	−23 41 19.89

CORRECTIONS.

Date.		Corr. of Clock.	Hourly rate.	m	n	e	Zenith Point.	Mic. Co.
1848, Jan. 19,	h. 0	s. . .	s. . .	s. . .	s. . .	s. . .	° ' '' 359 59 56.59	r. 29.9858

REMARKS.

(155) 17. Differs 17s in right ascension from Arg. Z. 313, 53; probably recorded over wrong threads.

INSTRUMENT READINGS.

	Date.		CIRCLE.							Barom.	THERMOM.				
			A.	B.	C.	D.	E.	F.	Mean.		At.	Ex.	U.	L.	I.
	1848,	h. m.	° ' ''						''	in.					
Zone 155	Jan. 19,	2 0	72 39 59.7	70.	67.	57.1	64.2	53.9	61.98	30.540	34.	28.2	36.3	35.5	40.
		2 20										27.2			
		3 0	59.7	69.5	68.1	56.6	64.2	52.9	61.83	30.534	33.7	26.5			
		3 40										26.3			
		3 20	59.6	69.2	68.2	56.2	66.2	52.5	62.02	30.532	33.	25.9		33.	
		0 40										25.4			
		0 0									30.526	32.5	24.4	31.	32.4	

Reading of micrometer E assumed as 63″.2.
[Observing book has 66″.2]

ZONE 156. JANUARY 20. S. $D_0 = -23° 17' 40''$.

| No. | Mag. | SECONDS OF TRANSIT | | | | | | | T. | a_1 | a_2 | MICROMETER | | | i | d_1 | d_2 | Mean Right Ascension, 1850.0 | Mean Declination, 1850.0 |
		I	II	III	IV	V	VI	VII	h. m. s.	s.	s.			r,	' "	"	"	h. m. s.	° ' "
1	8	56.		30.					4 47 46.66	+1.62	−0.79		3	32.750	−27 7.34	−1.85	−9.74	4 47 47.49	−23 44 58.93
2	8					46.			48 12.39	1.61	0.79		3	32.668	27 12.60	1.99	9.75	48 13.21	45 4.34
3	9					54.			49 20.39	1.60	0.97		4	47.660	11 31.83	2.18	8.15	49 21.02	29 22.16
4	8						59.		50 8.42	1.60	0.94		4	45.405	13 52.56	2.27	8.39	50 9.08	31 43.22
5	7	11.5	28.	45.					55 1.97	1.57	0.68		2	22.398	38 2.35	3.13	10.78	55 2.86	23 55 56.26
6	9		37.						56 10.90	1.57	0.64		1	18.320	42 12.17	3.34	11.22	56 11.63	24 0 6.73
7	9	57.5							58 47.85	1.54	0.88		3	38.095	21 31.50	3.80	9.14	58 48.51	23 39 24.44
8	9					29.			4 59 12.10	1.53	0.75		2	26.810	33 26.40	3.86	10.32	4 59 12.88	51 20.58
9	10					21.			5 0 47.40	1.50	0.94		3	43.024	16 22.52	4.15	8.61	5 0 47.99	34 15.28
10	9	46.		20.					4 36.66	1.50	0.80		3	32.025	27 52.89	4.64	9.78	4 37.36	23 45 47.51
11			17.5						6 51.45	1.49	0.56		1	10.142	50 44.93	5.24	12.12	6 52.38	24 8 42.29
12	9	2.5							9 52.81	1.47	0.94		4	42.630	16 47.88	5.79	8.66	9 53.34	23 34 42.33
13	9		9.						11 42.83	1.46	0.94		4	41.854	17 36.58	6.10	8.75	11 43.35	35 31.41
14	9			26.					15 42.95	1.44	0.95		4	42.430	17 0.68	6.84	8.68	15 43.44	34 56.20
15	9						58.		16 24.37	1.43	1.08		5	52.462	6 29.79	6.98	7.65	16 24.72	24 24.42
16	9	55.							20 45.23	1.40	1.03		4	48.246	10 55.54	7.78	8.08	20 45.60	28 51.40
17	8			47.					24 3.93	1.38	0.92		4	38.962	20 38.08	8.39	9.05	24 4.39	38 35.52
18	8					17.			25 0.23	1.37	0.99		5	44.755	14 34.12	8.58	8.61	25 0.61	32 31.14
19	7						24.		25 50.40	1.37	0.99		5	44.645	14 40.72	8.74	8.45	25 50.78	32 37.91
20	8			59.5					28 16.44	1.36	0.94		4	39.838	19 43.11	9.19	8.95	28 16.86	37 41.25
21	9							20.5	28 20.92	1.36	0.99		5	44.010	15 20.00	9.23	8.53	28 30.29	33 17.76
22	9						19.5		30 45.90	1.35	0.74		3	22.360	37 59.28	9.65	10.79	30 46.51	55 59.72
23	6	2.5		35.8					33 52.62	1.33	0.83		3	29.708	30 18.26	10.25	10.04	33 53.32	48 18.55
24	8			12.5					35 29.41	1.32	0.77		3	24.221	36 2.60	10.75	10.61	36 29.96	54 3.96
25	9			16.5					38 3.39	1.31	0.80		3	27.428	32 41.48	11.04	10.30	38 3.99	50 42.82
26	8					25.			39 8.07	1.31	0.78		3	24.390	35 52.07	11.25	10.64	39 8.60	53 53.90
27	7						34.		39 0.43	1.30	0.90		4	35.421	24 19.73	11.23	9.40	39 0.83	42 20.36
28	8	48.		31.5					42 48.48	1.29	0.79		3	25.430	34 46.82	11.96	10.52	42 48.98	52 49.30
29	9		6.8						48 42.70	1.26	0.74		2	19.742	40 48.00	13.10	11.09	48 43.22	23 58 52.19
30	8		33.5						50 7.44	1.25	0.64		1	12.105	48 41.79	13.38	11.90	50 8.05	24 6 47.07
31	9				56.5				51 56.36	1.25	0.85		3	29.430	30 35.95	13.73	10.08	51 56.76	23 48 39.76
32	8				20.5				53 20.37	1.24	0.92		3	34.936	24 50.23	14.02	9.46	53 20.69	42 53.71
33	8				55.5				54 55.39	1.23	0.80		2	24.288	36 4.37	14.32	10.61	54 55.82	54 9.30
34							59.		5 56 25.44	1.23	0.84		3	27.706	32 23.66	14.62	10.26	5 56 25.83	50 28.54
35	7		51.						6 0 24.82	1.21	1.06		4	45.682	13 36.38	15.41	8.30	6 0 24.97	37 40.09
36	8					12.			0 55.24	1.21	1.08		4	47.410	11 47.66	15.51	8.11	0 55.37	29 51.28
37	8				35.				2 34.87	1.20	0.90		3	32.628	27 15.18	15.84	9.71	2 35.17	45 20.73
38	7	28.		2.					5 18.66	1.19	0.91		3	32.825	27 2.63	16.39	9.69	5 18.94	45 8.71
39	8				59.5				6 16.50	1.18	1.13		5	50.831	8 13.07	16.58	7.79	6 16.55	26 17.44
40	8							19.5	6 28.92	1.18	1.06		4	44.625	14 42.03	16.63	8.45	6 29.04	32 47.11
41	6							24.	7 33.38	1.18	0.86		3	28.551	31 30.53	16.84	10.16	7 33.70	23 49 37.53
42	6		27.						10 0.91	1.17	0.75		2	17.488	43 9.75	17.33	11.37	11 1.33	24 1 18.45
43	8						36.		10 2.38	1.17	1.11		4	48.698	10 26.22	17.33	8.02	10 2.44	23 28 31.57
44	7			32.					12 49.00	1.16	1.11		4	48.770	10 22.46	17.89	8.02	12 49.05	28 28.57
45	7			33.					13 44.91	1.15	0.95		3	34.852	24 53.56	18.09	9.48	13 50.11	43 1.13
46	7			47.		38.	55.		14 21.31	1.15	1.05	V.	4	43.244	16 9.14	18.21	8.59	14 21.41	34 15.94
47	7				10.				16 9.88	1.14	1.08		4	46.172	13 5.55	18.56	8.29	16 9.94	31 12.42
48	9		57.			48.			21 31.00	1.13	0.97		3	35.695	24 2.61	19.65	9.38	21 31.16	42 11.64
49	8				12.				6 23 11.88	+1.12	−0.84		3	25.265	−34 57.24	−20.00	−10.52	6 23 12.16	−23 53 7.76

CORRECTIONS.

Date.	Corr. of Clock.	Hourly rate.	m	n	c	Zenith Point.	Mic. Co.
	h.	s.	s.	s.	s.	° ' "	r,
1848, Jan. 20,	0	. .	. .	. .	. .	359 59 57.11	29.9845

INSTRUMENT READINGS.

| Date. | CIRCLE. | | | | | | | Barom. | THERMOM. | | | | |
	A.	B.	C.	D.	E.	F.	Mean.		At.	Ex.	U.	L.	I.
	1848.								in.					
Zone 156	Jan. 20, 4 46	72 39 60.0	68.5	67.5	53.0	67.5	53.0	61.25	30.340	37.7	29.8			
	5 39								30.314	36.5	29.0			
	6 24								30.306	36.	29.			
	6 26								30.302	35.5	28.7			
	7 20								30.296	35.	28.			
	7 21								30.286	35.	28.			
	8 6								30.280	35.	28.			
	8 48								30.274	34.5	27.8			

REMARKS.

(156) 2. Transit over T. VI assumed to have been recorded as over T. V.

(156) 3. Transit over T. VI assumed to have been recorded as over T. V.

(156) 18. Right ascension differs 16s.5 from Arg. Z. 274, 40; probably recorded over wrong thread.

(156) 27. Right ascension differs 2s.5 and declination 41" from Arg. Z. 274, 62.

(156) 28. Time of transit over T. I assumed as 58s instead of 48s.

(156) 42. Minutes assumed as 10 instead of 11.

23—z

ZONE 156. JANUARY 20. S. $D_s = -23°\ 17'\ 40''$—Continued.

No.	Mag.	I.	II.	III.	IV.	V.	VI.	VII.	T. (h m s)	a₁ (s)	a₂ (s)	Mic.	n	r.	i (° ′ ″)	d₁ (″)	d₂ (″)	Mean Right Ascension, 1850.0 (h m s)	Mean Declination, 1850.0 (° ′ ″)
50							46.		6 24 12.34	+ 1.12	−0.73		2	15.295	−44 26.53	−20.21	−11.58	6 24 12.83	−24 2 38.32
51	8							14.	25 23.42	1.11	1.11		4	46.792	17 39.07	20.45	8.22	25 23.42	23 35 47.74
52	9				26.				28 0.15	1.11	0.93		3	32.370	27 31.43	21.02	9.74	28 0.33	45 42.19
53	6		25.				32.		48 58.64	1.06	0.98	II.	3	33.450	26 23.47	25.31	9.62	48 58.72	44 38.40
54	7	58.		31.					50 48.12	1.06	1.11	III.	4	44.202	15 9.46	25.68	8.48	50 48.07	33 23.62
55	5		47.						52 20.83	1.06	1.03		3	37.062	22 36.69	25.99	9.22	52 20.86	40 51.90
56	7	58.5							53 48.87	1.06	1.03		3	37.042	22 37.63	26.28	9.23	53 48.90	40 53.14
57	8				21.				54 20.88	1.05	1.06		3	38.940	20 38.96	26.39	9.04	54 20.87	38 54.39
58	3	55.		29.					56 45.64	1.05	1.08		4	40.742	18 46.44	26.92	8.83	56 45.61	23 37 2.19
59	7						39.		6 56 47.18	1.05	0.81		2	17.918	42 40.26	26.93	11.32	6 56 47.42	24 0 58.51
60	4	16.		50.					7 1 6.63	1.04	1.09	III.	4	41.282	18 12.67	27.82	8.78	7 1 6.68	23 36 29.27
61	7		38.						2 11.85	1.04	0.93		3	27.892	32 11.93	28.05	10.23	2 11.96	50 30.21
62	6				51.				3 50.86	1.04	0.96		3	29.925	30 4.64	28.37	10.00	3 50.94	48 23.01
63	9							17.5	4 26.83	1.04	0.91		3	26.025	34 8.93	28.50	10.43	4 26.96	52 27.86
64	7	58.							6 48.65	1.04	0.85		2	20.185	40 19.52	29.00	11.06	6 48.84	58 39.58
65	8					15.			6 58.04	1.04	0.87		2	22.498	37 57.71	29.05	10.81	6 58.21	56 17.57
66	8		41.						9 14.82	1.04	1.21		4	50.615	9 26.82	29.51	7.79	9 14.65	26 44.12
67	6						3.		9 29.38	1.04	1.20		4	48.720	10 24.84	29.56	7.98	9 29.22	28 42.38
68	7							9.	10 18.42	1.03	1.15		4	43.960	15 23.13	29.73	8.48	10 18.30	33 41.34
69	8			23.					12 39.98	1.03	1.18		5	47.213	12 0.38	30.21	8.15	12 39.83	23 30 18.74
70	7					4.5			13 47.35	1.03	0.69		2	5.932	55 15.72	30.45	12.62	13 47.01	24 13 38.79
71	6				25.				15 24.87	1.03	0.94		3	26.705	33 26.72	30.79	10.35	15 24.06	23 51 47.86
72	8			51.					17 7.93	1.03	1.10		5	39.282	20 18.18	31.15	8.09	17 7.86	23 38 38.32
73	8			26.5					18 43.48	1.03	0.76		2	11.292	49 38.78	31.47	12.03	18 43.75	24 8 2.26
74	6		47.5		21.				20 21.10	1.03	1.24		5	52.340	6 38.40	31.81	7.61	20 21.86	23 24 57.82
75				45.					1.88	1.03	0.95		3	29.275	30 45.61	..	10.07	(21) 1.93	48 35.68
76	8							53.	21 2.38	1.03	0.98		3	29.283	30 44.67	31.95	10.07	21 2.43	49 6.69
77	7		21.						29 54.83	1.03	1.08		4	37.080	22 36.32	33.77	9.23	29 54.78	40 50.32
78	9						41.5		30 24.65	1.03	1.02		3	31.744	28 10.52	33.58	9.81	30 24.66	46 34.21
79	7		36.5						10.37	1.03	0.95		3	25.314	34 53.92	..	10.51	(32) 10.45	52 44.43
80	6	40.5							34 31.07	1.03	0.93		3	23.622	36 39.62	34.72	10.68	34 31.17	55 5.02
81	7						2.		34 28.43	1.03	1.05		4	33.690	26 8.16	34.71	9.60	34 28.41	44 32.47
82	7						20.		35 46.44	1.03	1.03		3	32.409	27 28.85	34.98	9.74	35 46.44	45 53.57
83	6		13.						37 56.82	1.03	1.20		4	45.722	13 33.85	35.39	8.31	37 56.65	31 57.55
84	7						21.		37 4.05	1.03	1.20		4	46.132	13 7.37	35.39	8.27	38 3.91	31 31.03
85	5					32.			39 31.68	1.03	0.96		3	25.051	35 10.54	35.75	10.54	39 31.95	53 36.83
86	7						46.		40 12.45	1.03	1.03		3	31.140	28 48.35	35.89	9.88	40 12.45	47 14.12
87	8	13.							43 3.50	1.03	0.99		3	27.519	32 35.21	36.47	10.27	43 3.54	51 1.95
88	8	9.8							46 0.24	1.04	1.04		3	30.838	29 6.80	37.07	9.91	46 0.24	47 33.78
89	7					17.5			47 17.38	1.04	0.97		3	25.351	34 51.85	37.33	10.50	47 17.45	53 19.68
90	7						43.5		48 26.57	1.04	0.96		3	23.820	36 27.57	37.56	10.66	48 26.65	54 55.79
91	7							4.	49 13.41	1.04	1.13		4	35.190	21 25.41	37.72	9.11	49 13.32	23 39 52.24
92	7				21.				51 3.92	1.04	0.81		2	12.119	48 47.03	38.09	11.94	51 4.15	24 7 17.96
93	7				45.				52 54.88	1.04	1.22		4	45.230	14 4.74	38.43	8.37	52 54.70	23 32 31.54
94	8					58.75			55 15.49	1.05	1.26		4	48.042	11 8.23	38.94	8.00	55 15.28	29 35.23
95	7	25.	58.						7 58 15.26	1.05	0.95	3	2	22.419	38 1.03	39.54	10.82	7 58 15.36	56 31.39
96	3	18.5	52.	0.					8 1 8.94	1.06	1.00		3	26.235	33 56.32	40.12	10.42	8 1 9.00	52 26.86
97	7							34.	2 17.04	1.06	0.95		3	21.765	38 36.35	40.35	11.91	2 17.15	23 57 8.61
98	8							19.5	8 3 28.61	+ 1.07	−0.86		2	14.498	−46 19.44	−40.58	−11.71	8 3 28.82	−24 4 51.73

CORRECTIONS.

Date.	Corr. of Clock.	Hourly rate.	m	n	c	Zenith Point.	Mic. Co.
1848.	h. s.	s.	s.	s.	s.	° ′ ″	r.

INSTRUMENT READINGS.

Date.	A.	B.	C.	D.	E.	F.	Mean.	Barom.	At.	Ex.	U.	L.	I.
				CIRCLE.							THERMOM.		
1848. h. m.	° ′ ″							in.					

REMARKS.

(156) 50. Micrometer reading assumed as 16^s.295 instead of 15^s.295.

(156) 51. Micrometer reading assumed as 41^s.792 instead of 46^s.792.

(156) 83. Transit over T. II assumed as 23^s, not 13^s.

(156) 84. Transit over T. V assumed as recorded over T. VI, and minutes assumed as 38, not 37.

(156) 87. Right ascension differs 20^s.9 from Arg. Z. 362, 143; and Arg. probably wrong by 1 thread interval.

(156) 93. Transit over T. IV assumed as 55^s, not 45^s.

(156) 94. Declination differs 5′ from Arg. Z. 280, 146, and Z. 362, 165.

ZONE 156. JANUARY 23. S. $D_1 = -23°\ 17'\ 45''$ —Continued.

No.	Mag.	SECONDS OF TRANSIT.							T.	a_1	a_2	MICROMETER.		i	d_1	d_2	Mean Right Ascension, 1850.0.	Mean Declination, 1850.0.
		I.	II.	III.	IV.	V.	VI.	VII.	h. m. s.	s.	s.		r.	′ ″	″	″	h. m. s.	° ′ ″
99	8	98.							8 6 28.40	+1.07	−1.11	3	33.868	−25 56.69	−41.17	−9.58	8 6 28.36	−23 44 27.44
100	6					51.			6 50.87	1.07	1.04	3	28.065	32 1.46	41.24	10.21	6 50.90	23 50 32.91
101	8	19.	36.						33 9.81	1.14	0.94	2	16.560	44 7.94	46.38	11.48	33 10.01	24 2 45.80
102	8			6.					34 22.97	1.14	0.92	2	14.189	46 37.12	46.61	11.73	34 23.19	24 5 15.46
103	7		27.						36 0.83	1.15	1.20	4	37.674	21 59.04	46.93	9.16	36 0.78	23 40 35.13
104	7				33.				36 16.08	1.15	1.05	3	24.638	35 36.39	46.98	10.59	36 16.18	23 54 13.96
105	8			38.					37.95	1.16	. .	2	11.583	49 21.10	. .	12.03	(39)	24 7 13.13
106	8				5.				41 4.87*	1.17	1.09	3	25.072	32 1.03	47.89	10.27	41 4.95	23 50 39.13
107	9	35.							44 25.69	1.18	0.97	2	17.805	42 48.66	48.51	11.33	44 25.90	24 1 28.50
108	9		52.						8 48 25.85	+1.19	−1.11	3	28.825	−31 13.41	−49.26	−10.13	8 48 25.93	−23 49 52.80

ZONE 157. JANUARY 22. S. $D_0 = -25°\ 48'\ 0''$.

No.	Mag.	SECONDS OF TRANSIT.							T.	a_1	a_2		MICROMETER.		i	d_1	d_2	Mean Right Ascension, 1850.0.	Mean Declination, 1850.0.
		I.	II.	III.	IV.	V.	VI.	VII.	h. m. s.	s.	s.			r.	′ ″	″	″	h. m. s.	° ′ ″
1	7					29.			4 59 11.75	+0.21	−1.16	.	3	26.823	−33 19.19	−1.32	−6.39	4 59 10.80	−26 21 26.91
2	7	48.5	23.	39.5					5 4 39.83	0.17	0.97	IV.	4	41.560	17 55.03	2.30	4.63	5 4 39.03	6 1.96
3	9		46.						7 3.24	0.16	1.18	.	3	26.328	33 50.49	2.73	6.44	7 2.22	21 59.66
4	7				44.				8 26.73	0.14	1.20	.	3	25.472	34 44.19	2.99	6.55	8 25.67	22 53.73
5	9					39.8			10 39.71	0.13	1.31	.	3	18.408	42 7.34	3.39	7.40	10 38.53	30 18.13
6	7		7.8					16.	13 42.03	0.11	0.97	V.	4	42.383	17 3.19	3.96	4.53	13 41.17	5 4.68
7	9						19.8		20 2.60	0.06	1.13	.	3	31.545	28 23.13	5.13	5.82	20 1.53	16 34.08
8	9		57.5						22 32.15	0.05	1.41	.	1	11.132	49 42.79	5.61	8.29	22 30.79	37 56.69
9	9			38.5					22 55.72	0.04	1.15	.	3	30.314	29 40.43	5.68	5.06	22 54.61	17 52.07
10	10							45.	23 53.14	0.03	1.31	.	3	18.820	36 27.17	5.87	6.78	23 51.86	24 39.82
11	9		16.						26 50.56	0.02	1.22	.	3	26.068	34 6.42	6.43	6.47	26 49.36	26 22 19.32
12	9		57.8						30 32.30	+0.00	0 80	.	5	56.535	7 28.89	7.13	3.41	30 31.50	25 55 39.43
13	8			40.					35 57.23	−0.03	1.20	.	3	28.023	32 3.97	9.18	6.24	35 56.00	26 20 18.39
14	9				9.			0.	37 26.00	0.05	1.11	III.	4	35.048	24 43.76	8.46	5.40	37 24.84	12 57.62
15	8	53.4							40 28.02	0.07	1.29	III.	3	22.375	37 58.47	9.12	6.92	40 26.66	26 14.51
16	8							42.	41 7.75	0.07	1.19	.	3	29.389	30 38.21	9.19	6.08	41 6.49	18 53.48
17	7			1.3					43 35.87	0.08	1.25	.	3	24.823	35 24.46	9.68	6.62	43 34.54	26 23 40.76
18	9				57.				44 56.90	0.09	0.87	.	5	52.995	5 57.70	9.94	3.27	44 55.94	25 54 10.91
19	7				20.				46 2.90	0.10	0.96	.	4	48.294	10 52.15	10.10	3.83	46 1.84	25 59 6.14
20	8	42.		16.					50 33.54	0.13	1.40	.	2	16.182	44 32.14	11.06	7.67	50 32.01	26 32 50.87
21	9			1.				9.	52 17.36	0.14	1.13	III.	3	34.718	25 3.91	11.41	5.44	52 16.09	26 13 20.76
22	10		59.4						55 33.91	0.15	0.93	.	4	49.285	9 50.38	12.06	3.72	55 32.83	25 58 6.16
23	5		40.			31.5			57 14.42	0.16	1.19	.	3	31.070	28 52.93	12.40	5.88	57 13.07	26 17 11.21
24	10			30.					5 59 47.22	0.18	1.22	.	3	29.472	30 33.19	12.91	6.07	5 59 45.82	18 52.17
25	7				49.				6 3 48.06	0.20	1.52	.	1	8.789	52 9.20	13.72	8.61	6 3 47.24	40 31.53
26	5				31.				5 13.69	0.21	1.35	.	3	21.638	38 44.57	14.02	7.02	5 12.13	27 5.61
27	8		43.						8 17.53	0.22	1.08	.	4	40.475	19 3.37	14.63	4.75	8 16.23	7 22.75
28	9						10.		8 35.73	0.22	1.11	.	4	39.378	21 14.17	14.69	4.99	8 34.40	26 9 33.85
29	9			9.8			2.		11 27.14	0.23	0.96	.	5	49.120	10 0.56	15.28	3.71	11 25.95	25 58 19.55
30	10		40.		14.				12 44.80	0.24	1.20	.	3	32.095	27 48.56	15.54	5.75	12 43.36	26 16 9.85
31	8	40.		14.					15 14.20	0.25	1.26	IV.	3	28.323	36 59.11	16.06	6.67	15 12.69	25 21.84
32	7					42.			17 24.78	0.26	1.25	.	3	29.085	30 57.41	16.49	6.12	17 23.27	19 20.02
33	6						47.		18 12.73	0.26	1.30	.	3	26.484	33 40.52	16.60	6.44	18 11.17	26 22 3.62
34	9				22.4				6 20 22.26	−0.27	−1.17	.	3	35.372	−24 23.12	−17.10	−5.35	6 20 20.82	−26 12 45.57

CORRECTIONS.

Date.	Corr. of Clock.	Hourly rate.	m	n	c	Zenith Point.	Mic. Co.
1848.	h.	s.	s.	s.	s.	° ′ ″	r.
Jan. 22,	0	. .	. .	. .	. .	359 59 56.13	29.9862

INSTRUMENT READINGS.

Date.		A.	B.	C.	D.	E.	F.	Mean.	Barom.	THERMOM.				
										At.	Ex.	U.	L.	I.
	1848. h. m.	° ′ ″						″	in.	°	°	°	°	°
Zone 157 Jan. 22,	4 59	75 9 60.0	69.0	67.2	59.3	65.6	57.9	63.17	30.082	43.8	33.9			
	6 3								30.080	43.	33.8			
	6 5								30.096	41.8	33.1			
	6 57								30.082	41.8	33.2			
	7 19								30.084	41.0	32.8			
	7 44								30.078	40.8	32.8			
	8 38								30.070	40.2	32.0			
	9 0								30.072	40.	32.			

REMARKS.

(157) 10. Micrometer reading assumed as 23ʳ.820, not 18ʳ.820.

(157) 12. Micrometer reading assumed as 51ʳ.535, not 56ʳ.535.

(157) 18. Differs 2′ in declination from Arg. Z. 323, 101; and 1′ from Mer. Circle, 1849, February 16.

(157) 31. Micrometer reading assumed as 23ʳ.323, not 28ʳ.323.

(157) 32. Differs 1′ in declination from Arg. Z. 323, 60; and Z. 360, 31.

ZONE 157. JANUARY 22. S. $D_0 = -25°\ 48'\ 0''$—Continued.

No.	Mag.	I.	II.	III.	IV.	V.	VI.	VII.	T. (h. m. s.)	a_1 (s.)	a_2 (s.)	MICR.	n	r.	i	d_1	d_2	Mean Right Ascension, 1850.0. (h. m. s.)	Mean Declination, 1850.0. (° ′ ″)
35	10						4.		6 21 29.71	− 0.28	−0.90		4	48.252	−10 54.35	−17.34	− 3.81	6 21 28.44	−25 59 15.50
36	9						44.		23 9.72	0.29	1.03		4	46.229	13 1.34	17.68	4.06	23 8.40	26 1 23.08
37	7						22.		24 47.74	0.29	1.18		3	34.830	24 56.63	18.02	5.42	24 46.27	13 20.07
38	6			4.					27 38.54	0.30	1.18		3	35.050	24 42.88	18.61	5.40	27 37.06	13 6.89
39	6	27.5		1.5					30 18.94	0.31	1.34	III.	3	23.930	36 20.66	19.16	6.74	30 17.29	24 46.56
40	8		37.						33 11.59	0.32	1.37		3	22.313	38 2.10	19.77	6.93	33 9.90	26 28.80
41	8				9.				34 26.28	0.33	1.16		4	37.685	21 58.24	20.02	5.08	34 24.79	26 10 23.39
42	7			34.					36 8.66	0.34	1.00		5	48.670	10 35.14	20.52	3.78	37 7.34	25 58 59.44
43	7						52.5		18.24		1.27		3	29.068	30 58.29		6.12	38	26
44	6		23.		57.				41 57.21	0.35	1.32		3	26.296	33 52.56	21.60	6.46	41 55.54	22 20.62
45	8							27.	45 35.30	0.36	1.32		3	27.060	33 3.94	21.37	6.36	45 33.62	21 31.67
46	7		14.5						51 49.04	0.38	1.24		3	33.534	26 18.14	23.67	5.58	51 47.42	14 47.39
47	4			40.5					52 57.73	0.38	1.26		3	32.042	27 51.82	23.91	5.76	52 56.09	16 21.49
48	6			1.	19.				54 18.54	0.38	1.32		3	28.150	31 56.20	24.19	6.22	54 16.84	20 26.61
49	6				55.4				55 55.30	0.39	1.43		2	20.209	40 20.15	24.53	7.19	55 53.48	28 51.87
50	8					5.8			6 57 48.51	0.39	1.42		3	23.408	36 53.66	24.93	6.80	6 57 46.70	25 25.39
51	5			39.8					7 0 57.06	0.40	1.40		3	23.259	37 2.95	25.60	6.83	7 0 55.26	25 35.38
52	3			1.5		35.8			2 18.71	0.40	1.18	V.	4	38.658	20 56.86	25.87	4.94	2 17.13	9 27.67
53	8	23.							6 14.43	0.41	1.26		4	33.920	25 53.41	26.69	5.53	6 12.76	14 25.63
54	4		36.						8 10.53	0.41	1.14		4	42.145	17 18.45	27.11	4.53	8 8.98	5 50.09
55	4				45.			36.5	8 44.78	0.41	1.48	VII.	2	18.306	42 20.45	27.22	7.42	8 42.89	30 55.09
56	8							53.8	9 1.89	0.41	1.51		2	15.690	45 4.50	27.28	7.78	9 59.97	33 39.50
57	6					51.			11 43.65	0.42	1.50		2	17.528	43 8.79	27.80	7.55	11 41.73	31 44.14
58	5					58.5			12 46.29	0.42	1.32		3	29.742	30 16.12	25.05	6.06	12 44.55	18 50.23
59	6			11.					14 28.26	0.42	1.41		3	23.458	36 50.53	28.43	6.81	14 26.43	25 25.77
60	8		25.						16 42.31	0.42	1.14		5	43.152	16 15.24	28.90	4.42	16 40.75	4 48.56
61	7		56.5						18 31.07	0.42	1.39		5	25.520	34 40.93	29.27	6.56	18 29.26	23 16.76
62	6			10.5					19 27.73	0.43	1.34		3	28.806	31 14.79	29.47	6.16	19 25.96	19 50.42
63	7				17.5				20 0.17	0.43	1.48		2	19.525	41 3.55	29.58	7.28	19 58.26	29 40.41
64	5				56.5				21 56.42	0.43	1.51		2	17.137	43 32.81	29.99	7.60	21 54.48	32 10.40
65	8		56.						25 30.56	0.43	1.40		3	26.200	23 27.18	30.72	4.95	25 28.73	12 2.85
66	9							25.	25 32.78	0.43				.813	33 19.38	30.72	6.38	25 (32)	21 56.48
67	6		35.		26.				29 26.17	0.43	1.34	II.	3	30.504	29 28.25	31.56	5.94	29 24.40	18 5.75
68	7		22.						30 56.60	0.44	1.49		3	20.340	40 10.66	31.87	7.18	30 54.67	28 49.73
69	8	51.							32 42.69	0.44	1.48		3	21.104	39 17.49	32.23	7.09	32 40.77	27 56.81
70	5				42.			33.5	32 41.78	0.44	1.48	IV.	3	21.272	39 7.71	32.23	7.08	32 39.86	26 27 17.02
71	7	47.							36 38.25	0.44	1.10		5	47.843	11 20.54	33.05	3.83	36 36.71	25 59 57.42
72	8	14.							38 5.51	0.44	1.39		2	28.610	31 26.71	33.35	6.19	38 3.68	26 20 6.25
73	8		27.						40 1.61	0.44	1.53		2	18.248	42 21.83	33.76	7.46	39 59.64	31 3.05
74	9							49.	40 14.67	0.44	1.14		4	46.332	12 54.37	33.96	4.04	40 13.09	1 32.37
75	8				3.5				43 20.76	0.44	1.29		3	36.063	23 30.50	34.46	5.25	43 19.03	12 19.21
76	7						41.5		44 7.24	0.44	1.27		3	37.192	22 28.60	34.60	5.12	44 5.53	11 8.32
77	6		18.8						46 53.32	0.44	1.15		3	46.200	13 8.00	35.17	4.04	46 57.73	26 1 47.21
78	6								47	0.44	1.09		5	50.030	9 3.29	35.38	3.59	47	25 57 42.26
79	7				29.5				49 46.82	0.44	1.15		4	45.956	13 19.10	35.79	4.05	49 45.23	26 1 58.94
80	8					6.			54 5.87	0.43	1.28		3	37.370	22 17.74	36.69	4.98	54 4.16	10 59.41
81	9						30.5		56 13.36	0.43	1.17		4	44.942	14 22.38	37.14	4.17	56 11.78	3 3.69
82	8				22.				58 21.86	0.43	1.32		3	35.568	24 10.76	37.57	5.32	58 20.11	12 53.65
83	7							43.	7 59 8.75	−0.43	−1.41		3	28.592	−31 26.21	−38.72	− 6.19	7 59 6.91	−26 20 13.12

CORRECTIONS.

Date.	Corr. of Clock.	Hourly rate.	m	n	t	Zenith Point.	Mic. Co.
1848.	h. s.	s.	s.	s.	s.	′ ″	r.

INSTRUMENT READINGS.

Date.	CIRCLE.							Barom.	THERMOM.				
	A.	B.	C.	D.	E.	F.	Mean.		At.	Ex.	U.	L.	I.
1848. h. m.	° ′ ″						″	In.					

REMARKS.

(157) 42. Transit over T. II assumed as recorded over T. III; and minutes as 37, not 36.

(157) 56. Minutes assumed as 10, not 9.

(157) 57. Transit over T. V assumed as 1s, not 51s.

(157) 58. Transit over T. V assumed as 3s.5, not 58s.5, to agree with Arg. Z. 360, 140; and Transit Z., 1848, January 20.

(157) 65. Micrometer reading assumed as 36r.260, not 26r.260.

(157) 67. Transit at 35s assumed to have been over T. I.

(157) 74. Transit over T. VI assumed as recorded over T. VII.

(157) 81. Differs 1s in right ascension from Arg. Z. 290, 1.

ZONE 157. JANUARY 22. S. $D_0 = -25°\ 48'\ 0''$—Continued.

No.	Mag.	I.	II.	III.	IV.	V.	VI.	VII.	T.	a_1	a_2	Micr.		r.	i	d_1	d_2	Mean R.A. 1850.0	Mean Decl. 1850.0
84	7	2.6							8 31 54.17	−0.37	−1.28		4	41.188	−18 18.45	−44.32	−4.64	8 31 52.52	−26 7 7.41
85	9		9.						33 43.54	0.36	1.40		3	33.522	26 18.85	44.66	5.55	33 41.78	26 15 9.12
86	9				24.				38 6.92	0.35	1.17		4	49.500	9 36.37	45.53	3.62	38 5.40	25 58 25.52
87	6			45.8					39 45.68	0.34	1.25		4	44.128	15 13.85	45.84	4.27	39 44.09	26 4 3.98
88	8							54.	39 2.39	0.34	1.27		4	43.324	16 3.18	45.70	4.32	40 0.78	4 53.26
89	9	29.6			4.				46 21.28	0.32	1.52	IV.	3	25.968	34 12.68	47.06	6.51	46 19.43	23 6.45
90	10				36.				47 35.86	0.32	1.49		3	27.930	32 9.80	47.35	6.28	47 34.05	21 3.43
91	9		55.4						49 29.92	0.31	1.27		4	43.710	15 40.14	47.72	4.34	49 28.34	4 32.20
92	9			30.					51 47.25	0.31	1.40		4	34.828	24 57.51	48.14	5.42	51 45.54	13 51.07
93	6		8.						54 42.52	0.30	1.28		5	43.634	15 44.98	48.07	4.35	54 40.94	26 4 38.00
94	7				22.8				55 22.69	0.29	1.22		5	48.603	10 32.95	48.82	3.73	55 21.18	25 59 25.50
95	7			49.					8 58 6.28	0.28	1.62		2	19.840	40 42.54	49.33	7.27	8 58 4.38	26 29 39.14
96	9		36.						9 0 10.55	0.27	1.50		3	28.745	31 18.42	49.71	6.15	9 0 8.78	20 14.35
97	6		39.			30.			9 2 13.18	−0.27	−1.36		4	38.720	−20 53.15	−50.09	−4.92	9 2 11.55	−26 9 48.16

ZONE 158. MARCH 6. C. $D_0 = -27°\ 41'\ 30''$.

No.	Mag.	I.	II.	III.	IV.	V.	VI.	VII.	T.	a_1	a_2	Micr.		r.	i	d_1	d_2	Mean R.A. 1850.0	Mean Decl. 1850.0
1	8			42.5	59.5	16.7	34.4		10 59 59.59	−33.81	−0.81	IV.	4	45.743	−13 23.60	−0.32	−6.78	10 59 24.97	−27 55 0.79
2	9.10		31.6	49.3	6.5				11 11 6.68	33.76	0.78	III	2	21.298	39 2.26	1.72	11.80	11 10 32.14	28 20 45.78
3	9		28.	45.3	2.7	20.8			13 3.02	33.74	0.85	IV.	5	52.701	6 8.76	1.94	5.40	12 28.43	27 47 46.10
4	9			19.5	37.8				14 19.89	33.74	0.83	V.	4	45.648	13 30.09	2.09	6.83	13 45.32	27 55 9.01
5	8		42.	59.8	17.3	35.5	53.4		17 17.67	33.73	0.82	IV.	3	36.902	22 46.85	2.43	8.60	16 43.12	28 4 27.88
6	8			34.	52.	9.3	26.6		17 51.71	33.72	0.79	IV.	2	20.622	39 44.27	2.50	11.93	17 17.20	28 21 28.70
7	9							10.3	18 17.84	33.72	0.85	VII.	5	50.036	8 55.71	2.54	5.04	17 43.27	27 50 34.19
8	9		6.3	23.	41.3	59.5			20 41.28	33.71	0.82	IV.	3	33.076	20 47.07	2.81	9.36	20 6.75	28 8 20.24
9	9.10		58.1		33.			8.	22 33.09	33.70	0.80	IV.	3	22.606	37 43.92	2.99	11.51	21 58.59	28 19 28.42
10	8		37.2	55.3	12.8	20.8	47.5		24 12.58	33.69	0.85	V.	5	42.758	16 32.88	3.17	7.42	23 38.04	27 58 13.47
11	8.9							17.3	25 24.49	33.68	0.79	VII.	2	15.828	44 44.88	3.29	12.93	24 50.02	28 26 31.10
12	8.9							17.5	25 24.69	33.67	0.79	VII.	2	15.9	44 40.35	3.29	12.91	24 50.23	26 26.55
13	9.10			23.					30 22.84	33.65	0.83	IV.	3	29.036	31 0.46	3.79	10.19	29 48.37	13 44.46
14	9.10		39.3	56.3	14.7				33 14.37	33.63	0.79	III	2	12.189	48 32.82	4.05	13.60	32 39.95	30 20.56
15	7			59.2	16.5	34.4	51.5		34 16.56	33.63	0.81	IV.	3	19.820	40 38.53	4.14	12.00	33 42.12	22 24.76
16	9			11.8	28.5	46.4			39 29.84	33.61	0.81	IV.	2	15.066	44 55.04	4.62	12.97	38 54.42	26 42.63
17	9				9.2	26.8	44.6		39 51.65	33.60	0.80	V.	2	11.306	40 28.75	4.66	13.87	39 17.25	31 17.28
18	9.10			1.3	18.5	36.1			42 18.58	33.59	0.83	IV.	3	24.379	35 52.82	4.85	11.15	41 44.16	17 38.82
19	9.10			58.5			51.1		48 16.15	33.55	0.86	IV.	3	31.872	28 2.49	5.35	9.02	47 41.74	9 47.46
20	9.10		39.7		13.7				50 14.19	33.53	0.84	II.	3	25.964	34 13.07	5.51	10.83	49 39.82	15 59.41
21	8.9				4.5	22.5	39.6		56 4.64	33.50	0.85	IV.	3	16.795	43 44.10	5.94	12.74	55 30.31	28 25 32.78
22	9		27.2	46.2		10.8			57 45.62	33.49	0.91	IV.	4	51.156	7 45.86	6.07	5.71	57 11.22	27 49 27.66
23	9			46.5		11.	28.3		58 4.05	33.48	0.91	V.	4	48.871	10 7.64	6.10	6.18	57 29.66	27 51 49.92
24	9					30.6		3.5	11 59 44.91	33.48	0.86	V.	2	24.571	36 36.76	6.17	11.11	59 10.57	28 17 24.64
25	8.9							3.5	12 0 28.65	33.47	0.87	V.	3	28.278	31 48.04	6.29	10.36	11 59 54.31	13 34.69
26	7.8			37.5	54.5	12.			12 7 54.62	33.42	0.86	IV.	2	18.228	42 14.49	6.78	12.45	12 7 20.34	24 3.72
27	9		29.2	46.3	3.8				12 46.39	33.38	0.89	IV.	3	29.782	30 13.61	7.00	10.05	12 12.12	12 0.75
28	9				34.	51.6			13 16.48	33.38	0.86	IV.	2	15.848	44 43.68	7.13	12.95	12 42.24	26 33.76
29	9		6.5	23.4	41.3				17 23.70	33.35	0.91	IV.	3	34.	25 49.02	7.37	9.16	16 49.44	28 7 35.55
30	8			34.	51.8	8.9	26.6	43.9	12 30 9.11	−33.33	−0.94	IV.	4	47.689	−11 21.60	−7.55	−6.39	12 19 34.64	−27 53 5.54

CORRECTIONS.

Date.	Corr. of Clock.	Hourly rate.	m	n	e	Zenith Point.	Mic. Co.
1848. Mar. 6.	h. 0	s.	s.	s.	s.	350 59 61.73	29.9876

REMARKS.

(157) 88. Minutes assumed as 40, not 39.

(157) 89. Transit over T. III assumed to have been recorded over T. IV; and as 4s.0, not 0s.4.

(158) 22. Time of transit over T. VI assumed as 20s.8 instead of 10s.8.

(158) 23. T.'s II and III of following star assumed as recorded over T.'s IV and V.

(158) 24. T. VI assumed as recorded over T. V, and combined with its T.'s II and III, as above.

(158) 25. T. VI assumed as recorded over T. V.

INSTRUMENT READINGS.

Date	Circle	A.	B.	C.	D.	E.	F.	Mean.	Barom.	At.	Ex.	U.	L.	I.
Zone 158 Mar. 6, 11	77° 2′	32.9 / 31.6	31.7 / 30.8	39.2 / 39.2	33.3 / 34.8	35.8 / 35.5	30.9 / 31.3	33.92	30.148	37.8	31.9	37.5	.	35.2
11 25									30.152	30.5	37.			
11 40														
12		32.9 / 31.5	31.8 / 30.8	38.6 / 39.2	32.9 / 34.4	35.4 / 35.1	30.1 / 30.1	33.56	30.152	30.4	35.8			
12 20									30.152	36.5	30.8	34.		

ZONE 159. MARCH 7. S. $D_0 = -25°\ 10'\ 50''$.

No.	Mag.	I.	II.	III.	IV.	V.	VI.	VII.	T.	a_1	a_2	Mic.	N	r	i	d_1	d_2	Mean Right Ascension, 1850.0.	Mean Declination, 1850.0.
									h. m. s.	s.	s.			r.	' "	"	"	h. m. s.	° ' "
1	9		57.						9 4 31.33	−34.64	−1.62		5	45.590	−13 34.93	− 8.15	− 1.22	9 3 55.08	−25 24 34.30
2	7				29.8				4 29.66	34.63	1.53		3	29.311	29 40.68	8.15	4.07	3 53.50	40 42.90
3	9		44.						6 18.42	34.64	1.47		2	19.695	40 41.41	8.46	5.86	5 42.31	51 45.73
4	9			30.3					12 44.64	34.64	1.51		3	32.752	27 7.33	9.59	3.51	12 28.49	38 10.43
5	8			8.					15 42.34	34.64	1.53		4	37.792	21 42.22	10.04	2.60	15 6.17	32 44.86
6	9			3.					17 20.19	34.64	1.52		4	38.904	20 32.44	10.39	2.40	16 44.03	31 35.23
7	.				36.				20 35.93	34.64	1.40		2	15.892	44 40.73	10.92	6.54	19 59.89	55 48.19
8	.		2.						22 36.35	34.64	1.47		3	29.408	30 37.26	11.26	4.11	22 0.24	41 42.63
9	7						10.5		22 36.42	34.64	1.47		3	29.430	30 34.94	11.26	4.11	22 0.31	41 40.31
10	4					8.			23 50.71	34.64	1.39		2	15.642	44 56.72	11.45	6.59	23 14.68	56 4.76
11	7		52.						26 26.38	34.64	1.43		3	25.433	34 46.64	11.90	4.83	25 50.31	45 53.37
12	7			45.5					30 2.77	34.64	1.55		6	52.285	6 34.95	12.50	0.03	29 26.58	17 37.48
13	7					14.			30 56.98	34.64	1.52		4	44.945	14 14.10	12.65	1.32	30 20.82	25 18.07
14	8		33.5						34 24.69	34.64	1.44		3	32.772	27 6.01	13.18	3.51	33 48.61	38 12.70
15	7		16.				24.		39 50.12	34.64	1.44	II.	3	36.600	23 5.93	14.11	2.81	39 14.04	34 12.85
16	5		59.5				7.5		42 33.64	34.64	1.39		3	27.032	33 6.14	14.54	4.54	41 57.61	44 15.22
17	9					35.			44 17.90	34.63	1.40		3	32.945	26 55.03	14.83	3.48	43 41.87	38 3.34
18	9			33.5					46 50.72	34.63	1.46		4	43.045	16 12.73	15.23	1.67	46 14.63	27 19.63
19	8					12.5			48 55.28	34.63	1.35		2	21.750	38 33.59	15.55	5.49	48 19.30	49 44.63
20	6			17.			8.		50 34.02	34.62	1.34	III.	2	21.132	39 11.97	15.81	5.60	49 58.06	50 23.38
21	6		3.			34.			53 37.12	34.62	1.38		3	30.279	29 42.66	16.29	3.96	53 1.12	40 52.93
22	7		56.5				4.		9 55 30.40	34.62	1.38	V.	3	26.685	33 27.91	16.59	4.61	54 54.40	44 39.11
23	8			52.			43.		10 0 9.02	34.62	1.30	III.	2	19.495	40 54.71	17.30	5.91	9 59 33.10	52 7.92
24	9				21.5				5 21.45	34.61	1.25		2	13.532	47 8.91	18.09	7.00	10 4 45.59	58 24.00
25	.		7.						9 41.42	34.60	1.27		2	20.520	39 49.98	18.75	5.72	9 5.35	51 4.45
26	9		28.5				37.2		12 2.98	34.60	1.30		3	26.438	33 43.64	19.08	4.66	11 27.08	44 57.38
27	9		28.		1.5				15 1.86	34.59	1.36	IV.	4	40.095	19 18.26	19.53	2.19	14 25.91	30 29.98
28	8		32.		5.5				17 5.86	34.58	1.41		6	51.960	6 55.10	19.83	0.05	16 29.67	18 4.98
29	9			23.					18 40.16	34.58	1.32		3	35.058	24 42.69	20.07	3.08	18 4.26	35 55.84
30	9							49.	18 57.46	34.58	1.24		2	21.348	38 58.99	20.10	5.58	18 21.64	50 14.67
31	6		51.			42.			24 25.11	34.57	1.27		3	28.346	31 43.90	20.88	4.32	23 49.27	42 59.10
32	7			7.					10 26 24.18	−34.56	−1.22		2	21.198	−39 7.83	−21.17	− 5.60	10 25 48.40	−25 50 24.60

ZONE 160. MARCH 24. S. $D_0 = -25°\ 11'\ 0''$.

No.	Mag.	I.	II.	III.	IV.	V.	VI.	VII.	T.	a_1	a_2	Mic.	N	r	i	d_1	d_2	Mean Right Ascension, 1850.0.	Mean Declination, 1850.0.
1	6		36.						9 15 10.33	−17.80	−1.55		6	50.298	− 8 39.43	− 3.90	− 2.39	9 14 50.98	−25 19 45.72
2	9					42.5			15 25.43	17.80	1.52		4	37.850	21 37.40	3.94	4.60	15 6.11	32 47.94
3	9						30.8		17 2.71	17.80	1.50		4	39.042	20 24.91	4.21	4.38	16 45.41	31 33.50
4	10		45.5						20 19.95	17.81	1.46		2	15.012	44 32.78	4.77	8.47	20 0.68	55 46.02
5	9		5.						21 39.36	17.81	1.46		3	28.670	31 23.45	4.99	6.25	21 20.09	42 34.69
6	8			4.					22 21.14	17.81	1.46		3	32.350	27 32.80	5.10	5.59	22 1.87	38 43.49
7	7			4.					23 21.22	17.81	1.42		2	15.520	45 4.00	5.27	8.61	23 1.99	56 17.88
8	6					8.5			23 34.32	17.81	1.42		3	15.710	44 52.45	5.31	8.57	23 15.09	56 6.33
9	9		35.						26 9.38	17.82	1.42		3	25.523	34 41.00	5.74	6.81	25 50.14	45 53.55
10	10		11.						29 45.33	17.82	1.42		6	52.413	6 26.66	6.34	2.01	29 26.09	17 35.01
11	10			40.					30 39.88	17.82	1.40		4	45.050	14 6.85	6.54	3.32	30 20.66	25 16.69
12	10		33.						34 7.34	17.83	1.36		2	32.938	26 55.59	7.06	5.48	33 48.15	38 8.13
13	10		59.						9 38 33.43	−17.83	−1.31		2	19.065	−41 21.11	− 7.78	− 7.98	9 38 14.29	−25 52 36.87

CORRECTIONS.

Date.	Corr. of Clock.	Hourly rate.	m	n	c	Zenith Point.	Mic. Co.
	h.	s.	s.	s.	s.		r.
1848.							
Mar. 7,	o					359 59 60.99	29.9840
Mar. 24,	o					54.27	29.9819

INSTRUMENT READINGS.

Date.		CIRCLE.							Barom.	THERMOM.				
			A.	B.	C.	D.	E.	F.	Mean:		At.	Ex.	U.	L.	I.
	h. m.	° ' "							"	in.					
Zone 159	Mar. 7, 9 4	74 32	29.5	27.8	32.4	29.8	31.0	29.5	30.28	30.056	45.				40.3
			28.8	27.8	35.0	31.8	31.0	29.0							
	10 9									30.042	44.8				38.2
Zone 160	Mar. 24, 9 15	74 32	30.5	26.2	35.4	32.8	30.3	31.0	31.13	30.282	48.				39.
			30.0	26.8	37.0	33.8	29.0	30.8							
	9 45									30.300	47.				38.
	9 46									30.280	46.5				37.2
	10 48									30.280	45.8				35.8

REMARKS.

(159) 2. Micrometer reading assumed as 30ʳ.311, not 29ʳ.311.

(159) 4. Transit over T. II assumed to have been recorded as over T. III, and minutes assumed as 13 instead of 12.

(159) 5. Transit over T. II assumed to have been recorded as over T. III.

(159) 14. Transit over T. I assumed as recorded over T. II.

(159) 17. Transit over T. IV probably recorded as over T. V, to agree with Arg. Z. 288, 23.

(160) 4. Micrometer reading assumed as 16ʳ.012, not 15ʳ.012.

(160) 11. Transit over T. IV assumed as recorded over T. III.

ZONE 160. MARCH 24. S. D_o = −25° 11′ 0″—Continued.

No.	Mag.	I.	II.	III.	IV.	V.	VI.	VII.	T.	a_1	a_2	MICROMETER.	i	d_1	d_2	Mean Right Ascension, 1850.0	Mean Declination, 1850.0
									h. m. s.	s.	s.	r.	′ ″	″	″	h. m. s.	° ′ ″
14	8				33.				9 39 32.87	−17.84	−1.32	3　36.735	−22 57.39	− 7.94	− 4.79	9 39 13.71	−25 34 10.12
15	6		42.5				50.5		42 16.64	17.84	1.29	3　28.149	31 56.76	8.38	6.34	41 57.51	25 43 11.48
16	10		12.						45 46.48	17.84	1.24	1　9.840	50 58.41	8.93	9.66	45 27.40	26 2 17.00
17	7				28.				46 27.96	17.84	1.23	1　8.993	51 52.90	9.04	9.80	46 6.89	26 3 11.74
18	8				38.				48 37.87	17.84	1.24	3　26.932	38 26.12	9.37	7.44	48 18.70	25 49 42.93
19	7				18.				50 17.88	17.84	1.22	3　26.304	39 5.21	9.65	7.56	49 56.82	50 22.43
20	7					37.			52 19.88	17.84	1.21	3　30.450	29 31.76	9.96	5.93	52 0.83	40 47.65
21	8			35.			26.		9 59 52.02	17.85	1.12	2　19.634	40 46.18	11.12	7.87	9 59 43.05	52 5.17
22	10			15.					10 1 32.16	17.85	1.12	3　34.570	25 13.38	11.35	5.14	10 1 13.19	36 29.92
23	10		5.						3 39.33	17.85	1.12	5　49.645	9 20.30	11.66	2.46	3 20.36	20 34.44
24	10							55.	4 3.66	17.85	1.11	5　46.368	12 46.14	11.71	3.07	3 44.70	24 0.92
25	8				24.				9 23.91	17.85	1.04	2　20.758	39 35.62	12.50	7.68	9 5.02	50 55.80
26	8		11.5		45.				11 45.38	17.84	1.03	II.　3　26.523	33 38.26	12.63	6.62	11 26.51	44 57.71
27	7		27.5				18.		14 44.30	17.84	1.02	II.　5　40.305	19 6.71	13.25	4.15	14 25.54	30 24.71
28	9					27.5			16 10.22	17.84	0.99	2　16.020	43 36.45	13.45	8.38	15 51.39	54 58.28
29	10			23.					18 40.18	17.84	0.97	2　21.480	38 50.21	13.81	7.55	18 21.37	50 11.57
30	6			51.5	8.5	25.			21 8.29	17.84	0.93	V.　3　28.470	31 35.09	14.55	6.29	23 49.52	42 56.83
31	8				7.				26 6.90	17.84	0.91	3　21.490	38 53.97	14.80	7.54	25 48.15	50 16.31
32	7			0.				8.5	28 17.15	17.84	0.90	III.　3　34.715	25 4.22	15.10	5.15	27 58.41	36 24.47
33	7						36.		28 18.73	17.84	0.89	2　18.082	42 23.77	15.17	8.10	29 0.00	53 47.13
34	9			19.5					33 36.70	17.83	0.86	4　30.450	19 58.42	15.78	4.29	33 18.01	25 31 18.49
35	9			43.					34 0.24	17.83	0.83	1　11.902	48 49.81	15.84	9.29	33 41.58	26 0 14.94
36	10				43.5				35 43.38	17.83	0.84	4　42.736	16 32.44	16.06	3.71	35 24.71	25 27 52.21
37	8		22.		56.				39 56.10	17.82	0.79	II.　3　34.708	25 4.54	16.60	5.15	39 37.49	36 26.29
38	9			0.					41 17.16	17.82	0.78	3　34.762	25 1.21	16.78	5.15	40 58.56	25 36 23.14
39	9			8.					42 25.25	17.82	0.76	1　10.798	49 59.03	16.92	9.49	42 6.67	26 1 25.44
40	8				6.				47 5.94	17.81	0.72	2　15.155	45 27.14	17.49	8.70	46 47.41	25 56 53.33
41	10				45.				10 48 44.87	−17.81	−0.74	4　37.802	−21 42.09	−17.60	− 4.60	10 48 26.32	−25 33 4.38

ZONE 161. MARCH 29. S. D_o = −25° 56′ 0″.

No.	Mag.	I.	II.	III.	IV.	V.	VI.	VII.	T.	a_1	a_2	MICROMETER.	i	d_1	d_2	Mean Right Ascension, 1850.0	Mean Declination, 1850.0
1	9			18.					9 13 52.56	−19.51	−1.03	4　42.115	−17 10.47	− 3.75	− 1.81	9 13 32.02	−26 13 16.03
2	8		11.5	28.					16 45.70	19.51	1.66	3　24.182	36 5.18	4.22	5.08	16 24.53	32 14.48
3	8				27.				21 26.85	19.52	1.49	3　28.852	31 11.96	4.99	4.21	21 5.84	27 21.16
4	9			22.					23 39.30	19.52	1.77	2　20.928	39 24.64	5.34	5.67	23 18.01	35 35.65
5	8			5.	23.				25 39.92	19.53	1.56	3　27.225	32 54.28	5.67	4.52	25 18.83	29 4.47
6	9						56.		26 4.32	19.53	1.12	5　40.200	19 13.23	5.74	2.15	25 43.07	15 21.12
7	8			54.					30 11.31	19.54	1.91	2　17.585	42 54.44	6.40	6.29	29 49.86	39 7.13
8	9		32.5						34 7.05	19.55	0.89	5　47.272	11 49.41	7.02	0.89	33 46.61	7 57.32
9	6		25.			17.			40 59.64	19.56	1.79	II.　2　21.555	38 45.07	8.10	5.56	40 38.29	34 58.73
10	8		19.5						43 54.10	19.56	1.66	3　24.962	35 15.99	8.55	− 4.02	43 32.88	31 29.52
11					30.5				45 47.89	19.56	0.72	6　52.662	6 11.14	8.84	+ 0.09	45 27.61	2 19.89
12	6					47.			46 29.91	19.57	0.74	6　51.818	7 4.13	8.95	− 0.00	46 9.60	3 13.14
13	8			6.5					49 41.05	19.57	1.06	5　43.072	16 12.92	9.45	1.65	49 20.42	12 24.02
14	8			42.					50 59.26	19.57	1.60	3　27.228	32 54.09	9.64	4.52	50 38.09	29 8.25
15	7						30.		50 55.65	19.57	1.81	3　21.128	39 16.18	9.63	5.62	50 34.27	35 31.45
16	8			51.					54 8.24	19.57		F.Wire,　29 59.81		10.22	4.00	53 [47]	26 14.03
17	8			47.					9 56 21.56	−19.57	−1.24	3　38.102	−21 31.62	−10.44	− 2.54	9 56 0.75	−26 17 44.60

CORRECTIONS.

Date.	Corr. of Clock.	Hourly rate.	m	n	c	Zenith Point.	Mic. Co.
	h.	s.	s.	s.	s.	° ′ ″	r.
1848. Mar. 29,	0					359 59 55.39	30.0035

INSTRUMENT READINGS.

Date.		A.	B.	C.	D.	E.	F.	Mean.	Barom.	At.	Ex.	U.	L.	I.
		° ′ ″						″	in.	°	°	°	°	°
Zone 161	Mar. 29, 9 13	75 17 {29.5 / 30.0}	22.0 / 21.5	27.3 / 27.5	34.8 / 35.5	22.5 / 22.3	34.0 / 34.6	28.46	30.238	58.2	50.3			
	10 13								30.242	57.2	48.			
	10 17								30.256	57.	47.3			
	10 53								30.256	57.2	47.2			
	12 6								30.250	55.	45.3			
	12 8								30.250	55.	45.3			
	12 55								30.252	53.5	44.2			

REMARKS.

(160) 18. Micrometer reading assumed as 21′.932, not 26′.932.

(160) 19. Micrometer reading assumed as 21′.304, not 26′.304.

(160) 27. Transit over T. III assumed to have been recorded as over T. II.

(160) 33. Minutes assumed as 29, not 28; and transit over T. V as recorded over T. VI, to agree with Arg. Z. 288, 89, and Tran., 1848, March 29.

(161) 9. Minutes of transit assumed as 39 instead of 40.

ZONE 161. MARCH 29. S. D₀ = −25° 56′ 0″—Continued.

No.	Mag.	I	II	III	IV	V	VI	VII	T (h. m. s.)	a₁ (s.)	a₂ (s.)	MICROMETER mark	n	r	i (′ ″)	d₁ (″)	d₁ (″)	Mean Right Ascension, 1850.0 (h. m. s.)	Mean Declination, 1850.0 (° ′ ″)
18	9							22.	9 56 30.30	−19.57	−1.34	.	3	35.352	−24 23.51	−10.47	−3.05	9 56 9.30	−26 20 37.03
19	7			5.8					9 59 23.08	19.57	1.74	.	2	23.592	36 37.67	10.00	5.17	59 1.77	32 53.74
20	8			43.					10 0 0.26	19.57	1.45	.	3	31.875	28 2.36	10.99	3.68	9 59 39.24	24 17.03
21	8		4.5						5 39.10	19.58	1.70	.	3	25.162	35 3.58	11.81	4.90	10 5 17.82	31 20.29
22	6		12.		47.				6 46.72	19.58	1.24	.	4	38.337	21 8.71	11.98	2.51	6 25.90	17 23.20
23	8				20.5				8 20.38	19.58	1.79	.	3	22.695	37 38.27	12.21	5.34	7 59.01	33 55.82
24	8		2.5						11 37.07	19.58	1.50	.	3	29.650	30 21.96	12.67	4.06	11 15.99	26 38.69
25	8			48.5					13 5.74	19.58	1.50	.	3	30.228	29 45.88	12.88	3.96	12 44.66	06 2.72
26	9					42.			18 7.68	19.58	1.71	.	3	25.448	34 45.25	13.59	4.85	17 46.39	31 3.69
27	8		26.						22 0.63	19.58	1.87	.	2	21.190	39 8.02	14.13	5.62	21 39.18	35 27.77
28	7		36.5		10.5				27 10.76	19.58	1.85	.	2	22.048	38 14.02	14.83	5.47	26 49.33	34 34.32
29	5			15.8	33				30 33.01	19.57	1.97	IV.	2	16.580	41 52.35	15.29	6.09	30 11.47	38 13.73
30	8		14.						34 48.56	19.57	1.30	.	4	37.880	21 36.11	15.84	2.59	34 27.69	17 54.57
31	8		1.5		36.				36 35.98	19.57	1.72	.	3	25.705	34 29.38	16.08	4.79	36 14.69	30 50.23
32	9				0.		35.		39 0.26	19.57	2.18	.	2	13.470	47 12.87	16.39	7.03	38 38.51	43 36.29
33	9			27.					44 44.36	19.56	0.93	.	6	49.025	9 59.43	17.11	0.57	44 23.87	0 17.11
34	9		37.5						47 12.07	19.56	1.53	.	3	32.350	27 32.68	17.42	3.59	46 50.98	23 53.69
35	7			37.8				12.	1 37.68	19.55	1.17	.	5	44.722	14 29.54	17.6	1.34	48 16.96	10 48.48
36	8		5.2						52 39.86	19.55	2.09	.	2	16.152	44 23.85	18.08	6.55	52 18.22	40 48.48
37	7					28.8			53 11.55	19.55	1.68	.	3	27.780	32 19.08	18.15	4.43	52 50.32	28 41.66
38	7			50.				16.5	56 24.58	19.55	2.17	II.	2	14.331	46 18.12	18.52	6.87	56 2.86	42 43.51
39	8			53.		28.			58 27.72	19.54	1.70	.	3	27.460	32 39.47	18.76	4.49	58 6.48	29 2.72
40	9				3.	20.			10 58 2.80	19.54	1.70	.	3	27.808	32 17.46	18.83	4.42	10 58 41.56	28 40.71
41	10				37.				11 48 36.90	19.42	2.06	.	2	19.352	41 3.99	23.92	5.99	11 48 15.42	37 33.90
42	8						48.		50 13.68	19.42	1.20	.	4	42.654	16 38.21	24.07	1.71	49 53.00	13 3.99
43	10			15.5					52 50.06	19.41	1.36	.	4	39.818	19 34.50	24.29	2.24	52 29.29	16 1.03
44	10						2.		53 27.67	19.41	1.03	.	3	23.738	36 32.40	24.34	5.17	53 6.73	33 1.01
45	10				17.				11 58 34.24	19.39	1.74	.	3	29.322	30 42.79	24.77	4.13	11 58 13.11	27 11.69
46	9					15.5			12 0 58.20	19.38	1.96	.	3	23.512	36 46.05	24.96	5.21	12 0 36.86	33 17.12
47	10				42.5				4 59.87	19.38	1.04	.	6	49.480	9 31.07	25.11	0.47	2 39.45	5 56.65
48	8					27.			4 9.85	19.38	1.32	.	4	41.588	17 44.93	25.21	1.90	3 49.15	14 12.04
49	8				50.5				6 16.76	19.37	1.81	.	3	27.400	32 43.37	25.38	4.40	5 55.58	29 13.24
50	9			18.5					8 53.06	19.36	1.38	.	4	39.732	19 39.97	25.58	2.20	8 32.32	16 7.75
51	10				24.5				9 41.79	19.35	1.50	.	4	36.770	22 46.41	25.64	2.79	9 20.04	19 14.84
52	9			37.		29.			14 11.67	19.34	1.74	II.	3	30.092	29 51.23	25.96	4.00	13 50.50	26 24.19
53	10			34.		8.5			19 8.46	19.32	1.57	IV.	3	35.190	24 34.49	26.32	3.05	18 47.57	21 3.84
54	9			17.			26.		22 51.62	19.31	1.40	II.	4	40.478	16 53.34	26.57	2.06	22 30.01	15 21.97
55	9			5.8					26 40.36	19.29	1.58	.	4	34.938	24 40.75	26.80	3.09	26 19.46	21 10.64
56	9					13.			26 55.85	19.28	1.32	.	5	43.100	16 11.53	26.82	1.57	26 35.25	12 39.92
57	5				49.5				30 6.80	19.26	1.50	.	5	37.438	22 6.88	27.02	2.64	29 46.04	18 36.54
58	9					48.			33 47.92	19.25	2.27	.	2	15.848	44 43.19	27.24	6.65	33 26.40	41 17.38
59	10					57.			36 56.89	19.23	1.02	.	6	51.600	7 18.02	27.42	0.02	36 36.64	3 45.46
60	8			42.					40 16.64	19.22	2.00	.	2	19.760	47 56.75	27.61	7.24	39 55.42	44 31.60
61	9					48.		40.	40 47.94	19.22	2.46	IV.	.	10.886	50 2.23	27.64	7.49	40 26.26	46 37.36
62	9				37.5				54.82	19.19	1.38	.	5	41.570	17 47.51	27.84	1.90	44 34.28	14 17.25
63	8				51.				48 50.88	19.17	2.03	.	3	23.572	36 43.38	28.05	5.22	48 29.68	33 16.65
64	7							54.	49 2.16	19.17	2.05	.	3	22.802	37 30.61	28.06	5.35	48 40.94	34 4.02
65	8		12.				20.5		53 46.39	19.15	2.05	.	3	23.440	36 51.65	28.28	5.21	53 25.19	33 25.14
66	.							33.	12 54 58.68	−19.15	−1.34	.	6	43.554	−15 42.98	−28.33	−1.50	12 54 38.19	−26 12 12.81

CORRECTIONS.

Date.	Corr. of Clock.	Hourly rate.	m	n	c	Zenith Point.	Mic. Co.
1848.	h.	s.	s.	s.	s.	° ′ ″	r.

INSTRUMENT READINGS.

Date.	CIRCLE.							Barom.	THERMOM.				
	A.	B.	C.	D.	E.	F.	Mean.		At.	Ex.	U.	L.	I.
1848. h. m.	° ′ ″						″	in.	°				

REMARKS.

(161) 35. Transit over T. IV assumed to have been recorded as over T. III. Minutes of transit assumed as 48.

(161) 40. Minutes assumed as 59, not 58.

(161) 46. Minutes assumed as 0.

(161) 47. Minutes assumed as 2 instead of 4.

(161) 60. Micrometer reading assumed as 19ʳ.760, not 10ʳ.760, to agree with Arg. Z. 292, 80; 380, 10; and Mer. Circle, 1847, May 14.

(161) 61. Revolutions of micrometer instead of horizontal thread assumed as 10.

(161) 62. Minutes assumed as 44.

ZONE 162. APRIL 1.   C. $D_0 = -26° 26' 10''$.

No.	Mag.	\multicolumn{7}{SECONDS OF TRANSIT} I.	II.	III.	IV.	V.	VI.	VII.	T. (h. m. s.)	a_1 (s.)	n_1 (s.)	MICROMETER		(r.)	i (' ")	d_1 (")	d_2 (")	Mean Right Ascension, 1850.0 (h. m. s.)	Mean Declination, 1850.0 (° ' ")
1	7			8.	24.5	42.1	50.5		9 59 24.95	−22.03	−1.37	IV.	5	52.192	− 6 40.85	− 3.02	+ 0.14	9 59 1.55	−26 32 53.81
2	8,9		17.4		51.8	9.			10 2 51.82	22.03	1.91	IV.	2	16.898	43 37.64	3.64	− 6.48	10 2 27.89	27 9 57.76
3	8,9		6.7	74.1	41.3				5 41.39	22.03	1.34	III.	5	53.705	5 5.53	4.10	+ 0.42	5 18.02	26 31 19.21
4	9		33.2	56.4	13.3	31.2			7 13.44	22.03	1.95	IV.	2	13.766	46 54.12	4.33	− 7.08	6 49.46	27 13 15.53
5	8					39.7	56.3		8 23.42	22.03	1.35	IV.	5	51.261	7 39.36	4.52	0.05	7 59.01	26 33 53.93
6	8,9						49.8	8.	9 15.72	22.03	1.51	VI.	4	43.421	15 50.18	4.66	1.51	8 52.18	42 6.35
7	8				4.3	21.5	39.		11 21.60	22.04	1.60	IV.	3	37.634	22 1.05	4.99	2.58	10 57.96	48 18.62
8	9					34.	51.4	8.8	13 34.12	22.04	1.59	V.	3	38.130	21 29.74	5.34	2.48	13 10.49	26 47 47.56
9	9				19.5		54.5		16 36.95	22.04	1.98	IV.	2	11.605	49 9.69	5.81	7.48	16 12.93	27 15 32.98
10	8,9				38.2				17 35.08	22.04	1.48	IV.	5	45.369	13 49.23	5.97	− 1.15	17 14.56	26 40 6.34
11	8,9							43.5	18 9.01	22.04	1.33	VI.	5	54.015	4 46.13	5.05	+ 0.46	17 45.64	31 0.72
12	8,9								18	22.04	1.65	VIII+	3	34.361	25 25.43	5.05	− 3.18		51 38.61
13	9		28.2					37.	22 2.71	22.04	1.39	VI.	5	49.864	9 6.68	6.65	0.30	21 39.28	35 23.63
14	9,10		2.5		36.			21.7	23 36.77	22.04	1.55	IV.	5	40.541	18 52.21	6.89	2.04	23 13.18	26 45 11.74
15	9,10		21.7	39.	56.8				26 56.50	22.04	1.81	III.	3	23.069	37 14.93	7.40	5.31	26 12.65	27 3 37.64
16	6		28.8	46.	3.5	21.	38.2		30 3.53	22.04	1.66	IV.	3	33.388	26 27.62	7.87	3.37	29 39.83	26 52 48.86
17	9			26.5	43.5	1.5			32 43.78	22.04	1.93	IV.	2	16.691	43 50.75	8.27	6.52	32 19.84	27 10 15.54
18	8		3.4	20.7	37.2	55.			35 37.77	22.04	1.48	IV.	5	44.762	14 27.16	8.71	1.24	35 14.25	26 40 47.11
19	9,10				54.			28.3	35 53.86	22.04	1.52	IV.	5	42.076	17 15.82	8.75	1.76	35 30.30	43 36.33
20	9,10				19.5				38 19.39	22.04	1.44	IV.	5	46.722	12 24.12	9.10	0.89	37 55.90	38 44.11
21	8,9			1.5	19.3	36.			39 1.67	22.04	1.45	V.	5	47.092	12 0.96	9.21	0.83	38 38.18	26 38 21.00
22	7		39.8	57.	13.8	31.6	49.8		42 14.23	22.04	1.84	IV.	2	19.262	41 9.64	9.70	6.03	41 50.35	27 7 35.37
23	8		57.	14.5	31.3				44 31.61	22.03	1.81	III.	2	21.262	39 3.80	10.00	5.65	44 7.77	27 5 29.54
24	8			57.2	14.6	32.6			45 14.87	22.03	1.54	IV.	3	39.276	20 18.12	10.12	2.27	44 51.30	26 46 40.51
25	9				7.2		42.2		46 7.40	22.03	1.37	IV.	5	49.827	9 9.13	10.23	0.30	45 44.00	26 35 29.66
26	8		29.8	47.6	4.7				49 4.69	22.03	1.75	III.	3	25.355	34 51.66	10.65	4.88	48 40.91	27 1 17.19
27	9				41.5		16.5		53 41.70	22.03	1.46	IV.	5	44.816	14 23.70	11.09	1.23	52 18.21	26 40 46.02
28	8		52.2	9.4	26.5		1.1		57 26.68	22.03	1.49	IV.	5	42.985	16 18.69	11.63	− 1.58	56 3.16	42 41.90
29	4		45.3	12.4	30.				59 29.93	22.02	1.28	III.	5	55.965	2 43.60	11.93	+ 0.83	58 6.63	29 4.79
30	9				4.8	22.	39.8		10 59 4.86	22.02	1.28	V.	5	56.362	2 19.07	12.00	+ 0.90	10 58 41.56	26 28 40.17
31	5		17.8	35.2	52.2	9.5	27.2		11 1 52.46	22.02	1.08	IV.	2	11.206	49 34.77	12.36	− 7.58	11 1 28.46	27 16 4.71
32	9							6.	3 14.11	22.02	1.49	VII.	5	42.598	16 42.66	12.53	− 1.64	2 50.60	26 43 6.83
33	9				49.	6.5			7 49.12	22.01	1.29	V.	5	55.562	3 9.32	13.10	+ 0.78	7 25.82	26 29 31.64
34	8		2.2	10.8					9 37.16	22.01	2.01	III.	2	8.666	52 13.65	13.32	− 8.08	9 13.14	27 18 45.05
35	9,10		13.8		48.7				12 49.54	22.01	1.69	IV.	3	29.215	30 49.37	13.69	4.14	12 24.84	26 57 17.20
36	9			23.9	41.1		16.2		13 41.31	22.00	1.46	IV.	5	44.364	14 52.31	13.80	1.30	13 17.88	41 17.41
37	9								14	22.00	1.68	VIII+	3	29.372	32 37.08	13.81	4.10	14	57 4.99
38	9		24.				16.5		18 41.72	21.99	1.49	IV.	5	42.258	17 4.52	14.38	1.70	18 18.24	43 30.60
39	9			8.3		43.			19 25.72	21.99	1.52	IV.	5	40.198	19 13.74	14.45	2.00	19 2.21	45 40.28
40	9			1.					21 18.35	21.99	1.59	III.	4	35.578	24 1.34	14.67	2.96	20 54.77	50 28.97
41	9				53.	0.7	17.4		21 43.07	21.99	1.67	V.	3	30.515	29 27.63	14.72	3.90	21 19.41	26 55 56.25
42	7						10.5	28.	22 34.85	21.99	1.92	VI.	2	13.892	46 46.40	14.82	7.07	22 11.94	27 13 18.29
43	9		2.	18.8					25 36.43	21.98	1.65	III.	3	31.328	29 36.93	15.15	3.75	25 12.80	26 55 5.83
44	9				54.	10.			25 53.30	21.98	1.55	V.	4	38.268	21 13.36	15.18	2.45	25 29.77	26 47 40.99
45	9								26	21.97	1.80	VII.	3	21.482	38 53.59		5.63	26	27
46	9				42.				29 24.63	21.97	1.75	V.	3	24.632	35 36.64	15.56	− 5.03	29 0.91	27 2 7.23
47	9						32.	50.	31 57.83	21.96	1.29	VI.	5	55.050	3 41.15	15.82	+ 0.68	31 34.57	26 30 6.29
48	9		33.		8.2	42.5			34 7.97	21.95	1.92	IV.	2	13.738	46 55.83	16.06	− 7.11	33 44.10	27 13 29.05
49	8			9.2	25.8	13.			11 35 26.03	−21.95	−1.44	IV.	5	44.891	−14 19.00	−16.19	− 1.20	11 35 2.64	−26 40 46.39

CORRECTIONS.

Date.	Corr. of Clock.	Hourly rate.	m	n	c	Zenith Point.	Mic. Co.
	h. s.	s.	s.	s.	s.	° ' "	r.
1848, Apr. 1,	0	· ·	· ·	· ·	· ·	359 59 56.92	30.0060

INSTRUMENT READINGS.

Date	CIRCLE							Barom.	THERMOM.				
	A	B.	C.	D.	E.	F.	Mean.		At.	Ex.	U.	L.	I.
	° ' "						"	in.	°	°	°	°	°
Zone 162 Apr. 1, 10 0	75 47 31.1 / 31.2	22.2 / 21.8	28.2 / 30.1	34.1 / 35.8	21.9 / 22.1	33.8 / 35.8	28.55 / 29.13	30.292	56.5	46.5	53.0	55.8	61.2
10 20												45.6	
10 40												44.7	
11 0	32.9 / 32.9	22.0 / 21.1	29.6 / 31.	33.9 / 35.3	22.1 / 22.3	34.6 / 35.5	29.22 / 29.68	30.310		43.5	49.6	53.8	
11 21												43.0	
11 40								30.314				52.9	43.1

REMARKS.

(162) 27. Minutes assumed as 52, not 53.
(162) 28. Minutes assumed as 56, not 57.
(161) 29. Time of transit over T. II assumed as 55s.3 instead of 45s.3.
(162) 31. Minutes of transit assumed as 58, not 59.
(162) 36. Declination differs 5' from Arg. Z. 291, 22; probably micrometer 5' in error.
(162) 41. Time of transit over T. IV assumed as 43s instead of 53s.

ZONE 162. APRIL 1. C. D₀ = −26° 26′ 10″—Continued.

No.	Mag.	I.	II.	III.	IV.	V.	VI.	VII.	T. (h. m. s.)	a₁ (s.)	a₂ (s.)	MICROMETER		r.	i (′ ″)	d₁	d₂	Mean R.A. 1850.0 (h. m. s.)	Mean Decl. 1850.0 (° ′ ″)
50	9.10		34.	51.5					11 37 8.82	−21.94	−1.36	III.	5	49.670	− 9 18.99	−16.37	−0.31	11 36 45.52	−26 35 45.67
51	9.10				30.3	47.4			37 12.83	21.94	1.89	V.	2	15.408	45 11.52	16.38	6.77	36 49.00	27 11 44.67
52	7		37.5	55.	12.5	29.5	46.2		39 12.16	21.94	1.82	IV.	2	19.156	41 16.22	16.59	6.07	38 48.40	27 7 48.88
53	9			29.		3.5	20.5		41 46.24	21.94	1.51	IV.	5	45.088	14 6.76	16.85	1.21	41 22.79	26 40 34.82
54	9				39.3		13.8		42 39.26	21.93	1.50	V.	4	40.899	18 28.05	16.94	1.96	42 15.63	44 56.95
55	9				0.3	18.2			48 0.52	21.92	1.63	V.	3	32.295	27 36.01	17.47	3.58	47 36.97	54 7.06
56	9						13.7		48 39.22	21.92	1.39	V.	5	47.922	11 8.73	17.54	0.64	48 15.91	37 36.91
57	6.7		19.1	36.	53.				50 53.35	21.92	1.57	III.	3	35.498	24 15.21	17.76	2.98	50 29.86	50 45.95
58	9				29.	46.2			51 28.95	21.91	1.36	V.	5	49.271	9 44.23	17.82	−0.39	51 5.69	36 12.44
59	9			12.	28.8				53 29.07	21.90	1.32	III.	5	52.257	6 36.71	18.01	+0.17	53 5.85	33 4.55
60	9			39.7	56.2				11 54 56.56	21.89	1.54	III.	3	37.498	22 9.71	18.15	−2.59	54 33.13	48 40.45
61	9			43.2					12 0 0.65	21.86	1.38	III.	5	52.041	6 50.14	18.64	+0.13	59 37.39	33 18.65
62	9								0 .	21.88	1.45	.	4	43.1				59	
63	9					27.2	44.		0 9.76	21.84	1.45	V.	4	43.139	16 7.57	18.65	−1.53	11 59 46.43	26 42 37.75
64	7		57.3	14.8	32.	40.	6.5		12 3 31.95	−21.87	−1.91	IV.	2	13.409	−47 16.69	−18.98	−7.10	12 3 8.17	−27 13 52.85

ZONE 163. APRIL 20. C. D₀ = −25° 11′ 0″.

No.	Mag.	I.	II.	III.	IV.	V.	VI.	VII.	T. (h. m. s.)	a₁ (s.)	a₂ (s.)	MICROMETER		r.	i (′ ″)	d₁	d₂	Mean R.A. 1850.0 (h. m. s.)	Mean Decl. 1850.0 (° ′ ″)
1	7					55.5	29.3		10 41 55.28	+10.19	+0.55	IV.	2	15.645	−50 10.25	−1.06	−16.49	10 42 6.02	−26 1 27.80
2	8		46.3	4.1	20.9		55.		45 20.90	10.19	0.67	IV.	3	24.454	35 48.11	1.44	13.99	45 31.76	25 47 3.54
3	7			19.8	37.	54.			46 36.89	10.19	0.56	IV.	2	14.922	45 41.51	1.59	15.71	46 47.64	25 56 58.87
4	8				16.8	34.	51.		47 16.74	10.19	0.47	V.	2	11.408	49 22.35	1.66	16.34	47 27.40	26 0 40.35
5	8.9					49.3			47 15.21	10.19	0.84	VI.	4	37.585	21 56.40	1.66	11.65	47 26.24	25 33 9.71
6	8		25.4	43.	0.1	17.5	34.5		52 0.13	10.19	0.53	IV.	2	13.991	46 40.00	2.16	15.87	52 10.85	25 57 58.05
7	6		24.	41.3	58.2	15.7	32.6		54 58.38	10.18	0.45	IV.	2	10.869	49 55.71	2.50	16.43	55 9.01	26 1 14.64
8	9.10				24.2	41.3	50.2		10 57 41.54	10.18	0.43	V.	2	9.128	51 45.18	2.76	16.75	10 57 52.15	26 3 4.69
9	7				27.5	44.3	1.8	19.2	11 4 27.57	10.18	0.90	V.	5	50.951	7 58.57	3.50	9.29	11 4 38.74	25 19 11.36
10	7.8					59.2			5 42.09	10.18	0.75	V.	3	32.132	27 46.16	3.63	12.62	5 53.02	39 2.43
11	8			48.2		22.5	39.5	56.5	7 5.47	10.18	1.03	IV.	5	54.512	4 15.20	3.77	8.65	7 16.68	15 27.62
12	9		24.5	42.2	59.3				10 59.14	10.18	0.61	III.	3	24.882	35 21.09	4.17	13.92	11 9.93	46 39.18
13	8				53.	10.2	27.5		12 53.16	10.18	0.96	V.	5	50.221	8 44.59	4.36	9.42	13 4.30	19 58.37
14	9			25.6	42.7	59.3			14 42.48	10.18	0.54	IV.	2	21.286	39 2.70	4.53	14.57	14 53.20	25 50 21.80
15	9			24.5	42.				17 41.86	10.18	0.38	III.	2	9.357	51 30.51	4.63	16.73	17 52.42	26 2 52.07
16	8.9		33.8		7.7				21 7.86	10.19	0.77	III.	4	38.686	20 46.05	5.15	11.46	21 18.62	25 32 2.66
17	8.9		42.		16.1	33.			21 16.08	10.19	0.81	IV.	5	41.018	18 22.15	5.16	11.04	21 27.08	29 38.35
18	9					4.	21.1	38.5	22 47.06	10.19	0.76	V.	5	38.575	20 55.60	5.30	11.48	22 58.01	32 12.38
19	6				46.	3.4	20.1		24 46.19	10.19	0.46	V.	2	16.768	43 52.38	5.49	15.40	24 56.84	55 13.27
20	9				57.3		32.3		25 57.69	10.19	0.64	VI.	3	29.458	30 33.75	5.59	13.10	26 8.52	41 52.44
21	9			26.2	32.8				28 43.07	10.19	0.44	III.	2	16.178	44 22.67	5.85	15.49	28 53.70	55 44.01
22	9.10			25.	42.				30 42.05	10.19	0.92	III.	5	42.752	16 33.19	6.03	10.73	30 53.06	27 49.95
23	8			20.8	37.3	55.			31 37.65	10.19	0.43	IV.	2	16.314	44 14.52	6.11	15.46	31 48.27	55 36.09
24	8				18.2	35.7	52.7		32 18.39	10.19	0.54	V.	3	23.116	37 11.73	6.17	14.23	32 29.12	48 32.15
25	8			25.3	42.5	0.			33 42.55	10.19	0.51	IV.	3	21.486	38 54.21	6.29	14.53	33 53.25	25 50 15.03
26	9.10			3.5					36 20.76	10.20	0.33	III.	2	9.186	51 41.11	6.52	16.76	36 31.29	26 3 4.39
27	9.10			18.2	35.3				37 35.31	10.20	0.84	III.	5	46.119	13 1.91	6.63	10.14	37 46.35	25 24 18.68
28	3	9.3	26.	13.3	0.3	17.3	34.4	51.5	41 0.28	10.20	0.43	IV.	7	16.915	43 36.45	6.92	15.35	41 10.91	25 54 58.72
29	8			30.5	47.3	4.2			45 47.28	10.20	0.34	IV.	2	11.648	49 6.99	7.31	16.30	45 57.82	26 0 30.60
30	9		9.5	26.5		51.2	8.2		11 49 43.92	+10.21	+0.58	II.	3	29.256	−30 46.80	−7.53	−13.13	11 48 54.71	−25 42 7.46

CORRECTIONS.

Date.	Corr. of Clock.	Hourly rate.	m	n	c	Zenith Point.	Mic. Co.
	h.	s.	s.	s.	s.	° ′ ″	r.
1848. Apr. 20,	n					359 59 57.28	30.0131

INSTRUMENT READINGS.

Date.		CIRCLE.							Barom.	THERMOM.				
		A.	B.	C.	D.	E.	F.	Mean.		At.	Ex.	U.	L.	I.
	1848. h. m.	° ′ ″						″	in.	°	°	°	°	°
Zone 162	Apr. 1, 12 0	75 47 {31.0	24.1	30.2	35.5	23.0	34.8	29.77	30.320	52.5	41.7	48.8	52.8	60.0
		30.7	23.5	30.9	36.1	23.0	34.9}	29.85						
Zone 163	Apr. 20, 10 41								30.230	51.5	43.5			
	11 0	74 32 {30.4	24.1	31.5	35.0	21.8	29.5	28.76			43.	50.2	51.0	52.8
		30.7	22.9	32.3	35.9	20.9	30.1}							
	11 23											41.2		
	11 40								30.222	50.2	40.4			
	12 0											41.8		
	12 20								30.218	49.5	41.3			

REMARKS.

(163) 1. Micrometer reading assumed as 10ʳ.645, not 15ʳ.645.

(163) 8. Transit observations discordant and recorded over T.'s IV, V, and VI instead of T.'s III, IV, and V; the record over T. IV rejected.

(163) 18. Right ascension 1ᵐ discordant from Arg. Z. 291, 33; probably 23ᵐ.

(163) 19. Time of transits over T. V assumed as 3ˢ.4 instead of 5ˢ.4.

(163) 28. Time of transit over T. VI assumed as 34ˢ.4 instead of 31ˢ.4.

(163) 30. Transits over T.'s V and VII assumed as at 1ˢ.2 and 18ˢ.2 instead of 51ˢ.2 and 8ˢ.2, respectively, and minutes as 48, not 49.

ZONE 163. APRIL 20. C. $D_o = -25° 11' 0''$—Continued.

No.	Mag.	I	II	III	IV	V	VI	VII	T	a_1	a_2	Micrometer	r	i	d_1	d_2	Mean Right Ascension, 1850.0	Mean Declination, 1850.0
									h. m. s.	s.	s.			' ''	''	''	h. m. s.	° '' '
31	9.10			9.5	26.2				11 49 43.60	+10.21	+0.64	III. 3	33.671	−26 9.74	−7.63	−12.35	11 49 54.45	−25 37 29.72
32	9							36.	49 44.62	10.21	0.58	VII. 3	29.584	30 25.35	7.63	13.08	49 55.41	41 46.06
33	9			59.3			33.5		52 33.50	10.21	0.54	II. 4	38.698	20 44.86	7.84	11.46	52 44.25	32 4.16
34	8.9				53.2	10.5			53 10.36	10.21	0.61	III. 3	32.516	27 22.32	7.89	12.55	53 21.18	38 42.76
35	8.0					11.1		45.5	54 11.18	10.22	0.37	VI. 2	15.949	44 37.47	7.97	15.53	54 21.77	56 0.97
36	9.10				14.7	31.3			57 31.55	10.22	0.44	III. 2	20.938	39 24.02	8.22	14.63	57 42.21	50 46.87
37	9				28.3		3.		11 58 38.54	10.23	0.66	VI. 3	37.171	22 29.67	8.30	11.73	11 58 49.43	33 49.70
38	9			50.	7.	24.5			12 0 7.21	10.23	0.81	IV. 3	48.268	10 45.37	8.41	9.74	12 0 18.25	22 3.52
39	9			17.3	5.	22.			6 21.93	10.24	0.85	III. 5	52.649	6 11.97	8.83	8.96	6 33.02	17 29.76
40	9				13.8	1.	18.		6 43.86	10.24	0.82	V. 3	47.931	12 9.72	8.86	10.00	6 54.92	25 28.58
41	8					20.3	37.2		8 3.14	10.24	0.50	V. 3	27.728	32 22.36	8.95	13.41	8 13.68	43 44.72
42	7				55.	11.6	28.5		8 54.56	10.24	0.48	V. 3	25.787	34 24.11	9.01	13.77	9 5.28	45 46.89
43	9			40.7				31.2	10 57.52	10.24	0.75	VI. 5	46.379	12 45.70	9.15	10.09	11 8.51	24 4.94
44	9							19.	11 27.69	10.24	0.86	VII. 5	53.907	4 52.59	9.18	8.73	11 38.79	16 10.50
45	8						34.5	51.3	13 17.19	10.24	0.36	V. 2	17.928	42 33.24	9.30	15.19	13 27.70	53 57.73
46	8			18.5	5.5	22.		56.5	15 22.44	10.25	0.57	IV. 3	32.889	26 58.68	9.43	12.49	15 33.20	38 20.60
47	9.10			15.2		0.3			17 59.66	10.25	0.51	III. 3	28.942	31 6.37	9.60	13.20	18 10.62	42 29.17
48	8					14.	1.		17 26.78	10.25	0.35	IV. 2	18.412	42 2.94	9.57	15.10	17 37.39	53 27.61
49	8.9			30.	7.	24.6			21 24.34	10.26	0.68	III. 5	42.148	17 11.23	9.81	10.82	21 35.28	28 31.86
50	9					52.	9.3	26.3	21 52.10	10.26	0.59	V. 4	35.761	23 50.50	9.84	11.97	22 2.95	35 12.31
51	8			39.2		13.5	30.3		26 56.27	10.27	0.33	V. 2	16.787	41 39.37	10.13	15.04	27 6.87	53 4.54
52	9		8.7	25.2	42.3				30 42.51	10.29	0.48	IV. 3	29.928	30 4.45	10.35	13.02	30 53.28	25 41 27.82
53	9		2.2	19.	36.3				32 36.39	10.29	0.23	III. 2	11.825	48 55.52	10.44	16.30	32 46.91	26 0 22.26
54	9		14.2	2.2	19.3				35 19.02	10.30	0.50	II. 3	31.702	29 13.15	10.59	12.69	35 29.82	25 39 36.43
55	7.8				24.	40.7	57.6		35 23.68	10.30	0.64	V. 4	41.981	17 20.21	10.59	10.85	35 34.62	25 28 41.65
56	9				43.	0.5			36 25.94	10.30	0.15	V. 2	7.564	53 23.34	10.64	17.08	36 36.39	26 4 51.06
57	9		43.5	18.					42 17.91	10.31	0.33	II. 3	21.350	39 2.76	10.93	14.57	42 28.55	25 50 28.26
58	9			53.2	11.				42 53.48	10.31	0.49	V. 3	33.186	26 40.04	10.96	12.44	43 4.28	38 3.44
59	9			56.					43 55.87	10.32	0.49	IV. 3	32.938	26 55.59	11.01	12.48	44 6.68	38 19.08
60	6						21.	33.5	43 46.85	10.32	0.26	VI. 2	16.602	43 56.65	11.00	15.42	43 57.43	55 23.07
61	7			59.		33.	50.		49 15.99	10.34	0.47	IV. 3	32.527	27 21.57	11.25	12.55	49 26.80	38 45.37
62	9		13.			34.5	52.		49 17.53	10.34	0.37	IV. 3	25.260	34 57.49	11.25	13.86	49 28.24	46 22.60
63	8.9			18.5	5.4	23.2			54 5.65	10.35	0.19	IV. 2	13.899	46 45.71	11.45	15.93	54 16.19	58 13.09
64	9		31.			1.	39.3		56 5.28	10.36	0.27	II. 2	19.185	41 13.64	11.54	14.96	56 15.91	52 40.14
65	8		34.2		8.2	25.	42.7		12 56 8.28	10.36	0.43	IV. 3	30.960	28 59.70	11.54	12.83	12 56 19.07	40 24.07
66	6.7	28.3	45.3	2.6	19.7	36.6	54.	11.2	13 3 19.67	10.37	0.35	IV. 3	26.426	33 44.40	11.82	13.65	13 3 30.39	45 9.87
67	9.10					51.			4 16.91	10.38	0.57	VI. 5	42.087	17 15.00	11.85	10.84	4 27.86	28 37.69
68	9				40.7	57.5			5 23.46	10.39	0.37	V. 3	28.516	31 33.11	11.89	13.27	5 34.24	42 58.27
69	9.10			2.					8 19.18	10.40	0.26	III. 3	21.154	39 15.05	11.99	14.61	8 29.84	25 50 41.65
70	9.10			35.5					9 52.76	10.40	0.10	III. 2	9.344	51 31.33	12.04	16.78	10 3.26	26 3 0.15
71	9			16.5	3.2				11 3.40	10.41	0.59	III. 5	44.788	14 25.40	12.08	10.34	11 14.40	25 25 47.82
72	9			29.8	46.8				15 46.52	10.42	0.44	III. 3	35.229	24 32.09	12.21	12.07	15 57.68	35 56.37
73	8.9			23.5					17 40.68	10.43	0.26	III. 2	22.375	37 54.07	12.27	14.39	17 51.37	49 20.73
74	8.9					2.8	19.5		17 45.60	10.43	0.59	V. 4	46.348	12 46.26	12.27	10.07	17 56.62	24 8.60
75	8			17.8	34.9	52.			19 34.87	10.44	0.41	IV. 3	33.909	25 54.64	12.32	12.29	19 45.72	37 19.25
76	9			4.6	21.3				21 21.48	10.44	0.27	IV. 2	24.114	36 5.17	12.36	14.07	21 32.19	47 31.68
77	9							19.5	21 28.19	10.44	0.68	VII. 5	53.312	5 30.21	12.36	8.82	21 39.31	16 51.39
78	8				24.	41.3			23 24.10	10.45	0.63	IV. 4	49.899	9 2.79	12.41	9.43	23 35.18	20 24.63
79	9					16.2			13 23 42.07	+10.45	+0.71	VI. 5	56.018	−2 40.36	−12.42	−8.35	13 23 53.23	−25 14 1.13

CORRECTIONS.

Date.	Corr. of Clock.	Hourly rate.	m	n	c	Zenith Point.	Mic. Co.
	h.	s.	s.	s.	s.	° ' ''	r.
1848.							

REMARKS.

(163) 40. Micrometer reading assumed as 46r.931, not 47r.931.

(163) 45. Time of transit over T. V assumed as 34s.5 instead of 31s.5.

INSTRUMENT READINGS.

Date.	CIRCLE.							Barom.	THERMOM.				
	A.	B.	C.	D.	E.	F.	Mean.		At.	Ex.	U.	L.	I.
	1848. h. m.	° ''							in.					
Zone 163	Apr. 20, 12 30	74 32	30.4 24.2 31.9 31.9 22. 26.2 / 30.2 23.2 33.1 36.6 22.2 28.9					28.56				50.2	49.5
	12 40								30.218	49.4	41.2			
	13 0									41.				
	13 20									40.5				
	13 40									40.3				
	14 0	29.8 24.7 31.9 33.9 21.6 29.2 / 30.2 23.4 33.8 35.6 21.5 29.2						28.73	30.200	47.5	40.	49.	46.5	52.2

ZONE 163. APRIL 20. C. $D_o = -25^\circ 11' 0''$—Continued.

No.	Mag.	I.	II.	III.	IV.	V.	VI.	VII.	T. (h. m. s.)	a₁	a₂	Mic.	n	r	i	d₁	d₂	Mean Right Ascension, 1850.0	Mean Declination, 1850.0
80	9	..	44.	1.3	..	35.9	52.9	..	13 28 18.50	+10.47	+0.30	IV.	3	27.688	-32 25.06	-12.52	-13.43	13 28 29.36	-25 43 51.01
81	8.9	..	44.2	1.5	..	36.	53.1	..	28 18.77	10.47	0.30	IV.	3	27.859	32 14.27	12.52	13.39	28 29.54	43 40.18
82	8	..	20.3	37.3	54.	12.	..	..	32 54.46	10.48	0.26	IV.	3	25.456	34 45.25	12.59	13.82	33 5.20	25 46 11.66
83	9.10	..	..	47.	4.	..	..	..	56 4.10	10.49	0.05	III.	2	10.876	49 55.02	12.65	16.49	36 14.61	26 1 24.16
84	7	..	30.	47.	3.7	21.1	37.3	..	37 3.80	10.50	0.59	IV.	5	48.752	10 16.69	12.66	9.63	37 14.98	25 21 38.98
85	8.9	..	58.	15.	32.	..	..	..	39 32.13	10.51	0.41	IV.	3	37.628	22 1.43	12.70	11.63	39 43.05	33 25.76
86	8	..	17.8	..	52.5	..	..	..	40 52.26	10.52	0.38	IV.	3	35.269	24 29.53	12.72	12.06	41 3.16	35 54.31
87	9	..	..	2.	19.5	..	..	..	43 19.34	10.53	0.64	IV.	5	54.552	4 12.67	12.74	8.60	43 30.51	15 34.01
88	8	..	..	47.5	4.2	21.5	38.6	..	45 4.42	10.54	0.08	IV.	2	14.218	46 25.90	12.76	15.88	45 15.04	57 54.54
89	8.9	..	..	25.2	42.	..	16.3	..	46 42.14	10.55	0.29	IV.	3	29.952	30 1.73	12.77	13.00	46 52.98	41 26.90
90	7	..	..	3.5	20.3	37.4	51.6	..	49 20.48	10.56	0.63	IV.	5	54.295	4 28.37	12.79	8.65	49 31.67	15 50.31
91	8	..	22.6	39.4	56.8	13.6	30.8	..	51 56.73	10.56	0.41	IV.	3	39.179	20 24.10	12.80	11.36	52 7.70	31 48.32
92	9	..	23.	40.7	..	..	..	..	56 57.66	10.58	0.10	III.	4	18.427	41 57 35	12.82	15.12	57 8.34	53 25.30
93	9	..	..	..	19.2	..	53.5	10.8	57 36.44	10.59	0.13	IV.	2	20.299	40 4.59	12.82	14.77	57 47.16	51 32.18
94	4	..	..	..	23.	..	56.5	13.8	57 39.68	10.59	0.05	IV.	2	14.679	45 56.93	12.82	15.80	13 57 50.32	57 25.55
95	9	..	..	32.7	49.5	..	..	..	59 49.67	10.59	0.06	IV.	2	15.849	41 43.43	12.83	15.59	14 0 0.32	56 11.85
96	9	..	..	..	..	..	16.	..	13 59 41.91	10.59	0.30	VI.	3	33.239	26 36.46	12.83	12.42	13 59 52.80	38 1.71
97	9	..	..	..	..	..	48.7	..	14 0 14.62	10.60	0.27	VI.	3	31.347	25 35.24	12.83	12.77	14 0 25.49	40 0.84
98	9	..	3.	20.	37.2	..	..	..	2 37.19	10.61	0.30	IV.	2	33.212	26 38.59	12.84	12.42	2 48.10	38 3.85
99	7	..	..	11.	28.2	45.5	..	..	14 4 28.18	+10.62	+0.08	IV.	2	17.661	-42 49.92	-12.84	-15.27	14 4 38.88	-25 54 18.03

ZONE 164. MAY 3. C. $D_o = -27^\circ 41' 20''$.

No.	Mag.	I.	II.	III.	IV.	V.	VI.	VII.	T. (h. m. s.)	a₁	a₂	Mic.	n	r	i	d₁	d₂	Mean Right Ascension, 1850.0	Mean Declination, 1850.0
1	9	..	0.4	17.7	35.2	..	10.3	..	12 16 35.32	+13.67	+0.60	IV.	3	34.498	-25 17.90	-5.33	-4.11	12 16 49.59	-26 6 47.34
2	8	..	..	..	20.7	37.8	55.5	..	19 20.54	13.67	0.71	V.	4	47.394	11 40.61	5.52	1.60	19 34.92	27 53 7.73
3	9.10	..	..	..	..	5.2	..	..	21 5.14	13.67	0.40	IV.	2	12.505	48 13.38	5.64	8.43	21 19.21	28 29 47.45
4	8.9	..	..	..	41.3	58.3	16.6	..	22 41.14	13.68	0.42	V.	2	13.338	47 21.33	5.66	8.28	21 55.24	28 55.27
5	9	..	4.	21.3	39.3	56.2	..	..	33 38.95	13.69	0.60	IV.	3	31.452	28 29.09	6.41	4.71	33 53.24	28 10 0.21
6	9.10	..	39.	..	..	..	48.2	..	36 13.73	13.69	0.70	VI.	4	41.189	18 10.23	6.57	2.79	36 28.12	27 59 39.59
7	9	..	..	..	..	..	..	27.7	35 35.23	13.69	0.76	VII.	2	47.832	11 13.93	6.53	1.52	35 49.68	52 41.98
8	9	..	..	..	..	19.5	30.4	54.4	37 1.85	13.70	0.73	V.	4	44.054	15 10.09	6.62	2.25	.37 16.28	27 56 38.96
9	9	..	..	..	35.7	..	..	..	38 35.55	13.70	0.62	IV.	3	31.604	28 19.43	6.70	4.68	36 49.87	28 9 50.81
10	9	..	19.3	37.	54.	12.	..	..	40 54.35	13.70	0.69	IV.	4	38.765	20 41.66	6.84	3.30	41 8.74	2 11.80
11	9	..	14.	32.7	49.3	..	..	43.	42 49.58	13.70	0.53	IV.	2	20.308	40 4.03	6.94	6.39	43 3.81	21 37.86
12	9.10	..	..	46.	..	..	21.2	38.7	43 3.70	13.71	0.63	IV.	3	31.539	28 23.57	6.95	4.70	43 18.04	28 9 55.22
13	9	..	..	..	..	..	..	38.2	43 45.72	13.71	0.76	VII.	4	44.902	13 10.54	6.99	1.85	44 0.19	27 54 39.38
14	9	..	..	..	..	..	..	24.6	44 32.13	13.71	0.78	VII.	4	47.189	11 53.67	7.03	1.64	44 46.62	27 53 22.34
15	8	..	25.3	42.8	59.3	17.7	..	..	48 0.05	13.71	0.70	IV.	3	37.846	21 47.60	7.27	3.48	49 14.46	28 3 18.35
16	7.8	..	..	45.3	2.3	20.7	37.4	..	12 54 2.61	13.73	0.51	IV.	3	14.732	45 53.54	7.51	8.00	12 54 16.88	28 27 29.05
17	9.10	..	13.7	..	..	49.2	..	..	13 2 48.94	13.74	0.81	II.	4	43.971	15 13.85	7.90	2.28	13 3 3.49	27 56 44.03
18	9	..	56.	13.5	31.	48.3	5.6	..	4 30.95	13.75	0.62	IV.	3	23.720	36 33.97	7.97	-6.23	4 45.32	28 18 8.17
19	9	..	..	..	49.2	6.2	..	..	7 6.48	13.75	0.92	III.	5	55.808	2 53.47	8.08	+0.01	7 21.15	27 44 21.54
20	9.10	..	..	..	..	..	..	6.6	7 13.85	13.75	0.59	V.	2	18.582	41 52.41	8.09	-7.25	7 28.19	28 23 27.75
21	9	..	39.2	..	15.	..	..	..	10 14.59	13.76	0.86	II.	5	47.728	11 20.59	8.21	1.56	10 29.22	27 52 50.36
22	8.9	..	..	10.7	..	45.7	3.	..	10 28.24	13.76	0.80	IV.	4	11.288	18 3.51	8.21	2.81	10 42.80	59 34.53
23	9.10	..	57.2	15.8	..	..	..	..	16 32.86	13.77	0.88	III.	5	48.961	10 3.44	8.43	1.32	16 47.51	51 33.19
24	9	..	..	..	45.	2.5	19.5	..	13 16 44.89	+13.77	+0.94	V.	5	55.136	-3 35.94	-8.44	-0.12	13 16 59.60	-27 45 4.50

CORRECTIONS.

Date.	Corr. of Clock.	Hourly rate.	m	n	c	Zenith Point.	Mic. Co.	
1848. May 3.	h. 0	s. ..	s. ..	s. ..	s. ..	359 59 56.82	r. 30.0089	(163)

INSTRUMENT READINGS.

Date.	A.	B.	C.	D.	E.	F.	Mean.	Barom.	At.	Ex.	U.	L.	I.
Zone 164. 1848. May 3, 12 12		..	..	..	..	..	..	In. 29.880	63.4	56.2			
12 20	77 2 {32. / 31.8}	20.6 / 20.9	18.2 / 30.6	32.9 / 34.3	17.4 / 18.8	33.7 / 35.6	28.07	..	..	55.8	61.5	51.	60.7
12 45		..	..	..	..	..	..	..	..	54.8			
13 0		..	..	..	..	..	..	29.866	62.5	54.1			
13 20		..	..	..	..	..	..	29.866	62.	53.4			
13 40		..	..	..	..	..	..	..	..	53.3			
14 0		..	..	..	..	..	..	..	..	53.			
14 20		..	..	..	..	..	..	29.870	62.	52.			

REMARKS.

(163) 93. Transits over T.'s III, V, and VI assumed as recorded over T.'s IV, VI, and VII.

(163) 94. Transits over T.'s III, V, and VI assumed as recorded over T.'s IV, VI, and VII.

(164) 4. Minutes assumed as 21, not 22.

(164) 13. Micrometer reading assumed as 45r.962, not 44r.962, to agree with Arg. Z. 292, 86.

(164) 15. Minutes assumed as 49, not 48.

[(163) 92. Micrometer probably 2 18r.427.]

Zone 164. May 3. C. $D_o = -27° 41′ 20″$—Continued.

No.	Mag.	I.	II.	III.	IV.	V.	VI.	VII.	T.	a_1	a_2	Micrometer		r.	l	d_1	d_2	Mean Right Ascension, 1850.0.	Mean Declination, 1850.0.
									h. m. s.	s.	s.			r.	′ ″	″	″	h. m. s.	° ′ ″
25	9.10			18.	35.7				13 18 35.56	+13.78	+0.67	III.	2	24.838	−35 19.32	−8.50	−6.01	13 18 50.01	−28 16 53.83
26	9.10		43.	0.2	17.				21 17.57	13.79	0.74	IV.	3	31.441	28 29.76	8.59	4.72	21 32.10	10 3.09
27	9.10							33.	21 40.50	13.79	0.61	VII.	4	39.336	20 6.65	8.60	3.20	21 55.10	28 1 38.45
28	5		26.	43.4	1.	18.4	35.8	53.5	24 0.99	13.80	0.68	IV.	5	45.625	13 33.04	8.66	1.96	24 15.67	27 55 3.66
29	9.10		17.7		53.				26 52.90	13.80	0.63	IV.	2	18.879	41 33.40	8.74	7.19	27 7.33	28 23 9.33
30	9.10							43.?	27 8.11	13.81	0.68	VI.	2	21.861	38 26.62	8.75	6.60	27 22.60	28 20 1.97
31	8					54.8	12.2	30.2	28 37.49	13.81	0.89	V.	4	45.218	13 57.15	8.78	2.03	28 52.19	27 55 27.96
32	9			46.2	3.8	21.4			33 3.80	13.82	0.85	IV.	4	40.807	18 33.50	8 90	2.89	33 18.47	28 0 5.29
33	10				16.2				34 16.05	13.83	0.78	IV.	3	30.806	29 9.37	8.93	4.84	34 30.66	28 10 43.14
34	8.9				15.7		50.4		35 15.56	13.83	0.91	IV.	5	46.156	12 59.76	8.95	1.86	35 30.30	27 54 30.57
35	10		24.						39 59.09	13.64	0.96	II.	5	49.388	9 36.56	9.05	1.25	40 13.89	27 51 6.86
36	6			5.3		40.5	57.8	15.4	41 22.83	13.85	0.71	IV.	3	21.991	38 22.42	9.08	6.57	41 37.39	28 19 58.07
37	9			9.5	25.2	45.5			44 45.26	13.86	0.76	IV.	3	25.473	34 44.19	9.12	5.89	44 59.88	16 19.20
38	7			13.2	30.7	18.2		23.5	45 30.78	13.86	0.89	IV.	5	40.616	18 34.76	9.14	2.89	45 55.53	28 0 6.79
39	6.7			16.	33.7	50.3		25.5	45 33.30	13.86	0.99	VII.	5	50.889	8 2.02	9.14	0.94	45 48.15	27 49 32.10
40	8		55.2	13.5	30.7				45 30.07	13.87	0.95	IV.	4	46.665	12 25.67	9.16	1.76	48 45.49	27 53 56.81
41	9					19.3	35.5		48 1.64	13.87	0.73	V.	2	22.372	37 54.75	9.17	6.50	49 16.24	28 19 30.42
42	9.10			48.7		23.6			52 6.12	13.88	0.72	IV.	2	19.872	40 31.12	9.22	6.99	52 20.72	22 7.33
43	7.8			18.2	35.2		11.3		55 35.09	13.89	0.74	IV.	2	21.558	38 45.57	9.24	6.66	55 50.72	20 21.47
44	8				0.3		35.5		56 0.38	13.90	0.72	IV.	2	17.638	42 51.36	9.25	7.44	56 15.00	24 28.05
45	10				31.2				13 58 51.76	13.91	0.78	III.	3	23.372	36 55.98	9.27	6.30	13 59 6.45	18 31.55
46	8.9		8.2	25.7	43.4				14 2 43.29	13.92	0.90	IV.	3	36.319	23 23.70	9.23	3.76	14 2 58.17	4 56.74
47	9				10.2	28.	44.		3 9.91	13.92	0.86	IV.	3	30.618	29 21.29	9.28	4.68	3 24.69	10 55.45
48	9.10			1.5	18.3				5 35.35	13.93	0.68	III.	2	10.335	50 28.96	9.29	8.89	5 50.96	32 7.14
49	5			48.8	6.5	24.	41.4		6 6.33	13.93	0.66	IV.	2	7.922	53 0.55	9.29	9.42	6 20.92	34 39.26
50	9			38.7			31.3		8 56.33	13.94	0.75	IV.	2	17.992	42 29.10	9.29	7.38	9 11.02	24 5.77
51	9.10								10		0.79	IV.	2	21.083	39 15.30	9.29	6.77	10	20 51.36
52	9							13.5	10 20.77	13.95	0.78	V.	2	20.313	40 3.91	9.29	6.93	10 35.50	21 40.13
53	9				13.5	1.5	18.3		12 43.62	13.96	0.91	.	3	37.556	22 7.26	9.28	3.53	12 58.52	3 40.07
54	9.10					31.3			14 13.68	13.96	0.80	IV.	2	20.738	39 36.88	9.27	6.85	14 28.44	21 13.00
55	7.8			10.8	38.2	15.7	3.5		16 23.30	13.97	0.87	.	3	25.978	31 4.12	9.26	5.19	16 43.14	12 38.57
56	9			51.8	9.	26.7	44.2		20 9.14	13.98	0.77	.	2	15.788	44 47.32	9.24	7.83	20 23.89	28 26 24.39
57	9.10		58.5	15.8	33.3				23 33.39	14.00	1.03	.	5	43.424	15 51.21	9.20	2.37	23 46.42	27 57 22.78
58	9		9.2		41.2		18.8		27 44.13	14.02	0.79	.	2	15.730	44 50.96	9.15	7.84	27 58.94	28 26 27.95
59	9						33.2	51.2	27 58.52	14.02	0.98	.	4	37.226	22 19.94	9.15	3.59	28 13.52	28 3 51.68
60	9.10			23.8		58.			30 40.99	14.03	1.05	.	5	42.778	16 31.49	9.12	2.50	30 56.07	27 56 3.11
61	9		20.	37.5	55.2				32 55.07	14.04	0.94	III.	3	31.149	28 48.04	9.08	4.77	33 10.05	28 10 21.89
62	9			6.5	21.				33 0.42	14.04	0.92	.	3	28.516	31 33.11	9.08	5.29	33 21.38	13 7.48
63	8		14.3	32.8	10.8	7.7	25.		40 49.94	14.07	0.84	.	2	17.592	42 54.32	8.93	7.46	41 4.65	28 24 30.71
64	8			4.	21.2	38.6			44 35.98	14.08	1.18	.	5	53.061	5 46.10	8.85	−0.49	44 54.14	27 47 15.44
65	6.7			13.2	30.8	48.1			45 13.26	14.09	1.20	.	5	56.237	2 26.88	8.63	+0.13	45 23.55	27 43 55.58
66	7		27.5	45.4	2.8	20.6	38.		48 2.88	14.10	0.79	.	2	9.645	51 12.58	8.77	−9.06	48 17.77	28 32 50.41
67	9			3.2	21.2	38.3			49 20.85	14.11	1.03	.	4	35.104	24 25.88	8.74	3.97	49 36.02	5 58.59
68	9			35.5	53.	11.2			57 53.18	14.15	0.97	.	3	27.402	32 43.18	8.50	5.51	58 8.30	14 17.19
69	9				27.	44.7	2.		58 27.04	14.15	0.95	.	3	23.617	30 40.49	8.49	6.27	14 58 42.14	28 18 15.25
70	9				51.3	9.3	26.		14 59 51.41	+14.16	+1.22	.	5	53.296	−5 31.60	−8.45	−0.44	15 0 6.79	−27 47 0.49

CORRECTIONS.

Date.	Corr. of Clock.	Hourly rate.	m	n	c	Zenith Point.	Mic. Co.
	s.	s.	s.	s.	s.	° ′ ″	r.
1848. h.							

(164) 41. Minutes assumed as 49, not 48.
(164) 55. Time of transit over T. IV assumed as 28s.2 instead of 38s.2.

INSTRUMENT READINGS.

Date.	A.	B.	C.	D.	E.	F.	Mean.	Barom.	At.	Ex.	U.	L.	I.
	° ′ ″						″	in.	°	°	°	°	°
Zone 164 — 1848 May 3, 14 40 ... 15 11	77 2	30.8 / 31.1	21.6 / 20.6	28.2 / 30.2	33.8 / 33.5	18.3 / 19.1	32.1 / 33.2 — 27.87	29.865	60.	51.7 / 51.2 59.			58.5 60.8

ZONE 165. MAY 27. C. D₀ = —24° 33′ 20″.

No.	Mag.	SECONDS OF TRANSIT. I. II. III. IV. V. VI. VII.	T.	a_1	a_2	MICROMETER.	i	d_1	d_2	Mean Right Ascension, 1850.0.	Mean Declination, 1850.0.
			h. m. s.	s.	s.	r. ′ ″		′ ″	″	h. m. s.	° ′ ″
1	8	. . . . 26.7 43. 0.2 17.1 . .	13 1 43.29	+19.74	+0.94	IV. 5 48.391	—10 39.53	—3.21	—6.92	13 2 3.97	—24 44 9.66
2	9	. . . . 54.5	2 3 39	19.74	0.77	VI. 3 28.319	31 45.22	3.21	10.28	2 23.90	25 5 18.71
3	9.10	. . . . 42.7 59.3	6 59.46	19.74	0.84	III. 3 32.695	27 10.97	3.27	9.54	7 20.04	25 0 43.78
4	8.9	. . . . 29.7 46.6 4.1	9 46.84	19.74	0.98	IV. 5 48.758	10 16.30	3.30	6.86	10 7.56	24 43 46.46
5	8.9	. . . . . . 26.3 43.1 0.7 . .	10 26.37	19.74	0.94	V. 4 44.510	14 41.59	3.31	7.55	10 47.05	48 12.45
6	8.9	. . . . 24.7 41.7 . .	11 7.76	19.74	0.91	V. 4 40.575	18 48.51	3.32	8.23	11 28.41	24 52 20.06
7	8	. . 21.2 . . 55.3 12.5 29.3 . .	13 55.35	19.74	0.83	IV. 3 30.286	29 42.12	3.36	9.96	14 15.92	25 3 15.44
8	9.10	. . 1.8 . . 35.7	17 35.53	19.74	0.69	II. 2 10.258	50 33.52	3.40	13.34	17 55.96	25 24 10.26
9	9	. . . . . . 50.5	18 50.39	19.74	1.03	IV. 5 50.098	8 52.24	3.42	6.64	19 11.16	24 42 22.30
10	9	. . 44. 1.2 18.3	21 18.27	19.74	0.75	III. 2 17.222	43 17.26	3.44	12.16	21 38.76	25 16 52.86
11	8	. . . . 12.5 30. 47. 4.4 . .	22 30.00	19.74	0.94	IV. 4 40.146	19 15.12	3.46	8.30	22 50.68	24 52 46.88
12	9	. . 55.5 12.6 29.3	24 29.53	19.74	1.02	III. 5 46.814	12 18.15	3.49	7.18	24 50.24	24 45 48.62
13	9	. . 6. 23.8 40.5 57.8 . .	29 40.53	19.74	0.89	IV. 3 28.925	31 7.38	3.54	10.18	30 1.16	25 4 41.00
14	9	. . . . 42. 59.	30 59.00	19.74	0.82	III. 3 20.395	40 2.71	3.56	11.62	31 19.56	13 37.89
15	9	. . 0.5 17.7 34. 51.3 . .	34 34.39	19.74	0.87	IV. 3 27.074	33 3.63	3.61	10.49	34 55.00	25 6 37.73
16	7	. . 30.3 47. 4.3 21.3 38.5 55.5	36 4.36	19.74	1.06	IV. 5 47.956	11 6.66	3.62	6.99	36 25.16	24 44 37.27
17	7	. . . . 46.	36 54.57	19.74	0.78	VII. 2 12.676	48 2.72	3.63	12.93	37 15.04	25 21 39.28
18	9	. . 35.4 52.5 9. 20.6 . .	43 9.40	19.74	0.85	IV. 2 18.482	41 58.56	3.70	11.04	43 29.99	25 15 31.20
19	9	. . . . 14.2 30.8	46 31.04	19.74	1.15	III. 5 53.124	5 42.13	3.72	6.13	46 51.93	24 39 11.98
20	9	. . . . . . 2.7 19.7 . .	47 2.65	19.74	1.04	V. 3 40.428	19 5.63	3.73	8.25	47 23.43	24 52 37.61
21	9.10	. . . .	47			. 4 45.172		3.73	7.46		
22	7.8	. . . . . . 28. 45.5 2.	49 11.01	19.74	0.87	V. 2 18.258	42 12.80	3.75	11.98	49 31.62	25 15 48.53
23	9	. . 29.8 . . 14. 31. . .	13 58 3.93	19.75	0.92	IV. 2 19.606	40 48.00	3.81	11.75	13 58 24.60	25 14 23.56
24	8	. . . . 21.8 39. 55.3 . .	14 1 21.71	19.75	1.19	V. 5 51.		3.82	6.47	14 1 42.65	24
25	8	. . . . . . 20.3 37.2 . .	2 3.31	19.75	0.24	V. 5 55.645	3 3.97	3.82	5.71	2 24.32	36 33.50
26	8	. . 30.2 47.2 4.3 21.3 38.5 . .	4 4.30	19.75	0.14	IV. 3 45.052	14 15.48	3.83	7.47	4 26.25	24 47 46.78
27	7	. . 35.5 53.1 [19] 27. 44. 1.2	10 9.97	19.75	0.93	IV. 3 25.650	34 32.97	3.84	10.75	10 30.65	25 8 7.56
28	9	. . . . 56.2 12.6	14 12.96	19.76	1.04	III. 3 26.971	33 10.09	3.83	10.51	14 33.76	6 44.43
29	9	. . 52.5 . . . . 0.2 . .	14 26.50	19.76	1.03	VI. 3 25.238	34 58.43	3.83	10.82	14 47.29	8 33.08
30	7.8	. . . . 15.6 32.2 49.5 6.7 . .	20 32.46	19.76	0.96	IV. 2 13.851	46 48.72	3.81	12.75	20 53.16	25 20 25.28
31	8.9	. . . . 43.	20 51.92	19.76	1.18	VII 4 40.776	18 36.10	3.80	8.19	21 12.86	24 52 8.09
32	8.9	. . . . 53.7.	22 2.65	19.76	1.30	VII. 5 53.623	5 10.63	3.79	6.03	22 23.71	24 38 40.45
33	9	. . 29.5 . . 4.2 . . 37.8 . .	28 3.89	19.77	1.09	IV. 3 25.365	34 50.97	3.75	10.79	28 24.75	25 8 25.51
34	9	. . . . . . 57.8 . .	33 57.67	19.78	1.14	IV. 5 40.496	18 55.03	3.68	8.24	34 18.59	24 52 26.95
35	9	. . 26. 43. 50.5	35 59.91	19.78	0.88	III. 3 22.502	37 50.56	3.65	11.26	36 20.57	25 11 25.47
36	7	. . . . . . 8. . . 42. . .	37 57.95	19.78	1.16	IV. 4 39.583	14 36.84	3.64	7.49	37 18.92	24 43 7.97
37	9	. . . . . . 8.3 . . 42.3 . .	37 58.27	19.78	1.16	IV. 4 39.481	14 43.31	3.64	7.50	37 19.21	48 14.45
38	7	. . . . 9.?	38 17.90	19.79	1.07	VII. 3 33.589	25 55.11	3.63	9.35	38 35.76	59 28.09
39	8	. . . . 0.5 . .	39 26.58	19.79	1.21	VI. 4 41.069	18 17.70	3.61	8.13	39 47.58	51 49.44
40	9	. . . . . . 34. 51.5 8. . .	43 34.17	19.79	1.29	V. 4 43.002	16 16.12	3.53	7.80	43 55.25	24 49 47.45
41	9	. . 16.2 3.5 30.2 37.5 . .	46 20.37	19.79	1.17	IV. 3 33.282	26 34.26	3.49	9.46	46 41.33	25 0 7.21
42	7.8	. . 51. 8.1 25. 41.8 58.9 . .	48 25.02	19.80	1.34	IV. 5 42.775	16 31.88	3.44	7.85	48 46.16	24 50 3.17
43	2	6.5 . . 39.8 56.8 13.7 30.8 47.7	54 56.66	19.80	1.54	IV. 5 51.082	7 50.48	3.28	6.46	55 18.20	24 41 20.22
44	8	. . . . . . 37.5 54.8 11.6 . .	56 37.58	19.81	1.12	V. 2 22.762	38 32.84	3.24	11.22	56 58.51	25 12 7.30
45	9	. . 8.5 25.5 42.5 59.5 . .	14 58 42.58	19.82	1.60	IV. 5 52.991	5 50.56	3.19	6.13	14 59 4.00	24 39 19.88
46	9	. . . . 13.8 30.8 48.3 . .	15 1 30.92	19.82	0.99	IV. 2 10.955	49 50.38	3.11	13.23	15 1 51.73	25 23 26.72
47	8.9	. . 58.7 15.5 32.5 50. . .	3 32.69	19.82	1.28	IV. 3 26.724	33 25.52	3.05	10.56	3 53.79	25 6 59.13
48	8	. . . . . . 22.2 39.5 56.1 . .	4 22.27	19.82	1.60	V. 5 48.151	10 54.54	3.03	6.93	4 43.69	24 44 24.50
49	9	. . . . 10.8 27.2 44.9 . .	15 9 27.46	+19.83	+1.68	IV. 5 52.088	— 6 47.31	—2.87	—6.26	15 9 48.97	—24 40 16.44

CORRECTIONS.

Date.	Corr. of Clock.	Hourly rate.	m	n	c	Zenith Point.	Mic. Co.
1848. May 27,	h. s. 0	s.	s.	s.	s.	° ′ ″ 359 59 61.48	r. 29.9238

INSTRUMENT READINGS.

Date		CIRCLE.							Barom.	THERMOM.				
		A.	B.	C.	D.	E.	F.	Mean.		At.	Ex.	U.	L.	I.
Zone 165	1848. May 27, h. m. 13 0	73 54 61.6	59.8	63.1	58.1	59.1	59.9	60.27	in. 30.200	76.	72.2	75.	74.2	
	13 20	.	.	.	.	.	.	.	.	.	72.1			
	13 40	.	.	.	.	.	.	.	30.202	75.3	70.7			
	14 0	60.7	59.	63.	57.8	58.2	58.9	59.60	.	.	68.9	73.	73.5	
	14 24	.	.	.	.	.	.	.	30.194	74.	68.5			
	14 40	.	.	.	.	.	.	.	.	.	67.			
	15 0	.	.	.	.	.	.	.	.	.	66.			
	15 20	.	.	.	.	.	.	.	30.200	71.9	65.8			
	15 45	60.7	59.7	63.2	58.1	58.1	58.1	59.65	30.200	71.2	64.9	71.5	71.	73.8

REMARKS.

(165) 23. Time of transits over T.'s IV and V assumed as 4ˢ and 21ˢ instead of 14ˢ and 31ˢ.

(165) 36. Transits over T.'s IV and VI assumed as 58ˢ and 32ˢ, not 8ˢ and 42ˢ, and minutes as 36, not 37, and micrometer reading as 44ʳ.583, not 39ʳ.583, to agree with B. A. C. 4865; Arg. Z. 301, 52; and Transit Z., 1849, April 5.

(165) 37. Transits over T.'s IV and VI assumed as 58ˢ.3 and 32ˢ.3, not 8ˢ.3 and 42ˢ.3, and minutes as 36, not 37, and micrometer reading as 44ʳ.481, not 39ʳ.481, to agree with B. A. C. 4865; Arg. Z. 301, 52; and Transit Z., 1849, April 5.

(165) 44. Micrometer reading assumed as 21ʳ.762, not 22ʳ.762.

Zone 165. May 27. C. $D_0 = -24° 33' 20''$ — Continued.

No.	Mag.	I.	II.	III.	IV.	V.	VI.	VII.	T. (h. m. s.)	a_1 (s.)	a_2 (s.)	MICROMETER		$r.$	i (' '')	d_1 ('')	d_2 (')	Mean Right Ascension, 1850.0 (h. m. s.)	Mean Declination, 1850.0 (° ' '')
50	7.8			52.8	9.8	27.	44.1	1 5	15 11 27.06	+19.84	+1.05	IV.	2	8.338	−52 34.64	− 2.79	−13.73	15 11 47.95	−25 26 11.16
51	8.9			51.5	8.7	25.5			13 8.57	19.84	1.53	IV.	5	38.067	21 27.42	2.74	8.64	13 29.94	24 54 58.80
52	9		38.8	56.5	13.2				15 13.25	19.84	1.28	III.	3	20.415	40 1.45	2.65	11.64	15 34.37	25 13 35.74
53	8				41.8	59.			15 24.90	19.84	1.35	V.	3	25.919	34 15.77	2.64	10.70	15 46.09	7 49.11
54	9			50.7	7.	24.5			16 50.37	19.84	1.43	V.	3	28.560	31 30.26	2.59	10.25	17 11.64	25 5 3.12
55	8		16.		51.				18 33.66	19.85	1.82	IV.	5	53.768	5 1.77	2.53	5.98	18 55.33	24 38 30.28
56	7.8	16.3	33.6	50.	7.	24.4			23 50.29	19.86	1.32	IV.	2	16.905	43 37.20	2.31	12.24	24 11.47	25 17 11.75
57	7.8	24.3	11.3	58.2			32.5		25 58.40	19.86	1.39	IV.	2	20.328	40 2.78	2.22	11.66	26 19.65	25 13 36.66
58	9					55.2			26 21.24	19.86	1.92	VI.	5	53.664	5 8.22	2.21	5.99	26 43.02	24 38 36.42
59	9						T.		27 26.99	19.87	1.27	VI.	2	12.616	48 6.55	2.16	12.99	27 48.13	25 21 41.70
60	8.9		45.2	2.5	19.	36.5	53.6		31 19.43	19.87	1.37	IV.	3	27.617	32 29.58	1.99	10.41	31 40.67	25 6 1.98
61	7.8		16.4	35.5	52.	9.6	20.2		33 52.38	19.87	1.73	IV.	3	37.254	22 24.06	1.87	8.78	34 13.98	24 55 55.61
62	8		53.	10.	26.8	43.6	0.5		36 26.81	19.88	1.68	IV.	3	32.207	27 41.66	1.75	9.63	36 48.37	25 1 13.04
63	9			29.7					37 29.58	19.89	1.93	IV.	5	46.427	12 42.82	1.71	7.22	37 51.40	24 46 11.75
64	7.8			16.8	43.8	1.	17.9		38 43.92	19.89	1.95	IV.	5	47.788	11 17.14	1.65	6.99	39 5.76	24 44 45.78
65	3	16.1	3.2	20.4	37.	54.5	11.5	28.6	41 37.33	19.90	1.50	IV.	2	16.662	43 52.57	1.51	12.28	41 58.73	25 17 26.36
66	4	25.1	41.0	59.	16.	32.9	50.1	6.5	44 15.93	19.91	1.87	IV.	4	40.392	18 59.74	1.38	8.24	44 37.71	24 52 29.36
67	7.8				18.		52.4	9.5	15 45 18.26	+19.91	+2.03	IV.	5	50.029	−14 10.19	− 1.31	− 6.61	15 45 40.20	−24 47 38.11

Zone 166. May 30. S. $D_0 = -24° 33' 10''$.

No.	Mag.	I.	II.	III.	IV.	V.	VI.	VII.	T. (h. m. s.)	a_1 (s.)	a_2 (s.)	MICROMETER		$r.$	i (' '')	d_1 ('')	d_2 (')	Mean Right Ascension, 1850.0 (h. m. s.)	Mean Declination, 1850.0 (° ' '')
1	4						2.	18.8	16 11 44.84	+19.65	+0.47	VI.	2	20.202	−40 10.86	−10.09	− 9.67	16 12 4.96	−25 13 40.62
2	9				56.				14 55.90	19.66	0.19	IV.	5	52.998	6 52.87	9.90	4.11	15 15.75	24 40 16.88
3	8		13.			4.			18 47.08	19.67	0.44	IV.	3	26.770	33 22.58	9.67	8.55	19 7.19	25 6 50.80
4	7	41.5		16.					20 32.70	19.67	0.24	III.	4	43.930	15 17.05	9.57	5.65	20 52.66	24 48 42.27
5	5					2.5	19.5		20 45.56	19.67	0.27	V.	5	45.600	13 21.03	9.55	5.32	21 5.50	24 46 46.80
6	9		12.	29.				T.	24 46.16	19.68	0.23	.	6	51.500	7 23.98	9.30	4.36	25 6.07	24 40 47.64
7	9		50.		24.				26 24.02	19.68	0.41	.	3	29.600	30 25.16	9.21	8.07	26 44.11	25 3 52.44
8	10		17.		51.				30 51.02	19.69	0.39	.	4	34.802	24 49.39	8.93	7.18	31 11.10	24 58 15.40
9	10		42.						30 16.16	19.69	0.37	.	4	37.275	22 14.16	8.96	6.77	30 36.22	24 55 39.89
10	6		45.8		20.				37 19.98	19.71	0.54	.	2	18.895	41 31.71	8.50	9.90	37 40.23	25 15 0.11
11	8		31.			5.5			40 5.26	19.72	0.34	.	4	44.352	14 48.30	8.32	5.57	40 25.32	25 48 12.19
12	8				18.2				41 12.09	19.72	0.47	.	2	23.890	36 19.09	8.24	9.04	41 32.28	25 9 46.37
13	7				44.		18.		42 43.97	19.72	0.60	.	1	13.712	46 56.99	8.13	10.79	43 4.29	25 20 25.91
14	8					44.5			44 27.55	19.72	0.35	.	4	43.695	15 32.61	8.01	5.69	44 47.62	24 46 56.31
15	7			55.5		29.5			46 12.46	19.73	0.58	.	2	16.805	43 43.23	7.89	10.25	46 32.77	25 17 11.37
16	9			57.					48 14.14	19.73	0.35	.	5	45.228	13 57.91	7.75	5.43	48 34.22	24 47 21.09
17	5		53.		26.				50 26.52	19.74	0.38	.	4	41.108	18 13.68	7.59	6.12	50 46.64	51 37.39
18	5						55.5 12.		50 38.32	19.74	0.33	.	5	47.202	11 54.11	7.55	5.09	50 58.39	45 16.78
19	8			14.		48.			52 31.00	19.75	0.38	.	4	42.612	16 39.90	7.43	5.87	52 51.22	50 3.20
20	8					47.5			53 47.38	19.75	0.35	.	5	46.022	13 8.06	7.33	5.29	54 7.48	24 46 30.68
21	7		53.			27.			55 9.95	19.76	0.67	.	1	8.768	52 5.62	7.23	11.66	55 30.38	25 25 34.51
22	8		50.5						16 58 24.65	19.77	0.38	.	4	44.952	14 12.35	6.95	5.48	16 58 44.60	24 47 34.81
23	8		44.5						17 1 18.65	19.77	0.36	.	6	47.238	11 51.54	6.76	5.07	17 1 38.78	45 13.37
24	8				49.				1 48.67	19.77	0.40	.	5	42.428	16 53.83	6.72	5.88	2 9.04	24 50 16.43
25	7					58. 15.			2 41.04	19.78	0.51	.	3	29.588	30 25.79	6.64	8.09	3 1.33	25 3 50.52
26	9							18.5	3 27.40	19.78	0.49	.	3	33.989	25 48.84	6.58	7.32	3 47.67	24 59 12.74
27	7		20.		36.5				17 6 53.57	+19.79	+0.56	.	3	25.748	−34 26.75	− 6.32	− 7.74	17 7 14.24	−25 7 50.81

CORRECTIONS.

Date.	Corr. of Clock.	Hourly rate.	m	n	c	Zenith Point.	Mic. Co.
1848. (h.)	(s.)	(s.)	(s.)	(s.)	(s.)	(° ' '')	($r.$)
May 30, 0						359 59 61.08	29.9248

INSTRUMENT READINGS.

Date.	CIRCLE.							Barom.	THERMOM.				
	A.	B.	C.	D.	E.	F.	Mean.		At.	Ex.	U.	L.	l.
1848. (h. m.)	(° ' '')						('')	(in.)					
Zone 166 May 30, 16 0	73 54 60.	61.8	64.	58.8	59.2	58.	60.30	29.760	72.5	69.	73.8		
16 20								29.764	72.4	67.8			
16 40								29.772	72.	66.5			
17 0	59.8	61.8	64.2	57.5	59.0	58.	60.05	29.770	71.8	65.5			
17 20								29.786	71.5	64.5			

REMARKS.

(165) 67. Micrometer reading assumed as 45^r.029, not 50^r.029.

(166) 2. Micrometer reading assumed as 51^r.998 instead of 52^r.998.

(166) 9. Right ascension differs 4^m from Arg. Z. 387, too.

(166) 21. Transit over T. III assumed to have been recorded as over T. II.

(166) 27. Transit over T. III assumed as recorded over T. IV.

Zone 166. May 30. S. $D_s = -24°\ 35'\ 10''$ — Continued.

No.	Mag.	I.	II.	III.	IV.	V.	VI.	VII.	T.	a_1	a_2	Mic.		r.	i	d_1	d_2	Mean Right Ascension, 1850.0.	Mean Declination, 1870.0.
									h. m. s.	s.	s.			r.	′ ″	″	″	h. m. s.	° ′ ″
28	7		35.5		9.5				17 12 9.57 +19.81	+0.39		5	47.508	−11 34.60	− 5.85	− 5.01	17 12 29.72	−24 44 55.46
29	3				28.		1.5		12 27.72 19.81	0.43		4	42.020	17 17.45	5.82	5.95	12 47.91	50 39.22
30	7					10.			13 36.09 19.81	0.49		3	36.252	23 27.39	5.73	6.93	13 56.39	24 56 50.05
31	9							55.	19 3.54 19.83	0.72		1	11.498	49 17.29	5.25	11.20	19 24.09	25 22 43.74
32	10		47.		21.				30 21.07 19.86	0.50		4	40.585	18 46.56	4.20	6.19	30 41.38	24 52 6.95
33	11			38.5					55.54									
34	10			26.					35 43.12 19.88	0.72		2	16.662	43 52.25	3.67	10.31	36 3.72	25 17 16.23
35	10			9.5		43.5			37 26.58 19.88	0.49		4	41.720	17 35.77	3.51	6.00	37 46.95	24 50 55.28
36	8		21.5	38.5			29.5		40 55.62 19.89	0.49		4	44.440	14 45.23	3.17	5.54	41 16.00	48 3.94
37	6					36.5			17 45 19.54 +19.91	+0.52		4	41.550	−17 47.38	− 2.72	− 6.03	17 45 39.97	−24 51 6.13

Zone 167. June 2. C. $D_c = -25°\ 10'\ 50''$.

No.	Mag.	I.	II.	III.	IV.	V.	VI.	VII.	T.	a_1	a_2	Mic.		r.	i	d_1	d_2	Mean Right Ascension, 1850.0.	Mean Declination, 1870.0.
1	8		16.	33.5	50.	7.3	24.5		14 47 50.29 +18.92	+0.47	IV.	3	30.650	−29 19.29	− 8.44	− 9.90	14 48 9.68	−25 40 27.63
2	9		3.8	21.3	37.6		12.5		52 38.17 18.93	0.48	IV.	3	34.905	24 52.17	8.26	9.17	52 57.58	35 59.62
3	9.10						41.		53 6.87 18.93	0.50	VI.	5	54.246	4 31.75	8.27	5.89	53 26.30	15 35.91
4	9.10		0.4	18.	35.2				56 34.98 18.93	0.50	III.	3	31.588	28 20.49	8.15	9.73	56 54.41	39 28.37
5	9			10.8	28.6				57 11.10 18.93	0.53	V.	4	39.326	20 7.01	8.12	8.42	57 30.56	31 13.55
6	9.10							9.5	57 18.16 18.93	0.53	VII.	5	44.242	14 59.54	8.12	7.59	14 57 37.62	26 5.25
7	8		11.7	28.9	45.9	3.4	20.	37.6	14 59 46.00 18.93	0.53	IV.	2	16.641	43 55.83	8.04	12.30	15 0 5.46	55 6.17
8	7			7.3	24.5	51.6	8.4		15 1 7.24 18.93	0.53	V.	3	25.935	34 14.83	7.99	10.81	1 26.70	45 23.63
9	7		7.	24.	41.			15.8	3 41.27 18.93	0.54	IV.	3	33.320	26 31.32	7.89	9.44	5 0.71	37 38.65
10	9		9.6		43.5	1.7	17.8		4 43.92 18.93	0.55	IV.	4	41.318	18 1.63	7.85	8.00	5 3.40	29 7.46
11	10				59.3				7 16.54 18.94	0.56	III.	5	46.812	12 18.27	7.75	7.12	7 36.04	23 23.14
12	9			53.2	10.4	27.5		2.3	8 27.66 18.94	0.56	IV.	3	29.837	30 10.17	7.72	10.04	8 47.16	41 17.93
13	10			58.7					10 15.75 18.94	0.57	IV.	4	47.550	11 30.48	7.64	7.00	10 35.26	22 35.09
14	8		53.2	10.6	27.6	45.	2.3		11 27.80 18.94	0.58	IV.	3	44.231	15 6.44	7.59	7.57	11 47.32	26 11.60
15	9.10		52.	9.2	26.				13 26.23 18.94	0.58	III.	5	52.450	6 24.59	7.51	6.15	13 45.75	17 28.25
16	9.10		43.2	0.5	17.7				15 17.58 18.95	0.58	III.	3	30.805	29 9.50	7.43	9.86	15 37.11	40 16.79
17	9				48.				15 13.87 18.95	0.59	VI.	3	56.242	2 26.43	7.43	5.52	15 33.41	13 29.38
18	8		17.4	34.2	51.3	8.3	25.4		23 51.39 18.96	0.62	IV.	5	52.701	6 8.77	7.00	6.11	24 10.97	17 11.94
19	9.10		47.3	4.4	21.8				26 21.65 18.96	0.62	III.	3	23.656	30 38.10	6.96	11.11	26 41.23	47 46.17
20	8		13.	30.5	47.2				27 47.46 18.96	0.61	III.	2	12.422	48 18.26	6.89	13.06	28 7.03	59 28.21
21	7			9.1	26.4	43.4	0.9		28 9.23 18.96	0.62	V.	3	25.643	35 35.97	6.80	10.76	28 28.81	46 43.53
22	9		54.5	12.5	29.3				32 29.22 18.97	0.64	III.	3	31.320	28 37.37	6.67	9.78	32 48.63	39 43.82
23	9.10		30.5	48.	5.2				36 5.06 18.97	0.65	III.	3	22.237	38 7.18	6.50	11.36	36 24.68	49 15.04
24	9			23.4	40.2	57.8			37 40.42 18.98	0.65	IV.	3	20.775	33 38.44	6.42	11.61	38 0.05	50 46.47
25	6				37.2				38 3.10 18.98	0.67	VI.	3	46.471	12 39.93	6.40	7.18	38 22.75	23 43.51
26	7.8				9.3				38 35.21 18.98	0.67	VI.	4	39.496	19 56.54	6.37	8.35	38 54.86	31 1.26
27	7		38.5	56.2	13.2	30.6	47.4	4.5	41 13.17 18.98	0.67	IV.	3	21.861	38 30.52	6.24	11.42	41 32.82	49 38.16
28	6						29.		41 37.68 18.98	0.68	VII.	5	52.529	6 19.31	6.22	6.14	41 57.34	17 21.67
29	9		16.5	33.2	50.4				45 50.53 18.99	0.69	III.	5	50.025	8 56.65	6.00	6.57	46 10.21	19 59.22
30	8.9			25.8		59.5			46 42.73 18.99	0.69	IV.	4	41.035	18 19.27	5.95	8.11	47 2.41	29 23.33
31	9			24.8					46 50.05 18.99	0.69	VI.	5	45.472	10 34.33	5.95	6.81	47 10.36	21 37.09
32	2	36.1	53.2	10.9	27.	44.5	1.6	18.3	49 27.37 18.99	0.69	IV.	3	30.436	29 32.83	5.81	9.93	49 47.05	40 38.57
33	9				4.2				50 47.04 19.00	0.70	V.	3	26.551	33 16.32	5.74	10.60	51 6.74	44 42.66
34	8		29.5	47.2	4.	21.2	38.2		53 4.05 19.00	0.71	IV.	3	27.785	32 18.90	5.62	10.40	53 23.76	43 24.92
35	9		45.		19.2	36.	53.2		15 53 19.09 +19.00	+0.71	IV.	3	21.678	−38 42.06	− 5.60	−11.45	15 53 38.80	−25 49 49.11

CORRECTIONS.

Date.	Corr. of Clock.	Hourly rate.	m	n	c	Zenith Point.	Mic. Co.
1848, June 2,	h. s. 0	s.	s.	s.	s.	° ′ ″ 359 59 61.01	r. 29.9255

INSTRUMENT READINGS.

Date.		A.	B.	C.	D.	E.	F.	Mean.	Barom.	At.	Ex.	U.	L.	l.
	1848. h. m.	° ′ ″						″	In.	°	°	°	°	°
Zone 167	June 2, 14 40	74 32 {33.1 {34.	31.8 31.2	34. 34.4	30.8 31.1	32.9 32.9	30. 31.	32.26	29.998	71.5	68.	70.7	69.8	69.
	15 0										68.2			
	15 20								29.998	71.	67.9			
	15 40										66.			
	16 0								29.994	70.2	66.9			
	16 20										66.9			
	17 0	{32.8 {33.5	32.6 32.0	33.8 33.1	31.3 32.3	33.5 33.2	29.2 30.2	32.29	29.982	69.	62.6 69.	68.5	68.2	

REMARKS.

(167) 8. Transits over T.'s VI and VII assumed as at 41s.6 and 58s.4, not at 51s.6 and 8s.4.

(167) 9. Minutes of transit assumed as 4, not 5.

(167) 10. Right ascension differs 18s.5 from Arg. Z. 302, 69.

(167) 21. Micrometer reading assumed as 24r.643 instead of 25r.643.

Extern. therms. assumed as transposed.

Extern. therms. assumed as 64.9.

Zone 167. June 2. C. $D_0 = -25°\ 10'\ 50''$—Continued.

No.	Mag.	I.	II.	III.	IV.	V.	VI.	VII.	T. (h. m. s.)	a_1 (s.)	a_2 (s.)	Mic.		r.	i (' '')	d_1 ('')	d_2 ('')	Mean Right Ascension, 1850.0 (h. m. s.)	Mean Declination, 1850.0 (° ' '')
36	6							48.	15 54 56.66	+19.00	+0.72	VII.	5	43.790	−15 27.78	−5.51	−7.64	15 54 16.38	−25 26 30.93
37	9.10						13.		55 38.86	19.00	0.71	VI.	3	20.768	39 38.63	5.48	11.61	55 58.57	50 45.72
38	9.10				12.3				57 12.19	19.00	0.72	IV.	3	22.833	37 29.55	5.39	11.25	57 31.91	48 36.19
39	9.10				50.3				57 50.19	19.01	0.72	IV.	3	22.550	37 47.48	5.36	11.30	58 9.92	48 54.14
40	6				39.3	57.1	14.2	31.6	15 58 39.77	19.01	0.73	V.	2	16.488	44 3.80	5.31	12.35	15 58 59.51	25 55 11.46
41	9.10				18.6				16 0 16.56	19.01	0.72	IV.	2	9.708	51 8.57	5.22	13.57	16 0 38.29	26 2 17.36
42	9.10					11.2	28.		0 53.90	19.01	0.73	V.	2	18.451	42 0.69	5.19	12.03	1 13.64	25 53 7.91
43	8					43.5	0.7		2 26.53	19.02	0.74	V.	4	41.226	18 7.71	5.11	8.07	2 46.29	29 10.69
44	9.10		52.	9.	26.3				4 26.28	19.02	0.73	III.	2	17.595	42 53.63	5.00	12.17	4 46.03	54 0.80
45	9				23.8	41.			7 23.81	19.03	0.75	V.	4	41.366	17 58.86	4.83	8.04	7 43.59	29 1.73
46	9			22.5	39.3	56.3			9 56.52	19.03	0.75	III.	5	46.813	12 18.21	4.69	7.10	10 16.30	23 20.00
47	9.10					0.			10 43.03	19.03	0.75	IV.	5	53.171	5 39.37	4.64	6.01	11 2.81	16 40.02
48	2					1.5	18.4	35.6	11 44.37	19.03	0.76	V.	5	56.097	2 16.87	4.58	5.46	12 4.16	13 16.91
49	9		43.		17.8	35.			14 17.63	19.04	0.75	IV.	2	16.778	43 45.24	4.43	12.31	14 37.42	54 51.98
50	9			20.5	37.3	54.6			17 37.42	19.04	0.76	IV.	2	16.894	43 37.89	4.24	12.30	17 57.22	25 54 44.43
51	1	1.7	18.8	36.	53.4	10.8	27.6	45.2	19 53.36	19.05	0.76	IV.	2	6.479	54 31.19	4.11	14.12	20 13.17	26 5 39.42
52	9		50.5	7.	24.5				22 24.45	19.06	0.76	III.	3	30.102	29 53.73	3.96	9.98	22 44.26	25 40 57.67
53	9		0.	17.5	34.2				30 34.37	19.07	0.77	III.	3	25.706	31 29.45	3.48	10.75	30 54.22	25 45 33.68
54	9.10			30.8	48.	5.2			34 47.95	19.08	0.77	IV.	2	9.669	51 11.08	3.22	13.59	35 7.80	26 2 17.89
55	10				48.7				36 47.96	19.08	0.78	IV.	2	9.505	51 21.48	3.09	13.60	37 7.82	26 2 28.17
56	10						45.?		37 10.80	19.08	0.77	VI.	2	12.402	48 20.08	3.07	13.08	37 30.65	25 59 26.23
57	9				22.2				39 22.10	19.09	0.79	IV.	5	55.577	3 8.31	2.94	5.60	39 41.98	14 6.85
58	10				7.7				41 7.60	19.09	0.79	IV.	2	22.072	38 13.27	2.84	11.39	41 27.48	49 17.50
59	9				18.2				42 18.10	19.09	0.80	IV.	5	53.542	5 16.08	2.76	5.95	42 37.99	16 14.79
60	8					1.3	18.2		42 44.20	19.10	0.80	V.	4	49.531	9 26.41	2.74	6.64	43 4.10	20 25.79
61	8		14.3	31.3		5.5	22.8		44 48.56	19.10	0.80	IV.	3	36.212	23 30.34	2.60	8.93	45 8.46	34 31.87
62	9			42.6		17.	34.		44 59.93	19.10	0.80	IV.	3	37.052	22 37.57	2.59	8.78	45 19.83	33 38.94
63	8.9						46.3		46 12.18	19.11	0.80	VI.	5	52.687	6 9.53	2.52	6.10	46 32.09	17 8.15
64	8		8.	25.5	42.5	59.3	16.7		48 42.43	19.11	0.80	IV.	3	22.167	38 11.51	2.36	11.37	49 2.34	49 15.24
65	8		53.	10.	27.	44.5	1.3		54 27.22	19.12	0.81	IV.	4	41.626	17 42.24	2.00	7.97	54 47.15	28 42.21
66	8			53.2	10.2	27.2	44.3		55 10.22	19.13	0.81	IV.	4	44.683	14 30.30	1.95	7.48	55 30.16	25 29.73
67	9.10						52.		16 58 17.87	19.14	0.83	VI.	5	54.546	4 12.92	1.76	5.73	16 58 37.84	25 15 10.41
68	9		21.3		36.				17 0 55.88	19.14	0.81	III.	2	9.114	51 45.62	1.60	13.66	17 1 15.83	26 2 50.92
69	8		52.2	9.5	26.8		0.7		2 26.64	19.14	0.82	IV.	4	40.912	18 26.92	1.49	8.09	2 46.60	25 29 26.50
70	9				28.8		19.		17 2 45.46	+19.15	+0.82	V.	4	42.472	−16 49.57	−1.47	−7.82	17 3 5.43	−25 27 48.86

Zone 168. June 3. C. $D_0 = -28°\ 18'\ 50''$.

No.	Mag.	I.	II.	III.	IV.	V.	VI.	VII.	T. (h. m. s.)	a_1 (s.)	a_2 (s.)	Mic.		r.	i (' '')	d_1 ('')	d_2 ('')	Mean Right Ascension, 1850.0 (h. m. s.)	Mean Declination, 1850.0 (° ' '')
1	9		54.2		30.5				14 5 29.94	+18.89	+1.05	II.	5	46.006	−13 8.69	−1.28	−2.90	14 5 49.88	−28 32 2.87
2	8				18.6	36.1			6 11.06	18.89	1.02	V.	4	43.478	15 46.38	1.28	3.37	6 20.97	34 41.03
3	9			2.3	19.7		53.		9 37.49	18.89	0.98	IV.	4	39.997	19 24.41	1.27	4.06	9 57.36	38 19.74
4	8			15.2	32.7	50.3	7.5	25.2	14 50.20	18.89	0.77	IV.	2	19.939	40 26.99	1.22	7.95	15 9.66	59 26.16
5	9				32.	49.5	6.8		15 31.79	18.89	0.79	V.	3	23.201	37 6.46	1.20	7.31	15 51.47	56 4.97
6	6	12.	29.2	47.1	4.	22.4	39.5	57.5	19 4.53	18.90	0.84	IV.	3	30.092	29 54.29	1.17	5.98	19 24.27	58 51.44
7	8.9				21.5	39.			20 3.98	18.90	1.04	V.	5	51.396	7 30.86	1.16	1.87	20 23.92	26 23.91
8	8.9			29.5	47.6	5.			21 29.79	18.90	0.93	V.	3	40.098	19 26.23	1.13	4.04	21 49.62	28 38 21.40
9	9.10			34.	51.3				24 51.45	18.90	0.71	III.	2	19.002	41 25.44	1.08	8.15	25 11.06	29 0 24.67
10	9.10		6.7		41.8	59.3			14 26 41.79	+18.90	+0.80	IV.	3	27.729	−32 22.48	−1.04	−6.43	14 27 1.49	−28 51 19.95

CORRECTIONS.

Date.	Corr. of Clock.	Hourly rate.	m	n	c	Zenith Point.	Mic. Co.
	h. s. °	s.	s.	s.	s.	° ' ''	r.
1848. June 3.	o						359 59 61.47	29.9968

INSTRUMENT READINGS.

	Date.	A.	B.	C.	D.	E.	F.	Mean.	Barom.	At.	Ex.	U.	L.	I.
	1848. June 3, h. m.	° ' ''						''	in.					
Zone 168ª	14 5								29.884	75.	75.			
	14 20	77 39 62.5	60.5	64.1	56.7	60.7	59.9	60.73				74.9	76.2	73.5
	14 40								29.882	75.	74.9			
	14 50	61.7	60.0	64.2	57.3	60.8	59.8	60.63				75.7	73.5	71.

REMARKS.

(167) 36. Minutes of transit assumed as 53, not 54.

(167) 47. Right ascension differs 5^s from Arg. Z. 304, 44.

(167) 48. Declination differs 20'' from Arg. Z. 212, 38; 304, 45; 387, 71; and B. A. C. 5447.

(167) 66. Transit over T. IV assumed as 56^s, not 36^s.

(168) 3. Time of transit over T. V assumed as 53^s instead of 55^s.

* Readings of microscopes D and F assumed to be given 10'' too great.

ZONE 168. JUNE 3. C. $D_0 = -28° 18' 50''$.

No.	Mag.	I.	II.	III.	IV.	V.	VI.	VII.	T.	a_1	a_2	MICROMETER.	i	d_1	d_2	Mean Right Ascension, 1850.0	Mean Declination 1850.0
									h. m. s.	s.	s.	− r.	′ ″	″	″	h. m. s.	° ′ ″
11	9				39.2	56.2			14 27 38.92	+18.91	+1.02	V. 5 51.349	− 7 33.84	− 1.02	− 1.87	14 27 58.85	−28 26 26.73
12	9					36.			28 18.24	18.91	0.69	V. 2 17.920	42 33.74	1.01	8.35	28 37.84	29 1 33.10
13	8			58.	15.5	33.2			31 15.57	18.91	0.89	IV. 4 39.302	20 8.15	0.95	4.20	31 35.37	28 39 3.30
14	9		8.4	26.					32 43.70	18.91	0.86	III. 3 36.134	23 35.24	0.91	4.81	33 3.47	28 42 30.96
15	8						9.4		32 34.25	18.91	0.76	VI. 2 16.494	44 3.42	0.92	8.64	32 53.92	29 3 2.98
16	9.10				59.3				33 59.25	18.91	0.59	IV. 2 10.625	50 11.20	0.88	9.80	34 18.75	29 9 11.66
17	9				44.8	2.8			39 44.88	18.92	0.69	V. 3 23.460	36 50.27	0.75	7.26	40 4.49	28 55 48.28
18	8				44.5	2.3			40 41.62	18.92	0.99	V. 5 53.228	5 35.80	0.72	1.47	41 4.53	24 27.99
19	9.10			44.5		20.			46 2.21	18.92	0.68	IV. 3 24.031	36 14.46	0.57	7.18	46 21.85	55 12.21
20	8		22.5	39.5	57.2	14.8	32.6		14 47 57.39	+18.93	+0.86	IV. 5 45.257	−13 56.27	− 0.51	− 3.05	14 48 17.18	−28 32 49.83

ZONE 169. JUNE 5. C. $D_0 = -25° 48' 30'$.

No.	Mag.	I.	II.	III.	IV.	V.	VI.	VII.	T.	a_1	a_2	MICROMETER.	i	d_1	d_2	Mean Right Ascension, 1850.0	Mean Declination 1850.0
1	9					7.	23.8		14 47 49.68	+17.57	+1.61	V. 4 36.795	−22 45.60	− 7.04	− 6.81	14 48 8.86	−26 11 29.45
2	9			9.5	26.2	44.			55 26.52	17.58	2.48	IV. 2 20.373	39 59.95	6.83	9.71	55 46.58	28 46.49
3	8.9				27.3				56 10.11	17.58	1.85	V. 3 32.899	26 57.85	6.82	7.48	56 29.54	15 42.15
4	8			21.	37.3	55.			57 37.74	17.58	1.81	IV. 3 34.138	25 40.43	6.77	7.25	57 57.13	14 21.45
5	8*		35.1	52.2	9.2				59 9.40	17.58	1.52	III. 4 40.075	19 19.07	6.73	6.24	14 59 28.50	8 2.04
6	7			44.5			18.8		14 59 44.44	17.58	0.90	VI. 5 52.425	6 26.16	6.71	4.07	15 0 2.92	55 6.94
7	8		2.2	19.4	36.2		10.8		15 6 36.51	17.58	2.48	IV. 3 21.472	38 55.15	6.47	9.52	6 56.57	27 41.14
8	8		1.	18.2	35.2		9.5		8 35.33	17.59	2.44	IV. 3 22.627	37 42.60	6.40	9.31	8 55.36	26 28.31
9	8	46.	3.5	20.7	37.9				10 20.65	17.59	1.77	IV. 3 36.171	23 32.92	6.34	6.92	10 40.01	12 16.78
10	8		1.	17.8	35.5	52.5			11 18.08	17.59	2.56	IV. 2 20.608	39 45.15	6.30	9.67	11 38.23	28 31.12
11	8			36.	53.	10.4			12 53.11	17.59	2.52	IV. 2 21.425	38 53.96	6.23	9.53	13 13.22	27 39.72
12	8			39.2	55.8	13.5			13 38.98	17.59	1.62	IV. 2 39.393	20 10.60	6.21	6.33	13 58.19	8 53.14
13	8.9		16.5	34.		8.2	25.2		15 51.06	17.60	1.84	III. 3 35.390	24 22.00	6.12	7.05	16 10.50	13 5.17
14	9			34.5	51.5	9.	26.		15 51.70	17.60	1.34	IV. 4 45.510	13 38.52	6.12	5.27	16 10.64	2 19.91
15	9.10					6.2			16 49.04	17.60	1.72	V. 3 37.062	21 40.21	6.08	6.59	17 8.36	10 22.68
16	9		36.7		11.				19 11.05	17.60	2.20	III. 3 28.706	31 21.25	5.98	8.21	19 30.85	20 5.41
17	8.9			49.8	7.	24.2			20 7.02	17.60	1.48	IV. 4 43.023	16 14.49	5.95	5.70	20 26.10	4 56.14
18	9			11.8	28.3				23 11.41	17.60	1.66	V. 3 39.710	19 50.50	5.80	6.27	23 30.67	8 32.57
19	9		56.2		31.		5.5		25 30.97	17.60	3.12	IV. 2 10.865	49 55.96	5.70	11.41	25 51.69	38 43.07
20	7.8			29.	46.	3.2	20.9		27 46.24	17.61	1.27	IV. 5 48.255	10 48.08	5.60	4.76	28 5.12	59 28.46
21	9				37.3	54.3			28 20.10	17.61	1.64	IV. 4 40.891	18 28.55	5.58	6.08	28 39.35	7 10.21
22	9					55.5			29 21.24	17.61	2.27	VI. 3 28.224	31 51.11	5.53	8.30	29 41.12	20 34.94
23	9.10			36.8		11.7			33 54.12	17.61	1.27	IV. 5 48.222	10 50.09	5.30	4.78	34 13.00	59 30.17
24	9		41.3		15.3		50.		37 15.55	17.62	2.00	IV. 3 34.454	25 20.72	5.13	7.20	37 35.20	14 3.05
25	8					12.	29.3		37 54.74	17.62	3.09	V. 2 12.504	48 13.57	5.10	11.11	38 15.45	36 59.78
26	9				37.8	55.			39 37.77	17.62	1.59	V. 5 43.182	16 6.44	5.02	5.67	39 56.98	4 47.13
27	8.9			58.3	15.5	32.8			41 15.55	17.62	1.57	IV. 5 43.789	15 28.23	4.92	5.56	41 34.74	4 6.71
28	8			23.	40.1	57.	14.2		42 40.03	17.62	1.57	IV. 5 43.922	15 19.61	4.85	5.54	42 59.22	4 0.20
29	9						50.7		43 16.32	17.63	3.22	VI. 2 11.371	49 24.74	4.82	11.32	43 37.17	38 10.88
30	9			49.2		23.5			45 6.30	17.63	3.24	IV. 2 10.916	48 52.76	4.72	11.40	45 27.17	37 38.88
31	8.9			55.3	16.	33.7	49.8		46 15.70	17.63	2.25	IV. 3 30.752	29 12.82	4.66	7.86	46 35.55	17 55.34
32	8			28.3	45.3	2.6			49 45.40	17.63	1.85	IV. 4 39.219	20 13.37	4.46	6.36	50 4.88	8 54.19
33	7.8					16.5	34.		49 59.36	17.63	3.09	V. 2 14.450	46 11.60	4.45	10.76	50 20.08	34 56.81
34	8			18.8	36.	53.4	10.5		51 36.04	17.64	3.20	IV. 2 12.449	48 16.90	4.35	11.13	51 56.88	37 2.38
35	9			8.2	25.2		59.5		15 53 42.51	+17.64	+2.03	IV. 3 35.961	−23 45.96	− 4.23	− 6.95	15 54 2.18	−26 12 27.14

CORRECTIONS.

Date.	Corr. of Clock.	Hourly rate.	m	n	c	Zenith Point.	Mic. Co.
	h.	s.	s.	s.	s.	° ′ ″	r.
1848. June 5, · 0						359 59 61.34	29.9986

INSTRUMENT READINGS.

	Date.	CIRCLE.							Barom.	THERMOM.				
		A.	B.	C.	D.	E.	F.	Mean.		At.	Ex.	U.	L.	I.
	1848.	° ′ ″						″	in.	°	°	°	°	°
Zone 169	June 5, 14 50	75 9 64.6	61.2	66.1	59.8	60.1	61.4	62.20	29.890	75.5	69.3	74.4	74.2	
	15 0												68.9	
	15 20								29.888	74.5	68.			
	15 40												68.1	
	16 0								29.892			67.6		
	16 20												66.5	
	16 40	63.3	61.4	65.9	60.6	59.3	60.2	61.78	29.886	72.5	65.9	72.5	70.2	76.

REMARKS.

(169) 26. Right ascension differs $19^s.4$ from Arg. Z. 212, 8, and $18^s.7$ from Mer. Circle Z. 1848, May 27.

ZONE 169. JUNE 5. C. $D_0 = -25°\ 48'\ 30''$—Continued.

No.	Mag.	I.	II.	III.	IV.	V.	VI.	VII.	T.	a_1	a_2	Micr.		r.	i	d_1	d_2	Mean Right Ascension, 1850.0	Mean Declination, 1850.0
									h. m. s.	s.	s.			r.	′ ″	″	″	h. m. s.	° ′ ″
36	8		14.	31.5		5.5	22.4		15 53 48.43	+17.64	+2.26	IV.	3	31.378	−28 33.73	−4.22	−7.76	15 54 8.33	−26 17 15.71
37	9			15.	32.2				55 32.20	17.64	2.96	III.	2	17.361	43 8.54	4.12	10.23	55 52.80	31 52.89
38	9				0.2				56 0.12	17.64	3.01	IV.	2	16.657	43 52.89	4.10	10.36	56 20.77	26 32 37.35
39	9						14.2		55 39.83	17.65		VI.	3	14.		4.11		56 (0)	
40	7		4.3	21.5	39.3	55.8	13.		15 58 38.65	17.65	1.24	IV.	5	52.285	6 35.08	3.94	4.07	15 58 57.54	25 55 13.09
41	9			0.3	17.6				16 0 17.55	17.65	1.60	III.	4	45.479	13 40.02	3.84	5.26	16 0 36.80	26 2 19.12
42	7.8					3.	20.5	37.5	0 45.82	17.65	2.94	V.	2	18.676	41 46.39	3.82	10.00	1 6.41	30 30.21
43	9.10						39.2		2 4.85	17.65	3.10	VI.	2	15.573	45 1.18	3.74	10.56	2 25.60	26 33 45.48
44	9.10		42.2			33.8			14 16.72	17.67	1.36	IV.	5	52.544	6 18.75	2.96	4.01	14 35.75	25 54 55.72
45	9						42.5		15 8.20	17.68	2.87	V.	2	21.799	38 30.44	2.90	9.47	15 28.75	26 27 12.81
46	9					25.1	53.		16 18.35	17.68	2.19	V.	3	35.301	24 27.40	2.64	7.06	16 38.23	26 13 7.30
47	9					53.5			17 36.44	17.68	1.31	V.	5	52.722	6 7.44	2.75	3.98	17 55.46	25 54 44.17
48	1	0.8	17.5	35.	51.7	9.5	26.7	43.6	19 52.11	17.68	1.87	IV.	4	42.292	17 0.50	2.60	5.82	20 11.66	26 5 38.92
49	9			33.	50.	7.3			21 50.08	17.68	2.19	IV.	3	36.018	23 42.39	2.47	6.93	22 9.95	12 21.79
50	9			24.3		58.8			25 41.61	17.69	2.09	IV.	3	38.589	21 1.18	2.20	6.47	26 1.39	9 39.85
51	9		26.	43.2		17.8			28 0.51	17.69	3.60	IV.	2	8.680	52 13.08	2.05	11.80	28 21.80	40 56.93
52	8.9			20.7			12.		30 37.86	17.70	2.09	IV.	4	38.974	20 28.55	1.87	6.34	30 57.65	9 6.81
53	8.9			22.7			13.7	30.5	30 39.45	17.70	1.72	IV.	5	46.511	12 37.49	1.87	5.08	30 58.87	1 14.44
54	9		38.		12.6	30.	47.1		16 36 12.65	+17.71	+2.74	IV.	3	26.817	−33 19.63	−1.48	−8.57	16 36 33.10	−26 21 59.68

ZONE 170. JUNE 6. S. $D_0 = -23°\ 55'\ 30''$.

No.	Mag.	I.	II.	III.	IV.	V.	VI.	VII.	T.	a_1	a_2	Micr.		r.	i	d_1	d_2	Mean Right Ascension, 1850.0	Mean Declination, 1850.0
1	9			12.5		2.5			15 38 45.96	+18.42	+1.04	V.	2	12.088	−48 39.59	−30.81	−7.01	15 39 5.42	−24 44 47.41
2	9		7.5		41.				41 41.24	18.42	1.10	IV.	3	20.588	39 50.54	30.64	5.59	42 0.76	35 56.77
3	10				16.5				43 16.40	18.42	1.12	.	3	22.785	37 32.55	30.55	5.22	43 35.94	33 39.32
4	5					53.5			44 36.68	18.42	1.28	V.	6	50.046	8 55.39	30.49	0.68	44 56.38	4 56.56
5	7	41.5		15.5					49 15.44	18.42	1.17	.	3	32.322	27 34.50	30.23	3.61	49 35.03	23 38.34
6	9			18.					51 34.98	18.43	1.19	.	3	34.095	25 43.19	30.09	3.31	51 54.60	21 46.59
7	7				51.				54 34.09	18.43	1.19	.	3	37.300	22 21.95	29.92	2.78	54 53.71	18 24.65
8	9			48.					57 4.99	18.43	1.12	.	3	24.895	35 20.26	29.77	4.86	57 24.54	31 24.89
9	7			15.					15 58 32.10	18.44	1.27	.	6	52.600	7 17.84	29.68	0.24	15 58 51.81	3 17.76
10	7			15.5					16 0 50.02	18.44	1.22	.	5	44.390	14 50.56	29.56	1.59	16 1 9.68	10 51.71
11	9			21.					1 39.05	18.44	1.04	.	2	13.530	47 8.79	29.49	6.78	2 14.47	43 15.06
12	7	51.		24.5					4 24.69	18.44	1.28	.	6	52.795	6 2.47	29.31	0.18	4 44.41	2 1.96
13	8	49.5							6 23.60	18.45	1.03	.	1	12.668	48 1.15	29.19	6.94	6 43.08	44 7.28
14	8			45.					7 2.01	18.45	1.07	.	2	19.988	40 23.60	29.15	5.70	7 21.53	36 28.45
15	9			59.					12 33.06	18.45	1.06	.	1	19.038	41 22.43	28.81	5.87	12 52.57	37 27.11
16	10	23.							14 57.08	18.46	1.04	.	2	16.372	44 10.18	28.63	6.31	15 16.58	40 15.12
17	8			44.					16 1.08	18.46	1.23	.	5	48.265	10 47.33	28.56	0.94	16 20.77	6 46.83
18	7	27.							18 1.02	18.46	1.13	.	3	31.538	25 23.63	28.42	3.75	18 20.61	24 25.60
19	7			19.					19 36.04	18.46	1.20	.	4	43.720	15 30.24	28.32	1.79	19 55.70	11 30.26
20	4			29.5			20.5		20 46.60	18.46	0.99	.	1	10.122	50 41.55	28.23	7.40	21 6.05	46 47.18
21	8	12.					19.		24 45.64	18.47	1.03	II.	2	15.962	44 35.65	27.96	6.37	25 5.14	40 39.98
22	7		27.5						31 1.49	18.48	1.21	.	6	48.622	10 24.59	27.52	0.88	31 21.16	6 22.99
23	5					27.5			32 10.64	18.48	1.19	.	5	44.910	14 17.80	27.43	1.50	32 30.31	10 16.73
24	9		44.						37 18.06	18.49	1.04	.	5	20.975	39 21.25	27.05	5.50	37 37.59	35 23.80
25	6		13.	30.5					37 47.26	18.49	1.15	.	4	40.190	19 11.35	27.01	2.28	39 6.90	15 10.64
26	9		31.5						16 40 5.63	+18.50	+0.95	.	2	8.710	−52 10.45	−26.84	−7.59	16 40 25.08	−24 48 14.68

CORRECTIONS.

Date.	Corr. of Clock.	Hourly rate.	m	n	c	Zenith Point.	Mic. Co.
	h.	s.	s.	s.	s.	° ′ ″	r.
1848. June 6.	0					359 59 61.21	29.9986

INSTRUMENT READINGS.

Date.		CIRCLE.						Barom.	THERMOM.				
		A.	B.	C.	D.	E.	F.	Mean.		At.	Ex.	U.	L.	I.
	1848.	h. m.	° ′ ″						″	in.					
Zone 170	June 6. 15 38	73 17 {30. / 30.2}	{31.2 / 30.8}	{33.2 / 33.5}	{30.2 / 30.5}	{30. / 31.}	{26. / 26.}	30.21	30.058	68.0	58.	71.		71.5
	16 6								30.050	67.5	58.		70.	
	16 37								30.050	67.	58.			
	16 39								30.050	67.	58.			
	17 7								30.050	65.	57.8			
	17 50								30.048	64.8	56.8			
	17 51								30.042	64.	56.2			
	18 15								30.032	63.8	55.9			

REMARKS.

(169) 46. Time of transit over T. V assumed as 35ˢ.1 instead of 25ˢ.1.

(170) 9. Micrometer reading assumed as 51ʳ.600 instead of 52ʳ.600.

(170) 10. Transit over T. II assumed as recorded over T. III.

(170) 15. Transit over T. II assumed as recorded over T. III.

(170) 25. Minutes of transit assumed as 38, not 37.

ZONE 170. JUNE 6. S. $D_o = -23° 55' 30"$—Continued.

No.	Mag.	I	II	III	IV	V	VI	VII	T.	a_1	a_2	MICROMETER		r.	i	d_1	d_2	Mean Right Ascension, 1850.0	Mean Declination, 1850.0
									h. m. s.	s.	s.			r.	' "	"	"	h. m. s.	° ' "
27	7	·	·	·	·	34.	·	·	16 40 17.06	+18.50	+1.10	·	3	33.535	−26 18.14	−26.83	− 3.40	16 40 36.66	−24 22 18.37
28	6	·	·	35.5	·	·	·	·	41 52.50	18.50	1.03	·	2	22.042	38 14.84	26.71	5.35	42 12.03	34 16.90
29	8	·	·	11.	·	·	·	·	44 28.08	18.50	0.95	·	1	8.060	52 50.83	26.51	7.71	44 47.53	48 55.05
30	8	·	·	12.5	·	·	·	·	45 29.52	18.51	1.14	·	4	39.872	19 31.68	26.42	2.34	45 49.17	15 30.44
31	9	·	33.	·	·	24.	·	·	48 7.05	18.51	1.13	II.	4	37.768	21 43.22	26.22	2.70	48 26.60	17 42.14
32	5	·	4.8	22.	38.5	·	·	·	50 38.81	18.51	0.97	IV.	2	11.542	49 13.70	26.03	7.13	50 58.29	45 16.86
33	8	·	13.	·	46.5	·	·	·	52 46.69	18.52	1.12	IV.	4	38.685	20 46.74	25.86	2.55	53 6.33	16 45.15
34	8	·	55.	·	·	·	·	·	54 28.99	18.52	1.18	·	6	50.380	8 34.29	25.73	0.59	54 48.69	−4 30.61
35	7	·	·	·	·	16.	·	·	54 59.20	18.52	1.20	·	6	53.320	5 30.08	25.68	0.00	55 18.92	−1 25.85
36	7	·	·	7.	·	·	·	·	57 23.99	18.53	1.09	·	3	34.635	25 9.31	25.50	3.22	57 43.61	21 6.03
37	7	·	·	8.5	·	·	·	·	16 58 25.57	18.53	0.93	·	1	9.299	51 33.27	25.42	7.49	16 58 45.03	47 36.18
38	10	·	5.	·	·	·	·	·	17 7 39.07	18.54	0.98	·	2	17.960	42 30.36	24.67	6.05	17 7 58.59	38 31.08
39	10	·	·	·	·	·	0.5	·	9 43.58	18.55	1.08	·	3	35.540	24 12.33	24.49	3.08	10 3.21	20 9.90
40	7	·	36.5	·	10.	·	·	·	12 10.28	18.55	0.93	·	1	11.855	48 52.07	24.29	7.00	12 29.76	44 53.45
41	8	·	6.	·	40.	·	·	·	15 39.94	18.56	1.03	IV.	3	28.350	31 43.71	24.00	4.28	15 59.53	27 41.99
42	4	·	·	·	52.	·	·	·	16 51.90	18.56	1.18	·	6	52.812	6 1.72	23.90	0.15	17 11.64	1 55.77
43	9	·	56.	·	·	·	·	·	19 30.00	18.57	1.12	·	4	42.810	16 26.72	23.67	1.83	19 49.60	12 22.22
44	9	·	56.	·	·	·	·	·	23 30.00	18.58	1.12	·	4	42.962	16 17.25	23.33	1.80	23 49.70	12 12.38
45	9	·	·	·	42.	·	·	·	24 41.95	18.59	0.92	·	1	10.900	49 53.26	23.23	7.25	25 1.46	45 53.74
46	8	·	·	·	·	·	19.5	·	26 2.48	18.59	1.00	·	3	24.050	35 10.40	23.11	5.02	26 22.07	31 8.53
47	8	·	·	·	0.5	·	·	·	28 0.38	18.59	1.00	·	3	26.390	33 46.66	22.94	4.61	28 19.97	29 44.21
48	8	·	·	·	·	·	·	1.	40 27.24	18.62	1.09	·	6	43.843	13 19.42	21.84	1.38	40 46.05	9 12.64
49	8	·	54.5	28.	·	·	·	·	47 28.18	18.63	1.01	II.	3	32.210	27 41.47	21.20	3.63	47 47.82	23 36.30
50	6	·	5.5	39.5	·	·	·	·	50 30.44	18.64	1.05	II.	4	39.362	20 3.38	20.91	2.42	50 50.13	15 56.71
51	9	·	·	21.	·	·	·	·	51 20.88	18.65	1.07	·	5	43.482	15 47.69	20.85	1.72	51 40.60	11 40.26
52	7	·	33.	·	·	·	·	·	53 57.00	18.65	1.05	·	4	40.300	19 0.74	20.61	2.25	54 16.70	14 53.60
53	5	·	·	·	·	·	36.	·	53 19.10	18.65	1.05	·	4	38.858	20 36.13	20.66	2.51	53 38.80	16 29.30
54	6	·	·	·	·	·	37.	·	54 20.07	18.65	1.02	·	6	34.120	25 33.57	20.59	3.30	54 39.74	21 27.46
55	7	·	·	·	38.	·	·	·	55 37.86	18.66	1.00	·	4	31.672	28 6.82	20.44	3.72	55 57.52	24 0.08
56	8	·	·	·	·	50.	·	·	17 56 33.13	18.66	1.07	·	6	43.072	16 13.30	20.36	1.79	17 56 52.88	12 5.45
57	9	·	34.	·	·	·	·	·	18 0 8.11	18.67	0.88	·	2	12.730	47 58.40	20.03	6.07	18 0 27.66	43 55.40
58	8	·	·	·	·	4.	·	·	4 3.87	18.68	1.03	·	4	36.710	22 50.68	19.66	2.86	4 23.58	18 43.20
59	8	·	·	56.	·	·	·	·	7 13.10	18.69	1.11	·	6	51.490	7 24.86	19.36	0.35	7 32.00	3 14.57
60	8	·	24.	·	·	·	·	·	14 58.02	18.71	0.96	·	3	28.555	31 30.72	18.61	4.27	15 17.69	27 23.60
61	8	·	·	·	·	49.	·	·	15 32.01	18.71	0.95	·	3	26.708	33 26.34	18.55	4.57	15 51.67	29 19.46
62	7	·	10.	27.	·	·	·	·	19 44.02	18.72	0.93	·	6	23.568	36 43.63	18.15	5.13	20 3.67	32 36.91
63	6	·	·	36.3	·	·	·	·	20 53.36	18.72	1.06	·	6	45.552	13 37.58	18.03	1.37	21 13.14	9 26.98
64	5	·	10.	·	·	·	·	·	23 44.00	18.73	1.03	·	4	42.328	16 57.23	17.75	1.01	24 3.70	12 46.89
65	7	·	·	0.	·	·	·	·	24 17.03	18.73	1.03	·	5	41.418	17 57.11	17.69	2.06	24 36.70	13 46.86
66	4	·	·	·	·	56.5	·	·	24 22.74	18.73	1.06	·	6	46.562	12 34.20	17.60	1.10	24 42.53	8 23.14
67	6	·	·	·	·	·	·	52.	25 1.16	18.74	1.00	·	4	35.585	24 2.03	17.62	3.07	25 20.90	19 52.72
68	7	·	45.	·	18.5	·	·	·	32 18.70	18.75	0.92	·	3	26.630	33 31.50	16.90	4.59	32 38.37	29 22.99
69	7	·	·	11.	·	45.	·	·	32 28.12	18.75	1.06	·	6	48.288	10 45.88	16.88	0.89	32 47.93	6 33.65
70	9	·	·	24.5	·	·	·	·	35 41.46	18.76	0.94	·	3	29.640	30 22.72	16.55	4.08	36 1.16	26 13.35
71	8	·	27.	·	1.	·	·	·	38 0.50	18.77	0.92	II.	3	27.380	32 44.50	16.32	4.46	38 20.19	28 35.28
72	9	·	·	·	·	·	34.	·	39 0.77	18.78	0.84	·	2	14.302	46 20.94	16.22	6.70	39 19.79	42 13.86
73	7	·	·	·	4.	·	·	·	42 3.89	18.79	0.90	·	3	24.490	35 45.78	15.91	4.96	42 23.58	31 30.65
74	8	·	23.5	·	·	·	·	·	43 57.49	18.79	1.02	·	6	44.832	14 22.38	15.72	1.48	44 17.30	10 9.58
75	7	·	38.	·	·	·	·	·	18 47 12.13	+18.80	+0.79	·	1	8.200	−52 40.87	−15.39	−7.74	18 47 31.72	−24 48 34.00

CORRECTIONS.

Date.	Corr. of Clock.	Hourly rate.	m	n	c	Zenith Point.	Mic. Co.
1848.	h. s.	s.	s.	s.	s.	"	r.

INSTRUMENT READINGS.

Date.		CIRCLE							Barom.	THERMOM.				
		A.	B.	C.	D.	E.	F.	Mean.		At.	Ex.	U.	L.	I.
	1848,	° ' "						"	in.	°				
Zone 170	June 6, 18 47	·	·	·	·	·	·	·	30.040	63.8	55.3			
	19 1	·	·	·	·	·	·	·	30.050	64.0	54.8	67.	70.	
	19 24	·	·	·	·	·	·	·	30.052	64.5	54.0			
	20 0	73 17 {29.634 30.033}	34. 35.	35.5 30.5	30.8 32.5	32.5 25.5	25.5 25.8	31.22	30.050	64.2	53.5	67.		

REMARKS.

(170) 46. Micrometer reading assumed as 25ʳ.050 instead of 24ʳ.050.

(170) 47. Right ascension differs 16ˢ from Arg. Z. 222, 22; perhaps a thread interval in error.

(170) 48. Micrometer reading assumed as 45ʳ.842, not 43ʳ.842.

(170) 52. Right ascension differs 49ˢ.3 from mean of Arg. Z. 220, 72; 222, 56.

(170) 66. Transit over T. VI assumed as recorded over T. V.

ZONE 170. JUNE 6. S. $D_0 = -23^\circ\,55'\,30''$—Continued.

No.	Mag.	I.	II.	III.	IV.	V.	VI.	VII.	T.	a_1	a_2	Mic.	n	r.	i	d_1	d_2	Mean Right Ascension, 1850.0.	Mean Declination, 1850.0.
									h. m. s.	s.	s.			r.	′ ″	″	″	h. m. s.	° ′ ″
76	7		39.						18 53 13.06	+18.82	+0.87		2	21.698	−38 35.97	−14.77	−5.44	18 53 32.75	−24 34 26.18
77	8		45.5						54 19.49	18.82	1.02		4	46.102	13 0.21	14.66	1.26	54 39.33	8 46.13
78	8		50.		23.5				57 23.68	18.83	0.91	IV.	3	30.612	29 21.67	14.33	3.90	57 43.42	25 9.90
79	9						35.5		18 58 1.76	18.84	0.94		3	34.672	25 6.49	14.27	3.21	18 58 21.54	20 53.97
80	6		58.		31.6				19 1 31.84	18.84	0.91	IV.	3	30.328	29 39.61	13.90	3.95	19 1 51.59	25 27.46
81	8		42.						3 16.11	18.85	0.80		1	12.633	46 3.41	13.71	7.01	3 35.76	43 54.13
82	5		30.5	47.5		21.5			6 4.51	18.86	0.90			F. wire	30 0.09	13.42	4.00	6 24.27	25 47.51
83	8		44.				2.		9 18.12	18.87	1.00	II.	5	45.925	13 13.77	13.07	1.28	9 37.99	8 58.12
84	6		40.	57.					11 14.00	18.87	0.88	III.	3	26.255	32 52.34	12.88	4.66	11 33.75	28 39.93
85	4		14.5						15 48.57	18.88	0.82		1	9.015	51 51.65	12.40	5.92	16 8.27	47 39.97
86	4					21.			16 4.11	18.89	0.95		4	40.090	19 18.95	12.37	2.28	16 23.95	15 3.60
87	6						6.		17 32.26	18.89	0.92		3	35.078	24 41.00	12.22	3.13	17 52.07	20 26.35
88	7		32.						20 6.04	18.90	0.86		2	24.980	35 10.10	11.95	4.87	20 25.80	30 56.92
89	6			13.					21 29.96	18.91	0.88		3	39.812	30 11.80	11.80	4.03	21 49.75	25 57.63
90	7						19.5		21 45.77	18.91	0.89		3	31.578	28 20.68	11.77	3.75	22 5.57	24 6.20
91	6		36.					1.	25 10.08	18.92	0.96		4	44.200	14 59.66	11.40	1.57	25 29.96	10 42.63
92	9				12.				30 11.87	18.93	0.85		3	27.270	32 51.46	10.87	4.49	30 31.65	28 36.82
93	5		38.5		13.				33 12.78	18.94	0.77	IV.	2	13.015	47 41.28	10.55	6.94	33 32.49	43 28.77
94	4		24.	40.					44 57.50	18.97	0.89		4	36.700	22 50.25	9.28	2.85	45 17.36	18 32.38
95	7			33.		6.5			45 49.80	18.98	0.89		4	37.552	21 57.47	9.16	2.71	46 9.67	17 39.36
96	9					57.			47 39.85	18.99	0.75		2	12.788	47 55.57	9.01	6.98	47 59.59	43 41.56
97	8		26.						19 50 0.00	+19.00	+0.87		3	33.935	−25 53.03	−8.72	−3.34	19 51 19.87	−24 21 35.09

ZONE 171. JUNE 12. S. $D_0 = -23^\circ\,18'\,0''$.

No.	Mag.	I.	II.	III.	IV.	V.	VI.	VII.	T.	a_1	a_2	Mic.	n	r.	i	d_1	d_2	Mean Right Ascension, 1850.0.	Mean Declination, 1850.0.
1	6			43.					16 55 59.04	+18.47	+0.88		2	17.525	−42 58.27	−18.45	−6.06	16 55 19.29	−24 1 22.78
2	9				57.				55 56.89	18.47	1.31		5	47.378	11 43.13	18.45	1.19	56 16.67	23 30 2.77
3	8			57.5	31.				16 59 31.10	18.47	1.07		3	30.825	29 8.18	18.12	3.87	16 59 50.64	47 30.17
4	10			43.					17 4 59.92	18.48	1.15		4	36.742	22 48.18	17.60	2.90	17 5 19.55	41 8.68
5	7				20.		43.		5 19.65	18.48	1.00		3	25.778	34 24.80	17.57	4.71	5 39.13	23 52 47.08
6	3		59.						8 32.94	18.49	0.80	II.	2	12.092	48 38.46	17.26	6.98	8 52.23	24 7 2.70
7	5					55.			8 38.08	18.49	0.90		3	24.562	35 41.09	17.25	4.90	8 57.56	23 54 3.24
8	10		39.						11 12.94	18.49	0.81		2	12.402	48 19.14	17.00	6.93	11 32.24	24 6 43.07
9	9			23.					12 40.01	18.49	1.36		6	51.940	6 56.42	16.86	0.42	12 58.86	23 25 13.70
10	4		19.						14 35.92	18.49	1.14		3	36.260	23 27.39	16.66	2.97	14 55.55	41 47.02
11	7				23.5				15 23.36	18.49	1.07		3	31.358	28 34.99	16.58	3.79	15 42.92	46 55.36
12	5					57.			16 40.18	18.50	1.07		3	33.122	28 49.55	16.47	3.82	16 59.75	47 9.84
13	6		48.						21 21.83	18.50	1.12		3	34.992	24 46.78	15.99	3.19	21 41.45	43 5.06
14	3				56.5				21 56.30	18.50	1.03		3	28.015	32 4.54	15.94	4.33	22 15.89	23 50 24.81
15	8		42.						23 58.95	18.51	0.85		2	16.342	44 12.44	15.72	6.27	24 18.31	24 2 34.43
16	7			4.	38.				31 21.03	18.52	1.07	III.	3	33.202	26 39.29	14.97	3.49	31 40.62	23 44 57.75
17	6		15.5				6.		34 49.20	18.52	1.20	II.	4	41.356	17 58.24	14.61	2.15	35 8.98	23 36 15.00
18	8		21.5						36 55.42	18.53	0.83		2	14.558	46 3.89	14.38	6.56	37 14.78	24 4 24.83
19	5		54.		27.5				40 27.70	18.53	0.75		1	10.078	50 43.61	14.01	7.32	40 46.98	24 9 4.94
20	6		37.					44.	42 10.62	18.53	1.17		4	39.882	19 30.49	13.81	2.37	42 30.32	23 37 46.67
21	5		4.	21.		54.5			49 37.78	18.54	0.95	III.	3	23.91	36 22.04	13.23	5.01	47 57.27	54 40.28
22	8				7.				49 50.18	18.54	1.13		5	37.142	22 25.52	12.99	2.84	50 9.85	40 41.35
23	3					35.5	52.		17 50 18.54	+18.54	+1.03		3	30.492	−29 29.13	−12.93	−3.92	17 50 38.11	−23 47 45.98

CORRECTIONS.

Date.	Corr. of Clock.	Hourly rate.	m	n	c	Zenith Point.	Mic. Co.
	h.	s.	s.	s.	s.	° ′ ″	r.
1848. June 12.	0					359 59 64.08	30.0018

INSTRUMENT READINGS.

	Date.	CIRCLE.							Barom.	THERMOM.				
		A.	B.	C.	D.	E.	F.	Mean.		At.	Ex.	U.	L.	I.
	1848.	h. m.	° ′ ″						″	in.	°	°	°	°	°
Zone 171	June 12.	16 50	72 39 60.	62.3	64.2	58.3	56.8	57.2	59.80	30.074	73.0	60.8			70.
		17 21								30.078	67.8	60.		66.0	
		18 0			58.2					30.072	67.0	58.2			65.5
		18 20								30.066	66.8	58.5			
		18 43								30.060	66.2	57.2			
		19 15	59.5	64.5	64.5	59.8	58.5	57.0	60.63	30.062	66.2	56.8			

REMARKS.

(170) 83. Time of transit over T. IV assumed as 52ˢ instead of 2ˢ.
(170) 84. Micrometer reading assumed as 27ʳ, not 26ʳ.
(170) 85. Micrometer reading assumed as 0ʳ, not 19ʳ.
(170) 97. Minutes of transit assumed as 51 instead of 50.
(171) 1. Minutes of transit assumed as 54 instead of 55.
(171) 5. Time of transit over T. VI assumed as 53 instead of 43.
(171) 12. Declination differs 2′ from Arg. Z. 220, 25.
(171) 17. Transit over T. V assumed to have been recorded as over T. VI.
(171) 21. Minutes assumed as 47, not 49.

ZONE 171. JUNE 12. S. $D_0 = -23° 18' 0''$—Continued.

No.	Mag.	I.	II.	III.	IV.	V.	VI.	VII.	T.	a_1	a_2	Mic.	r.	i	d_1	d_2	Mean Right Ascension, 1850.0	Mean Declination, 1850.0
									h. m. s.	s.	s.		r.	' ''	''	''	h. m. s.	° ' ''
24	7		11.						17 54 44.96	+18.54	+0.72	1	8.340	−52 32.71	−12.42	−7.62	17 55 4.22	−24 10 52.75
25	10					19.			55 1.90	18.55	0.74	1	9.612	51 14.65	12.39	7.41	55 21.19	24 9 34.45
26	7						34.		55 0.43	18.55	1.09	4	34.805	24 50.73	12.39	3.20	17 55 20.07	23 43 6.32
27	5		14.						17 59 47.91	18.56	0.86	2	18.440	42 0.50	11.84	5.94	18 0 7.33	24 0 18.28
28	6					24.5			18 0 7.71	18.56	1.19	4	42.425	16 52.53	11.81	1.96	0 27.46	23 35 6.30
29	10						35.		1 1.41	18.56	1.19	4	42.376	16 55.85	11.70	1.96	1 21.16	35 9.51
30	3					31.2			2 14.37	18.56	1.09	3	34.518	25 16.52	11.57	3.25	2 34.02	23 43 31.34
31	10		2.5						5 36.41	18.57	0.83	1	16.654	43 51.25	11.17	6.24	5 55.81	24 2 8.66
32	8					36.			6 19.10	18.58	0.98	3	27.443	32 40.41	11.09	4.45	6 38.66	23 50 55.95
33	6						38.		7 4.40	18.58	0.90	3	22.052	38 18.22	10.99	5.35	7 23.88	23 56 34.56
34	10			34.					13 50.97	18.59	0.60	2	13.730	46 56.06	10.19	6.70	14 10.36	24 5 12.95
35	10		4.						16 37.82	18.59	1.21	5	43.842	15 24.51	9.86	1.69	16 57.62	23 33 36.06
36	6				14.				17 13.88	18.60	1.23	5	46.412	12 43.76	9.79	1.30	17 33.71	30 54.85
37	9		15.5	32.5					18 49.38	18.60	1.17	4	38.572	20 52.89	9.59	2.56	19 9.09	23 39 5.01
38	9		20.5		54.				20 54.20	18.60	0.71	1	9.722	51 7.19	9.34	7.40	21 13.51	24 9 23.93
39	7				53.5		27.		21 53.38	15.60	1.26	6	52.230	6 38.46	9.23	0.34	22 13.24	23 24 48.02
40	5		50.		24.				24 23.95	18.61	0.73	1	10.802	49 58.10	8.91	7.21	24 43.29	24 8 14.22
41	8			2.					27 18.90	18.62	0.94	3	25.671	34 31.65	8.56	4.73	27 38.46	23 52 44.94
42	8		50.						28 23.82	18.62	1.24	6	46.218	12 55.57	8.43	1.33	28 43.68	31 5.33
43	4				3.5		37.		29 3.40	18.62	1.14	4	39.995	19 24.54	8.35	2.34	29 23.16	37 35.23
44	5		50.3		23.				32 23.55	18.62	0.87	2	20.598	39 45.03	7.93	5.58	32 43.04	23 57 58.54
45	7			12.		45.			33 28.44	18.63	0.76	1	12.505	48 7.11	7.80	6.89	33 47.83	24 6 21.80
46	9		5.						35 38.81	18.63	1.32	6	53.342	5 28.32	7.53	0.16	35 58.76	23 23 36.01
47	9		50.						37 23.84	18.64	1.00	3	30.554	26 22.63	7.31	3.76	37 43.48	46 33.70
48	9		10.5						43 44.32	18.65	1.20	5	44.842	14 21.75	6.51	1.52	44 4.17	23 32 29.78
49	10					15.			43 57.89	18.65	0.71	1	9.052	51 49.70	6.47	7.54	44 17.25	24 10 3.71
50	10		57.						46 30.88	18.66	0.89	3	22.360	37 59.46	6.16	5.30	46 50.43	23 56 10.92
51	8		30.5			5.			50 4.60	18.67	1.26	6	49.322	9 40.70	4.70	0.77	50 24.53	27 46.17
52	7		25.		59.				51 58.86	18.67	1.27	6	51.040	7 52.74	4.45	0.50	52 18.80	25 57.69
53	6					8.			56 51.25	18.68	1.23	5	48.624	10 24.75	3.84	0.88	57 11.16	26 29.50
54	6			4.		37.			18 59 20.64	18.69	1.28	6	51.782	7 6.34	3.52	0.38	18 59 40.61	25 10.24
55	8						44.		19 0 10.37	18.69	1.28	6	51.552	7 20.91	3.41	0.42	19 0 30.34	25 24.74
56	7			21.5					2 38.43	18.70	0.85	2	19.710	40 41.10	3.09	5.73	2 57.98	58 49.92
57	8			23.					3 39.92	18.70	0.87	2	21.408	38 54.72	2.96	5.46	3 59.49	23 57 3.14
58	7		45.						9 18.95	18.71	0.70	1	9.989	50 49.13	2.22	7.37	9 38.36	24 8 53.72
59	6					10.			9 53.13	18.71	0.96	3	28.802	31 14.98	2.14	4.19	10 12.80	23 49 21.31
60	7				40.5				19 11 40.38	+18.71	+0.90	3	24.930	−35 18.00	−1.91	−4.85	19 11 59.99	−23 53 24.76

CORRECTIONS.

Date.	Corr. of Clock.	Hourly rate.	m	n	ϵ	Zenith Point.	Mic. Co.
1848.	h.	s.	s.	s.	s.	° ' ''	r.

REMARKS.

(171) 28. Right ascension differs 10s.4 from Arg. Z. 220, 29.

(171) 47. Micrometer reading assumed as 31r.554, not 30r.554.

INSTRUMENT READINGS.

Date.	CIRCLE.							Barom.	THERMOM.				
	A.	B.	C.	D.	E.	F.	Mean.		At.	Ex.	U.	L.	I.
1848. h. m.	° ' ''						''	In.	°				

ZONE 172. JUNE 15. C. $D_o = -26°\ 26'\ 0''$.

No.	Mag.	I.	II.	III.	IV.	V.	VI.	VII.	T. (h. m. s.)	a_1	a_2	Mic.	n	r	′ ″	i	d_1	d_2	Mean Right Ascension, 1850.0 (h. m. s.)	Mean Declination, 1850.0 (° ′ ″)
1	7			38.	55.3	11.6	28.5		14 30 54.79	+18.44	+1.38	IV.	5	50.959	− 2 44.13	7.49	+ 0.57		14 31 14.61	−26 28 51.07
2	8				19.3	37.	54.4		33 19.54	18.44	0.98	V.	2	18.092	42 23.08	7.43	6.12		33 38.96	27 8 36.63
3	9			18.2		53.3			34 35.72	18.44	0.98	V.	2	19.056	41 22.43	7.40	5.95		34 55.14	27 7 35.78
4	8.9			30.	47.	4.			37 47.04	18.44	1.26	IV.	4	48.479	10 32.14	7.32	0.75		38 6.74	26 36 40.21
5	8				36.	53.5	10.8		38 36.09	18.44	1.00	V.	2	22.516	37 45.54	7.31	5.33		38 55.53	27 3 58.18
6	5			53.2	10.5		45.		41 10.50	18.44	0.83	V.	2	7.205	53 45.62	7.24	8.07		41 29.77	20 0.93
7	9				17.2				42 17.07	18.44	1.00	IV.	2	25.532	34 40.43	7.20	4.80		42 36.51	27 0 52.43
8	9				45.2		19.8		42 45.20	18.44	1.03	VI.	3	27.878	32 12.63	7.19	4.38		43 1.67	26 58 24.20
9	9.10						21.5		42 47.03	18.44	1.01	VI.	3	25.635	34 33.47	7.19	4.78		43 6.48	27 0 45.44
10	9.10			44.1	1.		35.3		49 1.08	18.44	1.19	IV.	4	46.089	13 3.92	7.02	1.17		49 20.71	26 39 12.11
11	9				9.2	27.	44.		49 9.46	18.44	1.14	IV.	4	42.175	17 8.15	7.02	1.85		49 29.04	43 17.02
12	9.10							30.5	49 36.58	18.44	1.10	VII.	4	37.972	21 32.06	7.01	2.58		49 58.12	26 47 41.65
13	9.10				44.2	1.3			52 43.98	18.44	0.90	V.	2	18.791	41 39.12	6.92	5.99		53 3.32	27 7 52.03
14	9		45.9	3.5	20.		45.		54 20.51	18.44	0.82	IV.	2	12.277	48 27.68	6.85	7.17		54 39.77	14 41.70
15	9		46.		.2		.3		54 20.71	18.44	0.82	IV.	2	12.369	48 21.90	6.85	7.15		54 39.97	27 14 35.90
16	9		20.4	37.3	54.6	12.2	29.3		14 57 54.79	18.44	1.00	IV.	3	32.462	27 25.71	6.74	3.56		14 58 14.23	26 53 36.01
17	9.10				34.				15 4 33.85	18.44	0.93	IV.	3	27.848	32 14.96	6.50	4.39		15 4 53.22	26 58 25.85
18	8				23.	40.5	57.4		6 22.97	18.44	0.86	V.	3	24.290	35 56.20	6.43	− 5.02		6 42.29	27 2 9.65
19	8		45.	2.	19.2	36.2	53.5	10.8	11 19.22	18.44	1.18	IV.	5	56.312	2 22.21	6.24	+ 0.64		11 38.84	26 28 27.81
20	9						57.		12 22.50	18.44	0.82	VI.	2	21.154	39 11.09	6.19	− 5.58		12 41.76	27 5 22.86
21	9		43.4	1.	18.3			10.2	14 18.24	18.44	1.03	IV.	4	42.395	16 54.02	6.11	+ 1.80		14 37.71	26 43 1.93
22	8				44.	1.	18.		14 43.72	18.44	1.00	V.	4	39.631	19 47.74	6.09	2.29		15 3.16	45 56.12
23	9		16.	33.5	50.3				18 50.58	18.44	0.97	III.	4	37.849	21 38.64	5.90	2.61		19 9.99	47 47.15
24	9						27.		18 52.54	18.44	0.85	VI.	3	26.349	33 48.73	5.91	4.66		19 11.83	59 59.30
25	9					32.2			25 32.08	18.44	1.03	IV.	5	46.571	12 33.72	5.61	1.06		25 51.55	26 38 40.39
26	8		37.5	55.	12.2	29.7	47.1		30 12.32	18.44	0.70	IV.	2	17.703	42 47.22	5.39	6.21		30 31.46	27 8 58.82
27	8			38.8	56.1	13.2			37 56.08	18.44	0.98	IV.	5	48.166	10 53.60	4.99	0.79		38 15.50	26 36 59.38
28	9			42.	0.	17.			39 17.03	18.44	0.67	III.	2	19.049	41 22.56	4.92	5.97		39 36.14	27 7 33.45
29	9.10						16.8		39 42.33	18.44	0.75	VI.	3	25.591	34 36.22	4.90	4.80		40 1.52	27 0 45.92
30	9				0.2	34.6			43 17.51	18.44	0.94	IV.	2	47.085	12 1.39	4.72	0.97		43 36.89	26 38 7.08
31	7			46.5	3.3	21.	38.		45 3.56	18.44	0.79	IV.	3	32.723	27 9.15	4.62	3.51		45 22.79	53 17.28
32	9							59.3	45 7.42	18.44	0.93	VII.	5	46.602	12 31.33	4.62	1.07		45 26.79	26 38 37.02
33	8		11.2	26.6	46.	3.5	20.8	38.	47 46.00	18.44	0.59	IV.	2	14.841	45 46.65	4.47	6.74		48 5.03	27 11 57.86
34	8	9.5	26.4	43.2	0.9	18.4	35.4	52.7	50 0.93	18.45	0.95	IV.	5	50.112	8 51.36	4.35	0.43		50 20.33	26 34 56.14
35	8					37.3	54.8	11.9	51 37.41	18.45	0.92	V.	5	48.102	10 57.55	4.26	− 0.78		51 56.78	37 2.59
36	8	58.8	16.2	33.5					55 33.52	18.45	0.94	III.	5	53.029	5 48.05	4.04	+ 0.09		55 52.91	31 52.00
37	9				40.7		14.2		55 40.16	18.45	0.90	IV.	5	48.732	10 17.94	4.04	− 0.64		55 59.51	36 22.62
38	8.9					19.		53.2	56 1.58	18.45	0.93	V.	5	52.332	6 32.11	4.01	0.00		56 20.96	32 36.12
39	9					1.5			15 57 44.28	18.45	0.64	V.	4	43.942	15 17.09	3.91	− 1.52		15 58 3.57	41 22.45
40	7		12.5	30.	47.2	4.4	21.7		16 0 47.24	18.45	0.93	IV.	5	54.345	4 25.72	3.74	+ 0.35		16 1 6.62	30 29.11
41	8.9			46.2		21.			2 3.67	18.45	0.78	IV.	3	40.339	19 11.41	3.68	− 2.16		2 22.90	45 17.25
42	9				49.2	6.7	23.8		1 49.12	18.45	0.78	V.	4	40.302	19 5.76	3.68	2.16		2 8.35	45 11.60
43	9.10							57.2	2 5.33	18.45	0.89	VII.	5	51.320	7 35.21	3.66	0.19		2 24.67	26 33 39.06
44	9						13.8		3 56.43	18.45	0.62	V.	3	25.562	34 38.36	3.56	4.79		4 15.50	27 0 46.71
45	8				48.2	6.	23.5		5 48.61	18.45	0.73	V.	4	36.402	23 10.52	3.43	2.85		6 7.79	26 49 16.80
46	8			41.	57.8	15.6	32.4		14 58.08	18.46	0.71	IV.	3	37.917	21 43.16	2.92	2.58		15 17.25	47 48.66
47	8.9		22.	39.	56.3				17 39.08	18.46	0.66	IV.	3	35.210	24 33.22	2.76	3.07		17 58.20	50 39.05
48	8.9	26.1	43.8	1.	18.5				16 21 1.01	+18.47	+0.64	IV.	3	35.268	−24 29.64	2.50	− 3.06		16 21 20.12	−26 50 35.26

CORRECTIONS.

Date.	Corr. of Clock. (h.)	Hourly rate. (s.)	m (s.)	n (s.)	c (s.)	Zenith Point. (° ′ ″)	Mic. Co. (r.)
1848. June 15,	0 . .	. .	. .	. .	. .	359 59 61.83	29.9945

INSTRUMENT READINGS.

Date.	CIRCLE. A.	B.	C.	D.	E.	F.	Mean.	Barom. (In.)	THERMOM. At.	Ex.	U.	L.	I.
Zone 172 — 1848. June 15, 14 30								30.040	81.3	81.8			
14 40	75 47 {31.9 / 33.2}	{25.5 / 26.4}	{29.8 / 31.1}	{23.9 / 25.2}	{28. / 28.8}	{28.2 / 29.2}	28.43			81.7	82.	77.4	
15 0								30.040	81.2	80.9			
15 20									80.7				
15 40								30.038	80.7	81.2			
16 0									80.7				
16 20	{31.2 / 32.6}	{25.7 / 25.9}	{29.8 / 31.2}	{23.9 / 25.3}	{28.3 / 29.}	{27.5 / 29.2}	28.30	30.044	80.5	80.0	81.	77.	73.

REMARKS.

(172) 1. Micrometer reading assumed as 55ʳ.959, not 56ʳ.959.

(172) 15. Transits over T.'s IV and VI assumed as at 20ˢ.2 and 45ˢ.3 respectively, on the supposition that two components were observed.

(172) 17. Right ascension differs 9ˢ.5 from Arg. Z. 373. 54.

(172) 28. Declination in error about 40″.

(172) 41. Transits over T.'s III and V assumed as recorded over T.'s IV and VI, and minutes as 2, not 1.

Therm. readings assumed to be transposed.

ZONE 173.   JUNE 16, S. $D_a = -28°\ 18'\ 30''$.

No.	Mag.	I.	II.	III.	IV.	V.	VI.	VII.	T.	a_1	a_2	MICROMETER	r.	i	d_1	d_2	Mean Right Ascension, 1850.0.	Mean Declination, 1850.0.
									h. m. s.	s.	s.		r.	′ ″	″	″	h. m. s.	° ′ ″
1	7			3.					15 50 2.96	+18.30	+0.04	1	8.920	− 52 59.53	− 6.85	−14.34	15 50 21.30	−29 11 50.62
2	5		28.5			4.			52 3.85	18.30	0.55	II. 4	35.650	23 50.14	6.74	8.91	53 22.70	28 42 41.79
3	8		20.5						54 55.81	18.30	0.80	6	46.978	12 7.67	6.63	6.70	55 14.91	28 30 51.00
4	9		23.						56 58.45	18.31	0.15	2	15.648	44 55.41	6.53	12.83	57 16.91	29 3 44.77
5	9				53.				15 58 52.88	18.31	0.73	5	44.110	15 8.14	6.44	7.27	15 59 11.92	28 33 51.85
6	8		11.						16 0 46.37	18.31	0.35	3	25.960	34 13.32	6.35	10.79	16 1 5.03	28 53 0.46
7	3			7.5					1 25.19	18.31	0.17	2	18.368	42 5.39	6.32	12.28	1 43.67	29 0 53.99
8	9					58.			2 40.47	18.31	0.66	4	41.605	17 43.86	6.26	7.75	2 59.44	28 36 27.87
9	7				1.5				4 1.37	18.31	0.62	4	38.212	21 16.55	6.19	8.41	4 20.30	40 1.15
10	9			52.					6 9.68	18.32	0.64	4	40.400	18 58.80	6.07	7.97	6 28.64	28 37 42.84
11	6		18.				28.		10 53.14	18.32	0.03	1	10.728	50 2.73	5.83	13.81	11 11.49	29 8 52.37
12	5		22.5			15.5			15 57.82	18.33	0.12	II. 2	16.358	44 11.00	5.55	12.68	16 16.27	29 2 59.23
13	4		13.2		49.				17 48.74	18.33	0.22	2	22.404	37 51.80	5.45	11.49	18 7.29	28 56 38.74
14	7							35.	17 41.92	18.33	+0.14	1	17.720	42 46.59	5.45	12.41	18 0.39	29 1 34.45
15	6		24.		59.5				20 59.46	18.33	−0.01	1	10.668	50 6.56	5.27	13.82	21 17.76	29 8 55.65
16	7		7.8			50.8			22 43.18	18.33	+0.50	3	35.560	24 11.20	5.18	8.92	23 2.01	28 42 55.31
17	9				36.				26 35.86	18.33	0.33	3	27.982	32 6.61	4.96	10.39	26 54.52	50 51.96
18	9			31.					28 48.69	18.34	0.57	5	40.930	18 27.48	4.84	7.88	29 7.60	37 10.20
19	7				24.5				29 24.38	18.34	0.58	5	42.148	17 11.36	4.80	7.65	29 43.30	35 53.81
20	6				28.				30 27.87	18.35	0.56	4	39.832	19 34.69	4.73	8.11	30 46.78	38 17.53
21	6		48.						32 23.35	18.35	0.35	3	29.212	30 49.50	4.62	10.15	32 42.05	49 34.27
22	10							17.	32 24.20	18.35	0.56	4	39.958	19 27.36	4.62	8.07	32 43.11	38 10.05
23	7						35.		37 59.94	18.35	0.55	4	40.340	19 3.56	4.28	7.99	38 18.85	37 45.83
24	6					30.			38 12.44	18.36	0.46	4	37.305	22 13.85	4.27	8.58	38 31.26	40 56.70
25	9		49.						41 24.33	18.36	+0.37	3	33.010	26 51.08	4.08	9.40	41 43.06	28 45 34.56
26	7		14.5						43 59.09	18.36	−0.07	1	12.438	48 15.71	3.92	13.47	44 18.28	29 7 3.10
27	7				23.				44 22.04	18.36	−0.07	1	11.512	49 15.08	3.89	13.65	44 41.23	8 2.62
28	7					34.			45 16.21	18.37	+0.02	2	16.020	44 32.95	3.77	12.75	45 34.60	3 19.47
29	6							39.	46 45.91	18.37	0.04	2	17.594	42 54.25	3.74	12.43	47 4.32	29 1 40.42
30	9		13.5						48 48.81	18.37	0.55	4	43.013	16 14.05	3.61	7.48	49 7.73	28 34 55.14
31	7	9.	27.				29.		50 44.32	18.37	0.73	III. 6	53.232	5 35.41	3.50	5.50	51 3.42	24 14.41
32	8					24.			52 23.86	18.38	+0.37	3	33.388	26 27.70	3.39	9.33	52 42.61	28 45 10.42
33	8						24.		52 48.83	18.38	−0.02	2	14.218	46 26.15	3.36	13.11	53 7.19	29 5 12.62
34	6		35.						55 10.32	18.38	+0.46	4	38.512	20 56.67	3.21	8.35	56 29.16	28 39 38.23
35	9					42.			57 41.87	18.39	0.54	5	41.753	17 36.02	3.06	7.72	58 0.80	36 16.80
36	8							57.	16 58 39.43	+18.39	+0.39	4	36.246	−23 20.25	− 3.00	− 8.79	16 58 58.21	−28 42 2.04

CORRECTIONS.

Date.	Corr. of Clock.	Hourly rate.	m	n	c	Zenith Point.	Mic. Co.
	h.	s.	s.	s.	s.	° ′ ″	r.
1848. June 16,	0	. .	. .	. .	. .	359 59 60.65	29.9967

INSTRUMENT READINGS.

Date.		CIRCLE.							Barom.	THERMOM.				
		A.	B.	C.	D.	E.	F.	Mean.		At.	Ex.	U.	L.	I.
	1848. h. m.	° ′ ″						″	in.	°	°	°	°	°
Zone 173	June 16, 15 45	77 39 60.	52.2	58.2	48.0	49.8	56.5	54.12	30.008	78.	.	78.	79.5	.
	16 15								30.004	83.	78.8			82.
	16 41								30.006	82.9	77.9			
	17 0		58.0	54.0	57.8	49.8	50.6	55.7	54.32	30.000	81.6	76.9		

REMARKS.

(173) 1. Transit over T. IV assumed as recorded over T. III; and micrometer reading as $7^r.920$, not $8^r.920$, to agree with B. A. C. 5297; M. C. Z., 1846, May 4; M. C. Z., 1847, April 25.

(173) 2. Transit over T. IV assumed to have been recorded as over T. V; and minutes as 53, not 52.

(173) 16. Transit over T. V assumed as at $0^s.8$ instead of $50^s.8$.

(173) 26. Transit over T. II assumed as $24^s.5$, not $14^s.5$.

(173) 28. Minutes assumed as 45 instead of 46.

(173) 31. Time of transit over T. VI assumed as 19^s instead of 29^s.

(173) 34. Minutes assumed as 56, not 55.

Zone 174. June 20. C. $D_0 = -23° 18′ 0″.$

No.	Mag.	I.	II.	III.	IV.	V.	VI.	VII.	T. (h. m. s.)	a_1 (s.)	a_2 (s.)	Micrometer wire	n	r.	i (′ ″)	d_1 (″)	d_2 (″)	Mean R.A. 1850.0 (h. m. s.)	Mean Decl. 1850.0 (° ′ ″)
1	8			12.5	29.7	45.8	2.8	19.6	15 0 46.15	−19.30	+1.36	IV.	5	52.699	−6 8.89	−13.69	6.39	15 1 6.81	−23 24 28.07
2	8		54.2	11.	28.	4.7			4 11.11	19.29	1.34	IV.	5	50.879	8 3.08	13.53	6.69	4 31.74	26 23.30
3	9						3.	20.3	4 46.44	19.29	1.14	V.	3	29.712	30 17.88	13.50	10.05	5 6.87	48 41.43
4	9		7.7	23.1	40.7	57.3			7 40.69	19.29	1.33	IV.	5	50.198	8 46.03	13.36	6.79	8 1.31	27 6.18
5	9			11.4	27.6	44.7			9 27.89	19.29	1.20	IV.	3	36.433	23 16.54	13.28	8.98	9 48.38	.41 38.80
6	8				1.6	18.2	34.7		10 1.32	19.29	1.19	V.	3	35.355	24 24.00	13.25	9.15	10 21.80	42 46.40
7	8				32.7	49.2	5.5		10 32.29	19.29	1.19	V.	3	35.021	24 44.83	13.23	9.20	10 52.77	43 7.26
8	9.10					20.2	36.8		14 20.06	19.29	1.26	V.	4	44.459	14 44.85	13.04	7.70	14 40.63	33 5.59
9	8.9		24.4	41.3	58.5	15.5			19 58.36	19.29	1.06	IV.	3	23.107	37 12.48	12.76	11.10	20 18.71	55 36.34
10	9				42.5			16.	20 42.54	19.29	1.29	VI.	4	46.153	12 58.63	12.72	7.43	21 3.12	31 18.78
11	8				4.2	20.8	37.3		23 3.95	19.29	1.37	V.	5	55.166	3 34.11	12.60	6.01	23 24.61	21 52.72
12	9						57.		23 23.37	19.29	1.35	VI.	5	52.708	6 8.20	12.58	6.39	23 44.01	24 27.17
13	9								25	19.29	1.03	VII.	2	20.261	40 7.16	12.56	11.57	24 (16)	55 31.29
14	8.9					6.5	23.		25 49.55	19.29	1.22	V.	3	39.079	30 30.18	12.46	8.55	26 10.06	38 51.19
15	9				23.2			11.	27 23.26	19.29	1.31	VII.	4	48.842	10 9.83	12.38	7.00	27 43.66	28 29.21
16	9				25.7	13.		16.8	27 26.01	19.29	1.27	VII.	4	44.108	15 7.07	12.38	7.75	27 46.57	23 33 27.20
17	9							59.5	29 8.54	19.29	0.93	VI.	2	9.786	51 3.94	12.29	13.26	29 28.76	24 9 29.49
18	3			48.	4.3		38.		31 4.53	19.29	1.38	IV.	5	57.416	1 12.89	12.19	5.65	31 25.20	23 19 30.73
19	9				45.	1.5	17.6		32 44.52	19.29	1.12	V.	3	29.653	30 21.65	12.09	10.06	33 4.93	48 43.80
20	9					2.3	18.8		33 45.35	19.29	1.13	V.	3	31.421	28 30.84	12.04	9.78	34 5.77	46 52.66
21	9				3.2	20.2	36.5		35 3.00	19.29	1.06	V.	3	23.767	36 30.83	11.97	11.00	35 23.44	54 53.80
22	9.10				8.2	25.			37 8.14	19.29	1.20	V.	5	38.429	15 51.12	11.86	7.38	37 28.63	34 10.36
23	7		39.3	56.3	12.6	29.5	46.3		39 12.88	19.29	1.36	IV.	5	55.118	3 37.06	11.74	6.01	39 33.53	21 54.81
24	9			12.5	29.3				41 29.32	19.29	1.27	III	4	44.951	14 12.97	11.61	7.62	41 49.88	23 32 32.20
25	7		2.6	19.5	36.3	53.5	10.3		44 36.50	19.29	0.97	IV.	2	14.195	46 27.14	11.44	12.54	44 56.76	24 4 51.12
26	7							30.5	44 39.92	19.29	1.28	VII.	5	45.030	13 13.45	11.44	7.47	45 0.49	23 31 32.36
27	9.10		19.		53.5				46 53.10	19.29	1.30	II.	5	50.396	8 33.29	11.31	6.76	47 13.69	26 51.36
28	9		41.3	58.4	15.3	32.1			50 15.22	19.28	1.14	IV.	3	32.602	27 16.81	11.12	9.58	50 35.64	45 37.51
29	8.9		16.	33.2	50.2	6.3			51 49.85	19.28	1.09	IV.	3	28.182	31 54.19	11.02	10.29	52 10.22	50 15.58
30	9.10			17.					52 16.87	19.28	1.08	IV.	3	27.221	32 54.47	10.99	10.45	52 37.23	51 15.91
31	9.10					56.			52 22.42	19.28	1.06	VI.	3	34.749	35 28.95	10.99	10.85	52 42.76	53 50.82
32	9					55.8	12.7		53 39.05	19.28	1.14	V.	3	33.192	26 39.67	10.91	9.49	53 59.47	45 0.07
33	8		43.5	0.1	16.8	33.8	50.6		56 16.99	19.28	1.11	IV.	3	29.967	30 2.07	10.74	10.00	56 37.38	48 22.81
34	9.10			19.2	36.2				57 36.08	19.28	1.15	III.	3	33.679	26 9.24	10.66	9.42	57 56.51	44 29.32
35	9					11.	28.5		58 11.30	19.28	1.26	V.	4	45.030	14 8.83	10.63	7.61	58 31.84	23 32 27.07
36	7							22.3	15 58 31.44	19.28	0.98	VII.	2	15.738	44 50.65	10.61	12.29	15 58 51.70	24 3 13.55
37	7		15.6	32.5	49.2	6.2	23.2	40.	16 0 49.30	19.28	0.90	IV.	2	8.441	52 28.20	10.47	13.51	16 1 9.48	24 10 52.18
38	9		17.2	34.	50.7				2 50.86	19.29	1.27	III.	4	45.522	13 18.28	10.34	7.45	3 11.42	23 31 36.07
39	8				24.2	41.2	58.2		4 24.29	19.29	0.98	V.	2	16.942	43 35.14	10.23	12.12	4 44.56	24 1 57.49
40	9						1.2		4 27.63	19.29	1.07	VI.	3	26.518	33 38.13	10.23	10.57	4 47.99	23 51 58.93
41	8		31.7	48.8	5.3	22.	39.5		7 5.49	19.29	1.05	IV.	3	24.484	35 46.23	10.06	10.89	7 25.63	54 7.18
42	9.10				55.				7 54.67	19.29	1.09	IV.	3	27.708	32 23.79	10.00	10.38	8 15.25	50 44.17
43	9.10					43.5			8 26.65	19.29	1.12	V.	3	31.018	28 56.01	9.97	9.84	8 47.06	47 15.82
44	9			8.8	26.2				10 42.92	19.29	1.00	III.	2	19.002	41 25.50	9.82	11.78	11 3.21	59 47.10
45	6			59.5	16.2	33.4	50.2	7.3	11 16.47	19.29	1.11	IV.	3	30.189	29 48.27	9.75	9.07	11 36.87	48 8.02
46	9					32.2			11 58.56	19.29	1.36	VI.	5	56.386	2 17.44	9.73	5.79	12 19.21	23 20 32.96
47	9.10					30.5	47.2		13 13.53	19.29	0.97	IV.	2	17.511	42 59.45	9.65	12.02	13 33.79	24 1 21.12
48	9		27.	44.	0.7				16 0.86	19.29	0.94	III.	2	12.271	48 27.74	9.45	12.87	16 21.09	6 50.06
49	9			1.8	18.7	35.5			16 19 35.64	+19.29	+0.89	III.	2	7.812	−53 7.13	−9.20	−13.61	16 19 55.82	−24 11 29.94

CORRECTIONS.

Date	Corr. of Clock	Hourly rate	m	n	c	Zenith Point	Mic. Co.
	h.	s.	s.	s.	s.	′ ″	r.
1848 June 20,	0					359 59 65.00	29.9977

REMARKS.

(174) 2. Time of transit over T. VI assumed as 44ˢ.7 instead of 4ˢ.7.

(174) 13. Time of transit assumed as 23ᵐ 57ˢ, on supposition of identity with Arg. Z. 301, 115.

(174) 22. Micrometer reading assumed as 43ʳ.429, not 38ʳ.429.

INSTRUMENT READINGS.

Date	A.	B.	C.	D.	E.	F.	Mean.	Barom.	At.	Ex.	U.	L.	I.
	° ′ ″						″	in.	°	°	°	°	°
Zone 174 1848 June 20, 15 0								29.870	78.6	73.8	78.5	76.8	80.2
15 10	72 39 65.8	58.7	53.9	56.8	52.9	59.9	58.00						
15 20													
15 40								29.848	77.7	73.4	74.		
16 0										73.2			
16 20	65.2	59.1	53.8	57.8	52.1	59.5	57.92	29.854	77.	73.	77.	74.5	
16 40										72.8			
17 0								29.856	76.2	72.5			
17 20	63.9	59.2	53.4	57.8	51.4	58.9	57.43	29.858	76.	72.3	77.4	75.2	

Zone 174. June 20. C. $D_0 = -23° 18' 0''$—Continued.

No.	Mag.	SECONDS OF TRANSIT. I. II. III. IV. V. VI. VII.	T.	a_1	a_2	MICROMETER.		r	i	d_1	d_2	Mean Right Ascension, 1850.0	Mean Declination, 1850.0
			h. m. s.	s.	s.			r.	''	''	''	h. m. s.	° ' ''
50	9	.. 10.2 27. 44.3 ..	16 24 27.12	+19.29	+0.99	IV.	3	20.742	−39 40.76	− 8.84	−11.50	16 24 47.40	−23 58 1.10
51	9.10	.. 35.5 52.5 9.2 ..	29 9.26	19.29	1.09	III.	3	28.040	31 6.50	8.49	10.18	29 29.64	49 25.17
52	9	.. 20.5 37.3 54.2 ..	30 54.22	19.30	1.21	III.	4	41.909	17 23.91	8.36	8.09	31 14.73	23 35 40.36
53	9	.. 27.2 44.2 ..	32 1.15	19.30	0.93	III.	2	12.774	47 56.01	8.27	12.80	32 21.38	24 6 17.08
54	7	.. 37. .. 27.5 44.3 ..	32 10.65	19.30	0.89	V.	2	8.949	51 56.35	8.26	13.42	32 30.84	24 10 18.03
55	9.10	.. 5.7 22.8 39.2 ..	34 39.44	19.30	1.15	III.	3	34.624	25 10.00	8.06	9.26	34 59.89	23 43 27.32
56	9	.. 47.5 4.5 21.3 ..	38 21.31	19.30	1.15	III.	3	36.109	23 36.81	7.78	9.01	38 41.76	41 53.60
57	9	.. 12.2 29.2 46. 2.5 ..	40 45.93	19.30	1.18	IV.	3	39.165	20 25.04	7.58	8.53	41 6.41	38 41.75
58	9.10	.. 5.4 . 39.5 ..	46 22.47	19.30	1.11	IV.	3	31.608	28 19.18	7.10	9.74	46 42.88	46 36.02
59	9	.. 46.3 3.8 20.5 ..	49 20.40	19.31	1.12	III.	3	33.179	26 40.73	6.85	9.50	49 40.83	44 57.08
60	9	.. .. 43.2 0.5 ..	50 26.66	19.31	1.24	V.	5	46.975	12 8.26	6.83	7.29	49 47.21	23 30 22.38
61	8	.. 28.6 45.2 . 19.5 ..	54 2.38	19.31	0.96	III.	2	17.582	42 54.94	6.43	12.01	54 22.65	24 1 13.38
62	9	.. .. 45.7 ..	54 12.03	19.31	0.94	VI.	2	14.457	46 9.34	6.41	12.51	54 32.28	4 28.26
63	8	.. .. 33.4 ..	54 50.75	19.31	0.95	IV.	2	17.420	43 4.60	6.33	12.04	55 20.01	24 1 22.97
64	9	.. .. 46.5	55 55.92	19.31	1.24	VII.	3	47.295	11 47.84	6.25	7.23	56 16.47	23 30 1.32
65	10	.. 28.5 ..	58 45.49	19.32	1.26	III.	3	49.168	9 50.60	6.00	6.93	59 6.07	28 3.53
66	10	.. . 16.3 ..	58 59.58	19.32	1.31	V.	5	53.660	5 8.60	5.97	6.18	59 20.21	23 20.75
67	9	.. 20.5	16 59 29.90	19.32	1.09	VII.	3	30.729	29 13.44	5.93	9.89	16 59 50.31	47 20.26
68	9	.. 93? ..	17 0 35.75	19.32	1.07	VI.	3	29.299	30 43.73	5.83	10.12	17 0 56.14	48 59.68
69	9	.. 42.5 .. 18.8 35.5 ..	5 18.54	19.32	1.04	IV.	3	25.675	34 31.40	5.37	10.71	5 38.90	23 52 47.48
70	7	.. 58.1 14.8 31.8 48.5 ..	8 31.75	19.32	0.91	IV.	2	12.095	48 38.78	5.06	12.93	8 51.98	24 6 56.77
71	9	.. 58. 14.7 . 48.4 ..	8 31.65	19.32	0.91	IV.	2	12.158	48 35.08	5.06	12.92	8 51.88	24 6 53.06
72	9	.. . 0.2 28.5	8 37.21	19.32	1.02	VI.	3	24.440	35 48.55	5.06	10.90	8 57.55	23 54 4.51
73	9	.. 22.5 38.5 55.5 ..	12 38.89	19.33	1.29	IV.	3	51.932	6 56.98	4.66	6.47	12 59.51	25 8.11
74	8	.. 1.5 18. 34.5 51.7 ..	14 34.88	19.33	1.14	IV.	3	36.152	23 34.11	4.45	9.01	14 55.35	41 47.57
75	9	.. 22.5 39.5 55.8 ..	15 22.42	19.33	1.09	V.	3	31.282	28 39.57	4.37	9.80	15 42.84	23 46 53.74
76	5	.. 35.2 52. 9.5 25.7 ..	16 52.15	19.33	0.95	IV.	3	16.915	43 36.64	4.22	12.14	17 12.43	24 1 53.00
77	9	.. 47.2 4.5 20.5 ..	21 20.94	19.34	1.12	III.	3	34.806	24 52.81	3.76	9.22	21 41.40	23 43 5.79
78	7	.. 55.2 12.1 29.5 ..	17 21 55.41	+19.34	+1.05	V.	3	27.889	−32 12.25	− 3.69	−10.35	17 22 15.80	−23 50 26.29

Zone 175. June 24. C. $D. = -22° 40' 40''$.

No.	Mag.	SECONDS OF TRANSIT. I. II. III. IV. V. VI. VII.	T.	a_1	a_2	MICROMETER.		r	i	d_1	d_2	Mean Right Ascension, 1850.0	Mean Declination, 1850.0
1	7.8	.. 11.5 28.2 45.2 2.4 18.8 ..	15 0 45.25	+21.51	+0.17	IV.	2	17.004	−43 31.06	−15.06	− 6.04	15 1 6.93	−23 24 32.16
2	7.8	.. 53.7 10.3 27.4 ..	4 10.42	21.51	0.14	IV.	2	15.240	45 21.88	15.03	6.33	4 32.07	23 26 23.24
3	9	.. .. 13.7 ..	4 39.57	21.51	0.48	VI.	2	41.829	17 29.92	15.02	2.15	5 1.56	22 58 27.09
4	8.9	.. 23.3 . 57. 13.7 ..	7 46.14	21.51	0.12	IV.	2	14.530	46 6.33	14.97	6.43	8 1.77	23 27 7.73
5	8	.. 8.2 25.3 ..	15 42.02	21.50	0.48	III.	4	41.916	17 23.46	14.81	2.14	16 4.00	22 58 20.41
6	8	.. 28.7 45.2 2.2 18.3 ..	15 45.27	21.50	0.60	IV.	5	50.536	8 24.82	14.81	0.80	16 7.37	22 49 20.43
7	9	.. 25.5 41.3 . 15.5 ..	20 41.88	21.49	0.06	IV.	2	10.472	50 20.85	14.68	7.07	21 3.45	23 31 22.60
8	8	.. 39.7 56.3 13.6 30.1 ..	21 56.55	21.49	0.36	IV.	3	32.627	27 15.25	14.63	3.58	22 18.40	8 13.46
9	8	.. . 3.2 ..	23 3.12	21.49	0.20	IV.	2	19.464	40 56.97	14.59	5.65	23 24.81	21 57.21
10	9	.. .. 55.8	23 22.32	21.49	0.18	VI.	2	16.945	43 35.01	14.58	6.05	23 43.09	23 24 35.64
11	9	.. .. 54.7	23 4.36	21.49	0.50	VII.	4	43.032	16 14.61	14.59	1.96	23 26.35	22 57 11.16
12	9	.. 48.7 5.8 .. 56.5? ..	27 22.72	21.48	0.10	III.	2	12.169	48 34.08	14.44	6.81	27 44.30	23 29 35.33
13	9	.. . 25. .. 50.5 ..	27 25.46	21.48	0.07	VI.	2	8.397	52 31.20	14.44	7.40	27 47.01	33 33.04
14	9	.. .. 39.5 ..	29 56.39	21.48	0.12	III.	2	13.841	46 49.10	14.35	6.54	30 17.99	27 49.99
15	9	.. .. 5.3 ..	30 22.13	21.48	0.24	III.	3	22.901	37 25.34	14.34	5.11	30 43.85	18 24.79
16	9	.. .. 46.5 ..	15 30 29.68	+21.48	+0.30	V.	3	27.294	−32 49.76	−14.33	− 4.42	15 30 51.46	−23 13 48.51

CORRECTIONS.

Date.	Corr. of Clock.	Hourly rate.	m	n	t	Zenith Point.	Mic. Co.
	h.	s.	s.	s.	s.	° ' ''	r.
1848. June 24.	0					359 59 64.68	30.0043

REMARKS.

(174) 60. Minutes assumed as 49, not 50.
(174) 72. Time of transit over T. VI assumed as 10ˢ.2 instead of 0ˢ.2.
(175) 11. Minutes should probably be 24, not 23; *vide* Arg. Z. 209, 56.

INSTRUMENT READINGS.

Date.		CIRCLE. A.	B.	C.	D.	E.	F.	Mean.	Barom.	THERMOM. At.	Ex.	U.	L.	I.
	1848. h. m.	° ' ''						''	in.	°	°	°	°	°
Zone 175	June 24, 15 0 72	2 {39.7 / 40.2}	{32. / 31.9}	{37. / 37.7}	{32.1 / 34.1}	{29.1 / 29.5}	{35.0 / 36.0}	34.52	30.106	79.5	72.9	79.5	78.8	80.
	15 20												71.2	
	15 40								30.100	77.5	70.4			
	16 0	{38.5 / 39.3}	{33. / 33.1}	{37.5 / 37.7}	{33. / 34.2}	{29.9 / 30.3}	{34.2 / 35.5}	34.68				70.1	76.5	75.3
	16 20								30.102	76.	68.9			
	16 40										68.8			

ZONE 175. JUNE 24. C. $D_0 = -22° 40′ 40″$—Continued.

No.	Mag.	I.	II.	III.	IV.	V.	VI.	VII.	T.	a_1	a_2	MICROMETER.	i	d_1	d_2	Mean Right Ascension, 1850.0	Mean Declination, 1850.0
									h. m. s.	s.	s.	r ′ ″	″	″	″	h. m. s.	° ′ ″
17	8			47.		20.5	37.3		15 31 3.77	+21.48	+0.24	V. 3 21.796 −38 34.46	−14.31	5.29		15 31 25.49	−23 19 34.06
18	9				41.2	58.			32 41.22	21.48	0.64	V. 5 52.683 6 9.88	14.23	0.45		33 3.34	22 47 4.56
19	9		42.1	59.	15.2				36 15.57	21.48	0.47	III. 5 38.646 20 57.61	14.08	2.64		36 37.52	23 1 54.33
20	7.8		38.4	55.2	11.8		45.5		39 11.99	21.47	0.22	IV. 2 19.432 40 58.96	13.94	5.66		39 33.68	21 58.56
21	9						9.4		39 35.99	21.47	0.33	IV. 3 27.984 32 6.48	13.93	4.30		39 57.79	23 13 4.71
22	9				25.5	42.1			41 25.42	21.47	0.63	V. 5 52.020 6 51.53	13.84	0.56		41 47.52	22 47 45.93
23	7		5.5	22.1	39.3	56.	12.8		44 39.16	21.47	0.09	IV. 2 10.237 50 35.59	13.69	7.12		45 0.72	23 31 36.40
24	9			45.3	2.3				46 2.19	21.47	0.56	III. 5 44.798 14 24.70	13.62	1.67		46 24.22	22 55 19.99
25	9			36.3	53.1	9.8			46 53.06	21.47	0.45	IV. 4 38.470 21 0.37	13.58	2.67		47 14.98	23 1 56.62
26	9							42.5	46 51.67	21.47	0.15	VII. 2 14.684 45 56.80	13.58	6.40		47 13.49	26 56.78
27	8				32.3	49.5	6.		48 32.50	21.47	0.43	V. 3 35.387 24 21.99	13.50	3.17		48 54.40	23 5 18.66
28	9		55.4	12.1	29.				53 29.01	21.47	0.67	III. 5 54.182 4 35.77	13.24	0.21		53 51.15	22 45 29.22
29	8		27.2	44.	1.		34.5		56 0.92	21.46	0.29	IV. 4 24.957 34 13.56	13.10	4.62		56 22.67	23 15 11.28
30	7.8			31.3	48.2	5.7	22.1		56 48.44	21.46	0.35	IV. 3 29.428 30 36.07	13.06	4.08		57 10.25	11 33.21
31	9.10					51.	7.2		57 33.98	21.46	0.33	V. 3 26.938 33 11.91	13.01	4.48		57 55.77	14 9.40
32	7.8		51.3	7.8	25.1	41.8	58.5		59 24.93	21.46	0.28	IV. 3 24.412 35 50.76	12.91	4.87		59 46.67	23 16 48.54
33	9.10						30.3		15 59 5.83	21.46	0.66	VI. 5 53.162 5 39.81	12.93	0.38		15 59 27.95	22 46 33.12
34	10				57.?				16 1 56.89	21.46	0.63	IV. 5 51.368 7 33.09	12.77	0.64		16 2 18.98	22 48 26.50
35	9					6.5	23.5		2 49.72	21.46	0.10	V. 2 10.115 50 43.30	12.72	7.16		3 11.28	23 31 43.18
36	8.9		8.1	24.7	41.5				4 41.61	21.46	0.21	III. 2 18.239 42 13.49	12.61	5.87		5 3.28	23 23 11.97
37	9.10			43.2	0.1				7 0.08	21.46	0.05	III. 5 52.909 5 55.51	12.47	−0.39		7 22.19	22 46 48.37
38	9				34.5	51.3	8.		7 34.53	21.46	0.69	V. 5 55.650 3 3.66	12.44	+0.02		7 56.68	43 56.08
39	8				52.5	9.	25.5	42.6	9 9.06	21.46	0.56	IV. 4 45.988 13 8.38	12.35	−1.48		9 31.08	22 54 2.21
40	8				58.	15.2	31.7		11 58.16	21.46	0.24	V. 2 20.696 39 39.57	12.18	5.48		12 19.86	23 20 37.23
41	8.9			15.5	32.	48.8	5.5		13 32.13	21.46	0.67	IV. 5 54.102 4 40.85	12.08	0.20		13 54.96	22 45 33.13
42	8		29.3		3.				16 2.92	21.46	0.41	II. 3 34.189 25 37.27	11.92	3.33		16 24.79	23 6 32.52
43	7		40.6		14.	30.8		4.6	16 14.10	21.46	0.42	IV. 3 34.886 24 53.37	11.91	3.22		16 35.98	5 48.50
44	9		40.6		14.	30.8		4.6	16 14.10	21.46	0.46	IV. 3 37.301 22 22.07	11.91	2.85		16 36.03	3 16.83
45	9			33.5	50.3	7.2			31 50.33	21.45	0.50	IV. 3 38.835 20 45.55	10.87	2.85		32 12.28	23 1 39.27
46	9		53.5	10.1	26.5	43.7			34 26.90	21.45	0.63	IV. 5 49.421 9 34.87	10.69	0.94		34 48.98	22 50 26.50
47	8		11.8	20.9	34.5	3	2.5		35 45.64	21.45	0.58	IV. 4 46.016 13 6.62	10.59	1.48		36 7.67	22 53 58.69
48	9		18.2				8.2		40 34.90	21.45	0.38	VI. 3 29.970 30 1.44	10.25	4.00		40 56.73	23 10 55.69
49	8		52.	8.8	25.5	42.5	59.3		45 25.65	21.45	0.31	IV. 3 25.466 34 44.59	9.88	4.70		45 47.41	23 15 39.17
50	7		49.4	7.	23.8	40.4	57.	13.8	47 23.50	21.45	0.59	IV. 5 45.611 13 33.90	9.73	1.54		47 45.60	22 54 25.17
51	9			9.	26.	42.5			49 25.78	21.45	0.12	IV. 2 11.246 49 32.33	9.58	6.09		49 47.35	23 30 28.90
52	9		39.2	55.		29.			51 11.96	21.45	0.31	IV. 3 24.137 36 7.87	9.45	4.93		51 33.72	17 2.25
53	8.9		26.2	43.	59.3				52 42.81	21.45	0.48	IV. 3 36.804 22 53.01	9.34	2.93		53 4.74	23 3 45.28
54	8		39.5	56.		29.8			53 56.21	21.45	0.57	IV. 4 44.175 15 2.24	9.24	1.76		54 18.23	22 55 53.24
55	8		1.5	18.4	35.5				55 1.69	21.45	0.39	V. 3 30.465 29 30.82	9.14	3.93		55 23.53	23 10 23.89
56	9				12.				55 38.48	21.45	0.15	VI. 2 11.582 49 11.44	9.10	6.93		56 0.08	30 7.47
57	10			42.7					58 41.95	21.45	0.17	IV. 2 13.542 47 8.29	8.86	6.62		59 3.57	28 3.77
58	10				31.8				58 53.33	21.45	0.24	VI. 2 17.918 42 32.11	8.54	5.91		16 59 20.02	23 26.86
59	9								16 59	21.45	0.51	VII. 4 38.922 20 37.50	8.67	−2.59		17 0	23 1 23.76
60	9			14.7	30.5				17 2 57.54	21.45	0.72	V. 5 55.347 3 22.80	8.51	+0.01		3 19.71	22 44 11.30
61	9		49.9						12 5.75	21.45	0.69	III. 5 53.452 5 21.67	7.76	−0.27		12 27.89	22 46 9.70
62	9			54.3	11.7				12 37.78	21.45	0.20	V. 2 16.254 44 18.47	7.71	6.21		12 59.43	23 25 12.39
63	8		46.2	3.	20.				13 46.32	21.45	0.63	V. 5 48.292 10 45.75	7.61	1.09		14 8.40	22 51 34.45
64	8.9		18.	34.8	51.7	8.2			16 34.82	21.45	0.51	IV. 3 38.649 20 57.36	7.37	2.62		16 56.78	23 1 47.35
65	9		49.7	7.	23.3	40.7			17 19 23.57	+21.45	+0.30	IV. 3 22.504 −37 50.37	−7.13	−5.20		17 19 45.32	−23 18 42.70

CORRECTIONS.

Date.	Corr. of Clock.	Hourly rate.	m	n	c	Zenith Point.	Mic. Co.
1848.	h.	s.	s.	s.	s.	s.	° ′ ″	r
1848.	h.	s.	s.	s.	s.		° ′ ″	r

REMARKS.

(175) 29. Micrometer reading assumed as 25ˢ.957, not 24ˢ.957.

(175) 33. Right ascension differs 1ᵐ from Arg. Z. 397,49; should probably be 16ʰ 0ᵐ.

[(175) 59. 16ˢ after wire VII.]

INSTRUMENT READINGS.

Date.	CIRCLE.							Barom.	THERMOM.				
	A.	B.	C.	D.	E.	F.	Mean.		At.	Ex.	U.	L.	I.
1848. h. m.	° ′ ″						° ′ ″	in.	°	°	°	°	°
Zone 175 June 24, 17 0	72 2 {38.2 / 38.1}	{33.8 / 33.9}	{37.2 / 37.0}	{33.2 / 34.4}	{30.0 / 30.0}	{34.5 / 35.2}	34.67	30.100	74.3	68.4	76.2	75.7	
17 20										67.9			
17 40								30.100	72.5	67.3			
18 0	{38.1 / 38.2}	{33.1 / 32.9}	{37.5 / 38.1}	{33.9 / 34.4}	{30.0 / 29.7}	{33.8 / 34.2}	34.49	30.098	72.	67.	74.8	72.8	79.2

ZONE 175. JUNE 24. C. $D_0 = -22° 40' 40''$—Continued.

No.	Mag.	I.	II.	III.	IV.	V.	VI.	VII.	T.	a_1	a_2	MICROMETER.	i	d_1	d_2	Mean Right Ascension, 1850.0	Mean Declination, 1850.0
									h. m. s.	s.	s.	r. ′ ″	′ ″	″	″	h. m. s.	° ′ ″
66	9.10			22.7	39.5				17 20 39.50	+21.46	+0.66	III. 5 50.191	− 8 46.54	− 7.03	− 0.79	17 21 1.62	−22 49 34.16
67	8		2.3	18.3	35.1	52.2	8.3		24 35.30	21.46	0.59	IV. 4 44.913	14 15.78	0.68	1.63	24 57.35	22 55 4.09
68	9		2.	18.5	35.3				28 18.55	21.46	0.31	IV. 3 23.688	36 35.98	6.36	5.02	28 40.32	23 17 27.36
69	9.10	54.5	11.5	28.2					30 28.21	21.46	0.55	III. 4 41.861	17 26.86	6.16	2.12	30 50.22	22 58 15.14
70	8			36.	52.5	9.2	26.		32 52.53	21.46	0.33	IV. 3 24.852	35 22.89	5.94	4.83	33 14.32	23 16 13.66
71	9.10				37.4	54.			35 37.31	21.46	0.67	V. 5 50.636	8 16.50	5.69	0.72	35 59.44	22 49 4.91
72	9.10			7.1	23.2	40.5			38 23.61	21.46	0.60	IV. 4 45.308	13 51.18	5.43	1.56	38 45.67	22 54 38.17
73	8					10.2	27.2		38 53.60	21.46	0.42	V. 3 30.397	29 35.09	5.39	3.94	39 15.48	23 10 24.42
74	8					8.2	25.2		39 51.54	21.46	0.30	V. 3 22.405	37 56.45	5.30	5.22	40 13.30	18 46.97
75	8.9					3.5	20.2		40 46.76	21.46	0.48	V. 3 35.912	23 48.84	5.22	3.06	41 8.70	23 4 37.12
76	8					50.2	12.8		41 39.44	21.47	0.62	V. 4 47.696	11 21.50	5.14	1.18	42 1.53	22 52 7.82
77	9		58.8	15.7	32.4	49.1			45 32.43	21.47	0.57	IV. 4 43.261	15 59.67	4.76	1.69	45 54.47	22 56 46.32
78	8		44.	0.5	17.2				47 0.52	21.47	0.29	IV. 2 19.595	40 48.69	4.62	5.67	47 22.28	23 21 38.98
79	8.9		6.1	23.	39.4	56.3			49 39.59	21.47	0.32	IV. 3 23.326	36 55.87	4.37	5.07	50 1.38	17 48.31
80	9		6.8	23.8	40.5	57.2			51 40.48	21.47	0.15	IV. 2 9.179	51 41.86	4.18	7.35	52 2.10	32 33.39
81	8.9			16.5	33.5				51 16.54	21.47	0.42	V. 3 29.662	30 21.08	4.14	4.00	(52) 38.43	11 9.28
82	9					11.5	28.2		52 54.76	21.47	0.52	V. 4 38.	21	4.05	2.72	53 16.75	1 46.77
83	8					11.7	28.6		52 55.06	21.47	0.54	V. 4 38.857	20 36.20	4.05	2.59	53 17.07	23 1 22.84
84	8					25.			54 8.28	21.47	0.57	V. 4 42.052	17 15.82	3.93	2.09	54 30.32	22 58 1.84
85	7				2.7	18.5			54 45.54	21.47	0.67	V. 5 49.633	9 21.42	3.86	0.87	55 7.68	22 50 6.15
86	8	43.5	0.2	16.8		50.8			58 17.06	21.48	0.47	III. 4 33.612	26 13.49	3.51	3.42	58 39.01	23 7 0.42
87	7.8			22.8	39.3				58 22.64	21.48	0.64	V. 4 46.362	12 45.39	3.50	1.40	58 44.76	22 53 30.29
88	8			32.8	49.3	6.4	23.2		59 32.78	21.48	0.62	V. 4 45.498	13 39.58	3.39	1.53	59 54.88	22 54 24.50
89	8.9						10.5		17 59 19.85	21.48	0.21	VII. 2 13.897	46 46.09	3.41	6.59	17 59 41.54	23 27 36.09
90	8.9					56.	12.6		18 1 39.11	21.48	0.28	V. 2 18.749	41 41.80	3.19	5.84	18 2 0.87	22 30.83
91	7.8		0.5	17.5	34.	50.8	7.5		18 3 34.09	+21.48	+0.44	IV. 3 31.836	−38 4.75	− 2.98	− 3.71	18 3 56.01	−23 8 51.44

ZONE 176. JUNE 26. S. $D_0 = -26° 25' 40''$.

No.	Mag.	I.	II.	III.	IV.	V.	VI.	VII.	T.	a_1	a_2	MICROMETER.	i	d_1	d_2	Mean Right Ascension, 1850.0	Mean Declination, 1850.0
1	7				52.		27.		16 33 9.52	+20.09	+0.76	III. 3 32.170	−27 43.95	−20.48	− 3.61	16 33 30.37	−26 53 48.04
2	4			21.	38.				34 38.16	20.09	0.61	III. 2 16.514	44 1.66	20.38	6.44	34 58.86	27 10 8.48
3	7					45.5	3.		35 10.88	20.09	0.62	. 2 16.410	44 8.75	20.35	6.46	35 31.59	10 15.56
4	7					14.	31.5		36 56.73	20.09	0.60	. 2 14.603	46 1.86	20.25	6.79	37 17.42	27 12 8.90
5	8		16.5						42 8.32	20.09	0.72	. 6 28.334	31 37.49	19.90	4.31	42 29.13	26 57 41.70
6	5				13.				42 12.89	20.09	0.95	. 5 48.368	10 40.97	19.90	0.72	42 33.93	36 41.59
7	6					14.			42 39.54	20.09	0.87	. 4 40.108	19 18.01	19.87	2.19	43 0.50	26 45 20.07
8	7					38.			44 45.64	20.09	0.57	. 1 8.020	52 54.91	19.73	7.99	45 6.30	27 19 2.63
9	8			2.					47 19.40	20.09	0.92	. 5 42.782	16 31.24	19.57	1.72	47 40.41	26 42 32.53
10	9					8.5			48 51.21	20.09	0.82	. 3 33.515	26 19.46	19.48	3.37	49 12.12	52 22.31
11	9					18.			49 43.56	20.09	0.79	. 3 29.482	30 32.16	19.42	4.10	50 4.44	26 56 35.70
12	6			21.		13.			51 38.44	20.09	0.76	III. 3 24.966	35 15.80	19.30	4.92	51 59.29	27 1 20.02
13	8					39.			52 4.54	20.09	0.92	. 6 41.773	17 34.57	19.27	1.90	52 25.55	26 43 35.74
14	5					59.			53 24.55	20.09	0.84	. 3 33.342	26 30.00	19.18	3.41	53 45.48	52 32.59
15	8					10.	27.5		54 35.57	20.09	0.94	VI. 4 42.835	16 26.72	19.10	1.71	54 56.60	42 27.53
16	9		22.	39.		31.			16 58 56.55	20.09	0.99	. 5 47.098	12 0.20	18.90	0.95	16 59 17.63	35 0.05
17	8		22.		57.				17 0 56.79	20.09	0.90	IV. 4 37.014	22 31.61	18.69	2.73	17 1 17.78	48 33.03
18	4			13.5		48.			2 30.78	20.09	0.89	III. 4 34.718	24 55.19	18.59	3.15	2 51.76	50 56.93
19	8					29.5			17 2 55.05	+20.09	+0.90	. 4 35.802	−23 48.13	−18.56	− 2.95	17 3 16.04	−26 49 49.64

CORRECTIONS.

Date.	Corr. of Clock.	Hourly rate.	m	n	c	Zenith Point.	Mic. Co.
1848.	h.	s.	s.	s.	s.	s.	° ′ ″	r.
June 26,	0	. .	. .	. .	. .	. .	359 59 62.20	29.9988

REMARKS.

(175) 85. Declination differs 20′ from Arg. Arg. Z, 224, 33, and 307, 44; probably another star.

(176) 2. Transit over T. IV assumed to have been recorded as over T. V.

INSTRUMENT READINGS.

Date.		CIRCLE.							Barom.	THERMOM.				
		A.	B.	C.	D.	E.	F.	Mean.		At.	Ex.	U.	L.	I.
	1848. h. m.	° ′ ″						″	In.	°	°	°	°	°
Zone 176	June 26, 16 15	75 47 {28.4 / 30.0}	{22.4 / 22.4}	{28.2 / 29.2}	{21.8 / 23.5}	{21.5 / 22.5}	{25.2 / 26.6} {25.14}		30.118	78.8	74.0	70.	79.	
	16 34	.	.	. .	. .	. .	. .	. .	30.120	77.5	70.3	. .	. .	77.5
	17 25	.	.	. .	. .	. .	. .	. .	30.119	77.2	70.3			
	17 45	.	.	. .	. .	. .	. .	. .	30.116	76.8	69.			
	18 12	.	.	. .	. .	. .	. .	. .	*30.016	76.2	68.8	. .	. .	. .
	18 19	.	.	. .	. .	. .	. .	. .	30.116	75.8	68.			
	20 0	{28.5 / 30.0}	{25. / 24.5}	{30. / 31.}	{23.8 / 25.2}	{22. / 23.}	{24.8 / 26.2} {26.16}		30.110	75.	67.9	78.8	76.	

*Assumed as 30.116 inches.

ZONE 176. JUNE 26. S. $D_0 = -26° 25' 40''$—Continued.

No.	Mag.	I.	II.	III.	IV.	V.	VI.	VII.	T.	a_1	a_2	MICROMETER.			i	d_1	d_2	Mean Right Ascension, 1850.0.	Mean Declination, 1850.0.
									h. m. s.	s.	s.			r.	' ''	''	''	h. m. s.	° ' ''
20	5			33.				7.8	17 4 33.10	+20.09	+0.91	IV.	4	37.676	−21 50.09	−18.46	−2.61	17 4 54.10	−26 47 51.16
21	7		37.	54.					11 11.62	20.09	0.73	III.	2	15.603	44 58.73	18.01	6.62	11 32.44	27 11 3.36
22	5					39.8			11 22.26	20.09	0.69	.	1	11.229	49 33.30	18.00	7.43	11 43.04	27 15 38.73
23	9			36.					14 53.37	20.09	0.96	.	4	38.699	20 45.36	17.77	2.43	15 14.42	26 46 45.56
24	9			34.		8.			18 8.25	20.09	1.07	III.	6	49.090	9 55.40	17.50	0.57	19 29.41	26 35 53.47
25	9			33.			7.		20 49.98	20.09	0.80	III.	3	36.601	38 47.07	17.35	5.56	21 10.87	27 4 49.98
26	8		29.5	47.	5.				25 4.50	20.10	1.07	IV.	4	47.212	11 51.66	17.06	0.90	25 25.67	26 37 49.62
27	9		46.						27 20.74	20.10	0.80	.	3	26.328	33 50.49	16.90	4.68	27 41.73	59 52.07
28	6	31.5		56.	23.				29 23.14	20.10	0.98	III.	4	35.120	24 29.52	16.75	3.07	29 44.22	26 50 29.34
29	9		33.		8.				31 7.92	20.10	0.72	II.	2	8.449	52 26.94	16.63	7.96	31 28.74	27 18 31.53
30	6				5.	39.8			32 22.47	20.10	1.02	III.	4	39.654	19 45.49	16.54	2.26	32 43.59	26 45 44.29
31	8		26.5		1.5				35 1.36	20.10	0.82	IV.	4	17.195	43 19.20	16.34	6.34	35 22.28	27 9 21.88
32	0			1.		15.			36 18.02	20.10	0.96	III.	3	31.693	25 13.85	16.25	3.70	36 39.08	26 54 13.80
33	3			9.5	27.	44.5			38 44.30	20.10	0.97	IV.	3	31.040	28 54.75	16.07	3.82	39 5.37	26 54 54.64
34	4			3.		37.			40 37.32	20.10	0.92	IV.	3	25.780	34 24.68	15.93	4.77	40 58.34	27 0 25.38
35	6						57.		40 22.54	20.10	1.06	.	5	39.980	19 27.17	15.94	2.19	40 43.70	26 45 25.30
36	6				21.5				42 21.36	20.10	1.02	IV.	4	34.742	24 54.12	15.80	3.15	42 42.48	26 50 53.07
37	4			32.	49.	7.			43 49.28	20.10	0.80	IV.	2	12.242	48 29.95	15.68	7.25	44 10.18	27 14 32.88
38	7		19.		54.				45 53.79	20.11	1.00	IV.	3	32.038	27 52.14	15.51	3.64	46 14.00	26 53 51.29
39	4				41.5		16.		46 41.46	20.11	1.09	IV.	4	40.932	18 25.66	15.46	2.03	47 2.66	26 44 23.15
40	8							5.	47 12.87	20.11	0.89	.	2	19.965	40 25.48	15.42	5.83	47 33.87	27 6 26.73
41	6		17.5						49 52.27	20.11	0.93	.	2	23.151	37 4.89	15.22	5.27	50 13.31	27 3 5.38
42	8		5.			56.5			51 39.45	20.11	0.98	III.	3	27.362	32 45.75	15.07	4.49	52 0.54	26 58 45.31
43	8					19.			53 1.50	20.11	0.94	.	3	22.090	38 16.09	14.96	5.46	53 22.64	27 4 16.51
44	6					14.			53 56.71	20.11	1.05	.	4	33.778	25 54.92	14.89	3.32	54 17.87	26 51 53.13
45	5						20.8		54 46.35	20.11	1.05	.	4	34.702	24 57.20	14.82	3.15	55 7.51	50 55.17
46	7				14.				56 13.86	20.12	0.99	.	3	27.358	32 45.94	14.70	4.49	56 34.97	58 45.13
47	8					8.			17 56 33.54	20.12	1.11	.	4	37.788	21 43.47	14.67	2.59	17 56 54.77	26 47 40.73
48	8		59.5	17.		9.			18 3 34.40	20.12	0.88	III.	2	12.952	47 44.85	14.10	7.15	18 3 55.40	27 13 46.10
49	3		44.	2.	19.	36.			8 18.90	20.12	0.97	IV.	2	20.868	39 28.65	13.70	5.69	8 30.99	27 5 28.04
50	6		8.			0.			12 42.70	20.13	1.05	II.	3	2.756	32 33.12	13.32	4.45	13 3.88	26 58 30.89
51	6					21.	38.5		11 46.54	20.13	1.05	VI.	3	27.562	32 32.57	13.40	4.45	12 7.72	58 30.42
52	.						49.		14 57.07	20.13	1.29	.	.	.	. .	.	.	15	(37)
53	5			1.5					18 1.36	20.13	1.25	.	4	47.188	17 6.87	12.86	0.89	18 22.76	43 0.62
54	4				58.				18 23.55	20.13	1.15	.	3	35.208	24 32.90	12.83	3.05	18 44.83	50 28.78
55	5				50.				19 15.54	20.13	1.19	.	4	39.889	14 17.92	12.76	2.21	19 36.86	40 12.89
56	6		58.		32.5				22 32.54	20.14	1.29	IV.	5	49.400	9 36.19	12.47	0.49	22 53.97	35 29.15
57	7				24.		58.5		31 23.96	20.14	1.17	IV.	3	33.358	26 29.50	11.68	3.40	31 45.27	52 24.58
58	8				11.				32 53.77	20.14	1.24	.	4	40.792	18 34.76	11.55	2.04	33 15.15	26 44 28.35
59	1		22.	39.		13.5			35 56.41	20.15	1.02	III.	2	17.102	42 21.99	11.28	6.20	36 17.58	27 8 19.47
60	8		37.5			12.			37 54.68	20.15	0.98	.	1	12.182	48 31.60	11.16	7.29	38 15.81	14 30.14
61	9					18.			39 0.63	20.15	1.12	.	3	25.470	34 44.19	11.00	4.52	39 21.90	27 0 40.01
62	6		21.5	38.5	46.				40 55.97	20.15	1.16	IV.	3	29.789	30 13.17	10.83	4.05	41 17.28	26 56 8.05
63	4		13.		47.5	4.5			42 47.44	20.16	1.23	IV.	3	36.326	23 23.26	10.66	2.86	43 8.83	49 16.78
64	7					52.			43 17.52	20.16	1.35	.	5	50.928	7 59.89	10.60	0.21	43 39.03	33 50.70
65	8		13.		46.5				49 47.04	20.16	1.32	IV.	4	43.398	15 51.06	10.02	1.57	50 8.52	41 42.65
66	8		30.		5.				56 4.79	20.17	1.25	.	3	34.068	25 44.82	9.44	3.27	56 26.21	26 51 37.53
67	6		53.	28.					18 58 27.84	20.18	1.13	IV.	3	22.408	37 52.32	9.22	5.41	18 58 49.15	27 3 46.95
68	7		36.	53.					19 0 10.54	20.18	1.32	.	3	37.908	20 40.92	9.06	2.37	19 0 32.04	26 46 32.35
69	7							48.	19 1 13.55	+20.18	+1.27	.		32.768	−27 5.82	−8.97	−3.48	19 1 35.00	−26 52 58.27

CORRECTIONS.

Date.	Corr. of Clock.	Hourly rate.	m	n	c	Zenith Point.	Mic. Co.
1848.	h.	s.	s.	s.	s.	s.	° ' ''	r.

INSTRUMENT READINGS.

Date.	CIRCLE.							Barom.	THERMOM.				
		A.	B.	C.	D.	E.	F.	Mean.		At.	Ex.	U.	L.	I.
Zone 176	1848. June 26, 20 3 h. m.	° ' ''						''	in. 30.112	75.	67.0			75.

REMARKS.

(176) 24. Transits over T.'s II and IV assumed as recorded over T.'s III and V.

(176) 25. Micrometer reading assumed as 21r.601, not 36r.601, to agree with Arg. Z. 214, 95; 217, 29; 306, 34; 388, 126; and Transit Z., 1846, July 9.

(167) 28. Transit over T. III assumed as at 6s.0 instead of 56s.

(176) 53. Micrometer reading assumed as 42r.188, not 47r.188.

(176) 55. Micrometer reading assumed as 44r.889, not 39r.889.

(176) 59. Micrometer reading assumed as 18r.102, not 17r.102.

(176) 60. Transit over T. III assumed to have been recorded as over T. II.

(176) 62. Time of transit over T. IV assumed as 56s.0 instead of 46s.

(176) 68. Micrometer reading assumed as 38r.908, not 37r.908.

ZONE 176. JUNE 26. S. $D_0 = -26°\ 25'\ 40''$ — Continued.

Columns — No. | Mag. | Seconds of Transit (I.–VII.) | T. (h. m. s.) | a_1 (s.) | a_2 (s.) | Micrometer [ref | n | r] | i | d_1 | d_2 | Mean Right Ascension 1850.0 (h. m. s.) | Mean Declination 1850.0 (° ′ ″)

No.	Mag.	I.	II.	III.	IV.	V.	VI.	VII.	T.	a_1	a_2	Mic.	n	r	i	d_1	d_2	Mean R.A. 1850.0	Mean Decl. 1850.0
70	8		44.						19 3 18.84	+20.18	+1.07		1	11.968	−48 44.98	− 8.77	− 7.35	19 3 40.09	−27 14 41.10
71	6			10.			51.5		4 17.19	20.19	1.14	VI.	2	19.078	41 21.30	8.67	6.02	4 38.52	27 7 15.99
72	8		55.5		30.				10 30.04	20.19	1.39	IV.	4	41.946	17 22.02	8.11	1.82	10 51.62	26 43 11.95
73	9			7.5	42.				13 24.74	20.19	1.24		3	26.032	34 8.93	7.84	4.74	13 46.17	27 0 1.51
74	7		32.	49.5	6.8				17 6.77	20.20	1.47	IV.	6	48.122	10 56.29	7.50	0.69	17 28.44	26 36 44.48
75	4		40.	57.5	14.5				20 14.75	20.20	1.11	IV.	1	9.513	51 20.42	7.21	7.83	20 36.06	27 17 15.46
76	9							10.	20 17.82	20.20	1.18		2	16.730	43 48.37	7.20	6.47	20 39.20	27 8 42.04
77	7		45.		19.				26 19.29	20.21	1.50	IV.	5	47.440	11 39.24	6.64	0.82	26 41.00	26 37 26.70
78	9				57.5		50.		26 57.75	20.21	1.49	IV.	5	46.150	13 0.14	6.59	1.02	27 19.45	38 47.75
79	9		34.			9.			32 8.79	20.22	1.46	V.	4	41.485	17 51.40	6.04	1.91	32 30.47	43 39.35
80	7				50.	24.5			32 49.96	20.22	1.43	IV.	4	37.934	21 33.82	6.04	2.53	33 11.61	47 22.39
81	8		35.5						35 52.85	20.23	1.43		4	36.840	22 41.39	5.81	2.70	35 14.51	48 20.96
82	6		53.		27.5	2.			37 27.54	20.23	1.40	IV.	2	34.590	25 12.07	5.61	3.15	37 49.17	26 51 0.83
83	8					23.			37 48.45	20.23	1.21		2	15.220	45 23.31	5.58	6.74	38 9.89	27 11 15.63
84	7		49.8		24.5				40 24.44	20.23	1.48	IV.	2	41.208	18 8.53	5.33	7.95	40 46.15	26 43 55.81
85	7					6.	23.5		40 48.74	20.23	1.24		2	15.910	39 26.10	5.30	5.70	41 10.21	27 5 17.10
86	4		43.5		18.				46 18.04	20.24	1.52	IV.	5	43.430	15 50.94	4.78	1.51	46 39.80	26 41 37.23
87	6						55.5	13.	46 21.05	20.24	1.38		3	29.368	30 39.34	4.78	4.12	46 42.67	56 28.24
88	7						37.		47 45.13	20.24	1.58		6	47.935	11 7.54	4.65	0.68	48 6.95	36 52.87
89	4				27.	44.5			49 27.10	20.24	1.59	IV.	6	48.892	10 7.83	4.49	0.51	49 48.93	35 52.85
90	7		51.	8.	25.				51 25.33	20.25	1.58	IV.	5	47.058	12 3.10	4.31	0.88	51 47.16	37 48.29
91	8		14.	32.	49.	6.			54 48.93	20.25	1.52	IV.	5	40.522	18 51.59	3.99	2.06	55 10.70	26 44 37.64
92	6				42.		16.		55 41.68	20.25	1.26	IV.	2	12.615	48 6.42	3.91	7.27	56 3.19	27 13 57.60
93	6				18.	52.5			57 17.96	20.26	1.47	IV.	3	34.025	25 17.45	3.75	3.25	57 39.69	26 51 34.45
94	4			3.	20.	37.			19 59 37.33	20.26	1.60	IV.	3	45.695	13 26.77	3.54	1.12	19 59 59.19	39 11.43
95	8			12.					20 3 29.42	+20.26	+1.62		4	46.740	−12 20.66	− 3.17	− 0.91	20 3 51.30	−26 38 4.74

ZONE 177. JUNE 27. C. $D = -22°\ 3'\ 0''$.

No.	Mag.	I.	II.	III.	IV.	V.	VI.	VII.	T.	a_1	a_2	Mic.	n	r	i	d_1	d_2	Mean R.A. 1850.0	Mean Decl. 1850.0
1	8			16.5	33.	50.1	6.5		16 13 33.16	+22.78		IV.	2	18.225	−42 14.67	− 6.80	−11.82		−22 45 33.29
2	9			50.6		23.8	40.4		15 7.23	22.78		IV.	4	44.406	14 47.80	6.69	7.82		18 2.31
3	9.10			1.5	18.2	35.1			22 18.25	22.77		IV.	3	34.744	25 2.34	6.20	9.29		28 17.85
4	9.10			56.2	12.8	29.8			24 29.64	22.77		III.	3	32.863	27 0.37	6.03	9.57		30 15.97
5	8		25.8	42.8	59.2	16.	32.8		16 28 59.35	+22.77		IV.	3	28.322	−31 45.47	− 5.71	−10.26		−22 35 1.44

ZONE 178. JULY 10. S. $D_0 = -22°\ 40'\ 30''$.

No.	Mag.	I.	II.	III.	IV.	V.	VI.	VII.	T.	a_1	a_2	Mic.	n	r	i	d_1	d_2	Mean R.A. 1850.0	Mean Decl. 1850.0
1	9						2.		17 40 45.24	+23.28	+0.53		3	35.758	−23 58.52	− 5.57	− 3.08	17 41 9.05	−23 4 37.17
2	8						11.	28.	41 37.61	23.28	0.66		4	47.545	11 31.33	5.50	1.20	42 1.55	22 52 8.03
3	10			56.8	31.	47.			45 30.55	23.28	0.58		4	43.109	16 9.15	5.13	1.91	45 54.41	22 56 46.19
4	8				58.5	32.			46 58.48	23.28	0.30		2	19.460	40 56.65	5.01	5.69	47 22.06	23 21 37.35
5	9			4.	21.	38.			49 37.81	23.28	0.32		2	23.100	37 8.53	4.76	5.12	50 1.41	17 48.41
6	9			5.					51 38.80	23.28	0.14		1	9.014	51 50.27	4.58	7.42	52 2.22	32 32.27
7	9				15.				52 14.86	23.28	0.40		3	30.525	29 27.19	4.51	3.92	52 38.54	5.62
8	8				10.5				52 53.76	23.28	0.49		4	38.703	20 45.61	4.45	2.62	53 17.53	23 1 22.68
9	7				26.5				54 26.39	23.28	0.59		6	48.402	10 38.86	4.30	1.09	54 50.26	22 51 14.25
10	9			42.	15.				58 15.27	23.28	0.36		3	33.468	26 22.59	3.94	3.45	58 38.91	23 6 59.98
11	9					37.5		11.	17 58 20.73	23.28	0.52		5	46.252	12 53.81	3.94	1.41	17 58 44.53	22 53 29.16
12	10		3.5		37.	54.			18 1 37.08	+23.28	+0.19		2	17.590	−42 53.75	− 3.62	− 5.99	18 2 0.55	−23 23 33.36

CORRECTIONS.

Date.	Corr. of Clock.	Hourly rate.	m	n	c	Zenith Point.	Mic. Co.
1848.	h.	s.	s.	s.	s.	° ′ ″	r.
June 27,	0					359 59 64.19	30.0004
July 10,	0					62.40	30.0001

INSTRUMENT READINGS.

	Date.	Circle A.	B.	C.	D.	E.	F.	Mean.	Barom.	Therm. At.	Ex.	U.	L.	I.
	1848. h. m.	° ′ ″						″	in.	°	°	°	°	°
Zone 177	June 27, 16 10	71 24 67.4	57.6	64.6	56.6	54.2	62.2	60.43	30.080	82.4	80.4	81.5	81.2	79.8
	16 20										80.1			
	16 30								30.080	82.		79.9		
Zone 178	July 10, 17 30	72 2 {29.	24.4	24.5	21.2	20.8	24.2}	24.34	30.176	75.2	72.3			
		{30.	24.6	25.0	22.2	21.2	25.0}							
	18 8								30.172	75.2	72.			

REMARKS.

(176) 71. Transit over T. III assumed as 0ˢ, not 10ˢ, to agree with B. A. C. 6565, Transit, 1846, September 2, and 1848, July 20.

(176) 79. Transit over T. IV assumed to have been recorded as over T. V.

(176) 81. Transit over T. III assumed as recorded over T. II, and minutes as 34, not 35.

(176) 85. Micrometer reading assumed as 20ʳ.910, not 15ʳ.910.

Zone 178. July 10. S. $D_s = -22° 40' 30''$—Continued.

No.	Mag.	I.	II.	III.	IV.	V.	VI.	VII.	T.	a_1	a_4	Mic.		r.	′ ″	i	d_1	d_2	Mean Right Ascension, 1850.0	Mean Declination, 1850.0
13	7		58.5		32.	49.			18 3 32.09	+23.28	+0.33	.	3	31.658	−28 16.04	− 3.44	− 3.74		18 3 55.70	−23 8 53.22
14	11				43.				5 42.86	23.28	0.30	.	3	30.128	29 52.04	3.23	3.98		6 6.44	10 29.25
15	10		43.5		17.				18 8 17.06	+23.28	+0.16	.	2	21.433	−38 52.78	− 2.97	− 5.38		18 8 40.50	−23 19 31.13

Zone 179. July 11. C. $D_s = -22° 40' 30''$.

No.	Mag.	I.	II.	III.	IV.	V.	VI.	VII.	T.	a_1	a_4	Mic.		r.	′ ″	i	d_1	d_2	Mean Right Ascension, 1850.0	Mean Declination, 1850.0
1	8				35.2				18 2 35.12	+24.55	+0.78	IV.	2	18.739	−41 42.28	− 5.37	−11.79		18 3 0.45	−23 22 29.44
2	7			13.8	30.3	47.3	4.		3 30.47	24.55	0.84	IV.	3	31.798	28 7.13	5.28	9.72		3 55.86	23 8 52.13
3	9							39.2	3 48.87	24.55	0.90	VII.	5	47.845	11 13.24	5.25	7.19		4 14.32	22 51 55.68
4	8			58.5	15.3	32.2	48.5		8 15.23	24.55	0.75	IV.	2	21.572	38 44.69	4.81	11.34		8 40.53	23 19 30.84
5	8			5.3	22.	39.4	55.8		10 22.22	24.55	0.70	IV.	2	18.958	41 28.51	4.60	11.75		10 47.47	23 22 14.86
6	8			15.5	31.8	48.7			12 32.01	24.55	0.81	IV.	4	41.967	18 23.42	4.39	8.11		12 57.37	22 59 5.92
7	9			52.2					17 9.11	24.55	0.59	IV.	2	10.600	·50 12.76	3.92	13.08		17 34.25	23 30 50.76
8	7			19.4		52.2	9.1		18 35.78	24.55	0.70	IV.	3	35.287	24 28.45	3.78	9.17		19 1.03	5 11.40
9	7			40.2	57.1	14.3			20 57.15	24.55	0.63	IV.	2	20.423	39 56.81	3.56	11.53		21 22.33	20 41.90
10	7				48.	5.			18 21 47.99	+24.55	+0.59	V.	2	16.520	−44 1.73	− 3.50	−12.14		18 22 13.12	−23 24 47.37

Zone 180. July 17. S. $D_s = -22° 40' 20''$.

No.	Mag.	I.	II.	III.	IV.	V.	VI.	VII.	T.	a_1	a_4	Mic.		r.	′ ″	i	d_1	d_2	Mean Right Ascension, 1850.0	Mean Declination, 1850.0
1	9		33.		5.				18 7 5.79	+24.39	+0.73	.	3	25.238	−34 58.87	−13.02	− 4.77		18 7 30.91	−23 15 36.66
2	8				32.	49.			8 15.34	24.39	0.71	.	3	21.566	38 48.89	12.91	5.36		8 40.44	19 27.16
3	9			5.6			56.		10 22.50	24.39	0.72	.	2	18.868	41 33.84	12.72	5.79		10 47.61	23 22 12.35
4	7		58.		32.				12 31.78	24.38	0.81	.	4	40.842	18 30.30	12.53	2.28		12 56.97	22 59 5.11
5	10				38.				14 4.59	24.38	0.79	.	3	33.530	26 18.20	12.39	3.44		14 29.76	23 6 54.03
6	9			12.5		45.			16 11.98	24.38	0.78	.	3	30.078	28 52.43	12.18	3.80		16 37.14	9 28.41
7	7		2.	19.	36.				17 35.79	24.38	0.82	.	3	35.202	24 33.79	12.06	3.17		18 0.99	5 9.00
8	8		23.5			14.			20 57.16	24.37	0.77	V.	2	20.318	40 3.60	11.76	5.55		21 22.30	20 40.91
9	8			48.		21.5			21 47.97	24.37	0.75	.	1	16.378	44 9.12	11.68	6.19		22 13.09	24 46.99
10	8		22.						28 55.69	24.36	0.83	.	3	27.216	32 54.78	11.04	4.45		29 20.88	13 30.27
11	7			30.					29 29.00	24.36	0.82	.	3	22.586	37 45.16	10.98	5.19		29 55.08	18 21.33
12	8		9.		43.				32 42.85	24.35	0.80	.	2	15.506	45 5.20	10.69	6.32		33 8.00	23 25 42.21
13	9			14.					34 13.89	24.35	0.94	.	6	50.810	8 7.41	10.55	0.70		34 39.18	22 48 38.66
14	8		9.		42.8				40 42.68	24.34	0.94	.	4	39.168	20 15.50	9.97	2.54		41 7.96	23 0 48.01
15	5		7.9	41.5					44 41.42	24.34	0.98	.	5	44.332	14 53.95	9.61	1.72		45 6.74	22 55 25.28
16	5		21.		54.		29.		45 37.64	24.34	1.00	.	5	48.412	10 38.09	9.53	1.08		46 2.98	22 51 8.70
17	6				21.				46 30.45	24.33	0.88	.	2	19.482	40 56.02	9.44	5.69		46 55.66	23 21 31.15
18	9			59.					49 58.95	24.33	0.87	.	2	13.468	47 13.00	9.14	6.65		50 24.15	27 48.79
19	8		20.						51 53.79	24.33	0.88	.	1	10.152	50 38.97	8.96	7.18		52 19.00	23 31 15.11
20	7			10.		60.			52 9.77	24.33	1.02	.	4	45.593	13 33.29	8.04	1.53		52 35.12	22 54 3.76
21	8		29.		3.				54 46.02	24.33	0.98	III.	3	33.673	26 9.61	8.70	3.42		55 11.33	23 6 41.73
22	10		20.						56 53.67	24.32	1.06	.	5	50.198	8 45.72	8.51	0.80		57 19.05	22 49 15.03
23	8		42.		15.				18 59 15.35	24.32	0.93	IV.	1	15.938	44 37.34	8.30	6.25		18 59 40.60	23 25 11.89
24	9			6.		39.			19 0 5.72	24.32	0.93	.	1	15.752	44 49.02	8.21	6.39		19 0 30.97	23 25 23.52
25	9		55.						4 11.93	24.32	1.08	.	5	50.712	8 13.51	7.85	0.69		4 37.33	22 48 42.05
26	10		2.						14 35.76	24.31	1.00	.	1	15.	46	6.92			14 36.07	
27	9		14.5		39.				15 38.59	24.31	1.00	.	2	16.186	44 21.79	6.83	6.23		15 38.90	23 24 54.85
28	10*				37.5				18 37.36	24.30	1.08	.	3	30.245	29 44.75	6.56	3.97		19 1.74	10 15.28
29	9		59.						22 15.87	24.30	1.02	.	2	16.590	43 56.84	6.23	6.16		22 40.19	24 29.23
30	9			17.					19 23 0.20	+24.30	+1.10	.	4	36.896	−22 39.20	− 6.16	− 3.90		19 23 26.60	−23 3 9.32

CORRECTIONS.

Date.	Corr. of Clock.	Hourly rate.	m	n	c	Zenith Point.	Mic. Co.
	h. s.	s.	s.	s.	s.	° ′ ″	r.
1848. July 11.	0					359 59 63.49	30.0021
July 17.	0					63.77	30.0028

INSTRUMENT READINGS.

Date.	CIRCLE.							Barom.	THERMOM.				
	A.	B.	C.	D.	E.	F.	Mean.		At.	Ex.	U.	L.	I.
Zone 179 1848. July 11, 18 5								in. 30.160	76.4	72.7			
18 20	72 2 {37.9 / 37.7	32.5 / 33.0	34.7 / 34.5	31.5 / 32.8	29.8 / 30.2	32.9 / 34.1}	33.47	30.160		72.7	76.0	75.2	74.8
Zone 180 July 17, 18 0	72 2 28.3	22.	26.8	22.4	19.4	23.	23.65	30.100	72.8	62.2			75.6
18 20										62.8			
18 40										61.8			
19 0								30.104	70.8	61.2			
19 30	{27. / 28.	24. / 24.5	26. / 25.6	23.8 / 25.0	19.8 / 20.4	22.2 / 23.5}	24.15						

REMARKS.

(179) 6. Micrometer reading assumed as 40ˢ.967, not 41ˢ.967.

(179) 10. Transits over T.'s IV and V assumed as recorded over T.'s V and VI.

(180) 6. Micrometer reading assumed as 31ˢ.078, not 30ˢ.078.

(180) 27. Time of transit over T. II assumed as 4ˢ.5 instead of 14ˢ.5.

ZONE 181. JULY 18. C. $D_0 = -22° 2′ 50″$.

No.	Mag.	I.	II.	III.	IV.	V.	VI.	VII.
1	4	12.5	29.1	45.9	1.8	19.2	35.5	52.4
2	9				55.3	12.	28.2	
3	9							55.
4	10				29.?			
5	8		29.5	46.1				
6	8					20.7	37.5	
7	7.8				4.3	21.3	37.7	
8	8.9		23.		56.1			
9	8.9					47.5		
10	8.9						26.2	
11	8				5.	22.5	38.8	
12	9.10			12.5	29.2			
13	8	38.3	55.3	11.5	28.3	45.	2.5	19.3
14	8			46.1		19.7	35.6	
15	9							4.
16	8				25.1			15.5
17	8		21.5	38.	55.	11.6		
18	8	25.	41.7	58.5	14.8	31.5	48.6	4.3
19	8					10.6	26.5	43.5
20	8							32.5
21	9					20.5	37.	53.8
22	8.9			19.5	35.3	52.5	9.2	26.
23	6.7	29.7	46.4	3.6	19.7	37.2	53.6	10.6
24	8.9			36.3	52.8	10.	26.5	
25	8.9		21.3		55.	11.7	28.5	
26	9			45.5	2.2			
27	8.9		47.	3.5	20.	36.8	53.5	
28	8			26.2	43.3	0.1	17.	
29	9.10				54.5	11.	27.5	
30	8.9			15.6	32.2	49.	5.5	22.5
31	9			59.8	33.1			
32	9.10					17.2		
33	9			18.	34.5	51.3	8.	
34	10			55.3	12.2	28.8		
35	7		22.5	30.	55.5	12.3	28.7	45.8
36	9					48.	4.5	
37	7		43.	0.	16.3	33.3	49.5	6.3
38	8.9		2.5		36.3	53.3	9.3	
39	9			32.5	49.1	6.		
40	9					1.2	17.5	
41	9			12.5		45.7		
42	8.9				41.3	58.	14.6	31.5
43	8		54.5	11.5	27.5			
44	10		56.5		30.			
45	8							47.
46	8							21.5
47	7				23.8	40.8	57.1	
48	8				31.3			
49	9					11.5		

No.	T. (h m s)	a_1 (s)	a_2 (s)	MICROMETER (r)	i (′ ″)	d_1 (″)	d_2 (″)	Mean Right Ascension, 1850.0 (h m s)	Mean Declination, 1870.0 (° ′ ″)
1	15 51 2.34	+24.41	+0.61	IV. 5 50.798	− 8 8.17	−25.13	− 0.84	15 51 27.36	−22 11 24.14
2	52 55.16	24.40	0.61	V. 4 46.649	12 27.25	25.01	1.47	53 20.17	15 43.73
3	53 4.66	24.39	0.62	VII. 2 18.308	42 9.73	24.99	5.77	53 29.67	45 30.49
4	15 57 28.86	24.39	0.63	IV. 3 29.718	30 17.69	24.70	4.04	15 57 53.88	33 36.43
5	16 0 2.99	24.39	0.64	III. 2 17.269	43 14.32	24.53	5.06	16 0 28.02	46 34.81
6	0 4.12	24.39	0.64	V. 3 30.372	29 30.66	24.53	3.94	0 29.15	32 55.13
7	1 4.37	24.39	0.64	V. 3 21.329	39 3.95	24.46	5.33	1 29.40	42 23.74
8	6 56.31	24.38	0.66	IV. 2 17.082	43 26.23	24.06	5.99	7 21.35	46 46.28
9	7 30.68	24.37	0.66	IV. 2 19.806	40 35.27	24.02	5.58	7 55.71	43 54.87
10	7 52.96	24.37	0.66	VI. 3 30.572	29 23.80	24.00	3.92	8 17.99	32 41.72
11	9 5.32	24.37	0.67	V. 3 10.091	50 48.57	23.91	7.08	9 30.36	54 9.50
12	11 29.22	24.37	0.68	III. 5 48.584	10 27.24	23.74	1.16	11 54.27	13 42.14
13	13 28.60	24.36	0.68	IV. 2 18.223	42 14.79	23.61	5.85	13 53.64	45 34.25
14	15 2.76	24.35	0.69	IV. 4 44.404	14 47.93	23.49	1.76	15 27.80	18 3.18
15	22 13.88	24.34	0.71	VII. 5 34.752	24 55.07	22.98	3.27	22 38.93	28 11.32
16	24 25.18	24.34	0.72	VII. 3 32.873	26 58.86	22.81	3.57	24 50.24	30 15.24
17	28 54.87	24.33	0.73	IV. 3 28.318	31 45.72	22.49	4.27	29 19.93	35 2.48
18	34 14.91	24.31	0.75	IV. 3 36.155	23 33.86	22.08	3.06	34 39.97	26 49.00
19	34 53.53	24.31	0.75	IV. 4 48.085	10 56.73	22.02	1.24	35 18.59	14 9.99
20	35 42.02	24.31	0.75	VII. 2 10.122	50 42.92	21.96	7.08	36 7.08	54 1.96
21	37 3.75	24.30	0.75	V. 5 41.665	17 41.60	21.86	2.22	37 28.80	20 35.68
22	42 35.77	24.30	0.77	IV. 3 24.618	15 37.70	21.42	4.83	43 0.84	18 53.95
23	47 20.11	24.29	0.79	IV. 2 9.755	51 5.62	21.04	7.18	47 45.19	54 23.84
24	16 53 53.02	24.28	0.81	IV. 2 8.351	52 33.84	20.50	7.39	16 54 18.11	55 51.73
25	17 2 54.97	24.26	0.83	IV. 2 19.481	40 55.90	19.75	5.62	17 3 20.06	44 11.27
26	12 2.20	24.24	0.87	III. 2 17.619	12 52.31	18.04	5.92	12 27.31	46 7.17
27	12 20.19	24.24	0.87*	IV. 3 28.707	32 23.86	18.02	4.37	12 45.30	35 37.15
28	13 43.27	24.24	0.87	IV. 2 12.452	48 16.70	18.79	6.73	14 8.38	51 32.22
29	14 54.28	24.23	0.88	V. 3 24.182	36 4.92	18.69	4.90	15 19.30	39 18.51
30	24 32.16	24.22	0.91	IV. 2 9.055	51 49.58	17.81	7.29	24 57.29	55 4.68
31	26 33.14	24.21	0.92	III. 4 36.306	23 10.07	17.63	3.02	26 58.27	26 20.72
32	27 0.56	24.21	0.92	V. 2 42.158	17 9.22	17.59	2.13	27 25.69	30 18.94
33	28 34.62	24.21	0.92	V. 3 33.884	25 50.25	17.44	3.35	28 59.75	29 7.07
34	33 12.13	24.20	0.93	IV. 4 45.068	14 6.12	17.01	1.68	33 37.26	17 14.81
35	34 55.68	24.20	0.93	IV. 5 51.590	4 9.70	16.85	0.22	35 20.81	7 16.77
36	36 31.28	24.19	0.94	V. 3 29.762	30 14.76	16.70	4.04	36 56.41	33 25.50
37	38 16.42	24.19	0.96	IV. 4 37.684	21 49.57	16.54	2.85	38 41.57	24 58.94
38	41 36.18	24.19	0.97	IV. 2 11.845	48 54.52	16.21	6.63	42 1.34	52 7.56
39	42 49.15	24.19	0.97	V. 3 25.895	34 17.47	16.11	4.63	43 14.31	37 28.21
40	43 44.38	24.18	0.97	V. 3 33.307	26 32.51	16.02	3.47	44 9.53	29 42.00
41	45 29.04	24.18	0.98	IV. 2 7.371	53 35.29	15.84	7.52	45 54.20	56 48.65
42	47 11.30	24.18	0.99	V. 3 37.156	22 30.02	15.63	2.91	47 6.47	25 39.40
43	50 27.87	24.17	1.00	III. 3 33.175	26 40.08	15.36	3.50	49 52.04	29 49.84
44	50 29.95	24.17	1.00	VI. 4 41.982	18 23.14	15.36	2.28	49 55.12	21 30.78
45	50 56.88	24.17	1.00	VII. 3 35.966	23 44.83	15.31	3.08	50 22.05	26 53.22
46	50 31.37	24.17	1.00	VII. 2 31.175	28 45.59	15.35	3.82	50 56.54	31 54.76
47	52 23.82	24.17	1.00	V. 2 17.452	43 3.35	15.16	5.95	52 48.99	46 14.46
48	53 31.21	24.17	1.01	IV. 2 20.725	39 37.68	15.05	5.45	53 56.39	42 48.18
49	17 53 54.75	+24.17	+1.01	V. 3 26.555	−33 36.07	−15.01	− 4.53	17 54 19.93	−22 36 45.61

CORRECTIONS.

Date	Corr. of Clock	Hourly rate	m	n	c	Zenith Point	Mic. Co.
	h.	s.	s.	s.	s.	° ′ ″	r.
1848, July 18,	0					359 59 63.59	30.0029

INSTRUMENT READINGS.

Date			CIRCLE.					Barom.		THERMOM.			
	A.	B.	C.	D.	E.	F.	Mean.		At.	Ex.	U.	L.	I.
Zone 181, 1848 July 18, 15 50	71 24	65.3	57.1	62.8	57.1	51.3	60.	58.93	In.		72.1	77.5	76.	75.
16 0									30.202	77.	71.6			
16 20											70.9			
16 40									30.212	76.2	70.			
17 0		63.7	57.3	62.9	56.9	51.3	58.9	58.50	30.214	75.2	69.1	74.5	73.7	
17 20											68.0			
17 40									30.222	74.	67.7			
18 0											67.3			
18 20		63.7	57.8	62.7	57.1	50.0	58.2	58.25	30.228	73.3	67.0	73.4	72.	

REMARKS.

(181) 27. Micrometer reading assumed as 27ʳ.707, not 28ʳ.707.

(181) 42. Minutes assumed as 46, not 47.

(181) 43. Minutes assumed as 49, not 50.

(181) 44. Minutes assumed as 49, not 50; and micrometer reading as 40ʳ.982, not 41ʳ.982, to agree with Arg. Z. 224, 22, and 307, 33.

(181) 45. Minutes assumed as 49, not 50.

Zone 180. July 18. C. $D_0 = -22°\ 2'\ 50''$—Continued.

No.	Mag.	I.	II.	III.	IV.	V.	VI.	VII.	T. (h. m. s.)	a_1 (s.)	a_2 (s.)	Mic.	n	r.	i (′ ″)	d_1 (″)	d_2 (″)	Mean R.A. 1850.0 (h. m. s.)	Mean Decl. 1850.0 (° ′ ″)
50	8					59.5	16.		17 54 42.78	+24.16	+1.01	V.	3	33.031	−26 49.68	−14.93	−3.52	17 55 7.95	−22 29 58.13
51	8.9		43.5	0.2		33.5	49.7		57 16.81	24.16	1.02	IV.	3	34.592	25 11.94	14.69	3.27	57 41.99	28 19.90
52	9					30.5			58 19.57	24.16	1.02	V.	2	10.521	50 17.91	14.58	7.04	58 44.75	53 29.53
53	8.9							30.5	17 58 40.39	24.16	1.02	VII.	5	45.089	14 6.39	14.55	1.67	17 59 5.57	17 12.61
54	9		52.	8.8	25.3		58.5	5.	18 1 15.38	24.16	1.02	IV.	5	46.528	12 36.42	14.27	1.43	18 1 40.56	15 42.12
55	9		15.5	32.5	49.5				3 49.28	24.16	1.03	III.	2	11.986	48 45.50	14.03	6.83	4 14.47	51 56.36
56	9					11.7	28.5		3 55.02	24.16	1.03	V.	3	18.702	41 48.53	14.02	5.77	4 20.21	44 58.32
57	9		8.	24.3	41.5				7 41.35	24.15	1.04	III.	5	19.143	9 52.14	13.65	1.04	8 6.54	12 56.81
58	8.9			9.2	26.		59.		8 25.86	24.15	1.05	IV.	5	42.007	17 18.26	13.56	2.14	8 51.06	20 23.96
59	8 9			11.5	29.		1.5		8 28.46	24.15	1.05	V.	4	39.084	20 22.08	13.56	2.61	8 53.66	23 25.25
60	8.9		2.5	19.1			9.1		12 35.91	24.14	1.06	III.	4	40.818	18 32.37	13.14	2.32	13 1.11	21 37.83
61	8.9		8.3		41.3	58.2	14.6		12 41.46	24.14	1.06	IV.	5	44.156	15 3.43	13.13	1.82	13 6.66	18 8.38
62	10		55.2	11.8	29.			18.7	14 28.72	24.13	1.07	IV.	5	45.022	3 43.02	12.94	0.11	14 53.92	6 46.07
63	9				17.3	33.8	50.2		23 17.09	24.12	1.10	V.	4	57.847	11 11.92	12.04	1.24	23 42.31	14 15.20
64	9						25.2		23 51.90	24.12	1.10	VI.	2	20.046	40 20.59	11.98	5.57	24 17.12	43 28.14
65	9							11.	24 20.87	24.12	1.10	VII.	3	30.702	29 15.14	11.95	3.89	24 46.09	32 20.98
66	9						45.3		25 12.04	24.12	1.10	VI.	3	24.048	36 13.01	11.84	4.93	25 37.26	39 19.78
67	8.9							43.	25 52.90	24.12	1.10	VII.	5	49.862	9 6.62	11.77	0.90	26 18.12	12 9.29
68	10			25.	41.3	58.5			30 41.55	24.12	1.12	IV.	2	16.076	44 29.32	11.28	6.19	31 6.79	47 36.79
69	10			54.7	11.5	28.			33 11.19	24.12	1.13	IV.	5	43.786	15 28.34	11.03	1.86	33 36.44	18 31.25
70	8				52.	8.	25.5		33 51.80	24.12	1.13	V.		F. wire	29 55.12	10.95	2.44	34 17.05	33 1.51
71	9							4.5	34 14.11	24.12	1.13	VII.	2	15.134	45 28.71	10.92	6.34	34 39.36	48 35.97
72	6.7	2.3	19.	35.9	52.2	9.2	25.4	42.5	36 52.36	24.11	1.14	IV.	3	30.434	29 32.96	10.64	3.94	37 17.61	32 37.54
73	10						3.5		37 30.24	24.11	1.14	IV.	3	35.994	23 43.89	10.58	3.06	37 55.49	26 47.53
74	9			56.1					41 12.86	24.11	1.16	III.	3	36.761	22 55.76	10.20	2.05	41 38.13	25 58.91
75	7.8				23.8	40.5	57.		41 23.75	24.10	1.16	V.	4	42.637	16 39.00	10.18	2.05	41 49.01	19 41.32
76	9						29.1		41 55.85	24.10	1.16	VI.	3	33.118	26 44.00	10.13	3.50	42 21.11	29 47.69
77	8.9				10.8	27.6			43 10.79	24.10	1.16	V.	3	34.289	25 30.89	9.99	3.32	43 36.05	28 34.20
78	9						51.		43 17.75	24.10	1.16	VI.	3	29.097	30 56.28	9.98	4.14	43 43.01	34 0.40
79	9				39.5				44 39.42	24.10	1.17	IV.	3	18.665	41 51.09	9.84	5.78	45 4.69	44 56.71
80	7						15.		44 41.62	24.10	1.17	VI.	2	6.546	52 21.87	9.83	7.39	45 6.89	55 29.09
81	7					54.3	11.		45 37.52	24.10	1.17	V.	2	12.626	48 5.90	9.74	6.73	46 2.79	51 12.37
82	8		23.8	40.3	57.1	13.8	30.5	47.2	48 57.09	24.10	1.17	IV.	2	19.987	40 23.97	9.40	5.57	49 22.36	43 28.94
83	7.8	19.3	36.3	53.3	9.8	26.2			52 9.75	24.09	1.18	IV.	2	9.869	50 58.41	9.05	7.18	52 35.02	54 4.64
84	10					50.2			52 33.57	24.09	1.18	V.	5	44.241	14 59.97	9.01	1.77	52 58.84	18 0.75
85	10		11.5		45.				54 45.01	24.09	1.19	III.	2	17.097	43 25.04	8.79	6.03	55 10.29	46 29.86
86	9.10		20.8	37.3	54.				56 54.15	24.09	1.20	III.	2	14.383	46 15.30	8.57	6.46	57 19.44	49 20.33
87	9		58.5	15.	31.8	48.2	5.		18 57 31.73	24.09	1.20	IV.	3	20.196	40 15.13	8.50	5.54	18 57 57.02	43 19.77
88	9.10		31.	48.2	4.9	21.5			19 0 4.75	24.09	1.21	IV.	3	26.535	33 37.51	8.23	4.56	19 0 30.05	36 40.30
89	9		7.6	25.		58.			2 41.53	24.08	1.21	IV.	5	51.621	7 16.63	7.96	0.62	3 6.82	10 15.21
90	9		38.7	55.3	12.5				4 12.28	24.08	1.22	III.	2	14.842	45 46.40	7.80	6.40	4 37.58	48 50.60
91	8.9				44.1	1.	17.5		4 44.18	24.08	1.22	V.	5	43.664	15 36.13	7.75	1.84	5 9.48	18 35.72
92	9.10				10.				5 9.88	24.08	1.23	IV.	1	42.588	16 43.74	7.69	2.04	5 35.19	19 43.47
93	9		4.5	21.3	38.				7 38.01	24.08	1.23	III.	5	49.532	9 27.72	7.44	0.96	8 3.32	12 26.12
94	9		56.7		30.2				9 30.15	24.08	1.24	III.	4	40.182	19 12.42	7.23	2.40	9 55.47	22 12.05
95	9			3.1	19.5	36.3			10 19.61	24.05	1.24	IV.	3	35.492	24 15.52	7.16	3.13	10 44.93	27 15.81
96	7			56.5	13.2	30.2	46.3	3.5	11 13.21	24.08	1.25	IV.	3	22.787	37 32.43	7.05	5.15	11 38.54	40 34.63
97	9			35.	51.7	8.5			12 51.74	24.08	1.25	IV.	4	41.266	18 4.89	6.89	2.23	13 17.07	21 4.01
98	9.10			42.5		16.	[11]		19 15 59.20	+24.08	+1.26	III.	2	9.668	−51 10.83	−6.56	−7.24	19 15 24.54	−22 54 14.63

CORRECTIONS.

Date	Corr. of Clock	Hourly rate	m	n	c	Zenith Point	Mic. Co.
1848.	h.	s.	s.	s.	s.	° ′ ″	r.
	s.						

REMARKS.

(180) 54. Transits over T.'s II, III, IV, and VI assumed as 42.8, 58.8, 15.3, and 48.5, not 52., 8.8, 25.3, and 58.5, to agree with Arg. Z. 307, 59, and Mer. Circle, 1848, June 12.

(180) 98. Minutes assumed as 14, not 15, to agree with Arg. Z. 233, 28, and 240, 20.

INSTRUMENT READINGS.

Date	A.	B.	C.	D.	E.	F.	Mean.	Barom.	At.	Ex.	U.	L.	I.
			CIRCLE.							THERMOM.			
Zone 180 — July 18, 18 40								in.		66.8			
19 0										66.2			
19 20								30.218	72.2	65.8			
19 40										65.9			
20 0	71 24 61.6	57.7	60.9	57.2	49.3	58.1	57.47	30.210	72.	65.7	73.	71.5	

ZONES OBSERVED WITH THE MURAL CIRCLE, 1848.

ZONE 180. JULY 18. C. $D_0 = -22^\circ\ 2'\ 50''$—Continued.

No.	Mag.	I.	II.	III.	IV.	V.	VI.	VII.	T. (h. m. s.)	a_1 (s.)	a_2 (s.)
99	9			39.5			29.5		19 15 12.86	+24.08	+1.26
100	8		1.8	18.5	35.2	52.			16 18.52	24.08	1.26
101	9							46.2	16 56.10	24.08	1.26
102	10				47.2				20 47.08	24.07	1.28
103	10			0.5	17.5	34.2			23 34.13	24.07	1.29
104	9	11.5	28.5	45.	1.3				24 44.94	24.07	1.29
105	10						39.5		25 22.87	24.07	1.29
106	9					52.			26 18.75	24.07	1.30
107	8.9				33.5	50.2			27 33.50	24.07	1.30
108	8.9					21.3	37.5		28 4.44	24.07	1.30
109	8			1.2	17.5	34.3	51.	7.5	30 34.35	24.07	1.30
110	10				59.2	16.2		19.5	34 16.10	24.06	1.31
111	9							9.5	35 19.02	24.06	1.32
112	9						8.2		36 34.93	24.06	1.32
113	9			53.5	10.	26.5			38 10.05	24.06	1.33
114	9		41.5		14.8				49 14.88	24.06	1.36
115	9			38.3	55.3				49 55.14	24.06	1.36
116	7.8				32.	48.7	5.1		50 15.30	24.06	1.37
117	9					20.	36.5	53.2	52 19.87	24.06	1.38
118	8.9	35.2	52.	8.5	25.5	42.			19 55 8.67	24.06	1.38
119	9	35.	52.	9.	25.	42.			20 2 8.65	24.06	1.40
120	9	29.5	46.	2.5	19.6				20 5 2.76	+24.06	+1.41

No.	Micrometer	n	r	i	d_1	d_2	Mean Right Ascension, 1850.0.	Mean Declination, 1850.0.
99	IV.	2	12.289	-48 26.93	-6.64	-6.81	19 15 38.20	-22 51 30.38
100	IV.	3	19.190	41 18.23	6.53	5.71	16 43.86	44 20.47
101	VII.	5	48.129	10 55.60	0.47	1.17	17 21.44	13 53.24
102	IV.	4	45.195	13 58.28	6.06	1.61	21 12.43	16 55.95
103	III.	4	43.324	15 55.27	5.77	1.92	23 59.49	18 52.06
104	IV.	3	37.265	22 24.33	5.65	2.86	25 10.30	25 22.84
105	V.	3	43.991	15 14.04	5.57	1.79	25 48.23	18 11.40
106	VI.	3	33.468	26 22.15	5.48	3.45	26 44.12	20 21.08
107	V.	5	48.183	10 52.53	5.35	1.17	27 58.87	13 49.05
108	V.	5	45.172	14 1.55	5.29	1.62	28 29.81	16 58.46
109	IV.	4	38.442	21 2.12	5.04	2.60	30 59.72	23 59.85
110	V.	2	45.298	13 53.70	4.64	1.58	34 41.47	16 49.92
111	VII.	2	9.977	50 51.95	4.53	7.17	35 44.40	53 53.65
112	VI.	4	36.698	22 52.00	4.40	2.96	37 0.31	25 49.36
113	V.	5	50.449	8 30.31	4.23	0.77	38 35.44	11 25.34
114	II.	3	24.260	36 0.27	3.07	4.91	49 40.30	38 58.25
115	III.	5	42.878	16 25.21	3.01	2.00	50 20.56	19 20.22
116	V.	3	36.347	33 40.18	2.98	4.59	50 40.73	36 46.75
117	V.	3	31.790	28 7.51	2.76	3.72	52 45.31	31 3.99
118	IV.	3	26.795	33 21.01	2.47	3.52	19 55 34.11	36 17.00
119	IV.	4	39.902	20 33.04	1.76	2.43	20 2 34.11	23 27.23
120	IV.	3	33.542	-26 17.89	-1.46	-3.44	20 5 28.23	-22 29 12.79

ZONE 181. JULY 19. S. $D_0 = -21^\circ\ 25'\ 0''$.

No.	Mag.	I.	II.	III.	IV.	V.	VI.	VII.	T. (h. m. s.)	a_1 (s.)	a_2 (s.)
1	9					12.	45.		17 41 11.68	+24.17	+1.00
2	10					1.5			44 1.38	24.16	1.00
3	8			21.5		51.5	27.5		46 54.55	24.16	1.00
4	9			9.		42.			50 42.12	24.15	1.00
5	8			38.		12.			52 11.68	24.15	0.99
6	10						11.5		52 54.85	24.15	0.99
7	10			24.		57.			55 57.12	24.14	0.99
8	10						56.		56 22.80	24.14	0.98
9	9					13.			57 12.91	24.14	0.98
10	10							6.	17 58 16.10	24.14	0.98
11	10					22.			18 0 5.47	24.14	0.98
12	9							6.5	1 16.18	24.14	0.98
13	9			32.					4 5.37	24.13	0.98
14	9					28.			4 27.87	24.13	0.98
15	6						23.		4 49.87	24.13	0.98
16	9			8.5					7 41.96	24.12	0.98
17	10			35.5					10 8.94	24.12	0.98
18	10						58.		10 24.88	24.12	0.97
19	9			13.					12 29.70	24.12	0.97
20	10						15.		12 41.77	24.12	0.97
21	9					26.			14 9.43	24.12	0.97
22	10							44.	18 15 54.10	+24.11	+0.97

No.	Micrometer	n	r	i	d_1	d_2	Mean Right Ascension, 1850.0.	Mean Declination, 1850.0.
1		3	32.652	-27 13.67	-25.67	-9.61	17 41 37.05	-21 52 48.05
2		5	46.248	12 51.06	25.42	7.57	44 26.54	38 27.05
3	IV.	3	30.098	29 53.91	25.17	9.99	47 19.71	55 29.07
4		5	41.851	17 29.40	24.83	8.23	51 7.27	21 43 2.55
5	IV.	2	18.762	41 40.81	24.69	11.70	52 36.82	22 7 17.20
6			.353	31 43.33	24.63	10.29	53 19.99	21 40 17.76
7	IV.	5	44.472	14 45.57	24.36	7.83	56 22.25	22 12 35.99
8		2	13.690	46 59.19	24.33	12.47	56 47.92	22 5 16.68
9		2	20.672	39 41.02	24.25	11.41	58 38.03	21 52 18.20
10		3	33.105	26 44.50	24.16	9.54	17 58 41.22	21 35 27.15
11		5	49.082	9 56.04	23.99	7.12	18 0 30.59	21 45 33.20
12		1	5.680	50 8.02	23.89	12.92	1 41.30	51 12.52
13		4	39.400	20 0.99	23.63	8.48	4 30.48	22 12 59.30
14		3	34.152	25 39.55	23.60	9.37	4 52.98	51 12.52
15		4	40.095	19 20.22	23.57	8.48	5 14.98	22 44 52.27
16		2	13.290	47 23.44	23.30	12.56	8 7.06	22 12 59.30
17		2	17.038	43 28.30	23.08	11.98	10 34.04	22 9 3.36
18		4	37.702	21 49.00	23.06	8.84	10 49.97	21 47 20.90
19		7	20.840	39 30.18	22.86	11.40	12 54.79	22 5 4.44
20		1	8.322	52 35.97	22.85	13.32	13 6.86	22 18 12.14
21		5	40.879	18 30.80	22.71	8.36	14 34.52	21 44 1.87
22		4	36.279	-23 18.61	-22.55	-9.05	18 16 19.18	-21 48 50.21

CORRECTIONS.

Date.	Corr. of Clock.	Hourly rate.	m	n	e	Zenith Point.	Mic. Co.
	h.	s.	s.	s.	s.	° ' ''	r.
1848, July 19,	0					359 59 62.03	30.0014

REMARKS.

(180) 105. Declination differs 1' from Arg. Z. 238, 43.

(180) 119. Micrometer reading assumed as 38r.902 instead of 39r.902.

(181) 6. Micrometer reading assumed as 28r.353.

(181) 9. Minutes assumed as 58, not 57, to agree with Arg. Z. 224, 39; and 307, 52.

(181) 12. Micrometer reading assumed as 10r.680, not 5r.680.

* Corr. for runs +0″.07.

INSTRUMENT READINGS.

Date.	CIRCLE A.	B.	C.	D.	E.	F.	Mean.	Barom. (in.)	At.	Ex.	U.	L.	I.
Zone 181	1848 July 19, 17 40	70 47	29.2 / 30.0	24.5 / 25.0	28.2 / 28.4	23. / 24.2	21. / 22.2	26. / 27.	25.72	30.170	75.8	72.7	76.	75.
	18 21									30.160	75.	70.2	71.		76.5
	18 48													
	19 16									30.158	74.	69.5			
	20 0									30.158	73.6	69.			
	20 28		28.8 / 30.0	25. / 26.	29.2 / 29.0	24. / 25.	20.8 / 21.5	25.3 / 26.5	25.92	30.150	73.	68.2	74.		
	20 45									30.150	73.	68.			72.5

ZONE 181. JULY 19. S. $D_0 = -21°\ 25'\ 0''$—Continued.

No.	Mag.	I.	II.	III.	IV.	V.	VI.	VII.	T.	a_1	a_2	MICROMETER.	r.	i	d_1	d_2	Mean Right Ascension, 1850.0	Mean Declination, 1850.0
									h. m. s.	s.	s.		r.	' "	"	' "	h. m. s.	° ' "
23	9			18.					18 18 34.73	+24.11	+0.97	6	44.192	−15 3.92	−22.30	−7.86	18 18 59.81	−21 40 34.08
24	9		29.						20 2.37	24.11	0.97	5	41.235	18 8.35	22.17	8.31	20 27.45	43 38.83
25	8			53.					21 9.66	24.11	0.97	3	34.470	25 19.72	22.07	9.33	21 34.76	50 51.12
26	9					52.			21 35.46	24.10	0.97	4	47.270	11 48.40	22.03	7.39	22 0.53	37 17.82
27	9			34.					23 50.74	24.10	0.97	2	72.058	23 35.28	21.92	9.11	23 15.81	21 49 6.31
28	8		9.						25 42.42	24.10	0.96	2	20.416	39 56.56	21.64	11.46	26 7.48	22 5 29.66
29	9		37.						26 10.46	24.10	0.96	2	14.032	46 36.78	21.59	12.45	26 35.52	22 12 10.82
30	9		32.5						28 5.87	24.10	0.96	3	36.020	23 42.27	21.41	9.09	28 30.93	21 49 12.77
31	7				30.		3.5		28 30.11	24.10	0.96	5	53.295	5 31.66	21.37	6.49	28 55.17	21 30 59.52
32	8					20.			30 3.26	24.10	0.96	2	20.350	40 1.58	21.23	11.47	30 28.32	22 5 34.28
33	10					31.			31 14.46	24.09	0.96	4	47.008	12 5.04	21.11	7.43	31 39.51	21 37 33.58
34	10						31.		32 57.83	24.09	0.96	2	17.922	42 33.74	20.94	11.84	33 22.88	22 8 6.52
35	10		5.						35 38.37	24.09	0.96	4	44.160	15 2.17	20.69	7.87	36 3.42	21 40 30.73
36	10		20.		53.				41 53.20	24.08	0.95	IV. 2	14.858	45 45.58	20.08	12.33	42 18.23	22 11 17.99
37	6			25.8			15.8		43 42.57	24.08	0.95	III. 2	20.364	40 0.28	19.91	11.47	43 7.60	22 5 31.66
38	6		3.8		36.8				44 36.93	24.08	0.95	IV. 5	52.022	6 51.39	19.82	6.68	45 1.06	21 36 17.89
39	8		50.						48 23.37	24.07	0.95	3	29.593	30 25.60	19.45	10.07	48 48.39	55 55.12
40	9				50.				48 49.88	24.07	0.95	4	38.418	21 3.63	19.41	8.73	49 14.00	21 46 31.77
41	8			10.5					50 10.38	24.07	0.95	3	24.150	36 7.12	19.25	10.90	50 35.40	22 1 37.27
42	10		1.						52 34.49	24.07	0.95	1	8.368	52 30.06	19.04	13.32	52 59.51	22 18 3.32
43	8		23.5		57.				54 56.88	24.07	0.95	5	40.142	19 16.88	18.81	8.47	55 21.90	21 44 44.16
44	2				16.	33.	49.5		55 16.21	24.07	0.94	IV. 3	28.208	31 52.55	18.78	10.28	55 41.22	57 21.61
45	9		5.5						57 38.87	24.07	0.94	5	45.550	13 37.51	18.55	7.65	58 3.88	39 3.71
46	10				2.				58 1.87	24.06	0.94	4	34.695	24 57.14	18.51	9.30	58 26.87	50 24.95
47	.						11.		58 37.91	24.06	0.94		F.Wire.	29 59.91	18.46	10.00	59 2.91	21 55 28.37
48	9							37.	18 58 46.99	24.06	0.94	3	24.565	35 40.32	18.44	10.84	18 59 11.99	22 1 9.60
49	9		38.						19 1 11.37	24.06	0.94	3	30.800	29 9.75	18.19	9.88	19 1 36.37	21 54 37.82
50	9		9.						2 42.44	24.06	0.94	2	15.792	44 50.27	18.05	12.18	3 7.44	22 10 20.50
51	7			48.5		38.			3 5.03	24.06	0.94	III. 3	31.300	28 38.69	18.01	9.81	3 30.03	21 54 6.51
52	9					45.			4 28.19	24.06	0.94	2	14.545	46 5.58	17.88	12.40	4 53.19	22 11 35.86
53	9		0.5		33.5				6 33.66	24.06	0.94	IV. 2	20.242	40 8.18	17.67	11.51	6 58.66	5 37.36
54	9		5.2						7 25.46	24.05	0.94	1	13.668	46 59.63	17.59	12.50	7 50.45	12 29.72
55	9						19.		7 45.88	24.05	0.94	3	24.972	35 14.98	17.56	10.76	8 10.87	22 0 43.30
56	10							25.	8 35.10	24.05	0.94	5	38.740	20 44.80	17.48	8.68	9 0.11	21 46 10.96
57	10			47.					11 3.71	24.05	0.94	2	17.668	42 49.17	17.23	11.90	11 28.70	22 8 18.30
58	8				32.5				11 32.40	24.05	0.94	2	21.209	39 1.88	17.19	11.35	11 57.39	22 4 30.42
59	8					48.			12 31.37	24.05	0.94	3	30.189	29 48.15	17.09	9.98	12 56.36	21 55 15.22
60	9		3.						14 36.40	24.05	0.94	3	23.550	36 44.75	16.89	11.01	15 1.39	22 2 12.65
61	9						27.		14 36.98	24.05	0.94	2	23.458	36 46.75	16.89	10.98	15 1.97	22 2 14.62
62	8			30.					16 46.68	24.05	0.94	3	35.080	24 41.38	16.67	9.23	17 11.67	21 50 7.28
63	6						30.2		16 57.05	24.05	0.94	2	21.650	38 40.04	16.66	11.30	17 22.04	22 4 8.00
64	9						19.		17 45.91	24.05	0.94	3	20.238	29 44.81	16.58	9.97	18 10.90	21 55 11.36
65	.			7.					20 23.75	24.04	0.94	5	46.050	13 6.21	16.31	7.56	20 48.75	38 30.11
66	7		0.1						21 33.47	24.04	0.94	5	47.330	11 45.81	16.20	7.36	21 58.45	37 9.37
67	8					57.			21 40.42	24.04	0.94	4	40.458	18 55.98	16.19	8.41	22 5.40	44 20.58
68	7				56.				22 55.87	24.04	0.94	3	35.430	24 19.48	16.07	9.18	23 20.85	21 49 44.73
69	8		1.						27 33.56	24.04	0.94	1	12.355	48 21.09	15.61	12.73	27 58.54	22 13 49.43
70	8					0.1			27 44.35	24.04	0.94	2	28.002	31 59.58	15.60	10.30	28 9.33	21 57 25.48
71	10		52.		25.				19 30 25.12	+24.04	+0.94	IV. 3	28.862	−31 10.08	−15.33	−10.18	19 30 50.10	−21 56 35.59

CORRECTIONS.

Date.	Corr. of Clock.	Hourly rate.	m	n	c	Zenith Point.	Mic. Co.
1848.	h.	s.	s.	s.	s.	° ' "	r.

INSTRUMENT READINGS.

Date.	CIRCLE.							Barom.	THERMOM.				
	A.	H.	C.	D.	E.	F.	Mean.		At.	Ex.	U.	L.	I.
	h. m.	° ' "					"	in.	°	°	°	°	°
Zone 181	July 19, 21 8							30.150	72.8	67.5			

REMARKS.

(181) 27. Micrometer reading assumed as 36r.058, and minutes of transit as 22 instead of 23, to correspond with Arg. Z. 307, 96.

(181) 37. Minutes of transit assumed as 42, not 43.

(181) 41. Transit over T. IV assumed as recorded over T. III.

(181) 54. Right ascension differs 13s from Arg. Z. 238, 15; and Mural Z., 1848, July 18, and is wrong.

(181) 70. Transit over T. V assumed as 1s.0 instead of 0s.1, to agree with Transit Z., 1848, August 7.

ZONE 181. JULY 19. S. $D_o = -21° 25' 0''$—Continued.

No.	Mag.	I.	II.	III.	IV.	V.	VI.	VII.	T. (h. m. s.)	a_1 (s.)	a_2 (s.)	MICROMETER	r.	i (' '')	d_1 ('')	d_2 ('')	Mean Right Ascension, 1850.0 (h. m. s.)	Mean Declination, 1850.0 (° ' '')
72	8					15.			19 30 58.45	+24.04	+0.94	5	45.032	−14 10.28	−15.28	− 7.71	19 31 23.43	−21 39 33.27
73	9							5.	31 15.12	24.03	0.93	6	48.813	10 12.53	15.25	7.14	31 40.09	35 34.92
74	10			23.5					33 40.18	24.04	0.93	3	35.312	24 26.95	15.02	9.20	34 5.15	21 49 51.17
75	10					50.			34 16.78	24.04	0.93	1	9.428	51 26.62	14.96	13.19	34 41.75	22 16 54.77
76	8		38.5			28.5			37 11.88	24.04	0.93	3	32.558	27 19.63	14.07	9.62	37 36.85	21 52 43.92
77	9				11.	28.			38 11.06	24.03	0.93	IV 2	14.628	46 0.16	14.57	12.39	38 36.02	22 11 27.12
78	10				3.				41 2.91	24.03	0.93	3	19.770	35 27.97	14.30	10.75	41 27.87	22 0 53.02
79	10			5.					43 21.72	24.03	0.93	5	41.434	17 56.10	14.08	8.26	43 46.68	21 43 18.44
80	9		32.		15.				46 15.12	24.03	0.93	IV 3	31.639	28 17.24	13.81	9.76	46 40.08	21 53 40.81
81	10		13.	30.		3.5			50 46.62	24.03	0.93	III 2	15.552	45 2.00	13.37	12.22	51 11.58	22 10 27.59
82	9			36.5			26.		51 53.03	24.03	0.93	III 3	32.972	26 53.59	13.26	9.55	52 17.99	21 52 16.40
83	7				43.		16.		55 42.88	24.03	0.93	IV 4	40.782	18 35.07	12.90	8.36	56 7.84	21 43 56.33
84	9			3.			36.		19 57 19.48	24.03	0.93	III 2	19.938	40 26.74	12.74	11.54	19 57 44.44	22 5 51.02
85	10		7.5						20 0 40.88	24.03	0.93	3	28.043	32 2.78	12.43	10.33	20 1 5.84	21 57 25.54
86	8			22.					1 38.71	24.03	0.93	5	40.308	19 6.76	12.35	8.42	2 3.67	44 27.53
87	9							11.	1 21.10	24.03	0.93	5	39.738	19 42.16	12.37	8.50	1 46.06	45 3.03
88	10		27.5						4 0.87	24.03	0.93	3	31.090	27 48.04	12.11	9.84	4 25.83	21 53 10.89
89	10		44.						5 17.40	24.02	0.93	3	24.062	36 12.57	11.99	10.94	5 42.35	22 1 35.50
90	10				18.		51.		6 17.88	24.02	0.93	IV 3	30.490	29 29.38	11.90	9.93	6 42.83	21 54 51.21
91	8			54.					7 53.88	24.02	0.93	4	38.330	21 9.15	11.75	8.72	8 18.83	46 29.62
92	10			35.5		6.			10 8.38	24.02	0.93	IV 5	46.296	12 51.06	11.54	7.50	10 33.33	38 10.10
93	8			49.	6.	23.			12 22.63	24.02	0.94	IV 3	32.174	27 43.73	11.34	9.68	12 47.59	53 4.75
94	9				2.3				14 18.99	24.02	0.94	3	36.838	22 50.94	11.15	8.95	14 43.95	48 11.04
95	9					55.			14 54.88	24.02	0.94	4	45.502	13 39.01	11.10	7.62	15 19.84	21 38 57.73
96	9					21.5			16 21.43	24.02	0.94	1	17.252	43 15.13	10.97	11.99	16 46.39	22 8 38.09
97	10			49.5					19 22.87	24.02	0.94	4	47.190	11 51.98	10.69	7.36	19 47.83	21 37 10.03
98	10			54.					20 27.37	24.02	0.94	4	47.108	11 57.12	10.59	7.38	20 52.33	37 15.09
99	10						10.		20 53.42	24.02	0.94	3	39.698	19 51.33	10.55	8.52	21 18.38	45 10.40
100	8			54.5		28.			28 27.87	24.02	0.94	3	33.945	25 52.41	9.87	9.38	28 52.83	51 11.66
101	9					12.8			29 12.66	24.02	0.94	3	28.752	31 18.30	9.80	10.19	29 37.62	21 56 38.29
102	10			47.					31 22.44	24.02	0.95	2	16.853	43 39.78	9.61	12.05	31 47.41	22 9 1.44
103	10							58.5	31 8.60	24.02	0.95	4	40.085	19 19.64	9.63	8.46	31 33.57	21 44 37.73
104	11						15.5		32 58.00	24.02	0.95	4	36.632	22 55.95	9.46	8.98	33 23.87	48 14.39
105	10					41.			34 40.88	24.02	0.95	5	38.638	20 51.58	9.32	8.68	35 5.85	46 9.58
106	9							38.	35 4.87	24.02	0.95	5	40.950	18 26.29	9.28	8.32	35 29.84	43 43.89
107	10							41.6	36 8.46	24.02	0.95	5	43.080	16 12.73	9.19	8.00	36 33.43	21 41 29.92
108	7							52.5	37 2.45	24.02	0.95	3	22.370	37 58.02	9.11	11.20	37 27.42	22 3 18.33
109	7				32.		5.	22.	41 48.65	24.03	0.95	III 3	33.292	26 33.70	8.69	9.48	42 13.63	21 51 51.87
110	8					17.			43 16.87	24.03	0.95	4	37.352	22 10.53	8.56	8.87	43 41.85	47 27.96
111	9			7.	24.		56.5		45 40.39	24.03	0.95	III 6	53.150	5 40.56	8.35	7.46	46 5.37	21 30 56.37
112	9			9.		42.			48 42.18	24.03	0.95	IV 2	17.085	43 26.04	8.08	12.02	49 7.16	22 8 46.14
113	10						22.		48 48.88	24.03	0.95	3	37.304	22 15.80	8.08	8.86	49 13.86	21 47 32.74
114	10			37.					50 53.72	24.03	0.96	1	14.780	45 49.41	7.90	12.39	51 18.71	22 11 9.70
115	9			48.					53 4.64	24.03	0.96	3	30.298	29 41.55	7.71	9.96	53 29.63	21 54 59.22
116	9				4.5	37.5			54 20.98	24.03	0.96	2	18.278	42 11.04	7.61	11.84	54 45.97	22 7 30.49
117	10					10.8			56 10.68	24.03	0.96	4	38.783	20 40.53	7.45	8.63	56 35.67	21 45 56.61
118	5		59.	15.5	32.	49.			20 59 32.21	24.03	0.96	IV 4	37.235	22 17.87	7.16	8.89	20 59 57.20	47 33.92
119	11		27.						21 2 0.37	24.03	0.96	4	39.442	19 58.36	6.95	8.52	21 2 25.36	45 13.83
120	8			21.		54.			21 3 37.59	+24.04	+0.96	III 5	46.945	−12 10.00	−6.82	− 7.38	21 4 2.59	−21 37 24.20

CORRECTIONS.

Date.	Corr. of Clock.	Hourly rate.	m	n	c	Zenith Point.	Mic. Co.
1848.	h. s.	s.	s.	s.	s.	° ' ''	r.

INSTRUMENT READINGS.

Date.	CIRCLE.						Barom.	THERMOM.				
	A.	B.	C.	D.	E.	F.	Mean.		At.	Ex.	U.	L.	I.
1848. h. m.	° ' ''							in.	° ° ° ° °				

REMARKS.

(181) 78. Micrometer reading assumed as 24r.770, not 19r.770.

(181) 80. Time of transit over T. 11 assumed as 42s instead of 32s.

(181) 88. Micrometer reading assumed as 32r.090 instead of 31r.090.

(181) 103. Right ascension differs from Arg. Z, 237, 5 = 10s.4.

Zone 181. July 19. S. $D_o = -21° 25' 0''$—Continued.

No.	Mag.	I.	II.	III.	IV.	V.	VI.	VII.	T. (h. m. s.)	a₁ (s.)	a₂ (s.)	MICROMETER (r,)	i (' ")	d₁ (")	d₂ (")	Mean R.A. 1850.0 (h. m. s.)	Mean Decl. 1850.0 (° ' ")
121	8		41.	56.	14.5				21 5 14.46	+24.04	+0.96	. 3 30.502	−29 28.63	− 6.68	− 9.93	21 5 39.46	−21 54 45.24
122	9				52.				6 51.00	24.04	0.97	. 2 22.058	36 14.15	6.55	11.26	7 16.91	22 3 31.96
123	9				35.5		9.		21 8 35.62	+24.04	+0.97	. 1 12.575	−48 8.37	− 6.43	−12.75	21 9 0.63	−22 13 27.55

Zone 182. July 20. C. $D_o = -28° 18' 20''$.

No.	Mag.	I.	II.	III.	IV.	V.	VI.	VII.	T. (h. m. s.)	a₁ (s.)	a₂ (s.)	MICROMETER (r,)	i (' ")	d₁ (")	d₂ (")	Mean R.A. 1850.0 (h. m. s.)	Mean Decl. 1850.0 (° ' ")
1	8			25.2	42.2	0.5	17.7		17 48 42.62	+24.95	+1.02	IV. 3 34.295	−25 30.70	−18.05	− 3.17	17 49 8.59	−28 44 11.92
2	9.10					18.	35.6		49 0.43	24.95	0.83	V. 3 26.095	34 4.85	18.03	4.77	49 26.21	52 47.65
3	10				46.2		21.5		50 46.26	24.95	1.02	IV. 4 36.465	23 6.18	17.89	− 2.74	51 12.23	41 46.81
4	10					29.5	47.		52 11.98	24.94	1.35	V. 5 54.537	4 13.61	17.77	+ 0.77	52 38.27	22 50.61
5	9						25.2		53 50.15	24.94	0.99	VI. 3 34.606	25 10.60	17.64	− 3.10	54 16.08	43 51.34
6	9					37.5	54.5		55 19.70	24.94	1.03	V. 3 37.268	22 23.95	17.52	2.58	55 45.67	41 4.05
7	9					57.3	14.8		56 39.76	24.94	1.19	V. 4 45.485	13 35.39	17.41	0.99	57 5.89	32 13.79
8	7			51.7	9.2	26.2	54.2		58 9.10	24.93	1.27	IV. 5 49.558	9 26.22	17.29	0.18	58 35.30	28 3.69
9	9					12.8	30.5		17 58 55.33	24.93	0.92	V. 3 32.420	27 28.16	17.23	3.52	17 59 21.18	46 8.91
10	8		25.6	43.2	0.3				18 2 0.68	24.93	0.74	III. 3 23.381	36 55.42	16.96	5.30	18 2 26.35	28 55 37.68
11	9.10					35.3	53.5		2 17.92	24.93	0.60	V. 2 16.291	44 16.78	16.94	6.71	2 43.45	29 3 0.43
12	9.10		49.5						3 19.36	24.93	0.81	IV. 3 27.210	32 55.16	16.82	4.55	4 15.10	28 51 36.53
13	9			19.2	36.				4 35.86	24.93	0.79	III. 3 26.403	33 45.91	16.75	4.71	5 1.58	52 27.37
14	9					19.5		55.	5 2.06	24.92	0.98	V. 3 35.909	23 48.97	16.71	2.84	5 27.96	42 28.52
15	9						52.2		5 17.14	24.92	1.06	VI. 3 39.197	20 22.52	16.69	2.21	5 43.12	39 1.42
16	8		52.5	10.2	27.8	45.4	2.2		7 27.65	24.92	0.80	IV. 3 26.503	33 38.94	16.51	4.69	7 53.37	28 52 20.14
17	9		51.3	8.8	26.8				9 26.66	24.92	0.57	III. 2 16.085	44 28.44	16.34	6.76	9 52.15	29 3 11.54
18	9		52.	10.2	27.2				10 27.52	24.92	0.49	III. 2 12.052	48 41.35	16.26	7.56	10 52.93	29 7 25.17
19	9					2.3	19.5		11 12.04	24.92	0.90	V. 3 32.577	27 18.25	16.20	3.49	11 27.86	28 45 57.94
20	8			47.2	4.8	22.5	39.4		12 4.74	24.92	1.21	IV. 5 48.115	10 56.73	16.12	0.45	12 30.87	29 33.30
21	9.10				19.5	36.6			13 19.26	24.92	1.23	V. 5 48.986	10 2.00	16.01	0.30	13 45.41	28 28 38.31
22	9				14.3	31.5			14 13.94	24.92	0.44	V. 2 9.085	50 51.39	15.93	7.97	14 39.30	29 9 35.29
23	9			52.5	9.8	27.5			15 9.99	24.91	1.22	IV. 5 49.571	9 25.40	15.60	0.16	18 36.12	28 28 1.16
24	9						7.		18 31.93	24.91	0.76	VI. 3 26.872	33 15.68	15.57	4.62	18 57.60	51 55.87
25	8.9		50.7	17.5	34.8				20 34.97	24.91	0.73	III. 3 25.574	34 37.79	15.40	4.88	21 0.61	53 18.07
26	9				57.5	14.3	32.		21 57.03	24.91	1.05	V. 5 41.474	17 53.65	15.28	1.76	22 22.99	30 30.69
27	9					35.3			24 17.83	24.91	1.22	V. 5 50.369	8 35.35	15.08	0.03	24 43.96	27 10.46
28	8			50.5	8.2	26.	43.3		27 8.24	24.90	1.01	IV. 4 40.572	18 48.38	14.84	1.94	27 34.15	37 25.16
29	9				19.3	37.3	54.5		29 19.46	24.90	1.01	V. 4 40.723	19 41.89	14.65	− 2.10	29 45.37	38 18.64
30	9			54.2					31 11.07	24.90	1.27	III. 5 54.115	4 39.91	14.49	+ 0.72	31 38.14	23 13.71
31	9					40.5			31 22.77	24.90	0.62	V. 2 21.495	38 49.71	14.48	− 5.68	31 48.29	28 57 29.87
32	10						13.8		31 38.63	24.90	0.45	VI. 2 13.922	46 44.52	14.45	7.19	32 3.98	29 5 26.16
33	9				8.	25.5		0.5	33 55.50	24.90	1.04	IV. 4 42.549	16 44.36	14.31	− 1.54	33 51.44	28 36 20.21
34	9		41.	58.5					35 16.28	24.89	1.26	III. 5 55.258	3 28.28	14.14	+ 0.93	35 42.45	22 1.49
35	9				44.3	2.	19.5		35 44.29	24.89	0.64	V. 3 23.442	36 51.40	14.11	− 5.29	36 10.82	55 30.80
36	8		9.	26.	43.8	1.6	18.5		37 43.86	24.89	1.20	IV. 5 51.362	7 33.01	13.93	+ 0.17	38 9.95	26 7.77
37	9		52.5	10.5	27.5	45.3			40 27.75	24.89	0.98	IV. 3 32.148	27 45.29	13.71	− 3.57	40 53.62	46 22.57
38	9.10			23.5	41.3				44 41.16	24.89	0.66	III. 3 25.781	34 24.68	13.34	4.83	45 6.71	53 2.85
39	10				27.2				45 27.06	24.88	0.84	IV. 4 34.456	25 12.25	13.28	3.11	45 52.78	43 48.64
40	9.10		44.5	2.3	19.5				48 19.75	24.88	0.57	III. 3 22.252	38 6.24	13.04	5.53	48 45.20	56 44.81
41	9			56.5	14.2	32.2			49 14.26	24.88	0.75	IV. 3 31.223	28 43.39	12.96	3.76	49 39.89	47 20.11
42	9				10.	27.6	45.2		18 50 9.97	+24.88	+0.63	V. 3 24.808	−35 25.47	−12.88	− 5.02	18 50 35.48	−28 54 3.37

CORRECTIONS.

Date.	Corr. of Clock.	Hourly rate.	m	n	c	Zenith Point.	Mic. Co.
	h.	s.	s.	s.	s.	° ' "	r.
1848. July 20,	0	. .	. .	. .	. .	359 59 63.32	30.0010

REMARKS.

(182) 7. Declination 10' discordant from Arg. Z. 223, 41.

(182) 29. Micrometer reading assumed as 39'.723, not 40'.723.

INSTRUMENT READINGS.

	Date.	A.	B.	C.	D.	E.	F.	Mean.	Barom.	At.	Ex.	U.	L.	I.
		° ' "						"	in.	°	°	°	°	°
Zone 182	1848, July 20, 17 45	77 39 65.8	58.	64.3	57.3	52.4	61.	59.80	30.076	77.8	72.7	76.7	75.7	76.2
	18 0										72.3			
	18 20								30.072		71.8			
	18 40								30.070	76.	71.3			
	19 0										70.7			
	19 20	65.5	58.2	64.6	58.3	52.5	60.2	59.88	30.068	75.4	70.	75.5	73.5	

ZONE 182. JULY 20. C. $D_0 = -28°\ 18'\ 20''$—Continued.

No.	Mag.	I.	II.	III.	IV.	V.	VI.	VII.	T. (h. m. s.)	a_1	a_2	Micr.		r.	i (′ ″)	d_1	d_2	Mean Right Ascension, 1850.0 (h. m. s.)	Mean Declination, 1850.0 (° ′ ″)
43	9				12.5		47.5		18 51 12.40	+24.88	+0.61	VI.	3	24.088	−36 10.44	−12.79	−5.16	18 51 37.89	−28 54 48.39
44	9.10					43.5	8.		51 25.69	24.88	0.48	V.	2	17.656	42 50.42	12.78	6.44	51 51.05	29 1 29.64
45	9					57.		32.5	52 39.48	24.88	0.66	V.	3	27.785	32 18.78	12.67	4.43	53 5.02	28 50 55.88
46	9						56.2		53 21.14	24.88	0.67	VI.	3	27.467	32 38.60	12.61	4.50	53 46.69	28 51 15.71
47	9.10			29.2		4.6			54 46.86	24.88	0.43	IV.	2	14.587	46 2.76	12.50	7.05	55 12.17	29 4 42.31
48	9		49.2			43.			57 24.95	24.87	0.63	IV.	3	26.388	33 46.80	12.27	4.71	57 50.45	28 52 23.78
49	7.8			21.	38.1	56.	13.5		57 38.35	24.87	0.65	IV.	3	27.009	33 8.09	12.25	4.59	58 3.87	51 44.93
50	8.9				2.7	20.5	38.2		18 59 2.81	24.87	0.52	V.	3	20.902	39 30.47	12.13	5.80	18 59 28.20	28 58 8.40
51	9		24.	41.6	59.2				19 0 59.31	24.87	0.37	III.	2	13.512	47 9.92	11.97	7.29	19 1 24.55	29 5 49.18
52	9				37.7	55.7			1 20.38	24.87	0.74	V.	3	32.120	27 46.87	11.92	−3.58	1 45.09	28 46 22.37
53	9.10					31.3	49.3		2 31.53	24.87	1.18	V.	5	54.208	4 34.26	11.86	+0.76	2 57.58	23 5.36
54	10		2.8	20.2		55.1			4 37.85	24.87	0.85	IV.	3	38.367	21 15.17	11.67	−2.35	5 3.57	39 49.19
55	8			39.7	57.2	15.			6 57.25	24.86	0.54	IV.	3	23.397	36 54.41	11.47	5.32	7 22.65	55 31.20
56	9		27.2	45.2	2.5				9 2.61	24.86	1.03	III.	5	47.852	11 12.99	11.29	0.48	9 28.50	29 44.76
57	10		38.2		13.5				11 13.44	24.86	0.71	III.	3	31.938	27 58.41	11.11	3.62	11 39.01	46 33.14
58	9				26.2	44.	1.5		11 26.30	24.86	0.71	V.	3	32.383	27 30.49	11.10	3.52	11 51.87	46 5.11
59	9		13.8						13 49.20	24.86	0.51	II.	3	21.885	38 28.95	10.90	5.62	14 14.57	57 5.47
60	9		22.		39.8	14.5			13 57.21	24.86	0.49	V.	3	21.380	39 0.93	10.89	5.72	14 22.56	57 37.54
61	10						43.5		14 8.38	24.86	0.46	V.	3	19.830	40 37.72	10.87	6.03	14 33.70	59 14.62
62	9								15	24.85	0.76	VII.	3	34.825	24 56.07	10.80	3.04	15	43 29.01
63	9			6.5	24.	41.5			21 24.00	24.85	0.81	IV.	4	38.453	21 1.43	10.28	2.33	21 29.66	39 34.04
64	8.9			58.2	15.3	33.5			22 15.70	24.85	0.98	IV.	3	46.282	12 51.92	10.21	0.79	22 41.53	31 22.92
65	9							18.5	22 25.69	24.85	0.77	VII.	3	37.102	22 33.50	10.20	2.60	22 51.31	41 6.30
66	9					10.5	28.		23 52.91	24.85	0.59	V.	3	27.864	32 13.76	10.08	4.43	24 18.35	28 50 48.27
67	9.10			31.3					26 6.72	24.85	0.37	II.	2	17.571	42 54.88	9.90	6.48	26 31.94	29 1 31.26
68	9			57.2	15.	32.5	50.3		26 14.93	24.85	0.39	IV.	2	19.455	40 57.53	9.89	6.10	26 40.17	28 59 33.52
69	9					55.5	12.5		19 26 37.56	+24.85	+0.40	V.	2	19.026	−41 24.44	−9.86	−6.19	19 27 2.81	−29 0 0.49

ZONE 183. JULY 20. C. $D_0 = -23°\ 17'\ 50''$.

No.	Mag.	I.	II.	III.	IV.	V.	VI.	VII.	T. (h. m. s.)	a_1	a_2	Micr.		r.	i (′ ″)	d_1	d_2	Mean Right Ascension, 1850.0 (h. m. s.)	Mean Declination, 1850.0 (° ′ ″)
1	8			37.1	54.	10.8			20 12 10.87	+24.82	+0.42	III.	3	21.688	−38 41.49	−12.12	−5.37	20 12 36.11	−23 56 48.98
2	8		27.5	34.2	51.3	8.	25.		14 1.23	24.82	0.42	IV.	3	21.313	39 5.14	11.95	5.43	15 26.47	57 12.52
3	9.10				3.2		37.		16 3.24	24.82	0.41	VI.	3	20.838	39 34.24	11.88	5.51	16 28.47	57 41.63
4	9				51.3		25.7		18 51.64	24.82	0.38	VI.	5	46.922	12 11.44	11.71	1.25	19 16.84	30 14.40
5	10								21	24.82	0.38	.	3	35.953			3.03		
6	9		18.3	35.1	51.7	9.			24 51.96	24.82	0.38	IV.	3	32.542	27 20.63	11.33	3.60	25 17.16	23 45 25.56
7	9		38.5		12.5				26 12.43	24.82	0.39	II.	2	15.858	44 42.17	11.27	6.33	26 37.64	24 2 49.77
8	10		14.7		48.2				30 48.30	24.82	0.36	II.	5	43.916	15 19.87	11.00	1.72	31 13.48	23 33 22.59
9	9		4.8	21.8	38.7				32 38.65	24.82	0.36	III.	3	37.677	21 58.35	10.90	2.75	33 3.83	40 2.00
10	9				58.3	15.	32.		32 58.27	24.82	0.35	V.	4	45.264	13 54.39	10.88	1.51	33 23.44	23 31 56.78
11	9				8.3	25.1	32.3		34 25.19	24.82	0.37	IV.	2	18.273	42 11.67	10.80	5.94	34 50.38	24 0 18.41
12	9.10				9.2	26.	43.		35 26.04	24.82	0.36	IV.	3	34.321	25 29.07	10.74	3.31	35 51.22	23 43 33.12
13	10			47.6		21.			37 4.36	24.82	0.38	IV.	2	14.650	45 58.75	10.65	6.52	37 29.56	24 4 5.92
14	9			19.5		53.2			38 36.32	24.82	0.36	IV.	2	17.388	43 7.16	10.56	6.08	39 1.50	24 7 13.80
15	9					22.2	38.9		39 5.37	24.82	0.33	V.	5	53.263	5 33.59	10.54	0.22	39 30.52	23 23 34.35
16	10			38.					45 55.01	24.82	0.32	III.	4	51.848	6 59.93	10.15	0.45	46 20.15	25 0.53
17	9			50.3			41.3		52 7.49	24.81	0.30	III.	5	49.397	9 36.25	9.82	0.85	52 32.60	27 36.92
18	8.9				16.	33.5			20 52 16.28	+24.81	+0.31	V.	3	37.992	−21 38.33	−9.81	−2.70	20 52 41.40	−23 39 40.84

CORRECTIONS.

Date.	Corr. of Clock.	Hourly rate.	m	n	c	Zenith Point.	Mic. Co.
1848.	h.	s.	s.	s.	s.	° ′ ″	r.

INSTRUMENT READINGS.

Date.	CIRCLE							Barom.	THERMOM.				
	A.	B.	C.	D.	E.	F.	Mean.		At.	Ex.	U.	L.	I.
1848. July 20, 20 10	° ′ ″						″	in.		69.5			
20 20	72 39 69.4	63.9	68.	62.9	56.2	63.7	64.02	30.058	74.5	69.4	75.5	75.	76.2
20 40										68.9			
21 0								30.058		68.7			
21 20										68.5			
21 40	70.1	64.2	68.2	63.1	56.1	63.9	64.27	30.052	73.5	68.4	74.6	73.6	
21 52										68.2			

Zone 183.

REMARKS.

(182) 44. Time of transit over T. VI assumed as $0^s.8$ instead of 8^s.

(182) 52. Transits over T.'s V and VI assumed as recorded over T.'s IV and V.

(182) 53. Transits over T.'s IV and V assumed as recorded over T.'s V and VI.

(182) 60. Transit over T. III assumed to have been recorded as over T. IV.

(183) 2. Time of transits over T.'s III, IV, V, and VI assumed as $44^s.2$, $1^s.3$, 18^s, and 35^s instead of $34^s.2$, $51^s.3$, 8^s, and 25^s; and minutes as 15, not 14.

(183) 11. Time of transit over T. V assumed as $42^s.3$ instead of $52^s.3$.

ZONE 183. JULY 20. C. $D_o = -23°\ 17'\ 50''$—Continued.

No.	Mag.	I.	II.	III.	IV.	V.	VI.	VII.	T.	a_1	a_4	Micr.		r.	i	d_1	d_4	Mean Right Ascension, 1850.0	Mean Declination, 1850.0
									h. m. s.	s.	s.			r.	° ' ''	''	''	h. m. s.	° ' ''
19	8.9	..	9.6	26.3	43.2	..	17.5	..	20 57 43.41	+24.81	+0.30	IV.	3	29.278	−30 45.48	−9.51	−4.13	20 58 8.52	−23 48 49.12
20	8.9	..	21.7	..	..	12.	..	..	57 55.34	24.81	0.30	IV.	3	33.062	26 47.94	9.50	3.51	20 58 20.45	44 50.95
21	9 10	..	..	25.3	42.8	..	..	..	20 59 42.48	24.81	0.28	III.	4	45.272	13 53.00	9.40	1.50	21 0 7.57	31 53.90
22	9	..	..	16.3	32.9	49.8	..	..	21 1 32.95	24.81	0.31	IV.	3	23.518	36 46.77	9.31	5.06	1 58.07	54 51.14
23	9	..	..	11.8	27.6	..	1.	..	2 27.94	24.81	0.30	IV.	4	34.418	25 14.64	9.26	5.27	2 53.05	43 17.17
24	9	..	47.2	1.8	..	37.3	..	..	4 20.80	24.81	0.27	IV.	5	54.238	4 32.38	9.16	0.02	4 45.88	22 31.56
25	9	..	..	10.	27.	43.8	..	..	5 26.98	24.81	0.27	IV.	4	47.399	11 39.93	9.10	1.15	5 52.06	29 40.18
26	10	..	..	21.8	37.5	55.2	..	..	7 38.22	24.81	0.26	IV.	5	50.950	7 58.69	8.99	0.55	8 3.29	25 58.23
27	8.9	..	32.5	49.7	6.5	..	..	..	15 6.48	24.82	0.25	III.	5	53.575	5 13.89	8.60	0.14	15 31.55	23 12.63
28	9	..	..	..	..	27.	43.5	..	15 19.96	24.82	0.28	V.	2	22.458	37 49.37	8.59	5.27	15 45.06	55 53.23
29	10	..	..	..	54.?	..	..	..	20 53.88	24.82	0.26	IV.	3	24.541	35 42.59	8.29	4.91	21 18.96	53 45.79
30	10	..	..	..	..	..	22.7	..	20 46.43	24.82	0.25	VI.	3	26.364	33 46.61	8.30	4.61	21 13.50	51 49.52
31	9	..	40.8	..	14.7	31.6	..	..	23 14.66	24.82	0.24	IV.	3	34.738	25 2.72	8.18	3.21	23 39.72	23 43 4.11
32	8	..	41.6	58.3	15.5	..	..	..	26 15.43	24.82	0.25	III.	2	11.689	49 4.11	8.03	7.05	26 40.50	24 7 9.19
33	9	..	..	..	..	40.3	57.2	..	26 23.55	24.82	0.23	V.	3	30.941	29 0.77	8.02	3.86	26 48.60	23 47 2.65
34	9	..	26.	43.2	59.5	..	..	..	28 59.77	24.82	0.23	III.	3	33.606	26 13.88	7.89	3.42	29 24.82	44 15.19
35	9	..	..	42.5	59.1	16.3	..	..	30 59.25	24.82	0.23	IV.	3	25.730	34 27.88	7.79	4.72	31 24.30	52 30.39
36	7	12.1	29.	45.6	2.5	19.4	36.1	53.2	33 2.56	24.82	0.23	IV.	3	22.075	38 17.22	7.70	5.33	33 27.61	56 20.25
37	9	..	..	45.2	..	19.5	..	..	34 2.34	24.82	0.22	IV.	3	27.015	33 7.27	7.65	4.51	34 27.38	51 9.43
38	10	..	..	56.	12.2	29.2	..	..	40 12.50	24.82	0.18	IV.	5	46.295	12 51.11	7.36	1.32	40 37.50	30 49.79
39	8.9	..	52.7	9.4	26.3	43.5	..	..	42 26.42	24.82	0.20	IV.	3	20.497	39 56.25	7.27	5.56	42 51.44	57 59.10
40	9	..	0.3	..	34.3	..	..	..	46 34.21	24.82	0.20	II.	2	18.675	41 45.57	7.00	5.90	46 59.23	59 48.56
41	9	..	..	..	50.2	7.	24.	..	46 50.22	24.82	0.19	V.	3	32.285	27 36.64	7.08	3.63	47 15.23	45 37.35
42	9	..	45.8	2.9	19.5	36.3	..	..	49 19.48	24.82	0.19	IV.	3	21.835	38 32.15	6.96	5.37	49 44.49	56 34.48
43	8.9	..	..	8.8	25.2	42.5	59.	..	50 25.49	24.83	0.17	IV.	4	42.032	17 16.69	6.91	2.03	21 50 50.49	23 35 15.63
44	9	..	16.5	33.5	50.5	7.5	..	..	21 51 50.44	+24.83	+0.19	IV.	2	17.829	−42 39.27	−6.86	−6.03	22 52 15.46	−24 0 42.16

ZONE 184. JULY 24. S. $D_o = -20°\ 47'\ 30''$.

No.	Mag.	I.	II.	III.	IV.	V.	VI.	VII.	T.	a_1	a_4	Micr.		r.	i	d_1	d_4	Mean Right Ascension, 1850.0	Mean Declination, 1850.0
1	10	..	48.	..	21.	..	..	..	20 14 21.06	+25.25	+0.38	IV.	5	46.578	−12 33.28	−10.15	−7.48	20 14 46.69	−21 0 20.91
2	9	..	..	..	..	43.	..	..	15 10.02	25.25	0.38	.	3	24.571	35 40.27	10.07	10.84	15 35.65	23 31.18
3	9	..	..	25.	41.5	..	..	..	17 41.46	25.25	0.38	.	3	30.228	29 45.82	9.85	9.97	18 7.09	17 35.64
4	7	18.	34.5	51.	8.	..	..	..	20 51.15	25.25	0.38	.	3	24.462	35 47.61	9.63	10.86	20 16.78	23 38.10
5	7	..	..	16.5	49.5	..	..	..	21 49.55	25.25	0.38	.	4	35.065	24 33.47	9.48	9.23	22 15.18	12 22.18
6	10	..	..	2.	..	..	..	..	25 18.60	25.25	0.38	.	3	23.979	36 17.84	9.18	10.93	25 44.23	24 7.95
7	9	..	..	..	..	3.5	..	..	25 47.02	25.25	0.38	.	6	44.239	15 0.17	9.21	7.85	25 12.65	2 47.23
8	10	..	..	56.5	..	..	..	..	27 3.13	25.25	0.38	.	2	18.770	41 40.00	9.01	11.72	27 38.76	29 30.73
9	7	..	..	..	..	..	52.5	..	27 19.51	25.25	0.38	.	1	41.186	18 10.48	9.00	8.30	27 45.14	5 57.78
10	7	..	1.	..	..	..	..	..	29 17.63	25.25	0.38	.	2	17.618	42 52.00	8.80	11.90	29 43.26	30 42.70
11	10	..	..	49.5	..	..	..	..	34 6.09	25.24	0.38	.	3	27.420	32 42.12	8.41	10.40	34 31.71	20 30.93
12	8	..	..	27.	..	0.5	..	..	35 43.73	25.24	0.38	.	2	22.330	37 56.95	8.27	10.18	36 9.35	25 45.40
13	9	..	35.5	..	8.5	..	..	..	40 8.55	25.24	0.38	.	3	37.088	22 35.31	7.80	6.93	40 34.17	10 22.13
14	9	..	7.	..	40.	..	..	..	45 40.11	25.24	0.38	.	2	17.502	43 0.02	7.43	11.91	46 5.73	30 49.36
15	9	..	49.8	..	22.5	..	..	..	50 22.70	25.24	0.38	.	4	45.640	13 30.21	7.04	7.63	50 48.32	21 1 14.88
16	10	..	45.	..	..	..	..	..	53 18.36	25.24	0.37	.	1	5.552	7 19.55	6.80	7.00	53 43.97	20 55 3.35
17	9	..	..	..	35.5	..	8.5	..	54 52.00	25.24	0.38	.	3	27.710	32 23.73	6.67	10.35	55 17.62	21 20 10.75
18	9	..	..	..	3.5	36.5	..	..	20 58 20.08	25.24	0.38	.	4	41.210	18 7.96	6.39	8.30	20 58 45.70	21 5 52.65
19	6	..	59.	..	32.5	..	5.5	..	21 1 32.36	+25.24	+0.39	.	4	57.956	−0 35.91	−6.12	−5.75	21 1 57.99	−20 48 17.78

CORRECTIONS.

Date.	Corr. of Clock.	Hourly rate.	m	n	c	Zenith Point.	Mic. Co.
	h.	s.	s.	s.	s.	° ' ''	r.
1848. July 24.	o		.	.	.	359 59 62.89	30.0012

INSTRUMENT READINGS.

	Date.	A.	B.	C.	D.	E.	F.	Mean.	Barom.	At.	Ex.	U.	L.	I.
	1848. h. m.	° ' ''							in.	°	°	°	°	°
Zone 184	July 24, 20 10	70 9 60.	58.8	63.0	56.6	49.5	56.7	57.43	30.118	73.	65.6			
											65.			
	20 35													
	21 0								30.110	72.	64.			
											63.5			
	21 16													
	21 50	60.	58.8	63.0	58.0	49.3	56.7	57.63	30.104	74.2	63.8			

REMARKS.

(183) 19. Time of transit over T. VI assumed as 17s.5 instead of 47s.5.

(183) 28. Transits over T.'s V and VI assumed as 37s and 53s.5, not 27s and 43s.5.

(184) 4. Transits over T.'s II, III, IV, and V assumed as recorded over T.'s I, II, III, and IV, and minutes 19, not 20.

(184) 5. Transit over T. II assumed to have been recorded as over T. III.

(184) 7. Minutes assumed as 24, not 25.

(184) 10. Transit over T. III assumed as recorded over T. II.

(184) 13. Right ascension differs 18s.2 from Arg. Z. 243, 105; probably 1 thread interval in error.

(184) 16. Micrometer reading assumed as 49s.552, to agree with Mer. Circle, 1848, September 1, and Transit, July 24.

ZONE 184. JULY 24. S. D₀ = −20° 47′ 30″—Continued.

No.	Mag.	Seconds of Transit (I.–VII.)	T. (h. m. s.)	a₁	a_q	Mic.	n	r.	i (′ ″)	d₁	d₂	Mean R.A. 1850.0 (h. m. s.)	Mean Decl. 1850.0 (° ′ ″)
20	9	.. 31.5 .. 4.8	21 3 4.71	+25.25	+0.39	.	5	50.198	−8 45.72	−5.99	−6.92	21 3 30.35	−20 56 28.63
21	9	.. 26.5 .. 59.5 ..	5 59.58	25.25	0.38	.	2	23.878	36 19.22	5.75	10.97	6 25.21	21 24 5.94
22	5	...... 56. 12.5	6 39.50	25.25	0.38	.	3	31.495	28 26.20	5.70	9.78	7 5.13	21 16 11.68
23	8	.. 56.5 .. 29.5	9 29.56	25.25	0.39	.	5	49.120	9 53.33	5.46	7.08	9 55.20	20 57 35.87
24	8	.. 32.5 ... 5.8	12 5.74	25.25	0.38	.	2	21.088	39 14.29	5.25	11.39	12 31.37	21 27 0.93
25	.	. 40. 57. 13.5 .. 46.	15 13.33	25.25	0.38	.	2	19.040	41 22.75	5.00	11.71	15 38.06	29 9.46
26	8	. 52.5 .. 25.8	17 25.80	25.25	0.37	.	1	10.010	50 47.50	4.84	13.08	17 51.42	36 35.42
27	9	. 58.8 .. 32.	23 32.07	25.25	0.37	.	2	6.500	49 15.12	4.34	12.90	23 57.69	37 2.36
28	9	.... 16.5 ... 1.5	24 18.46	25.25	0.38	.	3	27.690	32 24.93	4.28	10.33	24 44.09	21 20 9.54
29	9	...... 3.	26 2.89	25.25	0.39	.	5	51.750	7 8.47	4.14	6.69	26 28.53	20 54 49.30
30	9	.. 11. 27.5 44.	28 44.09	25.25	0.39	.	4	41.031	18 18.51	3.92	8.31	29 9.73	21 6 0.74
31	10	.. 36. .. 8.5 25.	34 8.70	25.26	0.39	.	4	41.462	17 52.59	3.50	8.24	34 34.35	5 34.33
32	10	.. 17.5	40 50.73	25.26	0.39	.	3	35.280	24 28.89	2.97	9.19	41 16.38	12 11.05
33	10	... 3. ...	41 19.62	25.26	0.39	.	3	36.956	22 43.40	2.93	8.93	41 45.27	10 25.26
34	9	.... 2. 18.8 ..	42 2.06	25.26	0.39	.	3	33.280	26 34.39	2.87	9.51	42 27.71	14 16.77
35	9	. 16. ... 47. 6.	21 46 49.20	+25.27	−0.39	.	4	39.502	−19 55.60	−2.50	−8.56	21 47 14.86	−21 7 36.60

ZONE 185. AUGUST 1. C. D_v = −20° 48′ 0″.

No.	Mag.	Seconds of Transit (I.–VII.)	T. (h. m. s.)	a₁	a_q	Mic.	n	r.	i (′ ″)	d₁	d₂	Mean R.A. 1850.0 (h. m. s.)	Mean Decl. 1850.0 (° ′ ″)
1	8.9	... 34.2 .. 7.4 23.2 40.4 ..	17 50 7.21	+25.54	+0.95	IV.	4	45.608	−13 32.28	−4.05	−1.72	17 50 33.70	−21 1 38.05
2	9	... 17. 33.7 ..	51 33.29	25.54	0.95	III.	5	48.650	10 23.02	3.92	1.28	51 59.78	20 58 28.22
3	9	.... 13.2 30.	53 13.22	25.53	0.95	V.	2	18.506	41 57.24	3.77	5.69	53 39.70	21 30 6.70
4	9	. 31. 47. 4.1 ..	56 3.95	25.52	0.95	III.	3	38.800	20 39.92	3.52	2.70	56 30.42	8 45.24
5	9	. 52. 8.4 25.	57 25.08	25.52	0.95	III.	2	17.789	42 41.52	3.39	5.79	57 51.55	30 50.70
6	7	.... 44.5 1.2 ..	57 44.48	25.52	0.95	V.	2	21.245	39 5.45	3.37	5.29	58 10.95	27 14.11
7	9	.... 45.2	57 55.51	25.52	0.95	VII.	3	35.172	24 34.79	3.35	3.24	58 21.98	12 41.38
8	8	..... 20.	59 3.45	25.51	0.95	V.	3	31.977	27 55.77	3.25	3.70	59 29.91	16 2.72
9	7	.... 45.3	17 59 12.30	25.51	0.95	VI.	2	20.627	39 44.21	3.23	5.38	17 59 38.76	27 52.82
10	9	... 5.2 21.5 ..	18 1 21.58	25.51	0.95	III.	3	28.165	31 55.26	3.04	4.27	18 1 48.04	20 2.57
11	3	.. 48.1 5. 21.2 38. 54.4 ..	18 4 21.39	+25.51	+0.95	IV.	4	41.838	−17 28.80	−2.77	−2.25	18 4 47.85	−21 5 33.82

ZONE 186. AUGUST 4. S. D₀ = −22° 2′ 30″.

No.	Mag.	Seconds of Transit (I.–VII.)	T. (h. m. s.)	a₁	a_q	Mic.	n	r.	i (′ ″)	d₁	d₂	Mean R.A. 1850.0 (h. m. s.)	Mean Decl. 1850.0 (° ′ ″)
1	9	.. 36. 53.	20 2 9.64	+22.52	+1.92	.	4	38.810	−20 37.83	−11.21	−8.61	20 2 34.08	−22 23 27.65
2	10	.. 46. .. 19.	4 19.19	22.51	1.88	IV.	3	32.406	27 29.23	11.01	9.62	4 43.58	30 19.86
3	8	.... 13. .. 54.	4 3.42	22.51	1.88	.	3	33.452	26 23.41	10.98	9.45	5 27.81	29 13.84
4	8	.. 18.3 ..	8 51.82	22.50	1.87	.	3	35.136	24 37.89	10.60	9.20	9 16.19	27 27.69
5	6	.... 48. 4.5	8 47.88	22.50	1.92	.	4	45.829	13 18.28	10.60	7.53	9 12.30	16 6.41
6	7	.. 20.5 37.5 54.	12 54.10	22.50	1.91	IV.	4	56.642	·1 55.54	10.22	5.86	13 18.51	4 41.62
7	9	..... 57.	13 23.65	22.49	1.76	.	2	14.418	46 13.67	10.17	12.43	13 47.90	49 6.27
8	10	..... 42.	15 8.76	22.49	1.80	.	3	31.060	28 53.12	10.02	9.83	15 33.05	31 42.97
9	10	...... 12.	16 21.90	22.49	1.87	.	5	52.958	5 52.31	9.91	6.43	16 46.26	8 38.65
10	9	.... 10. 26.5 ..	18 53.28	22.48	1.78	V.	3	32.028	27 52.64	9.68	9.68	19 17.54	30 42.00
11	6	... 18.8 .. 52. ..	20 18.69	22.48	1.67	IV.	1	5.590	50 12.60	9.55	13.83	20 42.84	53 5.98
12	9	.. 28.5	23 2.11	22.48	1.68	.	2	13.578	36 37.91	9.32	12.56	23 26.27	39 29.82
13	9	.... 37.5 ..	23 4.15	22.48	1.68	.	2	13.180	37 3.84	9.32	12.62	23 28.31	39 55.78
14	8	... 54. ..	20 24 20.69	+22.48	+1.70	V.	1	19.090	−41 20.27	−9.20	−11.69	20 24 44.87	−22 44 11.16

CORRECTIONS.

Date.	Corr. of Clock. (h. s.)	Hourly rate. (s.)	m (s.)	n (s.)	c (s.)	Zenith Point. (° ′ ″)	Mic. Co. (r.)
1848. August 1,	0	.	.	.	.	359 59 64.10	30.0038
4,	.	.	.	.	.	63.36	30.0013

INSTRUMENT READINGS.

Date.	A.	B.	C.	D.	E.	F.	Mean.	Barom. (In.)	At.	Ex.	U.	L.	I.
Zone 185 Aug. 1, 17 45	70 9 68.1	62.2	67.9	62.8	52.9	63.6	62.92	30.058	75.8	70.2	75.7	74.2	77.
18 0	.	.	.	.	.	.	.	30.064	75.	69.8			
Zone 186 Aug. 4, 20 0	71 24 58.7	54.	60.	53.	47.	55.9	54.77	30.018	77.	73.8	.		
20 20	.	.	.	.	.	.	.	.	.	73.5			
20 40	.	.	.	.	.	.	.	30.010	76.8	73.2			
21 0	.	.	.	.	.	.	.	.	.	73.			
21 20	.	.	.	.	.	.	.	.	.	72.9			
21 40	.	.	.	.	.	.	.	30.004	76.	72.8			
22 0	58.8	54.	60.	53.7	47.	55.9	54.90	29.990	75.5	72.5			

REMARKS.

(184) 27. Micrometer reading assumed as 11r.506, not 6r.506.

(184) 28. Time of transit over T. VI assumed as 51s.5 instead of 1s.5.

(184) 35. Time of transit over T. IV assumed as 40s instead of 47s.

(186) 3. Transits over T. I assumed as recorded over T. V, and minutes as 5, not 4.

(186) 11. Micrometer reading assumed as 10r.590, not 5r.590.

(186) 12. Micrometer reading assumed as 23r.578, not 13r.578.

(186) 13. Micrometer reading assumed as 23r.180, not 13r.180.

ZONE 186. AUGUST 4. S. D. = −22° 30' 0″—Continued.

Seconds of Transit

No.	Mag.	I.	II.	III.	IV.	V.	VI.	VII.
15	8			27.7				
16	7				22.		55.	
17	9				43.5			
18	9			61.	44.5			
19	9				13.		46.	
20	7					4.	20.5	
21	9				57.5			
22	8			1.	34.5			
23	6			26.4	43.	0.	17.	
24	6					2.5	19.5	
25	8			43.8	0.		33.5	
26	9						9.5	
27	8.9			10.6	28.	45.		
28	8				17.	33.8		
29	9				59.			
30	5				45.5		19.	
31	9			3.	36.			
32	8			16.5	33.5		7.	
33	8				15.		48.	
34	8			2.8	36.5			
35	10					32.		
36	10			13.	47.			
37	10			8.	41.			
38	8			50.5	24.		57.	
39	6			32.3	40.	6.	22.5	

No.	T. (h. m. s.)	a₁ (s.)	a₂ (s.)	Mic.	N	r.	i	d₁	d₂	Mean Right Ascension 1850.0 (h. m. s.)	Mean Declination 1850.0
15	20 37 1.21	+22.46	+1.70	.	4	45.319	−13 49.48	−8.00	−7.61	20 37 25.37	−22 16 35.18
16	37 21.80	22.46	1.61	.	2	20.848	39 29.91	8.06	11.43	37 45.87	42 19.40
17	40 43.37	22.45	1.63		3	35.756	23 58.84	7.77	9.10	41 7.45	26 45.71
18	45 44.48	22.44	1.56	IV.	2	22.450	37 49.68	7.34	11.17	46 8.48	40 38.19
19	46 12.80	22.44	1.55	IV.	2	21.712	38 35.79	7.30	11.29	46 36.79	41 24.38
20	47 47.26	22.44	1.57	.	3	28.272	31 48.41	7.17	10.26	48 11.27	34 35.84
21	53 57.36	22.44	1.53		3	29.530	30 29.61	6.66	10.06	54 21.33	33 16.33
22	20 59 31.44	22.43	1.54	IV.	5	45.919	14 17.71	6.20	7.65	20 59 58.41	17 1.56
23	21 5 59.97	22.42	1.39	IV.	2	13.826	46 50.30	5.68	12.55	21 5 23.75	49 38.53
24	6 3.60	22.42	1.47	.	4	36.360	23 12.77	5.68	8.99	6 26.49	25 57.44
25	8 16.98	22.42	1.46	.	4	• 40.445	18 55.41	5.50	8.36	8 40.86	21 39.27
26	9 52.72	22.42	1.39	.	2	23.199	37 2.82	5.37	11.07	10 16.53	39 49.26
27	16 44.66	22.41	1.41	.	4	43.580	15 39.14	4.84	7.85	17 8.48	18 21.83
28	17 16.99	22.41	1.37	.	3	33.060	26 48.01	4.79	9.51	17 40.77	29 32.31
29	19 15.78	22.41	1.35	.	4	40.280	19 5.76	4.63	8.38	19 39.57	21 48.77
30	19 45.56	22.41	1.37	VI.	3	35.055	24 42.45	4.60	9.20	20 9.34	27 26.25
31	22 36.22	22.40	1.30	.	2	22.979	37 15.62	4.38	11.10	22 59.92	40 1.10
32	27 50.17	22.40	1.35	V.	5	51.459	7 26.93	3.98	6.63	28 13.92	10 7.54
33	30 14.80	22.40	1.30	IV.	3	39.046	20 32.37	3.80	8.57	30 38.50	23 14.74
34	32 36.36	22.40	1.25	IV.	3	26.308	33 51.81	3.62	10.58	33 0.01	36 36.01
35	38 15.36	22.39	1.26	.	5	41.508	17 51.53	3.21	8.18	38 39.01	20 32.92
36	44 46.70	22.39	1.20	IV.	4	36.872	22 40.46	2.76	8.91	45 10.29	25 22.13
37	47 41.27	22.39	1.09	.	2	14.729	45 53.04	2.55	12.41	48 4.75	48 38.00
38	55 23.88	22.39	1.10	IV.	3	32.360	27 32.12	2.04	9.03	55 47.37	30 13.79
39	21 59 5.84	+22.38	+1.10	.	4	42.640	−16 38.52	−1.80	−8.00	21 59 29.32	−22 19 16.32

ZONE 187. AUGUST 7. S. D. = −20° 10' 0″.

Seconds of Transit

No.	Mag.	I.	II.	III.	IV.	V.	VI.	VII.
1	10				17.5			
2	10						52.	
3	9			42.				
4	7						23.5	
5	9			0.				
6	9							31.
7	7		1.	18.	31.			
8	9			16.5	33.			
9	6				22.	38.		
10	7				42.	58.		
11	8					13.		
12	8		7.					
13	8			37.5				
14	4			28.5	45.			
15	7					52.8	9.	
16	5			51.5		24.		
17	9						5.	
18	9					18.		
19	10			30.8				
20						45.5		

No.	T. (h. m. s.)	a₁ (s.)	a₂ (s.)	Mic.	N	r.	i	d₁	d₂	Mean Right Ascension 1850.0 (h. m. s.)	Mean Declination 1850.0
1	18 29 34.06	+22.51	+1.31	.	4	38.809	−20 38.46	−25.59	−2.70	18 29 57.88	−20 31 6.75
2	30 19.14	22.51	1.03		2	22.520	37 45.53	25.53	5.08	30 42.68	48 16.14
3	33 58.51	22.50	1.19		3	31.187	28 45.70	25.30	3.82	33 22.20	39 14.82
4	32 7.08	22.50	1.39		4	42.890	16 23.33	25.36	2.12	33 30.07	26 50.75
5	35 16.63	22.48	1.48		5	48.092	10 58.07	25.08	1.35	35 40.59	21 24.50
6	35 58.15	22.48	1.05		2	23.020	37 14.05	25.04	5.01	36 21.68	47 44.10
7	38 34.19	22.48	1.40		4	43.778	15 26.58	24.79	1.97	38 58.07	25 53.34
8	39 33.02	22.48	1.52		4	50.510	8 24.19	24.60	1.02	39 57.02	18 49.80
9	40 21.72	22.48	1.36		3	40.558	18 57.61	24.62	2.46	40 45.56	29 24.69
10	41 58.23	22.47	1.38		4	41.938	17 22.09	24.48	2.25	42 22.08	27 48.82
11	42 42.12	22.47	1.47		5	46.980	12 9.05	24.41	1.51	43 6.06	22 34.97
12	45 40.09	22.46	1.36		4	40.923	18 25.28	24.13	2.40	46 3.91	28 51.81
13	45 54.09	22.46	1.40		4	43.210	16 2.43	24.11	2.06	46 17.95	26 28.60
14	48 1.60	22.45	1.01		2	20.065	40 18.46	23.91	5.48	48 25.06	50 47.82
15	48 52.61	22.45	1.23		3	33.292	26 33.45	23.86	3.51	49 16.29	37 0.52
16	53 24.23	22.44	1.24		3	33.142	26 42.93	23.42	3.53	53 47.91	37 9.88
17	53 32.10	22.44	0.93		1	14.955	45 39.88	23.41	6.19	53 55.47	56 9.48
18	54 45.12	22.43	1.51		5	48.987	10 1.87	23.30	1.21	55 9.06	20 26.35
19	59 3.89	22.41	1.36		4	39.580	−19 49.63	22.90	−2.58	59 27.66	−20 30 15.11
20	18 59 29.	+22.41	+1.40	.		.052		−22.86	.	18 59 (52)	

CORRECTIONS.

Date.	Corr. of Clock.	Hourly rate.	m	n	c	Zenith Point.	Mic. Co.
1848, August 7	h.	s.	s.	s.	s.	359 59 62.78	r. 30.0018

INSTRUMENT READINGS.

	Date.		CIRCLE.							Barom.	THERMOM.				
			A.	B.	C.	D.	E.	F.	Mean.		At.	Ex.	U.	L.	I.
	1848	h. m.								in.					
Zone 187	Aug. 7.	18 20	69.32	{31.5 26.9 32.9 28.2 21. 27. / 32.5 27.1 33.4 29.4 22. 28.2}					28.34	30.212	76.	66.3			
		18 50												65.	
		19 10												64.5	
		19 20								30.262	74.			63.9	
		19 40												63.6	
		20 0								30.260	72.8			62.9	
		20 50		{30. 28.2 33.8 28.8 22.2 26. / 31.5 28.2 34.5 29.5 23. 26.}					28.47					62.	

REMARKS.

(186) 22. Mic. reading assumed as 44ʳ.919, not 45ʳ.919, to agree with Arg. Z. 237, 38, and 247, 106.

(186) 23. Min. of transit assumed as 4, not 5.

(186) 32. Time of transit over T. V assumed as 6ˢ.7 instead of 0ˢ.7.

(187) 2. Right ascension differs 17ˢ.2 from Arg. Z. 227, 64; probably 1 thread interval in error.

(187) 3. Minutes assumed as 32, not 33, to agree with Arg. Z. 227, 67, and 310, 68.

(187) 4. Transit over T. V assumed as recorded over T. VI, and minutes as 33, not 34.

(187) 6. Transit over T. VI assumed as recorded over T. VII.

(187) 15. Transits over T.'s IV and V ass'd as recorded over T.'s V and VI.

(187) 17. Right ascension differs 17ˢ from Arg. Z. 224, 114; probably 1 thread interval in error.

(187) 18. Right ascension differs 28ˢ.3 from Arg. Z. 227, 99.

Zone 187. August 7. S. $D_0 = -20°\ 10'\ 0''$—Continued.

No.	Mag.	I.	II.	III.	IV.	V.	VI.	VII.	T. (h. m. s.)	a_1 (s.)	a_2 (s.)
21	·						39.		19 0 6.10	+22.41	+1.55
22	8		29.7				19.		1 46.20	22.41	1.28
23	9					36.	52.		2 19.35	22.40	1.25
24	8					50.			3 33.51	22.40	1.21
25	9		19.5	36.					6 52.56	22.39	1.16
26	9		22.5						7 55.63	22.39	1.07
27	9		32.		5.				9 4.98	22.38	1.16
28	9		44.	60.5					14 17.06	22.37	1.28
29	10						35.		14 2.17	22.37	1.28
30	10					20.			15 3.58	22.37	1.44
31	9					38.			16 21.46	22.36	1.14
32	9					17.			17 0.38	22.36	1.02
33	8					20.			18 19.86	22.35	1.23
34	9						7.		18 50.43	22.35	1.07
35	9		42.5						22 15.60	22.35	1.16
36	7			35.5	52.				22 51.94	22.35	1.18
37	9		34.5						25 7.59	22.34	1.56
38	9			44.					27 0.61	22.33	1.50
39	9					57.	13.5		27 56.94	22.33	1.21
40	9	16.	33.						31 5.62	22.32	1.54
41	7						12.		30 55.38	22.32	1.02
42	9					16.			31 15.88	22.32	1.47
43	10		38.						34 11.09	22.31	1.39
44	10						17.		42 44.18	22.29	1.28
45	10					59.			45 42.40	22.28	1.19
46	10					43.			47 47.95	22.27	0.95
47	10			34.					49 50.57	22.27	1.44
48	10							8.	50 18.52	22.26	1.32
49	9		16.5				36.		19 57 3.08	22.25	0.86
50	8				7.0	23.5	40.		20 0 6.94	22.24	0.93
51	9		20.5		3.				5 2.72	22.23	1.26
52	8			52.2					7 8.79	22.22	1.47
53	8				9.	25.3			8 8.88	22.22	1.53
54	8			11.		44.			10 27.61	22.21	1.57
55	9		50.5		23.5				14 23.57	22.20	0.95
56	9			36.		8.5			15 52.32	22.20	1.47
57	9		25.		58.				19 58.00	22.19	1.17
58	10		26.			59.5			23 42.80	22.18	1.39
59	10		46.5						28 19.59	22.17	1.60
60	9		30.	46.5					34 3.06	22.16	1.23
61	9						39.		51 56.12	22.12	1.51
62	4		55.	12.	28.	44.5	1.		55 28.15	22.12	1.56
63	7		12.	29.	45.	1.	18.		20 57 45.03	22.11	1.24
64	7		45.5	1.8	15.	35.			21 0 18.32	22.11	1.22
65	9					23.			3 6.34	22.10	1.08
66	8			46.					5 2.51	22.10	1.32
67	8			15.5	18.				6 1.75	22.10	1.34
68	8		12.5	45.5					7 45.50	22.09	1.24
69	8		59.		32.				21 9 32.06	+22.09	+1.07

No.	MICROMETER		r	i	d_1	d_2	Mean Right Ascension 1850.0 (h. m. s.)	Mean Declination 1850.0 (° ′ ″)
21		6	52.632	− 6 13.08	−22.80	− 0.73	19 0 30.09	−20 16 36.61
22		3	34.965	24 48.47	22.65	3.26	2 9.89	35 14.38
23		3	32.920	26 56.60	22.59	3.56	2 43.00	37 22.75
24		3	30.332	29 39.17	22.48	3.95	3 57.12	40 5.60
25		3	27.850	32 14.83	22.17	4.31	7 16.11	42 41.31
26		3	22.375	37 58.52	22.08	5.12	8 19.09	48 25.72
27		3	28.135	31 57.08	21.97	4.27	9 28.54	42 23.32
28		3	34.418	25 22.98	21.48	3.34	14 40.71	35 47.80
29		3	34.075	25 43.94	21.51	3.39	14 25.82	36 8.84
30		4	43.132	16 8.01	21.41	2.06	15 27.39	26 31.48
31		4	25.435	34 38.61	21.29	4.68	16 44.96	45 4.58
32		2	18.095	42 22.89	21.22	5.74	17 23.76	52 49.85
33		3	30.818	29 8.40	21.13	3.88	18 43.44	39 33.50
34		2	21.889	38 24.93	21.08	5.19	19 13.85	48 51.20
35		3	26.785	33 21.70	20.73	4.47	22 39.11	43 46.90
36		3	27.800	32 18.03	20.67	4.32	23 15.47	42 43.02
37		6	49.300	9 42.15	20.46	1.18	25 31.49	20 3.79
38		5	46.070	13 4.99	20.28	1.63	27 24.44	23 26.90
39		3	28.808	31 14.60	20.22	4.17	28 20.45	41 38.99
40		5	48.218	10 50.02	19.99	1.31	31 29.48	21 11.23
41		2	17.720	42 46.47	19.94	5.80	31 18.72	53 12.21
42		4	43.868	15 21.69	19.81	1.99	32 39.67	25 43.49
43		4	38.975	20 27.55	19.60	2.66	34 34.19	30 49.81
44		3	32.675	27 11.79	18.79	3.61	43 7.75	37 34.19
45		3	26.710	33 26.28	18.51	4.48	46 5.96	43 49.27
46		2	12.500	48 13.89	18.33	6.55	48 11.17	58 38.80
47		4	40.725	18 35.27	18.11	2.42	50 14.28	28 58.80
48		3	33.485	26 20.71	18.07	3.48	50 42.10	20 36 42.26
49		3	6.000	55 5.18	17.44	7.55	19 57 26.19	21 5 30.17
50		1	9.756	51 5.01	17.15	7.00	20 0 30.11	21 1 29.16
51		3	29.120	30 55.28	16.70	4.12	5 26.21	20 41 16.10
52		4	41.083	18 15.81	16.51	2.36	7 32.47	28 34.68
53		5	44.490	14 44.35	16.42	1.85	8 32.63	25 2.62
54		5	46.820	12 17.83	16.20	1.51	10 51.39	20 22 35.54
55		1	10.788	49 59.04	15.84	6.85	14 46.72	21 0 21.73
56		3	40.155	19 14.11	15.71	2.40	16 15.99	20 29 32.31
57		2	22.925	37 19.01	15.33	5.04	20 21.36	47 39.38
58		3	35.692	24 2.92	15.01	3.16	24 6.37	34 21.09
59		4	47.338	11 42.82	14.60	1.43	28 43.36	21 58.85
60		3	25.092	35 7.97	14.11	4.73	34 26.45	45 26.81
61		3	39.856	19 41.10	12.66	2.53	52 19.78	29 56.29
62		4	42.859	16 24.71	12.30	2.09	55 51.83	26 39.19
63	IV.	2	23.910	36 17.84	12.21	4.90	20 58 8.38	46 34.95
64	V.	2	22.752	37 30.74	12.01	5.09	21 0 41.65	47 47.84
65		1	14.450	46 11.35	11.80	6.33	3 29.52	56 29.48
66		3	28.179	31 54.44	11.66	4.27	5 25.93	42 10.37
67		3	29.011	31 2.05	11.59	4.15	6 25.19	41 17.79
68		3	23.006	37 18.75	11.46	5.05	8 8.83	47 35.26
69		2	13.345	−47 20.01	−11.32	− 6.50	21 9 55.22	−20 57 37.83

CORRECTIONS.

Date.	Corr. of Clock.	Hourly rate.	m	n	e	Zenith Point.	Mic. Co.
1847.	h.	s.	s.	s.	s.	° ′	r.
	s.						

INSTRUMENT READINGS.

Date.	A.	B.	C.	D.	E.	F.	Mean.	Barom.	At.	Ex.	U.	L.	I.
1848.	h. m.							in.	°	°	°	°	°
Zone 187 Aug. 7, 21 0								30.258	71.2	60.8			
21 20										60.			
21 40								30.250	70.	60.4			
22 0										59.6			
22 20										60.2			
22 30	69 32	30. / 30.2	33.9 / 34.3	30.6 / 30.6	24.2 / 24.2	25.8 / 26.0	29.23						

REMARKS.

(187) 22. Transit over T. III ass'd to have been recorded as over T. II.

(187) 30. Right ascension differs 16″.6 from Arg. Z. 310, 148; probably 1 thread interval in error.

(187) 33. Transit over T. IV assumed as recorded over T. V.

(187) 34. Transit over T. V ass'd as rec'ded over T. VI to agree with Arg. Z. 227, 133; 238, 32; and 310, 155.

(187) 39. Transits over T.'s IV and V assumed as recorded over T.'s V and VI.

(187) 41. Transit over T. V assumed as recorded over T. VI.

(187) 42. Transit over T. IV assumed as recorded over T. V.

(187) 46. Transit over T. IV assumed as recorded over T. V.

(187) 48. Right ascension differs 17″.7 from Arg. Z. 243, 36; probably 1 thread interval in error.

(187) 49. Transit over T. III ass'd to have been recorded as over T. II.

ZONE 187. AUGUST 7. S. $D_v = -20°\ 10'\ 0''$—Continued.

SECONDS OF TRANSIT.

No.	Mag.	I.	II.	III.	IV.	V.	VI.	VII.
70	10	.	.	.	.	.	28.5	.
71	11	.	.	.	30.	.	.	.
72	11	.	.	13.	.	46.	.	.
73	9	.	4.5	.	.	.	.	.
74	10	.	.	.	.	.	55.	.
75	10	.	9.	25.5	.	.	.	.
76	10	.	57.	.	.	.	.	.
77	7	32.	.	.	.	.	.	.
78	6	.	.	.	1.5	18.	.	.
79	8	20.	45.5	2.	.	.	.	.
80	9	.	.	.	.	26.	.	.
81	8	.	.	58.	14.5	31.	.	.
82	9	.	.	26.	42.	.	.	.
83	9	22.5	.	55.5	.	.	.	.
84	9	37.	.	10.5	.	.	.	.
85	9	.	45.	.	18.	.	.	.
86	10	2.	.	.	.	.	.	.
87	9	35.	.	8.	.	.	.	.
88	10	38.	.	11.	.	.	.	.
89	9	.	.	29.	.	.	.	.
90	10	.	.	.	.	.	37.8	.
91	9	53.	.	.	.	.	.	.
92	10	.	.	39.	.	.	.	.
93	9	.	27.	.	0.	.	.	.
94	9	38.	.	.	.	.	43.5	.
95	9	12.	28.5	15.	.	.	.	.
96	10	.	.	.	.	29.	.	.
97	8	.	56.	.	29.	15.	.	.
98	10	45.	.	17.8	.	.	.	.
99	8	36.5	.	9.	25.5	.	.	.

No.	T. (h. m. s.)	a_1 (s.)	a_2 (s.)	Mic.	r.	i (' '')	d_1	d_2	Mean R.A. 1850.0 (h. m. s.)	Mean Decl. 1850.0 (' '')
70	21 10 11.97	+22.09	+1.30	3	26.446	−33 42.96	−11.28	−4.54	21 10 35.36	−20 43 58.78
71	13 29.88	22.09	1.54	5	40.364	19 3.37	11.05	2.45	13 53.51	29 16.87
72	14 29.63	22.09	1.71	5	50.120	8 50.86	10.98	1.00	14 53.43	19 2.84
73	18 37.64	22.08	1.19	2	19.292	41 7.08	10.68	5.59	19 0.91	51 23.35
74	18 38.35	22.08	1.13	1	15.047	44 37.30	10.68	6.10	19 1.56	54 54.08
75	20 42.10	22.08	1.61	4	44.303	14 49.56	10.54	1.85	21 5.77	25 1.95
76	24 13.58	22.08	1.11	1	14.143	46 29.47	10.30	6.36	24 36.77	56 46.15
77	26 5.16	22.07	1.14	1	15.953	44 35.15	10.18	6.08	26 28.37	54 51.41
78	26 1.42	22.07	1.30	3	25.302	34 54.92	10.18	4.70	26 24.70	45 9.80
79	30 2.04	22.06	1.74	4	51.267	7 36.05	9.91	0.83	30 25.84	7 46.79
80	31 9.36	22.06	1.16	2	16.884	43 38.71	9.84	5.96	31 32.58	53 54.51
81	58.03	22.06	1.57	3	40.619	18 54.29	9.72	2.41	33 21.66	29 6.42
82	34 25.76	22.06	1.75	5	51.000	7 55.56	9.62	0.87	34 49.57	18 6.05
83	38 55.49	22.05	1.78	5	52.900	5 55.89	9.33	0.58	39 19.38	16 5.80
84	42 10.28	22.05	1.18	2	17.520	42 58.20	9.12	5.67	42 33.51	53 13.19
85	45 1.50	22.05	1.35	3	27.348	32 46.64	8.94	4.40	45 24.90	42 59.98
86	46 35.00	22.04	1.73	5	48.543	10 29.65	8.84	1.23	46 58.66	20 39.70
87	50 7.99	22.04	1.75	5	49.882	9 5.36	8.62	1.03	50 31.78	19 15.01
88	57 10.98	22.03	1.59	4	39.592	19 48.87	8.22	2.56	57 34.60	29 59.65
89	58 45.65	22.03	1.79	5	51.210	7 42.44	8.13	0.84	59 9.47	17 51.41
90	21 59 20.58	22.03	1.67	4	44.340	14 52.31	8.10	1.85	21 59 44.28	25 2.26
91	22 6 26.09	22.02	1.45	3	31.888	28 1.49	7.71	3.72	22 6 49.56	38 12.92
92	6 55.61	22.02	1.71	5	46.322	12 49.28	7.68	1.55	7 19.34	22 55.51
93	7 43.60	22.02	1.69	5	45.119	14 4.75	7.64	1.73	8 7.31	24 14.12
94	10 10.88	22.02	1.13	1	12.200	48 31.04	7.50	6.69	10 34.03	58 46.13
95	13 45.06	22.02	1.18	2	15.283	45 18.48	7.32	6.22	14 8.26	55 32.02
96	14 56.14	22.02	1.65	4	42.220	17 5.59	7.25	2.15	15 19.81	27 14.99
97	17 12.33	22.01	1.11	1	11.228	49 32.33	7.14	6.84	17 35.45	59 46.31
98	21 17.88	22.01	1.44	3	29.836	30 10.23	6.93	4.03	21 41.33	40 21.19
99	22 26 9.16	+22.00	+1.48	3	32.174	−27 43.73	−6.68	−3.68	22 26 32.64	−20 37 54.09

ZONE 188. AUGUST 14. S. $D_v = -19°\ 32'\ 38'$.

No.	Mag.	I.	II.	III.	IV.	V.	VI.	VII.
1	9	.	.	.	27.	.	0.	15.
2	8	.	12.	.	.	.	.	.
3	7	.	59.	.	.	.	.	.
4	9	.	.	.	.	38.5	55.	.
5	8	.	.	.	.	.	13.5	.
6	10	.	.	34.	50.	.	.	.
7	8	.	38.	54.5	11.	27.	.	.
8	10	.	59.	.	.	48.	.	.
9	9	.	13.	29.5	46.	.	.	.
10	10	.	23.5	40.	.	.	.	.
11	9	.	37.8	54.	.	27.	.	.
12	8	.	.	34.	51.	7.	23.	.
13	9	.	.	40.5	.	.	.	.
14	8	.	57.	13.8	30.	16.5	.	.
15	8	.	24.	40.5	56.8	.	.	.

No.	T. (h. m. s.)	a_1 (s.)	a_2 (s.)	Mic.	r.	i (' '')	d_1	d_2	Mean R.A. 1850.0 (h. m. s.)	Mean Decl. 1850.0 (' '')
1	18 57 43.06	+24.73	+0.49	2	15.683	−39 39.95	−11.69	−11.35	18 58 8.27	−20 12 32.99
2	18 59 45.03	24.73	0.49	2	14.278	46 21.51	11.48	12.22	19 0 10.25	19 15.21
3	19 0 31.06	24.73	0.61	3	30.718	29 14.92	11.41	9.90	0 57.30	2 6.23
4	0 22.09	24.73	0.50	2	16.850	43 40.83	11.43	11.89	0 47.32	16 34.15
5	1 40.76	24.72	0.53	2	20.483	39 53.37	11.30	11.37	2 6.01	20 12 46.04
6	3 50.22	24.72	0.76	4	47.835	11 11.02	11.08	7.43	4 15.70	19 44 0.43
7	6 10.83	24.71	0.63	3	30.420	29 33.83	10.85	9.94	6 36.17	20 2 24.62
8	8 31.79	24.70	0.71	4	39.873	20 33.88	10.62	8.74	8 57.20	19 53 23.24
9	10 45.98	24.70	0.82	5	53.406	5 24.56	10.40	6.67	11 11.50	19 38 11.63
10	13 56.50	24.69	0.57	2	19.085	41 19.92	10.09	11.50	14 21.76	20 14 11.60
11	15 10.60	24.68	0.68	3	32.696	27 10.85	9.96	9.60	15 35.96	20 0 0.41
12	18 50.61	24.67	0.85	4	53.173	5 36.97	9.61	6.66	19 16.13	19 38 23.24
13	20 57.07	24.67	0.81	4	50.260	8 39.88	9.40	7.10	21 22.58	41 26.38
14	22 30.10	24.66	0.84	4	49.930	8 59.84	9.24	7.11	22 55.60	41 46.19
15	19 23 56.88	+24.66	+0.76	4	38.895	−20 33.06	−9.00	−8.74	19 25 22.30	−19 53 20.80

CORRECTIONS.

Date.	Corr. of Clock.	Hourly rate.	m	n	c	Zenith Point.	Mic. Co.
	h.	s.	s.	s.	s.	s.	° ' ''	r.
1848. Aug. 14.	.	.	.	.	.	359 59 73.01	.

INSTRUMENT READINGS.

	Date.		CIRCLE. A.	B.	C.	D.	E.	F.	Mean.	Barom.	THERMOM. At.	Ex.	U.	L.	I.
	1848.	h. m.	° ' ''						''	in.	°	°	°	°	°
Zone 188	Aug. 14,	18 57	68 54 60. 57.0	63.4	55.7	53.3	56.0		57.57						
		19 0	.	.	.	.	.	.	.	30.200	78.	74.6			
		19 20	.	.	.	.	.	.	.	.	.	73.8			
		19 58	.	.	.	.	.	.	.	30.200	77.5	73.4			
		20	.	.	.	.	.	.	.	.	.	72.7			
		20 20	60.8 57.	63.4	55.7	52.8	56.		57.62	30.202	77.2	72.8	.	.	
		20 40	.	.	.	.	.	.	.	.	.	72.2			

REMARKS.

(187) 81. Minutes of transit assumed as 32.

(187) 83. Transit over T. IV ass'd to have been at 55s.5 instead of 35s.5.

(187) 90. Right ascension differs 16s.1 from Arg. Z. 255, 75; perhaps 1 thread interval in error.

(188) 1. Micrometer reading assumed as 20r.683, not 15r.683.

(188) 14. Time of transit over T. II assumed as 57s. instead of 37s.

(188) 15. Minutes assumed as 24, not 23, to agree with Arg. Z. 310, 165.

Extern. therm. assumed as 72°.8.

Zone 188. August 14. S. $D_0 = -19° 32' 30''$ — Continued.

No.	Mag.	SECONDS OF TRANSIT. I. II. III. IV. V. VI. VII.	T.	a_1	a_2	MICROMETER.		r.	i ′ ″	i	d_1	Mean Right Ascension, 1850.0.	Mean Declination, 1850.0.
			h. m. s.	s.	s.			r.	′ ″	″	″	h. m. s.	° ′ ″
16	10	. . . . . 43.	19 26 59.54	+24.65	+0.54		1	10.146	−50 40.09	− 8.80	−12.87	19 27 24.73	−20 23 31.76
17	9	. . 15. 32. 48.5	30 48.35	24.64	0.57		1	12.346	48 22.23	8.43	12.55	31 13.56	21 13.21
18	5	. . 38.8 55. 17.8 28. 44. . .	37 11.55	24.62	0.70		3	25.982	34 12.07	7.81	10.57	37 36.87	7 0.45
19	10	. . . . 28. . . .	37 55.25	24.62	0.64		2	18.775	41 40.23	7.74	1.64	38 20.51	14 29.61
20	10	. . 8. . . 41. . . 14. . . .	42 41.05	24.61	0.73	IV.	3	28.480	31 35.49	7.29	10.20	43 6.39	20 4 22.98
21	7	. . 41.5 58. 14. 30.5 . . .	46 14.28	24.60	0.93		5	51.789	8 8.71	6.95	7.00	46 39.81	19 40 52.66
22	9	. . 34.6 51.2 . . 24. . . .	50 7.60	24.59	0.80	V.	3	32.552	27 19.83	6.58	9.62	50 32.99	20 0 0.03
23	8	. . . . . 21. 37.5 44. . .	51 21.04	24.58	0.68		2	17.540	42 57.58	6.47	11.78	51 46.30	20 15 45.83
24	7	. . 33. 49. 5.5 . . 39. .	57 5.78	24.57	0.86		4	37.497	22 1.43	5.92	8.91	57 31.21	19 54 46.20
25	9	. . . . 29. . . .	19 58 12.58	24.57	0.82		3	32.680	27 11.73	5.82	9.60	19 58 37.97	59 57.15
26	8	. . . 2. 18.3 34.5 . . .	20 1 18.28	24.56	0.91		4	42.098	16 9.86	5.52	8.24	20 1 43.75	48 53.62
27	9	. . 4. 21. 37. 53.5 . . .	5 37.16	24.55	1.00		5	52.148	6 43.61	5.14	6.79	6 2.71	39 25.54
28	10	. . 42. 58. 16. 31.5 . .	8 14.89	24.55	0.98		4	47.509	11 33.02	4.89	7.46	8 40.42	19 44 15.37
29	9	. . 53.8 10. 26.5	11 26.61	24.54	0.70		1	10.990	49 46.43	4.60	12.77	11 51.85	20 22 33.80
30	6.7	. . . . . 22. 38.5 55. .	11 22.06	24.54	0.81	IV.	3	25.128	34 2.95	4.60	10.56	11 47.41	6 47.94
31	10	. . . . . 20.8 . . 53.5 . .	13 20.74	24.53	0.75		2	18.076	42 23.90	4.42	11.72	13 46.02	20 15 10.04
32	7	. . 26.8 43. 49.8 16. . .	15 59.63	24.52	0.92		3	37.468	22 11.65	4.18	8.90	16 25.07	19 54 54.73
33	9	. . 25.5 42.	17 58.45	24.52	0.87		3	30.724	29 14.57	4.00	9.89	18 23.84	20 1 58.46
34	9	. . . 51.3	25 7.83	24.50	1.00		4	44.182	15 1.33	3.35	7.92	25 33.33	19 47 42.60
35	8	. . . . 41. 57.5 . .	25 24.70	24.50	0.95		3	38.026	21 36.26	3.32	8.82	25 50.15	19 54 18.40
36	10	. . 46.	28 19.04	24.49	0.75		1	11.503	49 14.39	3.05	12.70	28 44.28	20 22 0.14
37	8	. . . 57.5 14. 30.5 . . .	31 14.02	24.49	1.02		4	43.842	15 23.00	2.79	7.98	31 39.53	19 48 3.77
38	10	. . 23. . . 56.	33 55.91	24.48	0.93		2	31.470	28 27.96	2.55	9.78	34 21.32	20 1 10.29
39	8	. . . 38. 54.3 11. 27. . .	34 54.49	24.48	1.00		2	39.472	19 56.98	2.46	8.60	35 19.88	19 52 38.04
40	8	. . 4.5 . 37.5 54. . . .	37 37.47	24.47	0.96		3	33.670	26 9.80	2.22	9.45	38 2.91	58 51.47
41	8	. . . 57. 13.5 30. . . .	39 13.52	24.47	1.04		4	43.499	15 44.73	2.07	8.03	39 39.03	19 48 24.83
42	7.8	. . 43.	20 43 16.02	+24.46	+0.84		2	15.910	−39 23.39	− 1.71	−11.30	20 43 41.32	−20 12 6.40

Zone 189. August 15. C. $D = -18° 55' 10''$.

No.	Mag.	SECONDS OF TRANSIT. I. II. III. IV. V. VI. VII.	T.	a_1	a_2	MICROMETER.		r.	i ′ ″	i	d_1	Mean Right Ascension, 1850.0.	Mean Declination, 1850.0.
1	8.9	. . . . . 18.6 . . 51.2 . .	18 0 18.55	+28.32	.	VI.	3	32.800	−27 3.86	−10.37	− 7.61	. .	−19 22 31.86
2	9	. . 44.9 1. 17.8	2 1.19	28.32	.	IV.	3	27.742	32 21.66	10.19	8.32	. .	27 50.17
3	8	. . 40.2 56.2 13.4 29.6 . .	2 56.68	28.32	.	IV.	3	27.876	32 13.20	10.10	8.30	. .	27 41.60
4	10	. . . . . 17.2	5 17.09	28.31	.	IV.	5	48.840	10 11.15	9.86	5.39	. .	5 36.39
5	8	. . . . . 59.5 . . .	5 59.30	28.30	.	IV.	5	52.343	6 31.42	9.78	4.90	. .	1 56.10
6	8	. . . . . . 27.2 . .	6 10.09	28.30	.	V.	5	56.199	2 29.24	9.70	4.36	. .	57 53.36
7	8.9	. . 9. 25.5 . . 14.5 . .	7 41.91	28.29	.	IV.	5	53.376	5 26.56	9.61	4.75	. .	0 50.92
8	8.9	. . . . 15.5 . .	7 42.88	28.29	.	VI.	5	47.186	11 54.03	9.61	5.60	. .	7 20.14
9	9	. . 9.6 26.5 42.3	11 48.57	28.28	.	III.	2	12.132	47 33.63	9.20	10.30	. .	43 3.13
10	9	. . . . . . 24.2 40.5 . .	12 7.99	28.28	.	VI.	3	35.242	21 30.84	9.16	7.27	. .	19 57.27
11	8.9	. . 13.1 29.3 45.9 . 18.6 . .	14 45.86	28.27	.	III.	3	27.645	32 27.81	8.89	8.33	. .	27 55.03
12	8.9	. . . . . 7.5 24.6 . .	14 51.48	28.27	.	V.	2	17.078	43 26.67	8.87	9.81	. .	38 55.35
13	9	. . . 3. 25.5 3. . 28. . .	17 55.42	28.26	.	IV.	5	52.002	6 52.66	8.57	4.94	. .	19 2 16.17
14	8	. . . 48. 4.6	22 4.52	28.24	.	III.	5	54.212	4 33.95	8.14	4.63	. .	18 59 56.72
15	9	. . . . 23.2 . .	22 6.89	28.24	.	V.	3	30.588	19 58.30	8.14	6.66	. .	19 15 23.10
16	8.9	. . . . . 53. 9.2 . .	22 36.65	28.24	.	V.	3	41.382	16 5.77	8.09	6.12	. .	13 30.28
17	8.9	. . . . . 56.2 13. . .	22 56.39	28.24	.	V.	3	41.382	18 5.77	8.06	6.42	. .	13 30.25
18	8	. . . . 45. . .	18 23 12.37	+28.24	.	VI.	4	40.860	− 9 4.61	− 8.02	− 5.23	. .	−19 4 27.86

CORRECTIONS.

Date.	Corr. of Clock.	Hourly rate.	m	n	c	Zenith Point.	Mic. Co.
	h.	s.	s.	s.	s.	s.	° ′ ″	r.
1848. Aug. 15.	. .	. .	. .	. .	. .	359 59 73.83	30.1597

INSTRUMENT READINGS.

Date.		CIRCLE.						Mean.	Barom.	THERMOM.				
		A.	B.	C.	D.	E.	F.			At.	Ex.	U.	L.	I.
	1848. h. m.	° ′ ″						″	In.	°	°	°	°	°
Zone 189 Aug. 15, 18 0	68 17	35.7 30.1 / 35.7 29.9	35.5 30. / 36.4 31.8	26.4 29.4 / 27.0 30.6				31.54	30.166	80.	76.5	78.8	78.5	77.8
18 20		. .	. .	. .	. .	. .	. .					75.3		
18 44		. .	. .	. .	. .	. .	. .					74.8		
19 0		. .	. .	. .	. .	. .	. .					74.3		
19 10		34.9 29.9 / 35.2 29.9	36.3 29.9 / 36.5 30.9	26.1 29.2 / 26.5 30.4				31.31	30.170	78.2	74.3	77.8	77.5	77.8

REMARKS.

(188) 21. Micrometer reading assumed as 50ʳ.789, not 51ʳ.789.

(188) 23. Time of transit over T. VI assumed as 54ˢ, instead of 44ˢ.

(188) 26. Micrometer reading assumed as 43ʳ.098 instead of 42ʳ.098.

(188) 30. Micrometer reading assumed as 26ʳ.128, not 25ʳ.128.

(188) 42. Micrometer reading assumed as 20ʳ.940, not 15ʳ.940.

(189) 9. Micrometer reading assumed as 13ʳ.132, not 12ʳ.132.

ZONE 189. AUGUST 15. C. $D_0 = -19^\circ\ 55'\ 10''$—Continued.

No.	Mag.	I.	II.	III.	IV.	V.	VI.	VII.	T. (h. m. s.)	a_1 (s.)	a_2 (s.)	MICROMETER		r.	i	d_1 ('')	d_2 ('')	Mean Right Ascension, 1850.0 (h. m. s.)	Mean Declination, 1850.0 (° ' '')
19	8.9		33.7	49.2			39.		18 26 6.18	+28.23		IV	3	32.476	−27 24.78	−7.73	7.65		−19 22 50.16
20	9.10			56.3	12.6		45.		26 12.53	28.23		VI	3	25.461	34 44.50	7.72	8.64		30 10.86
21	8.9				41.8		14.6		27 41.84	28.22		VI	4	39.356	20 5.38	7.57	6.69		15 29.64
22	8.9					36.2			28 19.86	28.22		V	4	35.345	24 16.84	7.50	7.26		19 41.60
23	9			20.5	36.3				29 36.56	28.22		III	4	40.942	18 24.60	7.37	6.48		13 48.45
24	10				55.7		28.5		31 55.75	28.21		VI	2	20.016	40 22.47	7.14	9.40		35 49.01
25	6			22.	38.1	55.			33 38.32	28.20		IV	3	30.063	29 56.11	6.96	7.99		25 21.06
26	7		19.	35.7	52.				34 51.92	28.20		III	3	27.763	32 20.95	6.84	8.32		27 45.52
27	9				25.2				35 25.07	28.20		IV	3	27.281	32 50.77	6.78	6.38		28 15.93
28	7		10.5	27.3	43.2	50.5			36 43.32	28.19		IV	2	10.738	50 4.00	6.65	10.71		45 31.36
29	9.10				43.2				? 43.08			VII	4	40.799	18 34.76	6.55	6.50		13 57.81
30	8		24.2		57.		29.6		38 56.98	28.19		IV	3	33.782	26 2.64	6.42	7.47		21 26.53
31	9			3.8					40 20.31	28.18		III	5	50.013	8 57.46	6.28	5.22		4 18.96
32	8					35.5	52.		40 19.30	28.18		V	3	36.732	22 57.39	6.28	7.06		18 20.73
33	9						33.5		40 0.91	28.18		VI	4	40.300	19 6.14	6.31	6.57		14 29.02
34	9						23.		41 50.34	28.18		VI	2	9.221	51 39.53	6.13	10.93		47 6.59
35	9				41.5	56.7			43 40.87	28.17		V	3	37.367	22 17.75	5.93	6.97		17 40.65
36	9.10				3.2				46 3.34	28.16		VI	4	44.853	14 20.16	5.69	5.94		9 41.81
37	7.8		47.5	3.8	19.3	36.3	52.5		48 19.92	28.15		IV	4	34.447	25 21.16	5.46	7.38		20 44.00
38	7.8		35.1	51.6	7.6	24.2	40.6		50 7.85	28.14		IV	3	26.922	33 13.04	5.27	8.43		28 36.74
39	9.10					1.5			50 45.08	28.14		V	3	25.353	34 51.53	5.21	8.65		30 15.39
40	9					5.			51 48.55	28.14		V	2	22.503	37 46.52	5.10	9.05		33 10.67
41	7		15.7	32.		5.	20.2		53 48.30	28.13		IV	3	28.057	32 1.97	4.89	8.27		27 25.13
42	7		19.2	35.5		8.	24.7		53 51.98	28.13		IV	3	36.212	23 30.34	4.88	7.13		18 52.35
43	9.10		9.	25.2	41.5				56 41.69	28.12		III	2	8.862	46 47.60	4.59	10.27		19 42 12.46
44	6		22.3	38.3	55.	11.	27.1		57 54.82	28.12		IV	5	56.106	2 29.43	4.46	4.36		18 57 48.25
45	8			13.3	29.5	46.	2.3		18 59 29.64	28.11		IV	4	43.512	15 43.94	4.30	6.12		18 11 4.36
46	9			14.	30.3				19 2 30.26	28.11		III	3	29.466	30 33.75	3.98	8.09		19 25 55.82
47	8.9		57.8	44.5	30.5	47.5			4 30.74	28.10		IV	3	26.947	33 11.47	3.77	8.44		28 33.68
48	9.10					27.			4 46.44	28.09		V	5	48.224	10 49.97	3.74	5.45		6 9.16
49	9					47.2	3.5		5 30.90	28.09		V	4	40.981	18 22.97	3.66	6.46		13 43.09
50	7		52.5	8.3	25.	47.5	57.2		8 24.95	28.08		IV	4	41.742	17 34.82	3.35	6.36		12 54.53
51	8.9						30.		19 8 57.38	+28.08		VI	5	46.787	−13 19.92	−3.29	5.64		−19 7 38.85

ZONE 190. AUGUST 16. S. D = −24° 33′ 0″.

No.	Mag.	I.	II.	III.	IV.	V.	VI.	VII.	T. (h. m. s.)	a_1 (s.)	a_2 (s.)	MICROMETER		r.	i	d_1 ('')	d_2 ('')	Mean Right Ascension, 1850.0 (h. m. s.)	Mean Declination, 1850.0 (° ' '')
1	10				6.				17 44 49.08	+25.97	+0.39	V	5	48.208	−10 50.97	−9.69	7.04	17 44 15.44	−24 44 7.70
2	7			57.	14.	31.			45 14.00	25.97	0.32	IV	5	41.502	17 50.08	9.58	8.13	45 40.29	21 51 7.79
3	10				40.5				46 40.41	25.96	0.14		2	19.822	40 34.27	9.47	11.69	47 6.51	25 13 55.43
4	9			37.		10.			47 53.50	25.96	0.23	III	3	29.914	30 5.45	9.36	10.00	48 19.69	3 24.81
5	9		39.						50 13.21	25.95	0.10		3	24.854	35 22.96	9.15	10.84	50 39.35	8 42.95
6	8				19.	36.	53.		50 18.98	25.95	0.23	IV	3	29.182	30 51.45	9.15	10.12	50 45.16	25 4 10.72
7	10					45.			51 11.06	25.95	0.38		4	45.972	13 9.69	9.07	7.39	51 37.39	24 46 26.15
8	8				56.				52 39.07	25.94	0.39		4	45.945	13 11.26	8.95	7.40	53 5.40	46 27.61
9	8		44.8	2.	18.5				55 18.84	25.93	0.44	IV	4	51.228	7 41.37	8.72	6.51	55 45.21	24 40 56.60
10	9		12.		46.				57 46.04	25.92	0.22	IV	3	26.575	33 35.00	8.51	10.57	58 12.18	25 6 54.08
11	10				42.	59.5			17 58 25.12	25.92	0.00	V	2	12.319	48 25.17	8.45	12.92	17 58 51.73	21 46.54
12	11			58.					18 0 15.13	+25.91	+0.12		2	15.575	−45 0.62	−8.29	−12.39	18 0 41.16	−25 18 21.30

CORRECTIONS.

Date.	Corr. of Clock. (h. s.)	Hourly rate. (s.)	m (s.)	n (s.)	c (s.)	Zenith Point. (° ' '')	Mic. Co. (r.)
1848. Aug. 16,						359 59 60.10	30.0100

REMARKS.

(189) 43. Micrometer reading assumed as 13r.862, not 8r.862.

(189) 48. Seconds of transit 10.74 or 46.44.

(190) 1. Transit over T. V assumed as recorded over T. VI, and minutes as 43, not 44.

[(189) 29. Same A. R. nearly as 28.]

INSTRUMENT READINGS.

Date.		A.	B.	C.	D.	E.	F.	Mean.	Barom. (In.)	At.	Ex.	U.	L.	I.
Zone 190	1848, Aug. 16, 17 40 (h. m.)	73.54 60.	56.8	60.5	55.8	48.6	54.2	55.98	30.076	80.9	78.5			
	18 0										77.2			
	18 20								30.080		76.5			
	18 40								30.086	80.	75.9	78.	79.0	79.4
	19 0										75.3			
	19 20								30.080	79.7	75.2			
Zone 191	Aug. 16, 20 40	75 9 60.	60.4 56.8	62.8	55.9	49.8	53.9	56.58	30.075	79.2	73.9	78.5	78.0	78.5
	21 20								30.078	78.8	73.5			
	21 40	60.	56.2	61.5	55.0	49.	53.2	55.82	30.072	78.5	73.1			

Zone 190. August 16. S. $D_o = -24° 33′ 0″$—Continued.

No.	Mag.	I	II	III	IV	V	VI	VII	T.	a_1	a_2	Mic.	n	r	′	″	i	d_1	d_2	Mean Right Ascension, 1850.0	Mean Declination, 1850.0
									h. m. s.	s.	s.			r.	′	″	″	″	″	h. m. s.	° ′ ″
13	8.9		7.	24.					18 3 41.15	+25.90	+0.18	III.	2	22.643	−37	37.26	7.99	11.22		18 4 7.23	−25 10 56.47
14	11		23.						4 57.15	25.90	0.40	.	4	47.166	11	53.67	7.88	7.19		5 23.45	24 45 8.74
15	10		36.5						7 10.67	25.89	0.26	.	3	30.302	29	41.36	7.68	9.95		7 36.82	25 2 58.99
16	10					36.			7 2.07	25.89	0.20	.	3	23.748	36	31.58	7.70	11.03		7 28.16	9 50.31
17	10		47.						9 21.29	25.88	0.09	.	2	41.442	49	19.46	7.51	13.08		9 47.26	22 40.05
18	11				29.5				10 29.30	25.88	0.29	.	3	33.113	26	44.75	7.40	9.50		10 55.53	25 0 1.65
19	6.7		17.	34.	51.				11 51.04	25.87	0.30	IV.	3	34.457	25	20.53	7.29	9.29		12 17.21	24 58 37.11
20	11			3.5		37.			14 20.33	25.86	0.38	.	4	42.080	17	13.36	7.08	8.01		14 46.57	50 28.45
21	8		52.		26.				18 26.02	25.85	0.48	IV.	5	53.160	5	40.06	6.72	6.22		18 52.35	24 38 53.10
22	8				16.				19 15.88	25.84	0.23	.	3	25.670	34	31.71	6.65	10.72		19 41.05	25 7 49.08
23	6.7					58.	15.		19 40.88	25.84	0.12	V.	2	13.175	47	31.36	6.62	12.78		20 6.84	25 20 50.76
24	7					39.	56.		21 22.05	25.84	0.32	.	3	33.800	26	1.27	6.47	9.39		21 48.21	24 59 17.13
25	.			56.					23 13.09	25.83	0.21	.	2	22.078	38	12.70	6.30	11.31		23 39.13	25 11 30.31
26	9					58.			23 24.00	25.83	0.16	.	2	16.718	43	49.72	6.27	12.20		23 49.91	25 17 7.59
27	10		16.						26 50.16	25.82	0.32	.	3	34.243	25	34.09	6.00	9.33		27 16.30	24 58 49.42
28	10						43.		27 9.09	25.82	0.34	.	3	36.842	22	50.00	5.97	8.89		27 35.24	56 4.86
29	10						51.		29 17.07	25.81	0.40	.	4	42.570	16	43.42	5.79	7.95		29 43.28	24 49 57.16
30	10				7.				31 6.88	25.80	0.24	.	3	24.882	35	21.01	5.63	10.85		31 32.92	25 8 37.49
31	8				57.	14.	31.		31 56.96	25.80	0.26	V.	3	26.003	34	4.92	5.56	10.66		32 23.02	7 21.14
32	9.8				14.	31.			33 13.89	25.79	+0.23	.	4	23.			5.45			33 39.91	
33	6.7		36.	53.	10.				35 10.06	25.79	0.24	IV.	4	24.070	36	3.72	5.28	10.97		35 36.00	9 19.97
34	10			57.					37 14.05	25.78	0.29	.	5	29.068	30	52.64	5.10	10.14		37 40.12	25 4 7.88
35	8			14.8		48.5			38 31.70	25.77	0.35	.	4	36.965	22	34.23	5.00	8.86		38 57.62	24 55 48.11
36	9		0.	17.					40 34.14	25.77	0.43	.	5	44.150	15	4.94	4.83	7.70		41 0.54	48 17.47
37	8		40.		14.				42 14.02	25.76	0.42	IV.	5	42.979	16	19.07	4.68	7.88		42 40.20	49 31.63
38	10			28.					43 45.15	25.76	0.45	.	5	46.778	12	20.55	4.56	7.26		44 11.36	45 32.37
39	8			28.5					44 45.59	25.75	0.36	.	3	36.018	23	42.52	4.47	9.02		45 11.70	56 56.01
40	10						28.		44 54.08	25.75	0.39	.	3	39.298	20	16.12	4.46	8.49		45 20.22	53 29.07
41	7		31.6	49.	6.				47 5.92	25.74	0.44	IV.	4	43.882	15	20.56	4.27	7.74		47 32.10	24 48 32.51
42	8		8.5	25.	42.				48 42.20	25.74	0.31	IV.	3	29.042	31	0.10	4.13	10.15		49 8.25	25 4 14.38
43	7		12.5	29.5	46.5		20.5		50 46.56	25.73	0.26	IV.	3	24.754	35	20.10	3.96	10.86		51 12.55	8 43.92
44	6.7		16.8	34.	51.	7.5			52 50.84	25.72	0.31	IV.	3	30.322	20	39.99	3.79	9.95		53 16.87	25 2 53.73
45	10			49.5					54 6.64	25.72	0.45	.	5	45.570	13	36.52	3.67	7.45		54 32.81	24 46 47.64
46	9			6.5					55 23.61	25.71	0.40	.	4	39.328	19	53.58	3.57	8.49		55 49.72	53 5.64
47	8					1.	18.		56 0.94	25.71	0.39	IV.	4	38.952	20	29.03	3.51	8.55		56 27.04	53 41.99
48	9		5.						57 39.15	25.70	0.47	.	5	47.289	11	48.53	3.38	7.18		58 5.32	44 50.09
49	8		4.8		38.				58 35.42	25.70	0.41	IV.	4	39.440	19	59.49	3.29	8.47		59 4.53	24 53 11.25
50	8					26.5	13.5		18 59 9.40	25.70	0.19	V.	2	15.202	45	24.31	3.24	12.46		18 59 35.29	25 18 40.01
51	9		36.			27.			19 3 10.12	25.69	0.48	II.	5	48.288	10	45.83	2.91	7.00		19 3 36.29	24 43 55.74
52	8.9		53.5	10.5	27.	44.			6 27.27	25.68	0.36	.	3	34.	26		2.64			6 53.31	
53	10		51.						8 25.25	25.67	0.19	.	2	13.779	46	52.74	2.47	12.70		8 51.14	25 20 7.91
54	9		9.	26.	43.				10 43.04	25.66	0.41	IV.	4	38.518	20	57.36	2.27	8.62		11 9.11	24 54 5.25
55	9		45.						12 19.15	25.65	0.51	.	5	50.120	8	50.74	2.14	6.69		12 45.31	41 59.57
56	7		8.5	25.	42.				19 15 42.22	+25.64	+0.17	IV.	4	44.635	−11	33.40	1.86	7.62		19 16 8.33	−24 47 42.88

CORRECTIONS.

Date.	Corr. of Clock.	Hourly rate.	m	n	c	Zenith Point.	Mic. Co.
1848.	h. s.	s.	s.	s.	s.	° ″	r.

INSTRUMENT READINGS.

Date.	CIRCLE.							Barom.	THERMOM.				
	A.	B.	C.	D.	E.	F.	Mean.		At.	Ex.	U.	L.	I.
1848. h. m.							″	in.	°				

REMARKS.

(190) 14. Declination differs 9″ from Arg. Z. 220, 98.

(190) 26. Transit over T. VI assumed as recorded over T. V.

(190) 46. Micrometer reading assumed as 39ʳ.528 instead of 39ʳ.328.

ZONE 191. AUGUST 16. S. $D_e = -25°\ 47'\ 50''$.

No.	Mag.	I.	II.	III.	IV.	V.	VI.	VII.	T. (h m s)	a_1 (s)	a_2 (s)	Mic.		r	i	d_1	d_i	Mean Right Ascension, 1850.0 (h m s)	Mean Declination, 1850.0 (° ′ ″)
1	9				51.				20 41 50.87	+23.41	+1.09		4	39.253	−20 11.22	−9.73	−8.36	20 42 15.37	−26 8 19.31
2	8		13.	30.	47.				44 47.23	23.40			4	39.220	12 12.11	9.26	8.36	48	0 20.03
3	10			9.		43.			49 25.96	23.39	2.14		2	13.893	46 45.90	9.14	12.83	49 51.49	34 57.87
4	11		37.						55 11.53	23.37	1.29		4	37.583	21 55.07	8.70	8.66	55 36.19	10 2.43
5	9		3.8	21.5	38.3				20 57 38.42	23.36	1.31		4	38.011	21 28.17	8.52	8.58	20 58 3.09	9 35.27
6	10		12.		46.				21 0 46.31	23.36	2.41		2	9.603	51 14.70	8.28	13.63	21 1 12.08	39 26.61
7	10				24.				2 6.74	23.35	1.82		3	26.436	33 43.52	8.18	10.64	2 31.91	21 52.34
8	9		57.5	14.5	32.				5 31.95	23.34	2.22	IV.	2	16.990	43 31.04	8.92	12.30	5 57.51	31 43.16
9	10		32.	6.					9 6.20	23.33	1.84		3	28.098	31 59.52	7.66	10.34	9 34.37	20 7.52
10	9		30.5	47.5	5.				15 4.88	23.32	1.61		3	35.832	23 54.01	7.23	8.97	15 29.81	12 0.21
11	8		58.5						19 33.04	23.31	1.86		3	30.432	29 33.21	6.91	9.93	19 58.21	17 40.05
12	8		2.5	19.9	36.5				21 36.72	23.30	2.05		3	26.405	33 45.72	6.77	10.64	22 2.07	21 53.13
13	7.8		10.	27.	44.				22 44.24	23.30	1.43		5	43.168	16 7.13	6.71	7.66	23 8.97	26 4 11.50
14	9		37.	54.	11.5				26 11.41	23.29	1.28		4	48.667	10 57.05	6.40	6.81	26 35.98	25 59 0.32
15	10				25.				27 24.94	23.29	2.57		2	13.640	41 48.38	6.39	12.02	27 50.80	26 29 56.79
16	6			49.8		23.			29 5.97	23.28	1.60		4	40.458	18 55.60	6.27	8.15	29 30.85	26 7 0.02
17	9			17.	34.	51.			30 54.07	23.28	1.13		5	53.080	5 44.96	6.17	5.93	31 18.48	25 53 47.06
18	9				56.5				31 56.12	23.28	2.50		2	17.262	43 15.07	6.08	12.26	32 22.20	26 31 23.41
19	9			43.	0.				33 0.11	23.27	2.55		2	16.330	44 13.33	6.01	12.43	33 25.93	32 21.77
20	9		22.						37 56.55	23.27	2.13	•	3	28.860	31 11.59	5.70	10.20	38 21.95	19 17.49
21	10				33.				38 32.04	23.26	2.73		2	12.815	47 53.70	5.66	13.06	38 58.93	36 2.42
22	8					24.8	41.5		39 7.27	23.26	2.68		2	14.560	46 4.59	5.62	12.74	39 33.21	34 12.95
23	10					18.			40 43.74	23.26	2.19		3	27.920	32 9.86	5.52	10.37	41 9.19	20 15.75
24	10			49.5					21 43 24.02	+23.25	+1.65		5	43.043	−16 14.90	−5.36	−7.69	21 43 48.92	−26 4 17.95

ZONE 192. AUGUST 18. P. $D_e = -22°\ 40'\ 0''$.

No.	Mag.	I.	II.	III.	IV.	V.	VI.	VII.	T. (h m s)	a_1 (s)	a_2	Mic.		r	i	d_1	d_i	Mean Right Ascension, 1850.0	Mean Declination, 1850.0 (° ′ ″)
1	11			6.	40.				19 7 22.95	+27.35			2	12.420	−18 17.35	−22.18	−12.75		−23 28 52.28
2	11				9.				8 52.02	27.35			2	13.510	47 9.14	22.04	12.57		27 43.75
3	10				31.				11 14.11	27.34			3	21.270	39 7.58	21.82	11.36		19 40.76
4	10		2.5						14 36.23	27.32			2	20.110	40 14.50	21.51	11.54		20 47.55
5	9			50.					15 6.89	27.32			2	13.650	46 59.88	21.46	12.55		27 33.69
6	9			38.5	55.5	12.			15 38.52	27.32		IV.	3	20.245	40 12.05	21.41	11.52		20 44.98
7	8			20.	37.	54.			18 36.96	27.31		IV.	3	30.158	29 50.22	21.14	9.98		10 21.34
8	8		41.5	58.	32.				22 15.06	27.30			2	11.559	49 10.52	20.80	12.88		29 44.50
9	9			59.5	16.	33.			22 59.40	27.29			4	36.819	22 43.02	20.73	8.93		3 12.68
10	10			47.	4.				27 3.84	27.27			3	31.840	28 4.50	20.36	9.71		8 34.57
11	9		47.5	4.	20.5				30 20.79	27.26			3	36.252	23 27.83	20.05	9.02		3 56.90
12	10			43.	17.				30 0.04	27.26			3	36.548	23 9.39	20.08	8.95		3 38.45
13	8.9		35.9	9.					35 9.03	27.24			3	28.043	32 2.79	19.62	10.30		23 12 32.70
14	10.9				36.	52.5			35 19.18	27.24			5	45.710	13 26.20	19.60	7.56		22 53 53.36
15	10		33.	6.	23.				38 6.25	27.23			3	30.078	29 55.17	19.35	9.99		23 10 24.51
16	9			37.	54.	10.5			40 53.80	27.22			3	31.278	28 40.00	19.11	9.80		9 8.91
17	8		54.	3.	27.5				43 27.62	27.21			2	9.178	51 40.09	18.88	13.25		32 12.22
18	10		41.5	18.					47 18.02	27.20			3	33.913	25 54.42	18.54	9.38		6 22.34
19	11			19.5					48 19.40	27.20			3	21.018	39 23.45	18.45	11.40		19 53.30
20	9.8		54.5	11.					51 28.00	27.19			3	32.492	27 23.95	18.17	9.60		7 51.72
21	6.7			47.	3.2	20.			19 52 3.36	+27.18		V.	3	31.652	−28 16.16	−18.12	−9.74		−23 8 44.02

CORRECTIONS.

Date.	Corr. of Clock.	Hourly rate.	m	n	c	Zenith Point.	Mic. Co.
1848. (h.)	(s.)	(s.)	(s.)	(s.)	(s.)	(° ′ ″)	(r.)
Aug. 18,	. .	. .	. .	. .	. .	359 59 61.75	30.0058

INSTRUMENT READINGS.

Date.		CIRCLE.						Barom.	THERMOM.				
		A.	B.	C.	D.	E.	F.	Mean.		At.	Ex.	U.	L.	I.
1848. (h. m.)		(° ′ ″)						(″)	(in.)	(°)				
Zone 192, Aug. 18, 19 0	72 2	{30. / 31.	26, / 25.5	28.8 / 29.3	22.8 / 24.2	21. / 21.8	25. / 25.}	25.86	29.924	77.8	70.2	79.2	78.5	78.
19 20														
19 40										60.9 / 60.2	79.	73.4	75.5	
20 0									29.930	76.	68.8			
20 40									29.932	75.5	67.7			
21 40									29.924	74.8	67.			
21 50		{30. / 31.	27. / 27.	30. / 30.2	23.2 / 24.0	22.2 / 22.8	24.8 / 24.0}	26.35						

REMARKS.

(191) 1. Right ascension differs $2^s.5$ from Arg. Z. 251, 19; wrong.

(191) 15. Micrometer reading assumed as $18^r.640$, not $13^r.640$.

(191) 17. Transits over T.'s III, IV, and V assumed as 37^s, 54^s, and 11^s, to agree with Arg. Z. 242, 721, and 251, 74; and Mur. October 14, 1848.

(192) 20. Declination differs $5'\ 19''$ from Arg. Z. 311, 35; micrometer probably 5^r in error.

ZONE 192. AUGUST 18. P. $D_e = -22°\ 40'\ 0''$—Continued.

No.	Mag.	I.	II.	III.	IV.	V.	VI.	VII.	T. (h. m. s.)	a_1 (s.)	a_2 (s.)	Micr.	n	r.	i (′ ″)	d_1 (″)	d_2 (″)	Mean R. A. 1850.0	Mean Decl. 1850.0
22	8	·	51.5	·	25.5	·	·	·	19 55 25.28	−27.17	·		4	39.146	−20 17.12	−17.82	− 8.56	· · ·	−23 0 43.50
23	10	·	·	46.	·	·	·	·	56 2.85	27.17	·		4	36.770	22 45.85	17.77	8.94	· · ·	3 12.56
24	11	·	57.	·	31.	·	·	·	19 59 30.77	27.16	·		3	32.830	27 2.56	17.47	9.55	· · ·	7 29.58
25	9	·	·	18.	·	52.	·	·	20 3 34.96	27.15	·	III.	2	15.360	45 12.84	17.12	12.30	· · ·	25 42.26
26	11	·	·	·	·	31.	·	·	4 57.55	27.14	·		3	21.155	39 14.36	17.01	11.39	· · ·	19 42.76
27	10	·	45.	·	·	18.8	·	·	10 18.67	27.12	·		3	28.759	31 17.86	16.55	10.19	· · ·	11 44.60
28	11	·	·	·	8.	·	·	·	12 7.88	27.11	·		2	25.338	34 47.19	16.39	10.73	· · ·	23 15 14.31
29	10	·	·	·	·	39.5	56.	·	14 22.68	27.11	·	V.	4	50.218	8 42.33	16.22	6.84	· · ·	22 49 3.39
30	11	·	·	·	23.	·	·	·	16 22.87	27.10	·		3	36.768	22 55.32	16.05	8.96	· · ·	23 3 20.33
31	10	·	·	·	46.	·	·	·	17 45.87	27.09	·		3	37.502	22 9.40	15.93	8.81	· · ·	0 34.14
32	9	·	·	·	·	10.	26.5	·	18 52.98	27.09	·	III.	2	10.940	49 49.76	15.84	13.01	· · ·	30 18.61
33	8	·	·	6.	23.	39.5	·	·	20 22.79	27.08	·	V.	3	20.450	39 59.01	15.71	11.50	· · ·	20 26.22
34	9	·	51.	·	25.	·	·	·	22 24.78	27.07	·	IV.	3	26.918	33 13.29	15.55	10.48	· · ·	13 39.32
35	11	·	·	·	51.	·	·	·	25 50.87	27.07	·		3	34.078	25 44.19	15.27	9.35	· · ·	6 8.81
36	10	·	·	·	10.5	27.5	·	·	27 10.53	27.06	·		3	27.048	33 5.20	15.16	10.46	· · ·	23 13 30.82
37	8	·	·	·	31.	48.	5.	·	28 31.24	27.06	·		5	42.015	17 18.20	15.04	8.11	· · ·	22 57 41.35
38	9	·	·	26.	·	0.	·	·	30 42.98	27.05	·		3	19.840	40 37.40	14.86	11.59	· · ·	23 21 3.85
39	10	·	·	42.5	·	·	·	·	32 59.41	27.05	·		3	9.330	51 30.96	14.68	13.26	· · ·	23 31 58.90
40	9	·	42.	·	16.	·	·	·	34 15.78	27.04	·	IV.	4	40.185	15 53.16	14.58	8.35	· · ·	22 59 16.09
41	10	·	·	·	·	·	·	·	· · ·	·	·		5	51.978	· · ·	14.44	6.58		
42	·	·	·	23.	·	·	·	·	37	27.03	·					14.30			
43	10	·	32.	·	·	·	·	·	39 5.75	27.02	·		2	17.268	43 12.81	14.19	12.00	· · ·	23 23 39.00
44	8	·	·	·	·	·	44.5	·	39 11.06	27.02	·		3	23.800	36 28.26	14.17	10.97	· · ·	16 53.40
45	10	·	·	·	47.	4.	·	·	42 47.02	27.01	·		3	25.043	35 10.98	13.90	10.78	· · ·	23 15 35.66
46	10	·	·	·	29.5	·	3.	·	44 29.48	27.00	·		5	40.428	18 57.92	13.76	8.36	· · ·	22 59 20.04
47	9	·	19.5	36.	·	·	·	·	50 53.02	26.99	·		3	23.669	36 37.35	13.26	10.99	· · ·	23 17 1.60
48	11	·	·	·	·	31.5	·	·	50 58.10	26.99	·		3	29.955	30 2.19	13.24	10.00	· · ·	10 25.43
49	9	·	·	·	·	25.	41.5	·	52 8.00	26.98	·		2	13.460	47 12.24	13.16	12.61	· · ·	23 27 38.01
50	8.9	·	·	34.8	·	8.	25.	·	20 53 51.51	26.97	·	V.	4	43.511	15 43.35	12.64	7.87	· · ·	22 56 3.86
51	9	·	21.5	38.	·	·	·	·	21 0 55.00	26.96	·		3	32.355	27 32.63	12.47	9.63	· · ·	23 7 54.73
52	7.8	·	·	9.5	26.	·	·	·	1 26.10	26.95	·		3	35.023	24 44.95	12.44	9.21	· · ·	5 6.60
53	8.9	·	50.	7.	·	·	·	·	4 23.74	26.94	·		3	30.838	29 7.55	12.21	9.87	· · ·	9 29.63
54	8.9	·	·	·	38.	55.	·	·	4 21.29	26.94	·		2	18.332	42 6.78	12.22	11.85	· · ·	22 30.85
55	10	·	·	·	·	56.	·	·	7 22.50	26.93	·		2	14.905	45 35.86	11.99	12.38	· · ·	26 0.23
56	8.9	·	7.5	24.	41.	57.5	·	·	11 40.92	26.92	·		3	38.798	20 47.88	11.67	8.60	· · ·	1 8.15
57	5	·	26.	42.5	59.	·	·	·	13 59.32	26.91	·		2	22.268	37 59.50	11.50	11.23	· · ·	18 22.23
58	8.7	·	·	51.	7.5	24.	·	·	15 7.45	26.90	·		2	17.658	42 48.60	11.42	11.96	· · ·	23 11.98
59	4.3	·	7.	24.	40.5	57.5	·	·	17 40.66	26.90	·		3	36.555	23 8.82	11.23	8.96	· · ·	3 29.01
60	9	·	51.	7.6	24.5	·	·	·	23 24.57	26.89	·	IV.	3	23.387	36 55.04	10.82	11.05	· · ·	23 17 16.91
61	11	·	·	·	57.5	·	·	·	28 14.43	26.68	·		5	49.630	9 20.18	10.49	6.89	· · ·	22 49 37.56
62	11	·	13.5	·	·	·	·	·	31 17.17	26.87	·		5	49.332	9 38.82	10.27	6.94	· · ·	22 49 56.03
63	9	·	37.	54.	10.5	27.5	·	·	36 10.04	26.86	·	IV.	3	25.592	34 36.60	9.95	10.69	· · ·	23 14 57.24
64	10	·	51.	·	·	8.	24.5	·	37 51.16	26.85	·			F.W.		9.84			
65	10	·	39.5	·	13.5	·	·	·	40 13.38	26.85	·	IV.	2	10.265	50 32.52	9.68	13.17	· · ·	23 30 55.37
66	11	·	·	23.	·	·	·	·	21 47 39.04	−27.83	·		5	50.582	− 8 20.41	− 9.21	− 6.72	· · ·	−22 48 36.34

CORRECTIONS.

Date.	Corr. of Clock.	Hourly rate.	m	n	c	Zenith Point.	Mic. Co.
1848.	h. s.	s.	s.	s.	s.	° ′	r.

REMARKS.

INSTRUMENT READINGS.

Date.	CIRCLE.							Barom.	THERMOM.				
	A.	B.	C.	D.	E.	F.	Mean.		At.	Ex.	U.	L.	I.
1848. h. m.	° ′ ″	°	°	°	°	°	° ″	in.	°	°	°	°	°

Zone 193. August 24. C. $D_e = -20° 10' 0''$.

No.	Mag.	I	II	III	IV	V	VI	VII	T. (h. m. s.)	a_1 (s.)	a_4 (s.)	MICROMETER	n	r.	i	d_1	d_4	Mean Right Ascension, 1850.0	Mean Declination, 1850.0
1	9					27.	44.		22 26 10.85	+23.11		V.	3	32.242	−27 39.27	−4.62	−9.67		−20 37 53.56
2	9		4.2		38.	54.5	10.8		31 37.78	23.10		IV.	3	23.328	36 58.74	4.39	11.01		47 14.14
3	8			50.7	7.2	23.5			39 7.16	23.08		IV.	5	45.730	13 21.95	4.08	7.64		20 23 36.67
4	9					46.1			41 29.35	23.08		V.	2	6.664	54 18.28	3.99	13.54		21 4 35.81
5	8		32.5	49.1	5.3	21.9	38.4		47 5.46	23.07		IV.	2	14.678	45 55.67	3.78	12.32		20 56 11.77
6	9		12.8	29.3	45.3	2.2			48 45.70	23.06		IV.	5	48.068	10 58.25	3.72	7.29		21 9.26
7	9				16.9	33.	49.7		58 16.75	23.05		V.	5	52.985	5 49.49	3.41	6.56		15 59.46
8	9								22 58	23.05		VII.	3	29.582	30 25.28	3.41	10.06		40 38.75
9	8			32.		4.5			23 5 48.31	23.04		IV.	4	38.967	20 28.24	3.16	8.65		30 40.05
10	9								6	23.04		VII.	3	20.606	39 48.35	3.15	11.43		50 2.93
11	9				20.	36.3			8 19.82	23.04		V.	3	23.738	36 32.58	3.07	11.07		46 46.74
12	9			53.4	9.7	26.			12 9.65	23.03		IV.	3	19.875	40 35.08	2.93	11.55		50 49.56
13	9		56.8	11.3	29.3				14 29.64	23.03		III.	4	39.344	20 4.57	2.84	8.59		30 16.00
14	4								23 15	+23.03		VII.	2	15.717	−44 50.46	−2.81	−12.13		−20 55 5.40

Zone 194. August 29. C. $D_e = -21° 25' 20'$.

No.	Mag.	I	II	III	IV	V	VI	VII	T. (h. m. s.)	a_1 (s.)	a_4 (s.)	MICROMETER	n	r.	i	d_1	d_4	Mean Right Ascension, 1850.0	Mean Declination, 1850.0
1	6.7			32.	48.	5.3	22.1	38.5	23 1 5.21	+23.22		IV.	3	26.301	−33 52.25	−6.42	−3.55		−21 59 22.22
2	9				14.2	30.7			2 30.72	23.21		III.	3	35.168	24 35.98	6.26	2.22		21 50 4.46
3	9			43.2		17.2		50.3	8 16.95	23.19		IV.	3	25.419	34 47.58	5.63	3.69		22 0 16.90
4	8.9				14.4		47.5		8 30.94	23.19		IV.	3	24.372	35 53.26	5.61	3.86		1 22.73
5	10					33.3	50.		14 49.97	23.18		III.	2	17.528	42 56.83	4.94	4.89		8 26.66
6	8.9			57.2		31.3	48.	4.	16 30.96	23.17		IV.	2	10.112	50 41.99	4.70	6.01		16 12.76
7	9					15.7	32.7		18 15.80	23.16		V.	3	25.606	34 35.50	4.56	3.66		0 3.72
8	8			55.2	12.2			2.3	23 28.90	23.15		IV.	2	14.112	46 31.17	4.02	5.41		12 0.60
9	8				19.	35.2		8.3	23 35.31	23.14		IV.	2	21.022	39 17.75	4.01	4.36		22 4 46.12
10	7						20.5	37.	25 3.90	23.13		V.	3	40.154	19 22.72	3.86	1.47		21 44 48.05
11	8.9			57.4	14.3	30.3	47.	3.8	23 30 30.63	+23.12		IV.	4	42.607	−16 39.90	−3.20	−1.10		−21 42 4.29

Zone 195. August 30. S. $D_e = -23° 17' 50''$.

No.	Mag.	I	II	III	IV	V	VI	VII	T. (h. m. s.)	a_1 (s.)	a_4 (s.)	MICROMETER	n	r.	i	d_1	d_4	Mean Right Ascension, 1850.0	Mean Declination, 1850.0
1	10			52.5		26.5			19 7 26.36	+20.05	+0.91	IV.	5	48.312	−10 43.05	−9.29	−3.10	19 7 47.32	−23 28 45.44
2	10				39.5				8 56.49	20.04	0.91		5	48.312	10 43.05	9.14	3.10	9 17.44	28 45.29
3	8				51.5		25.5		9 51.66	20.04	0.69	IV.	3	29.659	30 21.46	9.05	6.04	10 12.39	48 26.55
4	8				5.5				11 39.37	20.03	0.63		3	24.820	35 25.08	8.85	6.82	12 0.03	53 30.78
5	10							53.5	11 19.87	20.03	0.55		3	19.332	41 8.76	8.91	7.70	11 40.45	59 15.37
6	11						31.		13 14.10	20.02	0.67		3	20.717	33 25.71	8.72	6.52	13 34.79	51 30.95
7	10				23.				14 39.95	20.01	0.87		3	41.539	17 46.76	8.59	4.18	15 0.83	35 49.53
8	10					26.			15 9.26	20.01	0.99		3	49.478	9 28.77	8.51	2.91	15 30.26	27 30.22
9	8		21.				11.5		17 54.76	20.00	0.86	V.	3	39.132	20 26.79	8.28	4.55	18 15.62	38 29.62
10	10				35.				22 51.91	19.98	0.68		2	22.930	37 17.81	7.80	7.13	23 12.57	55 22.74
11	9						51.		22 34.08	19.98	0.70		3	25.072	35 8.97	7.83	6.78	22 54.76	23 53 13.58
12	8		36.	43					25 9.98	19.97	0.49	III.	2	8.289	52 36.28	7.50	9.48	25 30.42	24 10 43.26
13						16.			26 15.88	19.96	0.92			39.	20	7.48		26 36.76	23 37
14	7			53.5	10.5				30 27.37	19.94	0.86	III.	3	32.130	27 46.56	7.08	5.66	30 48.17	45 49.30
15	7				29.		2.		30 45.03	19.94	0.87	III.	3	32.910	28 0.22	7.06	5.54	31 5.84	46 2.82
16	9						34.		19 31 0.42	+19.93	+0.93		3	37.490	−22 9.58	−7.03	−4.81	19 31 21.20	−23 40 11.42

CORRECTIONS.

Date.	Corr. of Clock.	Hourly rate.	m	n	c	Zenith Point.	Mic. Co.
	h. s.	s.	s.	s.	s.	° ' ''	r.
1848. Aug. 24,						359 59 62.66	30.0089
29,						61.99	30.0118
30,						60.73	30.0139

REMARKS.

(194) 1. Perhaps micrometer 2r in error. (See Tables Δα and Δd.)

(195) 12. Minutes of transit assumed as 24 instead of 25. Time of transit over T. III assumed as 53s instead of 43s.

(195) 15. Micrometer reading assumed as 31r.910, instead of 32r.910

INSTRUMENT READINGS.

Date.	CIRCLE A.	B. C. D. E. F.	Mean.	Barom.	THERMOM. At.	Ex.	U.	L.	I.
	1848. h. m.	° ' ''	''	in.	°	°	°	°	°
Zone 193　Aug. 24, 22 20	69 32	{34.9 33.9 36.9 34.4 27.6 29.6} {34.5 34.3 37.1 34.9 28.5 30.4}	33.04	30.222	67.8	61.8	67.8	67.	
22 40						60.6			
23 0				30.226	67.2	59.5			
23 20		{34.4 34.4 37.2 34.2 28.2 28.9} {34.6 34.2 37.4 34.4 28.8 29.6}	33.02	30.226	67.	59.4	66.8	64.8	70.2
Zone 194　Aug 29,* 23 0	60 47	{34.2 29.9 34.2 29.8 26.3 29.6} {34.7 30.3 33.9 30.8 26.6 30.1}	30.87	29.964	73.2	67.5	73.5	73.4	74.2
23 20						67.8			
0 35				29.960	72.8	67.5			
Zone 195　Aug. 30, 19 0	72 39	60. 56.2 59.9 54.0 48.0 55.5	55.60	29.914	79.	71.8			

* Hour assumed as 20h instead of 23h, and degrees of circle reading as 70° instead of 60°.

29—z

ZONE 195. AUGUST 30. S. $D_0 = -23°\ 17'\ 50''$ — Continued.

No.	Mag.	I.	II.	III.	IV.	V.	VI.	VII.	T.	a_1	a_2	Wire	n	r.	i	d_1	d_2	Mean Right Ascension, 1850.0	Mean Declination, 1850.0
									h. m. s.	s.	s.			r.	° ' "	"	"	h. m. s.	° ' "
17	9						52.5		19 32 18.85	+19.93	+0.71		2	19.722	−40 39.35	−6.90	−7.64	19 32 39.52	−23 58 43.89
18	10						34.		34 0.38	19.92	0.73		2	20.565	39 46.60	6.75	7.50	34 21.03	57 50.85
19	10				19.5		53.6		35 19.70	19.92	1.01		3	40.415	19 6.64	6.62	4.36	35 40.63	23 37 7.62
20	9			28.5					37 45.47	19.90	0.64		2	12.963	47 42.90	6.41	8.71	38 6.01	24 5 48.02
21	9		1.	18.					40 34.05	19.89	0.66	III.	2	13.368	47 17.75	6.14	8.65	40 55.50	24 5 22.54
22	9		12.			3.			41 46.00	19.88	0.95		3	33.639	26 11.00	6.04	5.42	42 6.83	23 44 13.42
23	8		57.5		31.				43 31.10	19.87	0.97	IV.	3	35.000	14 18.68	5.87	3.63	43 51.94	32 18.38
24	8						55.		47 21.38	19.86	1.21		3	49.492	9 36.27	5.52	2.91	47 42.45	27 34.70
25	7					3.			49 2.87	19.85	1.00	VII.	2	34.008	25 43.00	5.36	5.36	49 23.72	43 43.72
26	7					59.	15.5		49 42.05	19.85	1.00		3	33.460	26 17.70	5.45	5.30	50 2.90	44 18.45
27	9			49.		2.			54 45.56	19.83	1.11	III.	3	39.078	20 30.55	4.84	4.58	55 6.50	23 38 20.97
28	7		45.		19.				19 50 16.92	19.81	0.87	IV.	2	17.516	42 57.74	4.43	7.99	19 59 39.60	24 1 0.16
29	8		50.		21.5				20 3 24.12	19.79	0.99	IV.	3	25.255	34 57.87	4.08	6.76	20 3 44.90	23 52 58.71
30	10		21.						6 54.86	19.77	1.03		3	26.875	33 19.93	3.78	6.51	7 15.66	51 20.22
31	6					11.5	28.		6 54.45	19.77	0.95	V.	3	20.562	39 51.92	3.78	7.51	7 15.17	57 53.21
32	9		41.5	59.		32.5			12 15.61	19.75	1.00	III.	3	21.552	38 50.21	3.31	7.35	12 36.36	56 50.87
33	9		32.	49.					15 5.90	19.73	1.02		3	21.155	39 15.11	3.07	7.42	15 26.65	57 15.60
34	10						13.5		15 56.69	19.73	1.24		4	37.758	21 44.23	3.00	4.78	16 17.66	39 42.01
35	9		23.	40.					18 56.90	19.72	1.39		4	46.773	12 17.73	2.74	3.34	19 18.01	30 13.81
36	10		11.						20 20 44.83	+19.71	+1.25		3	35.680	−24 3.80	−2.57	−5.10	20 21 5.79	−23 42 1.47

ZONE 196. AUGUST 30. S. $D_0 = -19\ 32'\ 20''$.

No.	Mag.	I.	II.	III.	IV.	V.	VI.	VII.	T.	a_1	a_2	Wire	n	r.	i	d_1	d_2	Mean Right Ascension, 1850.0	Mean Declination, 1850.0
1	9				4.	37.			20 43 20.48	+19.51		III.	2	20.899	−39 25.20	−11.75	−11.31	20 43	−20 12 6.26
2	8				38.	54.			49 37.80	19.48		IV.	4	50.990	7 53.61	11.35	7.02		19 40 31.98
3	8		19.5	36.		9.			53 52.54	19.47		III.	4	41.850	17 27.04	11.07	8.31		19 50 6.42
4	10			41.					57 57.52	19.45			2	15.130	45 27.14	10.82	12.12		20 18 10.08
5	11								20 58	19.45			3	27.765			10.30		
6	9		39.5		22.		55.		21 8 22.22	19.41		IV.	3	25.152	35 4.27	10.12	10.70		7 45.09
7	10		2.		34.5		57.		12 34.55	19.40		IV.	3	23.270	37 2.38	9.82	10.95		9 43.15
8	10		16.			16.5			14 49.03	19.39			2	13.345	47 18.88	9.67	12.39		20 19 59.94
9	9		43.5		16.5				18 16.42	19.38		IV.	4	49.362	9 36.00	9.42	7.20		19 42 12.62
10	8				43.	59.			18 26.45	19.38		V.	3	34.858	24 54.88	9.41	9.28		19 57 33.57
11	10		2.			51.			20 18.38	19.37			2	21.399	38 54.09	9.28	11.23		20 11 34.60
12	8	5.5	22.			55.			22 38.52	19.36		IV.	3	38.600	21 0.43	9.11	8.74		19 53 38.28
13	.			44.5					25 44.38	19.35			3	40.570	16 56.79	8.88	8.49		51 34.16
14	9					50.5	7.		26 34.20	19.35			3	37.679	21 57.98	8.81	8.88		19 54 35.67
15	5			3.5	20.				28 19.92	19.34			3	24.762	35 23.73	8.68	10.75		20 8 9.16
16	9				9.	26.			28 52.96	19.34			3	37.995	21 38.08	8.61	8.97		19 54 15.59
17	8				21.5	38.			30 5.08	19.34			2	15.338	45 14.54	8.56	12.11		20 17 55.21
18	6		56.5		27.	45.8			34 29.23	19.32			2	15.043	45 32.29	8.20	12.16		18 12.65
19	9				18.	35.			35 18.19	19.32			3	21.450	38 56.54	8.14	11.23		20 11 35.91
20	10			21.5					38 41.05	19.31			4	46.995	12 4.16	7.87	7.55		19 44 39.58
21	9				31.				38 58.24	19.31			2	16.993	43 30.56	7.85	11.86		20 16 10.27
22	8		26.5	43.					44 59.50	19.29			2	19.502	40 52.76	7.33	11.51		20 13 31.60
23	8			22.			54.		44 21.58	19.29			3	40.958	18 32.37	7.38	8.43		19 51 8.18
24	9		22.5		55.5				46 55.43	19.28			3	26.232	33 56.71	7.16	10.54		20 6 34.41
25	10		52.9		25.5	42.			21 48 25.59	+19.28			4	38.062	−21 24.58	−7.03	−8.87		−19 54 0.48

CORRECTIONS.

Date.	Corr. of Clock.	Hourly rate.	m	n	c	Zenith Point.	Mic. Co.
1848.	h.	s.	s.	s.	s.	° ' "	r.

REMARKS.

(195) 23. Micrometer reading assumed as ' 45ʳ.000, not 35ʳ.000.

(196) 6. Time of transit over T. II assumed as 49ˢ.5 instead of 39ˢ.5.

(196) 7. Time of transit over T. VI assumed as 7ˢ instead of 57ˢ.

INSTRUMENT READINGS.

Date.		A	B.	C.	D.	E.	F.	Mean.	Barom.	At.	Ex.	U.	L.	I.
	1848. h. m.	° ' "						"	in.	°	°	°	°	°
Zone 195	Aug. 30, 19 20								29.904	77.	71.2			
	20 0								29.900	76.4	70.4			
	20 20	72 39 61.	56.4	60.3	54.0	48.3	54.9	55.82						
Zone 196	Aug. 30, 20 40	68 54 60.	55.2	60.4	54.8	48.3	53.8	55.82	29.892	75.2	69.8			
	21 0								29.892	75.2	69.5			
	22 0	58.9	55.2	60.4	54.3	48.3	53.2	55.05			69.4			

ZONE 196. AUGUST 30. S. $D_0 = -19°\ 32'\ 20''$—Continued.

No.	Mag.	I.	II.	III.	IV.	V.	VI.	VII.	T.	m	a_1	MICROMETER.	i	d_1	d_2	Mean Right Ascension, 1850.0	Mean Declination, 1850.0
									h. m. s.	s.	s.	r.	' "	"	"	h. m. s.	° ' "
26	9						I.		21 50 28.32	+19.27		3 30.419	−29 33.33	− 6.85	− 9.94		−20 2 10.12
27	8		42.		15.				56 14.92	19.26		4 43.790	15 24.95	6.25	8.03		19 47 59.23
28	8		15.8		48.5				21 58 48.63	19.25		2 15.320	45 15.04	6.01	12.11		20 17 53.16
29							I.		22 0 44.68	+19.24		4 48.173	−10 50.65	− 5.82	− 7.35		−19 43 23.85

ZONE 197. AUGUST 30. S. $D_0 = -19°\ 32'\ 20''$.

No.	Mag.	I.	II.	III.	IV.	V.	VI.	VII.	T.	m	a_1	MICROMETER.	i	d_1	d_2	Mean Right Ascension, 1850.0	Mean Declination, 1850.0
1	9		50.5		23.	40.			22 43 23.29	+19.13	+1.72	IV. 2 17.302	−43 11.24	− 3.95	−11.84	22 43 44.14	−20 15 47.06
2					11.5	30.	16.5		44 13.60	19.13	1.82	4 41.934	17 22.02	3.95	8.26	44 34.55	19 49 54.23
3	6			26.		55.5			45 42.28	19.13	1.76	III. 3 34.042	25 46.57	3.89	9.40	46 3.17	19 58 19.86
4	8		15.		48.				48 48.00	19.12	1.64	IV. 2 12.129	48 35.57	3.77	12.60	49 8.76	20 21 11.94
5	9				41.5		14.		49 41.32	19.12	1.76	IV. 5 45.346	13 49.29	3.73	7.78	50 2.20	19 16 20.80
6	8		2.		34.5				52 34.69	19.12	1.63	IV. 3 23.800	36 28.89	3.62	10.91	52 55.44	20 9 3.42
7			2.						34.96								
8	9			41.		9.			53 57.61	19.11	1.72	III. 5 46.690	12 24.68	3.58	7.57	54 18.44	19 41 55.83
9	10						37.		55 4.29	19.11	1.61	2 25.590	34 31.40	3.53	10.64	55 25.01	20 7 5.57
10	9			2.5		35.			58 18.72	19.11	1.54	III. 2 17.052	43 26.61	3.41	11.88	22 58 39.37	16 1.90
11	10					0.5			22 59 44.08	19.10	1.57	3 31.500	29 26.00	3.36	9.78	23 0 4.75	20 0 50.14
12	10			59.5		31.			23 6 15.38	19.09	1.58	III. 5 50.088	8 51.42	3.14	7.07	6 36.05	19 41 21.63
13	8		10.	26.5	43.	59.5			8 43.03	19.09	1.55	IV. 5 49.989	8 57.65	3.05	7.08	9 3.67	41 27.78
14	6		41.5		14.2				10 14.25	19.08	1.54	V. 5 51.708	7 9.67	3.00	6.83	10 34.90	37 39.50
15	8		8.	24.	40.5				12 40.60	19.08	1.46	IV. 4 43.208	16 2.24	2.93	8.06	13 1.14	46 33.23
16	8		58.5		30.5				15 30.92	19.07	1.40	IV. 3 36.332	23 22.88	2.84	9.07	15 51.39	14 55 54.79
17	9		22.7		55.5				17 55.55	19.07	1.33	IV. 2 20.981	39 20.31	2.75	11.32	18 15.92	20 11 54.38
18	10		16.			6.5			22 49.47	19.06	1.22	V. 2 14.158	46 28.40	2.63	12.33	23 9.75	20 19 3.36
19	10				11.5		44.3		24 11.48	19.06	1.31	IV. 4 39.265	20 9.71	2.59	8.63	24 31.85	19 52 40.93
20	9					36.			25 19.59	19.06	1.27	3 33.952	25 51.79	2.56	9.41	25 39.92	58 23.76
21	10					44			27 43.88	19.06	1.29	4 45.126	14 1.79	2.50	7.78	28 4.23	46 32.07
22	10		43.						31 20.96	19.05	1.22	3 37.805	21 50.38	2.41	8.85	31 41.23	54 21.64
23	8		53.		26.	42.5			32 25.99	19.05	1.23	IV. 4 42.689	16 34.70	2.39	8.14	32 46.27	19 49 5.23
24	10			45.		17.			39 1.02	19.04	1.10	IV. 3 31.253	28 41.57	2.24	9.81	39 21.16	20 1 13.62
25	9			8.	24.	40.5	57.		22 40 24.22	+19.04	+1.16	5 48.499	−10 31.26	− 2.22	− 7.28	23 40 44.42	−19 43 0.76

ZONE 198. AUGUST 31. C. $D_0 = -23°\ 55'\ 20''$.

No.	Mag.	I.	II.	III.	IV.	V.	VI.	VII.	T.	m	a_1	MICROMETER.	i	d_1	d_2	Mean Right Ascension, 1850.0	Mean Declination, 1850.0
1	9.10				42.	59.2			19 31 42.16 1·22.72			V. 5 54.775	− 3 57.02	− 9.11	− 6.02		−23 59 32.15
2	9.10				35.3	52.			32 18.36 22.72			V. 5 55.487	3 12.51	9.05	5.90		23 58 47.46
3	9					45.7			33 11.86 22.71			VI. 2 12.844	47 50.62	8.96	12.78		24 43 32.38
4	9.10				34.2				19 40 34.00 22.68			IV. 5 49.199	9 47.37	8.18	6.91		5 22.46
5	9.10		20.		53.8	10.5			20 6 53.76 22.57			IV. 3 37.845	21 47.68	5.57	8.74		17 21.99
6	9		4.	20.8	37.5	55.	11.3		20 9 37.76 +22.55			IV. 3 33.915	−25 54.30	− 5.31	− 9.35		−24 21 28.96

CORRECTIONS.

Date.	Corr. of Clock.	Hourly rate.	m	n	c	Zenith Point.	Mic. Co.
	h.	s.	s.	s.	s.	° ' "	r.
1848. Aug. 31,						359 59 61.86	30.0094

REMARKS.

(197) 8. Time of transit over T. V assumed as 14ᵃ instead of 9ᵃ.

INSTRUMENT READINGS.

Date.	CIRCLE.							Barom.	THERMOM.				
	A.	B.	C.	D.	E.	F.	Mean.		At.	Ex.	U.	L.	I.
	° ' "						"	in.	°				
Zone 197　1848 Aug. 30, 22 40	69 54 60.0	56.0	67.3	56.2	49.4	54.8	56.28	29.882	75.0	68.9			
23 0								29.880	73.8	67.3			
23 20										67.5			
Zone 198　23 50	60.	56.	61.3	56.0	19.2	54.8	56.22	29.882	74.3	68.1	73.5	74.6	72.5
Aug. 31, 19 30	73 17 {32.7 27. 31.7 29.1 23.7 27.9 / 34.7 27.2 32.1 29.0 25.1 29.2}						29.19	29.828	78.2	75.4	78.	77.	75.8
19 40										75.3			
20 0								29.822	78.	74.5			

ZONE 199. AUGUST 31. C. $D_0 = -20°\ 10'\ 0''$.

No.	Mag.	I.	II.	III.	IV.	V.	VI.	VII.	T. (h. m. s.)	a_1 (s.)	a_2 (s.)	MICROMETER		r.	i (' ")	d_1 (")	d_2 (")	Mean Right Ascension, 1850.0 (h. m. s.)	Mean Declination, 1850.0 (° ' ")
1	8		30.2	56.	12.	28.8	45.2		22 26 12.27	+19.23	+1.53	IV.	3	32.128	−27 46.56	− 6.05	− 3.68	22 26 33.03	−20 37 56.29
2	10			1.5					31 18.07	19.22	1.62	III.	4	40.862	18 29.05	5.79	2.40	31 38.91	28 37.24
3	9					0.?			31 27.15	19.22	1.42	VII.	3	23.187	37 6.43	5.78	4.99	31 47.79	47 17.20
4	9					43.	59.4		35 26.54	19.20	1.48	V.	3	28.678	31 22.70	5.43	4.16	39 47.22	41 32.31
5	7								39	19.20	1.65	VII.	5	45.616	13 31.79	5.39	1.71		23 38.89
6	9								40	19.20	1.58	VII.	4	40.340	19 2.37	5.35	2.48		20 29 10.20
7	8			31.	47.5	4.3			41 31.03	19.19	1.22	V.	2	6.556	54 25.12	5.28	7.47	41 51.44	21 4 37.87
8	9			23.3					43 23.20	19.19	1.71	IV.	5	53.176	5 37.61	5.19	0.59	43 44.10	20 15 43.39
9	8		33.8	50.4	7.	23.3	39.9		47 6.90	19.18	1.25	IV.	2	14.564	46 2.89	5.01	6.27	47 27.36	56 14.17
10	9		14.2		47.2		20.1		22 48 47.20	19.18	1.65	IV.	5	47.965	11 4.65	4.93	1.36	22 49 8.03	21 10.94
11	8		21.3	37.3	54.				23 24 54.09	19.10	1.19	III.	2	15.824	44 43.49	3.50	6.11	23 25 14.38	54 53.10
12	8		4.3	20.7	37.1				33 37.20	19.09	1.36	III.	3	34.556	25 14.39	3.25	3.32	33 57.65	20 35 20.96
13	8.9					53.5	10.		33 36.93	19.09	1.10	VI.	2	10.818	49 57.87	3.25	6.86	33 57.12	21 0 7.98
14	8.9		55.2	12.	8.1	25.	41.4		42 8.36	19.08	1.04	IV.	2	7.121	53 49.51	3.05	6.42	42 28.48	21 3 58.98
15	9		21.2	37.3	54.	27.			46 54.06	19.07	1.14	IV.	2	17.876	42 34.09	2.95	5.80	47 14.27	20 52 43.74
16	9		14.8		18.	4.5			50 47.94	19.06	1.37	IV.	4	40.223	19 9.59	2.85	2.49	51 7.37	29 14.06
17	7				30.	53.5			51 20.00	19.06	1.14	V.	2	19.054	41 21.30	2.87	5.65	51 30.20	51 29.82
18	7		22.1	38.2	55.	11.4	27.9		23 54 54.94	19.05	1.12	IV.	2	17.547	42 55.82	2.82	5.85	23 55 14.11	53 4.49
19	9.10		51.8	8.5					0 8 25.04	19.04	1.48	III.	5	55.134	3 34.61	2.66	0.26	0 8 45.56	13 37.53
20	8				1.5	18.2			8 45.02	19.04	0.97	V.	2	8.372	52 31.33	2.65	7.26	9 5.03	2 41.24
21	9			40.	50.7				12 56.55	19.04	1.14	III.	3	24.664	35 34.91	2.63	4.80	13 16.73	45 42.37
22	5		17.3	34.	50.	7.	23.5		13 50.38	19.04	1.00	IV.	2	17.221	43 16.38	2.63	5.92	14 10.48	53 24.03
23	8.9		9.3	26.1	42.5	0.	16.		17 42.81	19.04	1.13	IV.	3	24.544	35 42.40	2.61	4.82	18 2.98	20 45 49.83
24	9		10.8	27.	43.7	0.5	16.6		19 43.74	19.04	0.98	IV.	2	12.912	47 46.29	2.60	6.56	20 3.76	57 55.45
25	9				26.8				25 26.69	19.03	1.37	IV.	5	49.492	9 28.98	2.61	1.09	25 47.09	19 32.68
26	8.9			15.3	32.	48.2			29 31.86	19.03	1.32	IV.	4	45.722	13 24.31	2.62	1.65	29 52.21	20 23 28.58
27	9		48.	4.3		37.7			31 21.03	19.03	0.97	IV.	2	15.		2.62		31 41.03	
28	7		19.7	35.3	52.	8.8	25.4		34 52.16	19.03	0.91	IV.	2	9.965	50 51.14	2.65	7.00	35 12.10	21 1 0.79
29	9					45.8	16).		44 45.92	19.03	1.09	VI.	3	27.612	32 29.33	2.75	4.35	45 6.04	20 42 36.43
30	9			28.3	45.		17.7		45 44.80	19.03	1.32	IV.	5	53.355	5 26.50	2.80	0.52	49 5.24	15 29.82
31	7.8				59.2		32.1		0 50 59.10	+19.03	+1.21	VI.	4	42.753	−16 30.80	− 2.84	− 2.09	0 51 19.40	−20 26 35.73

CORRECTIONS.

Date.	Corr. of Clock.	Hourly rate.	m	u	e	Zenith Point.	Mic. Co.
1848.	h.	s.	s.	s.	s.	s.	° ' "	r.

REMARKS.

(199) 14. Time of transits over T.'s II and III assumed as 20^s earlier than recorded.

INSTRUMENT READINGS.

Date.	A.	B.	C.	D.	E.	F.	Mean.	Barom.	At.	Ex.	U.	L.	I.
1848. h. m.	° ' "							in.	°	°	°	°	°
Zone 199 Aug. 31, 22 20	69 32 34.7 / 35.2	29.4 / 29.9	35.5 / 35.5	30.1 / 31.1	25.9 / 27.9	30.1 / 31.1	31.37	29.806	77.	72.7	76.5	76.	76.
22 40										72.2			
23 0								29.806	76.3	72.1			
23 25								29.800	76.2	73.2			
23 40										72.5			
0 0	33.8 / 34.7	29.4 / 29.8	34.7 / 35.1	30.2 / 31.5	26.3 / 26.8	29.9 / 30.9	31.09	29.790	76.	71.9	75.5	75.5	
0 20										71.6			

ZONE 200. SEPTEMBER 1. S. $D_s = -18°\,55'\,0''$.

No.	Mag.	I	II	III	IV	V	VI	VII	T. (h m s)	a_1	a_2	Mic.	n	r.	′	″	i	d_1	Mean R.A. 1850.0 (h m s)	Mean Decl. 1850.0 (° ′ ″)
1	9				29.				19 13 28.87	+19.14	+0.73		3	36.832	−22	51.25	−16.67	−2.05	19 13 48.74	−19 18 9.97
2	8		50.5	7.					15 23.39	19.14	0.79	III.	4	41.768	17	32.25	16.47	1.37	15 43.32	12 50.09
3	10			1).		51.5			16 35.25	19.13	0.66	III.	3	27.640	32	28.26	16.35	3.33	16 55.04	27 47.94
4	10		9.						18 41.83	19.12	0.87		5	50.261	8	40.39	16.13	0.18	19 1.82	3 56.70
5	8				56.5	29.			18 56.40	19.12	0.53	IV.	2	12.338	48	22.53	16.11	5.49	19 16.05	43 44.13
6	9		30.			35.			21 2.63	19.11	0.56		2	14.482	46	7.59	15.90	5.18	21 22.30	41 28.67
7	7		3.	19.5	36.				22 35.93	19.10	0.56	IV.	2	14.128	46	30.16	15.74	5.23	22 55.59	41 51.13
8	10		33.5						24 6.37	19.09	0.63		2	20.358	39	59.07	15.59	4.35	24 26.09	35 19.01
9	10			24.					24 40.47	19.09	0.85		4	43.825	15	23.07	15.53	1.08	25 0.41	10 39.68
10	9			35.5					25 52.00	19.08	0.89		5	48.940	10	2.81	15.41	0.36	26 11.97	5 18.58
11	7		48.		21.5				27 21.10	19.08	0.85	IV.	4	43.728	15	29.47	15.26	1.09	27 41.03	10 45.82
12	10						1.		27 44.73	19.08	0.89		5	47.640	11	24.92	15.25	0.54	28 4.70	6 40.71
13	9					29.			28 56.41	19.07	0.67		2	22.970	37	15.68	15.10	3.98	29 16.15	32 34.76
14	7			25.	41.				30 41.16	19.06	0.66	IV.	2	21.540	38	45.37	14.92	4.19	31 0.88	34 4.48
15	10			51.5					34 7.88	19.04	0.74		3	27.720	32	23.17	14.56	3.32	34 27.66	27 41.07
16	10			59.5		32.			36 15.83	19.03	0.87	V.	5	42.062	17	15.19	14.36	1.33	36 35.73	12 30.88
17	9		43.						38 15.83	19.02	0.93		4	47.990	11	1.39	14.16	0.49	38 35.78	6 16.04
18	9					53.5	14.5		39 41.97	19.02	0.70	V.	2	21.052	39	15.99	14.02	4.26	40 1.69	34 34.27
19	11				48.5				41 4.93	19.01	0.87		3	39.335	20	14.55	13.88	1.70	41 24.81	15 30.13
20	8			15.5					42 31.92	19.00	0.70		2	20.318	40	1.90	13.75	4.36	42 51.62	35 20.01
21	7,6			53.		25.3			43 9.16	19.00		V.	.	F.Wire.	29	59.36	13.69	1.61	43 (26)	25 14.66
22	8		55.					0.	45 27.63	18.99	0.85		3	35.756	23	59.02	13.46	2.20	45 47.47	19 14.68
23	7					36.	52.5		46 19.67	18.99	0.67		2	14.960	45	37.99	13.37	5.10	46 39.33	40 56.46
24	8		26.2		59.	15.5			52 59.00	18.95	0.79	IV.	3	24.958	35	16.30	12.72	3.70	53 18.74	30 32.72
25	8		29.		1.		34.		56 1.37	18.94	0.96	IV.	4	42.995	16	15.49	12.43	1.19	56 21.27	11 29.11
26	9					18.5			57 2.23	18.94	1.00	V.	5	46.650	12	27.25	12.33	0.70	57 22.17	7 40.28
27	7		40.5	57.	13.				19 59 13.22	18.92	0.95	IV.	4	40.573	18	47.57	12.12	0.95	59 33.09	14 1.22
28	9			35.					20 3 51.41	18.91	0.81		3	23.458	36	50.71	11.68	3.93	20 4 11.13	32 6.32
29	8						20.		3 47.40	18.91	1.00		6	44.708	14	28.97	11.69	0.94	4 7.31	9 41.60
30	8					59.	15.5		5 42.68	18.90	0.76	V.	2	16.312	44	13.45	11.51	4.94	6 2.34	39 29.90
31	10		47.8			37.			6 20.58	18.88	0.73	V.	2	11.683	49	3.54	11.26	5.61	8 40.10	44 20.41
32	5,6		51.5	8.	25.				10 24.57	18.87	0.82	IV.	2	20.630	39	42.40	11.06	4.33	10 44.26	34 57.79
33	10						59.		10 26.39	18.87	0.82		2	19.720	40	39.53	11.06	4.46	10 46.08	35 55.05
34	10				8.				11 51.54	18.87	0.85		2	21.420	38	53.09	10.93	4.21	12 11.26	34 8.23
35	10					5.			12 32.40	18.86	0.86		2	22.680	37	33.87	10.87	4.04	12 52.12	32 48.78
36	10						57.		13 24.39	18.86	1.07		4	44.726	14	26.06	10.79	0.94	13 44.32	9 38.69
37	10		34.	50.5					16 6.90	18.85	1.07	III.	4	43.485	15	44.67	10.54	1.11	16 26.82	10 56.32
38	8		51.	8.	24.				17 24.08	18.84	0.85	IV.	2	17.480	43	0.08	10.42	4.77	17 43.77	38 15.27
39	9					8.5	24.		17 51.80	18.84	1.00	V.	3	34.945	24	49.45	10.38	2.31	18 11.64	20 2.14
40	10		14.						20 46.87	18.83	0.88		2	20.593	39	44.27	10.12	4.33	21 6.58	34 58.72
41	6				58.				20 41.75	18.83	1.15		5	49.612	9	21.31	10.13	0.25	21 1.73	4 31.69
42	7					28.			20 55.37	18.83	1.15		5	49.450	9	31.42	10.11	0.27	21 15.35	4 41.80
43	9							37.	21 4.38	18.82	0.87		2	18.230	42	13.05	10.02	4.67	22 24.07	37 27.74
44	10				30.				25 13.40	18.81	0.81		2	8.322	52	34.44	9.72	6.10	25 33.02	47 50.26
45	9		13.	40.5					26 46.14	18.80	0.92		3	19.788	40	40.79	9.59	4.45	27 5.86	35 54.83
46	10			37.					28 53.42	18.79	1.08		4	36.978	22	32.87	9.39	2.03	29 13.29	17 44.29
47	9				16.8				29 10.67	18.79	1.09		4	37.005	23	34.11	9.36	2.03	29 36.55	18 45.56
48	9						5.		29 32.39	18.79	1.16		5	44.575	14	37.39	9.34	0.96	29 52.34	9 47.69
49	9	4.	21.8	38.	54.8				20 31 54.65	+18.78	+1.09	IV.	3	36.740	−22	57.08	−9.14	−2.07	20 32 14.52	−19 18 8.29

CORRECTIONS.

Date.	Corr. of Clock.	Hourly rate.	m	n	c	Zenith Point.	Mic. Co.
	h. s.	s.	s.	s.	s.	° ′ ″	r.
1848, Sept. 1.						359 59 60.81	30.0101

REMARKS.

(200) 12. Transit over T. V assumed as recorded over T. VI.

(200) 22. Transit over T. VI assumed to have been recorded as over T. VII.

(200) 43. Transit over T. VI assumed as recorded over T. VII.

(200) 47. Micrometer reading assumed as 36ʳ.005 instead of 37ʳ.005.

(200) 49. Time of transit over T. I assumed as 6ˢ instead of 4ˢ.

INSTRUMENT READINGS.

	Date.		CIRCLE. A.	B.	C.	D.	E.	F.	Mean.	Barom.	At.	Ex.	U.	L.	I.
	1848.	h. m.	° ′						″	in.					
Zone 199	Aug. 31,	0 40	69 32 {34.3	29.1	35.2	30.8	25.7	29.8	31.18	29.790	75.5	72.2	75.2	74.7	76.
			{35.	30.	35.5	31.5	27.1	30.2}							
		0 50										72.2			
Zone 200	Sept. 1,	19 0	68 17 {31.	24.9	31.8	24.8	20.8	26.	27.09			72.2			
			{32.3	25.3	33.	26.	22.	27.9}							
		19 13								29.950	78.5	71.7			
		19 40								29.956	77.8	71.1			
		26 0								29.964	77.2	70.8			
		20 20										70.3			

ZONE 200. SEPTEMBER 1. S. $D_0 = -18°\ 55'\ 0''$—Continued.

No.	Mag.	I.	II.	III.	IV.	V.	VI.	VII.	T.	a_1	a_2	MICROMETER	r	i	d_1	d_2	Mean Right Ascension, 1850.0	Mean Declination, 1870.0
50	10		49.		22.				20 33 21.86	+18.77	+1.15	IV. 4	41.650	−12 26.27	9.02	−0.63	20 33 41.75	−19 7 35.92
51	10						13.5		34 40.89	18.77	1.18	4	44.580	14 36.25	8.91	0.96	35 0.84	9 46.12
52	10		2.	18.	34.5				37 34.53	18.75	1.10	IV. 3	33.910	25 54.61	8.65	2.45	37 54.39	21 5.71
53	9			14.		46.5			38 30.35	18.75	1.20	4	44.402	14 47.11	8.55	0.98	38 50.30	9 56.67
54	10						53.		39 20.33	18.74	0.89	2	7.610	53 18.98	8.52	6.20	39 39.96	48 33.70
55	10		43.5						43 16.38	18.73	1.00	2	17.709	42 45.09	8.17	4.74	43 36.11	37 58.00
56	8				28.		0.		43 27.65	18.73	1.17	IV. 3	36.720	22 58.34	8.14	2.07	43 47.55	18 8.55
57	8				39.5				44 39.44	18.72	0.98	2	15.190	45 23.62	8.05	5.09	44 59.14	40 36.76
58	8					30.			45 13.54	18.72	1.03	2	21.592	35 42.16	8.00	4.19	45 33.29	33 54.37
59	7					11.	27.5		45 54.80	18.72	1.15	3	33.450	26 23.50	7.94	2.52	46 14.67	21 33.96
60	9						25.5		46 52.89	18.71	1.26	4	45.348	13 48.10	7.86	0.85	47 12.86	8 56.81
61	8.9		39.5						50 12.35	18.70	1.10	III. 3	25.998	34 11.19	7.58	3.57	50 32.15	29 22.34
62	6.7			28.5		1.	17.		50 44.61	18.70	1.04	2	18.810	41 36.23	7.54	4.59	51 4.45	36 48.36
63	10				35.5		8.5		52 35.65	18.69	1.11	IV. 3	25.309	34 54.48	7.39	3.67	52 55.45	30 5.54
64	9			8.	24.	40.			55 24.03	18.68	1.33	IV. 4	47.319	11 44.26	7.16	0.57	55 44.04	6 51.99
65	9		45.5						58 18.33	18.67	1.25	3	36.849	22 50.37	6.93	2.06	58 35.25	17 59.36
66	7			40.	56.	13.			20 58 56.29	18.66	1.05	IV. 2	14.712	45 53.59	6.88	5.18	20 59 16.00	41 5.65
67	9				1.5	34.5			21 0 18.00	18.66	1.25	3	35.149	24 37.00	6.77	2.27	21 0 37.91	19 46.04
68	9		53.	9.3	25.5				9 25.63	18.62	1.32	IV. 3	35.102	23 37.20	6.06	2.28	9 45.57	18 45.54
69	9.10		59.5	15.		48.5			11 31.94	18.61	1.20	III. 2	21.543	38 45.01	5.90	4.22	11 51.75	33 55.13
70	9			42.5		15.			12 58.76	18.61	1.31	III. 3	32.902	26 57.01	5.79	2.59	13 18.68	22 6.29
71	10		39.5		12.				16 12.12	18.59	1.22	IV. 2	19.843	40 31.63	5.56	4.47	16 31.93	35 41.66
72	9				58.5	14.5	31.		16 58.33	18.59	1.41	IV. 3	40.842	18 39.59	5.50	1.47	17 18.33	13 46.56
73	8						50.5		18 17.85	18.58	1.18	2	13.620	47 2.14	5.40	5.36	18 37.61	42 12.90
74	7		42.		16.		18.		21 15.41	18.57	1.14	IV. 2	8.042	52 51.77	5.18	6.17	21 35 12	48 3.12
75	10		33.		6.				24 5.86	18.56	1.46	IV. 4	40.112	19 16.50	4.98	1.57	24 25.88	14 23.05
76	9			30.5		3.			24 30.39	18.56	1.48	IV. 4	41.758	18 35.84	4.95	1.47	24 50.43	13 42.26
77	8		17.	33.5	49.5	6.5			26 49.80	18.55	1.38	IV. 3	28.980	31 3.43	4.79	3.14	27 9.73	26 11.36
78	7		0.	16.	32.5				28 16.13	18.55	1.40	IV. 5	30.150	29 31.95	4.60	2.04	28 36.08	24 39.55
79	8						11.5		28 38.88	18.55	1.56	5	47.742	11 18.48	4.66	0.46	28 58.99	6 23.60
80	9				16.	32.5			29 59.80	18.54	1.44	3	33.712	26 6.85	4.56	2.48	30 19.78	21 13.89
81	8		20.5	37.	55.5				31 53.39	18.54	1.33	IV. 2	21.120	39 11.65	4.44	4.28	32 13.26	34 20.37
82	4		24.5	41.	57.5				33 57.06	18.53	1.36	IV. 2	22.569	37 40.83	4.29	4.07	34 16.95	32 49.19
83	10		40.			29.			35 12.76	18.52	1.52	V. 3	38.383	21 13.02	4.21	1.79	35 32.80	16 19.92
84	10		40.5						38 13.33	18.51	1.64	2	48.845	10 7.64	4.01	0.30	38 33.48	5 11.95
85	10				1.5	34.			39 1.40	18.51	1.42	IV. 2	24.260	35 54.82	3.95	3.84	39 21.33	31 2.61
86	8								40			4	49.150	9 58.50	3.88	0.26		5 2.64
87	6		29.5		2.				43 2.10	18.50	1.54	IV. 3	35.660	24 4.93	3.68	2.20	43 22.14	19 10.81
88	10		59.		32.				45 31.84	18.48	1.54	IV. 3	29.658	30 21.52	3.33	3.06	45 51.66	25 27.91
89	9				57.	13.			48 40.45	18.48	1.43	V. 2	19.000	41 24.69	3.32	4.58	49 0.36	36 32.59
90	10				6.	22.5			49 49.80	18.47	1.57	V. 2	33.345	21 16.36	3.25	1.95	50 9.84	16 21.56
91	8		41.	57.5					57 13.86	18.45	1.60	III. 3	31.295	28 39.06	2.79	2.82	57 33.91	23 44.67
92	10				36.	52.5			21 57 19.68	18.45	1.48	V. 1	16.119	44 25.42	2.78	4.99	21 57 39.61	39 33.19
93	5		53.		9.5	25.5			22 0 25.72	18.44	1.71	IV. 4	39.362	20 3.69	2.59	1.67	22 0 45.87	15 7.95
94	9					49.	5.		22 0 32.56	+18.44	+1.72	V. 4	41.400	−17 55.91	−2.57	−1.37	22 0 52.72	−19 12 59.85

CORRECTIONS.

Date.	Corr. of Clock.	Hourly rate.	m	n	c	Zenith Point.	Mic. Co.
1848.	h.	s.	s.	s.	s.	°	r.

INSTRUMENT READINGS.

Date.	CIRCLE.							Barom.	THERMOM.				
		A.	B.	C.	D.	E.	F.	Mean.		At.	Ex.	U.	L.	I.
Zone 200	1848. Sept. 1, 20 20								In. 29.970	76.2	68.9			
	21 0								29.972	76.	68.3*			
	21 20										67.6			
	22 0	68 17	{30.2 / 31.2}	{26.4 / 25.6}	{32. / 33.4}	{26.8 / 27.0}	{20.8 / 21.8}	{25.2 / 26.8} 27.27			69.			

REMARKS.

(200) 50. Micrometer reading assumed as 46ʳ.650, not 41ʳ.650.

(200) 58. Declination differs 25″ from Arg. Z. 243, 111; perhaps micrometer reading should be 21ʳ.992, not 21ʳ.592.

(200) 67. Transit over T. III assumed to be recorded as over T. IV.

(200) 68. Micrometer reading assumed as 36ʳ.102 instead of 35ʳ.102.

(200) 76. Micrometer reading assumed as 40ʳ.758 instead of 41ʳ.758.

(200) 78. Transits over T.'s III, IV, and V assumed as recorded over T.'s II, III, and IV.

(200) 90. Micrometer reading assumed as 35ʳ.345, not 33ʳ.345.

* Assumed as 68.3.

ZONE 201. SEPTEMBER 1. S. $D_0 = -20°\ 10'\ 0''$.

Seconds of Transit

No.	Mag.	I.	II.	III.	IV.	V.	VI.	VII.
1	9	..	39.5	..	12.5	..	..	..
2	8	..	43.5	..	16.	32.	..	..
3	5	..	..	..	..	2.	18.5	..
4	10	..	10.5	..	43.	..	..	..
5	10	..	..	37.8	..	11.	..	..
6	10	..	..	..	..	7.	23.	..
7	9	..	..	39.	..	..	..	..
8	10	..	..	..	..	45.	1.	..
9	10	..	..	24.5	..	57.	..	..
10	8	..	5.5	..	..	..	..	..
11	9	..	..	..	38.	..	11.	..
12	10	..	..	22.	..	55.	..	..
13	10	..	17.5	..	..	7.5	..	..
14	10	..	..	..	56.	..	..	..
15	8	..	..	39.	55.	12.	..	..
16	8	..	16.5	33.	19.	55.	..	..
17	7	..	..	..	..	38.5	54.8	..
18	5	..	23.5	..	57.	13.	..	..
19	10	..	..	..	36.	..	..	..
20	10	..	40.	..	12.5	..	..	..
21	11	..	..	..	51.5	..	..	..
22	6	..	..	..	47.	..	19.	..
23	11	..	18.	..	52.	..	..	..
24	8	..	..	..	58.	..	..	..
25	5	..	..	..	22.	8.5	25.	..
26	9	..	..	47.	..	..	..	..
27	7	..	11.	..	44.	..	17.	..
28	5.6	..	28.5	45.	2.	..	..	..
29	10	..	58.	..	30.5	..	..	..
30	11	..	..	35.	..	..	1.	..
31	10	..	..	..	..	..	1.	..
32	10	..	51.	..	..	..	..	..
33	8	..	..	..	..	50.	6.5	..
34	9	..	..	6.	22.5	33.	..	..
35	10	..	..	35.	..	24.5	..	..
36	10	..	2.	..	34.5	..	..	..
37	9	..	..	..	33.5	..	..	..
38	5	..	14.5	..	47.	..	..	..
39	8	..	13.5	..	46.3	..	..	..
40	6	..	27.8	..	..	0.5	17.	..
41	7	..	25.5	..	59.	15.	..	..
42	8	..	51.	7.6	..	40.	..	..
43	8	..	59.8	..	33.	49.	..	..
44	8	..	..	13.5	..	53.	..	..

T., Micrometer, and Mean Places

No.	T. (h. m. s.)	a_1	a_2	Micrometer		r	i (' '')	d_1	d_2	Mean Right Ascension 1850.0 (h. m. s.)	Mean Declination 1850.0 (° ' '')
1	23 12 12.52	+18.26	+0.60	IV.	2	19.690	−40 41.29	−2.48	5.03	23 12 31.38	−20 50 48.80
2	15 16.01	18.26	0.72	IV.	3	39.342	20 13.98	2.39	2.00	15 34.99	30 18.46
3	14 45.47	18.26	0.57	.	2	15.600	44 57.98	2.41	5.64	15 4.30	55 6.03
4	19 43.23	18.25	0.71	IV.	3	37.452	22 12.60	2.25	2.38	20 2.19	32 17.23
5	21 54.34	18.24	0.54	.	2	10.999	49 46.28	2.19	6.33	22 13.12	59 54.80
6	22 50.36	18.24	0.78	V.	5	49.936	9 0.85	2.17	0.52	23 9.38	19 3.54
7	24 55.58	18.24	0.57	.	2	15.795	44 45.31	2.12	5.61	25 14.39	20 54 53.04
8	26 28.18	18.23	0.54	V.	2	10.879	49 53.89	2.07	6.35	26 46.95	21 0 2.31
9	29 40.82	18.23	0.73	V.	5	42.435	16 51.96	2.00	1.64	29 59.78	20 26 55.60
10	33 35.59	18.22	0.68	IV.	3	34.502	25 17.65	1.91	2.82	33 57.49	20 35 22.38
11	33 38.02	18.22	0.53	.	2	10.756	50 1.54	1.91	6.37	33 56.77	21 0 9.82
12	36 38.49	18.22	0.62	III.	3	25.469	34 44.56	1.84	4.16	36 57.33	20 44 50.56
13	38 50.81	18.21	+0.67	.	3	34.210	25 36.16	1.79	2.86	39 9.69	35 40.81
14	40 55.87	18.21	0.68	IV.	3	35.390	24 21.99	1.70	2.68	41 14.76	34 26.43
15	46 55.29	18.20	0.57	IV.	2	17.842	42 37.13	1.66	5.31	47 14.06	20 52 44.10
16	50 49.26	18.19	0.52	IV.	4	10.142	50 36.53	1.60	6.46	51 7.97	21 0 44.59
17	51 21.90	18.19	0.58	V.	2	19.000	41 24.69	1.60	5.13	51 40.67	20 51 31.42
18	54 56.31	18.19	0.56	IV.	2	17.480	43 0.07	1.56	5.36	55 15.06	53 6.99
19	23 56 35.89	18.19	0.77	.	5	52.480	6 21.38	1.53	0.15	23 56 54.85	16 23.06
20	0 2 12.76	18.18	0.58	IV.	2	21.268	39 2.51	1.49	4.81	0 2 31.52	49 8.81
21	3 51.37	18.18	0.68	.	3	37.325	22 20.57	1.48	2.38	4 10.23	20 32 24.43
22	8 46.51	18.17	0.51	.	2	8.269	52 37.06	1.45	6.79	9 5.19	21 2 45.90
23	11 51.48	18.17	0.70	IV.	4	41.310	18 1.43	1.44	1.78	12 10.35	20 28 4.65
24	12 57.68	18.17	0.60	.	3	24.610 ●	35 38.18	1.44	4.29	13 16.65	45 43.91
25	14 51.97	18.17	0.55	IV.	2	17	43	1.44	..	14 10.69	53
26	17 3.53	18.16	0.59	.	3	23.825	36 27.44	1.44	4.43	17 22.28	46 33.31
27	17 44.05	18.16	0.59	IV.	3	24.390	35 52.12	1.44	4.34	18 2.80	45 57.90
28	20 44.95	18.16	0.52	IV.	2	12.843	47 50.62	1.44	6.09	20 3.63	57 58.15
29	22 30.73	18.16	0.63	IV.	3	29.294	30 44.48	1.45	3.60	22 49.52	40 49.53
30	24 51.51	18.16	0.64	.	3	31.600	28 19.87	1.46	3.25	25 10.31	38 24.58
31	25 28.11	18.16	0.75	.	5	49.468	9 30.29	1.47	0.57	25 47.02	19 32.33
32	29 24.09	18.15	0.67	.	3	37.158	22 31.17	1.49	2.41	29 42.91	32 35.07
33	29 33.61	18.15	0.72	V.	4	45.703	13 25.63	1.49	1.14	29 52.48	23 28.26
34	31 22.45	18.15	0.53	IV.	2	15.632	44 43.18	1.51	5.63	31 41.13	54 50.32
35	34 51.61	18.15	0.69	V.	4	42.079	17 13.17	1.55	1.67	35 10.45	27 16.39
36	38 34.80	18.15	0.53	IV.	2	15.645	44 55.04	1.58	5.66	38 53.48	55 2.28
37	39 33.40	18.15	0.58	.	.	23.350	36 51.90	1.59	4.50	39 52.13	46 57.90
38	44 47.24	18.15	0.60	IV.	3	27.549	32 33.90	1.68	−3.84	45 5.90	42 39.42
39	48 46.39	18.15	0.76	IV.	5	53.340	5 28.16	1.75	+0.01	49 5.30	15 29.90
40	51 0.62	18.14	0.69	IV.	4	43.702	15 31.10	1.81	−1.43	51 19.45	25 34.34
41	52 58.65	18.14	0.53	IV.	2	16.623	43 53.70	1.85	5.51	53 17.32	54 1.06
42	54 23.94	18.14	0.67	III.	4	40.860	18 29.20	1.90	1.85	54 42.75	28 32.95
43	57 32.75	18.14	0.61	IV.	3	30.450	29 31.95	1.98	3.42	57 51.50	39 37.35
44	0 58 36.28	+18.14	+0.54	.	2	18.690	−41 43.82	−2.01	−5.20	0 58 54.90	−20 51 51.03

CORRECTIONS.

Date.	Corr. of Clock.	Hourly rate.	m	n	c	Zenith Point.	Mic. Co.
1848.	h.　　s.	s.	s.	s.	s.	°　'　''	r.

REMARKS.

(201) 25. Time of transit over T. IV assumed as 52ˢ instead of 22ˢ, and minutes as 13, not 14.

(201) 28. Transits over T.'s III, IV, and V assumed as recorded over T.'s II, III, and IV.

(201) 34. Declination differs 1' from Arg. Z.

(201) 35. Transit over T. VI assumed to have been recorded as over T. V.

INSTRUMENT READINGS.

Date.	CIRCLE.							Barom.	THERMOM.				
	A.	B.	C.	D.	E.	F.	Mean.		At.	Ex.	U.	L.	I.
1848.　h. m.	°　'　''						''	in.	°	°	°	°	°
Zone 201　Sept. 1, *23 10	69 32	29.4 26.5 30.8 26.8 21.2 25.8					27.17	29.980	74.2	66.4			
		30.8 26.8 32. 27.2 22.2 26.5											
		29. 25.2 31. 26. 20. 23.5					26.03						
		29.4 25. 31.5 26.2 21.2 24.4											
23 56								29.978	73.8	66.7 / 65.7			
0 20										65.7			
0 40								29.984	72.8	64.9			
1 0								29.986	72.9	63.9			

*The second set of double readings given for 23ʰ 10ᵐ is assumed to belong to 1ʰ 0ᵐ, making the mean for the former hour 27.16 and for the latter 26.03.

ZONE 202. SEPTEMBER 2. C. $D_o = -23°\ 55'\ 10''$.

No.	Mag.	I.	II.	III.	IV.	V.	VI.	VII.
1	10			26.2		0.1		
2	9					30.3		
3	10			29.5	46.3		20.	
4	9				36.			
5	9			25.7	42.3	59.5		
6	8	8.3	25.	42.	59.	15.8	32.7	
7	9				50.7	7.4	24.5	
8	9			6.7	41.	57.8		
9	9			44.2	0.7			
10	9				8.4	25.5	42.4	
11	8.9			6.	22.8	39.7	56.6	
12	9					36.9	53.5	
13	9						44.2	
14	9			38.7	45.2	12.3		
15	8.9		5.6	22.8	39.5		13.2	
16	10			21.8	38.		12.2	
17	10						2.	
18	9		27.8	44.3	1.3	18.7	35.8	
19	8.9				30.8		4.9	
20	8					32.7		
21	10					32.		
22	9		44.1	1.	18.	34.9		
23	10						57.7	
24	8		18.2	35.5	52.8	9.9	26.4	
25	8	6.3	22.8	40.	56.	13.	29.8	
26	8.9						43.2	
27	8		57.2		31.	47.5		
28	8			51.3	8.3	25.5	42.2	
29	9.10						38.	
30	9					58.9	15.7	
31	9		12.5	29.5				
32	8					10.5	27.1	
33	8					10.3	27.3	
34	8.9			54.3	11.3	28.5	45.3	
35	10			35.8			26.2	
36	8.9		55.	11.5		46.		
37	8					27.3	44.	
38	9			43.5	0.1		34.1	
39	9.10			28.2		2.3		
40	9.10					32.2		6.3
41	8	27.	43.4	0.9	17.5	34.7	51.3	
42	8		17.3	34.2	51.	8.7	25.	
43	8.9			11.3	28.1	45.	2.4	
44	7.8	31.	17.2		21.3	38.3	55.2	
45	9		14.6	31.9	48.8	5.5	22.	
46	9.10		14.3	32.	49.			
47	7.8		54.2		28.2	45.4	2.5	
48	9.10			46.	19.9			
49	7.8		58.8	16.7	32.7	49.	6.2	

No.	T. (h. m. s.)	a_1	a_2	Mic.		r	i	d_1	d_2	Mean Right Ascension, 1850.0	Mean Declination, 1850.0
1	19 31 43.32	+18.40	+0.92	IV.	5	54.814	− 3 54.64	−18.57	− 6.01	19 32 2.64	−23 59 29.22
2	33 13.15	18.39	0.32	V.	2	12.896	47 48.04	18.42	12.76	33 31.86	24 43 29.22
3	37 46.33	18.36	0.94	IV.	5	48.800	10 12.22	17.95	6.94	38 5.63	5 47.11
4	40 35.89	18.35	0.91	IV.	5	49.221	9 45.99	17.66	6.91	40 55.15	5 20.56
5	42 42.22	18.34	1.31	IV.	2	7.648	53 16.48	17.45	13.63	43 1.87	48 57.56
6	44 58.94	18.33	1.00	IV.	3	36.735	22 57.39	17.22	8.92	45 18.27	18 35.53
7	45 50.61	18.32	0.99	V.	3	37.527	22 7.63	17.13	8.76	46 9.92	17 43.72
8	47 40.80	18.31	1.23	IV.	2	12.627	48 4.30	16.04	12.81	48 0.34	43 44.05
9	51 0.88	18.30	1.00	III.	3	33.837	25 59.33	16.61	9.39	51 20.18	21 35.33
10	55 8.50	18.27	0.99	V.	3	31.563	28 21.81	16.21	9.75	55 27.76	23 57.77
11	58 22.83	18.26	0.92	IV.	3	36.688	23 0.36	15.90	8.92	58 42.01	18 35.18
12	19 59 19.91	18.25	0.75	V.	5	53.316	5 28.82	15.80	6.25	19 59 38.91	1 0.87
13	20 2 10.39	18.24	1.11	VI.	2	16.223	44 18.97	15.53	12.25	20 2 29.74	39 56.75
14	6 55.40	18.21	0.86	IV.	3	37.867	21 46.30	15.07	8.72	7 14.47	17 20.09
15	9 39.55	18.20	0.88	IV.	3	33.938	25 52.85	14.81	9.37	9 58.63	21 27.03
16	14 38.38	18.17	1.01	IV.	2	17.637	42 50.11	14.34	12.01	14 57.56	38 26.46
17	15 28.16	18.17	1.07	VI.	2	12.141	48 34.89	14.26	12.91	15 47.40	44 12.06
18	18 1.60	18.16	1.14	IV.	2	6.176	54 48.81	14.02	13.90	18 20.90	50 26.73
19	19 30.92	18.15	0.89	VI.	3	27.273	32 50.65	13.88	10.43	19 49.98	28 24.96
20	19 14.90	18.15	0.99	V.	2	17.056	43 26.48	13.90	12.10	19 34.04	39 2.48
21	23 15.02	18.13	0.87	V.	3	27.520	32 35.47	13.54	10.40	23 34.02	28 9.41
22	26 18.06	18.11	0.60	IV.	5	51.532	7 20.90	13.26	6.48	26 36.77	2 50.64
23	26 23.28	18.11	0.81	VI.	3	30.976	28 58.13	13.25	9.84	26 42.20	24 31.22
24	29 52.58	18.10	0.95	IV.	2	11.529	49 13.20	13.02	13.02	29 11.66	44 49.24
25	30 56.46	18.09	0.74	IV.	2	36.153	23 34.05	12.83	9.00	31 15.29	19 5.88
26	31 9.40	18.09	0.92	VI.	2	18.116	42 20.19	12.82	11.92	31 28.41	24 37 54.93
27	34 30.93	18.07	0.54	IV.	2	54.936	3 46.98	12.52	5.96	34 49.54	23 59 15.46
28	37 8.34	18.06	0.66	IV.	2	39.128	20 27.33	12.29	8.52	37 27.06	24 15 58.13
29	37 4.26	18.06	0.70	VI.	3	34.948	24 48.91	12.30	9.19	37 23.02	20 30.40
30	38 42.00	18.05	0.52	V.	5	53.054	5 45.53	12.15	6.22	39 0.57	1 13.90
31	43 46.60	18.03	0.90	III.	2	9.911	50 54.38	11.72	13.31	44 5.53	46 29.41
32	43 53.47	18.03	0.65	V.	3	34.789	24 59.20	11.71	9.24	44 12.15	20 30.15
33	44 53.24	18.02	0.96	V.	2	5.998	51 59.97	11.64	13.93	45 12.22	50 35.54
34	48 11.30	18.01	0.70	IV.	3	30.442	29 32.45	11.34	9.94	49 30.10	25 3.73
35	50 52.64	18.00	0.55	IV.	4	42.328	16 57.54	11.11	8.00	51 11.19	12 26.65
36	20 59 28.84	17.95	0.83	IV.	2	8.122	52 46.75	10.40	13.57	20 59 47.62	48 20.72
37	21 0 10.33	17.95	0.50	V.	4	40.986	18 21.79	10.35	8.20	21 0 28.78	13 50.34
38	3 0.29	17.94	0.77	IV.	2	12.357	48 21.35	10.13	12.90	3 19.00	13 54.38
39	9 45.26	17.91	0.56	IV.	3	29.461	30 34.00	9.61	10.07	10 3.73	26 3.68
40	10 32.32	17.90	0.53	V.	3	31.512	28 25.01	9.56	9.76	10 50.75	23 54.33
41	15 17.60	17.88	0.43	IV.	3	38.637	20 58.11	9.10	8.59	15 35.91	16 25.89
42	16 51.14	17.87	0.54	IV.	3	27.682	32 25.44	9.08	10.38	17 9.55	27 54.90
43	18 28.26	17.87	0.40	IV.	4	39.072	20 21.71	8.96	8.52	18 46.53	15 49.19
44	26 21.35	17.83	0.27	IV.	5	47.385	11 41.52	8.40	7.16	26 39.45	7 7.08
45	28 48.60	17.82	0.41	IV.	3	33.395	26 27.19	8.22	9.46	29 6.83	21 54.87
46	31 48.76	17.81	0.52	III.	2	20.799	39 31.48	8.03	11.52	32 7.09	35 1.03
47	31 28.33	17.80	0.65	IV.	2	7.048	53 54.09	7.85	13.70	34 46.76	49 25.73
48	39 19.98	17.77	0.64	II.	2	11.375	49 22.42	7.54	13.07	39 38.39	24 44 53.03
49	21 42 32.77	+17.76	+0.10	IV.	5	56.095	− 2 34.33	− 7.34	− 5.75	21 42 50.63	−23 57 57.42

CORRECTIONS.

Date.	Corr. of Clock.	Hourly rate.	m	n	c	Zenith Point.	Mic. Co.
	h. s.	s.	s.	s.	s.	° ' "	r
1848. Sept. 2,						359 59 2.47	30.0105

INSTRUMENT READINGS.

Date.		CIRCLE.							Barom.	THERMOM.				
		A.	B.	C.	D.	E.	F.	Mean.		At.	Ex.	U.	L.	I.
	1848. h. m.							"	in.	°	°	°	°	°
Zone 202 Sept. 2, 19 34										69.8	75.4	74.3	76.	
	19 40	73 17	33.7	28.3	33.9	29.8	23.9	26.2	29.64	30.080	75.8		69.2	
			35.1	27.5	34.4	30.4	24.8	27.7						
	20 0											68.8		
	20 20								30.076	75.		68.3		
	20 40											67.8		
	20 50	33.4	28.3	32.8	30.	23.2	25.6	29.22				74.	72.2	
		34.9	27.9	33.1	30.7	24.	26.8							
	21 0								30.076	74.		67.4		

REMARKS.

(202) 8. Transit over T. II assumed to have been recorded as over T. III.

(202) 14. Time of transit over T. IV assumed as 55ˢ.2 instead of 45ˢ.2.

(202) 40. Transits over T.'s IV and VI assumed as recorded over T.'s V and VII.

ZONE 202. SEPTEMBER 2. C. $D_0 = -23°\,55'\,10''$—Continued.

SECONDS OF TRANSIT

No.	Mag.	I.	II.	III.	IV.	V.	VI.	VII.
50	9	..	..	23.5	40.8	57.	14.	..
51	9	..	..	8.2	..	42.7	59.7	..
52	8.9	..	57.1	..	30.0	..	4.5	..
53	9	..	..	..	..	..	30.	..
54	8.9	..	..	..	27.7	44.5	1.5	..
55	9.10	..	..	18.3	..	..	..	..
56	9.10	..	..	..	..	13.	..	..
57	8.9	..	..	..	15.	31.8	18.9	..
58	8	..	..	29.2	45.8	3.	19.5	..
59	9.10	..	..	..	..	..	22.5	..
60	8	..	..	48.	4.9	21.9	..	..

No.	T. (h. m. s.)	a_1 (s.)	a_2 (s.)	MICROMETER.		r.	i (′ ″)	d_1 (″)	d_2 (″)	Mean Right Ascension, 1850.0 (h. m. s.)	Mean Declination, 1850.0 (° ′ ″)
50	21 46 40.41	+17.74	+0.12	IV.	5	54.365	− 4 23.02	− 7.09	− 6.04	21 46 58.30	−23 59 46.15
51	50 25.59	17.73	0.41	III.	2	19.603	40 46.62	6.87	11.73	50 43.73	24 36 15.22
52	50 30.89	17.73	0.38	IV.	2	22.901	37 19.82	6.86	11.16	50 49.00	32 47.84
53	51 56.21	17.72	0.00	VI.	5	53.502	5 16.96	6.79	6.17	52 13.93	0 39.92
54	53 27.64	17.71	0.22	V.	3	35.011	24 45.33	6.71	9.17	53 45.57	20 11.21
55	56 35.36	17.70	0.12	III.	4	44.944	14 12.85	6.54	7.57	56 53.18	9 36.96
56	56 56.11	17.70	0.16	V.	3	39.592	19 57.90	6.52	8.44	57 13.97	15 22.86
57	21 59 31.85	17.69	0.26	IV.	3	27.748	32 21.29	6.38	10.37	21 59 49.87	27 48.04
58	22 0 45.92	17.68	0.59	IV.	3	31.807	28 6.57	6.33	9.69	22 1 3.19	23 32.59
59	1 48.76	17.68	0.53	VI.	4	37.728	21 46.12	6.28	8.74	2 6.97	17 11.14
60	22 6 4.88	+17.66	+0.75	IV.	2	11.442	−49 18.72	− 6.07	−13.09	22 6 23.29	−24 44 47.88

ZONE 203. SEPTEMBER 7. C. $D_0 = -21°\,25'\,0'$.

No.	Mag.	I.	II.	III.	IV.	V.	VI.	VII.
1	9	..	..	..	..	..	19.3	..
2	9	..	..	7.	23.3	40.3	..	..
3	9	..	..	..	18.2	34.9	..	..
4	9	..	33.3	..	..	..	..	..
5	9	..	35.5	51.8	8.2	41.	..	..
6	6	..	40.3	6.	21.3	35.	..	..
7	8	..	1.7	18.3	34.3	..	..	..
8	7	..	..	11.5	28.	44.6	1.3	..
9	9.10	..	8.1	24.8	..	57.8	14.3	..
10	9.10	..	..	..	..	56.3	..	..
11	9	..	25.5	42.1	59.3	15.4	..	..
12	10	..	..	..	39.2	56.	..	..
13	8	..	26.3	..	0.	16.3	33.2	..
14	7	..	32.2	49.1	5.2	22.1	38.6	..
15	8	..	29.3	46.3	3.2	..	..	..
16	8.9	..	..	..	..	..	47.7	..
17	9	..	11.3	28.5	..	..	17.2	..
18	7.8	..	..	..	..	..	59.8	..
19	9	..	..	56.3	13.	..	..	..
20	9	..	..	..	..	52.1	..	..
21	8	..	..	..	16.	..	..	..
22	7.8	..	..	..	44.2	1.2	17.2	..
23	9.10	..	..	..	..	..	..	..
24	9.10	..	..	..	..	20.3	..	..
25	9	..	20.3	37.8	..	..	..	..
26	8	..	..	..	19.2	35.5	..	..
27	6	..	..	..	12.3	..	46.	..
28	8.9	..	..	28.	..	0.3	..	..
29	8.9	..	..	20.4	..	54.	..	..
30	9	..	40.2	57.3	13.3	30.3	..	..
31	9	..	..	..	..	59.	..	..
32	8	..	54.5	..	27.3	44.	0.7	..
33	9	..	..	..	20.3	37.	..	..
34	9.10	..	51.	..	..	..	49.3	..

No.	T. (h. m. s.)	a_1 (s.)	a_2 (s.)	MICROMETER.		r.	i (′ ″)	d_1 (″)	d_2 (″)	Mean Right Ascension, 1850.0 (h. m. s.)	Mean Declination, 1850.0 (° ′ ″)
1	21 3 46.15	+15.75	+0.32	VI.	5	47.062	−12 1.21	−15.21	− 7.40	21 4 2.22	−21 37 23.82
2	6 23.49	15.74	0.30	IV.	3	30.626	29 20.79	14.96	9.91	6 39.53	21 54 44.66
3	7 1.62	15.74	0.29	V.	3	22.257	39 5.61	14.90	11.20	7 17.65	22 3 31.71
4	9 6.67	15.72	0.30	II.	3	32.518	27 22.32	14.68	9.62	9 22.69	21 52 46.62
5	9 8.32	15.72	0.30	IV.	3	32.656	27 13.42	14.67	9.60	9 24.34	52 37.69
6	15 22.06	15.70	0.32	IV.	5	54.892	3 49.74	14.04	6.21	15 38.08	29 9.99
7	17 31.76	15.68	0.31	III.	4	45.869	13 14.77	13.53	7.55	17 50.75	38 36.18
8	18 28.00	15.68	0.29	IV.	3	34.687	25 5.92	13.73	9.30	18 44.03	50 28.95
9	23 41.36	15.66	0.31	IV.	4	47.753	11 16.90	13.24	7.30	23 57.33	36 37.44
10	24 39.66	15.65	0.29	V.	3	29.741	30 47.49	12.92	10.10	24 55.60	21 56 10.51
11	27 55.00	15.64	0.28	IV.	2	15.832	44 43.15	12.81	12.10	28 14.82	22 10 8.18
12	41 39.20	15.58	0.29	V.	3	27.040	33 5.46	11.55	10 47	41 55.07	21 58 27.46
13	47 59.83	15.55	0.28	IV.	3	34.406	25 23.73	10.94	9.33	48 15.60	50 43.00
14	50 5.47	15.54	0.28	IV.	3	31.525	28 24.45	10.68	9.77	50 21.20	53 44.80
15	59 2.06	15.50	0.30	III.	5	54.772	3 57.22	9.98	6.23	59 18.76	21 29 13.43
16	21 59 14.46	15.50	0.26	VI.	2	6.988	53 57.91	9.96	13.55	21 59 30.22	22 19 21.42
17	22 1 44.65	15.49	0.29	IV.	4	41.131	18 12.54	9.76	8.30	22 2 0.43	21 43 30.60
18	2 26.70	15.49	0.28	VI.	3	27.477	32 37.85	9.68	10.39	2 42.47	57 57.92
19	4 12.96	15.48	0.30	III.	5	46.840	12 15.20	9.57	7.41	4 28.74	21 37 32.21
20	4 35.32	15.48	0.27	V.	2	17.174	43 19.27	9.53	11.98	4 51.07	22 8 40.78
21	5 15.93	15.47	0.27	IV.	2	17.801	42 39.71	9.49	11.94	5 31.67	22 8 1.14
22	5 44.25	15.47	0.28	V.	3	35.975	23 44.83	9.44	9.08	6 0.00	21 49 3.35
23	5		0.29	VII.	4	43.466	15 46.13	9.43	7.83	(6)	21 41 3.39
24	6 47.18	15.47	0.27	VI.	3	24.402	35 50.75	9.37	10.86	7 22.92	22 1 10.95
25	9 54.00	15.46	0.29	III.	4	39.725	19 49.47	9.18	8.51	10 9.84	21 44 58.16
26	10 2.51	15.46	0.30	V.	5	51.803	3 55.26	9.10	6.22	10 18.27	29 10.58
27	26 12.50	15.39	0.29	VI.	5	55.485	3 12.45	8.02	6.12	26 28.18	28 26.59
28	27 27.52	15.39	0.28	VI.	3	42.208	17 13.42	7.95	8.14	27 43.19	42 29.51
29	28 20.58	15.38	0.27	VI.	3	33.192	26 39.22	7.89	9.50	28 36.23	51 56.61
30	34 13.62	15.36	0.28	IV.	4	40.927	18 25.34	7.62	8.35	34 29.26	43 41.31
31	34 25.90	15.36	0.27	VI.	3	27.678	32 25.12	7.61	10.43	34 41.57	57 43.16
32	38 27.52	15.35	0.29	IV.	3	49.407	9 34.31	7.29	6.06	38 43.16	34 48.36
33	39 3.80	15.35	0.27	V.	3	34.648	25 8.18	7.28	9.26	39 19.42	50 24.72
34	22 44 7.42	+15.33	+0.27	IV.	3	26.715	−33 26.09	− 7.10	−10.50	22 44 23.02	−21 58 43.69

CORRECTIONS.   **REMARKS.**

Date.	Corr. of Clock.	Hourly rate.	m	n	c	Zenith Point.	Mic. Co.
	h.	s.	s.	s.	s.	° ′ ″	r.
1848. Sept. 7.	h.	s.	s.	s.	s.	359 59 63.37	30.0134

(203) 5. Transit over T. VI assumed to have been recorded as over T. V.

(203) 24. Transit over T. VI assumed as 40s.3, not 20s.3, and minutes as 7, not 6.

INSTRUMENT READINGS.

ZONE 203. SEPTEMBER 7. C. D₀ = —21° 25′ 0″—Continued.

No.	Mag.	SECONDS OF TRANSIT (I. II. III. IV. V. VI. VII.)	T.	a₁	a₂	MICROMETER	i	d₁	d₂	Mean Right Ascension, 1850.0	Mean Declination, 1850.0
			h. m. s.	s.	s.	r.	′ ″	″	″	h. m. s.	° ′ ″
35	9.10	. . . 54.3 . . 27.4 . .	22 49 11.00	+15.31	+0.28	IV. 5 55.741	— 2 56.44	— 6.87	6.02	22 49 26.59	—21 28 9.33
36	10	. . . . 52.3 . .	50 35.74	15.31	0.27	V. 4 43.051	16 12.11	6.82	7.98	50 51.32	41 26.91
37	7	. . 54.2 11. . . 44. 0.5	22 54 27.52	15.29	0.27	IV. 4 44.175	15 1.48	6.70	7.83	22 54 43.06	40 16.01
38	4	21.3 37.8 54.2 10.8 27.4 44.5	23 1 11.00	15.27	0.26	IV. 3 26.342	33 49.68	6.41	10.74	23 1 26.53	59 6.73
39	9.10	. . . . 36.3 . . 9.6	2 36.33	15.27	0.27	VI. 3 35.202	24 33.09	6.35	9.20	2 51.87	21 49 48.67
40	9	. . . . 6. 23. . . 56.3	8 22.91	15.25	0.26	IV. 2 25.325	34 48.02	6.17	10.70	8 38.42	22 0 4.89
41	8.9	. . . . 20.3 . . 53.5	23 8 36.90	+15.25	+0.25	IV. 2 24.312	—35 51.57	—6.16	—10.85	23 8 52.40	—22 1 8.58

ZONE 204. SEPTEMBER 18. C. D = —18′ 17′ 20″.

No.	Mag.	SECONDS OF TRANSIT (I. II. III. IV. V. VI. VII.)	T.	a₁	a₂	MICROMETER	i	d₁	d₂	Mean Right Ascension, 1850.0	Mean Declination, 1850.0
1	8	. . 11.5 28. 44. 0.2 16.5 . .	19 18 44.09	+10.81	+1.68	. 4 38.491	—20 58.30	—20.36	— 8.87	19 19 56.58	—18 38 47.53
2	8	. . 36.5 . . 9.2 25.34 1.5 . .	19 9.09	10.81	1.67	. 4 37.868	21 37.20	20.31	8.96	19 21.57	39 26.47
3	9	. . 40.3 56.8 13.2	21 13.10	10.80	1.77	. 4 44.108	15 5.44	20.12	8.12	21 25.67	32 53.68
4	8	. . 29. 45.3 1.7 . .	21 45.34	10.80	1.70	. 3 39.376	20 2.81	20.08	8.75	21 57.84	37 51.64
5	9	. . . .	21		1.79	. 5 45.019	14 18.	20.06	7.99		
6	9	. . . . 38.3 54.5 10.7 . .	24 38.18	10.78	1.39	. 3 22.358	37 59.59	19.81	11.01	24 50.35	18 55 50.41
7	9	. . 43.5 0. 16.5 . .	26 59.95	10.77	1.22	. 2 13.223	47 26.66	19.70	12.21	26 11.94	5 18.60
8	7	. . 29.2 45.8 . .	27 29.21	10.76	1.12	. 2 7.066	52 56.47	19.55	12.95	27 41.09	10 48.97
9	9	. . . . 0.2 25.5 . .	27 52.84	10.76	1.19	. 2 11.877	48 51.32	19.51	12.43	28 4.79	19 6 43.26
10	7.8	. . . .	28		1.74	VII. 5 43.485	15 45.61	19.49	8.20	. . . .	18 33 33.30
11	9	. . . . 23.7 39.5 . .	36 7.24	10.72	1.77	. 5 46.588	12 31.14	18.75	7.77	36 19.73	18 30 17.66
12	8	. . 7.3 24.2 40. . .	38 23.79	10.70	1.16	. 2 12.264	48 27.18	18.54	12.37	38 35.65	19 6 18.09
13	8.9	. . . . 16.2 32.1 . .	38 59.78	10.70	1.50	. 3 31.618	28 18.30	18.48	9.78	39 11.98	18 46 6.56
14	9	. . 25. . . 57.3 13.5 . .	43 41.14	10.67	1.53	. 3 34.188	25 37.25	18.05	9.40	43 53.34	43 24.70
15	9	. . 40.2 . . 12.3 . .	47 56.34	10.65	1.68	. 4 43.848	20 35.32	17.67	8.82	48 8.67	38 21.61
16	9	. . . . 6.5 . . 29.2	48 6.56	10.65	1.48	. 3 32.316	27 31.88	17.65	9.68	48 18.69	45 22.21
17	9	. . . . 58.2 14.3 . .	49 41.88	10.64	1.45	. 3 30.881	29 4.41	17.50	9.88	49 53.97	46 51.79
18	9	18. 34.2 50.8 . . 23.2 . .	51 50.66	10.62	1.52	. 3 35.813	23 55.20	17.31	9.21	52 2.80	41 41.72
19	9	25.2 42.	54 58.15	10.61	1.63	. 2 42.918	16 18.55	17.01	8.25	55 10.39	34 3.81
20	8.9	. . . . 22. . . 54.3	54 21.86	10.61	1.55	. 3 37.987	21 38.83	17.07	8.91	54 34.02	16 39 24.81
21	9	. . 53.5 . . 26.2 . .	56 9.80	10.60	1.00	. 2 7.366	53 40.35	16.91	13.06	56 21.40	19 11 30.32
22	9.10	. . . . . . 41.8?	57 9.26	10.60	1.05	. 2 10.371	49 54.62	16.83	12.64	57 20.91	7 44.09
23	9	. . . .	19 57		1.07	VI. 2 10.016	49 51.58	.	12.56	19 57	19 7
24	10	. . . . 54.5 . .	19 59 54.39	10.58	1.74	IV. 5 48.806	10 11.84	16.56	7.46	20 0 6.71	18 27 55.86
25	9	. . . . 24. . .	20 0 51.57	10.57	1.41	VI. 3 30.874	29 4.54	16.47	9.88	1 3.55	46 50.89
26	9	. . . . 3.2 . .	3 30.77	10.56	1.40	VI. 3 30.778	29 10.56	16.23	9.89	3 42.73	46 56.68
27	9	. . . . 51.3 8.2 . .	4 51.52	10.55	1.33	V. 3 26.706	33 26.40	16.10	10.44	5 3.40	51 12.94
28	8.9	. . . . 38.3 . . 11.2 . .	5 38.44	10.55	1.64	VI. 4 44.271	14 55.70	16.04	8.05	5 50.63	32 39.79
29	9	38.1 54.5 11. 27.2 43.5 . .	8 10.88	10.53	1.28	IV. 3 24.065	35 31.75	15.80	10.71	8 22.69	53 21.26
30	8.9	. . . . 55.3 . . 28.1 44.2 . .	9 11.73	10.53	1.45	IV. 3 34.127	25 41.13	15.70	9.43	9 23.71	43 26.26
31	9.10	. . . . 28.8 . .	9 56.37	10.52	1.30	VI. 3 30.575	29 23.49	15.64	9.92	10 8.28	47 9.05
32	8.9	. . 32.5 18.3 . . 31.3 37.2 . .	12 4.92	10.51	1.56	IV. 4 39.709	19 41.72	15.44	8.66	12 16.99	37 25.82
33	8	. . 10. . . 12.5 29.2 45.4 . .	12 12.73	10.51	1.38	IV. 3 30.182	29 48.71	15.43	9.97	12 24.62	47 34.11
34	8.9	. . 17. 3.5 20. 36.2 52.3 . .	14 19.83	10.50	1.35	IV. 3 28.808	31 14.73	15.23	10.15	14 31.68	49 0.11
35	9.10	. . . . 2.3 18.5 . .	14 46.04	10.50	1.48	V. 3 35.937	23 47.22	15.19	9.19	14 58.02	41 31.60
36	9	. . 33.2 49.5 6. . . 38.3 . .	17 5.88	10.48	1.19	IV. 2 20.013	40 21.03	14.98	11.35	17 17.55	58 7.36
37	9	. . . . 36. 52.2 8.2 . .	17 35.83	10.48	1.32	V. 3 26.768	33 22.50	14.94	10.44	17 47.63	51 7.88
38	6.7	. . . . 48.2 4.3 . .	20 18 31.89	+10.48	+1.46	V. 4 35.385	—24 13.30	—14.85	—9.27	20 18 43.83	—18 41 57.51

CORRECTIONS.

Date.	Corr. of Clock.	Hourly rate.	m	n	c	Zenith Point.	Mic. Co.
	h.	s.	s.	s.	s.	° ′ ″	r.
1848. September 18.	.	. .	.	. .	. .	359 59 62.48	30.0150

INSTRUMENT READINGS.

Date.	CIRCLE A.	B.	C.	D.	E.	F.	Mean.	Barom.	THERMOM. At.	Ex.	U.	I.	I.
	° ′ ″						″	in.	°	°	°	°	°
Zone 203 Sept. 7. 22 10	. .	. .	. .	. .	. .	. .	. .	. .	. .	. .	55 6		
22 20	70 47 {33.1	33.1	36.2	33.5	25.1	28. / 33.3 32.6 36.7 34. 25.3 28.2}	31.54	. .	. .	55.6	65.	62.2	
22 40	. .	. .	. .	. .	. .	. .	. .	30.170	64.	55.6			
23 0	{32.9	33.2	36.0	34.1	25.4	27.6 / 32.9 32.9 36.0 34.5 25.3 27.8}	31.55	30.168	63.5	55.6	64.5	61.5	71.2
Zone 204 Sept. 18. 19 20	67 39 64.1	60.3	64.2	62.4	48.6	59.2	59.80	. .	. .	61.6	65.	64.3	63.5
19 30	. .	. .	. .	. .	. .	. .	. .	30.128	65.				
19 40	. .	. .	. .	. .	. .	. .	. .	. .	59.9				

[(204) 5. Precedes 4.2ˢ or 3ˢ.]

REMARKS.

(204) 7. Minutes assumed as 25, not 26.

(204) 14. Micrometer reading assumed as 34ʳ.188, not 34ʳ.688.

(204) 15. Micrometer reading assumed as 38ʳ.848, not 43ʳ.848.

(204) 16. Time of transit over T. VI assumed as 39ˢ.2 instead of 29ˢ.2.

(204) 19. Declination differs 1′ from Arg. Z. 252, 81.

(204) 22. Minutes assumed as 57, not 56, and micrometer reading as 10ʳ.871, not 10ʳ.371.

(204) 26. Declination differs 1′ from Arg. Z. 252, 96.

Zone 204. September 18. C. $D_0 = -18°\ 17'\ 20''$—Continued.

No.	Mag.	I.	II.	III.	IV.	V.	VI.	VII.	T. (h. m. s.)	a_1 (s.)	a_2 (s.)	MICROMETER.	r	i	d_1	d_2	Mean Right Ascension 1850.0 (h. m. s.)	Mean Declination 1850.0 (° ' '')
39	8				14.2		46.6		20 20 14.08	+10.47	+1.85	VI. 5	56.602	—4 7.78	—14.69	—6.42	20 20 26.40	—18 21 48.89
40	9					21.2	47.		21 4.61	10.46	1.07	V. 2	13.704	46 56.81	14.62	12.20	21 16.14	19 4 43.63
41	9					23.7	48.5		21 6.60	10.46	1.07	VI. 2	13.892	46 45.39	14.61	12.18	21 18.13	19 4 32.18
42	9					55.	11.2		22 38.74	10.45	1.56	V. 3	41.041	17 24.24	14.47	8.36	22 50.75	18 35 7.07
43	6	29.5	45.3	2.5	18.5	35.1	51.1		31 18.48	10.41	1.48	IV. 3	37.570	22 5.12	13.77	8.96	31 30.37	18 39 47.85
44	10					0.5			32 44.29	10.40	1.63	V. 4	46.364	12 44.33	13.56	7.78	32 56.32	30 25.67
45	10					31.			33 14.83	10.39	1.73	V. 4	51.899	6 56.60	13.51	7.03	33 26.95	24 37.14
46	8					28.			33 55.53	10.39	1.49	VI. 3	38.745	20 50.70	13.45	8.80	34 7.41	38 32.95
47	9		9.1	25.2		59.2	14.2		39 41.75	10.36	1.37	IV. 3	32.702	27 10.47	12.93	9.62	39 53.48	44 53.02
48	9		10.2	26.9		50.3	15.3		39 43.00	10.36	1.37	IV. 3	32.586	27 17.81	12.93	9.64	39 54.75	45 0.38
49	9					52.3			40 36.01	10.35	1.37	V. 3	32.436	27 27.10	12.85	9.66	40 47.73	45 9.61
50	7								40		1.53	VI. 4	41.858	17 27.14	12.85	8.39		35 5.38
51	7			51.2		23.3	39.3		46 7.17	10.32	1.62	IV. 5	47.462	11 36.41	12.37	7.62	46 19.11	18 29 16.40
52	9					18.	34.2		47 1.58	10.32	0.94	V. 2	9.648	51 11.20	12.29	12.70	47 12.84	19 6 56.25
53	8		19.2	5.3	22.				55 21.80	10.27	1.39	III. 3	35.378	24 22.83	11.59	9.27	55 33.46	18 42 3.69
54	9					49.	4.8		55 32.39	10.27	0.95	V. 2	11.618	49 7.69	11.57	12.50	55 43.60	19 6 51.76
55	8.9		23.3		56.	12.7			20 55 56.12	10.25	1.50	IV. 4	42.341	16 56.73	11.30	8.33	20 59 7.87	18 34 36.36
56	9.10		10.6	27.		59.8	15.7		21 1 43.32	10.24	1.01	III. 2	14.460	46 9.28	11.07	12.12	21 1 54.87	19 3 52.47
57	9				53.3		26.2		1 53.46	10.24	1.13	VI. 3	21.857	38 30.21	11.06	11.10	2 4.83	18 56 12.37
58	9			21.4		53.8	9.8		5 53.79	10.22	1.56	IV. 5	45.477	13 41.02	10.74	7.88	6 5.57	31 19.64
59	6	32.			4.5	20.	37.1	53.1	9 20.58	10.20	1.46	IV. 4	40.436	18 56.23	10.47	8.58	9 32.24	36 35.28
60	9.10			25.3	41.3				17 41.38	10.16	1.27	III. 3	30.037	29 57.67	9.84	10.00	17 52.51	18 47 37.71
61	9				33.	49.7		22.3	27 49.60	10.10	1.00	IV. 2	14.716	45 53.23	9.14	12.08	28 0.70	19 3 34.45
62	8	15.7		47.5	3.9	20.			29 47.70	10.10	0.95	IV. 2	12.035	48 41.41	9.05	12.46	28 58.75	19 6 22.92
63	9					20.2			37 20.07	10.06	1.39	IV. 4	37.079	22 26.78	8.51	9.03	37 31.52	18 40 4.32
64	8.9					13.8			37 57.55	10.05	1.45	V. 4	40.522	18 50.96	8.47	8.57	38 9.05	36 28.00
65	8				14.3	30.8	47.3		39 14.48	10.05	1.14	V. 3	23.638	36 38.93	8.39	10.86	39 25.67	18 54 18.16
66	8.9					49.5	6.2	22.1	40 49.58	10.04	0.96	V. 2	13.455	47 12.61	8.28	12.26	41 0.58	19 4 53.15
67	6				2.2	18.2	34.8	51.2	48 18.48	10.00	1.44	IV. 4	40.567	18 47.94	7.83	6.57	48 29.92	19 36 21.34
68	9			28.2	44.3	0.7	17.1		51 0.74	9.99	1.34	IV. 3	34.784	24 59.77	7.67	9.33	51 12.07	42 36.77
69	7	56.	12.2	28.2	44.8		16.8		53 44.63	9.98	1.43	IV. 3	39.882	19 39.84	7.53	8.64	53 56.04	37 16.01
70	9			12.8	29.	45.2			55 45.33	9.97	1.51	III. 4	44.552	14 37.64	7.42	8.01	55 56.81	32 13.07
71	9				11.3				59 27.66	9.95	1.38	III. 3	37.610	22 2.19	7.22	8.06	21 59 38.99	30 38.37
72	8.9			33.3	49.2	5.5	21.7		21 59 49.31	9.95	1.48	IV. 4	43.006	16 9.20	7.20	8.21	22 0 0.74	33 44.61
73	9				54.	10.2	26.8	43.	22 9 10.35	+9.90	+1.12	IV. 3	23.368	—36 56.23	—6.71	—10.91	22 9 21.37	—18 54 33.85

CORRECTIONS.

Date.	Corr. of Clock.	Hourly rate.	m	n	c	Zenith Point.	Mic. Co.
1848. h.	s.	s.	s.	s.	s.	° ' ''	r.

INSTRUMENT READINGS.

Date.	CIRCLE.							Barom.	THERMOM.				
	A.	B.	C.	D.	E.	F.	Mean.	in.	At.	Ex.	U.	L.	I.
Zone 204 Sept. 18, 1848 h. m. 20 0								30.130	64.7	58.7			
20 20										57.9			
20 40	63.7	60.3	65.2	63.1	49.3	59.	60.10	30.146	64.2	57.5	63.8	63.3	56.5
21 0													
21 20								30.152	63.5	55.3			
21 40										54.5			
22 0	63.7	60.7	65.1	63.5	49.3	58.4	60.12	30.146	63.	53.7	62.	60.3	63.5
22 10										53.2			

REMARKS.

(204) 39. Micrometer reading assumed as 54ʳ.602, not 56ʳ.602.

(204) 40. Time of transit over T. VI assumed as 37ˢ instead of 47ˢ.

(204) 41. Time of transit over T. VI assumed as 38ˢ.5 instead of 48ˢ.5.

(204) 42. Micrometer reading assumed as 42ʳ.041, not 41ʳ.041.

(204) 43. Minutes of transit assumed as 31 instead of 30.

(204) 49. Declination differs 1'' from Arg. Arg. Z. 244, 95.

(204) 62. Transits over T.'s IV, V, and VI assumed to have been recorded as over T.'s III, IV, and V, and minutes as 28, not 29.

Zone 205. October 7. C. D. = —16° 24' 50".

No.	Mag.	SECONDS OF TRANSIT (I. II. III. IV. V. VI. VII.)	T. (h. m. s.)	a₁ (s.)	a₂ (s.)	MICROMETER	i	d₁	Mean Right Ascension 1850.0	Mean Declination 1850.0
1	9	. . . 58.2	22 35 14.43	+4.77	+1.64	III. 4 43.288 —15 56.97	4.76—	2.28	22 35 20.84	—16 40 54.01
2	9	. . . . 55.2 . .	35 23.71	4.77	1.34	VI. 3 29.718 30 17.31	4.75	4.04	35 29.82	16 55 16.10
3	9.10	20.5 36.2 . .	38 52.67	4.75	1.00	III. 2 13.719 46 55.70	4.55	6.15	38 58.42	17 11 56.40
4	8.9	38. . 9.8 26. 42.	39 9.94	4.75	1.34	IV. 3 29.058 30 59.16	4.53	4.13	39 16.03	16 55 57.82
5	9	59.2 15.8 . .	41 59.34	4.73	1.13	V. 3 19.151 41 20.40	4.38	5.42	42 5.20	17 6 20.29
6	10	17.3 33. .	45 33.18	4.71	1.23	III. 3 23.105 37 12.67	4.19	4.91	45 39.12	2 11.77
7	7	10.2 26.3 42.2 58.5 15.	46 42.47	4.70	1.19	IV. 3 21.427 38 57.98	4.13	5.13	46 46.30	17 3 57.24
8	6		47	. .	1.75	VII. 5 46.992 12 5.61	4.10	1.79	47	16 37 1.50
9	10	34.2 50.3 3.	50 6.42	4.68	1.65	III. 4 41.878 17 25.22	3.96	2.46	50 12.75	16 42 21.64
10	9	10.4 26.3 42.8 58.8	22 51 42.64	4.67	1.02	IV. 2 13.041 47 38.33	3.88	6.24	22 51 48.33	17 12 38.45
11	9.10	30.2 46.5 2.8 18.9	23 2 2.66	4.61	1.31	IV. 3 25.175 35 2.64	3.41	4.64	23 2 8.58	0 0.69
12	9	56.2	3 24.06	4.61	1.24	IV. 2 21.704 38 40.43	3.35	5.11	3 29.91	17 3 38.89
13	9	17.	3 44.89	4.60	1.35	VI. 3 26.456 33 42.15	3.34	4.48	3 50.84	16 58 39.97
14	9	20.8 36.5 53. 9.2	6 52.94	4.59	1.26	IV. 3 22.083 38 16.72	3.21	5.06	6 58.79	17 3 14.99
15	8.9	56.7 13.1 29. 45.2 1.2	9 29.06	4.57	1.36	IV. 3 25.737 34 27.45	3.09	4.57	9 34.99	16 59 25.11
16	8.9	9.3 25.7 41.3 13.7	11 41.89	4.56	1.85	IV. 5 47.855 11 11.55	3.01	1.66	11 48.00	16 36 6.22
17	10	22. 38.3 54.2	13 54.34	4.55	1.18	III. 2 17.678 42 47.20	2.93	5.65	14 0.07	17 7 45.78
18	10	38.2	18 38.11	4.52	1.23	IV. 2 19.207 41 11.70	2.75	5.44	18 43.86	17 6 9.89
19	8.9	25.3 41.8 57.5 29.8	22 57.68	4.50	1.62	IV. 3 36.198 23 31.23	2.60	3.19	23 3.80	16 48 27.02
20	9	41.3 57.2 13.8 29.3	25 57.30	4.48	1.20	IV. 2 16.944 43 33.51	2.50	5.74	26 2.98	17 8 31.75
21	9	30.5 46. 2.8 19. 35.2	28 2.72	4.47	1.24	IV. 2 18.307 42 8.22	2.43	5.56	28 8.43	17 7 6.20
22	9	10.3 28. 43.8	30 43.50	4.41	1.65	III. 3 35.618 24 7.63	2.11	3.26	30 49.56	16 49 3.00
23	9	16.3 48.3	41 16.18	4.41	1.71	VI. 2 19.637 40 44.98	2.07	5.39	41 21.99	17 5 42.44
24	7		42	. .	1.81	VII. 4 42.566 16 42.92	2.	2.35	42	16 41 37.
25	8.9	19.2 35.5 52. 21.	44 51.73	4.39	1.17	IV. 2 13.182 47 31.69	1.98	6.25	41 57.29	17 12 29.92
26	8	15.5 31.5 47.9 3.3	50 31.53	4.36	1.85	IV. 5 43.216 16 2.93	1.86	2.26	50 37.74	16 40 57.05
27	9.10	4.4 20.3 37.	23 59 20.58	+4.32	+1.81	IV. 5 43.098 —16 10.42	1.71—	2.28	23 59 26.77	—16 41 4.41

Zone 206. October 10. S. D. = —17° 39' 40".

No.	Mag.	SECONDS OF TRANSIT (I. II. III. IV. V. VI. VII.)	T. (h. m. s.)	a₁ (s.)	a₂ (s.)	MICROMETER	i	d₁	Mean Right Ascension 1850.0	Mean Declination 1850.0
1	9	. . 5. . . 37. . .	22 49 37.24	+3.93	+0.41	5 44.785 —14 23.95	2.80—	8.01	22 49 41.58	—17 54 14.76
2	8	. . . . 38. .	50 5.58	3.93	—0.04	2 11.002 50 49.13	2.78	12.71	50 9.47	18 30 44.62
3	7	. . . 41. .	51 5.65	3.92	+0.37	5 41.433 17 54.85	2.74	8.45	51 12.94	17 57 46.04
4	9	. 22. . 54. .	54 54.22	3.90	0.26	3 32.182 27 43.23	2.58	9.70	54 58.38	18 7 35.51
5	6.5	. 15. 12. 27.8 44.	22 57 11.03	3.88	0.43	4 45.792 13 19.53	2.49	7.87	22 57 15.94	17 53 9.89
6	8	43.5 . 16. 32.	23 0 15.94	3.87	0.46	5 46.972 12 6.98	2.37	7.68	23 0 20.27	17 51 57.03
7		9. 29.	0							
8	8	22.	2 5.70	3.86	0.18	3 24.562 35 41.00	2.31	10.73	2 9.74	18 15 34.13
9	9	12.	2 39.62	3.85	0.08	3 17.070 42 34.18	2.29	11.63	2 43.55	22 28.10
10	8	10.	4 23.76	3.84	0.25	3 29.758 30 14.99	2.23	10.02	4 27.85	10 7.24
11	9	30.5	5 30.36	3.84	0.24	3 28.878 31 10.33	2.19	10.14	5 34.44	11 2.66
12	8	19.5 . 52.	8 51.98	3.82	0.30	3 33.658 26 10.55	2.08	9.49	8 56.10	6 2.12
13	9	27.	12 59.65	3.80	0.08	2 16.020 44 30.82	1.95	11.91	13 3.53	24 24.68
14	9	9. 25. 41.	13 24.95	3.79	0.14	2 20.000 40 21.59	1.94	11.37	13 28.88	18 20 14.90
15	10	8. 24.	14 51.73	3.78	0.39	4 39.292 20 8.27	1.90	8.71	14 55.90	17 59 58.88
16	9	12. 28. 43.5	16 27.79	3.77	0.29	3 31.283 28 39.69	1.85	9.82	16 31.85	18 8 34.26
17	9	24. . 56.	21 56.23	3.75	0.33	3 34.050 25 45.88	1.70	9.44	22 0.31	5 37.02
18	10	. . 37.	23 24 4.66	+3.73	+0.40	4 38.694 —23 45.74	1.65—	8.79	23 24 8.79	—18 0 36.15

CORRECTIONS.

Date	Corr. of Clock	Hourly rate	m	n	c	Zenith Point	Mic. Co.
1848.	h.	s.	s.	s.	s.	° ' "	r.
Oct. 7,	. .	. .	. .	. .	. .	350 59 63.45	30.0067
" 10,	. .	. .	. .	. .	. .	61.99	30.0051

REMARKS.

(205) 9. Time of transit over T. IV assumed as 6ˢ.3 instead of 0ˢ.3.
(206) 2. Declination differs 1' from Arg. Z. 253, 32.
(206) 5. Time of transit over T. III assumed as 55ˢ instead of 45ˢ.

INSTRUMENT READINGS.

Date	A.	B. C. D. E. F. (CIRCLE)	Mean.	Barom.	At. Ex U. L. I. (THERMOM.)
1847.	h. m.	° ' "	"	in.	°
Zone 205 Oct. 7.	22 30	65 47 {35.2 33.1 40.7 30.8 30.9 25.7 / 35.9 33.5 40.6 31.9 31.3 26.3}	32.99	30.234	63.2 56.1 63. 61.8 64.2
	22 40	. . .			56.0
	23 0	. . .		30.228	55.9
	23 20	. . .			55.6
	23 40	. . .		30.212	62.5 55.4
Zone 206 Oct. 10,	22 40	67 2 {26. 22.9 31.2 20.2 21.3 17. / 26. 22.8 31.7 20.8 22.3 18.2}	23.36		
	23 0	. . .		30.124	63.2 57. 62.2 61.3 62.5

ZONE 206. OCTOBER 10. S. $D_o = -17° 39' 40''$—Continued.

No.	Mag.	I	II	III	IV	V	VI	VII
19	8							15.
20	10		32.					
21	8					14.		
22	9		36.8		9.			
23	9						54.	
24	10		19.5			8.		
25	10			57.		39.5		
26	8.9		42. 58.5		31.			
27	10				17.5		50.	
28	9		50.3	23.				
29	9		51.	23.				
30	9		15.5	48.	4.5			
31	10			9.		41.		
32	9			29.5		1.8		
33	3.4		26.8	43.	59.			
34	9			30.	46.6			
35	6		2.	18.	34.5	50.5		
36	6		17.2	33.5	50.	6.		
37	10				4.			
38	10				47.			
39	9			20.				
40	8		59.	31.				
41	10				2.			
42	10			2.				
43	10			12.				
44	7		16.	48.5				
45	6				39.			
46	10		19.					
47	7		11.5 28.	34.	0.5 10.5			
48	10			8.		41.5		
49	10				42.			
50	10		39.		11.5			
51	9		25.		57.5			
52	9		21.			9.		
53	9		51.					
54	10				43.			
55	10			21.				
56	8		30. 55. 11.5 27.5					
57	8		5.		37.3 53.8			
58	8		19.					
59	7				58.2 14.2			
60	8		49.5	20.5				
61	8		30. 47. 2.					
62	10		20.					
63	9				39. 54.			
64	10		53.	30.				
65	9				28. 44.			
66	9				54.			
67	9				36. 52.			

No.	T. (h. m. s.)	a_1 (s.)	a_2 (s.)	MICROMETER (r.)	i (° ' ")	d_1 (")	d_2 (")	Mean Right Ascension, 1850.0 (h. m. s.)	Mean Declination, 1850.0 (° ' ")
19	23 24 42.60	+3.73	+0.09	2 14.153	−46 28.91	−1.63	−12.16	23 24 46.41	−18 26 22.70
20	26 31.88	3.72	0.46	4 42.634	16 38.21	1.59	8.27	26 36.06	17 56 28.07
21	26 41.61	3.72	0.55	5 49.180	9 48.50	1.59	7.42	26 45.88	17 49 37.51
22	29 9.20	3.71	0.13	2 16.942	43 33.00	1.52	11.78	29 13.04	18 23 26.30
23	29 21.63	3.70	0.51	4 45.767	13 21.79	1.52	7.86	29 25.84	17 53 11.17
24	31 51.97	3.69	0.53	4 46.612	12 27.82	1.46	7.74	31 56.19	17 52 17.02
25	33 13.23	3.68	0.17	2 18.789	41 37.49	1.44	11.52	33 17.08	18 21 30.45
26	38 14.75	3.66	0.36	4 41.090	18 14.42	1.34	8.48	38 18.77	17 58 4.24
27	39 17.51	3.65	0.49	4 43.132	16 6.94	1.32	8.19	39 21.65	17 55 56.45
28	42 22.88	3.63	0.29	3 27.419	32 42.12	1.27	10.34	42 26.80	18 12 33.73
29	44 23.24	3.61	0.29	3 25.795	34 23.74	1.24	10.57	44 27.14	14 15.55
30	48 48.08	3.60	0.39	3 33.592	26 14.81	1.18	9.50	48 52.07	18 6 5.49
31	49 8.76	3.60	0.58	5 47.820	11 13.74	1.17	7.57	49 12.94	17 51 2.48
32	51 29.40	3.59	0.64	5 51.975	6 52.91	1.14	7.00	51 33.63	17 46 41.05
33	55 59.16	3.57	0.36	3 29.646	30 22.29	1.09	10.03	56 3.09	18 10 13.40
34	56 30.09	3.56	0.28	3 24.546	35 42.28	1.09	10.74	56 33.93	15 34.11
35	23 59 34.37	3.55	0.32	3 26.642	33 30.74	1.06	10.45	23 59 38.24	13 22.25
36	0 0 49.80	3.54	0.19	2 15.760	44 47.13	1.05	11.94	0 0 53.53	24 40.12
37	1 47.77	3.54	0.40	3 31.891	28 1.17	1.04	9.74	1 51.71	7 51.95
38	3 14.67	3.53	0.44	3 34.660	25 7.24	1.03	9.35	3 18.64	4 57.62
39	4 3.61	3.53	0.21	2 16.845	43 39.84	1.03	11.82	4 7.35	23 32.69
40	5 31.24	3.52	0.50	3 38.250	21 22.45	1.02	8.89	5 35.20	1 12.36
41	5 45.80	3.52	0.50	3 39.275	20 17.99	1.02	8.75	5 49.82	18 0 7.76
42	7 1.98	3.51	0.51	3 40.090	19 26.92	1.01	8.61	7 5.90	17 59 16.54
43	10 11.93	3.50	0.21	2 16.385	44 8.74	0.99	11.88	10 15.64	18 24 1.61
44	11 48.56	3.49	0.13	2 9.880	50 55.78	0.99	12.79	11 52.18	30 49.56
45	12 22.54	3.49	0.13	2 8.740	52 8.13	0.99	12.91	12 26.16	18 32 2.03
46	14 51.59	3.48	0.56	5 42.232	17 4.54	0.98	8.31	14 55.03	17 56 53.83
47	17 44.12	3.46	0.34	3 24.700	35 32.49	0.98	10.72	17 47.92	18 15 24.19
48	20	3.45	0.69	5 51.532	7 20.90	0.97	7.04	20	17 47 8.91
49	22 9.66	3.44	0.51	3 37.340	22 19.19	0.97	8.98	22 13.61	18 2 9.14
50	26 55.22	3.43	0.26	2 20.702	39 37.56	0.99	11.28	26 58.90	19 29.83
51	28 41.22	3.41	0.22	2 14.302	46 19.12	0.99	12.17	28 44.85	26 12.28
52	32 35.96	3.40	0.24	2 15.390	45 10.89	1.01	12.02	32 40.60	25 3.92
53	37 23.59	3.38	0.53	3 36.165	23 33.36	1.05	9.14	37 27.50	3 23.55
54	37 15.65	3.38	0.36	2 23.578	36 37.79	1.05	10.88	37 19.39	16 29.72
55	38 48.66	3.37	0.52	3 37.664	21 58.74	1.06	8.93	38 52.55	1 48.73
56	41 11.38	3.36	0.30	2 18.372	42 4.44	1.08	11.66	41 15.04	21 56.82
57	45 37.43	3.35	0.24	2 12.499	48 12.44	1.14	12.42	45 41.02	28 6.00
58	47 35.28	3.34	0.39	3 24.685	35 33.50	1.16	10.73	47 39.01	18 15 25.39
59	47 41.94	3.34	0.76	5 52.012	6 50.64	1.16	6.97	47 46.04	17 46 38.77
60	51 20.76	3.33	0.38	2 22.365	37 53.06	1.21	11.05	51 24.47	18 17 45.32
61	53 2.61	3.32	0.69	4 45.752	13 21.73	1.24	7.84	53 6.62	17 53 10.81
62	56 36.31	3.31	0.61	3 38.922	20 40.15	1.30	8.75	56 40.23	18 0 30.20
63	0 57 21.66	3.30	0.41	2 23.306	36 54.85	1.32	10.92	0 57 25.37	16 47.09
64	1 0 30.30	3.29	0.29	2 13.585	47 3.65	1.38	12.29	1 0 33.88	18 26 57.32
65	1 11.74	3.29	0.72	5 46.992	12 5.80	1.39	7.54	1 15.75	17 51 54.73
66	2 21.64	3.29	0.37	2 19.676	40 42.48	1.42	11.44	2 25.30	18 20 35.34
67	1 4 19.64	+3.28	+0.38	2 20.073	−40 17.52	−1.46	−11.39	1 4 23.30	−18 20 10.37

CORRECTIONS.

Date.	Corr. of Clock.	Hourly rate.	w	n	c	Zenith Point.	Mic. Co.
1848.	h. s.	s.	s.	s.	s.	° ' "	r.

REMARKS.

(206) 23. Right ascension differs 1ᵐ from Arg. Z. 267, 25.
(206) 38. Right ascension differs 1ᵐ from Arg. Z. 268, 71.
(206) 47. Time of transit over T. IV assumed as 44ˢ instead of 34ˢ.
(206) 48. Transits discordant by 3ˢ.

INSTRUMENT READINGS.

Date.	A.	B.	C.	D.	E.	F.	Mean.	Barom.	At.	Ex.	U.	L.	I.
	°		"				"	in.	°	°	°	°	°
Zone 206 Oct. 10, 23 20										56.8	61.3	54.8	58.
23 30	67	2	25.2 24. 31.5 20.8 21.3 17.5				23.67						
			25.8 24.2 32.2 22.0 21.8 17.8										
23 40										56.2			
24 0								30.130	62.	55.2			
24 20										55.2			
24 40								30.134	61.8	55.			
1 40								30.152	61.2	54.2			

Zone 206. October 10. S. $D_0 = -17^\circ\,39'\,40''$ — Continued.

No.	Mag.	I	II	III	IV	V	VI	VII	T. (h. m. s.)	a_1	a_2	Micr.	r.	i (′ ″)	d_1	d_2	Mean R.A. 1850.0 (h. m. s.)	Mean Decl. 1850.0 (° ′ ″)
68	7			45.5		21.			1 7 20.98	+3.27	+0.61	3	37.386	−22 16.74	−1.53	−6.97	1 7 24.56	−18 2 7.24
69	8			6.5	23.5	39.			8 22.96	3.27	0.51	3	29.179	30 51.64	1.56	10.10	8 26.74	10 43.30
70	5			49.		21.5			10 5.22	3.26	0.39	2	20.435	39 54.43	1.60	11.33	10 8.87	18 19 47.36
71	9		53.	9.		41.			12 25.28	3.25	0.78	4	49.179	9 46.74	1.67	7.43	12 29.31	17 49 35.84
72	9		9.	25.	41.				18 41.24	3.23	0.59	3	34.189	25 37.35	1.85	9.43	18 45.06	18 5 28.63
73	7			27.8	43.5				20 43.73	3.23	0.63	3	37.058	22 37.26	1.91	9.02	20 47.59	2 28.19
74	9		30.5		2.				22 2.48	3.22	0.60	2	35.722	24 0.97	1.96	9.19	22 6.30	3 52.12
75	9			50.					23 6.30	3.22	0.42	2	19.535	40 50.88	2.00	11.46	23 9.94	20 44.34
76	8				57.				23 56.94	3.22	0.33	1	12.805	47 53.32	2.02	12.40	24 0.49	27 47.74
77	8				52.5				24 36.07	3.21	0.32	2	12.035	48 41.60	2.05	12.51	24 39.60	28 36.16
78	5			34.					25 33.93	3.21	0.38	2	17.315	43 10.24	2.08	11.77	25 37.52	23 4.09
79	9		35.						28 8.58	3.20	0.56	3	29.822	30 11.17	2.17	10.02	28 12.34	10 3.36
80	7			15.	31.	47.			28 30.96	3.20	0.46	3	22.685	37 38.90	2.19	11.02	28 34.62	17 32.11
81	9					50.5			29 34.29	3.20	0.64	4	36.538	23 1.04	2.22	9.09	29 38.13	2 52.35
82	.				8.5				31 8.37	3.20	0.66	4	36.810	22 43.59	2.28	9.05	31 12.23	2 34.92
83	7					19.5			32 3.25?	3.19			.413		2.32		32 (7)	
84	7						0.5		32 28.15	3.19	0.46	3	21.620	38 45.38	2.34	11.17	32 31.80	18 18 38.89
85	9					57.5			34 41.33	3.19	0.75	4	43.010	16 14.74	2.44	8.19	34 45.27	17 56 5.37
86	10				55.				38 54.87	3.18	0.54	3	27.502	32 36.85	2.61	10.34	38 58.59	18 18 29.80
87	7				59.5		32.		39 59.52	3.17	0.54	3	26.012	34 10.21	2.66	10.55	40 3.23	14 3.42
88	9		14.5			3.5			42 47.15	3.17	0.53	3	25.458	34 44.94	2.78	10.63	42 50.85	14 38.35
89	9		21.2	37.	53.5				45 53.47	3.16	0.63	3	32.092	27 48.87	2.94	9.72	45 57.26	18 7 41.53
90	9					6.			46 49.88	3.16	0.87	6	51.758	7 6.59	2.98	6.99	46 53.91	17 46 56.56
91	9			22.8					48 39.14	3.15	0.77	4	42.483	16 47.44	3.06	8.27	48 43.06	17 56 38.77
92	8			46.2					50 2.52	3.15	0.43	2	15.775	44 46.51	3.14	11.98	50 6.10	18 24 41.63
93	9				24.		56.5		50 24.02	3.15	0.37	2	13.215	47 27.74	3.16	12.34	50 27.54	27 23.24
94	10		35.						56 7.66	3.14	0.37	2	11.303	49 26.81	3.47	12.61	56 11.17	29 22.89
95	7		9.5	26.	48.				56 42.08	3.14	0.57	IV. 3	25.948	34 14.14	3.51	10.56	56 45.79	14 8.21
96	8				33.5		6.0		57 33.52	3.14	0.75	IV. 4	38.830	20 36.82	3.55	8.77	57 37.41	0 29.14
97	9					13.5			1 58 41.16	3.13	0.72	4	37.525	21 59.24	3.61	8.95	1 58 45.01	1 52.80
98	10		46.						2 1 18.59	3.13	0.60	3	28.243	31 50.42	3.77	10.25	2 1 22.32	11 44.44
99	8				33.5		6.3		1 33.68	3.13	0.67	IV. 3	33.429	26 25.16	3.78	9.52	1 37.48	18 6 18.46
100	9					20.2			3 4.04	3.12	0.82	4	44.546	14 38.46	3.87	7.97	3 7.98	17 54 30.30
101	7			23.					4 22.96	3.12	0.42	2	13.498	47 9.48	3.97	12.33	4 26.50	18 27 5.78
102	7					10.5	26.5		4 54.10	3.12	0.43	V. 2	14.412	46 12.67	3.98	12.20	4 57.65	26 8.85
103	10			5.					7 21.34	3.12	0.40	2	11.212	49 32.83	4.14	12.65	7 24.86	18 29 29.62
104	10		31.5		4.				14 3.99	3.11	0.93	IV. 5	51.603	7 16.38	4.56	6.98	14 8.03	17 47 7.92
105	6			41.5	57.5	14.			14 57.62	3.10	0.53	V. 2	19.512	40 52.76	4.62	11.48	15 1.25	18 20 48.86
106	10		30.						17 2.59	3.10	0.85	4	44.386	14 47.68	4.76	7.99	17 6.54	17 54 40.43
107	9					34.	50.		17 17.72	3.10	0.70	V. 3	31.850	28 3.74	4.78	9.75	17 21.52	18 7 58.27
108	10		11.8		44.				19 44.14	3.10	0.92	IV. 5	48.641	10 22.28	4.92	7.40	19 48.16	17 50 14.60
109	8		37.	54.			42.5		22 10.03	3.09	0.85	4	43.385	15 50.89	5.08	8.13	22 13.97	17 55 44.10
110	8		49.5		22.				26 21.99	3.09	0.61	IV. 3	24.920	35 18.62	5.38	10.72	26 25.69	18 15 14.72
111	7		25.5		58.				27 57.98	3.09	0.85	4	42.240	17 2.32	5.49	8.29	28 1.92	17 56 56.10
112	8		27.5		0.				29 59.90	3.08	0.96	IV. 5	50.688	8 13.75	5.64	7.10	30 4.03	17 48 6.49
113	9				45.5				29 45.37	3.08	0.77	3	36.496	23 12.51	5.62	9.09	29 49.22	18 3 7.22
114	8						35.		31 31.18	3.08	0.69	3	29.062	30 58.47	5.75	10.13	31 34.95	10 54.35
115	7			53.		25.5			34 9.36	3.08	0.49	2	12.773	47 54.75	5.94	12.44	34 12.03	27 53.13
116	9				54.				2 36 37.77	+3.08	+0.74	3	32.567	−27 18.87	−6.12	−9.65	2 36 41.59	−18 7 14.64

CORRECTIONS.

Date.	Corr. of Clock.	Hourly rate.	m	n	e	Zenith Point.	Mic. C0.
1848.	h. s.	s.	s.	s.	s.	° ′	r.

REMARKS.

(206) 71. Right ascension differs 10^s and declination $20'$ from Arg. Z. 331, 34.

(206) 76. Transit over T. IV assumed as recorded over T. V.

(206) 101. Transit over T. IV assumed as recorded over T. III.

(206) 112. Right ascension differs 1^m from Arg. Z. 318, 35.

INSTRUMENT READINGS.

Date.			CIRCLE.					Barom.		THERMOM.			
		A.	B.	C.	D.	E.	F.	Mean.		At.	Ex.	U. L.	L.
Zone 206 1848. Oct. 10, h. m.									In.				
2 0													52.9
2 20									30.160	60.3			52.3
2 40													51.2
3 0									30.166	60.2			51.2
3 20													50.6

ZONE 206, OCTOBER 10. S. $D_s = -17° 39' 40''$—Continued.

No.	Mag.	Seconds of Transit (I–VII)	T. (h. m. s.)	a_1	a_2	Micrometer		r.	i	d_1	d_2	Mean Right Ascension, 1850.0	Mean Declination, 1850.0
117	8	.. .. 59.5 .. 32.	2 37 59.52	+ 3.08	+0.67	IV.	3	27.195	−32 56.11	− 6.23	−10.39	2 38 3.27	−18 12 52.73
118	9	51. 7.	40 23.42	3.07	0.71	.	2	28.982	30 57.78	6.41	10.14	40 27.20	18 10 54.33
119	9	57.	40 40.81	3.07	0.84	.	4	39.362	20 3.88	6.43	8.69	40 44.72	17 59 59.00
120	8	7.5 24. 40.	42 40.11	3.07	0.91	.	5	44.790	14 23.82	6.58	7.93	42 44.09	54 18.33
121	8	15. 31.	44 47.48	3.07	0.95	.	5	46.762	12 19.85	6.74	7.67	44 51.50	17 52 14.26
122	10	13.	51 12.88	3.07	0.67	.	3	24.923	35 18.43	7.24	10.72	51 16.62	18 15 16.39
123	8	52.	54 8.33	3.07	0.53	.	2	12.889	47 47.48	7.47	12.42	54 11.93	27 47.37
124	8	58. 14.2	55 14.18	3.06	0.83	.	3	35.648	24 5.68	7.56	9.21	55 18.07	4 2.45
125	8	45. 1.	57 0.66	3.06	0.63	.	2	20.648	39 41.01	7.70	11.32	57 4.35	19 40.03
126	9	23. .. 55.8	2 59 39.43	3.06	0.84	.	3	36.253	23 27.83	7.91	9.13	2 59 43.33	3 24.87
127	9	18.	3 3 1.64	3.06	0.61	.	2	17.790	42 40.57	8.19	11.74	3 3 5.31	22 40.50
128	10	30.	4 13.80	3.06	0.49	.	3	39.195	20 22.97	8.29	8.72	4 17.75	0 19.98
129	8	39.8 .. 12.	6 12.12	3.06	0.74	.	3	28.340	31 44.34	8.44	10.25	6 15.92	11 43.03
130	9	52. .. 24.5	7 8.21	3.06	0.58	.	2	14.883	45 42.93	8.52	12.16	7 11.85	25 43.61
131	10	7.5	10 40.09	3.06	0.75	.	3	28.178	31 54.50	8.81	10.26	10 43.90	11 53.57
132	11	53.5	11 9.76	3.06	0.77	.	3	28.885	31 9.96	8.85	10.17	11 13.59	18 11 8.98
133	9	26.	12 25.88	3.06	0.93	.	4	40.948	18 23.91	8.96	8.46	12 29.87	17 58 21.33
134	9	32.5	13 48.79	3.06	0.87	.	3	35.779	23 57.39	9.07	9.18	13 52.72	18 3 55.64
135	7	48.8 .. 22. 38.	16 21.69	3.06	0.93	.	4	40.649	18 42.86	9.28	8.50	16 25.68	17 58 40.64
136	9	24. .. 56.	18 40.00	3.06	0.75	.	3	26.398	33 46.17	9.48	10.52	18 43.81	18 13 46.17
137	10	43.	19 42.89	3.06	1.06	.	5	49.828	9 7.68	9.57	7.21	19 47.01	17 49 4.46
138	10	56. .. 28.	22 28.30	3.06	0.61	.	2	15.474	45 5.25	9.82	12.06	22 31.97	18 25 7.13
139	11	22.	3 23 38.31	+ 3.06	+0.64	.	2	17.245	−43 14.51	− 9.91	−11.82	3 23 42.01	−18 23 16.24

ZONE 207. OCTOBER 11. C. $D_s = -16° 24' 50''$.

No.	Mag.	Seconds of Transit (I–VII)	T. (h. m. s.)	a_1	a_2	Micrometer		r.	i	d_1	d_2	Mean Right Ascension, 1850.0	Mean Declination, 1850.0
1	7.8	17.5 33.5	20 32 1.40	+ 4.14	+0.49	V.	4	45.036	−14 7.64	−13.07	− 2.05	20 32 6.03	−16 39 12.76
2	9.10	27. 42.8 .. 15.3	36 43.03	4.11	0.53	IV.	5	49.519	9 27.28	12.62	1.47	36 47.67	16 34 31.37
3	9	43.3 59.2 15.3 31.3	37 59.19	4.10	0.27	IV.	2	11.400	49 21.35	12.49	6.44	38 3.56	17 14 30.28
4	9	10.2	39 42.58	4.09	0.38	II.	3	24.650	35 35.76	12.32	4.71	39 47.05	17 0 42.79
5	8.9	53.2 9.	39 36.99	4.09	0.42	V.	3	31.437	28 29.84	12.33	3.82	39 41.50	16 53 35.99
6	8.9	13.7	39 40.87	4.09	0.35	VII.	3	21.494	38 53.03	12.32	5.12	39 45.31	17 4 0.47
7	9	35.3 41.	42 35.00	4.07	0.42	V.	3	27.039	33 5.64	12.05	4.39	42 39.49	16 58 12.08
8	9	47.5 .. 19.8 35.8	44 19.76	4.06	0.50	IV.	4	40.943	18 24.22	11.89	2.58	44 24.32	43 28.69
9	9.10	8.	46 40.37	4.05	0.52	II.	4	42.537	16 43.67	11.66	2.37	46 44.94	41 47.70
10	9.10	55.	46 54.89	4.04	0.57	IV.	5	47.269	11 48.53	11.64	1.76	46 59.50	16 36 51.93
11	9.10		46		0.37	VII.	2	18.361	42 5.14	11.64	5.53		17 7 12.31
12	9	26. .. 14.5	48 42.29	4.03	0.53	III.	4	39.772	19 37.39	11.47	2.73	48 46.85	16 44 41.59
13	7	11.5 27.2 43.2	49 11.20	4.03	0.58	V.	5	47.795	11 15.31	11.42	1.69	49 15.81	36 18.42
14	9.10	32.	50		0.43	VII.	2	25.964	34 8.05	11.34	4.52		59 13.91
15	9.10	58.2	51 58.07	4.01	0.46	IV.	3	28.252	31 49.79	11.16	4.23	52 2.54	16 56 55.18
16	8	51.2 7. 23.3 39.1	53 7.08	4.00	0.43	IV.	3	24.219	36 2.78	11.06	4.76	53 11.51	17 1 8.60
17	9.10	3. 19.	54 19.01	3.99	0.46	III.	3	27.432	32 41.35	10.94	4.34	54 23.46	16 57 46.63
18	8.9	36.4 53.1 9.3	55 52.88	3.98	0.43	IV.	3	24.215	36 3.04	10.80	4.76	55 57.29	17 1 8.60
19	9	36.3 53. 9.	56 36.65	3.98	0.53	V.	4	36.131	23 26.52	10.74	3.20	56 41.10	16 48 30.46
20	9.10	40.8 56.8	58 13.10	3.96	0.39	III.	2	17.251	43 14.13	10.59	5.67	58 17.45	17 8 20.39
21	8	47.2 .. 19.5	20 58 47.23	3.96	0.44	VI.	3	24.157	36 6.25	10.53	4.77	20 58 51.63	1 11.55
22	9	32.	21 0 59.86	+ 3.95	+0.41	VI.	3	20.671	−39 44.84	−10.33	− 5.23	21 1 4.22	−17 4 50.40

CORRECTIONS.

Date.	Corr. of Clock.	Hourly rate.	m	n	c	Zenith Point.	Mic. Co.
1848.	h.	s.	s.	s.	s.	° ' "	r.
Oct. 11,	. .	. .	. .	. .	. .	359 59 64.26	30.0139

REMARKS.

(207) 22. Right ascension differs 2^m from Arg. Z. 244, 115, and 256, 7.

INSTRUMENT READINGS.

Date.	CIRCLE.							Barom.	THERMOM.				
	A.	B.	C.	D.	E.	F.	Mean.		At.	Ex.	U.	L.	I.
1848. h. m.	° ' "						"	in.	°	°	°	°	°
Zone 207 Oct. 11, 20 30	65 47 32.7 / 33.8	31.2 / 30.6	36.7 / 36.8	29.9 / 30.4	28.1 / 28.5	23.8 / 23.9	30.53	30.232	60.	51.	60.	58.8	61.5
20 40	.	.	.	.	.	.	.	.	.	.	.	51.	
21 0	.	.	.	.	.	.	.	.	.	.	.	51.1	
21 40	.	.	.	.	.	.	.	.	.	.	.	46.5	
22 0	.	.	.	.	.	.	.	30.228	56.	.	.	45.7	
22 20	.	.	.	.	.	.	.	.	.	.	.	45.3	
22 40	65 47 32.2 / 32.9	31.6 / 31.2	37.4 / 37.3	30. / 30.3	28.8 / 29.3	22.1 / 22.1	30.43	30.232	55.3	44.1	54.	51.3	61.

ZONE 207. OCTOBER 11. C. $D_0 = -16°\ 24'\ 50''$—Continued.

No.	Mag.	I.	II.	III.	IV.	V.	VI.	VII.	T. (h. m. s.)
23	9		11.2	27.2					21 0 43.48
24	7				57.2	13.2	29.3		0 57.05
25	9			10.8					2 10.67
26	8			40.3	13.	28.7			2 56.68
27	9				43.5	0.2			6 59.93
28	8		37.2		25.3				6 9.40
29	9		54.5	11.2	27.	43.1			9 27.09
30	.7		17.3	33.9	49.8		22.2		10 49.88
31	9.10				2.				11 45.76
32	9		50.3				40.2		13 24.16
33	8						57.3		13 25.21
34	9					13.2	1.3		15 29.27
35	9				13.2	29.2			15 57.10
36	10				6.				16 33.84
37	9.10			26.	42.1		13.		18 42.10
38	8					55.8	11.9		19 39.74
39	9.10						46.		20 13.89
40	8			38.7	54.3		27.		21 54.64
41	9				51.2	38.			24 31.37
42	7.8					34.2	50.3		25 18.14
43	9					7.5	23.4		26 51.33
44	9			35.2	52.		24.5		29 8.02
45	8.9		55.2		27.5	43.2	59.		29 27.22
46	5				43.		14.5		31 42.64
47	9			26.8					35 59.17
48	8			27.	50.5	15.3	31.2		35 59.26
49	9								36
50	2			35.	41.2	57.	12.8		38 40.96
51	9					50.2	6.3		39 34.15
52	8.9			33.3	49.6		22.		42 5.76
53	9.10			44.1		16.6			44 16.47
54	9					37.2	53.2		44 21.10
55	10			43.3	59.2				48 15.57
56	9			42.	58.3				50 4.40
57	10					39.			51 22.80
58	9.10			39.2		12.5			54 11.96
59	9.10					5.5	22.		54 5.62
60	8				57.2	13.2	29.3		55 57.11
61	9			12.2		43.4			57 43.92
62	9			6.2	22.4	38.5			21 59 38.52
63	7					11.3	28.2	44.2	22 0 11.72
64	9				52.				2 8.23
65	9						38.2		2 6.01
66	10				50.2				5 6.42
67	9					56.2			5 56.06
68	7					25.7	57.5		6 25.46
69	9			6.2		37.3			8 37.92
70	9					10.2	42.		9 9.98
71	8					15.3	47.		22 9 15.02

No.	a_1 (s.)	a_2 (s.)	Mic.		r	i (′ ″)	d_1 (″)	d_2 (″)	Mean Right Ascension, 1850.0 (h. m. s.)	Mean Declination, 1850.0 (° ′ ″)
23	+3.95	+0.54	III.	4	38.788	−20 39.15	−10.36	−2.86	21 0 47.97	−16 15 42.37
24	3.95	0.36	V.	2	12.622	48 4.79	10.34	6.29	1 1.36	17 13 11.42
25	3.94	0.54	IV.	3	37.746	21 53.95	10.23	3.00	2 15.15	16 46 57.18
26	3.94	0.60	IV.	5	46.162	12 57.94	10.16	1.89	3 1.22	37 59.99
27	3.91	0.62	V.	5	47.985	11 3.46	9.83	1.66	7 4.46	36 4.95
28	3.91	0.58	IV.	4	41.773	17 32.12	9.81	2.47	7 13.89	42 34.40
29	3.89	0.66	IV.	5	52.906	5 51.28	9.58	1.00	9 31.64	30 51.86
30	3.88	0.49	IV.	3	26.308	23 18.78	9.47	3.20	10 54.25	16 48 21.45
31	3.88	0.45	V.	2	19.412	40 59.08	9.40	5.39	11 50.09	17 6 3.87
32	3.87	0.64	II.	4	47.392	11 38.98	9.27	1.73	13 28.67	16 36 39.98
33	3.87	0.52	VI.	5	30.968	28 58.82	9.25	3.87	13 29.60	16 54 1.94
34	3.85	0.46	V.	2	20.773	39 33.37	9.07	5.21	15 33.58	17 4 37.65
35	3.85	0.61	V.	4	42.190	17 6.33	9.03	2.41	16 1.56	16 42 7.77
36	3.84	0.65	VI.	5	46.772	12 19.53	8.95	1.81	16 38.33	16 37 20.32
37	3.83	0.47	IV.	2	20.610	39 43.71	8.79	5.23	18 46.40	17 4 47.73
38	3.82	0.55	IV.	2	31.428	28 30.40	8.72	3.82	19 44.11	16 53 32.94
39	3.82	0.60	VI.	3	36.721	22 57.90	8.66	3.13	20 18.11	47 59.69
40	3.81	0.53	IV.	3	27.674	32 26.00	8.53	4.30	21 58.94	57 28.83
41	3.79	0.64	VI.	3	41.746	17 35.01	8.31	2.47	24 35.80	42 35.70
42	3.79	0.58	V.	3	33.436	26 24.41	8.25	3.56	25 22.51	51 26.22
43	3.78	0.57	IV.	3	29.362	30 40.05	8.12	4.08	26 55.68	55 42.23
44	3.76	0.56	IV.	3	26.777	33 22.14	7.93	4.42	29 12.34	58 24.49
45	3.76	0.58	IV.	3	29.678	30 20.27	7.91	1.04	29 31.56	16 55 22.22
46	3.75	0.41	VI.	2	5.859	55 10.07	7.73	7.19	31 46.80	17 20 14.99
47	3.71	0.67	II.	4	39.837	10 32.94	7.30	2.72	36 3.55	16 44 33.05
48	3.71	0.70	IV.	5	44.913	14 16.23	7.30	2.06	36 3.67	16 39 15.68
49		0.48	VII.	2	13.056	47 37.70	7.39	6.24		17 12 41.33
50	3.69	0.64	IV.	3	36.419	23 17.42	7.18	3.17	38 45.29	16 48 17.77
51	3.69	0.67	VI.	3	38.458	21 9.92	7.13	2.90	39 38.51	46 9.05
52	3.67	0.63	IV.	3	31.702	28 13.21	6.91	3.78	42 10.06	53 13.99
53	3.66	0.60	II.	3	27.568	32 32.77	6.75	4.32	44 20.73	57 33.84
54	3.66	0.78	V.	5	53.439	5 21.22	6.75	0.05	44 25.54	30 18.92
55	3.63	0.77	III.	4	50.044	8 52.69	6.45	1.39	48 19.97	33 50.53
56	3.62	0.64	III.	3	28.338	31 44.53	6.38	4.22	49 8.66	16 56 45.13
57	3.61	0.60	V.	3	22.915	37 24.24	6.22	4.94	51 27.01	17 2 25.40
58	3.59	0.66	IV.	3	30.600	29 22.05	6.03	3.92	54 16.21	16 54 22.00
59	3.59	0.67	V.	3	31.267	28 40.51	6.04	3.84	54 9.88	53 40.30
60	3.58	0.67	V.	3	31.777	28 6.32	5.90	3.77	56 1.36	53 7.99
61	3.57	0.74	II.	4	40.948	18 23.49	5.77	2.57	57 48.23	43 27.63
62	3.56	0.75	III.	4	40.454	18 54.85	5.64	2.05	21 59 42.83	16 43 53.14
63	3.55	0.54	V.	2	9.476	51 22.17	5.60	0.73	22 0 15.81	17 16 24.50
64	3.54	0.78	III.	4	43.867	15 20.37	5.47	2.19	2 12.55	16 40 18.03
65	3.54	0.85	VI.	5	52.865	5 56.05	5.47	1.01	2 10.40	30 53.43
66	3.52	0.79	III.	4	42.531	16 44.43	5.26	2.36	5 10.73	41 42.05
67	3.52	0.70	IV.	3	29.537	30 29.17	5.21	4.07	6 0.28	55 28.45
68	3.52	0.85	VI.	5	51.125	7 46.30	5.18	1.23	6 29.83	16 32 42.80
69	3.50	0.62	II.	2	17.721	41 44.22	5.03	5.62	8 42.04	17 6 44.87
70	3.50	0.77	VI.	3	37.579	22 4.12	4.99	3.01	9 14.25	16 47 2.12
71	+3.50	+0.78	VI.	3	40.946	−18 32.68	−4.99	−2.57	22 9 19.30	−16 43 30.24

CORRECTIONS.

Date.	Corr. of Clock.	Hourly rate.	m	n	c	Zenith Point.	Mic. Co.
1848.	h.	s.	s.	s.	s.	° ′ ″	r.

INSTRUMENT READINGS.

Date.	CIRCLE.						Barom.	THERMOM.				
	A.	B.	C.	D.	E.	F.	Mean.		At.	Ex.	U.	L.	I.
1848. h. m.	° ′ ″						″	in.	°	°	°	°	°

REMARKS.

(207) 27. Transits over T.'s III and IV ass'd as recorded over T.'s IV and V.

(207) 28. Transit over T. II assumed to have been recorded as over T. III, and minutes as 7, not 6.

(207) 30. Micrometer reading assumed as 36r.308, not 26r.308.

(207) 32. Transit over T. V assumed as recorded over T. VI; T. II discordant and rejected.

(207) 34. Transit over T. VI assumed at 1s.3 instead of over T. V at 13s.

(207) 41. Transits assumed at 31s.2 and 3s.8 instead of 51s.2 and 38s, respectively.

(207) 50. Time of transit over T. III assumed as 25s instead of 35s.

(207) 51. Trans. ass'd as recorded over T.'s V and VI, as originally rec'ded, to agree with Arg. Z. 256, 54.

(207) 52. Transit over T. V ass'd to have been recorded as over T. VI.

(207) 56. Minutes assumed as 49, not 50; and transits over T.'s II and III as 32s and 48s.3, not 42s and 58s.3.

Zone 207.　October 11.　C.　$D_s = -16°\ 24'\ 50''$—Continued.

No.	Mag.	I	II	III	IV	V	VI	VII	T. (h. m. s.)	a_1 (s.)	a_2 (s.)	Micr.	r.	i (° ' ")	d_1 (")	d_2 (")	Mean Right Ascension, 1850.0 (h. m. s.)	Mean Declination, 1850.0 (° ' ")
72	9					4.7	20.5	35.3	22 14 20.64	+ 3.46	+0.85	IV. 4	47.737	−11 17.83	− 4.66	− 1.69	22 14 24.95	−16 36 14.18
73	9				7.3	23.2	39.3		15 23.26	3.46	0.81	IV. 3	41.131	18 21.59	4.59	2.54	15 27.55	43 18.72
74	9								21	.	.		F.Wire	29 59.13	4.21	2.68	. . .	54 56.02
75	9						16.7		20 44.60	3.42	0.74	VI. 3	28.202	31 52.55	4.26	4.24	20 48.76	16 56 51.05
76	7					33.	49.2		22 16.91	3.41	0.67	V. 2	18.538	41 53.86	4.17	5.51	22 20.99	17 6 53.54
77	7.8		26.8	42.6	58.9	15.3	31.3		27 59.00	3.38	0.67	IV. 2	15.848	44 42.17	3.83	5.86	28 3.05	9 41.86
78	9			8.2	24.2	40.8			29 24.35	3.37	0.69	IV. 2	16.731	43 46.87	3.75	5.75	29 28.41	8 46.37
79	9					38.3			30 21.97	3.36	0.64	V. 2	10.7	50 10.	3.69	6.56	30 25.97	17 15 10.25
80	8.9						34.2		32 2.07	3.35	0.86	VI. 4	40.110	19 16.94	3.60	2.65	32 6.23	16 44 13.22
81	8.9		44.3	0.0					35 16.90	3.33	0.89	III. 4	43.349	15 53.14	3.42	2.23	35 21.12	40 48.89
82	8.9		54.	10.3		41.3	57.6		35 25.87	3.33	0.80	IV. 3	29.780	30 13.74	3.41	4.04	35 30.00	55 11.19
83	9				14.2	30.1	45.9		37 13.97	3.32	0.96	V. 5	53.317	5 28.88	3.32	0.95	37 18.25	16 30 23.15
84	8			38.9	54.8				38 54.92	3.31	0.69	III. 2	13.731	46 54.56	3.22	6.16	38 58.92	17 11 53.91
85	7.8					28.2	44.4		39 12.18	3.31	0.81	V. 3	29.077	30 57.78	3.21	4.13	39 16.30	16 55 55.12
86	9		29.5	45.7	1.3	17.7	33.5		22 42 1.56	+ 3.29	+0.75	IV. 2	19.095	−41 18.67	− 3.06	− 5.45	22 42 5.60	−17 6 17.18

Zone 208.　October 14.　S.　$D_s = -25°\ 10'\ 20''$.

No.	Mag.	I	II	III	IV	V	VI	VII	T. (h. m. s.)	a_1 (s.)	a_2 (s.)	Micr.	r.	i (° ' ")	d_1 (")	d_2 (")	Mean Right Ascension, 1850.0 (h. m. s.)	Mean Declination, 1850.0 (° ' ")
1	8			18.	35.	52.			20 31 52.12	+ 1.95	+0.75	IV. 3	35.772	−23 57.77	−15.16	− 3.03	20 31 54.82	−25 34 35.06
2	10					48.			34 30.82	1.93	0.79	. 3	25.102	35 7.16	14.90	4.62	34 33.54	45 46.88
3	9		29.5						37 3.85	1.91	0.77	. 3	31.604	28 19.43	14.66	3.73	37 6.53	35 57.82
4	6				9.5				37 9.43	1.91	0.82	. 2	17.516	37 44.07	14.65	6.11	37 12.16	48 24.83
5	9					53.	10.		37 35.93	1.91	0.72	V. 3	42.041	16 37.96	14.61	1.89	37 38.56	27 11.46
6	8		2.	18.8	36.				41 36.00	1.87	0.73	IV. 3	38.293	21 19.81	14.23	2.60	41 38.66	31 56.64
7	10				59.5				46 16.67	1.84	0.78	. 3	21.195	36 4.37	13.80	4.98	46 19.29	46 43.15
8	9				15.				47 14.88	1.83	0.78	. 3	25.121	35 6.16	13.71	4.82	47 17.49	45 44.69
9	9			15.					48 49.34	1.82	0.71	. 5	42.342	16 57.67	13.59	1.94	48 51.87	27 33.20
10	9		36.	53.				44.8	50 10.42	1.81	0.80	III. 2	19.125	46 11.48	13.44	6.04	50 13.03	56 51.56
11	9			22.8					53 40.01	1.78	0.70	. 4	42.200	17 5.20	13.14	1.96	53 42.40	27 40.30
12	7				9.	26.			54 26.00	1.77	0.75	IV. 3	30.872	29 5.23	13.07	3.86	54 28.52	39 42.16
13	10			7.		42.			56 41.61	1.76	0.68	. 5	48.860	10 8.79	12.86	0.81	56 44.05	20 42.49
14	6			1.	18.	35.			20 58 17.97	1.74	0.73	IV. 4	34.302	35 30.26	12.73	3.27	20 58 20.44	36 6.26
15	9		47.		4.	21.			21 0 21.15	1.73	0.68	IV. 4	46.442	12 39.30	12.55	1.24	21 0 23.56	23 13.09
16	8				0.				1 17.24	1.72	0.69	. 5	44.178	15 2.36	12.47	1.62	1 19.65	25 36.45
17	8			56.	13.	31.			2 13.36	1.71	0.70	IV. 4	43.712	15 31.67	12.39	1.72	2 15.77	20 5.78
18	8		56.8	13.8					4 31.08	1.70	0.70	III. 4	42.342	16 56.35	12.20	1.92	4 33.45	27 30.47
19	9					40.2	57.2		4 40.10	1.70	0.71	IV. 2	40.637	18 43.75	12.19	2.22	4 42.51	29 15.16
20	9						47.	4.	5 29.78	1.69	0.80	. 2	16.603	43 55.21	12.12	6.28	5 32.27	54 33.61
21	10				28.				8 45.21	1.66	0.61	. 2	16.602	43 54.77	11.85	6.28	8 47.68	54 32.90
22	9			13.	30.	47.			9 47.12	1.65	0.75	IV. 3	31.423	28 30.91	11.76	3.76	9 49.52	30 6.43
23	10			10.	27.2				12 44.39	1.63	0.68	III. 5	49.055	9 56.16	11.54	0.79	12 46.70	20 28.49
24	10			3.		38.			14 37.64	1.62	0.78	IV. 3	23.000	37 19.18	11.39	5.19	14 40.04	47 55.76
25	6				53.	10.	26.7		15 9.85	1.61	0.80	IV. 3	20.602	39 49.60	11.31	5.60	15 12.26	50 26.54
26	8		26.						17 0.33	1.60	0.70	. 5	45.678	13 27.82	11.19	1.37	17 2.65	24 0.38
27	8						20.2	37.	17 2.90	1.60	0.81	. 2	18.198	42 15.10	11.19	6.01	17 5.31	52 52.30
28	9			49.8					19 24.25	1.58	0.83	. 2	15.084	45 29.28	11.01	6.54	19 26.66	56 6.83
29	9							56.	19 38.83	1.58	0.79	. 3	26.082	34 5.67	11.00	4.67	19 41.20	44 41.34
30	10							6.	21 20 48.96	+ 1.57	+0.72	. 5	42.702	−16 35.07	−10.90	− 1.86	21 20 51.25	−25 27 7.83

CORRECTIONS.

Date	Corr. of Clock	Hourly rate	m	n	c	Zenith Point	Mic. Co.
	h.	s.	s.	s.	s.	° ' "	r.
1848. Oct. 14	. .	. .	. .	. .	. .	359 59 61.28	.

INSTRUMENT READINGS.

	Date	A.	B.	C.	D.	E.	F.	Mean.	Barom.	At.	Ex.	U.	L.	I.
	1848. h. m.	° ' "						"	in.	°	°	°	°	°
Zone 208	Oct. 14, 20 20	74 32 {30.2 / 29.8}	29.8 / 30.	36.4 / 36.4	25. / 26.2	28. / 28.8	19. / 19.4	28.25	. .	. .	. .	60.5	. .	. .
	20 40								29.972	61.	53.2	. .	59.	60.
	21 0								. .	. .	52.6	. .	59.	55.
	22 0								. .	. .	51.	. .	. .	. .
	23 0								29.966	57.8	49.2			
	23 20								. .	. .	48.9			
	23 40								29.960	56.9	48.6			
	24 0								29.956	56.4	48.2			

REMARKS.

(207) 75.　Right ascension differs 12^s from Arg. Z. 256, 107; and Mer. Cir., 1848, October 14.

(208) 4.　Micrometer reading assumed as $22^r.516$, not $17^r.516$.

(208) 9.　Transit over T. II assumed as recorded over T. III.

(208) 10.　Micrometer reading assumed as $14^r.425$, not $19^r.425$.

[(207) 74.　Precedes 75. 6^s.]

ZONE 208. OCTOBER 14. S. $D_o = -25°\,10'\,20''$—Continued.

No.	Mag.	Seconds of Transit (I. II. III. IV. V. VI. VII.)	T. (h. m. s.)	a_1 (s.)	a_2 (s.)	Micrometer (r.)	i (' ")	d_1 (")	d_2 (")	Mean Right Ascension, 1850.0 (h. m. s)	Mean Declination, 1850.0 (° ' ")
31	9	0.2 17.	21 21 42.91	+ 1.56	+0.81	3 20.262	−40 10.87	−10.84	−5.65	21 21 45.28	−25 50 47.36
32	8	16.	23 58.69	1.54	0.84	2 13.748	46 54.17	10.67	6.77	24 1.07	57 31.55
33	10	2. 19.	25 1.82	1.53	0.82	2 17.225	43 16.01	10.59	6.18	25 4.19	53 52.78
34	8	1. 18. 9.8	26 35.44	1.52	0.84	2 12.298	48 24.35	10.48	7.01	26 37.80	59 1.84
35	9	24. 58.8	28 58.51	1.50	0.77	3 29.309	30 43.54	10.30	4.11	29 0.78	41 17.95
36	8	40.8 58.	31 15.22	1.48	0.83	2 17.285	43 11.62	10.14	6.16	31 17.53	53 47.92
37	9	32.2 40.	31 32.04	1.48	0.71	5 47.410	11 39.68	10.12	1.07	31 34.23	22 10.67
38	7	33. 40.	32 57.32	1.47	0.82	3 19.033	41 27.95	10.01	5.87	32 59.61	52 3.83
39	9	55.	33 20.88	1.47	0.70	5 49.562	9 24.45	9.99	0.71	33 23.05	19 55.15
40	7	20.2 37.5	35 54.60	1.45	0.76	3 34.799	24 58.83	9.81	3.19	35 56.81	35 31.83
41	8	2.6 36.5	37 36.66	1.43	0.74	4 39.627	19 46.19	9.69	2.37	37 38.03	30 18.25
42	9	22. 39.	38 21.85	1.43	0.80	3 25.170	35 3.14	9.64	4.81	38 24.08	45 37.59
43	9	42.8 0. 16.8	41 17.04	1.41	0.82	2 20.163	40 11.42	9.44	5.67	41 19.27	50 46.53
44	10	0.5	43 4.88	1.39	0.81	3 25.895	34 17.47	9.32	4.69	43 7.08	44 51.46
45	11	34.	45 16.77	1.37	0.83	3 21.002	39 24.27	9.18	5.68	45 18.97	49 59.13
46	11	45.	48 2.22	1.35	0.73	5 43.959	15 15.98	9.00	1.65	48 4.30	25 46.63
47	8	24. 58.5	50 58.36	1.33	0.72	5 48.293	10 43.86	8.81	0.92	50 0.41	21 13.59
48	8	7.	51 49.89	1.32	0.78	3 31.688	28 13.91	8.76	3.72	51 51.99	38 46.39
49	8	57.	52 39.84	1.31	0.80	3 27.122	33 0.44	8.71	4.49	52 41.95	43 33.64
50	9	43.	53 8.91	1.31	0.77	4 35.122	24 29.89	8.68	3.14	53 10.99	35 1.71
51	8	3.	55 20.17	1.29	0.78	4 35.950	23 37.25	8.55	2.99	55 22.24	34 8.79
52	9	53.	55 18.91	1.29	0.77	4 37.608	21 53.80	8.55	2.71	55 20.97	32 25.06
53	9	48.	56 13.86	1.28	0.84	2 20.400	39 57.13	8.49	5.64	56 15.98	50 31.26
54	9	44. 18.	21 59 18.10	1.26	0.76	4 44.140	15 2.93	8.30	1.62	21 59 20.12	25 32.85
55	10	7.	22 1 24.23	1.25	0.87	2 13.920	46 42.83	8.19	6.75	22 1 26.35	57 17.77
56	10	13.	2 55.88	1.23	0.80	3 30.588	29 23.05	8.10	3.91	2 57.91	39 55.06
57	6	42. 59.	5 16.33	1.21	0.87	2 15.829	44 42.67	7.97	6.42	5 18.41	55 17.06
58	8	52. 9.	5 34.94	1.21	0.74	4 47.628	11 24.91	7.95	1.03	5 36.89	21 53.89
59	9	9. 26.	6 51.86	1.20	0.82	3 26.672	33 28.67	7.88	4.57	6 53.88	44 1.12
60	8	49. 56.	8			.578	7			8	
61	10	42. 16.5	11 16.36	1.17	0.76	4 46.282	12 49.28	7.64	1.25	11 18.29	23 18.17
62	8.9	22.8	12 22.72	1.16	0.88	2 18.965	41 26.76	7.58	5.88	12 24.76	52 0.22
63	10	23.8	12 49.64	1.15	0.89	2 18.018	42 26.41	7.56	6.05	12 51.67	53 0.02
64	6	32. 49.5 6.3	15 6.40	1.14	0.80	3 39.960	20 37.76	7.44	2.31	15 8.34	31 7.51
65	10	43.5 17.5	17 17.60	1.12	0.50	4 40.619	18 43.93	7.33	2.21	17 19.52	29 13.47
66	10	22. 39.	20 55.30	1.09	0.77	5 49.705	9 15.04	7.14	0.67	20 58.16	19 42.85
67	10	36. 10.5	21 53.33	1.08	0.81	4 41.602	17 42.67	7.10	2.04	21 55.22	28 11.81
68	10	25.5	23 25.37	1.07	0.82	4 41.604	17 42.86	7.02	2.04	23 27.26	28 11.92
69	9	21.8 56.	24 21.79	1.06	0.79	5 46.452	12 39.80	6.98	1.22	24 23.64	23 8.00
70	10	38.2	27 55.41	1.03	0.92	2 17.445	43 1.97	6.81	6.15	27 57.36	53 34.93
71	9	49.	29 23.45	1.02	0.93	2 14.609	45 59.32	6.74	6.63	29 25.40	56 32.69
72	10	42. 59.	29 41.84	1.02	0.92	2 18.820	36 22.09	6.73	5.05	29 43.78	25 46 53.87
73	7.6	42.2 59.3 16.2 51.	37 16.54	0.96	0.97	2 9.909	50 53.90	6.40	7.44	37 18.47	26 1 27.74
74	7.8	13. 31.3 47. 4.2	40 47.45	0.94	0.94	3 17.932	32 9.54	6.26	4.34	40 49.33	25 42 40.14
75	10	51.5	44 25.91	0.91	0.96	2 17.509	42 57.52	6.12	6.14	44 27.81	25 53 29.78
76	9	40.	44 39.96	0.91	0.99	2 11.140	49 37.92	6.11	7.22	44 41.86	26 0 11.25
77	8	29.	44 54.82	0.90	0.97	2 14.570	46 2.70	6.10	6.64	44 56.69	25 56 35.44
78	7	24. 41.	46 6.84	0.90	0.94	3 24.058	36 12.64	6.05	5.03	46 8.68	46 43.72
79	10	12.5	22 49 55.29	+ 0.87	+0.95	3 22.772	−37 33.23	−5.91	−5.24	22 49 57.11	−25 48 4.38

CORRECTIONS.

Date.	Corr. of Clock.	Hourly rate.	m	n	c	Zenith Point.	Mic. Co.
1848. h.	s.	s.	s.	s.	s.	° ' "	r.

REMARKS.

(208) 39. Time of transit over T. II assumed as 23ˢ instead of 33ˢ.

(208) 64. Micrometer reading assumed as 38ʳ.960 instead of 39ʳ.960.

(208) 72. Micrometer reading assumed as 23ʳ.820, not 18ʳ.820.

(208) 74. Micrometer reading assumed as 27ʳ.932, not 17ʳ.932.

INSTRUMENT READINGS.

Date.	CIRCLE.							Barom.	THERMOM.				
	A.	B.	C.	D.	E.	F.	Mean.		At.	Ex.	U.	L.	l.
1848. h. m.	° ' "						"	In.	°	°	°	°	°
Zone 208 Oct. 14, 24 10	74 32 { 29. 28.6	31.8 31.8	37. 36.5	27.2 28.0	28.2 28.9	18.6 19.0 }	28.73					53.	

ZONE 208. OCTOBER 14. S. $D_o = -25° 10' 20''$—Continued.

No.	Mag.	I	II	III	IV	V	VI	VII	T	a_1	a_2	Micr.	r	i	d_1	d_2	Mean Right Ascension 1850.0	Mean Declination 1850.0
80	7.6		22	39	56				22 51 56.21	+0.85	+1.00	2	13.379	−47 16.93	−5.84	−6.84	22 51 58.06	−25 57 49.61
81	10					51	8		52 33.84	0.85	0.95	V. 3	23.382	36 55.17	5.82	5.14	52 35.64	47 26.13
82	9					22	39		54 4.77	0.84	0.99	V. 2	17.002	43 30.05	5.77	6.22	54 6.60	54 2.04
83	10				48	5			22 55 47.84	0.83	0.98	V. 2	20.336	40 1.14	5.72	5.66	22 55 49.65	50 32.52
84	9				50	7	23.8		23 2 49.84	0.77	0.93	· 4	37.563	21 56.54	5.50	2.72	23 2 51.54	25 32 24.76
85	·		17.5						6 51.98	0.74	1.05	1	9.460	51 23.18	5.39	7.53	6 53.77	26 1 56.10
86	6.7				16.5	33.5	50.5		7 16.39	0.74	0.97	IV. 3	30.362	29 37.48	5.37	3.94	7 18.10	25 40 6.79
87	9			5.2	22	39.5			10 22.19	0.71	1.02	IV. 3	21.632	38 45.01	5.28	5.44	10 23.92	49 15.73
88	10		48	5	22				12 22.13	0.70	0.96	IV. 3	38.056	21 34.57	5.24	2.63	12 23.79	32 2.44
89	7			5	22	39.6			13 22.16	0.69	1.00	IV. 3	28.900	31 8.95	5.21	4.20	13 23.85	41 38.36
90	8		40	57.2	14	37.5			15 14.27	0.68	0.96	IV. 4	43.548	15 41.07	5.17	1.71	15 15.91	26 7.95
91	8		0	17	34	51			19 34.13	0.65	0.95	IV. 5	51.502	7 22.79	5.06	0.37	19 35.73	17 48.22
92	9			27	44				23 44.06	0.62	0.98	IV. 4	46.630	12 27.38	4.99	1.19	23 45.66	22 53.56
93	10				52				24 51.88	0.61	1.07	2	25.145	34 59.25	4.97	4.84	24 53.56	45 29.06
94	7		30	47.2	5	23			26 4.86	0.60	1.06	IV. 3	29.222	30 48.94	4.94	4.15	26 6.52	41 18.03
95	8		24	40.5	58				29 57.95	0.57	1.08	IV. 3	28.214	31 52.18	4.87	4.32	29 59.60	25 42 21.37
96	10					32.3	49.5		30 15.10	0.57	1.17	V. 2	8.379	52 30.96	4.87	7.71	30 16.84	26 3 3.54
97	10		45						35 19.33	0.54	1.01	· 4	52.242	6 34.38	4.80	0.25	35 20.88	25 16 59.43
98	8				7	24.2	41.3		36 7.06	0.53	1.08	IV. 3	34.500	25 17.77	4.79	3.24	36 8.67	35 45.80
99	9		2	19	36				39 36.16	0.51	1.02	IV. 5	51.620	8 18.06	4.74	0.35	39 37.69	18 43.15
100	6		19.5	37	54	11	28		44 53.93	0.47	1.16	IV. 3	21.680	38 41.93	4.71	5.43	44 55.56	49 12.07
101	5.6		10	27.2	44	2			48 44.37	0.44	1.12	IV. 3	35.830	23 54.13	4.68	3.01	48 45.93	34 21.82
102	6		26	43	0				51 0.14	0.43	1.12	IV. 4	41.023	18 19.27	4.67	2.14	51 1.69	28 46.08
103	9						21		52 46.91	0.42	1.13	· 4	37.499	22 0.80	4.67	2.73	52 48.46	32 28.20
104	7		53.5	10	27	44			56 27.22	0.39	1.13	IV. 4	44.203	14 59.79	4.66	1.60	56 28.74	25 26.05
105	8		0	17					58 34.29	0.38	1.11	· 5	49.102	9 52.95	4.65	0.76	58 35.78	20 18.36
106	7				58.5	15.8	32		23 58 58.35	+0.38	+1.14	IV. 4	42.532	−16 44.68	−4.65	−1.88	23 58 59.87	−25 27 11.21

ZONE 209. NOVEMBER 28. C. $D_o = -27° 3' 0''$.

No.	Mag.	I	II	III	IV	V	VI	VII	T	a_1	a_2	Micr.	r	i	d_1	d_2	Mean Right Ascension 1850.0	Mean Declination 1850.0
1	10			37.2	45	12.5			0 27 12.31	−8.79	−0.47	III. 3	28.281	−31 45.04	−1.16	−10.31	0 27 3.05	−27 34 59.51
2	10					43.5			27 43.35	8.80	0.46	IV. 3	28.954	31 5.62	1.15	10.18	27 34.09	34 16.95
3	9				20.8	38.2			28 20.69	8.80	0.56	V. 3	22.538	37 48.04	1.14	11.35	28 11.33	41 0.53
4	9						30		28 55.35	8.81	0.46	VI. 3	28.051	32 1.84	1.13	10.35	28 46.08	35 13.32
5	10					57.3			31 57.18	8.84	0.15	IV. 5	47.326	11 44.95	1.11	6.91	31 48.19	14 52.07
6	9					58	15.1		32 40.53	8.85	0.45	V. 3	32.617	27 15.66	1.11	9.53	32 31.23	30 26.32
7	10					12.8			33 55.32	8.86	0.53	V. 3	23.689	36 35.72	1.10	11.15	33 45.93	39 47.97
8	9			26.2	42.8	0			35 42.98	8.88	0.33	IV. 3	35.758	23 58.71	1.09	8.98	35 33.77	27 8.78
9	8.9		52	9.2	26.5	44.0			37 9.27	8.89	0.23	IV. 4	41.790	17 31.05	1.08	7.90	37 0.15	20 40.03
10	9	54.3	11.8	29	46.6	4.1			40 29.19	8.93	0.64	IV. 2	16.007	44 32.26	1.06	12.52	40 19.62	47 45.84
11	8.9				35.8	54			41 18.92	8.93	0.10	V. 5	50.652	8 16.06	1.06	6.34	41 9.89	11 23.48
12	9		32.8	50.3	7.3	24.9	42.3		45 7.59	8.97	0.11	IV. 5	49.237	9 44.99	1.06	6.57	44 58.51	12 52.62
13	9.10			12.2	29.2	46.5			46 29.34	8.98	0.16	IV. 5	46.128	13 0.06	1.07	7.13	46 20.20	16 8.28
14	9		22	39.5	56.3				48 56.71	9.01	0.07	III. 5	52.274	6 34.19	1.07	6.01	48 47.63	9 41.27
15	9		35.4	52.8	10.2				51 10.32	9.03	0.73	III. 2	9.844	50 58.77	1.08	13.64	51 0.56	54 13.49
16	10				32.2	49.5			51 32.09	9.03	0.32	V. 3	35.806	23 55.45	1.08	8.97	51 22.74	27 5.50
17	10					19			54 18.90	9.06	0.57	IV. 2	20.419	39 55.80	1.10	11.73	54 9.27	43 8.63
18	10			5.7		39.3			0 55 39.97	−9.07	−0.65	II. 2	15.825	−44 42.92	−1.11	−12.56	0 55 30.25	−27 47 56.59

CORRECTIONS.

Date	Corr. of Clock.	Hourly rate.	m	n	ϵ	Zenith Point.	Mic. Co.
1848. Nov. 25.						359 59 57.23	30.0131

INSTRUMENT READINGS.

Date	A.	B.	C.	D.	E.	F.	Mean.	Barom.	At.	Ex.	U.	L.	I.
Zone 209 1848, Nov. 28, 0 25	76 24 58.7	61.5	68.2	57.6	56.4	45.7	58.52	30.255	45.2	33.4	43.8	40.5	47.5
0 40										32.7			
1 20										32.9			
1 25								30.246	42.		37.		
1 35	58.7	61.3	68.5	57.4	55.2	48.6	58.28					42.5	
1 50										32.7			
2 0								30.252	41.	32.2			
2 20										32.			
2 30	58.1	62.1	68.2	58.4	55.1	48.0	58.32	30.242	40.5	30.1	41.5	37.2	

REMARKS.

(208) 94. Time of transit over T. IV assumed as 5ˢ instead of 0ˢ.5.

(208) 99. Micrometer reading assumed as 50ʳ.620 instead of 51ʳ.620.

External thermometer assumed as 31°.9.

Zone 209. November 28. C. $D_0 = -27°\ 3'\ 0''$—Continued.

No.	Mag.	I.	II.	III.	IV.	V.	VI.	VII.
19	9.10	..	..	..	7.7	25.3	42.6	..
20	9	..	..	12.7	29.9	47.3	..	..
21	9	..	..	..	..	0.3	..	..
22	8.9	..	..	..	..	8.8	26.8	..
23	9	..	..	..	14.	..	19.2	..
24	9	..	2.	..	36.8	54.	..	..
25	9	..	..	..	9.8	27.	44.3	..
26	9.10	..	..	21.2	38.2	..	..	..
27	9	..	..	..	..	29.7	..	..
28	7	..	..	..	..	..	17.2	..
29	9	..	..	17.4	..	52.3	..	..
30	9	..	..	28.3	..	3.2	..	..
31	10	..	..	..	..	..	31.7	..
32	9	..	..	0.2	17.3	35.	52.3	..
33	7.8	..	32.9	50.6	8.	25.3	42.4	..
34	8.9	..	33.3	51.	8.3	26.	43.5	..
35	9.10	..	..	3.3	..	..	..	..
36	9	..	..	..	26.8	..	1.5	..
37	10	..	..	..	..	..	2.6	..
38	9	..	..	42.3	0.3	..	..	..
39	9.10	..	..	57.2	..	..	..	..
40	9	..	..	..	..	43.2	..	..
41	8.9	..	..	..	..	..	19.8	..
42	9	..	..	..	53.2	10.5	27.5	..
43	9.10	..	..	..	..	6.8	..	..
44	9	..	..	..	..	..	42.5	..
45	9	..	12.3	..	16.5	34.3	..	..
46	10	..	..	..	..	8.2	..	..
47	10	..	..	..	..	10.2	..	..
48	9	..	..	..	56.8	..	31.3	..
49	9	..	56.	13.2	30.7	..	..	..
50	10	..	..	..	..	..	57.7	..
51	9	..	..	..	..	..	17.	..
52	9	..	..	..	..	..	51.8	..
53	9	..	..	..	..	..	46.2	..
54	7.8	..	..	..	..	..	..	..
55	8	..	20.3	37.9	55.2	12.5	29.5	..
56	9.10	..	..	..	..	55.2	12.2	..
57	9.10	..	..	..	..	12.5	..	..
58	9.10	..	..	44.2	..	19.	..	..
59	10	..	..	..	26.8	13.6	..	..
60	10	..	..	..	9.1	..	..	..
61	9	..	..	6.5	23.9	41.7	18.5	..
62	9	..	..	..	40.7	..	16.3	..
63	8	..	37.5	45.3	2.5	19.0	37.1	..
64	8.9	..	..	13.2	30.5	18.	..	..
65	9	..	..	..	..	8.3	25.2	..
66	7	59.8	17.3	35.	51.0	9.3	26.3	..
67	9	..	37.2	55.1	12.2	29.8	17.3	..

No.	T. (h. m. s.)	a_1 (s.)	a_2 (s.)	MICROMETER		r.	i (' ")	d_1 (")	d_2 (")	Mean Right Ascension, 1850.0 (h. m. s.)	Mean Declination, 1850.0 (° ' ")
19	0 56 7.71	−9.07	−0.74	V.	2	9.175	51 40.98	−1.11	−13.76	0 55 57.00	−27 54 55.85
20	58 29.58	9.10	0.60	IV.	2	18.198	42 14.99	1.13	12.12	58 19.88	45 28.24
21	58 42.92	9.10	0.33	V.	3	31.951	24 49.16	1.13	9.11	58 33.49	27 59.40
22	0 58 51.78	9.10	0.39	V.	3	31.165	28 46.85	1.13	9.79	0 58 42.29	31 57.77
23	1 0 44.19	9.12	0.63	VI.	2	16.369	44 9.93	1.15	12.48	1 0 34.44	47 23.56
24	2 36.72	9.13	0.54	IV.	3	22.595	37 44.59	1.18	11.34	2 27.05	40 57.11
25	5 9.69	9.16	0.01	V.	5	55.402	3 14.61	1.21	5.46	5 0.52	6 21.48
26	10 38.42	9.21	0.64	III.	2	15.466	45 6.07	1.29	12.64	10 28.57	48 20.00
27	11 12.22	9.21	0.49	V.	3	24.426	35 49.68	1.30	11.02	11 2.52	39 2.00
28	11 42.54	9.22	0.17	VI.	5	41.291	14 55.33	1.31	7.44	11 33.15	18 4.08
29	13 34.86	9.24	0.38	IV.	3	31.059	28 53.62	1.35	9.81	13 25.24	32 4.78
30	14 45.78	9.25	0.32	V.	3	35.741	23 59.78	1.37	8.97	14 36.21	27 10.12
31	14 57.06	9.25	0.35	VI.	5	33.415	26 25.42	1.36	9.39	14 47.46	29 36.19
32	18 34.96	9.28	0.11	IV.	3	47.770	11 16.80	1.46	6.81	18 25.57	14 25.07
33	21 7.66	9.31	0.71	IV.	2	10.564	50 13.72	1.52	13.52	20 57.84	53 26.76
34	23 8.44	9.32	0.59	IV.	3	18.785	41 38.12	1.57	12.04	22 58.53	44 51.73
35	25 20.73	9.34	0.43	III.	3	28.372	31 42.38	1.64	10.31	25 10.96	34 54.33
36	25 26.76	9.34	0.19	VI.	3	43.097	16 10.21	1.64	7.66	25 17.23	19 19.51
37	25 27.94	9.34	0.19	VI.	5	43.187	16 4.63	1.64	7.64	25 18.41	19 13.91
38	35 0.03	9.43	0.02	III.	5	53.023	5 46.97	1.94	5.89	31 50.58	8 54.80
39	38 14.69	9.46	−0.21	III.	4	41.578	17 44.18	2.06	7.93	38 5.02	20 54.17
40	38 25.97	9.46	+0.04	V.	5	55.999	3 43.04	2.06	5.54	38 16.55	6 50.64
41	38 45.10	9.46	−0.01	VI.	5	53.921	5 53.33	2.07	5.07	38 35.63	9 1.31
42	40 53.01	9.48	0.34	V.	3	33.691	26 8.23	2.16	9.34	40 43.19	29 19.73
43	41 49.49	9.49	0.17	V.	4	44.146	15 3.49	2.19	7.47	41 39.85	18 13.15
44	43 7.78	9.50	0.58	VI.	2	18.408	42 2.20	2.25	12.11	42 57.70	45 16.56
45	45 16.82	9.52	0.67	IV.	2	12.597	48 6.24	2.34	13.15	45 6.63	51 21.73
46	45 50.89	9.53	0.17	V.	5	43.715	15 31.48	2.36	7.54	45 41.19	18 41.38
47	45 52.86	9.53	0.19	V.	5	42.265	17 2.63	2.36	7.81	45 43.16	20 12.80
48	48 56.66	9.55	0.10	VI.	5	48.541	10 28.55	2.49	6.65	48 47.01	13 37.72
49	50 30.72	9.56	0.22	III.	4	39.815	19 34.69	2.56	8.24	50 20.94	22 45.49
50	50 22.37	9.56	0.37	VI.	3	30.472	29 30.07	2.55	9.91	50 12.44	32 42.53
51	52 12.26	9.58	0.60	VI.	2	16.544	43 58.91	2.60	12.45	51 2.08	47 13.96
52	52 17.17	9.58	..	VI.	3	..	..	2.64	..	52	..
53	53 11.53	9.59	0.08	VI.	5	48.875	10 7.39	2.69	6.62	53 1.86	13 16.70
54	53	..	..	VII.	5	52.202	6 38.30	2.69	6.03	53	9 47.11
55	55 55.12	9.61	0.30	IV.	3	34.948	24 49.48	2.82	9.11	55 45.21	28 1.41
56	56 37.68	9.61	0.36	V.	3	31.281	28 39.63	2.86	9.77	56 27.71	31 52.26
57	57 55.18	9.63	0.17	V.	4	42.921	16 20.26	2.92	7.69	57 45.38	19 30.87
58	1 59 1.60	9.64	0.37	IV.	3	30.536	29 26.37	2.98	9.91	1 58 51.59	32 39.26
59	2 1 26.48	9.65	0.55	V.	2	19.154	41 15.15	3.11	11.99	2 1 16.20	44 30.25
60	3 9.02	9.67	0.62	IV.	2	15.017	45 34.36	3.20	12.73	2 58.73	48 50.29
61	4 23.91	9.68	0.73	IV.	2	8.372	52 31.21	3.27	13.97	4 13.50	55 48.45
62	5 41.11	9.69	0.19	VI.	4	41.780	17 31.37	3.34	7.88	5 31.23	20 42.59
63	9 2.53	9.72	−0.08	IV.	5	48.817	10 11.15	3.53	6.62	8 52.73	13 21.30
64	12 13.22	9.74	+0.01	V.	5	53.869	4 53.97	3.72	5.72	12 3.49	8 3.41
65	13 50.49	9.76	−0.76	V.	2	6.452	54 32.28	3.83	14.31	13 39.97	57 50.42
66	16 51.99	9.78	0.48	IV.	3	22.032	37 23.33	4.02	11.29	16 41.73	40 38.64
67	2 19 12.32	−9.80	−0.62	IV.	2	14.495	−46 7.27	−4.17	−12.83	2 19 1.90	−27 49 24.27

CORRECTIONS.

Date.	Corr. of Clock.	Hourly rate.	m	n	ε	Zenith Point.	Mic. Co.
1847.	h.	s.	s.	s.	s.	° ' "	r.

INSTRUMENT READINGS.

	Date.	CIRCLE.							Barom.	THERMOM.				
		A.	B.	C.	D.	E.	F.	Mean.		At.	Ex.	U.	I.	I.
Zone 209	1848, Nov. 28, 3 45	76 24 56.4	61.2	66.5	56.5	53.1	45.9	56.60	In. 30.232	39.5	31.5	41.5	37.7	
	4 0			..	..	..	..	..			31.1			
	4 20								30.224	39.	31.			
	4 45		55.3	60.6	66.	56.9	52.9	45.4	56.18	30.220	39.	30.9	40.5	37.2	46.5

REMARKS.

(209) 40. Micrometer reading assumed as 54^r.999, not 55^r.999.

(209) 41. Micrometer reading assumed as 52^r.921, not 53^r.921.

(209) 43. Declination differs from Arg. Z. 266, 29; 327, 32; 334, 4.

(209) 51. Minutes assumed as 51, not 52.

ZONE 209. NOVEMBER 28. C. $D_0 = -27°\ 3'\ 0''$—Continued.

No.	Mag.	I	II	III	IV	V	VI	VII	T. (h. m. s.)	n_1 (s.)	n_2 (s.)	Micr.		r.	i (' ")	d_1 ('')	d_2 ('')	Mean Right Ascension, 1850.0 (h. m. s.)	Mean Declination, 1850.0 (° ' ")
68	9			23.2	40.2	58.3			2 20 40.54	9.81	−0.32	IV.	3	33.326	−26 31.52	−4.26	−9.41	2 20 30.41	−27 29 45.19
69	8.9		24.				1.3	16.6	21 43.98	9.81	+0.04	V.	5	55.482	3 12.89	4.34	5.42	21 34.21	6 22.65
70	9.10		24.	41.7	59.2	16.4			23 58.80	9.83	−0.26	IV.	3	37.627	22 1.49	4.50	8.63	23 48.71	25 14.62
71	8			44.5	2.2	19.5	36.5		26 1.06	9.85	0.47	IV.	3	23.504	36 47.64	4.63	11.19	25 51.64	40 3.46
72	9.10						13.5		26 38.60	9.85	0.72	VI.	2	8.528	52 21.55	4.67	13.94	26 28.12	55 40.16
73	9				33.2				28 33.00	9.87	0.26	IV.	4	37.461	22 2.04	4.80	8.66	28 22.93	25 16.40
74	9				16.2				29 16.07	9.87	0.19	IV.	4	41.327	18 0.30	4.85	7.97	29 6.01	21 13.12
75	9.10						49.2		2 29 31.87	9.88	−0.19	V.	4	41.175	18 9.97	4.87	7.99	2 29 21.80	21 22.83
76	9.10			36.4	53.2	11.2			3 50 53.66	10.37	+0.02	IV.	3	51.055	7 50.73	10.22	7.19	3 50 43.31	11 8.14
77	10			16.2	33.	50.2			52 33.11	10.37	−0.23	IV.	3	35.511	21 14.34	10.38	9.00	52 22.51	27 33.72
78	10				23.7				53 10.64	10.38	0.21	V.	3	37.459	22 11.97	10.45	8.65	53 0.05	25 31.07
79	10				19.2				54 1.60	10.38	0.45	V.	3	21.988	38 22.42	10.53	11.47	53 50.86	41 44.42
80	9						58.		54 23.35	10.38	0.14	VI.	4	41.645	17 40.67	10.57	7.90	54 12.83	20 59.14
81	9		6.7	24.2	41.2				56 41.45	10.39	0.10	III.	3	37.978	21 39.46	10.81	8.55	56 30.87	24 58.72
82	10					7.2			3 56 49.88	10.39	0.13	III.	4	41.953	17 20.52	10.82	7.84	3 56 39.36	20 39.18
83	9.10			44.3	0.3	19.	36.1		4 1 1.24	10.41	0.32	V.	3	30.928	29 1.52	11.25	9.53	4 0 50.51	32 22.60
84	9.10								1		0.56	VII.	2	14.772	45 49.78	11.25	12.83	1	49 13.86
85	10		32.3		7.5				5 7.20	10.43	−0.02	II.	4	47.536	11 29.76	11.68	6.82	4 56.84	14 48.26
86	10						47.2		5 12.51	10.43	+0.05	VI.	5	53.046	5 45.59	11.69	5.82	5 2.13	9 3.10
87	10					36.2			6 18.83	10.43	−0.22	V.	3	36.182	23 32.04	11.80	8.87	6 8.18	26 52.71
88	10						10.7		6 35.34	10.44	−0.11	VI.	4	43.432	15 48.44	11.83	7.57	6 24.79	19 7.84
89	9.10	18.7			53.2				12 53.34	10.46	+0.10	II.	5	55.968	2 41.81	12.52	5.28	12 42.98	5 59.61
90	9.10						55.		13 20.33	10.46	−0.39	VI.	2	25.245	34 53.04	12.56	10.88	13 9.48	38 16.48
91	9		7.9	25.2	43.2	0.2			20 42.85	10.49	0.36	IV.	3	27.141	32 59.44	13.39	10.54	20 31.98	36 23.37
92	9.10				6.2		40.7		22 6.05	10.50	0.44	V.	3	22.371	37 58.59	13.55	11.41	21 55.11	41 23.55
93	9.10			24.3	42.	59.2			24.47			V.	4	42.435	16 51.13	13.	7.75	(24)	20 11.88
94	9.10	0.2	27.2						27 44.49	10.51	0.60	III.	2	12.346	48 21.71	14.19	13.27	27 33.38	51 49.17
95	10		11.3	28.2					28 28.45	10.51	0.50	III.	2	18.266	42 10.48	14.28	12.17	28 17.44	45 36.93
96	9.10			36.2					29 36.11	10.52	0.53	IV.	2	16.378	44 19.18	14.41	12.51	29 25.00	47 46.10
97	10			38.2					30 35.11	10.53	0.49	IV.	2	18.274	42 10.29	14.53	12.17	30 27.09	45 36.99
98	9								31		0.12	VII.	4	41.432	17 53.91	14.61	7.93	31	21 16.45
99	8.9				7.2	25.	42.3		32 7.44	10.53	0.31	V.	3	29.612	30 24.22	14.70	10.09	31 56.60	33 49.01
100	9						23.6		32 48.93	10.53	0.03	VI.	4	47.606	11 26.37	14.78	6.80	32 38.37	14 47.95
101	9.10				13.8				33 56.33	10.54	0.38	V.	3	24.961	35 15.92	14.91	10.95	33 45.41	38 41.78
102	9.10					22.8			34 48.07	10.54	0.49	VI.	3	18.689	41 49.02	15.02	12.10	34 37.04	45 16.14
103	9	25.3	43.2	0.3					37 0.36	10.54	0.08	III.	4	44.084	15 6.82	15.28	7.45	36 49.74	18 29.55
104	8	49.3	7.5	24.5	42.1	59.3			38 24.56	10.55	0.58	IV.	2	12.651	48 2.78	15.40	13.22	38 13.43	51 31.40
105	9		47.2	4.2					40 4.39	10.55	0.09	III.	4	43.186	16 3.25	15.64	7.61	39 53.75	19 26.50
106	10						5.5		40 30.87	10.55	0.29	VI.	3	30.908	29 2.46	15.69	9.84	40 20.03	32 27.99
107	8.9			22.5	39.5	57.2	14.8		44 39.76	10.56	0.13	IV.	4	41.048	18 17.70	16.19	8.00	44 29.07	21 41.89
108	9					31.3	48.2		4 45 13.60	−10.56	−0.51	V.	2	17.292	−43 12.06	−16.25	−12.35	4 45 2.53	−27 46 40.66

CORRECTIONS.

Date.	Corr. of Clock.	Hourly rate.	m	n	c	Zenith Point.	Mic. Co.
	h.	s.	s.	s.	s.	s.	° ' "	r.
1848. Aug. 18,								

REMARKS.

(209) 92. Transit over T. VI assumed to have been recorded as over T. V.

(209) 104. Times of transit over T.'s IV, V, and VI assumed as 24ˢ.5, 42ˢ.1, and 59ˢ.3, respectively.

INSTRUMENT READINGS.

Date.	CIRCLE.							Barom.	THERMOM.				
	A.	B.	C.	D.	E.	F.	Mean.		At.	Ex.	U.	L.	I.
1848.	h. m.	° ' "					''	in.	°	°	°	°	°

ZONE 210. NOVEMBER 28. C. $D_0 = -28°\ 18'\ 40''$.

No.	Mag.	I.	II.	III.	IV.	V.	VI.	VII.	T.	a_1	a_2
									h. m. s.	s.	s.
1	8			9.3		44.7	2.1		6 1 26.94	− 9.69	−0.91
2	9						58.1		2 23.01	9.69	0.12
3	9.10			57.					5 14.75	9.68	0.19
4	9				27.2	45.			5 27.28	9.68	0.33
5	8.9					35.	52.5		7 17.48	9.68	0.19
6	8.9				28.2				15 53.03	9.67	1.03
7	9			15.2		50.2	7.4		21 32.67	9.67	0.37
8	9		48.2	6.3	23.5	41.2			24 23.65	9.66	0.51
9	9		42.7	0.5	18.3	36.1	53.5		26 18.25	9.66	1.27
10	9					6.5			27 48.66	9.65	1.17
11	9						33.2		28 56.00	9.65	1.24
12	8		53.2	11.1	28.5	46.1			30 28.54	9.65	0.75
13	8			4.	21.3	39.3			31 21.55	9.65	0.61
14	9					34.3			32 34.17	9.64	0.99
15	9					0.7			32 43.15	9.64	0.72
16	10							39.5	33 4.44	9.64	0.68
17	9			47.	4.5	22.5			35 4.64	9.64	0.80
18	8		51.5	9.4		44.2			37 26.82	9.63	1.27
19	9.10				31.2	48.5			37 30.88	9.63	1.12
20	9			48.5	6.8	23.7			39 6.10	9.63	0.87
21	8.9		58.2	16.	33.5				40 15.90	9.63	0.79
22	9				4.5	22.3	39.6		41 4.50	9.63	1.05
23	9						9.		41 33.91	9.62	0.51
24	9						10.		41 34.91	9.62	0.52
25	9						36.2		43 1.13	9.62	0.74
26	8.9						18.3		43 43.22	9.62	0.62
27	9					14.2			45 14.08	9.61	0.70
28	9.10						39.5	57.	45 21.96	9.61	0.73
29	9						50.5		46 33.03	9.61	0.62
30	9			21.2	38.5				48 38.60	9.61	0.99
31	8			15.3	32.5				49 32.64	9.60	1.10
32	9						15.3		49 40.22	9.60	0.67
33	9			10.2	28.5				51 10.56	9.60	0.73
34	3		19.2	37.1	54.4	12.3	29.5		52 54.54	9.59	1.05
35	9		47.2	4.5		39.8			53 22.29	9.59	1.04
36	9.10			21.3					55 38.93	9.58	1.16
37	10				4.3				56 21.96	9.58	1.01
38	10					44.2			56 26.74	9.58	0.69
39	9.10			31.3	10.3				57 49.06	9.58	0.93
40	9						30.5		57 55.46	9.58	1.13
41	9							2.3	58 27.22	9.58	1.27
42	9				46.	3.8			6 59 46.01	9.57	1.21
43	9		22.9	40.5					7 2 58.18	9.56	1.14
44	9					9.5			2 9.46	9.56	1.63
45	9			48.3	6.2				3 5.99	9.56	1.16
46	9					39.			3 21.43	9.56	1.12
47	9					5.3	22.9		4 47.77	9.56	1.16
48	8.9						50.2		4 15.13	9.56	0.86
49	9						22.8		7 4 47.62	− 9.56	−1.56

No.	MICROMETER	i	r.	'	"	d_1	d_2	Mean Right Ascension, 1850.0	Mean Declination, 1850.0
			r.	'	"	"	"	h. m. s.	° ' "
1	IV.	2	12.982	−47	41.96	−1.07	−8.55	6 1 16.34	−29 6 31.58
2	VI.	5	53.015	5	47.48	1.21	0.21	2 13.20	28 24 28.90
3	III.	5	50.795	8	6.78	1.62	0.67	5 4.88	26 49.07
4	V.	4	43.841	15	22.50	1.66	2.11	5 17.27	34 6.27
5	V.	5	51.871	6	59.42	1.93	0.45	7 7.61	28 25 41.80
6	VI.	2	14.369	46	15.36	3.18	−8.26	15 42.33	29 5 6.80
7	IV.	5	49.861	3	51.91	4.03	+0.17	21 22.63	28 22 35.77
8	IV.	4	44.522	14	39.77	4.46	−1.96	24 13.48	28 33 26.19
9	IV.	2	7.619	53	18.29	4.75	9.69	26 7.32	29 12 12.73
10	V.	2	13.563	47	5.85	4.95	8.44	27 37.86	5 59.27
11	VI.	2	10.011	50	48.41	5.15	9.18	28 47.11	29 9 42.77
12	IV.	3	35.636	24	6.43	5.38	3.83	30 16.14	28 42 55.64
13	IV.	4	43.153	16	5.64	5.51	2.25	31 11.29	34 53.40
14	IV.	3	24.570	35	40.40	5.68	6.14	32 23.54	54 32.22
15	V.	5	38.499	20	58.99	5.70	3.23	32 32.79	39 47.92
16	VI.	5	40.607	18	46.69	5.76	2.78	32 54.12	37 35.23
17	IV.	4	35.475	24	7.56	6.06	3.87	34 54.20	28 42 57.49
18	IV.	2	13.026	46	36.46	6.40	8.36	37 15.92	29 5 31.22
19	V.	3	20.761	39	39.37	6.42	6.91	37 20.13	28 58 32.73
20	IV.	3	33.952	25	51.97	6.65	4.17	38 55.60	44 42.79
21	IV.	3	39.052	20	32.06	6.82	3.12	40 5.48	39 22.00
22	V.	3	26.748	33	23.83	6.94	5.60	40 53.82	52 16.46
23	VI.	5	53.721	5	3.15	7.01	0.06	41 23.76	23 50.22
24	VI.	5	52.840	5	58.39	7.01	0.25	41 24.77	24 45.65
25	VI.	3	43.172	16	12.98	7.23	2.25	42 50.77	35 2.46
26	VI.	4	48.719	10	16.38	7.32	1.10	43 32.98	29 4.80
27	IV.	4	45.585	13	14.02	7.55	1.70	45 3.77	32 3.27
28	V.	4	44.556	14	38.03	7.56	1.96	45 11.62	33 27.55
29	V.	5	50.372	8	33.78	7.75	0.77	46 22.80	27 22.30
30	III.	3	33.046	26	48.95	8.04	4.37	48 28.00	45 41.36
31	III.	3	28.178	31	54.44	8.16	5.39	49 21.94	50 47.99
32	VI.	5	49.901	9	2.92	8.18	0.88	49 29.95	27 51.98
33	V.	5	47.578	11	29.44	8.41	1.35	51 0.23	30 19.20
34	IV.	3	32.481	27	24.46	8.60	4.49	52 43.90	46 17.61
35	IV.	3	33.152	26	42.36	8.72	4.34	53 11.66	45 35.42
36	III.	3	28.266	31	49.98	9.04	5.37	55 28.19	50 43.39
37	III.	3	36.296	23	25.14	9.14	3.69	56 11.37	42 17.97
38	V.	5	51.891	6	58.17	9.15	0.46	56 16.47	25 47.78
39	III.	5	40.931	18	25.98	9.35	2.72	57 38.57	37 18.05
40	VI.	3	30.847	29	6.30	9.37	4.83	57 44.75	48 0.50
41	VI.	3	25.078	34	5.61	9.41	5.81	58 16.37	53 0.89
42	V.	3	28.255	31	49.42	9.63	5.37	6 59 35.23	50 44.42
43	III.	3	33.216	26	38.49	10.09	4.33	7 2 47.48	28 45 32.91
44	IV.	2	7.044	52	57.86	9.97	9.65	1 58.27	29 11 57.48
45	III.	3	31.864	28	3.05	10.10	4.61	2 55.27	28 46 57.76
46	V.	3	35.797	23	56.05	10.14	3.79	3 10.75	42 49.98
47	V.	3	33.			10.34		4 37.05	
48	VI.	5	47.457	11	36.60	10.27	1.38	4 4.71	28 30 28.25
49	VI.	2	13.272	−47	24.15	−10.34	−8.52	7 4 36.50	−29 6 23.01

CORRECTIONS.

Date.	Corr. of Clock.	Hourly rate.	m	n	c	Zenith Point.	Mic. Co.
1848.	h.	s.	s.	s.	s.	s.	° ' "	r.

INSTRUMENT READINGS.

	Date.		CIRCLE.							Barom.	THERMOM.				
			A.	B.	C.	D.	E.	F.	Mean.		At.	Ex.	U.	L.	I.
Zone 210	1848. Nov. 28,	h. m.	° ' "						"	in.	°	°	°	°	°
		6 0	77 39 56.	61.9	66.9	57.4	53.7	46.9	57.13	30.210	38.5	31.1	40.3	35.2	
		6 20										31.2			
		6 40										30.5			
		7 0										30.7			
		7 20								30.206	37.8				
		7 40	55.8	62.1	67.1	57.1	54.2	46.5	57.13	30.200	37.5	31.2	40.	35.7	45.

REMARKS.

(210) 7. Micrometer reading assumed as 54ʳ.861, not 49ʳ.861.

(210) 18. Micrometer reading assumed as 14ʳ.026, not 13ʳ.026.

(210) 41. Micrometer reading assumed as 26ʳ.078, not 25ʳ.078.

(210) 43. Minutes probably 1, not 2. See Transit Z., 1849, February 19.

ZONE 210. NOVEMBER 23. C. $D_a = -28°\ 18'\ 40''$—Continued.

No.	Mag.	I.	II.	III.	IV.	V.	VI.	VII.
50	9				8.5			
51	8.9		8.3	25.3	43.2			
52	8.9		34.9	52.3	9.8			
53	8			56.3	13.8	31.5		
54	8				37.5	55.5		
55	8.9				21.5			
56	8			8.2	25.2	43.4		
57	9				6.3	24.		
58	9						10.2	
59	8.9			50.2				
60	3				22.	38.3	56.2	
61	10					41.3		
62	10						13.3	
63	9.10					11.2		
64	7.8			55.3	12.9			
65	9.10					55.3		
66	8						29.	
67	10						17.5	
68	9					55.2	12.2	
69	9						16.5	
70	10						37.2	
71	9.10		23.2	40.9				
72	9.10				21.2			
73	9						18.5	
74	9					27.2		
75	9						57.3	
76	10						44.2	
77	9					35.	52.5	
78	9				38.2			
79	8.9						8.2	
80	9						42.3	
81	9					29.3		
82	9.10		27.2			2.5		
83	5		23.	40.5	57.7	15.5		
84	9					37.2	54.7	
85	9						30.7	
86	9			10.5	28.1	36.		

No.	T. (h. m. s.)	a₁ (s.)	a₂ (s.)	MICROMETER		r.	i	d₁	d	Mean Right Ascension, 1850.0 (h. m. s.)	Mean Declination, 1850.0 (° ′ ″)
50	7 6 8.36	9.55	−1.19	IV.	3	33.264	−26 35.39	−10.53	−4.32	7 5 57.62	−28 45 30.24
51	7 43.24	9.55	1.39	III.	3	23.449	36 51.14	10.76	6.38	7 32.30	55 48.28
52	9 9.95	9.54	1.14	III.	4	36.085	23 28.84	10.96	3.74	8 59.27	42 23.54
53	11 31.47	9.53	1.24	III.	3	32.145	27 45.55	11.29	4.55	11 20.70	46 41.39
54	11 37.60	9.53	1.35	V.	3	27.215	32 54.67	11.30	5.59	11 26.72	51 51.56
55	12 21.37	9.53	1.13	IV.	4	38.038	21 26.61	11.41	3.33	12 10.71	40 21.35
56	13 25.57	9.52	1.22	IV.	3	34.337	25 28.07	11.56	4.10	13 14.83	44 23.73
57	14 6.28	9.52	1.22	V.	3	34.453	25 20.59	11.65	4.07	13 55.54	28 44 16.31
58	14 35.05	9.52	1.60	VI.	2	15.784	44 46.38	11.72	7.99	14 23.93	29 3 46.09
59	18 7.89	9.51	1.56	III.	2	19.316	41 4.62	12.22	7.25	17 56.82	0 4.09
60	18 21.37	9.50	1.59	V.	2	18.594	41 50.28	12.26	7.40	18 10.28	29 0 49.94
61	19 23.50	9.50	1.52	V.	2	22.671	37 34.50	12.46	6.55	19 12.57	28 50 33.45
62	19 38.14	9.50	1.67	VI.	2	15.278	45 18.37	12.43	8.10	19 26.97	29 4 18.90
63	20 53.71	9.49	1.06	V.	5	46.056	13 4.54	12.61	1.67	20 43.16	28 31 58.62
64	22 12.84	9.49	1.43	III.	3	27.849	32 14.96	12.80	5.46	22 1.92	51 13.22
65	22 37.70	9.49	1.36	V.	3	32.026	27 52.70	12.85	4.58	22 26.85	46 50.13
66	22 53.96	9.49	1.40	VI.	3	30.189	29 47.77	12.89	4.96	22 43.07	48 45.62
67	23 42.42	9.48	0.98	VI.	5	51.651	7 13.18	13.01	0.52	23 31.96	26 6.71
68	24 37.42	9.48	1.11	V.	4	45.649	13 29.08	13.13	1.76	24 26.83	32 23.97
69	24 41.43	9.48	1.09	VI.	4	46.475	12 37.42	13.14	1.59	24 30.86	31 32.15
70	26 2.15	9.47	1.47	VI.	3	28.692	31 21.56	13.33	5.28	25 51.21	50 20.17
71	27 58.58	9.47	1.63	III.	3	21.240	39 9.71	13.61	6.84	27 47.48	58 10.16
72	28 21.09	9.46	1.09	IV.	5	48.117	10 55.23	13.66	1.24	28 10.54	28 29 50.13
73	29 0.70	9.46	1.75	V.	2	14.576	46 2.26	13.75	8.25	28 49.49	29 5 4.26
74	30 9.43	9.46	1.71	V.	2	17.732	42 44.29	13.91	7.58	29 58.26	29 1 45.78
75	30 22.21	9.45	1.59	VI.	3	24.164	36 5.68	13.93	6.23	30 11.17	28 55 5.84
76	31 9.16	9.45	1.48	VI.	3	29.715	30 17.38	14.05	5.06	30 58.23	49 16.49
77	32 17.48	9.45	1.02	V.	5	53.698	5 4.78	14.20	0.09	32 7.01	23 59.07
78	33 38.07	9.44	1.61	IV.	3	25.457	34 45.19	14.38	5.96	33 27.02	53 45.53
79	33 50.56	9.44	1.55	V.	3	28.078	32 0.46	14.41	5.41	33 39.57	51 0.28
80	34 7.21	9.44	1.63	VI.	3	24.041	36 13.33	14.45	6.25	33 56.14	55 14.03
81	35 11.78	9.43	1.28	V.	4	42.112	17 11.16	14.60	2.48	35 1.07	36 8.24
82	37 2.44	9.42	1.08	II.	5	53.114	5 41.07	14.86	0.21	36 51.94	24 36.14
83	37 58.02	9.42	1.31	IV.	3	42.396	17 2.38	14.99	2.42	37 47.29	35 59.73
84	38 19.67	9.42	1.19	V.	4	47.995	11 1.83	15.03	1.26	38 9.06	29 58.12
85	39 13.20	9.41	1.28	V.	4	44.674	14 30.29	15.16	1.05	39 2.51	33 27.40
86	7 40 28.23	−9.41	−1.28	IV.	4	45.235	−13 55.02	−15.33	−1.85	7 40 17.54	−28 32 52.20

CORRECTIONS.

Date.	Corr. of Clock.	Hourly rate.	m	n	c	Zenith Point,	Mic. Co.
1848.	h. s.	s.	s.	s.	s.	° ′ ″	r.

REMARKS.

(210) 86. Time of transit over T. V assumed as 46ˢ instead of 36ˢ.0.

INSTRUMENT READINGS.

Date.	CIRCLE							Barom.	THERMOM.				
	A.	B.	C.	D.	E.	F.	Mean.	At.	Ex.	U.	L.	I.	
1848. h. m.	° ′ ″						″	in.	°	°	°	°	°

ZONE 211. DECEMBER 2. C. $D_0 = -22°\,2'\,40''$.

No.	Mag.	I.	II.	III.	IV.	V.	VI.	VII.	T.	a_1	a_2	MICROMETER.	i	d_1	d_2	Mean Right Ascension, 1850.0	Mean Declination, 1850.0
									h. m. s.	s.	s.	r. ° ' "		"	"	h. m. s.	° ' "
1	9		24.	41.1	57.2	14.3	30.5		23 20 57.48	−8.75	−0.69	IV. 5 44.366	−14 50.75	−3.44	−1.84	23 20 48.04	−22 17 36.03
2	8					48.2	6.1		22 32.09	8.76	0.93	V. 2 20.523	39 49.30	3.38	5.44	22 22.40	42 38.18
3	8						21.3		22 47.95	8.76	0.99	VI. 2 13.442	47 13.56	3.37	6.52	22 38.20	50 3.45
4	8			10.3	26.3	43.8	0.3		24 26.80	8.78	0.88	IV. 3 25.172	35 3.02	3.29	4.73	24 17.14	37 51.04
5	8			51.3	8.8	25.4	42.1		25 8.56	8.78	0.81	IV. 3 31.794	28 7.38	3.27	3.73	25 58.97	30 54.38
6	10				18.5				27 18.38	8.80	0.86	IV. 3 26.715	33 26.09	3.18	4.51	27 8.72	36 13.78
7	10						53.		27 19.71	8.80	0.90	VI. 3 21.985	38 22.36	3.16	5.22	27 10.01	41 10.76
8	9.10						49.		28 15.75	8.81	0.79	VI. 3 33.288	25 30.70	3.13	3.51	28 6.15	28 17.34
9	9.10				22.	38.8			29 21.98	8.82	0.80	V. 3 32.298	27 35.83	3.09	3.66	29 12.36	30 22.59
10	9		14.3	31.2	48.				30 47.87	8.83	0.80	III. 3 32.547	27 20.39	3.04	3.62	30 38.24	30 7.05
11	8			19.7	36.3	53.2	9.2		31 36.24	8.84	0.93	IV. 2 17.989	42 27.97	3.01	5.83	31 26.47	45 16.81
12	8.9		12.2	28.3	45.3	2.2	18.3		35 45.29	8.89	0.82	IV. 3 30.440	29 32.58	2.86	3.93	35 35.59	32 19.37
13	9.10		16.5		50.3				37 50.14	8.90	0.89	II. 3 22.525	37 49.06	2.79	5.14	37 40.35	40 36.99
14	9.10		59.3		33.				39 32.85	8.92	0.71	II. 5 41.548	17 47.26	2.72	2.26	39 23.22	20 32.21
15	9					54.8	11.2		39 38.00	8.92	0.85	V. 3 26.552	33 36.25	2.72	4.53	39 28.23	36 23.50
16	7.8	0.3	17.	33.8	50.3	6.9	23.4		41 50.32	8.94	0.86	IV. 3 25.616	24 7.60	2.65	4.67	41 40.52	26 54.92
17	9			4.3		38.			45 21.24	8.97	0.69	IV. 4 43.181	16 3.87	2.54	2.01	45 11.58	18 48.42
18	10				9.3	26.5			46 9.50	8.98	0.77	V. 3 35.271	24 21.62	2.52	3.20	45 59.75	27 7.34
19	8			19.5	36.2				47 36.22	8.99	0.64	III. 4 48.929	10 2.62	2.47	1.15	47 26.59	12 46.24
20	8				33.5	50.6	7.3		48 33.77	9.00	0.97	V. 2 13.843	46 48.09	2.44	6.46	48 23.80	49 36.99
21	9.10					35.3			49 22.04	9.01	0.77	VI. 4 35.076	24 32.78	2.42	3.23	49 12.26	27 18.43
22	9					12.3	29.		49 55.66	9.01	0.78	V. 3 33.742	26 5.03	2.40	3.44	49 45.89	28 50.87
23	9					52.2			50 35.37	9.02	0.92	V. 2 19.044	41 21.99	2.39	5.68	50 25.43	14 10.06
24	9.10						25.4		50 52.09	9.02	0.92	VI. 3 19.138	41 16.28	2.38	5.66	50 42.15	44 4.32
25	9				42.2		15.3		53 42.04	9.05	0.65	VI. 5 47.444	11 37.47	2.32	1.37	53 32.34	14 21.16
26	9			56.3		30.2			55 13.22	9.06	0.92	IV. 2 19.	41	2.25	3.24	55 3.24	
27	8.9			33.2	49.8	6.3	23.		57 49.79	9.08	0.60	IV. 5 52.551	6 16.86	2.21	0.62	57 40.11	8 59.69
28	9.10				1.2				59 1.68	9.10	0.71	IV. 4 41.793	17 30.87	2.18	2.22	58 51.27	20 15.27
29	9					48.2	5.		23 59 31.57	9.10	0.88	V. 3 23.216	37 5.51	2.17	5.04	23 59 21.59	39 52.72
30	8.9			32.3	49.2	6.2			0 0 49.20	9.11	0.89	IV. 3 22.685	37 38.90	2.15	5.12	0 0 39.20	40 26.17
31	8						28.		0 54.70	9.11	0.65	VI. 5 47.092	11 59.44	2.15	1.43	0 44.94	14 43.02
32	8.9				6.5		39.3		2 6.19	9.12	0.63	VI. 5 48.718	10 17.37	2.14	1.18	1 56.44	13 0.69
33	7.8			2.3	18.2	35.2	52.5		3 18.69	9.14	0.94	IV. 2 17.232	43 15.64	2.13	5.95	3 8.60	46 3.72
34	9			14.2	0.3	17.3			5 0.55	9.15	1.01	IV. 2 9.778	51 2.87	2.11	7.09	4 50.39	53 52.07
35	9.10		19.2	36.3					6 52.90	9.17	0.74	III. 4 37.836	31 38.89	2.08	2.82	6 42.99	24 23.79
36	9.10		38.2	54.3	11.3				9 11.33	9.19	0.73	III. 4 39.216	20 12.48	2.06	2.61	9 1.41	22 57.15
37	9.10		38.2	54.3	11.3				9 11.32	9.19	0.76	III. 4 36.207	23 21.31	2.06	3.06	9 1.37	26 6.43
38	8			20.3	36.3	53.5	10.5		10 36.80	9.20	0.88	IV. 3 23.191	37 7.28	2.05	5.04	10 26.72	39 54.37
39	8		36.5	52.3	9.4	26.3	43.1		12 9.55	9.22	0.87	IV. 3 24.613	35 32.62	2.04	4.83	11 59.46	38 19.49
40	8		46.2	3.2	19.2		53.		18 19.62	9.27	0.77	IV. 3 34.732	25 3.10	2.02	3.29	18 9.58	27 48.41
41	6				53.8				18 53.66	9.28	0.80	IV. 3 32.394	27 29.99	2.01	3.64	18 43.58	30 15.64
42	9				16.				18		0.73	. 4 39.348	20 4.50	2.	2.59		22 49.09
43	9		15.3	32.2	49.				22 48.90	9.31	0.68	III. 4 44.313	14 52.57	2.03	1.84	22 38.91	17 36.44
44	8		17.2	34.1	50.9		23.5		23 50.66	9.32	0.62	IV. 5 49.846	8 3.81	2.04	0.87	23 40.72	10 46.72
45	9			40.3	57.	13.7	30.3		25 56.97	9.34	0.89	IV. 2 22.239	38 1.66	2.05	5.19	25 46.74	40 48.90
46	9					21.3	38.3		28 4.81	9.36	0.82	V. 3 28.525	71 32.48	2.07	4.23	27 54.63	34 18.78
47	9						26.		28 52.69	9.37	0.64	VI. 5 48.238	10 47.64	2.08	1.26	28 42.68	13 30.98
48	9.10			5.3		38.3			32 21.86	9.40	0.73	IV. 3 39.156	21 28.36	2.10	2.77	32 11.73	24 13.23
49	8.9		0.3	17.5	33.8		7.2		0 35 33.92	−9.43	−0.77	IV. 3 33.723	−26 6.41	−2.14	−3.44	0 35 23.72	−22 28 51.99

CORRECTIONS.

Date.	Corr. of Clock.	Hourly rate.	m	n	c	Zenith Point.	Mic. Co.
	h.	s.	s.	s.	s.	° ' "	r.
1848. Dec. 2						359 59 55.94	30.0086

INSTRUMENT READINGS.

Date.	CIRCLE. A.	B.	C.	D.	E.	F.	Mean.	Barom.	THERMOM. At.	Ex.	U.	L.	I.
	° ' "						"	in.	°	°	°	°	°
Zone 211 1848. Dec. 2, 23 20	71 24 63.2	65.2	70.3	58.8	61.1	55.7	62.38	29.858	53.2	48.	53.	50.8	
23 40								29.864	53.5	46.9			
0 0	62.6	65.6	70.2	59.3	60.8	54.7	62.20	29.868	52.	44.8			
0 20											44.3	50.8	50.0
0 40								29.872	51.5	41.6			
1 0								29.876	50.	40.6			
1 20	62.6	66.2	69.7	60.5	60.1	55.1	62.37	29.878	49.2	39.8	47.8	47.7	50.

REMARKS.

(211) 8. Micrometer reading assumed as 34ʳ.288 instead of 33ʳ.288.

(211) 16. Micrometer reading assumed as 35ʳ.616 instead of 25ʳ.616.

(211) 21. Right ascension differs 20ˢ.8 from Arg. Z. 269, 24.

(211) 44. Micrometer reading assumed as 50ʳ.846, not 49ʳ.846.

(211) 49. Transit over T. VI assumed to have been recorded as over T. V.

[(211) 42. Precedes 41. 2ˢ.]

ZONE 211. DECEMBER 2. C. D₀ = −22° 2′ 40″ —Continued.

No.	Mag.	I.	II.	III.	IV.	V.	VI.	VII.	T. (h m s)	a_1 (s)	a_2 (s)	MICROMETER		$r.$	i (′ ″)	d_1 (″)	d_9 (″)	Mean R.A. 1850.0 (h m s)	Mean Decl. 1850.0 (° ′ ″)
50	8.9		17.5	34.	7.5	24.			0 36 50.83	−9.44	−0.79	IV.	3	30.965	−28 59.58	2.15	3.85	0 35 40.60	−22 31 45.58
51	9				1.2		34.7		37 1.24	9.45	1.00	VI.	2	9.874	50 57.03	2.16	7.06	36 50.79	53 45.25
52	4				29.3	46.8	3.3		37 29.70	9.45	0.96	V.	2	13.648	47 0.45	2.17	6.50	37 19.29	49 49.12
53	6.7			29.3		3.	19.3		40 46.12	9.47	0.80	IV.	1	30.251	29 44.38	2.21	3.97	40 35.85	32 30.56
54	9.10				3.2		36.3		42 3.04	9.49	0.62	VI.	5	48.702	10 14.55	2.24	1.18	41 52.93	12 57.97
55	8.9						16.2		42 42.82	9.49	1.02	VI.	2	8.475	52 25.00	2.25	7.28	42 32.31	55 14.53
56	9.10				5.2	21.8			44 5.13	9.50	0.66	V.	5	45.455	13 42.46	2.28	1.68	43 54.97	16 26.42
57	7				26.5				45 26.38	9.51	0.64	IV.	5	46.711	12 23.42	2.31	1.49	45 16.23	15 7.22
58	9				42.				46 41.90	9.52	0.56	IV.	5	55.147	3 33.86	2.33	0.22	46 31.82	6 16.41
59	8.9				26.2		0.3		47 26.54	9.53	0.66	VI.	4	44.696	14 28.97	2.35	1.79	47 16.35	17 13.11
60	8					24.2	41.1		48 7.57	9.54	0.91	V.	2	18.473	41 57.99	2.36	5.76	47 57.12	44 46.11
61	8.9		27.5	44.7	1.1	18.3	34.		55 1.16	9.60	0.73	IV.	3	37.411	22 15.17	2.51	2.88	54 50.83	25 0.56
62	8.9		42.3		15.1	31.8	48.		55 15.16	9.60	0.73	IV.	3	37.411	22 15.17	2.51	2.88	55 4.83	25 0.56
63	9	53.1	9.2	26.	42.7				58 42.76	9.63	0.71	III.	3	39.978	19 33.94	2.59	2.49	58 32.42	22 19.02
64	9.10				12.2		45.4		0 59 12.10	9.64	0.76	VI.	3	33.984	25 49.58	2.60	3.40	0 59 1.70	28 35.58
65	9		23.2	40.2	56.7				1 0 56.76	9.65	0.72	III.	3	39.362	20 12.79	2.64	2.59	1 0 46.39	22 58.02
66	7.8		44.		0.8	17.3	34.2	51.	8 17.49	9.71	0.79	IV.	3	31.358	28 34.99	2.78	3.80	8 6.99	31 21.57
67	9.10					22.3	39.2		9 5.79	9.72	0.66	V.	3	45.306	13 51.62	2.80	1.70	8 55.41	16 36.12
68	9						14.?		9 40.74	9.73	0.83	VI.	3	26.608	33 32.43	2.81	4.52	9 30.18	36 19.76
69	9.10			27.2		0.7			12 44.06	9.75	0.64	III.	5	47.207	11 52.23	2.86	1.41	12 33.67	14 36.50
70	9		29.5		2.8				15 2.85	9.77	0.68	II.	4	42.778	16 28.28	2.90	2.08	14 52.40	19 13.26
71	8				21.5	41.	57.3	14.3	15 40.98	9.78	0.62	IV.	5	49.018	9 58.61	2.91	1.14	15 30.58	12 42.66
72	9				52.3		26.5		17 9.38	9.79	0.90	IV.	2	19.657	40 43.41	2.93	5.59	16 58.69	43 31.93
73	8					13.2	30.3	47.2	17 13.54	9.79	0.80	V.	3	30.622	29 20.85	2.93	3.91	17 2.95	32 7.69
74	6.7		26.2	43.	59.5	16.5	33.2		20 59.70	9.82	0.96	IV.	2	14.467	46 9.03	2.99	6.37	20 48.92	48 58.39
75	5.6				18.2	35.2	52.	8.8	1 22 35.23	−9.83	−0.72	IV.	3	37.992	−21 38.52	3.01	2.79	1 22 24.68	−22 24 24.32

ZONE 212. DECEMBER 4. S. D₀ = −20° 47′ 40″.

No.	Mag.	I.	II.	III.	IV.	V.	VI.	VII.	T. (h m s)	a_1 (s)	a_2 (s)	MICROMETER		$r.$	i (′ ″)	d_1 (″)	d_9 (″)	Mean R.A. 1850.0 (h m s)	Mean Decl. 1850.0 (° ′ ″)
1	8			16.	32.	49.			3 15 48.99	−11.93	−2.35	IV.	1	10.278	−50 31.70	1.89	5.87	3 15 34.71	−21 38 19.46
2	10					34.			16 17.23	11.93	2.32		1	11.062	49 42.61	1.93	5.75	16 2.98	37 30.29
3	7			24.	40.				17 40.26	11.94	1.99	IV.	3	20.320	40 7.42	2.04	4.39	17 26.33	27 53.85
4	8			29.	2.				18 45.46	11.94	2.30		1	12.128	48 35.33	2.11	5.59	18 31.22	36 23.03
5	10	59.5		32.5					26 32.54	11.98	1.65	IV.	3	30.299	29 41.43	2.76	2.96	26 18.91	17 27.15
6	10	28.	45.						31 1.43	12.01	1.85		3	24.369	35 53.45	3.14	3.79	30 47.57	23 40.38
7	9	24.5	41.	57.5					32 57.59	12.02	1.24	IV.	4	42.253	17 2.25	3.30	1.22	32 44.33	4 46.77
8	10	27.	44.						35 0.42	12.03	1.39		3	37.676	21 58.41	3.49	1.88	34 47.01	9 43.78
9	9				31.	47.5			36 14.51	12.03	1.13	V.	5	45.258	13 53.53	3.59	0.79	36 1.35	1 38.21
10	8			42.	15.2				37 58.56	12.04	2.25	III.	5	13.569	47 5.03	3.74	5.38	37 44.27	21 34.15
11	7				55.	12.			38 55.21	12.05	1.05	IV.	5	47.052	12 2.09	3.83	0.53	38 42.08	20 59 46.39
12	8					6.			39 33.00	12.05	1.98		1	20.885	30 26.52	3.87	4.31	39 18.97	21 27 14.70
13	6		40.	56.5	13.				42 13.07	12.06	1.80	IV.	3	26.071	34 6.56	4.12	3.56	41 59.21	21 54.24
14	9				14.5	31.			42 57.98	12.07	1.75	V.	3	27.680	32 25.44	4.18	3.32	42 44.16	20 12.94
15	10					45.			44 12.01	12.07	1.30		4	40.551	18 49.33	4.30	1.48	43 58.64	6 35.11
16	10			50.	23.3				46 6.60	12.08	2.31	III.	3	11.368	49 23.11	4.47	5.71	45 52.21	37 13.29
17	9				41.				47 7.99	12.09	1.99	.	3	20.453	39 58.63	4.57	4.37	46 53.91	27 47.57
18	8				49.				48 16.01	12.09	1.32		5	39.490	19 56.73	4.67	1.61	48 2.60	7 43.01
19	9	0.	17.	33.					3 54 33.26	−12.12	−1.34	IV.	4	38.915	−20 31.50	5.26	1.60	3 54 19.80	−21 8 18.45

CORRECTIONS.

Date.	Corr. of Clock.	Hourly rate.	m	n	c	Zenith Point.	Mic. Co.
1848. Dec. 4,	h.	s.	s.	s.	s.	359 59 55.26	30.0057

REMARKS.

(211) 50. Transits over T.'s V and VI assumed to have been recorded as over T.'s IV and V, respectively; and minutes as 35, not 36.

(211) 65. Declination differs 2′ from Arg. Z, 317, 1; micrometer reading probably should be 41ʳ.362.

INSTRUMENT READINGS.

	Date.	CIRCLE							Barom.	THERMOM.				
		A.	B.	C.	D.	E.	F.	Mean.		At.	Ex.	U.	L.	I.
Zone 212	1848 Dec. 4, 3 10	70 9 60.	62.0	67.7	56.2	56.0	50.8	58.78	in. 30.278	50.5	42.5			
	3 20								30.284		42.7			
	3 40								30.282					
	4 0	60.	62.3	67.8	55.8	56.2	50.8	58.82	30.282	50.4	41.0			

[(211) 56. ? + 1ˢ.]

ZONE 212. DECEMBER 4. S. $D_0 = -20°\ 47'\ 40''$—Continued.

No.	Mag.	I.	II.	III.	IV.	V.	VI.	VII.	T. (h. m. s.)	a_1	a_2
20	7	..	..	19.	..	52.	..	..	3 55 35.48	−12.12	−1.95
21	9	..	..	..	..	41.	..	..	56 24.49	12.13	1.35
22	6	..	52.	9.	25.	..	..	..	3 59 25.28	12.14	0.93
23	9	..	29.2	16.	3.	..	..	..	4 2 2.69	−12.15	−2.13

No.	Mag.	MICROMETER		r.	i	d_1	d_2	Mean Right Ascension, 1850.0	Mean Declination, 1850.0
20	7	III.	3	21.698	−38 40.86	− 5.36	− 4.19	3 55 21.41	−21 26 30.41
21	9	.	5	38.698	20 46.38	5.44	− 1.73	56 11.01	21 8 33.55
22	6	IV.	5	51.379	7 30.51	5.72	+ 0.08	3 59 12.21	20 55 16.15
23	9	IV.	1	16.582	−43 56.51	− 5.98	− 4.97	4 1 48.41	−21 31 47.46

ZONE 213. DECEMBER 18. C. $D_0 = -27°\ 40'\ 30''$.

No.	Mag.	I.	II.	III.	IV.	V.	VI.	VII.	T. (h. m. s.)	a_1	a_2
1	8	..	..	57.2	14.5	32.2	49.2	..	2 19 14.60	−11.72	− 0.89
2	8.9	..	..	..	3.5	21.5	38.8	..	21 3.73	11.73	1.52
3	9	..	..	23.2	..	..	15.5	..	22 40.70	11.74	1.26
4	8	..	..	..	..	..	23.5	..	22 49.64	11.75	1.06
5	9	..	31.2	..	..	6.2	..	..	25 6.19	11.77	1.24
6	8	..	33.5	..	..	9.2	..	43.3	25 8.71	11.77	1.32
7	8	..	..	..	..	..	7.3	25.3	25 49.96	11.78	1.68
8	7	..	..	..	27.5	44.8	2.4	..	32 44.84	11.84	1.71
9	9	..	..	..	..	..	..	..	33	..	1.29
10	9	..	36.2	54.7	11.2	28.9	46.2	..	35 11.35	11.86	1.29
11	8.9	..	..	..	..	48.	5.7	23.4	35 48.23	11.86	1.07
12	7.8	..	51.3	..	..	26.3	..	1.5	37 26.44	11.87	1.74
13	6	..	..	..	20.	..	55.5	12.8	43 37.72	11.93	1.76
14	9	..	..	..	55.	12.3	29.9	47.4	45 12.40	11.94	1.36
15	7	..	..	..	..	16.5	34.4	52.3	46 16.79	11.95	1.76
16	9	..	..	..	..	..	36.5	53.8	47 18.80	11.96	1.63
17	9	..	30.3	8.2	25.2	..	..	..	51 25.42	11.99	1.36
18	9	..	..	..	..	38.2	55.3	13.3	51 38.07	11.99	1.42
19	8	..	55.2	13.5	30.5	48.5	..	..	54 30.68	12.02	1.31
20	9	..	..	..	..	3.6	21.3	38.8	55 3.75	12.02	1.13
21	10	..	21.8	..	..	..	..	..	58 56.99	12.06	1.45
22	9	..	..	..	..	20.	38.	55.2	2 59 20.22	12.06	1.32
23	9.10	..	..	..	..	..	..	38.3	3 0 3.45	12.06	1.34
24	7	..	..	..	..	30.3	57.4	15.	1 39.66	12.07	1.52
25	10	..	..	..	..	44.2	..	..	4 44.08	12.10	0.90
26	10	..	..	..	..	55.3	..	30.3	5 55.31	12.11	1.18
27	7	..	..	..	..	11.5	29.4	46.4	7 11.61	12.12	1.17
28	9.10	..	..	35.2	..	10.	..	..	8 52.60	12.13	1.29
29	8.9	..	1.2	..	..	..	11.3	..	16 36.35	12.19	0.69
30	8.9	..	11.2	28.5	46.2	3.5	..	..	16 46.16	12.19	0.77
31	10	..	..	27.2	..	..	..	..	18 44.76	12.20	1.37
32	10	..	..	..	16.3	..	..	..	19 16.21	12.21	1.47
33	8	..	..	..	..	..	3.2	..	19 28.32	12.21	0.72
34	7	..	..	..	..	33.2	50.3	..	20 15.62	12.22	0.76
35	9.10	..	..	..	36.2	53.8	..	..	21 36.23	12.23	0.87
36	9	..	..	..	36.3	54.2	..	..	24 36.36	12.25	1.50
37	10	..	..	..	..	..	1.2	..	25 26.37	12.25	1.17
38	9.10	..	51.8	12.2	29.2	..	..	..	27 29.64	12.27	1.43
39	10	..	..	..	..	3.2	..	..	29 3.06	12.28	1.23
40	9.10	..	..	..	..	23.2	10.8	..	30 23.12	12.29	1.42
41	9.10	..	43.2	..	..	..	..	..	3 32 18.31	−12.30	− 0.91

No.	Mag.	MICROMETER		r.	i	d_1	d_2	Mean Right Ascension, 1850.0	Mean Declination, 1850.0
1	8	IV.	5	50.168	− 8 46.47	− 8.11	− 0.21	2 19 1.99	−27 49 24.79
2	8.9	V.	3	22.893	37 25.28	8.21	5.36	20 50.48	28 18 8.85
3	9	IV.	3	35.697	24 2.54	8.31	2.92	22 27.70	28 4 43.77
4	8	VI.	3	44.078	15 7.76	8.32	1.34	22 35.83	27 55 47.42
5	9	II.	3	37.058	22 37.13	8.45	2.67	24 53.18	28 3 18.25
6	8	IV.	3	30.368	29 37.10	8.45	3.93	24 55.62	10 19.48
7	8	V.	3	14.045	46 35.49	8.49	7.08	25 36.50	27 21.06
8	7	IV.	2	13.291	47 22.77	8.91	7.22	32 31.29	28 8.90
9	9	VII.	3	30.895	29 2.84	8.	3.83	33	9 44.67
10	9	IV.	3	30.052	29 56.80	9.07	4.00	34 58.20	10 39.87
11	8.9	V.	4	39.835	19 33.91	9.11	2.14	35 35.30	0 15.19
12	7.8	IV.	2	9.307	51 32.55	9.21	7.98	37 12.83	32 19.77
13	6	IV.	2	7.644	53 16.72	9.63	8.30	43 24.03	34 4.65
14	9	IV.	3	25.704	34 20.51	9.74	4.82	44 59.10	15 14.07
15	7	V.	2	7.175	53 46.38	9.82	8.39	46 3.08	34 34.59
16	9	V.	3	13.215	47 27.66	9.89	7.23	47 5.21	28 14.78
17	9	III.	3	24.718	35 31.42	10.18	5.02	51 12.07	16 16.62
18	9	V.	3	22.513	37 49.61	10.19	5.44	51 24.66	18 35.24
19	8	IV.	3	26.854	33 17.31	10.42	4.60	54 17.35	14 2.33
20	9	V.	4	35.018	24 34.43	10.46	3.05	54 50.60	8 17.94
21	10	II.	3	19.993	40 23.30	10.75	5.91	58 43.48	21 11.96
22	9	V.	3	26.245	33 55.54	10.77	4.73	59 6.84	14 41.04
23	9.10	VI.	3	26.626	33 31.21	10.83	4.65	2 59 50.05	14 16.72
24	7	V.	3	16.769	43 44.61	10.96	6.55	3 1 26.07	28 24 32.12
25	10	IV.	4	41.674	14 17.49	11.21	1.18	4 31.08	27 54 59.88
26	10	VI.	3	31.958	27 56.59	11.30	3.63	5 42.02	28 8 41.52
27	7	V.	3	32.294	27 36.07	11.40	3.57	6 58.32	8 21.04
28	9.10	IV.	3	36.683	33 28.10	11.54	4.64	8 39.18	28 14 14.28
29	8.9	IV.	4	52.872	5 55.38	12.19	+ 0.32	16 23.47	27 46 37.25
30	8.9	IV.	4	49.278	9 41.21	12.20	− 0.35	16 33.20	27 50 23.76
31	10	III.	2	22.887	37 20.44	12.37	5.37	18 31.19	28 18 8.18
32	10	IV.	2	17.241	43 15.07	12.41	6.46	19 2.53	28 24 3.94
33	8	VI.	6	51.317	7 32.35	12.43	+ 0.03	19 15.39	27 48 14.78
34	7	V.	6	48.778	10 13.60	12.50	− 0.41	20 2.64	50 56.54
35	9.10	V.	5	43.574	15 40.40	12.62	1.43	21 23.13	27 56 24.45
36	9	V.	2	14.887	45 42.63	12.89	6.93	24 22.61	28 32.45
37	10	V.	3	30.126	29 51.97	12.96	3.98	25 12.95	10 38.91
38	9.10	III.	2	17.679	42 47.16	13.14	6.38	27 15.94	23 36.68
39	10	IV.	3	27.305	32 49.08	13.27	4.52	28 40.55	13 36.87
40	9.10	V.	2	18.138	42 18.87	13.40	6.20	30 9.41	26 23 8.56
41	9.10	II.	4	41.175	−18 9.03	−13.59	− 1.87	3 32 5.10	−27 58 54.49

CORRECTIONS.

Date.	Corr. of Clock.	Hourly rate.	m	n	c	Zenith Point.	Mic. Co.
	h.	s.	s.	s.	s.	° ' "	r.
1848. Dec. 18,	. .	. .	. .	. .	. .	359 59 56.82	30.0063

REMARKS.

(212) 23. Time of transit over T. IV assumed as 3ˢ instead of 0ˢ.3.

(213) 25. Declination differs 1″ from Arg. Z. 322, 45.

(213) 39. Right ascension differs .18ˢ.4 from Arg. Z. 322, 75.

INSTRUMENT READINGS.

Date.		CIRCLE							Barom.	THERMOM.				
		A.	B.	C.	D.	E.	F.	Mean.		At.	Ex.	U.	L.	I.
	1848. h. m.	° ' "						"	in.	°	°	°	°	°
Zone 213	Dec. 18, 2 20	77 2 {33. 33.9	33.2 33.4	39.7 39.9	29.9 30.2	32.8 32.9	23.8 24.8}	32.29	29.978	56.2	49.8	54.	53.5	54.
	2 40										49.2			
	3 0								29.962	55.5	48.6			
	3 20								29.970		48.1			
	3 40								29.968	55.	47.9			
	4 0								29.970	55.	48.1			
	4 10								29.968	55.	48.8	54.5	54.	54.

ZONE 213. DECEMBER 18. C. $D_0 = -27° 40' 30''$—Continued.

SECONDS OF TRANSIT.

No.	Mag.	I.	II.	III.	IV.	V.	VI.	VII.
42	7	· ·	· ·	29.5	47.	· ·	23.	· ·
43	6	· ·	· ·	46.2	· ·	· ·	38.5	· ·
44	8	· ·	14.3	32.3	49.5	· ·	· ·	· ·
45	10	· ·	· ·	· ·	· ·	36.8	· ·	· ·
46	9	· ·	29.	46.3	· ·	· ·	· ·	· ·
47	9	· ·	· ·	· ·	10.3	· ·	45.8	· ·
48	9	· ·	· ·	· ·	· ·	· ·	37.2	· ·
49	8.9	· ·	· ·	· ·	· ·	· ·	· ·	· ·
50	10	· ·	· ·	· ·	· ·	· ·	50.3	· ·
51	8	· ·	44.2	1.3	19.2	36.5	· ·	· ·
52	10	· ·	· ·	· ·	· ·	· ·	· ·	· ·
53	9	· ·	21.5	41.3	59.2	17.2	· ·	· ·
54	8.9	· ·	· ·	· ·	56.	13.3	31.	· ·
55	9.10	· ·	· ·	· ·	8.2	25.	· ·	· ·
56	9	· ·	· ·	9.5	27.5	15.	· ·	· ·
57	9	· ·	· ·	· ·	· ·	· ·	31.2	· ·
58	9	· ·	· ·	· ·	· ·	31.2	· ·	· ·
59	9	· ·	· ·	· ·	45.1	2.8	19.5	· ·
60	9	· ·	· ·	59.2	17.2	· ·	· ·	· ·
61	7	· ·	21.5	39.6	57.5	14.8	· ·	· ·
62	9	· ·	8.	25.3	· ·	0.5	· ·	· ·
63	9	· ·	· ·	56.8	14.3	31.3	· ·	· ·
64	9	· ·	12.9	29.2	· ·	· ·	· ·	· ·
65	10	· ·	· ·	6.	· ·	· ·	41.	· ·
66	9.10	29.8	· ·	· ·	4.8	· ·	· ·	· ·
67	9.10	· ·	· ·	· ·	17.3	59.5	· ·	· ·
68	10	· ·	· ·	· ·	· ·	22.3	· ·	· ·
69	10	· ·	· ·	· ·	· ·	16.3	· ·	· ·
70	10	· ·	· ·	· ·	3.2	· ·	18.1	· ·
71	10	· ·	· ·	· ·	· ·	· ·	· ·	· ·
72	10	· ·	· ·	· ·	· ·	5.5	· ·	· ·
73	10	· ·	· ·	· ·	· ·	· ·	37.8	· ·
74	9	· ·	· ·	· ·	37.3	· ·	· ·	· ·
75	9.10	· ·	· ·	· ·	· ·	· ·	25.7	· ·
76	8	· ·	40.	· ·	· ·	14.5	· ·	· ·
77	6.9	· ·	46.3	4.	21.5	39.3	· ·	· ·
78	9.10	· ·	· ·	13.3	· ·	· ·	· ·	· ·
79	9.10	· ·	· ·	· ·	· ·	· ·	2.2	· ·
80	9.10	· ·	· ·	· ·	· ·	29.2	· ·	· ·
81	9.10	· ·	· ·	· ·	· ·	31.2	· ·	· ·
82	9.10	· ·	· ·	· ·	· ·	· ·	· ·	· ·
83	9.10	· ·	· ·	10.2	27.3	· ·	· ·	· ·
84	10	· ·	· ·	· ·	· ·	· ·	5.3	· ·
85	9	· ·	· ·	53.2	11.	28.3	· ·	· ·
86	10	· ·	· ·	· ·	31.3	· ·	· ·	· ·
87	9.10	55.3	13.4	30.4	· ·	· ·	· ·	· ·
88	10	· ·	· ·	24.3	· ·	59.3	· ·	· ·
89	10	· ·	· ·	· ·	· ·	· ·	50.7	· ·
90	9.10	· ·	· ·	· ·	18.7	36.3	· ·	· ·

No.	T. (h m s)	a_1	a_2	MICROMETER		r.	i (′ ″)	d_1	d_2	Mean Right Ascension, 1850.0 (h m s)	Mean Declination, 1850.0 (° ′ ″)
42	3 32 47.30	12.31	−1.48	IV.	2	15.239	−45 20.63	−13.63	− 6.84	3 32 33.57	−28 26 11.10
43	33 3.68	12.31	1.57	IV.	2	10.934	49 50.38	13.65	7.68	32 49.80	30 41.71
44	34 49.56	12.32	1.49	III.	2	14.208	46 24.95	13.81	7.06	34 35.75	27 15.82
45	35 19.13	12.32	1.43	V.	2	17.055	43 26.78	13.87	6.49	35 5.38	24 17.14
46	36 3.98	12.35	1.00	III.	3	35.675	24 3.99	14.21	2.91	38 50.63	4 51.11
47	39 10.55	12.35	1.22	VI.	3	26.398	33 45.66	14.23	4.70	38 56.98	14 34.59
48	39 2.32	12.35	1.28	VI.	3	23.617	36 39.99	14.21	5.24	38 48.69	17 29.44
49	39		1.33		3	20.746	39 40.59	14.21	5.78	39	20 30.58
50	43 15.45	12.38	0.92	VI.	4	39.380	20 2.75	14.61	2.21	43 2.15	0 49.57
51	48 19.06	12.41	1.04	IV.	3	33.687	26 8.67	15.10	3.30	48 5.61	28 6 57.07
52	48		0.76	VI.	4	46.495	12 36.17	15.10	0.88	· · ·	27 53 22.15
53	50 59.34	12.43	0.82	IV.	4	42.622	16 26.28	15.37	1.57	50 46.09	27 57 13.22
54	51 55.90	12.44	1.26	V.	2	22.692	37 33.18	15.46	5.41	51 42.20	28 18 24.05
55	53 7.86	12.44	0.71	V.	4	48.288	21 43.91	15.58	0.54	52 54.71	2 30.03
56	54 27.30	12.45	1.01	IV.	3	33.706	26 7.47	15.70	− 3.30	54 13.64	28 6 56.47
57	54 56.31	12.45	0.60	VI.	5	52.472	6 21.75	15.76	+ 0.25	54 43.26	27 47 7.26
58	55 13.83	12.45	0.65	VI.	5	49.771	9 11.14	15.79	− 0.25	55 0.73	49 57.18
59	56 3.95	12.46	0.75	V.	4	45.575	13 33.79	15.93	1.06	56 31.80	27 54 20.78
60	59 26.40	12.48	0.94	III.	3	36.528	23 10.58	16.08	2.74	58 12.96	28 3 59.40
61	3 59 39.68	12.48	0.94	IV.	3	36.374	23 7.63	16.22	2.75	3 59 26.26	28 3 56.60
62	4 1 25.48	12.49	0.64	IV.	5	50.508	8 25.20	16.40	0.10	4 1 12.35	27 49 11.70
63	1 56.66	12.50	0.84	V.	4	41.062	18 17.00	16.45	1.89	1 43.32	27 59 5.34
64	3 29.40	12.51	1.12	III.	3	28.447	31 37.93	16.61	4.31	3 15.77	28 12 28.85
65	4 6.01	12.51	0.89	VI.	4	38.121	21 21.70	16.67	2.45	3 52.61	28 2 10.82
66	6 4.79	12.52	0.77	II.	5	43.472	15 46.66	16.88	1.44	5 51.50	27 56 35.00
67	6 41.53	12.52	1.30	V.	2	19.048	41 21.74	16.84	− 6.13	6 27.71	28 22 14.81
68	9 3.95	12.54	0.55	IV.	5	52.696	6 7.69	17.17	+ 0.31	8 50.86	27 46 54.55
69	9 58.91	12.54	0.70	V.	4	46.536	12 33.53	17.27	− 0.85	9 45.67	53 21.65
70	11 3.16	12.55	0.79	VI.	4	41.781	17 31.87	17.37	1.75	10 49.82	27 56 20.99
71	11		0.89	VI.	4	37.672	21 49.82	17.	2.53	· · ·	28 2 39.35
72	12 47.73	12.56	1.51	V.	2	9.151	51 42.43	17.56	5.07	12 33.66	32 38.06
73	13 22.89	12.56	1.27	VI.	3	20.219	10 13.17	17.62	5.89	13 9.06	21 6.69
74	17 37.17	12.58	0.82	IV.	4	39.731	19 40.34	18.06	2.15	17 23.77	0 30.55
75	17 50.17	12.58	1.04	VI.	3	30.000	29 59.50	18.08	4.00	17 36.55	28 10 51.58
76	48 57.34	12.73	0.67	V.	5	43.142	16 7.51	21.49	1.49	48 43.94	27 57 0.49
77	50 3.82	12.74	0.66	IV.	5	43.392	15 52.52	21.63	1.45	49 50.42	27 56 45.69
78	51 13.16	12.74	1.02	IV.	3	26.868	33 16.43	21.76	4.61	50 59.40	28 14 12.80
79	52 27.33	12.74	1.06	VI.	3	25.001	35 13.11	21.90	4.96	52 13.53	16 9.97
80	52 54.35	12.74	1.02	VI.	3	27.218	32 54.16	21.96	4.54	52 40.59	13 50.66
81	52 56.31	12.74	1.10	VII.	3	23.271	37 1.31	21.97	5.31	52 42.47	17 58.59
82	54		0.80	VII.	3	36.906	22 45.66	22.	2.68	· · ·	3 40.34
83	56 27.47	12.76	1.07	III.	3	24.312	35 57.03	22.37	5.11	56 13.64	16 54.51
84	56 30.41	12.76	1.09	VI.	3	23.528	36 45.63	22.39	5.26	56 16.56	28 17 43.28
85	4 58 10.88	12.77	0.56	IV.	5	47.632	11 25.68	22.58	− 0.64	4 57 57.55	27 52 13.90
86	5 0 13.94	12.79	0.43	V.	5	52.805	6 0.78	22.82	+ 0.35	5 0 0.73	27 46 53.25
87	3 30.55	12.79	1.00	III.	3	26.670	33 28.98	23.22	− 4.66	3 16.76	28 14 26.66
88	5 41.92	12.79	0.54	IV.	5	47.497	11 34.53	23.48	0.65	5 25.59	27 52 28.66
89	6 15.77	12.80	1.20	VI.	2	17.071	43 25.79	23.55	6.52	6 1.77	28 24 25.86
90	9.10	5 7 1.38	−12.80	−0.51	V.	5	48.400	−10 37.59	−23.65	− 0.48	5 6 48.07	−27 51 31.72

CORRECTIONS.

Date.	Corr. of Clock.	Hourly rate.	m	n	c	Zenith Point.	Mic. Co.
1848.	h.　　s.	s.	s.	s.	s.	° ′ ″	r.

REMARKS.

(213) 60. Transits over T.'s III and IV assumed as 9s.2 and 27s.2, not 50s.2 and 17s.2, and minutes as 58, not 59, to agree with Arg. Z. 350, 1, and Mural October 18, 1847.

(213) 63. Declination differs 1′ from Arg. Z. 322, 117, and 350, 6; micrometer reading perhaps to be assumed as 42r.062.

INSTRUMENT READINGS.

Date.	CIRCLE							Mean.	Barom.	THERMOM.				
		A.	B.	C.	D.	E.	F.		in.	At.	Ex.	U.	L.	I.
Zone 213　Dec. 18, 4 20	77	2 {33.0 34.1 40. 30.0 33.0 22.9 / 33.6 34.1 40.1 30.9 33.2 23.1}						32.33						
4 50														
5 0									29.954		55	· ·	48.8	
5 20									29.940			· ·	48.8	
5 40									29.934			· ·	48.6	
5 50		{32.8 34.1 30.7 30.8 32.2 22.6 / 33.5 33.7 39.8 31. 32.4 22.9}						32.12	29.934	54.5	48.9	53.5	53.3	54.

ZONE 213. DECEMBER 18. C. $D_0 = -27°\,40'\,30''$ —Continued.

Seconds of Transit

No.	Mag.	I.	II.	III.	IV.	V.	VI.	VII.
91	8		55.2	13.2	30.3	48.2	5.2	
92	8.9			29.3	47.2	4.3	22.1	
93	9			49.2	7.	24.5		
94	10		51.3		26.3			
95	9.10				57.2	15.3		
96	9				40.3	57.5	15.5	
97	9						49.3	
98	10				17.			
99	9				54.2	11.2	28.3	
100	10			24.		59		
101	10		37.3	54.8	12.5			
102	9		56.3	16.3	33.2			
103	9						10.3	
104	9				59.7	17.2	34.3	
105	9.10						5.	
106	9.10				54.3	12.		
107	8.9						52.?	
108	9						46.8	
109	8				34.5	52.3	9.3	
110	9						38.5	
111	9.10					18.3	36.	
112	9			11.2			3.8	
113	9					41.3		
114	9						14.3	
115	9.10					21.3		
116	8.9					55.3	12.5	
117	8.9			10.5	28.3	46.	3.5	
118	9.10					33.5		
119	9		51.3?		25.5		0.9	
120	9		51.3	9.2	26.3	44.3		
121	10				33.8		10.	
122	9.10					8.8		
123	10					14.8		
124	10					14.5?		
125	9.10				14.2	19.5		

Measurements

No.	Mag.	T. (h. m. s.)	a_1 (s.)	a_2 (s.)	Micrometer		r.	i	d_1	d_2	Mean R.A. 1850.0 (h. m. s.)	Mean Decl. 1850.0 (° ' ")
91	8	5 9 30.44	−12.81	−1.33	IV.	2	11.241	−49 31.32	−23.95	− 7.67	5 9 16.30	−28 30 32.94
92	8.9	10 46.96	12.81	1.06	IV.	3	22.917	37 24.27	24.10	5.39	10 33.09	18 23.76
93	9	12 6.85	12.82	1.10	IV.	3	21.178	39 13.54	24.27	5.72	11 52.93	20 13.53
94	10	14 26.29	12.82	0.71	II.	3	38.092	21 32.25	24.56	2.45	14 12.76	28 2 29.26
95	9.10	14 57.48	12.82	0.60	V.	4	42.716	16 33.18	24.62	1.57	14 44.06	27 57 29.37
96	9	15 40.28	12.83	0.78	V.	3	34.735	25 2.72	24.72	3.10	15 26.67	28 6 0.54
97	9	16 14.42	12.83	1.02	VI.	3	23.941	36 19.53	24.78	5.19	16 0.57	28 17 19.50
98	10	17 46.89	12.83	0.50	V.	5	47.706	11 20.98	24.98	0.61	17 33.56	27 52 16.57
99	9	18 53.77	12.84	0.62	V.	4	41.845	17 27.79	25.13	1.74	18 40.31	27 58 24.66
100	10	21 41.56	12.84	0.70	IV.	4	38.185	21 17.43	25.48	2.43	21 28.02	28 2 15.34
101	10	23 12.40	12.85	0.54	III.	5	41.977	14 12.10	25.68	1.18	22 59.01	27 55 8.96
102	9	24 33.56	12.85	1.34	III.	2	6.588	52 17.29	25.84	8.20	24 19.37	28 33 21.33
103	9	24 35.46	12.85	0.89	VI.	3	29.171	30 51.64	25.85	4.17	24 21.72	11 51.96
104	9	25 59.57	12.86	0.91	V.	3	27.946	32 8.68	26.04	− 4.40	25 45.80	28 13 9.12
105	9.10	26 30.10	12.86	0.34	VI.	5	53.594	5 11.24	26.10	+ 0.50	26 10.90	27 46 6.84
106	9.10	27 54.39	12.86	0.53	V.	4	44.642	14 32.36	26.28	− 1.20	27 41.00	27 55 29.84
107	8.9	28 17.14	12.86	0.95	VII.	3	25.895	31 16.52	26.33	− 4.79	28 3.33	28 15 17.64
108	9	30 11.90	12.87	0.31	VI.	5	54.524	4 12.92	26.59	+ 0.68	29 58.72	27 45 8.83
109	8	31 34.57	12.87	0.58	V.	3	42.625	16 47.65	26.76	− 1.59	31 21.12	27 57 45.98
110	9	32 3.66	12.87	0.75	VI.	3	34.617	25 9.87	26.82	3.13	31 50.04	28 6 9.82
111	9.10	33 0.98	12.87	0.77	V.	3	33.731	26 5.72	26.96	3.30	32 47.34	28 7 5.98
112	9	34 28.85	12.88	0.47	IV.	5	47.112	11 58.31	27.15	0.73	34 15.53	27 52 56.19
113	9	34 23.93	12.88	0.40	V.	5	50.558	8 22.06	27.14	0.08	34 10.65	49 19.28
114	9	34 39.42	12.88	0.41	VI.	5	49.355	9 37.44	27.17	0.31	34 26.13	27 50 34.92
115	9.10	36 3.80	12.88	0.80	V.	3	32.128	27 46.37	27.35	− 3.60	35 50.12	25 8 47.32
116	8.9	36 37.78	12.88	0.34	V.	5	52.848	5 58.08	27.43	+ 0.35	36 24.56	27 46 55.16
117	8.9	38 28.32	12.88	0.98	IV.	3	23.618	36 40.43	27.68	− 5.26	38 14.46	28 17 43.37
118	9.10	39 16.15	12.89	0.30	V.	5	53.892	4 52.53	27.77	+ 0.58	39 2.96	27 45 49.72
119	9	41 25.96	12.89	0.99	IV.	2	21.805	38 28.56	28.07	− 5.60	41 12.08	28 19 32.25
120	9	43 26.54	12.89	1.13	IV.	2	15.861	44 41.36	28.33	6.75	43 12.52	25 46.44
121	10	45 35.39	12.90	1.18	VI.	2	13.687	46 57.94	28.52	7.20	45 21.30	3 3.76
122	9.10	45 51.15	12.90	1.09	V.	2	18.564	41 52.22	28.66	6.24	45 37.16	22 57.12
123	10	46 57.26	12.90	0.88	V.	3	27.271	32 51.22	28.82	4.53	46 43.48	13 54.57
124	10	47 56.85	12.90	1.06	V.	2	18.699	41 43.62	28.96	6.18	47 42.89	22 48.76
125	9.10	5 51 1.80	−12.91	−1.21	IV.	2	11.645	−49 5.87	−29.37	− 7.60	5 51 47.68	−28 30 12.84

ZONE 214. DECEMBER 30. C. $D_0 = -29°\,33'\,30''$.

No.	Mag.	I.	II.	III.	IV.	V.	VI.	VII.	T. (h. m. s.)	a_1 (s.)	a_2 (s.)	Micrometer		r.	i	d_1	d_2	Mean R.A.	Mean Decl.
1	10					6.3			2 1 6.15	−16.41		IV.	3	30.332	−29 39 36	− 4.76	− 3.95	2 0	−30 3 18.07
2	8				58.2	15.5	51.5		3 15.85	16.43		IV.	5	49	10	4.85		3	29 39 57.85
3	8				18.3	35.3	54.		5 35.92	16.45		IV.	5	52.462	6 22.52	4.97	+ 0.64	5	41 23.27
4	9						19.2		5 43.69	16.45		VI.	5	51.085	7 45.71	4.98	+ 0.42	5	
5	10					53.2			2 8 35.44	−16.48		V.	4	39.606	−19 48.43	− 5.10	− 1.96	2 8	−29 53 25.49

CORRECTIONS.

Date.	Corr. of Clock. (s.)	Hourly rate. (s.)	m (s.)	n (s.)	ε (s.)	Zenith Point. (° ' ")	Mic. Co. (r.)
1848. Dec. 30,						359 59 54.68	30.0095

INSTRUMENT READINGS.

Date.		Circle A.	B.	C.	D.	E.	F.	Mean.	Barom. (in.)	Therm. At.	Ex.	U.	L.	I.
Zone 214	1848. Dec. 30, 2 0	78 54 59.6	64.6	71.7	58.1	61.3	49.3	60.73	29.958	40.2	31.8	42.2	41.4	43.
	2 10										31.3			

REMARKS.

(213) 121. Transit over T. IV assumed as 35ˢ.8 instead of 33ˢ.8.

ZONE 215. JANUARY 23. C. $D_0 = -28^\circ\,56'\,40''$.

No.	Mag.	I.	II.	III.	IV.	V.	VI.	VII.	T.	a_1	a_2	Micrometer	r.	i	d_1	d_2	Mean Right Ascension, 1850.0	Mean Declination, 1850.0
									h. m. s.	s.	s.		r.	° ′ ″	″	″	h. m. s.	° ′ ″
1	9		52.3	8.5	25.7				5 22 26.65	−21.40	−1.04	IV. 2	15.376	−45 12.09	− 2.15	−12.99	5 22 4.21	−29 42 7.2
2	9				58.	15.3	33.2		22 57.78	21.40	1.09	IV. 3	27.804	32 17.71	2.20	10.46	22 35.25	29 10.4
3	9					22.			23 4.25	21.41	1.10	V. 3	28.344	31 44.02	2.24	10.35	22 41.74	28 36.6
4	9			50.3		26.3			26 8.25	21.43	1.00	IV. 2	11.425	49 19.89	2.63	13.93	25 45.82	46 16.4
5	9		45.4	3.3	21.3				28 21.08	21.45	1.15	IV. 5	49.370	9 36.80	2.92	5.97	27 58.48	6 25.7
6	8		47.4	4.9	22.8	40.2	58.1		32 22.76	21.46	1.14	IV. 5	53.842	4 55.84	3.46	5.04	32 0.16	1 44.3
7	9				51.3	8.5			33 50.88	21.47	0.97	IV. 2	9.862	50 57.65	3.67	14.27	33 28.44	47 55.6
8	9					58.			34 22.61	21.48	0.98	VI. 2	14.498	46 7.59	3.76	13.17	34 0.15	43 4.5
9	8					46.2	3.7		35 28.25	21.49	0.96	V. 2	9.694	51 8.57	3.90	14.38	35 5.8	46 6.8
10	8.9		52.2	0.5	27.2				37 27.35	21.50	1.04	IV. 3	32.566	27 19.13	4.18	9.46	37 4.8	24 12.8
11	9				25.3	43.			40 25.29	21.52	1.06	IV. 5	46.696	12 24.45	4.56	6.52	40 2.7	9 15.5
12	8.9		13.5	32.2	49.2	7.5	25.2		43 49.56	21.54	0.96	IV. 2	19.244	41 9.48	5.06	12.26	43 27.1	38 6.8
13	8.9		23.2		59.2		34.2		43 59.95	21.54	0.96	IV. 2	20.750	39 34.83	5.10	11.96	43 36.4	36 31.9
14	9					36.2	53.2		45 18.25	21.55	1.05	V. 4	46.279	12 49.93	5.28	6.61	44 55.6	9 41.8
15	9						57.8		45 22.51	21.55	1.05	VI. 4	47.162	11 54.64	5.28	6.43	44 59.9	8 46.3
16	7.8						9.5		46 34.22	21.56	0.97	VI. 3	27.729	32 22.29	5.45	10.43	46 11.7	29 18.2
17	9					59.5			48 41.90	21.57	1.02	V. 5	47.795	11 15.53	5.75	6.30	48 19.3	8 7.6
18	7.8			30.3			23.2		48 48.02	21.57	1.02	VI. 5	45.429	13 44.29	5.77	6.80	48 25.4	10 36.9
19	8						48.2		50 12.91	21.58	1.01	VI. 5	46.298	12 49.74	5.97	6.61	49 50.3	9 42.3
20	9.10			3.3					52 21.11	21.59	0.99	III. 4	43.999	15 12.03	6.28	7.09	51 58.5	12 5.4
21	8				48.2				52 48.09	21.59	1.02	IV. 4	48.294	10 43.08	6.35	6.19	52 25.5	7 35.6
22	8		1.3	16.3	36.4	54.3	12.		54 35.60	21.60	0.99	IV. 4	43.062	16 11.33	6.62	7.28	54 14.0	13 5.2
23	9.10			47.3	5.6				56 5.27	21.61	0.91	IV. 3	25.956	34 13.64	6.83	10.85	55 42.7	31 11.3
24	9.10						55.3		56 20.04	21.61	0.93	VI. 3	31.182	28 45.78	6.87	9.75	55 57.5	25 42.4
25	8		6.5	24.2	41.3	59.2			5 ▮ 41.66	−21.63	−0.90	IV. 3	26.581	−23 7.22	− 7.22	− 8.60	5 58 19.1	−29 20 3.1

ZONE 216. JANUARY 23. C. $D_0 = -29^\circ\,34'\,30''$.

No.	Mag.	I.	II.	III.	IV.	V.	VI.	VII.	T.	a_1	a_2	Micrometer	r.	i	d_1	d_2	Mean Right Ascension, 1850.0	Mean Declination, 1850.0
1	8					33.5	51.3		6 20 15.83	−21.76	−0.86	· 5	56.990	− 2 41.16	− 0.95	+ 0.65	6 19 53.2	−29 37 11.5
2	9		52.5		29.3	47.3			22 28.97	21.76	1.06	· 3	26.144	23 34.58	1.24	− 3.75	22 6.1	58 9.6
3	9				13.2	31.3			25 13.30	21.78	0.97	· 3	38.621	20 59.14	1.59	− 3.10	24 50.6	55 33.8
4	9			31.3	49.2				27 49.19	21.79	0.85	· 5	54.344	4 24.55	1.92	+ 0.33	27 26.5	29 58 56.2
5	8.9				41.3	59.5			28 41.38	21.79	1.09	· 2	21.538	38 45.53	2.02	− 6.86	28 18.5	30 13 24.4
6	7.8				30.3	48.3	6.5		29 30.52	21.80	1.06	· 3	25.775	23 57.61	2.14	3.83	29 7.7	29 58 33.6
7	9.10					37.2			30 19.18	21.80	1.13	V. 2	15.420	45 9.08	2.24	8.23	29 57.3	30 19 49.6
8	9.10				13.7				32 12.93	21.81	1.13	IV. 2	13.202	47 28.38	2.48	8.74	31 50.0	30 22 9.6
9	9.10		32.2			7.5			34 7.66	21.82	0.94	III. 4	39.641	19 45.55	2.73	2.89	33 44.9	29 54 21.2
10	6				30.5	38.5	56.2		34 20.49	21.82	1.12	IV. 2	15.542	45 1.63	2.76	8.20	33 57.5	30 19 42.6
11	9.10					37.5	14.2		35 38.01	21.82	1.15	IV. 2	10.572	50 13.32	2.92	9.31	35 15.0	24 55.5
12	9.10		22.3	40.3	58.				38 58.03	21.83	0.98	IV. 3	33.302	26 33.01	3.36	4.27	38 35.2	1 10.6
13	7.8					58.3	16.5		39 40.53	21.84	1.14	V. 2	9.487	51 21.74	3.46	9.53	39 17.5	26 4.7
14	9		2.	20.	37.3	55.5			42 37.63	21.85	1.07	IV. 3	16.878	41 37.64	3.84	7.46	42 14.7	16 18.9
15	9.10		48.2		24.2				45 24.13	21.86	1.12	IV. 2	11.149	49 37.13	4.21	0.19	45 1.1	24 20.5
16	9.10						54.2		45 18.59	21.86	1.10	VI. 2	15.295	45 17.68	4.20	8.26	44 55.6	20 0.2
17	8.9				46.2	4.3	21.9		46 46.27	21.86	1.06	IV. 2	20.021	40 20.56	4.38	7.21	46 23.3	15 2.2
18	9		12.6	30.2	48.1	6.2			48 48.22	21.87	1.12	IV. 2	9.827	50 59.85	4.65	9.48	48 25.2	25 44.0
19	10			45.2					49 3.12	21.87	1.06	III. 2	18.823	41 35.19	4.70	7.47	48 40.2	16 17.4
20	10			59.3					6 51 17.21	−21.88	−1.05	III. 2	20.430	−39 54.59	− 4.99	− 7.12	6 50 54.3	−30 14 36.7

CORRECTIONS.

Date.	Corr. of Clock.	Hourly rate.	m	n	c	Zenith Point.	Mic. Co.
1849. h.	s.	s.	s.	s.	s.	° ′ ″	r.

INSTRUMENT READINGS.

Date.	A.	B.	C.	D.	E.	F.	Mean.	Barom.	At.	Ex.	U.	L.	I.
1849. h. m.	° ′ ″						″	in.	°	°	°	°	°
Zone 215 Jan. 23, 5 20	88 17 {30.6 / 30.2	35.9 / 35.0	40.7 / 40.4	27.1 / 27.1	35.2 / 34.9	18.8 / 18.9}	31.23	30.282	38.8	30.3	39.2	38.8	40.3
5 40										29.7			
6 0	{31.1 / 30.6	36.9 / 36.0	41.9 / 41.4	27.5 / 27.8	36. / 35.7	17.6 / 17.3}	31.65	30.280	38.	28.9	38.8	37.5	
Zone 216 Jan. 23, 6 20										28.7			
6 30	88 54 61.3	67.7	72.6	57.4	67.2	49.7	62.68				38.	37.	
6 40								30.282	37.5	28.3			
7 0										28.2			

REMARKS.

(215) 25. Micrometer reading assumed as 36r.581, not 26r.581.

(216) 1. Micrometer reading assumed as 55r.990, not 56r.990.

(216) 2. Micrometer reading assumed as 36r.144, not 26r.144.

(216) 6. Micrometer reading assumed as 35r.775, not 25r.775.

(216) 9. Right ascension 18s discordant from Mural Z., 1847, February 12.

ZONE 216. JANUARY 23. C. $D_c = -29° 34' 30''$ —Continued.

No.	Mag.	I.	II.	III.	IV.	V.	VI.	VII.	T.	a_1	a_2	MICROMETER.		r.	i	d_1	d_2	Mean Right Ascension, 1850.0	Mean Declination, 1850.0
									h. m. s.	s.	s.				° ′ ″	″	′	h. m. s.	° ′ ″
21	9.10						48.2		6 51 48.71	−21.88	−1.07	IV.	2	17.365	−43 7.34	−5.05	−7.80	6 51 25.2	−30 17 50.2
22	9.10					46.2			52 28.25	21.89	1.04	V.	2	21.225	39 5.54	5.15	6.94	52 5.3	30 13 47.6
23	9			11.2		46.2	4.3		54 28.79	21.90	0.90	IV.	4	41.046	18 17.73	5.41	2.58	54 6.0	29 52 55.7
24	8.9			19.2			12.2		54 36.90	21.89	0.90	IV.	4	41.702	17 36.68	5.42	2.44	54 14.1	29 52 14.5
25	9							23.	55 47.33	21.89	1.13	VI.	2	8.258	52 38.93	5.56	9.82	55 24.3	30 27 24.3
26	9		45.8	3.2	21.3				58 21.37	21.90	1.08	IV.	2	12.902	47 47.00	5.92	8.80	57 58.4	22 31.7
27	9				57.3				6 59 57.21	21.91	1.05	IV.	2	17.469	43 0.81	6.13	7.78	59 34.2	30 17 44.7
28	9					33.2			7 0 15.52	21.91	0.81	V.	5	51.637	7 14.51	6.18	0.28	6 59 52.8	29 41 51.0
29	7.8						12.2		0 36.55	21.91	1.10	VI.	2	9.825	51 0.48	6.22	9.48	7 0 13.5	30 25 46.2
30	9.10				21.3	39.2			2 21.21	21.91	1.04	IV.	2	19.025	41 23.04	6.46	7.43	1 58.3	30 16 6.9
31	9.10					28.3			3 10.59	21.91	0.82	V.	5	48.172	10 52.06	6.57	1.02	2 47.9	29 45 29.6
32	9.10						19.2		3 43.69	21.91	0.84	VI.	5.	46.823	12 16.54	6.64	1.32	3 20.9	46 54.5
33	9				56.5	14.5			4 56.57	21.92	0.84	IV.	4	45.976	14 11.20	6.79	1.72	4 33.8	29 48 49.7
34	8.9						42.?		5 6.35	21.92	1.09	VII.	2	10.361	50 27.11	6.83	9.36	4 43.3	30 25 13.3
35	9				43.2	0.6			6 42.92	21.92	0.94	IV.	3	32.538	27 20.88	7.04	−4.44	6 20.1	30 2 2.4
36	9.10					40.2			7 22.55	21.93	0.79	V.	5	53.845	4 55.78	7.13	+0.20	.6 59.8	29 39 32.7
37	7.8			30.3	48.3	6.			8 30.35	21.93	0.95	IV.	3	29.632	30 23.10	7.26	−5.08	8 7.5	30 5 5.5
38	9			19.2	37.2				9 37.07	21.93	0.88	IV.	4	38.190	21 17.20	7.41	4.30	9 14.3	29 55 58.9
39	9			22.7					10 40.61	21.94	0.86	III.	4	41.767	17 32.04	7.59	2.42	10 17.8	29 52 12.0
40	8.9					57.3	16.2		10 40.04	21.94	0.98	V.	3	24.600	35 38.84	7.59	6.19	10 17.1	30 10 22.6
41	9					37.5			11 19.68	21.94	0.93	V.	3	32.206	27 41.72	7.65	4.52	10 56.8	2 23.9
42	9					55.3			12 37.38	21.94	0.99	V.	3	23.935	36 20.42	7.83	6.34	12 14.4	11 4.6
43	9			10.3	28.2				14 28.19	21.95	1.05	IV.	2	14.347	46 16.63	8.06	8.48	14 5.2	30 21 3.2
44	9						9.7		14 34.21	21.95	0.90	VI.	4	37.307	22 13.17	8.08	3.40	14 11.4	29 56 54.6
45	9				58.5				15 58.39	21.95	0.99	IV.	3	22.608	37 13.8	8.28	6.61	15 35.4	30 12 28.7
46	9						40.2		16 4.69	21.95	0.84	VI.	5	44.465	14 44.79	8.26	1.84	15 41.9	29 49 24.9
47	8			49.2	7.3	25.2	42.3		18 24.04	21.96	0.87	IV.	4	38.448	21 1.01	8.50	3.15	18 2.1	55 42.7
48	9				47.7	5.3			18 47.56	21.96	0.85	IV.	4	42.576	16 41.06	8.55	2.25	18 24.8	29 51 22.7
49	9					8.3			19 50.39	21.96	0.97	V.	3	24.262	36 0.11	8.80	6.26	19 27.5	30 10 45.2
50	9				47.7	15.3			20 29.86	21.96	0.89	V.	4	35.589	24 0.73	8.88	3.78	20 7.0	29 58 43.4
51	8.9		10.3	28.1	46.3				23 46.16	21.96	1.03	IV.	2	15.099	45 29.34	9.31	8.30	23 23.2	30 20 17.0
52	9.10					23.			24 5.22	21.97	0.87	V.	4	37.136	22 23.65	9.36	3.43	23 42.4	29 57 6.4
53	9.10						48.2		24 12.70	21.97	0.85	VI.	4	41.085	18 15.07	9.38	2.57	23 49.9	29 52 57.0
54	9				50.3		26.		25 50.33	21.97	0.92	IV.	3	20.412	30 37.05	9.66	5.13	25 27.4	30 5 21.8
55	9						22.3		26 46.76	21.97	0.98	VI.	3	22.794	37 31.81	9.50	6.59	25 23.8	12 18.0
56	9			57.5	15.	33.3			28 15.22	21.98	0.91	V.	3	30.772	29 11.50	9.92	−4.83	27 52.3	30 3 56.3
57	9		26.5	44.2		35.			30 2.29	21.98	0.74	III.	5	53.100	5 42.23	10.16	+0.04	29 39.6	29 40 22.4
58	9					30.3			30 12.61	21.98	0.76	V.	4	49.816	9 7.68	10.19	−0.68	29 49.9	29 43 48.6
59	9.10			49.3					32 7.23	21.98	0.99	III.	2	17.576	42 53.42	10.45	7.75	31 44.3	30 17 41.6
60	9		42.	59.0	17.5				33 17.54	21.99	0.92	IV.	3	27.496	32 37.21	10.60	5.55	32 54.6	30 7 23.4
61	9					15.			33 27.27	21.99	0.79	V.	5	45.896	13 14.73	10.62	1.52	33 4.5	29 47 56.9
62	8.9				13.2				34 31.13	21.99	0.80	III.	5	44.340	14 52.12	10.77	1.80	34 5.3	49 34.8
63	9					53.2		29.2	34 53.38	21.99	0.76	IV.	5	49.516	9 27.58	10.81	0.75	34 30.6	44 9.1
64	9				56.2	13.2	32.3		34 56.12	21.98	0.75	IV.	5	51.292	7 36.10	10.82	0.35	34 33.4	42 17.3
65	8.9					51.3			36 33.56	21.99	0.60	V.	4	43.760	15 27.85	11.05	2.00	36 10.8	50 10.9
66	9						22.3		36 46.80	21.99	0.82	VI.	4	40.682	18 41.26	11.07	2.66	36 24.0	53 25.0
67	9			12.3	30.5		6.2		38 48.30	21.99	0.81	IV.	4	41.402	17 55.64	11.34	2.50	38 25.5	52 39.5
68	9.10					0.2			38 42.42	21.99	0.85	V.	4	36.674	22 52.59	11.33	3.53	38 19.6	29 57 37.5
69	9				45.	3.			7 42 2.88	−21.99	−0.92	IV.	3	24.228	−36 2.24	−11.79	−6.27	7 41 40.0	−30 10 50.3

CORRECTIONS.

Date.	Corr. of Clock.	Hourly rate.	m	n	c	Zenith Point.	Mic. Co.
1849.	h.	s.	s.	s.	s.	° ′ ″	r.

REMARKS.

(216) 33. Micrometer reading assumed as 44″.976, not 45″.976.

(216) 50. Transit over T. VI assumed as at 5ˢ.3 instead of 15ˢ.3.

INSTRUMENT READINGS.

Date.		CIRCLE.							Barom.	THERMOM.				
		A.	B.	C.	D.	E.	F.	Mean.		At.	Ex.	U.	L.	I.
	1849. h. m.	° ′ ″						″	in.	°	°	°	°	°
Zone 216	Jan. 23, 7 40													
	7 50	88 54 60.5	67.7	72.5	57.2	66.6	19.	62.25	30.272	37.	28.1	36.	35.5	42.2

ZONE 216. JANUARY 23. C. $D_0 = -29^\circ\,34'\,30''$—Continued.

No.	Mag.	I.	II.	III.	IV.	V.	VI.	VII.
70	9.10				33.			
71	8.9				11.2	46.5		
72	8.9					8.7	26.2	
73	8.9			51.3	9.2			
74	9.10				47.2	5.		
75	8		16.3	34.5	52.	10.		
76	8			29.2	47.	4.7		
77	6			46.3	3.8	22.	39.5	

No.	T. (h. m. s.)	a_1	a_2	Micrometer	i (r)	i (′ ″)	d_1	d_2	Mean Right Ascension, 1850.0	Mean Declination, 1850.0
70	7 42 16.29	−21.99	−0.76	V. 5	47.831	−11 13.27	−11.82	−1.10	7 41 53.5	−29 45 56.2
71	43 11.03	21.99	0.81	IV. 4	40.666	18 41.70	11.94	2.66	42 48.2	29 53 26.3
72	43 50.72	21.99	0.92	V. 3	24.078	36 11.52	12.02	6.31	43 27.8	30 10 59.9
73	46 9.13	22.00	0.82	IV. 4	37.862	21 37.59	12.35	3.27	45 46.3	29 56 23.2
74	47 4.94	22.00	0.87	IV. 3	29.426	30 36.20	12.46	5.12	46 42.1	30 5 23.8
75	49 52.13	22.00	0.82	IV. 3	36.961	22 43.23	12.84	3.47	49 29.3	29 57 29.5
76	50 46.97	22.00	0.80	IV. 4	40.884	18 27.95	12.96	2.02	50 24.2	53 13.5
77	7 52 4.02	−22.00	−0.81	IV. 3	38.358	−21 15.76	−13.14	−3.16	7 51 41.2	−29 56 2.1

ZONE 217. JANUARY 23. C. $D_0 = -28^\circ\,19'\,40''$.

No.	Mag.	I.	II.	III.	IV.	V.	VI.	VII.
1	9					0.2	17.4	
2	9		25.4	43.5	1.2			
3	8			19.2	36.3	54.4		
4	9					23.2		
5	9						0.3	
6	9			1.2	18.6	36.2		
7	9					57.2		
8	9					42.2	59.2	
9	9						8.2	
10	9			6.				
11	8.9					36.5		
12	8.9						11.3	
13	9		23.5	10.7				
14	9				12.2	47.4		
15	9					40.3		
16	8.9					37.5	50.5	
17	8.9						0.7	
18	9					9.2		
19	9					12.5		
20	9				55.2	12.5		
21	9		16.5	52.				
22	9.10		9.1	27.2	44.5			
23	9.10			10.2				
24	9.10				3.2	21.		
25	9							
26	9				7.5	43.1		
27	10				35.7			
28	10				31.3			
29	7	32.5	50.5					
30	9.10				24.5		59.2	
31	9.10					23.5		
32	9					49.2		
33	9					49.5		
34	9			23.		3.1		
35	9			20.5	38.			
36	9		13.5		48.	23.3		
37	10				48.2	11.2		

No.	T. (h. m. s.)	a_1	a_2	Micrometer	i (r)	i (′ ″)	d_1	d_2	Mean Right Ascension, 1850.0	Mean Declination, 1850.0
1	9 3 0.04	−21.87	−0.82	IV. 4	57.065	−1 32.39	−0.74	−0.41	9 2 37.4	−28 21 13.5
2	7 0.98	21.85	0.80	IV. 3	33.841	25 58.94	1.28	5.12	6 38.3	28 45 45.3
3	7 18.96	21.85	0.77	IV. 2	17.365	43 7.34	1.33	8.65	6 56.3	29 2 57.3
4	7 48.16	21.85	0.79	VI. 3	29.668	30 20.71	1.38	6.07	7 25.5	28 50 8.2
5	8 25.09	21.85	0.75	VI. 2	9.498	51 21.24	1.47	10.31	8 2.5	29 11 13.0
6	11 36.27	21.84	0.81	IV. 3	32.307	27 35.45	1.89	5.52	11 13.6	28 47 22.9
7	11 39.71	21.84	0.85	V. 5	48.245	10 47.54	1.90	2.22	11 17.0	30 31.7
8	12 24.38	21.83	0.82	V. 3	32.818	27 3.13	2.00	5.41	12 1.7	46 50.5
9	12 33.15	21.83	0.82	VI. 3	36.222	23 29.54	2.02	4.70	12 10.5	43 16.3
10	14 5.87	21.83	0.83	IV. 4	41.536	17 47.24	2.22	3.60	13 43.2	37 33.1
11	14 19.02	21.83	0.86	V. 5	49.178	9 42.65	2.25	2.05	13 56.3	29 27.0
12	14 36.23	21.83	0.85	VI. 4	43.837	15 23.10	2.29	3.12	14 13.6	35 8.6
13	16 58.60	21.82	0.86	III. 4	40.578	18 46.84	2.59	3.81	16 35.9	38 33.2
14	17 12.21	21.82	0.88	IV. 4	50.528	8 24.06	2.63	1.76	16 49.5	28 8.4
15	17 22.54	21.82	0.88	V. 5	52.389	6 27.43	2.65	1.37	17 0.1	26 11.4
16	18 15.22	21.82	0.87	V. 4	46.589	12 30.42	2.76	2.57	17 52.5	32 15.7
17	18 24.91	21.82	0.89	VI. 5	53.031	5 47.00	2.78	1.23	18 2.2	25 31.0
18	19 34.14	21.82	0.85	VI. 3	38.082	21 32.76	2.94	4.34	19 11.5	41 20.0
19	19 37.44	21.82	0.87	VI. 3	39.				19 14.7	40
20	25 55.03	21.81	0.91	IV. 5	55.199	3 30.85	3.74	0.80	25 32.4	28 23 15.4
21	27 51.94	21.80	0.64	IV. 2	15.968	44 34.77	3.98	8.95	27 29.3	29 4 27.7
22	29 44.65	21.79	0.90	IV. 3	35.028	24 44.52	4.23	4.96	29 22.0	28 44 33.7
23	30 10.07	21.78	0.91	IV. 3	41.108	18 23.06	4.29	3.70	29 53.4	38 11.1
24	31 3.24	21.78	0.90	IV. 3	35.508	24 14.53	4.39	4.85	30 40.6	28 44 3.8
25	31		0.86	VII. 3	12.770	47 55.84	4.41	9.63	30	29 7 49.9
26	33 25.24	21.77	0.87	IV. 2	8.998	51 51.90	4.68	10.42	33 2.6	29 11 47.0
27	34 15.36	21.76	0.91	V. 3	27.917	32 10.62	4.77	6.44	33 52.7	28 52 1.9
28	35 21.17	21.76	0.92	IV. 4	37.681	21 49.01	4.92	4.40	34 58.5	28 41 38.3
29	37 8.10	21.75	0.89	III. 5	13.284	47 22.80	5.15	9.52	36 45.5	29 7 17.5
30	37 24.26	21.75	0.96	IV. 5	50.001	8 57.02	5.19	1.87	37 1.5	28 28 44.1
31	37 49.44	21.75	0.94	VI. 4	40.416	18 58.05	5.23	3.85	37 25.8	38 47.2
32	38 14.11	21.75	0.91	VI. 3	24.162	36 6.20	5.29	7.23	37 51.5	55 55.7
33	39 14.45	21.74	0.93	VI. 3	28.712	31 20.62	5.42	6.27	38 51.8	51 12.3
34	40 27.95	21.74	0.94	IV. 3	32.457	27 26.03	5.57	5.49	40 5.3	47 17.1
35	41 20.33	21.74	0.92	IV. 2	20.451	39 53.77	5.67	8.01	40 57.7	28 59 47.5
36	43 18.33	21.73	0.90	IV. 2	8.503	52 23.13	5.98	10.52	43 25.7	29 12 19.6
37	9 46 5.98	−21.72	−0.93	IV. 2	16.308	−44 13.64	−6.26	−8.88	9 45 43.3	−29 4 8.8

CORRECTIONS.

Date.	Corr. of Clock.	Hourly rate.	m	n	c	Zenith Point.	Mic. Co.
1849.	h.	s.	s.	s.	s.	° ′ ″	r.

REMARKS.

INSTRUMENT READINGS.

Date.		CIRCLE.							Barom.	THERMOM.				
		A.	B.	C.	D.	E.	F.	Mean.		At.	Ex.	U.	L.	I.
	1849. (h. m.)	° ′ ″						″	in.	°	°	°	°	°
Zone 217 Jan. 23,	9 0	87 39 59.5	65.6	70.8	56.6	63.8	47.1	60.57	30.256	36.	27.4	36.2	36.	
	9 20										27.7			
	9 40										27.3			
	10 0	60.3	64.9	71.1	57.	63.2	47.4	60.65	30.250	36.	27.	35.5	33.5	42.8

ZONE 217. JANUARY 23. C. $D_0 = -28°\ 19'\ 40''$—Continued.

No.	Mag.	I.	II.	III.	IV.	V.	VI.	VII.	T.	a_1	a_2	MICROMETER.		i	d_1	d_2	Mean Right Ascension, 1850.0	Mean Declination, 1850.0
									h. m. s.	s.	s.		r.	' ''	''	''	h. m. s.	° ' ''
38	9.10				15.7				9 46 15.61	−21.72	− 0.94	IV.	2	18.451	−41 59.22	− 6.28	− 8.43	9 45 53.0	− 29 1 53.9
39	9		54.7	29.5					48 29.76	21.71	0.95	IV.	2	27.195	40 9.76	6.56	8.06	48 7.1	29 0 4.4
40	9						33.		49 57.93	21.70	1.01	VI.	5	45.132	14 2.86	6.74	2.87	49 35.2	28 33 52.5
41	9				44.5	2.5			50 27.21	21.70	1.00	V.	5	45.622	13 32.05	6.81	2.77	50 4.5	33 21.6
42	9.10			30.5	48.2				51 48.11	21.69	0.97	IV.	3	25.605	34 35.80	6.97	6.92	51 25.5	54 29.7
43	8.9				40.3	57.8			52 22.75	21.68	1.02	V.	5	43.695	15 32.92	7.04	3.15	52 0.0	35 23.1
44	10		55.2	30.7					56 30.55	21.66	1.03	IV.	5	43.782	15 27.27	7.54	3.14	56 7.9	35 18.0
45	10		28.5			3.5			58 46.03	21.65	1.02	IV.	3	34.542	25 15.15	7.81	2.98	58 23.4	45 5.9
46	9				41.5	59.3			9 59 41.63	21.65	1.07	IV.	5	55.002	3 43.10	7.93	0.82	59 18.9	23 31.0
47	9				32.5				10 0 15.05	−21.65	− 1.07	V.	5	54.182	− 4 34.82	− 8.00	− 1.00	9 59 52.3	− 28 24 23.8

ZONE 218. JANUARY 27. C. $D_0 = -23°\ 18'\ 30''$.

No.	Mag.	I.	II.	III.	IV.	V.	VI.	VII.	T.	a_1	a_2	MICROMETER.		i	d_1	d_2	Mean Right Ascension, 1850.0	Mean Declination, 1850.0
1	8.9			52.5	8.3	42.5			4 0 8.84	−21.09	− 1.69	IV.	4	36.858	−22 40.60	− 0.61	− 6.87	3 59 46.1	− 23 41 18.1
2	8.9					27.2 44.5			0 10.60	21.10	1.53	V.	3	25.548	34 39.43	0.61	8.73	3 59 48.0	53 18.8
3	10					1.3			1 44.55	21.11	1.82	V.	4	47.192	11 52.57	0.74	5.23	4 1 21.6	30 28.5
4	9			40.3 56.5	14.				4 56.90	21.13	1.58	IV.	3	31.830	28 5.13	1.04	7.71	4 34.2	46 43.9
5	8	28.4 45.3	2.4						7 2.27	21.14	1.78	IV.	5	46.915	12 8.77	1.23	6.20	6 39.3	23 30 46.2
6	8					23.8			6 50.10	21.14	1.24	VI.	2	7.168	53 47.35	1.21	11.73	6 27.7	24 12 30.3
7	8		28.2	2.3					9 45.32	21.17	1.68	IV.	4	41.048	18 17.73	1.47	6.22	9 22.5	23 36 55.4
8	8.9			46.3	3.5				10 29.64	21.17	1.42	V.	3	24.419	35 50.32	1.53	8.91	10 7.0	54 30.8
9	8		2.5 13.4	35.5 53.		9.4			12 35.85	21.19	1.87	IV.	5	56.899	1 43.91	1.72	3.66	12 12.8	23 20 19.3
10	9			40.4 56.5 14.4					17 57.05	21.23	1.23	IV.	2	14.082	46 33.12	2.20	10.62	17 34.6	24 5 15.9
11	10		33.2		20.2				20 7.03	21.25	1.72	IV.	5	50.135	8 48.66	2.41	4.76	19 44.0	23 27 25.8
12	8.9			16.2 32.2 49.1					20 32.56	21.25	1.71	IV.	4	49.072	9 54.14	2.45	4.94	20 9.6	28 31.5
13	10				35.3				21 18.37	21.25	1.36	V.	3	25.185	35 2.20	2.52	8.78	20 55.8	53 43.5
14	9			23.5					22 23.36	21.26	1.44	IV.	3	31.872	28 2.49	2.62	7.70	22 0 7	46 42.8
15	9								22	21.26	1.71	VII.	5	51.248	7 39.12	2.68	4.58	22	26 16.4
16	9				9.2 25.7 42.3				24 8.87	21.28	1.36	IV.	3	27.372	32 45.06	2.78	8.43	22 46.2	51 26.3
17	9				42.3				24 25.42	21.29	1.41	V.	3	29.378	30 39.21	2.81	8.10	24 2.7	49 20.1
18	8.9				7.8 23.8				24 50.59	21.29	1.47	V.	3	34.365	25 26.32	2.84	7.29	24 27.8	44 6.5
19	10			47.5	22.				27 21.63	21.31	1.31	IV.	3	25.000	35 13.68	3.08	8.81	26 59.0	53 55.6
20	9			46.5		37.3			29 20.43	21.33	1.52	IV.	5	41.905	17 25.08	3.28	6.06	28 57.6	36 4.4
21	8			45.5 2.3 19.	36.2 52.4				31 19.17	21.34	1.72	IV.	5	56.008	2 39.94	3.47	3.81	30 56.1	21 17.2
22	9.10		44. 59.3						35 17.03	21.37	1.25	III.	3	26.241	33 55.89	3.85	8.61	34 54.4	52 38.4
23	8			25.3 42.5 59.5					36 25.61	21.38	1.59	IV.	5	49.713	0 15.09	3.95	4.82	36 2.6	27 53.9
24	8			38.3 55.2					37 21.48	21.39	1.22	V.	2	24.167	36 0.92	4.07	8.06	36 58.9	54 44.0
25	9.10				16.3				41 42.74	21.41	1.27	VI.	3	31.135	28 48.73	4.49	7.82	41 20.1	47 31.0
26	8.9				10.2				42 53.43	21.43	1.47	V.	3	45.503	13 32.55	4.61	5.17	42 30.5	32 12.6
27	10			22.7	56.5				44 39.70	21.45	1.46	IV.	4	44.858	14 18.55	4.79	5.60	44 16.8	32 58.9
28	9				9.5	43.5			48 9.65	21.47	1.26	IV.	3	33.614	26 13.31	5.14	7.42	47 46.9	34 55.9
29	8.9			35.2					48 35.07	21.47	1.26	IV.	3	33.528	26 18.77	5.18	7.44	48 11.3	45 1.4
30	8.9				11.5				48 54.64	21.48	1.24	V.	3	32.288	27 36.64	5.21	7.63	48 31.9	46 19.5
31	8.9					51.3			49 17.71	21.48	1.35	VI.	3	39.648	19 54.57	5.26	6.43	48 54.9	38 36.3
32	8					5.3			4 50 31.70	−21.49	− 1.42	VI.	3	46.159	−13 6.01	− 5.38	− 5.37	4 50 8.8	− 23 31 46.8

CORRECTIONS.

REMARKS.

Date.	Corr. of Clock.	Hourly rate.	m	n	c	Zenith Point.	Mic. Co.
1849.	h.	s.	s.	s.	s.	° ' ''	r.

INSTRUMENT READINGS.

Date.		CIRCLE.							Barom.	THERMOM.				
		A.	B.	C.	D.	E.	F.	Mean.		At.	Ex.	U.	L.	I.
Zone 218	1849. h. m. Jan. 27, 3 55	82 30 66.8	65.6	69.2	58.	61.2	50.0	60.80	in.	°	°	°	°	°
	4 0								30.378	44.6	32.1	44.2	42.8	50.
	4 20										30.8			
	4 40								30.386	42.5	30.4			
	4 50	60.2 66.1	71.1	57.5	63.	47.8		60.95						

ZONE 219.   JANUARY 27.   C. $D_0 = -23°\ 13'\ 50''$.

Seconds of Transit

No.	Mag.	I.	II.	III.	IV.	V.	VI.	VII.
1	9.10				33.5			
2	9.10				21.5			
3	9.10		21.		54.3	11.3	27.5	
4	10				19.2		53.	
5	9.10				36.2	53.5	9.7	
6	9				35.7	52.3		
7	9.10				22.			
8	9				48.2			
9	9.10						30.3	
10	9					3.5		
11	9					43.2		
12	9.10					49.7		
13	9.10						34.	
14	8.9				16.3	33.2	50.1	
15	9.10		43.5	0.7				
16	8				31.3	48.6	5.4	
17	8			29.2		2.2		
18	9				5.	21.3		
19	9						51.	
20	10					34.8		
21	10						37.5	
22	9.10					10.2		
23	8.9			45.	2.2	19.1		
24	9.10					48.2	5.6	
25	9				31.8	48.3		
26	9.10				27.2			
27	9.10					46.2		
28	9		15.			48.5		
29	9		15.1			48.6		
30	8						11.	27.2
31	9							14.3
32	9							7.
33	9							
34	9					23.	40.	
35	9						42.3	
36	5				18.2	35.2		
37	9						55.2	
38	9				55.2	12.2		
39	9.10						44.8	
40	8					44.2	1.5	17.6
41	9.10				55.3		29.3	
42	9.10						1.5	
43	9					46.2		
44	9.10						23.	
45	9							
46	5					26.	42.8	
47	9						11.8	
48	8			56.2	13.2	30.	47.3	
49	8.9a			23.2	40.6	57.5		
50	9				34.2		8.5	

(continued)

No.	T. (h m s)	a_1	a_2	Micrometer		r.	i (' '')	d_1 ('')	d_2 ('')	Mean Right Ascension, 1850.0 (h m s)	Mean Declination, 1850.0 (° ' '')
1	6 19 33.44	22.03	−0.99	IV.	2	12.922	−47 45.75	0.90−	7.93	6 19 10.4	24 1 44.6
2	20 21.38	22.03	1.07	IV.	3	26.725	33 25.40	0.99	5.56	19 58.3	23 47 22.0
3	21 54.34	22.03	1.12	IV.	3	31.686	28 14.22	1.18	4.72	21 31.2	42 10.1
4	23 19.25	22.04	1.07	IV.	3	20.712	39 42.67	1.35	6.59	22 56.1	53 40.6
5	23 36.24	22.05	1.08	IV.	3	21.250	39 9.04	1.38	6.50	23 13.1	23 53 6.9
6	24 35.44	22.05	1.04	IV.	2	12.102	48 37.31	1.50	8.07	24 12.4	24 2 36.9
7	25 21.67	22.05	1.13	IV.	3	27.618	32 29.51	1.59	5.41	24 58.7	23 46 26.5
8	25 48.08	22.05	1.18	IV.	4	37.712	21 47.08	1.65	3.69	25 24.8	35 42.4
9	25 56.68	22.05	1.09	VI.	3	20.054	40 23.82	1.66	6.70	25 33.5	54 22.2
10	26 46.71	22.06	1.21	V.	5	41.795	17 32.16	1.79	3.01	26 23.4	31 27.0
11	27 26.28	22.06	1.14	V.	3	25.908	34 12.95	1.85	5.69	27 3.1	48 10.5
12	28 32.81	22.06	1.16	V.	3	28.354	31 43.33	1.98	5.28	28 9.6	45 40.6
13	29 0.38	22.07	1.28	VI.	4	50.721	8 11.26	2.04	1.51	28 37.0	22 4.6
14	30 16.28	22.07	1.11	IV.	2	14.719	45 53.11	2.19	7.62	29 53.1	59 52.9
15	32 17.65	22.08	1.27	III.	4	41.800	17 29.96	2.44	3.00	31 54.3	31 25.4
16	32 31.61	22.08	1.29	IV.	5	45.952	13 11.09	2.47	2.31	32 8.2	27 5.9
17	33 45.27	22.08	1.27	III.	4	39.968	19 25.01	2.62	3.32	33 21.9	33 21.0
18	34 4.69	22.08	1.27	IV.	4	39.148	20 17.02	2.66	3.46	33 41.3	34 13.1
19	34 17.44	22.08	1.24	VI.	3	31.965	27 56.59	2.68	4.67	33 54.1	41 53.9
20	36 31.69	22.09	1.22	IV.	3	24.315	35 56.85	2.97	5.97	36 11.4	49 55.8
21	37 3.94	22.09	1.27	VI.	4	31.757	28 9.64	3.03	4.70	36 40.6	42 7.4
22	37 53.37	22.09	1.29	V.	3	35.755	23 58.92	3.13	4.03	37 30.0	37 56.1
23	39 2.07	22.10	1.29	IV.	3	31.327	28 36.93	3.27	4.78	38 38.7	23 42 35.0
24	39 48.44	22.11	1.19	IV.	2	12.922	47 45.75	3.37	7.93	39 25.1	24 1 47.1
25	40 48.50	22.11	1.22	IV.	2	15.421	45 9.27	3.49	7.50	40 25.2	23 59 10.3
26	41 44.09	22.11	1.31	VI.	3	31.972	27 56.15	3.60	4.67	41 20.7	41 54.4
27	41 46.11	22.11	1.26	IV.	2	20.684	39 39.03	3.60	6.59	41 22.7	53 39.2
28	43 48.65	22.12	1.25	IV.	2	16.108	44 26.05	3.87	7.35	43 25.3	58 27.3
29	43 48.78	22.12	1.25	IV.	2	16.555	43 58.08	3.87	7.41	43 25.4	57 59.4
30	43 53.80	22.12	1.27	V.	2	19.996	40 22.50	3.88	6.71	43 30.4	54 23.1
31	44 40.70	22.13		VI.	4	43.892	15 19.81	3.97	2.65	44 17.3	29 16.4
32	45 33.40	22.13	1.41	VI.	4	44.863	14 18.80	4.09	2.49	45 9.9	28 15.4
33	46	22.13	1.33	VII.	3	26.052	34 7.44	4.20	5.67	46	48 7.3
34	47 22.94	22.14	1.29	IV.	2	15.478	45 5.69	4.31	7.49	46 59.5	59 7.5
35	47 25.30	22.14	1.30	V.	2	18.364	42 5.05	4.32	7.00	47 1.9	56 6.4
36	48 18.15	22.14	1.29	IV.	2	14.695	45 54.61	4.45	7.62	47 54.7	59 56.7
37	48 21.64	22.14	1.37	VI.	3	29.438	30 35.32	4.45	5.09	47 55.1	44 34.9
38	51 12.11	22.15	1.45	IV.	4	40.000	19 23.50	4.80	3.31	50 48.5	33 21.6
39	51 28.09	22.15	1.52	V.	5	54.532	4 12.92	4.84	0.86	51 4.4	18 8.6
40	52 44.25	22.16	1.43	IV.	3	32.014	27 53.64	5.00	4.66	52 20.7	41 53.3
41	54 12.32	22.16	1.45	IV.	3	32.038	27 52.14	5.18	4.65	53 48.7	41 52.0
42	54 44.66	22.16	1.46	V.	3	34.898	24 52.63	5.25	4.17	54 21.0	38 52.1
43	55 46.09	22.17	1.58	IV.	5	55.218	3 29.66	5.38	0.75	55 22.3	17 25.8
44	55 49.37	22.17	1.58	VI.	5	53.342	5 27.73	5.39	1.09	55 25.6	19 24.2
45	56			VI.	5	55.534	3 10.07	5.50	0.69	56 13.8	17 6.3
46	57 9.16	22.18	1.46	V.	3	26.658	33 29.73	5.57	5.57	56 45.5	23 47 30.9
47	6 57 54.69	22.18	1.38	V.	2	9.349	51 30.46	5.66	8.56	6 57 31.1	24 5 34.7
48	7 1 30.13	22.19	1.55	IV.	3	36.092	23 37.82	6.12	3.97	7 1 6.4	23 37 37.9
49	2 57.39	22.19	1.51	IV.	3	25.785	34 24.37	6.30	5.72	2 33.7	48 26.4
50	7 3 51.37	−22.20	−1.55	IV.	3	31.823	−28 5.56−	−6.42−	−4.60	7 3 27.6	−23 42 6.7

CORRECTIONS.

Date.	Corr. of Clock.	Hourly rate.	m	n	c	Zenith Point.	Mic. Co.
1849.	h. s.	s.	s.	s.	s.	° ' ''	r.

INSTRUMENT READINGS.

Date	CIRCLE							Barom.	THERMOM.				
		A.	B.	C.	D.	E.	F.	Mean.		At.	Ex.	U.	L.	I.
Zone 219	1849. Jan. 27.* 6 20	82 39 61.2	69.5	72.3	62.	64.5	50.7	63.37	in. 30.392	39.5	28.4	38.2	37.3
	7 0	61.1	68.9	73.2	61.	65.9	48.9	63.17	30.394	38.	27.7	37.2	36.8

*Minutes of circle reading assumed as 34 instead of 39.

REMARKS.

(219) 11. Declination differs 9' 37" from Arg. Z. 274, 129, and Transit Z. January 22, 1848.

(219) 17. Declination differs 24" from Arg. Z. 274, 137, and Transit Z. January 22, 1849; micrometer reading perhaps 39.668.

[(219) 10. Doubtful 10ˢ.]

ZONE 220. FEBRUARY 9. S. $D_s = -28°\ 19'\ 0''$.

SECONDS OF TRANSIT / T / a_1 / a_2:

No.	Mag.	I.	II.	III.	IV.	V.	VI.	VII.	T.	a_1	a_2
									h. m. s.	s.	s.
1	9		22.		57.				4 42 57.10	−28.01	−0.82
2	9						6.		42 30.88	28.03	0.75
3	8					11.			44 53.35	28.04	0.78
4	7		49.		14.5				49 14.45	28.08	0.71
5	7			45.	13.	30.			50 12.63	28.09	0.78
6	7		33.	50.2	8.				53 8.11	28.12	0.71
7	6					41.	58.		53 40.66	28.13	0.82
8	8		19.						56 54.43	28.16	0.72
9	9			40.					57 57.74	28.17	0.70
10	9							42.5	4 58 7.31	28.17	0.70
11	9		31.	48.					5 1 5.98	28.18	0.78
12	9					51.			1 33.38	28.19	0.76
13	8						50.		2 14.79	28.19	0.69
14	9						41.		3 5.95	28.20	0.80
15	9		52.						6 27.38	28.23	0.74
16	9						39.5		7 21.96	28.23	0.80
17	6		10.	28.	45.5				9 45.48	28.25	0.83
18	7		18.	5.	22.5				13 22.85	28.27	0.71
19	8		57.8		32.6				15 32.89	28.29	0.81
20	7		50.	7.	25.				17 24.98	28.31	0.82
21	8				14.5				19 14.43	28.33	0.68
22	9		9.						21 44.38	28.34	0.73
23	9		24.						22 59.31	28.35	0 81
24	10					50.			23 38.45	28.36	0.78
25	7						6.		24 48.49	28.37	0.81
26	7					55.	13.		25 37.70	28.37	0.78
27	8		45.						28 20.34	28.39	0.74
28	8				37.				28 36.86	28.39	0.76
29	4		12.5	30.	48.				30 47.77	28.41	0.74
30	7		11.5						32 16.83	28.43	0.76
31	5				22.3	41.			32 22.78	28.43	0.75
32	7			12.	29.				33 11.59	28.44	0.72
33	8		14.	32.					35 49.50	28.45	0.77
34	8				14.				36 26.37	28.45	0.72
35	9				47.				38 46.87	28.47	0.76
36	9						6.		39 30.95	28.48	0.75
37	5		7.	25.	43.				41 42.62	28.49	0.76
38	8				27.2	45.			42 27.28	28.50	0.78
39	8					59.	16.8		43 41.64	28.50	0.82
40	8				31.				45 48.75	28.52	0.80
41	7			37.	54.				46 54.26	28.53	0.75
42	7			9.					48 26.70	28.54	0.67
43	7				12.				48 54.12	28.55	0.64
44	7			2.					50 19.75	28.55	0.64
45	6					49.			50 13.93	28.55	0.70
46	6				37.				51 36.85	28.56	0.73
47	6					27.			51 51.93	28.56	0.70
48	6					30.			52 54.81	28.57	0.65
49	8				47.				5 56 46.89	−28.60	−0.78

MICROMETER / i / d_1 / d_2 / Mean Right Ascension, 1850.0 / Mean Declination, 1850.0:

No.	MICROMETER.		r.	i	d_1	d_2	Mean R.A. 1850.0	Mean Decl. 1850.0
			r,	′ ″	″	″	h. m. s.	° ′ ″
1	IV.	4	37.285	−22 13.99	−2.08	−6.53	4 42 28.3	−28 41 22.6
2	.	3	20.121	40 10.74	2.04	10.00	42 2.1	59 37.8
3	.	3	27.471	32 38.84	2.27	8.52	44 24.5	28 51 49.6
4	IV.	2	12.	49	2.66	11.66	48 45.7	29 8
5	V.	3	31.358	28 35.05	2.76	7.73	49 43.8	28 47 45.5
6	IV.	2	12.822	47 52.02	3.04	11.49	52 39.3	29 7 6.6
7	IV.	4	38.355	21 6.91	3.10	6.32	53 11.7	28 40 16.3
8	.	2	17.668	42 46.06	3.42	10.50	56 25.6	29 2 0.9
9	.	2	11.955	48 45.89	3.53	11.67	57 26.9	8 1.1
10	.	2	12.532	48 11.03	3.54	11.55	4 57 38.4	29 7 26.1
11	II.	3	33.202	26 38.72	3.83	7.36	5 0 37.0	28 45 49.9
12	.	3	27.902	32 11.37	3.88	8.43	1 4.4	28 51 23.7
13	.	2	9.543	51 18.58	3.94	12.18	1 45.9	29 10 33.6
14	.	4	37.030	22 30.57	4.03	6.59	2 37.0	28 41 41.2
15	.	3	25.089	35 7.66	4.38	9.00	5 58.4	54 21.0
16	.	4	39.835	19 34.16	4.47	6.02	6 52.9	38 44.7
17	.	5	47.745	11 18.56	4.71	4.44	9 16.4	28 30 27.7
18	IV.	2	17.893	42 33.97	5.09	10.44	12 53.9	29 1 49.5
19	IV.	4	46.323	12 46.79	5.31	4.73	15 3.8	28 31 56.8
20	IV.	4	48.220	10 47.73	5.52	4.35	16 55.9	28 29 57.6
21	.	2	12.911	47 46.44	5.71	11.47	18 45.4	29 7 3.6
22	.	3	24.070	36 11.45	5.97	9.20	21 15.3	28 55 26.6
23	.	5	44.955	14 12.78	6.11	5.00	22 30.2	33 23.9
24	.	4	38.550	20 54.99	6.17	6.28	23 9.3	40 7.4
25	.	5	45.078	14 6.26	6.30	4.97	24 19.3	33 17.5
26	.	4	39.653	19 45.70	6.39	6.06	25 8.6	38 58.1
27	.	3	29.333	30 41.54	6.68	8.12	27 51.2	49 56.3
28	.	3	34.603	25 11.26	6.71	7.07	28 7.7	44 25.0
29	IV.	3	30.940	29 0.96	6.95	7.81	30 18.6	48 15.7
30	.	3	35.918	23 48.12	7.12	6.81	31 47.6	43 2.0
31	.	3	32.206	27 41.72	7.13	7.56	31 53.6	46 56.4
32	.	3	23.972	36 18.16	7.22	9.20	32 42.4	55 34.6
33	III.	4	39.752	10 38.42	7.51	6.04	35 20.3	38 52.0
34	.	3	28.668	31 23.64	7.58	8.24	35 57.2	50 39.5
35	.	4	38.005	21 23.69	7.84	6.39	36 17.6	40 42.9
36	.	4	35.852	23 44.41	7.93	6.82	39 1.7	42 59.2
37	.	3	37.122	22 33.20	8.16	6.57	41 13.4	41 47.9
38	V.	4	42.393	16 53.88	8.26	5.51	41 58.0	36 7.6
39	.	5	52.340	6 30.57	8.40	3.53	43 12.3	28 42.5
40	.	4	50.119	8 47.91	8.65	3.98	45 19.4	28 0.5
41	IV.	3	37.200	22 22.77	8.77	5.53	46 25.0	28 41 37.1
42	.	2	17.582	42 53.10	8.94	10.51	47 57.5	29 2 12.6
43	.	2	9.589	51 15.31	9.00	12.17	48 24.9	10 36.5
44	.	2	10.428	50 21.91	9.16	11.99	49 50.6	29 9 43.1
45	.	3	25.900	39 30.50	9.15	9.82	49 44.7	28 58 49.8
46	.	3	32.270	27 37.77	9.31	7.54	51 7.6	46 54.6
47	.	3	25.608	34 35.55	9.31	8.89	51 23.7	28 53 53.8
48	.	2	12.470	48 14.07	9.46	11.56	52 25.6	29 7 36.0
49	.	5	48.643	−10 22.25	−9.91	−3.25	5 56 17.5	−28 29 35.4

CORRECTIONS.

Date.	Corr. of Clock.	Hourly rate.	m	n	c	Zenith Point.	Mic. Co.
1849.	h. s.	s.	s.	s.	s.	° ′ ″	r.

REMARKS.

(220) 4. Transit over T. II assumed as at 39ˢ instead of 49ˢ.

(220) 5. Transit over T. III assumed as at 55ˢ instead of 45ˢ.

(220) 31. Transit 1ˢᵗ discordant.

(220) 45. Micrometer reading assumed as 20ʳ.900, not 25ʳ.900, to agree with Arg. Z. 350, 149; 353, 33; and 357, 89.

INSTRUMENT READINGS.

Date.		CIRCLE.							Barom.	THERMOM.				
		A.	B.	C.	D.	E.	F.	Mean.		At.	Ex.	U.	L.	I.
	1849. h. m.	° ′ ″						″	In.					
Zone 220	Feb. 9. 4 40	87 39 60.	64.8	70.6	56.5	64.0	48.	60.65	29.972	38.3	26.7	40.	40.	40.8
	5 0	.	.	.	.	.	.	.			26.1			
	5 20	.	.	.	.	.	.	.			25.5	40.	33.	33.5
	5 40	.	.	.	.	.	.	.	29.984	35.9	24.9			
	6 0	.	.	.	.	.	.	.			24.4			
	6 20	.	.	.	.	.	.	.			23.9			
	6 30	60.	65.3	70.6	56.5	64.3	46.8	60.58			23.9			

ZONE 220. FEBRUARY 9. S. $D_o = -28° 19' 0''$ — Continued.

No.	Mag.	I.	II.	III.	IV.	V.	VI.	VII.	T.	a₁	a₂	Mic.	n	r	i	d₁	d₂	Mean Right Ascension, 1850.0.	Mean Declination, 1850.0.
									h. m. s.	s.	s.			r.		''	''	h. m. s.	° ' ''
50	8			59.	16.				5 58 16.27	−28.62	−0.69	IV.	3	25.023	−35 12.24	−10.00	−9.01	5 57 47.0	−28 54 31.3
51	6					34.5			5 59 16.97	28.62	0.75	.	4	41.933	17 22.57	10.20	5.60	58 47.6	36 38.4
52	.							35.	6 0 2.94	28.62	0.74	.	4	38.852	20 36.15	10.29	6.22	5 59 33.6	39 52.7
53	7						41.		1 8.92	28.63	0.79	.	5	51.570	7 16.91	10.43	3.69	6 0 39.5	26 33.0
54	8						30.		2 54.95	28.63	0.74	.	3	37.240	22 25.79	10.64	6.54	2 25.6	41 43.0
55	8		58.						5 33.30	28.65	0.78	.	5	51.378	7 29.83	10.95	3.52	5 3.9	26 44.3
56	7					3.			5 45.52	28.65	0.78	.	4	49.450	11 44.67	10.98	5.09	5 16.1	34 0.7
57	6			19.	36.				7 36.33	28.66	0.79	IV.	5	52.468	6 22.28	11.21	3.51	7 6.9	25 37.0
58	7		21.						8 59.30	28.67	0.78	.	4	49.438	9 30.03	11.38	4.11	8 29.9	28 45.5
59	6					23.			9 5.48	28.68	0.75	.	3	42.623	16 48.05	11.39	5.47	8 36.0	36 4.9
60	6						8.		9 32.95	28.68	0.73	.	3	37.178	22 29.69	11.44	6.55	9 3.5	41 47.7
61	7			8.5	26.				11 26.01	28.69	0.68	IV.	3	26.528	33 37.95	11.67	8.69	10 56.6	28 52 58.3
62	8		17.						12 52.47	28.71	0.63	.	2	12.480	48 12.47	11.85	11.56	12 23.1	29 7 35.9
63	8		5.						13 40.37	28.72	0.66	.	3	26.423	33 44.03	11.95	8.72	13 11.0	28 53 4.7
64	7				50.				13 49.89	28.72	0.67	.	3	22.412	37 56.22	11.97	9.53	13 20.5	28 57 17.7
65	7				54.	11.	29.		17 11.28	28.73	0.63	.	2	14.042	45 30.12	12.26	11.06	15 41.9	29 5 2.4
66	8		38.	56.					18 13.63	28.73	0.60	.	8	8.586	52 17.30	12.52	12.37	17 44.3	29 11 42.2
67	5			7.	24.				19 24.27	28.74	0.72	.	3	37.330	22 20.27	12.67	6.52	18 54.8	28 41 30.5
68	8						20.		19 44.94	28.74	0.73	.	3	41.792	17 39.94	12.71	5.63	19 15.5	36 58.3
69	9				17.	35.			21 17.10	28.75	0.67	V.	3	24.738	35 30.12	12.90	9.06	20 47.7	54 52.1
70	9		58.						24 33.33	28.77	0.71	.	3	35.350	24 24.01	13.30	6.92	24 3.8	43 44.2
71	7					0.	17.6		24 42.51	28.77	0.75	V.	4	45.118	14 2.74	13.33	4.97	24 13.0	28 33 21.0
72	6			19.	36.5				26 36.61	28.78	0.59	IV.	2	8.142	52 45.71	13.57	12.46	26 7.2	29 12 11.7
73	7		32.	49.8					28 7.50	28.79	0.62	III.	2	14.148	46 28.48	13.77	11.21	27 38.1	5 53.5
74	9						56.		29 20.79	28.80	0.60	.	2	10.635	50 9.93	13.80	11.94	27 51.4	29 9 35.7
75	7			12.	30.	47.			6 30 47.29	−28.81	−0.70	IV.	3	36.245	−23 28.28	−14.11	−6.74	6 30 17.8	−28 42 49.1

ZONE 221. FEBRUARY 9. S. $D_o = -26° 29' 10''$.

No.	Mag.	I.	II.	III.	IV.	V.	VI.	VII.	T.	a₁	a₂	Mic.	n	r	i	d₁	d₂	Mean Right Ascension, 1850.0.	Mean Declination, 1850.0.
1	8			57.5					7 42 32.23	−29.02	−1.51		3	40.159	−19 22.18	−2.36	−8.09	7 42 1.7	−26 48 42.6
2	7					56.			42 55.89	29.02	1.63		4	51.813	5 4.75	2.41	6.16	42 25.2	37 23.3
3	8						44.8		44 10.34	29.03	1.46		3	36.250	23 27.97	2.58	8.82	43 39.9	52 49.4
4	7			43.					46 0.35	29.04	1.15		3	34.623	25 9.82	2.82	9.13	45 29.9	54 31.8
5	7						41.		46 6.55	29.04	1.40		3	30.275	29 42.47	2.83	9.95	45 36.1	59 5.2
6	7			20.5					47 55.24	29.04	1.44		3	35.510	24 13.91	3.06	8.96	47 24.8	53 35.9
7	8			9.					48 43.73	29.05	1.46		3	37.679	21 57.68	3.17	8.56	48 13.2	26 51 19.4
8	8					24.	12.		49 6.43	29.05	1.17		1	8.892	51 58.92	3.23	14.02	48 36.2	27 21 26.2
9	7						40.5		50 6.01	29.05	1.52		5	45.532	13 37.95	3.35	7.08	49 35.4	26 42 58.4
10	9					35.5			51 18.22	29.05	1.42		3	35.382	24 22.57	3.51	8.99	50 47.8	26 53 45.1
11	5		24.	41.					52 58.60	29.05	1.27		2	19.488	40 53.61	3.73	12.00	52 28.3	27 10 19.3
12	8						40.		53 5.53	29.05	1.34		3	26.693	33 27.48	3.75	10.63	52 35.2	27 2 51.9
13	7						41.		54 6.54	29.06	1.43		4	36.362	23 12.66	3.88	8.80	53 36.0	26 52 35.3
14	7					30.			55 12.76	29.06	1.47		4	39.502	19 38.55	4.03	8.16	54 42.2	49 0.7
15	6					15.			56 14.88	29.06	1.51		4	45.679	18 40.79	4.17	8.01	55 44.3	48 3.0
16	7						55.8		56 21.32	29.06	1.45		4	38.613	20 51.29	4.18	8.38	55 50.8	50 13.9
17	8						50.5		57 33.24	29.07	1.43		4	37.743	21 45.51	4.34	8.53	57 2.7	26 51 8.4
18	8		23.	42.					7 59 57.75	−29.07	−1.32		3	28.501	−31 34.05	−4.67	−10.29	7 59 27.4	−27 0 59.0

CORRECTIONS.

Date.	Corr. of Clock.	Hourly rate.	m	n	r	Zenith Point.	Mic. Co.
1849.	h.	s.	s.	s.	s.	° ' ''	r.

INSTRUMENT READINGS.

Date.		CIRCLE.							Barom.	THERMOM.				
		A.	B.	C.	D.	E.	F.	Mean.		At.	Ex.	U.	L.	I.
	1849.	h. m.	° ' ''						''	in.	°	°	°	°	°
Zone 221	Feb. 9. 7 40	85 49 60.	68.8	75.3	60.5	69.	48.8	63.73	30.040	31.4	23.4	..	32.	29.
	8 0										23.7			
	8 20										23.9			
	9 0	61.0	68.9	75.8	60.8	69.	48.8	64.05	30.110	31.5	24.0	40.	31.	29.

REMARKS.

(220) 56. Micrometer reading assumed as 44ʳ.450, not 49ʳ.450.

(220) 65. Minutes assumed as 16, not 17.

(220) 69. Declination differs 10' 28'' from Arg. Z. 357, 141; micrometer reading probably 34ʳ.738.

(221) 2. Micrometer reading assumed as 50ʳ.813, not 51ʳ.813.

(221) 8. Transits discordant; T. VI rejected.

(221) 15. Micrometer reading assumed as 40ʳ.679, not 45ʳ.679, to agree with Arg. Z. 352, 62, and 360, 231.

ZONE 221. FEBRUARY 9. S. $D_0 = -26°\,29'\,10''$—Continued.

No.	Mag.	I.	II.	III.	IV.	V.	VI.	VII.	T. (h. m. s.)	a_1 (s.)	a_1 (s.)	Micr.	n	r.	i (' ")	d_1 (")	d_2 (")	Mean Right Ascension, 1850.0 (h. m. s.)	Mean Declination, 1850.0 (° ' ")
19	5		33.2	51.					8 1 8.18	−29.07	−1.51		4	47.350	−11 41.83	−4.82	−6.73	8 0 37.6	−26 41 3.4
20	9					28.	45.5		1 10.91	29.07	1.52		4	48.358	10 39.51	4.82	6.54	0 40.3	26 40 0.9
21	7			32.					3 49.33	29.07	1.34		3	28.719	31 20.18	5.17	10.25	3 18.9	27 0 45.6
22	8*					12.5			3 55.30	29.07	1.48		5	46.916	12 10.71	5.18	6.82	3 24.8	26 41 32.7
23	7		32.5	50.					6 7.32	29.08	1.27		3	24.968	35 15.50	5.38	10.96	5 37.0	27 4 41.8
24	9						41.		6 6.50	29.09	1.50		5	48.755	10 15.35	5.48	6.49	5 35.9	26 39 37.3
25	8				2.				8 1.88	29.09	1.26		3	24.990	35 14.30	5.74	10.95	7 31.5	27 4 41.0
26	7					4.5	23.		8 47.87	29.09	1.32		3	31.575	28 21.31	5.83	9.70	8 17.5	26 57 46.8
27	9						18.		9 43.47	29.09	1.20		2	18.952	41 28.24	5.98	12.10	9 13.2	27 10 56.3
28	7				41.				11 40.87	29.09	1.40		4	40.189	19 11.76	6.23	8.00	11 10.4	26 49 36.1
29	6						34.		12 59.50	29.09	1.48		5	47.912	11 8.38	6.41	6.63	12 28.9	40 31.4
30	5		22.	39.					13 56.59	29.09	1.51		5	51.515	7 21.73	6.54	5.96	13 26.0	36 44.2
31	7				30.				14 29.88	29.09	1.44		4	45.165	13 59.41	6.61	7.15	13 59.3	26 43 23.2
32	8					23.			15 5.56	29.09	1.19		2	19.910	40 27.89	6.70	11.91	14 35.3	27 9 56.5
33	7				24.				16 23.89	29.10	1.44		4	45.494	13 36.83	6.88	7.09	15 53.3	26 43 2.8
34	6		14.	31.					17 48.67	29.10	1.08		2	9.942	50 52.14	7.06	13.82	17 18.5	27 20 23.0
35	9					20.6			18 3.54	29.10	1.34		4	38.160	21 19.46	7.11	8.46	17 33.1	26 50 45.0
36	7		38.2	56.					20 13.15	29.10	1.33		3	36.456	23 14.92	7.40	8.78	19 42.7	52 41.1
37	5					46.	3.5		20 28.91	29.10	1.45		4	48.198	10 49.49	7.43	6.57	19 58.4	40 13.5
38	7				48.8				21 48.65	29.10	1.29		3	31.999	27 54.55	7.61	9.62	21 16.3	26 57 21.8
39	5					43.	0.		22 25.57	29.10	1.22		3	25.452	34 45.58	7.69	10.86	21 55.2	27 4 14.1
40	5					57.	14.		23 39.64	29.10	1.35		4	38.848	20 36.09	7.85	8.33	23 9.2	26 50 2.3
41	6					8.			24 50.44	29.11	1.06		2	10.402	50 24.41	8.01	13.73	24 20.3	27 19 56.1
42	7						51.		26 16.54	29.11	1.24		3	29.188	30 51.01	8.21	10.15	25 46.2	27 0 19.4
43	5		5.	22.8					28 40.00	29.11	1.49		6	53.982	4 46.75	8.53	5.49	28 9.4	26 34 10.8
44	8				10.				32 9.89	29.11	1.45		6	52.460	6 22.78	9.01	5.78	31 39.3	35 47.6
45	8					13.5			32 56.30	29.11	1.39		5	46.450	12 40.27	9.10	6.90	32 25.8	42 6.3
46	7			18.					34 35.41	29.11	1.37		4	44.843	14 18.92	9.33	7.21	34 4.9	43 45.5
47	6				23.	40.			35 22.79	29.11	1.26		3	34.665	25 7.37	9.45	9.12	34 52.4	26 54 35.9
48	7		0.	17.					37 34.64	29.12	1.05		2	14.150	46 28.37	9.74	13.02	37 4.5	27 16 1.1
49	8		45.						39 19.80	29.12	1.11		3	21.477	38 54.37	9.99	11.62	38 49.6	8 26.0
50	7					47.	4.		39 29.60	29.12	1.18		3	25.100	31 59.33	10.01	10.36	38 59.3	1 29.7
51	7		10.8						41 45.63	29.12	1.02	II.	2	17.018	43 27.72	10.29	12.47	41 15.5	13 0.5
52	8			7.					42 24.40	29.12	1.02	II.	2	17.020	43 27.60	10.39	12.47	41 54.3	13 0.5
53	8				57.				42 50.91	29.12	1.03	II.	2	18.742	41 39.59	10.45	11.66	42 20.8	11 11.7
54	4		5.5	23.	10.				44 40.19	29.12	1.08	IV.	3	20.650	39 46.63	10.69	11.77	44 10.0	9 19.1
55	7					22.			46 4.62	29.12	1.13	III.	3	24.952	35 16.50	10.88	10.96	45 34.4	4 48.3
56	4		1.	18.	36.				49 35.68	29.12	1.10	IV.	3	23.419	36 53.05	11.36	11.25	49 5.4	6 25.7
57	7		3.	29.					51 37.58	29.12	1.07	III.	3	21.603	38 46.72	11.62	11.60	51 7.4	27 8 19.9
58	8		16.	33.					52 50.55	29.12	1.25	III.	4	39.163	20 15.58	11.78	8.27	52 20.2	26 49 45.6
59	6			30.					53 47.41	29.12	1.01	II.	2	16.148	44 22.42	11.91	12.63	53 17.3	27 13 57.0
60	6		34.2	52.					55 9.14	29.12	1.17	III.	3	33.554	26 16.95	12.10	9.32	54 38.9	26 55 48.4
61	7			39.	46.				56 46.15	29.12	1.30	III.	4	46.745	12 19.62	12.30	6.84	56 15.7	41 48.8
62	8					28.			58 10.68	29.12	1.13	III.	3	29.680	30 20.14	12.50	10.06	57 40.4	59 52.7
63	8			34.	52.				8 59 51.64	29.12	1.27	IV.	5	44.617	14 35.00	12.73	7.25	8 59 21.3	44 5.0
64	8		28.5	56.					9 1 3.23	−29.12	−1.27	II.	5	46.455	−12 38.83	−12.89	−6.90	9 0 32.8	−26 42 8.6

CORRECTIONS.

Date.	Corr. of Clock.	Hourly rate.	m	n	c	Zenith Point.	Mic. Co.
1849.	h.	s.	s.	s.	s.	° ' "	r.

INSTRUMENT READINGS.

Date.	CIRCLE.							Barom.	THERMOM.				
	A.	B.	C.	D.	E.	F.	Mean.		At.	Ex.	U.	L.	I.
1849. h. m.	° ' "						"	in.	°	°	°	°	°

REMARKS.

(221) 53. Transit over T. III assumed as 51ˢ, not 57ˢ, to agree with Arg. Z. 352, 143, and Mural, 1849, March 12.

(221) 56. Transit over T. II assumed as at 1ˢ instead of 0ˢ.1.

(221) 61. Transit over T. III assumed as at 29ˢ instead of 39ˢ.

ZONE 222. FEBRUARY 10. C. $D_0 = -28°\ 19'\ 0''$.

SECONDS OF TRANSIT.

No.	Mag.	I.	II.	III.	IV.	V.	VI.	VII.
1	8					27.3		2.2
2	7						51.6	
3	8.9				59.2		34.1	
4	8		26.2	14.4	2.2	19.8	37.4	
5	9						15.5	33.2
6	9.10						44.	1.5
7	9			14.5	32.2		7.5	25.3
8	8.9					25.2		1.3
9	7.8					45.2	2.4	20.3
10	8		32.8	50.2	7.4	42.2		
11	9.10				39.2		15.2	
12	9			26.5	43.2			
13	8.9		7.4	25.7	13.3	1.4	18.6	
14	9.10			11.2				
15	8			7.5	25.5		0.2	
16	9.10							
17	9				44.2	1.2		
18	9			35.7			14.5	31.3
19	9.10		27.5			3.2		
20	8						19.5	
21	8.9				15.5	33.2	50.3	
22	8			1.2	18.2	36.		
23	9					1.2	18.3	
24	9					21.3		
25	9						6.3	
26	9				2.3		37.3	
27	9					39.3		
28	7.8					51.2	9.2	
29	7.8				53.2	10.5		
30	9.10						53.	
31	7.8				32.2		7.3	
32	9							
33	9			47.2		22.		
34	9.10			49.8				
35	8		36.3	54.3	12.		17.1	
36	9		31.	48.5	6.1			
37	9				36.	53.6		
38	8		37.2	55.2	12.5	30.5		
39	9			39.7		14.8		
40	9						7.3	
41	9			43.2	11.5	24.8		
42	8		39.3	57.3	15.2	32.8	50.3	
43	8				30.3	48.		
44	7.8		33.	50.7	8.5	26.4		
45	8			42.	59.6	17.1		
46	9						9.5	
47	9			39.2				
48	9.10			50.2		25.3		
49	9		31.3	49.	6.2		41.4	
50	9				33.2		9.3	

No.	T. (h. m. s.)	a_1 (s.)	a_2 (s.)	MICROMETER.		(r.)	i (° ′ ″)	d_1 (″)	d_2 (″)	Mean Right Ascension, 1850.0. (h. m. s.)	Mean Declination, 1850.0. (° ′ ″)
1	3 37 27.16	−27.86	−1.64	IV.	4	41.245	−18 5.49	+ 0.09	− 1.74	3 36 57.6	− 28 37 7.1
2	38 16.42	27.88	1.77	VI.	2	13.557	47 6.74	+ 0.05	7.33	37 46.8	29 6 14.0
3	40 59.06	27.89	1.65	IV.	4	39.255	20 10.37	− 0.09	2.14	40 29.5	28 39 12.6
4	43 2.04	27.92	1.73	IV.	3	23.598	36 41.69	0.21	5.30	42 32.4	55 47.2
5	47 58.03	27.96	1.68	V.	3	33.653	26 10.93	0.49	3.27	47 28.4	45 14.7
6	49 26.44	27.98	1.67	V.	3	35.166	24 35.99	0.57	2.97	48 56.8	28 43 39.5
7	53 49.91	28.00	1.82	IV.	2	7.823	53 5.52	0.84	8.49	53 20.1	29 12 14.8
8	55 25.65	28.03	1.69	IV.	4	35.942	23 38.07	0.94	2.81	54 55.9	28 42 41.8
9	56 45.00	28.04	1.75	IV.	3	22.515	37 40.69	1.02	5.52	56 15.2	56 56.2
10	59 7.59	28.07	1.69	IV.	3	33.278	26 34.51	1.16	3.34	58 37.8	45 39.0
11	3 59 39.61	28.08	1.69	IV.	3	33.238	26 36.96	1.21	3.35	3 59 9.8	28 45 41.5
12	4 1 43.67	28.09	1.79	IV.	2	14.147	46 29.11	1.35	7.20	4 1 13.8	29 5 37.7
13	3 43.20	28.11	1.82	IV.	2	8.876	51 59.80	1.40	8.26	3 13.3	29 11 9.6
14	6 28.82	28.14	1.71	III.	3	29.441	30 35.67	1.67	4.11	5 59.0	28 49 40.9
15	7 25.33	28.15	1.74	IV.	3	23.727	36 33.54	1.74	5.27	6 55.4	55 40.5
16	7 .	28.15	1.70	VII.	3	32.798	27 4.07	1.78	3.44	7 . .	46 9.3
17	10 1.45	28.17	1.71	IV.	3	32.621	27 15.62	1.92	3.48	9 31.6	46 21.0
18	10 56.50	28.18	1.71	IV.	3	31.807	28 6.57	1.98	3.64	10 26.6	47 12.2
19	13 2.94	28.21	1.64	IV.	5	45.635	13 31.11	2.14	0.85	12 33.1	28 32 34.1
20	14 1.64	28.22	1.80	V.	2	10.794	49 59.64	2.22	7.88	13 31.6	29 9 9.7
21	17 32.95	28.24	1.66	IV.	4	42.046	16 18.55	2.48	1.40	17 3.0	28 35 22.4
22	19 18.53	28.26	1.60	IV.	4	49.931	14 13.85	2.62	1.00	18 48.7	33 17.5
23	20 0.86	28.27	1.70	IV.	3	29.439	30 35.36	2.67	4.11	19 30.9	28 49 42.2
24	21 3.54	28.28	1.78	V.	2	18.802	41 37.33	2.75	6.26	20 33.5	29 0 46.3
25	21 31.17	28.28	1.78	VI.	2	18.906	41 31.05	2.79	6.24	21 1.1	29 0 40.1
26	24 2.20	28.30	1.70	IV.	3	35.845	23 53.20	2.99	2.83	23 32.2	28 42 59.0
27	24 21.71	28.31	1.71	V.	3	33.185	26 40.29	3.01	3.36	23 51.7	28 45 45.7
28	25 51.23	28.32	1.84	IV.	2	7.705	53 12.99	3.13	8.50	25 21.1	29 12 24.6
29	26 35.34	28.33	1.82	V.	2	12.443	48 16.41	3.20	7.55	26 5.2	29 7 27.2
30	27 17.96	28.34	1.72	VI.	3	31.475	28 27.58	3.26	3.70	26 47.9	28 47 34.5
31	28 32.16	28.35	1.71	IV.	3	33.142	26 42.94	3.36	3.37	28 2.1	45 49.7
32	29	28.35	1.67	VII.	4	46.581	12 31.36	3.45	0.66	29	31 35.5
33	32 4.73	28.37	1.64	IV.	5	48.607	10 24.58	3.65	0.26	31 34.7	29 28.5
34	34 7.53	28.39	1.64	III.	5	48.195	10 50.12	3.83	0.34	33 37.5	27 54.3
35	35 11.69	28.40	1.63	IV.	5	49.072	9 55.33	3.92	0.18	34 41.9	28 59.4
36	37 6.18	28.42	1.77	III.	2	22.563	37 53.27	4.09	5.51	36 30.0	57 2.9
37	37 35.90	28.42	1.77	IV.	2	21.627	38 39.87	4.13	5.69	37 5.7	57 49.8
38	40 12.65	28.45	1.77	IV.	3	23.443	36 51.54	4.35	5.33	39 42.4	56 1.2
39	42 57.30	28.46	1.70	IV.	3	37.482	22 10.66	4.60	2.50	42 27.1	41 17.9
40	43 32.18	28.47	1.79	VI.	2	20.177	40 11.52	4.65	5.98	43 1.9	59 22.2
41	44 53.55	28.48	1.76	IV.	3	27.522	32 35.60	4.77	4.51	44 23.3	28 51 44.9
42	49 15.00	28.52	1.83	IV.	2	12.237	48 28.96	5.16	7.59	48 44.6	29 7 41.7
43	50 12.83	28.53	1.73	III.	3	31.358	28 34.80	5.26	3.73	49 42.6	28 47 43.8
44	53 8.47	28.56	1.84	IV.	2	12.766	47 55.59	5.55	7.49	52 38.1	29 7 8.6
45	53 41.98	28.56	1.71	IV.	4	38.317	21 9.23	5.60	2.34	53 11.7	28 40 17.2
46	54 34.32	28.57	1.83	VI.	2	14.118	46 31.49	5.68	7.22	54 3.9	29 5 44.4
47	57 56.94	28.59	1.84	III.	2	11.858	48 51.97	6.00	7.67	57 26.5	8 5.6
48	4 58 7.70	28.60	1.84	IV.	2	12.455	48 15.29	6.03	7.55	4 57 37.3	29 7 28.9
49	5 1 6.42	28.62	1.73	IV.	3	33.205	26 39.03	6.37	3.36	5 0 36.1	28 45 48.7
50	5 1 33.65	−28.63	−1.76	IV.	3	27.802	−32 17.84	− 6.36	− 4.45	5 1 3.3	− 28 51 28.7

CORRECTIONS.

Date.	Corr. of Clock.	Hourly rate.	m	n	c	Zenith Point.	Mic. Co.
1849.	h. s.	s.	s.	s.	s.	° ′ ″	r..

INSTRUMENT READINGS.

Date.	CIRCLE.							Barom.	THERMOM.				
	A.	B.	C.	D.	E.	F.	Mean.		At.	Ex.	U.	L.	I.
	1849. h. m.							in.					
Zone 222	Feb. 10, 3 40	87 39 61.2	63.1	70.8	55.8	63.1	48.6	60.43	30.040	40.	32.	36.6	38.2	38.8
	4 0										31.7			
	4 20										31.2			
	4 40										30.6			
	4 45								30.020	39.	30.5			
	5 0	61.4	63.8	71.	56.	62.8	47.6	60.43	30.002*	36.5	30.	36.	33.8

REMARKS.

(222) 10. Transit over T. VI assumed to have been recorded as over T. V.

(222) 22. Micrometer reading assumed as 44r.931, not 49r.931.

(222) 37. Right ascension differs 1m from Arg. Z. 351, 47.

(222) 41. Time of transit over T. IV assumed as at 53s.2 instead of 43s.2.

[(222) 16. Precedes 15. 10s.]

*Barom. assumed as 30.020; at. therm., 38.5.

ZONE 223.　FEBRUARY 13.　C.　$D_0 = -32°\ 4'\ 50''$.

No.	Mag.	I	II	III	IV	V	VI	VII	T. (h m s)	a_1 (s)	a_4 (s)	Mic.	n	r	(° ′ ″)	i (″)	d_1 (″)	d_4 (″)	Mean R.A. 1850.0 (h m s)	Mean Decl. 1850.0 (° ′ ″)
1	9.10		39.3		16.3				7 51 16.15	-30.69	-0.91	IV.	2	21.751	-38 32.04	-3.60	-12.17		7 50 44.6	-32 43 36.8
2	8				54.		31.2		51 54.27	30.69	0.91	IV.	2	14.665	45 56.55	2.67	14.02		51 22.7	51 3.2
3	8				57.1		33.5		51 56.99	30.69	0.91	VI.	2	21.009	39 19.20	2.68	12.35		51 25.4	44 24.2
4	9.10				31.2				53 31.09	30.69	0.99	IV.	5	53.416	5 22.77	2.85	4.01		52 59.4	10 19.6
5	10				37.2				53 37.09	30.69	0.99	VII.	5	54.460	4 17.43	2.86	3.75		53 5.4	9 14.0
6	9								55	30.70	0.97	VII.	5	46.971	12 7.32	3.05	5.63		55	17 6.0
7	9			20.	38.5		44.5		56 38.25	30.70	0.93	IV.	2	19.662	40 43.14	3.22	12.74		56 6.6	45 49.1
8	9				39.	27.2	45.		56 8.53	30.70	0.91	IV.	2	12.675	48 1.36	3.16	14.58		55 36.9	53 9.1
9	8.9					55.3	13.3		57 36.83	30.70	0.93	V.	3	21.331	39 4.03	3.33	12.27		57 5.2	44 9.6
10	8				56.5	15.3			7 58 56.74	30.71	0.99	IV.	5	48.797	10 12.52	3.48	5.18		58 25.0	13 11.2
11	9			11.5	29.7				8 0 29.80	30.71	0.92	III.	2	11.512	49 13.87	3.66	14.83		7 59 58.2	54 22.4
12	9						9.5		0 33.02	30.71	0.95	VI.	3	24.568	35 40.78	3.67	11.40		8 0 1.4	40 45.9
13	9.10		51.4						2 23.17	30.72	0.95	II.	3	25.744	34 26.44	3.89	11.11		1 56.5	39 31.4
14	8.9			39.3	57.3				2 57.50	30.72	0.93	IV.	2	11.527	49 13.43	3.94	14.82		2 25.8	54 22.2
15	9						34.3		3 57.81	30.72	0.96	VI.	3	23.862	36 24.58	4.05	11.59		3 26.1	41 30.5
16	8.9					56.2			3 37.71	30.72	0.94	V.	3	17.021	43 34.25	4.01	13.38		3 6.1	48 41.6
17	8.9				40.3	4.8			4 46.34	30.72	0.98	IV.	3	36.068	23 39.33	4.15	8.45		4 14.6	28 41.9
18	9						30.5		4 54.05	30.72	1.00	VI.	4	46.004	13 7.33	4.17	6.43		4 22.3	18 7.9
19	9						2.3		5 46.53	30.72	1.03	VI.	5	54.038	4 43.87	4.26	3.90		5 14.8	9 42.0
20	9		22.4	40.8					7 59.14	30.73	0.99	III.	3	33.725	26 6.09	4.51	9.04		7 27.4	31 9.6
21	9					31.3	49.3		8 12.75	30.73	0.96	V.	2	14.873	45 43.76	4.54	13.93		7 47.1	50 52.2
22	9				18.3				11 18.19	30.73	0.98	IV.	3	22.454	37 53.58	4.89	11.07		10 46.5	43 0.4
23	8.9					0.5			11 42.20	30.73	1.00	V.	3	32.184	27 43.11	4.93	9.44		11 10.5	32 47.5
24	8					24.3	42.0		12 6.27	30.73	1.03	V.	4	44.985	14 11.03	4.98	6.17		11 34.5	19 12.2
25	9			29.4	47.3				47.46			IV.	3	26.868	33 16.43	5.25	10.81		(13 16)	38 22.4
26	9					17.3	35.4		14 58.99	30.74	1.01	V.	3	31.663	28 15.73	5.31	9.58		14 27.2	33 20.6
27	9			10.3	28.2				15 28.39	30.74	1.04	III.	4	44.864	14 17.61	5.37	6.21		14 55.6	19 19.2
28	7				0.3	18.3	37.2		16 0.30	30.74	1.01	IV.	3	30.268	29 43.37	5.42	9.94		15 28.6	34 48.7
29	9.10				12.2				16 12.05	30.74	1.01	V.	3	39.215	29 46.70	5.44	9.95		15 40.3	34 52.1
30	10						32.3		16 55.77	30.74	0.99	VI.	2	18.945	41 27.36	5.53	12.87		16 24.0	46 35.8
31	8			16.3	34.5		11.3		18 31.64	30.75	1.04	IV.	4	39.570	30 18.00	5.72	7.55		18 2.8	35 21.3
32	9.10						3.2		18 26.77	30.75	1.03	VI.	3	35.122	24 38.63	5.70	8.69		17 55.0	29 43.0
33	9						52.5		19 16.06	30.75	1.04	VI.	3	38.303	21 19.18	5.79	7.84		18 44.3	26 22.8
34	9			35.3	53.3	11.4			20 53.32	30.75	1.04	IV.	3	37.201	22 28.31	5.98	8.15		20 21.5	27 32.4
35	8.9					26.2	44.5		21 7.89	30.75	1.01	V.	2	22.032	38 14.86	6.00	12.07		20 36.1	43 22.9
36	10				12.3				22 12.20	30.75	1.01	IV.	2	19.079	41 19.71	6.13	12.83		21 40.4	16 28.7
37	9						55.8		22 19.20	30.75	0.99	VI.	2	12.498	48 13.16	6.15	14.57		21 47.5	53 23.9
38	9				17.3				24 17.18	30.75	1.08	IV.	5	49.036	9 57.59	6.36	5.16		23 45.3	14 59.1
39	9				55.2				24 55.08	30.75	1.08	IV.	5	49.451	9 31.66	6.44	5.04		24 23.2	14 33.1
40	8.9								24	30.75	1.04	VI.	3	30.637	29 19.98	6.50	9.84		24	34 26.3
41	9						8.3		25 31.47	30.76	1.02	VI.	2	18.918	41 30.30	6.51	12.80		25 59.7	46 39.7
42	9		40.1	50.2	17.4	35.4			30 17.18	30.76	1.06	IV.	3	27.674	32 26.00	7.04	10.63		29 45.4	37 33.7
43	9		17.5	36.	54.2	12.5			31 54.20	30.76	1.06	IV.	3	32.354	27 32.50	7.21	9.30		31 22.4	32 39.1
44	10					33.2			32 14.69	30.76	1.04	V.	2	15.691	44 52.52	7.25	13.71		31 42.9	50 3.5
45	9		12.8	31.3	49.2				35 49.46	30.76	1.07	IV.	3	23.122	37 11.56	7.31	11.81		35 17.6	42 20.7
46	10				5.2				36 5.11	30.76	1.05	IV.	2	17		8.	13.		35 35.3	48
47	9		28.3	46.2					38 4.80	30.77	1.09	III.	3	28.154	31 55.70	7.91	10.47		37 32.9	37 4.1
48	5		29.	47.2	6.		42.2		38 5.73	30.77	1.08	IV.	3	26.462	33 42.15	7.91	10.02		37 33.9	38 51.0
49	9		30.5	48.8	6.5				8 41 6.06	-30.77	-1.09	IV.	3	23.449	-36 51.16	-8.24	-11.69		8 40 35.1	-32 42 1.1

CORRECTIONS.

Date.	Corr. of Clock.	Hourly rate.	m	u	r	Zenith Point.	Mic. Co.
1849.	h.	s.	s.	s.	s.	° ′ ″	r.

REMARKS. — (223) 7. Transit over T. VI assumed as at 14ˢ.5 instead of 44ˢ.5.

INSTRUMENT READINGS.

Date.		A.	B.	C.	D.	E.	F.	Mean.	Barom.	At.	Ex	U.	L.	I.
Zone 223	1849. Feb. 13, 7 45	91 24 59.9	65.7	70.4	55.4	63.	47.6	60.50	in.					
	7 50								30.036	39.	29.	40.7	35.9	36.3
	8 10										29.8			
	8 20										30.2			
	7 50								30.026	37.5	31.			
	9 0	60.1	65.0	71.2	55.4	63.1	46.	60.13			31.8		34.5	36.
	9 20										32.4			
	9 40								30.016		32.6			
	10 0	59.6	64.1	71.2	55.4	61.4	46.5	59.70	30.022	37.	32.2		34.8	36.3

[(223) 40. Precedes 39. 2ˢ or 3ˢ.]

ZONE 223. FEBRUARY 13. C. $D_0 = -32° 4' 50''$ —Continued.

No.	Mag.	I.	II.	III.	IV.	V.	VI.	VII.	T.	a_1	a_i
									h. m. s.	s.	s.
50	9							34.5	6 41 58.04	−30.77	−1.14
51	8			20.3					42 20.22	30.77	1.07
52	9							44.2	42 7.68	30.77	1.08
53	9			53.2		30.5	48.3		44 11.92	30.77	1.14
54	7				17.5		54.		44 17.46	30.77	1.15
55	9					27.	45.3		45 8.79	30.77	1.12
56	9.10		36.2	54.3	12.5				47 12.65	30.77	1.14
57	9		42.5	1.3	19.3				48 19.34	30.77	1.12
58	9					49.2	8.2		49 31.15	30.77	1.09
59	8					10.5	28.2		49 51.82	30.77	1.09
60	10						11.8		53 35.37	30.77	1.15
61	10					59.			53 40.70	30.77	1.14
62	9						3.2		54 26.69	30.77	1.12
63	9				43.5	1.9	20.3		8 58 43.61	30.77	1.16
64	9.10			49.2	7.8				9 0 7.62	30.77	1.18
65	10				37.2	55.2			0 18.90	30.77	1.21
66	9				17.2	5.2			1 46.98	30.77	1.16
67	9		21.3		57.5				4 57.69	30.77	1.18
68	9				17.2			11.8	8 35.43	30.76	1.15
69	9			29.3		6.24			8 47.63	30.76	1.16
70	8.9				52.3	11.	39.3		9 52.53	30.76	1.18
71	9.10				30.8				12 30.66	30.76	1.22
72	10				25.?				13 24.85	30.76	1.21
73	9						26.3		13 49.85	30.76	1.23
74	8		17.4	35.6	53.8		30.6		17 23.08	30.76	1.22
75	9.10						54.8		18 18.34	30.76	1.26
76	9				57.3	15.8	34.2		19 57.47	30.75	1.23
77	9				31.2		7.2		20 30.00	30.75	1.22
78	9.10						8.3		21 31.64	30.75	1.27
79	9.10			9.8	27.5				23 9.16	30.75	1.26
80	8.9				13.3	31.8			23 55.11	30.75	1.23
81	8				49.8	8.2			24 31.52	30.75	1.22
82	9					22.2			25 45.61	30.74	1.21
83	9						53.3		26 16.77	30.74	1.23
84	9					40.3			28 3.85	30.74	1.28
85	9		15.7	34.2					30 34.16	30.74	1.22
86	9				19.8				31 1.48	30.74	1.25
87	9				46.	4.2			31 27.71	30.74	1.26
88	9.10		32.8		9.5				34 51.28	30.73	1.31
89	9		21.5	40.	16.5				34 58.32	30.73	1.31
90	9			35.4	53.5				35 17.14	30.73	1.32
91	8			39.2	57.3	16.2			36 57.52	30.72	1.26
92	9			11.5	30.				38 11.55	30.72	1.31
93	8		44.2	2.8	21.	39.5			40 21.05	30.72	1.26
94	8		2.8	21.	39.5	57.2			41 39.28	30.72	1.30
95	9.10					38.1			43 1.56	30.71	1.28
96	9						6.3		43 29.80	30.71	1.29
97	9					57.2			44 35.90	30.71	1.31
98	9.10					31.			9 44 54.52	−30.71	−1.30

No.	MICROMETER.		r.	i	d_1	d_i	Mean Right Ascension, 1850.0.	Mean Declination, 1850.0.
			r.	' "	"	"	h. m. s.	° ' "
50	VI.	5	51.532	− 7 21.29	− 8.34	− 4.52	8 41 26.1	−. 32 12 24.2
51	IV.	2	14.925	45 40.12	8.37	13.91	41 48.4	50 52.4
52	VI.	2	19.520	40 52.73	8.35	12.73	41 35.8	46 3.8
53	IV.	4	45.419	13 43.53	8.58	6.08	43 40.0	18 48.2
54	IV.	5	50.621	6 18.16	8.59	4.75	43 45.5	13 21.5
55	V.	3	34.538	25 15.40	8.68	8.85	44 36.9	30 22.9
56	IV.	3	39.455	20 6.92	8.91	7.58	46 40.7	25 13.4
57	IV.	3	31.748	28 10.33	9.03	9.55	47 47.5	33 18.9
58	V.	2	14.564	46 3.34	9.17	14.00	48 50.3	51 16.5
59	V.	2	15.002	44 39.35	9.20	13.66	49 20.0	49 52.2
60	IV.	3	33.543	26 17.83	9.61	9.08	53 3.4	31 26.5
61	V.	3	31.165	28 47.04	9.62	9.70	53 8.8	33 56.4
62	VI.	2	21.049	39 16.70	9.70	12.32	53 54.8	44 28.7
63	IV.	3	34.492	25 18.28	10.17	8.85	58 11.7	30 27.3
64	IV.	4	42.152	17 8.50	10.33	7.90	59 35.7	22 16.7
65	V.	5	54.988	3 44.16	10.35	3.69	8 59 46.9	8 48.2
66	IV.	3	31.189	28 45.53	10.51	9.69	9 1 15.1	33 55.7
67	IV.	3	35.415	24 20.43	10.85	8.62	4 25.7	33 29.9
68	IV.	2	12.117	48 36.36	11.25	14.63	8 3.5	53 52.2
69	IV.	2	17.480	43 0.12	11.27	13.23	8 15.7	48 14.6
70	IV.	3	23.458	36 50.60	11.40	11.69	9 20.6	42 3.7
71	IV.	4	40.525	18 50.61	11.68	7.33	11 58.7	23 59.6
72	IV.	3	35.363	24 23.70	11.78	8.65	12 51.9	29 34.1
73	VI.	4	46.196	12 55.39	11.82	5.89	13 17.9	18 3.1
74	IV.	3	31.556	28 22.50	12.27	9.60	17 22.0	33 34.4
75	VI.	5	52.004	6 51.54	12.32	4.42	17 46.3	11 58.3
76	IV.	3	33.358	26 29.50	12.50	9.19	19 25.5	31 41.2
77	V.	3	24.107	36 9.84	12.56	11.52	19 58.9	41 23.9
78	VI.	5	50.612	8 56.58	12.67	4.94	20 59.8	14 4.2
79	IV.	4	41.375	17 57.33	12.85	7.10	22 37.2	23 7.3
80	V.	3	24.057	36 12.91	12.93	11.55	23 23.1	41 27.4
81	V.	2	20.754	39 34.95	13.01	12.30	23 59.5	44 50.4
82	VI.	2	13.278	47 24.24	13.16	14.34	25 13.7	52 41.7
83	VI.	2	19.275	41 8.10	13.23	12.77	25 44.8	46 24.1
84	VI.	4	46.962	12 7.13	13.42	5.69	27 31.6	17 16.2
85	III.	2	10.208	50 35.65	13.70	15.12	30 2.2	55 54.5
86	V.	3	25.585	34 37.11	13.75	11.13	30 29.4	39 52.0
87	V.	3	28.636	31 25.64	13.81	10.34	30 55.7	36 39.8
88	IV.	5	48.822	10 10.95	14.19	5.25	34 19.2	15 20.4
89	IV.	5	49.446	9 31.97	14.20	5.11	34 26.3	14 41.3
90	IV.	5	50.183	9 45.65	14.24	4.90	34 45.1	13 54.8
91	IV.	2	22.474	37 46.87	14.44	11.93	36 25.5	43 3.2
92	IV.	3	38.922	20 40.11	14.58	7.75	37 39.5	25 52.4
93	IV.	2	16.796	43 42.78	14.83	13.39	39 49.1	49 1.0
94	IV.	3	32.260	27 38.33	14.99	9.41	41 7.3	32 52.7
95	V.	2	18.142	42 18.91	15.15	13.04	42 29.6	47 37.1
96	VI.	2	22.920	37 19.27	15.21	11.81	42 57.8	42 36.3
97	V.	3	31.005	28 57.01	15.35	9.74	44 6.9	35 12.1
98	VI.	3	25.025	− 35 12.05	− 15.38	− 11.28	9 44 22.5	− 32 41 28.7

CORRECTIONS.

Date.	Corr. of Clock.	Hourly rate.	m	n	c	Zenith Point.	Mic. Co.
	h.	s.	s.	s.	s.	s.	° ' "	r.
1849.								

REMARKS.

(223) 58. Transits 1st discordant.
(223) 70. Time of transit over T. VI assumed as 29ˢ.3 instead of 39ˢ.3.

INSTRUMENT READINGS.

Date.	CIRCLE.							Barom.	THERMOM.				
	A.	B.	C.	D.	E.	F.	Mean.		At.	Ex.	U.	L.	I.
1849. h. m.	° ' "							in.	°				

ZONE 223. FEBRUARY 13. C. $D_o = -32° 4' 50''$—Continued.

No.	Mag.	I.	II.	III.	IV.	V.	VI.	VII.	T. (h. m. s.)	a_1	a_2	Mic.	n	r.	i (' '')	d_1 ('')	d_2 ('')	Mean Right Ascension, 1850.0 (h. m. s.)	Mean Declination, 1850.0 (° ' '')
99	8.9	·	·	·	·	·	32.3	·	9 45 55.84	−30.71	−1.34	VI.	5	47.607	−11 27.59	−15.50	−5.54	9 45 23.8	− 32 16 38.6
100	9	·	·	38.	55.3	·	·	·	47 55.74	30.70	1.32	IV.	3	33.320	26 31.82	15.74	9.14	47 23.7	31 46.7
101	9	·	·	·	34.	52.3	·	·	48 15.76	30.70	1.31	V.	3	28.693	31 22.07	15.76	10.32	47 43.8	36 38.2
102	8	·	·	·	30.9	49.	·	·	49 12.53	30.70	1.30	V.	3	26.224	33 57.08	15.90	10.97	48 40.5	39 14.0
103	7	·	·	16.3	34.3	53.2	11.3	·	50 34.62	30.70	1.31	IV.	3	23.094	32 13.32	16.06	11.77	50 2.6	42 31.2
104	9	·	·	·	47.3	·	24.1	·	51 47.41	30.70	1.32	IV.	3	31.915	27 59.79	16.21	9.50	51 15.4	33 15.5
105	9	·	·	·	·	1.3	·	·	52 42.70	30.69	1.28	V.	2	9.094	51 46.33	16.32	15.40	52 10.7	57 8.0
106	9	·	·	·	·	·	44.8	·	53 8.26	30.69	1.31	VI.	2	17.692	42 47.26	16.39	13.16	52 36.3	48 6.8
107	9.10	·	·	·	3.2	·	·	·	55 3.06	30.68	1.35	IV.	4	40.534	18 50.11	16.63	7.33	54 31.0	24 4.1
108	9.10	·	·	·	1.3	·	·	·	56 1.16	30.68	1.36	IV.	4	38.564	20 53.73	16.75	6.81	55 29.1	26 7.3
109	7.8	·	43.	1.3	19.2	38.1	56.2	·	57 19.60	30.68	1.35	IV.	3	34.208	25 36.10	16.92	8.94	56 47.6	30 52.0
110	10	·	·	28.	·	·	4.2	·	58 27.81	30.67	1.38	IV.	4	47.840	11 10.82	17.07	5.52	57 55.8	16 23.4
111	8	·	·	·	·	47.2	5.5	·	9 59 28.93	30.67	1.34	V.	3	25.675	34 31.41	17.21	11.11	9 58 56.9	39 49.7
112	9.10	·	53.	11.4	29.3	·	·	·	10 1 29.54	30.67	1.36	IV.	3	34.265	25 32.59	17.44	8.92	10 0 57.5	30 49.0
113	9	·	·	43.	1.3	19.3	·	·	10 3 1.25	−30.66	−1.39	IV.	5	49.862	− 9 5.67	−17.64	−5.00	10 2 29.2	− 32 14 18.3

ZONE 224. FEBRUARY 13. C. $D_o = -32° 5' 20'$.

No.	Mag.	I.	II.	III.	IV.	V.	VI.	VII.	T. (h. m. s.)	a_1	a_2	Mic.	n	r.	i (' '')	d_1 ('')	d_2 ('')	Mean Right Ascension, 1850.0 (h. m. s.)	Mean Declination, 1850.0 (° ' '')
1	9	·	·	·	·	·	33.3	·	11 43 56.86	−31.14	−0.37	VI.	4	41.389	−17 56.64	−1.96	−4.06	11 43 25.35	− 32 23 22.7
2	9.10	·	·	2.8	21.1	39.3	·	·	46 21.02	31.13	0.24	IV.	2	16.513	44 0.71	2.18	10.54	45 49.65	40 33.4
3	9	·	·	·	20.2	38.2	·	·	47 1.65	31.12	0.23	V.	2	14.826	45 46.71	2.24	11.00	46 30.30	51 19.9
4	9	·	·	4.9	23.	41.5	·	·	48 23.09	31.11	0.35	IV.	3	28.638	31 26.15	2.35	7.35	47 51.63	36 55.9
5	8	·	21.8	40.5	58.5	16.5	14.6	·	49 55.43	31.10	0.35	IV.	3	36.368	23 20.63	2.50	5.34	49 26.98	28 18.5
6	9	·	·	36.5	54.8	13.2	31.1	·	11 58 54.85	31.02	0.51	IV.	5	56.951	1 40.68	3.28	0.05	11 58 23.32	7 4.0
7	9.10	·	15.7	34.3	52.5	·	·	·	12 1 52.50	31.02	0.47	IV.	4	49.393	9 34.10	3.52	1.93	12 1 21.01	14 59.5
8	9.10	·	·	27.6	45.3	·	·	·	2 45.57	31.01	0.41	IV.	4	40.901	18 26.88	3.60	4.16	2 14.15	23 54.6
9	9	·	·	·	·	·	11.3	·	2 34.84	31.01	0.33	VI.	3	26.569	33 35.25	3.59	7.90	2 3.50	39 6.7
10	9	·	·	·	57.2	·	34.	·	3 57.28	31.00	0.29	IV.	3	18.958	41 32.62	3.71	9.91	3 25.99	47 6.2
11	9	·	·	36.2	·	32.9	·	·	4 14.56	30.99	0.34	IV.	3	31.237	28 42.51	3.72	6.70	3 43.23	34 13.0
12	9	·	·	·	59.2	·	35.5	·	5 59.33	30.98	0.33	IV.	3	24.341	35 55.22	3.88	7.18	5 28.02	41 26.3
13	9.10	·	·	·	3.5	·	40.	·	5 3.46	30.99	0.35	V.	3	26.949	33 11.41	3.80	7.79	4 32.12	38 43.0
14	9	·	·	·	·	·	21.5	39.6	7 2.94	30.97	0.21	VI.	2	9.773	51 3.87	3.97	12.30	6 31.73	56 40.1
15	9	·	·	·	·	·	·	·	7	30.97	0.27	VII.	2	15.406	45 10.83	4.02	10.84	· · ·	41 45.7
16	10	·	·	·	·	2.2	·	·	8 43.97	30.96	0.42	V.	4	41.618	17 48.68	4.11	4.00	8 12.59	23 16.8
17	9	·	·	4.7	23.5	·	·	·	11 41.64	30.94	0.42	III.	3	37.630	22 1.13	4.36	5.02	11 10.28	27 30.5
18	9	·	·	·	·	47.2	·	·	11 47.14	30.94	0.26	IV.	2	11.659	49 5.08	4.37	11.82	11 15.94	54 41.3
19	10	·	·	·	·	22.	·	·	12 3.39	30.93	0.24	V.	2	8.630	52 15.41	4.39	12.61	11 32.22	57 52.4
20	9.10	·	·	·	35.5	53.6	·	·	14 53.65	30.91	0.40	III.	3	35.888	23 50.32	4.62	5.48	14 22.34	29 20.4
21	9	·	·	·	17.2	35.5	53.5	·	15 17.06	30.91	0.33	IV.	3	22.206	38 6.82	4.65	9.05	14 45.82	43 40.5
22	9.10	·	13.5	32.1	50.2	·	·	·	17 50.26	30.89	0.51	IV.	5	48.827	10 10.63	4.86	2.16	17 18.86	15 37.7
23	10	·	·	·	31.8	·	·	·	19 31.69	30.87	0.58	IV.	5	55.206	3 30.41	5.00	0.54	19 0.24	8 56.0
24	9	·	5.	23.1	41.3	50.6	·	·	21 41.42	30.86	0.40	IV.	3	35.422	24 19.90	5.17	5.61	21 10.16	29 50.8
25	9	·	33.	51.3	9.2	28.2	46.2	·	24 9.61	30.84	0.31	IV.	2	15.758	44 47.95	5.36	10.75	23 38.46	50 24.1
26	9.10	·	·	·	6.8	·	43.2	·	25 6.71	30.83	0.47	IV.	4	43.231	16 0.66	5.44	3.57	24 35.41	21 29.9
27	10	·	·	·	·	46.3	·	·	25 28.09	30.82	0.48	IV.	4	43.879	15 19.99	5.46	3.42	24 56.79	20 48.9
28	9	·	·	·	·	·	·	53.	26 16.56	30.82	0.46	VI.	3	38.618	20 59.26	5.53	4.77	25 45.28	26 29.6
29	10	·	·	11.2	·	·	·	5.5	28 29.33	30.80	0.49	VI.	4	44.691	14 29.73	5.70	3.21	27 58.04	19 58.6
30	9.10	·	·	·	32.2	50.2	8.3	·	28 32.00	30.80	0.51	IV.	4	47.492	11 33.43	5.70	2.48	28 0.69	17 1.6
31	10	·	4.5	·	·	59.2	·	·	12 32 41.08	−30.77	−0.46	V.	3	38.175	−21 27.18	−6.01	−4.89	12 32 9.85	− 32 26 58.1

CORRECTIONS.

Date.	Corr. of Clock.	Hourly rate.	m	n	c	Zenith Point.	Mic. Co.
1849.	h.	s.	s.	s.	s.	° ' ''	r.

REMARKS.

(224) 11. Time of transit over T. III assumed as 56ˢ.2 instead of 36ˢ.2.

INSTRUMENT READINGS.

Date.		CIRCLE.						THERMOM.				
	A.	B.	C.	D.	E.	F.	Mean.	Barom.	At.	Ex.	U. L.	I.
Zone 224 Feb. 13, 11 44	° ' ''						''	in. 30.052	37.	30.7		
11 50	91 24	59.1	64.8 71.3	56.1 62.1	46.3		59.95	· · ·	·	30.2	35.8 36.5	
12 10								· · ·		30.1		
12 20								30.054	37.	29.1		
12 40								· · ·		29.6		
13 0								30.054	36.5	29.6		
13 20								· · ·		27.9		
13 40	58.9	65.8	71.1 56.2	63.	45.2		60.03	30.060	35.5	28,	35.7 33.5	

External Thermometer assumed as 29°.5, 28°.6, and 28°.

ZONE 224. FEBRUARY 13. C. $D_0 = -32°\ 5'\ 20''$—Continued.

No.	Mag.	I.	II.	III.	IV.	V.	VI.	VII.	T. (h. m. s.)	a_1 (s.)	a_2 (s.)
32	9.10			29.		5.2			12 33 47.10	−30.76	−0.40
33	10					3.3			34 26.82	30.75	0.38
34	7.8		35.2		11.3	30.2	48.3		39 11.71	30.71	0.45
35	9		42.1	0.8	18.8				42 18.91	30.68	0.39
36	9				43.2		19.8		42 43.19	30.67	0.35
37	9.10				45.8				43 45.66	30.68	0.49
38	9					25.3			44 7.01	30.67	0.45
39	9.10					51.			44 32.72	30.67	0.46
40	9.10				39.2	57.5			45 57.44	30.67	0.44
41	9.10					32.3			46 14.09	30.67	0.51
42	9.10				44.6	3.	21.5		48 2.98	30.63	0.34
43	9		12.5	30.8	48.5	7.3			49 48.96	30.62	0.53
44	10				21.2				50 21.05	30.61	0.40
45	9				11.4	30.2			51 11.57	30.61	0.45
46	7.8		14.8	33.	51.5				52 51.45	30.59	0.42
47	8.9			4.5		41.5	59.5		53 23.01	30.59	0.42
48	8					39.	57.5		53 20.74	30.59	0.37
49	9			42.3					56 0.73	30.56	0.57
50	9					25.7	43.2		57 7.12	30.55	0.55
51	10			15.8	34.				12 59 52.45	30.53	0.54
52	8		37.3	55.5	14.	32.3			13 1 13.94	30.52	0.43
53	10				5.2				5 23.62	30.48	0.38
54	9			56.2		33.			6 14.61	30.47	0.46
55	9			58.3	17.	34.7			8 35.00	30.45	0.44
56	9				6.5	24.8			9 24.73	30.44	0.47
57	9				5.		41.5		10 4.96	30.44	0.46
58	9						23.5		10 47.05	30.43	0.57
59	9			18.4	36.0	55.3			12 36.81	30.42	0.30
60	9.10		50.2		26.8				14 26.90	30.40	0.39
61	9.10					7.2	25.3		14 48.68	30.40	0.37
62	8								15	30.39	0.54
63	9					12.2	30.6		16 53.98	30.37	0.45
64	9					4.2	22.5		17 46.01	30.36	0.54
65	9			50.	8.2				20 8.20	30.34	0.53
66	9					35.3			20 16.73	30.34	0.38
67	9						14.6		20 38.11	30.34	0.47
68	9					45.3	3.		22 26.79	30.32	0.51
69	9				15.8	34.3			24 15.84	30.30	0.55
70	8		7.	25.2	43.3	2.1	20.2		26 43.60	30.28	0.53
71	9			48.3	6.5		43.4		28 6.67	30.27	0.47
72	8		11.9	30.1	48.1	6.4			30 48.32	30.24	0.61
73	10				5.5				33 23.95	30.22	0.43
74	8.9				41.2				33 41.12	30.22	0.42
75	9						28.2		33 51.77	30.21	0.54
76	9.10				41.2				35 41.06	30.20	0.57
77	9.10					29.8			36 11.55	30.19	0.56
78	9					29.			37 10.71	30.18	0.54
79	6					59.1			37 40.92	30.17	0.62
80	10				41.8				39 41.68	30.15	0.50
81	9.10			32.6					13 40 50.93	−30.14	−0.53

No.	MICROMETER.	i	r	′	″	d_1 ('')	d ('')	Mean Right Ascension, 1850.0 (h. m. s.)	Mean Declination, 1850.0 (° ′ ″)
32	V.	3	28.513	−31	33.48	6.09	−7.39	12 33 15.94	− 32 37 7.0
33	VI.	3	24.878	35	21.21	6.13	8.33	33 55.60	40 55.7
34	IV.	3	35.712	24	1.61	6.47	5.53	38 40.55	29 33.6
35	IV.	3	24.652	35	35.58	6.68	8.39	41 47.64	41 10.6
36	IV.	2	18.586	41	50.70	6.71	10.00	42 12.17	47 27.4
37	IV.	4	41.586	17	44.03	6.77	3.99	43 14.49	23 14.8
38	V.	3	33.711	26	7.16	6.80	6.04	43 35.89	31 40.0
39	V.	3	35.306	24	27.27	6.82	5.62	44 1.59	29 59.7
40	IV.	3	32.186	27	42.98	6.91	6.44	45 26.33	33 16.3
41	V.	4	43.508	15	43.85	6.93	3.50	45 42.91	21 14.3
42	IV.	2	14.146	46	29.18	7.05	11.16	47 32.01	52 7.4
43	IV.	5	44.225	14	59.66	7.17	3.33	49 17.81	20 30.2
44	IV.	5	31.872	28	2.49	7.20	6.51	49 49.98	33 36.2
45	IV.	3	30.830	29	7.67	7.25	6.79	50 40.51	34 41.9
46	IV.	3	24.352	35	54.53	7.34	8.46	52 20.44	41 30.3
47	III.	3	25.710	34	28.95	7.37	8.12	52 52.00	40 4.4
48	V.	2	17.361	43	7.96	7.37	10.34	52 49.78	48 45.7
49	III.	5	48.545	10	28.09	7.53	2.20	55 29.60	15 57.8
50	V.	4	44.888	14	17.05	7.60	3.16	56 36.02	19 47.8
51	III.	4	43.957	15	14.54	7.75	3.30	12 59 21.38	20 45.7
52	IV.	3	23.956	36	19.10	7.82	8.59	13 0 42.99	41 55.5
53	III.	2	17.096	43	23.58	8.02	10.41	4 52.76	49 2.0
54	IV.	3	30.156	29	50.44	8.06	6.96	5 43.68	35 25.5
55	IV.	3	25.846	34	20.55	8.10	8.08	8 4.11	39 56.8
56	IV.	3	29.626	30	23.53	8.22	7.12	8 53.82	35 58.9
57	IV.	3	28.001	32	5.42	8.25	7.52	9 34.06	37 41.2
58	V.	5	46.820	12	16.79	8.29	2.68	10 16.05	17 47.8
59	V.	2	14.205	46	25.85	8.36	11.16	12 6.00	52 5.4
60	IV.	2	14.673	45	56.06	8.43	11.04	13 56.11	51 35.5
61	IV.	2	12.884	47	48.51	8.44	11.53	14 47.91	53 28.5
62	VII.	4	40.715	18	39.32	8.48	4.23	15	24 12.0
63	V.	3	25.964	34	13.20	8.54	8.07	16 23.16	39 49.8
64	V.	5	40.305	19	5.91	8.57	4.35	17 15.11	24 38.8
65	IV.	3	35.563	24	11.08	8.66	5.55	19 37.33	29 45.3
66	IV.	2	11.094	49	40.90	8.67	12.00	19 46.01	55 21.6
67	VI.	3	23.841	36	26.20	8.68	8.62	20 7.30	42 3.5
68	IV.	3	32.317	27	34.82	8.73	6.40	21 55.96	33 10.0
69	IV.	3	36.788	22	54.03	8.80	5.23	23 44.99	28 28.1
70	IV.	3	33.112	26	44.81	8.87	6.19	26 12.79	32 19.9
71	IV.	3	23.361	36	56.69	8.91	8.76	27 35.93	42 34.4
72	IV.	4	44.032	15	10.46	9.00	3.37	30 17.47	20 42.8
73	III.	2	18.704	47	53.28	9.05	11.56	32 53.30	53 33.9
74	IV.	2	16.018	44	31.64	9.05	10.70	33 10.48	50 11.4
75	VI.	3	34.380	25	25.25	9.06	5.85	33 21.02	31 0.2
76	IV.	3	40.588	18	55.75	9.09	4.25	35 10.29	24 29.1
77	V.	3	38.646	20	57.57	9.11	4.75	35 40.80	26 31.4
78	V.	3	34.340	25	27.89	9.13	5.87	36 39.99	31 2.9
79	V.	4	47.658	11	23.32	9.14	2.40	37 10.13	16 54.9
80	IV.	3	25.619	34	34.92	9.18	8.17	39 11.03	40 12.3
81	III.	3	29.219	−30	48.91	− 9.21	− 7.20	13 40 20.26	− 32 36 25.4

CORRECTIONS.

Date.	Corr. of Clock.	Hourly rate.	m	n	c	Zenith Point.	Mic. Co.
1849.	h.　　　s.	s.	s.	s,	s,	° ′ ″	r.

REMARKS.

(224) 72. Time of transit over T. IV assumed as 48ˢ.1 instead of 45ˢ.1.

INSTRUMENT READINGS.

Date.	CIRCLE.							Barom.	THERMOM.				
	A.	B.	C.	D.	E.	F.	Mean.		At.	Ex.	U.	L.	I.
1849.　h. m.	° ′ ″						″	in.	°	°	°	°	°

ZONE 225. FEBRUARY 15. C. $D_s = -30° 49' 30''.$

No.	Mag.	I.	II.	III.	IV.	V.	VI.	VII.	T.	a_1	a_2	MICR.	n	r	i	d_1	d_2	Mean Right Ascension, 1850.0	Mean Declination, 1850.0
									h. m. s.	s.	s.			r.	′ ″	″	″	h. m. s.	° ′ ″
1	9			27.	44.5	2.6			5 22 44.70	−30.19	−0.94	IV.	4	40.237	−19 8.74	−2.18	−3.60	5 22 13.6	−31 8 44.5
2	9				26.7	44.3			23 26.42	30.20	0.94	IV.	4	36.561	22 58.10	2.25	4.45	22 55.3	12 34.8
3	9					31.6	49.6		24 13.63	30.21	0.94	IV.	4	44.178	15 2.55	2.33	2.70	23 42.5	31 4 37.6
4	9.10		48.7	6.8					26 24.94	30.23	0.95	III.	5	49.200	9 46.98	2.56	1.53	25 53.7	30 59 21.1
5	10				50.4	9.			29 50.57	30.25	0.95	IV.	3	23.498	36 48.03	2.90	7.54	29 19.4	31 20 28.5
6	10								30	30.25	0.95	VII.	2	18.915	41 31.55	3.00	8.63	30	31 13.2
7	9			3.3	21.8	39.3			32 21.47	30.27	0.95	IV.	3	39.928	19 36.98	3.17	3.65	31 50.2	9 13.8
8	10						53.5		32 17.54	30.27	0.95	V.	3	37.476	22 11.10	3.16	4.24	31 46.3	11 48.5
9	9		22.2		58.	16.2			34 58.15	30.29	0.95	IV.	3	29.968	30 2.00	3.43	6.01	34 26.9	19 41.4
10	9.10					59.3			35 41.11	30.30	0.96	V.	3	21.245	39 9.41	3.50	8.07	35 9.9	28 51.0
11	9						20.3		35 44.31	30.30	0.96	VI.	3	24.985	35 14.49	3.50	7.18	35 13.1	24 55.2
12	8			49.		25.5			40 7.18	30.33	0.96	IV.	2	6.689	54 16.68	3.96	11.56	39 35.9	44 2.2
13	9					52.2	10.2		40 34.03	30.33	0.96	V.	2	15.608	44 57.79	4.01	9.43	40 2.7	34 41.2
14	9.10			11.3	29.2				42 29.23	30.34	0.96	IV.	2	28.468	31 30.85	4.21	6.37	41 57.9	31 21 11.4
15	9.10						29.2		42 53.23	30.34	0.96	VI.	5	50.188	8 45.65	4.25	1.29	42 21.9	30 58 21.2
16	9.10						45.5		44 9.54	30.35	0.96	VI.	4	40.523	18 51.43	4.39	3.54	43 38.2	31 8 29.4
17	10		47.2	6.2					46 23.95	30.37	0.97	III.	2	17.599	42 52.04	4.62	8.96	45 52.6	32 35.6
18	10				55.2				46 55.11	30.38	0.97	IV.	2	17.968	42 29.33	4.67	9.87	46 23.8	32 13.9
19	9			57.3		33.4			49 15.42	30.40	0.97	IV.	3	39.162	20 25.25	4.92	3.86	48 44.1	10 4.0
20	7.8		16.3	31.3	52.3		28.3		50 52.39	30.40	0.97	IV.	2	16.801	43 42.47	5.09	9.15	50 21.0	33 26.7
21	7				13.3	32.0	49.5		51 13.52	30.41	0.97	IV.	3	25.528	34 40.69	5.13	7.06	50 42.1	24 22.9
22	9						34.5		52 58.55	30.41	0.97	VI.	3	32.976	26 53.15	5.32	5.28	52 27.2	16 33.8
23	9.10						51.3		53 15.33	30.42	0.97	VI.	4	46.573	12 31.74	5.35	2.10	52 43.9	2 9.2
24	8.9			58.3	16.	33.8	52.		55 16.06	30.43	0.98	IV.	4	45.378	13 46.11	5.57	2.42	54 44.6	3 24.1
25	9					22.5	40.3		56 4.14	30.44	0.98	V.	2	6.718	54 15.25	5.66	11.59	55 32.7	44 2.5
26	10			20.	38.	55.3			58 37.81	30.46	0.98	IV.	5	47.778	11 14.21	5.92	1.84	58 6.4	0 52.0
27	10				29.2	46.2			5 59 28.65	30.47	0.98	IV.	4	42.714	16 33.17	6.03	3.02	5 58 57.2	6 12.2
28	10				34.1	52.3			6 0 34.07	30.47	0.98	IV.	3	26.988	33 8.96	6.14	6.70	6 0 2.6	22 51.8
29	7.8			20.3	38.3	56.3			1 38.26	30.48	0.98	IV.	3	25.746	34 26.88	6.25	7.00	1 6.8	24 10.1
30	10						22.		1 45.07	30.48	0.98	VI.	2	20.046	40 19.62	6.27	8.38	1 14.5	30 4.3
31	9.10						25.6		2 49.85	30.49	0.98	VI.	3	29.126	30 54.84	6.39	6.21	2 18.4	31 20 37.4
32	9					38.8	57.		4 20.95	30.49	0.98	V.	5	48.682	10 19.90	6.58	1.63	3 49.5	30 59 58.2
33	9						33.3		4 57.32	30.50	0.98	VI.	5	55.349	3 27.74	6.64	0.00	4 25.6	30 52 58.5
34	10				44.5				6 44.40	30.51	0.99	IV.	2	20.832	39 29.62	6.85	8.18	6 12.9	31 29 14.6
35	10					58.7			8 40.08	30.53	0.99	V.	5	50.503	5 25.82	7.07	1.21	8 8.6	30 58 4.1
36	9.10			21.5	39.5		16.2		11 39.74	30.54	0.99	IV.	2	13.611	47 2.73	7.42	9.93	11 8.2	31 36 50.1
37	9				43.5	1.3	18.8		11 43.08	30.54	0.99	IV.	2	18.969	41 26.54	7.43	8.63	11 11.5	31 31 12.6
38	8.9					0.3	18.4		12 42.41	30.55	0.99	V.	5	51.246	7 39.18	7.54	1.03	12 10.9	30 57 17.7
39	9			46.3		22.5			15 4.34	30.57	1.00	IV.	2	10.565	50 16.58	7.83	10.66	14 32.8	31 40 5.1
40	10			7.2	25.2				17 25.18	30.58	1.00	IV.	3	33.962	25 51.41	8.11	5.08	16 53.6	15 34.6
41	8				9.2	27.5	45.3		18 9.15	30.59	1.00	IV.	2	7.782	53 7.96	8.20	11.33	17 37.6	42 57.5
42	9			59.3	16.8				20 17.07	30.60	1.00	IV.	5	44.702	14 29.60	8.45	2.56	19 45.5	4 10.6
43	8						6.3		6 20 30.32	30.60	1.00	VI.	3	26.085	34 5.62	8.48	6.92	6 19 58.7	23 51.0
44	10				41.3				7 12 41.18	30.87	1.05	IV.	3	24.686	35 33.38	15.41	7.27	7 12 9.3	31 25 26.1
45	9					47.5	5.2		13 29.41	30.87	1.05	V.	5	51.385	7 30.52	15.52	0.93	12 57.5	30 57 17.0
46	9.10				11.9	29.8	47.5		15 11.63	30.88	1.06	IV.	3	27.268	32 51.58	15.75	6.66	14 39.7	31 22 44.0
47	9		47.5	5.7					17 23.80	30.89	1.06	III.	4	51.062	7 47.66	16.06	1.06	16 51.8	30 57 34.8
48	7				48.3	6.6	24.8		17 48.47	30.89	1.06	IV.	2	12.348	−48 21.99	−16.11	−10.25	17 16.5	−31 38 18.3
49	9				51.5	8.3			7 19 51.	−30.90	−1.06	IV.	2	.238				7 19 19.	

CORRECTIONS.

Date.	Corr. of Clock.	Hourly rate.	m	n	c	Zenith Point.	Mic. Co.
1849.	h. s.	s.	s.	s.	s.	° ′ ″	r.

REMARKS.

INSTRUMENT READINGS.

Date.	A.	B.	C.	D.	E.	F.	Mean.	Barom.	At.	Ex.	U.	L.	I.	Remarks.
	° ′ ″						″	in.	°	°	°	°	°	
Zone 225 Feb. 15, 1849 5 20								29.992	27.5	18.5	36.7	23.5	28.	
5 30	90 9 61.7	66.1	71.8	59.6	61.2	48.2	61.43							
5 40									18.					
6 0								29.996	26.5	17.7				
6 20	59.8 67.1	71.9	59.2	62.1	46.8	61.15		29.982	25.2	17.5		22.	23.2	Barometer reading rejected.
7 10								30.608	23.	15.5				
7 20	58.7 67.9	71.9	59.8	62.2	46.8	61.22						20.3	22.	
7 40								30.008	22.8	14.9				
8 32								30.006	22.	13.6				

ZONE 225. FEBRUARY 15. C. $D_0 = -30°\,49'\,30''$—Continued.

No.	Mag.	I.	II.	III.	IV.	V.	VI.	VII.
50	9				28.2			
51	8						6.3	
52	8					32.3		
53	10				28.8			
54	8.9		0.8		37.3	55.3	13.8	
55	9.10				38.2	56.3	14.3	
56	9		4.8		40.3		16.5	
57	9.10				35.8		29.6	
58	9			58.	15.8			
59	10					53.2		
60	9		.·.		35.2	53.1	11.2	
61	9.10					27.2		
62	9					18.7	36.5	
63	9			12.2				
64	8					53.2	11.3	
65	9					48.5		
66	9.10					24.3		
67	9			27.2	45.5			
68	9						27.4	
69	8.9			46.7	4.8	22.7	41.	58.9
70	9			9.5	27.3	45.6	3.7	.·.
71	9.10				16.3		52.7	
72	9.10				34.	52.		
73	9.10				28.2	16.3		
74	9			36.3	54.2	12.3		
75	9.10				35.5		10.8	
76	9.10				21.5	39.2		
77	10		54.2		30.8			
78	10			18.9	36.4	54.3		
79	8.9		15.2			51.5		
80	9.10				47.3	5.2		
81	9		36.3	54.3	12.2			
82	9				42.	59.7		
83	9							43.5
84	9.10			53.5	10.8	29.3		
85	9.10		42.3	0.5	18.5			
86	9.10		57.3	15.5	33.5			
87	9				16.6	34.3	52.7	
88	9					26.	43.6	

No.	Mag.	T. (h. m. s.)	a_1 (s.)	a_2 (s.)	MICROMETER		r.	i (′ ″)	d_1 (″)	d_2 (″)	Mean Right Ascension, 1850.0 (h. m. s.)	Mean Declination 1850.0 (° ′ ″)
50	9	7 20 28.10	−30.90	−1.06	IV.	3	20.764	−36 31.12	−16.48	−7.72	7 19 56.1	− 31 26 25.3
51	8	19 30.26	30.90	1.06	VI.	2	19.262	41 8.92	16.35	8.57	18 58.3	31 3.8
52	8	20 56.35	30.90	1.06	VI.	3	29.103	30 56.28	16.56	6.21	20 24.4	20 49.0
53	10	22 10.72	30.91	1.06	V.	3	28.762	31 17.67	16.72	6.30	21 33.7	21 10.7
54	8.9	23 37.29	30.91	1.06	IV.	2	17.822	42 38.42	16.91	8.93	23 5.3	32 34.3
55	9.10	23 38.14	30.91	1.06	IV.	2	17.906	42 33.15	16.91	8.92	23 6.2	32 29.0
56	9	27 40.58	30.93	1.07	IV.	4	40.754	18 36.11	17.47	3.46	27 8.6	8 27.0
57	9.10	28 53.78	30.94	1.07	IV.	4	38.317	21 9.23	17.63	4.04	28 21.8	31 11 0.9
58	9	31 15.94	30.95	1.07	IV.	5	49.488	9 29.34	17.97	1.40	30 44.6	30 59 18.7
59	10	31 35.27	30.95	1.07	V.	5	48.768	10 14.59	18.01	1.64	31 3.3	31 0 4.2
60	9	32 53.18	30.95	1.07	IV.	4	42.191	17 6.12	18.19	3.13	32 21.2	6 54.4
61	9.10	33 9.20	30.95	1.07	V.	4	38.631	20 49.84	18.23	3.96	32 37.2	31 10 42.0
62	9	34 0.65	30.96	1.07	V.	5	51.068	7 50.61	18.36	1.06	33 28.6	30 57 40.0
63	9	35 30.34	30.96	1.08	III.	3	39.042	20 32.46	18.55	3.86	34 58.3	31 10 24.9
64	8	35 35.25	30.96	1.08	V.	3	30.952	29 0.27	18.56	5.78	35 3.2	18 54.6
65	9	36 30.44	30.96	1.08	IV.	3	29.672	30 11.55	18.69	6.08	35 58.4	20 6.3
66	9.10	37 6.20	30.97	1.08	VI.	3	26.685	33 27.73	18.78	6.78	36 34.2	31 23 23.3
67	9	38 45.39	30.97	1.08	IV.	5	50.238	8 42.26	19.00	1.23	38 13.3	30 58 32.5
68	9	38 51.46	30.97	1.08	VI.	3	30.456	29 31.45	19.02	5.90	38 19.4	31 19 26.4
69	8.9	7 43 22.92	30.99	1.08	IV.	3	34.912	24 51.73	19.65	4.84	7 42 50.9	14 46.2
70	9	8 34 45.59	31.08	1.13	IV.	2	12.605	48 5.82	26.78	10.21	8 34 13.4	38 12.8
71	9.10	35 16.45	31.08	1.14	IV.	3	33.012	26 51.02	26.86	5.28	34 44.2	16 53.2
72	9.10	36 33.90	31.08	1.14	IV.	3	37.018	22 39.66	27.04	4.35	36 1.7	12 41.1
73	9.10	37 28.21	31.08	1.14	IV.	4	45.649	13 28.98	27.17	2.31	36 56.0	3 23.5
74	9	38 54.22	31.08	1.14	IV.	2	21.516	38 46.78	27.36	8.04	38 22.0	28 52.2
75	9.10	39 35.10	31.08	1.14	IV.	4	45.731	13 23.83	27.47	2.29	39 2.9	31 3 23.6
76	9.10	40 39.41	31.08	1.14	IV.	5	53.201	5 36.27	27.60	0.54	40 7.2	30 55 31.4
77	10	43 30.72	31.09	1.15	IV.	2	7.626	53 18.00	27.98	11.41	42 59.5	31 43 27.4
78	10	47 36.48	31.09	1.15	IV.	3	26.261	33 54.76	28.54	6.89	47 4.2	24 0.2
79	8.9	48 33.31	31.09	1.15	IV.	2	15.354	45 13.47	28.68	9.60	48 1.1	35 21.7
80	9.10	50 5.30	31.09	1.15	IV.	2	14.228	46 24.03	28.89	9.80	49 33.1	36 32.7
81	9	52 12.34	31.09	1.15	IV.	4	43.647	15 34.62	29.18	2.76	51 40.1	5 36.6
82	9	52 41.68	31.09	1.15	IV.	2	16.908	43 35.75	29.23	9.17	52 9.4	33 44.2
83	9	53 7.53	31.09	1.15	VI.	3	27.078	33 3.32	29.30	6.70	52 35.3	23 9.3
84	9.10	57 11.16	31.09	1.16	IV.	3	31.459	28 28.65	29.84	5.66	56 38.9	18 34.2
85	9.10	8 58 18.49	31.09	1.16	IV.	3	30.923	29 2.02	30.00	5.78	8 57 46.2	31 19 7.8
86	9.10	9 0 33.52	31.09	1.16	IV.	5	49.354	9 37.80	30.30	1.50	9 0 1.3	30 50 39.6
87	9	1 34.50	31.09	1.16	IV.	3	31.228	28 43.08	30.43	5.71	1 2.3	31 18 49.2
88	9	9 2 7.73	−31.09	−1.16	IV.	3	24.238	−36 2.30	−30.52	−7.36	9 1 35.5	− 31 26 10.2

ZONE 226. FEBRUARY 16. S. $D_0 = -25°\,13'\,50''$.

No.	Mag.	I.	II.	III.	IV.	V.	VI.	VII.
1	9			45.	2.	19.		
2	9			22.				
3	9						9.	
4	9					23.		
5	9				13.5			
6	8					7.5		

No.	Mag.	T. (h. m. s.)	a_1 (s.)	a_2 (s.)	MICROMETER		r.	i (′ ″)	d_1 (″)	d_2 (″)	Mean Right Ascension, 1850.0 (h. m. s.)	Mean Declination 1850.0 (° ′ ″)
1	9	4 58 19.25	−29.52	−1.39	IV.	.	8.465	−52 25.52	− 0.07	−9.86	4 57 48.34	− 26 6 25.4
2	9	4 59 39.15	29.52	1.30	.	3	30.960	28 59.58	0.19	3.83	4 59 8.33	25 42 55.6
3	9	5 0 34.89	29.53	1.24	.	4	42.460	16 49.90	0.27	3.79	5 0 4.12	30 44.0
4	9	1 48.86	29.54	1.33	.	3	23.202	37 6.60	0.37	7.20	1 17.99	51 4.2
5	9	3 13.36	29.55	1.31	.	3	31.978	27 55.90	0.50	5.64	2 42.50	41 52.0
6	8	5 3 50.43	−29.56	−1.27	.	3	38.848	−20 44.82	− 0.55	−4.42	5 3 19.60	− 25 34 39.8

CORRECTIONS.

Date.	Corr. of Clock.	Hourly rate.	m	n	c	Zenith Point.	Mic. Co.
1849.	h.	s.	s.	s.	s.	° ′ ″	r.

REMARKS.

(225) 50. Micrometer reading assumed as 23ʳ.764, not 20ʳ.764, to agree with February 23 and Mer. Circle, January 23, 1849.

INSTRUMENT READINGS.

	Date.		CIRCLE.							Barom.	THERMOM.				
			A.	B.	C.	D.	E.	F.	Mean.		At.	Ex.	U.	L.	I.
	1849.	h. m.	° ′ ″						″	in.	°	°	°	°	°
Zone 225	Feb. 15,	8 45	90 9 58.1	68.5	72.5	60.1	62.2	45.5	61.15	30.004	22.	13.1	13.5	34.2	18.5 21.
		9 0													
Zone 226	Feb. 16,	4 50	84 34 60.	65.9	74.3	57.2	65.2	46.	61.43						
		6	60.	66.5	74.2	57.2	65.2	45.5	61.43						

Zone 226. February 16. S. $D_c = -25°\ 13'\ 50''$—Continued.

No.	Mag.	I.	II.	III.	IV.	V.	VI.	VII.	T. (h. m. s.)	a_1 (s.)	m_1 (s.)	Micrometer		r.	i.	d_1	d_2	Mean Right Ascension 1850.0 (h. m. s.)	Mean Declination 1850.0
7	9			35.					5 6 52.20	−29.58	−1.29	.	3	40.000	−19 32.34	−0.80	−4.21	5 6 21.35	−25 33 27.4
8	10			43.					7 0.21	29.58	1.30		4	41.848	17 26.90	0.82	3.99	6 29.33	31 21.6
9	7		25.	42.	59.				10 59.15	29.61	1.34	IV.	4	43.116	16 8.01	1.15	3.67	10 28.20	30 2.8
10	8		6.						12 40.35	29.62	1.26		4	60.365		1.31	..	12 9.47	
11	6				39.	56.			12 38.94	29.62	1.32	IV.	4	48.114	10 54.32	1.30	2.82	12 8.00	24 48.4
12	8			49.	6.				14 6.07	29.63	1.34	IV.	4	48.212	10 48.23	1.43	2.81	13 35.10	24 42.5
13	7		25.5	41.	58.				16 58.63	29.65	1.45		3	30.119	29 52.60	1.69	5.98	16 27.53	43 50.3
14	9						6.		18 31.83	29.66	1.52		2	18.880	41 32.74	1.82	7.98	18 0.65	55 32.5
15	7		36.2	53.2		27.2			22 10.33	29.69	1.51	V.	3	28.160	31 55.57	2.16	6.32	21 39.13	45 54.0
16	8		7.		41.2				23 41.22	29.70	1.42	IV.	5	48.220	10 48.92	2.30	2.80	23 10.10	24 44.0
17	10		28.	45.					26 2.30	29.71	1.56	III.	3	24.142	36 7.45	2.51	7.03	25 31.03	50 7.0
18	6		52.	9.	26.				27 26.16	29.72	1.47		4	44.560	14 37.44	2.64	3.43	26 54.97	28 33.5
19	9				15.5				28 15.39	29.73	1.46		4	47.963	11 3.68	2.72	2.85	27 44.20	24 59.3
20	9						31.5		28 57.41	29.73	1.53		3	34.690	25 5.74	2.78	5.16	28 26.15	39 3.7
21	7					31.			30 13.80	29.74	1.58		3	23.922	36 21.30	2.89	7.07	29 42.48	50 21.3
22	7					21.5	36.5		31 2.28	29.75	1.61		2	18.806	41 37.14	2.97	7.99	30 30.92	55 38.1
23	7		8.2						33 42.56	29.77	1.53		3	37.842	21 47.39	3.23	4.60	33 11.26	35 45.2
24	7				49.				33 48.87	29.77	1.55		3	36.482	23 13.41	3.24	4.84	33 17.55	37 11.5
25	7						44.		34 9.92	29.77	1.56		3	31.488	28 26.76	3.26	5.73	33 38.59	42 25.7
26	6					45.			35 27.92	29.78	1.55	VI.	3	38.329	21 17.58	3.40	4.51	34 56.59	35 15.5
27	7		21.	38.	55.				37 55.13	29.80	1.60	VII.	3	32.372	27 31.18	3.63	5.57	37 23.73	41 30.4
28	9				37.5				40 37.42	29.82	1.76	IX.	3	18.182	42 16.04	3.80	8.10	40 5.00	56 18.0
29	8					42.8	n.		41 25.77	29.82	1.66		3	28.199	31 53.10	3.97	6.31	40 54.30	45 53.5
30	9			37.					43 54.18	29.84	1.65		3	23.173	37 8.24	4.21	7.21	43 22.69	51 9.6
31	8				58.				44 40.80	29.84	1.65		3	24.406	35 45.49	4.29	6.98	44 9.31	49 46.8
32	8					32.3			45 35.17	29.85	1.67		3	29.752	30 15.56	4.35	6.04	45 3.65	44 16.0
33	6.5					50.5	8.		46 33.50	29.86	1.77	V.	2	15.552	45 1.37	4.48	8.57	46 1.87	59 4.4
34	7		11.	28.					48 45.28	29.87	1.63	III.	4	39.868	19 31.15	4.60	4.25	48 13.78	33 30.1
35	.				15.5	33.			49 15.67	29.87	1.62	IV.	5	44.790	14 24.01	4.73	3.37	48 44.18	28 22.1
36	9		43.5		17.				53 17.37	29.90	1.62	IV.	5	49.505	−9 28.27	5.15	2.56	52 45.85	23 26.0
37	9		5.5						54 39.85	29.91	1.63		3	49.939	8 58.46	5.29	2.49	54 8.31	22 56.2
38	8				14.5				55 14.35	29.91	1.70		3	40.712	18 47.85	5.34	4.11	54 42.77	32 47.3
39	4					56.	13.		55 38.93	29.91	1.67	V.	4	47.638	11 24.57	5.38	2.67	55 7.35	25 23.8
40	9		35.						5 58 9.36	−29.93	−1.75	.	3	38.175	−21 26.68	−5.65	−4.54	5 57 37.68	−25 35 26.9

Zone 227. February 16. S. $D_n = -30°\ 49'\ 30''$.

No.	Mag.	I.	II.	III.	IV.	V.	VI.	VII.	T. (h. m. s.)	a_1 (s.)	m_1 (s.)	Micrometer		r.	i.	d_1	d_2	Mean Right Ascension 1850.0 (h. m. s.)	Mean Declination 1850.0
1	8			25.		1.			6 12 43.14	−30.22	−1.73	III.	5	51.289	−7 35.91	−2.80	−5.03	6 12 11.19	−30 57 13.7
2	7			46.5		23.			15 4.69	30.24	1.38	V.	2	10.576	50 13.45	3.07	14.65	14 33.07	31 40 1.2
3	9		49.						17 25.24	30.26	1.60	.	3	33.942	25 52.10	3.34	9.07	16 53.38	15 34.5
4	6			9.	28.				18 27.50	30.26	1.37	.	2	7.780	53 8.21	3.45	15.34	17 55.96	42 57.0
5	7			51.					20 9.14	30.28	1.49	.	3	21.382	39 0.65	3.65	12.05	19 37.37	28 46.4
6	6				50.	7.			20 31.45	30.28	1.54	.	3	26.089	33 59.16	3.69	10.94	19 59.63	23 43.8
7	7		16.	34.	52.				24 52.08	30.30	1.72	.	4	44.329	14 52.00	4.19	6.64	24 20.06	4 32.8
8	7		13.	31.	49.				29 49.07	30.34	1.69	IV.	3	38.786	20 48.64	4.77	7.96	29 17.04	10 31.4
9	8						56.		30 19.95	30.34	1.54	.	2	21.700	38 35.86	4.83	11.97	29 48.10	28 22.7
10	9			33.					33 51.10	30.36	1.66	.	3	33.208	26 38.91	5.25	9.23	33 19.08	16 23.4
11	9		47.						6 36 23.31	−30.37	−1.57	.	2	22.330	−37 54.65	−5.56	−11.82	6 35 51.37	−31 27 42.0

CORRECTIONS.

Date.	Corr. of Clock.	Hourly rate.	m	n	ε	Zenith Point.	Mic. Co.
1849.	h.	s.	s.	s.	s.	° '	r.

INSTRUMENT READINGS.

	Date.		CIRCLE.							Barom.	THERMOM.				
			A.	B.	C.	D.	E.	F.	Mean.		At.	Ex.	U.	L.	I.
Zone 227	1849. Feb. 16,	6 10	90 9 60.	66.6	71.6	56.9	64.3	44.3	60.62	in.					
		6 20								29.928	23.9	17.5			
		6 40										17.5			
		7 0										17.3			
		7 20								29.936	23.	16.			
		7 25	60.	66.6	72.	56.9	64.3	44.3	60.68						

ZONE 227. FEBRUARY 16. S. $D_0 = -30°\ 49'\ 30''$—Continued.

Seconds of transit

No.	Mag.	I.	II.	III.	IV.	V.	VI.	VII.
12	7			54.				
13	9					37.	15.	
14	7		23.5					
15	5				18.	37.	54.	
16	7		53.		29.			
17	8				31.			
18	7				29.			
19	7		9.2					
20	6				12.			
21	9						13.	
22	5					4.	23.	
23	8				17.	34.5		
24	8		15.2					
25	5				58.		34.	
26	7			31.		7.5		
27	8		37.5					
28	8					39.5		
29	6			41.	59.5			
30	8			14.	32.			
31	7		15.	33.5	51.			
32	7					41.5	58.	
33	8					15.		
34	8			23.5				
35	7				30.	48.		
36	8			54.				
37	9		14.					
38	7				6.5	24.		
39	6				20.	38.		
40	5				31.			
41	5				30.			
42	6					14.5	32.5	

Micrometer and reductions

No.	T.	a_1	a_2	Mic.	No.	r	i	d_1	d_2	Mean Right Ascension, 1850.0	Mean Declination, 1850.0
		h. m. s.	s.	s.			r.	''	''	''	h. m. s	° ' ''
12	6 37 12.15	—30.38	—1.54		2	18.829	—41 34.75	5.65	—12.66	6 36 40.23	—31 31 23.1
13	37 38.91	30.38	1.57		2	22.362	37 54.27	5.71	11.82	37 6.96	27 41.8
14	40 59.83	30.40	1.57		2	20.102	40 14.28	6.11	12.36	40 27.86	30 2.8
15	40 18.18	30.40	1.51		2	12.993	47 41.36	6.02	14.07	39 46.27	37 32.4
16	43 29.05	30.41	1.74	IV.	3	37.840	21 48.02	6.42	8.17	42 56.90	11 32.6
17	44 30.87	30.42	1.79		4	43.550	15 40.84	6.54	6.83	43 58.66	5 24.2
18	45 28.87	30.42	1.79		4	42.752	16 30.72	6.67	7.01	44 56.67	6 14.4
19	48 45.50	30.44	1.64		3	24.160	36 5.97	7.06	11.39	48 13.42	25 54.4
20	49 11.93	30.44	1.54		2	13.532	47 7.68	7.12	13.94	48 39.95	31 36 58.7
21	49 37.03	30.45	1.87		6	50.002	8 57.21	7.17	5.32	49 4.71	30 58 39.7
22	50 46.32	30.45	1.57		2	14.546	46 4.46	7.31	13.69	50 14.30	31 35 55.5
23	52 16.68	30.46	1.69		4	37.708	21 47.33	7.50	8.20	51 44.53	11 33.0
24	54 51.40	30.47	1.88		4	47.385	11 38.88	7.82	5.93	54 19.05	31 1 22.6
25	54 57.96	30.47	1.92		5	52.398	6 26.67	7.83	4.77	54 25.57	30 56 9.3
26	6 59 49.27	30.50	1.75		3	31.600	28 19.68	8.45	9.62	6 59 17.02	31 18 7.8
27	7 2 13.89	30.51	1.60		2	13.125	47 31.95	8.77	14.04	7 1 41.78	37 24.8
28	2 21.24	30.51	1.62		2	15.943	44 36.71	8.79	13.37	1 49.11	34 28.9
29	3 59.34	30.52	1.56		2	8.959	51 54.34	8.99	15.06	3 27.26	41 48.4
30	5 32.00	30.53	1.85		4	39.022	19 28.33	9.18	7.66	5 59.62	9 15.2
31	8 51.24	30.54	1.74		3	26.783	33 21.76	9.60	10.77	8 18.96	23 12.1
32	9 22.76	30.54	1.83		4	35.250	24 22.06	9.64	8.76	8 50.39	14 10.5
33	10 57.06	30.55	1.95		6	48.083	10 57.65	9.88	5.76	10 24.56	0 43.3
34	12 41.61	30.56	1.74		3	24.722	35 30.93	10.10	11.25	12 19.31	31 25 22.3
35	13 29.98	30.56	1.99		5	51.403	7 29.14	10.21	4.98	12 57.43	30 57 14.3
36	15 12.10	30.56	1.78		3	27.332	32 47.20	10.42	10.63	14 39.76	31 22 38.3
37	16 50.22	30.57	1.80		3	30.056	20 31.26	10.63	7.87	16 17.76	31 10 19.8
38	17 24.29	30.57	2.00		4	51.043	7 50.42	10.71	5.06	16 51.72	30 57 10.2
39	18 19.97	30.58	1.98	V.	4	48.120	10 54.32	10.83	5.74	17 47.41	31 0 40.9
40	19 30.00	30.58	1.73		2	19.333	41 3.89	10.99	12.54	18 55.59	30 57.4
41	20 29.88	30.59	1.76		3	23.603	36 41.39	11.11	11.52	19 57.53	26 34.0
42	7 20 56.49	—30.59	—1.81		3	29.116	—30 55.59	—11.16	—10.21	7 20 24.09	—31 20 47.0

ZONE 228. FEBRUARY 16. S. $D_0 = -23°\ 19'\ 0''$.

Seconds of transit

No.	Mag.	I.	II.	III.	IV.	V.	VI.	VII.
1	3				41.5	58.5	15.	
2	7				0.2	17.	34.	
3	8			8.				
4	7				51.			
5	6					56.8		
6	9		19.					
7	7			11.				
8	8		26.5					
9	8				32.			
10	8					19.		
11	9			58.				
12	8				59.	16.		
13	5					23.	40.	
14	7			49.				

Micrometer and reductions

No.	T.	a_1	a_2	Mic.	No.	r	i	d_1	d_2	Mean Right Ascension, 1850.0	Mean Declination, 1850.0
1	8 1 41.45	—30.39	—1.84	IV.	3	26.808	—33 20.20	—1.73	—4.52	8 1 9.2	—23 52 26.5
2	4 0.14	30.40	1.88	IV.	2	14.892	45 42.19	2.02	6.51	3 27.9	24 4 50.7
3	6 24.91	30.40	1.77		3	35.123	24 38.44	2.32	3.15	5 52.7	23 43 43.9
4	6 0.87	30.40	1.77		3	34.468	25 19.85	2.37	3.26	6 28.7	44 25.5
5	7 23.23	30.41	1.80		3	28.627	31 26.21	2.44	4.22	6 51.0	50 32.9
6	11 52.90	30.41	1.81		3	21.328	39 3.78	2.98	5.44	11 20.7	58 12.2
7	12 10.87	30.41	1.79		3	28.680	31 22.82	3.03	4.23	11 38.7	50 30.1
8	14 0.34	30.42	1.76		3	29.508	30 30.55	3.26	4.09	13 28.2	49 37.9
9	14 15.02	30.42	1.81		2	20.592	39 45.25	3.29	5.56	13 42.8	58 54.1
10	14 45.41	30.42	1.71		3	41.100	18 23.56	3.35	2.17	14 13.3	37 29.1
11	17 14.93	30.43	1.79		2	22.516	37 43.68	3.66	5.24	16 42.7	56 52.6
12	17 42.29	30.43	1.74	V.	3	31.689	28 14.10	3.72	3.71	17 10.1	47 21.5
13	19 6.32	30.43	1.67	V.	4	44.550	14 38.45	3.89	1.60	18 34.2	33 43.9
14	8 21 5.99	—30.43	—1.65		4	47.253	—11 47.92	—4.14	—1.17	8 20 33.9	—23 30 53.2

CORRECTIONS.

Date.	Corr. of Clock.	Hourly rate.	m	n	c	Zenith Point.	Mic. Co.
1849.	h.	s.	s.	s.	s.	° ' ''	r.

REMARKS.

(228) 4. Transit over T. IV assumed as 1s, not 51s, and minutes as 7, not 6.

INSTRUMENT READINGS.

Date.	CIRCLE.							Barom.	THERMOM.				
	A.	B.	C.	D.	E.	F.	Mean.		At.	Ex.	U.	L.	I.
	° ' ''						''	in.	°				
Zone 228 Feb. 16, 8 0	82 39 60.	67.2	68.3	58.3	65.5	44.	60.55	29.934	23.4	16.3			
8 20										16.2			
8 40										15.3			
9 0	60.	67.2	68.3	59.2	65.5	44.	60.70	29.934	23.5	15.			

ZONE 228. FEBRUARY 16, S. $D_a = -23°\ 19'\ 0''$—Continued.

No.	Mag.	I.	II.	III.	IV.	V.	VI.	VII.	T. h. m. s.	a₁ s.	a₂ s.	MICROMETER	n	r	i ' "	d₁ "	d₂ "	Mean Right Ascension, 1850.0 h. m. s.	Mean Declination, 1850.0 ° ' "
15	8			5.					8 24 21.91	−30.43	−1.75	.	3	24.152	−36 6.82	−4.54	−4.96	8 23 49.7	−23 55 16.3
16	9			55.					25 12.04	30.43	1.60	.	5	53.852	4 58.60	4.65	0.10	24 40.0	24 3.3
17	8		44.5			47.			25 13.40	30.43	1.64	.	4	45.738	13 17.80	4.65	1.41	24 41.3	32 23.9
18	9								27 18.34	30.44	1.63	.	4	46.820	12 13.47	4.95	1.24	26 46.3	31 19.7
19	7				40.				27 23.18	30.44	1.67	.	3	38.292	21 19.06	4.93	2.67	26 51.1	40 27.5
20	8		55.						29 28.84	30.44	1.67	.	3	36.538	23 9.46	5.20	2.91	28 56.7	42 17.6
21	8			37.					29 53.92	30.44	1.67	.	3	36.494	23 12.53	5.24	2.92	29 21.8	42 20.7
22	7		47.	4.	21.				31 20.87	30.44	1.68	IV.	3	32.203	27 41.01	5.43	3.63	30 48.7	23 46 51.0
23	8		8.	25.					33 41.94	30.45	1.75	III.	2	16.992	43 30.04	5.73	6.15	33 9.7	24 2 41.9
24	8		20.						34 53.93	30.45	1.76	.	2	14.683	45 54.24	5.89	6.55	34 21.7	24 5 6.7
25	8					20.8			35 3.91	30.45	1.68	.	3	28.690	31 22.26	5.91	4.22	34 31.8	23 50 32.4
26	7			16.					36 32.93	30.45	1.63	.	4	39.064	21 24.48	6.08	2.65	36 0.8	40 33.2
27	8					22.			36 48.41	30.45	1.69	.	3	25.266	34 57.19	6.13	4.79	36 16.3	54 8.1
28	8					9.			37 35.38	30.45	1.72	.	3	20.312	40 7.96	6.23	5.63	37 3.2	59 19.8
29	9		3.						41 35.85	30.46	1.66	.	3	26.635	31 25.27	6.75	4.23	41 4.7	50 36.3
30	9					59.			41 25.41	30.46	1.60	.	4	39.878	19 31.84	6.73	2.37	40 53.4	23 38 40.9
31	8		23.8						43 57.71	30.46	1.70	.	2	18.210	42 13.15	7.06	5.95	43 25.5	24 1 26.2
32	.				12.5	29.			43 55.57	30.46	1.48	VI.	.	.149	4 48	7.	0.	43 23.6	23 23 55.0
33	9			47.					48 3.01	30.46	1.59	.	3	35.810	23 55.21	7.58	3.03	47 31.9	43 5.8
34	8				57.3	14.5			48 57.39	30.46	1.62	.	3	29.428	30 36.07	7.70	4.10	48 25.3	49 47.9
35	8		37.5		13.				52 10.84	30.46	1.61	.	3	28.292	31 47.35	8.17	4.27	51 38.77	23 50 59.8
36	8			59.					53 15.99	30.46	1.69	.	2	11.325	49 25.65	8.26	7.10	52 43.8	24 8 41.0
37	7						8.5		53 34.91	30.46	1.55	.	4	39.330	20 6.42	8.30	2.45	53 2.9	23 39 17.2
38	5				48.		5.	22.	54 48.17	30.46	1.52	.	5	44.278	14 56.33	8.46	1.65	54 16.2	34 6.4
39	7		13.	30.3	47.				56 46.99	30.46	1.54	.	4	39.660	19 44.83	8.70	2.41	56 15.0	38 56.0
40	7				7.				58 6.88	30.46	1.53	.	4	39.765	19 38.17	8.92	2.39	57 34.9	38 49.5
41	7				58.				8 58 57.88	30.46	1.51	.	4	42.830	16 25.82	8.09	1.69	58 25.9	35 35.7
42	6		50.	7.	24.				9 0 23.90	−30.46	−1.50	.	4	44.836	−14 19.93	−9.18	−1.56	8 59 51.9	−23 33 30.7

ZONE 229. FEBRUARY 19. C. $D_a = -28°\ 54'\ 20''$.

No.	Mag.	I.	II.	III.	IV.	V.	VI.	VII.	T. h. m. s.	a₁ s.	a₂ s.	MICROMETER	n	r	i ' "	d₁ "	d₂ "	Mean Right Ascension, 1850.0 h. m. s.	Mean Declination, 1850.0 ° ' "
1	7			26.3	43.5		19.5		5 46 43.88	−31.33	−0.55	IV.	3	25.381	−34 49.98	−2.71	−6.99	5 46 12.0	−29 29 19.7
2	9,10		10.5	33.5					48 51.17	31.35	0.48	III.	5	45.401	13 45.50	2.92	2.75	48 19.3	8 11.2
3	7			39.7	56.7	14.9	32.6		48 57.17	31.35	0.49	IV.	4	43.072	16 10.71	2.95	3.24	48 25.3	10 36.9
4	9			22.	39.7	57.5			50 22.05	31.36	0.49	IV.	4	43.925	15 17.11	3.11	3.05	49 50.2	9 43.3
5	8,9			39.3	8.5	16.3			53 58.07	31.38	0.50	IV.	4	45.961	13 9.33	3.50	2.63	53 26.2	7 35.5
6	8,9		10.5	28.2	45.9	3.5			54 45.91	31.38	0.51	IV.	4	40.718	18 38.44	3.58	3.73	54 14.0	13 5.7
7	9				51.	8.5			5 58 50.79	31.42	0.58	IV.	3	24.222	25 35.22	4.01	5.12	5 58 19.0	20 4.4
8	7		15.5	33.5	50.8	9.4			6 0 51.18	31.43	0.65	IV.	2	10.595	50 11.88	4.26	10.18	6 0 19.1	44 46.3
9	10					39.2			1 21.32	31.44	0.62	VII.	3	18.001	42 32.40	4.30	8.59	0 49.2	37 5.3
10	9,10		54.	12.1	29.3				4 29.53	31.46	0.59	IV.	3	28.472	31 36.05	4.65	6.34	3 57.5	26 7.0
11	9			53.2	11.5	28.8			4 53.34	31.46	0.67	IV.	2	7.941	52 58.18	4.69	10.74	4 21.2	47 33.6
12	9,10		35.5	53.3					7 11.05	31.48	0.58	III.	3	29.204	30 49.88	4.95	6.17	6 39.0	29 25 21.0
13	8,9				14.2	31.7			7 14.11	31.48	0.49	IV.	5	54.362	4 23.45	4.95	0.86	6 42.1	28 58 49.3
14	9					14.			7 56.28	31.49	0.58	V.	3	30.576	29 23.99	5.02	5.88	7 24.2	29 23 54.9
15	7,8								8	31.49	0.57	VI.	3	32.935	26 55.72	5.08	5.38	8	21 26.2
16	8				45.3	3.3			9 45.39	31.50	0.57	IV.	3	35.024	24 44.77	5.23	4.94	9 13.3	19 14.9
17	7,8				43.	0.8			6 10 42.89	−31.51	−0.67	IV.	2	10.885	−49 53.50	−5.33	−10.11	6 10 10.7	−29 44 28.9

CORRECTIONS.

Date.	Corr. of Clock.	Hourly rate.	m	n	c	Zenith Point.	Mic. Co.
1849.	h.	s.	s.	s.	s.	° ' "	r.

INSTRUMENT READINGS.

Date.		CIRCLE.							Barom.	THERMOM.				
		A.	B.	C.	D.	E.	F.	Mean.		At.	Ex.	U.	L.	I.
Zone 229	1849 Feb. 19, 5 10	88 14 62.2	68.8	73.8	59.4	65.9	49.0	63.18	in.			21.	32.2	
	5 50													
	5 58								30.572	28.	20.5	25.5		
	6 20										20.3	27.2		
	6 40								30.568	27.5	19.8			

REMARKS.

(228) 16. Declination differs 1' from Arg. Z. 368, 44.

(228) 18. Transit over T. II assumed as recorded over T. I.

(228) 19. Right ascension differs 10s from Arg. Z. 368, 48.

(228) 32. Micrometer reading assumed as 54r.149.

(228) 35. Transits 2s discordant.

(229) 4. Time of transit over T. II assumed as 15s.5 instead of 10s.5.

(229) 5. Time of transit over T. IV assumed as 58s.5 instead of 8s.5.

(229) 7. Micrometer reading assumed as 34r.222, not 24r.222.

ZONE 229. FEBRUARY 19. C. $D_0 = -28° 54′ 20″$—Continued.

No.	Mag.	I.	II.	III.	IV.	V.	VI.	VII.	T.	a_1	a_2	Micrometer (r / ″)	i	d_1	d_2	Mean Right Ascension, 1850.0	Mean Declination, 1850.0
									h. m. s.	s.	s.	″ / ′ ″	″	″	″	h. m. s.	° ′ ″
18	10		19.2		54.8				6 12 54.70	−31.52	−0.53	IV. 6 45.938 −13 11.96	−5.59	−2.63		6 12 22.7	−29 7 40.2
19	10					52.2			13 34.42	31.53	0.61	V. 3 25.570 34 38.04	5.66	6.95		13 2.3	29 10.6
20	9			46.2		21.5			15 3.83	31.54	0.63	IV. 2 21.776 38 30.40	5.83	7.77		14 31.6	33 4.0
21	8.9					58.3	16.5		15 40.79	31.54	0.64	V. 2 18.868 41 33.18	5.90	8.41		15 8.6	36 7.5
22	9						50.?		16 14.70	31.55	0.53	VI. 5 48.441 10 35.37	5.96	2.11		15 42.6	5 3.4
23	9			58.3	16.2				18 16.09	31.56	0.55	IV. 4 42.028 17 16.23	6.19	3.46		17 44.0	11 45.9
24	8.9						50.8		18 15.36	31.56	0.69	VI. 2 8.302 52 36.37	6.19	10.66		17 43.1	47 13.2
25	8		49.5		25.5	13.2			20 25.30	31.57	0.66	IV. 2 17.829 42 37.08	6.43	8.62		19 53.1	37 13.0
26	10			0.5		36.3			23 18.48	31.59	0.57	IV. 4 42.058 17 13.22	6.76	3.45		22 46.3	11 43.4
27	8.9			21.5	30.1	56.8			26 39.15	31.61	0.57	IV. 4 41.642 17 40.51	7.14	3.54		26 7.0	12 11.2
28	10					27.3			27 9.47	31.62	0.66	V. 3 21.682 38 41.89	7.20	7.79		26 37.2	33 16.9
29	10						58.		27 22.71	31.62	0.64	VI. 3 26.279 33 53.57	7.22	6.86		26 50.5	28 27.6
30	9				52.	9.8	27.4		28 51.99	31.63	0.66	IV. 3 23.015 36 15.47	7.40	7.14		28 19.7	30 50.0
31	9.10		12.9		48.				33 48.15	31.65	0.56	IV. 5 51.649 7 13.57	8.00	1.44		33 15.9	1 43.0
32	8.9		12.2	30.	47.7	5.3	23.		37 47.71	31.68	0.57	IV. 4 48.032 10 59.41	8.49	2.20		37 15.5	5 30.1
33	9.10						49.2		38 13.90	31.69	0.67	VI. 3 25.476 34 43.95	8.54	6.97		37 41.5	29 19.5
34	8.9		34.2		59.2	16.5	34.4		40 59.18	31.70	0.65	IV. 3 30.306 29 40.99	8.88	5.94		40 26.9	24 15.8
35	10					55.2	12.5		6 41 37.34	−31.70	−0.66	V. 3 28.032 −32 3.54	−8.96	−6.42		6 41 5.0	−29 26 38.9

ZONE 230. FEBRUARY 19. C. $D_0 = -30° 49′ 50″$.

No.	Mag.	I.	II.	III.	IV.	V.	VI.	VII.	T.	a_1	a_2	Micrometer (r / ″)	i	d_1	d_2	Mean Right Ascension, 1850.0	Mean Declination, 1850.0
1	9					59.2			7 27 41.21	−30.02	−2.95	V. 5 40.862 −18 30.72	−2.83	−3.42		7 27 8.24	−31 8 27.0
2	9.10		28.2		54.5	12.4			29 54.40	30.03	2.94	IV. 4 38.366 21 4.90	3.12	4.02		29 21.43	31 11 2.0
3	9		40.5	48.3	16.8				31 16.62	30.04	2.95	IV. 5 49.542 9 25.95	3.30	1.36		30 43.63	30 59 20.6
4	10					51.5			31 33.57	30.04	2.95	V. 5 48.810 10 11.89	3.34	1.53		31 0.58	31 0 6.8
5	8.9			36.1	54.	11.8			32 53.96	30.05	2.93	IV. 5 42.252 17 3.48	3.51	3.09		32 20.98	7 0.1
6	9					28.3			33 10.30	30.05	2.93	IV. 3 38.905 20 41.24	3.55	3.86		32 37.32	10 38.7
7	9					19.5			34 1.55	30.05	2.93	IV. 4 46.114 12 59.85	3.67	2.17		33 28.57	2 55.7
8	9			12.5		48.6			35 30.62	30.06	2.91	IV. 3 39.168 20 24.87	3.87	3.81		34 57.65	10 22.6
9	8						11.8		35 35.86	30.06	2.89	VI. 3 31.041 28 54.62	3.88	5.75		35 2.91	18 54.3
10	9.10					48.2			36 30.14	30.06	2.89	V. 3 29.752 30 15.56	4.00	6.06		35 57.19	20 15.6
11	9.10					23.8	42.5		37 6.12	30.07	2.88	V. 3 26.742 33 24.39	4.09	6.79		36 33.17	23 25.3
12	8.9			34.5	52.3				38 52.37	30.07	2.87	IV. 3 30.542 29 26.12	4.32	5.87		38 19.43	19 20.3
13	10					30.7			39 12.62	30.07	2.86	V. 3 28.566 31 30.09	4.38	6.34		38 39.69	21 30.8
14	10					22.1	39.5		40 3.66	30.07	2.85	V. 2 17.723 42 45.08	4.49	8.96		39 30.74	32 48.5
15	8		46.8		23.5	41.6	59.6		43 23.40	30.09	2.84	IV. 3 34.985 24 47.22	4.95	4.80		42 50.47	31 14 47.0
16	10					45.5			44 45.39	30.09	2.85	IV. 5 52.058 5 51.34	5.15	0.50		44 12.45	30 55 47.0
17	9			41.2	9.3	27.	35.2		46 9.16	30.10	2.82	IV. 3 34.565 25 13.71	5.34	4.90		45 36.24	31 15 14.0
18	9				38.5	56.4	14.1		46 38.29	30.10	2.82	IV. 3 34.542 25 15.15	5.42	4.90		46 5.37	15 15.5
19	9				54.3	12.6	30.5		47 54.39	30.11	2.80	IV. 3 24.066 35 15.81	5.59	7.22		47 21.48	25 18.6
20	9				47.2	5.3			48 47.15	30.11	2.80	IV. 3 29.984 30 1.00	5.72	6.00		48 14.24	20 2.7
21	8.9				31.	49.2	6.5		49 30.87	30.11	2.80	IV. 4 40.761 18 32.29	5.81	3.79		48 57.96	8 31.9
22	9.10						53.7		49 17.05	30.11	2.79	VI. 3 35.500 24 14.97	5.77	4.68		48 44.15	14 15.4
23	9		50.	7.9	26.2	44.4			52 26.17	30.12	2.76	VI. 2 21.121 39 11.62	6.23	8.15		51 53.29	29 16.0
24	9.10					10.5			52 52.56	30.12	2.78	V. 4 47.217 11 51.06	6.30	1.92		52 19.66	1 49.3
25	10			17.5					54 35.70	30.13	2.73	III. 2 10.965 49 47.98	6.54	10.63		54 2.84	39 55.2
26	10				45.8		21.8		54 45.75	30.13	2.75	IV. 3 27.951 32 8.49	6.56	6.49		54 12.87	22 11.6
27	10					5.	22.5		7 54 46.64	−30.13	−2.74	V. 3 20.216 −40 13.96	−6.56	−8.38		7 54 13.77	−31 30 18.9

CORRECTIONS.

Date.	Corr. of Clock.	Hourly rate.	m	n	e	Zenith Point.	Mic. Co.
1849.	h. s.	s.	s.	s.	s.	° ′ ″	r.

REMARKS.

(229) 30. Micrometer reading assumed as 24ʳ.015 instead of 23ʳ.015.
(230) 2. Time of transit over T. II assumed as 18ˢ.2 instead of 28ˢ.2.
(230) 3. Time of transit over T. III assumed as 58ˢ.3 instead of 48ˢ.3.
(230) 17. Time of transit over T. III assumed as 51ˢ.2 instead of 41ˢ.2.

INSTRUMENT READINGS.

Date.		CIRCLE.							Barom.	THERMOM.				
		A.	B.	C.	D.	E.	F.	Mean.		At.	Ex.	U.	L.	I.
	1849. h. m.	° ′ ″						″	in.	°	°	°	°	°
Zone 230	Feb. 19, 7 26	90 9 62.7	70.7	74.5	61.7	68.3	49.8	64.62	30.566	26.5	18.		24.8	26.
	7 40										17.8			
	8 0								30.570	26.	17.			
	8 40	62.5	71.2	75.2	62.	68.8	49.1	64.80	30.560	25.5	16.2		24.5	25.

ZONE 230. FEBRUARY 19. C. $D_o = -30°\ 49'\ 50''$—Continued.

No.	Mag.	I.	II.	III.	IV.	V.	VI.	VII.	T.	a_1	a_2	Micrometer	r.	i	d_1	d_2	Mean Right Ascension, 1850.0	Mean Declination, 1850.0
									h. m. s.	s.	s.		r.	′ ″	″	″	h. m. s.	° ′ ″
28	9.10						25.2		7 55 49.23	−30.13	−2.76	VI. 3	44.366	−14 58.65	−6.72	−2.58	7 55 16.34	−31 4 58.0
29	9.10					4.5	22.3		56 46.45	30.13	2.76	V. 5	47.825	11 13.71	6.65	1.78	56 13.56	1 12.3
30	9			50.5	8.3				58 8.38	30.14	2.73	IV. 3	33.748	26 4.84	7.04	5.10	57 35.51	16 7.0
31	9.10					49.8	7.9		7 58 31.88	30.14	2.74	V. 4	41.565	17 45.78	7.10	3.23	7 57 59.00	7 46.1
32	10			47.2	5.1				8 2 5.20	30.15	2.69	IV. 2	15.923	44 37.53	7.61	9.42	8 1 32.36	34 44.6
33	10					52.3			2 34.36	30.15	2.73	V. 5	47.906	11 8.63	7.68	1.72	2 1.48	1 8.0
34	8.9			27.8		4.	21.9		3 45.95	30.16	2.71	IV. 3	37.167	22 30.44	7.85	4.28	3 13.08	12 32.6
35	10			25.3		1.5			5 43.36	30.16	2.66	IV. 2	14.951	45 38.56	8.14	9.66	5 10.54	35 46.4
36	9				34.4				7 34.36	30.17	2.64	IV. 2	8.628	52 15.16	8.40	11.23	7 1.55	42 24.8
37	8			55.2	13.5	31.8			8 13.47	30.17	2.66	IV. 3	32.508	27 22.77	8.49	5.40	7 40.64	17 26.7
38	10.11						54.5		8 18.53	30.17	2.67	VI. 4	43.404	15 50.68	8.50	2.79	7 45.69	5 52.0
39	9.10			48.2		25.			10 6.56	30.17	2.64	V. 2	19.186	41 13.43	8.76	8.63	9 33.75	31 20.8
40	10					1.	18.6		10 42.83	30.18	2.65	V. 2	42.725	16 32.86	8.85	2.97	10 10.00	6 34.7
41	10					18.3			12 0.06	30.18	2.63	V. 2	17.068	43 26.22	9.03	9.14	11 27.25	33 34.4
42	10					59.			12 40.67	30.18	2.60	V. 2	10.443	50 21.84	9.13	10.79	12 7.89	40 31.8
43	9.10			54.2	11.9	29.8			14 11.93	30.18	2.62	IV. 3	28.870	31 10.84	9.35	6.27	13 39.13	21 16.5
44	9.10				54.8	13.1			14 54.80	30.19	2.61	IV. 3	18.779	41 38.40	9.45	8.73	14 22.00	31 46.6
45	9.10			49.6	8.1	26.			16 26.05	30.19	2.58	III. 2	16.487	44 1.84	9.66	9.29	15 53.28	34 10.8
46	8.9			31.3	49.2	7.4			16 49.26	30.19	2.59	IV. 3	23.735	36 33.03	9.72	7.51	16 16.48	26 40.3
47	9						53.8		17 17.84	30.19	2.61	VI. 4	41.644	17 41.01	9.78	3.99	16 45.04	7 44.8
48	8			25.7	13.2	1.1			19 43.28	30.20	2.57	IV. 3	23.161	37 9.18	10.14	7.67	19 10.51	27 17.0
49	9			4.2			58.2		21 22.27	30.20	2.56	IV. 3	18.421	42 6.56	10.36	8.81	20 49.51	32 15.7
50	8.9				37.2	55.3			21 37.06	30.20	2.54	IV. 2	9.489	51 21.36	10.40	11.02	21 4.32	41 32.8
51	8						14.3		21 38.27	30.20	2.56	VI. 2	20.451	39 54.40	10.40	8.33	21 5.51	30 3.1
52	10			47.2		24.3			24 5.80	30.20	2.56	IV. 3	36.232	23 29.10	10.74	4.50	23 33.04	13 34.3
53	7					18.3	36.8		25 0.34	30.21	2.51	V. 3	11.410	49 21.20	10.86	10.55	24 27.62	39 32.6
54	9					28.3			26 10.24	30.21	2.54	V. 3	29.975	30 1.56	11.02	6.01	25 37.49	20 8.6
55	9					40.3	8.5		26 22.42	30.21	2.55	V. 3	37.402	22 15.76	11.05	4.23	25 49.66	12 21.0
56	7.8						9.		27 33.03	30.21	2.56	VI. 4	47.652	11 23.97	11.22	1.73	27 0.26	1 26.9
57	9		36.5	54.8		31.2			30 12.93	30.22	2.48	IV. 2	9.155	51 42.18	11.59	11.12	29 40.23	41 55.0
58	8				52.8	11.2			30 52.79	30.22	2.46	IV. 2	6.464	54 30.99	11.67	11.78	30 20.11	44 44.4
59	8.9						1.8		31 25.84	30.22	2.51	VI. 4	37.425	22 5.90	11.75	4.22	30 53.11	12 11.9
60	9		9.5	28.2	46.2				34 46.14	30.23	2.45	IV. 2	12.677	48 1.24	12.21	10.23	34 13.46	31 38 13.7
61	9				17.2	35.			35 17.00	30.23	2.50	IV. 3	53.118	5 49.27	12.27	0.50	34 44.36	30 55 52.0
62	9			16.7	34.2				36 34.44	30.23	2.47	IV. 3	37.102	22 34.45	12.44	4.30	36 1.74	31 12 41.2
63	9			11.2	28.3				37 28.77	30.23	2.47	IV. 4	45.722	13 24.39	12.57	2.23	36 56.07	3 29.3
64	8.9		18.5	36.7	54.8				38 54.78	30.23	2.44	IV. 2	21.616	38 40.57	12.75	8.05	38 22.11	28 51.4
65	10			36.2	54.2				8 39 54.22	−30.23	−2.46	IV. 4	45.808	−13 18.92	−12.90	−2.22	8 39 21.53	−31 3 24.0

CORRECTIONS.

Date.	Corr. of Clock.	Hourly rate.	m	n	c	Zenith Point.	Mic. Co.
1849.	h. s.	s.	s.	s.	s.	° ′ ″	r.

REMARKS.

(230) 55. Time of transit over T. VI assumed as 58s.5 instead of 8s.5.
(230) 56. Micrometer reading assumed as 47r.652, not 46r.652.

INSTRUMENT READINGS.

Date.	CIRCLE.							Barom.	THERMOM.				
	A.	B.	C.	D.	E.	F.	Mean.		At.	Ex.	U.	L.	I.
1849. h. m.	° ′ ″						″	in.	°	°	°	°	°

ZONE 231.　FEBRUARY 23.　S.　$D_0 = -30° 49' 30''$.

No.	Mag.	I.	II.	III.	IV.	V.	VI.	VII.	T. (h. m. s.)	a_1 (s.)	a_2 (s.)	Mic.		r.	i (' '')	d_1 ('')	d_2 (')	Mean Right Ascension, 1850.0. (h. m. s.)	Mean Declination, 1850.0. ('' ' '')
1	7.8			2.2					6 1 20.31	−31.70	+0.02		3	25.670	−34 31.47	−1.68	−7.01	6 0 48.63	−31 14 10.2
2	9					23.			2 4.80	31.71	+0.04	IV.	3	20.119	40 19.99	1.78	8.32	1 33.13	31 30 0.1
3	8		45.5		21.				4 21.29	31.72	−0.03	IV.	5	48.618	10 23.88	2.08	1.70	3 49.54	30 59 56.7
4	9					26.5			5 6.41	31.73	−0.00		3	27.985	32 6.42	2.19	6.48	4 36.68	31 21 45.1
5	10						32.		5 55.99	31.73	+0.01		3	22.358	37 57.66	2.28	7.80	5 24.27	31 27 37.7
6	10		5.						8 41.19	31.75	−0.06		4	50.448	8 26.64	2.66	1.29	8 9.38	30 58 0.6
7	7		8.	26.	43.				11 43.80	31.77	0.01		2	18.885	41 31.74	3.07	8.64	11 12.02	31 31 13.4
8	7					1.	19.		12 43.06	31.78	0.08		4	51.228	7 39.30	3.20	1.11	12 11.20	30 57 13.6
9	8				5.	23.	41.		15 4.84	31.80	0.01	V.	3	10.510	50 17.65	3.51	10.61	14 33.03	31 40 1.8
10	6			52.	10.				18 10.09	31.82	0.01	IV.	2	7.718	53 12.18	3.92	11.31	17 38.26	42 57.4
11	9		32.5						20 8.82	31.83	0.05		4	21.320	39 4.16	4.18	8.05	19 36.94	28 46.4
12	8.7				31.2				20 31.07	31.84	0.07		4	26.068	34 6.75	4.22	6.93	19 59.16	23 47.9
13	7.8		16.2	33	52.				24 51.81	31.86	0.13		4	44.336	14 51.56	4.78	2.69	24 19.82	4 29.0
14	9.8		13.	31.					26 49.18	31.87	0.13	III.	4	40.343	19 1.59	5.03	3.60	26 17.18	8 40.2
15	8		13.	31.5	49.				29 40.24	31.89	0.15	IV.	4	38.628	20 49.66	5.42	4.01	29 17.20	10 29.1
16	8				20.	38.			30 19.86	31.90	0.10	IV.	3	21.703	38 40.50	5.48	7.90	29 47.86	28 23.9
17	9					40.	58.		32 22.00	31.91	0.14		3	30.169	29 53.29	5.73	5.98	31 49.95	19 35.0
18	8				9.	27.			34 8.80	31.92	0.10		2	8.440	52 27.08	5.96	11.14	33 36.78	42 14.2
19	8		35.8	54.	12.				37 12.06	31.94	0.14		2	18.763	41 39.46	6.35	8.67	36 39.98	31 31 24.5
20	5		42.5	59.8					39 18.35	31.95	0.23		2	54.242	5 31.91	6.62	1.00	38 46.17	30 55 9.5
21	9					18.			40 59.80	31.96	0.15		2	20.072	40 17.80	6.82	8.33	40 27.69	31 30 3.0
22	6						54.		41 17.90	31.96	0.14		2	12.910	47 47.13	6.75	10.06	39 45.80	37 33.9
23	9		53.5		29.				43 29.30	31.98	0.22	IV.	3	37.839	21 48.08	7.13	4.34	42 57.10	11 29.6
24	5		39.5						45 15.85	31.99	0.18		3	18.146	42 16.91	7.35	8.78	44 43.68	32 3.0
25	8				29.2				45 20.07	31.99	0.23		4	42.719	16 32.86	7.37	3.06	44 56.85	6 13.3
26	9		10.						48 46.30	32.01	0.20		4	24.083	36 10.71	7.76	7.30	48 14.09	25 55.9
27	6				12.5				49 12.43	32.01	0.19		2	13.518	47 8.56	7.84	9.92	48 40.23	36 56.3
28	10					18.5			50 0.29	32.01	0.20		2	19.328	41 4.58	7.94	8.51	49 28.08	30 51.0
29	6					5.	23.		50 46.82	32.02	0.19	V.	4	14.529	46 5.53	8.03	8.66	50 14.61	35 52.2
30	9					34.2			52 16.19	32.03	0.25		4	37.692	21 48.71	8.21	4.22	51 43.91	11 31.1
31	9		16.						54 52.20	32.04	0.28		4	47.332	11 42.21	8.53	1.99	54 19.88	31 1 22.7
32	6				58.2	16.			54 58.09	32.04	0.30		4	52.362	6 29.00	8.55	0.85	54 25.75	30 56 8.4
33	7.8		13.5	32.	50.				6 59 49.90	32.07	0.27	IV.	5	31.543	28 23.32	9.14	5.65	6 59 17.56	31 18 8.1
34	9		37.						7 2 13.39	32.08	0.25		2	13.099	47 33.52	9.44	10.02	7 1 41.06	37 23.0
35	9				21.				2 20.92	32.08	0.25		2	15.883	44 40.04	9.45	9.34	1 48.59	34 28.8
36	6					17.			2 58.99	32.09	0.30		2	37.888	21 45.07	9.53	4.18	2 26.60	11 28.8
37	7					17.			3 58.65	32.09	0.25		2	8.883	51 59.42	9.66	11.06	3 26.31	41 50.1
38	7			14.3					5 32.44	32.10	0.32		2	39.908	19 28.64	9.84	3.70	5 0.02	9 12.2
39	8			33.	51.				8 50.99	32.12	0.30	IV.	3	26.719	33 25.84	10.30	6.75	8 18.57	23 12.9
40	8						58.5		9 22.55	32.12	0.33		4	35.180	24 26.71	10.33	4.80	8 50.10	14 11.8
41	9			23.8					12 41.91	32.14	0.32		2	24.731	35 30.37	10.75	7.23	12 9.45	31 25 18.3
42	9					48.			13 30.09	32.14	0.38		5	51.353	7 32.52	10.86	1.06	12 57.57	30 57 14.4
43	10						21.		14 45.02	32.15	0.39	IV.	5	52.785	6 2.44	11.03	0.73	14 12.48	55 44.2
44	9		48.		24.				17 24.03	32.16	0.40		5	51.046	7 51.30	11.36	1.13	16 51.47	30 57 33.8
45	8		2.	20.					18 38.19	32.16	0.40		5	48.068	10 56.58	11.52	1.81	18 5.63	31 0 39.9
46	6			13.5					19 31.64	32.17	0.35		2	20.228	41 9.93	11.64	8.60	18 59.12	31 0.2
47	9							5.	19 10.59	32.17	0.35		2	20.725	39 37.09	11.60	8.18	18 38.07	29 26.9
48	5					48.			20 29.85	32.17	0.36		3	23.510	36 46.78	11.76	7.54	19 57.32	26 36.1
49	7						33.		7 20 57.05	−32.17	−0.37		3	28.985	−31 3.55	−11.83	−6.23	7 20 24.51	−31 20 51.6

CORRECTIONS.

Date.	Corr. of Clock.	Hourly rate.	m	n	c	Zenith Point.	Nic. Co.
1849.	h.　　s.	s.	s.	s.	s.	°　'　''	r.

REMARKS.

(231) 20. Micrometer reading assumed as 53ʳ.242, not 54ʳ.242.

(231) 22. Minutes assumed as 40, not 41.

(231) 46. Micrometer reading assumed as 19ʳ.228, not 20ʳ.228.

INSTRUMENT READINGS.

Date.		A.	B.	C.	D.	E.	F.	Mean.	Barom.	At.	Ex.	U.	L.	I.
	1849.	° ' ''						''	in.	°	°	°	°	°
Zone 231	Feb. 23, 6 0	90 9 60.	65.	70.3	54.9	63.8	46.8	60.13	30.406	39.2	32.4	38.	39.	
	6 20										31.			
	6 40										30.4			
	7 0	60.	65.	70.5	54.9	65.	46.8	60.37	30.398	37.	30.0			
	7 20										29.8			
	7 40										29.4			
	8 0								30.391	36.	29.			
	8 30	60.	65.6	71.0	54.9	65.	46.8	60.55	30.384	35.2	28.5			

ZONE 231. FEBRUARY 23. S. $D_0 = -30°\ 49'\ 30''$—Continued.

No.	Mag.	I.	II.	III.	IV.	V.	VI.	VII.	T.	a_1	a_2	Mic.	n	r,	i	d_1	d_2	Mean Right Ascension, 1850.0	Mean Declination, 1850.0
									h. m. s.	s.	s.			r,	′ ″	″	″	h. m. s.	° ′ ″
50	6		2,	20.					7 23 38.25	−32.19	−0.36		2	17.765	−42 41.50	−12.17	−8.90	7 23 5.70	−31 32 32.6
51	9						14.3		23 38.25	32.19	0.36		2	17.635	42 28.33	12.17	8.89	23 5.70	32 19.4
52	8		5.3		41.5	59.			27 41.30	32.20	0.43	V.	4	40.678	18 40.39	12.69	3.52	27 8.67	8 26.6
53	10		18.						29 54.23	32.21	0.44		4	38.263	21 11.36	12.99	4.09	29 21.58	31 10 58.4
54	9		40.5						31 16.69	32.22	0.47		5	49.438	9 31.59	13.16	1.49	30 44.00	30 59 16.2
55	10				36.				31 35.88	32.22	0.47		5	48.709	10 18.11	13.20	1.66	31 3.19	31 0 3.0
56	8			35.8					32 53.95	32.23	0.45		4	42.133	17 9.13	13.37	3.19	32 21.27	31 6 55.7
57	10			43.5					33 1.71	32.23	0.48		5	50.982	7 55.00	13.39	1.13	32 29.00	30 57 39.5
58	10		54.8						35 31.02	32.24	0.47		3	39.000	20 34.72	13.72	3.91	34 58.31	31 10 22.3
59	6					54.			35 35.94	32.24	0.45		3	30.898	29 3.66	13.73	5.79	35 3.25	18 53.2
60	8					48.			36 29.94	32.24	0.45		3	29.608	30 24.72	13.85	6.09	35 57.25	20 14.7
61	9						42.		37 6.03	32.24	0.45		3	26.612	33 32.56	13.93	6.79	36 33.34	23 23.3
62	7			34.5					38 10.75	32.25	0.46		3	30.394	29 34.90	14.00	5.91	37 38.04	31 19 24.9
63	8						22.		38 46.03	32.25	0.50		6	50.139	8 48.72	14.14	1.33	38 13.28	30 58 34.2
64	10				29.				41 28.89	32.26	0.54		5	54.108	4 39.27	14.50	0.42	40 50.09	30 55 24.2
65	7		47.			41.5			43 23.35	32.27	0.50	V.	3	34.823	24 56.79	14.75	4.88	43 50.58	31 14 46.4
66	7.8		23.	41.					45 59.17	32.28	0.51	III.	3	34.442	25 21.29	15.10	4.97	45 26.38	15 11.4
67	7		2.	20.2	38.				46 38.13	32.28	0.51	IV.	3	34.425	25 22.55	15.18	4.98	46 5.34	15 12.7
68	7		18.	36.5					47 54.45	32.28	0.50	III.	3	24.830	35 24.10	15.34	7.21	47 21.67	25 16.7
69	8				46.				48 45.85	32.29	0.51		3	29.793	30 12.92	15.46	6.05	48 13.05	20 4.4
70	7.6				31.				49 30.86	32.29	0.54		4	40.650	18 42.70	15.57	3.52	48 58.03	8 31.8
71	9			8.					52 26.10	32.30	0.52		2	26.059	34 1.29	15.94	6.93	51 53.28	23 54.2
72	9					10.8			52 52.86	32.30	0.56		4	47.092	11 58.84	15.99	2.02	52 20.00	1 46.9
73	8			17.					54 35.17	32.31	0.51		2	15.820	44 43.49	16.23	9.35	54 2.35	34 39.1
74	8						5.		54 28.97	32.31	0.52		2	20.112	40 15.54	16.22	8.33	53 56.14	30 10.1
75	8			49.					56 7.17	32.31	0.58		4	44.200	14 59.47	16.43	2.71	55 34.28	4 58.6
76	8			46.5					57 4.64	32.31	0.54		6	20.447	39 51.26	16.56	8.25	56 31.79	29 46.1
77	8			8.8					58 26.90	32.32	0.57		3	33.540	26 17.83	16.72	5.19	57 54.01	16 9.7
78	9						8.		7 58 32.04	32.32	0.58		4	41.432	17 54.45	16.74	3.35	7 57 59.14	7 44.5
79	8		29.	47.					8 2 5.27	32.33	0.53		2	15.739	44 48.57	17.23	9.38	8 1 32.41	34 45.2
80	9				34.8				2 34.68	32.33	0.60		4	47.773	11 15.59	17.29	1.87	2 1.75	1 4.8
81	6					4.	21.		3 45.52	32.34	0.59		2	37.028	22 34.01	17.44	4.38	3 12.59	12 25.8
82	8						19.		5 42.92	32.34	0.55		2	14.894	45 42.60	17.72	9.58	5 10.03	35 40.0
83	6		16.						7 52.42	32.35	0.55		2	8.416	52 27.34	17.99	11.19	7 19.52	42 26.5
84	5			56.	14.				8 13.97	32.35	0.60	IV.	3	32.360	27 32.12	18.04	5.48	7 41.02	17 25.6
85	5				48.	6.2	24.		8 47.90	32.35	0.55		2	9.473	51 22.30	18.11	10.89	8 15.00	41 21.3
86	8					24.5			10 6.29	32.35	0.58		3	19.072	41 25.61	18.29	8.62	9 33.36	31 22.5
87	9						19.		10 43.03	32.35	0.63		6	42.518	16 47.11	18.37	3.16	10 10.05	6 38.7
88	10						59.		12 22.88	32.36	0.57		2	10.208	50 36.77	18.60	10.72	11 49.95	40 36.1
89	9			54.					14 12.09	32.36	0.63		3	28.779	31 16.35	18.85	6.29	13 39.10	21 11.5
90	9				55.	13.			14 54.84	32.37	0.63		2	18.658	41 46.11	18.93	8.71	14 21.84	31 43.7
91	9			8.					16 26.17	32.37	0.60		2	16.360	44 9.87	19.13	9.25	15 53.20	34 8.3
92	8				49.				16 48.88	32.37	0.62		3	23.599	36 41.63	19.17	7.52	16 15.89	20 38.3
93	7						53.5		17 17.54	32.37	0.67		4	41.495	17 50.44	19.26	3.32	16 44.50	7 43.0
94	9				54.				18 53.86	32.37	0.67		4	39.679	19 43.64	19.45	3.74	18 20.82	9 36.8
95	6				43.				19 42.89	32.38	0.64		3	23.002	37 19.02	19.58	7.67	19 9.87	27 16.3
96	6				35.				20 34.95	32.38	0.61		2	9.843	50 58.85	19.68	10.81	20 1.90	40 59.3
97	6				36.				21 35.95	32.38	0.62		2	9.190	51 39.98	19.81	10.98	21 2.95	41 40.8
98	5						23.		8 21 47.04	−32.38	−0.69		4	38.332	−21 8.98	−19.83	−4.07	8 21 13.97	−31 11 2.9

CORRECTIONS.

Date.	Corr. of Clock.	Hourly rate.	m	n	c	Zenith Point.	Mic. Co.
1849.	h.	s.	s.	s.	s.	° ′ ″	r,
	s.	s.					

REMARKS.

(231) 97. Right ascension 2ˢ discordant from Mural February 19, 1849, and Transit March 23, 1849; perhaps T. IV should be 38ˢ.

INSTRUMENT READINGS.

Date.	CIRCLE.							Barom.	THERMOM.				
	A.	B.	C.	D.	E.	F.	Mean.		At.	Ex.	U.	L.	I.
1849. h. m.	° ′ ″						″	In.	°				

Zone 231. February 23. S. $D_0 = -30°\ 49'\ 30''$ — Continued.

Zone 232. March 7. C. $D_0 = -34°\ 35'\ 0''$.

Seconds of transit, T, a_1, a_2

No.	Mag.	I.	II.	III.	IV.	V.	VI.	VII.	T. (h. m. s.)	a_1 (s.)	a_2 (s.)
99	3.4	..	..	24.	42.5	..	19.	..	8 24 42.51	−32.39	−0.63
100	6	..	57.	15.	..	..	..	..	26 33.18	32.39	0.70
101	8.9	..	..	15.	33.	..	..	..	8 27 33.03	−32.40	−0.73
1	6	..	22.3	41.5	49.5	19.1	37.9	..	7 48 0.24	−21.47	−1.80
2	8.9	..	15.3	34.3	..	..	30.5	..	51 53.10	21.48	1.26
3	8.9	..	20.8	39.2	57.8	16.3	35.5	..	51 57.97	21.48	1.39
4	8.9	..	..	..	48.5	7.3	26.3	..	53 48.56	21.49	1.30
5	9	..	..	..	..	4.2	23.	..	54 45.41	21.50	1.45
6	9	..	..	..	..	..	47.2	..	55 9.68	21.50	1.30
7	8.9	..	..	..	14.	32.5	51.5	..	56 13.84	21.50	1.37
8	9	..	..	..	..	..	19.2	..	56 41.68	21.51	1.30
9	9	..	..	..	..	8.5	26.5	..	7 57 49.40	21.52	1.10
10	7	..	4.4	23.1	42.1	0.4	..	..	8 2 41.99	21.53	1.19
11	6.7	..	15.1	33.5	52.5	11.4	..	..	3 52.56	21.54	1.35
12	9.10	..	..	..	53.5	..	..	..	4 53.38	21.54	1.50
13	9.10	..	..	..	..	27.2	..	..	5 8.28	21.55	1.46
14	7	..	..	..	..	36.2	55.3	14.5	6 36.40	21.55	1.60
15	6	..	..	..	..	..	9.5	..	6 50.48	27.55	1.58
16	9	..	..	..	..	..	55.2	..	7 36.40	21.50	1.28
17	9.10	..	..	..	..	..	42.3	..	8 4.78	21.56	1.24
18	7	..	..	..	..	..	..	7.3	8 29.77	21.56	1.12
19	7	..	..	..	..	..	..	..	9	21.57	1.34
20	8	..	..	..	..	..	..	..	10	21.57	1.51
21	8	..	..	..	..	..	32.	..	10 54.28	21.57	1.65
22	6.7	..	..	..	..	56.2	15.2	33.5	12 56.14	21.58	1.29
23	9	..	..	..	..	..	40.5	59.3	14 21.76	21.59	1.16
24	9.10	..	56.1	15.3	34.	53.1	..	..	17 34.10	21.60	1.53
25	8.9	..	9.	28.	46.2	5.3	..	..	18 46.56	21.60	1.28
26	9	..	..	..	30.3	49.3	..	..	19 30.28	21.61	1.36
27	9.10	..	..	..	10.2	29.1	48.	..	20 10.21	21.61	1.42
28	9.10	..	55.3	..	33.4	52.3	..	..	24 30.28	21.63	1.27
29	10	..	..	..	..	..	25.3	..	24 47.67	21.63	1.46
30	9	..	..	..	..	..	10.5	..	25 32.97	21.63	1.01
31	10	..	..	..	..	..	47 ?	..	26 9.47	21.64	0.98
32	9	..	..	41.3	0.	18.7	..	..	32 0.03	21.65	1.03
33	2	..	59.2	18.2	36.3	55.5	14.1	..	34 36.73	21.66	1.00
34	9	..	..	..	..	54.5	..	32.3	35 54.51	21.66	1.51
35	8	..	..	10.5	29.1	..	..	7.3	37 29.39	21.67	1.40
36	10	..	..	48.8	7.	..	..	..	41 7.27	21.68	1.18
37	10	..	..	..	..	52.7	11.2	..	41 33.80	21.68	1.14
38	9.10	..	..	..	..	44.7	..	..	42 25.77	21.68	1.27
39	9.10	..	..	..	..	37.2	..	15.	43 37.27	21.68	1.03
40	7.8	..	..	..	..	52.5	11.6	30.2	44 52.48	21.69	1.45
41	10	..	..	..	59.2	..	..	..	46 18.16	21.69	0.97
42	10	..	..	..	..	53.	11.5	..	8 46 34.16	−21.69	−0.86

Micrometer, i, d_1, d_2, Mean Right Ascension and Declination 1850.0

No.	Micr.	r.	i (° ')	d_1 (″)	d_2 (″)	Mean R.A. 1850.0 (h. m. s.)	Mean Decl. 1850.0 (° ′ ″)
99	. 2	11.265	−49 29.93	−20.24	−10.48	8 24 9.49	− 31 39 30.7
100	4	37.095	22 25.20	20.48	4.36	26 0.09	11 20.1
101	IV. 4	47.518	−11 31.80	−20.61	−1.91	8 26 59.90	− 31 1 24.3
1	IV. 2	7.124	−53 49.47	− 6.84	−16.78	7 47 37.0	− 35 29 13.1
2	III. 5	45.262	13 54.20	7.39	5.61	51 30.4	34 49 7.2
3	IV. 3	36.274	23 26.53	7.40	8.18	51 35.1	58 42.1
4	IV. 4	40.689	18 40.26	7.65	6.91	53 25.8	34 53 54.8
5	V. 3	29.843	30 9.79	7.78	10.05	54 22.4	35 5 27.6
6	VI. 4	39.524	19 54.13	7.84	7.26	54 46.9	34 55 9.2
7	VI. 3	36.974	22 42.42	7.98	7.98	55 51.0	57 58.4
8	VI. 4	41.238	18 6.56	8.05	6.75	56 18.9	53 21.4
9	V. 5	53.784	4 59.67	8.21	3.16	7 57 26.8	40 11.0
10	IV. 4	47.651	11 23.31	8.89	4.88	8 2 19.3	34 46 37.1
11	IV. 3	31.024	25 47.52	9.06	8.84	3 29.7	35 1 5.4
12	IV. 3	23.262	37 2.90	9.19	11.96	4 30.3	12 24.1
13	V. 2	26.368	33 48.05	9.23	11.08	4 45.3	9 8.4
14	IV 2	16.270	44 16.02	9.42	14.05	6 13.3	19 39.5
15	V. 2	18.561	41 52.64	9.47	13.36	6 27.3	35 17 15.5
16	V. 3	38.185	21 26.55	9.57	7.63	7 13.6	34 56 43.8
17	VI. 3	39.605	19 53.50	9.62	7.21	7 42.0	35 55 10.3
18	VI. 4	48.008	10 4.93	9.69	4.55	8 7.1	34 45 19.2
19	VII. 3	32.874	26 59.18	9.8	9.16	9	35 2 18.2
20	VII. 2	21.536	38 46.22	10.0	12.48	10	14 6.6
21	VI. 2	10.673	50 7.48	10.03	15.74	10 31.1	35 25 33.3
22	IV. 3	35.854	23 52.64	10.31	8.30	12 33.3	34 59 11.2
23	V. 4	43.699	15 32.74	10.50	6.06	13 59.0	34 50 49.3
24	IV. 2	16.766	43 44.72	10.06	13.93	17 11.0	35 19 9.6
25	IV. 3	33.606	20 13.82	11.12	8.96	18 23.7	1 33.9
26	IV. 3	28.154	31 55.96	11.21	10.55	19 7.3	7 17.7
27	IV. 3	23.278	37 1.89	11.31	11.99	19 47.2	12 25.2
28	IV. 3	32.318	27 34.95	11.91	9.32	24 10.4	2 56.2
29	VI. 2	18.877	41 32.81	11.95	13.27	24 24.6	35 16 58.0
30	VI. 5	49.778	9 11.19	12.04	4.30	25 10.9	34 44 27.5
31	VI. 5	52.531	6 18.52	12.12	3.52	25 46.8	41 34.2
32	IV. 4	46.361	12 44.48	12.92	5.26	31 37.4	48 2.7
33	IV. 4	47.672	11 22.01	13.28	4.87	34 14.1	34 46 40.2
34	IV. 2	10.829	49 57.01	13.45	15.70	35 31.3	35 24 26.2
35	IV. 2	11.767	48 58.25	13.66	15.41	37 6.2	24 27.3
36	IV. 3	32.778	27 5.63	14.15	9.19	40 44.4	35 2 9.0
37	V. 4	40.434	18 56.82	14.21	6.98	41 11.1	34 54 18.0
38	V. 3	25.079	35 8.79	14.33	11.45	42 2.8	35 10 34.6
39	IV. 5	44.185	15 2.17	14.46	5.89	43 14.6	34 50 22.5
40	IV. 5	13.725	46 55.46	14.65	14.63	44 29.3	35 22 24.9
41	III. 5	45.932	13 11.96	14.84	5.38	45 55.5	34 48 32.2
42	V. 5	54.598	− 4 8.70	−14.87	−2.92	8 46 11.6	− 34 39 26.5

CORRECTIONS.

Date.	Corr. of Clock.	Hourly rate.	m	n	c	Zenith Point.	Mic. Co.
	h.	s.	s.	s.	s.	° ′ ″	r.
1849.	h.	s.	s.	s.	s.	s.		r.

REMARKS.

(232) 1. Time of transit over T. IV assumed as 59″.5 instead of 49″.5.

(232) 22. Declination differs 10′ from B. A. C. 2794.

INSTRUMENT READINGS.

Date.	A.	B.	C.	D.	E.	F.	Mean.	Barom. (in.)	At.	Ex.	U.	L.	I.
Zone 232, 1849, Mar. 7, 7 0	03 54 58.5	51.6	66.5	51.4	60.4	46.6	57.50		48.4	46.7	44.3	38.0	45.7
7 45	.	.	.	.	.	.	.	29.988		46.2			
8 0	.	.	.	.	.	.	.		48.	45.1			
8 20	.	.	.	.	.	.	.	30.010	47.6	45.2			
8 38	.	.	.	.	.	.	.	30.012		44.4			
9 0	.	.	.	.	.	.	.	30.018	47.4	44.4			
9 20										44.0			
9 40	58.1	61.4	66.6	51.6	60.4	46.6	57.45			43.7			
9 53	.	.	.	.	.	.	.	30.026	46.5	43.	46.3	45.	

[(232) 19. Precedes 18. 20ˢ.]

ZONE 232. MARCH 7. C. D₀ = −34° 35′ 0″.

Seconds of Transit (columns I–VII):

No.	Mag.	I.	II.	III.	IV.	V.	VI.	VII.
43	9.10						2.8	21.3
44	8.9						47.2	
45	9						49.2	
46	9.10				55.4	14.2	33.3	
47	9.10		20.3		39.	7.2		
48	8.9			29.5		7.	25.2	
49	8					44.	2.8	
50	8.9						57.8	
51	9.10		18.8		16.4			
52	8					27.3		
53	8.9						52.5	
54	9.10					3.	21.5	
55	8.9				45.2	4.2	23.1	
56	9				49.3	8.4	27.3	
57	10					50.2		
58	8.9			46.	4.8	21.2	42.5	
59	10						45.2	
60	8		25.2	44.	3.1			
61	9					27.3	46.2	
62	9					22.		
63	8			53.3	12.3	31.1	49.4	
64	8			24.3	43.	1.5		
65	8			45.1	3.3	22.5	41.2	
66	8.9			55.5		33.2	51.8	
67	9			32.2	51.			
68	8.9			15.7	31.9	53.5		
69	9				22.2	41.		
70	8.9			35.2	53.8			
71	3			20.3	45.2	4.2		
72	9		43.2	2.		39.5		
73	6.7		21.5	40.2	50.2	17.5		
74	9					4.2		
75	9.10			44.8	22.			
76	7	1.8	20.8	38.7	58.3			
77	10			38.7	16.3			
78	9				58.2			
79	7			36.3	14.2			
80	8			40.2	58.9			
81	9.10		35.2	54.2				
82	9			44.8	3.5			
83	8.9			36.3	54.8			
84	9		14.4	12.2		20.3		
85	8			24.6	43.6	22.4		
86	9							
87	8			43.8	2.5	21.5	40.4	
88	10			35.2				
89	9		20.		39.8	57.4		
90	10				2.8	21.3		
91	9		16.8	36.	54.8	13.3	32.3	

No.	T. (h. m. s.)	a₁ (s.)	a₂ (s.)	MICROMETER.		r.	i (′ ″)	d₁ (″)	d₂ (″)	Mean Right Ascension, 1850.0 (h. m. s.)	Mean Declination, 1850.0 (° ′ ″)
43	8 47 43.90	−21.70	−1.04	V.	3	40.026	−19 30.96	−15.02	− 7.10	8 47 21.2	− 34 54 53.1
44	48 28.34	21.70	1.18	V.	3	30.046	29 57.18	15.13	9.99	48 5.5	35 5 22.3
45	49 11.68	21.70	1.00	VI.	4	38.656	20 48.40	15.24	7.50	48 49.0	34 56 11.2
46	52 14.25	21.71	1.42	IV.	2	11.125	49 38.57	15.63	15.62	51 51.1	35 25 9.8
47	53 38.32	21.71	0.86	IV.	5	50.527	8 24.13	15.82	4.07	53 15.75	34 43 44.0
48	55 48.12	21.72	0.94	IV.	4	44.125	15 4.68	16.10	5.89	55 25.5	34 50 26.7
49	8 56 25.20	21.72	1.15	V.	3	29.414	30 36.95	16.18	10.17	56 2.3	35 6 3.3
50	9 0 20.03	21.73	1.45	VI.	2	6.636	54 20.52	16.70	16.96	8 59 56.9	29 54.2
51	2 56.45	21.73	1.13	IV.	3	28.678	31 22.95	17.03	10.40	9 2 33.6	35 6 50.4
52	3 8.61	21.73	0.82	V.	5	49.684	9 17.10	17.07	4.31	2 46.1	34 44 38.5
53	3 14.97	21.73	0.80	VI.	5	51.718	7 9.43	17.08	3.72	2 52.4	34 42 30.2
54	4 43.91	21.74	1.28	V.	2	17.572	42 54.67	17.27	13.67	4 20.9	35 18 25.6
55	5 45.31	21.74	1.13	IV.	3	27.456	32 39.78	17.40	10.75	5 22.4	8 7.9
56	6 49.49	21.74	1.07	IV.	3	31.278	28 40.00	17.55	9.62	6 26.7	4 7.2
57	7 40.11	21.75	1.31	V.	2	14.467	46 9.48	17.66	14.63	7 17.1	21 41.8
58	9 4.91	21.75	1.28	IV.	2	15.610	44 57.35	17.85	14.27	8 41.9	35 20 29.5
59	10 7.07	21.75	0.78	VI.	5	50.757	8 9.75	17.93	4.09	10 45.1	34 43 31.7
60	12 2.95	21.75	1.04	IV.	3	31.568	28 1.75	18.17	9.55	11 40.2	35 3 29.5
61	12 8.64	21.75	0.77	V.	5	50.292	8 39.40	18.19	4.10	11 46.1	34 44 1.7
62	12 44.47	21.75	1.06	VI.	3	29.364	30 39.97	18.26	10.20	12 21.7	35 6 8.4
63	15 12.16	21.75	0.87	IV.	4	42.598	16 40.52	18.59	6.32	14 49.5	34 52 5.4
64	15 24.15	21.75	0.75	V.	5	50.970	7 56.38	18.61	3.43	15 1.7	43 18.9
65	17 3.65	21.76	0.87	IV.	4	41.946	17 21.31	18.84	6.53	16 41.9	34 52 46.7
66	19 14.27	21.76	1.15	IV.	2	20.206	40 9.07	19.19	12.90	18 51.4	35 15 41.1
67	19 32.04	21.76	1.20	IV.	2	18.395	42 2.73	19.22	13.45	19 9.1	17 35.4
68	20 15.77	21.76	1.20	IV.	2	16.725	43 47.20	19.31	13.96	19 52.8	35 19 20.5
69	21 3.22	21.76	1.23	V.	2	14.851	45 45.14	19.42	14.52	20 40.2	34 21 19.1
70	22 53.89	21.76	0.92	IV.	3	37.462	22 11.08	19.65	7.82	22 31.2	34 57 39.4
71	23 26.31	21.77	1.18	IV.	2	18.184	42 15.91	19.72	13.50	23 3.4	35 17 49.1
72	25 20.86	21.77	1.13	IV.	2	19.808	40 33.86	19.97	13.02	24 58.0	16 6.9
73	25 40.19	21.77	0.96	IV.	3	32.465	27 25.53	20.01	9.29	25 17.5	2 54.8
74	26 26.52	21.77	1.20	VI.	2	14.705	47 54.55	20.12	14.57	26 3.6	35 23 29.2
75	27 44.57	21.77	0.93	IV.	3	33.106	26 26.48	20.29	9.01	27 21.9	34 51 55.8
76	29 20.47	21.77	1.03	IV.	3	26.305	33 52.01	20.51	11.09	28 57.7	35 9 23.6
77	29 38.65	21.77	1.03	IV.	3	26.778	33 22.07	20.54	10.96	29 15.9	8 53.6
78	30 20.51	21.77	1.19	VI.	2	14.343	46 17.44	20.63	14.68	29 57.5	21 52.8
79	31 36.37	21.77	1.23	IV.	2	10.963	49 48.67	20.79	15.68	31 13.4	35 25 25.1
80	32 21.44	21.77	0.69	V.	5	49.061	9 56.28	20.89	4.58	31 59.0	34 45 21.7
81	33 54.19	21.78	1.21	IV.	2	11.446	49 18.57	21.09	15.54	33 31.2	35 24 55.2
82	34 44.60	21.78	1.07	IV.	3	21.192	39 12.69	21.18	12.61	34 21.8	15 46.5
83	35 17.17	21.78	1.15	V.	2	15.123	45 28.21	21.28	14.44	34 54.2	35 21 3.9
84	36	21.78	. .	IV.	5	41.041	18 19.36	21.4	6.79	35	34 53 47.6
85	36 24.73	21.78	0.73	IV.	5	45.491	13 40.02	21.42	5.49	36 2.2	49 6.9
86	37	21.78	. .	VII.	4	36.684	22 39.60	21.4	7.97	37	34 58 9.1
87	40 2.61	21.78	0.99	IV.	3	25.545	34 39.62	21.90	11.31	39 39.8	35 10 12.8
88	42 35.05	21.78	0.96	IV.	3	27.985	32 6.42	22.22	10.60	42 12.3	7 39.2
89	43 19.82	21.78	1.04	IV.	2	20.078	40 17.05	22.33	12.95	42 57.0	16 52.3
90	47 2.50	21.78	1.02	IV.	2	20.117	40 14.59	22.81	12.94	46 39.7	35 15 50.3
91	9 48 54.70	−21.78	−0.74	IV.	3	39.664	−19 53.69	−23.04	− 7.18	9 48 32.2	− 34 55 23.9

CORRECTIONS.

Date.	Corr. of Clock.	Hourly rate.	m	n	c	Zenith Point.	Mic. Co.
1849.	h.	s.	s.	s.	s.	° ′ ″	r.

INSTRUMENT READINGS.

Date.	CIRCLE.							Barom.	THERMOM.				
	A.	B.	C.	D.	E.	F.	Mean.		At.	Ex.	U.	L.	I.
1849. h. m.	° ′ ″						″	in.					

REMARKS.

(232) 47. Transits over T.'s III and V assumed as 0s.3 and 57s, not 20s.3 and 7s, to agree with Transit Z., March 7, 1849.

(232) 84. The only means of harmonizing these transits is to suppose transit over T. II recorded over T. III, and as 31s.4, not 11s.4; and transit over T. VI as 50s.3 and not 20s.3.

(232) 85. Time of transit over T. VI assumed as 2s.4 instead of 22s.4.

ZONE 232. MARCH 7. C. $D_e = -34^\circ 35' 0''$—Continued.

No.	Mag.	I.	II.	III.	IV.	V.	VI.	VII.	T.	a₁	a₂	MICROMETER		r	i	d₁	d₂	Mean Right Ascension, 1850.0.	Mean Declination, 1850.0.
									h. m. s.	s.	s.			r.	′ ″	″	″	h. m. s.	° ′ ″
92	10			31.3	50.5				9 48 50.29	−21.78	−0.74	V	3	39.869	−19 40.69	−23.03	−7.13	9 48 27.8	− 34 55 10.9
93	9.10				56.2		34.		50 56.27	21.78	0.79	IV	3	36.376	23 20.13	23.30	8.13	50 33.7	58 51.6
94	9.10			59.3					52 18.28	21.78	1.07	III	2	15.595	44 57.73	23.49	14.29	51 55.4	35 20 35.5
95	7			30.2	49.2	8.2	26.4		9 52 49.12	−21.78	−0.93	IV	3	25.309	−34 51.11	−23.55	−11.38	9 52 26.4	− 35 10 26.0

ZONE 233. MARCH 12. S. $D_e = -26^\circ 24' 0''$.

No.	Mag.	I.	II.	III.	IV.	V.	VI.	VII.	T.	a₁	a₂	MICROMETER		r	i	d₁	d₂	Mean Right Ascension, 1850.0.	Mean Declination, 1850.0.
1	9			37.					8 26 11.75	−22.94	−2.55		3	25.149	−35 3.96	− 2.20	− 8.83	8 25 46.3	− 26 59 15.0
2	10					28.			25 53.56	22.94	2.52		3	28.272	31 48.54	2.16	8.31	25 28.1	55 59.0
3	8		0.5	17.					28 34.81	22.95	2.24		4	47.972	11 2.61	2.50	4.93	28 9.6	26 35 10.0
4	10					23.			32 5.53	22.97	2.54		2	16.772	43 44.72	2.93	10.31	31 40.0	27 7 58.0
5	9			23.		57.6			33 40.38	22.98	2.42		3	23.810	36 28.27	3.13	9.08	33 15.0	27 0 40.5
6	8					47.5			34 30.26	22.98	2.21		5	39.888	19 31.90	3.22	6.27	34 5.1	26 43 41.8
7	8						51.		35 16.57	22.97	2.36		3	29.668	30 20.83	3.32	8.06	34 51.3	26 54 32.2
8	9		55.	12.5			4.8		37 30.00	23.00	2.50		2	9.079	51 47.51	3.59	11.67	37 4.5	27 16 2.8
9	10				53.2	10.5			38 53.14	23.00	2.20		4	33.345	26 21.27	3.79	7.43	38 27.9	26 50 32.5
10	11		40.		15.				41 14.78	23.01	2.13		3	36.290	23 25.52	4.05	6.92	40 49.6	26 47 36.5
11	9						58.		41 23.44	23.01	2.41		2	11.930	48 44.65	4.07	11.13	40 58.0	27 12 59.9
12	9					3.			42 45.49	23.02	2.37		2	13.612	47 3.04	4.22	10.85	42 20.1	11 18.1
13	·					12.			43 54.60	23.02	2.25		2	21.958	38 19.43	4.37	9.40	43 39.3	2 33.8
14	4					52.	9.5		44 34.73	23.02	2.33		2	15.198	45 4.81	4.45	10.53	44 9.4	9 19.8
15	8				0.				46 59.90	23.03	2.21		2	19.802	40 34.23	4.73	9.77	46 34.7	4 48.7
16	9		26.				35.5		47 0.89	23.03	2.27		2	15.048	45 32.54	4.73	10.80	46 35.6	9 47.9
17	5		56.	13.5	31.				49 30.87	23.04	2.17	IV	2	18.292	42 9.20	5.03	10.05	49 5.7	6 24.3
18	7				32.5	50.			51 32.48	23.05	2.16		2	16.488	44 2.28	5.27	10.36	51 7.3	8 17.9
19	6		7.8	25.	42.				53 42.35	23.06	2.19		2	11.078	49 1.52	5.52	11.31	53 17.1	27 13 18.4
20	9					21.2			55 3.88	23.06	1.96		3	28.503	31 34.11	5.68	8.26	54 38.9	26 55 48.0
21	9						37.8		56 3.23	23.06	2.14		5	11.540	49 13.30	5.80	11.22	55 38.0	27 13 30.3
22	8		55.5	13.					58 30.32	23.07	1.59		5	53.303	5 29.56	6.09	3.99	58 5.7	26 29 39.6
23	9			29.8		4.			8 59 46.97	23.07	1.72		4	39.508	19 54.50	6.23	6.35	8 59 22.2	26 44 7.1
24	9			44.5					9 2 1.91	23.08	1.97		2	15.833	44 42.95	6.49	10.48	9 1 36.9	27 8 59.9
25	9						32.		1 57.54	23.08	1.66		4	41.417	17 55.45	6.49	6.03	1 32.8	26 42 8.0
26	9					0.5	17.		5 0.04	23.09	1.68		3	34.210	25 35.98	6.84	7.30	4 35.3	49 50.1
27	7				32.3	50.	8.		9 50.15	23.10	1.43	IV	4	48.833	10 9.07	7.40	4.75	9 45.6	34 21.2
28	7		25.	13.					12 0.05	23.11	1.44		2	44.176	15 0.85	7.65	5.56	11 35.5	26 39 14.1
29	9			33.			8.5		13 50.72	23.11	1.74		2	16.193	44 20.79	7.86	10.42	13 25.9	27 8 39.1
30	8						27.		13 52.55	23.11	1.61		3	26.792	33 21.32	7.86	8.55	13 27.8	26 57 37.8
31	9						57.2		15 22.66	23.12	1.22		2	14.598	46 1.45	8.05	10.69	14 57.8	27 10 20.2
32	9						24.5		16 50.02	23.12	1.26		5	50.978	7 56.00	8.21	4.39	16 25.6	26 32 8.6
33	9			56.					9 19 13.31	−23.13	−1.45		3	31.353	−28 35.11	− 8.48	− 7.77	9 18 48.7	− 26 52 51.4

CORRECTIONS.

Date.	Corr. of Clock.	Hourly rate.	m	n	c	Zenith Point.	Mic. Co.
1849.	h.	s.	s.	s.	s.	s.	° ′ ″	r. °

INSTRUMENT READINGS.

	Date.		CIRCLE.							Barom.	THERMOM.				
			A.	B.	C.	D.	E.	F.	Mean.		At.	Ex.	U.	L.	I.
	1849.	h. m.	° ′ ″						″	in.	°	°	°	°	°
Zone 233	Mar. 12,	8 20	85 44 58.2	60.1	66.2	53.3	59.5	46.8	57.35	29.834	51.4	43.3	49.5	48.8	50.
		8 40										42.			
		9 0								29.826	50.	42.			
		9 10										42.1			
		9 19	58.2	60.1	67.0	53.3	59.5	46.2	57.38						

ZONE 234. MARCH 16. S. $D_0 = -37°\,5'\,40''$.

Columns under **SECONDS OF TRANSIT** are I.–VII. The **MICROMETER** group carries a roman-numeral column and a count column.

No.	Mag.	I.	II.	III.	IV.	V.	VI.	VII.	T. (h. m. s.)	a_1 (s.)	a_2 (s.)	Micr.	n	r.	i (′ ″)	d_1	d_2	Mean R.A. 1850.0 (h. m. s.)	Mean Decl. 1850.0 (° ′ ″)
1	7		15.	35.	54.8				7 32 54.44	−25.42	−2.41	IV.	3	25.468	−34 44.51	−2.66	−10.68	7 32 26.6	−37 40 37.8
2	6		57.8						34 37.11	25.43	2.46		2	8.868	51 58.67	2.89	17.02	34 9.2	57 54.6
3	6			38.2					34 57.85	25.43	2.46		2	11.635	49 6.02	2.94	15.98	34 30.0	55 4.9
4	5					13.	32.5		34 53.49	25.43	2.43	VI.	3	13.636	41 52.77	2.93	13.29	34 25.6	47 49.0
5	8		57.						38 36.03	25.46	2.33		4	41.358	17 57.08	3.42	4.84	38 8.2	23 45.3
6	6			32.2					38 51.82	25.46	2.43		2	15.723	44 49.58	3.45	14.30	38 23.9	50 47.1
7	6			22.					39 41.49	25.47	2.36		3	30.790	29 10.18	3.58	8.71	39 13.7	35 2.5
8	5				22.				40 21.84	25.48	2.36		3	29.440	30 35.32	3.66	9.20	39 54.0	36 28.2
9	7						50.		40 11.25	25.48	2.34		3	33.988	25 49.59	3.65	7.52	39 43.4	31 40.8
10	6					37.			41 17.53	25.49	2.35		3	31.592	28 20.24	3.80	8.41	40 49.7	34 12.5
11	6						18.		41 39.26	25.49	2.31		4	40.878	18 28.89	3.86	5.00	41 11.5	24 17.7
12	7						57.5		42 18.75	25.49	2.34		3	29.668	30 20.71	3.94	9.12	41 50.9	36 13.8
13	7			38.	57.2				43 57.38	25.50	2.41		2	16.719	43 47.67	4.16	14.01	43 29.5	49 45.8
14	10		23.	42.					51 1.79	25.55	2.27		3	37.705	21 56.36	5.14	6.16	50 34.0	27 47.7
15	8		32.	52.	11.		49.5		7 54 11.05	25.57	2.30	IV.	3	27.220	32 54.53	5.60	10.05	7 53 43.2	38 50.2
16	10		20.2	40.	50.5				8 2 59.37	25.60	2.26	IV.	3	31.409	28 31.78	6.86	8.48	8 2 31.5	34 27.1
17	7				35.	55.			3 35.29	25.61	2.17	IV.	5	49.974	8 58.65	6.95	1.67	3 7.5	14 47.3
18	10						48.		4 9.26	25.62	2.19		4	43.416	15 49.87	7.02	4.09	3 41.5	21 41.0
19	9						50.2		5 11.37	25.62	2.27		2	22.820	37 25.48	7.17	11.72	4 43.5	43 24.4
20	9						26.		5 47.11	25.63	2.30		2	16.875	43 38.38	7.26	13.94	5 19.2	49 39.6
21	7			30.	49.				7 49.22	25.64	2.16		3	47.002	12 13.10	7.56	2.77	7 21.4	18 3.4
22	9				43.				8 42.87	25.64	2.16		4	48.454	10 33.05	7.69	2.27	8 15.1	16 23.0
23	10						29.		8 50.26	25.64	2.15		4	51.093	7 47.91	7.71	1.28	8 22.5	13 36.9
24	10						20.		9 41.26	25.65	2.16		4	47.738	11 18.37	7.84	2.50	9 13.4	17 8.7
25	11		36.	56.					13 15.29	25.67	2.20		3	36.935	22 44.61	8.36	6.45	12 47.4	28 39.4
26	9					24.	44.		14 4.80	25.68	2.23	V.	2	23.655	36 33.03	8.49	11.41	13 36.9	42 32.9
27	10		58.	18.	37.5				16 37.36	25.69	2.23	IV.	2	22.814	37 25.30	8.87	11.72	16 9.4	43 25.9
28	11			39.5					17 59.08	25.70	2.23		2	20.373	39 58.10	9.08	12.63	17 31.2	45 59.8
29	7					31.6			18 11.94	25.70	2.24		2	18.153	42 18.16	9.11	13.48	17 44.0	48 20.8
30	11		58.			55.5			20 36.58	25.71	2.12		4	45.672	13 27.53	9.47	3.25	20 8.8	19 20.3
31	7			35.5	56.				21 55.45	25.71	2.13	IV.	3	38.365	21 15.32	9.67	5.91	21 27.6	27 10.9
32	10				3.				23 2.87	25.72	2.08		4	50.662	8 14.33	9.85	1.43	22 35.1	14 5.6
33	8		27.	47.					27 6.29	25.74	2.11	III.	4	40.586	18 46.22	10.45	5.10	26 38.4	24 41.8
34	7				45.				27 44.86	25.74	2.17		3	26.218	33 57.40	10.55	10.42	27 17.0	39 58.4
35	6				31.				28 11.29	25.74	2.20		2	15.053	45 32.54	10.62	14.66	27 43.3	51 37.8
36	8				9.				28 49.44	25.75	2.16		3	25.029	35 11.86	10.71	10.86	28 21.5	41 13.4
37	8			24.5					30 44.08	25.76	2.17		3	19.600	40 46.21	11.01	12.88	30 16.2	46 50.1
38	7				13.8	33.			31 13.49	25.76	2.22		2	10.580	50 12.82	11.00	16.38	30 45.5	56 20.3
39	9					15.5			31 56.12	25.76	2.09		4	41.872	17 27.33	11.19	4.60	31 28.3	23 23.1
40	6				53.	13.			32 53.21	25.77	2.11	V.	4	36.407	23 9.52	11.35	6.65	32 25.3	29 7.5
41	10	13.5	32.	52.					35 52.10	25.77	2.17	IV.	2	14.692	45 54.80	11.79	14.79	35 24.2	52 1.4
42	11					59.	19.		36 39.98	25.78	2.03		3	51.422	7 28.20	11.91	1.16	36 10.2	13 21.3
43	7		40.						39 19.03	25.80	2.05		3	40.112	19 24.04	12.33	5.26	38 51.2	25 22.5
44	10					29.2			39 29.06	25.80	2.06		3	37.972	21 39.78	12.35	6.05	39 1.2	27 35.2
45	8					14.2			39 54.82	25.80	2.05		3	41.410	18 4.23	12.41	4.81	39 27.0	24 1.5
46	6					54.2	13.8		40 34.96	25.80	2.03	V.	4	45.143	14 1.16	12.52	3.44	40 7.1	19 57.1
47	8				0.2				42 0.04	25.81	2.09		3	31.683	28 14.41	12.73	8.39	41 32.1	34 15.5
48	8							15.8	42 37.06	25.81	2.05		4	39.082	20 21.73	12.82	5.64	42 9.2	26 20.2
49	7							5.	8 43 26.26	−25.82	−2.06		4	38.402	−21 4.53	−12.95	−5.90	8 42 58.4	−37 27 3.4

CORRECTIONS.

Date.	Corr. of Clock.	Hourly rate.	m	n	c	Zenith Point.	Mic. Co.
1849. h.	s.	s.	s.	s.	s.	° ′ ″	r.

INSTRUMENT READINGS.

Date.		CIRCLE.							Barom.	THERMOM.				
		A.	B.	C.	D.	E.	F.	Mean.	In.	At.	Ex.	U.	L.	I.
Zone 234	1849. Mar. 16, 7 30	96 24 60.	63.9	69.	55.5	61.6	50.	60.00						
	7 40								29.962	52.3	49.2	52.5		50.8
	8 0	61.6	63.9	70.3	55.5	62.	50.	60.55			49.			
	8 20										48.8			
	8 40								29.984	51.8	46.2			
	9 0								29.988	51.6	45.5			
	9 20										43.9			
	9 40										42.8			
	10 0	61.6	64.2	69.5	55.5	62.5	50.	60.55	29.994	50.	42.2	49.5	50.3	50.

Ex. therm. assumed as 45.0

ZONE 234.   MARCH 16.   S. $D_o = -37° 5' 40''$—Continued.

SECONDS OF TRANSIT.

No.	Mag.	I.	II.	III.	IV.	V.	VI.	VII.
50	10					10.3		
51	8			13.5	33.			
52	7		52.8	12.				
53	6				0.	19.8	30.	
54	8					10.2	30.	
55	8			53.				
56	9		46.2		20.			
57	10					59.6	19.5	
58	8					47.5		
59	9						58.5	
60	9		14.8	34.	54.			
61	5.6		30.8	50.3	10.	29.		
62	11				44.			
63	9		26.8	46.2				
64	10			33.2		12.		
65	9		22.8	42.5				
66	9			30.2				
67	9			13.			11.3	
68	9.8		4.8	24.2				
69	7					9.	28.5	
70	9			39.8				
71	10.9						50.	
72	8				53.			
73	7				42.5			
74	9				40.5			
75	10					43.5		
76	10			3.				
77	10						12.5	
78	11		31.2					
79	7		16.2	36.	55.3			
80	8.7		42.		1.5	21.		
81	9						20.	
82	6		10.5	29.	49.			
83	7					35.	54.5	
84	8						16.2	
85	8				26.			
86	6					8.8		
87	7				58.			
88	6					54.	13.3	
89	8					59.		
90	7					25.8	45.2	
91	8			51.	10.8	30.		
92	10						55.5	15.
93	11			54.				
94	9			19.5	39.			
95	10				30.5	50.		
96	8			31.	50.6			
97	8						34.8	54.

No.	T. (h. m. s.)	a_1 (s.)	a_2 (s.)	MICROMETER		r.	i (' '')	d_1 ('')	d_2 ('')	Mean Right Ascension, 1850.0 (h. m. s.)	Mean Declination, 1850.0 (° ' '')
50	8 44 50.98	25.82	−2.01		5	43.203	−10 50.18	−13.17	−2.33	8 44 23.1	−37 16 25.7
51	47 32.93	25.83	2.07		3	28.082	30 57.66	13.57	9.73	47 5.0	37 1.0
52	49 31.82	25.84	2.11	III.	2	16.328	44 11.81	13.88	14.17	49 3.9	50 19.9
53	50 0.07	25.84	2.09	IV.	2	20.962	39 20.27	13.95	12.41	49 32.1	45 26.6
54	53 50.95	25.85	2.04		3	27.286	32 50.45	14.52	10.01	53 23.1	38 55.0
55	54 12.52	25.65	2.01		3	35.607	24 6.07	14.58	6.93	53 44.7	30 9.6
56	55 20.06	25.87	2.01	IV.	3	30.385	29 36.04	15.19	8.86	57 52.2	35 40.1
57	8 58 40.45	25.67	2.00	V.	3	33.475	26 22.15	15.24	7.71	8 58 12.6	32 25.1
58	9 0 27.98	25.88	2.02	V.	3	27.346	32 46.69	15.51	9.99	9 0 0.1	38 52.2
59	1 19.42	25.88	2.08		2	9.681	51 9.64	15.63	16.76	0 51.6	57 22.0
60	8 53.58	25.90	2.04	IV.	2	12.258	48 27.64	16.76	15.78	8 25.9	54 40.2
61	10 9.80	25.91	2.04	IV.	2	10.180	50 37.90	16.94	16.57	9 41.8	56 51.4
62	11 43.86	25.91	1.92		4	41.962	17 20.31	17.17	4.58	10 16.0	23 22.1
63	14 5.79	25.92	1.93	III.	3	34.929	24 50.48	17.52	7.18	13 37.9	30 55.2
64	14 52.75	25.92	1.87	III.	5	51.185	7 42.39	17.63	1.23	14 25.0	13 41.2
65	17 2.05	25.93	2.00	III.	2	17.209	43 16.50	17.95	13.84	16 34.1	49 28.3
66	17 49.74	25.93	1.96		3	25.300	34 54.80	18.07	10.75	17 21.8	41 3.6
67	19 32.55	25.93	1.88		4	39.370	20 3.22	18.32	5.54	19 4.7	26 7.1
68	22 43.79	25.94	1.90	III.	3	32.150	27 44.99	18.78	8.20	22 16.0	33 52.0
69	22 49.68	25.94	1.87	V.	4	39.135	20 18.21	18.30	5.62	22 21.9	26 22.6
70	24 59.34	25.94	1.92		3	24.203	36 3.62	19.11	11.16	24 31.5	42 13.9
71	25 11.15	25.94	1.94		3	21.148	39 15.26	19.14	12.35	24 43.3	44 26.7
72	26 52.86	25.95	1.90		3	27.058	33 4.63	19.39	10.10	26 25.0	39 14.1
73	27 42.46	25.95	1.97		2	8.538	52 20.88	19.51	17.19	27 14.5	58 37.6
74	28 40.36	25.95	1.84		4	40.182	19 12.19	19.65	5.23	28 12.6	25 17.1
75	29 24.11	25.96	1.84		4	39.735	19 40.50	19.75	5.39	28 56.3	25 45.6
76	31 22.50	25.96	1.87		3	29.203	30 49.94	20.03	9.30	30 54.7	36 59.3
77	31 33.76	25.96	1.80		4	47.032	12 2.75	20.06	2.75	31 6.0	18 5.6
78	34 13.27	25.97	1.84		3	33.638	26 11.19	20.44	7.65	33 45.5	32 19.3
79	35 55.41	25.97	1.90	IV.	2	17.592	42 53.04	20.69	13.69	35 27.5	49 7.4
80	39 21.11	25.98	1.90	IV.	2	13.038	47 38.60	21.16	15.43	38 53.2	53 55.2
81	39 41.26	25.98	1.75		5	51.380	7 30.83	21.21	1.16	39 13.5	13 33.2
82	41 48.98	25.98	1.80	IV.	3	36.103	23 37.14	21.50	6.74	41 21.2	29 45.4
83	42 15.58	25.98	1.84	V.	2	25.630	34 29.13	21.57	10.62	41 47.8	40 41.3
84	43 37.42	25.98	1.83		3	27.208	32 55.10	21.76	10.05	43 9.6	39 6.9
85	45 25.86	25.99	1.74		4	44.740	14 25.96	22.01	3.56	44 58.1	20 31.5
86	45 49.37	25.99	1.79		3	36.503	23 6.45	22.06	6.57	45 21.6	29 15.1
87	46 57.86	25.99	1.77		3	39.293	20 17.09	22.21	5.53	46 30.1	26 24.8
88	47 34.46	25.99	1.83	V.	3	24.183	36 5.07	22.30	11.17	47 6.6	42 18.5
89	48 39.57	25.99	1.78		4	36.825	22 43.04	22.45	6.47	48 11.8	28 52.0
90	50 25.63	25.99	1.84	IV.	2	18.813	41 36.26	22.70	13.27	49 57.8	47 52.2
91	55 30.08	26.00	1.73	IV.	4	42.710	16 33.42	23.38	4.32	55 2.3	22 41.1
92	9 55 36.19	26.00	1.73		4	43.085	16 16.42	23.39	4.19	9 55 8.5	22 24.0
93	10 0 33.06	26.00	1.73		3	36.180	23 31.74	24.06	6.71	10 0 5.3	29 42.5
94	1 58.54	26.01	1.75	III.	3	28.572	31 29.47	24.26	9.53	1 30.8	37 43.3
95	2 49.95	26.01	1.70	IV.	4	39.028	20 24.49	24.36	5.66	2 22.2	26 34.5
96	6 10.09	26.01	1.68	III.	4	39.912	19 28.39	24.81	5.32	5 42.4	25 38.5
97	10 6 15.30	−26.01	−1.72	V.	3	29.442	−30 35.19	−24.82	−9.20	10 5 47.6	−37 36 49.2

CORRECTIONS.

Date.	Corr. of Clock.	Hourly rate.	m	u	ε	Zenith Point.	Mic. Co.
1849.	h. s.	s.	s.	s.	s.	° ' ''	r.

REMARKS.

INSTRUMENT READINGS.

Date.	CIRCLE.							Barom.	THERMOM.				
	A.	B.	C.	D.	E.	F.	Mean.		At.	Ex.	U.	L.	I.
1849, h. m.	° ' ''						''	in.	°	°	°	°	°

ZONE 235.   MARCH 16.   S. $D_0 = -34^\circ\,35'\,30''$.

Seconds of Transit, T, a_1, a_2

No.	Mag.	I.	II.	III.	IV.	V.	VI.	VII.	T. (h m s)	a_1	a_2
1	5.4		3.5	22.	41.5				11 18 41.26	−25.84	−1.93
2	6		27.5	46.3	5.2				21 5.21	25.83	1.92
3	9				8.	27.			22 8.06	25.83	1.92
4	7		42.2		20.2				24 20.02	25.82	1.92
5	6		22.	41.		18.6			25 59.90	25.82	1.94
6	7		48.5	8.	26.				27 26.47	25.82	1.94
7	6				19.	37.5			28 18.84	25.81	1.92
8	7				39.				29 38.90	25.81	1.94
9	8					27.2	16.		30 8.48	25.81	1.92
10	7		46.	5.	23.4				34 23.67	25.80	1.93
11	9		56.5	15.5					35 34.39	25.79	1.94
12	10						40.5		36 2.93	25.79	1.94
13	9					38.			37 0.25	25.79	1.95
14	8				35.5	54.			38 35.33	25.78	1.93
15	7.6			45.	4.	22.			40 3.62	25.78	1.94
16	7			16.8	35.2				41 35.37	25.77	1.94
17	7		25.	44.	2.8				47 2.81	25.76	1.95
18	9		28.	47.	6.				53 6.00	25.74	1.96
19	10				28.				54 27.88	25.73	1.95
20	10					54.			55 35.15	25.73	1.96
21	10.9		9.						57 46.78	25.72	1.95
22	6.7		4.8	23.8	42.4				11 58 42.53	25.72	1.95
23	6.7		2.	20.8	39.6	58.6			12 7 39.74	25.70	1.97
24	5		47.8	7.					10 25.84	25.68	1.97
25	8				33.				10 32.85	25.68	1.97
26	8		31.	49.5					12 8.61	25.67	1.96
27	9			52.					13 10.00	25.66	1.97
28	8							2.5	13 24.61	25.66	1.98
29	7						3.	21.5	14 44.26	25.66	1.97
30	9			8.5	27.2			23.7	16 46.20	25.65	1.96
31	11					27.	46.5		18 27.18	25.64	1.99
32	10			32.	50.8				21 9.75	25.63	1.98
33	9				27.2				21 46.10	25.63	1.98
34	10				23.2	42.8			22 23.52	25.62	1.98
35	11			45.5					26 4.43	25.61	1.98
36	9.10		26.8	46.					28 4.76	25.60	1.98
37	11			14.5	33.8				28 33.53	25.60	1.98
38	7.8		57.8	16.5	35.6				35 35.52	25.57	1.99
39	8.9		14.	32.8	52.				36 51.91	25.56	2.00
40	8.9		48.2		27.5				12 40 25.96	−25.54	−1.98

Micrometer, i, d_1, d_2, Mean Right Ascension and Mean Declination 1850.0

No.	Micrometer		r	i (° ′ ″)	d_1 (″)	d_2 (″)	Mean R.A. 1850.0 (h m s)	Mean Decl. 1850.0 (° ′ ″)
1		3	21.722	−38 39.31	−4.16	−12.49	11 18 13.5	− 35 14 26.0
2		5	51.043	7 51.61	4.38	3.82	20 37.5	34 43 29.8
3		4	44.312	14 53.00	4.48	5.78	21 40.3	50 33.3
4		4	45.542	13 35.82	4.68	5.43	23 52.3	34 49 15.9
5		2	13.608	47 2.92	4.84	14.94	25 32.1	35 22 52.7
6		2	13.923	46 42.97	4.97	14.85	26 58.7	35 22 32.8
7		4	47.705	11 19.94	5.05	4.80	27 51.1	34 46 59.8
8		2	19.733	40 38.63	5.18	13.09	29 11.2	35 16 26.9
9	VI.	5	49.302	9 41.26	5.22	4.29	29 40.7	34 45 20.8
10		4	48.350	10 39.63	5.60	4.60	33 56.0	34 46 19.8
11		3	26.320	33 50.88	5.71	11.10	35 6.7	35 9 37.7
12		3	24.61	35 37.46	5.75	11.60	35 35.2	11 24.8
13		2	8.729	52 9.34	5.84	16.46	36 32.8	35 28 1.6
14		5	48.389	10 38.32	5.98	4.59	38 7.6	34 46 18.9
15	V.	3	31.340	28 36.12	6.11	9.60	39 35.9	35 4 21.8
16		3	26.743	33 24.33	6.25	10.99	41 7.7	9 11.6
17		3	26.573	33 35.13	6.72	11.02	46 35.1	9 22.9
18		2	9.753	51 1.56	7.24	16.15	52 38.3	35 26 57.9
19		5	49.778	9 10.94	7.36	4.18	54 0.2	34 44 52.5
20		3	31.243	25 42.20	7.45	9.63	55 7.4	35 4 29.3
21		5	46.072	13 2.68	7.63	5.26	57 19.1	34 48 45.6
22		4	43.412	15 49.62	7.70	6.02	11 58 14.9	34 51 33.3
23		2	13.355	47 18.84	8.42	15.05	12 7 12.1	35 23 13.3
24		2	20.601	39 43.74	8.64	12.84	9 58.2	35 15 35.2
25		3	35.823	23 44.56	8.65	8.26	10 5.2	34 59 41.5
26	III.	4	42.453	16 49.12	8.77	6.30	11 41.0	34 52 34.2
27		3	24.328	35 55.84	8.85	11.71	12 43.3	35 11 46.4
28		2	14.262	46 22.53	8.87	13.26	12 57.2	35 22 14.7
29			.745	5 13.	9.	3.	14 16.6	34 40 55.0
30	III.	4	46.700	12 22.44	9.13	5.07	16 18.6	34 48 6.6
31	IV.	2	17.069	43 25.78	9.26	13.91	17 59.5	35 19 19.0
32		3	29.789	30 12.99	9.46	10.07	20 42.1	6 2.5
33		3	26.075	34 6.12	9.51	11.19	21 18.5	9 56.8
34		3	35.520	24 13.76	9.56	8.35	21 55.9	0 1.7
35		2	21.672	38 36.55	9.82	12.52	25 36.8	35 14 26.9
36	III.	3	35.743	23 59.41	9.96	8.29	27 37.2	34 59 47.7
37	IV.	3	35.705	24 2.05	10.00	8.28	28 6.0	34 59 50.3
38	IV.	3	24.900	35 19.89	10.49	11.54	35 8.0	35 11 11.9
39	IV.	2	12.752	47 56.47	10.58	15.22	36 24.4	35 23 52.3
40	IV.	4	41.852	−17 27.20	−10.82	−6.49	12 39 58.4	− 34 53 14.5

CORRECTIONS.

Date	Corr. of Clock	Hourly rate	m	n	e	Zenith Point	Mic. Co.
1849.	h.	s.	s.	s.	s.	° ″	r.

REMARKS.

(235) 28. Right ascension differs 4ˢ.4 from Mural Z. April 2, 1849.

(235) 29. Micrometer reading assumed as 53ʳ.745.

(235) 40. Transit over T. IV rejected.

INSTRUMENT READINGS.

Date	A.	B.	C.	D.	E.	F.	Mean.	Barom.	At.	Ex.	U.	L.	I.
Zone 235 1849. March 16, 11 15	93 54 60.	62.8	66.8	54.3	60.5	47.8	58.70	30.000 in.	49.	39.		49.8	50.
11 40										38.9			
12 0	60.	62.8	66.8	54.3	60.8	47.2	58.65	29.990	49.3	38.2			
12 20										38.			
12 40	60.	62.8	66.8	54.3	60.8	46.9	58.60			37.4			

Zone 236. MARCH 19. C. $D_0 = -30°\ 14'\ 50''$.

No.	Mag.	I.	II.	III.	IV.	V.	VI.	VII.	T (h m s)	a_1 (s)	a_2 (s)	MICROMETER (r)	i (' ")	d_1 (")	d_2 (")	Mean Right Ascension 1850.0 (h m s)	Mean Declination 1850.0 (° ' ")
1	9			54.5	12.8		48.		11 2 12.49	−26.50	−0.61	IV. 5 43.264	−16 6.25	− 0.55	2.16	11 1 45.4	− 30 30 59.0
2	9.10		33.4		9.2	27.			4 9.17	26.50	0.60	IV. 3 25.215	35 0.31	0.74	6.05	3 42.1	49 57.1
3	9		7.5	26.	43.8				5 43.76	26.50	0.62	IV. 5 54.465	4 17.35	0.90	+ 0.23	5 16.6	19 8.0
4	9		44.2	2.8	20.7	38.3			7 20.50	26.50	0.60	IV. 3 40.948	18 32.97	1.06	2.64	6 53.4	30 33 26.7
5	10				45.2	22.			8 45.63	26.50	0.57	IV. 2 14.533	46 4.90	1.21	6.38	8 18.6	31 1 4.5
6	9		43.4	1.6	19.6				11 19.50	26.50	0.59	III. 5 44.531	14 40.09	1.47	1.87	10 52.4	30 29 33.4
7	9					37.8			11 19.71	26.50	0.57	V. 2 19.474	40 55.43	1.47	7.29	10 52.6	55 54.2
8	9					14.2			11 56.33	26.50	0.59	V. 4 41.925	17 23.00	1.52	2.44	11 29.2	32 17.0
9	10		21.2		57.				13 57.03	26.49	0.59	IV. 4 44.788	14 22.94	1.72	1.62	13 29.9	29 16.5
10	9			22.8	40.				14 40.36	26.49	0.58	IV. 4 44.645	14 31.99	1.80	1.84	14 13.3	29 25.6
11	8.9					1.3	19.4		14 43.52	26.49	0.57	V. 3 32.737	27 8.27	1.80	4.40	14 16.4	42 4.5
12	10		23.		59.1				16 59.02	26.49	0.57	IV. 3 25.661	34 32.29	2.02	5.95	16 32.0	49 30.3
13	9.10				20.	37.8	56.		17 19.93	26.49	0.55	IV. 2 18.535	41 53.90	2.05	7.50	16 52.9	56 53.5
14	9.10			56.9	14.6				21 14.73	26.48	0.57	IV. 5 49.188	9 48.11	2.43	0.90	20 47.7	30 24 41.4
15	9				35.3	53.2	11.4		21 35.26	26.48	0.53	IV. 2 13.757	46 53.45	2.46	8.58	21 8.3	31 1 54.5
16	10			54.?	11.8		47.3		25 11.75	26.48	0.55	IV. 4 39.763	19 38.30	2.80	2.89	24 44.7	30 34 34.0
17	10		42.8		36.2	54.3			25 18.56	26.48	0.55	V. 4 41.099	18 14.96	2.81	2.61	24 51.5	30 33 10.4
18	3					41.3			26 5.42	26.48	0.52	VI. 2 13.971	46 40.65	2.88	8.52	25 38.4	31 1 42.2
19	10		19.3	37.3	55.2				29 55.28	26.47	0.52	IV. 2 19.888	40 28.83	3.24	7.21	29 23.3	30 55 29.3
20	8			29.8	47.3	5.	23.2		30 47.42	26.47	0.55	IV. 5 50.649	8 16.64	3.31	0.55	30 20.4	23 10.5
21	9.10					11.	29.		32 53.22	26.46	0.54	IV. 5 51.182	7 42.95	3.49	0.44	32 26.2	22 36.9
22	9		40.5	58.2	16.2	34.2			37 16.25	26.46	0.51	IV. 3 27.508	32 36.47	3.91	5.54	36 49.3	47 35.9
23	8.9				0.1	18.3			38 0.10	26.45	0.50	IV. 2 18.820	41 35.82	3.96	7.44	37 33.1	56 37.2
24	10							57.2	38 21.41	26.45	0.50	VII. 3 22.604	37 43.74	4.01	7.62	37 54.5	52 45.4
25	8.9			3.3	21.	39.2			40 21.21	26.45	0.53	IV. 5 48.664	10 20.93	4.19	0.97	39 54.2	25 16.1
26	10						58.2		40 22.43	26.45	0.53	VI. 5 52.708	6 7.35	4.19	0.12	39 55.4	21 1.7
27	9.10		45.	3.	21.				44 20.96	26.44	0.50	IV. 3 27.511	32 36.29	4.53	5.54	43 54.0	47 36.4
28	9.10			14.3	32.	50.2			46 32.13	26.44	0.49	IV. 3 27.222	32 54.41	4.72	5.61	46 5.2	47 54.7
29	9		2.3	20.5	38.2	56.3			47 38.30	26.43	0.48	IV. 3 25.266	34 57.19	4.81	6.05	47 11.4	49 58.0
30	9.10		37.4		13.2		49.		49 13.25	26.43	0.50	IV. 5 52.486	6 21.16	4.95	0.17	48 46.3	21 16.3
31	8		16.2	35.8	54.2		30.1		50 54.11	26.42	0.48	IV. 3 26.316	33 51.31	5.10	5.80	50 27.2	48 52.2
32	8		12.2	30.2	48.2	6.7			55 48.31	26.41	0.45	IV. 3 23.964	36 18.66	5.11	6.32	55 21.4	51 20.5
33	8.9					30.2	48.2		56 12.38	26.41	0.46	VI. 3 34.288	25 31.08	5.54	4.08	55 45.5	40 30.7
34	9					37.2	55.3		57 19.47	26.41	0.46	V. 5 52.633	6 12.05	5.63	0.13	56 52.6	21 7.8
35	10				8.	26.1			11 59 8.00	26.40	0.45	IV. 3 31.262	28 41.01	5.78	4.72	58 41.2	43 41.5
36	7			3.	21.	39.1	56.5		12 0 20.97	26.40	0.45	IV. 4 40.098	19 17.41	5.86	2.81	11 59 54.1	34 16.1
37	9			17.3		3.3			5 35.41	26.39	0.44	IV. 5 45.856	13 17.11	6.30	1.58	12 5 8.6	28 15.0
38	8.9				14.				5 46.08	26.38	0.43	V. 3 33.792	26 2.08	6.32	4.18	5 19.3	41 2.6
39	8.9		38.5	56.5	14.3				8 14.42	26.38	0.42	IV. 3 23.965	36 18.60	6.51	6.32	7 47.6	51 21.4
40	10					56.	13.8		8 37.94	26.38	0.42	V. 3 19.384	41 6.16	6.54	7.33	8 11.1	56 10.0
41	9			49.8	7.8	25.3			10 25.62	26.37	0.43	IV. 5 51.670	7 12.25	6.68	0.32	9 58.8	22 9.2
42	8.9					23.2	41.2		12 11 5.38	−26.37	−0.42	V. 3 35.224	−24 32.41	− 6.74	− 3.87	12 10 38.6	− 30 39 33.0

CORRECTIONS.

Date.	Corr. of Clock.	Hourly rate.	m	n	c	Zenith Point.	Mic. Co.
1849.	h. s.	s.	s.	s.	s.	° ' "	r.

REMARKS.

(236) 37. Time of transit over T. V assumed as 53s.3 instead of 3s.3.

(236) 38. Time of transit over T. V assumed as 4s.0 instead of 14s.

INSTRUMENT READINGS.

	Date.	A.	B.	C.	D.	E.	F.	Mean.	Barom.	At.	Ex.	U.	L.	I.
	1849. h. m.	° ' "						"	in.	°	°	°	°	°
Zone 236	Mar. 19, 11 0	89 34 60.0	62.8	64.8	57.3	54.3	51.4	58.43	30.190	48.2	40.2	52.2	48.8	48.5
	11 20										40.			
	11 40								30.180	46.5	39.5			
	12 0										39.7			
	12 10	60.2	63.2	64.9	51.	54.2	58.4	58.65	30.168	45.5	39.6		43.5	46.2

ZONE 237. MARCH 22. S. $D_0 = -35°\,10'\,20''$.

No.	Mag.	I.	II.	III.	IV.	V.	VI.	VII.	T. (h. m. s.)	a₁ (s.)	a₂ (s.)	MICROMETER.		r.	i	d₁	d₂	Mean Right Ascension, 1850.0	Mean Declination, 1850.0
1	8		36.3	55.2					8 11 14.33	−26.49	−3.30	III.	3	26.091	−34 5.13	−2.28	−11.25	8 10 44.5	− 35 44 38.6
2	7		56.5	15.3	34.2				12 34.32	26.50	3.23	IV.	3	34.041	25 46.46	2.48	8.73	12 4.0	35 36 17.7
3	4.5		32.	51.					16 10.22	26.52	3.30	·	2	10.809	49 57.77	2.98	16.13	15 40.4	36 0 36.9
4	9					53.8			16 15.89	26.52	3.27	·	2	18.015	42 26.95	2.99	13.78	15 46.1	35 53 3.7
5	9			9.	27.				23 28.02	26.56	3.20	IV.	2	9.366	51 28.89	4.02	16.56	22 58.3	36 2 9.5
6	9				8.				26 7.85	26.58	3.08	·	3	28.748	31 18.55	4.38	10.39	25 38.2	35 41 53.3
7	7		13.5	34.	52.5				30 52.34	26.60	3.05	IV.	3	25.992	34 11.45	5.07	11.26	30 22.7	44 47.8
8	6.7				45.3	5.			32 4.59	26.60	2.98	IV.	3	33.552	36 17.26	5.23	8.76	31 35.0	36 51.3
9	9			7.2	26.				33 45.16	26.61	2.89	III.	5	51.560	7 16.84	5.48	3.35	33 15.7	17 47.7
10	9					39.			35 20.08	26.62	2.92	·	3	38.029	21 36.27	5.70	7.50	34 50.6	32 9.5
11	7						39.		36 1.21	26.62	2.88	·	3	44.552	14 46.86	5.79	5.49	35 31.7	25 18.1
12	6.5				35.5	54.5			37 35.51	26.63	2.86	IV.	4	45.372	13 46.54	6.01	5.24	37 6.0	24 17.6
13	8			0.	18.				39 18.43	26.64	2.89	·	3	32.735	27 8.39	6.26	9.16	38 48.9	37 43.8
14	11.10				43.				40 42.87	26.64	2.82	·	4	41.120	15 5.00	6.46	5.61	40 13.4	25 37.1
15	10		52.8	11.5					43 30.71	26.65	2.77	III.	5	49.392	9 34.98	6.85	4.00	43 1.3	20 5.8
16	10			19.					44 8.11	26.66	2.75	·	5	51.420	7 27.70	6.94	3.40	43 38.7	17 58.0
17	6			40.2	58.8	18.			44 59.05	26.66	2.75	V.	4	47.209	11 51.57	7.06	4.68	44 29.6	22 23.3
18	6.5		37.	56.8					47 15.60	26.67	2.87	III.	3	12.508	48 11.41	7.39	15.60	46 46.1	58 54.4
19	8		40.2						48 13.25	26.67	2.73	·	5	42.722	16 32.86	7.54	6.04	47 48.8	27 6.4
20	7		48.8	7.8					49 26.86	26.68	2.73	III.	4	40.602	18 45.21	7.69	6.70	48 57.4	29 19.6
21	8		42.8	2.	20.8				52 20.86	26.69	2.67	IV.	4	44.620	14 33.62	8.09	5.46	51 51.5	25 7.3
22	8		25.	44.	3.5				54 3.20	26.70	2.74	IV.	5	23.005	37 18.83	8.32	12.19	53 33.8	47 59.3
23	11		47.	6.					56 25.06	26.71	2.63	III.	5	40.895	18 28.01	8.65	6.60	55 55.7	29 3.3
24	10				12.				8 57 11.88	26.71	2.57	·	5	51.829	7 2.20	8.70	3.20	56 42.6	17 34.2
25	11		33.						9 0 11.09	26.72	2.62	·	3	32.963	26 59.74	9.18	9.08	59 41.7	37 38.0
26	7				26.	45.2			0 26.08	26.72	2.58	V.	3	40.285	19 14.83	9.21	6.78	8 59 56.8	29 50.8
27	8						19.		1 41.17	26.73	2.63	·	3	25.540	34 35.05	9.38	11.41	9 1 11.8	21 19.3
28	10				39.5				3 39.36	26.74	2.55	·	3	38.134	21 29.69	9.64	7.46	3 10.1	32 6.8
29	8		41.2						5 19.25	26.74	2.50	·	4	41.720	17 34.17	9.88	6.36	4 50.0	28 10.4
30	8				28.8				5 28.66	26.74	2.51	·	4	40.362	19 0.06	9.90	6.76	4 59.4	29 37.6
31	9						21.		5 43.22	26.74	2.53	·	5	34.579	25 12.64	9.93	8.56	5 14.0	35 51.1
32	9						30.5		6 52.72	26.75	2.52	·	3	35.122	24 38.57	10.08	8.39	6 23.5	35 17.0
33	10						23.		7 45.21	26.75	2.45	·	5	48.012	11 1.23	10.21	4.44	7 16.0	21 35.9
34	5.6				11.5	30.5			9 11.53	26.75	2.42	IV.	5	49.070	9 54.25	10.43	4.10	8 42.4	20 26.8
35	9			35.8					11 57.84	26.76	2.49	·	3	26.093	34 4.99	10.80	11.26	11 28.6	44 47.0
36	9				55.2				12 55.05	26.77	2.38	·	4	48.278	10 44.09	10.91	4.28	12 25.9	21 19.3
37	8				30.	49.			14 29.86	26.77	2.50	IV.	2	15.380	45 11.83	11.15	15.66	14 0.6	35 55 56.6
38	9		33.2	52.					18 11.32	26.78	2.47	·	2	10.099	50 42.35	11.65	16.38	17 42.1	36 1 30.4
39	7		1.8	20.8					19 39.89	26.79	2.40	·	3	26.137	34 2.23	11.85	11.22	19 10.7	35 44 55.3
40	8				13.				20 12.85	26.79	2.37	·	3	28.410	31 39.94	11.92	10.52	19 43.7	42 22.4
41	8				10.				21 9.88	26.79	2.27	·	5	48.325	10 42.33	12.04	4.32	20 40.8	21 18.7
42	7				53.5	12.			21 53.21	26.80	2.31	IV.	3	27.132	22 32.58	12.14	7.77	21 24.1	33 12.5
43	7				48.8				22 48.66	26.80	2.30	·	3	38.593	21 0.89	12.26	7.30	22 19.6	31 40.5
44	4.3					57.8	10.8		23 33.00	26.80	2.22	·	4	51.632	7 13.88	12.36	3.31	23 4.0	17 49.6
45	9						39.5		25 1.52	26.81	2.37	·	2	12.275	48 27.14	12.56	15.69	24 32.3	59 15.4
46	7					51.5			26 32.66	26.81	2.20	·	5	48.210	10 49.65	12.75	4.33	26 3.7	21 26.7
47	6						5.		27 27.18	26.81	2.29	·	3	26.398	33 46.04	12.87	11.14	26 57.1	44 30.0
48	6					38.	46.8		28 9.06	26.82	2.21	V.	5	41.413	17 56.39	12.98	6.43	27 40.0	28 35.8
49	7		48.8						9 30 26.83	−26.82	−2.15	·	5	47.778	−11 15.47	−13.27	−4.48	9 29 57.8	− 35 21 53.2

CORRECTIONS.

Date.	Corr. of Clock.	Hourly rate.	m	n	c	Zenith Point.	Mic. Co.
1849.	h.	s.	s.	s.	s.	° ' "	r.

INSTRUMENT READINGS.

Date.	CIRCLE							Barom.	THERMOM.				
	A.	B.	C.	D.	E.	F.	Mean.	in.	At.	Ex.	U.	L.	I.
Zone 237 1849 Mar. 22, 8 0	94 29 60.	64.	66.2	60.9	59.3	53.6	60.67						
8 20								30.318	49.	40.	48.5		49.
8 40										39.			
9 20								30.334	47.5	37.8			
9 40	62.5	64.2	67.8	60.5	61.5	52.8	61.55			37.2			
10 0								30.338	46.5	36.8			
10 20										36.2			
10 40										35.8			
11 0	62.5	65.2	67.8	61.0	61.2	52.8	61.75	30.340	45.	35.	43.5	51.	46.

REMARKS.

(237) 5. Transit over T. IV rejected; declination differs 1' from Mer. Circle Z. March 19, 1849.

(237) 20. Declination differs about 15" from Mer. Circle Z. March 19, 1849, and Transit Z. March 12, 1849.

(237) 48. Time of transit over T. V assumed as 28ˢ instead of 38ˢ.

ZONE 237.　MARCH 22.　S.　$D_o = -35°\ 10'\ 20''$—Continued.

No.	Mag.	I.	II.	III.	IV.	V.	VI.	VII.	T. (h m s)	a_1 (s)	a_q (s)	Mic.		r	i	d_1	d_q	Mean Right Ascension, 1850.0 (h m s)	Mean Declination, 1850.0 (° ' ")
50	7							58.	9 30 1.04	−26.82	−2.22	.	3	32.778	−27 5.19	−13.22	−9.14	9 29 32.0	− 35 37 57.5
51	5						20.		31 42.21	26.83	2.14	.	4	44.420	14 46.86	13.43	5.50	31 13.2	25 25.8
52	7						38.		34 0.21	26.83	2.11	.	4	44.943	14 13.85	13.74	5.34	33 31.3	24 52.9
53	6				42.8	1.			35 23.59	26.83	2.08	V.	4	48.638	10 21.80	13.93	4.21	34 54.7	20 59.9
54	10		55.						43 33.10	26.85	2.05	.	3	31.260	28 40.51	14.98	9.61	43 4.2	39 25.1
55	5			41.	59.5				43 59.69	26.85	2.03	IV.	3	36.168	23 33.12	15.04	8.07	43 30.8	34 16.2
56	6				40.	59.			44 39.90	26.85	2.01	.	3	36.606	23 5.58	15.12	7.93	44 11.1	33 48.6
57	8			30.					47 49.00	26.86	1.99	.	3	29.555	30 27.86	15.57	10.14	47 20.2	41 13.6
58	9		47.	6.8					52 25.46	26.87	1.85	III.	4	49.013	9 57.28	16.11	4.09	51 56.7	20 37.5
59	6		32.8	52.					54 10.96	26.87	1.82	III.	4	49.914	9 0.65	16.33	3.81	53 42.3	35 19 40.8
60	8						59.		54 21.00	26.87	1.99	.	2	10.433	50 22.66	16.35	16.29	53 52.1	36 1 15.3
61	11						36.		56 58.22	26.88	1.82	.	5	41.133	16 13.89	16.69	6.55	56 29.5	35 28 57.1
62	8				9.				59 8.93	26.88	1.91	.	2	14.973	45 37.18	16.96	14.80	58 40.1	56 29.0
63	5						53.		9 59 15.22	26.88	1.84	.	3	31.289	28 39.19	16.97	9.60	58 46.5	39 25.8
64	7						49.5		10 0 11.72	26.88	1.83	.	3	31.343	28 35.80	17.09	9.59	9 59 43.0	39 22.6
65	7					39.2			1 19.99	26.88	1.89	.	2	15.049	45 32.85	17.23	14.80	10 0 51.2	· 56 24.9
66	9		48.						3 26.10	26.89	1.79	.	3	31.088	28 51.17	17.49	9.66	2 57.4	35 39 38.3
67	6			33.					3 52.16	26.89	1.87	.	2	9.582	51 14.64	17.54	16.54	3 23.4	36 2 8.9
68	7				36.				4 35.90	26.89	1.81	.	3	19.809	40 39.25	17.64	13.24	4 7.2	35 51 30.1
69	7					48.			5 28.69	26.89	1.86	.	2	8.118	52 47.52	17.73	16.94	4 59.0	36 3 42.2
70	8					52.5			6 33.60	26.89	1.70	.	4	40.630	18 44.40	17.88	6.71	6 5.0	35 29 29.0
71	7					38.			7 0.21	26.89	1.65	.	5	49.860	9 5.98	17.94	3.82	6 31.7	19 47.7
72	8				35.8				8 35.72	26.89	1.78	.	2	17.018	43 28.92	18.13	14.15	8 7.1	54 21.2
73	6.5					35.	53.8		9 15.95	26.89	1.73	V.	3	24.623	35 37.46	18.22	11.69	8 47.3	46 27.4
74	8				54.		32.		10 54.00	26.90	1.76	.	2	16.482	44 2.72	18.42	14.30	10 25.3	35 54 55.4
75	5				32.				12 31.96	26.90	1.76	.	2	8.530	52 21.38	18.61	16.88	12 3.3	36 3 16.9
76	8						29.		12 51.22	26.90	1.66	.	3	31.402	28 32.10	18.65	9.57	12 22.7	35 39 20.3
77	7				13.	32.			14 13.00	26.90	1.58	IV.	4	43.023	16 13.79	18.83	5.93	13 44.5	26 58.5
78	7		13.2	32.					15 51.16	26.90	1.56	.	4	41.963	17 19.68	19.02	6.27	15 22.7	28 5.0
79	8			22.					16 41.00	26.90	1.61	.	3	30.570	29 24.11	19.12	9.82	16 12.5	40 13.0
80	7				57.2		54.3		17 16.37	26.90	1.59	.	3	33.023	26 50.33	19.19	9.06	16 47.9	37 38.6
81	9				14.				19 13.92	26.91	1.64	.	2	16.978	43 31.42	19.44	14.17	18 45.4	54 25.0
82	7.6		23.5	42.5	1.5				22 1.49	26.91	1.48	IV.	4	43.772	15 26.70	19.77	5.67	21 33.1	26 12.1
83	8			46.					23 5.10	26.91	1.58	.	2	16.232	42 12.40	19.90	13.73	22 36.6	53 6.0
84	8				58.				23 57.92	26.91	1.58	.	2	16.003	44 32.57	20.01	14.49	23 29.4	55 27.1
85	7					55.			24 36.10	26.91	1.45	.	4	40.579	18 47.66	20.10	6.68	24 7.7	29 34.4
86	7						36.		25 58.21	26.91	1.43	.	4	42.800	16 28.33	20.26	6.02	25 29.9	27 14.6
87	9				26.				26 25.84	26.91	1.48	.	3	29.693	30 19.27	20.31	10.09	25 57.4	41 9.7
88	9						5.2		26 27.39	26.91	1.49	.	3	27.132	32 59.87	20.31	10.91	25 59.0	43 51.1
89	7						50.		27 12.21	26.91	1.37	.	5	51.893	6 58.54	20.40	3.20	26 44.0	17 42.1
90	9			15.					29 34.03	26.91	1.43	.	3	33.958	25 51.41	20.69	8.75	29 5.7	36 40.8
91	7					14.			29 55.06	26.91	1.41	.	3	35.108	24 39.57	20.73	8.40	29 26.7	35 28.7
92	8			48.6	7.				32 7.26	26.91	1.35	IV.	4	39.769	19 37.92	20.99	6.94	31 39.0	30 25.8
93	5			39.	58.	17.			32 57.95	26.91	1.45	IV.	2	17.510	42 58.18	21.10	14.01	32 29.6	53 53.3
94	8			11.2					34 30.26	26.91	1.41	.	2	22.668	37 33.94	21.28	12.36	34 1.9	48 27.6
95	6				37.				35 36.88	26.91	1.38	.	3	22.748	37 41.23	21.41	12.32	35 8.6	48 35.0
96	8					17.5	37.		36 58.92	26.91	1.27	V.	4	44.779	14 23.94	21.59	5.39	36 30.7	35 25 10.9
97	9						41.2		37 3.21	26.91	1.38	.	2	10.692	50 6.23	21.60	16.21	36 34.9	36 1 4.0
98	8						33.		10 38 55.00	−26.91	−1.40	.	2	9.328	−51 32.06	−21.82	−16.63	10 38 26.7	− 36 2 30.5

CORRECTIONS.

Date.	Corr. of Clock.	Hourly rate.	m	n	ϵ	Zenith Point.	Mic. Co.
1849.	h,	s,	s,	s,	s,	° ' "	r.
	s.	s.	s.				

INSTRUMENT READINGS.

Date.	CIRCLE.							Barom.	THERMOM.				
	A.	B.	C.	D.	E.	F.	Mean.		At.	Ex.	U.	L.	I.
1849. h. m.	° ' "					"		in.	°	°	°	°	°

REMARKS.

ZONE 237. MARCH 22. S. $D_0 = -35^\circ\ 10'\ 20''$—Continued.

No.	Mag.	I.	II.	III.	IV.	V.	VI.	VII.	T. (h. m. s.)	a_1 (s.)	a_2 (s.)
99	8			32.5					10 40 10.56	−26.91	−1.25
100	8			16.5		54.			40 35.40	26.91	1.21
101	6.7						48.5		41 10.71	26.91	1.19
102	10				7.8				46 26.91	26.91	1.29
103	6			11.8	30.5	47.			47 30.38	26.91	1.19
104	8			34.					48 53.16	26.91	1.27
105	8			52.					50 11.04	26.91	1.18
106	7					20.5			50 42.71	26.91	1.09
107	7.6			20.	39.				52 38.93	26.91	1.13
108	9		14.8						54 52.84	26.91	1.04
109	8			42.					56 1.08	26.91	1.12
110	6				43.				57 42.92	26.91	1.13
111	9					19.5			10 57 41.50	−26.91	−1.16

No.	MICROMETER.		r.	l (′ ″)	d_1 (″)	d_2 (″)	Mean Right Ascension, 1850.0 (h. m. s.)	Mean Declination, 1850.0 (° ′ ″)
99	.	4	40.762	−18 34.29	−21.97	− 6.62	10 39 42.4	− 35 29 22.9
100	V.	5	51.220	7 40.81	22.02	3.41	40 7.3	18 26.2
101	.	5	49.595	9 22.81	22.09	3.90	40 42.6	20 8.8
102	.	2	16.112	44 25.30	22.73	14.44	45 58.7	55 22.5
103	IV.	3	31.205	28 44.33	22.86	9.63	47 2.3	35 39 36.8
104	.	2	9.713	51 6.51	23.04	16.51	48 25.0	36 2 6.1
105	.	3	24.112	36 9.27	23.19	11.84	49 43.0	35 47 4.3
106	.	5	45.140	14 2.43	23.25	5.28	50 14.7	24 51.0
107	IV.	3	28.658	31 24.26	23.50	10.41	52 10.9	42 38.2
108	.	4	43.869	15 19.24	23.78	5.65	54 24.9	26 8.7
109	.	2	19.922	40 26.20	23.91	13.22	55 43.0	51 23.3
110	.	2	16.611	43 54.51	24.12	14.29	57 14.9	35 54 52.9
111	.	2	9.832	−51 0.10	−24.12	−16.49	10 57 13.4	− 36 2 0.7

ZONE 238. MARCH 22. S. $D_0 = -34^\circ\ 0'\ 30''$.

No.	Mag.	I.	II.	III.	IV.	V.	VI.	VII.	T. (h. m. s.)	a_1 (s.)	a_2 (s.)
1	10			42.	59.				12 25 19.72	−27.66	−0.91
2	8			42.2	1.				29 19.79	27.65	0.90
3	9					1.			29 42.38	27.65	0.67
4	7				48.6	7.			31 7.12	27.64	0.72
5	10				28.				33 27.88	27.63	0.60
6	7.8			26.2	45.2				36 3.89	27.62	0.91
7	9					23.	41.		36 22.62	27.62	0.71
8	8			19.2	8.	27.			40 26.94	27.60	1.11
9	7			38.5	57.3	16.			44 15.99	27.58	0.72
10	10				1.	19.2			46 38.20	27.57	0.74
11	9						33.		47 14.36	27.57	0.76
12	7				30.	48.3			48 48.45	27.56	0.76
13	8			10.2	29.5				51 48.16	27.55	1.13
14	10						27.		51 49.57	27.55	1.22
15	9			8.5	27.2				54 46.01	27.53	0.79
16	9			11.	30.				57 48.65	27.51	0.86
17	7					57.5	16.8	35.	12 57 57.76	27.51	0.82
18	8				45.8	4.	22.5		13 0 3.76	27.50	0.85
19	8						30.		0 52.62	27.50	1.11
20	8					49.			2 48.87	27.49	0.78
21	5						56.8		3 39.16	27.48	0.84
22	9					19.2			5 19.08	27.48	0.76
23	8						23.	41.5	6 4.20	27.47	0.86
24	9				51.				8 9.80	27.46	0.86
25	8			5.5	24.	42.8			13 42.85	27.45	0.73
26	9				44.		40.		16 2.72	27.43	1.19
27	7.6				38.5	57.			17 57.05	27.42	0.87
28	9					59.			18 58.92	27.41	1.19
29	9						57.5		19 38.75	27.41	1.06
30	5.6				1.2	19.3		57.	21 19.63	27.40	1.22
31	10				4.	23.			26 4.04	27.37	1.11
32	7			50.	9.	27.3			13 29 27.49	−27.35	−0.91

No.	MICROMETER.		r.	l (′ ″)	d_1 (″)	d_2 (″)	Mean Right Ascension, 1850.0 (h. m. s.)	Mean Declination, 1850.0 (° ′ ″)
1	III.	3	21.902	−38 27.76	− 0.67	−17.35	12 24 51.1	− 34 39 15.8
2	III.	3	24.830	35 24.10	0.88	16.51	28 51.2	36 11.5
3	.	4	43.450	15 47.55	0.90	11.12	29 14.1	16 29.6
4	IV.	4	39.788	19 36.73	0.98	12.18	30 38.8	20 19.9
5	III.	5	51.202	7 41.75	1.10	8.93	32 59.7	8 21.8
6	III.	3	25.560	34 37.87	1.25	16.30	35 35.3	35 25.4
7	IV.	4	42.300	16 59.27	1.27	11.45	35 54.3	17 42.0
8	IV.	2	8.559	52 19.56	1.49	21.33	39 58.2	53 12.4
9	IV.	4	44.032	15 11.65	1.71	10.96	43 47.6	15 54.3
10	III.	3	43.053	16 12.72	1.84	11.26	46 10.0	16 55.8
11	.	4	40.528	18 50.86	1.88	11.97	46 46.0	19 34.7
12	IV.	4	41.722	17 35.43	1.97	11.63	48 20.2	18 19.0
13	III.	2	11.310	49 26.53	2.14	20.52	51 19.5	50 19.2
14	.	2	12.240	48 29.28	2.14	20.25	51 20.8	49 21.7
15	.	4	41.580	17 43.84	2.31	11.65	54 17.7	18 27.8
16	.	3	56.320	23 23.46	2.48	13.18	57 20.3	24 9.1
17	IV.	4	41.702	17 36.68	2.49	11.63	57 29.4	18 20.8
18	IV.	4	37.998	21 29.12	2.61	12.69	12 59 35.4	22 14.4
19	.	2	17.170	43 20.06	2.66	18.77	13 0 24.0	44 11.5
20	.	5	45.442	13 43.28	2.77	10.55	2 20.6	14 26.6
21	.	5	40.342	19 2.78	2.81	12.03	3 9.8	19 47.6
22	IV.	4	47.760	11 17.61	2.91	9.90	4 50.8	12 0.4
23	V.	4	38.892	20 33.34	2.94	12.43	5 36.0	21 18.7
24	.	4	41.302	18 1.34	3.06	11.74	7 41.5	18 46.9
25	IV.	5	53.026	5 47.14	3.36	8.40	13 14.7	6 18.9
26	III.	2	15.236	45 20.31	3.48	19.34	15 34.1	46 13.1
27	IV.	2	42.479	16 48.05	3.58	11.40	17 28.6	17 33.0
28	.	2	16.380	44 9.11	3.64	18.99	18 30.3	45 1.7
29	.	3	27.705	32 24.11	3.67	15.68	19 10.3	33 13.5
30	IV.	2	14.190	46 26.41	3.76	19.66	20 51.0	47 19.8
31	IV.	4	26.472	33 41.46	4.00	16.09	25 35.6	34 31.5
32	IV.	4	43.140	−16 6.50	−4.18	−11.20	13 28 59.2	− 34 16 51.9

CORRECTIONS.

Date.	Cort. of Clock.	Hourly rate.	m	n	c	Zenith Point.	Mic. Co.
1849.	h. s.	s.	s.	s.	s.	° ′ ″	r.

REMARKS.

(238) 1. Time of transit over T. III assumed as 1ˢ instead of 59ˢ.

INSTRUMENT READINGS.

Date.	CIRCLE.							Barom.	THERMOM.				
	A.	B.	C.	D.	E.	F.	Mean.		At.	Ex	U.	L.	I.
Zone 238 1849. Mar. 22, 12 20	93 19 60.	65.3	65.8	59.3	57.8	50.5	59.78	In.					
12 40										32.9			
13 0										33.8			
13 40										33.4			
14 20		60.	65.3	65.8	60.2	58.	50.5	59.97				42.8	43.5

Zone 238. March 22. S. $D_0 = -34°\ 0'\ 30''$—Continued.

No.	Mag.	I.	II.	III.	IV.	V.	VI.	VII.	T. (h. m. s.)	a_1 (s.)	a_2 (s.)	MICROMETER		r.	i	d_1	d_2	Mean R.A. 1850.0	Mean Decl. 1850.0
33	7					0.	18.5		13 29 41.31	−27.35	−0.92	V.	4	42.239	−17 3.48	−4.19	−11.48	13 29 13.0	− 34 17 49.2
34	9				12.8	31.	50.2		31 12.61	27.34	1.11	IV.	3	27.102	33 1.88	4.27	15.85	30 44.2	33 52.0
35	10		1.						34 38.49	27.32	0.85	.	5	49.595	9 21.62	4.44	9.36	34 10.3	10 5.4
36	7				2.3				35 2.15	27.31	1.10	.	3	29.018	31 1.61	4.46	15.29	34 33.7	31 51.4
37						8.	27.		35 49.48	27.31	1.12	VI.	3	27.386	32 44.06	4.50	15.77	35 21.1	33 34.3
38	8		22.	41.					37 59.65	27.30	1.03	.	3	35.420	24 19.93	4.61	13.44	37 31.3	25 8.0
39	9		59.	18.	36.2				39 36.46	27.29	1.01	IV.	3	38.663	20 56.50	4.69	12.49	39 8.2	21 43.7
40	10			16.					42 4.76	27.28	1.19	.	2	24.240	35 55.53	4.80	16.67	41 36.3	36 47.0
41	8		41.	59.	18.				44 18.06	27.26	1.00	IV.	3	40.752	18 45.34	4.91	11.90	43 49.8	19 32.1
42	4			1.	20.				45 38.68	27.25	1.17	.	3	26.802	33 20.38	4.97	15.94	45 10.3	34 11.3
43	8					22.			46 3.16	27.24	1.23	.	3	21.975	38 23.43	4.99	17.36	45 34.7	39 15.8
44	8			28.5		6.			48 5.94	27.23	1.08	IV.	4	35.278	24 19.93	5.08	13.48	47 37.6	25 8.5
45	7				51.				48 50.88	27.23	0.92	.	5	49.685	9 16.85	5.13	9.34	48 22.7	10 1.3
46	8				5.	24.			50 23.85	27.22	0.97	IV.	4	46.565	12 31.61	5.19	10.25	49 55.6	13 17.1
47	9				45.				52 3.75	27.21	1.18	.	3	27.043	32 8.80	5.25	15.61	51 35.4	32 59.7
48	8			56.5	34.				54 33.95	27.20	1.14	IV.	3	33.392	26 27.37	5.35	14.02	54 5.6	27 16.7
49	7.6			30.2	49.	8.2			58 7.87	27.17	0.95	IV.	5	49.050	9 56.71	5.51	9.55	57 39.7	10 41.8
50	7					43.5			58 43.43	27.17	1.37	.	2	15.136	45 27.07	5.53	19.39	58 14.9	46 22.0
51	6					43.			59 24.41	27.16	1.00	.	5	46.005	13 8.02	5.56	10.38	58 56.2	13 54.0
52	8						33.2		13 59 55.94	27.16	1.01	.	5	44.642	14 33.68	5.58	10.77	13 59 27.8	15 20.0
53	7					30.2			14 1 1.64	27.15	0.95	.	5	49.710	9 15.47	5.62	9.31	14 0 33.5	10 0.4
54	9			29.2					4 6.86	27.12	1.34	.	2	19.208	41 10.42	5.73	18.18	3 38.4	42 4.3
55	9					21.8			4 21.69	27.12	1.30	.	2	21.493	39 48.41	5.74	17.50	3 53.3	39 41.6
56	9					5.5			6 5.35	27.10	1.13	.	3	36.772	22 55.03	5.80	13.05	5 37.1	23 43.9
57	8.7			37.2	56.	15.			8 14.79	27.09	1.08	IV.	4	41.636	17 40.89	5.89	11.72	7 46.6	18 28.5
58	10		28.						11 5.57	27.08	1.24	.	3	29.176	30 51.07	5.98	15.25	10 37.2	31 42.3
59	10					8.			11 7.85	27.08	1.15	.	4	36.768	22 46.24	5.99	13.05	10 39.6	23 35.3
60	8						23.5		11 46.15	27.07	1.36	.	3	19.513	40 57.87	6.01	18.05	11 17.7	41 51.9
61	10			13.5		51.			14 50.95	27.05	1.23	IV.	3	32.801	27 4.20	6.10	14.10	14 22.7	27 54.5
62	10			11.	29.5	45.			14 16 48.28	−27.04	−1.35	IV.	2	21.689	−38 35.92	−6.17	−17.45	14 16 19.0	− 34 39 29.5

Zone 239. March 23. C. $D_0 = -32°\ 42'\ 30''$.

No.	Mag.	I.	II.	III.	IV.	V.	VI.	VII.	T. (h. m. s.)	a_1 (s.)	a_2 (s.)	MICROMETER		r.	i	d_1	d_2	Mean R.A. 1850.0	Mean Decl. 1850.0
1	10				42.	2.2	39.3		9 33 2.39	−28.14	−1.03	III.	3	37.606	−22 2.64	−2.79	−4.10	9 32 33.2	− 33 4 39.5
2	10				46.5	4.5	41.7		33 4.79	28.14	1.03	IV.	3	37.945	21 41.41	2.79	4.02	32 35.6	4 18.2
3	10			36.2	54.7	13.3			34 36.31	28.14	1.06	IV.	3	32.972	26 55.52	2.97	5.26	34 7.1	9 31.7
4	9.10		45.2		22.1				38 22.07	28.15	1.06	IV.	3	32.761	27 6.70	3.35	5.31	37 52.9	9 45.4
5	9.10		50.7	9.2	27.2	45.3			39 27.33	28.16	1.04	IV.	3	35.861	23 52.20	3.49	4.54	38 58.1	33 6 30.2
6	9.10						52.5		39 15.80	28.16	1.00	VI.	4	43.289	15 57.90	3.47	2.67	38 46.6	32 58 34.0
7	10				38.2				44 19.91	28.17	0.97	III.	5	49.041	9 56.90	4.03	1.24	43 50.8	32 52 32.2
8	10				19.2				44 19.11	28.17	1.13	IV.	2	16.222	42 13.53	4.03	9.01	43 49.8	33 24 56.6
9	10		47.2	5.3	13.7				47 23.92	28.17	1.13	IV.	2	18.261	42 11.15	4.30	9.00	46 54.6	33 24 54.5
10	8.9		51.3	9.1	27.2	46.2			49 9.29	28.18	1.01	IV.	4	42.934	16 19.30	4.57	2.76	48 40.1	32 58 56.6
11	9			17.5	35.2		12.4		50 35.59	28.18	1.02	IV.	4	39.717	19 41.25	4.71	3.56	50 6.4	33 2 19.5
12	10				45.8	4.3	23.2		51 45.90	28.18	1.15	IV.	2	13.263	47 24.62	4.85	10.30	51 16.6	33 30 9.8
13	9						16.5		52 39.80	28.19	1.00	VI.	5	44.688	14 30.73	4.95	2.31	52 10.6	32 57 8.0
14	10					48.			53 11.30	28.19	1.00	VI.	5	44.135	15 5.40	5.00	2.45	52 42.1	32 57 42.9
15	9		20.4	38.7	57.4	15.8	34.3		55 57.35	28.19		IV.	2	16.086	44 27.43	5.31	9.57	55 28.0	33 27 12.3
16	10.11				50.7	9.1			9 58 9.16	−28.20	−1.15	IV.	2	13.562	−47 5.80	−5.56	−10.23	9 57 39.8	− 33 29 51.6

CORRECTIONS.

Date.	Corr. of Clock.	Hourly rate.	m	n	c	Zenith Point.	Mic. Co.
1849.	h. s.	s.	s.	s.	s.	° ′ ″	r.

REMARKS.

(239) 1. Time of transit over T. III assumed as 44ˢ instead of 42ˢ.

(239) 9. Time of transit over T. IV assumed as 23ˢ.7 instead of 13ˢ.7.

INSTRUMENT READINGS.

	Date.	A.	B.	C.	D.	E.	F.	Mean.	Barom. (in.)	At.	Ex.	U.	L.	I.
Zone 239	1849. Mar. 23, 9 30	92 2 { 28.6 { 28.1	32 31.3	34.1 34.2	29.5 30.6	27.7 27.9	18.8 18.9	28.48	30.364	48.	42.1	50.	44.8	48.8
	9 40										42.			
	10 0								30.358		41.8			
	10 20										41.3			
	10 50										41.1			
	11 0								30.342	45.2	41.2			
	11 12	27.9 27.7	31.4 31.9	34.2 33.9	29.8 30.6	26.3 26.8	18.7 18.4	28.14			41.1		43.5	45.5

ZONE 239. MARCH 23. C. $D_s = -32°\ 42'\ 30''$ — Continued.

No.	Mag.	I.	II.	III.	IV.	V.	VI.	VII.	T.	a_1	a_8	Mic.	n	r	i	d_1	d_8	Mean R.A. 1850.0	Mean Decl. 1850.0
									h. m. s.	s.	s.			r.	′ ″	″	″	h. m. s.	° ′ ″
17	10		5.2	43.5	42.				9 59 42.17	−28.20	−1.14	IV.	2	15.987	−44 33.55	−5.73	0.59	9 59 12.8	− 33 27 18.9
18	10			53.6	11.7	30.2	48.3		10 2 11.72	28.20	1.12	IV.	2	19.813	40 33.54	6.00	8.61	10 1 42.4	33 23 15.1
19	9.10					36.2			4 17.93	28.21	0.96	V.	5	51.632	7 14.88	6.23	0.58	3 48.8	32 49 51.7
20	10				43.2				5 43.07	28.21	1.00	IV.	4	43.521	15 42.66	6.38	2.60	5 13.9	32 58 21.6
21	9					24.2	42.6		6 5.84	28.21	1.06	V.	3	32.252	27 38.90	6.42	5.44	5 36.6	33 10 20.8
22	10.11			35.7		12.5			8 54.12	28.22	1.06	IV.	3	32.286	27 36.76	6.72	5.43	8 24.8	10 18.9
23	9			22.2	40.2	58.3	17.3		10 40.26	28.22	1.12	IV.	2	20.265	40 5.45	6.92	8.49	10 10.9	22 50.9
24	10					39.2	57.5		11 20.85	28.22	0.99	V.	4	47.525	11 37.73	6.99	1.61	10 51.6	33 54 10.3
25	9.10		57.5	15.9	34.5				14 34.43	28.22	0.97	IV.	4	49.971	8 57.65	7.34	1.00	14 5.2	32 51 36.0
26	10			14.3	33.				16 32.58	28.22	0.97	IV.	5	50.024	8 55.58	7.54	0.99	16 3.7	51 34.1
27	10				8.2		44.8		17 8.09	28.22	0.99	IV.	4	45.176	14 2.49	7.61	2.21	16 38.9	56 42.3
28	10					36.5	54.8		17 18.14	28.22	1.00	V.	4	44.784	15 1.42	7.63	2.44	16 48.9	32 57 41.5
29	9		46.2	4.4	22.8	11.5			19 22.97	28.23	1.01	IV.	4	41.833	17 28.40	7.86	3.03	18 53.7	33 0 9.3
30	9			4.4	22.7	11.2	59.5		20 22.80	28.23	0.99	IV.	5	46.517	12 35.82	7.96	1.87	19 53.6	32 55 15.6
31	9			22.8	41.2		17.8		21 41.13	28.23	1.10	IV.	3	24.756	35 28.99	8.09	7.34	21 11.8	33 18 14.4
32	10						52.6		22 15.93	28.23	1.16	VI.	2	11.942	45 47.94	8.16	10.62	21 46.6	33 31 36.6
33	8.9		41.6		18.4	37.2	55.4		28 18.60	28.23	1.01	IV.	4	42.511	16 46.04	8.79	2.85	27 49.4	32 59 27.7
34	9.10				40.3	8.2			31 7.96	28.24	1.12	IV.	2	19.230	41 10.30	9.08	8.75	30 38.6	33 23 59.1
35	9.10				33.2		9.5		31 32.92	28.24	1.07	IV.	3	30.615	29 21.48	9.12	5.85	31 3.6	12 6.4
36	8.9		27.5	46.		4.7	22.5		32 45.98	28.24	1.06	IV.	3	32.776	27 5.63	9.25	5.31	32 16.7	33 9 50.2
37	8.9				16.2	4.6			33 27.91	28.24	0.96	V.	5	51.573	7 18.67	9.32	0.59	32 58.7	32 49 58.6
38	9		46.2	4.2	12.3				35 4.26	28.24	0.99	IV.	4	46.611	12 28.65	9.49	1.83	34 35.0	55 10.0
39	10				43.3	2.2			35 43.53	28.24	0.99	IV.	4	46.161	12 56.90	9.56	1.94	35 14.3	55 38.4
40	10					6.2			35 47.89	28.24	0.99	V.	4	46.492	12 36.57	9.57	1.86	35 18.6	55 18.0
41	9					38.2			36 1.40	28.24	0.97	VI.	5	49.335	9 39.25	9.50	1.13	35 32.3	32 52 20.0
42	10				56.5		23.5		37 56.54	28.24	1.15	IV.	2	15.052	45 32.29	9.77	0.85	37 27.2	33 28 21.9
43	10					3.5	21.7		39 45.09	28.24	1.00	IV.	5	41.706	14 29.35	9.97	2.30	39 15.8*	32 57 11.6
44	9.10				54.	12.4			40 53.93	28.24	1.08	IV.	3	28.666	31 23.76	10.09	6.37	40 24.6	33 14 10.2
45	10					10.7			41 21.56	28.24	1.07	V.	3	30.624	29 20.98	10.13	5.84	40 52.2	12 7.0
46	8			9.2	28.2	16.3	4.3		43 27.78	28.24	1.09	IV.	3	26.971	33 10.03	10.35	6.77	42 58.4	15 57.2
47	9								43	28.24	1.02		4	39.384	20 2.28	10.35	3.63	43	33 2 46.3
48	9				57.2		33.6		45 56.98	28.24	0.97	IV.	5	50.047	8 54.13	10.58	0.96	45 27.8	32 51 35.7
49	10					12.7	31.3		46 54.44	28.24	1.07	VI.	3	30.854	29 6.23	10.68	5.79	46 25.1	33 11 52.7
50	10					15.2			48 26.52	28.24	1.03	V.	3	37.639	22 0.76	10.83	1.07	47 57.6	33 4 45.7
51	7		2.1	20.6	8.8	57.3			52 38.96	28.24	0.99	IV.	4	45.850	13 16.20	11.24	2.01	52 9.7	32 55 59.5
52	9							9.2	52 32.41	28.24	1.17	VI.	2	9.721	51 7.12	11.23	11.24	52 3.0	33 33 59.6
53	9				50.3		27.5	46.2	55 9.13	28.24	1.04	IV.	3	36.176	23 32.62	11.48	4.41	54 39.8	32 56 18.5
54	9.10			32.8		9.5			57 9.56	28.24	0.98	IV.	5	47.337	11 44.41	11.68	1.64	56 40.3	32 54 27.7
55	10				8.3		45.3		58 8.38	28.24	1.04	IV.	3	36.832	22 51.27	11.75	4.27	57 39.1	33 3 37.3
56	10					32.9	51.		10 59 14.17	28.24	1.17	V.	2	16.057	43 33.56	11.86	9.38	10 58 44.8	26 24.8
57	10			32.3	50.8	9.5			11 0 50.82	28.24	1.11	IV.	3	22.913	37 24.54	12.01	7.85	11 0 21.4	33 20 14.4
58	9					47.2	23.5		1 46.93	28.24	0.97	IV.	5	50.065	8 53.00	12.10	0.95	1 17.7	32 51 36.0
59	10				21.8	10.8			4	28.24	1.09	IV.	3	25.362	34 50.89	12.35	7.20	3	33 17 40.4
60	10								4	28.24	1.07		3	30.872	29 5.23	12.35	5.78	3	11 53.4
61	10						27.	45.3	6 8.32	28.24	1.18	V.	2	8.361	52 32.41	12.49	11.61	5 38.9	35 26.5
62	9						17.7		6 40.31	28.23	1.05	VI.	4	34.398	25 15.84	12.54	4.90	6 11.0	8 3.3
63	10					11.3			7 52.68	28.23	1.13	IV.	3	17.017	43 34.50	12.64	9.35	7 23.3	26 20.5
64	10				25.2	14.2			9 25.37	28.23	1.11	IV.	3	22.912	37 24.60	12.80	7.82	8 56.0	33 20 15.2
65	9	15.3	33.4	52.		28.3			11 51.92	28.23	0.99	IV.	4	45.766	13 21.56	13.01	2.03	11 22.7	32 56 6.6
66	10			11.2					11 12 11.08	−28.23	−0.97	IV.	5	50.669	− 8 15.08	−13.05	0.80	11 11 41.9	32 50 58.0

CORRECTIONS.

Date.	Corr. of Clock.	Hourly rate.	m	n	c	Zenith Point.	Mic. Co.
1849.	h.	s.	s.	s.	s.	s.	° ′ ″	r.

INSTRUMENT READINGS.

Date.	CIRCLE.							Barom.	THERMOM.				
	A.	B.	C.	D.	E.	F.	Mean.		At.	Ex.	U.	L.	I.
1849. h. m.	° ′ ″						″	In.	°		°		°

REMARKS.

ZONE 240. MARCH 23. C. $D_0 = -32°\ 42'\ 30''$.

No.	Mag.	I.	II.	III.	IV.	V.	VI.	VII.	T.	a_1	a_2	MICR.	n	r	i	d_1	d_2	Mean Right Ascension 1850.0	Mean Declination 1850.0
									h. m. s.	s.	s.			r	' "	"	"	h. m. s.	° ' "
1	9			0.1	18.4	37			12 40 18.45	28.01	−1.23	IV.	3	28.599	−31 27.96	−16.11	−6.35	12 39 49.2	− 33 14 20.4
2	9		29.	48.	6.3				42 6.22	28.00	1.22	IV.	3	26.204	33 58.27	16.25	6.98	41 37.0	16 51.5
3	7		26.2	14.2	2.3	21.3	39.4		43 2.72	28.00	1.22	IV.	3	32.028	27 52.76	16.28	5.48	42 33.5	10 44.5
4	10			1.2		38.0			45 19.59	27.99	1.21	IV.	3	26.727	33 25.34	16.43	6.85	44 50.4	33 16 18.6
5	10		24.3		1.3	19.5			48 1.21	27.98	1.25	IV.	5	49.678	9 17.31	16.60	0.99	47 32.0	32 52 4.9
6	10		38.2		15.		51.6		50 15.07	27.97	1.18	IV.	2	15.414	45 9.70	16.75	9.81	49 45.9	33 28 6.3
7	9.10					11.3			49 52.93	27.97	1.23	V.	4	38.821	20 37.79	16.72	3.76	49 23.7	3 28.3
8	9		16.5	35.5	54.	12.4			52 53.83	27.96	1.19	IV.	3	21.634	38 44.90	16.90	8.18	52 24.7	33 21 40.0
9	8.9					37.	55.2		53 18.61	27.96	1.24	V.	5	52.871	5 56.95	16.94	0.19	52 49.4	32 48 44.1
10	9.10				34.2				56 15.55	27.94	1.17	V.	2	14.586	46 1.96	17.12	10.01	55 46.4	33 28 59.1
11	9			52.3	10.2	29.3	17.4		12 59 10.57	27.92	1.18	IV.	3	24.388	35 52.27	17.30	7.45	12 58 41.5	18 47.0
12	9.10			16.4	35.1		11.5		13 0 34.86	27.92	1.18	IV.	3	24.287	35 58.60	17.38	7.46	13 0 5.8	18 53.5
13	9					29.2	47.4		1 10.51	27.91	1.15	V.	2	11.086	49 41.40	17.42	10.96	0 41.5	33 32 39.8
14	10.11		45.2		21.8		57.		5 21.37	27.90	1.23	IV.	5	52.614	6 13.06	17.67	0.25	4 52.2	32 49 1.0
15	9.10			17.2	35.3				5 35.41	27.90	1.19	IV.	3	34.713	25 4.29	17.69	4.79	5 6.3	33 7 56.8
16	9.10					56.5	15.2		6 38.41	27.90	1.18	V.	3	27.806	32 17.65	17.75	6.58	6 9.3	15 12.0
17	9						59.3		7 22.53	27.90	1.16	VI.	3	21.912	38 27.20	17.79	8.13	6 53.5	21 23.1
18	10						20.2		7 43.44	27.89	1.17	VI.	3	23.478	36 49.22	17.81	7.71	7 14.4	19 44.7
19	10		29.2		6.3				10 6.22	27.87	1.16	IV.	3	23.468	36 49.97	17.96	7.71	9 37.2	33 19 45.6
20	9		58.5	17.	35.2	53.4			12 35.30	27.86	1.21	IV.	5	49.712	9 15.15	18.14	0.97	12 6.2	32 52 4.3
21	10				28.8				13 28.64	27.86	1.16	IV.	3	31.861	28 3.18	18.15	5.53	12 59.6	33 10 36.9
22	10				27.2		4.7		14 27.53	27.85	1.17	IV.	3	32.968	26 53.77	18.21	5.20	13 58.5	9 47.2
23	9		13.3	31.9	50.2	8.2			16 50.15	27.84	1.13	IV.	2	13.376	47 17.53	18.40	10.37	16 21.2	30 16.3
24	10				54.3				17 54.15	27.83	1.02	IV.	3	27.366	32 45.44	18.41	6.60	17 25.3	15 40.5
25	8.9				28.	46.3	4.7		18 27.90	27.83	1.15	IV.	3	29.776	30 13.99	18.44	6.06	17 58.9	33 13 8.5
26	9		38.3	56.8	15.2	33.8			20 15.29	27.82	1.18	IV.	5	46.631	12 28.60	18.55	1.75	19 46.3	32 55 18.9
27	9			33.	51.	9.5	27.7		22 51.08	27.81	1.13	IV.	3	24.509	35 44.61	18.60	7.43	22 22.1	33 18 40.7
28	9		31.1	49.3	8.				26 7.93	27.79	1.13	IV.	3	25.396	34 49.03	18.87	7.40	25 39.0	17 45.3
29	9					29.5	48.3		26 11.06	27.79	1.09	V.	2	7.066	53 53.49	18.67	11.97	25 42.2	30 24.3
30	9				25.7	44.	2.6		27 25.73	27.78	1.11	IV.	3	28.238	31 50.67	18.94	6.44	26 56.8	14 46.1
31	10			15.3			11.		29 34.01	27.77	1.09	IV.	2	11.479	49 17.50	19.05	10.87	29 5.1	32 17.4
32	8.9			5.3	23.5	42.2	60.6		32 23.63	27.79	1.09	IV.	2	8.244	52 39.37	19.20	11.69	31 54.8	33 35 40.3
33	8			21.3	39.3	58.1			33 37.63	27.75	1.17	IV.	5	51.558	7 19.36	19.28	0.47	33 10.7	32 50 9.1
34	10						15.2		33 38.50	27.75	1.14	VI.	4	42.992	16 16.36	19.28	2.73	33 9.6	32 59 8.4
35	8.9								34	27.74	1.12	VII.+	3	29.755	30 14.93	19.32	6.06	. . .	33 13 10.3
36	10					23.	41.8		37 23.10	27.73	1.12	IV.	3	29.938	30 3.82	19.46	6.02	36 54.3	33 12 59.3
37	9				20.	38.4	56.5		38 19.91	27.73	1.14	IV.	4	45.105	14 3.18	19.51	2.13	37 51.0	32 56 54.8
38	9			53.8	12.2	30.5	49.3		41 12.27	27.71	1.13	IV.	3	35.158	21 28.25	19.66	3.91	40 43.1	33 4 21.8
39	9.10			36.3	54.9		31.3		42 54.73	27.70	1.12	IV.	3	40.168	19 22.12	19.71	3.38	42 25.9	2 15.2
40	9.10					23.2	41.7		43 4.90	27.69	1.11	V.	3	33.946	25 52.41	19.75	5.04	42 36.1	8 47.2
41	10						25.3		43 48.61	27.69	1.10	VI.	3	32.074	27 49.81	19.78	5.48	43 19.8	33 10 45.1
42	9.10					23.1	41.3		45 23.00	27.68	1.14	IV.	5	51.456	7 25.69	19.85	0.52	44 54.2	32 50 16.1
43	9.10		21.1	39.4	57.6				47 57.87	27.67	1.10	IV.	3	34.520	25 16.53	19.98	4.83	47 29.1	33 8 11.3
44	9		6.0	24.2	43.				49 42.94	27.66	1.06	III.	2	16.223	44 18.41	20.05	9.62	49 14.2	27 18.1
45	9				48.8	7.	25.3		49 48.60	27.66	1.09	IV.	3	28.527	31 32.54	20.06	6.40	49 19.9	14 29.0
46	9					44.8	3.5		50 26.56	27.65	1.08	IV.	3	27.825	32 16.21	20.09	6.59	49 57.8	33 15 12.9
47	9					46.3			51 28.04	27.64	1.14	V.	5	53.265	5 32.45	20.13	0.05	50 59.2	32 48 22.6
48	9.10				35.2	53.8	12.4		52 35.31	27.63	1.06	IV.	2	19.558	40 49.73	20.17	8.74	52 6.6	33 23 48.6
49	10		59.3						13 55 56.41	−27.62	−1.06	II.	2	17.794	−42 38.93	−20.30	−9.12	13 55 7.8	− 33 25 38.4

CORRECTIONS.

Date.	Corr. of Clock.	Hourly rate.	m	n	c	Zenith Point.	Mic. Co.
1849.	h.	s.	s.	s.	s.	° ' "	r.

REMARKS.

INSTRUMENT READINGS.

Date.	A.	B.	C.	D.	E.	F.	Mean.	Barom.	At.	Ex.	U.	L.	I.
	° ... "						"	in.	°				
Zone 240 1849. Mar. 23, 12 20								30.340	44.8	39.9		43.5	45.
12 40	92 2 27.4 27.3	32.2 32.0	34.3 33.8	30.2 30.7	26.4 26.2	17.9 18.1	28.05						
13 0													
13 20								30.340	44.8	39.1			
13 40										38.5			
14 0								30.336	44.8	37.9			
14 20										37.2			
14 40	27.6 27.4	31.7 31.2	33.2 33.1	29.2 29.8	26.1 26.4	16.7 16.5	27.43	30.330	44.8	36.9	49.	43.	45.5

Zone 240. March 23. C. $D_e = -32° 42' 30''$—Continued.

No.	Mag.	I.	II.	III.	IV.	V.	VI.	VII.	T.	a_1	a_3	MICROMETER.	i	d_1	d_3	Mean Right Ascension, 1850.0	Mean Declination, 1850.0
									h. m. s.	s.	s.	r.	′ ″	″	″	h. m. s.	° ′ ″
50	9					17.5	36.	54.3	13 56 17.54	−27.61	−1.10	IV. 3 39.411	−20 9.68	−20.33	−3.56	13 55 48.8	− 33 3 3.6
51	9		11.2	29.3			6.3		13 57 29.50	27.60	1.11	IV. 4 43.708	15 30.79	20.38	2.48	57 0.8	32 58 23.7
52	10			59.3					14 0 17.86	27.59	1.11	III. 5 48.036	10 59.98	20.50	1.38	13 59 49.2	53 51.8
53	10					49.2			0 30.92	27.59	1.11	V. 5 49.804	9 9.50	20.51	0.92	14 0 2.2	32 52 0.9
54	10								1	27.58	1.07	VI. 29.880	30 7.34	20.55	6.03	1	33 13 3.9
55	9.10	14.7	33.2						4 51.70	27.56	1.10	III. 5 50.143	8 47.79	20.67	−0.83	4 23.0	32 51 39.3
56	9.10			54.7		21.2			4 54.54	27.56	1.11	IV. 5 53.572	5 12.93	20.06	+0.02	4 25.9	48 3.6
57	9.10			20.5	38.5				5 2.02	27.56	1.11	V. 5 53.075	5 43.99	20.68	−0.10	4 33.4	48 34.8
58	10	58.5	16.5	35.2					10 35.18	27.53	1.06	IV. 4 43.861	15 21.12	20.88	2.44	10 6.6	32 58 14.4
59	10			36.5					11 36.35	27.52	1.05	IV. 3 28.102	31 59.15	20.91	6.50	11 7.8	33 14 56.6
60	10					49.8			12 13.10	27.51	1.08	V. 4 42.594	16 41.15	20.93	2.76	11 44.5	32 59 34.8
61	10				27.5				12 50.61	27.50	1.00	VI. 2 10.128	50 41.73	20.95	11.25	12 22.1	33 33 43.9
62	10.11		59.4						15 17.87	27.48	1.05	III. 3 32.698	27 10.54	21.03	5.30	14 49.3	10 6.9
63	10			5.					15 42.04	27.48	1.04	V. 5 28.492	31 34.80	21.04	6.39	15 13.5	14 32.2
64	9.10	14.	51.1	9.4					19 50.97	27.46	1.03	IV. 3 31.856	28 3.49	21.17	5.53	19 22.5	33 11 0.2
65	8.9	8.1	26.6	44.6	3.4	21.3			21 44.91	27.45	1.06	IV. 4 45.294	13 50.37	21.23	2.07	21 16.4	32 56 43.7
66	10.11				4.3				23 45.98	27.43	1.04	V. 5 45.736	13 23.89	21.27	1.96	23 17.5	32 56 17.1
67	10		29.5				43.2		27 6.49	27.40	1.02	IV. 3 35.738	23 59.98	21.36	4.52	26 38.1	33 6 55.9
68	9.10		10.8			6.5	24.8		32 47.96	27.38	1.01	IV. 3 25.195	35 5.90	21.40	7.28	32 19.6	33 18 4.7
69	9					58.3	16.5		33 39.88	27.37	1.03	V. 3 42.891	16 22.38	21.51	2.69	33 11.5	32 59 16.6
70	9.10		5.7	24.4	43.		1.5	20.	37 42.96	27.33	1.00	IV. 4 34.904	24 48.53	21.59	4.71	37 14.6	33 7 44.8
71	10		59.8	36.2	55.				40 36.47	27.32	0.97	IV. 2 19.995	40 22.10	21.65	8.64	40 8.2	23 22.5
72	9		33.5	52.3	10.5	29.			44 10.57	27.29	1.00	IV. 4 41.877	17 25.64	21.69	2.93	43 42.3	0 20.3
73	9			47.2		24.2	42.8		45 5.87	27.27	1.00	IV. 4 38.021	21 27.68	21.71	3.85	44 37.6	4 23.2
74	9				12.1	30.8	49.2		45 12.30	27.27	1.00	IV. 4 40.866	18 29.08	21.71	3.18	44 44.0	1 24.0
75	6.7			43.1	1.3	20.2	38.2		14 47 1.49	−27.26	−0.98	IV. 3 28.558	−31 30.60	−21.74	−6.37	14 46 33.2	− 33 14 28.7

Zone 241. March 29. C. $D_e = -29° 34' 40''$.

No.	Mag.	I.	II.	III.	IV.	V.	VI.	VII.	T.	a_1	a_3	MICROMETER.	i	d_1	d_3	Mean Right Ascension, 1850.0	Mean Declination, 1850.0
1	10				4.2	22.5			11 52 40.19	−32.36	−0.18	III. 5 48.011	−10 59.66	− 2.12	− 6.32	11 52 7.6	− 29 45 48.1
2	8.9				0.2	18.2	35.8	53.4	53 18.05	32.36	0.18	IV. 5 47.834	11 12.96	2.17	6.36	52 45.5	46 1.5
3	8.9		31.5	48.	5.8	23.3	41.3		55 5.84	32.35	0.18	IV. 5 47.632	11 25.77	2.32	6.40	54 33.3	46 14.5
4	9.10				32.3	50.2			56 50.15	32.35	0.21	IV. 5 46.586	12 31.42	2.47	6.61	56 17.6	29 47 20.5
5	8				25.2	43.3	0.8		57 25.19	32.35	0.76	IV. 2 14.442	46 10.67	2.52	13.23	56 52.1	30 21 6.4
6	10				43.3	1.3			59 1.19	32.35	0.61	IV. 3 23.656	36 38.06	2.64	11.31	58 28.2	11 32.0
7	10					29.2			11 59 11.30	32.35	0.61	V. 3 24.687	35 33.38	2.66	11.09	58 38.3	30 10 27.1
8	10					22.3			12 0 4.55	32.35	0.28	V. 5 41.749	17 35.12	2.74	7.60	11 59 31.9	29 52 25.5
9	8					8.7	26.6		0 50.85	32.35	0.71	V. 2 17.071	43 26.03	2.80	12.69	12 0 17.8	30 18 21.5
10	9						47.5		1 12.00	32.35	0.53	VI. 3 27.428	32 41.48	2.83	10.53	0 39.1	30 7 34.8
11	8			12.3	30.1	47.7	5.6		4 30.08	32.34	0.17	IV. 5 47.770	11 16.99	3.08	6.38	3 57.6	29 46 6.5
12	9					59.2			5 41.06	32.34	0.87	V. 2 7.656	53 16.49	3.17	14.66	5 7.9	30 28 14.3
13	10			9.2	26.		1.8		6 43.93	32.33	0.57	III. 3 24.998	35 13.62	3.40	11.03	8 11.0	10 8.1
14	9.10				44.2	2.	20.5		8 44.35	32.33	0.68	IV. 2 18.795	41 37.39	3.40	12.32	8 11.4	16 33.1
15	9		55.2		31.1	49.2	6.4		10 31.02	32.33	0.78	IV. 2 13.481	47 10 94	3.54	13.44	9 57.9	22 7.9
16	9.10			3.5	21.3		57.		12 21.34	32.33	0.46	IV. 3 30.015	29 59.06	3.66	10.00	11 48.5	30 4 52.7
17	9				31.5	49.2	6.8		13 31.39	32.32	0.14	IV. 5 49.156	9 50.11	3.75	6.10	12 58.9	29 44 40.0
18	9				12.8	30.7			14 12.86	32.32	0.05	IV. 5 54.436	4 18.75	3.80	5.02	13 40.5	29 39 7.6
19	9.10					30.7			12 14 55.09	−32.32	−0.74	VI. 2 14.867	−45 44.39	− 3.85	−13.15	12 14 22.0	− 30 20 41.4

CORRECTIONS.

Date.	Corr. of Clock.	Hourly rate.	m	n	c	Zenith Point.	Mic. Co.
1849. h.	s.	s.	s.	s.	s.	° ′ ″	r.

REMARKS.

(240) 56. Time of transit over T. VI assumed as 31ˢ.2 instead of 21 .2.

INSTRUMENT READINGS.

Date.	A.	B.	C.	D.	E.	F.	Mean.	Barom.	At.	Ex.	U.	L.	I.
1849. h. m.	° ′ ″						″	in.	°	°	°	°	°
Zone 241 Mar. 29, 11 50	88 54 61.9	63.7	66.2	58.8	58.9	53.8	60.55	30.050	51.5	49.1	49.	50.7	50.
12 0										48.8			
12 20								30.050	51.3	48.2			
12 40										48.6			
13 0										48.5			
13 20										48 3			
13 45								30.036	51.	46.9			
13 50	61.6	63.9	66.8	58.1	58.9	53.4	60.45					48.5	49.

ZONE 241. MARCH 29. C. $D_0 = -29° 34' 40''$—Continued.

No.	Mag.	I.	II.	III.	IV.	V.	VI.	VII.	T.	a_1	a_2	Micrometer		r	i	d_1	d_2	Mean Right Ascension, 1850.0	Mean Declination, 1850.0
									h. m. s.	s.	s.			r.	' "	"	"	h. m. s.	° ' "
20	10				27.3				12 16 27.17	−32.32	−0.24	IV.	4	42.737	−16 31.67	−3.96	−7.40	12 15 54.6	− 29 51 23.0
21	9.10						19.2		16 43.67	32.32	0.06	VI.	5	53.287	5 31.19	4.02	5.24	16 11.3	29 40 20.5
22	9					22.3	40.4		18 4.56	32.31	0.64	V.	2	17.515	42 58.31	4.08	12.60	17 31.6	30 17 55.0
23	10			31.3		6.5			19 49.00	32.31	0.22	IV.	4	44.225	14 58.47	4.21	7.09	19 16.5	29 49 49.8
24	9.10			37.2		12.5			21 54.88	32.31	0.38	IV.	3	34.895	24 52.82	4.35	8.99	21 22.2	29 59 46.2
25	9					11.2			22 23.18	32.31	0.71	V.	2	16.302	44 10.02	4.38	12.84	21 50.2	30 19 7.8
26	9.10						24.3		22 48.78	32.30	0.12	VI.	5	50.421	8 31.16	4.41	5.82	22 16.4	29 43 21.4
27	8						8.3		23 32.79	32.30	0.23	VI.	4	43.283	15 56.27	4.46	7.30	23 0.3	29 50 50.0
28	8					33.	50.5		24 15.04	32.30	0.54	V.	3	25.943	34 14.52	4.51	10.83	23 42.2	30 0 9.8
29	10						16.2		24 40.72	32.30	0.49	VI.	3	29.071	30 58.29	4.53	10.20	24 7.9	30 5 53.0
30	10				8.7				30 8.58	32.29	0.12	IV.	5	49.264	9 43.40	4.91	6.05	29 36.2	29 44 34.4
31	9				52.3	9.9	27.6		30 52.13	32.29	0.31	IV.	3	38.006	21 0.08	4.96	8.23	30 19.5	29 55 53.3
32	8		13.3		19.5	37.3	55.4		35 19.45	32.28	0.51	IV.	3	27.652	32 27.36	5.24	10.46	34 46.6	30 7 23.1
33	10				20.8	38.6			38 20.83	32.27	0.36	IV.	3	35.314	24 26.77	5.44	8.91	37 48.2	29 59 21.1
34	10			45.4	2.2		38.2		40 2.69	32.26	0.27	IV.	4	40.120	19 16.03	5.55	7.93	34 30.2	29 54 9.5
35	9.10				22.8		59.5		41 23.30	32.26	0.76	IV.	2	12.712	47 58.96	5.63	13.62	40 50.3	30 22 58.2
36	9.10						57.5		41 21.89	32.26	0.71	VI.	2	15.310	45 16.48	5.63	13.07	40 48.9	30 20 15.2
37	8				53.2	11.			42 53.19	32.25	0.12	IV.	5	48.321	10 42.58	5.72	6.26	42 20.8	29 45 34.6
38	8.9		59.2	17.2	34.8	52.4			44 34.87	32.25	0.10	IV.	4	44.398	14 47.61	5.83	7.00	44 2.4	29 49 40.4
39	8								44	32.25	0.63	VII.	2	19.398	41 0.51		12.19	44	30 15 56.5
40	9		36.5	54.3	12.7		48.5		49 12.53	32.23	0.62	IV.	2	19.208	41 11.68	6.12	12.24	48 39.7	16 10.0
41	9			30.6	48.5	6.5			50 48.48	32.23	0.55	IV.	3	24.098	36 14.66	6.22	11.24	50 15.7	30 11 12.1
42	9			15.3	33.4		8.4		52 33.13	32.23	0.15	IV.	3	46.496	12 43.41	6.32	6.62	52 0.8	29 47 36.4
43	8		34.9	53.2	10.8	28.6	45.9		54 10.71	32.22	0.40	IV.	3	32.359	27 32.19	6.42	9.51	53 38.1	30 2 28.1
44	10		28.3	46.1	4.				56 3.99	32.21	0.12	IV.	5	47.491	11 34.68	6.53	6.41	55 31.7	29 46 27.6
45	10			43.	0.5		35.5		58 0.42	32.20	0.31	IV.	3	36.552	23 9.02	6.64	8.65	57 27.9	54 4.3
46	10		38.2			32.2	49.3		58 14.05	32.20	−0.31	IV.	3	36.066	22 42.92	6.65	8.57	57 41.6	57 38.1
47	8.9				58.5	16.3	34.1		12 59 58.54	32.20	+0.03	IV.	5	55.608	2 50.41	6.76	4.74	12 59 26.4	37 50.9
48	9.10			25.4	42.0	0.8			13 1 13.05	32.19	−0.15	IV.	4	45.618	13 30.98	6.86	6.79	13 1 10.7	29 48 24.6
49	9					34.2	53.3		3 34.20	32.19	0.67	IV.	2	16.305	44 19.29	6.96	12.83	3 1.3	30 19 19.1
50	8.9				23.	43.2	1.		4 43.02	32.18	0.61	IV.	2	19.472	40 55.18	7.03	12.16	4 10.2	15 54.4
51	9					24.2	41.6		5 6.31	32.18	0.48	V.	3	26.066	33 10.26	7.05	10.63	4 33.7	30 8 8.0
52	8.9								5		0.26	VII.	4	39.169	20 16.52	7.09	8.11	5	29 55 11.7
53	10				40.2				7 40.08	32.17	0.10	IV.	5	48.256	10 46.66	7.20	6.26	7 7.8	45 40.1
54	8		33.	50.8	8.3	26.4	43.8		9 8.52	32.17	0.13	IV.	5	46.145	12 59.09	7.28	6.68	8 36.2	47 53.1
55	8.9			2.	19.7	37.3	55.4		10 19.72	32.16	0.28	IV.	3	38.150	21 28.75	7.35	8.33	9 47.3	29 56 24.4
56	8			12.3	29.9	47.4	5.6		11 30.02	32.16	0.43	IV.	3	29.266	30 46.17	7.44	10.15	10 57.4	30 5 43.8
57	9		3.8	21.3	39.3	57.4	15.4		14 39.47	32.15	0.36	IV.	3	33.576	26 15.69	7.58	9.28	14 7.0	1 12.6
58	8.9		44.3		20.		55.5		17 20.01	32.14	0.74	IV.	2	11.024	49 44.85	7.74	13 99	16 47.1	24 46.6
59	9.10				36.5	54.6	12.3		18 36.54	32.13	0.74	IV.	2	11.086	49 41.02	7.80	13.97	18 3.7	24 42.8
60	8.9				55.7	13.6	31.5		19 55.79	32.12	0.33	IV.	3	34.391	25 24.69	7.88	9.08	19 23.3	0 21.6
61	9				6.2	25.	42.3		21 6.63	32.12	0.59	V.	2	19.535	40 51.54	7.94	12.18	20 33.9	15 51.7
62	8		19.2	37.5	55.	12.8	30.4		23 55.01	32.11	0.61	IV.	2	18.645	41 46.93	8.09	12.36	23 22.3	30 16 47.4
63	9.10		10.3		46.		4.3		25 46.17	32.10	0.18	IV.	4	42.632	16 38.37	8.19	7.41	25 13.9	29 51 34.0
64	9.10				49.8	7.5	25.3		28 7.48	32.09	0.57	IV.	2	19.883	40 29.15	8.32	12.10	27 31.8	30 15 29.6
65	10					57.5	15.3		28 39.69	32.09	0.47	VI.	3	25.368	34 50.73	8.35	10.97	28 7.1	30 9 50.1
66	9.10		32.3	50.5	8.3				31 8.20	32.08	0.30	IV.	3	35.048	24 5.69	8.48	7.83	30 35.8	29 59 2.0
67	9					46.5	4.3		31 28.72	32.08	0.43	V.	3	27.806	32 17.65	8.49	10.49	30 56.2	30 7 16.6
68	10				7.2	25.1			13 33 25.03	−32.07	−0.40	IV.	3	25.855	−34 19.99	−8.60	−10.87	13 32 52.5	− 30 9 19.5

CORRECTIONS.

Date.	Corr. of Clock.	Hourly rate.	m	n	c	Zenith Point.	Mic. Co.
1849.	h.	s.	s.	s.	s.	s.	° ' "	r.

INSTRUMENT READINGS.

Date.	Circle							Barom.	Thermom.				
	A.	B.	C.	D.	E.	F.	Mean.		At.	Ex.	U.	L.	I.
1849. h. m.	° ' "						"	in.	°	°	°	°	°

ZONE 241. MARCH 29. C. $D_z = -29° 34' 40''$—Continued.

No.	Mag.	I	II	III	IV	V	VI	VII	T (h m s)	a_1	a_2	Mic.	n	r	i (' ")	d_1	d_2	Mean Right Ascension, 1850.0 (h m s)	Mean Declination, 1850.0 (° ' ")
69	10						4.2		13 34 28.70	−32.06	−0.22	VI.	4	40.475	−18 54.50	−8.65	−7.84	13 33 56.4	− 29 53 51.0
70	9		56.1	13.3	31.9	49.3			37 31.62	32.05	+0.01	IV.	5	52.629	6 12.11	8.82	5.34	36 59.6	41 6.3
71	9				18.5	36.5	54.2		38 18.62	32.05	−0.02	IV.	5	50.646	8 16.53	8.86	5.73	37 46.5	43 11.1
72	8.9		48.1	6.2	24.		59.6		40 23.98	32.04	0.30	IV.	3	34.841	24 56.10	8.97	8.99	39 51.6	50 54.1
73	8			42.5	0.2	17.5	35.4		41 0.01	32.03	0.28	IV.	3	36.001	22 40.70	9.00	8.55	40 27.7	29 57 36.3
74	8					37.6	55.2		42 19.60	32.03	0.63	V.	2	16.417	44 7.17	9.07	12.86	41 46.9	30 19 9.1
75	8					56.2	14.2		42 38.33	32.03	0.77	V.	2	8.476	52 25.20	9.05	14.54	42 5.5	27 28.8
76	8				16.2	34.	51.5		44 16.09	32.02	0.35	IV.	3	32.440	27 27.10	9.17	9.49	43 43.7	30 2 25.8
77	9						11.8		44 36.28	32.02	0.03	VI.	5	49.963	8 59.65	9.19	5.87	44 4.2	29 43 54.7
78	8				51.	8.5	26.3		47 50.80	32.00	0.14	IV.	4	43.768	15 26.95	9.35	7.19	47 18.7	29 50 23.5
79	8			20.	37.3	55.2			49 37.45	31.99	0.63	IV.	2	15.573	44 59.67	9.45	13.03	49 4.8	30 20 2.2
80	8					8.2	26.3		13 49 50.50	−31.99	−0.52	V.	2	21.646	−38 39.06	−9.46	−11.64	13 49 18.0	− 30 13 40.2

ZONE 242. MARCH 30. S. $D_z = -36° 30' 50''$.

No.	Mag.	I	II	III	IV	V	VI	VII	T (h m s)	a_1	a_2	Mic.	n	r	i (' ")	d_1	d_2	Mean Right Ascension, 1850.0 (h m s)	Mean Declination, 1850.0 (° ' ")
1	6					54.	13.		11 39 34.66	−33.08	−0.96		4	42.978	−16 16.99	−1.11	−11.49	11 39 0.62	− 36 47 19.6
2	9				52.		31.		40 52.16	33.08	0.47	VI.	2	14.600	46 1.20	1.24	21.44	40 18.61	37 17 13.9
3	9				30.				42 29.94	33.08	0.41	.	2	12.212	48 30.46	1.42	22.43	41 56.45	37 19 44.3
4	6			18.	37.2				43 37.23	33.08	0.91	IV.	4	39.658	19 44.96	1.53	12.62	43 3.24	36 50 49.1
5	9					22.			44 2.78	33.07	0.04	.	4	42.573	16 42.46	1.58	11.60	43 28.77	47 45.6
6	6.7				16.8				45 16.65	33.07	0.84	.	3	35.770	23 57.91	1.72	13.98	44 42.74	36 55 3.6
7	7					2.	21.5		45 42.76	33.07	0.59	V.	2	22.332	37 56.15	1.76	18.75	45 9.10	37 9 6.7
8	6				13.5				47 13.37	33.07	0.96	.	4	44.336	14 51.56	1.93	11.01	46 39.34	36 45 54.5
9	6.5						7.2		47 28.75	33.07	0.82	.	3	35.833	23 54.27	1.96	13.90	46 54.86	55 0.1
10	9		1.8	21.	40.				50 40.20	33.06	0.93	IV.	4	41.482	17 50.62	2.30	12.00	50 6.37	46 54.9
11	10						36.5		51 58.05	33.06	1.10	.	5	52.122	6 44.13	2.43	8.30	51 23.89	37 44.9
12	8			24.8	13.8				53 43.97	33.06	1.09	IV.	5	51.230	7 40.00	2.60	8.60	53 9.82	36 38 41.2
13	10			41.					55 0.44	33.05	0.54	.	2	18.080	42 21.80	2.73	20.28	54 26.85	37 13 34.8
14	10						24.		56 45.55	33.05	0.93	.	4	42.322	16 58.52	2.92	11.67	56 11.57	36 48 3.1
15	6				20.				58 19.87	33.04	1.05	.	4	47.121	11 56.64	3.07	10.03	57 45.78	36 42 50.7
16	5				29.	48.			11 59 28.76	33.04	0.73	IV.	4	29.650	30 16.56	3.19	16.12	11 58 54.99	37 1 25.0
17	9			9.	28.5				12 1 28.36	33.04	0.84	IV.	4	36.382	23 10.65	3.37	13.76	12 0 54.48	36 54 17.8
18	4		42.5	2.5	21.5				3 21.49	33.04	0.73	IV.	3	29.108	30 56.03	3.55	16.31	2 47.72	37 2 5.9
19	8			41.					4 0.43	33.04	1.00	.	4	45.450	13 41.03	3.61	10.61	3 26.39	36 44 45.2
20	6				35.		13		5 34.74	33.03	1.07	IV.	5	48.550	10 25.16	3.75	9.51	5 0.61	41 31.4
21	10			12.5			10.2		7 31.81	33.02	0.81	III.	3	34.518	25 17.47	3.93	14.42	6 57.98	36 56 25.8
22	11				45.				9 44.89	33.02	0.58	.	3	22.226	38 2.37	4.15	18.79	9 11.29	37 9 15.3
23	5		10.2	29.8	48.8				12 48.92	33.01	0.76	IV.	3	33.082	26 46.69	4.41	14.93	12 15.15	36 57 56.0
24	6.5				55.	14.	33.5		15 54.03	33.00	1.09	.	4	50.522	8 23.25	4.68	8.85	15 20.84	39 26.8
25	10		12.6		51.2				18 51.29	33.00	0.91	IV.	3	39.162	20 25.24	4.94	12.79	18 17.38	36 51 32.9
26	7			35.					20 54.46	32.99	0.47	V.	2	15.632	44 56.29	5.10	21.17	20 21.00	37 15 22.6
27	6.5					49.	8.6	?	21 29.82	32.99	0.59	.	3	23.358	36 50.88	5.15	18.36	20 56.24	8 10.4
28	10			55.8					24 15.17	32.98	0.65	.	3	26.322	33 50.75	5.37	17.30	23 41.54	5 3.4
29	6				20.	39.2			25 19.79	32.98	0.47	IV.	2	16.912	43 33.66	5.44	20.72	24 46.34	37 14 49.8
30	10			21.					28 40.37	32.97	0.79	.	3	34.218	25 35.29	5.71	14.53	28 6.61	36 56 45.5
31	9			16.		54.8			30 35.33	32.96	0.36	III.	2	8.949	51 54.41	5.86	23.62	30 2.01	37 23 13.9
32	6		6.3	25.2	45.				32 44.83	32.95	0.71	IV.	3	29.293	30 44.54	6.02	16.24	32 11.17	1 56.8
33	7				14.2				12 34 14.05	−32.95	−0.69	.	3	−27.553	−32 33.65	−6.13	−16.88	12 33 40.41	− 37 3 46.7

CORRECTIONS.

Date.	Corr. of Clock.	Hourly rate.	m	n	c	Zenith Point.	Mic. Co.
1849.	h.	s.	s.	s.	s.	s.	° ' "	r.

REMARKS.

(241) 73. Micrometer revolutions assumed as 37.001, not 35.001.

INSTRUMENT READINGS.

Date.	A.	B.	C.	D.	E.	F.	Mean.	Barom.	At.	Ex.	U.	L.	I.	
Zone 242 1849. Mar. 30, 11 30	95 49 60.	63.2	65.	57.0	57.5	54.0	59.45	In.	55.	49.2			52.5	
11 40								30.070		49.7				
12 0										49.7				
12 15	63.	63.6	66.2	57.0	59.2	53.	60.33							
12 20										49.3				
13 0								30.052		48.9				Ex. therm. assumed 49.5.
13 40										49.6				
14 20										50.6				
14 45	62.8	63.6	66.2	57.0	59.0	53.	60.27							

ZONE 242. MARCH 30. S. $D_0 = -36°\ 30'\ 50''$—Continued.

No.	Mag.	I.	II.	III.	IV.	V.	VI.	VII.	T. (h. m. s.)	n₁ (s.)
34	7				17.		8.		12 31 29.47	−32.95
35	7				17.				36 16.86	32.94
36	9						36.5		37 58.05	32.93
37	6					23.5	42.5		38 4.12	32.93
38	8		20.3	39.7					41 59.05	32.92
39	6			14.					42 33.45	32.92
40	6,7					17.5			42 58.09	32.92
41	7,6						12.		43 33.55	32.92
42	9				46.5				45 46.43	32.90
43	9		19.		57.5				50 57.55	32.88
44	9				41.8	4.			54 44.77	32.87
45	6,7		7.2		46.				56 45.97	32.86
46	7					33.			57 13.82	32.86
47	8			52.8					59 12.17	32.85
48	6,7					25.7	45.		12 59 6.53	32.85
49	6					6.2			13 0 46.65	32.85
50	3,2			37.2	56.3				4 15.80	32.83
51	9						31.		3 55.39	32.83
52	7		42.8	2.		40.2			7 21.33	32.82
53	9		33.	52.	12.				11 11.66	32.80
54	10			39.2	58.8				14 18.08	32.79
55	10			56.					15 31.70	32.78
56	7,6					42.			16 22.47	32.77
57	8					31.3	51.		17 12.17	32.77
58	9			36.5	56.				21 15.30	32.75
59	10						12.		21 33.55	32.75
60	9				26.				23 45.44	32.74
61	10				47.				25 6.43	32.73
62	8		20.		39.8	59.			26 58.93	32.72
63	10				0.				28 10.43	32.71
64	9				57.2				28 57.07	32.71
65	7						54.6		29 16.35	32.71
66	8						10.		30 1.55	32.70
67	7				35.8		14.3		31 35.74	32.69
68	8			38.5					31 17.17	32.68
69	8,9					44.8			34 25.60	32.68
70	10				23.				38 42.38	32.65
71	7			54.					42 32.99	32.64
72	7				47.	6.			43 6.14	32.63
73	9					3.	22.		45 2.84	32.62
74	8,9				30.8				46 30.70	32.61
75	9			21.	10.				48 59.56	32.60
76	7,6			9.5	27.2				50 49.41	32.59
77	9						27.2		51 8.	32.58
78	7						20.5		52 1.35	32.58
79	8					5.			52 45.81	32.57
80	8				0.	19.5			55 19.35	32.56
81	9				41.				56 0.37	32.56
82	6,7					32.3	51.3		13 57 32.06	−32.55

No.	a₁ (s.)	MICROMETER		r.	i (′ ″)	d₁ (″)	d₂ (″)	Mean Right Ascension, 1850.0 (h. m. s.)	Mean Declination, 1850.0 (° ′ ″)
34	−0.63	·	3	24.272	−35 59.35	−6.15	−18.04	12 33 55.91	− 37 7 13.5
35	0.87	·	4	38.062	21 25.10	6.28	13.18	35 43.05	36 52 34.6
36	0.79	·	3	33.625	26 12.44	6.40	14.73	37 24.33	57 23.6
37	0.74	·	3	31.202	28 44.71	6.41	15.56	37 30.45	36 59 56.7
38	0.69	·	3	28.202	31 52.74	6.68	16.65	41 25.44	37 3 6.1
39	1.05	·	5	50.302	8 37.87	6.72	8.91	41 59.45	36 39 43.5
40	0.63	·	3	24.439	35 49.06	6.75	17.96	42 24.54	37 7 3.8
41	1.03	·	5	48.419	10 37.06	6.79	9.60	42 59.60	36 41 43.4
42	0.43	·	2	13.950	46 41.34	6.93	21.78	45 13.10	37 18 0.1
43	0.73	·	3	30.650	29 19.29	7.28	15.77	50 23.94	37 0 32.3
44	1.10	·	5	51.678	7 11.75	7.52	8.42	54 10.80	36 38 17.7
45	0.75	·	3	31.992	27 55.02	7.64	15.30	56 12.29	59 8.0
46	1.03	·	5	47.179	11 54.45	7.66	10.00	56 39.93	43 2.1
47	0.80	·	3	34.770	25 0.46	7.79	14.33	58 38.52	56 12.6
48	0.99	·	4	45.582	13 33.62	7.79	10.54	12 58 32.69	36 44 41.9
49	0.46	·	2	14.487	46 8.16	7.90	21.60	13 0 13.34	37 17 27.7
50	0.73	III.	3	30.840	29 7.05	8 08	15.70	3 42.24	0 20.8
51	0.46	·	2	16.202	44 20.78	8.06	20.97	3 22.16	37 15 39.8
52	1.11	III.	5	52.223	6 37.22	8.26	8.25	6 47.40	36 37 43.7
53	0.87	IV.	3	38.275	21 20.96	8.47	13.11	10 37.99	36 52 32.5
54	0.66	III.	3	25.920	33 12.41	8.64	17.04	13 44.64	37 4 28.1
55	0.96	·	5	43.876	15 20.25	8.70	11.13	15 0.96	36 46 30.1
56	0.48	·	2	16.953	43 33.30	8.75	20.71	15 49.22	37 14 52.8
57	0.60	V.	3	23.096	37 13.19	8.79	16.50	16 38.80	37 8 30.5
58	0.77	·	3	32.728	27 8.58	9.00	15.05	20 41.78	36 58 22.6
59	0.93	·	4	43.570	15 39.64	9.02	11.26	20 59.85	46 49.9
60	1.04	·	5	47.889	11 9.07	9.11	9.77	23 11.06	36 42 16.0
61	0.52	·	2	18.625	41 47.62	9.18	20.12	24 33.18	37 13 6.9
62	0.96	IV.	4	43.362	15 52.69	9.27	11.34	26 25.25	36 47 3.3
63	0.99	·	4	45.235	13 54.51	9.33	10.67	27 45.73	45 4.5
64	0.99	·	4	46.028	13 5.19	9.36	10.39	28 23.37	44 14.9
65	0.80	·	3	34.290	25 30.83	9.38	14.49	28 42.84	56 44.7
66	1.00	·	4	47.202	11 52.19	9.41	10.00	29 27.85	36 43 1.6
67	0.72	·	3	31.072	28 52.81	9.47	15.62	31 2.33	37 0 7.9
68	1.12	·	5	52.972	5 49.52	9.59	7.98	33 43.37	36 36 57.1
69	0.97	·	4	44.765	14 24.76	9.60	10.84	33 51.95	36 45 35.2
70	0.63	·	3	25.465	34 44.45	9.76	17.60	38 9.10	37 6 1.8
71	0.35	·	2	8.882	51 57.79	9.92	23.65	42 0.00	23 21.4
72	0.56	IV.	3	21.692	38 41.20	9.94	19.00	42 32.95	37 10 0.1
73	1.01	V.	5	46.593	12 31.23	10.01	10.21	44 29.21	36 43 41.5
74	0.55	·	2	20.608	39 43.80	10.07	19.36	45 57.54	37 11 3.2
75	0.80	III.	3	35.880	23 50.82	10.15	13.94	48 26.16	36 55 4.9
76	0.96	III.	3	44.070	15 16.92	10.21	11.06	50 14.86	46 28.2
77		·		.493				50 35.	
78	1.06	·	4	50.112	8 49.30	10.25	8.95	51 27.71	39 58.5
79	1.00	·	3	46.109	13 4.69	10.29	10.35	52 12.24	36 44 15.3
80	0.69	·	3	28.465	31 36.49	10.35	16.54	54 46.10	37 2 53.4
81	0.79	·	3	34.508	25 17.09	10.37	14.42	55 27.02	36 56 31.9
82	−0.72	IV.	3	30.778	−29 11.12	−10.42	−15.73	13 56 58.79	− 37 0 27.3

CORRECTIONS.

Date.	Corr. of Clock.	Hourly rate.	m	n	c	Zenith Point.	Mic. Co.
1849.	h.	s.	s.	s.	s.	s.	° ′ ″	r.

INSTRUMENT READINGS.

Date.	CIRCLE							Barom.	THERMOM.				
	A.	B.	C.	D.	E.	F.	Mean.		At.	Ex.	U.	L.	I.
1849.	h. m.	° ′ ″						″	in.	°	°	°	°	°

REMARKS.

ZONE 242. MARCH 30. S. $D_0 = -36° 30' 50''$—Continued.

No.	Mag.	SECONDS OF TRANSIT						
		I.	II.	III.	IV.	V.	VI.	VII
83	10			7.	26.			
84	8		2.	21.3	41.			
85	10			38.				
86	10.9		23.2					
87	8			59.				
88	9		56.					
89	6				44.	3.5		
90	7.8				19.8	39.		
91	3				41.	0.5		
92	8		28.8	48.				
93	9				12.	31.		
94	6				26.5			
95	8							31.
96	9						19.6	
97	10					52.3		
98	11							6.
99	9		13.2					
100	10		5.5					
101	7.8			8.8				
102	9			41.	0.			
103	10		25.5					
104	2.3			53.	12.3			
105	9			12.				
106	9						53.	
107	9						3.	
108	7.8					4.		
109	9		12.0					
110	8				4.8			
111	7			59.5	18.5			
112	9		28.					
113	4						38.8	
114	8		54.	13.8				

No.	T. (h. m. s.)	a_1 (s.)	a_2 (s.)	MICROMETER		i (r.)	i (′ ″)	d_1 (″)	d_2 (″)	Mean Right Ascension, 1850.0 (h. m. s.)	Mean Declination, 1850.0 (° ′ ″)
83	13 59 26.12	−32.53	−0.85		3	38.273	−21 20.77	−10.46	−13.00	13 58 52.74	− 36 52 34.3
84	14 2 40.83	32.52	0.54	IV.	2	20.130	40 13.78	10.56	19.57	14 2 7.77	37 11 33.9
85	4 57.34	32.50	0.71		3	29.565	30 26.98	10.61	16.15	4 24.13	37 1 43.7
86	6 1.92	32.49	0.69		4	40.162	19 12.08	10.64	12.41	5 28.53	36 50 25.1
87	7 18.38	32.49	0.84		3	37.062	22 36.71	10.67	13.52	6 45.05	53 50.9
88	8 34.74	32.48	0.79		3	34.702	25 4.3	10.70	14.34	8 1.47	36 56 19.4
89	8 43.91	32.48	0.49	IV.	2	16.892	43 36.75	10.71	20.77	8 10.97	37 14 55.3
90	10 19.77	32.47	1.09	IV.	5	52.008	6 51.04	10.75	8.20	9 46.21	36 38 0.0
91	11 0.51	32.46	0.54	IV.	2	20.165	40 11.61	10.77	19.55	11 27.51	37 11 32.0
92	15 7.47	32.44	0.98	III.	4	45.613	13 30.72	10.85	10.52	14 34.05	36 44 42.1
93	15 11.83	32.41	0.96	IV.	4	43.953	15 15.35	10.85	11.08	14 38.43	46 27.3
94	16 26.37	32.42	0.97		4	44.638	14 36.06	10.78	10.84	15 52.95	45 47.7
95	16 52.55	32.42	0.63		3	36.190	23 31.55	10.79	13.81	16 19.30	54 46.2
96	17 41.15	32.42	0.91			41.160	18 11.33	10.90	12.05	17 7.82	49 24.3
97	22 33.05	32.39	0.87			38.635	20 4.50	10.99	12.95	21 59.70	52 3.5
98	23 27.55	32.38	0.86			38.370	21 6.54	11.00	13.06	22 54.31	52 20.6
99	25 51.94	32.36	0.81			36.072	23 38.57	11.04	13.87	25 18.77	54 53.5
100	27 44.18	32.35	1.11			51.390	7 26.88	11.06	8.58	27 10.72	35 36.5
101	28 28.19	32.34	0.86		3	38.388	21 13.63	11.08	13.00	27 54.99	36 52 27.6
102	30 0.27	32.34	0.22			1.405	59 48.47	11.10	26.41	29 27.71	37 31 16.0
103	31 4.20	32.33	0.95			44.142	15 2.24	11.11	11.05	30 30.92	36 46 11.4
104	33 12.29	32.32	0.58	IV.	3	22.872	37 27.12	11.14	18.61	32 39.39	37 8 46.9
105	34 31.38	32.31	0.83		4	36.945	22 34.58	11.15	13.55	33 58.24	36 53 49.3
106	34 14.55	32.31	1.03		5	45.272	10 45.91	11.15	9.56	33 41.21	41 56.6
107	35 24.55	32.30	1.05		5	49.832	9 7.74	11.16	8.92	34 51.20	36 40 17.8
108	36 44.40	32.29	0.41			13.093	47 36.16	11.17	22.15	36 11.70	37 18 59.5
109	39 40.10	32.27	0.48			17.610	42 50.59	11.21	20.52	39 7.35	14 12.3
110	40 5.64	32.27	0.72			31.042	28 54.62	11.21	15.64	39 32.65	37 0 11.5
111	41 18.65	32.26	0.96	IV.	4	44.420	14 46.23	11.22	10.91	40 45.43	36 45 58.4
112	44 6.69	32.24	1.05		5	48.082	10 56.46	11.24	9.59	43 33.40	36 42 7.3
113	44 0.24	32.24	0.54		2	20.793	39 32.63	11.24	19.34	43 27.46	37 10 53.2
114	14 46 32.98	−32.22	−1.10		5	52.843	− 5 58.11	−11.26	− 8.00	14 45 59.66	− 36 37 7.4

ZONE 243. APRIL 2. S. $D_0 = -34° 35' 20''$.

No.	Mag.	SECONDS OF TRANSIT						
		I.	II.	III.	IV.	V.	VI.	VII
1	9				14.8			
2	9				50.5		23.3	
3	5			2.2	21.2			
4	10.9					57.		
5	10			17.2	36.2			
6	8					7.	26.	
7	7.8			55.6	14.		51.8	
8	11						11.	
9	8.7			55.	14.		51.5	
10	9				8.2			
11	10			19.5	38.5		35.2	
12	9			34.6	43.			

No.	T. (h. m. s.)	a_1 (s.)	a_2 (s.)	MICROMETER		i (r.)	i (′ ″)	d_1 (″)	d_2 (″)	Mean Right Ascension, 1850.0 (h. m. s.)	Mean Declination, 1850.0 (° ′ ″)
1	9 59 52.64	−34.44	−1.06		3	31.210	−28 43.64	− 0.04	− 7.65	9 59 17.1	− 35 4 11.3
2	9 59 50.54	34.44	1.14		2	21.042	39 16.57	0.04	10.65	9 59 15.0	14 47.3
3	10 3 40.07	34.45	1.07	III.	3	28.169	31 54.76	0.48	8.54	10 3 4.5	35 7 23.8
4	3 38.21	34.45	1.00		4	39.278	20 9.36	0.48	5.30	3 2.8	34 55 35.1
5	5 55.09	34.45	1.12	III.	3	24.822	35 24.60	0.75	9.52	5 19.5	35 10 54.9
6	7 6.92	34.46	1.20	IV.	2	16.263	44 16.46	0.89	12.09	6 31.3	35 19 49.4
7	9 33.14	34.47	0.93	III.	5	50.162	8 46.59	1.19	2.15	9 57.7	34 44 9.9
8	10 52.13	34.47	1.10		3	29.061	30 58.98	1.34	8.27	10 16.6	35 5 28.6
9	12 33.80	34.47	1.05	III.	3	34.608	25 10.76	1.54	6.66	11 57.3	0 39.0
10	14 27.08	34.48	1.11		3	28.243	31 50.17	1.77	8.53	13 51.5	7 20.5
11	15 57.51	34.48	1.27	III.	2	8.352	52 32.04	1.96	14.48	15 21.6	35 28 8.5
12	10 17 2.16	−34.49	−1.01	III.	4	41.450	−17 52.07	− 2.08	− 4.67	10 16 26.7	− 34 53 18.8

CORRECTIONS.

Date.	Corr. of Clock.	Hourly rate.	m	n	c	Zenith Point.	Mic. Co.
1849.	h.	s.	s.	s.	s.	° ′ ″	r.

INSTRUMENT READINGS.

Date.	CIRCLE							Barom.	THERMOM.				
	A.	B.	C.	D.	E.	F.	Mean.		At.	Ex.	U.	L.	I.
Zone 243, April 2, 9 50	93 54 59.3	59.2	60.8	56.3	52.3	50.8	56.45	In.					
10 0								30.148	53.4	45.8	53.	52.	
10 20										44.			
11 10	59.3	59.2	61.2	56.3	52.3	50.8	56.52						
12 0								30.140	49.5	40.3			
12 20										39.8			
12 40								30.148	48.5	39.8			
13 20	59.3	59.2	61.2	58.2	52.3	50.8	56.83						

REMARKS.

(242) 91. Transits over T.'s III and IV assumed as recorded over T.'s IV and V, and minutes as 12, not 11.

(243) 2. Time of transit over T. VI assumed as 28ˢ.3 instead of 23ˢ.3.

(243) 12. Time of transit over T. II assumed as 24ˢ.6 instead of 34ˢ.6.

ZONE 243. APRIL 2. S. $D_0 = -34° 35' 20''$—Continued.

No.	Mag.	I.	II.	III.	IV.	V.	VI.	VII.	T.	a_1	a_2			r.	i	d_1	d_2	Mean Right Ascension, 1850.0	Mean Declination, 1850.0
									h. m. s.	s.	s.			r.	' "	"	"	h. m. s.	° ' "
13	11.10				33.5				10 18 33.37	−34.49	−1.00		4	42.753	−16 30.66	−2.27	−4.32	10 17 57.9	−34 51 57.3
14	8		49.2				44.8		22 7.61	34.50	1.28		2	9.192	51 39.86	2.69	14.22	21 31.9	35 27 16.8
15	9	8.	27.	46.		24.			25 4.97	34.51	1.29	III.	2	9.176	51 40.17	3.05	14.22	24 29.2	27 17.4
16	10		10.	29.					26 47.86	34.51	1.10	III.	3	32.508	27 22.58	3.26	7.27	26 12.2	1 53.1
17	7				0.8	18.5			27 19.24	34.51	1.21	IV.	2	18.332	42 6.69	3.32	11.46	26 43.5	17 41.5
18	7		31.						29 8.83	34.52	1.11		2	32.330	27 27.29	3.54	7.32	28 33.2	35 2 58.2
19	9				20.8				29 29.67	34.52	0.99		5	46.750	12 21.00	3.58	3.14	28 54.2	34 47 47.7
20	6.7		51.		28.8				31 28.73	34.52	1.06	IV.	4	33.418	21 2.90	3.82	5.56	30 53.2	34 56 32.3
21	8		47.2						34 25.11	34.52	1.19		3	22.708	37 36.83	4.17	10.15	33 49.4	35 13 11.2
22	6.7				36.8				34 35.65	34.52	1.07		4	37.412	22 6.02	4.19	5.84	34 1.1	34 57 36.1
23	6.7	i			15.5	33.8			35 15.18	34.52	1.07	IV.	4	39.070	21 24.60	4.27	5.65	34 39.6	34 56 54.5
24	9					24.2			36 5.06	34.53	1.29		2	11.206	49 33.81	4.37	13.63	35 29.2	35 25 11.8
25	8					8.5			36 49.76	34.53	1.02		5	44.983	14 12.16	4.46	3.63	36 14.2	34 49 40.2
26	9.8		4.	23.2					40 42.05	34.54	1.24		2	17.580	42 53.23	4.92	11.69	40 6.3	35 18 9.8
27	8.7			59.					41 17.97	34.54	1.26		2	15.931	44 36.53	4.99	12.19	40 42.2	20 13.7
28	9			16.					42 36.89	34.54	1.18		3	26.760	33 23.01	5.15	8.97	42 1.2	8 57.1
29	9					9.			42 50.09	34.54	1.18		3	26.515	33 38.83	5.18	9.03	42 14.4	9 13.0
30	8					53.5			43 34.68	34.54	1.12		3	34.612	25 10.76	5.27	6.64	42 59.0	35 0 42.7
31	7				51.				44 32.19	34.54	1.11		3	36.153	23 34.06	5.37	6.20	43 56.5	34 59 5.6
32	10					44.			45 6.48	34.55	1.09		3	37.868	21 46.14	5.44	5.70	44 30.8	57 17.3
33	6.5				38.6	57.5			46 35.76	34.55	0.97	IV.	5	52.701	6 7.53	5.63	1.43	46 3.2	41 34.6
34	7.8		18.	37.2					48 55.95	34.55	0.98	III.	5	52.374	6 27.80	5.89	1.53	48 20.5	34 41 55.2
35	7.8		11.2	30.3					50 49.26	34.55	1.31	III.	2	11.518	49 13.49	6.12	13.54	50 13.4	35 24 53.2
36	8			6.8					51 25.75	34.55	1.05		5	44.352	14 51.31	6.19	3.82	50 50.1	34 50 21.3
37	8				47.				51 46.87	34.55	1.06		5	42.730	16 33.30	6.23	4.29	51 11.3	52 3.8
38	9						18.5		51 40.97	34.55	1.01		5	48.738	10 16.48	6.22	2.58	51 5.4	45 45.3
39	10		16.	8.5				1.5	54 24.07	34.55	1.03	III.	5	49.122	9 51.87	6.53	0.93	53 48.5	34 45 19.3
40	9			5.5	24.				56 43.11	34.56	1.14	III.	3	34.456	25 20.42	6.80	6.69	56 7.4	35 0 53.9
41	10		36.						58 13.82	34.56	1.15		3	35.280	24 18.27	6.97	6.45	57 38.1	34 59 51.7
42	5				25.3				58 25.15	34.56	1.15		3	35.490	24 15.66	7.00	6.40	57 49.4	34 59 49.1
43	10						10.		58 32.48	34.56	1.18		3	31.218	28 43.58	7.01	7.65	57 56.7	35 4 18.2
44	10						4.		10 59 26.47	34.56	1.03		5	49.913	9 2.72	7.11	2.20	58 50.9	34 44 32.0
45	10						6.		11 0 28.45	34.56	1.18		3	31.392	28 32.73	7.23	7.60	10 59 52.7	35 4 7.6
46	8				40.				3 39.67	34.56	1.24		3	24.712	35 31.75	7.59	9.57	11 3 4.1	11 8.9
47	6.7					27.2			3 49.57	34.56	1.27		3	19.200	41 17.51	7.61	11.19	3 13.7	16 56.3
48	6.7					7.			4 29.28	34.56	1.34		2	11.761	48 59.19	7.68	13.46	3 53.4	24 40.3
49	11			25.5					7 44.52	34.57	1.36		2	10.193	50 36.52	8.05	13.94	7 8.6	26 18.5
50	8				7.				8 6.91	34.57	1.30		3	18.300	42 14.14	8.09	11.48	7 31.0	35 17 53.7
51	8				20.				9 1.33	34.57	1.03		5	52.662	6 10.22	8.20	1.44	8 25.7	34 41 39.9
52	10					30.5			9 52.95	34.57	1.18		3	32.927	26 56.16	8.29	7.15	9 17.2	35 2 31.6
53	7		25.5						14 3.28	34.57	1.09		3	46.263	12 59.03	8.75	3.27	13 27.6	34 48 31.0
54	6.7				30.8				14 30.68	34.57	1.04		4	52.112	6 43.37	•8.80	1.58	13 55.1	34 42 13.8
55	10					43.			15 23.86	34.57	1.37		2	11.120	49 39.26	8.89	13.67	14 47.9	35 25 21.8
56	8					27.8			16 8.66	34.57	1.37		2	11.240	49 31.81	8.97	13.62	15 32.7	25 14.4
57	5						11.		16 33.33	34.57	1.33		2	15.712	44 51.39	9.02	12.27	15 57.4	20 32.7
58	7						45.		17 7.38	34.57	1.30		2	20.032	40 20.50	9.08	10.97	16 31.5	16 0.6
59	8					35.			18 16.14	34.57	1.23		2	29.850	30 4.26	9.21	8.05	17 40.3	5 41.5
60	5					8.	27.		18 49.20	34.57	1.30		3	21.	39	9.	11.	18 13.3	15
61	8		27.3						11 21 5.23	−34.57	−1.30		3	21.222	−39 10.23	−9.52	−10.61	11 20 29.4	−35 14 50.4

CORRECTIONS.

Date.	Corr. of Clock.	Hourly rate.	m	n	e	Zenith Point.	Mic. Co.
1849.	h.	s.	s.	s,	s.	° ' "	r.

REMARKS.

(243) 41. Right ascension discordant 12ˢ by B. A. C. 3792, and Mural Z., April 18, 1846.

INSTRUMENT READINGS.

Date.	CIRCLE.							Barom.	THERMOM.				
	A.	B.	C.	D.	E.	F.	Mean.		At.	Ex.	U.	L.	I.
1849. h. m.	° ' "						"	in.	°	°	°	°	°

ZONE 243. APRIL 2. S. $D_s = -34°\ 35'\ 20''$—Continued.

No.	Mag.	I.	II.	III.	IV.	V.	VI.	VII.	T.	a_1	a_2	MICROMETER		r.	i	d_1	d_2	Mean Right Ascension, 1850.0	Mean Declination, 1850.0
									h. m. s.	s.	s.			r.	′ ″	″	″	h. m. s.	° ′ ″
62	8.9						50.		11 21 12.47	−34.57	−1.07	·	5	50.938	− 8 1.77	− 9.53	− 1.91	11 20 36.8	− 34 43 33.2
63	8			9.8					24 28.75	34.57	1.12	·	4	45.453	13 40.64	9.68	3.49	23 53.1	34 49 14.2
64	5.6	29.8	49.				27.2		26 7.96	34.57	1.37	III.	2	13.566	47 4.99	10.05	12.94	25 32.0	35 22 48.0
65	6.7		57.	16.	34.8				27 34.91	34.57	1.38	IV.	2	13.841	46 48.11	10.21	12.66	26 59.0	35 22 31.2
66	6				27.				28 26.86	34.57	1.11	·	5	47.626	11 19.86	10.30	2.87	27 51.2	34 46 53.0
67	6.7				28.5				29 47.45	34.57	1.33	·	2	18.625	41 47.68	10.45	12.40	29 11.5	35 17 30.5
68	8.9				16.8				30 16.68	34.57	1.09	·	5	49.185	9 48.30	10.50	2.42	29 41.0	34 45 21.2
69	9		53.8	13.					33 31.76	34.57	1.22	III.	3	34.492	25 18.10	10.84	6.68	32 56.0	35 0 55.6
70	7.6		53.8	13.2					34 31.87	34.57	1.11	III.	5	48.251	10 46.60	10.94	2.70	33 56.2	34 46 20.2
71	8		4.5						35 42.38	34.57	1.29	·	3	26.162	34 0.29	11.06	9.14	35 6.5	35 9 40.5
72	9			6.					36 24.92	34.57	1.18	·	4	40.583	18 46.40	11.14	4.91	35 49.2	34 54 22.5
73	9					8.8	27.8		37 8.69	34.57	1.43	IV.	2	8.608	52 16.42	11.22	14.48	36 32.7	35 28 2.1
74	7.8			24.5	43.				38 43.17	34.57	1.11	IV.	5	48.265	10 46.10	11.38	2.66	38 7.5	34 46 20.1
75	5.6			53.			49.2		40 11.77	34.57	1.26	·	3	31.192	28 45.34	11.54	7.65	39 35.9	35 4 24.5
76	7.8			24.8	43.5				41 43.52	34.57	1.30	IV.	3	26.650	33 30.24	11.69	9.01	41 7.7	0 10.9
77	11		2.8						44 40.62	34.57	1.23	·	4	34.780	24 49.66	11.99	6.60	44 4.6	35 0 28.3
78	11		9.5						45 47.31	34.57	1.22	·	4	36.688	22 50.01	12.10	6.06	45 11.5	34 58 28.2
79	10				22.5				46 22.38	34.56	1.33	·	3	23.268	37 2.52	12.17	9.99	45 46.5	35 12 44.7
80	6.7					30.	48.5		47 11.01	34.56	1.31	V.	2	26.435	33 38.95	12.25	9.07	46 35.1	35 9 20.3
81	9						5.5		48 27.97	34.56	1.17	·	5	44.693	14 30.41	12.38	3.70	47 52.2	34 50 6.5
82	11					30.			50 11.01	34.56	1.36	·	3	21.300	39 5.07	12.55	10.59	49 35.1	35 14 49.1
83	11		10.8		48.5				52 48.59	34.56	1.39	IV.	2	17.380	43 6.30	12.80	11.79	52 12.6	35 18 51.0
84	10	59.				55.2			54 36.63	34.56	1.14	·	5	49.683	9 16.97	13.07	2.25	54 0.9	34 44 52.2
85	8					2.	21.		55 43.31	34.56	1.29	·	3	31.125	28 49.55	13.08	7.67	55 7.5	35 4 30.3
86	9	16.8							57 54.58	34.55	1.18	·	5	46.018	13 0.01	13.29	3.32	57 18.9	34 48 42.6
87	4	12.8	31.5	50.8					11 58 50.56	34.55	1.20	IV.	4	43.369	15 52.25	13.38	4.10	11 58 14.9	34 51 29.7
88	10			19.					12 2 18.84	34.55	1.30	·	3	31.315	28 37.50	13.70	7.62	12 1 43.0	35 4 18.8
89	10		18.8						4 37.75	34.55	1.19	·	4	45.513	13 43.34	13.92	3.46	4 2.0	34 49 20.7
90	10				57.8				5 57.65	34.54	1.33	·	3	28.620	31 26.08	14.04	8.44	5 21.8	35 7 8.6
91	8	10.2	29.2	48.					7 48.11	34.54	1.46	IV.	2	13.302	47 22.17	14.20	13.04	7 12.1	23 9.4
92	6.7	56.2							10 34.14	34.53	1.40	·	3	20.602	39 49.07	14.46	10.81	9 58.2	15 34.3
93	10			39.5					10 39.37	34.53	1.37	·	3	24.740	35 29.99	14.47	9.56	10 3.5	35 11 14.0
94	8	38.6	47.6						12 16.46	34.53	1.23	III.	4	42.356	17 4.55	14.61	4.38	11 40.7	34 52 43.5
95	7.8		9.8						13 25.79	34.53	1.47	·	3	14.198	46 25.34	14.71	12.76	12 52.8	35 22 12.8
96	9					56.			13 18.42	34.53	1.39	·	3	24.188	36 4.63	14.70	9.74	− 12 42.5	11 49.1
97	10		35.	54.3					15 54.02	34.53	1.30	IV.	3	35.435	24 19.17	14.93	6.39	15 18.2	35 0 0.5
98	9			54.5					16 54.37	34.52	1.20	·	3	46.668	12 35.02	15.02	3.11	16 18.6	34 45 3.2
99	10		58.	17.					18 35.97	34.52	1.45	III.	2	16.930	43 33.87	15.16	11.92	18 0.0	35 19 21.0
100	8	40.2	59.						21 17.95	34.52	1.35	·	3	29.730	30 16.75	15.39	8.08	20 42.1	6 0.2
101	9			35.					21 53.89	34.52	1.39	·	3	20.003	34 10.58	15.43	9.20	21 18.0	35 9 55.2
102	10				31.6	50.8			22 31.72	34.52	1.32	IV.	3	35.453	24 18.04	15.49	6.39	21 55.9	34 59 59.0
103	11		16.					·	24 34.95	34.51	1.23	·	4	45.556	13 34.16	15.67	3.44	24 59.2	49 13.3
104	10	35.	54.						25 12.86	34.50	1.31	III.	3	35.622	24 7.13	15.96	6.34	27 37.0	59 49.4
105	10		23.	41.5	0.5				25 41.64	34.50	1.31	IV.	3	35.622	24 7.32	16.01	6.34	28 5.8	59 49.7
106	11		35.						30 53.91	34.50	1.29	·	3	38.363	21 15.26	16.16	6.55	30 18.1	34 56 55.0
107	8	5.8	25.	44.					35 43.82	34.49	1.42	IV.	2	24.740	35 29.61	16.54	9.57	35 7.9	35 11 15.7
108	8			59.8		37.3			36 59.66	34.49	1.51	·	2	12.640	48 2.99	16.64	13.25	36 23.7	35 23 52.9
109	7.8		15.7	34.					39 34.24	34.48	−1.29	IV.	4	41.762	−17 32.85	−16.84	−4.57	39 58.5	− 34 53 14.3
110	10			39.					12 42 58.	−34.47		·	·	.482				12 42 24.	

CORRECTIONS.

Date.	Corr. of Clock.	Hourly rate.	m	n	c	Zenith Point.	Mic. Co.
1849.	h.	s.	s.	s.	s.	° ′ ″	r.

REMARKS.

(243) 95. Right ascension differs 4ˢ.4 from Mural Z. March 16, 1849.

(243) 109. Minutes assumed as 40, not 39.

INSTRUMENT READINGS.

Date.	CIRCLE.							Barom.	THERMOM.				
	A.	B.	C.	D.	E.	F.	Mean.		At.	Ex.	U.	L.	I.
1849. h. m.	° ′ ″						″	In.	°	°	°	°	°

ZONE 243. · APRIL 2. S. $D_0 = -34°\ 35'\ 20''$—Continued.

Columns: No. | Mag. | SECONDS OF TRANSIT (I–VII) | T. (h. m. s.) | a_1 (s.) | a_2 (s.) | MICROMETER (wire, n, r.) | i (′ ″) | d_1 (″) | d_2 (″) | Mean Right Ascension, 1850.0 (h. m. s) | Mean Declination, 1850.0 (° ′ ″)

No.	Mag.	I	II	III	IV	V	VI	VII	T.	a_1	a_2	Mic.	n	r.	i	d_1	d_2	Mean R.A. 1850.0	Mean Decl. 1850.0
111	9					32.			12 43 12.98	−34.47	−1.48		2	18.753	−41 40.47	−17.10	−11.39	12 42 37.0	−35 17 28.9
112	9						15.8		43 38.28	34.46	1.39		3	30.732	29 13.95	17.13	7.79	43 2.4	4 58.9
113	9							18.5	44 21.88	34.46	1.40		3	28.680	31 22.36	17.17	8.42	43 46.0	7 8.0
114	3		32.	51.	10.	28.8			12 59 9.68	34.41	1.41	IV.	3	32.376	27 31.12	18.17	7.31	12 58 34.1	3 16.6
115	6.7			19.	37.8				13 0 37.89	34.41	1.58	IV.	2	11.302	49 27.60	18.27	13.66	13 0 1.9	25 19.5
116	6.7		20.	39.	58.				1 59.96	34.41	1.55	IV.	2	14.893	45 42.13	18.35	12.55	1 24.0	35 21 33.0
117	7				57.				2 56.87	34.40	1.32		4	44.560	14 37.45	18.41	3.71	2 21.1	34 50 19.6
118	9			41.					3 59.95	34.40	1.31		4	45.770	13 20.74	18.47	3.37	3 21.2	34 48 42.6
119	8.7		17.5	36.8					5 55.53	34.39	1.46	III.	3	27.026	33 6.39	18.59	8.02	5 19.7	35 8 53.9
120	10		12.3	31.2					12 50.10	34.37	1.44	III.	3	31.878	28 1.93	18.99	7.38	12 14.3	3 48.3
121	8		19.5						13 57.47	34.36	1.56		2	16.928	43 33.24	19.06	11.94	13 21.5	35 19 24.2
122	9					21.5			14 21.36	34.36	1.38		4	40.505	18 51.93	19.08	4.92	13 45.6	34 54 35.9
123	10				51.				15 50.88	34.35	1.31		5	48.508	10 30.86	19.17	2.57	15 15.2	34 46 12.6
124	10						56.		16 18.26	34.35	1.63		2	9.228	51 35.91	19.19	14.29	15 42.3	35 27 29.4
125	9			29.	47.7	6.2			13 19 6.50	−34.34	−1.35	IV.	4	44.673	−14 30.16	−19.35	−3.47	13 18 30.8	−34 50 13.0

ZONE 244. APRIL 5. C. $D_0 = -25°\ 49'\ 0''$.

No.	Mag.	I	II	III	IV	V	VI	VII	T.	a_1	a_2	Mic.	n	r.	i	d_1	d_2	Mean R.A. 1850.0	Mean Decl. 1850.0
1	9		37.2	48.	12.	29.5	46.4		9 12 11.97	−35.64	−0.86	IV.	2	10.829	−49 57.01	−1.98	−13.24	9 11 35.5	−26 39 12.2
2	9				49.2	5.9			14 6.14	35.65	0.90	IV.	5	43.083	16 11.21	2.21	7.81	13 29.6	5 21.9
3	8.9					26.2	43.2		14 8.98	35.65	0.91	V.	3	35.712	24 1.67	2.21	9.04	13 32.4	13 12.3
4	8.9		27.2	44.8	2.8	19.4	36.6		17 2.19	35.66	0.92	IV.	2	17.519	42 57.62	2.57	12.10	16 25.6	26 32 12.6
5	9.10			31.3	47.8	5.5			20 35.26	35.68	0.97	IV.	5	52.262	6 35.22	3.04	6.29	20 1.6	25 55 44.0
6	8.9				43.2	0.5	17.3		21 43.10	35.68	0.97	IV.	2	22.219	38 0.55	3.15	11.30	21 6.5	26 27 15.6
7	8			5.	22.2	39.5	56.5	13.5	23 39.42	35.69	1.01	IV.	5	51.740	7 7.80	3.39	6.38	23 2.7	25 56 17.3
8	7				35.5	52.3		27.3	23 52.68	35.69	1.01	III.	5	51.978	6 52.55	3.41	6.34	23 16.0	25 56 2.5
9	9						14.4		24 40.12	35.70	1.01	VI.	3	39.475	20 5.60	3.51	8.42	24 3.4	26 9 17.3
10	9					55.3	13.5		25 55.68	35.70	1.01	IV.	2	20.573	39 46.06	3.66	11.58	25 19.0	29 1.1
11	10						54.?		26 19.74	35.71	1.00	VI.	3	33.713	26 7.03	3.71	9.37	25 43.0	15 20.7
12	9		53.2	10.3	27.2	45.2			30 27.61	35.72	1.01	IV.	2	11.002	49 46.23	4.22	13.21	29 50.9	30 3.5
13	8.9						23.2		30 48.93	35.72	1.04	V.	4	37.538	21 58.50	4.26	8.73	30 12.1	11 11.5
14	9		49.3	6.2	23.2	41.			34 23.56	35.74	1.06	IV.	4	40.652	18 42.58	4.69	8.22	33 46.8	7 55.9
15	10					36.3			37 36.20	35.75	1.06	IV.	3	21.198	39 12.31	5.08	11.48	37 59.4	28 28.3
16	8.9				15.	32.2	49.5	6.2	38 32.14	35.76	1.09	IV.	3	36.801	22 53.22	5.19	8.85	37 55.3	12 7.8
17	9					46.6	3.3	20.3	39 46.22	35.76	1.09	V.	4	42.357	16 55.52	5.34	7.93	39 9.4	6 8.6
18	8								40	35.76	1.06	VII.	3	14.921	45 45.04	5.5	12.54	40	35 3.5
19	9.10					10.5	45.5		44 10.79	35.78	1.09	IV.	2	18.316	42 7.69	5.87	11.97	43 33.9	31 25.8
20	10			30.	47.5		11.8		46 4.68	35.79	1.13	III.	4	46.046	13 3.43	6.09	7.32	45 27.8	2 16.5
21	10		31.5	49.2		23.8			46 6.41	35.79	1.13	IV.	4	40.461	12 38.14	6.09	7.25	45 29.4	1 51.5
22	8.9						3.2	20.3	46 16.04	35.79	1.14	V.	4	45.238	13 55.33	6.17	7.46	46 9.1	3 9.0
23	9		22.5	40.2	57.2		31.5		49 57.20	35.80	1.14	IV.	3	36.592	23 6.45	6.55	8.89	49 20.3	12 21.9
24	9				42.	56.8	16.2	33.5	49 59.03	35.80	1.15	IV.	3	29.175	30 51.89	6.56	10.15	49 22.1	26 20 8.6
25	10						49.2		51 14.67	35.81	1.28	VI.	5	54.080	4 41.35	6.70	5.98	50 37.8	25 53 54.0
26	8.9				7.4	24.3	41.4	58.7	54 24.33	35.82	1.29	IV.	3	23.386	30 55.12	7.12	11.11	53 47.2	26 26 13.3
27	10				20.0	35.			56 37.99	35.83	1.33	IV.	3	31.472	28 27.77	7.33	9.75	56 0.8	17 44.8
28	10					46.3	3.5		56 46.22	35.83	1.33	IV.	3	28.666	31 23.76	7.35	10.23	56 9.1	20 41.3
29	8					26.8	43.5	1.4	57 26.71	35.83	1.33	IV.	3	37.788	21 51.28	7.43	8.69	56 49.5	11 7.4
30	8			4.3		19.3	56.6	13.5	9 59 39.13	−35.84	−1.36	IV.	2	16.946	−43 33.43	−7.69	−12.21	9 59 1.9	−26 32 53.3

CORRECTIONS.

Date.	Corr. of Clock.	Hourly rate.	m	n	c	Zenith Point.	Mic. Co.
1849. h.	s.	s.	s.	s.	s.	° ′ ″	r.

INSTRUMENT READINGS.

Date.	A.	B.	C.	D.	E.	F.	Mean.	Barom.	At.	Ex.	U.	L.	I.
Zone 244 — 1849. April 5. 9 0								30.110	61	52.	59.	56.8	
9 10	85 9 63.4	61.7	66.0	62.5	55.	58.9	61.25						
9 20										50.?			
9 40								30.132	59	49.?			
10 0								30.140	58.2	48.0			
10 20								30.146	57.2	47.0			
10 40										47.0			
11 0								30.148	55.8	47.0			
11 20								30.160	55.4	46.8	34.5	53.2	

REMARKS.

(244) 1. Transit over T. III discordant and rejected.

(244) 5. Transits over T.'s III, IV, and V assumed as 21s.3, 37s.8, and 55s.5 instead of 31s.3, 47s.8, and 5s.5.

ZONE 244. APRIL 5. C. $D_0 = -25°\ 49'\ 0''$—Continued.

No.	Mag.	I.	II.	III.	IV.	V.	VI.	VII.	. T. (h. m. s.)	a_1 (s.)	a_2 (s.)	Micr.	n	r.	i (' '')	d_1 ('')	d_2 ('')	Mean Right Ascension, 1850.0 (h. m. s.)	Mean Declination, 1850.0 (° ' '')
31	9					27.3	44.		10 0 9.95	−35.84	−1.37	VI.	5	55.802	− 2 53.12	− 7.75	− 5.69	9 59 32.9	− 25 32 6.6
32	9						50.4		1 16.12	35.85	1.36	VI.	3	25.266	34 57.11	7.87	10.80	10 0 38.9	26 24 15.8
33	9			6.3	23.8	40.4			5 23.55	35.66	1.39	IV.	5	49.845	9 6.74	8.34	6.68	4 46.3	25 58 21.8
34	9				55.3	12.5	30.3		5 55.44	35.86	1.39	IV.	2	18.452	41 59.16	8.40	12.95	5 18.2	26 31 20.5
35	6			45.2	3.4	20.6	37.7		7 3.13	35.87	1.39	IV.	3	31.853	28 3.68	8.53	9.69	6 25.9	17 21.9
36	9			19.2	36.2		11.5		8 36.59	35.87	1.40	IV.	2	16.015	44 31.20	8.70	12.36	7 59.3	33 52.3
37	9.10		22.8	40.5	57.3				10 57.43	35.88	1.42	IV.	4	41.652	17 39.83	8.96	8.03	10 20.1	0 50.8
38	9			36.2	53.3	10.5			11 53.28	35.88	1.41	IV.	3	22.972	37 20.90	9.06	11.19	11 16.0	26 41.2
39	9.10			4.8	22.1	39.5	56.5		13 22.11	35.89	1.42	IV.	3	23.613	36 40.76	9.22	11.08	12 44.8	26 1.1
40	10		35.3	53.2					16 10.17	35.90	1.44	III.	4	43.078	16 9.83	9.53	7.81	15 32.8	26 5 27.2
41	9				29.	46.2	3.2		16 28.94	35.90	1.44	IV.	5	53.021	5 47.45	9.57	6.14	15 51.6	25 55 3.2
42	9				53.4				17 53.36	35.90	1.43	IV.	2	10.088	50 43.61	9.71	13.39	17 16.0	26 40 6.7
43	9					41.2	58.2		18 23.56	35.90	1.44	V.	3	18.805	41 42.29	9.76	12.89	17 46.5	31 4.9
44	9				42.2		16.3		19 42.05	35.91	1.46	IV.	4	35.351	24 15.41	9.91	9.10	19 4.7	13 34.4
45	9			59.2	16.8				22 16.63	35.92	1.45	IV.	2	14.575	46 2.27	10.17	12.61	21 39.3	35 25.0
46	9					23.8			22 49.51	35.92	1.47	VI.	4	42.180	16 48.74	10.22	7.90	22 12.1	6 6.9
47	9.10					10.5			24 36.21	35.92	1.48	VI.	4	42.702	16 34.61	10.41	7.86	23 58.8	5 52.9
48	9.10				49.1		23.3		26 48.19	35.93	1.49	IV.	4	45.898	13 13.28	10.63	7.34	26 11.6	2 31.3
49	9				55.2		32.3		26 58.04	35.93	1.49	V.	4	46.151	12 57.97	10.65	7.29	26 20.6	26 2 15.9
50	7		3.2	21.2	38.1	55.			29 38.08	35.94	1.50	IV.	5	54.255	4 30.12	10.92	5.94	29 0.6	25 53 47.0
51	8					16.2	33.5		29 59.15	35.94	1.50	V.	5	50.749	8 10.26	10.96	6.53	29 21.7	25 57 27.8
52	6						23.2?		30 48.80	35.94	1.48	VI.	2	10.945	48 47.68	11.04	13.24	30 11.4	26 38 12.0
53	10					43.1	0.3		32 43.12	35.94	1.51	IV.	5	54.495	4 15.05	11.22	5.90	31 5.7	25 53 32.2
54	8.9		44.2	2.	18.9	35.8			34 18.89	35.95	1.52	IV.	4	48.007	10 55.39	11.37	7.01	33 41.4	26 0 13.8
55	9		17.5	34.8	52.3	9.5			35 52.15	35.95	1.51	IV.	2	9.471	51 22.43	11.52	13.50	35 14.7	40 47.4
56	8.9		18.	35.2	52.3	9.8	26.8		36 52.45	35.96	1.52	IV.	2	18.984	41 25.61	11.63	11.66	36 15.0	30 49.1
57	9		41.8	58.2	16.2				39 16.08	35.96	1.52	IV.	2	6.785	54 10.02	11.87	13.97	38 38.6	26 43 36.5
58	8				47.3	4.2	21.1		39 47.03	35.96	1.54	IV.	5	51.894	6 58.13	11.92	6.32	39 9.5	25 56 16.4
59	8		9.3	26.5	43.5	0.9	18.		42 43.70	35.97	1.55	IV.	4	46.946	12 7.51	12.20	7.14	42 6.2	26 1 26.9
60	9		26.2	43.2	0.2		34.5		45 0.38	35.97	1.57	IV.	4	42.429	16 51.19	12.42	7.90	44 22.9	+6 11.5
61	9.10				21.8		56.		46 21.69	35.98	1.55	IV.	2	14.520	46 5.72	12.55	12.61	45 44.2	26 35 30.9
62	8				25.2	42.3	59.4		47 25.13	35.98	1.57	V.	5	51.246	7 38.99	12.65	6.44	46 47.6	25 56 58.1
63	9					22.4	39.3		48 5.14	35.98	1.58	V.	4	47.748	11 18.61	12.71	7.02	47 27.6	26 0 38.3
64	7.8				54.3	11.5	28.4		48 54.22	35.98	1.58	IV.	3	35.191	21 26.18	12.79	8.61	48 16.7	10 47.6
65	9.10			22.3		56.2			51 39.30	35.99	1.60	IV.	3	38.107	21 31.38	13.06	8.63	51 1.7	26 10 53.1
66	8			31.4	48.2	5.4			52 48.38	35.99	1.60	IV.	3	35.302	8 38.24	13.17	6.60	52 10.8	25 57 58.0
67	9.10					30.5			52 56.10	35.99	1.58	VI.	2	9.468	51 23.24	13.18	13.50	52 18.5	26 40 49.9
68	9						2.2		53 27.88	35.99	1.59	VI.	3	21.111	39 17.70	13.24	11.51	52 50.3	28 42.5
69	7		12.2	29.3	46.7	4.1	21.		55 46.72	36.00	1.62	VI.	4	47.175	11 53.32	13.47	7.11	55 9.1	1 13.9
70	9					57.5			56 40.01	36.00	1.60	V.	2	7.672	53 15.49	13.55	13.78	56 2.4	42 42.8
71	9.10					6.5			57 49.17	36.00	1.60	V.	3	21.099	39 18.51	13.66	11.52	57 11.6	28 43.7
72	6			27.1	44.5	1.5		▼	58 44.32	36.00	1.61	IV.	3	20.761	39 39.53	13.75	11.56	58 6.7	29 4.9
73	6		45.	2.	19.2	36.	53.6		10 59 19.19	36.00	1.62	IV.	3	21.153	39 15.14	13.81	11.49	10 58 41.6	28 40.4
74	10					52.8	9.5		11 1 35.41	36.01	1.63	V.	3	30.699	29 16.21	14.04	9.88	11 0 57.8	26 18 40.1
75	8			0.2	16.9	34.4			5 17.21	36.01	1.64	IV.	4	48.808	10 11.83	14.41	6.85	4 39.6	25 59 23.1
76	9.10			45.	2.2		36.2		7 2.10	36.02	1.64	III.	4	46.091	13 0.73	14.58	7.30	6 24.4	26 2 22.6
77	9				12.2		46.4		7 12.09	36.02	1.64	IV.	5	53.268	5 32.07	14.61	6.08	6 34.4	25 54 52.8
78	8.9						11.?		7 36.74	36.02	1.63	VI.	3	34.480	25 19.04	14.65	9.23	6 59.1	26 14 42.9
79	9								11 8	−36.02	−1.63	VII.	2	20.242	−40 12.08	−14.7	−11.66	11 7	− 26 29 38.5

CORRECTIONS.

Date.	Corr. of Clock.	Hourly rate.	m	n	c	Zenith Point.	Mic. Co.
1849.　h.	s.	s.	s.	s.	s.	° ' ''	r.

INSTRUMENT READINGS.

Date.		CIRCLE.							Barom.	THERMOM.				
		A.	B.	C.	D.	E.	F.	Mean.		At.	Ex.	U.	L.	I.
	1849.　h. m.	° ' ''						''	in.	°	°	°	°	°
Zone 244	April 5, 11 40	85 9 63.9	63.8	67.1	64.9	56.2	58.9	62.47	30.170	55.	46.0			

REMARKS.

(244) 52. Micrometer reading assumed as 11ʳ.945 instead of 10ʳ.945.

ZONE 244.　APRIL 5.　C.　$D_o = -25° 49' 0''$—Continued.

No.	Mag.	I.	II.	III.	IV.	V.	VI.	VII.	T.	a_1	a_2	MICROMETER.	i	d_1	d_2	Mean Right Ascension, 1850.0	Mean Declination, 1850.0
									h. m. s.	s.	s.	r.	′ ″	″	″	h. m. s.	° ′ ″
80	9.10	.	.	.	.	.	42.8	.	11 9 8.51	−36.02	−1.64	VI 4 42.980	−16 17.17	−14.80	−7.80	11 8 30.9	−26 5 39.8
81	8.9	.	.	.	.	26.5	43.3	.	10 9.12	36.02	1.63	V 3 24.452	35 48.31	14.91	10.95	9 31.5	25 14.2
82	9.10	.	.	5.2	.	39.5	.	.	12 22.44	36.02	1.64	IV 4 43.895	15 18.99	15.14	7.65	11 44.8	4 41.8
83	10	.	.	21.2	37.5	.	13.2	.	15 38.25	36.03	1.63	IV 3 24.491	35 45.74	15.47	10.94	15 0.6	25 12.1
84	8	.	.	50.4	7.7	25.2	.	.	18 7.76	36.03	1.64	IV 4 40.575	18 47.47	15.60	8.21	16 30.1	8 11.3
85	9	.	.	.	37.2	.	.	.	18 37.06	36.03	1.64	IV 4 37.126	22 23.91	15.77	8.79	17 59.4	11 48.5
86	8.9	.	.	.	.	.	.	.	19 .	36.03	1.64	VI 4 45.699	13 26.52	16.97	7.37	18	26 2 50.7
87	8	.	0.3	17.5	34.4	51.5	8.9	.	25 34.60	36.04	1.66	IV 4 53.017	5 46.51	16.49	6.12	24 56.9	25 55 9.1
88	9.10	.	.	.	.	17.8	34.5	.	26 0.45	36.04	1.66	IV 4 49.137	9 50.55	16.64	6.84	25 22.7	25 59 14.0
89	10	.	23.5	.	.	.	.	.	28 58.04	36.04	1.65	IV 4 30.441	29 32.52	16.85	9.93	28 20.4	26 18 59.3
90	9	.	.	.	31.7	18.5	5.3	.	29 31.33	36.04	1.66	IV 5 52.521	6 18.96	16.90	6.19	28 53.6	25 55 42.1
91	9.10	.	.	55.3	.	30.3	.	.	31 12.78	36.05	1.64	IV 2 19.691	40 41.26	17.07	11.75	30 35.1	26 30 10.1
92	8.9	.	.	8.8	26.2	.	0.4	.	32 26.11	36.05	1.66	IV 4 47.594	11 26.96	17.20	7.04	31 48.4	26 0 51.2
93	9.10	.	.	46.3	3.2	.	.	.	34 3.37	36.05	1.66	IV 4 49.685	9 19.23	17.38	6.68	33 25.7	25 58 43.3
94	9	.	.	.	40.8	.	15.4	.	35 40.88	36.05	1.64	IV 2 9.579	51 15.59	17.54	13.50	35 3.2	26 40 46.6
95	9	.	.	.	9.2	26.2	43.5	.	37 9.12	36.05	1.66	IV 4 45.495	13 38.77	17.70	7.40	36 31.4	3 3.9
96	9.10	.	50.5	7.5	21.8	12.2	.	.	39 24.87	36.05	1.66	IV 3 35.321	21 26.33	17.93	9.11	38 47.2	26 13 53.4
97	4	.	14.5	31.5	49.	6.1	23.1	.	41 48.92	36.06	1.67	IV 5 53.255	5 32.80	18.17	6.07	41 11.2	25 54 57.1
98	8	.	6.2	23.5	40.5	57.8	.	.	43 40.60	36.06	1.65	IV 3 23.135	37 10.75	18.37	11.17	43 2.9	26 26 40.3
99	8.9	.	.	.	.	25.4	42.2	.	44 8.07	36.06	1.66	V 3 34.511	25 17.16	18.41	9.24	43 30.3	14 44.8
100	9.10	.	.	52.2	9.5	.	.	.	46 9.44	36.06	1.65	IV 2 21.388	38 58.99	18.63	11.47	45 31.7	28 29.1
101	9	.	.	.	.	53.	9.8	.	11 46 35.69	−36.06	−1.67	V 4 47.955	−11 4.62	−18.67	−6.98	11 46 58.0	−26 0 30.3

ZONE 245.　APRIL 5.　C.　$D_o = -37° 43' 50''$.

No.	Mag.	I.	II.	III.	IV.	V.	VI.	VII.	T.	a_1	a_2	MICROMETER.	i	d_1	d_2	Mean Right Ascension, 1850.0	Mean Declination, 1850.0
1	9	.	.	.	49.8	9.5	49.2	.	12 45 9.65	−38.32	.	IV 2 15.098	−45 29.40	−1.52	−22.22	.	−38 29 43.1
2	8	.	.	.	.	55.2	.	.	45 35.24	38.32	.	V 2 10.576	50 13.26	1.56	24.14	.	34 29.0
3	8	.	42.1	2.	21.2	.	.	.	50 21.40	38.30	.	IV 3 37.264	22 24.43	1.96	13.04	.	6 29.4
4	8.9	.	.	.	.	52.6	.	.	50 13.37	38.30	.	VI 2 17.416	43 4.51	1.95	21.25	.	27 17.7
5	8	.	.	.	.	51.8	.	.	51 12.68	38.30	.	VI 3 26.688	33 27.95	2.03	17.37	.	17 37.4
6	9.10	.	.	.	3.	22.8	42.6	.	53 3.13	38.29	.	IV 2 15.685	44 52.52	2.18	21.97	.	29 6.7
7	9	.	.	34.2	53.5	13.1	32.6	.	12 55 53.56	38.28	.	IV 3 34.279	25 31.71	2.42	14.25	.	9 38.4
8	9	46.2	6.3	25.3	14.9	4.5	.	.	13 3 25.47	38.26	.	IV 4 31.890	28 1.36	3.03	15.22	.	38 12 9.6
9	8	10.8	30.7	49.5	9.7	29.3	.	.	6 50.09	38.24	.	IV 4 51.513	7 21.04	3.31	7.34	.	37 51 21.7
10	9.10	15.5	35.5	55.7	14.5	34.2	.	.	8 55.00	38.24	.	IV 3 · 33 45.98	3.48	17.40	.	38 17 56.0	
11	8	22.7	42.3	2.1	21.5	41.1	.	.	14 2.00	38.22	.	IV 4 39.602	19 48.53	3.89	12.09	.	3 54.5
12	10	17.8	.	.	.	57.2	.	.	16 57.11	38.21	.	IV 2 38.495	21 1.70	4.12	12.54	.	38 5 8.4
13	10	59.2	19.2	.	.	.	.	.	21 38.74	38.19	.	III 1 46.478	12 36.51	4.50	9.33	.	37 56 40.3
14	8.9	.	.	17.2	36.3	.	.	.	22 36.52	38.18	.	IV 3 37.451	22 12.67	4.58	12.96	.	38 6 20.2
15	5	.	.	.	.	.	19.5	39.5	23 59.83	38.18	.	VI 2 7.446	53 29.70	4.61	25.40	.	37 49.9
16	8.9	.	.	.	1.5	21.1	10.5	59.2	25 20.80	38.17	.	IV 3 37.908	21 43.75	4.80	12.77	.	5 51.3
17	6	.	.	.	3.2	22.5	12.3	2.1	26 22.74	38.17	.	IV 3 36.658	23 2.31	4.88	13.29	.	6 10.5
18	9	.	.	.	.	50.2	10.2	.	26 30.90	38.17	.	V 4 43.851	15 59.97	4.89	10.63	.	0 5.5
19	8.9	.	.	.	46.2	5.5	25.5	.	29 46.12	38.15	.	IV 3 36.046	23 40.52	5.13	13.54	.	7 49.2
20	8.9	55.4	15.3	35.	.	.	.	.	33 34.88	38.14	.	IV 3 28.992	31 3.24	5.45	16.41	.	15 15.1
21	10	.	.	.	.	12.2	.	.	32 52.22	38.14	.	V 2 8.491	52 24.20	5.30	25.02	.	30 44.6
22	9.10	.	12.5	.	.	51.5	11.	.	35 32.04	38.13	.	IV 4 43.092	16 9.51	5.61	10.66	.	0 15.8
23	10	.	.	.	23.2	.	.	.	13 36 3.07	−38.13	.	V 4 42.293	−17 0.15	−5.64	−11.01	.	−38 1 6.8

CORRECTIONS.

Date.	Corr. of Clock.	Hourly rate.	m	n	c	Zenith Point.	Mic. Co.
						° ′ ″	r.
1849.	h.	s.	s.	s.	s.		
	s.	s.	s.	s.	s.		

REMARKS.

(244) 83. Time of transit over T. IV assumed as 37s.5 instead of 57s.5.
(244) 84. Minutes of transit assumed as 17s instead of 18s.
(244) 88. Minutes assumed as 27, not 26.
(245) 15. Minutes assumed as 22, not 23.

INSTRUMENT READINGS.

Date.		CIRCLE.							Barom.	THERMOM.				
		A.	B.	C.	D.	E.	F.	Mean.		At.	Ex.	U.	L.	I.
	1849. h. m.	° ′ ″						″	in.	°				
Zone 245	April 5, 12 40	97 2 {50.9 / 31.6}	{34.9 / 35.0}	{34.0 / 34.4}	{33.9 / 35.0}	{28.4 / 28.8}	{26.8 / 27.2}	31.74	30.174	54.	44.5	.	50.	53.2
	13 0	.	.	.	.	.	.	.	30.188	53.	44.0			
	13 20	.	.	.	.	.	.	.	.	.	44.			
	13 40	.	.	.	.	.	.	.	.	.	43.5			
	14 0	.	.	.	.	.	.	.	30.188	52.	42.			
	14 20	{31.7 / 31.9}	{36. / 35.9}	{31.9 / 35.2}	{35.0 / 36.0}	{29.2 / 29.2}	{26.4 / 27.2}	32.38	30.192	51.	41.2	58.5	50.7	48.5

ZONE 245.   APRIL 5.   C. $D_s = -37°\ 43'\ 50''$—Continued.

No.	Mag.	I	II	III	IV	V	VI	VII	T.	a_1	a_2	Micrometer			i	d_1	d_2	Mean Right Ascension 1850.0	Mean Declination 1850.0
									h. m. s.	s.	s.			r.	' "	"	"	h. m. s.	° ' "
24	9							40.5	13 37 20.53	−38.12		V.	2	9.045	−51 49.33	− 5.75	−24.80		− 38 36 9.9
25	10		43.2	3.2	22.8				40 3.11	38.11		IV.	5	53.715	5 4.51	5.96	6.45		37 49 6.9
26	10				19.3				41 19.17	38.10		IV.	4	48.495	10 30.48	6.06	8.52		37 54 35.6
27	8.9			13.5	33.2	52.9			42 13.52	38.09		IV.	3	23.646	36 38.69	6.14	18.66		38 20 53.5
28	9		44.2	3.7	23.4	42.7			44 3.78	38.09		IV.	5	50.489	8 26.51	6.27	7.73		37 52 30.5
29	8.9			52.	11.5				45 11.53	38.08		IV.	3	25.602	34 35.08	6.36	17.82		38 18 40.2
30	8.9	19.3	38.8	55.2	17.7				47 58.37	38.07		IV.	5	47.675	11 23.00	6.58	8.86		37 55 28.4
31	9		28.2	48.2					48 48.01	38.07		IV.	2	21.549	38 44.84	6.66	19.53		38 23 1.0
32	9						6.		49 26.67	38.06		VI.	2	9.285	51 34.59	6.70	24.69		35 56.0
33	10		22.8	42.5	2.				52 2.25	38.05		IV.	2	8.798	52 4.38	6.90	24.89		36 26.2
34	9				55.0	15.			52 55.01	38.05		IV.	2	13.572	47 5.17	6.97	22.87		31 25.0
35	10						12.2		13 53 33.12	38.05		VI.	3	29.659	30 21.27	7.01	16.14		14 24.4
36	9.10		45.2	5.2	24.5				14 2 24.72	38.00		IV.	2	16.413	44 7.04	7.70	21.69		28 26.2
37	10		5.5	44.8					5 44.90	37.98		IV.	2	13.554	47 6.30	7.96	22.92		31 27.2
38	9.10			32.5	52.	11.8			6 32.36	37.97		IV.	2	15.745	44 48.76	8.02	22.58		29 9.4
39	10			4.2					8 24.00	37.96		III.	2	13.492	47 9.69	8.17	22.04		31 30.8
40	9.10				37.2				8 37.13	37.96		IV.	2	13.302	47 22.17	8.19	23.01		31 43.4
41	9.10						16.5		8 37.18	37.96		VI.	2	10.000	50 49.63	8.19	24.40		35 12.2
42	8								10	37.95		VII.	3	32.862	26 59.80	8.34	14.83		38 11 13.0
43	8.9		36.3	56.2	15.8				13 15.74	37.94		IV.	4	43.932	15 16.67	8.54	10.34		37 59 25.6
44	10				52.5				13 52.36	37.93		IV.	4	45.666	13 27.90	8.59	9.64		37 57 36.1
45	10			27.8					15 47.49	37.92		III.	3	37.997	21 38.04	8.73	12.73		38 5 49.5
46	10			3.2					16 22.89	37.92		III.	3	37.577	22 4.45	8.78	12.90		6 16.1
47	10				31.3				16 31.15	37.92		IV.	3	41.251	18 14.15	8.79	11.42		38 2 24.4
48	9			27.5	47.1				17 47.10	37.91		IV.	4	47.081	11 59.10	8.88	9.06		37 56 7.1
49	9					42.2	1.7		18 22.60	37.91		V.	3	33.752	26 4.50	8.93	14.47		38 10 18.0
50	9			31.2	50.8	10.5			19 50.89	37.90		IV.	5	50.213	8 43.83	9.04	7.84		37 52 50.7
51	7					52.			14 22 32.38	−37.88		V.	3	32.109	−27 47.75	−9.23	−15.14		− 38 12 2.1

ZONE 246.   APRIL 10.   C. $D_u = -30°\ 12'\ 10''$.

No.	Mag.	I	II	III	IV	V	VI	VII	T.	a_1	a_2	Micrometer			i	d_1	d_2	Mean Right Ascension 1850.0	Mean Declination 1850.0
1	8			17.3	35.3	53.2	11.2		11 55 53.23	−30.60	−1.59	IV.	2	21.382	−38 55.37	− 3.09	− 7.80	11 55 21.04	− 30 51 16.3
2	8.9								56			V.	3	31.732	28 11.33	3.15	5.64	56	40 30.1
3	8				42.3	59.8			57 24.26	30.60	1.75	V.	5	50.076	8 52.56	3.23	1.88	56 51.91	21 7.7
4	9.10			55.2	12.7				11 59 12.87	30.60	1.50	IV.	3	28.681	31 22.76	3.42	6.27	58 40.77	43 42.4
5	8		49.2	25.5	43.4				12 0 25.37	30.60	1.51	IV.	3	37.671	21 58.69	3.50	4.40	11 59 53.26	34 16.6
6	9				8.2	26.			0 50.32	30.60	1.61	V.	5	56.692	6 8.28	3.53	1.35	12 0 18.11	18 23.2
7	10			23.5					2 5.55	30.59	1.34	V.	3	30.487	29 29.63	3.66	5.00	1 33.62	41 49.2
8	10			23.5					3 5.65	30.59	1.40	V.	4	43.913	15 18.24	3.75	3.15	2 33.66	27 35.1
9	8.9		4.2	22.1					5 40.17	30.59	1.24	III.	4	43.268	15 58.02	3.99	3.28	5 8.34	28 15.3
10	6				51.1	8.6	26.3		5 50.73	30.59	1.12	IV.	3	31.250	28 41.70	4.00	5.74	5 19.02	41 1.4
11	10				29.8				7 29.71	30.59	0.95	IV.	2	18.935	41 28.68	4.15	8.31	6 58.17	53 51.1
12	8			18.					12 8 17.89	−30.59	−0.93	IV.	2	21.302	−39 0.39	− 4.22	− 7.82	12 7 46.47	− 30 51 22.4

CORRECTIONS.

Date.	Corr. of Clock.	Hourly rate.	m	n	c	Zenith Point.	Mic. Co.
1849.	h. s.	s.	s.	s.	s.	° ' "	r.

INSTRUMENT READINGS.

Date.	Circle A.	B.	C.	D.	E.	F.	Mean.	Barom.	Thermom. At.	Ex.	U.	L.	I.
	1849. h. m.							in.	°	°	°	°	°
Zone 246	April 10, 11 50 89 32 32.1 / 33.1	31.1 / 31.2	34.2 / 34.2	31.1 / 32.1	24.8 / 25.9	25.3 / 25.9	29.84		60.6	60.	62.	60.5	
	12 10							29.822	61.	59.5			

REMARKS.

Zone 247. April 11. S. $D_0 = -39°\ 36'\ 30''$.

No.	Mag.	I.	II.	III.	IV.	V.	VI.	VII.	T.	a_1	a_2	Mic.	n	r	i	d_1	d_2	Mean Right Ascension, 1850.0	Mean Declination, 1850.0
									h. m. s.	s.	s.			r	′ ″	″	″	h. m. s.	° ′ ″
1	10		28.				48.5		9 37 8.40	−31.42	−0.70	II.	3	36.523	−23 10.15	−2.21	−12.71	9 36 36.3	−39 59 55.1
2	9						47.		38 6.59	31.42	0.84	·	2	8.583	52 18.49	2.32	27.21	37 34.3	40 29 18.0
3	9				38.				39 37.95	31.42	0.85	·	2	9.398	51 27.01	2.49	26.77	39 5.7	40 28 26.3
4	9				39.				40 38.85	31.42	0.69	·	5	39.218	20 13.89	2.62	11.36	40 6.7	39 56 57.8
5	8					22.	42.3		41 2.03	31.43	0.70	V.	4	36.928	22 36.59	2.66	12.50	40 29.9	39 59 21.8
6	10					31.	50.6		42 10.61	31.43	0.74	V.	3	27.302	32 49.45	2.80	17.39	41 38.4	40 9 39.6
7	10				37.				43 36.85	31.44	0.67	·	4	39.222	20 12.44	2.97	11.35	43 4.7	39 56 56.8
8	11						24.8		44 44.64	31.44	0.73	·	3	27.219	32 54.41	3.11	17.43	44 12.5	40 9 45.0
9	11			49.	9.				48 9.06	31.45	0.64	IV.	5	45.230	13 56.58	3.51	8.36	47 37.0	39 50 38.4
10	9		47.2		28.				49 27.75	31.46	0.70	IV.	3	33.280	26 34.39	3.66	14.33	48 55.6	40 3 22.4
11	9					10.8			49 50.83	31.46	0.61	·	5	51.946	6 55.05	3.71	5.09	49 18.8	39 43 33.8
12	6.7						7.		50 26.87	31.46	0.72	·	3	30.023	29 58.37	3.78	16.00	49 54.7	40 5 48.1
13	10			18.	39.				52 38.02	31.47	0.70	IV.	3	33.740	26 5.34	4.05	14.10	52 5.9	40 2 53.5
14	11			21.					54 41.27	31.47	0.63	·	4	44.472	14 42.41	4.30	8.74	54 9.2	39 51 25.5
15	10		24.	44.					57 4.32	31.48	0.63	III.	4	43.396	15 49.93	4.59	9.27	56 32.2	39 52 33.8
16	9.8		38.						58 18.57	31.48	0.74	·	2	22.112	38 8.14	4.75	20.06	57 46.3	40 15 3.0
17	9.8					45.	5.2		9 58 24.84	31.48	0.74	·	2	22.508	37 45.05	4.76	19.87	9 57 52.6	40 14 40.7
18	9		37.8	58.					10 1 18.22	31.49	0.66	III.	3	33.512	21 5.84	5.11	11.71	10 0 46.1	39 57 52.7
19	10			38.	58.				1 58.06	31.49	0.63	IV.	4	43.660	15 33.80	5.19	9.15	1 25.9	40 52 18.1
20	9			20.					3 40.29	31.50	0.59	·	5	51.122	7 46.27	5.40	5.48	3 8.2	39 44 27.2
21	11						49.		4 8.82	31.50	0.72	·	3	26.365	33 48.05	5.46	17.87	3 36.6	40 10 41.3
22	5.6				3.	23.2	43.		6 2.91	31.51	0.70	IV.	3	28.752	31 18.30	5.69	16.65	5 30.7	40 8 10.7
23	10			27.					10 47.26	31.52	0.63	·	4	42.688	16 34.17	6.26	9.60	10 15.1	39 53 20.0
24	8.9		31.5	52.					12 12.07	31.52	0.61	III.	4	46.442	12 38.77	6.45	7.76	11 39.9	49 23.0
25	8.9					45.5	5.8		12 25.61	31.52	0.58	V.	5	51.100	7 48.26	6.48	5.49	11 53.5	39 44 30.3
26	11			58.					15 18.32	31.53	0.76	·	2	16.792	43 42.47	6.84	22.87	14 46.0	40 20 42.2
27	11			11.2					16 31.44	31.53	0.72	·	2	23.578	36 36.99	7.00	19.29	15 59.2	40 13 33.3
28	7.6			0.	20.2				17 20.14	31.54	0.64	IV.	3	40.042	19 29.89	7.09	10.93	16 48.0	39 56 17.9
29	8				37.8				18 37.72	31.54	0.76	·	2	14.692	45 54.79	7.25	23.96	18 5.4	40 22 56.0
30	8.9			46.					21 6.34	31.55	0.76	·	2	14.152	46 28.22	7.55	24.24	20 34.0	23 30.0
31	8		44.2		4.2				24 24.58	31.55	0.70	III.	3	25.368	34 50.53	7.97	18.38	23 52.3	11 46.9
32	8			15.8					25 36.01	31.56	0.66	·	3	34.182	25 37.49	8.11	13.87	25 3.8	2 29.5
33	10				17.				26 16.84	31.56	0.65	·	3	36.172	23 32.87	8.20	12.87	25 44.6	0 23.9
34	9			35.8		15.8			28 55.77	31.57	0.72	III.	2	21.685	38 35.67	8.53	20.27	28 23.5	15 34.5
35	8.9		26.						32 6.65	31.57	0.75	·	2	15.052	45 30.91	8.93	23.77	31 34.3	40 22 33.6
36	8				40.2	0.5			32 40.25	31.57	0.61	IV.	3	42.689	16 43.79	8.99	9.63	32 8.1	39 53 32.4
37	9				3.2				34 3.05	31.57	0.63	·	3	38.780	20 49.03	9.18	11.56	33 30.8	57 39.8
38	10					22.			35 1.91	31.58	0.63	·	3	38.918	20 40.36	9.30	11.49	34 29.7	57 31.2
39	8					8.	27.8		35 47.80	31.58	0.61	V.	3	41.752	17 42.58	9.40	10.09	35 15.6	39 54 32.1
40	7.6		58.5	19.	39.		20.		39 39.23	31.58	0.69	IV.	3	26.002	34 10.83	9.89	18.05	39 7.0	40 11 8.8
41	9				39.				45 38.00	31.58	0.72	·	2	18.100	42 21.11	10.63	22.17	45 6.6	40 19 23.9
42	10						11.		46 30.88	31.59	0.58	·	4	45.289	13 52.25	10.74	8.32	45 58.7	39 50 41.3
43	8.9			24.5					49 44.84	31.59	0.74	·	2	13.652	46 59.52	11.15	24.57	49 12.5	40 24 5.2
44	8.9			24.					50 44.22	31.60	0.68	·	3	26.992	33 8.46	11.27	17.54	50 11.9	10 7.3
45	9.8				16.5	36.6			51 16.42	31.60	0.72	IV.	2	17.770	42 41.75	11.33	22.38	50 44.1	19 45.4
46	6.7		10.	30.2	50.5				55 50.50	31.60	0.69	IV.	2	19.045	41 21.85	11.89	21.67	55 18.2	18 25.4
47	9.10						51.		56 10.87	31.61	0.64	·	3	30.778	29 10.94	11.93	15.61	55 38.6	6 8.5
48	8.9						56.		10 57 15.73	31.61	0.69	·	2	19.455	40 56.75	12.06	21.44	10 56 43.4	18 0.2
49	8.9		50.2	10.8	31.				11 1 30.84	−31.61	−0.64	IV.	3	29.447	−30 34.88	−12.58	−16.27	11 0 58.6	−40 7 33.7

CORRECTIONS.

Date.	Corr. of Clock.	Hourly rate.	m	n	c	Zenith Point.	Mic. Co.
1849.	h.	s.	s.	s.	s.	° ′ ″	r.

REMARKS.

INSTRUMENT READINGS.

Date.	CIRCLE.							Barom.	THERMOM.				
	A.	B.	C.	D.	E.	F.	Mean.		At.	Ex.	U.	L.	I.
Zone 247 1849. April 11, 9 35	98 54 58.8	57.2	59.8	54.8	48.5	51.3	55.07	30.152	59.7	53.3			
10 0										52.7			
10 20								30.162	58.2	51.9			
10 40	58.8	57.2	60.1	54.8	48.3	50.4	54.93	30.162	58.2	50.7			
11 0										49.9			
11 20										49.2			
11 40	58.8	57.8	60.1	54.8	48.3	50.2	54.95	30.166	56.	48.7			
12 0										47.5			
12 20								30.164	55.	46.4			

ZONE 247. APRIL 11. S. $D_o = -39°\ 36'\ 30''$—Continued.

No.	Mag.	I.	II.	III.	IV.	V.	VI.	VII.	T.	a_1	a_2
									h. m. s.	s.	s.
50	10			25.	45.				11 4 45.08	−31.61	−0.53
51	10			59.					7 19.35	31.61	0.72
52	7		16.	36.2					8 56.51	31.61	0.67
53	7				34.2	54.5			9 34.15	31.61	0.66
54	9					41.	1.5		11 21.21	31.62	0.53
55	10		43.8						19 24.39	31.62	0.67
56	10					32.	52.5		20 12.10	31.62	0.61
57	10				38.2	58.8			22 38.32	31.62	0.63
58	5.4		11.8	32.					26 52.22	31.61	0.52
59	5			9.2	29.2		9.5		27 29.26	31.61	0.68
60	9.8		34.2	54.8					31 14.90	31.61	0.64
61	9.10				46.5	0.7			31 46.41	31.61	0.58
62	7.8		33.8						34 14.25	31.61	0.59
63	10				20.				34 19.84	31.61	0.53
64	6.7						11.5		34 31.32	31.61	0.63
65	10				18.				39 17.85	31.61	0.55
66	9						7.		38 26.88	31.61	0.53
67	10				37.				40 36.91	31.61	0.68
68	8.9				45.2				43 45.04	31.61	0.58
69	10			43.					43 3.19	31.61	0.61
70	8				33.	53.			44 32.91	31.61	0.53
71	8.9		2.	22.3					49 42.45	31.60	0.60
72	7.6			36.	56.2	16.5	37.		50 56.35	31.60	0.60
73	11		37.						58 17.44	31.59	0.55
74	10					54.			11 58 33.90	31.59	0.54
75	10		46.			26.			12 1 6.08	31.59	0.53
76	5.6						22.		1 41.66	31.59	0.66
77	8			27.		7.			3 47.01	31.59	0.55
78	10.9			18.					6 38.21	31.58	0.55
79	7.8				24.2	44.5			7 44.44	31.58	0.67
80	9.8		50.5	11.					9 31.15	31.57	0.60
81	8					40.	0.5		10 19.94	31.57	0.62
82	9				13.				12 12.84	31.57	0.54
83	9		56.8	17.					15 37.29	31.56	0.60
84	8		3.5		44.				15 43.91	31.56	0.60
85	8.9		49.	9.					17 29.33	31.55	0.49
86	7		48.5		29.				24 28.96	31.54	0.59
87	9		3.	23.					26 43.33	31.54	0.53
88	10				20.				27 19.92	31.53	0.63
89	3				14.2	34.4			28 14.10	31.53	0.58
90	8				45.	5.			29 44.88	31.53	0.52
91	9		45.3	5.8					32 25.88	31.52	0.50
92	10				46.3	6.5			32 46.33	31.52	0.46
93	7		12.	32.3					35 52.72	31.51	0.66
94	10		29.						41 9.56	31.50	0.50
95	7.6				40.5				41 40.35	31.50	0.50
96	10				59.5				44 59.34	31.49	0.52
97	8					10.			44 49.83	31.49	0.51
98	9		34.5						12 48 14.91	−31.48	−0.49

No.	MICROMETER.		r.	i	d_1	d_2	Mean Right Ascension, 1850.0.	Mean Declination, 1850.0.
			r.	′ ″	″	″	h. m. s.	° ′ ″
50	IV.	5	52.116	− 6 44.32	−12.97	− 5.00	11 4 12.9	− 39 43 32.3
51		2	12.138	48 34.54	13.29	25.37	6 47.0	40 25 43.2
52	III.+	3	22.956	37 21.66	13.46	19.66	8 24.2	14 24.8
53	IV.	3	25.038	35 11.30	13.56	18.55	9 1.9	40 12 13.4
54		5	50.682	8 20.73	13.77	5.66	10 49.1	39 45 10.2
55		2	20.670	39 37.96	14.74	20.84	18 52.1	40 16 43.5
56	V.	3	31.729	28 11.52	14.95	15.13	19 39.9	5 11.6
57		5	27.050	32 8.55	15.13	17.06	22 6.1	40 9 10.7
58		5	50.220	8 42.95	15.62	5.89	26 20.1	39 45 34.5
59	IV.	2	18.045	42 24.57	15.70	22.24	26 57.0	40 19 32.5
60		2	23.632	36 33.54	16.15	19.30	30 42.6	13 39.0
61	IV.	3	35.053	24 42.95	16.20	13.41	31 14.2	1 42.6
62		3	33.610	26 12.94	16.50	14.17	33 42.1	3 13.6
63		3	36.598	23 6.07	16.51	12.66	33 47.7	0 5.2
64		3	26.329	33 50.31	16.53	17.89	33 59.1	40 10 54.7
65		5	41.453	17 53.63	16.97	10.23	37 45.7	39 54 50.8
66		5	46.326	12 47.95	10.49	7.80	37 54.7	39 49 42.8
67		2	16.560	43 57.77	17.24	23.00	40 4.6	40 21 8.0
68		3	34.678	25 6.50	17.61	13.62	43 12.9	2 7.7
69		3	28.663	31 23.70	17.53	16.68	42 31.0	40 8 27.9
70	IV.	4	44.892	14 16.52	17.70	8.51	44 0.8	39 51 12.7
71		3	30.660	29 18.41	18.29	15.67	49 10.3	40 6 22.4
72	IV.	3	30.272	29 43.12	18.44	15.86	50 24.2	6 47.4
73		3	35.493	24 14.84	19.30	13.21	57 45.3	40 1 17.4
74		3	37.905	21 43.93	19.33	12.00	11 58 1.8	39 58 45.3
75	V.	3	39.662	19 53.81	19.61	11.11	12 0 34.0	39 56 54.5
76		2	14.082	46 33.63	19.68	24.34	1 9.4	40 23 47.6
77		3	30.038	29 57.62	19.92	15.98	3 14.8	7 3.5
78		3	34.816	24 57.58	20.25	13.56	6 6.1	2 1.4
79	IV.	2	19.429	40 57.87	20.38	21.47	7 12.2	18 9.7
80	III.	3	23.369	36 55.94	20.57	19.44	8 59.0	14 5.9
81	V.	2	19.408	40 59.56	20.67	21.48	9 47.8	18 11.7
82		3	36.387	23 19.31	20.87	12.67	11 40.7	0 23.0
83	III.	3	24.035	36 13.85	21.27	19.07	15 5.1	13 24.2
84	IV.	3	24.661	35 35.02	21.28	18.73	15 11.8	40 12 45.0
85		5	45.789	13 20.93	21.47	8.05	16 57.3	39 50 20.4
86	IV.	3	23.930	36 20.74	22.23	19.12	23 56.8	40 13 32.1
87	III.	3	36.736	22 57.10	22.47	12.60	26 11.3	0 2.2
88		2	15.352	45 13.59	22.54	23.66	26 47.8	22 29.8
89	IV.	3	25.666	34 30.65	22.63	18.22	27 42.0	40 11 41.5
90	IV.	4	37.432	22 4.77	22.80	12.24	29 12.8	39 59 9.8
91		4	40.518	18 50.40	23.08	10.70	31 53.9	55 54.3
92	IV.	5	47.760	11 17.60	23.12	7.11	32 14.3	39 48 17.8
93	III.	2	8.182	52 42.62	23.44	27.47	35 20.5	40 30 3.5
94		2	22.486	37 44.74	23.98	19.91	40 37.5	40 14 58.6
95		3	39.200	20 22.86	24.04	11.33	41 8.4	39 57 28.2
96		3	34.828	24 57.01	24.37	13.55	44 17.3	40 2 4.9
97		3	29.708	30 18.32	24.35	16.15	44 17.8	40 7 28.8
98		4	40.786	−18 32.06	−24.65	−10.60	12 47 42.9	− 39 55 37.9

CORRECTIONS.

Date.	Corr. of Clock.	Hourly rate.	m	n	t	Zenith Point.	Mic. Co.
1849.	h.	s.	s.	s.	s.	° ′ ″	r.

REMARKS.

(247) 61. Time of transit over T. V assumed as $0^s.7$ instead of $0^s.7$.

(247) 75. Transit over T. III assumed to have been recorded as over T. II.

INSTRUMENT READINGS.

Date.	A.	B.	C.	D.	E.	F.	Mean	Barom.	At.	Ex.	U.	L.	I.
	° ′ ″	″					″	in.	°	°			
Zone 247 1849 April 11, 12 40													
13 0								30.168	54.	46.5			
13 35	98 54 58.8	58.2	60.2	55.8	48.3	49.5	55.13			46.3			

ZONE 247. APRIL 11. S. $D_0 = -39° 36' 30''$—Continued.

No.	Mag.	I.	II.	III.	IV.	V.	VI.	VII.	T. (h. m. s.)	a_1	a_2	Mic.	n	r.	i	d_1	d_4	Mean Right Ascension, 1850.0	Mean Declination, 1850.0
99	8					34.7	5.		12 48 14.64	−31.48	−0.56	V.	3	26.348	−33 49.31	−24.68	−17.88	12 47	− 40 11 1.9
100	8		12.8	33.					50 53.26	31.47	0.56	III.	3	26.883	33 15.30	24.95	17.61	50 21.2	10 27.9
101	9				18.				51 17.85	31.47	0.56		3	26.630	33 31.49	24.97	17.73	50 45.8	10 44.2
102	8				10.8	31.			52 10.75	31.47	0.53	IV.	3	32.640	27 14.42	25.06	14.66	51 38.8	40 4 24.1
103	10							23.5	54 43.39	31.46	0.42		5	50.312	8 37.80	25.29	5.62	54 11.5	34 45 38.9
104	9				30.5				54 50.70	31.46	0.46		4	42.468	16 48.18	25.30	9.72	54 18.8	34 53 53.2
105	8					20.8			55 0.63	31.45	0.52		3	30.196	29 47.83	25.33	15.90	54 29.7	40 6 59.1
106	5.6					15.			55 54.87	31.45	0.50		3	34.302	23 30.27	25.41	13.81	55 22.9	2 30.5
107	8.7				53.5	13.			12 56 53.16	31.45	0.45	IV.	4	43.707	15 30.85	25.50	9.08	12 56 21.3	52 35.4
108	7		22.8	43.		3.		3.5	13 1 3.14	31.43	0.55	IV.	3	24.455	35 48.06	25.88	18.83	13 0 31.2	13 2.8
109	10		44.5						3 25.03	31.42	0.55		3	24.863	35 21.52	26.08	18.63	2 53.1	12 36.2
110	11				56.				3 55.87	31.42	0.55		3	23.772	36 30.65	26.13	19.19	3 23.9	40 13 46.0
111	10				53.				4 52.85	31.41	0.47		5	30.700	19 43.51	26.22	11.06	4 21.0	39 56 50.8
112	9					36.5			6 16.04	31.41	0.60		2	13.152	47 1.82	26.34	24.87	5 44.0	40 24 23.0
113	8				35.5				7 35.41	31.40	0.58		2	17.018	43 28.92	26.46	22.80	7 3.4	20 48.2
114	6					4.	24.		8 43.53	31.40	0.63	V.	2	8.655	52 13.66	26.55	27.24	8 11.5	29 37.4
115	6		17.						11 57.66	31.39	0.60		2	13.905	46 42.72	26.83	24.44	11 25.7	24 4.0
116	8			59.			59.5		12 19.28	31.38	0.52	III.	3	27.130	32 59.56	26.87	17.49	11 47.4	10 14.0
117	9		36.8	57.					19 17.36	31.36	0.57	III.	3	18.092	42 21.05	27.45	22.23	18 45.4	19 40.7
118	11.10				32.				22 31.90	31.35	0.57		2	17.880	12 34.72	27.70	22.33	21 0.0	40 19 54.6
119	11							18.5	23 38.38	31.34	0.45		4	39.360	20 3.79	27.78	11.24	23 6.6	39 57 12.8
120	9		17.5	38.					25 58.13	31.33	0.53	III.	3	24.782	35 27.10	27.95	18.66	25 26.3	39 12 43.7
121	9		41.	1.					27 21.35	31.32	0.51	III.	3	28.070	32 0.90	28.06	16.98	26 49.5	40 9 15.9
122	7		21.	41.5					29 1.58	31.31	0.50	III.	3	29.438	30 35.19	28.18	16.28	28 29.8	7 49.7
123	10		12.	32.5					13 30 52.61	−31.31	−0.61	III.	2	8.620	−52 15.10	−28.30	−17.27	13 30 20.9	− 40 29 40.7

ZONE 248. APRIL 12. C. $D_0 = -23° 56' 10''$.

No.	Mag.	I.	II.	III.	IV.	V.	VI.	VII.	T. (h. m. s.)	a_1	a_2	Mic.	n	r.	i	d_1	d_4	Mean Right Ascension, 1850.0	Mean Declination, 1850.0
1	10			59.8		33.5			9 41 16.63	−30.63	−2.08	IV.	3	20.416	−40 1.42	−2.89	−11.48	9 40 43.9	− 24 36 25.8
2	9			59.2	16.5	33.5			41 59.44	30.63	1.95	IV.	3	25.883	34 18.23	2.96	10.66	41 26.9	30 41.8
3	9.10					8.3	25.5		42 51.52	30.63	1.98	V.	3	24.974	35 15.31	3.05	10.77	42 18.9	31 39.1
4	9				30.3	46.8	4.4	21.5	47 47.25	30.65	2.24	IV.	2	11.485	49 16.12	3.57	12.86	47 14.4	45 42.5
5	8.9			19.8	36.9	54.1	11.2		49 53.99	30.66	1.76	IV.	3	34.121	25 41.51	3.75	9.36	49 21.6	22 4.6
6	9					36.5			50 19.44	30.66	2.05	V.	2	19.576	40 48.97	3.82	11.60	49 46.7	37 4.4
7	8				35.3	52.5		26.3	51 52.41	30.67	1.80	IV.	3	31.411	28 31.66	3.98	9.79	51 19.9	24 55.4
8	7.8			44.8	1.3	18.3	35.	52.2	9 57 18.35	30.68	1.97	IV.	3	21.363	39 2.03	4.53	11.35	56 45.7	24 35 27.9
9	7.8			51.5	8.6	25.2	42.		10 0 25.38	30.70	1.28	IV.	5	56.076	2 35.67	4.84	6.02	9 59 53.4	23 58 56.5
10	9					15.3	33.8		0 58.73	30.70	1.52	V.	3	43.589	15 47.42	4.90	7.92	10 0 26.5	24 2 10.2
11	9					53.5	10.5		1 36.68	30.70	1.54	V.	3	42.015	17 26.14	4.96	6.16	1 4.4	13 49.3
12	8.9					34.1	50.3		2 16.89	30.70	1.57	V.	3	40.726	18 47.03	5.03	6.35	1 44.6	15 10.4
13	9						6.3		2 32.56	30.70	1.65	VI.	3	36.604	23 5.70	5.05	8.98	2 0.2	19 29.7
14	10				47.9				5 47.79	30.71	1.46	IV.	4	45.223	13 55.83	5.38	7.66	5 15.6	10 18.9
15	9					28.1	45.2		6 11.32	30.71	1.71	V.	3	32.486	27 24.09	5.42	9.63	5 38.9	23 49.1
16	9			59.3	16.3				8 33.34	30.72	1.94	III.	2	20.501	39 50.07	5.66	11.47	6 0.7	36 17.2
17	10				40.2	57.2			8 57.16	30.73	1.94	IV.	3	20.681	39 44.62	5.70	11.45	8 24.5	36 11.8
18	9								8	30.72	1.53	VII.	4	41.216	18 8.25	5.7	8.23	8	14 32.2
19	9.10				33.	49.5	6.3		10 49.59	30.73	1.62	IV.	3	36.353	23 21.57	5.88	9.02	10 17.2	19 46.5
20	9.10			21.3	38.2	55.1			10 12 55.17	−30.74	−1.84	IV.	3	24.618	−35 37.71	−6.09	−10.84	10 12 22.6	− 24 32 4.6

CORRECTIONS.

Date.	Corr. of Clock.	Hourly rate.	m	n	ε	Zenith Point.	Mic. Co.
1849.	h.	s.	s.	s.	s.	° ′ ″	r.

INSTRUMENT READINGS.

	Date.		A.	B.	C.	D.	E.	F.	Mean.	Barom.	At.	Ex.	U.	L.	I.
			° ′						″	in.					
Zone 248	1849. April 12,	9 40	83 17 {31.9 / 32.5	30.8 / 31.1	34.3 / 34.9	31.6 / 32.8	25.3 / 26.9	24.5 / 25.9}	30.22	30.184	60.3	53.6	59.	60.5	59.
		10 0										52.9			
		10 20								30.186	59.	51.6			
		10 40										50.8		58.5	58.4
		10 50	{38.2 / 33.1	30.9 / 31.9	34.8 / 35.2	31.9 / 32.7	25.6 / 26.4	24.1 / 24.9}	30.31						
		11 0								30.182	58.5	50.2		59.	57.5
		11 50								30.172	57.5	48.8		59.	57.5

REMARKS.

(247) 99. Time of transit over T. VI assumed as 55s instead of 5s.

(247) 108. Transit over T. VII assumed to have been recorded as over T. VI.

Zone 248. April 12. C. $D_c = -23°\ 56'\ 10''$—Continued.

No.	Mag.	I.	II.	III.	IV.	V.	VI.	VII.	T. (h. m. s.)	a_1 (s.)	a_3 (s.)	Micr.	r. (r.)	i (′ ″)	d_1 (″)	d_2 (″)	Mean R.A. 1850.0 (h. m. s.)	Mean Decl. 1850.0 (° ′ ″)
21	9.10				14.2		48.2		10 13 14.27	−30.74	−1.76	IV. 3	27.637	−32 15.65	6.12	11.33	10 12 41.8	−24 28 43.0
22	7		19.3	35.2	52.2	9.2	25.9		14 52.19	30.74	1.92	IV. 3	19.902	40 33.41	6.29	11.56	14 19.5	37 1.3
23	8.9		22.3	39.2	56.5				17 56.39	30.75	2.11	IV. 2	8.971	51 53.59	6.59	13.25	17 23.5	48 23.4
24	9						52.5		18 18.74	30.75	1.44	VI. 4	43.063	16 12.03	6.63	8.00	17 46.6	12 36.7
25	10				6.8				23 6.68	30.77	1.52	IV. 3	37.576	22 4.64	7.11	8.33	22 34.4	18 30.6
26	10					4.0			23 48.06	30.77	1.90	V. 4	48.758	10 14.22	7.18	7.12	23 16.0	6 38.5
27	9.10						49.7		24 15.28	30.77	1.69	VII. 3	29.315	30 42.98	7.23	10.09	23 42.8	27 10.3
28	10			4.3	20.3				26 20.73	30.78	1.58	IV. 3	33.872	25 57.00	7.42	9.42	25 48.4	22 23.8
29	10		41.0	57.8	14.8				28 14.82	30.78	1.52	IV. 3	36.878	22 48.35	7.61	8.94	27 42.5	19 14.9
30	10				34.5				33 34.37	30.79	1.54	IV. 3	34.611	25 10.76	8.14	9.28	33 2.0	21 38.2
31	9		6.2	23.4	40.2		13.4		35 40.09	30.80	1.28	IV. 4	46.359	13 47.35	6.34	7.48	35 8.0	10 13.2
32	9.10				59.1	16.0			36 59.04	30.81	1.45	IV. 3	38.075	21 33.39	8.47	8.70	36 26.8	18 0.6
33	7.8		20.4	37.2	54.0	11.1	27.7		38 54.11	30.81	1.37	IV. 4	41.532	17 47.49	8.66	8.23	38 21.9	14 14.4
34	8.9			51.2	8.2	25.3			41 8.19	30.81	1.92	IV. 2	12.663	48 2.12	8.86	12.71	40 35.5	44 33.7
35	7						53.2		10 56 19.35	30.85	1.88	VI. 2	11.281	49 29.61	10.25	12.92	10 55 46.6	46 2.8
36	8		43.5	0.4	17.2	34.2	51.2		11 3 17.32	30.86	1.86	IV. 2	9.923	50 53.83	10.86	13.12	11 2 44.6	47 27.8
37	7.8			7.3	25.0				48 24.65	30.91	0.78	IV. 5	53.962	4 48.32	14.45	6.31	48 53.0	1 19.1
38	8						24.1		48 50.32	30.91	0.86	VI. 4	50.279	8 39.25	14.48	6.89	49 18.6	5 10.6
39	9						29.5		48 55.70	30.91	1.46	VI. 2	18.525	41 55.21	14.57	11.79	49 23.3	38 31.6
40	10			14.5	31.5		5.3		56 31.50	30.91	0.78	IV. 5	51.665	7 12.56	15.14	6.66	56 59.8	3 44.4
41	10				14.5				11 59 14.44	30.91	1.46	IV. 2	15.917	44 37.91	15.26	12.23	11 59 42.1	41 15.4
42	8		42.8	59.3	16.3	33.5	50.2		12 3 16.49	30.91	0.80	IV. 5	48.317	10 42.83	15.55	7.15	12 2 44.8	7 15.5
43	10				32.3		6.3		6 32.37	30.91	1.23	IV. 3	26.025	34 9.38	15.79	10.65	6 0.2	30 45.8
44	9.10			32.4	49.3	6.5			12 49.36	30.91	1.15	IV. 2	13.600	47 3.42	16.22	12.60	12 17.0	43 42.2
45	10			48.4	5.1	21.7			15 5.05	30.91	1.01	IV. 3	34.772	25 0.53	16.38	9.23	14 33.1	21 36.1
46	8					0.2			15 43.39	30.91	0.66	V. 5	53.091	5 43.30	16.42	6.44	15 11.8	2 16.2
47	7					22.0			16 5.20	30.91	0.62	V. 5	54.967	3 45.48	16.45	6.13	15 33.7	0 18.1
48	8.9						35.2		17 4.47	30.91	1.03	VI. 3	33.912	25 54.48	16.52	9.36	16 32.5	22 30.4
49	10					42.8			18 25.65	30.91	1.43	V. 2	13.125	47 33.58	16.60	12.67	17 53.3	44 12.9
50	10						35.5		19 4.76	30.91	0.95	VI. 4	37.105	22 25.73	16.65	8.89	18 32.9	19 1.3
51	10				32.5	49.5			20 32.45	30.91	1.14	IV. 3	27.163	32 58.11	16.74	10.47	20 0.4	29 35.3
52	10				21.0				22 20.87	30.91	1.11	IV. 3	28.154	31 55.95	16.86	10.32	21 48.5	28 33.1
53	10					58.2			22 41.26	30.91	1.06	V. 3	31.196	30 50.64	16.88	9.62	22 9.3	27 27.3
54	10			43.1		16.4			24 59.69	30.91	1.47	IV. 2	9.212	51 38.60	17.03	13.26	24 27.3	48 19.9
55	9				57.4	14.2	31.1		25 57.30	30.91	1.03	IV. 3	31.475	28 27.58	17.09	9.78	25 25.4	25 4.4
56	10			25.2	42.0				29 42.02	30.90	0.98	IV. 3	33.100	26 45.56	17.33	9.54	29 10.1	23 22.4
57	9						23.0		29 49.21	30.90	0.62	VI. 5	51.600	7 17.08	17.34	6.65	29 17.7	3 51.1
58	10				11.5	28.3			31 11.32	30.90	1.27	IV. 2	17.629	42 50.65	17.42	11.99	30 39.2	39 30.0
59	9.10		29.5	46.3	3.2		36.5		34 3.16	30.90	0.71	IV. 4	45.715	13 24.83	17.59	7.54	33 31.6	10 0.0
60	8		14.1	31.0	47.5	4.7	21.3		35 47.78	30.90	0.70	IV. 4	45.849	13 16.35	17.70	7.51	35 16.2	9 51.6
61	9				27.8		1.3		36 27.61	30.90	0.76	IV. 4	42.891	16 22.00	17.73	8.00	35 56.0	12 57.7
62	8.9		45.4		19.2		53.1		38 19.27	30.90	0.67	IV. 4	46.511	12 35.00	17.85	7.41	37 47.7	9 0.3
63	8		52.5	9.7	26.2				40 26.44	30.89	0.70	III. 4	44.272	14 55.01	17.97	7.75	39 54.8	11 30.7
64	7				26.7	43.5	0.7		40 26.83	30.89	0.53	IV. 5	53.537	5 15.19	17.97	6.36	39 55.4	−24 1 49.5
65	9.10						27.5		40 53.69	30.89	0.47	VI. 5	56.719	1 55.62	17.99	5.85	40 22.3	−23 58 29.5
66	9						32.3		41 58.57	30.89	1.00	VI. 3	28.388	31 41.33	18.05	10.29	41 26.7	−24 28 19.7
67	10				36.8	53.3			43 36.52	30.89	0.92	IV. 3	32.536	27 21.01	18.13	9.62	43 4.7	23 58.8
68	9		48.3	5.1	22.2	38.5	56.2		47 22.09	30.89	1.13	IV. 2	20.446	39 54.09	18.34	11.51	46 50.1	36 33.9
69	8						14.4		12 47 40.63	−30.89	−0.60	VI. 4	47.386	−11 40.83	−18.36	−7.28	12 47 9.1	−24 8 16.5

CORRECTIONS.

Date.	Corr. of Clock.	Hourly rate.	m	n	c	Zenith Point.	Mic. Co.
1849.	h.	s.	s.	s.	s.	° ′ ″	r.

INSTRUMENT READINGS.

Date.	CIRCLE A.	B.	C.	D.	E.	F.	Mean.	Barom. (In.)	Thermom. At.	Ex.	U.	L.	I.
Zone 248 — 1849 April 12, 12 0	83 17 {31.6 / 32.1}	31.3 / 32.0	34.9 / 35.	32. / 33.	25.9 / 26.6	24.3 / 24.5	30.31				48.5		
12 20											48.2		
12 45								30.160	56.5	47.3			
13 0											46.8		
13 20	{30.8 / 31.4}	31.5 / 31.9	34.7 / 34.8	32.6 / 33.3	25.5 / 26.4	24.2 / 24.5	30.13	30.154	55.7	47.2	56.	56.	
13 30											46.9		
13 53								30.144	55.1	46.3			

REMARKS.

(248) 21. Transit over T. VI assumed to have been recorded as over T. V.

(248) 31. Micrometer reading assumed as 45ʳ.359 instead of 46ʳ.359.

(248) 35. Clouds suspected.

(248) 36. Mist obscuring small stars, stopped.

(248) 37. Apparently clear; perhaps a little mist remaining.

ZONE 248. APRIL 12. C. $D_0 = -23° 56' 10''$—Continued.

No.	Mag.	I.	II.	III.	IV.	V.	VI.	VII.	T. (h. m. s.)	a_1 (s.)	a_2 (s.)	MICROMETER	r.	i (' '')	d_1 ('')	d_2 ('')	Mean Right Ascension, 1850.0 (h. m. s.)	Mean Declination, 1850.0 (° ' '')
70	8.9		14.2	30.8	47.3		21.5		12 50 47.74	−30.88	−0.83	IV. 3	35.343	−24 24.95	−18.53	−9.15	12 50 16.0	− 24 21 2.6
71	9.10		18.5		52.1				52 52.24	30.88	0.66	IV. 4	42.526	16 45.10	18.65	8.00	52 20.7	13 21.8
72	9.10			29.2		3.3			12 56 46.25	30.87	0.99	IV. 3	25.605	34 35.80	18.85	10.78	12 56 14.4	31 15.4
73	9.10			22.5	39.5	6.2			13 0 39.37	30.87	0.88	IV. 3	30.897	29 3.66	19.05	9.87	13 0 7.6	25 42.6
74	9.10				51.3				1 51.17	30.87	0.80	IV. 3	32.072	25 44.59	19.11	9.35	1 19.5	22 23.0
75	9			35.5	55.5	12.7	29.5		2 45.62	30.87	0.63	IV. 4	42.361	16 55.52	19.17	8.07	2 14.1	13 32.8
76	9.10		7.9	15.2	41.8	58.5			6 41.82	30.86	0.83	IV. 3	31.682	28 14.48	19.35	9.75	6 10.1	24 53.6
77	10				24.2				7 24.09	30.86	0.46	IV. 5	50.151	8 47.65	19.39	6.83	6 53.8	5 23.9
78	9		59.8		33.3	50.5	7.4		9 33.56	30.85	0.60	IV. 4	41.977	17 19.43	19.50	8.12	9 2.1	13 57.0
79	9				38.9	13.			10 39.00	30.85	1.16	IV. 2	13.789	46 51.38	19.55	12.61	10 7.0	43 33.6
80	10					36.5			11 19.55	30.85	0.83	V. 3	29.341	30 41.60	19.58	10.10	10 47.0	27 21.3
81	9.10						0.3		11 26.55	30.85	0.66	VI. 4	38.724	20 44.25	19.59	8.68	10 55.0	17 22.5
82	9		18.2	35.4	51.5	8.7	25.6		13 51.95	30.85	0.47	IV. 5	47.312	11 45.91	19.70	7.29	13 20.6	8 22.9
83	10		52.1				0.2		16 27.19	30.84	0.73	VI. 3	34.149	25 39.75	19.82	9.33	15 55.6	22 18.9
84	8.9			17.3	34.2	51.5	8.3		16 34.38	30.84	0.70	IV. 3	35.854	23 52.64	19.82	9.08	16 2.8	20 31.5
85	9						6.8		17 33.02	30.84	0.97	VI. 2	21.086	39 14.50	19.86	11.44	17 1.2	35 55.8
86	10						28.3		18 54.57	30.83	0.73	VI. 3	33.343	26 30.44	19.93	9.56	18 23.0	23 9.8
87	9.10					59.2			19 42.08	30.83	1.09	V. 2	15.056	45 32.41	19.96	12.38	19 10.2	42 14.7
88	8.9				44.4	1.2	17.9		20 44.23	30.83	0.78	IV. 3	30.765	29 11.94	20.01	9.88	20 12.6	25 51.8
89	10					21.8	35.2		25 21.40	30.82	1.12	IV. 2	11.794	48 56.50	20.20	12.92	24 49.5	45 39.6
90	10					49.5			26 32.44	30.82	0.94	V. 3	20.685	39 44.43	20.27	11.50	26 0.7	36 26.2
91	10					36.2			27 19.20	30.82	0.84	V. 3	25.051	35 10.54	20.30	10.82	26 47.5	31 51.7
92	8		41.8	59.2		32.5			31 15.88	30.81	0.53	IV. 2	39.915	19 29.96	20.48	8.43	30 44.5	16 8.9
93	7				7.3	24.2	41.5		52 7.41	30.75	0.44	IV. 4	39.064	19 44.58	21.33	8.46	51 36.2	16 24.4
94	9		53.3	10.	26.8	43.7			55 27.01	30.74	0.19	IV. 5	51.965	6 53.67	21.44	6.53	54 56.1	3 31.6
95	8		41.5	58.5	15.2	32.4	49.5		58 15.50	30.73	0.12	IV. 5	54.321	4 25.96	21.53	6.16	57 44.7	1 3.7
96	9			42.4		16.5			13 59 59.50	30.72	0.45	IV. 3	36.941	22 44.42	21.59	8.91	13 59 28.3	19 24.9
97	8		40.7	57.4	14.3	31.5			14 2 14.46	30.72	0.65	IV. 2	16.152	44 23.36	21.66	12.23	14 1 42.9	41 7.3
98	8				56.	13.3	29.8		2 56.05	30.71	0.76	IV. 2	20.665	39 40.22	21.67	11.50	2 24.6	36 23.4
99	9					54.2	11.5		3 37.51	30.71	0.59	V. 3	28.666	31 23.76	21.69	10.28	3 6.2	28 5.7
100	8				56.3	13.5			4 56.29	30.71	0.96	IV. 2	9.939	50 52.83	21.70	13.21	4 24.6	47 37.7
101	9.10		39.5	56.5	13.2				8 13.41	30.70	0.79	IV. 2	17.480	43 0.12	21.82	12.03	7 41.9	39 44.0
102	9				9.7	26.5	43.5		9 9.57	30.69	0.44	IV. 3	35.232	24 31.85	21.85	9.16	8 38.4	21 12.9
103	9		9.	25.9	42.8				12 42.85	30.68	0.49	IV. 3	32.128	27 46.56	21.92	9.68	12 11.7	24 28.2
104	6			30.1	46.2	3.5	20.4		16 46.64	30.67	0.14	IV. 5	48.527	10 29.66	22.02	7.09	16 15.8	7 8.8
105	9.10			21.1			11.4		19 37.89	30.66	0.19	IV. 3	45.198	13 57.40	22.08	7.59	19 7.0	10 37.1
106	9.10			37.	53.8	21.1			20 53.93	30.66	0.74	IV. 2	17.221	43 16.31	22.11	12.07	20 22.5	40 0.5
107	9		21.5		55.2		29.3		14 22 55.40	−30.65	−0.70	IV. 2	18.624	−41 48.24	−22.14	−11.81	14 22 24.0	− 24 38 32.2

CORRECTIONS.

Date.	Corr. of Clock.	Hourly rate.	m	n	c	Zenith Point.	Mic. Co.
	h.	s.	s.	s.	s.	° ' ''	r.
1849.							

INSTRUMENT READINGS.

Date.	CIRCLE.							Barom.	THERMOM.				
	A.	B.	C.	D.	E.	F.	Mean.		At.	Ex.	U.	L.	I.
	h. m.	° ' ''						''	in.	°	°	°	°	°
Zone 248	1849, April 12, 14 5										46.4			
	14 20	83 17 {31.1 31.5 34.9 33.4 25.1 24.3 / 31.5 31.7 34.9 34.1 25.7 24.5}						30.22	30.132	55.	46.3	59.	55.4	56.

REMARKS.

(248) 73. Time of transit over T. V assumed as 56s.2 instead of 6s.2.

(248) 75. Transits over T.'s III, IV, V, and VI assumed as 28s.5, 45s.5, 2s.7, and 19s.5, respectively, not 38s.5, 55s.5, 12s.7 and 29s.5.

(248) 89. Transit over T.'s IV and V assumed as recorded over T.'s V and VI.

(248) 106. Time of transit over T. V assumed as 11s.1 instead of 21s.1.

ZONE 249. APRIL 14. C. $D_s = -23°\ 56'\ 30''$.

No.	Mag.	I.	II.	III.	IV.	V.	VI.	VII.	T.	a_1	a_2	Micr.	r.	i	d_1	d_2	Mean Right Ascension, 1850.0	Mean Declination, 1850.0
									h. m. s.	s.	s.		r.	′ ″	″	″	h. m. s.	° ′ ″
1	10						45.3		10 31 11.54	−29.13	−0.72	VI. 4	42.005	−17 18.37	−2.29	−2.10	10 30 41.7	−24 13 52.8
2	10					0.2			32 43.31	29.13	0.72	V. 4	39.625	19 47.52	2.44	2.48	32 13.5	16 22.4
3	10					51.2	7.8		33 34.17	29.13	0.71	V. 3	34.702	25 5.04	2.52	3.26	33 4.3	21 40.8
4	8.9			23.1	30.5	56.4	13.4		35 39.68	29.14	0.78	IV. 4	45.498	13 38.58	1.55	1.55	35 9.8	10 12.9
5	8.9			41.3	58.3	15.4			36 56.33	29.14	0.77	IV. 3	38.194	21 25.99	2.86	2.70	36 28.4	18 1.6
6	9						1.5		37 27.72	29.15	0.72	VI. 2	21.350	38 58.07	2.90	5.37	36 57.8	35 36.3
7	10						52.5		38 18.76	29.15	0.79	VI. 3	37.088	22 35.33	2.08	2.88	37 48.8	19 11.2
8	8						27.5		38 53.74	29.15	0.82	VI. 4	41.655	17 40.20	3.04	2.16	38 23.8	14 15.4
9	8					24.3			40 7.15	29.15	0.74	V. 2	12.808	47 53.34	3.16	6.71	39 37.3	44 33.2
10	10			30.3	55.5				41 55.83	29.16	0.82	IV. 3	34.355	25 20.05	3.34	3.31	41 25.8	22 3.6
11	9.10		27.7	44.3		19.5			44 1.34	29.16	0.79	IV. 2	13.713	46 56.21	3.54	6.60	43 31.29	43 36.3
12	8.9			43.2	59.5	16.6	33.4		46 59.75	29.17	0.92	IV. 5	54.101	4 39.71	3.83	0.21	46 29.7	1 13.7
13	9.10					15.3	32.4		47 58.55	29.17	0.93	V. 5	54.668	4 4.31	3.93	0.12	47 28.4	0 38.4
14	9			16.5	33.7		7.7		49 33.69	29.18	0.84	IV. 2	9.462	50 20.25	4.08	7.10	49 3.7	47 1.4
15	10					56.4	13.5		50 39.59	29.18	0.91	V. 3	27.247	32 52.90	4.19	4.43	50 9.5	29 31.5
16	10					27.1	43.5		53 9.80	29.18	0.90	V. 2	13.752	46 54.14	4.42	6.59	52 39.7	43 35.1
17	7		46.2	3.5	20.8	37.3	54.4		56 20.46	29.19	0.94	IV. 2	11.403	49 21.26	4.70	6.97	55 50.3	46 2.9
18	10		13.2	30.3	47.5				10 58 47.31	29.20	1.05	IV. 4	43.282	15 57.64	4.94	1.90	10 58 17.1	13 34.5
19	7		43.5	0.7			51.5		11 3 17.68	29.21	0.97	IV. 2	9.991	50 40.63	5.38	7.19	11 2 47.5	47 32.2
20	10			56.3	12.5	29.4			9 12.69	29.22	0.99	IV. 3	26.064	34 7.00	5.92	4.62	8 42.5	30 47.5
21	8.9		35.7	52.7	9.2		43.3		12 9.50	29.23	0.99	IV. 3	32.221	27 40.78	6.18	3.65	11 39.3	24 20.6
22	9		20.2	36.7	54.2	10.7			13 53.92	29.23	0.98	IV. 4	30.442	29 32.45	6.33	3.93	13 23.7	26 12.7
23	9.10				28.1	45.2			14 28.15	29.23	1.00	IV. 4	41.575	17 44.72	6.38	2.17	13 57.9	14 23.3
24	8				23.4	40.2	56.9		15 23.23	29.23	0.98	IV. 3	34.112	25 42.07	6.46	3.35	14 53.0	22 21.9
25	9				26.3	43.2	0.2		16 26.15	29.23	0.93	IV. 2	12.533	48 10.34	6.56	0.79	15 56.0	44 53.7
26	10		59.7	16.3	33.5				19 33.45	29.24	0.96	IV. 3	31.476	28 27.52	6.83	3.76	19 3.2	25 8.1
27	9		54.						21 27.95	29.24	1.02	IV. 5	52.440	6 21.04	7.00	0.46	20 57.7	3 1.5
28	8			32.5	49.2	6.2	23.1		22 49.32	29.24	1.00	IV. 4	45.328	13 49.30	7.12	1.58	22 19.1	10 28.0
29	10			14.3		48.8			24 31.57	29.25	0.95	IV. 3	32.935	26 55.59	7.25	3.53	24 1.4	23 36.4
30	9.10		56.5		30.4	47.2			27 30.33	29.25	0.92	IV. 3	27.751	32 21.10	7.51	4.35	27 0.2	29 3.0
31	9				1.5		35.5	52.8	31 18.42	29.26	0.86	IV. 2	11.982	49 41.76	7.84	6.87	30 48.3	48 29.5
32	9.10						37.5	54.1	31 20.23	29.26	0.86	V. 2	10.316	50 20.81	7.84	7.15	31 50.2	47 14.8
33	8								32		0.97	VII. 5	51.698	7 10.86	8.0	0.57	32	3 49.4
34	10				44.	60.2			36 43.50	29.26	0.84	IV. 2	7.885	53 1.63	8.29	7.53	36 13.4	49 47.5
35	9					38.5			38 21.64	29.26	0.94	V. 4	45.202	13 57.53	8.42	1.60	37 51.4	10 37.5
36	9						16.5		38 42.75	29.26	0.91	VI. 4	40.493	18 53.44	8.46	2.50	38 12.6	15 34.4
37	8						40.5		39 6.71	29.26	0.95	VI. 5	53.228	5 34.96	8.49	0.32	38 36.5	2 13.8
38	8								39		0.93	VI. 4	47.328	11 44.47	8.5	1.26	39	8 24.3
39	9					53.2			40 36.13	29.27	0.84	V. 3	18.845	41 30.78	8.61	5.78	40 6.0	38 24.2
40	10						25.5		40 51.78	29.27	0.88	VI.	F.Wire.	29 50.13	8.64	4.00	40 21.63	26 41.8
41	8.9						0.2		41 26.45	29.27	0.90	VI. 4	41.021	18 20.17	8.67	2.26	40 56.3	15 1.1
42	10			48.3	5.2				45 5.19	29.27	0.88	IV. 4	37.423	22 5.33	8.97	2.83	44 35.0	18 47.1
43	10				0.5				46 0.42	29.27	0.82	IV. 2	18.275	42 10.27	9.04	5.87	45 30.3	38 55.2
44	8		6.5	24.2	41.				48 40.86	29.27	0.87	III. 3	37.882	21 45.19	9.25	2.75	48 10.7	18 27.2
45	8				50.2		23.8		48 50.05	29.27	0.91	IV. 4	50.555	8 21.17	9.26	0.75	48 19.9	5 1.2
46	8						58.5		48 24.70	29.27	0.92	VII. 5	54.061	4 42.57	9.23	0.20	47 54.5	1 22.0
47	10				37.2				51 37.08	29.28	0.87	IV. 4	41.972	17 19.68	9.49	2.09	51 6.9	14 1.2
48	10			47.2	3.2				53 3.61	29.28	0.83	IV. 3	30.301	29 41.12	9.59	3.95	52 33.5	26 24.7
49	10			20.2	37.2				11 54 37.16	−29.28	−0.85	IV. 4	42.348	−16 56.33	−9.72	−2.04	11 54 7.0	−24 13 38.1

CORRECTIONS.

Date.	Corr. of Clock.	Hourly rate.	m	n	ε	Zenith Point.	Mic. Co.
1849.	h.	s.	s.	s.	s.	° ′ ″	r.

REMARKS.

(249) 11. T. V assumed as 18ˢ.5, not 19ˢ.5.
(249) 14. Micrometer revolutions assumed as 10.462, not 9.462.

INSTRUMENT READINGS.

	Date.	CIRCLE.							Barom.	THERMOM.				
		A.	B.	C.	D.	E.	F.	Mean.		At.	Ex.	U.	L.	I.
	1849. h. m.	° ′ ″						″	in.	°	°	°	°	°
Zone 249	April 14, 10 30	83 17	32.9 / 32.7	35.1 / 34.6	36.3 / 36.2	36.2 / 36.5	26.1 / 26.5	26.3 / 26.6	32.17	30.070	46.5	33.1	48.5	47.5	48.8
	10 40											32.8			
	11 0									30.070	44.8	32.5			
	11 20											32.2			
	11 40									30.064	42.6	32.			
	12 0	32.6 / 32.1	36.5 / 35.8	39.1 / 35.7	37.1 / 37.3	27.1 / 27.5	25.1 / 25.4	32.86		30.060	42.2	31.8	48.	37.5	45.3

ZONE 249. APRIL 14. C. D_0 = −23° 56′ 30″ — Continued.

No.	Mag.	I.	II.	III.	IV.	V.	VI.	VII.	T.	a_1	a_2	MICROMETER		r	i	d_1	d_4	Mean Right Ascension, 1850.0	Mean Declination, 1850.0
									h. m. s.	s.	s.			r	′ ″	″	″	h. m. s.	° ′ ″
50	9.10			14.2	31.5				11 57 31.34	−29.28	−0.87	IV.	5	51.762	− 7 6.42	− 9.95	− 0.55	11 57 1.2	− 24 3 46.9
51	9.10			46.2	2.5				11 59 2.46	29.28	0.87	IV.	5	53.823	4 57.04	10.06	0.22	11 58 32.3	1 37.3
52	10			15.2					12 0 32.19	29.28	0.81	III.	3	34.204	25 36.17	10.18	3.33	12 0 2.1	22 19.7
53	10					52.5			0 35.51	29.28	0.79	V.	3	26.716	33 26.09	10.16	4.52	0 5.4	30 10.8
54	8				16.5	33.3			12 3 16.43	−29.28	−0.85	IV.	3	48.423	−10 36.18	−10.39	− 1.08	12 21 46.3	− 24 7 17.7

ZONE 250. APRIL 16. S. D_0 = −22° 43′ 40″.

No.	Mag.	I.	II.	III.	IV.	V.	VI.	VII.	T.	a_1	a_2	MICROMETER		r	i	d_1	d_4	Mean Right Ascension, 1850.0	Mean Declination, 1850.0
1	4.5			25.	42.	59.	15.5		9 52 41.00	−28.80	−3.10	.	3	29.840	−30 9.98	− 3.45	−10.03	9 52 10.1	− 23 14 3.5
2	7		45.	2.					55 18.76	28.82	3.18	.	4	35.200	21 16.01	3.69	8.74	54 46.8	23 5 8.4
3	9					35.			55 18.33	28.82	3.31	.	5	50.575	8 21.30	3.69	6.86	54 46.2	22 52 11.9
4	7		14.5						57 48.24	28.83	2.95	.	3	20.783	39 37.71	3.91	11.42	57 16.5	23 23 33.0
5	4.5					56.5			57 56.46	28.83	2.84	.	2	11.172	49 35.69	3.92	12.81	57 24.8	33 32.4
6	9						48.		58 14.56	28.83	3.00	.	3	26.388	33 46.80	3.95	10.55	57 42.7	17 41.3
7	8					31.			9 59 14.07	28.83	2.51	.	2	17.860	42 33.97	4.04	11.89	58 42.4	23 20 29.9
8	9					28.5			10 0 28.39	28.84	3.33	.	.	.808	5 6.29	4.15	6.66	9 59 56.22	22 48 57.1
9	7.6						43.		1 26.16	28.84	2.97		3	24.678	35 33.95	4.24	10.81	10 0 54.4	23 19 29.0
10	9					43.			2 42.87	28.85	3.06		3	32.653	27 13.61	4.35	9.60	2 11.0	11 7.6
11	9						29.5		3 12.74	28.85	3.08		3	34.555	25 14.40	4.40	9.31	2 40.8	9 8.1
12	10							11.5	3 38.05	28.85	3.18		3	43.103	16 9.55	4.43	8.01	3 6.0	0 2.0
13	9				31.				5 47.85	28.86	2.90		2	22.298	37 57.41	4.63	11.20	5 16.1	21 53.2
14	4		5.5	22.	39.				7 38.97	28.87	3.11		3	39.172	20 24.62	4.79	8.59	7 7.0	4 18.0
15	5		29.	46.					11 2.76	28.88	3.03		5	35.985	23 44.28	5.10	9.09	10 30.9	23 7 38.5
16	8					48.8			11 48.68	28.88	3.13		4	44.372	14 49.30	5.17	7.81	11 16.7	22 58 42.3
17	10			22.5					13 39.38	28.89	3.10		4	42.771	16 26.96	5.34	8.05	13 7.4	23 0 22.4
18	7						18.		14 1.33	28.89	3.17		5	49.734	9 13.96	5.37	6.99	13 29.3	22 53 6.3
19	6.5					56.8			14 56.68	28.89	3.12		4	45.618	13 30.98	5.45	7.62	14 24.7	22 57 24.5
20	7.6		53.	10.	27.				16 26.89	28.89	2.69		2	10.210	50 36.02	5.60	13.06	15 55.3	23 34 34.7
21	7		12.						20 45.68	28.91	3.04		3	42.035	17 14.60	5.98	8.17	20 13.7	1 8.8
22	9.8				59.5				21 16.34	28.91	2.97		3	37.150	22 31.32	6.03	8.91	20 44.5	6 26.3
23	8.9		16.						23 49.68	28.92	2.96		3	28.580	21 1.26	6.26	8.70	23 17.8	23 4 16.2
24	9			55.					24 11.89	28.92	3.04		3	45.372	13 45.98	6.30	7.66	23 39.9	22 57 39.9
25	7							3.5	24 30.02	28.92	2.74		2	19.770	40 36.09	6.32	11.57	25 58.4	23 24 34.9
26	3				7.5				27 24.39	28.93	3.02		4	44.724	14 26.46	6.58	7.75	26 52.4	22 58 20.8
27	7						54.5	11.	27 37.50	28.93	2.63		2	12.974	47 42.93	6.60	12.55	27 5.9	23 31 42.1
28	8			13.5					30 30.34	28.94	2.90		3	36.709	22 58.86	6.86	8.99	29 58.5	6 54.7
29	10			43.					31 59.81	28.95	2.78		3	28.298	31 46.78	7.00	10.27	31 28.1	23 5 44.0
30	9					3.			33 2.89	28.95	2.99		5	48.972	10 1.54	7.09	7.19	32 31.0	22 53 55.8
31	7							53.5	33 20.02	28.95	3.04		5	52.325	6 31.70	7.12	6.69	32 48.0	22 50 25.5
32	6		14.8	32.					37 48.65	28.97	2.78		3	31.952	27 57.34	7.51	9.71	37 16.9	23 11 54.6
33	8		5.2	22.					44 38.90	28.98	2.93		5	49.388	9 35.30	8.12	7.13	44 7.0	22 53 30.6
34	8				18.				45 17.96	28.99	2.46		2	10.340	50 27.92	8.18	12.95	44 46.5	23 34 29.1
35	8		27.8						47 1.58	28.99	2.47		2	12.649	48 1.86	8.34	12.60	46 30.1	32 2.8
36	10					7.			47 6.88	28.99	2.63		3	26.015	34 10.01	8.35	10.59	46 35.3	18 9.0
37	9		13.5						48 47.19	29.00	2.67		3	30.515	29 27.38	8.50	9.92	48 15.5	13 25.8
38	7			1.2					49 18.00	29.00	2.66		3	29.556	30 27.79	8.55	10.07	48 46.3	14 26.4
39	10			27.5					50 44.33	29.00	2.71		3	35.526	24 13.22	8.67	9.18	50 12.6	8 11.1
40	8						20.8		10 51 4.01	−29.00	−2.65		3	29.860	−30 8.79	− 8.71	−10.03	10 50 32.4	− 23 14 7.5

CORRECTIONS.

Date	Corr. of Clock	Hourly rate	m	n	c	Zenith Point	Mic. Co.
1849. h.	s.	s.	s.	s.	s.	° ′ ″	r.

INSTRUMENT READINGS.

Date	CIRCLE. A.	B.	C.	D.	E.	F.	Mean.	Barom.	THERMOM. At.	Ex.	U.	L.	I.
	° ′ ″						″	In.	°	°	°	°	°
Zone 250 — 1849. April 16, 9 50	82 4 61.2	61.2	66.	59.0	52.	52.2	58.60	29.838	48.	41.5	47.5	51.8	49.0
10 0										41.4			
10 20								29.848		40.8			
10 40								29.850	46.5	40.2			
11 0	61.2	61.2	66.	59.0	52.	51.6	58.50	29.858	46.2	40.			
11 20										39.5			
11 40	61.2	62.2	66.3	60.5	52.8	51.6	59.10			38.8			
12 0										38.5			
12 20								29.856	45.	37.3			

REMARKS.

(249) 51. Transit over T. III assumed as at 45ˢ.2, not 46ˢ.2.

(250) 8. Micrometer reading assumed as ˢ53ʳ.808.

(250) 26. Minutes of transit assumed as 26, not 27.

ZONE 250. APRIL 16. S. D₀ = −22° 43′ 40″—Continued.

No.	Mag.	I.	II.	III.	IV.	V.	VI.	VII.	T. (h m s)	n_1	n_2
41	7					6.	22.8		10 51 49.21	−29.00	−2.53
42	7		35.3		9.				56 8.93	29.01	2.65
43	9					53.5	10.		10 56 36.67	29.01	2.80
44	7.8		35.8	52.8					11 0 9.58	29.02	2.51
45	7.6				10.	27.			1 10.08	29.03	2.70
46	9			40.					5 56.88	29.04	2.69
47	10						34.		6 0.56	29.04	2.66
48	10.9			38.3					7 55.25	29.04	2.79
49	9		57.	14.	30.5				9 30.62	29.04	2.51
50	9			13.8					10 30.71	29.05	2.28
51	6.7		10.5	27.5					11 44.34	29.05	2.30
52	9.8				28.				12 11.26	29.05	2.59
53	7				25.7				13 25.59	29.05	2.70
54	7				33.				14 32.87	29.05	2.51
55	8					12.2			14 55.32	29.06	2.36
56	7					57.			15 40.32	29.06	2.69
57	6					47.			16 24.32	29.06	2.67
58	10		48.						19 21.68	29.06	2.65
59	9			8.					20 24.88	29.07	2.59
60	6		53.3		27.				21 26.93	29.07	2.57
61	9		54.5		27.8				24 28.00	29.07	2.23
62	8.7		17.8	34.5					25 51.42	29.07	2.48
63	8					20.	36.8		26 3.31	29.07	2.49
64	10					46.5			27 29.83	29.08	2.60
65	8					37.8	54.5		28 21.07	29.08	2.51
66	5				47.	4.			29 46.97	29.08	2.10
67	10			21.					31 37.88	29.08	2.49
68	8					20.	36.8		32 3.17	29.08	2.17
69	9		38.						34 11.78	29.09	2.12
70	10					35.			34 18.21	29.09	2.31
71	6.7					13.5	30.5		34 56.73	29.09	2.10
72	9			17.8					36 34.66	29.09	2.21
73	10		36.5						44 10.26	29.10	2.09
74	8					39.			44 22.29	29.10	2.39
75	10						19.		44 45.56	29.10	2.36
76	9		32.3	49.2					51 6.01	29.11	2.28
77	10						46.		51 12.49	29.11	2.01
78	9		39.5						53 13.18	29.11	2.30
79	10			49.					55 5.91	29.11	2.35
80	9						54.		55 20.59	29.11	2.15
81	9		20.8	37.8					57 54.56	29.11	2.09
82	10					55.5			58 38.81	29.12	2.31
83	6				51.3				11 59 51.18	29.12	2.31
84	5					43.2	60.		12 0 26.53	29.12	2.42
85	10		30.						7 3.69	29.12	2.08
86	10		39.2						8 12.88	29.12	2.24
87	10					53.			8 36.29	29.12	2.20
88	7			24.					10 40.82	29.12	2.07
89	9					39.			12 11 22.17	−29.12	−1.97

No.	MICROMETER		r.	t (′ ″)	d_1 (″)	d_2 (″)	Mean Right Ascension, 1850.0 (h m s)	Mean Declination, 1850.0 (° ′ ″)
41	VI.	2	20.479	−39 52.71	−8.77	−11.43	10 51 17.7	− 23 23 52.9
42	·	3	32.905	26 52.08	9.15	10.55	55 37.3	23 10 51.8
43	·	4	44.637	14 32.93	9.18	7.81	56 4.9	22 58 39.9
44	·	3	23.928	36 20.74	9.51	10.90	10 59 38.1	23 20 21.2
45	·	4	40.580	18 47.16	9.60	8.42	11 0 38.3	2 45.2
46	·	4	42.953	16 17.55	10.03	8.07	5 25.2	0 15.6
47	·	4	41.107	18 14.84	10.04	8.35	5 28.8	23 2 13.2
48	·	5	52.970	5 50.28	10.21	6.58	7 23.4	22 49 47.1
49	·	3	30.253	29 44.25	10.36	9.96	8 59.1	22 13 44.6
50	·	2	11.253	49 30.11	10.45	12.82	9 59.4	23 33 33.4
51	·	2	13.318	47 20.66	10.55	12.51	11 13.0	31 23.7
52	·	4	38.058	21 25.80	10.60	8.80	11 39.6	23 5 25.2
53	·	5	40.800	10 12.33	10.71	7.19	12 53.8	22 54 10.2
54	·	3	33.553	26 17.20	10.81	9.47	14 1.3	23 10 17.5
55	·	2	22.283	37 59.23	10.84	11.16	14 23.9	23 22 1.2
56	·	4	48.530	10 28.72	10.90	7.23	15 8.6	22 54 36.8
57	·	4	47.860	9 5.09	10.96	7.02	15 52.6	53 3.1
58	·	4	48.032	10 58.22	11.23	7.31	18 50.0	55 6.8
59	·	4	43.745	15 27.90	11.32	7.91	19 53.2	59 27.2
60	·	4	43.278	15 57.90	11.41	8.02	20 55.3	22 59 57.3
61	·	2	16.488	44 2.34	11.69	12.04	23 56.7	23 28 6.1
62	·	4	38.250	21 12.93	11.81	8.77	25 19.9	5 13.5
63	·	4	38.768	20 37.79	11.82	8.69	25 31.8	23 4 38.3
64	·	5	50.142	8 48.47	11.95	7.00	26 58.2	22 52 47.4
65	·	4	43.082	16 10.52	12.03	8.05	27 49.5	23 0 10.6
66	·	2	8.570	52 18.87	12.16	13.25	29 15.8	36 24.3
67	·	5	42.653	16 37.88	12.32	8.11	31 6.3	0 38.3
68	·	2	16.196	44 21.03	12.36	12.07	31 31.9	28 25.5
69	·	2	13.466	47 10.69	12.55	12.50	33 40.6	31 15.7
70	·	3	29.413	30 31.99	12.56	10.09	33 46.8	14 34.6
71	·	2	11.679	49 4.20	12.61	12.77	34 25.5	33 9.6
72	·	3	21.429	38 57.69	12.76	11.29	36 3.4	23 1.7
73	·	2	16.658	43 50.42	13.41	12.02	43 39.1	27 55.9
74	·	4	42.680	16 35.74	13.43	8.11	43 50.8	0 37.3
75	·	4	40.	19	13.	8.	44 14.1	3
76	·	4	38.370	21 5.41	14.01	8.76	50 34.6	5 8.2
77	·	2	14.638	45 58.94	14.02	12.32	50 41.4	30 5.3
78	·	4	42.402	16 51.69	14.19	8.15	52 41.8	23 0 54.0
79	·	5	47.520	11 32.49	14.35	7.37	54 34.4	22 55 34.2
80	·	3	30.708	29 15.58	14.37	9.00	54 49.3	23 13 19.9
81	·	3	27.383	32 44.18	14.59	10.38	57 23.4	23 16 49.2
82	·	5	46.472	12 38.89	14.65	7.54	58 7.4	22 56 41.1
83	·	5	47.228	11 51.19	14.75	7.41	59 19.8	55 53.4
84	·	3	56.000	2 48.36	14.80	6.12	11 59 55.0	22 46 49.3
85	·	3	31.516	28 24.57	15.33	9.77	12 6 32.5	23 12 29.7
86	·	5	46.190	12 55.46	15.44	7.56	7 41.5	22 56 58.5
87	·	4	42.869	16 23.82	15.47	8.08	8 5.0	23 0 27.4
88	·	3	33.232	26 37.21	15.63	9.51	10 9.6	10 42.4
89	·	3	26.419	−33 44.91	−15.69	−10.53	12 10 51.1	− 23 17 51.1

CORRECTIONS.

Date.	Corr. of Clock.	Hourly rate.	m	n	ε	Zenith Point.	Mic. Co.
1849. h.	s.	s.	s.	s.	s.	° ′ ″	r.

REMARKS.

(250) 57. Micrometer reading assumed as 49ʳ.860, not 47ʳ.860.

INSTRUMENT READINGS.

Date.	CIRCLE.							Barom.	THERMOM.				
	A.	B.	C.	D.	E.	F.	Mean.		At.	Ex.	U.	L.	I.
1849. h. m.	° ′ ″						″	In.	°	°	°	°	°
Zone 250 April 16, 12 40	82 4 61.0	63.2	66.3	61.0	52.8	51.6	59.32				35.9		
13 0								29.866	43.7	35.5			
13 20										34.3			
13 40								29.858	42.2	34.2			

ZONE 250. APRIL 16. S. $D_o = -22^\circ\ 43'\ 40''$—Continued.

SECONDS OF TRANSIT.

No.	Mag.	I.	II.	III.	IV.	V.	VI.	VII.
90	9			59.8				
91	6				10.			
92	8			33.				
93	9				31.5			
94	9					16.		
95	7					16,2		
96	6		24.8	41.8	59.			
97	7			59.5		33.		
98	8		30.					
99	9				12.5			
100	9				33.5			
101	7.6				23.2			
102	9				6.			
103	7						45.8	
104	8			1.8	18.2			
105	7			24.	40.3			
106	8				24.8	41.5		
107	8			56.				
108	7				52.			
109	9		41.	58.				
110	10		20.3		53.			
111	7.8			9.	25.2			
112	9						1.6	
113	8			0.5	17.5			
114	10		59.	16.5				
115	7						24.	
116	8		13.					
117	9						11.	
118	7							48.
119	7		45.2	2.				
120	8				27.	44.		
121	10						55.	
122	9			58.5				
123	9						58.	
124	6.7				51.		24.5	
125	9		47.3	59.				
126	8		28.5	45.3				
127	8				25.	42.		
128	6.7				31.	48.		
129	10				14.8			
130	9						8.3	
131	7.6				10.5			
132	9				6.8			
133	8						48.	4.8
134	9				25.8			
135	10					28.		
136	10		47.2		21.			

No.	Mag.	T. (h m s)	a_1	a_i	MICROMETER	r.	i	d_1	d_2	Mean Right Ascension, 1850.0 (h m s)	Mean Declination, 1850.0 (° ' ")
90	9	12 14 16.66	29.12	−1.89	3	21.279	−39 7.10	−15.91	−11.32	12 13 45.7	− 23 23 14.3
91	6	15 9.91	29.12	1.67	3	20.400	40 2.43	15.98	11.45	14 38.9	24 9.9
92	8	16 49.86	29.12	1.86	3	19.948	40 30.40	16.11	11.52	16 18.9	24 35.0
93	9	17 31.38	29.12	2.13	5	43.202	16 3.86	16.17	8.02	17 0.1	0 8.0
94	9	17 58.99	29.12	1.75	2	11.318	49 25.59	16.20	11.84	17 28.1	33 33.6
95	7	19 1.28	29.13	1.83	2	18.315	42 6.75	16.28	11.78	18 30.3	23 26 14.8
96	6	22 58.70	29.13	2.18	5	51.015	7 53.37	16.59	6.85	22 27.4	22 51 56.8
97	7	25 16.24	29.13	1.62	3	22.248	38 6.43	16.75	11.17	24 45.3	23 22 14.3
98	8	26 53.76	29.13	1.75	2	17.189	43 17.10	16.87	11.95	26 22.9	27 26.0
99	9	27 12.38	29.13	1.85	3	25.779	34 24.75	16.89	10.62	26 41.4	18 32.3
100	9	28 33.38	29.13	2.05	5	42.913	16 21.81	16.99	8.06	28 2.2	0 26.9
101	7.6	29 33.08	29.13	1.82	3	25.088	35 8.22	17.07	10.73	29 2.1	19 16.0
102	9	32 5.86	29.13	1.88	5	31.820	27 57.90	17.25	9.73	31 34.9	23 12 4.9
103	7	32 12.34	29.13	2.04	4	44.292	14 55.01	17.25	7.83	31 41.2	22 59 0.1
104	8	34 18.37	29.12	1.97	4	40.740	18 37.00	17.40	8.38	33 47.2	23 2 42.8
105	7	35 40.53	29.12	1.97	4	42.340	16 56.90	17.49	8.15	35 9.4	1 2.5
106	8	36 24.64	29.12	1.68	2	16.960	43 37.55	17.55	12.00	35 53.8	27 42.1
107	8	42 12.91	29.12	1.54	2	9.489	51 20.74	17.95	13.13	41 42.3	35 31.8
108	7	42 51.91	29.12	1.62	3	20.930	39 28.93	18.00	11.37	42 21.2	23 38.3
109	9	45 14.81	29.12	1.58	2	18.812	41 35.82	18.15	11.71	44 44.1	23 25 45.7
110	10	47 53.43	29.12	1.97	5	49.792	9 10.06	18.33	7.03	47 22.3	22 53 15.4
111	7.8	52 42.36	29.12	1.79	4	37.540	21 57.43	18.65	8.90	52 11.5	23 6 5.0
112	9	52 44.77	29.12	1.65	3	25.960	34 13.46	18.65	10.60	52 14.0	18 22.7
113	8	55 34.27	29.11	1.61	3	24.050	36 13.16	18.84	10.88	55 3.5	23 20 22.9
114	10	12 58 33.06	29.11	1.91	5	51.706	7 9.62	19.03	6.73	12 58 2.0	22 51 15.4
115	7	13 1 7.28	29.11	1.77	4	42.323	16 58.27	19.21	8.13	13 0 36.4	23 1 5.6
116	8	2 46.68	29.11	1.74	4	39.933	19 26.44	19.31	8.49	2 15.8	3 34.2
117	9	2 54.25	29.11	1.69	3	36.372	23 20.44	19.31	9.04	2 23.4	7 28.8
118	7	3 14.53	29.11	1.52	2	21.863	38 25.63	19.33	11.26	2 43.9	22 36.2
119	7	7 18.87	29.10	1.71	4	40.202	19 10.37	19.57	8.45	6 48.1	3 18.4
120	8	7 43.83	29.10	1.60	3	31.816	28 6.00	19.59	9.73	7 13.1	12 15.3
121	10	8 21.53	29.10	1.48	2	21.752	38 32.66	19.63	11.26	7 51.0	22 43.5
122	9	10 15.40	29.10	1.36	2	13.276	47 23.30	19.74	12.58	9 44.9	31 35.6
123	9	10 24.54	29.10	1.46	3	22.538	37 48.25	19.75	11.15	9 54.0	23 21 59.2
124	6.7	13 7.84	29.10	1.72	4	44.978	14 11.11	19.90	7.73	12 37.0	22 58 18.7
125	9	15 15.95	29.09	1.76	5	50.312	8 37.30	20.01	6.92	14 45.1	22 52 44.2
126	8	19 2.23	29.09	1.31	2	14.340	46 16.56	20.22	12.39	18 31.8	23 30 29.2
127	8	19 24.99	29.09	1.31	2	14.472	46 8.79	20.24	12.37	18 54.6	23 30 19.4
128	6.7	22 47.90	29.08	1.71	5	50.766	8 8.94	20.39	6.85	22 17.1	22 52 16.2
129	10	24 31.66	29.08	1.57	3	39.499	20 3.97	20.47	8.56	24 1.0	23 4 13.0
130	9	25 34.77	29.08	1.26	2	13.472	47 12.20	20.52	12.56	25 4.4	23 31 25.3
131	7.6	29 27.44	29.07	1.67	5	52.248	6 35.72	20.69	6.62	28 56.7	22 50 43.0
132	9	30 6.69	29.07	1.32	2	22.692	37 33.00	20.72	11.14	29 36.3	23 21 44.9
133	8	30 31.32	29.07	1.62	4	47.655	11 23.51	20.74	7.32	30 0.6	22 55 31.6
134	9	32 25.74	29.07	1.20	2	14.712	45 53.54	20.80	12.35	31 55.5	23 30 6.7
135	10	35 11.05	29.06	1.20	2	16.598	43 55.76	20.90	12.06	34 40.8	28 8.7
136	10	13 38 20.94	−29.06	−1.21	2	17.670	−42 48.08	−21.01	−11.91	13 37 50.7	− 23 27 1.0

CORRECTIONS.

Date.	Corr. of Clock.	Hourly rate.	m	n	c	Zenith Point.	Mic. Co.
1849.	h.	s.	s.	s.	s.	° ' "	r.

INSTRUMENT READINGS.

Date.	CIRCLE.							Barom.	THERMOM.				
	A.	B.	C.	D.	E.	F.	Mean.		At.	Ex.	U.	L.	I.
1849. h. m.	° ' "						"	in.	°	°	°	°	°

REMARKS.

ZONE 251. APRIL 20. S. $D_0 = -24° 34' 0''$.

No.	Mag.	I.	II.	III.	IV.	V.	VI.	VII.
1	8			16.	33.			
2	9		22.8	39.				
3	10			4.				
4	7			49.5				
5	7					32.8		
6	6			39.				
7	5				19.9			
8	7.6					12.5		
9	10		48.					
10	10					51.		
11	7.8		5.	23.				
12	6		5.6					
13	8				7.			
14	7					45.2		
15	6						43.	
16	8						33.	
17	6.7			30.				
18	7			55.				
19	9			54.5				
20	8		0.5	17.3			8.8	
21	10					2.		
22	9						54.8	
23	8					42.		
24	10		34.6					
25	7			37.3				
26	9				42.3			
27	5					39.5		
28	9						54.	
29	4				7.5			
30	7					6.		
31	6						38.	
32	10						9.5	
33	10						37.	
34	9				35.			
35	10					33.		
36	8				17.			
37	9					53.		
38	8		26.					
39	10			46.8				7.
40	10			46.8				
41	9.8				41.6			
42	9		43.					
43	10				33.5			
44	9		28.					
45	6					16.8		
46	8					55.5		
47	·					48.8		
48	8						22.5	
49	10		31.8					

No.	T.	a_1	a_2	MICROMETER (r)	i	d_1	d_2	Mean Right Ascension, 1850.0.	Mean Declination, 1850.0.
	h. m. s.	s.	s.	r.	' "	"	"	h. m. s.	° ' "
1	10 49 33.01	−27.99	−2.20	· 5 46.203	−12 51.13	− 0.25	− 7.41	10 49 2.8	− 24 46 58.8
2	51 56.60	28.00	2.24	· 2 16.163	44 22.09	0.46	12.23	51 26.4	25 18 34.8
3	52 21.10	28.00	2.23	· 2 20.992	39 19.14	0.51	11.45	51 50.9	13 31.3
4	54 49.36	28.00	2.22	·· 3 31.090	28 51.49	0.67	9.83	53 19.1	25 3 2.0
5	53 58.89	28.00	2.21	· 4 38.895	20 33.46	0.66	8.57	53 28.6	24 54 42.7
6	55 56.05	28.01	2.22	· 3 29.300	30 43.92	0.84	10.11	55 25.8	25 4 54.9
7	56 19.78	28.01	2.20	· 5 47.090	11 59.78	0.87	7.27	55 49.6	24 46 7.9
8	10 56 55.53	28.01	2.21	· 4 42.300	16 59.71	0.93	8.04	56 25.3	24 51 8.7
9	11 0 22.25	28.02	2.23	· 2 17.960	42 28.64	1.26	11.93	10 59 52.0	25 16 41.8
10	0 33.94	28.02	2.22	· 3 28.128	31 57.58	1.28	10.30	11 0 3.7	6 9.2
11	2 39.65	28.02	2.23	· 3 23.956	36 18.98	1.47	10.97	2 9.4	10 31.4
12	3 39.82	28.03	2.23	· 3 23.689	36 35.49	1.56	11.03	3 9.5	25 10 48.1
13	4 6.87	28.03	2.22	· 4 35.590	24 0.29	1.60	9.10	3 36.6	24 58 11.0
14	4 28.13	28.03	2.22	· 3 27.692	32 24.87	1.63	10.37	3 57.9	25 6 36.9
15	5 9.00	28.03	2.23	· 2 15.613	44 57.79	1.69	12.32	4 38.7	25 19 11.8
16	5 59.10	28.03	2.22	· 3 35.478	24 16.41	1.77	9.12	5 28.9	24 58 27.3
17	7 47.10	28.04	2.23	· 2 19.162	41 14.00	1.93	11.75	7 16.8	25 15 27.7
18	10 12.13	28.04	2.23	· 2 15.992	44 32.76	2.15	12.26	9 41.9	18 47.2
19	11 11.59	28.04	2.23	· 3 21.818	38 33.04	2.23	11.32	10 41.3	12 46.6
20	13 34.67	28.05	2.24	· 2 14.820	45 46.71	2.44	12.45	13 4.4	25 20 1.6
21	14 45.07	28.05	2.20	· 5 47.102	11 59.22	2.53	7.26	14 14.8	24 46 9.0
22	15 20.86	28.05	2.20	· 5 47.963	11 5.24	2.59	7.12	14 50.6	45 14.9
23	16 25.07	28.05	2.20	· 5 48.250	10 47.29	2.68	7.08	15 54.8	24 44 57.0
24	18 8.89	28.06	2.23	· 2 11.532	49 11.98	2.83	12.99	17 38.6	25 23 27.8
25	18 54.39	28.06	2.22	· 3 22.286	38 3.93	2.89	11.24	18 24.1	25 12 18.1
26	19 25.80	28.06	2.20	c 4 37.870	21 37.09	2.96	8.74	18 55.54	24 55 48.8
27	20 22.47	28.06	2.21	· 3 31.932	27 58.78	3.02	9.69	19 52.2	25 2 11.5
28	21 20.09	28.06	2.20	· 4 38.378	21 9.29	3.10	8.67	20 49.8	24 55 21.1
29	23 24.58	28.07	2.20	· 3 35.629	24 6.70	3.27	9.10	22 54.3	58 19.1
30	23 49.02	28.07	2.20	· 4 40.063	19 19.98	3.31	8.39	23 18.7	24 53 31.7
31	24 4.11	28.07	2.21	· 3 29.850	30 9.35	3.33	10.02	23 33.8	25 4 22.7
32	26 35.60	28.07	2.21	· 3 34.870	24 54.38	3.54	9.22	26 5.3	24 50 7.1
33	28 3.06	28.08	2.19	· 4 48.360	10 39.69	3.66	7.07	27 32.8	44 50.4
34	29 18.01	28.08	2.20	· 3 38.642	20 57.88	3.77	8.62	28 47.7	24 55 10.3
35	29 58.99	28.08	2.23	· 2 14.089	46 33.37	3.83	12.57	29 28.7	25 20 49.9
36	31 16.89	28.08	2.19	· 5 47.703	11 21.25	3.93	7.17	30 46.6	24 45 32.4
37	31 19.07	28.08	2.19	· 5 46.182	12 57.15	3.95	7.41	30 48.8	24 47 8.5
38	34 0.30	28.09	2.23	· 3 10.632	50 8.36	4.16	13.13	33 30.0	25 24 25.6
39	33 49.84	28.09	2.22	· 3 20.623	39 48.38	4.14	11.51	33 19.5	.25 14 4.0
40	36 20.96	28.09	2.19	· 5 49.898	9 2.54	4.35	6.81	35 50.7	24 43 13.7
41	36 41.68	28.09	2.20	· 4 43.580	15 38.89	4.39	7.83	36 11.4	24 49 51.1
42	38 17.30	28.09	2.23	· 3 10.808	49 57.20	4.51	13.11	37 47.0	25 24 14.8
43	38 16.37	28.09	2.22	· 3 23.359	36 56.88	4.51	11.08	37 46.1	11 12.5
44	40 2.21	28.09	2.20	· 3 25.348	34 51.54	4.65	10.75	39 31.9	9 6.9
45	40 16.67	28.10	2.20	· 3 26.730	33 25.15	4.67	10.52	39 46.4	7 40.3
46	40 38.41	28.10	2.20	· 3 25.959	34 13.52	4.72	10.65	40 8.1	8 28.9
47	41 31.76	28.10	2.20	· F.wire	29 59.13	4.77	10.00	41 1.5	4 13.9
48	41 48.55	28.10	2.21	· 2 21.672	38 37.74	4.79	11.35	41 18.2	25 12 53.9
49	11 46 5.97	−28.10	−2.19	· 3 41.056	−18 25.82	− 5.13	− 8.23	11 45 35.7	− 24 52 39.2

CORRECTIONS.

Date.	Corr. of Clock.	Hourly rate.	m	n	c	Zenith Point.	Mic. Co.
1849.	h.	s.	s.	s.	s.	° ' "	r.

INSTRUMENT READINGS.

Date.	A.	B.	C.	D.	E.	F.	Mean.	Barom.	At.	Ex.	U.	L.	I.
	° ' "						"	in.	°	'	°	'	°
Zone 251 1849 April 20, 11 0								30.018	50.	43.8	50.	48.2	50.
11 20										43.9			
11 45	83 54 60.	59.8	66.9	57.0	53.2	50.	57.82			42.			
12 0								30.028	49.	41.8			
12 20	60.	60.	66.9	57.0	53.2	50.	57.85			40.8			
12 40										59.3			
13 0								30.050	47.5	39.3		43.5	47.5

REMARKS.

(251) 3. Right ascension 1ᵐ different from Arg. Z. 288, 123.

(251) 4. Transit over T. IV assumed as recorded over T. III, and minutes as 53, not 54.

(251) 12. Right ascension differs 3ˢ from Arg. Z. 281, 115; 293, 7, and Mer. Cir. Z., April 11, 1849. Transit over T. II probably 8ˢ.6.

(251) 26. Transit over T. V assumed as recorded over T. IV.

Ex. therm. assumed as 42.9.

ZONE 251. APRIL 20. S. $D_0 = -24°\ 34'\ 0''$—Continued.

No.	Mag.	I.	II.	III.	IV.	V.	VI.	VII.	T.	a_1	a_2	Mic.	No.	r.	i	d_1	d_2	Mean Right Ascension, 1850.0	Mean Declination, 1850.0
									h. m. s.	s.	s.			r.	′ ″	″	″	h. m. s.	° ′ ″
50	8.7				44.6				11 46 44.47	−28.10	−2.20	·	3	33.970	−25 50.91	−5.18	−9.36	11 46 14.2	−25 0 5.5
51	2					52.	9.		47 35.06	28.10	2.19	·	4	40.690	18 40.64	5.24	8.29	47 4.8	24 52 54.2
52	8		38.	55.					50 12.20	28.11	2.22	·	2	16.092	44 26.55	5.45	12.25	49 41.9	25 18 44.2
53	3.4			12.	29.	46.			51 46.03	28.11	2.20	·	3	29.918	30 0.69	5.57	10.01	51 15.7	25 4 16.3
54	10					30.			51 56.00	28.11	2.19	·	4	38.269	21 13.00	5.58	8.68	51 25.8	24 55 27.3
55	9		26.						57 0.18	28.12	2.19	·	3	35.943	23 46.61	5.95	9.05	56 29.9	58 1.6
56	8.7			34.	50.5				58 50.75	28.12	2.19	·	3	36.664	23 1.94	6.10	8.94	58 20.4	57 17.0
57	9						47.8		11 59 13.84	28.12	2.18	·	5	51.743	7 7.99	6.12	6.51	11 58 43.5	24 41 20.6
58	8					5.5			12 0 48.26	28.12	2.22	·	2	12.952	47 44.31	6.24	12.75	12 0 17.9	25 22 3.3
59	6		11.	28.					4 45.12	28.12	2.20	·	3	27.970	32 7.17	6.53	10.32	4 14.8	6 24.0
60	8.7				13.2				5 13.07	28.12	2.20	·	3	32.483	27 24.34	6.56	9.60	4 41.6	25 1 40.5
61	8						1.		5 27.10	28.12	2.20	·	3	34.849	24 55.69	6.57	9.23	4 56.3	24 59 11.5
62	8			45.5					7 2.62	28.12	2.21	·	2	17.328	43 9.16	6.68	12.06	6 32.3	25 17 27.9
63	9				42.				7 24.74	28.12	2.22	·	2	11.580	49 10.48	6.71	13.00	6 54.4	23 30.2
64	8					35.7			8 1.80	28.13	2.20	·	3	33.083	26 46.63	6.75	9.51	7 31.5	25 1 2.9
65	8			33.					9 50.08	28.13	2.20	·	4	34.663	24 57.89	6.89	9.25	9 19.5	24 59 14.0
66	8					19.8			9 45.87	28.13	2.20	·	3	25.968	34 12.89	6.88	10.64	9 15.5	25 8 30.4
67	9				39.				11 38.96	28.13	2.22	·	2	10.932	49 50.56	7.02	13.10	11 8.6	24 10.7
68	7.8					25.8	43.		12 8.83	28.13	2.21	·	3	18.599	41 55.33	7.05	11.84	11 38.5	16 14.2
69	7.8		8.6			0.			14 42.87	28.13	2.20	·	3	29.446	30 35.00	7.23	10.08	14 12.5	25 4 52.3
70	8			15.	32.				15 32.00	28.13	2.19	·	4	41.453	17 52.44	7.29	8.17	15 1.7	24 52 7.9
71	7.8			28.					16 45.08	28.13	2.21	·	3	23.679	36 36.43	7.37	11.01	16 14.7	25 10 54.8
72	7.8					33.8			16 59.85	28.13	2.18	·	5	49.832	9 7.86	7.39	6.84	16 29.5	24 43 22.1
73	5.6					30.			17 56.07	28.13	2.20	·	3	25.089	35 8.16	7.45	10.79	17 25.7	25 9 26.4
74	9.8		1.2	18.2					19 35.35	28.13	2.19	·	5	43.440	15 48.24	7.63	7.85	20 5.0	24 50 3.7
75	·			42.					24 59.14	28.13	2.18	·	5	45.028	14 8.77	7.93	7.61	24 28.8	48 24.3
76	10		36.8		11.				27 10.92	28.13	2.19	·	4	41.520	17 48.24	8.08	8.15	26 40.5	24 52 4.5
77	9			7.8	24.9				28 41.94	28.13	2.20	III.	3	24.720	35 31.06	8.19	10.84	28 11.6	25 9 50.1
78	9			15.5	32.3				29 49.55	28.13	2.21	III.	3	23.146	37 9.93	8.26	11.12	29 19.2	25 11 29.3
79	9					28.5			30 11.55	28.13	2.19	·	5	45.666	13 29.34	8.28	7.49	29 41.2	24 47 45.1
80	·					44.			31 10.03	28.13	2.16	·		.612	5 18.59	8.35	6.20	30 39.7	24 39 33.1
81	9			36.7		30.			33 53.76	28.13	2.20	·	3	32.178	27 43.48	8.51	9.65	33 23.4	25 2 1.6
82	9				41.5				35 24.54	28.13	2.19	·	4	42.732	16 32.42	8.61	7.96	34 54.2	24 50 49.0
83	9.10			9.8	44.				39 43.95	28.13	2.21	·	3	24.305	35 57.48	8.88	10.91	39 13.6	25 10 17.3
84	8				52.				40 51.86	28.13	2.19	·	3	29.830	30 10.61	8.95	10.03	40 21.5	4 29.6
85	8				35.2				41 35.06	28.13	2.19	·	3	31.610	28 19.05	9.00	9.75	41 4.7	2 37.8
86	8.7			23.		13.5			42 39.83	28.13	2.19	III.	3	32.908	26 57.29	9.06	9.54	42 9.5	1 15.9
87	8				1.				44 0.87	28.13	2.20	·	3	27.650	32 27.51	9.14	10.38	43 30.5	6 47.0
88	9.6					41.2			44 7.30	28.13	2.18	·	3	33.313	26 32.32	9.15	9.47	43 37.0	25 0 50.9
89	9					48.8			45 14.84	28.13	2.16	·	5	53.228	5 34.96	9.21	6.26	44 44.6	24 39 50.4
90	7.8					47.	4.		46 30.05	28.13	2.17	V.	3	37.718	21 55.79	9.28	8.77	45 59.7	56 13.8
91	10					52.			47 18.04	28.13	2.16	·	3	53.030	5 54.54	9.33	6.30	46 47.8	40 10.2
92	10			5.2					55 22.29	28.12	2.17	·	3	37.623	22 1.57	9.79	8.78	54 52.0	56 20.1
93	5.6			0.5	17.2				56 17.32	28.12	2.18	IV.	3	34.432	25 22.11	9.84	9.30	55 47.0	24 59 41.2
94	9				57.				57 56.90	28.12	2.19	·	2	21.816	38 27.89	9.92	11.34	57 26.6	25 12 49.1
95	8					8.			12 58 34.06	28.12	2.19	·	2	22.608	37 39.03	9.96	11.21	12 58 3.7	25 12 0.2
96	7.8				34.				13 2 33.89	28.12	2.16	·	4	49.110	9 51.80	10.17	6.91	13 2 3.6	24 44 8.9
97	7.8					28.5			13 2 54.60	−28.12	−2.18	·	3	29.070	−30 58.35	−10.19	−10.15	13 2 24.3	−25 5 18.7

CORRECTIONS.

Date.	Corr. of Clock.	Hourly rate.	m	n	c	Zenith Point.	Mic. Co.
	h.	s.	s.	s.	s.	° ′ ″	r.
1849.							

REMARKS.

(251) 74. Minutes assumed as 20, not 19.
(251) 80. Micrometer reading assumed as 53r.612.
(251) 81. Transits discordant; T. VI rejected.

INSTRUMENT READINGS.

Date.	CIRCLE.							Barom.	THERMOM.				
	A.	B.	C.	D.	E.	F.	Mean.		At.	Ex.	U.	L.	I.
1849. h. m.	° ′ ″					″		in.	°	°	°	°	°

ZONE 252. MAY 2. S. $D_0 = -21° 24' 0''$.

No.	Mag.	I.	II.	III.	IV.	V.	VI.	VII.	T.	a_1	a_2	Micrometer	i	d_1	d_2	Mean Right Ascension, 1850.0	Mean Declination, 1850.0
									h. m. s.	s.	s.	r.	' ''	''	''	h. m. s.	° ' ''
1	7.8		37.	54.					14 49 10.56	−15.66	−2.15	4 50.422	− 8 29.02	− 0.63	− 0.04	14 48 52.7	− 21 32 29.7
2	7.8		51.2	9.					50 25.12	15.66	2.29	3 36.098	23 37.26	0.65	2.11	50 7.2	21 47 40.0
3	7.8		38.	55.		28.5			52 11.62	15.66	2.49	2 9.955	50 51.88	0.67	5.05	51 53.5	22 14 58.5
4	9.8				27.	43.8			53 10.56	15.66	2.31	5 45.140	14 2.43	0.68	0.80	52 52.6	21 38 3.9
5	10					7.			53 33.84	15.66	2.43	2 18.502	41 56.71	0.69	4.69	53 15.7	22 6 2.1
6	9						5.5		55 32.40	15.65	2.50	3 28.485	31 35.24	0.72	3.23	55 14.2	21 55 39.2
7	10							11.	56 37.86	15.65	2.42	5 45.260	13 55.14	0.73	0.78	56 29.8	37 56.7
8	7				1.2				57 44.60	15.65	2.52	3 34.782	24 59.97	0.75	2.31	57 26.4	21 49 3.0
9	9			11.					14 59 27.71	15.65	2.71	2 17.572	42 53.78	0.77	− 4.81	59 9.4	22 6 59.4
10	7				3.				15 0 2.89	15.64	2.50	5 51.899	6 57.81	0.78	+ 0.16	14 59 44.7	21 30 58.4
11	8					54.			0 37.46	15.64	2.55	4 45.018	14 9.02	0.79	− 0.82	15 0 19.3	21 38 10.6
12	8					56.5			1 39.71	15.64	2.77	2 16.048	44 30.19	0.80	− 5.05	1 21.3	22 8 36.0
13	8				46.				2 45.89	15.64	2.59	5 52.678	6 8.97	0.81	+ 0.28	2 27.7	21 30 9.5
14	10					19.			3 45.89	15.63	2.71	3 36.144	23 34.62	0.82	− 2.10	3 27.6	47 37.5
15	10		27.5	44.					5 0.75	15.63	2.79	3 29.736	30 16.37	0.83	3.04	4 42.3	54 20.3
16	11					43.			6 26.35	15.63	2.84	3 27.950	32 8.61	0.84	3.20	6 7.9	56 12.7
17	3			45.5	2.				8 2.01	15.63	2.87	3 33.464	26 22.84	0.86	2.48	7 43.5	50 26.2
18	8		31.						12 4.36	15.62	2.96	4 40.715	18 37.44	0.89	1.44	11 45.8	42 39.8
19	9					12.5			11 55.87	15.62	3.02	3 30.408	29 34.65	0.89	2.94	11 37.2	53 38.5
20	9					1.5			12 44.95	15.61	2.96	4 43.091	16 9.95	0.90	1.11	12 26.4	40 12.0
21	10						44.5		13 11.39	15.61	3.02	3 35.842	23 53.39	0.90	2.15	12 52.8	21 47 56.4
22	9						36.		14 2.87	15.61	3.14	2 22.870	37 22.53	0.91	4.03	13 44.1	22 1 27.5
23	9				30.5				15 30.37	15.61	3.10	2 35.052	24 43.08	0.92	2.26	15 11.6	21 48 46.3
24	8					20.3			15 47.11	15.61	3.24	2 13.615	47 3.17	0.92	− 5.41	15 29.2	22 11 9.5
25	8					8.5			16 35.33	15.60	3.02	2 52.390	6 27.61	0.93	+ 0.23	16 16.7	21 30 25.3
26	7			21.					18 20.85	15.60	3.25	3 25.800	34 23.51	0.94	− 3.61	18 2.0	58 28.1
27	8				21.				20 4.45	15.60	3.20	4 43.270	15 58.84	0.95	1.08	19 45.6	40 0.9
28	10				5.5				22 5.37	15.59	3.31	4 36.220	23 29.85	0.96	1.09	21 46.5	47 32.9
29	7.8							54.	22 20.86	15.59	3.30	4 43.042	16 13.60	0.96	1.12	22 4.0	40 15.7
30	10.9		14.	30.5					26 47.29	15.57	3.40	4 45.060	14 5.44	0.97	0.81	26 28.3	38 7.2
31	5		32.5	49.2	6.				29 5.89	15.57	3.48	4 46.100	13 0.73	0.98	0.67	28 46.8	37 2.4
32	7		1.5	18.2					30 34.88	15.57	3.64	3 25.550	34 39.12	0.98	3.65	30 15.7	58 43.8
33	10			23.					31 39.64	15.56	3.65	3 29.190	30 50.76	0.98	3.12	31 20.4	54 54.9
34	11						12.		31 38.89	15.56	3.63	3 33.953	25 51.97	0.98	2.41	31 19.7	21 49 55.4
35	9		2.8	19.5					35 36.26	15.55	3.91	2 11.462	49 17.06	0.99	5.72	35 16.8	22 13 23.8
36	10					9.	26.		35 52.64	15.55	3.79	3 30.252	29 44.38	0.99	2.96	35 33.3	21 53 48.4
37	7.6				31.				37 14.13	15.55	3.98	2 8.324	52 34.73	0.99	6.06	36 54.6	22 10 41.8
38	10			38.					39 54.71	15.54	3.87	4 41.422	17 53.89	0.99	1.33	39 35.3	21 41 56.2
39	9				40.				40 39.87	15.54	3.92	3 33.710	26 7.82	0.99	2.46	40 20.4	21 50 10.7
40	7				36.				42 35.94	15.53	3.10	2 14.733	45 52.24	0.98	5.25	42 17.3	22 9 58.5
41	9					12.3	29.		42 55.68	15.53	3.12	2 10.613	43 54.82	0.97	− 4.97	42 37.0	22 8 0.8
42	8		20.8	37.3					44 54.12	15.52	3.96	5 51.785	7 4.58	0.96	+ 0.14	44 34.6	21 31 5.4
43	11					59.5			45 42.87	15.52	4.10	2 29.724	30 17.38	0.96	− 3.04	45 23.3	54 21.4
44	8		38.2	55.					47 11.66	15.52	4.05	4 47.955	11 3.68	0.95	0.39	46 52.1	35 5.0
45	8.					54.5			48 21.39	15.51	4.16	3 37.102	22 34.45	0.95	2.06	48 1.7	21 40 38.4
46	9					2.3			49 29.15	15.51	4.34	2 18.073	42 23.56	0.94	4.75	49 9.3	22 6 29.2
47	10				5.				51 21.72	15.50	4.40	2 16.475	44 2.66	0.93	4.99	51 1.8	8 8.6
48	2				48.	5.			51 48.06	15.50	4.41	2 13.390	47 16.65	0.92	5.45	51 28.2	22 11 23.0
49	9					54.3			15 52 37.73	−15.50	−4.27	4 39.048	− 20 23.68	− 0.91	− 1.67	15 52 18.0	− 21 44 26.3

CORRECTIONS.

Date.	Corr. of Clock.	Hourly rate.	m	n	c	Zenith Point.	Mic. Co.
1849.	h.	s.	s.	s.	s.	° ' ''	r.

INSTRUMENT READINGS.

Date.		A.	B.	C.	D.	E.	F.	Mean.	Barom.	At.	Ex.	U.	L.	I.
	1849. h. m.	° ' ''						''	In.	°	°	°	°	°
Zone 252	May 2, 14 40	80 44	59.3 / 59.8	60.5 / 60.5	63.0 / 64.3	58.8 / 59.	47.2 / 47.2	53.2 / 53.2 } 57.17	30.438	..	50.9			
	15 0								30.436	56.2	50.4			
	15 10											52.5	63.	56.5
	15 20										50.			
	15 40										49.3			
	16 0								30.420	55.2	49.2			

REMARKS.

(252) 11. Right ascension differs 10^s from Arg. Z. 295, 138.

(252) 29. Transit over T. VI assumed as recorded over T. VII.

(252) 46. Transit over T. VI assumed as $2^s.3$, not 23^s.

ZONE 252. MAY 2. S. $D_o = -21^\circ\,24'\,0''$—Continued.

No.	Mag.	I.	II.	III.	IV.	V.	VI.	VII.	T.	a_1	a_2	Mic.	n	r.	i	d_1	d_2	Mean Right Ascension, 1850.0.	Mean Declination, 1850.0.
									h. m. s.	s.	s.			r.	′ ″	″	″	h. m. s.	° ′ ″
50	7					42.			15 53 25.49	−15.50	−4.24	.	5	49.772	− 9 11.57	− 0.91	− 0.14	15 53 5.7	− 21 33 12.6
51	8			19.2	36.				55 35.93	15.49	4.31	.	5	52.850	5 58.11	0.88	+ 0.27	55 16.1	21 29 58.7
52	10		52.	9.					57 25.58	15.48	4.60	.	2	13.580	47 4.17	0.87	− 5.41	57 5.5	22 11 10.5
53	10				5.				58 4.88	15.48	4.45	.	4	38.912	20 31.70	0.86	1.68	57 45.0	21 44 34.2
54	·					3.	19.5		58 46.41	15.48	4.44	.	4	44.202	15 0.35	0.85	0.92	58 26.5	21 39 2.1
55	9					13.			15 59 56.31	15.48	4.62	.	2	24.130	36 3.30	0.84	3.88	15 59 36.2	22 0 8.0
56	7			8.5					16 1 25.18	15.47	4.67	.	2	23.783	36 24.00	0.82	3.92	16 1 5.0	22 0 28.7
57	6					4.8			1 48.22	15.47	4.56	.	3	38.242	21 23.03	0.82	1.77	1 28.2	21 45 25.6
58	8						51.		2 17.89	15.47	4.64	.	3	35.780	23 57.33	0.81	2.14	1 57.8	21 48 0.3
59	8						52.		3 18.82	15.46	4.79	.	2	15.620	44 57.41	0.79	5.13	2 58.6	22 9 3.3
60	9					54.8			4 38.05	15.46	4.80	.	2	18.850	41 34.38	0.77	4.68	4 17.8	22 5 39.8
61	7				48.				5 47.88	15.45	4.70	.	3	38.655	20 57.00	0.75	1.71	5 27.7	21 44 59.7
62	6.7					36.5	53.		16 6 19.85	−15.45	−4.82	.	3	24.628	−35 37.15	− 0.74	− 3.79	16 5 59.6	− 21 59 41.7

ZONE 253. MAY 11. S. $D_o = -24^\circ\,59'\,0''$.

No.	Mag.	I.	II.	III.	IV.	V.	VI.	VII.	T.	a_1	a_2	Mic.	n	r.	i	d_1	d_2	Mean Right Ascension, 1850.0.	Mean Declination, 1850.0.
1	8			48.	5.				14 15 4.99	−16.63	−0.42	IV.	5	49.653	− 9 18.86	− 3.89	− 2.96	14 14 47.94	− 25 8 25.7
2	8				54.				15 53.86	16.63	0.44	.	3	31.202	28 44.71	3.92	5.81	15 36.79	27 54.4
3	10		2.						17 36.28	16.63	0.45	.	2	18.652	41 45.36	3.98	7.77	17 19.20	40 57.1
4	11					49.			18 31.58	16.63	0.48	.	2	15.599	44 58.43	4.02	5.25	18 14.77	44 10.7
5	7			11.	28.				21 11.00	16.62	0.43	IV.	3	38.479	21 8.10	4.13	4.70	20 53.95	20 16.9
6	10					33.5			22 16.33	16.62	0.49	.	2	11.312	49 27.35	4.15	8.94	21 59.22	48 40.4
7	9		57.	14.					26 30.98	16.62	0.51	III.	3	30.365	29 37.10	4.30	5.94	26 13.85	28 47.3
8	8					19.5			26 32.58	16.62	0.50	.	3	35.372	24 23.19	4.30	5.16	26 15.46	23 32.6
9	10						47.5		27 13.75	16.62	0.51	.	4	39.653	19 46.03	4.32	4.50	26 56.62	18 54.8
10	8				42.5				28 42.39	16.62	0.50	.	4	49.770	9 11.45	4.37	2.93	28 25.27	8 18.7
11	5		26.						31 0.05	16.62	0.54	.	3	23.242	37 3.65	4.48	7.06	31 42.89	36 15.2
12	9					22.5			32 5.48	16.62	0.54	.	3	23.632	36 39.63	4.49	6.99	31 48.32	35 51.1
13	6						5.		32 31.16	16.60	0.56	.	2	13.052	47 38.42	4.51	8.66	32 13.98	46 51.6
14	9					21.			34 4.18	16.61	0.52	.	5	52.345	6 30.25	4.55	2.54	33 47.05	5 37.3
15	7				24.5				35 24.37	16.61	0.54	.	3	36.668	23 1.69	4.59	4.97	35 7.22	22 11.3
16	10					14.6			35 57.73	16.61	0.54	.	4	43.354	15 53.57	4.61	3.94	35 40.58	15 2.1
17	6.7					54.6			36 37.75	16.61	0.56	.	4	46.902	12 10.71	4.63	3.39	36 20.58	11 18.7
18	3		43.2		17.5				39 17.28	16.61	0.60	.	3	31.906	28 0.35	4.72	5.70	39 0.07	27 10.8
19	10					20.			43 3.06	16.60	0.63	.	3	32.004	27 54.33	4.83	5.66	42 45.83	27 4.8
20	10				20.				44 19.87	16.60	0.63	.	3	33.913	25 54.42	4.87	5.37	44 2.64	25 4.7
21	11						10.5		44 36.73	16.60	0.61	.	5	47.397	11 40.90	4.86	3.31	44 19.52	10 49.1
22	11						8.		46 34.21	16.60	0.64	.	2	20.340	40 1.42	4.94	7.52	46 16.97	39 13.9
23	5			10.5	27.2				48 27.32	16.59	0.66	III.	2	19.248	41 8.67	4.98	7.69	48 10.07	40 21.3
24	9.8			4.5			55.2		51 21.50	16.59	0.65	.	5	47.710	11 20.81	5.06	3.26	51 4.26	10 29.1
25	7		41.	58.			48.5		53 14.93	16.59	0.68	III.	3	23.602	36 41.32	5.11	7.00	52 57.66	35 53.4
26	10			34.					54 51.06	16.59	0.67	.	5	46.439	12 40.40	5.13	3.45	54 33.80	11 49.0
27	5.4			59.2					57 16.26	16.58	0.69	.	5	46.260	12 51.63	5.18	3.47	56 58.99	12 0.3
28	9			37.					57 53.96	16.58	0.72	.	3	30.770	29 11.50	5.20	5.88	57 36.66	28 22.6
29	7						22.5		57 48.77	16.58	0.72	.	3	28.132	31 57.27	5.20	6.29	57 31.47	31 8.8
30	9						39.5		14 59 5.78	16.58	0.73	.	3	32.229	27 40.28	5.23	5.62	14 58 48.47	26 51.1
31	8		36.						15 1 10.03	16.58	0.73	.	3	27.069	33 3.45	5.27	6.46	15 0 52.72	32 15.2
32	5				44.2				15 1 44.14	−16.58	−0.75	.	2	14.479	−46 8.35	− 5.28	− 8.45	15 1 26.81	− 25 45 22.1

CORRECTIONS.

Date.	Corr. of Clock.	Hourly rate.	m	n	c	Zenith Point.	Mic. Co.
1849.	h. s.	s.	s.	s.	s.	° ′ ″	r.

REMARKS.

(252) 51. Declination differs from Arg. Z. 209, 92; 213, 1; micrometer reading perhaps 52r.650.

(253) 5. Transits over T.'s IV and V assumed as recorded over T.'s III and IV.

(253) 11. Minutes assumed as 32, not 31.

INSTRUMENT READINGS.

Date.	CIRCLE.							Barom.	THERMOM.				
	A.	B.	C.	D.	E.	F.	Mean.		At.	Ex.	U.	L.	I.
	1849. h. m.	° ′ ″						″	in.	°	°	°	°	°
Zone 253 — May 11, 14 20	83 19 {59.2 / 59.2}	59.2 / 59.8	62.2 / 62.7	60.2 / 61.2	45.6 / 45.9	52.2 / 52.2	56.63	29.858	55.2	49.2	56.9	62.	53.8
14 40										48.3			
15 0								29.858	54.5	47.5			
15 20										47.2			
15 40								29.870	53.5	47.1			

ZONE 253. MAY 11. S. $D_0 = -24° 59' 0''$—Continued.

No.	Mag.	I.	II.	III.	IV.	V.	VI.	VII.	T.	a₁	a₂	Mic.	r.	i	d₁	d₂	Mean Right Ascension, 1850.0	Mean Declination, 1850.0
									h. m. s.	s.	s.		r.	' "	"	"	h. m. s.	° ' "
33	8					25.8			15 2 8.88	−16.58	−0.72	3	35.590	−24 9.39	5.28	−5.11	15 1 51.58	−25 23 19.8
34	6		36.8						4 10.79	16.57	0.73	5	51.178	7 42.38	5.31	2.70	3 53.49	6 50.4
35	8				47.2				4 47.08	16.57	0.75	3	25.672	34 31.53	5.33	6.69	4 29.76	33 43.5
36	5					35.			5 18.02	16.57	0.76	3	27.020	38 20.72	5.33	7.24	5 0.69	37 33.3
37	7					21.5			9 4.42	16.56	0.80	2	18.428	42 1.04	5.38	7.83	5 47.00	41 14.3
38	9				45.				10 44.88	16.56	0.81	3	26.252	33 55.26	5.42	6.59	10 27.51	33 7.3
39	9						29.5		10 55.74	16.56	0.83	3	23.572	36 43.39	5.42	7.01	10 38.35	35 55.8
40	8					22.			12 5.07	16.56	0.81	3	32.918	26 56.91	5.43	5.53	11 47.70	26 7.9
41	8			46.					14 3.02	16.55	0.82	4	41.092	18 14.46	5.45	4.27	13 45.65	17 24.2
42	9				35.				14 31.86	16.55	0.83	3	30.616	29 21.80	5.46	5.90	14 17.46	28 33.2
43	8.7			37.5			28.8		15 54.76	16.55	0.84	III 2	19.392	40 59.69	5.48	7.67	15 37.37	40 12.8
44	9		54.5		29.8				17 28.60	16.55	0.86	5	53.015	5 47.83	5.49	2.42	17 11.23	4 55.7
45	9			6.5					19 23.54	16.54	0.87	2	17.233	43 15.06	5.51	8.00	19 6.13	42 26.6
46	6.7			11.5	28.5		2.5		24 28.55	16.53	0.90	IV 4	41.376	17 57.27	5.55	4.23	24 11.12	17 7.0
47	7.8		2.5	19.5		52.5			25 36.23	16.53	0.92	III 4	44.788	14 22.37	5.56	3.70	26 18.78	13 31.6
48	8.9					32.			26 58.15	16.53	0.94	2	12.222	48 30.52	5.57	8.83	26 40.68	47 44.9
49	9					39.			28 22.09	16.53	0.91	4	37.112	22 25.22	5.58	4.87	28 4.65	21 35.7
50	5						20.5		28 46.65	16.52	0.94	2	13.208	47 28.69	5.58	8.67	28 29.19	46 42.9
51	8			40.5		14.			31 57.39	16.52	0.91	V 5	52.069	6 47.46	5.60	2.56	31 39.90	5 55.0
52	9				6.8	23.5			33 6.57	16.51	0.94	IV 2	19.908	40 27.58	3.60	7.60	32 49.12	39 40.8
53	10.9			25.					36 42.06	16.50	0.98	2	11.770	50 0.24	5.61	9.00	36 24.58	49 14.8
54	8			47.					38 3.96	16.50	0.98	3	29.286	30 44.79	5.61	6.11	37 46.48	29 56.5
55	8				19.				38 18.86	16.50	0.98	3	31.153	28 47.70	5.61	5.82	38 1.38	27 59.2
56	6					57.5			38 40.58	16.50	0.98	3	35.278	24 29.09	5.62	5.17	38 23.10	23 39.9
57	5					29.	46.2		39 12.25	16.50	0.99	V 3	28.329	31 45.09	5.62	6.26	38 54.76	30 57.0
58	6		16.						41 50.13	16.49	1.01	2	10.275	50 30.82	5.62	9.15	41 32.63	49 45.6
59	4				15.				42 14.88	16.49	0.98	5	41.189	18 10.13	5.62	4.24	41 57.41	17 20.0
60	8				17.5				43 17.41	16.49	0.99	3	19.770	40 41.70	5.62	7.62	42 59.93	39 54.9
61	10.9				4.				44 3.89	16.48	1.03	3	22.802	37 31.51	5.62	7.12	43 46.38	36 44.2
62	8		21.						45 55.04	16.48	1.03	3	25.775	34 24.56	5.63	6.67	45 37.53	33 36.9
63	7			10.8					46 27.81	16.48	1.04	4	38.670	20 46.15	5.63	4.66	46 10.29	19 56.7
64	6			3.2					47 20.16	16.47	1.04	3	29.860	30 8.53	5.63	6.02	47 2.65	29 20.2
65	8					45.			47 28.09	16.47	1.03	4	37.160	22 22.21	5.63	4.87	47 10.59	21 32.7
66	2		30.	47.2	64.5				15 49 4.23	−16.47	−1.05	IV 2	19.102	−41 18.27	−5.63	−7.72	15 48 46.71	−25 40 31.6

CORRECTIONS.

Date.	Corr. of Clock.	Hourly rate.	m	n	c	Zenith Point.	Mic. Co.
	h. s.	s.	s.	s.	s.	° ' "	r.
1849.							

INSTRUMENT READINGS.

Date.	CIRCLE.							Barom.	THERMOM.				
	A.	B.	C.	D.	E.	F.	Mean.		At.	Ex.	U.	L.	I.
1849. h. m.	° ' "						"	in.	°	°	°	°	°

REMARKS.

(253) 36. Micrometer reading assumed as 22ʳ.020, not 27ʳ.020.
(253) 47. Minutes assumed as 26, not 25.
(253) 53. Micrometer reading assumed as 10ʳ.770, not 11ʳ.770.

ZONE 254. JUNE 16. C. $D_0 = -19°\,33'\,40''$.

No.	Mag.	I.	II.	III.	IV.	V.	VI.	VII.	T.	a_1	a_2	Micr.		r.	i	d_1	d_2	Mean Right Ascension, 1850.0	Mean Declination, 1850.0
									h. m. s.	s.	s.			r.	′ ″	″	″	h. m. s.	° ′ ″
1	9			57.2	13.2				15 32 56.96	+4.99	+0.74	IV.	5	53.307	−5 38.78	−1.83	−2.04	15 33 27.9	−19 39 22.7
2	9	33.2	49.6	16.2	22.6	38.5			6.02	4.		IV.	4	47.265	11 58.15	1.8	3.08		45 43.1
3	8	1.6	17.6	33.7	50.5	6.5			38 33.98	4.98	0.75	IV.	3	33.976	25 50.53	1.86	5.32	38 39.7	59 37.7
4	9			35.2	51.8				39 35.28	4.98	0.75	IV.	3	37.782	21 51.72	1.88	4.68	39 41.0	55 38.3
5	8			7.2	23.9				40 7.33	4.98	0.73	IV.	3	33.631	26 12.31	1.86	5.43	40 13.1	59 59.6
6	8				51.5	8.3			40 35.40	4.98	0.74	IV.	4	43.943	15 26.35	1.88	3.63	40 41.1	49 11.9
7	9.10					20.2			41 47.62	4.98	0.74	V.	3	33.545	20 11.43	1.90	5.40	41 53.3	19 59 58.7
8	9					14.2			41 41.53	4.95	0.78	V.	1	11.509	49 19.20	1.90	9.17	41 47.3	20 23 10.3
9	8				57.4	14.3			42 41.27	4.98	0.75	IV.	3	26.234	33 56.46	1.91	6.64	42 47.0	20 7 45.0
10	5	0.3	16.5	32.8	49.2	5.2			44 32.78	4.97	0.70	IV.	5	50.045	9 3.35	1.93	2.60	44 38.4	19 42 47.9
11	9					37.1			45 4.54	4.97	0.71	V.	4	41.435	18 4.42	1.93	4.06	45 10.2	19 51 50.4
12	9.10				15.2				46 58.61	4.97	0.75	IV.	1	12.424	48 22.93	1.95	9.01	47 4.3	20 22 13.9
13	9.10				30.2				46 13.62	4.97	0.76	IV.	1	13.899	46 50.19	1.95	8.75	46 19.3	20 40.9
14	8.9		15.2	32.2	48.5	4.5			47 31.90	4.97	0.74	IV.	2	14.662	46 2.59	1.96	8.62	47 37.6	19 53.2
15	9					20.7			48	4.97	0.70	V.	4	33.321	26 33.76		5.43	48	0 21.2
16	7.8			23.3	39.2	55.4	12.5		49 39.40	4.97	0.73	IV.	1	7.495	53 31.98	1.98	9.87	49 45.1	27 23.8
17	10		55.		30.8	47.			53 14.29	4.97	0.71	IV.	2	14.701	46 0.14	2.02	8.61	53 20.0	20 19 50.7
18	9			45.8	2.3				56 2.23	4.96	0.66	III.	5	40.077	19 23.89	2.02	4.29	56 7.8	19 53 15.2
19	8		46.5	3.5	59.7				57 46.89	4.96	0.67	IV.	3	[illegible]	27 27.22	2.04	5.59	57 52.5	20 1 14.8
20	3	40.8	56.2	13.2	29.8				58 56.81	4.96	0.68	IV.	3	18.89	41 37.71	2.04	7.89	58 2.4	15 27.6
21	6				47.5	4.3			58 31.26	4.96	0.70	IV.	1	7.398	53 38.13	2.04	9.88	58 36.9	27 30.0
22	9		43.2	59.4					15 59 43.08	4.96	0.69	IV.	3	[illegible]	47 18.47	2.05	8.82	15 59 48.7	21 9.3
23	9	26.3	43.2	59.6	16.1				16 0 43.11	4.96	0.65	IV.	3	20.468	38 55.42	2.05	7.62	16 0 48.7	12 45.1
24	9			39.2					2 6.61	4.95	0.65	V.	3	33.518	26 17.51	2.06	5.40	2 12.2	20 0 5.0
25	9.10	15.5	31.5	58.5	4.6				6 48.16	4.96	0.61	IV.	4	42.378	17 4.86	2.08	3.90	6 53.7	19 50 50.8
26	9		42.3	59.5	15.3	32.3			7 59.20	4.95	0.59	V.	5	51.205	7 50.67	2.09	2.41	8 4.7	41 35.2
27	7		6.8	24.6	40.9				8 8.23	4.95	0.58	IV.	5	49.316	9 47.32	2.09	2.73	8 13.8	43 32.1
28	7	43.5	59.7	15.8	32.4	48.4			10 15.90	4.95	0.59	IV.	5	42.435	17 1.28	2.10	3.89	16 21.5	19 50 47.3
29	9			1.7	18.	34.5			11 1.70	4.95	0.62	IV.	1	9.937	50 53.66	2.10	9.43	11 7.3	20 24 50.2
30	9				11.2				11 35.65	4.95	0.58	V.	5	42.952	11 14.70	2.10	2.95	11 44.7	19 44 59.8
31	9.10				12.0				11 37.45	4.95	0.58	VI.	5	43.170	11 2.22	2.10	2.93	11 45.0	44 47.2
32	6	42.2	58.3	14.8	30.9	47.2			15 14.69	4.95	0.58	IV	5	51.893	7 7.30	2.11	2.29	15 20.2	19 40 51.7
33	9		14.3		46.5	3.4			23 30.41	4.95	0.59	IV.	1	9.286	51 37.73	2.12	9.55	23 35.0	20 25 31.4
34	10		25.2	42.5	59.2				27 42.26	4.95	0.54	IV.	4	37.066	22 38.09	2.11	4.80	26 47.8	19 56 25.0
35	10				29.2				28 56.54	4.94	0.58	V.	2	15.209	45 28.53	2.11	8.54	29 2.1	20 19 19.2
36	6.7		22.8	39.	55.7	11.7			31 32.11	4.94	0.53	IV.	3	27.318	32 49.45	2.11	6.46	31 44.6	20 6 37.0
37	7		43.2	59.2	16.	32.6			33 59.61	4.94	0.49	IV.	5	54.763	4 7.19	2.10	1.80	33 5.0	19 37 51.1
38	9.10					54.2			33 21.66	4.94	0.49	V.	4	46.928	12 19.68	2.10	3.12	33 27.1	19 46 4.9
39	9					13.4			34 40.72	4.94	0.55	V.	1	10.308	50 35.71	2.10	9.31	34 46.2	20 24 27.2
40	8	29.4	45.3	1.8	18.2	34.7			38 1.87	4.94	0.49	IV.	4	43.942	15 26.52	2.09	3.62	38 7.3	19 49 12.2
41	9.10	19.9	35.	52.5					40 52.46	4.94	0.49	III.	4	45.439	13 51.81	2.09	3.37	39 57.9	19 47 37.3
42	9.10				21.4				40 4.85	4.94	0.52	IV.	2	23.039	37 17.77	2.09	7.20	40 10.3	20 11 7.0
43	9			10.3	27.				42 10.43	4.94	0.52	IV.	1	12.818	47 57.99	2.07	8.96	42 15.0	20 21 49.0
44	10		44.2	0.3					44 0.43	4.94	0.47	II.	4	37.859	21 47.50	2.06	4.67	44 5.8	19 55 34.2
45	6		12.2	28.8	45.3	1.5			44 28.76	4.94	0.49	IV.	3	24.526	35 43.61	2.06	6.93	44 34.2	20 9 32.6
46	9.10	11.5	27.8	44.2					47 44.17	4.94	0.45	III.	4	41.914	17 31.28	2.04	3.96	47 49.6	19 51 17.3
47	10	17.5	34.1	50.5					50 50.38	4.94	0.44	III.	4	39.458	20 7.49	2.02	4.38	50 55.7	19 53 53.9
48	10	3.8	36.2						52 36.47	4.94	0.52	II.	2	13.499	47 15.20	2.00	8.85	52 41.9	20 21 6.0
49	7.8	44.7	0.2	17.2		49.8			16 53 17.12	+4.94	+0.47	IV.	3	21.711	−38 40.06	−1.99	−7.42	16 53 22.5	−20 12 29.5

CORRECTIONS.

Date.	Corr. of Clock.	Hourly rate.	*m*	*n*	*c*	Zenith Point.	Mic. Co.
1849. h.	s.	s.	s.	s.	s.	° ′ ″	r.

INSTRUMENT READINGS.

Date	A.	B.	C.	D.	E.	F.	Mean.	Barom.	At.	Ex.	U.	L.	I.
	° ′ ″						″	in.					
Zone 254 1849. June 16, 15 30	78 54 61.	59.5	64.8	56.5	63.3	55.1	60.03	30.122		66.7	73	70.8	72
15 50								30.122	74.3	66.1			
16 0										65.9			
16 20										65.1			
16 40										65.1			
17 0								30.130	72.	64.7			
17 10	61.4	60.4	65.6	58.7	63.2	54.6	60.65	30.136		65.		69.2	70.4

REMARKS.

(254) 12. Right ascension differs 1^m from Arg. Z. 208, 99.

(254) 20. Minutes of transit assumed as 57, not 58.

(254) 23. Micrometer reading assumed as $21^r.468$ instead of $20^r.468$.

(254) 25. Transit over T. III assumed as at $48^s.5$ instead of $58^s.5$.

(254) 26. Right ascension differs 1^m from Arg. Z. 211, 16; 305, 12; minutes probably 6.

(254) 30. Micrometer reading assumed as $47^r.952$, not $42^r.952$.

(254) 31. Micrometer reading assumed as $48^r.170$, not $43^r.170$.

(254) 34. Minutes assumed as 26, not 27.

(254) 37. Minutes of transit assumed as 32, not 33.

(254) 41. Minutes assumed as 39, not 40.

(254) 49. Assumed transit over T. III at $36^s.2$.

ZONE 254. JUNE 16. C. $D_0 = -19° 33' 40''$—Continued.

Left portion (seconds of transit):

No.	Mag.	I	II	III	IV	V	VI	VII	T. (h. m. s.)	a_1 (s.)	a_2 (s.)
50	8.9	..	..	..	..	20.2	36.2	..	16 53 3.57	+ 4.94	+ 0.46
51	9.10	16.2	32.8	..	..	..	..	..	55 49.02	4.95	0.45
52	9	..	..	59.1	16.2	..	..	..	55 59.43	4.95	0.45
53	7.8	..	33.8	50.2	..	19.8	..	..	56 47.16	4.95	0.44
54	9.10	27.3	43.8	59.8	..	..	..	..	58 59.96	4.95	0.38
55	8.9	2.5	..	34.8	51.3	7.4	..	..	16 59 34.93	4.95	0.41
56	8.9	..	..	5.2	21.5	..	..	..	17 2 5.14	4.95	0.43
57	8.9	..	..	..	40.	56.5	..	..	2 23.65	4.95	0.42
58	9.10	24.5	40.7	57.2	13.3	29.6	..	..	6 57.06	4.95	0.35
59	10	15.3	31.8	..	..	..	..	..	10 48.08	4.96	0.38
60	9.10	..	..	52.3	..	25.5	..	..	10 52.64	4.96	0.38
61	10	..	..	..	..	35.3	..	..	10 2.62	4.96	0.38
62	9	..	..	..	..	36.2	..	..	17 11 3.66	+ 4.96	+ 0.32

Right portion (micrometer and results):

No.	MICROMETER		r.	i (′ ″)	d_1 (″)	d_2 (″)	Mean Right Ascension, 1850.0 (h. m. s.)	Mean Declination, 1850.0 (° ′ ″)
50	IV	1	12.456	− 48 20.93	− 1.99	− 9.03	16 53 9.0	− 20 22 11.9
51	II	3	23.907	36 22.05	1.97	7.05	54 54.4	10 11.1
52	IV	3	18.995	41 30.42	1.96	7.89	55 4.8	15 20.3
53	IV	2	17.719	42 50.77	1.95	8.12	55 52.6	20 16 40.8
54	III	5	48.623	10 32.68	1.93	2.82	58 5.3	19 44 17.4
55	IV	3	32.765	27 6.51	1.92	5.54	16 59 40.3	20 0 54.0
56	IV	1	7.528	53 29.92	1.89	9.90	17 2 10.5	27 21.7
57	IV	3	20.364	40 4.76	1.89	7.66	2 29.0	20 13 54.3
58	IV	5	51.767	7 15.20	1.83	2.29	7 2.4	19 40 59.3
59	II	2	22.342	38 0.61	1.80	7.32	9 53.4	20 11 49.7
60	IV	2	14.530	46 10.98	1.80	8.66	9 58.0	20 1.4
61	IV	1	10.523	50 22.16	1.79	9.36	10 8.0	20 24 13.3
62	V	5	44.029	− 15 20.94	− 1.81	− 3.60	17 11 8.9	− 19 49 6.3

ZONE 255. JUNE 18. C. $D_0 = -20° 48' 40''$.

Left portion (seconds of transit):

No.	Mag.	I	II	III	IV	V	VI	VII	T. (h. m. s.)	a_1 (s.)	a_2 (s.)
1	9	..	..	4.2	20.6	37.3	..	..	14 43 4.21	+ 5.40	+ 1.23
2	9	..	..	38.3	55.2	..	..	..	44 38.44	5.40	0.86
3	9	..	..	20.2	36.5	..	..	..	45 3.64	5.39	0.95
4	8.9	10.5	26.6	43.2	59.6	..	..	..	47 43.20	5.39	1.17
5	8	..	27.7	43.3	0.3	17.	..	..	49 43.81	5.38	1.29
6	8.9	40.3	56.8	13.5	29.6	46.3	..	..	51 13.30	5.38	1.17
7	10	2.5	18.5	..	..	..	..	..	53 35.22	5.37	1.09
8	8	..	..	46.5	3.4	19.7	..	..	54 46.72	5.37	1.18
9	9	..	..	..	..	36.9	..	..	54 4.04	5.37	1.04
10	9.10	..	54.2	..	27.	..	..	..	56 10.46	5.36	1.35
11	9	9.2	25.5	..	..	..	..	..	57 42.07	5.36	1.06
12	7.8	..	..	41.8	58.8	15.4	..	..	57 42.18	5.36	1.21
13	8	..	19.5	36.5	53.2	9.4	..	..	14 59 36.39	5.36	1.25
14	9.10	..	..	..	34.7	51.4	..	..	15 0 18.32	5.36	0.97
15	9	..	..	..	17.5	34.5	..	..	1 1.26	5.36	0.95
16	9	..	..	..	..	52.5	..	..	2 19.59	5.35	1.24
17	9.10	48.5	5.3	..	38.2	..	..	..	8 21.60	5.34	1.05
18	9.10	..	..	..	..	31.3	..	..	9 58.49	5.33	0.84
19	9	4.8	21.3	37.5	54.2	10.5	..	..	11 37.66	5.33	1.39
20	9.10	..	..	..	34.8	..	..	..	12 18.07	5.33	1.36
21	9.10	..	..	..	..	3.3	..	..	12 30.38	5.33	1.23
22	9.10	..	..	31.3	..	4.4	..	..	14 31.44	5.32	0.93
23	8	36.4	52.8	8.2	24.	..	..	..	16 6.58	5.32	1.22
24	10	..	..	33.3	..	7.0	..	..	16 33.77	5.32	1.20
25	9.10	..	..	33.4	..	7.1	..	..	16 33.87	5.32	1.20
26	9.10	..	..	..	34.2	..	..	..	18 17.53	5.32	1.11
27	9.10	..	..	38.2	..	11.5	..	..	20 38.44	5.31	0.93
28	9.10	..	..	..	..	18.5	..	..	20 45.49	5.31	1.03
29	8.9	21.4	37.5	..	10.6	27.1	..	..	22 54.13	5.31	1.09
30	9	..	..	..	..	27.5	..	..	22 54.55	5.31	1.33
31	7	..	3.5	20.4	37.2	53.2	..	..	23 20.32	5.30	1.15
32	10	..	..	..	..	25.2	..	..	15 24 52.33	+ 5.30	+ 1.02

Right portion (micrometer and results):

No.	MICROMETER		r.	i (′ ″)	d_1 (″)	d_2 (″)	Mean Right Ascension, 1850.0 (h. m. s.)	Mean Declination, 1850.0 (° ′ ″)
1	IV	2	22.631	− 37 42.80	− 0.70	− 11.35	14 43 10.8	− 21 26 34.9
2	IV	5	48.777	10 22.87	0.74	6.61	44 44.7	20 59 10.2
3	IV	4	42.581	16 52.06	0.76	7.72	45 10.0	21 5 40.5
4	IV	3	26.556	33 36.19	0.84	10.63	47 49.7	22 27.7
5	IV	2	17.014	43 35.06	0.88	12.36	48 50.5	32 28.3
6	IV	3	25.686	34 30.72	0.92	10.79	51 19.8	23 22.4
7	II	3	30.499	29 28.69	0.98	9.91	53 41.7	18 19.6
8	IV	3	24.033	36 14.41	1.01	11.09	54 53.3	25 6.5
9	V	3	34.515	25 16.78	1.00	9.18	54 10.5	14 7.0
10	IV	1	11.806	49 1.45	1.04	13.30	56 17.2	37 55.8
11	II	3	32.616	27 15.80	1.09	9.53	57 48.5	16 6.4
12	IV	2	22.584	37 45.74	1.09	11.35	57 48.7	26 38.2
13	IV	2	18.469	41 32.37	1.12	12.00	14 59 43.0	30 25.5
14	IV	4	39.605	19 58.83	1.15	8.26	15 0 24.6	8 48.2
15	IV	4	38.628	21 0.08	1.16	8.43	1 7.6	9 49.7
16	IV	2	19.228	41 16.32	1.19	11.96	2 26.2	30 9.5
17	III	3	33.800	26 1.52	1.33	9.31	8 28.0	14 52.2
18	V	5	47.044	12 11.84	1.36	6.93	10 4.6	1 0.1
19	IV	1	7.345	53 41.46	1.39	14.11	11 44.4	42 37.0
20	IV	1	9.656	51 16.41	1.42	13.68	12 24.8	40 11.5
21	V	2	18.217	47 19.79	1.41	12.14	12 36.9	31 13.3
22	IV	4	40.439	19 6.54	1.45	8.12	14 37.7	7 56.1
23	IV	2	18.952	41 33.43	1.47	12.01	16 15.1	30 26.9
24	IV	3	25.278	34 56.42	1.48	10.86	16 40.3	23 48.8
25	IV	3	25.464	34 44.76	1.48	10.82	16 40.4	23 37.1
26	IV	3	28.318	31 45.78	1.52	10.31	18 24.0	20 37.6
27	IV	4	39.475	20 7.04	1.56	8.28	20 44.7	8 56.9
28	V	3	31.514	28 25.14	1.56	9.73	20 51.8	17 16.4
29	IV	3	27.396	32 43.56	1.59	11.48	22 0.5	21 36.6
30	V	1	9.612	51 19.23	1.59	13.69	22 1.2	40 14.5
31	IV	3	22.238	38 7.13	1.61	11.42	23 26.8	27 0.2
32	V	3	31.238	− 28 42.45	− 1.63	− 9.78	15 24 58.6	− 21 17 33.9

CORRECTIONS.

Date.	Corr. of Clock.	Hourly rate.	m	n	c	Zenith Point.	Mic. Co.
1849.	h. s.	s.	s.	s.	s.	° ′ ″	r.

INSTRUMENT READINGS.

	Date.	CIRCLE.							Barom.	THERMOM.				
	1849. h. m.	A.	B.	C.	D.	E.	F.	Menn.		At.	Ex.	U.	L.	I.
Zone 255	June 18, 14 40	80 9 62.2	58.6	63.9	56.1	61.3	54.5	59.43	in. 30.348	75.8	71.4			
	15 0										70.4			
	15 20										69.4			
	15 40									30.344	74.5	68.5			
	16 0											67.7			
	16 20											67.			
	16 40	61.7 59.	64.7	57.9	61.5	54.6		59.90	30.340	72.5	66.2			
	17 0								30.332	72.	66.1	74.2	69.8	72.3

REMARKS.

(254) 51. Minutes assumed as 54, not 55.
(254) 52. Minutes assumed as 54, not 55.
(254) 53. Minutes assumed as 55, not 56; transits discordant; those over T.'s II and III rejected.
(254) 54. Minutes assumed as 57, not 58.
(254) 59. Minutes assumed as 9, not 10.
(254) 60. Minutes assumed as 9, not 10.
(255) 1. Declination differs 2″ from Arg. Z. 209, 15; micrometer reading perhaps 24r.631.
(255) 5. Minutes assumed as 48, not 49.
(255) 8. Right ascension differs 1s from Arg. Z. 209, 27.
(255) 13. Declination differs 35″ from Arg. Z. 209, 31; micrometer reading perhaps 18r.469.
(255) 17. Transit over T. IV assumed as 38s.2.
(255) 28. Transit over T. IV assumed as at 2s.
(255) 29. Minutes assumed as 21, not 22.
(255) 30. Minutes assumed as 21, not 22.

ZONE 255. JUNE 18. S. $D_0 = -20°\ 48'\ 40''$—Continued.

No.	Mag.	I.	II.	III.	IV.	V.	VI.	VII.	T.	a_1	a_2	Micr.	n	r.	i (' ")	d_1	d_2	Mean Right Ascension, 1850.0	Mean Declination, 1850.0
									h. m. s.	s.	s.			r.	' "	"	"	h. m. s.	° ' "
33	8		23.5	39.2	56.2	12.6			15 25 39.62	+5.30	+1.12	IV.	3	24.569	−35 40.85	−1.64	−10.98	15 25 46.0	−21 24 33.5
34	8			17.7	34.3	50.7			27 17.75	5.30	0.98	IV.	4	34.334	25 29.65	1.68	9.21	27 24.0	21 14 20.5
35	10			29.2	45.4				28 28.99	5.30	0.72	IV.	5	52.735	6 14.50	1.69	5.90	28 35.0	20 55 2.1
36	9.10						34.7		29 1.87	5.29	0.87	V.	4	41.949	17 32.10	1.70	7.84	29 8.0	21 6 21.6
37	8.9				0.5	17.3			30 44.19	5.29	0.87	IV.	4	42.165	17 18.18	1.73	7.80	30 50.3	6 7.7
38	8.9	20.7	37.3	53.7	9.8	26.6			32 53.52	5.29	0.88	IV.	4	41.488	18 0.72	1.76	7.92	32 59.7	6 50.4
39	8.9	45.2	1.7	18.2	34.6				33 18.15	5.29	1.10	IV.	3	24.398	35 51.64	1.76	11.02	33 24.5	24 44.4
40	10				4.3				34 4.42	5.29	1.11	III.	3	23.378	36 55.62	1.78	11.21	34 10.8	25 48.6
41	9	31.5	48.	4.6	21.	37.6			36 4.54	5.28	1.04	IV.	3	28.725	31 20.05	1.80	9.33	36 10.9	20 11.2
42	10	45.2	1.7						38?18.16	5.28	0.82	III.	5	44.527	14 49.74	1.83	7.38	37 24.3	3 38.9
43	8.9				4.3	21.1	37.5		41 4.49	5.27	0.79	IV.	5	46.477	12 47.42	1.87	7.02	41 10.5	1 36.3
44	8.9		59.3	15.8	32.3				43 15.76	5.27	0.93	IV.	3	35.064	24 42.33	1.90	9.08	43 22.0	13 33.3
45	9			27.4	44.2	0.3			44 27.47	5.27	1.16	IV.	2	18.374	42 9.95	1.91	12.11	44 33.9	31 4.0
46	9.10						12.8?		44 39.93	5.27	0.99	V.	3	30.760	29 12.25	1.92	9.87	44 46.2	18 4.0
47	9.10								45	5.27	0.98	VI.	3	31.622	28 17.55	1.9	9.71	45	17 9.2
48	9		54.5	11.2	27.5				47 11.03	5.26	0.82	IV.	4	43.400	16 0.72	1.94	7.58	47 17.1	4 50.2
49	9	42.2	58.2				47.9		48 14.96	5.26	0.86	II.	4	40.061	19 29.46	1.96	8.18	48 21.1	6 19.6
50	8			19.5	35.5	52.6			48 19.39	5.26	0.78	IV.	5	45.480	13 49.80	1.96	7.20	48 25.4	21 2 39.0
51	9.10			36.2		8.8			49 36.08	5.26	0.72	IV.	5	50.091	9 0.53	1.98	6.37	49 42.1	20 57 48.9
52	10	54.8	10.4						51 27.31	5.26	0.80	II.	4	44.528	14 49.18	1.99	7.38	51 33.4	21 3 38.5
53	8		42.5	59.5	15.6	32.3			53 59.21	5.26	1.17	IV.	2	16.536	44 5.17	2.02	12.46	54 5.6	32 59.6
54	9	36.7	53.6	9.6	26.6				55 9.85	5.25	1.13	IV.	2	19.242	41 15.44	2.02	11.96	55 16.2	21 30 9.4
55	9.10			41.5	57.5				55 41.20	5.25	0.68	IV.	5	51.795	7 13.44	2.03	6.05	55 47.1	20 56 1.5
56	8			47.3		20.4			57 47.46	5.25	1.07	IV.	2	23.738	36 33.22	2.04	11.14	56 53.8	21 25 26.4
57	8.9			54.2	10.6				58 54.12	5.25	1.09	IV.	2	22.066	38 18.18	2.06	11.46	58 0.5	27 11.7
58	9					25.2			58 52.29	5.25	1.14	V.	2	18.837	41 40.72	2.06	12.04	57 58.7	30 34.8
59	8.9					22.8			15 59 49.99	5.25	0.74	V.	5	47.776	11 25.64	2.07	6.78	15 58 56.0	0 14.5
60	10			17.8	34.				16 0 17.61	5.25	1.15	IV.	2	17.474	43 6.33	2.07	12.29	16 0 24.0	21 22 0.7
61	10				28.2?				3 11.64	5.24	0.71	IV.	5	48.536	10 38.19	2.09	6.64	3 17.6	20 59 26.9
62	7			45.5	2.6	18.3			5 45.66	5.24	0.73	IV.	5	47.342	11 53.20	2.11	6.89	4 51.6	21 0 42.2
63	9.10	58.8	15.4	31.9		5.3			7 32.01	5.24	0.88	IV.	3	36.252	23 27.91	2.12	8.87	6 38.1	21 12 18.9
64	7.8	30.2	46.3	2.8	19.4	35.3			8 2.80	5.24	0.65	IV.	5	52.299	6 42.05	2.13	5.96	8 8.7	20 55 30.1
65	8			48.5	5.3	21.4			9 48.57	5.24	1.11	IV.	2	18.009	42 32.66	2.14	12.18	8 54.9	21 31 27.0
66	9	59.3		32.3	48.7				10 32.21	5.24	0.73	IV.	4	46.146	13 8.33	2.14	7.10	10 38.2	1 57.6
67	9		14.2		47.3	3.4			11 30.64	5.23	0.82	IV.	4	39.930	19 38.30	2.15	8.19	11 36.7	8 28.6
68	10				48.	4.			11 31.29	5.23	0.78	V.	4	43.321	16 6.18	2.15	7.58	11 37.3	4 55.9
69	9				28.2	44.5			13 11.58	5.23	0.93	IV.	3	31.240	28 42.39	2.15	9.78	13 17.7	21 17 34.3
70	9.10			13.2	29.6?				14 13.10	5.23	0.63	IV.	5	52.282	6 43.12	2.16	5.96	14 19.0	20 55 31.2
71	9.10	51.6		24.5					16 24.61	5.23	0.97	III.	3	28.688	31 22.32	2.16	10.24	16 30.8	21 20 14.7
72	9	45.7	5.3	21.3					20 21.60	5.23	0.88	III.	3	34.764	25 1.03	2.18	9.14	20 27.7	13 52.3
73	9				4.3				21 47.70	5.22	0.77	IV.	4	41.701	17 47.17	2.18	7.87	20 53.7	6 37.2
74	6	36.2	52.6	9.		42.			24 9.10	5.22	0.81	IV.	4	39.002	19 33.79	2.18	8.19	23 15.1	8 24.2
75	10				51.				24 34.42	5.22	0.70	IV.	4	46.206	13 4.57	2.18	7.08	24 40.3	1 53.8
76	9	55.6	11.9		45.5				26 28.59	5.22	1.11	IV.	2	16.159	44 28.75	2.19	12.53	26 34.9	33 23.5
77	9.10	28.7		1.7	18.3	34.5			34 1.67	5.22	0.69	IV.	5	45.121	14 12.47	2.19	7.26	34 7.6	3 1.9
78	9.10	40.	56.7	12.8	29.6				39 12.98	5.21	0.75	IV.	4	40.906	18 37.06	2.19	8.02	39 18.9	7 27.3
79	9.10				49.3	6.8			39 33.21	5.21	1.18	IV.	1	9.729	51 11.76	2.19	13.68	39 39.6	40 7.6
80	9.10					32.			40 59.17	5.21	0.73	V.	5	41.900	17 34.43	2.19	7.83	40 5.1	6 24.4
81	8.9					5.2			16 40 32.27	+5.21	+1.11	V.	2	14.647	−46 3.65	−2.19	−12.80	16 40 38.6	−21 34 56.6

CORRECTIONS.

Date.	Corr. of Clock.	Hourly rate.	m	n	c	Zenith Point.	Mic. Co.
1849.	h.	s.	s.	s.	s.	s.	° ' "	r.

INSTRUMENT READINGS.

Date.	CIRCLE.							Barom.	THERMOM.				
	A.	B.	C.	D.	E.	F.	Mean.		At.	Ex.	U.	L.	I.
1849. h. m.	° ' "						"	in.	°	°	°	°	°

REMARKS.

(255) 42. Minutes assumed as 37.
(255) 56. Minutes assumed as 56, not 57.
(255) 57. Minutes assumed as 57, not 58.
(255) 58. Minutes assumed as 57, not 58.
(255) 59. Minutes assumed as 58, not 59.
(255) 62. Minutes assumed as 4, not 5.
(255) 63. Minutes assumed as 6, not 7.
(255) 65. Minutes assumed as 8, not 9.
(255) 73. Minutes assumed as 20, not 21.
(255) 74. Minutes assumed as 23, not 24, and micrometer reading as 40'.002, not 39'.002.
(255) 80. Minutes assumed as 39, not 40.

Zone 255. June 18. C. $D_s = -20°\ 48'\ 40''$—Continued.

No.	Mag.	I	II	III	IV	V	VI	VII	T. (h m s)	a_1	a_2	Mic.	No.	r	i	d_1	d_2	Mean Right Ascension, 1850.0	Mean Declination, 1850.0
82	9	55.3	12.3	..	45.3	..	..	..	16 43 28.50	+5.21	+0.95	IV.	3	25.562	−34 38.56	−2.18	−10.81	16 42 34.7	− 21 23 31.6
83	9.10	..	..	10.5	..	..	..	..	45 10.48	5.21	0.66	III.	5	40.155	13 7.39	2.18	7.06	45 16.4	1 56.6
84	9	..	..	..	51.5	7.3	..	..	45 34.56	5.21	1.14	IV.*	1	12.049	48 46.64	2.18	13.29	45 40.9	37 42.1
85	9.10	..	..	20.2	36.2	..	..	..	46 19.92	5.21	0.98	IV.	3	23.465	36 50.10	2.18	11.18	46 26.1	25 43.5
86	8	..	..	..	..	3.5	..	..	46 30.63	5.21	0.90	V.	3	29.623	30 23.47	2.18	10.06	46 36.7	19 15.7
87	9	..	..	..	58.3	14.6	..	..	47 41.62	5.21	1.07	IV.	2	16.366	44 15.96	2.19	12.51	47 47.9	33 10.6
88	9	..	..	38.6	..	..	..	..	48 38.74	5.21	1.04	III.	2	17.494	43 5.01	2.17	12.28	48 45.0	31 59.5
89	9	..	..	58.7	..	..	..	..	49 58.82	5.21	0.93	III.	3	26.436	33 43.78	2.17	10.66	49 5.0	22 36.0
90	9	..	..	..	..	29.2	..	..	49 55.36	5.21	0.75	V.	4	39.606	19 59.71	2.17	8.25	50 1.3	8 50.1
91	10	..	..	..	..	8.5	..	..	50 35.64	5.21	0.80	V.	3	35.456	24 17.00	2.17	9.01	50 41.6	13 8.8
92	8	..	..	..	44.	0.5	..	..	51 27.50	5.21	0.81	IV.	3	34.974	24 47.84	2.16	9.09	51 33.5	13 39.1
93	10	..	17.5	..	..	..	..	..	54 33.97	5.21	0.75	II.	3	36.362	21 15.51	2.15	8.48	54 39.9	10 6.1
94	10	..	..	..	56.2	..	..	..	54 39.58	5.21	0.77	IV.	3	36.925	22 45.37	2.15	8.74	54 45.6	11 36.3
95	10	..	..	..	..	17.5	..	..	55 44.63	5.21	0.86	V.	3	30.478	29 29.04	2.14	9.91	55 50.7	18 22.0
96	8	..	..	40.7	56.5	..	..	..	56 40.30	5.21	0.67	IV.	4	44.162	15 13.35	2.14	7.40	56 46.2	4 3.0
97	9.10	..	..	8.	..	..	..	..	57 8.01	5.21	0.70	IV.	3	42.032	17 25.01	2.13	7.81	57 13.9	6 14.9
98	8.9	..	..	12.3	45.2	..	..	..	16 57 12.33	5.21	0.65	IV.	3	44.864	14 27.15	2.13	7.30	16 57 18.2	3 16.0
99	.	..	..	45.5	..	18.7	..	..	17 0 45.85	+5.21	+1.09	IV.	1	13.918	−46 48.99	−2.12	−12.94	17 0 52.1	− 21 35 44.1

Zone 256. June 19. S. $D_s = -21°\ 23'\ 40''$.

[Throughout this zone transits over T.'s I–V assumed to have been recorded as over II–VI, respectively.]

No.	Mag.	I	II	III	IV	V	VI	VII	T. (h m s)	a_1	a_2	Mic.	No.	r	i	d_1	d_2	Mean Right Ascension, 1850.0	Mean Declination, 1850.0
1	10.9	..	..	..	..	45.	..	..	15 47 44.96	+5.36	+1.13	.	5	47.918	−11 16.79	−2.15	−2.85	15 47 51.4	− 21 35 1.8
2	10	..	..	..	..	28.	..	..	50 28.16	5.36	1.20	.	1	9.802	51 7.13	2.16	9.61	50 34.7	22 14 58.9
3	1	..	..	21.5	38.	55.	..	..	51 21.59	5.35	1.18	IV.	2	13.222	47 33.01	2.16	9.02	51 28.1	22 11 24.2
4	9	..	..	..	59.	..	..	..	52 58.95	5.35	1.09	.	5	49.610	9 30.72	2.16	2.55	53 5.4	21 33 15.4
5	9.8	..	..	..	..	58.	..	..	53 41.20	5.35	1.17	.	1	9.028	51 55.79	2.17	9.75	53 47.7	22 15 47.7
6	10	..	..	..	..	53.	..	..	15 58 20.05	5.35	1.08	.	5	44.050	15 17.74	2.18	3.56	15 58 26.5	21 30 3.5
7	8	..	25.	..	..	..	..	..	16 0 58.13	5.34	1.10	.	2	23.570	36 43.51	2.18	7.17	16 1 4.6	22 0 32.9
8	7.8	..	..	..	21.5	..	..	..	1 21.54	5.34	1.06	.	3	38.018	21 36.96	2.18	4.50	1 27.0	21 45 23.7
9	9	..	..	..	..	24.5	..	..	2 51.51	5.34	1.07	.	3	35.610	24 8.08	2.18	5.05	1 57.0	21 47 55.3
10	10	..	..	..	..	25.7	..	..	3 51.92	5.34	1.10	.	1	15.508	45 9.52	2.18	8.63	2 59.4	22 9 0.3
11	9	..	48.	5.	..	..	..	..	5 21.31	5.34	1.04	III.	4	38.460	21 10.11	2.18	4.50	5 27.7	21 44 56.5
12	8	..	..	37.	53.5	..	..	..	5 53.56	5.34	1.06	IV.	3	24.382	35 52.64	2.16	7.04	6 0.0	59 41.9
13	10	..	16.	..	..	5.5	..	..	8 48.94	5.33	1.00	.	5	51.300	7 44.39	2.18	2.26	8 55.3	21 31 28.8
14	11	..	2.5	..	..	..	..	..	10 35.69	5.33	1.05	.	1	20.243	40 12.02	2.18	7.74	10 42.1	22 4 1.9
15	11	..	15.	31.5	..	..	..	..	11 48.12	5.33	1.06	.	1	10.980	49 53.19	2.18	9.39	11 54.5	22 13 44.8
16	9	..	..	..	21.	..	..	..	12 21.03	5.33	0.99	.	4	38.695	20 55.81	2.18	4.46	12 27.3	21 44 42.4
17	11	18.	..	..	..	..	..	..	14 51.18	5.33	1.01	.	2	23.310	36 55.94	2.18	7.23	14 57.5	22 0 45.3
18	8	..	..	36.	52.5	..	..	..	15 52.54	5.32	0.99	IV.	3	30.788	29 10.56	2.17	5.87	15 58.8	21 52 58.6
19	8	..	42.2	58.5	..	..	47.8	..	18 15.05	5.32	0.96	III.	3	37.213	22 25.06	2.17	4.73	18 21.3	46 12.6
20	10	..	..	11.	29.	..	..	..	26 27.78	5.32	0.89	IV.	4	49.470	9 39.50	2.15	2.58	26 34.0	33 24.2
21	11	..	4.	..	36.	..	..	..	28 36.56	5.31	0.89	.	3	38.728	20 52.35	2.14	4.48	28 42.8	44 39.0
22	11	..	..	41.5	..	..	..	..	29 58.04	5.31	0.88	.	3	39.005	20 34.97	2.13	4.42	30 4.2	21 44 21.5
23	8	..	40.	56.3	13.	..	..	..	35 13.07	5.31	0.90	IV.	1	10.332	50 34.14	2.09	9.51	35 19.3	22 14 25.7
24	10	..	..	8.5	..	..	..	..	38 24.99	5.31	0.86	.	3	29.900	30 6.21	2.07	6.02	38 31.2	21 53 54.3
25	9	..	..	..	33.	..	..	..	39 33.00	5.31	0.80	.	4	43.083	16 20.50	2.06	3.71	39 39.1	40 6.3
26	7	..	..	..	32.5	..	5.5	..	40 32.52	5.31	0.80	IV.	5	42.969	11 13.76	2.06	2.66	40 38.6	21 34 58.7
27	10	..	24.	..	..	..	30.	..	16 42 57.07	+5.30	+0.84	IV.	2	20.842	−39 34.89	−2.03	−7.63	16 43 3.2	− 22 3 24.6

CORRECTIONS.

Date.	Corr. of Clock.	Hourly rate.	m	n	e	Zenith Point.	Mic. Co.
1849.	h.	s.	s.	s.	s.	° ' "	r.

INSTRUMENT READINGS.

Date.		CIRCLE.						Barom.	THERMOM.				
		A.	B.	C.	D.	E.	F.	Mean.		At.	Ex.	U.	L.	I.
Zone 256 June 19, 1849	h. m.	° ' "						"	in.					
	15 40	80 44 50.9	53.6	57.3	52.9	55.2	51.2	55.02						
	16 0								30.234	75.5	72.5	74.	75.	75.
	16 20										72.		74.	73.5
	16 40								30.232	75.	72.			
	17 0	59.3	54.	57.6	52.9	55.6	51.2	55.10						71.9
	17 20								30.228	74.2	71.9			
	17 40													71.9
	17 50	59.0	54.5	57.8	52.9	55.8	50.8	55.13						

REMARKS.

(255) 82. Minutes assumed as 42, not 43.

(255) 89. Minutes assumed as 48, not 49, to agree with Arg. Z. 392, 19; 393, 12.

(255) 98. Time of transit over T. V assumed as 45s.2.

(256) 2. Right ascension differs 16s from Arg. Z. 209, 87; perhaps one thread interval in error.

(256) 6. Transit over T. V assumed as recorded over T. IV.

(256) 9. Transit over T. V assumed as recorded over T. IV, and minutes as 1, not 2.

(256) 10. Transit over T. V assumed as recorded over T. IV, and minutes as 2, not 3.

(256) 23. Declination differs 16" from Arg. Z. 213, 46; 302, 3; micrometer reading, perhaps, 10r.532.

(256) 26. Micrometer reading assumed as 47r.969, not 42r.969.

[(*255) From 84 to 99, inclusive, under Micrometer, add I to IV, IV, V, etc.]

ZONE 256. JUNE 19. S. $D_a = -21°\ 23'\ 40''$—Continued.

No.	Mag.	I.	II.	III.	IV.	V.	VI.	VII.	T.	a_1	a_2	MICROMETER.	i	d_1	d_2	Mean Right Ascension, 1850.0	Mean Declination, 1850.0
									h. m. s.	s.	s.	r.	' "	"	"	h. m. s.	° ' "
28	10		3.						16 45 36.12	+5.31	+0.80	II. 3 36.000	−23 43.41	−2.01	−4.97	16 45 42.2	−21 47 30.4
29	8					51.5			45 34.84	5.31	0.78	V. 4 45.430	13 53.82	2.01	3.31	45 40.9	37 39.1
30	7		9.	25.8	42.				47 42.12	5.30	0.77	IV. 5 49.718	9 23.88	1.99	2.52	47 48.2	33 8.4
31	10.9				39.				48 38.95	5.30	0.74	IV. 5 50.792	8 16.41	1.98	2.33	48 45.0	32 0.7
32	7		52.		25.		58.		16 56 25.08	5.30	0.74	IV. 3 32.148	27 45.36	1.88	5.63	16 56 31.1	51 32.9
33	10			21.5					17 1 38.02	5.30	0.70	III. 3 35.003	24 46.09	1.82	5.15	17 1 44.0	48 33.1
34	10			4.					2 20.55	5.30	0.68	III. 4 40.990	18 31.21	1.80	4.05	2 26.5	42 17.0
35	10				0.		33.		3 0.01	5.30	0.68	IV. 5 47.133	12 6.20	1.79	2.98	3 6.0	35 51.0
36	10			35.5					5 52.00	5.30	0.67	III. 3 31.639	28 17.24	1.75	5.71	5 58.0	52 4.7
37	8			3.	19.2				7 19.38	5.30	0.64	IV. 4 42.603	16 50.68	1.73	3.79	7 25.3	50 36.2
38	9		58.5		31.2				14 31.24	5.30	0.59	IV. 5 48.958	10 11.51	1.62	2.66	14 37.1	33 55.8
39	9						16.		14 43.08	5.30	0.58	VI. 5 53.082	5 52.72	1.61	1.94	14 48.9	29 36.3
40	9				31.5				16 31.41	5.30	0.56	IV. 5 56.360	5 35.36	1.58	1.63	16 37.3	29 19.8
41	9			16.8					23 33.37	5.31	0.54	III. 3 37.948	21 41.24	1.46	4.59	23 39.1	45 27.3
42	10					11.			23 54.32	5.31	0.54	V. 4 40.816	18 43.20	1.46	4.08	24 0.2	42 28.7
43	7.6		38.	54.		27.3			26 10.74	5.31	0.56	III. 3 27.703	32 24.11	1.39	6.44	26 16.6	56 11.9
44	6		5.	21.6	37.3				29 37.87	5.31	0.51	IV. 3 34.485	25 18.79	1.33	5.24	29 43.7	49 5.4
45	11			7.					32 23.50	5.31	0.51	III. 3 32.088	27 49.06	1.28	5.65	32 29.3	51 36.0
46	4		47.	4.	20.	37.			34 20.23	5.32	0.46	IV. 4 46.730	12 31.55	1.24	3.04	34 26.0	21 36 15.8
47	8.7				15.				35 15.17	5.32	0.53	IV. 2 7.132	43 27.47	1.20	7.95	35 21.0	22 7 16.6
48	10						7.		17 35 33.97	+5.32	+0.49	VI. 3 26.958	−33 10.78	−1.19	−6.57	17 35 39.8	−21 56 58.5

ZONE 257. JUNE 20. C. $D_a = -20°\ 11'\ 10''$.

No.	Mag.	I.	II.	III.	IV.	V.	VI.	VII.	T.	a_1	a_2	MICROMETER.	i	d_1	d_2	Mean Right Ascension, 1850.0	Mean Declination, 1850.0
1	9.10				55.8	11.7	28.6		16 3 55.62	+6.14	+0.89	IV. 3 31.108	−28 50.61	−3.75	−5.82	16 4 2.64	−20 40 10.2
2	7			28.6	44.2	1.5	17.8		5 44.64	6.13	0.88	IV. 1 11.505	49 20.51	3.74	9.19	5 51.85	21 0 43.4
3	7			19.2			5.8		5 32.84	6.13	0.89	IV. 3 28.165	31 55.26	3.74	6.32	5 39.86	20 43 15.3
4	8		29.	45.0	1.7	18.5	34.7		8 1.90	6.13	0.88	IV. 2 16.451	44 10.49	3.73	8.34	8 8.91	55 32.6
5	9.10		27.3	43.5	59.5		32.7		11 59.88	6.12	0.90	IV. 5 45.745	13 33.24	3.71	3.32	11 6.90	24 50.3
6	10						46.7		14 13.21	6.12	0.89	V. 2 16.416	44 12.82	3.70	8.34	14 20.22	55 34.9
7	9.10		55.9	12.4	28.6	45.4	1.2		24 28.70	6.11	0.92	IV. 5 45.071	14 15.60	3.64	3.43	23 35.73	20 25 32.7
8	10		27.3	44.3	0.4	16.8	33.2		34 0.40	6.11	0.94	IV. 1 9.264	51 41.05	3.56	9.57	34 7.45	21 3 4.2
9	9						11.6		34 39.12	6.11	0.92	V. 5 46.127	13 9.27	3.56	3.24	34 46.15	20 24 26.1
10	9			56.6	12.8	29.4			39 12.89	6.10	0.95	IV. 3 30.961	28 59.70	3.52	5.83	39 19.94	40 19.1
11	9			52.7	8.2	25.2			42 8.68	6.10	0.95	IV. 5 48.625	10 32.55	3.49	2.80	42 15.73	21 48.8
12	10			35.3	51.3	7.6	24.2		46 51.39	6.10	0.96	IV. 3 38.285	21 20.31	3.44	4.58	46 58.45	32 38.4
13	9.10		54.6		27.2	43.5			49 27.20	6.10	0.96	IV. 3 38.013	21 37.28	3.41	4.63	49 34.26	32 55.3
14	10		2.2		34.5		7.2		51 34.64	6.10	0.97	IV. 5 49.333	9 47.92	3.39	2.69	51 41.71	21 4.0
15	8.9		29.2	45.3	2.	18.3	34.9		53 1.94	6.10	0.97	IV. 5 48.235	10 57.08	3.36	2.86	53 9.01	22 13.3
16	9		25.3	41.3	58.2				55 57.97	6.10	0.98	III. 5 54.786	4 5.62	3.32	1.75	55 5.05	15 20.7
17	9.10				13.2	29.2			55 12.96	6.10	0.97	IV. 2 22.217	38 8.83	3.34	7.35	55 20.03	49 29.5
18	7					1.9	18.2		16 56 45.48	6.10	0.98	V. 5 53.524	5 25.03	3.31	1.96	16 56 52.56	16 40.3
19	9.10		53.7	10.2	26.7				17 0 26.62	6.10	0.98	III. 3 36.532	23 10.28	3.27	4.87	17 0 33.70	34 28.4
20	9				56.4		29.3		1 56.50	6.10	0.98	IV. 4 41.815	17 40.02	3.25	3.97	2 3.58	28 57.2
21	9.10					24.3			1 7.74	6.10	0.98	IV. 4 35.774	23 59.10	3.26	5.01	1 14.82	35 17.4
22	8.9					19.3			2 2.77	6.10	0.98	IV. 5 43.339	16 4.56	3.24	3.71	2 9.85	27 21.5
23	9						36.2		17 2 3.48	+6.10	+0.98	V. 3 33.438	−26 24.41	−3.24	−5.39	17 2 10.56	−20 37 43.0

CORRECTIONS.

Date.	Corr. of Clock.	Hourly rate.	m	n	c	Zenith Point.	Mic. Co.
1849.	h.	s.	s.	s.	s.	° ' "	r.

INSTRUMENT READINGS.

Date.		A.	B.	C.	D.	E.	F.	Mean.	Barom.	At.	Ex.	U.	L.	I.
	1849, h. m.	° ' "						"	in.	°	°	°	°	°
Zone 257	June 20, *16 0	79.32 {33.7 / 35.1}	28.9 / 29.4	32.2 / 33.6	30.4 / 32.1	33.8 / 35.5	28.8 / 30.9	32.03	30.166	80.5	76.1		76.8	82.2
	16 20													
	16 40								30.166	79.8	75.5		75.6	
	17 0								30.166			74.5		
	17 20								30.168	78.5	75.			
	17 30	33.6 / 34.2	28.9 / 29.9	32.2 / 32.8	30.8 / 33.0	33.5 / 35.1	28.8 / 30.4	31.93					76.8	78.5
	17 40											73.4		

REMARKS.

(256) 40. Micrometer reading assumed as 53r.360, not 56r.360.

(256) 47. Micrometer reading assumed as 17r.132, not 7r.132.

(257) 5. Minutes assumed as 10, not 11.

(257) 7. Minutes assumed as 23, not 24.

(257) 12. Right ascension differs 1m from Arg. Z. 211, 51; minutes probably 45, not 46.

(257) 16. Minutes assumed as 54, not 55.

*Minutes of circle reading assumed as 33 instead of 32.

ZONE 257. JUNE 20. C. $D_0=-20°\ 11'\ 10''$—Continued.

No.	Mag.	I.	II.	III.	IV.	V.	VI.	VII.	T. (h m s)	a_1	a_2
24	10	45.2			18.4				17 4 18.18	+6.10	+0.98
25	8.9	17.7	34.3	50.3		7.1	23.6		6 50.60	6.10	0.98
26	10	20.2		53.2					9 53.04	6.10	1.00
27	9.10				46.3	3.4			10 46.59	6.10	0.99
28	9.10							24.7	10 52.04	6.10	0.99
29	9.10					17.3			10 0.78	6.10	0.99
30	5			54.2	10.3	26.8			12 54.00	6.10	0.98
31	9				6.3	22.3			13 49.70	6.10	0.99
32	9.10					34.2			13 1.48	6.10	0.99
33	10			41.3					15 41.23	6.10	1.01
34	10			49.3					17 49.38	6.10	1.01
35	10	48.5	4.8	21.2					18 21.23	6.10	1.01
36	9		56.2	12.3	29.1	45.4			20 12.53	6.10	1.00
37	10			22.7					24 22.80	6.11	1.02
38	10				52.2	8.1			26 35.49	6.11	1.02
39	9.10				35.2				27 18.58	6.11	1.01
40	9					14.6			27 41.83	6.11	1.01
41	9							0.7	28 27.98	6.11	1.02
42	10				47.2	3.8			32 47.26	6.11	1.02
43	8.9	54.5	10.4	27.4	43.6	59.5			38 27.08	6.11	1.02
44	9		6.2	23.2	39.2	56.3			40 23.01	6.12	1.04
45	10				7.8				42 7.94	6.12	1.04
46	10			44.5					43 44.66	6.12	1.04
47	10					25.6			43 52.93	6.12	1.06
48	10					15.3			44 58.69	6.12	1.05
49	9.10				52.3	8.5			45 35.67	6.12	1.04
50	10					32.			46 59.33	6.12	1.06
51	10	1.6		34.2					48 34.35	6.12	1.06
52	8.9				9.9	26.2			50 26.32	6.13	1.05
53	7.8				57.6	13.8	30.7		51 57.63	6.13	1.06
54	9.10					4.2	21.2		52 4.44	6.13	1.06
55	8			16.8	33.2	49.8	6.5		53 33.36	6.13	1.07
56	10			22.3					55 38.67	6.13	1.07
57	10				45.8		18.6		56 45.86	6.13	1.07
58	10	47.3	3.8						57 30.16	6.13	1.08
59	10.11						1.8?		57 29.13'	6.13	1.08
60	10					14.8			17 59 14.93	6.14	1.07
61	9					3.6	20.3		18 0 47.24	6.14	1.07
62	10					18.6			2 1.97	6.14	1.07
63	9.10								2'	6.14	1.08
64	9								3	6.14	1.08
65	10					22.			4 49.28	6.14	1.08
66	6					56.2	13.2		4 39.95	6.14	1.07
67	9				57.4				6 57.54	6.15	1.08
68	7					25.3	41.5		6 8.72	6.14	1.08
69	8								6	6.14	1.09
70	8				32.1		5.4		7 32.42	6.15	1.10
71	10				30.2				8 30.30	6.15	1.10
72	10						4.2		18 8 31.48	+6.15	+1.10

No.	MICROMETER		r.	i	d_1	d_2	Mean Right Ascension, 1850.0 (h m s)	Mean Declination, 1850.0 (° ' ")
24	III.	5	46.425	−12 50.37	−3.21	−3.18	17 4 25.26	−20 24 6.8
25	IV.	3	23.252	37 3.53	3.17	7.16	6 57.68	48 23.9
26	III.	5	52.489	6 29.75	3.12	2.14	10 0.14	17 45.0
27	IV.	4	41.187	17 16.81	3.11	3.95	9 53.68	28 33.9
28	V.	5	50.336	8 45.21	3.11	2.50	9 59.13	20 0.8
29	VII.	5	46.324	12 56.40	3.12	3.19	10 7.87	24 12.7
30	IV.	2	15.222	45 27.57	3.07	8.57	13 1.08	56 49.2
31	IV.	2	45.675	13 37.64	3.05	3.30	13 56.79	24 54.0
32	V.	3	35.770	23 57.91	3.07	5.02	13 8.57	35 16.0
33	III.	5	52.723	6 15.19	3.03	2.10	15 48.34	17 30.3
34	III.	3	32.844	27 1.50	2.99	5.52	17 56.49	38 20.0
35	III.	5	47.603	11 36.69	2.97	2.98	18 28.34	22 52.6
36	IV.	2	21.729	38 39.25	2.95	7.44	20 19.63	49 59.6
37	III.	3	31.457	28 28.77	2.87	5.75	24 29.93	39 47.4
38	IV.	3	29.055	30 59.35	2.93	6.16	26 42.62	42 18.3
39	IV.	2	19.305	41 11.49	2.81	7.85	27 25.70	52 32.2
40	V.	2	20.481	39 57.85	2.81	7.65	27 48.95	51 18.3
41	V.	3	35.618	24 7.51	2.80	5.03	28 35.11	35 25.3
42	IV.	3	24.854	35 22.84	2.72	6.90	31 54.39	46 42.5
43	IV.	3	25.048	35 10.73	2.62	6.87	38 34.21	46 30.2
44	IV.	3	25.013	35 12.93	2.60	6.87	40 30.17	46 32.4
45	III.	2	16.949	43 38.63	2.55	6.27	42 15.10	20 54 59.4
46	III.	1	11.425	49 25.47	2.53	9.20	43 51.82	21 0 47.2
47	V.	5	47.051	12 11.84	2.52	3.08	44 0.11	20 23 27.4
48	IV.	2	23.229	37 5.35	2.50	7.18	45 5.86	48 25.0
49	III.	1	12.902	47 52.59	2.49	8.99	45 42.83	59 14.1
50	V.	5	48.172	11 0.92	2.46	2.86	46 6.51	22 16.2
51	III.	3	34.878	24 53.87	2.43	5.15	48 41.53	20 36 11.4
52	III.	1	10.581	50 18.09	2.39	9.30	50 33.50	21 1 39.9
53	IV.	5	50.990	8 4.03	2.36	2.51	51 4.82	20 19 18.9
54	IV.	4	40.351	19 12.07	2.36	4.22	52 11.63	30 28.6
55	IV.	3	27.577	32 32.14	2.32	6.43	53 40.56	43 50.9
56	II.	2	15.228	45 26.76	2.28	8.55	55 45.87	56 47.6
57	IV.	3	22.323	38 1.81	2.25	7.33	55 53.06	49 21.4
58	II.	5	42.809	16 37.19	2.24	3.79	57 37.37	27 53.2
59	V.	5	47.517	11 42.09	2.24	2.95	57 36.34	22 57.3
60	III.	2	20.335	40 6.70	2.20	7.68	59 22.14	51 26.6
61	IV.	2	15.942	44 42.23	2.17	8.46	17 59 54.45	56 2.9
62	IV.	2	17.472	43 6.46	2.13	8.20	18 2 9.18	54 26.8
63	VI.	3	27.164	32 57.80	2.12	6.51	. . .	44 16.4
64		5	43.628	15 46.11	2.10	3.63	. . .	27 1.8
65	V.	4	36.424	23 19.00	2.07	4.88	4 56.50	20 34 36.0
66	IV.	1	6.798	54 15.50	2.08	10.08	4 47.16	21 5 37.7
67	III.	2	17.374	43 12.42	2.02	8.22	6 4.77	20 54 32.7
68	IV.	3	25.478	34 43.88	2.04	6.80	6 15.94	46 2.7
69	VI.	5	45.022	14 18.36	2.03	3.40	. . .	25 33.6
70	IV.	3	35.734	24 0.23	2.01	5.00	7 39.67	35 17.2
71	III.	3	29.748	30 15.81	1.99	6.04	8 37.55	41 33.8
72	V.	3	32.672	−27 12.35	−1.99	−5.54	18 8 38.73	−20 38 29.9

CORRECTIONS.

Date.	Corr. of Clock.	Hourly rate.	m	n	c	Zenith Point.	Mic. Co.
1849.	h.	s.	s.	s.	s.	° ' "	r.

INSTRUMENT READINGS.

Date.	CIRCLE							Baróm.	THERMOM.				
		A.	B.	C.	D.	E.	F.	Mean.	in.	At.	Ex.	U.	L.	I.
Zone 257	1849. June 20, 18 0								30.168			73.6		
	18 20											72.5		
	18 40	79.32 {33.8 29.2 32.1 31.6 32.4 28.9 / 32.7 29.8 33.1 33.4 33.7 30.6}					31.79	30.164	76.8	71.8	77.2	76.	

REMARKS.

(257) 26. Transits discordant. Assumed observation on T. I as 20s.2 instead of 26s.2, when R. A. differs 20s from Arg. Z. 211, 78.

(257) 27. Minutes assumed as 9, not 10; and mic. reading as 42r.187, not 41r.187, to agree with Arg. Z.

(257) 28. Minutes assumed as 9, not 10.

(257) 36. R. A. differs 1m from Arg. Z. 213, 95; minutes probably 19, not 20.

(257) 42. Minutes assumed as 31, not 32.

(257) 50. Minutes assumed as 45, not 46.

(257) 53. Minutes assumed as 50, not 51.

(257) 57. Minutes assumed as 55, not 56.

(257) 58. Transits over T.'s I and II ass'd as 57s.3 and 13s.8, not 47s.3 and 3s.8.

(257) 59. Transit over T. V perhaps belongs to preceding reading; and declination, with 1 mic. rev. in error, to Arg. Z. 310, 7.

(257) 61. R. A. assumed as 17h 59m.

(257) 65. R. A. differs 1m from Arg. Z. 310, 19; minutes probably 3.

(257) 67. Minutes ass'd as 5, not 6, to agree with Arg. Z. 307. 66; 310, 22.

ZONE 257. JUNE 20. C. $D_s = -20°\ 11'\ 10''$—Continued.

No.	Mag.	I.	II.	III.	IV.	V.	VI.	VII.	T. (h. m. s.)	a_1 (s.)	a_2 (s.)
73	9		14.7		47.7				18 11 31.21	+6.15	+1.10
74	9.10			6.2		38.8			12 6.15	6.15	1.10
75	9			16.2	32.3				16.01	6.15	1.10
76	9.10		37.3	54.1					16 53.94	6.16	1.09
77	6			17.3		50.7			16 17.67	6.16	1.10
78	10			4.2					19 4.33	6.16	1.10
79	8.9	13.7	29.9	46.5	3.4				21 46.58	6.17	1.10
80	9		15.5	31.4	48.1	4.3			21 31.64	6.17	1.11
81	9	53.5	10.5	26.5	43.5				24 26.67	6.17	1.12
82	10.11			19.5					25 19.47	6.18	1.12
83	8			17.3	33.6	49.7			26 17.10	6.18	1.11
84	9		21.4	37.2					27 37.51	6.18	1.13
85	9				1.7	18.3			28 45.43	6.18	1.13
86	9.10	18.5		50.8					30 51.03	6.19	1.13
87	9.10			10.2	26.5				30 10.08	6.19	1.13
88	10					6.5			30 33.69	6.19	1.12
89	9								31	6.19	1.12
90	10					23.			32 50.28	6.19	1.13
91	8		7.6	23.8		56.8			33 23.98	6.19	1.13
92	9.10								34	6.19	1.13
93	9					1.4			34 28.58	6.19	1.12
94	8.9	41.8	57.7	14.3	31.2				36 14.44	6.20	1.13
95	9.10				40.5	56.3			36 23.69	6.20	1.13
96	10					43.8			37 11.01	6.20	1.13
97	9.10				12.2				38 55.64	6.20	1.14
98	10								38	6.20	1.14
99	8.9					23.8			39 51.12	6.20	1.14
100	7	5.8	24.2	39.2	54.9	11.3			18 40 39.45	+6.21	+1.14

No.	MICROMETER (r)	i (′ ″)	d_1 (″)	d_2 (″)	Mean Right Ascension, 1850.0 (h. m. s.)	Mean Declination, 1850.0 (° ′ ″)
73	IV. 5 53.729	− 5 12.11	− 1.02	− 1.90	18 11 38.46	− 20 16 25.9
74	IV. 4 49.508	9 37.39	1.90	2.62	12 13.40	20 51.9
75	IV. 3 28.041	32 2.97	. .	6.37	14 23.26	43 21.2
76	III. 2 20.331	40 6.94	1.77	7.68	17 1.19	51 26.4
77	IV. 3 34.110	25 42.26	1.79	5.26	16 24.93	36 59.3
78	III. 1 18.600	41 55.33	1.73	7.98	19 11.59	20 53 15.0
79	IV. 1 9.665	51 15.85	1.66	9.56	20 53.85	21 2 37.1
80	IV. 5 47.588	11 37.69	1.65	2.95	21 38.42	20 22 52.3
81	IV. 4 42.325	17 8.19	1.58	3.87	24 33.96	28 23.6
82	III. 5 47.430	11 47.04	1.56	2.97	25 26.77	23 1.6
83	IV. 2 14.880	45 45.85	1.53	8.65	26 24.30	57 9.0
84	III. 5 44.743	14 35.75	1.50	3.43	27 44.82	25 50.7
85	IV. 5 52.716	6 15.70	1.46	2.06	28 52.74	17 29.2
86	III. 4 45.688	13 36.33	1.40	3.28	30 58.35	24 51.1
87	IV. 4 42.998	16 25.76	1.43	3.75	30 17.40	20 27 40.9
88	V. 1 10.218	50 41.23	1.41	9.48	30 41.00	21 2 2.1
89	VI. 3 23.451	36 50.79	1.4	7.14	. . .	20 48 9.3
90	V. 3 33.539	26 18.02	1.34	5.37	32 57.60	37 34.7
91	IV. 4 43.676	15 43.28	1.33	3.64	33 31.30	26 58.3
92	VII. 3 31.940	27 57.78	1.3	5.67	. . .	20 39 14.8
93	V. 1 8.673	52 21.82	1.30	9.75	34 35.89	21 3 42.9
94	IV. 3 23.868	36 24.69	1.29	7.08	36 21.77	20 47 43.0
95	IV. 2 16.031	44 30.71	1.23	8.46	36 31.01	55 56.4
96	V. 2 16.548	44 4.22	1.21	8.38	37 18.34	55 23.8
97	IV. 3 34.041	24 49.98	1.15	5.13	39 2.98	36 6.3
98	VI. 3 37.935	21 41.66	1.14	4.62	39	32 57.6
99	V. 4 44.709	14 38.89	1.13	3.44	38 58.46	25 53.5
100	IV. 4 41.364	− 18 8.50	− 1.12	− 4.04	18 40 45.80	− 20 29 23.7

ZONE 258. JUNE 21. S. $D_s = -18°\ 53'\ 20''$.

[The column T for this zone has been computed on the supposition that the transits over T.'s I–V have been recorded as over II–VI, respectively, throughout the zone.]

No.	Mag.	I.	II.	III.	IV.	V.	VI.	VII.	T. (h. m. s.)	a_1 (s.)	a_2 (s.)
1	9			11.					16 11 11.14	+6.49	+0.24
2	8					45.			11 12.46	6.49	0.24
3	9					33.			12 16.50	6.49	0.23
4	6		40.	56.	12.				15 12.35	6.49	0.24
5	10			17.					16 33.23	6.48	0.21
6	11		14.		47.				23 46.80	6.47	0.22
7	10		20.	16.2					25 52.54	6.47	0.26
8	11		13.	29.4					27 45.62	6.47	0.23
9	12				34.				31 34.13	6.47	0.27
10	7			42.5	58.	14.			32 58.12	6.47	0.28
11	10		57.		29.2				35 29.48	6.46	0.28
12	10		19.	35.	51.4				38 51.47	6.46	0.28
13	9			50.					39 50.09	6.46	0.24
14	9					40.5			40 8.06	6.46	0.25
15	9				59.5				41 59.63	6.46	0.29
16	8			11.	27.				43 27.14	6.46	0.23
17	9			44.	0.2				16 45 0.25	+6.46	+0.23

No.	MICROMETER (r)	i (′ ″)	d_1 (″)	d_2 (″)	Mean Right Ascension, 1850.0 (h. m. s.)	Mean Declination, 1850.0 (° ′ ″)
1	. 1 13.818	− 46 55.14	− 8.34	− 12.70	16 11 17.9	− 19 40 36.2
2	. 1 13.122	47 39.11	8.34	12.79	11 19.2	41 20.2
3	. 2 19.842	40 37.75	8.34	11.69	12 23.2	34 17.8
4	IV. 2 13.543	47 12.64	8.37	12.74	15 19.1	40 53.7
5	. 3 20.714	35 31.46	8.37	10.90	16 39.0	29 10.7
6	IV. 4 37.373	22 18.32	8.41	8.77	23 53.5	15 55.5
7	III. 2 16.932	43 39.70	8.41	12.16	25 59.3	37 20.3
8	III. 3 35.989	23 44.09	8.41	9.00	27 52.3	17 21.5
9	. 1 20.810	39 36.59	8.42	11.52	31 40.9	33 16.5
10	IV. 1 16.039	44 32.20	8.41	12.31	33 4.9	38 12.9
11	IV. 2 20.293	40 9.33	8.40	11.61	35 30.2	33 49.3
12	IV. 2 18.192	42 21.05	8.40	11.94	38 58.2	36 1.4
13	. 3 33.379	26 28.18	8.39	9.43	39 56.8	20 6.0
14	. 4 41.458	18 3.09	8.39	6.09	40 14.8	11 39.6
15	. 2 19.685	40 47.28	8.38	11.72	42 6.4	34 27.4
16	IV. 5 47.041	12 11.90	8.37	7.18	43 33.8	5 47.5
17	IV. 5 49.212	− 9 55.77	− 8.35	− 6.80	16 45 6.9	− 19 3 30.9

CORRECTIONS.

Date	Corr. of Clock	Hourly rate	m	n	c	Zenith Point	Mic. Co.
1849.	h. s.	s.	s.	s.	s.	° ′ ″	r.

INSTRUMENT READINGS.

Date	A.	B.	C.	D.	E.	F.	Mean.	Barom.	At.	Ex.	U.	L.	I.
Zone 258. 1849. June 21, 16 0	78 14 60.	54.1	58.5	54.3	55.8	55.	56.28	30.164	83.	81.5	79.5	83.5	81.
16 20										*81.2			
16 40										77.2			
17 0								30.156	81.9	76.8			
17 20										75.8			
17 40	60.5	54.1	58.5	54.3	55.3	54.5	56.20			75.4			
18 0								30.154	79.9	75.2			
18 20										74.9			
18 40										74.8			

REMARKS.

(257) 75. Minutes assumed as 14.

(257) 79. Minutes assumed as 20, not 21.

(257) 82. Right ascension differs 36s from Arg. Z. 310, 56.

(257) 85. Right ascension differs 1m from Arg. Z. 310, 61; minutes probably 27, not 28.

(257) 90. Right ascension differs 1m from Arg. Z. 310, 67; and minutes probably 31, not 32.

(257) 91. Transit over T. V assumed to have been recorded over T. IV.

(257) 99. Minutes assumed as 38, not 39.

(258) 3. Transit over T. IV assumed to have been recorded over T. VI.

(258) 5. Micrometer reading assumed as 24r.714, not 20r.714, to agree with Arg. Z. 211, 25, and 305, 25.

(258) 13. Right ascension differs 17s from Arg. Z. 300, 53; transit over T. II perhaps recorded over T. III.

* Used as 79°.2.

ZONE 258. JUNE 21. S. $D_0 = -18°\ 53'\ 20''$—Continued.

No.	Mag.	I.	II.	III.	IV.	V.	VI.	VII.	T.	a_1	a_3
									h. m. s.	s.	s.
18	10					44.5	61.		16 46 25.31	+ 6.46	+ 0.27
19	8			52.	8.5				48 8.40	6.46	0.27
20	9						29.3		48 56.78	6.46	0.30
21	10						53.8		50 21.36	6.45	0.27
22	7		51.2	7.2	23.3				54 23.53	6.45	0.28
23	11				6.				57 6.13	6.45	0.32
24	.				11.				58 11.06	6.45	0.30
25	8					47.			16 58 30.62	6.45	0.27
26	9						44.		17 0 11.50	6.45	0.32
27	7.8					35.	51.		1 18.57	6.45	0.29
28	11				12.5				5 12.47	6.45	0.29
29	9			15.8	32.				7 32.05	6.45	0.29
30	11		20.	36.					9 52.41	6.45	0.29
31	8.7		6.8	23.	30.				11 39.21	6.45	0.31
32	9.8			20.					13 36.22	6.45	0.35
33	9			2.8			51.5		14 19.05	6.45	0.33
34	9		57.8	14.2					16 30.44	6.45	0.37
35	10					7.5			16 51.09	6.45	0.32
36	11					2.5			18 46.12	6.45	0.32
37	9		13.	29.6	45.5				20 45.67	6.45	0.35
38	9				40.				21 40.11	6.45	0.37
39	9		40.	56.		28.			25 12.15	6.46	0.32
40	10		20.3	36.2			25.		29 52.62	6.46	0.38
41	10		47.2	3.5	19.5				32 19.71	6.46	0.37
42	11						43.		34 10.51	6.46	0.39
43	9		9.	25.	41.				39 41.36	6.46	0.43
44	9		11.						42 43.67	6.46	0.41
45	7				49.5	6.			42 49.57	6.46	0.41
46	8						55.		43 22.59	6.47	0.36
47	8.9				22.				46 22.04	6.47	0.40
48	10		23.		55.2				47 55.42	6.47	0.40
49	10						18.5		48 46.01	6.47	0.42
50	9			10.5					51 26.81	6.47	0.39
51	10					57.5	14.		51 41.22	6.47	0.45
52	6					11.	27.2		52 54.70	6.47	0.39
53	9			45.8	2.				55 2.07	6.48	0.44
54	11			56.					56 12.23	6.48	0.45
55	8					49.2			56 32.67	6.48	0.47
56	10						57.		57 57.14	6.48	0.47
57	9			36.					17 59 52.36	6.48	0.39
58	8				38.	54.			18 0 37.82	6.49	0.44
59	10		4.5						2 37.13	6.49	0.45
60	8			59.2		28.3			3 15.62	6.49	0.45
61	10			38.					4 54.34	6.49	0.40
62	9			21.					5 37.33	6.49	0.41
63	7			3.5					6 3.46	6.49	0.40
64	8						52.3		6 19.89	6.49	0.41
65	9					45.			7 28.64	6.49	0.41
66	7		13.	29.6	45.5		34.5		18 8 2.09	+ 6.49	+ 0.42

No.	MICROMETER		r,	i	d_1	d_3	Mean Right Ascension, 1850.0.	Mean Declination, 1850.0.
			r,	′ ″	″	″	h. m. s.	° ′ ″
18		3	36.898	− 22 47.19 −	8.35 −	8.85	16 46 35.0	− 19 16 24.4
19	IV.	3	35.549	24 11.96	8.33	9.08	48 15.1	17 49.4
20	.	2	20.980	39 26.42	8.33	11.49	49 3.5	33 6.2
21		4	41.420	18 5.55	8.32	8.10	50 28.1	11 42.0
22	IV.	3	37.078	22 35.96	8.28	8.82	54 30.3	16 13.1
23	.	2	19.602	40 52.54	8.24	11.74	57 12.9	34 32.5
24		3	35.651	24 5.50	8.23	9.04	58 17.8	17 42.3
25	.	4	47.000	11 18.11	8.23	7.03	16 58 37.3	4 53.4
26	.	3	25.058	35 10.01	8.21	10.83	17 0 18.3	28 49.1
27	V.	4	38.810	20 48.58	8.20	8.53	1 25.3	14 25.3
28	.	5	47.872	11 19.62	8.14	7.03	5 19.2	4 54.8
29	IV.	4	43.202	16 12.47	8.11	7.79	7 38.8	9 48.4
30	.	5	47.630	11 34.43	8.07	7.07	9 59.1	5 9.6
31	IV.	4	42.903	16 31.10	8.05	7.84	11 46.0	10 7.0
32	.	3	26.285	33 53.13	8.01	10.62	13 43.0	27 31.8
33	III.	4	35.449	24 19.05	8.01	9.08	14 25.8	17 56.1
34	III.	2	18.232	42 18.35	7.96	11.96	16 37.3	35 58.3
35	.	4	43.732	15 39.70	7.96	7.70	16 57.8	9 15.4
36	.	4	47.514	11 42.34	7.93	7.09	18 52.9	5 17.4
37	IV.	3	32.695	27 10.91	7.90	9.54	20 52.5	20 48.3
38	.	3	27.650	32 27.57	7.89	10.38	21 46.9	26 5.8
39	III.	5	48.848	10 18.17	7.82	6.84	25 18.9	3 52.8
40	III.	3	27.083	33 2.95	7.73	10.49	29 59.5	26 41.2
41	IV.	3	30.310	29 40.71	7.69	9.95	32 26.5	23 18.4
42	.	3	27.949	32 8.61	7.65	10.34	34 17.3	25 46.0
43	IV.	1	11.132	49 42.47	7.54	13.18	39 48.2	43 23.2
44	.	2	10.802	50 3.86	7.48	13.24	42 50.6	43 44.6
45	IV.	3	25.275	34 56.43	7.48	10.80	42 56.4	28 34.7
46	.	5	48.221	10 56.78	7.45	6.95	43 29.4	4 31.2
47	I.	3	37.680	21 58.12	7.40	8.71	46 28.9	15 34.2
48	IV.	3	31.984	24 47.28	7.37	9.16	48 2.3	18 23.8
49	.	3	28.188	31 53.81	7.34	10.32	48 52.9	25 31.5
50	.	4	45.190	14 7.64	7.28	7.45	51 33.7	7 42.4
51	V.	2	12.695	48 5.95	7.28	12.92	51 48.1	41 46.2
52	V.	5	47.042	12 11.84	7.34	7.15	53 1.6	5 46.2
53	IV.	3	26.373	33 47.74	7.19	10.61	55 9.0	27 25.5
54	.	2	18.930	41 34.38	7.17	11.86	56 19.2	35 13.4
55	.	1	9.058	51 53.90	7.16	13.55	56 39.6	45 34.6
56	.	1	11.590	49 15.13	7.14	13.12	57 4.1	19 42 55.4
57	.	3	53.072	5 56.86	7.08	6.15	17 59 59.2	18 59 30.1
58	IV.	3	31.042	28 54.62	7.07	9.83	18 0 44.7	19 22 31.5
59	.	4	25.990	34 12.20	7.02	10.68	2 44.1	31 49.9
60	III.	3	26.135	34 2.42	7.01	10.62	3 22.6	27 40.0
61	.	5	51.203	7 50.55	6.97	6.44	5 1.2	1 24.0
62	.	4	47.208	12 0.99	6.95	7.12	5 44.2	19 5 35.1
63	.	5	53.580	5 21.27	6.93	6.07	6 10.4	18 58 54.3
64	.	5	50.745	8 19.35	6.93	6.51	6 26.8	19 1 52.8
65	.	5	51.623	7 24.37	6.90	6.37	7 35.5	0 57.6
66	.	5	51.779	− 7 14.51	6.89 −	6.35	18 8 9.0	− 19 0 47.7

CORRECTIONS.

Date.	Corr. of Clock.	Hourly rate.	m	n	c	Zenith Point.	Mic. Co.
1849.	h.	s.	s.	s.	s.	s.	° ′ ″	r,

INSTRUMENT READINGS.

Date.	CIRCLE.							Barom.	THERMOM.				
	A.	B.	C.	D.	E.	F.	Mean.		At.	Ex.	U.	L.	I.
	° ′ ″						″	In.	°				
Zone 258 June 21, 1849. 19 0								30.150	79.	74.2			
19 20										73.9			
19 30	78 14 60.5	54.1	58.5	55.8	55.8	54.5	56.53						

REMARKS.

(258) 41. Declination differs 1′ from Arg. Z. 211, 107.

(258) 56. Transit over T. III assumed as recorded over T. V ; and minutes as 56, not 57.

(258) 60. Time of transit over T. III assumed as 32s.3 instead of 28s.3.

(258) 63. Transit over T. III assumed as recorded over T. II, to agree with Arg. Z. 218, 50 ; 219, 42 ; 227, 21 ; and 391, 129.

ZONE 258. JUNE 21. S. $D_o = -18°\ 53'\ 20''$—Continued.

Seconds of transit, time, corrections

No.	Mag.	I.	II.	III.	IV.	V.	VI.	VII.	T. (h. m. s.)	a_1 (s.)	a_2 (s.)
67	9			45.2					18 12 1.44	+6.50	+0.52
68	9		32.3	49.					15 5.07	6.50	0.49
69	10					26.			15 9.48	6.50	0.51
70	10		12.5	59.5			47.5		18 15.31	6.51	0.44
71	11						32.5		18 0.09	6.51	0.45
72	8			11.					22 27.27	6.51	0.47
73	7				56.				22 56.02	6.51	0.47
74	9					32.			23 15.58	6.51	0.47
75	8		53.	10.		32.			26 25.79	6.52	0.49
76	9			45.					28 1.27	6.52	0.48
77	8					26.			28 9.55	6.52	0.49
78	9			40.					30 56.28	6.53	0.49
79	10			58.5					32 14.73	6.53	0.54
80	8		25.3	41.	57.5				33 57.58	6.53	0.51
81	10					37.			34 20.54	6.53	0.52
82	8.7					27.8			35 11.32	6.53	0.53
83	10						17.		35 44.50	6.54	0.53
84	7				2.8				37 2.96	6.54	0.57
85	7.8		44.5		16.3				39 16.75	6.54	0.52
86	7		6.2						40 38.79	6.54	0.52
87	8					56.			40 39.62	6.54	0.49
88	9					47.5			41 31.02	6.55	0.54
89	10			44.2	0.5				44 0.50	6.55	0.53
90	9			7.	23.				46 23.15	6.56	0.51
91	7.8			7.	23.	39.		12.2	48 39.41	6.56	0.54
92	7.8		10.6	26.6	43.				50 26.69	6.57	0.56
93	9					20.			51 3.52	6.57	0.57
94	9				8.				52 8.13	6.57	0.57
95	7		35.	51.					54 7.42	6.57	0.57
96	7			11.	27.				54 10.81	6.57	0.55
97	9			44.2	0.2				57 0.40	6.58	0.62
98	11	8.							58 40.65	6.59	0.61
99	5.6					20.5	37.		18 59 20.57	6.59	0.59
100	10				33.5				19 0 33.64	6.59	0.61
101	9				50.				2 50.11	6.60	0.59
102	9			33.	50.				3 49.67	6.60	0.60
103	10					46.5			4 30.11	6.60	0.56
104	10			34.			23.		5 50.42	6.60	0.57
105	10		13.8	30.					7 46.35	6.61	0.62
106	7.6			28.2					8 44.48	6.61	0.58
107	8			1.					9 17.34	6.61	0.55
108	10						41.3		9 8.82	6.61	0.60
109	9			46.3					11 4.54	6.62	0.64
110	10				35.				11 35.04	6.62	0.60
111	6.7			26.					12 42.22	6.62	0.62
112	10				9.5				13 9.60	6.62	0.61
113	10					57.8			13 41.36	6.62	0.58
114	10			20.3					15 36.58	6.63	0.59
115	11				27.				19 16 10.55	+6.63	+0.61

Micrometer, instrumental corrections and mean places

No.	Micrometer		r	i ($'\ ''$)	d_1 ($''$)	d_2 ($''$)	Mean Right Ascension, 1850.0 (h. m. s.)	Mean Declination, 1850.0 (° ' ")
67		1	11.468	−49 22.39	−6.79	−13.14	18 12 8.5	−19 43 2.3
68	III.	3	25.860	34 18.98	6.71	10.70	15 12.1	27 56.4
69		1	15.356	45 19.06	6.71	12.47	15 16.5	38 58.2
70	III.	5	50.470	8 36.55	6.62	6.54	18 22.3	2 9.7
71		4	47.653	11 34.24	6.63	7.00	18 7.1	5 7.8
72		3	37.813	21 49.59	6.51	8.67	22 34.3	15 24.8
73		3	39.672	19 53.19	6.50	8.37	23 3.0	13 28.1
74		3	39.852	19 41.82	6.49	8.34	23 22.6	13 16.6
75	IV.	2	30.730	29 14.39	6.41	9.88	26 32.8	22 50.7
76		3	30.783	21 51.46	6.36	8.65	28 8.3	15 26.5
77		3	33.789	26 2.27	6.36	9.37	28 16.6	19 38.0
78		4	39.380	20 18.59	6.29	8.41	31 3.3	13 53.3
79		2	18.388	42 8.64	6.25	11.98	32 21.8	35 46.9
80	IV.	3	28.388	31 41.33	6.20	10.29	34 4.6	25 17.8
81		3	31.525	28 22.51	6.19	9.74	34 27.6	22 0.4
82		3	26.078	34 6.12	6.16	10.67	35 18.4	27 42.9
83		3	25.631	34 34.17	6.14	10.75	35 51.6	28 11.1
84		1	9.122	51 49.78	6.11	13.55	37 10.1	45 29.4
85	IV.	3	32.075	27 49.88	6.04	9.65	39 23.8	21 25.6
86		3	35.053	24 42.64	6.00	9.14	40 45.8	18 17.8
87		4	48.480	10 41.89	6.00	6.90	40 46.6	4 14.8
88		3	45.920	34 15.97	5.97	10.69	41 38.1	27 52.6
89	IV.	3	35.703	24 2.17	5.90	9.03	44 7.6	17 37.1
90		4	43.353	16 3.05	5.83	7.75	46 30.2	9 36.6
91	IV.	3	32.753	27 7.26	5.76	9.54	48 46.5	20 42.6
92	IV.	3	35.243	34 58.57	5.71	10.81	50 33.8	25 35.1
93		3	23.692	36 35.80	5.69	11.08	51 10.7	30 12.6
94		3	20.912	39 30.05	5.66	11.54	52 15.3	33 7.2
95	III.	3	26.383	33 46.99	5.59	10.63	54 14.6	27 23.2
96		3	34.518	25 16.66	5.59	9.22	54 17.9	18 51.5
97	IV.	1	12.263	48 32.84	5.50	13.04	57 7.6	42 11.4
98		3	17.980	42 33.72	5.44	12.04	58 47.8	36 11.2
99	IV.	3	22.760	37 34.20	5.42	11.24	18 59 27.7	31 10.9
100		2	15.603	45 3.37	5.39	12.45	19 0 40.8	38 41.2
101		3	27.838	32 15.58	5.30	10.38	2 57.3	25 51.3
102	IV.	3	25.295	34 55.37	5.27	10.81	3 56.9	28 31.4
103		5	46.719	12 32.12	5.25	7.16	4 37.3	6 4.5
104		3	39.455	20 7.67	5.20	8.40	5 57.6	13 41.3
105	III.	2	15.082	45 35.86	5.14	12.54	7 53.6	39 13.5
106		3	40.245	19 18.04	5.11	8.26	8 51.7	12 51.4
107		5	49.245	9 53.44	5.09	6.72	9 24.5	3 25.2
108		3	29.390	30 38.46	5.09	10.10	9 16.0	24 13.6
109		2	16.061	44 34.46	5.03	12.37	11 11.8	58 11.9
110		4	37.150	22 32.26	5.01	8.77	11 42.3	16 6.0
111		3	26.290	37 1.05	4.97	11.40	12 49.5	30 37.4
112		3	29.622	30 23.75	4.95	10.06	13 16.8	23 58.8
113		3	35.248	24 30.91	4.94	9.10	13 48.6	18 5.0
114		3	40.302	19 13.64	4.87	8.25	15 43.8	12 46.8
115		3	32.985	−26 52.58	−4.84	−9.49	19 16 17.6	−19 20 26.9

CORRECTIONS.

Date.	Corr. of Clock.	Hourly rate.	m	n	c	Zenith Point.	Mic. Co.
	h. s.	s.	s.	s.	s.	° ' "	r.
1849.							

INSTRUMENT READINGS.

Date.	CIRCLE.							Barom.	THERMOM.				
	A.	B.	C.	D.	E.	F.	Mean.		At.	Ex.	U.	L.	I.
1849.	h. m.	° ' "					"	In.	°	°	°	°	°

REMARKS.

(258) 73. Declination differs 10″ from Arg. Z. 227, 51; micrometer reading perhaps 39ʳ.752, not 39ʳ.852.

(258) 75. Time of transit over T. V assumed as 42ˢ instead of 32ˢ.

(258) 105. Declination differs 5′ 15″ from Arg. Z. 227, 117; micrometer reading probably 20ʳ.082, not 15ʳ.082.

(258) 109. Transit over T. II assumed as 48ˢ.3, not 46ˢ.3, to agree with Meridian Circle Z., August 25, 1849, and Transit August 14, 1848.

(258) 111. Micrometer reading assumed as 23ʳ.290, not 26ʳ.290.

ZONE 258. JUNE 21. S. D_0 = −78° 53′ 20″—Continued.

No.	Mag.	I.	II.	III.	IV.	V.	VI.	VII.	T.	a_1	a_2
									h. m. s.	s.	s.
116	11						20.5		19 16 48.00	+ 6.63	+0.63
117	10		36.	52.3					19 8.60	6.64	0.65
118	11						27.5		18 55.09	6.64	0.57
119	10				34.5				20 34.50	6.64	0.60
120	10					37.5			21 14.98	6.64	0.66
121	9			31.8					22 48.04	6.65	0.66
122	11			36.8	53.				24 53.05	6.65	0.61
123	10		48.5	5.	21.				26 21.10	6.66	0.58
124	7			17.	34.	50.8			19 27 33.89	+ 6.66	+0.62

No.	MICROMETER.		r.	i	d_1	d_2	Mean Right Ascension, 1850.0.	Mean Declination, 1850.0.
			r.	° ′ ″	″	″	h. m. s.	° ′ ″
116	.	3	26.030	−34 9.07	− 4.82	−10.69	19 16 55.3	− 19 27 44.6
117	III.	2	15.813	44 49.89	4.74	12.41	19 15.9	38 27.0
118	.	5	48.833	10 19.30	4.75	6.78	19 2.3	3 50.8
119	.	4	43.509	15 53.25	4.69	7.71	20 41.7	9 25.6
120	.	2	12.948	47 50.01	4.66	12.93	21 22.3	41 27.6
121	.	2	12.619	48 10.34	4.61	12.99	22 55.3	41 47.9
122	IV.	4	42.379	17 4.17	4.53	7.86	25 0.3	10 36.6
123	IV.	4	47.290	11 55.95	4.48	7.08	26 28.3	5 27.5
124	IV.	4	42.260	−17 11.65	− 4.42	− 7.92	19 27 41.2	− 19 10 44.0

ZONE 259. JUNE 22. C. D_0 = −20° 8′ 40′.

No.	Mag.	I.	II.	III.	IV.	V.	VI.	VII.	T.	a_1	a_2
									h. m. s.	s.	s.
1	9.10		32.2	48.3	3.6	21.			15 3 48.06	+ 6.85	+0.92
2	10					28.?			4 55.32	6.84	0.84
3	9.10	30.1	45.2	2.	18.2	34.7			7 2.04	6.84	0.83
4	8.9	2.4	18.5	35.2	51.7				9 35.12	6.83	0.80
5	8.9				14.2	30.3			10 57.61	6.83	0.86
6	8.9			4.2	20.7	36.3			11 4.00	6.83	0.80
7	10		7.7	24.3		56.5			15 24.09	6.82	0.79
8	8	44.8	0.7	17.3	14.1	30.6			17 17.50	6.81	0.91
9	9.10			19.5		52.4			18 19.59	6.81	0.76
10	8			30.5	46.7	3.3			19 30.43	6.81	0.87
11	8	16.3	32.5	49.2					22 49.04	6.80	0.76
12	9	46.7	3.5	19.8	36.1	52.5			25 19.72	6.80	0.68
13	9.10			23.	38.7				26 22.59	6.80	0.80
14	10			26.8		0.2			28 27.17	6.79	0.89
15	7								30	6.79	0.80
16	9				6.5	23.5			31 50.37	6.78	0.80
17	10	55.5			45.	1.4			34 28.48	6.78	0.82
18	8	6.4	22.4	39.	55.8	11.5			38 39.02	6.77	0.83
19	9		37.6	54.1	10.5	27.1			40 54.10	6.76	0.83
20	8.9			3.1	19.4	36.			41 3.06	6.76	0.88
21	8.9					11.8			41 39.12	6.76	0.72
22	9.10	23.0	40.5	56.6		29.5			46 56.75	6.75	0.72
23	9.10		55.5		28.1	44.1			46 11.66	6.75	0.71
24	9			29.5	46.3				47 29.63	6.75	0.70
25	6.7		31.7	47.2	3.5				49 47.23	6.75	0.76
26	8				53.8				49 37.26	6.75	0.74
27	8.9				23.	39.5			50 6.60	6.75	0.77
28	8	39.2	55.5	11.5	28.2	44.4			52 11.76	6.74	0.79
29	10					45.3			53 12.63	6.74	0.69
30	9	28.6	45.3	7.3	18.4	34.2			56 1.60	6.74	0.72
31	10				15.7	32.5			57 59.43	6.74	0.77
32	4		12.3	29.3	45.3	2.3			58 29.10	6.74	0.71
33	9				47.3	4.5			58 31.26	6.74	0.73
34	9.10					13.3			15 59 40.63	6.73	0.69
35	9.10				57.3	14.			16 0 41.10	6.73	0.65
36	9.10		38.3			28.			16 3 54.95	+ 6.73	+0.74

No.	MICROMETER.		r.	i	d_1	d_2	Mean Right Ascension, 1850.0.	Mean Declination, 1850.0.
			r.	° ′ ″	″	″	h. m. s.	° ′ ″
1	IV.	3	24.735	−35 29.18	− 0.20	− 6.89	15 3 55.83	− 20 44 16.3
2	V.	5	45.596	13 42.59	0.22	3.37	5 3.00	22 26.2
3	IV.	5	45.360	13 57.59	0.26	3.41	7 9.71	22 41.3
4	IV.	5	49.430	9 42.74	0.30	2.75	9 42.75	18 25.2
5	IV.	3	35.415	24 20.43	0.32	5.09	11 5.30	33 5.8
6	IV.	5	48.782	10 22.57	0.32	2.84	11 11.63	19 5.7
7	IV.	5	49.495	9 38.06	0.38	2.71	15 31.70	18 21.2
8	IV.	2	18.392	42 8.76	0.40	7.97	17 25.22	50 57.1
9	IV.	5	55.051	3 49.12	0.41	1.70	18 27.16	12 31.3
10	IV.	3	27.856	32 14.52	0.43	6.37	19 38.11	41 1.3
11	III.	5	55.096	3 46.29	0.46	1.78	21 36.60	12 28.5
12	IV.	4	31.069	39 20.71	0.48	7.52	25 27.40	48 8.7
13	IV.	4	38.299	21 20.84	0.49	4.60	26 30.19	30 5.9
14	V.	2	14.423	46 17.82	0.51	8.65	28 34.85	55 7.0
15	VII.	4	37.436	22 15.85	0.53	4.74	30	31 1.1
16	IV.	4	36.986	22 43.04	0.54	4.81	30 57.95	31 28.4
17	IV.	3	30.728	29 14.32	0.55	5.89	34 36.06	38 0.7
18	IV.	5	23.258	37 3.15	0.58	7.15	38 46.62	45 50.9
19	IV.	3	23.886	36 23.56	0.59	7.04	41 1.69	20 45 11.2
20	IV.	1	8.108	52 53.48	0.59	9.74	41 10.70	21 1 43.8
21	V.	5	44.891	14 26.71	0.59	3.48	41 46.66	20 23 10.8
22	IV.	5	45.781	13 30.91	0.60	3.31	47 4.22	22 14.8
23	IV.	5	47.262	11 58.15	0.60	3.08	46 19.12	20 41.8
24	IV.	5	48.011	11 11.01	0.60	2.95	47 37.06	19 54.6
25	IV.	3	35.877	23 51.26	0.61	5.01	48 54.74	32 36.9
26	IV.	4	40.876	18 38.94	0.61	4.17	49 44.75	27 23.7
27	IV.	5	33.667	26 9.09	0.61	5.37	50 14.12	34 56.0
28	IV.	3	25.372	34 50.54	0.61	6.80	52 19.29	43 37.9
29	V.	5	48.085	11 6.43	0.61	2.93	53 20.66	19 50.0
30	IV.	4	39.347	20 14.83	0.61	4.42	56 9.66	28 59.9
31	IV.	3	24.554	35 41.79	0.61	6.94	58 6.94	44 20.3
32	IV.	4	40.700	18 50.00	0.61	4.18	58 36.55	27 34.8
33	IV.	3	36.466	23 14.49	0.61	4.89	58 38.73	32 0.0
34	V.	4	46.818	12 26.46	0.61	3.14	15 59 48.05	31 10.2
35	IV.	5	54.800	4 4.81	0.61	1.80	16 0 48.48	12 47.2
36	IV.	3	28.625	−31 26.40	− 0.60	− 6.23	16 4 2.42	− 20 40 13.2

CORRECTIONS.

Date.	Corr. of Clock.	Hourly rate.	m	n	c	Zenith Point.	Mic. Co.
1849. h.	s.	s.	s.	s.	° s.	° ′ ″	r.

INSTRUMENT READINGS.

Date.	CIRCLE.							Barom.	THERMOM.				
	A.	B.	C.	D.	E.	F.	Mean.		At.	Ex.	U.	L.	I.
	° ′ ″						″	in.					
Zone 259 1849. June 22, 15 0	79 29 64.6	57.1	61.1	58.1	57.9	59.5	59.72	30.070	84.5	80.4	81.7	84.	82.2
15 20										79.4			
15 40										78.7			
16 0								30.070	82.7	78.2			
16 20	63.8	57.3	61.0	58.9	57.7	59.1	59.63	30.072	82.5	77.9		83.	81.5

REMARKS.

(259) 1. Right ascen. differs 1ᵐ from Arg. Z. 365, 42; min. probably 2.

(259) 2. Right ascension differs 1ᵐ from Arg. Z. 208, 41; minutes perhaps 3, and transit over T. V 25ˢ, not 28ˢ.

(259) 5. Right ascen. differs 1ᵐ from Arg. Z. 208, 52; min. probably 9.

(259) 8. Assumed the transits over T.'s IV and V as 34ˢ.1 and 50ˢ.6 instead of 14ˢ.1 and 30ˢ.6, respectively.

(259) 11. Minutes assumed as 21, not 22, to agree with Arg. Z. 208, 66; 385, 69.

(259) 16. Assumed the minutes as 30 instead of 31.

(259) 22. Right ascension differs 1ᵐ from Arg. Z. 208, 99.

(259) 25. Minutes assumed as 48, not 49.

(259) 27. Declination differs 10′ from Arg. Z. 208, 84.

(259) 31. Right ascen. differs 1ᵐ from Arg. Z. 209, 94; min. probably 56.

Zone 259. June 22. C. $D_0 = -20°\ 8'\ 40''$—Continued.

Seconds of Transit

No.	Mag.	I.	II.	III.	IV.	V.	VI.	VII.
37	9.10					32.5		
38	8			44.2	0.3			
39	7			32.5	49.	5.4		
40	7.8		44.8		17.5	34.4		
41	9					32.3		
42	10.11			54.2				
43	10		7.2			59.		
44	9			28.	44.3	1.2		
45	10.11				50.2			
46	9.10					59.2		
47	9	27.3	43.1	0.3		33.4		

No.	T.	a_1	a_2	Mic.	n	r.	i	d_1	d_2	Mean R.A. 1850.0	Mean Decl. 1850.0
37	16 3 59.75	+ 6.73	+ 0.76	IV.	3	26.289	− 33 53.00	− 0.60	− 6.64	16 4 7.24	− 20 42 40.2
38	5 44.00	6.73	0.82	IV.	1	8.976	51 58.98	0.59	9.61	5 51.55	21 0 49.2
39	5 32.56	6.73	0.76	IV.	1	25.721	34 28.45	0.60	6.74	5 40.05	20 43 15.8
40	8 1.21	6.72	0.80	IV.	2	13.934	46 48.17	0.59	8.75	8 8.73	55 37.5
41	11 59.61	6.72	0.67	V.	5	43.282	16 7.88	0.57	3.75	11 7.00	24 52.2
42	22 54.33	6.71	0.74	III.	1	18.904	41 36.13	0.49	7.89	23 1.78	50 24.5
43	23 23.96	6.71	0.66	IV.	4	40.871	18 39.19	0.49	4.16	23 31.33	27 23.8
44	23 28.09	6.71	0.63	IV.	5	42.611	16 49.99	0.49	3.86	23 35.43	25 24.3
45	27 17.44	6.70	0.71	V.	2	21.542	38 51.11	0.46	7.45	27 24.85	47 30.0
46	28 26.56	6.70	0.57	V.	5	55.027	3 50.56	0.45	1.77	28 33.83	20 12 32.8
47	16(?33) 0.19	+ 6.70	+ 0.78	IV.	1	6.745	− 54 18.89	0.40	− 10.00	16 33 7.67	− 21 3 9.3

Zone 260. June 22. C. $D_0 = -19°\ 33'\ 30''$.

Seconds of Transit

No.	Mag.	I.	II.	III.	IV.	V.	VI.	VII.
1	9.10			42.	58.2			
2	8.9				48.2	5.3		
3	7.8		46.2	2.5		35.7		
4	7.6				21.3	37.5	54.3	
5	10		45.3		17.9	34.1		
6	9		22.2		54.2	11.	27.3	
7	10.11							
8	10			29.7				
9	10				7.2	23.4		
10	10					33.3		
11	9				17.4			
12	10				2.2		35.2	
13	10				5.8	21.6	37.7	
14	8.9				41.2		13.5	
15	8.9				55.2	12.5		
16	10				40.		13.4	
17	10						42.5	
18	10					37.2		
19	10						54.3	
20	9.10		5.3	21.6	37.3			
21	10		0.5		33.2			
22	10						25.3	
23	9.10					52.3		
24	9			52.		24.4		
25	10.11			39.5		12.2		
26	8		58.3	14.3	30.8	47.1		
27	9.10		5.8		38.3			
28	8.9			24.3	41.	57.2		
29	8				34.2	50.3		
30	10.11						27.7	
31	9			27.2				
32	10.11			56.8				
33	8.9						40.8	
34	8			29.5	46.2		18.5	

No.	T.	a_1	a_2	Mic.	n	r.	i	d_1	d_2	Mean R.A. 1850.0	Mean Decl. 1850.0
1	16 58 58.27	+ 6.68	+ 0.90	III.	5	48.550	− 10 37.25	− 5.37	− 6.86	16 58 5.8	− 19 44 19.5
2	16 59 32.20	6.68	0.93	IV.	3	32.710	27 10.03	5.37	9.54	16 59 39.8	20 0 54.9
3	17 2 2.73	6.68	1.00	IV.	1	7.424	53 36.49	5.33	13.86	17 2 10.4	27 25.7
4	2 21.34	6.68	0.96	IV.	3	20.270	40 10.58	5.33	11.66	2 29.0	13 57.6
5	4 17.89	6.68	1.00	IV.	2	10.498	50 23.85	5.30	13.33	4 25.5	20 24 12.5
6	6 54.57	6.68	0.90	IV.	5	51.671	7 21.36	5.26	6.32	7 2.2	19 41 2.9
7	6	6.68	0.95	VI.	3	28.135	31 56.95	5.26	10.31	7	20 5 42.5
8	9 46.00	6.68	0.98	II.	2	22.212	38 8.70	5.21	11.33	9 53.7	11 55.2
9	10 50.69	6.68	0.97	IV.	1	14.408	46 18.51	5.20	12.65	9 58.3	20 6.4
10	10 0.62	6.68	1.01	V.	1	10.376	50 31.44	5.21	13.35	10 8.3	20 24 20.0
11	11 0.94	6.68	0.93	IV.	5	43.946	15 26.08	5.19	7.63	11 8.6	19 49 8.9
12	12 2.44	6.68	0.99	IV.	2	15.761	44 53.50	5.18	12.43	12 10.1	20 18 41.2
13	12 5.13	6.68	0.99	IV.	2	14.738	45 57.74	5.13	12.59	12 12.8	19 45.5
14	13 41.10	6.68	0.96	IV.	3	29.272	30 45.86	5.15	10.12	13 48.7	4 37.1
15	14 55.64	6.68	0.97	IV.	3	29.879	30 7.59	5.13	10.02	15 3.3	3 52.7
16	15 40.44	6.68	1.02	IV.	2	11.808	43 47.82	5.12	12.23	15 48.1	20 17 35.2
17	16 9.93	6.68	0.96	V.	4	36.664	24 6.62	5.11	8.86	16 17.6	19 57 50.6
18	18 20.61	6.68	1.03	IV.	1	11.681	49 9.35	5.07	13.12	18 28.3	20 22 57.5
19	19 21.66	6.68	1.00	V.	3	20.252	40 11.64	5.05	11.66	19 29.3	13 58.3
20	25 37.80	6.68	1.00	III.	3	23.331	36 55.44	4.95	11.13	25 45.5	20 10 41.5
21	26 33.16	6.68	0.96	III.	5	45.557	13 45.10	4.93	7.36	26 40.9	19 47 27.4
22	27 52.67	6.68	1.00	V.	3	23.022	37 17.77	4.90	11.19	28 0.4	20 11 3.9
23	27 35.80	.6.65	0.98	IV.	4	35.075	24 43.02	4.90	9.14	27 43.5	19 58 27.0
24	29 8.13	6.68	0.98	IV.	4	40.562	18 58.77	4.98	8.21	29 15.8	52 41.9
25	32 55.78	6.69	0.98	IV.	4	39.918	19 39.00	4.81	8.31	33 3.4	19 53 22.2
26	33 30.78	6.69	1.01	IV.	3	32.131	27 46.43	4.80	9.64	33 38.5	20 1 30.9
27	36 38.49	6.69	1.02	III.	3	25.831	34 21.49	4.75	10.70	36 46.2	20 8 6.9
28	39 40.81	6.69	0.96	IV.	5	49.475	9 39.31	4.69	6.68	39 48.5	19 43 20.7
29	40 34.02	6.69	1.01	IV.	3	36.349	23 21.89	4.67	8.92	40 41.7	57 5.5
30	41 54.45	6.69	1.00	V.	4	42.271	17 11.46	4.64	7.92	42 2.1	50 54.0
31	42 43.59	6.69	0.97	II.	5	49.176	9 57.72	4.63	6.74	42 51.2	43 39.1
32	43 13.18	6.69	0.98	II.	5	48.250	10 55.89	4.62	6.89	43 20.8	19 44 37.4
33	43 8.21	6.69	1.03	V.	3	31.672	28 15.10	4.62	9.71	43 15.9	20 1 59.4
34	17 45 46.00	+ 6.69	+ 1.01	IV.	4	42.268	− 17 12.77	− 4.57	− 7.92	17 44 53.7	− 19 50 55.3

CORRECTIONS.

Date.	Corr. of Clock.	Hourly rate.	m	n	c	Zenith Point.	Mic. Co.
1849. h.	s.	s.	s.	s.	s.	° ' ''	r.

INSTRUMENT READINGS.

Date.		CIRCLE.							Barom.	THERMOM.				
		A.	B.	C.	D.	E.	F.	Mean.		At.	Ex.	U.	L.	I.
	1849. h. m.	° ' ''						''	in.					
Zone 260	June 22, 17 0	78 54 64.9	58.5	63.	60.5	58.4	59.9	60.87	30.070	81.3	77.		81.	80.7
	17 20								30.074	80.5	77.			
	17 40									76.6				
	15 0								30.068	80.	76.			
	18 20									75.6				
	19 0	64.7	58.5	63.	61.9	58.4		61.05*	30.060	79.5	75.8	82.	79.8	79.8

REMARKS.

(259) 39. The number (25) of micrometer revolutions deduced from comparison with zone of June 20.

(259) 41. Minutes assumed as 10, not 11.

(259) 43. Time of transit over T. V assumed as 57s.0 instead of 59s.0.

(260) 1. Minutes assumed as 57 instead of 58.

(260) 9. Minutes assumed as 9, not 10.

(260) 16. Micrometer reading assumed as 16r.808, not 11r.808.

(260) 17. Micrometer reading assumed as 35r.664 instead of 30r.664.

(260) 30. Right ascension differs 1m 3s from Arg. Z. 219, 7; minutes perhaps 40, not 41; and transit over T. V 24s, not 27s.

(260) 34. Minutes assumed as 44, not 45.

*The mean 61''.30 is corrected by −0''.25 in order to reduce the mean of five microscopes to the mean of six.

ZONES OBSERVED WITH THE MURAL CIRCLE, 1849.

ZONE 260. JUNE 22. C. $D_0 = -19° 33' 30''$—Continued.

No.	Mag.	I.	II.	III.	IV.	V.	VI.	VII.	T. (h. m. s.)	a₁ (s.)	a₂ (s.)
35	10		42.2	58.5					17 46 58.58	+6.70	+1.08
36	10			58.					46 41.55	6.70	0.99
37	9			42.2					48 25.71	6.70	1.01
38	9.10				49.5	6.2			48 33.33	6.70	1.02
39	9			18.3	34.3				50 1.74	6.70	1.04
40	7			57.2	13.5	30.1			51 57.23	6.70	1.08
41	10			28.					52 3.53	6.70	1.02
42	9				42.1				52 5.52	6.70	1.03
43	9.10	31.2	47.6	4.					55 3.93	6.70	1.02
44	8	0.5	16.7	33.2		5.2			56 33.01	6.70	1.01
45	9			39.7					57 56.10	6.71	1.00
46	9.10				14.2	30.			57 57.52	6.71	1.06
47	9.10	51.2	8.1						59 24.18	6.71	1.07
48	9				26.				59 26.02	6.71	1.03
49	9					56.2			17 59 39.67	6.71	1.07
50	9.10					36.2			18 0 3.64	6.71	1.03
51	10					39.7			0 7.14	6.71	1.03
52	7.8			57.7	13.5	46.5			2 13.83	6.71	1.04
53	9				10.1				3 53.50	6.71	1.11
54	9				11.4	27.8			4 55.10	6.71	1.03
55	8			53.3	26.				6 9.51	6.71	1.11
56	9.10					12.			6 39.36	6.72	1.09
57	9				39.5	56.2	12.5		8 39.73	6.72	1.02
58	9				33.5				10 33.47	6.72	1.04
59	9			12.	27.5				11 27.93	6.72	1.05
60	8.9					46.5	2.5		11 29.69	6.72	1.11
61	8.9					33.5			12 0.97	6.72	1.03
62	10					10.5			14 54.03	6.73	1.06
63	8.9				9.6				15 9.53	6.73	1.03
64	8.9				37.2				15 37.18	6.73	1.05
65	9	1.4	18.2			50.5			19 34.21	6.73	1.07
66	10		26.5						21 42.91	6.74	1.05
67	9					47.5	3.5		21 30.87	6.74	1.13
68	10				59.2				24 59.30	6.74	1.11
69	8.9	53.5	9.3						24 25.96	6.74	1.16
70	9.10					53.2			24 36.70	6.74	1.09
71	8				24.2		57.2		25 24.43	6.74	1.08
72	9.10						4.5		25 31.95	6.74	1.08
73	9			57.3	13.2				27 13.44	6.75	1.09
74	10						4.5		27 31.97	6.75	1.06
75	9.10						37.2		28 4.64	6.75	1.09
76	9						25.4		29 52.87	6.75	1.07
77	7.8	19.3	35.3	52.1			24.6		31 51.96	6.75	1.14
78	10					31.8			32 15.40	6.75	1.06
79	8					39.6			33 23.01	6.76	1.17
80	9				55.2	11.5	27.5		35 55.06	6.76	1.13
81	7.8	29.4	45.2	2.	18.5	34.6			37 1.94	6.76	1.08
82	9.10	5.3			38.7				38 38.41	6.77	1.14
83	8					6.3	23.4		18 39 50.22	+6.77	+1.18

No.	Mag.	MICROMETER.		r.	i (′ ″)	d₁ (″)	d₂ (″)	Mean Right Ascension, 1850.0. (h. m. s.)	Mean Declination, 1850.0. (° ′ ″)
35	10	III.	1	12.332	−48 28.50	4.54	−13.03	17 46 6.3	− 20 22 16.2
36	10	IV.	5	45.676	13 37.58	4.55	7.32	46 49.2	19 47 19.5
37	9	III.	4	37.919	21 43.87	4.51	8.65	48 33.4	55 27.0
38	9.10	IV.	4	41.364	18 8.50	4.51	8.07	48 41.0	19 51 51.1
39	9	IV.	3	31.161	28 47.29	4.48	9.80	50 9.5	20 2 31.6
40	7	IV.	2	15.095	45 35.48	4.44	12.54	51 5.0	20 19 22.5
41	10	IV.	5	41.641	17 50.88	4.44	8.01	52 11.3	19 51 33.3
42	9	V.	4	36.325	23 25.27	4.44	8.92	52 13.3	57 8.6
43	9.10	III.	5	44.542	14 48.80	4.37	7.52	55 11.6	48 30.7
44	8	II.	5	47.422	11 47.86	4.35	7.01	56 40.7	45 29.2
45	9	II.	5	49.028	9 10.37	4.31	6.59	57 3.8	19 42 51.3
46	9.10	IV.	3	25.892	34 17.73	4.31	10.71	58 5.3	20 8 2.7
47	9.10	II.	3	25.832	34 21.30	4.28	10.70	59 31.9	20 8 6.3
48	9	III.	3	40.231	19 18.16	4.28	8.25	59 33.8	19 53 0.7
49	9	IV.	2	27.691	32 25.31	4.28	10.40	17 59 47.4	20 6 10.0
50	9.10	V.	4	39.755	19 49.79	4.27	8.33	18 0 11.4	19 53 32.4
51	10	V.	4	40.462	19 5.67	4.27	8.21	0 14.8	52 48.2
52	7.8	IV.	4	41.285	18 13.47	4.22	8.07	2 21.6	19 51 55.8
53	9	IV.	1	7.664	53 21.33	4.18	13.84	3 1.3	20 27 9.3
54	9	IV.	5	46.414	12 51.44	4.16	7.19	4 2.8	19 46 32.8
55	8	IV.	1	9.074	51 52.90	4.13	13.60	6 17.3	20 25 40.6
56	9.10	V.	3	20.847	39 34.14	4.12	11.57	6 47.2	20 13 19.8
57	9	IV.	5	49.606	9 30.97	4.08	6.65	8 47.5	19 43 11.7
58	9	III.	4	45.828	13 27.53	4.03	7.29	10 41.2	47 8.8
59	9	II.	3	39.242	20 20.09	4.01	8.41	11 35.7	19 54 2.5
60	8.9	IV.	2	17.832	42 43.70	4.01	12.08	11 37.7	20 16 29.8
61	8.9	V.	5	49.769	9 20.61	3.99	6.62	12 8.7	19 43 1.2
62	10	IV.	4	43.213	16 12.28	3.91	7.75	15 1.8	49 53.9
63	8.9	III.	5	53.704	5 13.68	3.91	5.96	15 17.3	38 53.5
64	8.9	III.	4	44.668	14 40.40	3.90	7.49	15 44.9	48 21.8
65	9	IV.	4	41.421	18 4.67	3.80	8.05	19 42.0	51 46.5
66	10	II.	5	50.984	8 4.09	3.75	6.40	21 50.7	19 41 44.2
67	9	V.	1	11.685	49 9.16	3.74	13.16	21 38.7	20 22 56.1
68	10	III.	3	30.549	29 25.68	3.64	9.91	25 7.2	3 9.2
69	8.9	II.	1	6.374	54 42.16	3.66	14.08	24 33.9	20 28 29.9
70	9.10	IV.	4	36.396	23 20.26	3.65	8.90	24 44.5	19 57 2.8
71	8	IV.	4	39.670	20 7.23	3.63	8.35	25 32.2	53 49.2
72	9.10	V.	4	41.593	17 54.57	3.62	8.02	25 39.7	51 36.2
73	9	III.	3	36.105	23 37.01	3.58	8.95	27 21.3	57 19.5
74	10	V.	4	48.158	11 2.55	3.57	6.89	27 39.8	44 43.0
75	9.10	V.	3	39.448	20 7.29	3.56	8.38	28 12.5	53 49.2
76	9	V.	4	−49.371	9 46.54	3.49	6.69	29 0.7	19 43 26.7
77	7.8	IV.	2	22.168	38 11.72	3.46	11.34	30 59.9	20 11 56.5
78	10	III.	5	56.671	2 7.43	3.43	5.44	32 23.2	19 35 46.3
79	8	IV.	2	7.713	53 14.99	3.39	13.85	33 30.9	20 17 2.2
80	9	IV.	3	31.568	28 21.75	3.32	9.74	36 2.9	20 2 4.8
81	7.8	IV.	4	47.437	11 47.36	3.28	7.02	37 9.8	19 45 27.7
82	9.10	III.	3	32.271	27 36.45	3.23	9.62	38 46.3	20 1 19.3
83	8	IV.	1	8.750	−52 13.15	−3.18	−13.67	18 38 58.2	− 20 26 0.0

CORRECTIONS.

Date.	Corr. of Clock.	Hourly rate.	m	n	c	Zenith Point.	Mic. Co.
1849.	h. s.	s.	s.	.s.	s.	° ′ ″	r.

INSTRUMENT READINGS.

Date.	CIRCLE.							Barom.	THERMOM.				
	A.	B.	C.	D.	E.	F.	Mean.		At.	Ex.	U.	L.	I.
1849. h. m.	° ′ ″						″	In.					

REMARKS.

(260) 35. Minutes assumed as 45, not 46.
(260) 40. Minutes of transit assumed as 50, not 51.
(260) 41. Transit over T. IV assumed as 20s, not 28s, to agree with Transit Z, June 26, 1848, and Arg. Z.
(260) 42. Transit over T. IV assumed as 38s.1, not 48s, to agree with Transit Z, June 26, 1848, and Arg. Z.
(260) 45. Minutes assumed as 56, not 57.
(260) 53. Minutes assumed as 2, not 3.
(260) 54. Minutes assumed as 3, not 4.
(260) 76. Minutes assumed as 28, not 29.
(260) 77. Minutes assumed as 30, not 31.
(260) 83. Minutes assumed as 38, not 39.

ZONE 260. JUNE 22. C. $D_o = -19° 33' 30''$—Continued.

No.	Mag.	I.	II.	III.	IV.	V.	VI.	VII.	T.	a_1	a_2	MICROMETER.	r.	i	d_1	d_2	Mean Right Ascension, 1850.0	Mean Declination, 1850.0
84	5.9			49.		21.4			18 40 48.94	+ 6.77	+ 1.17	IV. 2	15.492	− 45 10.64	− 3.16	− 12.48	18 39 56.0	− 20 18 56.3
85	9			45.5					41 45.62	6.77	1.15	III. 3	23.485	36 48.84	3.13	11.12	41 53.5	20 10 33.1
86	9		52.5			41.3			42 8.82	6.77	1.10	II. 5	45.911	13 22.51	3.12	7.27	42 16.7	19 47 2.9
87	9			31.		3.4			42 30.92	6.77	1.10	IV. 5	44.498	14 51.62	3.10	7.51	42 38.8	19 48 32.2
88	10					35.2			43 2.56	6.77	1.17	V. 2	19.175	41 19.71	3.09	11.88	43 10.5	20 15 4.7
89	10					1.3			43 28.68	6.77	1.16	V. 3	24.562	35 41.29	3.07	11.94	43 36.6	20 9 26.3
90	8.9			49.2					45 49.26	6.78	1.14	III. 4	34.985	24 47.07	2.99	9.14	45 57.2	19 58 30.1
91	9				34.3				45 17.76	6.78	1.16	IV. 3	27.075	33 3.58	3.01	10.51	45 25.7	20 6 47.1
92	9			2.2		35.3			46 2.47	6.78	1.11	IV. 5	43.821	15 33.09	2.98	7.63	46 10.6	19 49 14.6
93	10					59.5?			46 26.97	6.78	1.10	V. 5	50.282	8 48.60	2.97	6.52	46 34.9	42 28.1
94	9.10				5.2	22.			49 49.08	6.79	1.13	IV. 4	39.248	20 21.29	2.85	8.41	49 57.0	54 2.6
95	8	4.5	21.4	37.3	53.4				51 37.29	6.79	1.13	IV. 4	41.532	17 57.90	2.78	8.03	51 45.2	19 51 38.7
96	9				22.3	38.6			52 5.89	6.79	1.16	IV. 3	28.354	31 43.52	2.76	10.29	52 13.8	20 5 26.6
97	9.10					10.2			52 37.61	6.79	1.15	V. 3	31.581	28 20.87	2.74	9.73	52 45.5	20 2 3.3
98	10		11.5		44.7				54 28.08	6.80	1.12	IV. 5	49.135	10 0.54	2.66	6.71	54 36.0	19 43 39.9
99	9				34.2	50.8			55 17.87	6.80	1.20	IV. 1	12.992	47 47.13	2.63	12.95	55 25.9	20 21 32.7
100	9		44.1	0.3		33.1			57 0.44	6.80	1.12	IV. 5	50.541	8 32.35	2.55	6.46	57 8.4	19 42 11.4
101	9.10			44.2	0.2				58 0.44	6.81	1.19	IV. 2	21.568	38 48.22	2.47	11.45	58 9.44	20 12 32.1
102	10		58.3						18 59 14.66	6.81	1.14	II. 2	42.641	16 47.55	2.46	7.82	18 59 22.6	19 50 27.8
103	9			54.2					19 0 54.29	6.81	1.17	III. 3	30.808	29 9.25	2.39	9.86	19 0 2.3	20 2 51.5
104	9				19.2				0 2.64	6.81	1.19	IV. 2	20.184	40 16.29	2.43	11.69	0 10.6	14 0.4
105	7.8			49.2	5.2				1 48.99	6.81	1.17	IV. 3	31.160	28 47.35	2.36	9.80	0 57.0	2 29.5
106	9					12.4			0 39.75	6.81	1.20	V. 1	17.715	42 50.06	2.41	12.13	0 47.8	16 35.5
107	9.10		42.						19 2 58.30	+ 6.81	+ 1.19	II. 2	21.368	− 39 1.71	− 2.30	− 11.51	19 3 6.3	− 20 12 45.5

ZONE 261. JULY 2. C. $D_o = -28° 59' 20''$.

No.	Mag.	I.	II.	III.	IV.	V.	VI.	VII.	T.	a_1	a_2	MICROMETER.	r.	i	d_1	d_2	Mean Right Ascension, 1850.0	Mean Declination, 1850.0
1	8			17.5					18 1 17.66	+ 9.69	+ 0.86	III. 1	13.939	− 46 47.55	− 3.19	− 9.72	18 1 28.2	− 29 46 20.5
2	8				48.2				1 30.34	9.69	0.85	IV. 2	20.276	40 10.51	3.19	8.24	1 40.9	39 41.9
3	8			45.3	33.2				2 15.39	9.69	0.85	IV. 3	24.026	36 14.66	3.19	7.38	2 25.9	35 45.2
4	9		53.2	11.3	29.2				4 11.18	9.69	0.84	IV. 3	25.621	34 34.73	3.17	7.01	4 21.7	34 4.9
5	9	31.	48.2	6.2					6 6.14	9.69	0.94	III. 3	23.972	30 18.16	3.16	7.39	6 16.7	35 48.7
6	9.10				31.3	49.2			6 13.67	9.69	0.81	IV. 5	47.014	12 13.47	3.16	2.13	6 24.4	11 38.8
7	9		55.1	12.5					8 12.62	7.69	0.82	III. 4	40.709	18 48.79	3.14	3.56	8 23.1	18 15.5
8	9				40.2	57.5			8 22.26	9.69	0.85	IV. 1	14.655	46 2.77	3.14	9.54	8 32.8	45 35.4
9	9			27.5	45.4				9 27.50	9.69	0.83	IV. 2	16.227	44 21.42	3.14	9.18	9 38.1	43 56.8
10	9				14.6				10 56.74	9.69	0.83	IV. 2	19.655	40 49.29	3.12	8.38	10 7.3	40 20.8
11	8.9			12.3					10 42.24	9.69	0.80	III. 5	51.107	7 56.69	3.12	1.21	10 52.7	7 21.0
12	3				30.2	48.4			11 12.70	9.69	0.84	IV. 1	7.448	53 34.86	3.12	11.20	11 23.2	53 9.2
13	9					16.5			11 41.31	9.69	0.83	V. 3	24.049	30 13.09	3.12	7.37	11 51.8	35 43.6
14	10				58.6	16.4			12 40.96	9.69	0.83	IV. 5	20.188	40 15.54	3.11	8.26	12 51.5	39 46.9
15	9		54.2		29.2				14 29.24	9.70	0.80	III. 5	49.056	10 5.43	3.10	1.68	14 39.7	9 30.2
16	8.9					9.3			15 51.46	9.70	0.82	IV. 2	24.157	36 6.95	3.09	7.35	16 2.0	35 37.4
17	8.9		45.3	2.4	20.5				17 20.41	9.70	0.82	III. 2	24.473	35 47.12	3.07	7.27	17 30.9	35 17.4
18	9		53.2	10.2					19 28.12	9.70	0.80	II. 2	33.148	26 42.49	3.06	5.27	19 38.6	26 10.8
19	7.8		53.7	10.8	28.3		4.2		19 28.69	9.70	0.79	IV. 4	38.372	21 16.13	3.06	4.11	19 39.2	20 43.3
20	8					5.3			20 47.51	9.70	0.79	IV. 3	35.151	24 36.81	3.05	4.82	20 58.0	24 4.7
21	10			4.2		39.7			18 22 21.91	+ 9.70	+ 0.77	IV. 4	46.098	− 13 10.58	− 3.04	− 2.34	18 22 32.4	− 29 12 36.0

CORRECTIONS.

Date.	Corr. of Clock.	Hourly rate.	m	n	c	Zenith Point.	Mic. Co.
1849.	h.	s.	s.	s.	s.	° ' ''	r.

INSTRUMENT READINGS.

Date.		CIRCLE.							Barom.	THERMOM.				
		A.	B.	C.	D.	E.	F.	Mean.		At.	Ex.	U.	L.	I.
	1849. h. m.	° ' ''						''	in.	°	°	°	°	°
Zone 261	July 2, 18 0	88 19 61.4	59.1	60.2	63.	53.5	55.1	58.72	30.080	69.5	60.2	77.7	68.2	70.7
	18 20										59.9			
	18 40								30.082		58.9			
	19 0	60.7	60.1	60.1	64.2	53.2	54.5	58.80	30.078	65.8	58.4		70.	69.4

REMARKS.

(260) 84. Minutes assumed as 39, not 40.
(260) 101. Transits over T.'s II and III assumed as recorded over T.'s III and IV.
(260) 103. Minutes assumed as 59, not 0.
(260) 105. Minutes assumed as 0, not 1.
(261) 10. Minutes assumed as 9, not 10.

ZONE 261. JULY 2. C. D = −28° 59′ 20″—Continued.

No.	Mag.	I.	II.	III.	IV.	V.	VI.	VII.	T. (h. m. s.)	a_1	a_2
22	7.8			30.6		6.3			18 22 31.01	+9.70	+0.78
23	7	39.2	56.8	14.2	32.3	49.6			26 14.42	9.71	0.81
24	9		9.3	27.3					27 27.12	9.71	0.78
25	7.8					9.			27 33.81	9.71	0.80
26	8		45.7	3.5		38.8			29 3.50	9.71	0.81
27	10	36.2		11.3		47.			31 11.57	9.71	0.78
28	10	43.5	0.9		36.2	54.2			31 18.70	9.71	0.78
29	8.9				14.7	32.2			33 56.92	9.71	0.78
30	9					9.5			33 34.24	9.71	0.79
31	8.9			38.2	56.3				34 38.39	9.72	0.78
32	8.9				32.3				35 14.44	9.72	0.78
33	9	8.1	25.3						36 43.17	9.72	0.78
34	9		42.2			36.2			37 0.38	9.72	0.78
35	7.8			3.3	21.3	39.3			37 3.63	9.72	0.79
36	10				2.8				40 45.07	9.72	0.75
37	9.10	57.2	15.3	32.7					41 32.74	9.72	0.77
38	10			1.3					42 1.40	9.73	0.76
39	7		37.3	54.3	12.	29.6			43 54.47	9.73	0.75
40	10				57.3				43 39.58	9.73	0.73
41	8				44.5	1.7			44 26.68	9.73	0.74
42	7.8		26.6	44.3	2.6				46 44.45	9.73	0.74
43	8			26.1	44.	1.6			46 26.25	9.73	0.76
44	10				13.2				47 55.36	9.73	0.76
45	10	44.3	1.9	19.2					49 19.41	9.74	0.73
46	8.9	3.3	20.9	38.5	56.4				51 38.57	9.74	0.74
47	9.10			51.3		26.2			54 51.20	9.75	0.76
48	9	7.2	24.3						55 42.18	9.75	0.73
49	7.8			7.3	25.	42.5			56 7.32	9.75	0.72
50	9		9.3	26.3	44.6				57 26.69	9.75	0.72
51	9.10				29.8				18 58 12.06	9.75	0.71
52	10	3.2							19 0 38.30	9.75	0.70
53	9		56.4	14.	31.5	49.2			1 14.00	9.76	0.70
54	7					13.2			1 37.96	9.76	0.73
55	9.10					49.3			2 14.04	9.76	0.74
56	9	11.3	28.3	46.8					5 46.46	9.77	0.71
57	8		43.5	0.2	18.2	35.8			5 0.59	9.76	0.71
58	8	14.3	32.2	49.3					19 9 49.54	+9.77	+0.69

No.	MICROMETER	r	(′ ″)	i	d_1	d_2	Mean Right Ascension, 1850.0 (h. m. s.)	Mean Declination, 1850.0 (° ′ ″)
22	IV. 4	41.562	−17 55.89	−3.04		−3.36	18 22 41.5	−29 17 22.3
23	IV. 1	11.694	49 8.41	3.01		10.24	26 24.9	48 41.7
24	III. 4	37.876	22 5.52	3.00		4.27	27 37.6	21 32.8
25	V. 3	24.311	35 56.78	3.00		7.31	27 44.3	35 27.1
26	IV. 2	13.818	46 55.33	2.99		9.74	29 14.0	46 28.0
27	IV. 3	31.981	27 55.58	2.97		5.54	31 22.1	27 24.1
28	IV. 3	32.563	27 19.19	2.97		5.41	31 29.2	26 47.6
29	IV. 2	22.983	37 20.46	2.95		7.61	33 7.4	36 51.0
30	V. 1	12.823	47 57.42	2.96		9.98	33 44.7	47 30.4
31	IV. 3	25.497	34 42.57	2.95		7.03	34 48.9	34 12.5
32	IV. 3	21.372	39 1.40	2.94		7.99	35 24.9	38 32.3
33	II. 3	19.705	40 45.77	2.93		8.37	36 53.7	40 17.1
34	II. 3	21.072	39 20.05	2.92		8.05	37 10.9	38 51.1
35	IV. 3	13.382	47 22.68	2.92		9.86	37 14.1	46 55.5
36	IV. 5	44.491	14 51.94	2.89		2.70	40 55.5	14 17.5
37	III. 3	24.466	35 47.37	2.88		7.28	41 43.2	35 17.5
38	III. 3	30.305	29 41.06	2.87		5.93	42 11.9	29 9.9
39	IV. 3	26.625	33 31.74	2.84		6.77	43 4.9	33 1.3
40	IV. 5	45.568	13 44.35	2.86		2.46	43 50.0	13 9.7
41	IV. 4	43.237	16 10.83	2.85		2.97	44 37.2	15 36.6
42	IV. 3	35.472	24 16.73	2.81		4.75	45 54.9	23 44.3
43	IV. 1	20.294	40 9.20	2.82		8.23	46 36.7	39 40.2
44	IV. 2	24.678	35 34.20	2.79		7.23	47 5.8	35 4.2
45	III. 1	43.400	16 0.10	2.77		2.95	49 29.9	15 25.8
46	IV. 3	26.805	33 20.32	2.74		6.74	51 40.0	32 49.8
47	IV. 1	10.872	49 59.91	2.70		10.43	54 1.7	49 33.0
48	II. 3	33.717	26 6.72	2.69		5.16	55 52.6	25 34.6
49	IV. 4	40.944	18 34.54	2.68		3.50	56 17.8	18 0.7
50	IV. 3	36.133	23 35.19	2.67		4.60	57 37.2	23 2.5
51	IV. 4	42.579	16 52.06	2.66		3.12	18 58 22.5	16 17.8
52	III. 5	52.012	6 59.82	2.63		0.97	19 0 48.7	6 23.4
53	IV. 5	52.585	6 23.91	2.62		0.84	1 24.5	5 47.4
54	V. 1	15.808	44 50.21	2.62		9.30	1 48.4	44 22.1
55	V. 1	13.636	47 6.55	2.61		9.79	2 24.5	46 39.0
56	III. 3	28.190	31 53.69	2.58		6.41	5 56.9	31 22.7
57	IV. 3	29.972	30 1.63	2.59		6.01	5 11.1	29 30.2
58	III. 4	41.636	−17 50.69	−2.55		−3.33	19 10 0.0	−29 17 16.6

ZONE 262. JULY 3. C. D = −29° 14′ 20″.

No.	Mag.	I.	II.	III.	IV.	V.	VI.	VII.	T. (h. m. s.)	a_1	a_2
1	8	14.2	31.6	49.2	7.2	24.5			15 48 49.34	+9.65	+0.86
2	9.10				48.	7.2			48 30.96	9.65	1.04
3	8.9			46.5	4.4	22.3			50 46.69	9.65	1.04
4	8					45.2			50 9.97	9.65	0.89
5	9					12.4			50 37.20	9.65	0.86
6	8.9	56.	13.4	31.3	49.				53 31.15	9.64	0.96
7	9			2.3	20.1	37.5			54 2.29	9.64	0.93
8	9		42.3	0.3	17.8				15 59 0.09	+9.63	+0.88

No.	MICROMETER	r	(′ ″)	i	d_1	d_2	Mean Right Ascension, 1850.0 (h. m. s.)	Mean Declination, 1850.0 (° ′ ″)
1	IV. 4	40.768	−18 45.58	−0.86		2.54	15 48 59.85	−29 33 9.0
2	IV. 1	12.937	47 50.39	0.85		8.93	48 41.65	30 2 20.2
3	IV. 1	11.941	48 52.85	0.90		9.17	50 57.38	30 3 22.9
4	V. 4	35.296	24 29.53	0.88		3.79	50 20.51	29 38 54.2
5	V. 4	40.582	13 57.76	0.89		2.60	50 47.71	33 21.2
6	IV. 3	24.362	35 53.84	0.96		6.30	53 41.75	50 21.1
7	IV. 3	31.496	28 26.20	0.97		4.66	54 12.86	42 51.8
8	IV. 4	38.095	−21 33.39	−1.09		−3.15	15 59 10.60	−29 35 57.6

CORRECTIONS.

Date.	Corr. of Clock.	Hourly rate.	m	n	c	Zenith Point.	Mic. Co.
1849.	h.	s.	s.	s.	s.	° ′ ″	r.

INSTRUMENT READINGS.

Date.		CIRCLE.						Barom.	THERMOM.				
1849. (h. m.)	A.	B.	C.	D.	E.	F.	Mean.	in.	At.	Ex.	U.	L.	I.
Zone 262 July 3, 15 45	88 34 60.8	56.4	58.9	59.8	52.6	53.6	57.02	30.218	71.8	66.5	..	69.7	71.
16 0										66.8			
16 20	60.9	56.9	59.9	60.9	52.4	53.8	57.47	30.224	70.7	65.7	73.	67.5	70.

REMARKS.

(261) 29. Minutes assumed as 32, not 33.
(261) 32. Right ascension differs 10^s from Arg. Z. 221, 119.
(261) 39. Minutes assumed as 42, not 43.
(261) 42. Minutes assumed as 45, not 46.
(261) 44. Minutes assumed as 46, not 47.
(261) 47. Minutes assumed as 53, not 54.
(262) 2. Transit observations discordant by 2^s; their mean doubtless 1^s in error.
(262) 6. Time of transit over T. I assumed as $55^s.6$ instead of $5^s.6$.

ZONE 262. JULY 3. C. $D_0 = -29°\,14'\,20''$—Continued.

No.	Mag.	I.	II.	III.	IV.	V.	VI.	VII.	T. (h. m. s.)	a_1	a_2	Micrometer	r.	i	d_1	d_2	Mean Right Ascension, 1850.0	Mean Declination, 1850.0
9	8.9				48.4	15.7			15 59 30.45	+9.63	+0.97	IV. 3	23.462	−36 50.22	−1.10	−6.49	15 59 41.05	−29 51 17.8
10	9.10				39.5	57.4			16 0 21.85	9.63	0.98	IV. 3	22.011	38 21.13	1.12	6.83	16 0 32.46	52 49.1
11	8	31.1	48.6	6.2		41.6			3 6.35	9.62	0.93	IV. 3	28.971	31 4.43	1.21	5.24	3 16.90	45 30.9
12	8		59.3	17.	34.4	52.6			4 16.97	9.62	0.96	IV. 3	25.372	34 50.48	1.26	6.05	4 27.55	49 17.8
13	8.9	44.6		19.7	37.4	55.2			7 19.79	9.62	0.80	IV. 5	51.536	7 29.77	1.36	0.12	7 30.21	21 51.2
14	9				28.2	45.5			8 10.33	9.62	0.88	IV. 4	36.429	10 45.15	1.39	0.81	8 20.83	29 25 7.4
15	8.9			18.2		53.3			9 18.14	9.61	1.07	IV. 1	7.971	53 1.88	1.44	10.10	9 28.82	30 7 33.4
16	8.9		10.6		46.2	3.8			9 28.32	9.61	1.05	IV. 2	12.113	48 42.38	1.44	9.12	9 38.98	30 3 12.9
17	9		22.4	40.1	58.	15.5			11 40.14	9.61	0.93	IV. 3	30.242	29 44.66	1.51	4.94	11 50.68	29 44 11.3
18	9.10		5.2	22.	40.				13 22.35	9.61	0.93	IV. 3	30.174	29 49.09	1.57	4.06	13 32.89	44 15.6
19	8.9			15.5		50.3			14 15.32	9.60	0.97	IV. 3	25.161	35 3.56	1.61	6.10	14 25.89	49 31.3
20	8.9		13.2		48.2	6.3			14 30.72	9.60	0.97	IV. 3	26.392	33 46.42	1.61	5.82	14 41.29	48 13.8
21	8				30.3	48.			16 12.64	9.60	0.88	IV. 4	39.659	19 55.26	1.66	2.81	16 23.12	34 19.7
22	8.9	27.1	44.3	2.3	20.1	37.4			20 2.24	9.60	0.90	IV. 4	42.076	17 23.57	1.80	2.25	20 12.74	31 47.6
23	8.9		16.2	34.2	52.				21 34.08	9.59	0.94	IV. 3	32.362	27 31.94	1.83	4.46	21 44.61	41 58.2
24	9			5.5	23.4	41.3			22 5.73	9.59	0.89	IV. 4	40.479	19 3.91	1.84	2.62	22 16.21	33 28.4
25	9.10					34.5			16 23 59.19	+9.59	+0.99	V. 2	22.285	−38 4.44	−1.88	−6.77	16 24 9.77	−29 52 33.1

ZONE 263. JULY 5. C. $D_0 = -28°\,54'\,10''$.

No.	Mag.	I.	II.	III.	IV.	V.	VI.	VII.	T. (h. m. s.)	a_1	a_2	Micrometer	r.	i	d_1	d_2	Mean Right Ascension, 1850.0	Mean Declination, 1850.0
1	8			9.7	27.2	44.6			15 50 9.58	+9.95	+1.10	IV. 2	16.125	−44 30.76	−3.12	−13.12	15 50 20.63	−29 38 57.0
2	9.10		44.4	2.0		37.3			54 2.07	9.94	1.17	IV. 2	12.368	48 26.52	3.17	13.97	54 13.18	42 53.7
3	9	31.5	49.2	6.3	24.2				58 6.56	9.93	0.52	IV. 5	49.707	9 24.57	3.22	5.63	15 58 17.01	3 43.4
4	9		42.2	59.7	17.2	35.3			15 59 59.76	9.93	1.04	IV. 2	18.974	41 31.93	3.24	12.49	16 0 10.73	35 57.7
5	6	57.2	14.6	32.3	50.1	7.9			16 1 32.46	9.92	0.47	IV. 5	52.389	6 36.28	3.25	5.03	1 42.85	0 54.6
6	8.9	30.4	48.	5.2	23.6	40.9			3 5.62	9.92	1.24	IV. 1	9.846	51 4.25	3.28	14.55	3 16.78	45 32.1
7	9					12.8			3 37.69	9.92	0.75	V. 4	38.608	21 1.58	3.29	8.08	3 48.36	15 22.9
8	9					52.3			4 17.00	9.92	1.30	V. 1	6.206	54 51.30	3.29	15.37	4 28.22	49 20.0
9	8	44.2	1.7	19.2	37.3	54.6			7 19.40	9.91	0.86	IV. 3	32.394	27 29.87	3.33	9.47	7 30.17	21 52.7
10	8.9		52.5	9.2	27.8	45.4			8 9.89	9.91	0.93	IV. 3	29.276	30 45.48	3.34	10.18	8 20.73	25 9.0
11	9	22.8	40.4	58.2	16.	33.5			10 58.18	9.91	1.02	IV. 2	20.287	40 9.76	3.38	12.18	11 9.11	34 35.3
12	9		43.3	0.5	18.5	35.8			11 0.73	9.91	0.82	IV. 5	44.812	14 31.61	3.38	6.70	11 11.46	8 51.7
13	9					14.8			11 39.55	9.91	1.20	V. 1	11.116	49 44.60	3.39	14.25	11 50.64	41 12.2
14	8.9	29.1	46.5		21.4	39.1			15 4.00	9.90	0.84	II. 3	33.466	26 22.65	3.44	9.22	15 14.74	20 45.3
15	8	29.2	46.6		21.5	39.2			15 4.10	9.90	0.84	IV. 3	33.368	26 28.81	3.44	9.24	15 14.84	20 51.5
16	8.9					41.?			16 5.96	9.90	0.52	V. 5	50.432	8 38.87	3.45	5.46	16 16.38	2 57.8
17	9.10			26.2	43.6				18 43.71	9.89	0.60	III. 4	46.489	12 46.23	3.48	6.33	17 54.20	7 6.0
18	9.10					7.4			18 49.72	9.89	0.47	IV. 5	51.814	7 12.12	3.48	5.15	18 0.08	29 1 30.7
19	8					21.3			19 56.40	9.89	0.39	V. 5	56.455	2 20.79	3.48	4.13	18 6.68	28 56 38.4
20	9		26.2	44.5	1.9				20 1.88	9.89	0.96	III. 3	22.939	37 22.91	3.50	11.58	20 12.73	29 31 48.0
21	9.10				31.3				20 13.40	9.89	1.19	IV. 2	11.300	49 33.43	3.50	14.22	20 24.48	44 1.1
22	8.9				25.	42.5			21 7.35	9.89	0.61	IV. 5	44.761	14 34.87	3.51	6.71	21 17.85	8 55.1
23	9					9.1			21 33.85	9.89	1.11	V. 2	15.184	45 29.78	3.52	13.34	21 44.85	39 56.6
24	8.9					40.5			22 5.29	9.89	0.99	V. 3	21.314	39 4.79	3.52	11.95	22 16.16	33 30.3
25	9	56.6	14.5	32.					24 32.04	9.88	0.93	III. 3	24.139	36 7.77	3.55	11.33	24 42.85	30 32.7
26	9.10				2.4				16 25 44.58	+9.88	+0.89	IV. 3	30.871	−29 5.23	−3.57	−9.79	16 25 55.35	−29 23 28.6

CORRECTIONS.

Date.	Corr. of Clock.	Hourly rate.	m	n	c	Zenith Point.	Mic. Co.
1849.	h.	s.	s.	s.	s.	° ' "	r.

REMARKS.

(262) 9. Transit over T. V assumed to have been observed at 5s.7 instead of 15s.7.
(262) 14. Micrometer reading assumed as 48r.429, not 38r.429.
(263) 17. Minutes assumed as 17, not 18.
(263) 18. Minutes assumed as 17, not 18.
(263) 19. Transit over T. I assumed as recorded over T. IV, and minutes as 17, not 18.

INSTRUMENT READINGS.

Date.	CIRCLE							Barom.	THERMOM.				
	A.	B.	C.	D.	E.	F.	Mean.		At.	Ex.	U.	L.	I.
1849 July 5, (h. m.)	° ' "						"	in.	°				
Zone 263　15 50	88 14 62.0	56.1	57.8	59.9	52.1	53.7	56.93	30.192	72.5	69.8	..	70.3	71.5
16 0										69.5			
16 25	62.0	56.0	58.1	59.8	52.1	53.1	56.85	30.198	71.5	68.5	72.5	69.2	70.5

Zone 264. July 5. C. D₀ = −20° 48′ 40″.

Seconds of Transit:

No.	Mag.	I.	II.	III.	IV.	V.	VI.	VII.
1	9				51.3			
2	9.10				12.			
3	8			35.2	52.3			
4	8				20.2	36.5		
5	9					42.7		
6	10					41.2		
7	10	34.6			7.4			
8	9				27.2			
9	8.9			54.3	11.4			
10	8			46.5	3.			
11	10			33.2	50.2			
12	8.9					45.2		
13	8.9			14.7	31.3			
14	8		57.6	14.2	30.9	47.		
15	10	56.6	13.2	29.3				
16	10	15.9	32.					
17	10.11				12.2			
18	10				9.4			
19	10				46.2			
20	10				27.3			
21	8			9.8	26.4	43.5		
22	8.9			22.	38.2	11.3		
23	6.7					49.2	6.1	
24	8					49.3	6.2	
25	8.9					7.5		

Reductions:

No.	T. (h. m. s.)	a₁ (s.)	a₂ (s.)	Micrometer	r.	i (′ ″)	d₁ (″)	d₂ (″)	Mean Right Ascension, 1850.0 (h. m. s.)	Mean Declination, 1850.0 (° ′ ″)
1	16 54 34.67	+9.82	+1.10	IV. 3	36.806	−22 52.84	−0.43	−3.83	16 54 45.6	−21 11 37.1
2	54 39.13	9.82	1.04	VI. 3	30.351	29 37.67	0.43	4.94	54 50.0	18 23.0
3	56 35.45	9.82	1.10	IV. 5	44.056	15 12.91	0.41	2.58	56 46.4	3 55.9
4	57 3.58	9.82	1.00	IV. 3	27.806	32 17.53	0.41	5.38	57 14.4	21 3.3
5	16 57 9.18	9.82	1.15	V. 5	44.774	14 33.86	0.41	2.46	16 57 20.2	3 16.7
6	17 0 41.34	9.81	0.84	IV. 1	13.795	46 56.65	0.39	7.78	17 0 52.0	35 44.8
7	2 7.43	9.81	1.12	III. 5	46.622	12 38.27	0.38	2.14	2 18.4	1 20.8
8	2 10.58	9.81	1.04	IV. 4	37.550	22 7.72	0.38	3.71	2 21.4	10 51.8
9	3 54.56	9.81	0.80	IV. 1	13.646	47 6.05	0.36	7.81	3 5.2	35 54.2
10	3 29.96	9.81	0.90	IV. 3	23.035	36 20.36	0.37	6.05	3 40.7	21 25 6.8
11	4 17.01	9.81	1.12	VI. 5	48.906	10 14.22	0.36	1.76	4 27.9	20 58 56.3
12	5 12.35	9.81	1.02	V. 3	37.672	21 58.43	0.35	3.68	5 23.2	21 10 42.5
13	6 58.26	9.80	1.01	IV. 3	36.917	22 45.87	0.34	3.82	6 9.1	11 30.0
14	7 14.16	9.80	0.87	IV. 1	9.152	51 47.95	0.34	8.60	7 24.8	40 36.9
15	9 29.56	9.80	0.85	III. 3	23.678	36 36.02	0.33	6.09	9 40.2	25 23.0
16	11 48.68	9.80	0.86	II. 3	26.694	33 27.41	0.31	5.57	11 50.3	22 13.3
17	11 12.32	9.80	0.83	III. 3	23.342	36 57.68	0.31	6.15	11 23.0	25 44.3
18	12 52.76	9.80	0.93	IV. 4	34.588	25 13.52	0.30	4.21	13 3.5	13 55.0
19	12 13.31	9.80	0.85	IV. 3	25.026	35 11.99	0.31	5.86	12 24.0	23 58.2
20	13 54.46	9.80	0.07	IV. 4	39.899	19 40.12	0.30	3.30	13 5.2	8 23.7
21	14 26.52	9.80	0.73	IV. 1	15.497	45 10.08	0.29	7.50	14 37.1	33 57.9
22	14 38.39	9.80	0.78	IV. 2	19.635	40 50.61	0.29	6.78	14 49.0	29 37.7
23	15 32.68	9.80	0.85	IV. 3	30.954	29 0.02	0.28	4.64	15 43.5	17 45.1
24	17 32.98	9.79	0.83	IV. 3	28.932	31 6.88	0.27	5.18	17 43.6	19 52.3
25	17 17 34.63	+9.79	+0.86	V. 3	32.065	−27 50.25	−0.27	−4.65	17 17 45.3	−21 16 35.2

Zone 265. July 11. C. D₀ = −20° 48′ 30″.

Seconds of Transit:

No.	Mag.	I.	II.	III.	IV.	V.	VI.	VII.
1	8	51.4	7.3	24.5		57.3		
2	9	33.	49.6	5.4	22.5			
3	9		35.3	52.	8.4	25.		
4	8.9		51.6	7.9	24.9	11.4		
5	10			22.8				
6	6.7	11.1	27.4	43.8	60.5	16.9		
7	10					39.3		
8	9	47.6	4.		36.8	53.3		
9	9.10		15.5	32.2		5.4		
10	7.8					59.2		
11	9				36.8	53.4		
12	8		10.2		43.2	59.8		
13	9				44.5	1.5		
14	10	14.2		47.6	4.			
15	10.11					43.2		
16	10	32.2	48.4	5.1				
17	10.11			44.2	3.3			
18	10				0.2	17.		
19	8.9			33.3	50.3			
20	8.9				25.4	42.3		

Reductions:

No.	T. (h. m. s.)	a₁ (s.)	a₂ (s.)	Micrometer	r.	i (′ ″)	d₁ (″)	d₂ (″)	Mean Right Ascension, 1850.0 (h. m. s.)	Mean Declination, 1850.0 (° ′ ″)
1	17 3 24.30	+16.78	+0.18	IV. 3	23.925	−36 20.99	−8.29	−5.04	17 3 41.3	−21 25 4.3
2	5 5.84	16.78	0.23	IV. 3	37.631	22 1.20	8.26	2.70	5 22.8	10 42.2
3	6 51.93	16.78	0.23	IV. 3	36.888	22 47.69	8.24	2.83	6 8.9	11 28.8
4	7 8.18	16.78	0.11	IV. 3	9.102	51 49.71	8.24	7.55	7 25.1	40 35.5
5	9 22.92	16.77	0.18	III. 3	23.624	36 40.07	8.21	5.09	9 39.9	21 25 23.4
6	11 43.94	16.77	0.29	IV. 5	50.938	8 7.17	8.18	0.47	12 1.0	20 56 45.8
7	12 6.41	16.77	0.18	V. 2	24.985	35 14.93	8.17	4.85	12 23.4	21 23 58.0
8	14 20.39	16.76	0.13	IV. 1	15.454	45 12.52	8.15	6.48	14 37.3	33 57.1
9	14 32.25	16.76	0.16	IV. 2	19.582	40 53.98	8.15	5.77	14 49.2	29 37.9
10	15 26.33	16.76	0.20	V. 3	30.898	29 3.34	8.13	3.85	15 43.3	17 45.3
11	16 20.30	16.76	0.16	IV. 2	19.864	40 36.12	8.12	5.72	16 37.2	29 20.0
12	17 26.70	16.76	0.20	II. 3	28.916	31 7.88	8.11	4.19	17 43.7	19 50.2
13	17 28.24	16.76	0.21	IV. 3	32.030	27 52.58	8.11	3.66	17 45.2	16 34.4
14	22 47.42	16.75	0.19	IV. 3	27.154	32 58.55	8.03	4.48	22 4.4	21 41.1
15	22 10.30	16.75	0.17	V. 3	22.419	37 55.53	8.04	5.29	22 27.2	26 38.9
16	24 5.05	16.75	0.23	III. 4	37.032	22 39.54	8.02	2.81	24 22.0	11 20.4
17	25 45.45	16.75	0.25	IV. 4	43.346	16 4.05	7.99	1.76	26 2.5	4 43.8
18	26 43.88	16.75	0.25	IV. 4	41.734	17 45.03	7.98	2.02	26 0.9	6 25.0
19	26 33.50	16.75	0.25	IV. 4	42.332	17 7.70	7.98	−1.91	26 50.5	21 5 47.6
20	17 27 9.20	+16.75	+0.31	IV. 5	55.021	−3 49.68	−7.98	+0.21	17 27 26.3	−20 52 27.4

CORRECTIONS.

Date.	Corr. of Clock.	Hourly rate.	m	n	e	Zenith Point.	Mic. Co.
1849.	h. s.	s.	s.	s.	s.	° ′ ″	r.

INSTRUMENT READINGS.

Date.	A.	B.	C.	D.	E.	F.	Mean.	Barom.	At.	Ex.	U.	L.	I.
	1849. h. m.	° ′ ″						″	in.					
Zone 264 July 5, 17 0	80 9 63.2	59.2	61.8	62.6	55.2	55.2	59.53	30.206	71.	67.		70.8	70.7
17 20	63.5	59.0	61.9	63.0	55.1	55.1	59.60	30.206	70.5	66.5		67.7	
Zone 265 July 11, 17 0	80 9 65.1	56.9	60.3	59.6	55.7	57.1	59.12	30.314	81.8	79.5	79.	81.	79.5
										79.1			
17 20													
17 40								30.304	80.8	78.4		79.1	
18 0										78.0			
18 40								30.320	79.5	77.8			
19	64.4	57.3	60.7	59.9	55.2	57.1	59.10	30.326	79.2	77.5		78.8	78.5

REMARKS.

(264) 6. Transit over T. III assumed as recorded over T. IV.

(264) 9. Minutes assumed as 2, not 3.

(264) 13. Minutes assumed as 5, not 6.

(264) 18. Right ascension differs 1ᵐ from Arg. Z. 213, 85; minutes probably 11, not 12.

(264) 19. Transit over T. V assumed as recorded over T. IV.

(264) 20. Transit over T. V assumed as recorded over T. IV, to agree with Arg. Z. 393, 50, and minutes as 12, not 13.

(265) 3. Minutes of transit assumed as 5, not 6.

(265) 14. Minutes assumed as 21, not 22.

(265) 17. Transits discordant by 2ˢ; their mean probably 1ˢ in error.

(265) 18. Minutes assumed as 25, not 26.

ZONE 265.　JULY 11.　C,　$D_0 = -20°\ 48'\ 33''$ —Continued.

SECONDS OF TRANSIT · T · a₁ · a₂

No.	Mag.	I.	II.	III.	IV.	V.	VI.	VII.	T. (h. m. s.)	a₁ (s.)	a₂ (s.)
21	8					5.			17 27 32.22	+16.74	+0.32
22	8.9					58.5			28 25.66	16.74	0.23
23	6.7	36.4		9.5	25.8	42.4			34 9.41	16.74	0.12
24	9.10				4.5	21.1			35 4.52	16.74	0.18
25	9.10				54.8		28.		35 53.01	16.73	0.12
26	9.10				54.2		27.		37 54.20	16.73	0.16
27	9					56.5			37 23.60	16.73	0.17
28	9.10		11.8		14.6				42 58.30	16.73	0.36
29	9					7.2			43 34.39	16.73	0.25
30	10	14.3		18.	34.8				44 17.82	16.73	0.26
31	9		25.5	42.	58.5				45 25.53	16.72	0.28
32	8.9	43.5	0.2	10.3	32.1	49.2			50 16.26	16.72	0.27
33	9.10			22.5	39.2				51 6.05	16.72	0.17
34	8.9	49.1	5.6	22.1	38.4	55.			53 22.04	16.72	0.16
35	10.11			16.8	33.5				54 0.48	16.72	0.30
36	9.10			28.5					55 28.45	16.72	0.30
37	8.9		13.1		46.3				56 13.29	16.72	0.25
38	10				10.				57 53.30	16.71	0.16
39	8				50.5				57 33.79	16.71	0.15
40	7				11.1	27.2			58 54.35	16.71	0.17
41	8		56.	12.5					59 12.50	16.71	0.21
42	7		21.8	38.3	54.2				59 21.61	16.71	0.17
43	9			55.	21.8				59 11.67	16.71	0.17
44	10	14.							17 59 25.	16.71	0.17
45	8.9				14.2				18 1 57.53	16.71	0.19
46	8.9				47.8	3.3			1 30.48	16.71	0.19
47	9				24.2				2 51.41	16.71	0.30
48	10			25.	41.2				3 24.80	16.71	0.28
49	6			30.3	47.3	3.6			4 30.57	16.71	0.26
50	9				4.2	20.6			6 47.71	16.71	0.28
51	10			52.3					11 52.44	16.71	0.14
52	10				32.3				11 59.37	16.71	0.14
53	9.10				17.8	33.8			12 1.00	16.71	0.17
54	9.10			13.5	29.4				13 13.17	16.71	0.17
55	9		7.5	24.	40.5	56.9			16 23.99	16.70	0.26
56	10.11			33.5					17 33.65	16.70	0.13
57	9		34.2	51.5					19 51.13	16.70	0.17
58	9				27.2				19 54.33	16.70	0.20
59	9				51.3	8.1			19 34.85	16.70	0.17
60	9				9.4				20 36.58	16.70	0.27
61	8.9			43.2	59.5	16.6			21 43.26	16.70	0.13
62	8.9				46.5				22 13.62	16.70	0.19
63	9		22.						23 22.11	16.70	0.19
64	9		20.2		53.3				24 20.37	16.70	0.20
65	7.8	34.3	50.3	7.1	23.6	39.9			26 7.06	16.70	0.29
66	9	38.3	54.2	11.2					28 11.12	16.70	0.13
67	9		34.2		57.5				28 24.46	16.70	0.16
68	7.8			55.	11.2				28 33.29	16.70	0.15
69	7.8			56.	12.5				18 29 39.51	+16.70	+0.24

MICROMETER · i · d₁ · d₂ · Mean Right Ascension 1850.0 · Mean Declination 1850.0

No.	Micrometer		r.	i (′ ″)	d₁ (″)	d₂ (″)	Mean R. A. (h. m. s.)	Mean Decl. (° ′ ″)
21	V.	5	56.205	− 2 36.50	− 7.97	+ 0.41	17 27 49.3	− 20 51 14.1
22	V.	3	38.724	20 52.35	7.96	− 2.53	28 42.6	21 9 32.8
23	IV.	1	13.232	47 31.95	7.88	6.65	34 26.3	30 16.7
24	IV.	3	25.779	34 24.69	7.87	4.72	35 21.4	23 7.3
25	IV.	2	11.265	49 35.69	7.85	7.19	37 11.9	38 20.7
26	IV.	2	17.524	43 3.07	7.83	6.12	37 11.1	31 47.0
27	V.	2	22.314	38 2.68	7.84	5.31	37 40.5	21 56 45.8
28	IV.	5	52.668	6 18.65	7.76	0.15	43 15.3	20 54 56.6
29	V.	4	47.145	22 5.95	7.76	1.10	42 51.4	21 0 44.8
30	IV.	4	41.339	18 9.76	7.74	2.03	44 34.8	21 6 49.6
31	IV.	5	46.610	10 33.05	7.72	0.84	45 42.5	20 59 11.6
32	IV.	5	46.304	12 58.21	7.65	1.24	50 33.3	21 1 37.1
33	IV.	2	22.006	38 21.81	7.63	5.36	51 22.9	27 4.8
34	IV.	2	19.115	41 23.23	7.60	5.84	53 38.9	21 30 6.7
35	IV.	5	51.599	7 25.81	7.58	0.34	54 47.5	20 56 3.7
36	III.	5	50.900	8 9.19	7.56	0.46	55 45.5	20 56 47.2
37	IV.	3	39.502	20 3.85	7.54	2.39	56 30.3	21 8 43.8
38	IV.	2	21.073	39 20.40	7.51	5.52	58 10.2	28 3.4
39	IV.	2	18.436	42 4.68	7.52	5.97	57 50.7	30 48.2
40	IV.	2	21.870	38 30.28	7.49	5.36	59 11.2	27 13.1
41	II.	3	32.517	27 22.20	7.47	3.57	59 29.4	16 3.2
42	IV.	2	21.250	39 9.26	7.47	5.50	17 58 38.5	17 52.2
43	IV.	3	23.576	36 43.07	7.47	5.09	18 0 28.5	25 25.6
44	II.	3	23.591	36 42.13	7.45	5.09	0 42.	25 24.7
45	IV.	3	27.928	32 9.87	7.43	4.35	1 14.4	20 51.6
46	IV.	3	28.715	31 20.56	7.45	4.22	1 47.4	21 20 2.2
47	V.	5	53.155	5 47.96	7.42	0.06	2 8.4	20 54 25.4
48	IV.	4	46.845	12 24.20	7.41	1.14	3 41.8	21 1 2.7
49	IV.	4	42.562	16 53.19	7.38	1.86	4 47.5	21 5 32.4
50	IV.	5	48.049	11 6.57	7.34	0.94	7 4.7	20 59 46.8
51	III.	2	15.751	44 54.02	7.22	6.45	12 9.3	21 33 37.7
52	V.	2	16.400	44 13.26	7.21	6.33	12 16.2	32 56.8
53	IV.	3	23.046	37 16.26	7.21	5.19	12 17.9	25 58.7
54	IV.	3	22.808	37 31.07	7.19	5.24	13 30.1	26 13.5
55	IV.	4	41.330	18 10.58	7.11	2.07	16 41.0	6 49.8
56	III.	1	13.372	47 23.37	7.09	6.86	17 50.5	36 7.3
57	III.	3	22.956	37 21.84	7.02	5.21	19 8.0	26 4.1
58	V.	3	29.255	30 46.61	7.02	4.12	19 11.2	19 27.7
59	IV.	1	21.738	38 38.43	7.03	5.41	19 51.7	27 20.9
60	V.	4	45.362	13 57.90	7.01	1.39	20 53.6	2 36.3
61	IV.	1	12.191	48 37.36	6.98	7.06	22 0.1	37 21.4
62	V.	3	27.936	32 9.18	6.97	4.36	22 30.5	10 50.5
63	III.	3	28.106	31 58.00	6.93	4.32	23 39.0	20 40.2
64	IV.	3	28.398	31 40.64	6.91	4.27	24 37.3	21 20 21.8
65	IV.	3	50.567	8 28.07	6.86	0.49	26 24.1	20 57 5.4
66	III.	1	12.620	48 10.40	6.82	6.99	28 27.9	21 36 54.2
67	IV.	2	17.159	43 25.97	6.81	6.20	28 41.3	32 9.0
68	IV.	2	18.294	42 14.84	6.81	6.03	28 55.1	30 57.7
69	IV.	4	38.080	− 21 34.39	− 6.79	− 2.62	18 29 56.5	− 21 10 13.8

CORRECTIONS.

Date.	Corr. of Clock.	Hourly rate.	m	n	c	Zenith Point.	Mic. Co.
1849.	h.	s.	s.	s.	s.	° ′ ″	r.

INSTRUMENT READINGS.

Date.	A.	B.	C.	D.	E.	F.	Mean.	Barom.	At.	Ex.	U.	L.	I.
	CIRCLE.								THERMOM.				
1849. h. m.	° ′ ″							In.					

REMARKS.

(265) 26. Minutes assumed as 36, not 37.

(265) 43. Transits over T.'s II and III assumed as recorded over T.'s IV and V, and transit over T. III as 11ˢ.8, not 21ˢ.8, and minutes as 0, not 1.

(265) 45. Minutes of transit ass'd as 0ᵐ instead of 1ᵐ.

(265) 47. Minutes assumed as 1, not 2.

(265) 57. Minutes assumed as 18, not 19.

(265) 58. Minutes assumed as 18, not 19, to agree with Arg. Z. 310, 47.

ZONE 265. JULY 11. C. $D_0 = -20°\ 48'\ 30''$ — Continued.

No.	Mag.	I	II	III	IV	V	VI	VII	T (h. m. s.)	a_1 (s.)	a_2 (s.)	Mic.	r	i (′ ″)	d_1 (″)	d_2 (″)	Mean Right Ascension, 1850.0 (h. m. s.)	Mean Declination, 1850.0 (° ′ ″)
70	8.9					56.?			18 30 23.19	+16.70	+0.27	IV. 5	45.938	−13 21.00	−6.77	−1.28	18 30 40.2	−21 1 59.0
71	8.9					21.5			31 48.67	16.70	0.26	V. 4	42.442	17 1.16	6.74	1.88	32 5.6	5 39.8
72	9					56.			31 23.06	16.70	0.13	V. 1	12.002	48 49.03	6.75	7.10	31 39.9	37 32.9
73	9			43.2		16.5			32 43.46	16.70	0.17	IV. 2	21.661	38 43.52	6.71	5.41	33 0.3	27 25.6
74	9				23.2				34 6.50	16.70	0.16	IV. 2	21.491	38 54.05	6.68	5.45	34 23.4	27 36.2
75	8					51.4			34 16.58	16.70	0.27	V. 4	44.366	15 0.41	6.67	1.58	34 35.6	3 38.7
76	8				40.8	56.6			35 23.97	16.70	0.25	IV. 4	41.115	18 23.94	6.65	2.11	35 40.9	7 2.7
77	7.8				20.7	37.2			36 4.22	16.70	0.25	IV. 4	39.342	20 15.33	6.63	2.42	36 21.2	8 54.4
78	10				5.5				37 48.83	16.70	0.20	IV. 3	38.305	31 46.47	6.59	4.29	37 5.7	20 27.4
79	10		50.2	7.2					38 6.96	16.70	0.21	III. 3	31.054	28 53.93	6.58	3.82	38 23.9	17 34.3
80	10			42.3					38 42.32	16.70	0.25	III. 4	40.930	18 34.92	6.56	2.14	38 59.3	7 13.6
81	10	51.	7.2						42 23.81	16.70	0.27	II. 4	43.675	15 42.72	6.47	1.67	42 40.8	4 20.9
82	9.10			36.6	53.2				42 36.60	16.70	0.28	IV. 4	46.068	13 13.09	6.46	1.27	42 53.6	1 50.8
83	10.11	34.1							44 7.15	16.70	0.16	I. 2	19.562	40 54.81	6.43	5.79	44 24.0	29 37.0
84	7	12.2	28.2	44.9					45 44.98	16.70	0.15	III. 2	17.022	43 34.31	6.39	6.24	45 1.8	32 16.9
85	9				12.2	29.2			45 55.98	16.70	0.25	IV. 4	41.456	18 2.66	6.38	2.03	45 12.9	6 41.1
86	9.10	49.8	6.2		39.2	56.1			48 22.80	16.70	0.20	II. 3	28.232	31 51.05	6.32	4.29	48 39.7	20 31.7
87	6		13.2	29.2	46.2	2.8			48 29.60	16.70	0.21	IV. 3	30.750	29 12.88	6.32	3.88	48 46.5	17 53.1
88	9		42.2		15.5				50 58.72	16.71	0.18	IV. 3	23.328	36 58.70	6.26	5.14	50 15.6	25 40.1
89	9.10	2.4		34.3					52 34.84	16.71	0.25	III. 4	39.706	19 51.74	6.22	2.36	52 51.8	21 8 30.3
90	9	22.3	38.4	55.1					54 55.05	16.71	0.29	III. 5	51.518	7 31.02	6.16	0.34	55 12.1	20 56 7.5
91	9.10				33.				54 16.36	16.71	0.22	IV. 3	35.249	24 30.72	6.18−	3.11	54 33.3	21 13 10.0
92	9.10				57.2				54 40.66	16.71	0.30	IV. 5	53.665	5 16.06	6.17+	0.05	54 57.7	20 53 52.2
93	9					31.2			55 58.39	16.71	0.28	V. 4	46.954	12 17.80	6.14−	1.11	56 15.4	21 0 55.0
94	8				7.2	24.2			56 50.97	16.71	0.24	IV. 3	38.404	21 12.81	6.12	2.55	57 7.9	9 51.5
95	9				50.3	6.5			56 33.67	16.71	0.25	IV. 3	39.952	19 35.41	6.13	2.29	56 50.6	8 13.8
96	9			46.5					58 46.66	16.71	0.12	III. 1	10.552	50 20.15	6.07	7.35	58 3.5	39 3.6
97	8.9			32.5			5.6		58 32.66	16.71	0.16	IV. 3	20.769	39 38.97	6.08	5.60	58 49.5	28 20.7
98	8.9				58.2				18 59 21.54	16.71	0.22	IV. 4	35.242	24 32.54	6.05	3.11	18 59 38.5	13 11.7
99	4		16.3	33.3	49.7	6.3			19 0 33.15	16.71	0.21	IV. 3	33.121	26 44.18	6.03	3.47	19 0 50.1	21 15 23.7
100	9				53.2				19 1 20.41	+16.71	+0.30	V. 5	53.114	−5 50.52	−6.02	−0.04	19 1 37.4	−20 54 26.6

ZONE 266. JULY 17. C. $D_0 = -30°\ 49'\ 30''$.

No.	Mag.	I	II	III	IV	V	VI	VII	T (h. m. s.)	a_1 (s.)	a_2 (s.)	Mic.	r	i (′ ″)	d_1 (″)	d_2 (″)	Mean Right Ascension, 1850.0 (h. m. s.)	Mean Declination, 1850.0 (° ′ ″)
1	9	27.1	45.2		20.8				17 9 2.96	+18.37	−0.15	IV. 4	47.529	−11 41.39	−2.24	−0.73	17 9 21.18	−31 1 14.4
2	9			2.8	20.9				9 2.80	18.37	0.15	IV. 5	51.838	7 10.62	2.24	+0.32	9 21.02	30 56 42.5
3	8					54.			9 18.21	18.37	0.16	V. 3	37.532	22 7.21	2.24	−3.16	9 36.42	31 11 32.6
4	8.9		7.5	25.8	44.1				11 25.75	18.37	0.16	IV. 3	24.476	35 46.61	2.24	6.37	11 43.96	25 25.2
5	8.9			15.5	34.1				12 15.76	18.37	0.16	IV. 3	24.059	36 12.66	2.24	6.48	12 33.97	25 51.4
6	10					49.3			12 13.30	18.37	0.16	V. 2	20.029	40 25.76	2.24	7.48	12 31.60	30 5.5
7	10				32.?				13 13.83	18.37	0.16	IV. 3	29.296	30 44.23	2.23	5.17	13 32.04	20 21.6
8	8.9				49.2	7.4			13 31.22	18.37	0.16	IV. 2	17.301	43 17.06	2.23	8.16	13 49.43	32 57.5
9	10	39.5	57.1	15.1					16 15.28	18.36	0.16	III. 2	20.057	40 24.00	2.23	7.47	16 33.48	30 3.7
10	8.9			36.8	54.8				16 36.76	18.36	0.16	IV. 2	21.812	38 33.92	2.23	7.03	16 54.96	31 28 13.2
11	9					33.5			17 57.79	18.36	0.15	V. 5	51.338	7 42.00	2.22	0.20	18 16.00	30 57 14.4
12	8		12.5	31.3					18 12.86	18.36	0.16	IV. 4	44.486	14 52.44	2.22	1.45	18 31.06	31 4 26.1
13	8			59.3	17.5				18 41.42	18.36	0.16	IV. 3	34.292	25 30.77	2.22	3.94	18 59.62	15 6.9
14	8			30.3	48.5				17 19 12.37	+18.35	−0.16	IV. 3	25.567	−34 38.12	−2.22	−6.10	17 19 30.56	−31 24 16.4

CORRECTIONS.

Date.	Corr. of Clock.	Hourly rate.	m	n	c	Zenith Point.	Mic. Co.
1849.	h.	s.	s.	s.	s.	° ′ ″	r.

INSTRUMENT READINGS.

Date.	CIRCLE. A.	B.	C.	D.	E.	F.	Mean.	Barom.	THERMOM. At.	Ex.	U.	L.	I.
	1849. h. m.							In.					
Zone 266	July 17, 17 10 90 9 64.5	57.6	61.2	63.1	51.4	55.6	58.93	30.156	75.5	70.5	..	75.7	76.7
	17 30								..	70.1			
	17 40							30.158	74.5	70.0			

REMARKS.

(265) 78. Minutes assumed as 36, not 37.
(265) 84. Minutes assumed as 44, not 45.
(265) 85. Minutes assumed as 44, not 45, to agree with Mer. Cir. Z., 1848, July 19.
(265) 88. Minutes assumed as 49, not 50.
(265) 96. Minutes assumed as 57, not 58.
(265) 98. Transit over T. IV assumed as 38ˢ.2, not 58ˢ.2.
(266) Wind fresh; sometimes difficult to hear the clock.

ZONE 266. JULY 17. C. $D_s = -30° 49' 30''$—Continued.

No.	Mag.	I.	II.	III.	IV.	V.	VI.	VII.	T.	a_1	a_q	MIC.	No.	r	i	d_1	d_u	Mean Right Ascension, 1850.0.	Mean Declination, 1850.0.
									h. m. s.	s.	s.				′ ″	″	″	h. m. s.	° ′ ″
15	10	..	..	..	37.2	55.3	..	..	17 20 19.25	+18.35	−0.16	IV.	3	29.976	−30 1.38	− 2.22	− 5.01	17 20 37.44	− 31 19 38.6
16	8.9	30.3	48.2	6.5	..	..	..	..	22 6.36	18.35	0.16	III.	3	24.114	36 9.33	2.22	6.45	22 24.55	25 48.0
17	9	..	..	..	..	35.5	..	..	22 59.51	18.35	0.17	V.	1	8.215	52 46.58	2.21	10.43	23 17.69	31 42 29.2
18	10	..	..	23.2	..	..	..	..	23 23.14	18.35	0.15	III.	5	49.807	9 18.16	2.21	− 0.17	23 41.34	30 58 50.5
19	9.10	..	..	8.5	..	..	..	..	24 8.44	18.35	0.15	III.	5	51.314	7 43.82	2.21	+ 0.19	24 26.64	30 57 15.8
20	9	..	..	40.5	58.6	..	..	..	24 40.50	18.35	0.16	IV.	3	37.167	22 30.32	2.21	− 3.25	24 58.70	31 12 5.8
21	10	..	..	55.2	12.4	..	..	..	17 28 54.76	+18.34	−0.16	IV.	1	22.302	−38 3.24	− 2.20	− 6.91	17 29 12.94	− 31 27 42.3

ZONE 267. JULY 17. C. $D_s = -21° 23' 30''$.

No.	Mag.	I.	II.	III.	IV.	V.	VI.	VII.	T.	a_1	a_q	MIC.	No.	r	i	d_1	d_u	Mean Right Ascension, 1850.0.	Mean Declination, 1850.0.
									h. m. s.	s.	s.				′ ″	″	″	h. m. s.	° ′ ″
1	7.8	..	..	9.5	26.	42.8	9.5	..	17 29 26.17	+16.30	+1.21	IV.	3	34.428	−25 22.30	7.46	5.24	17 29 43.7	− 21 49 5.0
2	9.10	38.5	..	11.5	26.1	..	..	..	32 11.53	16.29	1.23	IV.	3	32.011	27 53.77	7.42	5.66	32 29.1	21 51 36.8
3	9.10	..	..	..	53.8	10.3	..	..	32 37.10	16.29	1.29	IV.	1	10.592	49 58.71	7.41	9.31	32 54.7	22 13 45.4
4	7	..	..	52.3	8.3	26.3	41.5	..	34 8.59	16.29	1.19	IV.	5	46.657	12 35.95	7.39	3.14	34 26.1	21 36 16.5
5	8	..	..	..	3.3	19.5	36.3	..	35 3.13	16.29	1.27	IV.	2	17.088	43 30.36	7.37	8.25	35 20.7	22 7 16.0
6	9.10	..	..	..	..	55.2	..	..	35 22.17	16.29	1.25	IV.	3	26.865	33 16.56	7.36	6.55	35 39.7	21 57 0.5
7	9.10	..	..	53.2	..	26.3	..	..	37 53.26	16.28	1.19	V.	5	50.941	8 6.79	7.33	2.39	38 10.7	31 46.5
8	9.10	..	..	..	39.2	..	..	..	37 22.59	16.28	1.17	IV.	5	55.772	3 3.73	7.34	1.59	37 40.0	21 26 42.7
9	10	..	..	..	..	29.5	..	..	38 56.45	16.28	1.24	V.	2	22.931	37 23.79	7.31	7.22	39 14.0	22 1 8.3
10	9.10	..	..	19.5	36.3	..	..	..	41 19.58	16.28	1.27	IV.	3	30.858	29 6.05	7.27	5.85	41 37.1	21 52 49.2
11	9	..	..	..	..	..	1.5	..	41 28.53	16.28	1.25	5.	4	39.857	20 46.07	7.27	4.48	41 46.1	44 27.8
12	10	37.5	..	10.5	..	..	..	..	44 10.55	16.27	1.25	III.	4	39.549	20 1.71	7.22	4.36	44 28.1	43 43.3
13	7.8	28.6	45.5	1.8	18.5	34.7	..	..	47 1.82	16.27	1.39	IV.	3	28.330	31 44.90	7.17	6.29	47 19.5	55 28.4
14	9.10	..	..	6.4	23.	39.4	..	..	49 22.89	16.27	1.46	IV.	1	12.061	48 45.45	7.15	9.12	48 40.6	12 31.7
15	10	..	..	..	10.1	..	..	..	49 53.34	16.26	1.42	IV.	3	25.254	34 57.80	7.12	6.82	50 11.0	21 58 41.7
16	8	..	45.5	2.0	18.3	..	..	..	52 18.55	16.26	1.42	III.	2	17.065	43 31.67	7.08	8.24	52 36.2	22 7 17.0
17	9	..	45.2	2.1	18.4	..	..	..	53 1.85	16.26	1.41	IV.	3	26.562	33 35.76	7.07	6.40	53 19.5	21 57 19.2
18	8.9	..	..	..	..	54.3	..	..	53 21.38	16.26	1.33	V.	5	52.548	6 26.11	7.06	2.13	53 39.0	21 30 5.3
19	9	..	..	..	..	..	1.5	..	54 28.40	16.26	1.48	V.	1	10.591	50 17.65	7.04	9.37	54 46.1	22 14 4.1
20	9	..	48.3	4.8	..	..	..	..	56 4.82	16.26	1.40	III.	4	42.837	16 33.99	7.01	3.80	56 22.5	21 40 14.8
21	9	..	..	44.7	1.7	..	..	..	57 44.88	16.25	1.47	IV.	2	17.016	43 34.81	6.99	8.26	58 2.6	22 7 20.1
22	9	..	..	..	..	..	3.5	..	56 30.41	16.25	1.48	III.	1	12.016	48 48.21	7.00	9.14	56 48.1	12 34.3
23	8.9	..	..	..	45.7	2.2	..	..	57 29.04	16.25	1.46	IV.	2	20.891	39 31.69	6.98	7.57	57 46.8	22 3 16.2
24	8.9	..	..	23.	..	56.3	..	..	58 23.19	16.25	1.45	IV.	3	31.317	28 37.50	6.97	5.78	58 40.9	21 52 20.3
25	9	..	..	24.2	..	..	..	..	59 24.34	16.25	1.49	III.	2	13.919	46 48.86	6.95	8.77	59 42.1	22 10 34.6
26	9	..	..	..	52.3	8.5	..	..	17 59 35.46	16.25	1.49	IV.	2	12.992	47 47.19	6.94	8.94	17 59 53.2	11 33.1
27	9	..	..	..	..	8.2	24.3	..	18 0 51.31	16.25	1.49	IV.	2	12.702	48 5.38	6.94	9.02	18 0 9.1	11 51.3
28	8.9	..	..	22.5	39.5	56.3	..	..	18 1 22.85	+16.25	+1.50	IV.	2	8.959	−52 0.05	6.93	9.66	18 1 40.6	− 22 15 46.6

CORRECTIONS.

Date.	Corr. of Clock.	Hourly rate.	m	n	c	Zenith Point.	Mic. Co.
1849.	h. s.	s.	s.	s.	s.	° ′ ″	r.

INSTRUMENT READINGS.

Date.		CIRCLE.							Barom.	THERMOM.				
		A.	B.	C.	D.	E.	F.	Mean.		At.	Ex.	U.	L.	I.
Zone 267	1849. h. m. July 17, 18 0	80 44 62.5	56.9	60.5	62.7	50.6	54.3	57.92	in. 30.156	74.	69.7	78.	72.	74.5

REMARKS.

(266) 17. Right ascension differs 1ᵐ from B. A. C. 5908, depending only on Lacaille 6108.

(267) 1. Transit over T. V assumed to have been at 59ˢ.5 instead of 9ˢ.5.

(267) 27. Right ascension assumed as 17ʰ 59ᵐ, to agree with Arg. Z. 24.44; 307. 56.

www.ingramcontent.com/pod-product-compliance
Lightning Source LLC
Chambersburg PA
CBHW051125120726
47905CB00005B/1434